A Honky Tonk Night and Murder

Sharon E. Buck

Southern Chick Lit

Copyright © 2016 Sharon E. Buck

All rights reserved.

No portion of this book may be reproduced in any form without written permission from the publisher or author, except as permitted by U.S. copyright law.

Contents

1. Chapter 1 — 1
2. Chapter 2 — 23
3. Chapter 3 — 61
4. Chapter 4 — 72
5. Chapter 5 — 158
6. Chapter 6 — 165
7. Chapter 7 — 175
8. Chapter 8 — 195

9.	Chapter 9	202
10.	Chapter 10	212
11.	Chapter 11	218
12.	Chapter 12	230
13.	Chapter 13	237
14.	Chapter 14	255
15.	Chapter 15	260
16.	Chapter 16	281
17.	Chapter 17	301
18.	Chapter 18	338
19.	Chapter 19	365
20.	Chapter 20	396
21.	Chapter21	411

22.	Chapter 22	432
23.	Chapter 23	443
24.	Chapter 24	459
25.	Chapter 25	467
26.	Chapter 26	481
27.	Chapter 27	496
28.	Chapter 28	523
29.	Chapter 29	550
30.	Chapter 30	586
31.	Chapter 31	605
32.	Chapter 32	626
33.	Chapter 33	704
34.	ABOUT THE AUTHOR	713

35. ACKNOWLEDGMENTS 716

Chapter 1

"Is there really anything such as a honky tonk night anymore," I mused, "or is it just karaoke gone bad?"

This is what happens when my brain engages with caffeine first thing in the morning. Random thoughts emerge with no apparent connection to anything going on in my life. Then the universe decides to play a cruel joke on me by dragging up something from the deep morasses of my mind and it suddenly appears in a weird life form in front of me. I love music.

My cell phone rang interrupting a perfectly good train of thought going nowhere. Reaching for it on my kitchen's Ooba Tuba granite countertop, I chuckled to myself. The real reason why I had purchased this granite countertop was because I just flat out liked the name. I mean, come on, who couldn't like a name like Ooba Tuba?

Pink's "So What" was still merrily playing when I picked up the cell phone. I groaned as I recognized the number on caller I.D.. I seriously debated about whether or not to answer the phone but I knew the caller would just call me every fifteen minutes if I didn't answer.

"Hello, Dewitt." I chugged some of my freshly brewed nectar of the gods better known as the latest offering from the coffee-of- the-month club, Moroccan Heaven. It was delicious.

"Parker, Parker! How are you, girl?" Dewitt Munster, yes, that really is his name, is the local sheriff in River County, Florida. He wasn't the brightest bulb in the box and had barely skated through on his last election. He won by one vote over the local drug dealer who had run against him...twice. The drug dealer demanded a re-count and it showed the drug dealer winning by two votes. Ballot box counting was not at its finest in River County, especially when it showed two different results two different times.

The case zoomed up all the way to the Florida Supreme Court where the great and almighty justices decided it was probably better to have the bumbling incumbent sheriff in office versus a known drug dealer who had twenty-seven pages of arrests. There might have been, allegedly, some fairly hefty campaign contributions made to a couple of the justices.

This, of course, made national news and the drug dealer was on every major daytime television show. Screaming he was being discriminated against, here he was now trying to go on the straight and narrow road of the great American Dream and mainstream America did not want him and others like him succeeding.

It made for great television. Unfortunately, he was arrested twice more for alleged threats of intimidation on female hosts. Still, it did put River County back in the national news.

I answered cautiously, "I'm good, Dewitt."

"So, when are you coming back to Po'thole?"

And there it was. The dreaded question of going back to my hometown. I live in Atlanta and I love Atlanta but Po'thole -- technically pronounced Poat Hole, called Po Ho by the natives and Pot Hole by anyone north of the Georgia border -- seemed to have an umbilical cord attached to me during the past however many months and I couldn't seem to get loose of it.

Carefully drinking some more of the delicious dark aromatic brew in front of me, I replied, "Well, I hadn't really planned on going down there, Dewitt."

"Parker," he cleared his throat, "ah, you know we've had a little problem down here and..."

I snorted, "A little problem, Dewitt? Let's see, you had three murders back in May. Still unresolved. You have a major disappearance of a well-known CPA. Your election went all the way to the Florida Supreme Court because of voter count issues. They determined you only won by two votes, and that was against a known drug dealer. Problems, Dewitt? You've got a boatload of them."

He became defensive. "Well, we know who murdered them people."

I interrupted him, "You have no, I repeat, no evidence against Misty Dawn. It was circumstantial and you still haven't found her. All you're doing is speculating."

I sighed, "Cut to the chase, Dewitt. What do you want?"

Long silence. I drank some more coffee.

"There's been another murder."

I really wasn't surprised. Small towns out in the middle of

God's green acres in Northeast Florida were ripe for all sorts of craziness. People disappeared all the time. Usually the story line was someone fell out of a boat or off the bank fishing and a gator ate them. River County must have some really fat gators out in the St. Johns River then.

I didn't say anything.

"Parker? You still there?"

"Yes, Dewitt, I'm here." I sighed, "I know I'm going to regret this but who was murdered and why does it have anything to do with me?"

"Well, it was Scooter Travis and he was found dead at The Last Drop Saloon. And, I thought that maybe, um, you might come down and, um, see what was going on."

I started to laugh. After being a New York Times bestseller on my last book A Dose of Nice, I knew it was just a matter of time before Dewitt called me.

"No."

"What do you mean no?"

"No, Dewitt, I am not coming back down to Po'thole. I don't like Po'thole and, besides which, you arrested me over nothing. Nope, I am NOT coming back down to Po'thole."

"You mean you're not going to help Gracie Blanche with the Harvest Full Moon Festival?"

Po'thole had more full moon festivals than pagans did from the Middle Ages. Sad to say, many of the full moon festivals were not held on full moon nights.

"Dewitt, I have absolutely no, I repeat, no desire to come back to Po'thole. Have a great day. Besides, what the heck is a county sheriff doing calling a bestselling author for advice?! That's just crazy!" I pushed End on my cell phone.

Thank goodness for Moroccan Heaven; otherwise, I would have thrown my coffee cup across the room. Also, since I had just paid an exorbitant amount of money to make my condo look like something out of Architectural Digest, throwing a cup of coffee against my newly painted wall would be foolish at best, stupid at the worst.

I'm Parker Bell, owner of a computer security consulting firm and national bestselling crime author. After escaping from the confines of a rural, economically depressed, and limited thinking little town located on the beautiful St. Johns River in Northeast Florida, I had created a very successful computer security consulting company in Atlanta. Believing that both sides of my brain needed to be balanced, I started writing true crime novels. No one was more surprised than I was when my first and second books became New York Times bestsellers.

My third book, A Dose of Nice, had been written about the three murders in Po'thole. It had all the makings of a good movie: a young beer tycoon also the youngest mayor of Po'thole had been found all trussed up like a turkey roasting on a spit at his men only hunting camp, then the local delicatessen owner had been found dead in his riverfront home, and the local used car salesman – everyone's friend, it said so right on his business card – was found dead at his desk with a car purchase application under his hand. The only thing the murders had in common was they all had eaten barbeque dinners.

Well, there was one other thing they had in common and that was the Lady Gatorettes. It was highly rumored and speculated that the five hormonal, sugar-and-caffeine-infused women had murdered the afore-mentioned community leaders. Specifically, it had all the appearances that Misty Dawn, during one of her out-of-control menopausal moments, might have been the one who created the untimely death of them all.

The evidence, at best, against her was circumstantial and Dewitt had never been able to find or arrest her.

There was also the disappearance of my former first love boyfriend Joe D. Savannah, owner of We Make Money, CPAs. No one had seen hide nor hair of him since ground had been broken for the Florida Fishing Resort and that had opened on time, unlike anything else in River County.

The Middle Eastern owners had been interviewed extensively by the FBI, Homeland Security, and the afore-mentioned Sheriff Dewitt Munster regarding the murders and the disappearance of Joe D. The owners were making money hand over fist, the local economy was booming with all of the new folks coming into River County and Po'thole. Things had settled back down into a dull roar, according to my best friend since fourth grade Gracie Blanche.

I blamed Gracie Blanche for turning my life upside down earlier in the year. My life had been calm until she called me to come help her out for the Florida Full Moon Crappy Festival held every Memorial Day weekend since World War II for the Old Fashion Antique Show and Sale. Little did I know I was going to be embroiled with Homeland Security, the FBI, a Middle Eastern real estate development group, three murders, and the disappearance of a well-known thrice married CPA. Oh, yeah, did I mention the Lady Gatorettes who terrorized anyone who got within one hundred yards of them?

Still, I mused, why would Scooter Travis be murdered? Even though I wasn't wild about Po'thole I did keep up with their latest news on the internet. It had been heavily rumored for years that Scooter had murdered his first two wives and had gotten away with it. He had also been mayor at one point and his personal net worth had grown exponentially while he was in office. But, of course, that was because he was such a "good" businessman although he had filed bankruptcy in his first three businesses. No one talked about that out loud anymore either.

He was just a good ole boy and had played on the only high school football team that had won a state title back in 1971. To say the guys that played on that team were tighter than super glue was an understatement.

I wondered if some of the team were covering up the local mayor's murder and it was really something else. Taking another sip of Moroccan Heaven, I said, "Not my circus, not my monkey." Little did I know.

Chapter 2

"I didn't do it," a whispered voice said after I had mumbled a very sleepy hello on my cell phone at three a.m.

"Yeah, okay. You didn't do what?" My brain, normally clicking along at two hundred miles per hour, wasn't functioning in the middle of the night and I didn't have any real reason to get up and fix coffee. I was all snuggled up in my newly purchased, very expensive 800-thread count sheets and was sleeping the dreams of angels until this strange phone call.

"It's me and I didn't have anything to do with Scooter's murder. They're going to try to frame me on this one too."

I snapped wide awake. "Misty Dawn, is that you? Why would anyone think you did it?" My warm snuggly sheets were thrown back as I struggled to sit up on the edge of the bed. Being a couple of pounds overweight and having that fat chunky monkey wrapped around my waistline did not make for a smooth transition out of the bed. I ended up on the floor unintentionally.

Silence.

"Hello! Misty Dawn, are you still there?"

More silence. I silently cursed. The line was still live.

"Misty Dawn, what the heck is going on?"

A mumbled, "I didn't do it, and I didn't do them other ones either."

Total silence for about five seconds, then she had hung up.

Since it was three a.m. and I was barely awake, sleep called my name and I succumbed to my heavy eyelids closing once again.

My landline phone jarred me out of a very sexy dream with Mark Wahlberg around eight a.m. This was not starting off to be a promising good day.

"Hello," I mumbled.

"Parker, darling! How are you?"

My day just took a major turn south. It was Saffron Woo, my New York book agent. Saffron claims to be first-generation American of Chinese immigrant parents. I have it on good authority her real name is Delilah Brooke, she's Jewish, and she's from Greenville, South Carolina. Whatever, I didn't care if she was purple and hung upside down. She's a book agent extraordinaire, fashion diva, and has made me a ton of money. I love her but just not first thing in the morning. She makes the

Energizer Bunny look like he's on Valium.

"What, Saffron?" I groaned.

"Parker, girl, A Dose of Nice is selling very, very well and the new editor Keegan Valarr is interested in another book from you."

"Why?"

"Why what, Parker?"

"Why does this Keegan guy want a new book from me? I haven't even looked at any other crimes or murders. What would I write on?"

"Have you had coffee yet?" Saffron's voice purred through the line.

"No!" I was never going to be voted Miss Congeniality without my coffee.

"Call me after you have had your first cup."

"Wait!" I interrupted her as an unwanted thought exploded in my brain but it was too late. She had already hung up.

I dragged my unwilling body into the kitchen where the only thing of any real value or substance was my coffee maker. I pushed all other thoughts out of my mind.

In less than twenty-four hours I received two calls before I had my first cup of coffee. This is never a good sign and I vaguely wondered if I needed to visit a voodoo store to get some type of magic potion to wave over me, my condo, and my phone to get rid of the obviously nasty, evil, and wicked spirits that attacked me at the crack of dawn. I don't give a rat's pa-tootie what time the weatherman says is dawn, anything before nine a.m. and my precious first cup of coffee is the crack of dawn to me.

Slurping down the hot, dark brown nectar, I was standing at the kitchen's countertop ledge checking my email when I remembered why I was trying to interrupt Saffron. In the excitement of my remembering, I inadvertently sloshed some of my coffee on my keyboard. It blinked twice and then the screen went black.

"No!!!!" I screamed. "Flipping a! Are you flipping kidding me?! No, no, noooo!!!!!"

The phone rang. I hate the phone.

"What?" I snarled into the receiver. I didn't even look at caller I.D., it could have been the president for all I cared and my response would be the same.

"Parker? Are you okay?" It was Missy, my office manager. She sounded slightly worried.

"Yeah, well, I, um, had a little accident and, um..."

She started to laugh, not the "we're all in this together" laugh. No, it was the more humiliating laugh of "I can't believe you did it again to your laptop" type.

"If you're coming into the office, I'll have a new laptop for you. If you're not coming into the office, then I'll have someone run it over to you.

"You know," she coughed slightly, "you're averaging a new laptop every month now, don't you?"

"Whatever, Missy, I had planned on working from home today anyway. So, just send it over."

"Okay. Parker, what's going on down in Po'thole? Dwight called at seven thirty this morning looking for you. I told him you never come in before ten and he snorted."

"I hung up the phone on him."

"Yes, he said so," she paused. "Does he want you to do another book?"

"I guess. Actually, I think he's looking for more publicity. Ever since Rob got that cushy job at CNN for doing those murder stories through the eyes of a cop, Dewitt calls me periodically. I never take his calls and I haven't returned any of them up to now. He thinks I got Rob that job. Rob got it all on his own."

"Parker, you helped by getting him dressed up nice and all."

"Saffron did that." I ignored her. "Anyway, I think Dewitt wants a job like that and I think he thinks if another book was written on what's happening in Po'thole, he might get a cushy job at a major network."

Missy snickered. "I guess he doesn't realize he doesn't fit the profile, does he?"

"No."

"Saffron called here this morning also."

"What's up with everyone calling the office? Yeah, she called me too and told me that the new editor – Keegan somebody or other – wanted me to write a new book. She said to call her after I've had a cup of coffee."

"Parker, do I need to make plane reservations?"

"No, I'm not going anywhere." My eyes narrowed, my head started pounding, I poured another cup of coffee. Then it dawned on me.

"Did that weasel call Saffron?!" I yelled.

"Um."

Taking a deep breath, I said, "I'm guessing Dewitt called Saffron to see if she could get me to go to that godforsaken place. Plus, I don't have a house anymore since it was blown up. I AM NOT GOING BACK TO PO'THOLE!"

"Did you ever figure out who blew up your house, Parker?"

"Not exactly," I admitted. At first, everyone thought it might have been the Lady Gatorettes or it could have been the crazy Middle Eastern/Homeland Security guys. No one knew except that it had been arson and the insurance company had been generous with a check.

I guess this isn't the time to admit that I might have inadvertently blown up my own childhood home. I had booby-trapped the house and I may have accidently set the timer wrong. Well, I had all sorts of crazy people after me and making death threats. What was I supposed to do – let them kill me? I think not!

We talked for a few more minutes about company business and then, taking a deep breath, I returned Saffron's call.

"Girl, how long does it take you to drink coffee?" Saffron laughed. Well, it was more of a cackle but whatever.

"Saffron, why does the new editor want a new book from me?" Drinking a new cup of Moroccan Heaven, I waited for her answer.

"A Dose of Nice has done so well and he wants to capitalize on those sales with another book."

"And, pray tell, Saffron, what would this new book be on?" I was going to drag it out of her one way or another.

"There's another murder in Po'thole…"

"Yeah, so? There's all sorts of murders all over the country and what makes this so special about another murder in Po'thole?"

"Parker, Dewitt thinks…"

I interrupted her again and enunciated very slowly. "I do not care what Dewitt thinks. The man cannot find his way out of a paper bag with two hands. He did not solve or arrest anyone for the last three murders."

"Parker…"

"What would the book be about, Saffron? How about an incompetent, goober sheriff who can't solve murders or would it be Rednecks Take Over River County or would it be Po'thole Murders R Us? Huh, what would it be? There is not a book here!" I didn't realize I was shouting until Saffron gently reminded me.

"Shut up, Parker!" She screamed into the phone. "Shut up a minute!"

"I'm not doing another book on Po'thole. I hate Po'thole!" And with that I disconnected Saffron. I was stewed. I spent my teenage years plotting and planning on how to escape the little ratty town that time had stomped all over. I did not want to spend any more time there this year...or any other year. The people were nice enough but there was absolutely no ambition in that town and, if it weren't for inbreeding, some of the local families would have died out a long time ago. No, Po'thole was not on my top one hundred places to visit again.

Close to noon time, just after I received my new laptop, Gracie Blanche called me. Gracie Blanche is my oldest friend since the fourth grade. She thinks the sun rises and falls on

Po'thole. It does, like every other town and city in America, but our viewpoints are at the opposite end of the spectrum. Gracie Blanche runs most of the antique shows at the various festivals throughout the year. She's a baby female Napoleon and can be quite mean at times.

"Good morning, Gracie Blanche. How you doing today?"

"What do you mean you're not going to help me with the Harvest Full Moon Festival?"

"And a gracious good morning to you too! Since when have I ever helped you with that thing, Gracie Blanche? Get off my back! What do you really want?" I gritted my teeth.

"You helped earlier this year!"

"Yeah, that was accident. In a moment of weakness, I agreed to help you. It's caused me more grief and agony than I care to share."

"You made a boatload of money from coming back here." Her tone was accusatory, almost like I owed her something.

"That I did but I'm not coming back." I could already see me drawing the line in the sand on not going back to that dinky little town where everyone knew everyone else's business. It should have been named Gossip Central.

"Scooter's dead." She was quiet for a moment. Although she and Scooter had both been married to other folks at the time, as she explained it later to me, the snake from the Garden of Eden had tempted both she and Scooter beyond human endurance or capabilities to ward it off. I might have believed her if the meeting of their flesh had been just one time. But, no, their fleshly desire apparently consumed them for a number of years. I strongly suspected they were still asking God for forgiveness up until Scooter's untimely death. But, then again, what death is ever timely?

I was still steamed. "I'm sorry about Scooter but who called you? Dewitt?"

"Yes, Parker, he called me. He said he thought you were good for the community."

"Bull hinky! What he really wants is for me to come back down there and write a book featuring him!" I exploded. "That idiot doesn't seem to realize that my last book didn't do him any favors. He came off as a bumbling Barney Fife, which he is, and HE DID NOT SOLVE ANYTHING!"

Gracie Blanche, bless her heart, said, "I really think Dewitt wants to get one of them tv jobs like you got Rob."

It was a conspiracy! I had to give Dewitt credit. The man had been busy taking action to get everyone he thought who might have any influence on me call me. The bad news is he doesn't have the sense God gave a goose. I had been as gentle as I possibly could in my book but he still came across as looking like a buffoon. I can't imagine why Dewitt thinks a major news channel would want to use him for anything.

The phone again. I recognized the area code but not the number. What had I done to seriously annoy the Po'thole spirits? I was beginning to wonder if I needed to call Rey-Rey, the friendly Atlanta Jamaican voodoo queen. Her store Spirits B Gone was heavily rumored to be very effective in getting rid of unwanted ghosts. Mind you, I had only seen her ads in the glossy, high-end magazines, I didn't actually know anyone who claimed to use her services. So, obviously, she was making enough money to cover those ridiculously expensive ads.

I was receiving more than phone calls from Northeast Florida than I was from my own office. I cursed everyone and everything that I could think of while pouring another cup of my super-charged go-go juice. I was still wearing my Screw You tee shirt from last night. What's the point in putting on clothes if you're not going to leave your house?

After the sixth ring and my voicemail not picking up, I answered the phone.

"Parker here."

"Hey, I haven't talked to you in a coon's age. Ya gotta minute?"

I answered cautiously, recognizing the voice. "Yes."

"Something weird is going on in Po'thole. I think we need your help."

"But I'm not a private eye or even a detective. I'm just a writer who writes about true crime stories. I own a computer consulting company. Why does everyone and his brother want me to come back to Po'thole? I hate it there!" I wailed. "Did Dewitt ask you to call me?"

I was on the verge of hanging up the phone.

"Dewitt? What does he have to do with anything? I'm calling

you 'cas you live up north in a big city and have more experience with bigger fish playing in a pond."

"I do not live up 'north,' as you put it. Atlanta is not north. It's still the South, the deep South." I archly replied.

"It's north of Po'thole and that's I meant." A slight pause. "Parker, I think I'm being followed. I'm pretty sure my phones are tapped and I think someone's spying on me on my computer. I need your help. I don't trust anyone here."

I was suspicious. "Dewitt's not involved on any of this?"

Sigh, "Parker, the man is denser than a box of bricks, you know that. If he knows anything about anything, it's by accident and he probably doesn't even realize he knows anything."

"Why me?" I wailed. "I hate it there. I escaped as soon as I got out of high school and until Gracie Blanche somehow, and I still don't understand how, got me to come back and help her with the Full Moon Crappie Festival, I haven't been back there in twenty years and look at what happened! Besides which, where were you the entire time I was there? I never saw or heard from you at all."

Silence.

"Parker, I need your help."

"Tabitha, what about Tony Bugs? Can he help you?"

"Think about that for a minute, Parker, and then ask me again."

Ding, ding, ding! Could the police chief be in on whatever is going on in Po'thole?

"Tabitha, are you still in Po'thole or have you finally driven out of the county? You know there are some really nice places in the world outside of Po'thole." I laughed.

"I'm in downtown Po'thole and, yes, I am fully aware there are things that exist outside of our little town. I get National Geographic and the Smithsonian magazines." She snipped at me. "Are you coming down here to help me out or not?"

I sighed. Apparently the Universe was playing a cruel and unusual trick on me. I wondered why I need to go back to Po'thole? Twice in one year was waaay too much. Especially since I had not been in there in the twenty years prior to this year.

"No!"

"Parker, you uppity Yankee! Get your fanny back down here to help me!" Tabitha shouted.

"I. AM. NOT. A. YANKEE!! Let me get this straight, I haven't been back to Po'thole since I left high school and finally Gracie Blanche talks me into coming back ONE TIME, I repeat ONE TIME, for that stinking antique show. There were three murders, none solved by that incompetent dim wit you have for a sheriff. I write a best-selling book where NO ONE, repeat NO ONE comes off looking good except for, maybe, the Middle Eastern guys, and now you want me to come back down, twice in one year, to help you?! Are you guys flipping looney tunes down there? Are you smoking the funny weed? Pray tell, how did you manage to survive all those years without me? You don't need me! Get someone else to figure out your problems. They're not mine and I AM NOT COMING

BACK TO PO'THOLE!" I slammed the phone down, sweating profusely.

The phone rang again.

"Leave. Me. Alone. I. Am. Not. Coming. Back. To. Po'thole."

"Parker."

"What?" I snapped. I hadn't looked at my caller I.D. because I was so sure it was Tabitha calling me back. Turns out it was my office calling. I told Missy about the phone calls from Po'thole.

Missy laughed, "Sure you don't want to go down there? After

all, you had such a great time the last time and you made a lot of money from your book about it."

I slammed the phone down. Normally, I never hang up on anyone but my nerves felt like they'd been dipped in sugar and then flung into a hot fryer. There was NOTHING that was going to make me go to Po'thole! I was wrong.

Chapter 3

My day got considerably better after all of the phone calls from Northeast Florida. I changed clothes. The sun had come out, rare in Atlanta, and I pushed away all of the morning's phone calls.

"So What" started playing on my cell phone. I glanced at the caller I.D. and it showed an unknown number. This was nothing unusual. Due to the nature of my computer consulting work, I had clients who often didn't want anyone knowing what their phone numbers were.

"Hello."

"Parker," a long pause, then, "I don't care what you hear, I didn't do it. I didn't kill Scooter or Tabitha."

Whoa! You could slap me and call me Sally and gotten the same response.

"Misty Dawn? Is that you?" I was stunned to put it mildly, and what the heck was she doing calling me again? What was she saying about Tabitha? My mind had completely clouded over.

"I didn't do it!"

"Wait, wait! Don't hang up, Misty Dawn!" I shouted. Tears were springing to my eyes unannounced. "What did you just say about Tabitha?"

"She's dead, murdered."

I thought I detected a note of sadness in Misty Dawn's voice.

"Wait! What do you mean dead? I talked with her a few hours ago."

"She's dead. You were the last call she made on her cell phone."

I tried to capture my thoughts that were bouncing around in my head like a pinball machine. Nothing was making sense.

"Misty Dawn, what are you talking about?" My mind was racing. "Wait! How do you know what the last call on her cell phone was unless you were there?"

Horrified, I wondered if this was some sort of sick joke Misty Dawn was playing. Maybe she really had gone off the deep end. Maybe the sugar and caffeine combination had truly pushed her into menopausal hell.

"I was supposed to meet with her and the door was open. I went in, she was on the floor, and she was dead. I wondered who she might have talked to last. It was you." Her voice was flat, emotionless. "I wiped off my fingerprints."

The phone disconnected.

Tabitha and I had been friends since grade school. She was the first person I ever told that Mikey had kissed me, on the lips, in second grade. Turns out Mikey kissed every girl on the lips in the second grade. It probably wouldn't surprise you to know that at last count Mikey was on his fourth wife.

Tabitha was one of my sources of Po'thole information. Although we could go months on end and not talk when we did it was like putting on a pair of old comfortable slippers. We picked right back up where we had left off.

I made another phone call.

"Gracie Blanche speaking. How may I help you?"

"Gracie Blanche, it's Parker…"

"Ooooh, I knew you'd come back to help me at…"

"Gracie Blanche, I need you to call Tony Bugs and tell him that Tabitha is dead. At her house."

Silence, then, "Parker, girl, you had better get yourself a good attorney 'cas nobody in Po'thole is going to be happy about you killing Tabitha. She was a very nice person and a member of First Baptist and we protect our own. You know what I mean."

I sighed, "Gracie Blanche, I didn't do it. I'm in Atlanta. I just received an anonymous phone call saying she was dead. Would you pu-lease call the cops and find out if she is actually dead?"

"Parker Louise Bell, you do try my patience at times. You know that?"

Once again, I was staring at a blank phone. I do not like

it when someone just disconnects without saying goodbye. It's okay for me to do it, but no one had better do that to me.

I called the office and told Missy to get the party wagon ready to go to Po'thole. I needed to hit the road first thing in two days.

"Where are you going to stay since your house blew up the last time you were down there?"

"Um, I don't suppose a new one could be built overnight, could it?" I didn't even think about my house...or lack thereof.

"Of course, it can be. It's just a question of how much money do you want to spend and what you want it to look like." Missy paused and then said, "What about a double-wide mobile home? That can be set up and done by the time you get down there."

I groaned. Living in mobile homes when I was growing up meant you were poor, white, trashy, and your mental light bulb was never going to glow in the darkness of the world. I am fully aware that this is not necessarily the case now and

I have seen some lovely double-wides...however.

"Missy. I don't care what you do. I don't care if it's a popup tent. Whatever you do, it's just got to have air conditioning and heat. The weather's weird this time of year down there."

"Give me three days, Parker, and it will be done."

"What am I supposed to do for three days?" I almost shouted.

"Um, come into the office and see all of the new clients we have because of the publicity from the last trip to Po'thole?"

Chapter 4

Two days later, I was on my way to Po'thole. My heart isn't going pitty-pat, my stomach isn't doing the tap dance of the seven fat ugly women, there's a travel mug full of coffee in my car cup container, and I am actually in a good mood. Darn it! The earth must have spun on its axis backwards.

I punched Gracie Blanche's number.

"Gracie Blanche speaking. How may I help you?"

"It's Parker."

"It's about time you called back."

"Tony knew I was coming back. I talked to him right after you told him to call me. Thanks for that."

She sniffed, "You'd think my close personal friend Parker

Bell would have thought to call me and tell me that also, wouldn't you? But, nooo, apparently not.

"What do you want?" Gracie Blanche's tone was anything but friendly and to think the girl worked in customer service.

"I'll be back in town later today."

"You're not staying with me."

"Since when have I ever stayed with you, Gracie Blanche?!" I snipped back. "I'm staying at my house. Well, on my property. Guess I'll see you around." I punched the End button on my cell phone.

Missy didn't tell me anything about my new abode except that she was "pretty sure" I was going to like it. As long as it had air conditioning, I didn't care. Apparently, I was in denial.

Driving up the street and seeing a double-wide mobile home on my property caused me to burst into tears. Let me hasten to add, I cry once every four years for five minutes whether I need to or not. The word "cry" is not in my vocabulary.

I felt like my guts had been ripped out inch by inch. My house, while I never lived there after leaving Po'thole, was the last thing that semi-tied me to the semblance that my parents weren't really dead. They were just at the grocery store and hadn't come home yet. It's amazing what our brains can use as an excuse.

That double-wide brought out sobs and heaving that I didn't know existed within my body. My brain completely shut down. My vehicle rolled into the driveway and I fell over in the front seat in the fetal position. I didn't know how long I had been laying there when Bill Weeble, the elderly next door neighbor who is the nosiest person I had ever met, tapped on my window.

I ignored him. The man couldn't hear jack poo-poo and talked in circles. The last person I wanted to talk to right now was him. Apparently that wasn't meant to be.

"Parker, Parker." He tapped again and slightly raised his voice from a raspy whisper to a subdued level. "Parker, Parker. Are you drunk and passed out?"

Yeah, like if I was drunk and passed out, why would I answer a stupid question like that?

"No. Leave me alone. I'm fine." I refuse to get up and engage in what Bill calls normal conversation. I call it talking in circles and going nowhere. It's kind of like sitting in a rocking chair, it's all motion. Three hours later, you're still in the same spot. Same thing talking to Bill.

Tap, tap, tap. "Parker, if you're drunk and dead in there, I'm going to go to the police."

"Bill," I shouted. "I'm fine, go away."

"Parker, I think you're dead. I'm going to call the police now."

I laid there for a few more seconds when it dawned on me that having the police here wasn't a good thing. I hauled myself up. Bill had the speed of a pregnant turtle. He had only walked eight feet when I jumped out of the car.

"Bill," I shouted. Those so-called state-of-the-art hearing aids he had gotten from the Veterans Administration apparently had been purchased in bulk at a closeout-discount place in Southeast Asia somewhere because Bill sure couldn't hear with them.

He didn't respond. I tapped him on the shoulder. He jumped.

"Parker, I thought you were passed out drunk in your car."

"Bill." I was almost shouting at the top of my outdoor voice. "It's a van. I don't get drunk and

I'm fine. You don't need to call the police. I'm fine."

"Then why were you laid out in your car? Did you know some folks came by here and put up that trashy trailer on your property?"

He puffed out his skinny, sunken in chest. Heck, maybe he was just taking a really deep breath. I couldn't tell. "I tried to stop them but they ignored me."

"It's a van. You tried to stop them from putting up something on my property, Bill? Now why would that be?" I know better than to ask him questions but somehow I just can't help myself.

"Because it's a trailer and trailers have no business in our neighborhood." He paused, "Besides which, it will bring down the value of our property."

He waved his hand at me in a very dismissive fashion. "Only white trash live in these things and your mom and dad would have a fit if they knew you did this."

While I knew my parents wouldn't be happy, it was really crappy that he brought it up. I was not feeling warm, compassionate thoughts about Bill Weeble.

"Bill, it is a modular home, not a double-wide mobile home. It does have landscaping…"

He interrupted me, "It doesn't have those pretty azalea bushes out front like your mom had."

I gritted my teeth. "That's true, Bill, but I don't like azalea bushes and…"

Elizabeth Weeble poked her head out of the house. "YOU DON'T LIKE AZALEA BUSHES?! WHAT IS WRONG WITH YOU?"

I'm sure that everyone in Po'thole now knows I'm back and I'm reasonably sure someone from the garden club will be prancing by my property any moment with tips on how to speed up the process of having fully blooming weed bushes aka azaleas in February although it was only October. The darn things are as ugly as home-made sin to me. They only bloom two weeks out of the year and the rest of the time give inspiration to the camouflage manufacturers. Oh, wait, the manufacturers haven't changed the color or pattern of camouflage in decades. Azaleas are just ugly and serve no useful purpose to mankind.

"Bill and Elizabeth, it's nice to see you're up and about. I'll catch up with you at another time." Being polite and courteous isn't one of my stronger gifts but I do try. I thought I came across as a polite neighbor but who knows what the Weebles thought?

Entering the modular home, and, yes, it was a modular home and not a double-wide as I had first thought, Missy had done a great job in having it decorated and with furniture that suited my personality. Everything had that new smell. I had a coffee table to put my feet on. The air conditioning was cold, food and coffee were in the kitchen, the water worked, I was a happy camper. There was actually a land line for my computer and, bless Missy's heart, I had a new laptop on the countertop.

I called Tony. He was out and would call me upon his return.

I realized Missy had been kind enough to have someone leave me a week's worth of the Po'thole Daily News. Not having anything else better to do, I caught up on all of the local happenings.

Scooter Travis being murdered and not having a clue as to motive or who did it captured a good portion of the paper's space for the past week. There was a lot of re-hashing of what Scooter was known for and some of the projects that he was working on including the plans for a casino.

I darn near dropped my teeth out of my head when I read that. Casino? What would a casino want with a rural, economically depressed, little town where the IQ barely rated over the mentally challenged level?

Of course, a casino would be perfect for the local economy and for laundering money. Cash is extremely hard to trace. But what was the connection with Scooter? According to Gracie Blanche, during one of her many "is he ever going to leave his wife" calls, Scooter was a capitalist from the get-go. He believed in God, apple pie, and a fat bank account, including one in the Cayman Islands that his latest wife didn't know about but Gracie Blanche did.

Casino people would definitely not want to knock off someone who was on their side and especially not a mayor who was pushing their agenda.

Tabitha, while very popular in town, only had one day's worth of free publicity. Odd that a city commissioner had only one day's coverage while a former mayor, allegedly crooked, got several days' worth. Sad to know that it probably wouldn't help any of her many worthwhile charities and causes. I felt an ache in my heart that I probably wasn't the best friend Tabitha had because I wouldn't move back to the town time forgot but I always returned her phone calls and we did talk about three or four times a year on the phone. What I really ached for was the knowing of one of my childhood friends was no longer here on earth, that I would never hear her laughter again.

It was a not so subtle reminder that I was getting older and that time is fleeting. Wait! I started to shake it out. I wasn't that old and things happen. Why I came back here was still puzzling to me. It was like I was drawn to come back here and find out what happened to my friends.

Okay, it was bad enough that Bobby, Buddy, and Jack had been murdered when I was here the first time but I didn't have a warm, fuzzy friendship with any of them. Scooter and Tabitha were a different story. I knew them well and in some small way I wanted to help find whoever had murdered them.

Oh, heck, who am I kidding? I did want to help find their murderers and why they were killed but I was also wondering if there might another book in it for me. The Murderous Little Town in the South had a nice ring to it.

I decided to go over to the house before the funeral tomorrow morning. Nothing looked out of place at Tabitha's house. I went to the back porch door and looked in. Newspapers and old magazines were scattered all over the floor. That looked normal. The back door was locked. I pounded on the door. No answer. Although Sox and Cutie Pie, the cats, were sitting on the kitchen countertop looking bored, that was also normal. I couldn't see anything out of place. Although I vaguely wondered what the cats were still doing in the house.

Tabitha's house looked just liked I remembered...magazines strewn all over the sofa, coffee table, and floor. Ironically, these were Architectural Digest, Better Homes & Garden, and the bible of all Southern women, Southern Living magazines. One would think she might have applied some of their decorating tips to her own home but apparently it was just better reading and thinking about it versus actually doing something.

The parlor room, better known as the formal living room to

anyone under the age of fifty, was covered in a fine layer of dust and looked like it did the day Tabitha's mother had passed on over to the other side. The room was a shrine. Clear plastic furniture covers protected the fabric from the everyday dirt and grime of someone's clothes. I was so glad no one did this anymore.

Tony Bugs had told me on the phone that she had been shot in the parlor. This brought up a whole slew of questions. What was Misty Dawn doing in the parlor? Tabitha never went into that room. It was a shrine to her late mother. The room hadn't been changed, dusted, or vacuumed in probably thirty years. The sofa was still wrapped in vinyl and the lace doilies were on the sofa's armrests for Sunday company. This was an allergy sufferer's worse nightmare. If Tabitha were found in that room, then she had definitely been murdered.

Tabitha also had a close personal relationship with Mr. Smith and Mr. Wesson and I seriously doubted she would have ventured into that room without either one of them in her hand. If she had done that, then something was seriously wrong. Well, let me hasten to add, any death is seriously wrong but to have Tabitha in that shrine room to her mother something very unusual had to happen. Tabitha was petrified of ghosts and she was sure ghosts were in that room to protect her mother's ashes. Nope, Tabitha wouldn't have gone into that room willingly.

I walked outside and around to the front of the house. Standing on my tiptoes, I tried peering in through the windows. The blinds were closed. I couldn't see anything. I decided to go around to the side of the house. The blinds had been pulled up and the window was shattered.

From this angle I could see where she had been shot and fallen. The blood stain was clearly visible from the window. I imagined the last thing Tabitha did was to put her left hand around the little cross she always wore. Her mother had given it to her when she was thirteen.

The tears started to flow. I managed to get them wiped away as a police cruiser stopped in front of the house. I recognized the chief of police getting out of the car.

"When did you get back into town?" Tony displayed all of the charm of a displaced New Jerseyite, which he was.

"Oh, about thirty minutes ago."

Tony smiled, showing the dimple in his left cheek and twinkling puppy dog eyes. "You know, you still owe me a dinner."

Holy freaking cow! There was a city commissioner who had been murdered and the only thing Tony could think about was a forgotten dinner I had promised him the last time I was in Po'thole?!

"Um, yeah, okay. What about Tabitha though?"

He chuckled. "Well, I don't expect her to go with us."

Men!

I glared at him.

Tabitha had been facing the window, the blinds were up, and the glass had exploded inward because there were tons of it all over the area rug...along with the blood stains. The life of my friend splattered on a rug.

I have witnessed a number of crime scenes in my life and seen god knows how many crime scene photos, but my reaction was one I never anticipated. I burst into tears...again.

Tony Bugs turned and put his arms around me. I felt unexpected warmth and compassion from him. I literally melted into him...in a platonic way, of course. Deep sobs escaped from my normally you-can't-make-me-feel-anything lips. I was vaguely aware that Tony had led me into the house to the dining room and sat me down on a chair.

"Parker," he said gently. "I am so sorry for your loss and I know you're hurting right now but you do know I'm going to have to ask you some questions."

I numbly nodded my head. There was a void inside my brain, everything had slowed down like a snake in winter...sluggish, vapid, and my body seemed to be totally separate from my brain.

I guess I must have fainted because the pungent, nauseating smell of an ammonia capsule was under my nose. Jerking my head away from the capsule, I heard someone say, "She's coming around, Chief."

"Parker, Parker, can you hear me?" Alas, instead of Fabio whispering in my ear and enticing me to run away with him in a steamy dream, it was the professional, detached voice of Chief Buglia prodding me to come back to reality.

"What?" I snapped, sitting up so fast I touched noses with

the EMT holding the ammonia capsule. He's probably going to have nightmares for a while.

Scrambling up, probably not very ladylike – I had not been blessed with that Southern gene of ladylikeness much to my mother's chagrin, I said, "Chief, here's what I know." I told him everything including Tabitha's concern about her phone tapped and being followed.

Tony scratched his head. "Why didn't she come to me about this?"

"What were you going to do about it, Tony? You don't have enough officers to give her twenty-four hour protection. She couldn't afford to pay your off-duty officers to watch her. What? What, pray tell, could you do about it?" Admittedly, my voice had risen and it was full of anger. Realistically, I knew he didn't have an answer.

"Filing a report isn't really going to help much anyway. You know that." I was grumpy.

"Since you seem to have all the answers, do you know who did this?" Tony snapped.

After a few more minutes of terse verbal exchanges, I stomped out of the house and drove back to my new house. I couldn't call it home because it wasn't. Home had blown up the last time I was in Po'thole. This place was merely a poor substitution for home.

The coolness of the air conditioning put a dose of nice back into my attitude. Popping a top, Missy was thoughtful enough to have had a case of my favorite adult frothy liquid libation put in the refrigerator, I wondered what was going on in this tiny little town in Northeast Florida. There were now a total of five murders in less than twelve months. There had never been that many murders in one year since the town was established in 1821. Was there some new discharge being dumped into the once pristine but now contaminated St. Johns River that was affecting only certain members of Po'hole society? Much as I hoped that would be the simple answer, it didn't make any sense.

The newspaper wasn't going to provide all of the little details people talk about. Tony wasn't going to share his findings, he was more interested in our going out to dinner. I strongly suspected I wouldn't get any information from him during dinner either. Dewitt would be over the moon if he knew I was back in Po'thole. He was a last resort. The only two people I knew well enough anymore who probably had a good idea of what was going on was the vice mayor Shelley George and city commissioner Celesta Summers. Gracie Blanche didn't count because she was only interested in what was going on in her world and the Old Fashioned Antique Show and Sale during the Full Moon Crappie Festival.

Celesta is a short woman built like a small high school fullback and wears her curly, reddish, brownish, and grayish hair in a style reminiscent of the 1950's. You definitely want her on your side when it comes to a throw-down involving justice. A pit bull doesn't stand a chance against her.

"You have reached the Summers residence. We don't have

caller I.D. If you would like a return phone call, leave your name and telephone number. I serve the people. God bless Po'thole!"

I laughed. That phone message is a new spin for politicians.

I left my name and telephone number. The next one to call is Shelley George. Shelley has been in local politics since the early seventies. She seems to be the only one on the city commission who is actually interested in trying to move Po'thole forward.

"You've reached vice mayor Shelley George. Leave me a message and I'll return it within the next twenty-four hours. Together we can make Po'thole a better place!"

Maybe it's just me being cynical and not living here anymore, but even for small town politics these phone messages seemed a little strange. Plus, this isn't even an election year.

I left a message on her voicemail also. Apparently I'm the only one in this part of the country who actually answers her phone.

As I am guzzling down my adult foamy liquid libation, "So what" started playing on my cell phone.

"Parker here."

"Hey, it's Celesta. What's going on?" Bam! No nonsense, straight to the point. I love that about Celesta. I explained everything that had happened up to this point.

"Darn! Excuse my cussing!" Nothing like a Southern Baptist swearing. "You know I liked Tabitha. I really did. So, do you think I'm next on the list?"

My ears stood at attention. "List? Celesta, what list? Wait! You don't know her funeral is tomorrow?"

"Someone keeps taking my newspaper and I haven't actually read it in a couple of days. Well, I'm assuming there's probably a list of names and since anyone who knows me knows I'm against a casino coming in here, I'm assuming I'm next on the list. Probably Shelley too."

She chuckled, "If the guys had a pair, they'd be on the list too; but, god forbid, they act like men."

I rolled my eyes, although I didn't disagree with her and was glad that she couldn't see me rolling my eyes. "What makes you think Tabitha's murder has anything to do with a casino?"

"Because that's what's on everyone's mind right now."

"Is it just the women on the city commission that are against the casino? Plus, I thought there are five of you on the commission and if Tabitha, you, and Shelley vote against the casino, then so what?"

"Yeah, but that's the problem, Parker. We haven't voted yet. If something happens to us, it's very possible the casino may go through anyway."

"Wait, wait! With Scooter and Tabitha being murdered, are you sure this is just about the casino or could it be something else?"

"Well, you know, for a small town we always have something coming up." She was thinking, I could hear the wheels turning in her head. "Maybe it's because some of the organizers of the Full Moon

Crappie Festival want to move the beer tents down to the riverfront and some of us don't."

"How did Scooter vote on that?"

She laughed. "Oh, you know Scooter. He voted for it. He sits, well sat, on the board of directors for Bobby Derlicter's Beer Barn."

I knew I was going to regret but I had to ask anyway. "So why don't you want the beer tents down by the riverfront?"

I heard Celesta's teeth start to grind and the big inhale of air certainly indicted I may have unknowingly fallen into one of the seven deadly sins.

"I do not want any beer sold downtown. There are families that come to the festival and children do not need to be subjected to drunks and alcoholics."

"You do realize that most festivals in the United States have beer at them and they rarely have a problem with drunk and disorderly patrons which is what you are suggesting, don't you?" I waited on the explosion.

"We, the citizens of Po'thole who I serve honorably, do not want beer around our children."

"What you really mean, Celesta, is that if you see any First Baptist folks down there having a beer, you think God is going to send them directly to Hades and you don't want that on your conscious." I was almost giggling. Of course, having a beer in my hand that Celesta couldn't see helped a great deal as well.

"Parker, you are really trying my patience! What do you want?"

"I want to know what is going on down here. You've had five people die in less than twelve months. All under suspicious circumstances and, surprisingly, this doesn't seem to upset the sheriff or the chief of police very much. What the heck is going?"

Celesta was silent for a moment. "The library, back room in an hour."

Still chewing on a mint to hide the possible delectable aroma of the beer I had consumed, I found Celesta in the back room. She had on a big floppy hat, sunglasses, and wearing a scarf that looked like it had been her mother's...and her mother had been dead for years. This was not a stylish look. I could only assume she thought she was wearing a disguise and thought she would be unrecognizable. She was wrong.

"Trade places with me. I'm sitting with my back to the glass. If anybody tries to do anything, you just shoot them."

I started to laugh. "Seriously, Celesta, you want me to shoot someone?"

Indignantly, she replied, "Yes, of course, I do. I would much rather you shoot and kill someone rather just watch me get killed. I would like to think you'd protect a friend."

"I'm not carrying a gun and what makes you think someone wants you dead?"

She put her hand to her mouth in shock. "You're not carrying a gun? What's wrong with you?! I always carry one! Trade places with me. You're pretty worthless sometimes, Parker!"

"Well, Celesta, better folks than you have told me that. Regardless, let's get down to brass tacks. What the heck is going on here?"

We swopped places. Glancing continuously at the glass window behind me, Celesta filled me in on the very slight possibility of a casino coming into the city. Her concern, keeping in mind that she is "old" Po'thole, loves it the way it is, and therefore isn't looking for any type of real growth inside the city, is that it will bring in "undesirables."

I shall say we had a very healthy discussion on the potential income that a casino could bring into the city. We finally agreed to disagree with her having the last word. This brought us back to the beginning of the conversation.

"What makes you think someone wants you dead, Celesta?"

"Shelley has received some very strange emails, as have I. Scooter received some too. I don't know about Johnny "Ten Fingers"...."

"Wait! What is Johnny "Ten Fingers" doing as a city commissioner? I thought once he lost the election to Dewitt he was out of the picture."

"Well, you know, he won a chunk of change when he went before the Florida Supreme Court on the election count with Dewitt. It turns out that he actually lives inside the city limits, he qualified to run at the last minute, and beat out Sammy Youell. There were rumors," she wiggled her eyebrows, "that he used his, ah, influence for getting enough votes to win."

I laughed, "I'll bet. So, let me guess, he wouldn't say anything anyway about getting threats because, after all, he gets threats all the time."

She nodded her head. "Yes, if you threaten Johnny "Ten Fingers" on anything, that's pretty much it. You never hear from that person ever again. Supposedly they move out of town but because it's on the north side, you know the cops just don't care and they're not going to do anything much about it.

"They have their own brand of justice over there, if you know what I mean." She nodded her head conspiratorially. "I think Tony Bugs has some sort of agreement with him too."

Unfortunately, nothing she said shocked me. I saw it everywhere, subtle but very effective forms of discrimination...the color of someone's skin, if someone was perceived poorer than the accuser, female. You pretty much didn't get much of a break on anything. Yet if you stood up for yourself, it could be a rough row to hoe.

"So, is Johnny "Ten Fingers" actually running Po'thole?" This could be a very scary thought. Forget the casino, running massive quantities of drugs through town and not having to worry about law enforcement interference was huge. If he had cut a deal with Dewitt, not likely because the man was already too stupid to understand what was going on in his county, or Tony Bugs, this could be bad. According to local scuttlebutt from when I was here the last time, Tony might have mafia connections in New Jersey and if he was looking the other way when Johnny "Ten Fingers" might be doing something illegal, it could appear that he was on the take. Unfortunately, many members of this small, sleepy Southern town on the beautiful St. Johns already strongly suspected that simply because Tony was from New Jersey.

Suddenly Celesta gasped. "I absolutely deplore those gals!" She was frantically pawing through her oversized handbag.

I whipped around and there, with their faces pressed up against the glass window and their tongues leaving unsanitary prints, were the Lady Gatorettes minus one.

Myrtle Sue, Flo, Rhonda Jean, Mary Jane and Misty Dawn, were five married hormonal women and had been friends since elementary school. They wreaked havoc everywhere they went. Believing that caffeine and sugar was an important daily ritual, they consumed more than their fair share. One or the other of them was always on a sugar roller coaster.

In all honesty, I was surprised to see them at the library. Other than being rabid Gator football fans and knowing all of the statistics by heart, I didn't know they were all that interested in the printed word and could read much less visit the library.

Here's the short rundown on these gals.

Myrtle Sue bragged that she had tracked her husband down during hunting season when he had "escaped"— her words—from the house without asking her permission. Southern boys during hunting season don't believe it's necessary to ask their wives for permission to go hunting or explain why they go off in the woods with other men to get sweaty, nasty, dirty, stinky, and still don't have a dead animal to show for what they were doing over the weekend.

Apparently, it was that time of the month for Myrtle Sue and she had come home from a particularly bad time at Wal-Mart and discovered that her husband, the erstwhile J.W., had gone off for the weekend with the boys and left her a note saying he would see her Monday morning before he went to work. And, oh, yes, could he have clean clothes to wear on Monday?

Myrtle Sue saw red. She vowed that J.W. wouldn't have clean clothes for the remainder of hunting season because he'd made the fatal error of not saying "I love you" on his note.

After becoming a graduate of the 90-day Myrtle Sue School of Doing Your Own Laundry, J.W. now leaves notes with a great big I Love You.

Flo is a tall, slim waitress with long blond hair who is now on her sixth husband and makes one mean strawberry pie. Flo's reason for having so many husbands was because not one of them appreciated and loved the Gators as much as she did.

"Humph," she sniffed. "If my husband doesn't have a clue as to who the quarterback is, what type of offense the Gators are running, and who the coaches are, then what good is he to me?"

She also only dates men when it is not football season and that probably explains why she's never noticed that's why they knew nothing about Gator football.

Mary Jane, a very attractive brunette way back when, went to Atlanta for a weekend with some out-of-town cousins upon graduating from high school and upon her return has never seemed quite right. There was much speculation that she had indulged in some cheap street pharmaceuticals and that was the reason why she's just never been quite right. No one knows for sure—she's never explained—and her out-of-town cousins disavow knowledge of anything. They also have never visited her ever again.

Apparently not realizing New York City is bigger than Atlanta, she moved there for a brief moment in time. She thought she was in love with the city that never sleeps at night, changed her mind after a year, and came back. She's still a redneck but now has an educated palate. She also dates guys that she meets on the Internet. While the rest of the Lady Gatorettes occasionally scold her for surfing for men on the Internet, they are all secretly envious of her.

Rhonda Jean is the trick play master. She knows every trick play that has been in a Gator game for the past thirty-five years. She also annoys the heck out of the coaches at Florida because she creates and sends in new trick plays every week during spring practice and the regular season. Rhonda Jean's fervent wish is that one of her plays will be used during a televised game and the Gators will run in for a touchdown. So far it hasn't happened.

Her husband, Big T, short for Thomas the Third, is pleased as a pig in mud and mighty proud of his wife every time she receives a letter from the coaches. He just knows that one day one of his wife's plays will be used and then they will both be national celebrities. That's the reason why Big T gave up chewing for dipping. Dipping didn't turn your teeth as brown and he's very proud of his big smile. Also, he doesn't want to look like a big old Southern redneck on national TV. The bad news is, Big T poaches game and all the Fish & Game Commission people know him all too well.

Misty Dawn, the only Lady Gatorette not plastered up against the window is in their version of the Witness Protection Program. Misty Dawn is a good person to have on your side. Why she called to tell me about Tabitha still has me puzzled.

She was so named because that's what the morning looked like the day she was born and her mother took that as a naming sign. She sends encouraging cards and notes to all of the football players who play in each game. She was tickled pink when one of the players mentioned on national TV that it was her cards and letters that helped him during the difficult ordeal of his brother being arrested for dog fighting.

Misty Dawn, unfortunately, isn't quite as dainty as what her name might indicate. She has the vocabulary of a cross-country truck driver. And, oh, yes, she has a very short fuse on a very hot temper. The woman carries grudges like Christians forgive sins.

It's too bad that Misty Dawn didn't joined the Navy. Swift, silent, and deadly, she would've made a natural Navy Seal. The only person she's never gotten mad at is her husband John Boy. She thinks he walks on water.

John Boy works construction and is afraid of no one; however, he absolutely quivers when she walks in the house with that death-to-the-world glint in her eye.

The one time he had not let her vent, she had gone out to the chicken house and they ended up eating chicken for a month. He was glad that the only thing she had killed was fifteen chickens. As he confided to J.W. one night over beer, he was mighty happy he didn't have pigs or cattle on his ranchette because Misty Dawn might've killed them, too.

Leaning back from the glass, the gals broke out in raucous laughter and started waving at me. Celesta by this time had drawn out her Lady Smith .38 gun. This made the Lady Gatorettes laugh even louder.

They charged into the room. I honestly thought Celesta was going to shoot one of them but instead she started to laugh also. A little nervously perhaps but she laughed. I, on the other hand, cringed because I knew it was me they wanted to talk to not Celesta. Although with her big ego I was pretty darn sure she was convinced they had come to see her. After all, she "represented the wishes of the people." I was merely a turncoat who had left the beautiful, thriving metropolis of Po'thole.

They all turned to me and started jabbering up a storm. I had absolutely no clue what they were saying.

"Wait, wait, ladies!" I threw up my non-coffee drinking hand in a stop motion. "Y'all take a deep breath and then one, ONE, of you tell me what's going on."

"Misty Dawn couldn't be here," started Myrtle Sue.

I cocked an eyebrow at her.

"But she did tell me she had called you."

"What?!" exploded Celesta. "You didn't tell me that, Parker!"

I shrugged.

The Lady Gatorettes turned and stared, hard, at Celesta before turning back to me.

"Misty Dawn does have her good side and she does have a high moral sense of justice," stated Myrtle Sue. Noticing my quizzical expression, she hurried on, "It might not be the same as yours or Celesta's but she does have one."

"Anyway, she did not kill Buddy, Bobby, or Happy Jack. She also did not kill Scooter or Tabitha. Tabitha was always nice to us."

Celesta just couldn't help herself and blurted out, "Tabitha thought all of you were looney tunes."

Rhonda Jean whipped around, eyed Celesta like she might view the devil invading upon her territory, and said, "Mama always told me if you can't say something nice, you shouldn't open your mouth. Let me point out, we ALL voted for you and Tabitha. Not once did Tabitha ever say anything mean about us.

"Also, let me point out, you sure don't have any problems with taking our money when you're running for office and you need some of them purty signs put up.

"You might," glared Rhonda Jean, "want to be nice to us."

The other Lady Gatorettes nodded their heads up and down vigorously. Celesta did not grovel, back down, or otherwise acquiesce. In fact, the woman fueled the fire by saying, "I return your phone calls when no other city commissioner will and I..."

Jumping into the fray before parts of dead bodies started being flung around the room, I said, "Ladies, stop! Myrtle Sue, please finish telling me what's going on."

"Tabitha had gotten word to Misty Dawn that she needed to talk to her."

Flo popped up with, "Tabitha wanted us to be her protection squad."

"Flo! How could you!"

"Flo, hush your mouth!"

"Flo, I'm gonna...."

I vaguely wondered why the library didn't put a Keurig in each room. I needed some coffee.

"Okay, enough! Myrtle Sue, finish your story before I get up and walk out of here."

"Parker, some of the city commissioners have been getting death threats." She looked over at Celesta. "Tony Bugs told us we had better stop doing that or he was going to lock us up during football season and wouldn't let us watch Gator football!"

They all wailed in unison. I swear it sounded just like a wolf pack. "Nooooo, nooooo, noooo!"

"Then Dimwit, ah, Dewitt, told us the same thing and, Parker, we didn't do it. We're being framed!" Tears were flowing down their cheeks like a faucet had been turned on.

Oh, I could easily understand why Tony Bugs and Dewitt had told them that but what neither of them didn't understand was that the Lady Gatorettes would escape from their pitiful jails within two nanoseconds if they were locked up during Gator football season.

That new construction both of them wanted done on their respective jails? Done. The Lady Gatorettes would simply find a way to ramrod through the concrete blocks so they could see their beloved Gator games on time. And trust me when I say it would be done in less than two hours.

The combined IQ on both of these law enforcement officers was starting to edge close to that of a turkey.

"Okay, okay. You do understand why someone might think you had something to do with all of these murders, don't you?"

A chorus of Nos erupted from them and they all looked at each other like a calf looks at a new gate. They didn't have a clue. I was really longing for Atlanta now. It must be something in the water that makes the residents of Po'thole dumber than dirt.

"Um, y'all do realize you create havoc everywhere you go, right?" I tried another tactic.

"Things just happen to us, Parker. Weird things, you know that."

Celesta snorted. I rolled my eyes.

"Really? You're taking absolutely no responsibility for any of your actions, you're playing the victim role, and you expect me to believe that. Come on now!" I stood up. I was going back to Atlanta. The devil could hang onto what was or was not happening in this crappy little town. I was going home.

"Misty Dawn thinks she knows who killed Bobby, Buddy, and Happy Jack."

I was halfway out the door. "Great! Go tell Tony Bugs or Dewitt. I'm going back to Atlanta."

Then, "Joe D., Parker, Joe D. killed them."

I almost sank to the floor right there. The world that was looking brighter and brighter because I was going back to Atlanta suddenly dimmed and I felt like I had been sucked through a black hole in the universe.

"Wh...what?"

"Misty Dawn thinks Joe D. killed them. Think about it, he's run off and hasn't been seen since all of the murders. No one has heard from him."

Much as I hated to admit it, and I certainly wasn't going to with this group of women, the thought had crossed my mind as well.

Joe D. Savannah, my first love boyfriend, was the owner of We Make Money, CPAs. While he always professed his undying love for me, he couldn't keep his pants zipped up and had been married numerous times. He did come visit me in Atlanta between wives for "a high school reunion." There was a very special spot in my heart for Joe D.

"Have you heard from him, Parker?"

I shook my head no. I was still trying to process that Joe D. might have had a part in three murders.

"Do you think he had anything to do with Scooter or Tabitha?" I didn't realize the words had inadvertently materialized and escaped out of my mouth.

The Lady Gatorettes looked at each other and shrugged. Celesta banged her hand on the table. "Let's go find that son-of-a-gun and throw away the key."

As the remaining four Lady Gatorettes and a city commissioner rushed out the door to find and crush a circumstantial suspect in three maybe five murders, it suddenly occurred to me that I might be the only sane one in the group. My therapist was going to have a field day with that.

Chapter 5

"I told you I didn't kill anyone."

Unless I was in the middle of a horrifying nightmare, Misty Dawn was standing in the middle of my bedroom. I supposedly have a state-of-the-art security system in this house and there was dead silence in my room. No alarms, no frantic beeping, no nothing. My heart, on the other hand, was pounding like crazy.

"Misty Dawn, how the heck did you get in my house without the security system going off and what do you want?" I was throwing covers off and struggling to get out of bed.

"You might want to stay put, Parker. I have Dirty Bertha aimed at you."

Talk about another heart stopper! Dirty Bertha was Misty Dawn's renaming of the .44 Magnum Smith & Wesson Model 29 gun made famous in the Dirty Harry movies starring Clint Eastwood. She's the only female, make that a person, I know who can hold and shoot that baby cannon with only one hand.

I eased myself back into bed. I surmised that if she shot me it would be a lot easier and cheaper to remove the bed with bloodstains than it would be to replace the carpet. Also, the house resale value would be better.

Barely making out her dark silhouette in the room, I reached for the lamp.

"Nope. You don't need that light on. You know who I am and you don't need to see anything else."

"Come on, Misty Dawn, what is going on in this stinking town? This whole thing is becoming very annoying. I hate Po'thole and I want to go back to Atlanta!" I was almost sniveling at this point.

"Shut your eyes."

"No! If you're going to kill me, you're going to have to do it with my eyes open and when you do, the last darn thing you'll ever see are my eyes and I'll be placing a Biblical curse for generations to come on you and your descendants!" I was mad.

She chuckled, "Just shut your eyes, Parker, I'm not going to shoot you. I coulda done that when I first came in here."

Okay, I'm not normally a rule-follower but in this case it seemed like a wise thing to do. I counted to sixty, rather quickly but I did count to sixty and wondered the entire time if this was going to be the last thing I ever did.

Cracking an eye open, I didn't see any dark shadows. Opening both eyes and turning on the lamp, there was no Misty Dawn standing before me.

I jumped up and ran from room to room and all of the little security system contacts were still in place and the panel showed everything safe and secure. I now realized what a fallacy that was. What a false sense of safety and security those systems are and how the American public had bought into it. A multi-billion dollar a year business preying on the fears of people knowing full-well their systems could be hacked, apparently very easily, by a female redneck. I wondered if Misty Dawn could do the same thing with my computer system. A fleeting thought crossed my mind that maybe I should put her on payroll and let her hack into things for me. I dismissed it almost immediately because I was pretty sure she had no clue on what to do with computers.

I was wrong.

Chapter 6

"What, Parker?" A very sleepy Missy answered her cell phone. "Do you realize it's three a.m.? If you need a new laptop, I can overnight it to you when I get in the office."

"That's not it."

"You mean you're actually calling me about something other than killing off another laptop?"

"Missy, I need one of the guys to troubleshoot my laptop remotely. I need to find out if anything is being re-routed or hijacked from my laptop. I also need to know how this new top-of-the-line security system you had installed here can be hacked." I then told her everything that had gone on.

"I'm on it." I could hear her getting out of bed. "I'm going to send Denny down with the new party wagon."

"Really? Two of the party wagons here in Po'thole? Don't you think that's going to wave flags with Homeland Security, the FBI, the CIA, ah...." I spluttered.

"They already know you're there."

"What? How? Who told them?"

"I guess they tracked you by satellite once you were more than an hour out from Atlanta."

"Missy, how do you know these things?"

"Don't ask."

"Is there anything painted on top of the party wagon?"

"Not that I'm aware of but that doesn't mean anything."

"Missy, you're supposed to make sure of these things!" I needed coffee because I sure wasn't going back to sleep at this point.

"Let me re-phrase that, Parker. There was nothing painted on top of the party wagon when it left Atlanta. However, if a flock of birds flew over it and deposited their waste on top, then, yes, there might have been a bug planted in that poop. How the heck am I supposed to know?" She was seriously annoyed and Missy rarely got upset with me.

"Okay," I grumbled. "Talk to you later."

This whole thing kept getting bigger and bigger...and, what was worst, nothing made any sense. None of the murders seemed to have any connection. The only common factor in the first three murders was barbeque. With Scooter and Tabitha, possibly a casino connection or maybe a drug connection with Johnny "Ten Fingers." But, it still didn't make any sense.

Finally, Hawaiian Delight finished making. I took a mouthful, swallowed it, and realized immediately this coffee was meant for little old ladies eating cookies at a church social. It was weak and nasty. I promptly poured the rest of it down the sink. Scrambling around in the cupboards I found African Dark. God bless Missy for having the cabinets stocked with five different premium coffees.

Finally, a decent brew worthy of being included in the nectar of the gods. I inhaled the first cup. The mist from my sleep deprived brain lifted. The second cup brought some clarity back into my life.

While Joe D. had disappeared, I didn't believe he had anything to do with the other murders much less Scooter and Tabitha. I didn't think all of them were clients and that he murdered them to cover up any financial wrongdoings on his part.

Johnny "Ten Fingers", while more on the criminal intent side, didn't seem to have any real interest in doing away with these folks. It appeared to me that he was trying to turn his life around. I was pretty sure no one else in town would agree with me but it was a possibility. At the very least, he was trying to look legitimate.

The Lady Gatorettes did know everyone and they were hormonal and sugar-and-caffeine infused every day. You just never knew what they were capable of. There was a distinct possibility that they had gotten royally ticked off at each person and decided it was time for them to go meet their maker. I could see them...maybe...killing off one person but not everyone else.

Misty Dawn was a loose cannon at best; however, if she told you she didn't do something, then I believed her. The Lady Gatorettes might be nuttier than a house of squirrels but they did tell the truth.

I heard some noise outside. I flipped on the porch lights just as Bon Jovi's "Livin' on a Prayer" blasted through speakers the size of a small pickup three feet from my door.

Oh, great! Things just kept getting better and better. Either someone was trying to send me a warning message or they were telling me time was short. Regardless, I was pretty sure it wasn't Jehovah's Witnesses commenting on my less than sterling life.

Chapter 7

I was more than delighted to see Denny Rowe roll up in the driveway in the new party wagon, so named because we could all live uncomfortably in the vehicle for a couple of days. We had been scrunched up together the last time I was in Po'thole. I did not have fond memories of that time, especially since I might have been the one who blew up my childhood home by accident but I was never going to admit that to anyone.

Denny Rowe, ex-FBI, ex-black ops, stood about six three and weighed in the neighborhood of two-hundred and thirty-five pounds. He was sort of on payroll but I wasn't exactly sure what he did and, in all honesty, I probably didn't want to know. I think he might do "specialty" security work for some of our clients. Regardless, he was on my team and I knew he always had my back.

Potus, a very large blond Akita, bounded out of the party wagon like he was chasing a new ball.

"Nooo!" Denny and I both shouted at the same time as Potus unleased his massive body into a welcoming dog hug. As one hundred twenty-five pounds of sheer muscle landed on me before I could curl up into the fetal position, I hoped there would be no broken bones.

I woke up on the couch with a cup of coffee on the table. Slowly I took inventory of my body and concluded that nothing was broken, I wasn't any more swimmy headed than I was before, and Denny had been thoughtful enough to have coffee ready for me. The bad news was I was probably out for about ten minutes and that could indicate a concussion. Rats! The last thing I wanted to do was go back to the ER in Po'thole.

"So, yeah, we're going to the ER." Denny made the decision for me.

"Denny, you've been here less than ten minutes and already

you're wanting to put me away." I was trying to make a joke.

"Parker, you've been out for almost ten minutes and, as much as I would like to blame this on Potus, I think something else must be going on in your brain. You need to be checked." This last was stated with no hope of my charming him into not going.

An hour later I was home resting on the couch. Amazingly, there was no one else in the ER. Yes, I had a concussion and, yes, I probably could have gotten several days of rest IF I were in Atlanta. Being in Po'thole, not so much. No one ever left me alone when I was here.

The phone went off. Unknown popped up on caller I.D.. I cringed and debated whether to answer it or not.

Not feeling like Miss Congeniality, I snapped, "Yeah, what do you want?"

"That dog loves you."

Great! Misty Dawn was apparently now stalking me and watching every move I made.

"Yes, he does." Exasperated. "What do you want Misty Dawn?

You 'bout scared me out of my ever-loving mind last night. Why don't you just come out with it and either tell me what you know or just go away and leave me alone?"

"Ok."

"Ok, what?!"

"Things are not what they seem here, Parker. You should know that."

"Aw, come on, Misty Dawn! You keep talking in circles and aren't making any sense. Just flipping tell what's going on or what you think is going on or I'm not going to answer my phone anymore when you call. I'll just let everything roll over into voicemail and I'll pick it up at my leisure."

Nothing, silence. I looked at my screen, it was blank. That crazy woman had hung up on me! I was furious and questioned her ancestry back as far as I could remember with the most colorful language I could come up with.

Denny suddenly appeared in my line of vision as I was letting loose with a particularly descriptive string of the English language regarding Misty Dawn. He waved a piece of paper at me and put his finger to his lips.

"What?! You've heard me curse before!" It simply didn't register what he was trying to tell me.

He handed me the piece of paper and tapped his finger to his lips again. Potus was sitting at attention in front of me. Ears straight up.

Reading the note, I looked up at Denny. "Really? I have to go back to the hospital? Why?"

"They called on my cell phone and said I needed to bring you back."

I let loose with another string of colorful descriptions on life in general. Other than a construction work site, I was pretty sure none of them would ever be allowed in a family establishment.

After getting comfortable in the party wagon, I asked him, "Are you sure the entire place is bugged?"

Denny nodded. "Yeah, this is all stuff you can't buy here.

Whoever did this got their stuff off some really specialized websites or they know people in the business. This is definitely a pro who set this stuff up. You've been videoed and recorded from the minute you set foot in the house."

"You mean my naked body could be flashed all over the internet?!" I felt nauseous. As a bestselling crime author, the last thing I needed was to have my naked body on the internet. I could see the porn websites having a field day with this..."Crime does pay," "Read

This," or "Ring my bell." Get it, my name being Parker Bell?

"Nah, that's not what this is about. This is about keeping track of your every move."

"Do you think the FBI or Homeland Security is involved?"

"I can't imagine why, Parker, but I'll make a few phone calls and see what I can find out."

"Are you sure no one can hear or see what we're doing right now?"

"Yep. They can see the party wagon but no one can hear or see what's going on inside of here. Checks are run every fifteen minutes, the reports go into Atlanta, and someone sees them. If something looks out of the ordinary, I'll be notified within another ten minutes."

"Let's double check that. Put some type of recording device in here that you know will trip the sensors and let's see how fast someone responds." I growled, "For your sake, it had better be quick, otherwise, I'm firing people today. We're only as good as our weakest link."

Denny nodded. We went to Radio Shack and picked up the

most expensive listening device they had, installed it in the party wagon, made sure it was working, sat back and waited. Forty-five minutes later, I called the office.

"Missy, who handles the security monitoring for Denny's party wagon?"

"Hold on, I think it's Donna and her backup is Timmy. Do you want me to connect you?"

"No. What I want you to do is go back there and find out what they're doing and why no one has picked up on anything. Call me back."

Less than eight minutes later, Missy called me back. "She's sitting back in the bullpen, laughing and joking. I went over to the printer and looked at the report. It shows a lot of red warning text. What do you want me to do?"

I loved Missy, she has been with me since the beginning and she knew what was coming up. My fuse, never long to begin with, was lit and burning down quickly to the explosion.

"Who else is in the bullpen with her? Do we have backups in place for them?"

"Thad, David, Donna, Timmy, and Sally."

"Doesn't that printer make noise, a ding or something, when there is a breach?"

"Yes."

"Okay, I'm going to have Denny add another device in the next couple of minutes. I want you to go back, hang out with them for a few minutes, and see if you can hear the printer going off.

Then I want you to call me when you're back in your office."

Denny was already installing another device.

"How long should it take, Denny?"

"No longer than three minutes, tops."

Eight minutes later, Missy called. "Oh, you can definitely hear it go off and I wasn't blocking her line of vision or hearing."

"What did she do, Missy?"

"She glanced over at it, laughed, and said, "they're playing around again." Then she went back to chatting with everyone." She paused, "Do you want me to fire her?"

I exploded, "She is not taking the security of our company seriously! Fire every single one of them in the bullpen! Have our guys escort them out now. We can mail their personal items to them. Make sure we have their current addresses. Make sure HR makes them sign a notice before leaving the building.

"We're in the security business and these morons can't even properly monitor their boss's vehicle! Geez, Louise, this had never ever better get out! This could affect our clients' confidence in us!"

"Flipping A!" I shouted as I turned back around to Denny. "I pay some of the best money in the country to have these people work for us and they can't even be bothered to check the printer when it dings! Flipping A!"

"Parker, you're firing them. Let it go and let's focus on the problem at hand."

Chapter 8

Denny and I hashed over every detail possible on the case and didn't come up with anything different than what I had. This case was beyond frustrating!

"Maybe I should just call Johnny "Ten Fingers" and see what he has to say." I couldn't think of anything else.

"Do you really think this guy is just going to fall down and confess? Seriously, Parker, this guy has an arrest record of twenty-seven pages! None, I repeat, none of his charges have ever stuck. This guy has never done more than an overnight stay in jail. What do you think you can do with him?"

Denny had a point. Johnny "Ten Fingers" wasn't going to fall down on the ground and spill his guts. He wasn't going to be on the Jerry Springer show any time soon confessing to anything. I would probably end up as gator bait before that occurred. That was not a pleasant thought.

"Denny, why does this guy have all of these arrests and he's never served any time?"

"Probably because he's got a really great attorney that he pays a boatload of money to. You know how this works, Parker."

"Yeah, but I'm guessing there's a connection somewhere between the attorney, Johnny "Ten Fingers" and the government. How else would he keep getting off?"

Denny stared right through me for several minutes, his way of concentrating, and said, "I need to make some phone calls. You need to get out of the party wagon."

As I stepped out of the vehicle, a splotch of red exploded next to my head. Being the ever brave soul that I am, I screamed, grabbed my head, and fell forward onto the ground. I was sure that the red I saw was probably my brains falling out. Turns out it was a red paint pellet hitting the side of the modified camper.

Then I heard it, the very faint sounds of Jon Bon Jovi's "Livin' on a Prayer." Let me be the first to say I love Jon Bon Jovi's music, I think he's cute as a button, and he's got a tush that can lay on my bed anytime BUT his music playing as I think I'm about to be killed is not what I want to hear!

Gun in hand, crouched, Denny appeared in the doorway. Reaching down, he grabbed me with his free hand and lifted me back in the camper. I shouldn't have been but I was surprised that Denny could lift me up with one hand and not feel like he was straining.

"You know, someone really doesn't like you." He growled, "The good news is they have decided not to kill you for whatever reason."

"Two times in less than twenty-four hours," I muttered.

"Parker, what do you know that no one else knows? It's either that or they don't want you back here for any reason, which totally leads back into you know something that you're not supposed to know. I would guess it stretches back to the first three murders. There's a connection here somewhere. What is it?"

"I have absolutely no clue."

"Come on, Parker, think. You gotta have some idea."

I truly had no idea. I spent the better part of the morning thinking about any connections. Most people would call it sleeping.

Chapter 9

People were so packed in the funeral home that if someone fainted they wouldn't hit the floor for two days. The service for Tabitha was very tasteful. Apparently she had had the foresight to actually plan everything out. Charlie, the funeral home director, told me she was the most organized person he had ever met. She had her entire funeral planned for at least five years with annual updates to her obituary. While others might call it organized, I called it for what it was - obsessive compulsive.

There were so many people crammed in there that there was no way I was going to be able to figure out who might have been the murderer.

It was like old home week. I saw people I hadn't seen since high school. There's a reason for that. Whatever they were like in high school they've now had twenty years to perfect those annoying traits. Sad to say, some of them had taken it to the next level.

"Girl, I haven't seen you in a month of Sundays! How you doing?" Most people would stop right there and wait for an answer but nooo, Sally Ann kept right on going. "Did you hear that Tabitha was a member of some devil worshipping cult and that's the reason why she died? She was practicing against God and God smote her down! And..."

I couldn't stand it. "Sally Ann, you know perfectly well that Tabitha was a fine, upstanding member of First Baptist. Do you even listen to what you say? All of that is untrue and you know it. All you're trying to do is make it look like you know something when you don't. Dare I say liar, liar, pants on fire!" I was fuming.

Unfortunately, while there had been the low murmurings usually heard at the end of a funeral service, it was now incredibly quiet. Apparently, my voice had risen when I was going off on Sally Ann and the ever nosy community of folks all wanted to hear what I had to say to Sally Ann. I glanced around when I realized all eyes were on me and saw a couple of bemused looks.

"I never, Parker Bell!"

"Well, yeah, you have, Sally Ann," I retorted. "You gossip every opportunity you get...whether it's true or not. All because you have low self-esteem and you want to seem important to others."

Sally Ann turned beet red and before I knew what had happened, she sprayed me with Cajun Death mace. To say it burned was a major understatement. I howled and dug at my eyes. I couldn't see anything. I was pushing people out of the way and frantically trying to find the ladies restroom.

I heard Sally Ann shouting, "I had to protect myself! I HAD TO! Y'all saw how she was getting ready to attack me!"

I wondered if I turned the Lady Gatorettes on her if that would shut her up. Let me hasten to add, I don't mean forever but maybe have a direct, meaningful experience with Jesus. It was a thought, and one that ran through my head as I was splashing water into my eyes trying to see again.

There was a knocking at the Ladies Restroom door.

"Ladies, it's Charlie. I need to come in there and see how Parker is. Y'all make sure you're decent."

Since I was the only person in there, I hollered out, "Come on in. My eyes are still burning!"

Charlie was handing me a very soft towel to dry my face and

hands on. I'm taking a wild guess and saying it was from the embalming room. I didn't care, it was certainly way softer than the paper towels in the restroom.

"Parker, it's going to take about thirty minutes before that stuff dissipates entirely. Just keep flushing your eyes." He cleared his throat. "Um, the next time you attend one of our services, we do have a private room off to the side for those truly bereaved at the loss of a loved one. You'll be able to see the service but no one can see you.

I think you might be more comfortable there during the services. It has a private exit door as well."

I started to laugh. Finally! A place where I could observe others and not be seen. Of course, the sad part about this was...another person had died.

"Parker, are you okay? We do have smelling salts. A glass of water, perhaps?"

"I'm good, Charlie, I'm good. I was thinking that's perfect. The sad part is another person will have died and I really don't want that."

Charlie smiled, "Death is just a part of life, Parker."

Chapter 10

I was still laughing as I told Denny what happened at the funeral when Tony Bugs showed up. He wasn't amused.

"Parker, did you know Sally Ann wants to press charges against you?"

"For what?! She maced ME! I did not touch or make any threatening moves toward her!" I screeched.

He started to laugh. "Yeah, I heard. 'Bout time somebody called her out."

We all laughed.

"So what brings you over? I'm sure it's not just because of Sally Ann."

"Dinner."

"What?"

"Dinner. You owe me a dinner. What day this week do you want to go out?" He was smiling.

Oh, good lord! I can't find anyone to date in Atlanta, the internet dating sites are full of losers, and the only person who wants to ask me out lives in Po'thole. God truly does have a sense of humor. I don't particularly care for it myself.

Denny was laughing and doing a fist bump with Tony. It's a very sad state of affairs when the "boys" gang up on me. I knew it was coming to this, I really was going to have to go out with Tony Bugs. I was pretty sure I could get him to take me to St. Augustine for dinner so we wouldn't have twenty thousand prying eyes on us and spreading rumors. That could happen on its own and I didn't want to contribute to or make those rumors spread any faster.

"Tomorrow night? Sixish and let's go to St. Augustine?"

"Sure, Parker. Any particular place or do you want me to choose?"

"As long as it's not fast food, anywhere is good with me. Before you ask, yes, I'm a foodie and, yes, I know good food and wine."

"Ooo, she's already talking wine, Denny." Tony winked at him.

"Enough! Tomorrow, pick me up here at six. Now, go away!" I was laughing as he left the house.

"You know, Denny, I think I want to have some fun with Sally Ann."

He groaned, "Don't do it, Parker, don't do it. This could drive her to suicide and how would you feel?"

"I guess 'relieved' isn't an option, is it?"

We were both laughing so hard that Potus just kept quizzically cocking his head back and forth looking at us. I was glad we could humor him.

Chapter 11

The next morning, before nine a.m. and before coffee, there was a pounding on my door. I vaguely wondered why Potus and Denny hadn't stopped whoever it was banging on my door but that didn't register in the sleeping part of my brain.

Various whoops and laughter still didn't register as I stumbled to the door and opened it. There they were, all dressed out in the latest Gator wear. I give you, ladies and gentlemen, the Lady Gatorettes.

That's right, Myrtle Sue, Flo, Rhonda Jean, and Mary Jane were standing there pleased as punch. I might have been angry had they not brought two, count them two, boxes of coffee and two dozen donuts. Denny was standing behind them and grinning like he had won the Florida Lottery.

Ever the gracious hostess, I threw the door wide open. "Ladies, do come in."

Laughing and squealing, they didn't need a second invitation. They poured into the living room. The next thing I knew they were rooting around in the kitchen like French pigs on a truffle hunt. They found the coffee cups and a couple of plates. It was breakfast Southern style. Okay, redneck Southern style but I didn't care because they had brought coffee over. The donuts were a bonus.

Potus had trooped in behind Denny and out of the corner of my eye I saw him go into high alert mode. A very soft growl deep in his throat alerted Denny.

Denny eased around the Lady Gatorettes who were chowing down on the donuts like they had never seen one before. He threw open the back door and almost knocked Misty Dawn off the steps.

More squeals of delight from the ladies and Misty Dawn had donuts and coffee thrust in her hands. I knew the rest of them were still in touch with her!

"Misty Dawn, what the h-e-double toothpick is going on?" Curiosity was about to kill me.

"Can't talk about it right now." She had consumed three donuts pretty much all at one time.

"Sally Ann must be punished," stated Flo in one of her few authoritative voices. Most of the time she sounded a little like a squeaky mouse.

"Yep."

"Yes."

"I don't like her anyway."

"Don't kill her." The last from Misty Dawn as she slurped coffee. Good lord, Miss Manners would have a field day with these gals...or she'd be visiting a therapist on a regular basis, possibly even taking Valium daily.

Denny, laughing, looked over at me. "You really did call them, didn't you?"

Misty Dawn, ever the ladylike individual that she is, reached over and attempted to take Rhonda Jean's custard filled donut. Now Rhonda Jean is the most laid back of the Lady Gatorettes but this very thing had set off a major problem the last time I was here and I had visions of my entire house being destroyed in moments.

Rhonda Jean slammed her meaty fist down on Misty Dawn's hand. Glares were exchanged and then a slow grin on each of their faces. Misty Dawn got the donut and, basically, Rhonda Jean lived to see another day. There was no doubt in my mind that Misty Dawn might could kill Rhonda

Jean, or anyone for that matter, if provoked enough. Of course, killing a friend who's saved your life on a couple of occasions might give you a pass for life with Misty Dawn. I, for one, was not going to find that out.

"Misty Dawn, Sally Ann maced Parker for no reason except, well, she mighta called her out for gossiping but Parker never touched her."

I didn't recall seeing Myrtle Sue or any of the Lady Gatorettes at the funeral but it was so packed the Pope could have been there and I wouldn't have seen him. If they were there and not making a scene, then they truly did like Tabitha.

"Um, ladies, do you think…" I didn't get all of the words out before they were plotting and planning on how to drive Sally Ann crazy.

Misty Dawn stood up. "Don't do anything that's going to cost her a ton of money, don't kill her." She glared at them. "Don't do something every day. Do it every other day. Do something indoors and then do something outdoors. Do Not, I repeat, Do Not make her bathroom blow up and no cherry bombs in the toilet."

They tried to look repentant but it didn't work. They were laughing, I was laughing, Denny was laughing, and I swear I thought I saw Potus was laughing. Misty Dawn got up, laughing with all of the rest of us, waved goodbye, and disappeared out the door. I ran over, opened it, and no Misty Dawn anywhere.

"How does she do that?" I asked.

They looked at each other, shrugged, and Mary Jane said,

"She's one with nature. She just sorta blends in. She does it better than we do. We can blend in but Misty Dawn just seems to have a natural talent for it."

"We can't even see her sometimes," piped up Flo.

Denny thanked them for coming over and bringing coffee and donuts. He also gave them his "emergency" contact number. I'm guessing he's hoping they'll bother him versus me but I kind of doubt that.

"Well?"

"Well, what?"

"Do you think Sally Ann is going to go off the deep end?"

"Don't know, Denny, but I'm pretty sure she'll call Tony on me...again."

"Yeah, speaking of that, don't you have a dinner date with him tonight?" Denny grinned.

It occurred to me that maybe this had been a setup along with the two guys ganging up on me. While I'm sure dinner would be nice with Tony, I had more important things to focus on...like why were so many people being murdered in Po'thole?

Chapter 12

I decided to pay an unannounced visit to Joe D.'s office and speak with Murphy, his partner.

Deciding I probably wouldn't get anywhere if I walked in through the front door. The back door seemed like the best option to me. I very gently and softly knocked on the back door. No answer. Gee, what a surprise!

Taking out my lock picking tools, a jumbo paperclip in this case, I jimmied it while lifting up on the door handle. Least you think I'm a pro at this, Joe D. had actually showed me this little trick the last time I was in Po'thole when he had accidently forgotten his keys. That probably explained why he had jumbo paperclips in one of the cup holders in his car.

I eased on in, carefully shutting the door. I didn't hear any noise which was a little odd but then again it was an accounting office and they are not normally loud folks anyway. Walking down the hallway, I peeked in the main office. No one was there. I guessed the secretary might have been in the ladies restroom. I never could remember her name. Turns out she was in Murphy's office. On his desk. Riding him like a monkey that had escaped from the circus.

Okay, while not appropriate, I burst out laughing. Probably not a good thing to do in case they wanted to charge me with breaking and entering but I was pretty sure they weren't going to do that.

She screamed and wiggled off of him. Murphy rolled off the desk and fell on the floor smacking his head on the desk chair on the way down. He was out cold.

She hissed at me, "I'll kill you if you ever breathe a word of this to my husband or his wife."

I was laughing so hard that all I could do was nod.

"Murphy, Murphy." I had turned him over and was gently slapping his face. Looking up at her, I said, "Help me get his pants back up. We're going to have to call 911 and it would be best if his pants were up and his shirt tucked in. You do it since you're probably, ah, more familiar with his clothing, but hurry."

If looks could kill, I'd be dead. "Or you have the choice of letting them find him like this."

She was trying to get everything tucked in, away, and whatever else while I called 911. I explained that his secretary and I had come into his office and found him lying on the floor.

They asked a lot of questions. Yes, he was bleeding from the forehead. No, I don't know what happened to him. Yes, an ambulance is needed. No, I don't know if he is a diabetic or hypoglycemic. Yes, he's still out cold. The guy could be dead by the time I finished answering all of their questions.

As the EMTs were putting Murphy in the ambulance, I leaned over to his secretary and said, "Don't you think you need to call his wife?"

"You're not my boss."

"Okay, no problem I'll do it." I smiled wickedly.

It was amazing how fast she whipped out her cell phone and called Murphy's wife. I smiled and waved goodbye knowing full well I would never be voted Miss Congeniality by her.

Chapter 13

Other than my diagramming all of the connections to everything that was going on – with no satisfactory answers, I might add – it was turning into a boring afternoon. I decided to pay Murphy a visit in the hospital.

There he was all propped up watching tv. He started twitching when I walked into his room.

"Get out!"

I ignored him. "Murphy, we need to have a short chat and then I'll leave you alone."

He snorted.

"You know you caused me to have a concussion, a severe whiplash, four stitches, and a black eye. I ought to sue your fanny!"

Seriously? This guy is playing the victim in all of this?!

"Really, Murphy? It's MY fault you were doing the nasty-nasty on your desk, cheating on YOUR wife and HER husband AND you left the office doors unlocked? And you're threatening to sue me? For what, you moron?"

Unfortunately, Mona, Murphy's wife, was standing behind me, unbeknownst to either one of us.

"Again? Murphy, you promised!" She wailed. "I truly am telling the paper everything this time! AND, I am filing for divorce."

As she wheeled around to leave the room, me being the ever helpful soul that I am, said, "Mona, here's the paper's phone number."

She took it, glared back at Murphy who was now whiter than the hospital bed sheets, and almost ran out of the room.

"And you've now caused me a divorce."

"Murphy, you need to learn to take responsibility for your actions. Where's Joe D. and what the fon-goo is going on?"

Hoping that Murphy was going to overlook the little white lie I told about the doors being unlocked; but, then again, he probably thought Miss Suzie Cream Cheese had done it. I would imagine Murphy was too focused on the good thing that was going to happen in his office to pay any attention to something as mundane as making sure the doors were locked. Judging from Mona's reaction, this was not the first dalliance he had been caught in either.

Murphy squirmed in the bed. Not looking at me, he murmured, "I dunno."

"Yeah, you do and I'm not leaving until you tell me."

"I'm not telling you anything."

Exasperated and my patience wearing thin, I snapped. "You do realize you could fall out of bed again and damage a lot more of your body, don't you? Like, oh, gee, I don't know, a broken leg?"

That seemed to get Murphy's attention. After all, I hadn't even touched him and he was in the hospital. I could see the wheels spinning in his head.

"Joe D.'s in the Islands."

"Why? What's the connection with him and Bobby, Buddy, and Happy Jack?"

"He started getting threatening letters. You know, death threats. He's scared to death of Misty Dawn, you know."

Why does everything keep going back to Misty Dawn I wondered. I honestly didn't think she had anything to do with any of the murders but that was only a gut feeling and I didn't have any proof one way or another.

"Why is he afraid of Misty Dawn, Murphy?"

"Well, he made a small mistake on her taxes a couple of years ago and the IRS audited her and John Boy. She had to pay a one hundred forty-five dollar penalty. She told Joe D. she was going to cut pieces parts off his body if he ever cost her money again. Then John Boy leaned across Joe D.'s desk and told him he'd better watch himself. Ever since then, Joe D.'s been very, very careful with their tax returns."

I harrumphed. "If she were going to kill him, he'd be dead by now."

Murphy nodded. "You know that and I know that but Joe D. spent several sleepless nights after that. He's finally calmed down now but, during tax season, that boy chews antacids like eating peanuts down at the Beer Barn."

"Where did Joe D. get the money to go stay in the Islands for months on end? I am right in assuming you're not talking about the islands in the St. Johns River, right?"

"You're right. He's in the Virgin Islands." Murphy responded reluctantly.

Another thought came to me. "He didn't take a woman down there with him, did he?" When Murphy didn't answer immediately, I knew what had happened. Joe D. was a complete and utter idiot when it came to women, me withstanding.

"Let me guess, it's someone he met online and he's trying to impress her. That or he's trying to impress someone in a business deal. I'm betting it's the first." If Murphy couldn't see, hear, or feel the frost coming off my words, he was a moron. Oh, wait, I already knew that about him!

Murphy mumbled something I couldn't quite make out.

"WHAT!"

Poor guy, he jumped in the bed. "Ah, online and she's from Norway. She looks like Tiger Woods ex-wife."

Okay, I can't compete with a woman that gorgeous. Regardless, I made a decision that Joe D. and I would not have any more "reunions"…ever. I knew that eventually he'd come crying on my doorstep begging forgiveness and I was the only woman he had ever truly loved, blah, blah, blah. Piglet!

"The money, Murphy, the money. Focus. How did Joe D. get enough money for a long, and I'm betting, lavish vacation in the Islands?" I knew Joe D. was absolutely paranoid about using credit cards because of the interest rates. He wasn't remotely interested in the points and the rewards. He was concerned about the interest rates.

"Well, he might have come into some money."

Danger, Will Robinson, Danger!

"You and I both know his parents didn't leave him any money when they died. We both know he's been divorced umpteen times and didn't fare well in them. We both know he's never going to use credit cards for more than twenty-seven days to avoid the interest charges. So what is it? Did he steal or embezzle the money? I'm taking a wild guess and say he didn't win the lottery."

My tone would have melted ice in Alaska during January.

Murphy shook his head, looking everywhere to see if someone would magically drop in on him and save him from me.

"Or one of y'all's clients needed to launder some funds and since you're both CPAs, Joe D. knows how to do that."

An idea formed in my head. "Does this have anything to do with Johnny "Ten Fingers"?"

Murphy actually started to laugh. "Good god, no. Joe D. might take some chances on different things but he wouldn't dare do anything to Johnny "Ten Fingers". Plus, although I'm not supposed to say, but Johnny's not one of our clients."

My patience level, already very thin at best, exploded. "Where did he get the money, Murphy? I swear I'm going to hold a pillow over your head until you suffocate if you don't tell me!"

Murphy looked scared. "Okay, okay. He found the money."

I glared at him. Not with my mere mortal eyes, but with the eye of the tiger. I was seeing

Murphy shredded, possibly in a quesadilla.

Hurrying on, he said, "He found a bag with one hundred thousand dollars in it in front of..."

I saw a red dot on Murphy's head. Between his eyes. Then the red dot started dribbling down on his nose. It didn't register at first what I was seeing and then it dawned on me that Murphy had been shot. I whipped around, no one. I ran out into the hallway, no one. Only the nurses at the station twelve steps from Murphy's room were there.

"Did you see anyone?" I was frantic. "Murphy's been shot. Did you see anyone?"

Alarms went off, the nurses were scrambling out from behind the nurses station and running into his room. It sounded like they had hit the nuclear war panic button.

Elsa, the head nurse, came back out and confronted me with a cold stare. "He's dead, he was shot."

"Do you think I didn't know that when I came running out to get you?" I snapped.

"You were the only one in that room."

Oh, great! Then it dawned on me, especially since I could now see the security guards approaching me from two different hallways, they thought I had killed Murphy.

Chapter 14

"You're in a world of hurt, Parker." I nodded. I was sitting in Tony's office. I guess the good news was I wasn't sitting in one of the questioning rooms.

"I'm going to share this with you although I shouldn't. There's no one on the security tape in that hallway. No one, from the time you went in until the time you came out, was in the hallway. No one heard anything, no one saw anything."

Tipping back in his chair, he said, "If someone other than you, of course, shot Murphy, then it would have had to come from behind the nurses' station or from the ceiling. The nurses were hustling around like they normally do on their shift, so it's really not possible for someone to shoot from behind them without hitting one of them. The ceiling is so lightweight it couldn't hold the weight of an adult."

I was miserable. I was going to be hung out to dry on something I really didn't do. It's one thing to be blamed for something I did do or maybe have a hand in, but it's a totally different thing when I'm totally innocent. Nothing was making any sense.

"Parker, you know I'm going to have to hold you overnight, don't you?"

I nodded. I had made my one phone call to Denny and he was

supposed to be getting me an attorney but so far no one had showed up. I also wasn't talking until I had one present.

"You know, it's really strange how every time you're around people start dying, Parker. This little town has had more murders in less than a year than we've had in twenty-odd years. Don't you find that a little strange?"

Yeah, actually I did but I wasn't going to say anything until my attorney got here. I knew at this point, if Tony wanted to, and I sure hoped he didn't want to, he could charge me with six murders. I could be sitting here a long time. I wasn't looking forward to the next twenty-four hours.

"Got anything to say for yourself, Parker?"

I nodded. "Guess we aren't going out for dinner, are we?"

Chapter 15

Although I had a private cell, this was not my idea of having fun. I wanted to stay as far away as possible from those other women and I definitely did not want to become anyone's new girlfriend or a friend with benefits.

They glared at me. They didn't look too bad, more like scared baby mamas. I'm guessing that's close to the truth but I didn't see any point to striking up a conversation. They left me alone and I was definitely going to leave them alone.

Breakfast was not enticing and the coffee was the weakest hot brown liquid I had ever put in my mouth. I could barely tell if there was any caffeine in it. I was becoming increasingly cranky.

The deputies soon came down and presented us to the court. It was strangely quiet. Most women I know talk incessantly, these gals acted like they had been given a gag order for a tv show.

Standing before the Honorable Joseph Paul Hungert, I knew that orange is not the new black. It was still dog ugly and identified me as a criminal. I've done a lot of wild and wacky things over the years but never once have I ever spent the night in jail. Let me point out that it has never been on my bucket list either.

The prosecutor made his case.

"Parker Bell, you have been charged with the murder of Murphy Twilla. How do you plead?"

I looked around, no one came charging in through the doors at the last minute like they do on tv. I looked over at the prosecutor who was ignoring me.

"How do you plead?"

"Not guilty."

The prosecutor said, "Your honor, we would like to recommend no bail be set for Parker Bell."

Panic set in. I had to get out. The walls were starting to close in on me. Air was becoming scarce.

"Your honor, put whatever bond amount you want on me but please let me go home. I promise I won't leave town, the state, the country. I'll give you my passport, I'll do anything but please let me go home." I didn't care how desperate I sounded, I wanted to go home.

The Honorable Joseph Paul Hungert had attended church with my parents. I hoped for a little of God's grace and mercy to be on him.

"Two million dollars and turn your passport in."

"Thank you, Lord! Thank you, Jesus!"

Denny finally showed up, paid the two hundred thousand dollar bail, and an hour later I was breathing fresh free air.

"This is a mess, Parker."

"What took you so long, Denny?" He'd shown up about twenty minutes after the preliminary hearing.

"There's evil at work here, Parker."

I knew that, you didn't have to be a rocket scientist to figure that one out. It definitely was something more tangible than an imaginary little person running around in a red suit carrying a pitchfork.

"Murphy was just lying there and the next thing I knew he was dead. He was in the process of telling me Joe D. had found a bag with one hundred thousand dollars in front of…gee, I don't know. That's when he was shot."

I was in a state of shock. Crime book authors aren't supposed to be in the middle of a murder. I could just see this now. Saffron Woo was going to have a field day with the publicity and would be hawking my new book before I had even written the first word. Of course, the good news is that it's almost guaranteed to be a bestseller and I'll make a boatload of money. The bad news is I might not have any place to spend it if I'm sitting in jail for the rest of my life.

"Parker, I'll see if I can get the hallway security tapes from the hospital."

"There's nothing there. I guarantee it. Tony Bugs already told me that. The shot had to come from the ceiling but it's not strong enough to hold up a person."

Denny looked thoughtful. "What if someone had it set up remotely? Those little units don't weigh more than about four or five pounds. It's a one-time use type of thing. I think I'll go take a look after I get you home."

Home had never looked so good. Well, except that the Lady Gatorettes without Misty Dawn were sitting in my living room. I could feel steam starting to build in my head.

Myrtle Sue jumped up when I entered the door. "Parker, we're going to be your bodyguards."

Flo handed me a cup of steaming Mocha Docha Delight. Rhonda Jean was busy diagraming something on a notepad. Mary Jane was folding my clothes.

Okay, maybe these gals could be useful for something; although I admit I was a little shaken seeing two empty doughnut boxes sitting on the dining room table. I didn't know how much sugar they had had and I was a wee bit concerned someone might explode with a new found burst of energy doing God knows what.

"What's that smell?" Since I rarely cooked and I knew Denny liked eating C-rations out of a can I wasn't sure what that delicious aroma was emanating from my kitchen. I knew there was a stove in there but since I only used the microwave I didn't even know if the stove worked.

Mary Jane laughed. "Well, honey, we've got to eat and keep our strength up! I made a beef bourguignon that is to die for."

"That's fancy beef stew for the rest of us," murmured Flo.

"You sure don't have any problems going back for seconds on it, missy!"

Before their squabbling escalated into something disastrous, I jumped in there. "I'm sure it's delicious, Mary Jane, and I appreciate your doing that for me. It's very sweet of you."

They all looked at each other. Their eyes threatened to leak tears down their faces.

"What? What did I do now?" I was completely puzzled, I was nice to them and actually was sincere in paying them a compliment. Plus, I was tired of eating fast food and frozen dinners all the time. I was pretty darn sure it would taste a sight better than six chick burgers for five dollars at the local fast food place.

"You appreciate something we're doing for you?" asked Mary Jane in a very subdued voice, almost like a child's voice.

"Yes, I do." I nodded and then grinned, "But don't let it go to your head."

They all looked at each other again, burst into laughter, and started chattering again...much like monkeys who have found a new stash of coconuts.

The food was out of this world! Southern gals and their food, it was heaven on earth. Mary Jane did know how to throw down some seriously good food. There might be some redeeming grace on being back in Po'thole, especially if the Lady Gatorettes were cooking for me.

After the table had been cleared and the dishes stacked in the dishwasher – I had a dishwasher? Who knew? – Rhonda Jean rapped her pen on the table.

"I think I've figured out something." Every head whipped around to her.

Rhonda Jean cleared her throat, kind of sounded like a baby elephant snorting, "Parker's not the only common denominator in all these murders. Neither is Misty Dawn."

The girls started the chattering again. I couldn't understand a word they were saying. Oh, it was Southern English alright but the dialect was a wee bit off and then, duh, I understood. They had their own little language. Made sense, I guess, one for all and all for one.

I waved my hands. "What? What have you figured out, Rhonda

Jean? I'm lost here. I've been trying to figure out what's going on here and why I keep getting caught up in all of this."

"Do you remember the trick play from November 6, 1986?"

I was stunned. "Like Rhonda Jean, how old do you think I am?! And, no, I don't remember Gator football plays."

The feeling of camaraderie was slipping into thin air, I could literally feel it dissipating. I needed a save, a big one. "Well, of course, I remember Tebow's jump pass on the goal line but it wasn't in 1986." I smiled broadly, hoping that was going to work. The last thing I wanted to have happen was to have these gals turn on me.

Big smiles all around. Rhonda Jean nodded. Life was copasetic again.

"Okay, so when you diagram the murders out with the players, you are obviously one of the main players. So is Misty Dawn but we know she didn't do it."

The gals nodded and murmurs of "she's being framed" were heard.

"You've got Dimwit involved but he hasn't got the sense a cat does on jumping on a hot stove, so he's pretty much out. BUT, you've got Tony Bugs involved. He's there on absolutely everything." Rhonda Jean leaned back in her chair. "Did you know Tony Bugs before coming back to Po'thole?"

I nodded no. "Not that I'm aware of."

"Did you ever do any work for him or his city or whatever it was he was doing in New Jersey?"

Still shaking my head no, I said, "Pretty sure not."

"What about teaching one of those fancy computer security seminars? I know you've done some of those for different cities."

I was surprised Rhonda Jean knew that but, then again, my appearances have appeared all over the internet and I had done a bunch of training for various law enforcement agencies. I guess it was possible I had run into Tony Bugs but I didn't remember.

"I'll call my office and see if they can find out anything."

Chapter 16

Pink's "So What" song went off on my phone. Going from chattering monkeys to dead silence was unreal.

I looked at caller I.D.. Thankfully, it was Denny. "Parker, ask those girls if they know anyone who has a camouflaged remote gun trigger. I found how Murphy was murdered. It was jury rigged out the wahzoo but would be good for only one shot. Ask them."

"Um, ladies, Denny wants to know if any of you have a camouflaged remote gun trigger?" I wasn't even sure what that was but Denny did and that was good enough for me.

Myrtle Sue seemed to be a little perplexed too. "Do you mean one of them things that will shoot automatically and that you can set it up from another location? Like during hunting season?"

"Yeah, I guess so." Ask me about software packages and I could tell you everything and more than you never wanted to know but this was way out of my wheelhouse.

The Lady Gatorettes looked at each other, I could tell they were silently debating whether to let me in on whatever secret they were trying to hide.

Flo finally said, "Well, you know our men are hunters and we all might have, um, some experience in that area but we all…"

"Categorically deny that any of us would do this awful thing." Rhonda Jean finished.

Suddenly it dawned on me, like, duh! Of course! Some of their husbands were poachers or certainly dangled on the border of what was legal and illegal to do in Northeast Florida. They weren't about to give up their husbands! After all, good old Southern boys are hard to find, get 'em trained right, and then keep them.

I started to laugh, "Okay, okay, I gotcha. I'm not asking you to divulge any secrets but do any of you know how it's done? Set it up, then remotely fire it, and without it making a ton of noise?"

They all nodded collectively. Well, this wasn't getting me anywhere except I now knew they knew a LOT about killing that I had never previously thought of. I definitely wanted these gals on my side!

"Is it legal to buy this stuff or is it law enforcement only?" Heck, who knew about these things?

"Anyone can buy it on the internet if you have a Paypal account or a debit or credit card," offered Mary Jane. "But I personally do not know how to set one of those things up."

I was scared to ask but plunged forward anyway. Actually, I was dreading the response I thought I might get.

"Is there any one of you who does know how to do it?"

Suddenly they were looking everywhere but at me. A couple of nudges between them.

"Well, Misty Dawn does but she wouldn't kill Murphy."

This was looking really bad for Misty Dawn. The woman apparently had way too many hidden skill sets. Admirable but not at this time.

"Misty Dawn hates hospitals and would never go in there." Rhonda Jean was emphatic. "Wouldn't make any difference if her mama was in there, she wouldn't go. The smells make her sick and there's not any fresh air in there either. She'd die."

Denny came through the door about then, had a box in his hands, and grimaced.

"What?!" I shouted. I was a wee bit tense plus he scared me when the door suddenly popped open. "I thought you were on the phone?"

"I was but you're only a couple of minutes from the hospital and it was just easier to come back."

He opened the box, spilling out all sorts of tubes, rods, and god knows what out on the table. It looked like a tinker toy set had exploded.

"Don't touch anything." He looked solemnly at them. "I

mean it. I need to see if I can find fingerprints on this."

Glancing up at me, he said, "I shot video on this showing it up in the ceiling, how it was set up, and how easy it was to get up and down in the ceiling. This is definitely how Murphy was killed but I need to see if there are any fingerprints on this."

"Do you want to overnight it to Gene at the FBI?" I had a lot of contacts and didn't mind using them if the need arose. In fact, I was kind of surprised I hadn't heard from anyone about the murder spree going on in Po'thole.

He shook his head. "I want you guys to video this and then I'll send it to Carl."

This was tedious work and boring. Patience is not my strong point. While Denny continued to do his magic with Scotch tape and god knows whatever else, the Lady Gatorettes were in a quiet huddle videoing Denny, and I called the office again to see if Missy had an updates on Tony Bugs attending any of my seminars. I thought this might be a bit of a stretch at best.

"Hey, Missy. What's going on?"

A deep sigh. "Do you need another laptop, Parker?"

"Nope."

"Really?"

"Nope, I was calling to see what was going on in the office and to see if you found out anything on if Tony Bugs had attended any of the seminars."

"Seriously, Parker, I'm up to my eyeballs in alligator poo and it's been less than two hours since you called the last time. You must be bored. It's probably going to be tomorrow before I can get that information to you."

This didn't sound like my super confident, super-efficient right-hand gal. The one person I depended upon for everything. Something was up.

"What's wrong, Missy? Do I need to come back?" While most people think of me as tough, uncaring, and unfeeling, nothing could be further from the truth when it came to people I care about. Missy has been with me since the beginning of my company. I regularly fire her about three times a year.

It doesn't stick because she ignores it and continues to show up for work.

"Parker, make Dewitt stop calling me. He's driving me up a wall, I can't get any work done. I've told him and told him if he wants something from you, he needs to call you directly." A long sigh. "In fact, I told him not to ever call me again."

New turn of events, what on earth could possess Dewitt to call Missy instead of me...and on a consistent basis. This was weird.

"Is he sweet on you, Missy?" Only thing I could think of.

"Nope, because he keeps asking questions about you, Rob, book deals, tv, whatever, you name it. I know you need to work with him down there but MAKE HIM LEAVE ME ALONE!"

Wow! She was upset and Missy didn't get upset easily.

"Next time he calls, tell him 'no comment' and hang up on him. I don't care what he says, hang up on him. I'm not going to have you harassed because Demwit is bored."

The next phone call was to Dewitt. I drummed my fingers on the countertop while waiting to be connected.

"Sheriff Munster."

"Dewitt, Parker here, do not ever call my Atlanta office ever again. You are harassing Missy, jeopardizing the smooth running of my office, and, in short, have turned into a stalker. You so much as punch the numbers into your phone, I'll file charges on you. Do you understand me?" I was spitting mad.

"Parker, I can explain."

"No, you can't. Leave Missy alone, you have any problems with anything you've got my phone number, use it. Anything else?"

"Um.."

"Wrong answer." I disconnected.

The phone rang back. It was Dewitt. I let it roll into voicemail. If necessary, I'd have Denny go over and talk to him. I was not a happy camper.

The phone rang again. Dewitt was going to be persistent.

"What."

"Parker, I'm, um, sorry about calling her all the time. I want to get out of this rat hole and do what you and Rob are doing on the national scene." He sounded pathetic.

"Dewitt, I'm going to be really honest here and tell you that you aren't smart enough, good looking enough, and you still haven't solved any crimes that would make the national media pay any attention to you in a positive light.

"You will come across as a struggling, redneck buffoon and I hardly think that's what you want." Just call me no filters Parker. "Focus on the things you like to do, Dewitt, and don't chase the national spotlight. I will tell you from firsthand experience, it's not easy, it's not pretty, and is pretty nasty at times. I don't recommend it."

"But you do it so well and you make a lot of money from it." He was sounding more and more pitiful. Thank goodness I don't ride on that pity train!

"I make a lot of money from my computer security consulting business. Everything else is gravy money. Focus on what you know, Dewitt. I'm not going to help you."

I probably should have felt bad about taking the proverbial two-by-four to Dewitt and pounding him into the sand but I didn't. In all honesty, I thought I was doing him a favor by telling him that.

Unfortunately, I knew my mother was probably rolling over in her grave right now because I had not used the good Southern manners she had taught me. Oh, well, I was never politically correct while she was alive. I assumed it made no difference now.

Chapter 17

I've been in Po'thole less than a week and have had more wacky things happen here than it ever does to me in Atlanta. I swear I think it must be the water. The St. Johns River is beyond beautiful and is a nature lover's mecca but I do wonder about the quality of the water from the river to the houses.

Nothing was popping up at me that I absolutely needed to do. Well, except for finding out why there have been so many murders and what does it have in connection with me. While my ego is big enough for three Gator football players, I really hoped that I wasn't the only thing tying all of these murders together.

Potus was sitting quietly on the sofa, tongue hanging out and giving me a cheesy smile. Denny stayed in the party wagon but had left Potus to protect me. He would defend me to his death with anyone except Misty Dawn. That dog absolutely adored her and basically threw out the welcome mat for her when she made sudden and unexplained appearances. No noise, no nothing except for the wagging of his tail. This, of course, made me wonder how many times she had been inside my new home. The security system was worthless around her. She had even figured out how to make the cameras not work at all. Amazing talent, scary, but still amazing skills.

I vaguely wondered if the Lady Gatorettes had done anything to Sally Ann. I hadn't heard anything but, then again, why would I? Tony Bugs hadn't called since I'd been sprung from jail. Maybe that dinner was on the back burner. Nah, he's a guy and he's going to want to do that dinner at some point in the near future.

As far as I knew, there was no connection to the two of us but weirder things have happened. Our paths very easily could have crossed and I wouldn't be aware of it. In the course of doing book tours and doing seminars for my company, we might have met and it simply would not have registered with me.

While the public can be very adoring...and I love them because they buy my books...they will remember everything I do and I, seeing hundreds and thousands of people, have absolutely no clue who they are or what they do. I try to be as polite as I can be while flashing my unique brand of humor but, unfortunately, not everyone loves me. Oh, well, as long as they spend their money on my book I don't care. It's just business.

Deciding that Angels Delight coffee was a weak and insipid blend of water and leftover coffee grounds, I inadvertently knocked the cup over and swiped some liquid into my laptop. I heard a small hissing sound and knew that I had killed off another computer.

"Aarrgghh! Why me, Lord, why?" I cursed and then called Missy.

"Good morning, Parker."

"Um."

"I'll overnight it to you." She giggled. "We'll still looking for some type of connection between you and Tony. So far, I'm not finding anything but you do know it's kind of looking for a needle in a haystack, don't you?"

"Yes." We discussed a few more things pertinent to the running of the office and that was it.

Denny rapped on the door and stepped inside. "I've been thinking."

"Never a good thing," I quipped.

Ignoring me, he plopped down on the sofa causing Potus to stretch way out and plunk down on the floor. He didn't look amused.

"Did Tony Bugs have any connections with casinos in Jersey?"

"Probably, I don't know. Why?"

"What if Tony Bugs was sent down here to pave the way for a casino, i.e., have everything already lined up, law enforcement wise, to be able to either blame things on others...like Johnny "Ten Fingers" or be able to turn a blind eye to the corruption that always follows casinos?"

Well, it did make for an interesting premise.

"Bear with me on this. What if all of these murders are just a smoke screen? To divert attention away from the casinos coming in?"

"But why kill all of these people, Denny? It just doesn't make any sense."

"He's got the perfect fall guys…the Lady Gatorettes and, specifically, Misty Dawn. Everyone knows they're crazier than looney tunes. They're the perfect foil for him."

I argued, "But what about Johnny "Ten Fingers"? Where does he fit into all of this?"

"Is he truly a local guy or is he a guy that just suddenly showed up a couple of years ago and is now running drugs and girls through Po'thole? We already know that Dewitt couldn't find his fanny if he were holding onto it with both hands.

"This is a small town and, usually with small towns, by the

time law enforcement is truly aware of the connections in the crime community, it's already profit time and they can only hope to impact the illegal activities in a small way. Yeah, I know they'll put big articles out saying how they're catching this criminal and busting up that drug ring but you and I both know that's only to assure the community that their tax dollars are hard at work and they're being diligently protected."

I shook my head. "I really don't know anything about Johnny "Ten Fingers". Remember, I left here umpteen years ago. He really might not have any connection at all to any of this. He's only just showed up on my radar."

There was a very slight tapping at the back door. Potus went straight into the attention mode and then he started wagging his tail.

"Come on in, Misty Dawn," I yelled.

The woman looked like she had just gotten out of the shower. Freshly washed hair, a scrubbed face, and clean cammies on. I did notice she was wearing New Balance sneakers.

She helped herself to a cup of coffee and then plopped down on the chair opposite the sofa.

Looking directly at Denny, "You wanted to know if I know how to use a remote gun control trigger." It was a statement, not a question.

I could tell from looking at Denny that he had a newfound respect for Misty Dawn. She came to him, he didn't have to go looking for her, and she was totally prepared to answer questions. He might be in love. So few women wanted someone like him; however, she was married to John Boy and I knew if she'd stuck with him for twenty-odd years she was never going to leave him for someone else. Also, being the Southern redneck she was, John Boy was hers and hers alone. She wasn't going to mess around on her husband.

"The short answer is yes, of course, I do. The other answer is I have all of my stuff, it's not been stolen, and it's at the house. John Boy said to tell you if you wanted to see it you could come out there but you'd have to show him your Lord Lovat Officer's Model Knife."

Denny looked shocked. The man usually wore a poker face that any military man would be proud of but she had totally caught him off guard.

"Um, how did you know I have one, Misty Dawn? There's only supposed to be five in existence. They're pretty rare."

Misty Dawn smiled, "I have my ways and John Boy really wants to see it. Actually, I want you to let him hold it."

The poker face was back on. "What if I told you I don't have it here?"

"What if I told you I knew you have it on your right calf?"

They stared at each other for about fifteen seconds and then sly grins slowly etched across their faces. Denny stuck his hand out and Misty Dawn shook it. I felt like we were at a United Nations peace agreement union.

"Okay, the unit that you have only weighs about four to six pounds which means it's good for one shot, and one shot only. I'm betting you that unit was installed right about the time Murphy was brought in, probably under the guise of a maintenance guy changing out a light bulb or something like that."

Snapping her fingers, she said, "In fact, I'm betting you Tony Bugs or one of his guys asked for that room because," she wiggled her fingers in quote marks, "that room would be easier to secure."

Denny nodded. "You and I are on the same page, exactly what I thought. The question is why would Murphy be important enough to kill? What did he know or someone thought he knew that was worth dying for?"

She shook her head and shrugged her shoulders.

"Murphy told me that Joe D. had found one hundred thousand dollars in front of something but he didn't actually finish the sentence." I was thinking out loud again.

They whipped both of their heads around so fast I vaguely wondered if there was an exorcism ritual that was about to be performed.

"What? You never said anything about one hundred thousand dollars, Parker. You only said a bag of money. That's a lot of money and certainly a good enough reason to get killed over."

Misty Dawn's eyes had grown slits in them. Her lips were tight. Her fists were balled up. This was way more than a high interest level. This had all the makings of a raging inferno about to bust open.

"How much did you say? One hundred thousand dollars?"

I nodded.

"But Murphy only said they, Joe D., had found it in front of something?"

I nodded again.

Turning to Denny, Misty Dawn said, "You coming with me? Parker, you stay put or at least don't go anywhere with Tony Bugs or his guys."

Dialing her phone, "I'm calling the Lady Gatorettes in to protect you."

Visions of that delightful beef bourguignon danced through my mind. "Will Mary Jane cook again?"

Misty Dawn was busy giving her orders to one of the gals and made sure that they would be fixing another great meal for me. I could get used to this. No wonder men let women wait on them, it's fun!

"They'll be here in twenty minutes. Denny and I have things

to do." Turning her attention to Potus, "Guard Parker."

I swear that dog nodded his head. He ignores me but obeys Misty Dawn and Denny. Whatever.

They left through the back door. I gave it about two seconds and opened it so I could see what direction they had headed off in. Gone. No sign of them anywhere. I was envious. I wanted to be able to do that but apparently I don't have the skill set for it. I tripped down the stairs and ended up in a heap on the ground. Potus appeared at the door and smiled. His ears were at attention. A low growl started in his throat and he turned around in the doorway.

Coming back in, I heard the doorbell. Looking through the peephole, I saw Tony Bugs. I decided not to open the door. Even though I had my suspicions about him, I didn't really think he'd do anything to me. On the other hand, I was out on a two million dollar bond and he could make me disappear if he wanted to.

He rang the doorbell again, waited a few more moments, and then turned on his heel and left.

I could see the Lady Gatorettes coming down the street and hoped they wouldn't turn into the driveway while Tony Bugs was leaving because for sure he'd know something was up. Thankfully, they rode on past and waved at Tony Bugs. A few minutes later, they were behind my house and dancing through the door.

Flo said, "We saw Tony and decided to come around the

back way. Even if he shows back up at your front door, he won't know we're here protecting you. He isn't getting you at all!"

Nods of agreement were acknowledged.

Myrtle Sue, ever the domestic goddess, was running into my bedroom. "Parker, girl, you didn't make your bed! I need to clean your house. Ladies, take her somewhere for a couple of hours. I need to clean this house, do her laundry, and Mary Jane needs to get a meal going!"

"Um, I need some coffee."

"Flo, get coffee while you're out. Get her some of the good stuff, not this wimpy flavored crap she's been drinking."

"Un, huh, no, you're not! I like my gourmet coffees. If you guys don't like it, get your own coffee but leave mine alone." Okay, it's wonderful that I now have four wives but they are not going to mess with my coffee! Plus, a spoon in their coffee screamed for help. I mean, literally, a spoon could stand up straight in their coffee it was that strong.

Totally ignoring me, I was hustled out the door and into Mary Jane's Lexus. The Secret Service probably didn't provide as much body coverage as the Lady Gatorettes did. Scary thought though it was, they were impressing me. I just kept having to remind myself that they could flip at any moment.

I got the scenic tour. They drove me down River Street, beautiful homes from the early 1900's with magnificently landscaped yards dotted the street with views of the St. Johns River that were to die for. You could sit on your front porch and watch boats sail along, people fishing, water skiers, and still have that feeling of peace and relaxation. I almost wished I had a home on the river.

Jerking myself back into reality as my phone rang, I realized I wanted to do nothing except ride around and not have to worry about anything. To say this was a new feeling for me was an understatement! Geez, maybe there was something in those power plant emissions that had infiltrated my brain through my lungs and was making me more receptive to the Po'thole way of life.

"Parker, that's your phone going off."

"Yeah, I know and I've decided I'm not going to answer it."

"Might be something important."

"Might not be either."

Flo giggled, "I know what it is...you're tired of all the technology in our lives and you are taking a moment to appreciate life."

Dang! Was she inside my head or what?

"Yeah, something like that."

In a show of solidarity, everyone turned their phones off. I mean completely off, not on vibrate. Nope, completely off. Well, it was the least I could do as well.

It was a very nice two hours of riding around town with the colorful descriptions of what was going on in the town, new wall murals, businesses closing versus being sold, new businesses trying to make it in the poorest town in Florida, ideas on how to make Po'thole more vibrant, and why the Bingo Palace did such great business.

During that two hour ride, not once did the gals bring up or gossip about any other person. They were proud to show off the town. I realized that had I been riding with anyone else, my friends, it would have been all about the gossip.

I remembered Thomas Henry Buckles quote, "Great minds discuss ideas. Average minds discuss events. Small minds discuss people." The Lady

Gatorettes definitely were not small-minded people when it came to their town.

"Okay, we've been off the grid long enough," announced Rhonda Jean. "Time to turn the phones back on and head back."

I discovered I had five messages waiting on me. Two from Tony Bugs, probably not a good sign. I didn't think he was calling me to remind me that I still owed him dinner. One from Denny and two from the office.

I returned Denny's call first. "Yo, what's up?"

He chuckled, "Thought you'd like to know, no fingerprints."

"Yeah, I thought as much. If someone were going to take the time to set all of that up, the last thing they would want to get tripped up on is having fingerprints on the little machine."

We hung up.

"Hey, Missy, it's Parker. Whatcha got for me?"

"For starters, you did have Tony Bugs attend one of your seminars a couple of years ago."

I was stunned. There might be a connection here that I never knew about…and that might not be good. It did open up a world of possibilities that I hadn't even considered before.

"Which one?"

"It was in Newark."

I remembered that conference. It was awful. Newark was not on my top ten list to ever go back there again. The weather was awful, the meeting rooms were something from a third world country, none of the technical stuff worked, the people were ruder than normal, and the only reason why most of those people attended that particular seminar was because their city government had mandated it. Oh, yeah, it was such a win-win for everyone. Not!

"I think I spoke on being hacked from the inside or is your co-worker spying on your work. Was that the topic?"

"Yes. There were one hundred people who signed the sign-in sheet saying they attended. Tony was number eighty-six on the list."

"Okay, see what else you can find out about that conference. Did we video tape it? Maybe he's on there somewhere."

"We probably did. Let me see what I can find." Then we caught up on other business.

A little wary, I listened to Tony Bugs messages. I was right, they weren't good. Sally Ann was going to file charges against me. The little twit! And, surprise, surprise, he wanted to know when we could go out for dinner.

I really wasn't sure I wanted to go out with him. He could be dangerous.

Chapter 18

Celesta called me and sounded a little rattled. "Parker, another death note. This time it was under the windshield wiper on my car."

"Have you called Tony or Dewitt? I can't ever remember if you're inside the city limits or out."

"In and, no, on calling the cops. I don't trust Tony. I think he's got something to do with this."

Well, at least, I had another person who was thinking along the same lines as I was. "What do you know about Johnny "Ten Fingers"? Is he a local guy or what? How did he suddenly appear on the political scene?"

She laughed. "He's been around for a while. Went to high school here, I think he might have been from Jacksonville originally but I don't know for sure. I do know he graduated from here. He went to some vo-tech training place for something and was back here within a couple of months.

"At that point, I guess he fell off the radar because I didn't hear or know anything about him until just a couple of years ago. The rumor on the street was that he found God and God wanted him to be a positive role model for others."

"Yeah but wait a minute. You never heard anything about this guy for a couple of years and then he suddenly shows up wanting to run for office?" I paused, "Celesta, something doesn't make any sense here. The guy's got a rap sheet as long as my arm and you watch the arrest log like it's going out of style, right?"

"Yes."

"How on God's green earth could he have twenty-seven pages of arrests without it being in the newspaper and you not knowing about it? This doesn't sound kosher."

"You're Presbyterian or Assembly of God, I can't remember which, being Jewish kosher has nothing to do with it. He was allegedly arrested in St. Johns County all those times but," she emphasized the word but, "when I looked up everything online, it was all redacted."

"What? How could that be?"

"Don't know, I strongly suspect he's got some sort of tie-in, agreement, call it what you want, with either the FBI, DEA, something so that he keeps skating on everything. Maybe he's an informant."

"If that's the case, why would he suddenly be in the limelight? Usually those guys want their informants to keep a very low profile. Johnny "Ten Fingers" is doing anything but being a low profile."

"True, Parker, but he's still in a small town and I can't imagine why he would be on anyone's radar."

I shook my head. "Seriously, Celesta, do you really believe that?" My tone dripped contempt. "You've got a guy, a black guy, who has twenty-seven pages of arrests with not one conviction or one night spent in jail, he runs for sheriff, screams discrimination, goes all the way to the Florida Supreme Court, he comes back, runs and is elected as a city commissioner. Does that not strike you as odd and waving flags at people? You don't think every major law enforcement agency in this country hasn't looked at him at least once and wondered the same thing you and I do? Seriously, Celesta, you do need to get out in the world a little bit and East Po'thole doesn't count!"

"I watch Fox News and that's all I need to know." She was a wee bit on the huffy side.

I knew this was never going to go anywhere. Celesta would never leave Po'thole. I vaguely wondered if the Eastern sky split open and Christ came down to pick her up if she'd go willingly. She's a Baptist, so maybe.

"Let's get back to the death note. What did it say, Celesta?"

"You will die, witch."

"Witch and not the ever popular b word?"

"Nope, witch because I wondered the same thing," she giggled.

"Are you going to call the cops?"

"Why? You and I both know nothing's going to come from it."

"Well, um, Celesta, in case something happens to you, they will at least have a record of it."

"And, what, Parker, do you think that's going to do? Bring me back from an untimely death? I really don't think so." The good news is she was laughing.

"Celesta, we haven't really talked about what's going on

here. Tell me about the possible casino, why you think Tony might have something to do with what's going on, how are the Lady Gatorettes tied up in this, and what's up with all these deaths? What's the connection because I sure can't figure any out."

"I've been racking my brain on all of this stuff too, Parker, and the only thing I keep coming up with is that someone wants the casino to come to Po'thole. The big drawback is that everyone thinks the Seminole Indians can do this but they can't because they don't actually have any land that is deeded to them in the city. In the county they do but it's all the way out to the new fishing world lodge and those guys aren't going to sell or give them that land.

"If it's not the Seminoles, then I'm guessing it's Mafia based."

Oh, my, from one extreme to the other with Celesta. There would be no happy middle ground. While she might be right, chances were just as good that she was wrong; however, I wasn't going to be the one to tell her that.

"What do the Lady Gatorettes think about the casino?"

"I don't know and, honestly, I don't care. A casino should not be here in Po'thole! All of my phone calls want them to stay far, far away. We don't need prostitution, illegal activities, drinking on Sundays, Mafia, child sex trafficking. Do I need to go on, Parker?"

"What about the new jobs it would bring in? What about helping the town to grow and thrive? What about all of the new taxes it would bring? Celesta, there are good things about a casino. Not everything is negative."

"Yes, it is! Gambling is a sin!"

Oh, lord, did I ever open a hornet's nest on this. While I was just messing with Celesta, she took it as a serious matter and was about ready to go to war over this. I needed to do something that would nip it in the bud quickly.

"What about Shelley? Is she in favor of or against the casino? What about the other city commissioners?"

"Scooter was in favor of it, predominantly because he owned the property where it might go. Tabitha was against it for the same reasons I have and Shelley is still on the fence. It really depends on who gets to her last because that's the way she'll vote. And who knows how Johnny "Ten Fingers" will vote."

"So, you and Tabitha against, Scooter for, Shelley and Johnny "Ten Fingers" are iffy at best. I'm betting Scooter, since he was the mayor, was going to vote for anything that is going to help the tax base. I'm betting Shelley and Johnny "Ten Fingers" will go along with the mayor for the same reason on getting the taxes. So, in essence, you're outvoted at the moment."

Sigh, "Yes, but I think I can get Shelley on board with me but, here's the real issue. We have four city commissioners including the mayor. The mayor is the one that can throw the vote in a crazy direction.

"Also, we have to have a new city commissioner and a new mayor elected before anything can come up for a vote and that's going to be several months away. Who knows who's going to run and what their thoughts are on this. The next meeting is Thursday night and I'm assuming we're going to put it out there for new commissioners."

"Who do you think will run? In fact," I mused, "do you actually have to replace Tabitha and Scooter?"

"Good point, I don't know. I guess I'll need to talk with the city attorney about it. Let me go and I'll speak with you later."

This whole thing was puzzling me more and more. It looked like a lot of loose ends going nowhere but I knew a slew of coincidences that were not coincidences. There had to be a connection somewhere.

Skimming down all of my phone connects, I pushed Greg's number and hoped I could get him on the first try.

"Greg Sherman."

"Greg, Parker Bell here. How you doing?"

"Good. How's Po'thole?"

Laughing, I answered, "It's always amazing to me that I'm important enough that you want to keep close ties on my location."

Greg was a typical FBI guy, buttoned down, uptight white guy with virtually no sense of humor. But for some reason I was always able to make him laugh. He was in his mid-forties, on his third marriage, had no clue as to when his kids' birthdays were, and probably saw them once a year. He didn't seem to realize that he was married to the FBI. Human flesh and blood would never do it for him. That was just for fun but with zero attachments. Why he kept thinking marriage was going to work for him was beyond me but, then again, we stayed in touch because I had helped him locate and dissolve a terrorist cell that was moving money out of this country at an astounding rate. Surprisingly, it was so low key and low tech I almost overlooked it. It was brilliant in its simplicity. Greg won several in-house awards for the bust.

"So, turning to a little bit of a more serious manner, Greg.

What do you know of Johnny "Ten Fingers" in Po'thole?"

Cautiously, he answered, "What makes you think I know anything about him?"

"Well, he has twenty-seven pages of arrests, not one conviction, not one night in jail, and he's always over in St. Johns County when these alleged arrests occur. Something just doesn't seem like he's the normal criminal.

"So, to me, that means he's either an informant or works for you guys in some capacity. BUT, he's not a criminal. So what gives?"

Silence, then a chuckle. "Let me get back with you on that."

And...there's my sign. Johnny "Ten Fingers" is definitely working in some capacity of law enforcement.

Knowing that I was going to have to eventually return Tony Bugs call, I decided to get it over with it.

I called and left a message for him. The doorbell rang and there he was. Outside my front door. This probably wasn't a good thing. Contrary to popular belief, you do not have to let law enforcement in your home if they "just want to talk with you." You can make them stand outside the door and talk.

"Yes, Tony. What do you want?"

"Open the door, Parker."

"Why?"

"I need to speak with you."

"Do it through the door."

"Parker, let's do this the easy way. Sally Ann is filing charges against you and I need to serve the papers."

"Put them in the door and I'll do it that way. You can back off the porch and watch me do it. I have no intentions of getting arrested again until we get all of this mess straightened out."

"Are you saying you don't trust me, Parker? I'm hurt." He was laughing.

"Yeah, pretty much, Tony. Put the papers in the door, step off the porch, take my picture getting and reading them. I'll stand still long enough for you to get good pictures."

I didn't hear anything. I looked out the window and Tony was standing on the ground looking up at me grinning. He waved for me to come out.

Opening the door, the papers were stuck in there. Basically, I did a couple of posed shots for Tony to show whoever he needed to show them to.

Sure enough, that twit Sally Ann was filing a complaint against me for threatening her, assaulting her, and a couple of fluff charges.

"What do I have to do to file charges against her?" I shouted to Tony.

"Come on down to the office and do the paperwork."

Going to the police station of my own accord when I was out on bail did not for a happy Parker make. Therefore, I decided to get the Lady Gatorettes involved. Misty Dawn had already told them what to do but since I hadn't heard anything I made the dangerous assumption that either they hadn't done anything yet – unlikely – or they were bidding their time, more likely, or that they were doing a few little things here and there and were building up to something really good, the most likely scenario.

I wanted them to create enough stress in her life that she would drop all charges against me. I was going to turn into her pimp where she would do whatever I wanted her to do...and I really just wanted her to go away.

"Nah, some other time. Catch ya later, Tony." I went back inside and he left in his squad car.

The good news was he didn't ask me out for dinner.

Chapter 19

Popping a top off a frothy adult liquid libation, I was conjuring all sorts of naughty and vicious thoughts on how to drive Sally Ann crazy when Misty Dawn, Denny, and Potus were suddenly standing in my living room.

"How the heck do you guys do that?!" I screamed.

They laughed and grabbed a couple of Yuenglings from the refrigerator. They plopped down on the sofa and I brought them up to speed on what happened earlier.

"Good thing you didn't go with him," stated Denny. "Did Missy ever get back with you on the video stuff? I'm betting you Tony's the connection to everything and somehow you're a major piece of this puzzle."

Holding his hands up, he said, "Don't ask me how, but you're central to all of this."

Misty Dawn killed off half of the beer in one gulp and nodded. "I'm getting blamed for a lot of stuff that I've never done."

"Sorry about that, Misty Dawn."

She shrugged. "Sally Ann is going to pay for what she's doing to you. Give me a couple of days and everything will be dropped and taken care of. She won't bother you ever again."

"Don't kill her!"

Misty Dawn smiled. "Won't have to. She'll be a good girl from here on out. I believe Jesus is going to have a meeting with her and she will repent of her evil ways."

While I was very curious as to what might take place, I figured I'd be better off not knowing. Hearing Misty Dawn talk about a come-to-Jesus meeting with Sally Ann made the hair on my arms stand up, and I don't mean in the biblical sense.

"Misty Dawn, why do you think Bobby, Buddy, and Happy Jack were murdered?"

"Don't know."

Great! Suddenly she has nothing to say.

"But I didn't do it."

Denny nodded.

"What? What does that mean, Denny?"

"She didn't do it. Didn't have any real reason to. No motive, no reason. In the wrong place at the wrong time. Misty Dawn and the Lady Gatorettes are an easy blame. Besides, who was it that started that rumor anyway? It was Dewitt, wasn't it?"

We both nodded.

"Where is that Barney Fife look alike? Haven't seen or heard from him in a couple of days."

She and I looked at each other and shrugged.

"No news is good news." I got us each another beer and tossed a bag of chips on the coffee table. Never let it be said I don't entertain my beer-drinking guests properly. Potus glared at me until I gave him a bone the size of Rhode Island to gnaw on.

"What's important about the barbeque dinners?" I asked. "That's the only thing that's different about Scooter and Tabitha. Maybe it's two different killers."

"Nope, I think it's all tied in together but made to look different." Misty Dawn was draining her second adult libation in two gulps. If I did that, I'd pass out on the floor fairly quickly. She got up to get another one. She looked at Denny, he nodded yes, and me, being the ever weak one in the group, nodded yes also. I could sleep it off later.

"Did Buddy, Bobby, and Happy Jack know each other? Like were they friends, did they do business together?"

"Aw, heck, Parker, it's Po'thole. We all know each other and do business with each other. If you can't connect with someone in two ways, then you're not from here. But, if you want to know if they were close friends, I don't think so."

"What's the connection between them then? There's got to be a connection!" I was frustrated and feeling the beers.

"We're all Southern rednecks? Geez, I don't know."

Denny said, "We need a break. Let's go to one of those honky tonk bars, sing karaoke, have a few more beers, and have a good time."

He looked at us, we looked at him...shoot, it seemed like a good idea at the time.

As we were riding over to The Capt'n's Table, it occurred to me that I didn't know Denny liked honky tonk, I didn't know he liked karaoke much less singing, and it was extraordinarily rare that we had ever gone to a bar and...gasp...shock...had fun. There was a new word creeping around in my brain that was so ugly and so foreign to me that it took a few moments for me to grasp it.

Taking a deep breath and shaking my head, I didn't even want to acknowledge the thought and feeling that was hovering around in my already over-crowded brain. But the word just wouldn't let go. Inhaling slowly and slowly releasing it through my mouth, I closed my eyes and silently admitted it. I was jealous of Misty Dawn and her relationship with Denny. He never would have gone to a karaoke club with me but he was willing to do so with Misty Dawn.

The woman was totally secure, knowing full well that no one was going to call the sheriff's department and report her being at The Capt'n's Table. For sure, no one was going to report her singing either. Me, on the other hand, there was absolutely no doubt in my mind that Tony Bugs and Dewitt Munster would know about it by the end of the evening along with all sorts of innuendos whether true or not.

The Capt'n's Table was packed and it was early yet. Smells of deep fried oil wafted through the air outside and stale beer permeated the inside of the bar area. The karaoke stage was at the far end of the bar. Flashing spotlights danced around the stage creating the effect that you too could be a rock star...at least for a few minutes and only in the delusion of your own mind. But, hey, illusion is everything and after a couple of beers the world did look a little better.

We found a table just far enough from the stage that we could talk but not so close that we had to hear every bad note that was sung. As soon as we sat down, John Boy appeared, leaned over and smooched on Misty Dawn, leaving absolutely no doubt to anyone who she belonged to. Denny was surveying the room but I knew he had seen John Boy kiss Misty Dawn. John Boy, sporting new gold tips on his otherwise spiked black hair, went over to Denny and did a bro-hug. Apparently Denny showing him his Lord Lovat Officer's Model Knife earlier in the day bonded them as kindred spirits.

It also occurred to me that our being at The Capt'n's Table might have been pre-planned. For what I wasn't sure but me, being the ever cynical individual that I am, decided I probably should eat some food and slow down on my adult frothy liquid libations. Just going out to have some fun with no strings attached never entered my mind.

We ordered stuffed potato skins, ten million different types of wings and their accompanying sauces, Fritos covered in taco meat and slathered in very heart healthy Velveeta cheese sauce covered with jalapenos, and two pitchers of beer. I knew I was going to have serious heartburn in the morning but did I care? Nope. I was actually laughing and having a good time. Something that was somewhat foreign to me OR buried so deep that I had forgotten what it was like. To say I'm a Type A personality and continually focused is a bit of an understatement. Whereas most Type A's function at a level ten or eleven, I was pretty much at a level fifteen just sleeping.

People were getting up and singing to different songs. There were a few really good singers but most were of the "I've had five drinks, think I can sing, and will now prove it to you" variety. They were all having a good time.

Then Denny popped up with, "It's time for us to get up there and sing 'Wild Thing'."

John Boy said, "What about 'Born to be Wild'? I love that song."

Misty Dawn, cramming another stuff potato skin in her mouth, mumbled, "I want Pink's "So What, I'm a Rock Star."

I was in shock with these three but definitely agreed with Misty Dawn's selection. After all, "So What" is what I have on my cell phone.

Denny jumped up and walked purposefully to the stage, wrote his name down on the clipboard, turned around, saw our waitress, server, whatever the heck is the politically correct word now for the twenty-something girl with her boobs pretty much hanging out of her tank top and her Daisy Dukes leaving nothing to the imagination, did a circular motion over his head, and came back to our table.

"We're number three on the list, so we need to have more beer." Denny was the most relaxed I had ever seen him. I'd say he was definitely feeling good, but, then, we all were.

"Son, I like the way you think!" shouted John Boy, finishing up the last bit of his beer.

I'd lost count of how many pitchers of beer had been deposited and consumed at our table. Our server made sure no empty containers were left on our table. Since we had been sitting there awhile, I knew I had consumed at least one whole pitcher by myself...and I was the underdog in this beer drinking fest. Everyone else had probably consumed at least two pitchers each. We were not going to feel good in the morning but, right now, the world was great.

Denny's name was called and we all trouped up to the stage laughing. Pink's "So What" started and we all joined in singing at the top of our lungs. Misty Dawn and I were doing our dance moves. Pink has nothing to worry about!

Just as our second song of "Born to be Wild" came on, someone in the very back of the room yelled, "Alert, alert! Repeat, alert, alert!"

Misty Dawn jumped off the stage, blended right in with the other patrons, and disappeared. I saw it with my own two eyes. She literally just disappeared in the crowd. First she's there and then she's not. I am envious of her talent.

Dewitt entered the room, the noise level barely changed. He was about six feet in the room, people were going around him to leave when I spotted Misty Dawn. She had just passed Dewitt, did a half turn, smiled at me or maybe it was John Boy, and then was out the door. She had literally just walked past Dewitt and he didn't even know she was there. Hence, his nickname of Dimwit.

Turning to John Boy, who had now drained Misty Dawn's beer, placed it in front of him, and stacked her empty food plates next to his, I asked, "How the heck does she do that, blending into whatever she's around?"

Dewitt spotted us and was making his way toward our table.

"She's one with whatever environment she's in." He drained his beer mug. "Yo, Dim…er, Dewitt. Whatcha doing here?"

Dewitt did not appear to be in a good mood. "Where's Misty Dawn?"

We all looked at each other and shrugged.

"Dewitt, would you like to join us for a beer?" Denny was being far more gracious than I was. I simply wanted him to leave. Now that I was having fun at this party and not stressing my brain about all of the murders, I wanted him to just...go...away.

Ignoring him, Dewitt glared at us. "Where is Misty Dawn?"

"Don't know." John Boy did have his own moments of brevity.

I shrugged, "No clue."

"Who?" Denny was grinning.

"You know, I could have all three of you arrested for public intoxication, drunk and disorderly conduct, and driving under the influence. Let's see how you like them apples." Dewitt's face looked just like Barney Fife's when he got upset about something.

I started to giggle. Probably not the wisest thing to do with a law enforcement officer especially since I was out on bond but everything was funny at this point.

"Parker, you think that's funny, huh? You have…"

Denny pushed Misty Dawn's chair out with his foot. "Dewitt, sit down. You're wound up too tight. You know you can't arrest us for anything. We're sitting in a club minding our own business. We sang a couple of songs and that's it.

"As far as driving goes, we have someone picking us up. So there's no DUI involved. Come on now, have a beer with us or leave us alone. We're just having a honky tonk night, a little singing, a little drinking, and a little relaxing."

Dewitt was like a dog with a new bone, he wasn't going to let go. Through clenched teeth, he said, "I know Misty Dawn was here. I got a call. Where is she now?"

In unison, we all three said, "Don't know."

He gave us the stink eye. "Y'all had better not be driving 'cas you'll be looking like dead hawk meat if you do." He stomped out the door.

We were laughing so hard that we almost missed Flo sashaying across the room towards us.

"Dimwit's something else, isn't he?" She was laughing. "Alright you guys, y'all need to settle up your bill and we're gonna take you home. Dimwit's got three patrol cars stationed between here and your house, Parker. I'm guessing it's not because you're the grand marshal of some parade."

That created more roars of laughter. Denny waved for Miss Hotty Totty to make her way back to the table.

"So, what's the damage?"

She gave him a teeny tiny piece of paper that I was pretty sure Denny couldn't read at this point. Heck, we'd all be in remedial reading at this point. I seriously doubted I could have even signed my name at this juncture.

Denny gave her two one hundred bills and told her to keep the change, but with one caveat. "There were only three of us tonight, right?"

She was looking at the one hundred dollar tip, comprehension spread across her face, she smiled. "Of course, only three of y'all were here. Friends stopped by but y'all three were only here all night."

Denny nodded and winked.

Flo had to help me walk straight. John Boy managed to get through the door without walking into it and Denny bumped into the wall next to the door jam but managed to turn sideways and get out through the door.

Thankfully, Flo had brought her SUV and we somehow managed to get in it without destroying anything.

We stumbled into my humble abode a little worse for the wear and discovered Misty Dawn with two sleeping bags on the floor.

"John Boy, there's your sleeping bag. Denny, that empty bedroom now has sheets on the bed, that's yours. Flo, help Parker to her bedroom."

We all muttered some type of thank yous to Flo and Misty Dawn. I promptly passed out in my bed.

Chapter 20

I smelled coffee. Unfortunately, I couldn't roll over to get out of bed to get to the coffee. I could barely move my eyeballs to see where I was. To say the night before was a little hazy was a massive understatement.

Groaning, I tried to move my head. It wouldn't move. I wondered if I had had a stroke or something worse. I was pretty sure I hadn't died because I could feel my eyelashes aching. I didn't think you would probably feel pain in heaven. I'm guessing you would probably feel good all the time.

A cheerful looking woman popped her head through the doorway, I hated her immediately.

"Aha, I thought I heard you moving around."

I groaned again, the words didn't make any sense.

"Okay, I know you're Parker and I'm a friend of Mary Jane's. I'm an RN and, if you would like, I can give you some go-go juice and you'll feel great in about twenty-thirty minutes. Do you want some?"

Yeah, maybe that's why she's so darn cheerful. She's been sucking on that go-go juice, whatever it is.

I groaned again.

"What's in it you ask? It's a standard saline solution for dehydration and some B50. I'm going to hook you up and you'll feel great shortly."

Flo was back and said, "Girl, you look like your favorite dog got run over. John Boy is getting his go-go juice right now. Denny's still sleeping and that big old dog of yours is laying on Misty Dawn and won't let Sandy hook up the IVs to her."

I managed to whisper, "Potus" while snapping my fingers, which required a great deal of coordination and strength on my part.

He appeared in the doorway. He was definitely in protection mode. His ears were at attention, he was anxious, and kept looking between me and Misty Dawn in the living room.

"Stand down from Misty Dawn."

I swear that dog shook his head no. Gaining a little strength in my voice, I said it louder and more firmly, "Stand down from Misty Dawn."

He left the room.

Flo looked out and said, "He's laying by Denny's door."

Sandy rolled in an IV stand and drip bag that looked like it had temporarily escaped from the hospital. After rolling me over on my back and cleaning my arm, she inserted the needle and I felt a warm sensation almost immediately. I went back to sleep hoping that I wasn't being given an overdose of something deadly.

Waking up about an hour later, I vaguely wondered if last night had all been a dream. The IV drip was no longer in my arm and I wasn't even sure if it had been there in the first place. I felt like I always did first thing in the morning, a little slow and in dire need of coffee.

Making my way into the kitchen, I discovered the Lady Gatorettes playing cards very quietly. They were holding up little index cards to communicate with each other. Most of what I could see on the cards involved some type of insult and a curse word. Okay, so they were being considerate and creative at the same time.

Misty Dawn and John Boy were still sleeping on the floor and

Potus was guarding Denny's room.

"Um."

A cup of streaming hot coffee was thrust in my hands and gentle hands lead me to the table with a chair already waiting for me.

Rhonda Jean gave me an index card that read, "We moved everything around behind the house and put a big sign up on the front door that says Gone Fishing. Tony Bugs came by about ten, saw the note, and left. We didn't make any noise."

There was a little happy face. She handed me my cell phone. It had been turned to vibrate.

Honestly, as crazy and loony tunes as these hormonal women normally were, they were doing a nice job of taking care of me. I looked at four empty boxes of doughnuts on my countertop. It was only a matter of time before one of them went whacko.

"Myrtle Sue, are you cheating?"

Her eyes were big as saucers. "Um, no, Misty Dawn, I was not. Besides which, I thought you were sleeping and you can't see that far over here anyway."

Misty Dawn snorted, still with her eyes closed, "I know how you are."

John Boy groaned, "Oh, baby. What time is it? I gotta get a few things done today."

Denny opened the door, standing there in his tighty-whities. I could have sworn he'd told me he went commando. Maybe he'd put on something to keep the girls from ogling him. It didn't work. They ogled.

He groaned. Sandy appeared from nowhere, Misty Dawn snapped her fingers and Potus obediently went over to her, covering her with his body. Sandy rolled the IV stand into the bedroom, shutting the door firmly behind her. I knew Denny would be feeling pretty good shortly.

I felt my cell phone starting to vibrate. Caller I.D. showed it to be my office. I managed to croak out good morning.

"Parker, do you know what time it is? I've been worried about you...and Denny. Neither one of you guys have answered your phone in over eight hours."

"Yeah, well, I'll explain later. Any emergencies?"

"Not an emergency but something you definitely need to know. I found the seminar video, the one that Tony Bugs was in. I've sent the link over to you via email.

"Apparently, you made fun of him or, rather, his question, and the group laughed. He got up a few minutes later and left. I'm guessing he's harboring a grudge against you.

"Also, when you look at the video, you might not recognize him. He looks quite different now versus then. Apparently, he was in a serious car accident a couple of months later and had a lot of plastic surgery done."

"Really? He doesn't look like he's had any done."

"He must have had a really good doctor then."

"Are you sure it's the same guy?" My brain was starting to whir on all sixty watts of energy.

"Well, here's the thing, Parker. I personally don't think so. Your Tony Bugs has a slightly different body type than the guy in the video but you need to figure that out. Read the report I sent you and then you tell me what you think is going on."

Hanging up, I wondered what would be the point in killing a real police officer and then substituting someone else in his place? It would be far cheaper and easier to put a cop on the illicit payroll of the crime families.

Everything was getting more confusing, not clearer.

Chapter 21

Firing up my laptop, I quickly found the information Missy had emailed me. Trying to compare the photos on the computer isn't the same as having the printed version in front of me. In my haste to move my coffee cup over so that the computer would have a clear wireless connection with the printer, I watched in horror as my coffee cup...of its own accord, let me add...magically slopped some over into the laptop's keyboard. I watched as the screen slowly turned to black.

"Oh, flipping a!" I shouted. I just want to know if the universe is trying to send me a message about my drinking coffee. Have I royally annoyed a cherubic flying coffee angel who causes me to spill the nectar of the gods on my computers? Or is it some serious evil plot that was hatched prior to my birth and I'm now cursed for the rest of my mortal life?

"Why me? Why now?" I wailed.

I hated making this phone call, although, realistically, I could have just texted Missy to overnight me a new computer. But, nooo, apparently I felt the need to punish myself even more by calling her.

"Um, Missy, I, um..."

Laughing, she said, "I'll overnight it to you. That's two just since you've been there, what, a week. Anything else?"

"No."

Well, the good news is she didn't give me any grief and aggravation about it. However, Denny, emerging from his cocoon, looked at me and rolled his eyes.

"Already? Another one?"

I was irritated. "Enough. Is your laptop in the party wagon or here in the house? Missy thinks the guy from the seminar and this Tony Bugs is not the same person. It looks like a possible switch."

Bringing him up to speed, I ended with, "What would the

point be to have a similar but different Tony Bugs come to Po'thole?"

"Parker, I know you tend to be a bit of a conspiratorialist, but in this case, I think you could be right. If you are right, then that means this whole thing has been planned for a while...and probably not on a local level.

"But there's got to be a connection here somewhere. The question is where and what is it?"

Forgetting that the Lady Gatorettes were still here;

mainly, because they were being so quiet, Rhonda Jean popped up with, "Is there grant money involved for the city in any way? Did Scooter or Tabitha or any of the city commissioners go to any conventions in the last year or so where grants for Native Americans might have been on the agenda? Specifically, for business grants?"

I shrugged. "I can call Celesta and ask her but, then again, she doesn't go to those things because they are out of the county and she refuses to leave the county. Heck, I can barely get her to cross the bridge to go eat pizza in East Po'thole."

We all laughed.

"What about Shelley George?" asked Mary Jane. "She goes to all those things and she's a lot more progressive than Celesta. She might know something."

Finally answering her phone after letting it ring six times and my patience to the point where I wanted to throw the phone across the room, I heard, "Hello, Shelley George."

"Shelley, it's Parker."

"Girl, how you doing?"

I didn't have the time or the desire to get drawn into a long discussion on everything going on in Po'thole.

"Shelley, out of all the conventions and seminars you've gone to out of state and, specifically, the ones you've gone to in New Jersey, New York, and Washington, has anything ever come up about Native American grants and business grants?"

"Sure, of course, it has. Native American applies to the Seminole Indians as well as those Indians out West. I've been looking for years to get some of that grant money for us. Why..."

"Shelley, did Tony Bugs go with you on any of those trips? Did Johnny "Ten Fingers"? Did you make any deals up there?"

"Parker, you have to understand how the political process works. To answer your questions, though, Tony never went with us, neither did Johnny. Yes, I was working on deals for us here. No, I didn't sell out or make any agreements that can't be justified."

"Whoa! Wait!" I shouted, "What agreements?"

"Parker, Parker, calm down. We have ten acres of beautiful riverfront property that can be developed where the businesses would be on the city tax rolls."

I had Shelley on speaker phone and the Lady Gatorettes went wild. It sounded like screaming monkeys at a coconut love fest. Accusations were flung at Shelley for being a traitor to our hometown, maybe she was on the take, you name it – the Lady

Gatorettes were putting it out there.

Finally I heard Shelley shouting.

"Wait, wait! Everyone, wait!" I screamed. "Let Shelley talk."

Shelley, ever the calm individual and a true politician, said, "Everyone, listen. We need new businesses for the city's tax rolls. We need new businesses to bring more people downtown. We need new businesses to heighten our awareness statewide.

"I have talked to many groups and folks about different grants but nothing about a casino."

I rolled my eyes, took a deep breath, and said, "If grant money were available for various businesses to come and develop the riverfront something like the boardwalk at Daytona Beach and then those businesses had to close or go out of business because of lack of sales, then they could sell their individual businesses to one large owner who could do with it what he wanted, right? Like it's a front or set-up for a casino to come in a couple of years down the road, right, Shelley?"

There was silence. That's when I knew she hadn't thought past just getting new businesses downtown. Shelley, unknowingly, was the weak link.

"Possibly. We can't stop individual businesses from selling to someone else." She said slowly, "That would take a lot of money to set up."

Small town thinking. Locals were only thinking of thousands of dollars when outside interests were thinking millions.

"Shelley, what's a couple of million dollars to set up something when you're going to make a couple HUNDRED MILLION dollars on the back end? It's peanuts!

"Plus, protection money collected from each business is where Tony Bugs comes in. The protection money becomes too much for the small business owner to pay, then they take out a loan from loan sharks. They can't pay that off, then then the business goes to who?

Outside interests who in turn can sell it to casinos down the road."

"I doubt it would ever come to that."

Misty Dawn exploded. "Are you a special kind of stupid, Shelley?! Of course, that's how it's going to happen!"

Denny, trying to be a diplomat, said, "Let's not have any name calling here."

"Shelley, you always go along with whatever is the majority vote. What Parker said is probably exactly what is going to happen.

"We have all of this beautiful riverfront property and nobody but nobody has ever figured out that the river is what this city should be promoting to bring people and dollars here. But, nooo, our fine, upstanding city commissioners want to bring in new businesses, businesses that will block the view of the river. Y'all are just stupid!" Misty Dawn was getting that wild look in her eyes. I didn't know if that meant she needed medication or what but she was making me nervous.

I mean, if you thought about it, the Lady Gatorettes could wreck major havoc on whatever buildings might be built on the riverfront. They could sabotage the site, the building materials, the tools, and blow up things...which might not be such a bad idea. I need to let thoughts like that do a slide and glide in my brain. They certainly didn't need to stay there and percolate...although it was tempting.

"Misty Dawn, I have the best interests of the citizens at heart and anything that will help this town to grow, I will do it!" Shelley huffed over the phone.

Before things could escalate even more, Denny waded into the estrogen-laded conversation. "Ladies, let's take a break, think things over and then have this conversation tomorrow. Let's meet at the park at ten, okay?"

Suspicion was in Shelley's voice. "Why the park?"

"Because you guys can get as loud as you want and no one is going to throw us out or call the police," explained Denny.

"Okay, see you at ten at the park."

Denny turned to Misty Dawn who was now slurping another cup of coffee. "You might want to re-think calling a city commissioner, or anyone for that matter, a special kind of stupid. If they weren't aggravated before with you, they definitely will be after being called stupid; particularly since you are indicating that they may be just shy of having a full house of brains."

Misty Dawn looked at Denny for a moment and then turned back to whispering with the Lady Gatorettes. After a few minutes of whispered conversations, occasional glances at me and Denny, they all said goodbye and left.

"Do you think I had any effect on them, Parker?"

"Probably not. They're probably plotting and planning on how to make sure the casino doesn't come in and, more realistically, on how to get rid of Tony Bugs."

Little did I know how close to the truth I was.

Chapter 22

Saffron Woo was not the first person I ever wanted to talk to first thing in the morning. Unfortunately, it happened on a fairly regular basis. The woman apparently got up at the crack of dawn, worked really hard until noon, had lunch at a fancy, high-priced restaurant in New York City, and then did socialite stuff for the rest of the day. I did know she wouldn't answer any of her phones after seven thirty at night.

"Yeah." Miss Congeniality I was never going to be first thing in the morning. Some would argue that I would never be voted for that regardless of what it was.

"Parker, darling, how are you today?" Never pausing for a moment, she merrily continued. "You'll be so happy to know that I have gotten you a huge advance on your next book. You can say 'thank you' now."

My brain was not in gear, I hadn't had any coffee, I hated her perky voice first thing in the morning, and I hung up the phone on her. Oh, yeah, I pushed the button to vibrate, and shoved the cell phone under my other pillow so I couldn't hear it. I went back to sleep for a couple more hours.

A continuous pounding on my front door finally woke me up. I stumbled to the door and turned the doorknob. It wouldn't turn. I peeked out the keyhole. Denny was standing there holding a cup of coffee and he didn't look happy. I twisted the doorknob again, nothing. I couldn't get it to turn.

"Hold on, Denny." I went to the back door and that doorknob was jammed also. For all intents and purposes, I was locked in my own house.

"Denny, I'm locked in." I shouted through the door.

"You know, if you didn't want me to be able to come in your house, all you had to do was say so. Gluing the lock is even a little beneath you." His voice was very controlled which meant he was furious.

"Find a way to open this door now."

"Parker, why give me a key if you didn't want me to come in your house?"

"Denny, I'm starting to get really ticked off here! I didn't glue anything and get this door OPEN NOW!" I was shouting.

"Then back away from the door, Parker."

A couple of hard kicks from Denny, the door bent inwards and the doorknob was left sitting in the doorframe casing. So much for strong secure doors.

"What is going on here?" His voice was still very controlled.

"Listen, I'm not happy about this either. I don't have the foggiest notion what is going on but I do know I need coffee."

He thrust a cup at me. "It's probably cooled down considerably since I first got here."

It had but God knows I sure wasn't going to complain about it at this point. I needed the coffee and starting another battle with Denny wasn't worth it.

"You're going to need to go to Lowe's or Home Depot for another door."

"Parker, call the folks who installed this mobile home…"

"It's a modular home."

"I don't care if the three little pigs built this place! Call them and tell them to replace the door! I'm not your stinking handyman!" Denny shouted. "You act like I'm supposed to clean up all of your messes. You're a pain, Parker Bell!"

Losing my temper, I shouted, "Fine! Considering how much

you're paid, you should be taking care of my stuff! You know what? You're fired! Get out of my house now, leave the party wagon and you figure out how to get back to Atlanta or wherever it is you roost on your own stinking nickel!"

We stared at each other for a moment. He turned around and left. I found my cell phone under the pillow. It had ten messages on it. I ignored them and called Missy.

"Hi, Parker, how you doing today?" She was chipper.

"Cancel everything that Denny is associated with, his passwords, the credit cards, the expense account, everything. He's not to have access to anything. Have Anthony write his last check, severance pay, etc. Have Jimmy check for any back door access to any of our programs and our servers. If he finds anything suspicious, have him eliminate it or shut it down completely. This is a priority one. Do it now!"

Stunned silence then, "Parker, are you just mad about something or do you think Denny has actually violated something, become a security risk?"

"Just get it done now, Missy. Get everything done ASAP. This is a priority one." I punched the end button on my phone. I was still fuming. Denny and I both had short fuses and they had both exploded at the same time.

I dialed another number. "It's Parker. I want you to monitor all calls for Missy and Denny for the next three hours. Call me if they have any communication between the two of them. Specifically, if Missy calls Denny. Thanks."

If Missy called Denny, then that was it. I really would fire her and not take her back this time. I had never fired Denny before so I was assuming, always a dangerous thing, that Missy would believe I was serious and proceed to do what I had told her to do.

I made a pot of coffee and started returning messages.

Chapter 23

"Good morning, Saffron. What do you mean you got me an advance on my next book?" I snarled.

"Parker, darling, not any old advance but a huge advance! And you're welcome!"

I could feel Saffron beaming at me through the phone. Let's be honest, money does revive a girl.

"How much?"

I whistled when she told me the number. "I must have sold more books than I realized to get an advance that big."

"Yes, my dear, you did. What's going on down there in that little godforsaken town?"

I brought her up to speed only leaving out that I had just fired Denny. She had the hots for Denny. Heck, she had the hots for any male of legal age who was breathing on a regular basis and didn't need assistance from an oxygen tank.

Meanwhile, my mind was racing fifty million miles an hour between what was happening in Po'thole and what kind of book I should write on all of this frivolity.

Checking my messages as soon as I had hung up with Saffron, I found the one I was looking for.

"Nothing from Denny to Missy on their regular phones. A two minute call came into Missy from a burner phone. I pulled the conversation. Denny was asking Missy what was going on. He was mad. She was very businesslike with him. No code words were used. She explained several times that his services were no longer needed. She finally thanked him for his services and hung up the phone."

I was relieved about Missy. She had been with me since the beginning and I didn't really want to fire her. Oh, yeah, we'd had several explosions over the years but she knew when I was serious. I was serious about Denny.

The next message was from her. "Everything has been taken care of. The subject did call in, I explained his services were no longer required and we appreciated what he had done for us. I hung up."

I was even more glad she had explained what had happened on the phone call with Denny. I mentally made a note to give her a raise upon my return.

Rhonda Jean had left me a message. "Saw Denny walking, gave him a ride to the rental car place, he wouldn't talk. Do you need us?"

Suspecting that the Lady Gatorettes had been keeping an eye on my place even with Denny here actually gave me a sense of relief.

I texted back, "Yes, when can you be here?"

Within thirty seconds I heard a truck pull up in the yard. Since I no longer had a front door, I watched with some amusement as the ladies filed out of the truck. They looked almost like the clowns in the circus where they just keep coming out.

Rhonda Jean clucked, "Look at that door! We need to get that fixed now. Parker, what size is that door?"

Probably looking like Bambi in the headlights, I just stood there and shrugged. Geez, it never occurred to me that there might be different door sizes. I thought they were all a standard size. Being mechanically handy is not one of my basic skill sets.

Whipping a measuring tape out of her purse, Rhonda Jean quickly measured it and started back down the steps.

"Wait!" I hesitated to even ask but I did need to know. "Did any of y'all put glue in the keyholes to keep me from getting out?"

They all looked at each other. Apparently they have a secret way of communicating with each other because I couldn't pick up any "tells," micro-expressions, from their faces or body language.

"Nope, not us and that's not a good thing, Parker," said Rhonda Jean. I guess it was her turn today to be the leader of the group. "Was your back door also glued?"

I nodded.

"I'm going to the store and getting two doors. Myrtle Sue, since you're our domestic goddess," everyone smiled at Myrtle Sue who blushed, "Get all this stuff cleaned up. Mary Jane and Flo, figure out the perimeter and then let Misty Dawn know the details. We need to keep our gal safe!" She bounced down to the truck and took off.

Oh, yay! I was now officially adopted by the Lady Gatorettes. There were worse things in life, I suppose, and they were probably going to be a lot cheaper than Denny but I did need to ask.

"Um, Myrtle Sue…"

"I'm cleaning, Parker, ask someone else." Ooookay, the woman was focused I had to give her credit for that.

"Um, Flo, how much do I need to pay you guys for all of this and for being my security detail? Also, aren't your husbands going to be worried about you?"

Flo was getting ready to go outside and secure the perimeter. I did know what that meant and

I hoped it did not involve land mines.

"Ask Misty Dawn the next time she calls." She was out in the yard in a flash.

Myrtle Sue thrust a fresh cup of coffee in my hands and pointed for me to go back into the bedroom.

Grabbing my laptop, I went back into the bedroom. I must have dozed off or Myrtle Sue drugged me, not out of the realm of possibilities, I woke up with the bedroom looking like a Martha Stewart showroom.

I stumbled out into the living room, slightly dazed at the sight. Myrtle Sue had a gift for interior design. Who knew?! She had completely re-arranged my living room and, I must admit, it did look a lot better. The room was more open and airy looking. In fact, it looked downright spacious. Sigh, I really don't have the girly-girl gene for decorating or really doing anything domestic.

A cup of coffee was thrust into my hand. "Wow! This is great! It's...it's beautiful!"

Myrtle Sue smiled. "This is what I do when everybody will leave me alone. Notice how easy it is to move around now. Plus, it looks nice."

"Myrtle Sue, you did an outstanding job!" I figured a couple of compliments would go a long way with her...and also probably with the other Lady Gatorettes as well. She beamed.

"Any news on anything?" I asked.

"Nope."

"Any phone calls?"

"Nope."

I sighed inwardly. Myrtle Sue was back to her normal chatty self. I tried another tactic. "Anyone come to the door?"

"Nope."

"Myrtle Sue, did you drug me so I would sleep during all of this cleaning up and interior decorating?"

"Nope." A slight pause, "What's your definition of drugging?"

I glared at Myrtle Sue, which had absolutely no effect on her, but, then again, why would it? She hung out with the Lady

Gatorettes and they all could give the stink eye to the devil and he would have backed down.

"Never mind. We need to go out and find out who's killing all of these people!" I went to grab my purse but I couldn't find it.

"Myrtle Sue, where is my purse?" I exploded.

"Parker, you aren't supposed to leave the house, remember? And I can't let you giddy up and get outta here. Misty Dawn would kill me dead."

"When are they coming back?"

A shrug of the shoulders. I called Missy to see what was happening with my company in Atlanta. Everything was flowing smoothly, according to her. I was a little annoyed. Apparently no one needed or wanted me for anything. Even Potus was ignoring me.

I should have known this was the calm before the storm.

Chapter 24

After promising Myrtle Sue I wasn't going to run away, she let me out of the house so I could wander around the yard. She had warned me that I shouldn't get too close to the edge of the property because that's where Flo and the girls had set up booby traps. She indicated that parts of my body might fly off on their own if I stepped on the barely seen thin wire running from tiny little azalea bush to tiny little azalea bush.

She also warned against trying to jump over the azalea bushes because there might be an infrared beam that would be broken and as she said "that wouldn't be a good thing." The good news was that all of this kept people out of my yard or, at the very least, would hurt them badly. The bad news was it kept me a prisoner in my own yard.

Bill Weeble, my elderly, hard-of-hearing next door neighbor waved at me. I waved and then turned my back hoping he would stay on his property and not wander over to talk to me. Alas, this was not to be.

"Parker, Parker!" He hoarsely shouted, although it really sounded more like a loud whisper. "Parker, what's going on at your house?"

I tried to ignore him and continued walking around the perimeter line of my property. I watched Bill out of the corner of my eye. Much as he annoyed me, I didn't want to watch him get blown to bits.

When he finally decided to walk, at a snail's pace because he was using a walker, over to see me I had to break my resolve and trot over to the property line.

"Bill, don't cross the property line. There's..."

"You can't tell me what to do," he snapped. "Your mom and dad let me come over any time I wanted and I want to right now."

Oh, yeah, this is the reason why I love old people. They won't listen to anything.

"Bill, mom and dad are dead. Don't come over here right now because..."

"I want to see that thing you're calling a house and you can't stop me!"

Losing my temper, I snapped back at him. "Bill, it's called trespassing. I do not want you on my property. There are explosives lining the perimeter. You could get blown to bits. Stay off my property!"

He harrumphed. "All you had to do was say you didn't want me over there."

Aarrgghh! The good news is that I watched him hobble back indoors. As aggravating and nosy as he was, I didn't want him blown up. That would be really hard to explain in light of all of the other stuff going on in my life here.

As I was standing there contemplating life and Bill, I caught a whiff of something. I wasn't sure what it was. Then a loud boom!

The line of explosives on the far side of my property had been detonated. Rushing over to see if anyone was hurt, I made a note to myself, the next time I smell that smell I'll know that it is lighter fluid being lit.

I couldn't see that anyone had crossed into my yard. There was a pink sneaker laying about ten feet from the line. I knew that it wasn't one of the Lady Gatorettes because none of them would be caught dead wearing anything other than blue and orange. That was a relief.

Gently picking up the sneaker, I saw a note stuck inside the shoe. It was typed.

"Next time it's your house with you in it. Stop messing around in stuff that's none of your business."

Now I was mad. I was mad before but now I had done a slow burn, no pun intended, and it was time to solve all of these murders. I strongly suspected it was the work of one person, and I was pretty sure it was a man. There was only one name on that list.

Chapter 25

I stomped back in the house, dialing a little used number. I wasn't even sure if the number was still good. I kind of suspected that it was a burner cell phone, one that was used once or twice and then tossed.

"Yeah." Businesslike, no nonsense.

"I need to know what you have on..." and I gave the name. "Is he involved on any cases that you guys are working?"

"Why?"

"I strongly suspect he's involved or connected to all of the murders in Po'thole. I think it's because of..."

I heard what sounded like a soft cough sound, a dropping of the phone, and then it was disconnected. Shaking my head, I knew this wasn't good. No point in calling back, my contact was probably dead. I read enough thrillers, worked with enough law enforcement agencies, and shot enough guns with suppressors to know what a soft cough sound meant.

What could possibly be so important about this little dinky town out in the middle of nowhere? Too many people had already died and now my contact in Washington. Well, he could have been anywhere since I called him on his cell phone.

Also, in all fairness, he might have been killed because of a case he was working on. This might have had nothing to do with me, although it seemed strangely coincidental....and I don't believe in coincidences.

Fixing a cup of coffee, I was wondering if I should alert the news media and have them swarm over this area. While I love the news media, particularly when I have a new book coming out, they weren't always the best method of finding answers. Although having another however many hands and eyes trying to find answers might be helpful.

I inwardly groaned when I realized it might play really well into the Lady Gatorettes hands. Rhonda Jean would demand that the Florida football coaches pay attention to her trick plays. It would also give all of the ladies an opportunity to give a big old redneck shout out to their favorite players. Was it really worth it I mused?

On the flip side of the coin Saffron Woo would have a field day with this. So would the national media if it was a slow news week. Guess I'd better start looking at what was going on in the world...or call Missy and let her give me the quick updates.

"Hey, Missy."

"Hey, yourself, Parker Bell." Missy was her normal chipper self. "Need another computer?"

"Nope. Tell me what's going on statewide, nationwide, and international wise in terms of the news."

"What are you looking for? Murders, nightclub shootings, what?"

"The short version is do you think this week and next are going to be a slow news week?"

"Parker," a small sigh, "do I look like I have a crystal ball in front of me? I know you think I'm the great and all-knowing Wizard of Oz but there's no way of knowing what's going to happen in the next seven to ten days. What is it that you're trying to do or find out?"

I explained the situation down here and gave her my idea on getting the national news media involved.

"You know," she mused. "You could get Saffron to approach it from one or two angles and we could get some of our computer guys on it. We could blast it out all over the internet."

"Let's do it and here's the strategy."

For the next few minutes we discussed various ways to get as much coverage as possible on Po'thole.

Much as I dreaded speaking to Saffron, we had a love-hate relationship, she was going to be key to getting a lot of buzz going on these murders.

I truly admired several things about Saffron. Whenever I called her she answered within three rings and she never put me on hold when she had incoming calls. Of course, I truly suspected that was because I made her a LOT of money on my books and that she had a cell phone she used just for me.

Taking a deep breath and wondering vaguely why I didn't smoke, I called Saffron.

"Parker, darling, how are you?" She always sounded genuinely glad to hear from me. "What's new wherever you are? You know I've gotten Rob a book deal?"

I didn't care about Rob at the moment, I was more interested in having her help me. Okay, so I'm self-centered and self-focused. I personally thought those were some of my more enduring qualities. Missy informed me that was not so but refused to elaborate on what my best qualities were. I'm sure I have some...somewhere.

"I'm great, Saffron. I need your help." I paused, knowing that was like teasing a dog with a bone that had meat on it.

"I'm on it, dear. What can I do for you?" I could almost see her doing the happy dance. I rarely if ever called her for help. She knew this would be big.

"I've got a situation down here in Po'thole…"

"I need to come down and see what this delightful little town is all about."

"You'd hate it. There have been more murders here than

Carter's got little green pills and I think the police chief is tied in with the Mafia in some way. But, and that's a big but, I can't seem to find out anything about him. I've called my contacts at the FBI and CIA and they all shut down when I ask about this guy. I don't know if he's involved in an on-going case, if he's a secret informant or if he is in the witness protection program. Although that would seem a little odd to put him in a quasi-high profile job like a police chief even if it's in a dinky little town. I don't know if he is being investigated.

"Regardless, I want to get some publicity going down here. Many hands make light work or whatever that saying is. I need some help with this."

"Okay, darling, this is what Saffron can do for you. I can get hold of your publisher and put out some of these scrumptious details for your next book. I'll put out the word to some of my journalist friends."

I interrupted, "Not the ones you have lunch and cocktails with, Saffron. I need real ones."

She ignored me. "I'll get this out on the AP wire. Will you be doing the virtual internet thing?"

"Yes, Missy is already on it."

"Great! Within forty-eight hours, I guarantee you people will be all over that little town of yours. Okay, I need to run. Taa taa!"

I smiled as I punched the end button. This town was not going to know what hit them.

Chapter 26

Within twelve minutes I received my first hostile phone call from Dewitt. "Parker, what have you done?" I could hear the tightness in his chest as he struggled to maintain composure.

"In reference to what?" I replied sweetly, while struggling to keep from laughing.

"I've just had two phone calls from reporters wanting to know about the status of our serial murderer here. What did you have to do with this?" He was seething. While I suppose I should say I have compassion and mercy for him, sadly, I do not. The poor man should never have been sheriff to begin with. He truly embraced the philosophy of Peter Drucker in that you rise to the highest level of your incompetency, one level higher or lower in life you might be great. Unfortunately, I strongly suspected Dewitt had already hit the Peter Principle at several different levels.

"Dewitt, what makes you think I had anything to do with this? The truth is there have been six, count them, six murders here in less than a year. Don't you think somebody somewhere was going to pick up that this isn't the vacation spot of the world? There have been way too many murders here for someone not to notice."

He grumbled. "I still think you had something to do with it."

"Dewitt, much as I am enjoying the conversation I have another call coming in. Have a great day." I started to laugh and managed to get myself under control while answering the next call.

"Hello."

"Parker, I'm pretty upset with you," growled Tony Bugs.

"Um, why?" I was having a hard time keeping the laughter out of my voice. Meanwhile, I had laugh tears streaming down my face. It was a glorious time for me.

"I'm getting phone calls from reporters all across the country. I strongly suspect you got some of your cronies to set this up." His voice was tight and starting to rise.

"Now why would I do that, Tony?" I was now biting my tongue to keep from laughing.

"Probably because you think we're all idiots down here. I'm from New Jersey and I know more than these yahoos!" He was starting to shout.

I decided to push his buttons a little bit. "Yeah, about that,

Tony. You took one of my seminars, didn't you? Or, I guess I should say someone who looked incredibly similar to you. But it wasn't you, was it?"

A brief silence and then there was no illusion about Tony. "You have no idea what you're up against, Parker. You think you're so smart but you're not. You've been warned!"

"So, I guess this means I don't have to go dinner with you now, does it?" I couldn't keep the laughter contained at this point.

He slammed his phone down. I literally was laughing so hard that I had to get a tissue to contain all of the fluids oozing from my eyeballs and nose.

After settling down, I called Rhonda Jean. The Lady Gatorettes had thoughtfully inputted their names and cell phone numbers into my phone with the exception of Misty Dawn and she was really the one I wanted to talk to.

"Hey, hey, Parker! What can I do you for?" Rhonda Jean sounded way too happy. I guessed that she had probably inhaled a couple of doughnuts or some other highly sugared item within the past thirty minutes or so.

"Rhonda Jean, would you have Misty Dawn call me as soon as possible?"

I could hear Rhonda Jean licking her fingers. I was right, she had been eating doughnuts. "She's not happy with you."

That caught me a little off-guard. "Why? What did I do?"

"You fired Denny and she really liked him. She thinks you're an idiot for doing that."

Okay, the good news about being on a sugar high is that it's equivalent to having a couple of stiff drinks. In other words, loose lips. The bad news is I needed the Lady Gatorettes on my side and, specifically, watching my back. If they wouldn't or couldn't, I'd need to hire some security people and that wouldn't be the same thing.

"Okay, I might be an idiot but I had my reasons." I needed to pacify her. Then it dawned on me. "Is Denny still here?"

"Maybe, maybe not." She was cautious. Maybe the sugar high

was wearing off a little bit. That or she knew Misty Dawn would kill her for telling me that she liked Denny and that Denny may still be in the area.

"Rhonda Jean, are y'all still going to help me or are y'all through with me?" I wanted to lay it out on the line. I needed to know.

A big sigh. "Yes, of course, Parker. We still have your back. We promised and we don't go back on our promises. Well, of course, unless you do something mean or nasty or hurt one of us but since you haven't done that, we're still protecting you."

I looked out the front window and then the window over the sink. "I don't see you guys out there."

A sigh. "Parker, you know we all hunt, right?"

"Yes."

"We don't have to be out in the open or on top of you to protect you. Right now, you're standing in front of the kitchen sink and you have on a blue shirt. Don't you think I could hit someone before they got through any part of the back of your house?"

She had a point.

"Gotcha and I appreciate it. Ask Misty Dawn to contact me, please. I need to tell her what's going on."

"We are already know about the internet stuff and you getting the news reporters."

"How?" Dang! I thought all of my conversations were secure.

"I put Google alerts on anything that came up about this area and on you. Easy peasy."

Something so simple and yet something I had totally overlooked. I might need to hire Rhonda Jean for my security company.

"Smart on your part, Rhonda Jean." I sounded appreciative.

"Yep, that's what I do." She sounded proud. "I'll get Misty Dawn for you. It might be a couple of hours. I think she's fishing."

"Okay, just have her get in touch with me before eight tonight."

I started to giggle again until it became an outrageously loud laugh. I now had confirmation that Tony Bugs was involved somehow in the murders and what was going on in town. Denny was probably still in town. Although I was still really upset with him, there was a slight possibility we could work things out and he would come back. I had the Lady Gatorettes on my side and protecting my back. I had the news media and social media buzzing about the serial murders. And, most importantly, things were starting to change for the better.

It never occurred to me that revenge would be served so quickly.

Chapter 27

There was a loud pounding on my front door. I didn't bother to look out and see who it was. I made the dangerous assumption it was Misty Dawn. I was wrong. It was Tony Bugs and Dewitt with their team of merry idiots in swat team uniforms.

"Yes, gentlemen, what can I do for you today?" I asked sweetly. Meanwhile, my heart was thumping against my chest. I hoped they couldn't see it. My cell phone which was usually connected to me like an umbilical cord was laying on the countertop. I couldn't buzz anyone for help.

"Parker Bell, you are under arrest for hindering the process of an on-going investigation. You are also under arrest for the murder of Tabitha Smith. You are a person of interest in the Scooter Travis murder.

Your bond for the murder of Murphy has been revoked. You are under arrest." Tony Bugs pronounced this in a very formal, deep voice. Dewitt looked like Bambi in the headlights.

As Tony continued with my Miranda rights, my brain had whirred into action after the first six words.

My smart mouth took over, I couldn't help it, and what was worse was that I started to laugh. They were not amused.

"So, gentlemen, who's actually arresting me and who's jurisdiction is it? Think on that a moment while I get my cell phone."

Tony and Dewitt turned and looked at each other. A somewhat confused look on their faces. I pushed the door to while hightailing back to the counter. Rhonda Jean suddenly appeared. It was like a magic act. She almost caused me to drop my cell phone.

"Quick! Come with me!" She bounced gently on a large tile in the kitchen floor and a trap door opened up. "Down, now!"

I didn't need a second invitation. I dropped through the trap door and moved off to the side. It wouldn't do me any good if Rhonda Jean dropped down on top of me and smushed me dead. Although, in all fairness, I'd rather be dead that way instead of sitting in some jail rotting.

"Come!" She pointed her finger at two large containers on the side of the house. We shimmied and crab crawled over to them. There was a vertical cut in the plastic. Rhonda Jean opened it. "Get in there and I'll tell you what to do when I get in the other one. Be really quiet!"

She didn't have to tell me twice. I scooted in real quick and she pushed the plastic opening closed. A few mili-seconds later I could barely hear her in the other container. I almost screamed when I felt her hand touch my arm. It was dark and I couldn't see anything, in my defense.

She pulled me closer to a small opening in the wall between the two containers. "These are the compost and trash bins. If they bring dogs in, they won't be able to smell us in here." She whispered.

"I don't smell any garbage or rotting leaves," I whispered back.

"There's an air freshener in each of our bins. Plus, there's deer musk oil that's been sprinkled around the outside of these. Shh! They're walking around now."

I could hear the guys stomping around outside cursing. They were having a fit. Dewitt kept repeating while shouting, "How could she disappear like that?

How could she disappear like that?"

Tony Bugs was definitely in charge. Standing less than two feet from my container, he shouted, "Check the attic, the closets, under the house, anywhere she could be hiding. She couldn't have disappeared into thin air. She's got to be somewhere close."

Well, he was right about being close. I almost giggled. Then I saw a red dot from Rhonda Jean's container.

Boom! Then another Boom! I knew that Rhonda Jean had detonated some of the perimeter's explosives. They were never designed to kill anyone but to scare off people. This is apparently all it took for the merry men of law enforcement to decide that I had run through my own homemade security system to escape from them. They took off like a hound on a coon hunt.

Rhonda Jean whispered. "We're going to have to be here for a while. They've still got to come back and get their vehicles. Mary Jane will let me know when we can leave. We're going to have to make a run for it when she gives me the signal. Follow my instructions."

"Absolutely!" As far as I was concerned, Rhonda Jean now walked on water for saving me.

It seemed like we sat there for an hour but, of course, my looking at my cell phone every five minutes didn't help either. I saw two quick flashes of red dots from Rhonda Jean's hole, then another two red dots. I braced for another set of explosions which never came.

"We can go now," said Rhonda Jean, speaking in a normal tone of voice. "They're gone."

Easing out of the tight container and crab crawling under the house, I came out by the back door. Rhonda Jean was right behind me.

Entering my home, I discovered River County's finest had made a mess. They had thrown all of the pillows from the sofa on the floor and upturned all of the furniture. Heck, I was impressed they thought I was small enough to hide underneath the sofa cushions or that

I could slide under the chair in my quest not to be found by them. However, I strongly suspected it was just their male ego that suffered a blow since I had escaped from them and they were showing their displeasure by tearing up my place.

"Myrtle Sue needs to get in here," harrumphed Rhonda Jean. "Them boys are pigs."

"Ah, look at all the dirt they drug in too." Okay, so I was playing the pity hand. I was hoping Myrtle Sue would vacuum the entire house.

Rhonda Jean was punching her cell phone like crazy texting to Myrtle Sue.

"You know, you can do voice to text on your cell phone, right?" I thought I was being helpful. Rhonda Jean barely glanced up from fingers dancing over the phone.

"Yeah, I know how to do that but I didn't want you hearing what I was saying to Myrtle Sue."

Oh. Nothing like being put into place by someone who's IQ could be measured in doughnuts. Yes, I was still grateful for her saving me but the 'tude could go.

"Did you ever get hold of Misty Dawn?"

Rhonda Jean looked up. "Well, I have been a little busy saving you from the cops but, yes, she knows you want to talk with her."

I was starting to get irritated now. Two verbal slap downs from a redneck gal in less than two minutes was beyond my limit of being nice.

"Listen, Rhonda Jean, I don't really need you or the other Lady Gatorettes. Yes, I'd rather have you on my side than not but…"

Rhonda Jean looked at me, glanced at her cell phone, and said, "Okay." She walked out of the house.

I was still irritated, probably because she was right but, heck, I wasn't going to admit that. I'd fired Denny and now I guess I'd fired the Lady Gatorettes. I wasn't doing too well with my leadership skills.

Calling Missy, I explained everything that had happened including my repartee with Rhonda Jean.

Missy sighed, "Parker, you are running off all of the people who could actually protect you. Why?"

"I dunno." Sad to say, I really didn't. "Maybe it's the water here."

"You don't drink water, Parker. You drink coffee, you drink iced tea, and you drink beer. That's it. The plain variety of water has never once passed through your lips since I've known you. You cannot use that as an excuse. Why are you doing this?"

Rats! Why did I have to have someone on my team who could bust my chops? Maybe I was being hormonal. Nah! Not any more than normal. Then the answer came to me and it wasn't pretty.

"Do you know the answer, Missy?" Hoping that she would say she didn't have a clue.

"Yes."

Inwardly I groaned. Oh, great, and she was probably going to hit it right on the head. Better to get it over with and move forward than to dwell on woulda, coulda, shoulda.

"And that would be...."

"You always want to be in control and don't like it very much when someone disagrees with you."

Yeah, that would be it. My defensive chip-on-the-shoulder popped up. "So? That's what makes me a successful businesswoman." I could justify pretty much anything...in my head, anyway.

"True, it does," she agreed. "But, when you're not running your own company, it doesn't serve you well and that's what's happening down there. You need their help, you're not used to being dependent upon someone helping you out.

"Plus," she smirked, "it's why you never have a boyfriend for very long."

Ouch, that hurt! True but it still hurt.

She continued on, "Denny's still down there. I can track him. He doesn't know that but I can."

"Is he with Misty Dawn?" I interrupted her.

"Parker," she sighed, "it doesn't tell me who he's with, just where he is. He was out on the river fishing. At least, I assume he was fishing because he was on the river and his location didn't change for quite a while."

I exploded. "He's with Misty Dawn! That low down, stinking son of a…"

"Parker, you fired him. He's free to do whatever he wants to do."

Just because the Bible says the truth will make you free doesn't mean I like having it thrown back up into my face.

"True. I'm going to need some time to think about things."

"Don't take too long. You've got reporters fixing to descend upon you and I would imagine Dewitt and Tony are going to come back after you. Also, you don't know if any crazies are going to pop up on your doorstep."

Oops! I hadn't thought about that part. Terminating our phone call after a few seconds, I had to admit to myself

I probably did need the Lady Gatorettes and maybe Denny. I needed more eyes and ears so I could avoid having an unpleasant stay-cation in the local jail.

Pink's "So What" started playing on my phone. I didn't recognize the number but decided to answer it anyway.

A very formal voice asked, "Is this Parker Bell?"

"Yes." It didn't have the same authoritative tone that the FBI or other law enforcement people used. My curiosity was piqued.

"This is a friendly phone call. You need to back off from Tony, the proposed casino, and all of the other riverfront business development."

I don't deal real well with authority or anyone telling me what I can and cannot do. "Or what?"

Silence, then. "You don't want to pursue this."

"I'm guessing you're not law enforcement so you threatening me doesn't mean a whole lot. I'll do…"

"We're the permanent law enforcement folks. We don't threaten, we make promises."

I could almost hear a smile in his voice. So I took a different tactic. "Sweetie, you've made your phone call for the day. You don't scare me. In fact, take this as fair warning. You will start having problems if you start or continue to mess with me. How's them apples?"

He chuckled, "You're feisty but you don't know what you're stepping into. I will tell you this much, it's probably not what you think." He paused.

I can be hot-headed and impulsive but I do have the sense God gave a goose. I wasn't going to help him out by divulging anything. So, I didn't say anything.

"Okay, you've been warned."

I was sweating as he hung up. I analyzed his voice. It was educated, formal, quasi-FBI sounding, probably from the Northeast somewhere, maybe in the Pennsylvania area, and it sounded like he was well-informed. No overt threat but definitely an implied one. It actually sounded like he was a corporate executive. That definitely would take a whole new twist on things. If it wasn't the Mafia that was tied in with Tony Bugs, then who was it? What corporation could it be?

My brain was starting to feel like a washing machine with all of the agitation going on. I needed to get to the rinse, spin, and done cycle.

Who could I trust and ask questions about possible corporations or other interested parties in the riverfront development? While I sort of knew the other city commissioners, the two that popped into my mind were Celesta and Shelley.

Calling them, I invited them over to the house since I couldn't be seen in public without getting arrested and asked them to park their cars behind my house. I was beyond shocked when both said they had an opening in their busy schedules today and would be over later. Will wonders never cease!

Chapter 28

Surprisingly, they both showed up with five minutes of each other. Knowing the two of them from way back I knew punctuality was not either's strong suit so they were really interested in what I had to say.

Shelley got down to brass tacks. "Parker, there's all sorts of rumors flying around town about you. Tell me what's going on."

Celesta jumped in there too, nodding sagely. "Yes, there's a rumor that you are going to be arrested for all of the murders here.

"Now," she leaned forward, winking at me, "what gives?"

Thank goodness I had fixed coffee; otherwise, the two of them could cause me to have a nuclear meltdown because of their frosty stares.

"Tony Bugs is definitely involved in something. I'm not sure if he's Mafia."

The two of them exchanged a knowing glance.

"But, here's the wild thing. The phone call I got sounded like it was from a corporate executive and he did tell me it's not what I think is going on. I guess my real question is," I looked at both of them carefully, "what IS going on? There's something here that either you guys know about or are involved with or have major suspicions on. Tell me what it is because I can't believe either of you would have had someone kill Tabitha and Scooter. Oh, yeah, let's not forget about Buddy, Bobby, Happy Jack, or even Murphy. I just don't see you doing that. So what's going on?"

I stood up. I had laid out my cards on the table with them. If they were going to try and kill me, I stood a good chance of getting to the kitchen floor first and disappearing before they could do that.

Celesta looked over at Shelley who barely nodded her head. "Right after you left the first time, Shelley, Tabitha, and I started getting these strange phone calls."

"What kind of strange phone calls?" I asked.

"Someone with a gruff voice would say 'you know what you need to do to develop the riverfront' and sometimes they would just go 'vote right.' I had absolutely no clue what they were talking about because nothing was really coming up before the city commission on actually doing anything with the riverfront," Celesta said.

"She doesn't have caller I.D. so she couldn't see who it was calling. Me, on the other hand," Shelley was smiling. "I'm in today's world and I have caller I.D.."

And that's when their squabbling started.

"I'm not paying extra money to the phone company to find out who's calling me. They want a return phone call, they can jolly well leave their name and number." Celesta was starting to build up a full head of steam in mili-seconds.

"Then you need to quit complaining about how many hang ups you have and how many callers you can't identify because people won't leave their name and number. And why, girl, do you still have an answering machine and not voice mail? You're way too old fashion and you are younger than me."

Celesta was fuming. I knew there was a fire extinguisher in the kitchen if smoke and fire came out of her head because of an internal explosion.

"I'm not paying good money for something that still works.

I don't need or want voicemail. I've heard way too many things that can go wrong with it. People should have the common sense to leave their name and phone numbers when they get an answering machine."

Shelley harrumphed.

I jumped in there before a free-for-all started. And to think they were always so cordial to each other during the city commission meetings.

"Ladies, let's get back to the strange phone calls." I turned to Shelley. "Since you have caller

I.D., did you try calling the number back?"

"Yep. Must be one of those burner cell phones." She smirked at Celesta. "That's a disposable cell phone to you."

Celesta was clenching and unclenching her fists. I could see her grinding her teeth. Dr. Steve was going to be happy to put her back in his chair for more dental work.

Shelley continued on merrily, "No answer, no voicemail, no nothing. The calls were coming about once a week and every time I tried calling it back almost immediately but no answer. I had one of my grandkids try to find out where it was coming from.

"The calls were coming in from all over the country. First New Jersey, then California, then the Chicago area, then the Miami area. All that made me think of was that someone was either doing a lot of flying around or they were having someone call me from those places."

"Was it the same voice each time or was it different?" I was very curious as to what was going on.

"Different voices but it sounded very mechanical. You know, like it was done being through a scrambler machine."

I turned to Celesta. "Same thing with you?"

She nodded her head. I could see the wheels spinning in her head trying to think of things to get back at Shelley on.

"Yes, first couple of weeks it was about voting right. Then it became 'you know what to do when the vote comes up.' Honestly, I didn't know what they were referring to at that point."

I mused, "Someone has been planning this a long time. Is there anything that came up before the other four murders and you guys either listened to a proposal or shot one down? Maybe it's a revenge thing?"

They looked at each other, I couldn't tell if they were sending telepathic messages to each other or not. However, they were signaling to each other but I wasn't privy to that method. They sat there for a few more minutes running their fingers around the coffee cup edge. Then I noticed Celesta started running her fingers around in a different direction than Shelley. That went on for another ten to fifteen seconds, then Shelley tapped her fore finger twice on the edge of the cup. Celesta responded with one tap on the side of her cup.

I exploded, my patience level isn't real high on a good day and I knew our time was limited. "Stop your secret signaling and tell me what's going on!"

They looked at each other again and then they both tapped the top of their cups.

"Okay, the reason why we didn't want to say anything is because you know who the other person is," said Shelley slowly.

Celesta said softly, "You might have even dated him."

I was stunned. Joe D. Savannah, the illustrious owner of We Make Money, CPAs and my first love boyfriend, was involved in all of this?

So I answered in the only intelligent way I knew how. "Do what?"

They both nodded. I felt like throwing up. Instead, being ever the gracious hostess my mother had hoped I'd be, I stood up, wiggled my coffee cup, and said, "Y'all want more coffee?"

"Could I have more cream in mine?" asked Shelley.

"It's a bit on the, ah, strong side," added Celesta.

Do I look like a waitress to them? This is probably the gracious part my mother worked so hard to instill in me but that never took. So I brought over the coffee pot, poured in the delicious nectar of the gods, and plopped down the creamer in its cute little store container. They could add the creamer to their own likeness.

Shelley laughed, "I love being treated like family."

Celesta barely glanced up. "Didn't make it in Little Women, did you?"

Some background for those of you who have never lived in a

small town and do not understand their ways of high society. Little Women was an offshoot of the Woman's Club of Po'thole and only high school sophomores, juniors, and seniors were invited and allowed. Not just anyone was invited.

Apparently you had to be of a certain socio-economic background. The whole thing was beyond hoity-toity in my estimation. However, to my mother's delight, I was invited to join their little sister club thus ensuring my initiation into the proper society of Po'thole.

Their afternoon high tea to meet and greet the potential members ended up in a disaster. I didn't wear white gloves or high heeled shoes or jewelry and I didn't hold up my pinky finger when I slurped the incredibly hot tea from their delicate tea cup. This was cause for immediate concern in their pristine world.

The coup de'grace was that my stomach had been upset earlier in the day and I thought everything was now fine. I was wrong.

Eating a cute cucumber sandwich, I passed gas. Not a soft ladylike genteel sound but one that sounded like a sonic boom. Yes, I was highly embarrassed but I did what my mother had always said to do. "Excuse me."

Unfortunately, that wasn't good enough for the high fluting upper echelon of this illustrious little town. They asked me to leave as their eyes were heavily watering and they were gasping for air.

I was truly sorry, I didn't do it intentionally, things just happen sometimes, and my mother was beyond mortified when I told her. She shopped at the grocery store for a month at six a.m. so she wouldn't run into anyone she knew.

Answering Celesta with a curt "no" I sputtered out, "Joe D. is involved in all of this? How? He didn't have anything to do with the other murders though, right?"

I felt nauseous. The coffee, which normally helped to clear my errant thoughts, was having absolutely no effect upon the information that was swirling around in my head. While Joe

D. might skate along the fine edge of tax legality as far as the IRS was concerned and as much as he might annoy me with marrying other women because he "couldn't have me," I didn't see him doing anything outrageously illegal.

"No," answered Shelley. "I don't think he had anything to do with the first three murders but he looks like the number one candidate for Scooter and Tabitha and maybe Murphy but him I don't think so."

I interrupted her. "But does he have to gain with all of this? I don't get it. Was he the CPA for some new group coming in or what?"

Celesta jumped in there. "I don't think Joe D. has the resources to purchase everything outright. BUT we all know that CPAs come across all sorts of interesting businesses and I think he got into bed with one of those nefarious types. He was bent and determined that he was going to destroy our riverfront. Why..."

Oh, good lord, Celesta was off on another tangent about how people, anyone, was trying to destroy the quaintness of this little town. Unfortunately, Celesta never left living in the past. What she remembers as a child does not equate to the modern day world. Yes, she's right on a couple of points but she is either unwilling or is unable to move anything forward toward progress in this area. She thinks everything is just fine and dandy with the way everything is. Why change anything? In short, she was part of the problem for the lack of progress and new jobs in the area. She was not part of the solution.

The really unfortunate part was that she did not recognize that she was part of the problem. I had tried discussing things, progressive ideas, with her and it was like talking to a brick wall. She had informed me in no uncertain terms that "many, many citizens" looked to her for guidance in keeping Po'thole the way it was. In reality, she only had a handful of people who communicated with her on a thrice weekly basis...and they were all in their late 80's. Old people don't want change, they want consistency.

"Celesta!" Both Shelley and I shouted at the same time.

"What! You both know I'm right! What is your problem?"

Ever the noble individual who will fall on her sword to save others, not true, I growled back at her through clenched teeth. "You have absolutely no proof about any of that. You're just making stuff up. I want facts...and you don't have any so that means we're back to square one."

Celesta's face was flushed, she set her coffee cup down, and stood up. "I have other things to do. Nice seeing you, Parker, and I hope you figure out what's really happening in our town because I know the truth whether either of you will admit it or not."

Yes, she did let the door slam behind her. Shelley and I both rolled our eyes.

"Well, at least, she has the strength of her convictions. I do admire her for that," I said.

We discussed a number of other possibilities but nothing that added up to Joe D. other than some very loose circumstantial evidence.

I wondered if the Lady Gatorettes knew anything.

Chapter 29

Early the next morning, any time prior to nine a.m. is early for me, my phone rang. Much as I love Pink's "So What" as my ring tone, at seven a.m. I'm not prepared to be even remotely nice.

"Yeah," I mumbled sleepily.

"You wanted to talk to me." A statement, not a question.

Scrambling out of bed, an early morning lovely fashion statement I would never make since I wear a long tee shirt to bed, I asked. "Misty Dawn?"

"Yeah, Sunshine, that's me. Don't you ever get up before mid-morning?" Misty Dawn's voice was flat. I was never going to vote for her for Miss Congeniality but then again she probably would never vote that for me either.

Trying to be nice, I invited her over. "I'll put a pot of coffee on. Come over..."

"No." A slight intake of air. "Tell me what you want 'cas I'm not particularly happy with you right now. I'm giving you two minutes and then I'm pulling the plug on you, including your security detail of the Lady Gatorettes."

I don't like to be threatened first thing in the morning...or any time for that matter...but I actually needed her and I didn't want her to know that.

"Okay, here goes." At ninety to nothing, I told her all of my suppositions of what was going on.

I finished with, "What do you think or know?"

A long pause and then I realized I had been disconnected. A moment of panic set in. Did this mean that Misty Dawn was truly pulling the plug or did it mean she was coming over? I never knew with these gals and Misty Dawn was a particular enigma to me.

Putting on the coffee pot, I figured I might as well get a head start on the day. I called my office.

"Parker! Thought you had fallen off the face of the earth!" Missy was always so happy to hear from me. "How's all of the reporters doing down there?"

Oops! I had forgotten about them. Since I couldn't leave the house because of fear of being arrested, I really didn't know what was going on in the outside world.

"I guess okay. Hey, have you talked with Denny?"

"Maybe but if I did, it was a personal call and not business-related."

It never occurred to me that Missy might have a life outside of work nor did it ever occur to me that she and Denny might be dating. Since Missy always answered my phone calls I assumed, perhaps wrongly, that she was always at work. Now I had a new thought that popped up in my mind wondering how much work she was actually getting done. Was she really working or was she goofing off?

I shook my head. No point in even going in that direction. Considering how often I called her, and not during normal working hours, she deserved every penny I paid her. Oh, yeah, I fire her about once or twice a year sometimes even three times and she totally ignores me. That had to be worth something, right?

"Sooo, is he still in this area?"

"Maybe."

Okay, I knew how this game was played. She wanted me to draw it out of her, bit by bit, piece by piece. My patience was at one already and it wasn't even nine a.m.

"Missy, just give me the details and stop making me drag it out of you!"

"Have you had coffee yet, Parker?"

"It's making even as we speak," I growled. "Tell me the details. Now!"

"Yes, he's still down there. He actually likes that area because of the great fishing. Misty Dawn is showing him some great fishing holes in the St. Johns River. And, yes, John Boy is fully aware that Denny is fishing with his wife. And, no, he's not remotely worried about her because he's secure in knowing that she loves him totally. John Boy that is, not Denny. There! No soap opera, no nothing. Denny's not on your payroll anymore and..."

"Wait! What happened to it being 'our' payroll? Do you have feelings for him?" One way or the other, I was going to find out.

"Denny's a nice guy." Smooth as silk, no defensiveness. Also, no acknowledgement of her emotional state with him. "As to 'our' versus 'your' payroll, it was just a slip."

That sounded okay but I was definitely picking up something else going. Why can't people just be honest and tell me exactly what they're upset about.

"Missy, are you unhappy about something?" Then a horrible thought dawned on me. "You're not thinking of leaving me, are you?" If she was, this would really ruin my morning.

She laughed. "Really? That's what you think because I inadvertently said 'your' versus 'our'? If you must know, I was reading an email from Noah down in the mailroom and he was concerned that Sophia in R&D was getting mail from Russia on a regular basis. So, yeah, I wasn't really paying a whole lot of attention to you at that particular moment. I was multi-tasking.

"Why would I leave you when I'm having this much fun?" She laughed louder. "Parker, I've been with you since the beginning. Haven't you realized yet that we are joined at the hip?"

Somewhat mollified, I said, "Well, okay, as long as you're happy."

Then Boom! Shak-a-laka! "I want a raise."

Knowing that she had me over a barrel, a soft barrel but still a barrel, I said, "How much? Wait! What are you making now?"

She told me. Taking a deep breath, I quickly ran some numbers in my head. "Okay, a fifteen percent increase, effective immediately. You already own five percent equity in the company and you get a week's vacation every three months."

"I want seven working days every three months, which you

know I never take because I'm always on call."

"Okay, deal. Have Thomas send me over the paperwork and I'll sign it."

Now that we had agreed to the basics. I tried again, "Regarding Denny, do you think he might consider coming back?"

"Nope."

"Nope, what?"

"He's happy fishing."

Ungrateful so-and-so. I wanted to use other language but Missy always jumped all over me for that. It's one of the disadvantages of having a hard-core Bible-belt Christian working for me.

"Alright. Do you know if the Lady Gatorettes are totally out of the picture or what?"

About that time I turned around to get more coffee and Misty Dawn rose from the kitchen floor like Michael Jackson did in concert. I screamed and dropped my mug.

Missy was shouting something in the phone. I couldn't tell what she was saying because I was trying really hard not to pee in my pants from the scare Misty Dawn just gave me. I also dropped the phone.

Misty Dawn started to laugh. "That was worth it alone just to see your face. God, Parker, that was funny. I never would have taken you for a screamer!"

Laugh tears were running down her face. I hated her intensely at that moment and surprisingly grateful that she had shown up. I grinned and then started to laugh also.

She pointed at the cell phone still laughing. "Better tell Missy that you're okay."

I picked up the phone and heard Missy barking orders at someone on her other line. "Run the scanner cameras, find out if Parker is still standing."

"Missy, I'm fine," I sputtered out, laughing. "Misty Dawn just came up out of my kitchen floor and scared the holy flipping be-jesus out of me. I'll talk to you later but get Thomas to email the proper forms for you. Bye."

Misty Dawn was wiping the tears from her face and drying her hands on her jeans. Redneck women, you've got to love them. She picked up the coffee pot, poured herself a cup, and then wiggled it to see if I wanted any. Does a bear poop in the woods? Of course, I wanted…no, I NEEDED…the coffee, the delicious nectar of the gods.

"Parker Bell, you've really tried my patience." Misty Dawn looked like she was getting ready to drop kick me through the goalposts of life. The good news was that she was wearing a U of F tee shirt.

"Go Gators!" I said weakly and gave the Gator chomp.

"Really? That's your best shot at me?" Shaking her head, "Pitiful, Parker, just pitiful but yes, Go Gators!" She smiled.

"We do have a situation here. There's reporters swarming all over town. Dimwit and Tony are beside themselves with all of the standard interruptions plus the reporters raining down on them. I think it's a corporation that's pulling all of the strings on the riverfront development but I don't know which one it is or even if it's a legitimate one. Tony's definitely involved." Shaking her head, "that boy's definitely out to get me."

"Um, what did you do to him to make him go after you on a personal basis?"

"Might have been that time I ran into him at The Capt'n's Table and he challenged me to a drinking contest in front of half of his squad. Flipping wimp! He bet me I couldn't drink three beers and three shots and make it to the door before he did."

Un oh, Tony was challenging her, and in front of a bunch of guys. Foolish man. That's what happens when you're not a Po'thole native. You don't know how some of these folks were brought up. I daresay Misty Dawn could do that by the time she was a sophomore in high school and still go to classes reasonably sober...or at least enough to fake the teachers out.

"How far did he make it before passing out?"

She laughed, "He was probably eight feet from the door. Of course," she grinned wickedly, "I went back and pounded three more beers and three more shots. Then I left."

"Who was the bartender?" I had already figured out how Misty Dawn could do that and not pass out cold.

Grinning even bigger and giving me a wink, she said, "Us girls have to know how to beat the guys at their own game, Parker. Some of them are just dumber than dirt. Let's just say that Patsy made out like a bandit in her tip."

"Speaking of beating guys at their own game, what are we going to do about this riverfront development project? That is unless you're for it."

"Nope, that riverfront needs to be left alone. I don't care about development a block up but the riverfront needs to be left alone.

"Those idiots," she snorted, "who want to call it the Florida Riviera aka the Redneck Riviera don't understand that gators will call it tourist hors d'oeuvres. On the flip side of the coin, it would bring in a lot of tax dollars to our area. Of course, Celesta's going to get her knickers in a wad because 'things aren't the same' but whatever. She's part of the problem in growing this area."

I was amazed at Misty Dawn's actual knowledge of the city. I guess she did know about something other than hunting, fishing, and Gator football. Who knew?

"Do you think any of the city commissioners are on the

take?" Inquiring minds wanted to know.

"Scooter, of course, was. He just never got caught outright. My understanding is that he was paying off Tony Bugs but who really knows. Gracie Blanche, mean as the little midget is, would turn her mother in to the cops in a heartbeat."

I interrupted her. "How could she and Scooter be carrying on when she had to know that he was on the take?"

She shrugged, "Love is blind, I guess. Plus, once that mean

little Hitler woman latched her fingernails into him she didn't want to know nothing about nothing on him.

"Celesta thinks she knows where the dirt is here but she doesn't and you know how she is once she's got her mind made up about something. You can't change it even if you can prove her wrong. Shelley truly wants to see the area grow and while she might vote soft on something, she isn't going to take any bribes. And Tabitha, God bless her soul, wouldn't have taken any bribes either.

"So based on all of that, if the city commissioners can't be bought, then you turn to the cops in charge. Because everyone knows they can be bought...and for not much money."

"You ever bought any of them, Misty Dawn?"

Another grin, "Not me personally but you know...."

Probably John Boy, I surmised. I opened my mouth and Misty Dawn suddenly said urgently, "We've got to get out of here now!"

She flung open the back door and took off running across the back yard. Once the initial shock wore off, about two seconds, I was right behind her. Although I normally look like a turtle in heat trying to run, I was actually not that far behind her.

Huffing and puffing as we reached the tree line, I managed to gasp out, "Wha...what's going on?"

She turned and pointed her finger at my house. Sure enough, River County's finest were circling the house in their swat team gear. They looked dangerously ready to shoot whoever was going to come out of any door or window.

Tony Bugs was walking around the house shouting through his bullhorn, "This is the police! Parker Bell, come out of the house with your hands in the air! You are under arrest!"

Bless their hearts, the elderly Weebles next door were trying to come out their back door with their hands in the air. Elizabeth held onto to the hand rail while holding her purse and had one arm raised. Bill was waving his cane in the air and had one hand at waist level. Could he raise his arm all the way up? Yes, but I could hear him now saying, "I didn't want to put my hands up in the air. I'm not a common criminal!" Tony Bugs was going to have fun with him.

Tony marched over to the Weebles and tried to shoo them into the house. I could see Bill doing his standard talking in circles, not making any points, waving his cane, and pointing his bony finger at Tony. Misty Dawn and I looked at each other and started to laugh until we both remembered not to make any noise.

Misty Dawn texted something on her cell phone and a few minutes later I saw a drone flying over my house. The ever alert swat team failed to notice anything unusual over their heads.

She poked me and nodded her head for me to follow her. The good news was that I was wearing my Po'hole standard of jeans, blousy shirt, and sneakers. The bad news was I wasn't as adept as Misty Dawn on going through the woods. Better news was we ended up on a dirt road about a hundred yards from my house that I didn't know existed.

The Lady Gatorettes were waiting on us and Flo, bless her heart, thrust a cup of coffee in my hands. I nodded my thanks, internally cringed when I took the first sip and realized it was some of her coffee that would eat the enamel off my teeth. Gratitude, which should have been high on my list, wasn't even in the top five at the moment. It did occur to me that God might smite me or wave

His magic wand over me and reduce me to nothing but ashes since I wasn't truly grateful for the coffee but I was pretty sure my mother's prayers from heaven would save me.

Breaking into this never-ending stream of monkey chatter in my head, Rhonda Jean said, "I got a call from Shelley to go check on Celesta."

"What's up with that?"

"Why her?"

"Dang! That girl don't like us none." All of the Lady

Gatorettes had jumped in there with both feet.

"Y'all wait up!" commanded Rhonda Jean. "Shelley said the man on the phone said Celesta was being uncooperative…"

"Yeah, like that's anything new," I snorted. They all glared at me.

Continuing, she said, "and that her, Celesta, health might not be that good."

Misty Dawn took over. "Rhonda Jean, you and Myrtle Sue go check on her. If she's okay, tell her we're setting up a watch on her to keep her safe. Ignore whatever she has to say 'cas you know she's gonna be mouthy.

"Flo, you and Mary Jane go check on Shelley. I know she's got security cameras around her house. See if you can tap her phone.

"You," pointing at me, "get to stay with me." Well, much as I hate to admit it, I actually like Misty Dawn and I did feel very safe with her.

There were two short blasts on a whistle. I whipped my head around trying to see where it came from. My arm was grabbed by Misty Dawn and she pulled me toward her truck.

I saw the rear truck wheel start to deflate before I heard the shot. Someone was shooting from a bit of a distance for me not to hear the shot first. Cursing the shooter's mother, I was barely in the truck before it took off.

Misty Dawn was calm, way too calm for what had just happened to her truck. Then, "Whoever did that to my truck is going to pay for it...dearly."

I shuttered. I knew she didn't mean pay for the tire.

Chapter 30

"Ah, who do you think did that, Misty Dawn?" I asked. I was still a little unnerved that I saw the tire deflate before I heard the sound of a bullet whizzing past my head. Realistically that meant someone had to be at least three hundred yards away, pretty much back at my house.

I couldn't see my house from here so someone had a powerful eagle eye. The good news was that it wasn't Denny shooting at us because if it had been, he would have killed all of us before we could have responded.

Looking over at me while driving like a maniac on three wheels, she lifted her left eyebrow. "It's Tony or one of his goons from up north. God knows, there ain't a one of his deputies who could hit anything from that far away."

Reaching down between the bucket seats she pulled up a

stainless container of coffee. "Want some?"

I greedily grabbed it from her hand and sucked down a large mouthful. Not the brightest thing I've ever done. Gagging and almost spitting it out, I realized it was old fashion moonshine or some of the cheapest whiskey the local ABC sold.

Roaring with laughter, Misty Dawn skidded sideways onto the paved road. The tire was completely shot and was grinding on the pavement. It didn't seem to matter to Misty Dawn.

Taking a big guzzle out of the coffee cup that she had offered to me, she said, "See that road up there? I'm pulling in there and you're going to jump out and I'll catch up with you later."

Sputtering and still trying to get my breath back after that moonshine exploded in my head, I shook my head no.

"Girl, you don't have a choice in this. You can jump out willingly or I can shove your pa-tootie out the door. We've got to keep you safe."

She turned and grinned at me. "You're the only one who thinks we didn't have anything to do with all these murders."

Before I could stop my big mouth out shot, "Well, you don't, do you?"

She laughed. "Nope. But Tony's going to find himself in a world of hurt over the next day or so."

She turned so suddenly, my door flew open and I fell out of the truck. Guess I should have been wearing my seatbelt but noooo why would I do that? I was unceremoniously sitting on the ground as I watched Misty Dawn go screeching down the road. Standing up, I noticed a car pulled off to the side. As I limped over to it, my right hinny cheek was going to be bruised for a week and I probably wouldn't be able to sit comfortably on it for at least that long, the passenger door swung open.

If I'd had a grain of sense, which apparently I didn't, I would have looked before I got in the car.

Flo was sitting in the driver's seat and Myrtle Sue was sitting in the back. She was holding a gun and it was pointing at me.

Going for a bit of humor, I said, "That color doesn't match my outfit."

"Since when did you become a fashionista?" snarled Myrtle Sue.

"Whoa! Okay, I'm not." I was clearly thrown for a loop. I thought the Lady Gatorettes were on my side. I slowly raised my hands showing complete humbleness and servitude, better known as I'm a complete coward and will do whatever they say.

"What's going on? Did I do something to piss you guys off?"

Myrtle Sue snarled again, "You showed up here...again."

I vaguely wondered if the Lady Gatorettes had a division in their ranks.

"It's that time of month," loudly whispered Flo, shooting me a warning glance. "Also, Myrtle Sue didn't get her coffee and doughnut this morning."

Clapping my hands, I gaily announced, "Well, then let's go to the doughnut shop and change that frown into a smile. I'll buy."

"Did you forget you're hiding from the law or are you a special kind of stupid?" snarled Myrtle Sue. "Plus, I don't see you with a purse and that means I'm going to have to pay for my own coffee and doughnut! What makes you think you're so special, huh?"

Okay, so I'm now seeing the dark side of a Lady Gatorette and it wasn't pretty. As a matter of fact, she was making me nervous...plus, she had a gun. I didn't want her trigger finger to inadvertently tighten and shoot me by accident.

I also vaguely wondered who I was leaving everything to in the event of my untimely demise. At this particular point in time, my memory was failing me and I had no clue. For all I remembered, it might be the elephant sanctuary at the zoo.

"Myrtle Sue, put that gun down! Parker isn't going anywhere 'cas...oops! Parker, get down on the floor right now!"

My brain didn't make the connection quite as quickly as Flo had hoped. Grabbing the front of my shirt, she jerked me down to the floorboard and started throwing papers all over me.

"Be still and you don't say anything or we'll all end up in jail!" She warned.

I could hear Myrtle Sue throwing stuff around. I felt the car slowing down and my heart was pounding. I still wasn't sure what was going on.

The car came to a complete stop.

"Well, hey there, Tommy!" Flo was using her come-hither, super friendly voice. I was guessing she'd had a fling with this Tommy.

"Flo, Myrtle Sue." Typical law enforcement voice, flat, not warm and friendly. "What are y'all doing out this way? Little far for a doughnut run, isn't it? Oh, yeah, the doughnut shop is in the opposite direction."

"Now, Tommy…"

"Get out of the car and keep your hands where I can see them."

I was sweating bullets. If he decided to poke and prod the newspapers tossed and wadded up all over me, I'd be arrested and in jail faster than you could say Tony Buglia.

The gals were mumbling, most of the words weren't fit for the First Baptist Church Sunday School group. I was praying God was going to have pity on me, I guess it's called grace and favor in religious circles, and that no one could hear my beating heart...or smell my fear sweat. I don't know what term the religious would call that.

I could sort of see Tommy poking his head in the car through a tiny, little space between the newspapers. Hopefully, he couldn't see me.

"Good golly, your car looks like a drunk pig got loose in here, Flo. Since when is your car this trashed?"

Myrtle Sue snarled, "What's it to you, Tommy? You got your doughnut and your coffee, didn't you? Probably even had someone bring it to you, didn't you?

"I didn't!" she suddenly screamed. "J.W. is sick and I couldn't find where he hid the coffee. I didn't get MY coffee this morning and because that worthless so-and-so is worshipping the porcelain goddess even as we are standing here he didn't bring it to me either. I didn't get MY doughnut!"

Myrtle Sue was in a full-blown hormonal rage. The thought crossed my mind that she might be diabetic and needed the sugar infusion.

"Wha, what?" stuttered Tommy. I could hear him shutting the car door. I imagined he was backing up as well and probably wondering if he needed to call back-up since the Lady Gatorettes rampages were well-documented in River County.

"Tommy," Flo was still using her sexy voice. "It's Myrtle Sue's time of the month and…"

"Yeah, yeah, y'all go on. If you see Parker Bell, tell her Tony needs to see her at the station."

I heard his car peel out. In the interest of my health, I decided not to move until Flo told me it was safe.

"Myrtle Sue, you were wonderful! Honey, thank you for jumping in there and saving us!" Flo was all giggly. "And, guess what? I have some day old doughnuts in that box on the floor back there."

I felt Myrtle Sue jump on the backseat and she was thrashing around trying to find the doughnuts. Figuring it was probably safe to raise my head, I was trying to unwind my body from the floorboard. Writers and computer consultants are not bendy people.

"That's the cobra pose," laughed Flo. "I didn't take you for a yoga person, Parker." It never occurred to me that the position I was in on the floor might qualify as a yoga pose.

"Yeah, well, me neither." To say I was stiff was an understatement.

Myrtle Sue raised her head from the backseat, white doughnut powder all over her face. "Flo, you're a lifesaver." She grinned.

"Guys, this isn't good if Tony's setting up roadblocks trying to find me. That means he's really serious."

"It also means he's really worried about what you do or don't know about the riverfront development."

"Flo, Myrtle Sue, what is really going on at the riverfront? God knows, Po'thole could sure use an infusion of money and improve the area."

The two of them looked at each other and said in unison, "You need to talk to Misty Dawn."

Chapter 31

Fifteen minutes later we were out in the middle of nowhere. In fact, I was real sure I had never seen this part of River County before. We were deep in a wooded area. If they dropped me off here by my lonesome, I wasn't sure I could even find my way to a paved road much less to safety.

Pulling up to a small cabin, although probably now politically correct called a tiny house, I could hear people singing. The song? "Don't go breaking my heart" by Elton John and Kiki Dee. Good lord, the Lady Gatorettes were singing karaoke.

It must be their version of a honky tonk night…in the woods…away from civilization. I only hoped they had not consumed vast quantities of sugar, caffeine, or alcohol. In all honesty, I really knew that was probably way too much to ask for. I strongly suspected there's only so much God was going to answer on my wish list...and I was already probably pushing His limits.

Walking into the cabin with fear and trepidation, I realized I should have feared nothing. They were all just dancing around and singing. Not a sign of doughnuts or alcohol anywhere. They did have two big pots of coffee on though.

These were just happy women having a good time. I joined in the merriment. After a couple more songs, Misty Dawn turned off the karaoke machine and announced, "We need to wrap up this whole thing with Tony Bugs and the riverfront development."

Everyone nodded. I was ecstatic. Now, finally, maybe I'd find out what's going on.

"Parker," everyone turned to me, "what do you think is going on?"

Aw, come on! They're flipping it back to me?! God was punishing me for asking for His help. See if I was going to go back to church again any time soon!

Thinking through everything carefully for a moment, I decided to take the plunge and see what popped up.

"I think a corporation of sorts," making quote marks in the air around corporation, "found a hook to use on Tony to get him to come to Po'thole.

"The really strange thing is the real Tony Buglia attended one of my seminars about a year ago in New Jersey. We have a video of him signing in first thing in the morning but after lunch it's not the same guy signing back in. They are very, very similar looking but it's definitely not the same guy when you study the pictures."

All of the gals looked at each other. I swear they must have some kind of telepathic communication between them, probably all of the sugar and caffeine has short-circuited their brains, because all five of them got this strange knowing look on their faces.

"Go on," said Rhonda Jean.

"Then this town gets the new Tony Bugs. Bobby Derlicter dies in a very strange accident, then

Buddy Walker dies eating barbecue from some restaurant that the whole town knows he'd never be caught in much less eating a meal from them, and finally Happy Jack Canaday."

"Everyone's friend because it says so on his card," shouted the girls in unison. Never under-estimate the power of advertising and a business card. Everyone burst into laughter.

"You get the Middle Eastern guys that come in and start a big theme fishing resort. Although, in all honesty, I don't think anyone had anything to do with them coming in."

"Except Joe D.," murmured Mary Jane. I ignored her. I was still having problems thinking Joe D. might have been involved in anything really nefarious. A little shady? Yes. Walking on a fence and skating through the finer nuances of the law? Yes. Doing anything truly outrageous and having people die over it? Nope, not in a million years. But...I could be wrong. I wasn't right all of the time.

"I think someone took great pains to set you guys up to take the fall. And someone, specifically," I looked directly at Misty Dawn and pointed at her, "you were targeted. For what reason, I'm not sure but you either know something or saw something you shouldn't have and someone, Tony probably, thinks you know more than you do. Therefore, you need to be put out of commission. The only thing he has on any of you is circumstantial evidence. Although, unfortunately, in this area that's almost good enough to put you away for life."

Myrtle Sue's sugar high was starting to wear off. "Are you ever going to get to the riverfront development?"

I grinned. "Of course. I would imagine y'all are aware that this riverfront is the only undeveloped city-owned piece of property on the St. Johns River. It's basically already developed for buildings and businesses because the infrastructure is in place. You've got water, sewer, sidewalks, paved roads, and it sits right next to a marina that can't seem to figure out how to make money. It's absolutely perfect for someone to come in and make it a mini-boardwalk slash tourist area.

"The only real problem is you have the city commissioners where half of them are for development because it will bring in dollars to the city and the other half of them who are scared to death any type of development is going to ruin the quaintness of Po'thole. The ones who don't want any progress in the city are the ones who are receiving death threats and or who have died."

I shook my head, frowning. "Tabitha was such a sweet person and for her to die over something like this..." My voice trailed off.

"With Scooter dying, the one person it would affect the most is Gracie Blanche. Everyone but her knew he could be bought off. So it really doesn't make any sense why he was murdered."

"Even though Gracie Blanche can be a little Hitler, we don't know anyone who hated her enough to kill off a love affair that had been going on for years." Although Mary Jane was trying hard to keep from laughing out loud, she didn't succeed and the other girls joined in. Heck, I couldn't help myself, I started to laugh also.

Wiping the tears from my eyes, I finally managed to sputter out, "I never could figure out if her husband knew she had an affair going with Scooter or if he even cared."

Misty Dawn giggled, "Oh, he knew but he didn't care. He, um, has a friend over in St. Augustine...a special friend...a very creative friend."

"His friend has a boatload of sugar in his tank, if you get my drift," laughed Rhonda Jean.

"Really? Wow, I didn't know that! Did Gracie Blanche know?"

"Good lord, Parker, you must think everyone in this town is a special kind of stupid!" snapped Flo. "Of course, she knew. Between the two of them, they have a fair chunk of change. If they split up, it won't be the same thing. Besides, it's no different than some guy having a trophy wife. She gets to do what she wants and he does what he wants while they both are playing charades with each other. They both know what's going on but as long as they don't acknowledge anything out loud, it doesn't exist. Gracie Blanche's marriage with Sam is the same way. Besides, which, it works for them and ain't nobody's business but their own. Although First Baptist would probably disagree with that 'cas everything in this town is their business...or they'd like to think so."

I was laughing so hard I fell out of my chair. Everyone else was laughing and snorting so loud I thought probably the sheriff's department could probably hear us miles off. But, then again, we probably just sounded like wild pigs rutting around. In this area, that wouldn't mean jack poo-poo. We were safe.

After a few minutes of raucous laughter, Misty Dawn did the Gator Chomp and everyone quieted down immediately.

"So what's the rest of your thought process, Parker?"

Gosh, these women didn't give up! I was really hoping someone was going to share some of the love and tell me what they thought was going on.

"If it was the Mafia, then they would definitely need someone like Tony to help enforce things. At the very least, they would need someone like him to give them the lowdown on people and the area.

"If it's not the Mafia, then it has to be some type of large development company. Regardless of who it is, I'm guessing, they want something where there is a lot of cash coming in, i.e., flowing through their hands, so it can be laundered. While some of the banks did this for the CIA in Miami back in the late '70's, I can't imagine they would still be trying to do that in this day and time."

I looked at each Lady Gatorette and said, "Okay, I've told y'all everything I know and what I think. Now it's time for you to tell me what you think is going on."

All of a sudden a high pitched whistle pierced the inside of the cabin. Everyone started scrambling. It looked like a battle station alert. Everyone was flying around grabbing things and then disappearing. I had yet to figure out how they did that on a consistent basis. You could be looking at them one moment and then the next they were gone. Even after examining the floors, my own included, it was almost impossible to figure out how they were doing it.

Misty Dawn grabbed me at the collar and dragged me backwards into a closet. "Down you go!" I dropped about six feet in a mini-elevator. I couldn't see a thing. Dark was an understatement.

A hand clamped over my mouth. The good news is I had the good sense not to struggle. The bad news was "Don't make a sound or we'll be dead. Got it."

Whoever it was didn't have to tell me twice. I was thrust in what felt like a nylon chair. A soft voice whispered in my ear, "You better hope no one decides to set the cabin on fire. If that happens, John Boy's gonna do a grab and drag. You'll be with him. Do what he says and you should be fine."

That was the last thing I heard before an explosion of light blinded me. I vaguely wondered if it was God telling me my time on earth was up, then everything went black.

CHAPTER 32

I don't know how long it was before I came to. It was still pitch black and I could smell smoke. I gingerly moved my fingers and arms. They seemed to be working okay. Trying to determine if my legs and feet were in working order, I discovered there was a lot of something on top of me. It was heavy. Trying to wiggle my way out from under the weight, I realized I had a slight headache. I also had leaves all over my face. The good news was I didn't feel any blood.

I could hear laughter and voices approaching. They didn't sound like the Lady Gatorettes and considering that I had just been in a cabin that was blown up, I didn't think it prudent on my part to draw attention to myself.

Almost gasping out loud, I heard Tony Bugs laughingly say, "You know, for country girls they don't seem to think I know anything. That ought to teach them."

Tommy laughed also. "Well, when you have a local native here, me, who knows how them girls operate, it's pretty easy to blow up their cabin. It's even easier to set them up for all those murders too."

Tony was still laughing. "Yep, those murders are going to be pinned on them and, in particular, that witch Misty Dawn."

"Speaking of things, when am I gonna get my money?" asked Tommy.

"Probably never."

The gunshot couldn't have been more than eight feet from me. I jumped when I heard it but the good news was Tony couldn't see me because of the darkness and there was enough crackling from the cabin fire that he probably didn't think anything about the additional rustling sound when I jumped; otherwise, I'm sure I would have been making love to the next bullet.

"Stupid redneck deputy. Did he really think he was going to get paid? Dumb! Well, that's another murder Misty Dawn's gonna be blamed for."

I could hear Tony stomping off. I slowly counted to one hundred before I started to wiggle out of the cocoon-like encasement. Trying to pull my legs out from the dead weight turned out to be an accurate statement. There was a body laying across my legs, and it wasn't Tommy.

Finally managing to get to my feet, I cautiously looked around to make sure Tony and his band of merry deputies weren't lying in wait for me. Clearing my throat quietly, I whispered loudly, "Hey, is anyone out there? Misty Dawn? Rhonda Jean? Flo, Mary Jane? Myrtle Sue? Anybody?"

Crickets weren't even chirping. It was quiet except for the crackling of the smoldering embers of the cabin. How I had not burned up in the explosion was beyond me. Whatever incendiary device Tony had used was one that exploded and then caused all of the flames to burn back into themselves. I was guessing it was probably a black market item. The whole thing from start to finish was probably fifteen minutes or less.

Not hearing any human noise, I was suddenly engulfed with sadness. What if all of the Lady Gatorettes had been burned up trying to save my life? I mean, they were crazy as looney tunes but they were my crazy looney tunes. I felt one of my eyeballs starting to sweat as a liquid drop eased its way down my check.

"Do you think you could help me up?" said a whisper from near my feet as I felt a hand grab my ankle.

I screamed. My nerves were shot, no pun intended, I was miles from anywhere, no clue how to get back to town, I had a warrant out for my arrest, Tony had already proved he wasn't above killing someone, I had people dying right and left, there was obviously a bounty on my head, I couldn't find any of the Lady Gatorettes, and now a hand grabbing my ankle. I could only take so much before I came completely unglued.

"Shhh! Do you really want Tony to come back here and finish you off?"

"Denny, is that you?" Relief flooded through my veins. His sins were forgiven and I'd put him back on payroll in a heartbeat if he would get me out of here.

"Nope, it's John Boy." He stood up, dressed completely in camouflage and black stuff smeared all over his face. I wasn't sure if it was soot or some goo that he had intentionally smeared. While it was not a lovely fashion statement, I was beyond thrilled there was another safe, live human being next to me.

"Where, where is everybody?" I stuttered, hoping he had an answer and the girls wouldn't be dead.

Very calmly, John Boy answered, "Tony's going to have to die. You understand that, don't you? He has tried to kill my beloved one time too many."

I nodded my head 'yes,' although I couldn't see in the dark I was pretty sure John Boy could.

"Come on." He grabbed my hand and started pulling me deeper into the woods.

"What, where...?"

"They're probably fine. We were the only ones actually caught still in the cabin. The rest of them were already out." Pausing, he said, "I've seen you run. You look like a turtle in heat and I had to make sure Tony didn't catch you."

Stumbling and getting whacked in the face by tree branches as I was being dragged behind John Boy was no fun; however, if it meant I'd still be alive tomorrow, I say let's go for it.

Suddenly, John Boy let go of my hand. "Stop and don't move. I'll be right back."

He was gone and I heard absolutely no sound. No twigs snapping, no birds, not even a gnat or a mosquito. I needed to learn how to do this.

"Squat down but don't sit," came a whisper.

I did as I was told. So far the girls and one husband had kept me alive. I wasn't about to ignore what they told me to do.

I felt something fly over the top of my head. I really hoped it wasn't a rabid FSU fan not having a sense of humor about my trash talking their lousy football team a couple of weeks ago.

"Okay, you can stand up now."

"What was that, John Boy?"

"Um, you don't want to know."

A flashlight was lit under my face and then other flashlights were turned on. I could see all of the Lady Gatorettes with black smudges under their eyes and a Gator football sticker on their forehead. The sight was a little unnerving at best.

Misty Dawn was the first to speak. "Tony is dead meat."

Bobbing heads in the glow of the flashlights looked like a Halloween party gone bad. They all started hissing. I assumed this sound was not the mating call of gators.

"That jerk has tried to kill me for the last time."

They hissed some more and bobbed their heads up and down.

Breaking the spell, I said, "Who is he really working for? And why, Misty Dawn, is he so bent and determined to frame you for all of the murders?"

John Boy cleared his throat, "Because Happy Jack told her that not only was Tony collecting 'fire protection money' from all three of them, he was also collecting it from other successful business owners. He wanted Misty Dawn and the ladies to help him make Tony stop bleeding them dry.

"I'm guessing that Tony saw her leave Happy Jack's place and figured she was a good one to pin the blame on. After all, her car loan application was sitting on his desk and everyone knows Misty Dawn don't drive no car. It's always a truck."

I was stunned. "Really? That's it? Come on, there's gotta be more to this story than that."

Rhonda Jean said slowly, "Well, it might have been 'cas Tabitha told her that Tony threatened to kill her if she didn't vote for the riverfront development. Misty Dawn might have left all four of his tires gasping for air when he was some place he wasn't supposed to be."

"Like where?"

"Like over in Lincolnville at Miss Rose D'light's house of ill repute. She might have taken a couple of pictures of him and Miss Rose D'light doing the naughty naughty. And maybe she left a note on his windshield and told him to lay off of Tabitha or those photos would be mailed to his wife."

I started to laugh. Pretty soon we were all laughing. "Oh, good lord! Really? That's just flat out funny. So it really wasn't about drinking Tony under the table then?"

Mary Jane snorted. "Nope. We thought it was funny. Apparently Tony doesn't have the same sense of humor."

"Do you think Tony killed Tabitha though? Was it really worth him killing Tabitha even after Misty Dawn warned him?" I wasn't getting the connection. All it seemed like to me was a retaliation for getting even with

Misty Dawn and that seemed like very slim grounds to kill a very sweet human being. There had to be more to this story. Then I had a brain flash.

"Has anyone even seen what the plans are for the riverfront?" I asked.

They all looked at each other, still with the flashlights under their chins. They shook their heads 'no.'

"I think Tabitha might have seen them," Misty Dawn said slowly.

I exploded. "Good god, people! Are you telling me all of

the craziness that is happening in this town and nobody's even seen the riverfront plans? This might be the greatest thing since sliced bread and everybody's in an uproar when you don't even have a clue as to what the plans are! Good golly, Miss Molly!"

Small town bumpkins! Typical small town thought mentality. Grrr.

"Parker, the original plans were submitted to the city commissioners last year and they were turned down. The whole thing is who's going to buy the riverfront property, not so much as what is going to be built." Rhonda Jean explained.

"Well, supposedly, it's going to be a hotel and a boardwalk, with lots of little businesses. That's what the talk is anyway," mumbled Mary Jane.

"Somewhere, there has to be a set of plans." My brain was going in forty million different directions. Then, "Did Tabitha have a set of plans or had she seen them? What about Celesta or Shelley? The other city commissioners?"

"Planning and zoning had a set of plans 'cas I saw them," said John Boy.

Everyone whipped their head to look at him.

"Sweetums," said Misty Dawn quietly. The girls all took one giant step back without saying Simon sez. "When did you plan on telling me that?"

"Honey, I was down at that office looking at the way the river goes up into the old cypress company area to see if I might spot any good fishing holes. Ted had the plans out and was showing me how there was going to be boat slips all the way from the bridge down to the cove. That's not exactly the riverfront development y'all are talking about. You're talking about building stuff on the riverbank. That's a totally different thing." John Boy weakly explained.

Keep in mind, John Boy works in construction and is liable to get into a fight with almost anyone but he's afraid of his wife's temper. The 'sweetums' was a dead giveaway that she wasn't happy and that he probably would be paying for his forgetfulness for quite a while.

"Did you ask Ted if they were going to put bids out for construction work? Work that you might make some money at?" Her voice was still very quiet. I had to lean slightly forward to hear her. I felt a hand tugging my shirttail backwards. The rest of the gals took another small step back. This definitely wasn't an homage to Neil Armstrong's "One small step for man" speech when he landed on the moon.

"Yes. Yes, I did."

A collective groan went up from the girls. I assumed that meant John Boy had just signed his death warrant with his wife.

"So, you asked if they, the city, the new owners, whoever was going to need to have construction work done on the riverbank? Am I understanding you right, John Boy?"

I felt myself being tugged into a line formation behind Misty Dawn. Since everybody still had their flashlights up and under their chin, the dark smudges were still under their eyes, and the Gator sticker still on their forehead, I wondered when John Boy was going to realize he was fresh meat for a pack of rabid, sugar-infused and caffeine-laded, hormonal women who were ready to shred him to pieces to protect the leader of their pack.

Apparently the thought kicked in when he suddenly said, "Ohhh. I, ah, um…"

"Do you think you can remember the name that was on the lower right corner of the plans, John William?" Misty Dawn's voice was icy. I shuddered, and she wasn't even talking to me.

The Lady Gatorettes took one step forward. The good news I was on the end of the line. The bad news was if they decided to kill or permanently maim John Boy, I had a perfect view of everything.

"Now, honey, listen, I wasn't really paying that much attention to writing on the plans." John Boy was scrambling to find something, anything that would keep him from being killed by his wife. "But, it looked like restaurants and little stores like they have down to Daytona."

Silence. I was discovering that wasn't necessarily a good thing with the Lady Gatorettes and I knew for sure that wasn't a good thing with Misty Dawn.

"You. Stupid. Imbecile. We had already guessed that part. You've known about this for how long and didn't bother to tell me? John Boy, I think it best you go stay with your mama for a while...a long while."

"Aw, come on, Misty Dawn! Don't make me go stay with her. She's mean."

"You mean she makes you make up your bed, makes you clean up the floor when you stomp in with those dirty boots on, and, oh yeah, you have a curfew. You shoulda thought about all those things before you forgot to tell me about the riverfront."

The next thing I knew Misty Dawn had hurled something at John Boy. Judging from the thwack sound, I was guessing it was a semi-dry cow patty. Where she got it out here was beyond me but I wasn't going to ask any questions.

John Boy howled and said a few choice words that I was real sure Misty Dawn had heard on several different occasions. These were not your garden variety choice of curse words. These were more along the lines of creative sailor verbiage.

Myrtle Sue snapped at him, "Listen, you dip weed, you better zip it before we all start throwing stuff at you."

John Boy growled and then stomped off, disappearing into the dark.

Misty Dawn turned around to face us. "I think we need to go to Tabitha's house and see if there are any plans over there.

"Parker, call Celesta and Shelley and see if they have seen any plans. Real plans, not guesswork. Myrtle Sue, y'all go back to Parker's house and see if it's still standing. Make sure you've got the night goggles. I don't want any of us to be surprised by Tony."

"Um, how about not killing him until we figure out what's going on?" I was hoping we'd figure it out before he made any of our demises permanent. They ignored me.

Myrtle Sue was quiet on the ride back to my house. I was pretty sure it had been totally blown up, trashed at the very least. She drove up to the back property line and snapped her night goggles on like she was on a black ops mission. I think the government really needs to hire these gals for some of their more clandestine work. They seemed to have a real knack for it.

"There." She pointed at some tiny little red dot to the left of my house. "One of those idiots is smoking."

She whispered into her cell, "Can I take these bozos out? What do you mean I can't kill anybody? They're trying to kill us and Parker! I think it's only fair. Yeah, okay. There's only one I can see. Yeah, yeah, I got it."

I looked at her. She refused to look back. "I can't kill anybody. No, that's not right. I'm not allowed to kill anybody." She started pulling out what looked like remote controlled baby airplanes out of the backseat and continued to grumble as she launched a drone, then another one, and then a last one.

"Uh, what are you going to do with those?"

"God, Parker, don't you know anything?" Myrtle Sue was working the controls on the drones. "We can see who's over there and how many are over there. I can also see if Tony and Dewitt have others stationed around your house. And, finally, I can create a diversion that will cause them to move away from your house so I can get you back in there."

Watching her work the controls on three drones was impressive. She looked like a tiny Ninja warrior with her modern day technology. I was trying to look over her shoulder but she kept shrugging me off. Just as well, she needed a shower. Badly.

"Geez, Parker, the first thing you need to do is take a shower. Please stand downwind from me."

As irritating as this was from a stinky female, she was probably right. After all, it had been a long day starting with escaping from my own house hours earlier, then a romp through the woods, being chased, getting blown up and almost set on fire at the cabin. Between the various adrenaline rushes combined with the sweat of pure out-and-out fear, my odor d'jour was probably not going to be made into a popular perfume worn by a major celebrity any time soon.

My scent was odoriferous even to me. Plus, it would just feel beyond wonderful to lather up with my Tahitian Wonder and have it wash away all of the dirt, grime, and who knows what else off of me. Yes, those four brilliant marketing words never sounded better bouncing around in my head: wash, lather, rinse, repeat. I figured three cleansings would make me feel like a normal human being again, along with a frothy liquid libation.

"Watch this." Myrtle Sue pushed some buttons on the control whizmo and little red streaks could be seen coming down from the heavens. Okay, it was the drones and they were about twelve feet above the deputy smoking.

I could hear the poor guy scream as the mini-rockets, although Myrtle Sue swore later it was just some fireworks she'd fired at him, exploded around him. He took off running, jumped in his truck, and roared off. Oh, yeah, River County's finest is going to be a big help if it is ever invaded by aliens.

Myrtle Sue calmly walked to the back of my house, opened the door, flipped the light switch, and snarled, "You're home."

My nerves were a wee bit on the frazzled side. "Listen, Myrtle Sue, what's your stinking problem, huh? Until the last twenty-four hours, you've always been really nice to me and me to you. I get it that this isn't much fun for you. Trust me, it isn't any fun for me either. What is your problem?"

Myrtle Sue glared back at me. I could see the wheels turning in her head. She started blinking her eyes quickly. It almost looked like she was going to cry but I was pretty sure that was against the Lady Gatorettes code of ethics. She sniffed instead.

"J.W. wants to join the Marines and I don't know why."

"Really? The Marines? I don't get it. He's got the perfect life with you here."

She smiled.

"Y'all own property, he hunts and fishes all the time, he worships the ground you walk on. Why would he want to join the Marines? Did he give you a reason?" I was flummoxed but now

I understood why she was so upset.

"He said he wanted to kill things on two legs instead of four. That's all," she gestured weakly.

Rut row! Could it be that J.W. was killing everyone, practicing to go into the Marines?

"Um, he isn't...he didn't...he..."

"Parker Bell! You know J.W. wouldn't kill anyone around here! Well, unless, of course, they were going to hurt me or the other girls, then he would." From the look on her face, I could tell she had wondered the same thing. "He just says he wants to kill some of them furriners to keep them away from America."

My cell phone vibrated in the back left pocket of my jeans. I pulled it out and read the text message.

"Myrtle Sue, Misty Dawn wants to know why you're still here. She says you're not answering your phone and says you need to go to your station now. Now is in all capital letters."

Looking like Bambi in the headlights, Myrtle Sue took off running to her car. I didn't understand these girls at all. I grabbed a longneck from the refrigerator and turned on the hot water for a shower that could not wait. Peeling off my clothes and soaping up with Tahitian Wonder, it suddenly occurred to me I had turned on the lights in my house. Lights that could be seen by the local law enforcement people. People like Tony Bugs. The Tony Bugs who wanted to arrest me on trumped up charges. The lights on probably were not a good thing, especially since Myrtle Sue had taken off running. A moment of panic attacked me when it registered that I might not have the protection I so desperately needed from Po'thole's finest group of hormonal women.

Taking a long pull from the beer, yes I took the beer into the shower with me, I made the decision to turn off the lights after I finished this wonderful shower. I watched the mud and dirt wash down the drain hoping that the plumbing system wouldn't clog up because of all the nasty stuff that was being washed off of me.

Twenty minutes later when the hot water ceased to be my friend and invited cold water to viciously attack my naked body, I got out of the shower. Toweling off, I thought I heard a noise in the living room. Since I was unarmed and was now only wearing a Gator tee-shirt, I was a bit hesitant to rush out and confront whomever or whatever it was. Plus, I was tired. I just wanted to go to bed to go to sleep.

Forcing my tired body to take a pro-active approach, I peeked around the door. I didn't see anything. I cautiously checked the entire house, including the closets, and not finding a boogie man, I flopped in bed and immediately passed out.

It only seemed like minutes since I had gone to sleep when I was awakened by a raspy laugh.

"Did you really think you could escape from the long arms of the law?" asked a dark figure standing at the end of my bed.

I screamed.

He laughed again. "Really, Parker, you thought you knew it all, didn't you?"

"Wha...what the?" Okay, I'm not really good at being woken up during normal non-stress times. With everything that had been going on the past several days, my stress level was off the charts.

"Who are you and what do you want?" I screeched.

"Hoop, holler, scream as loud as you want, Parker, no one can hear you."

"You didn't hurt the Weebles did you?" Out of everything that could happen, I didn't want the old people next door hurt.

"What? No, of course not. They can't hear anything with their hearing aids in much less when they're sleeping and they're not wearing them."

"Tony?" I cautiously asked, since I still wasn't one hundred percent sure it was him. "Why this? Why the murders? Why everything?"

He snickered. "Really? You haven't figured it out yet, Miz

Hotshot? Since you're going to die anyway, by Misty Dawn's own gun, I'll lay it all out to you. We've got several hours before the sun comes up and your untimely death by a former schoolmate.

"And, since you're so darn nosy, yes, I'll answer your questions."

I was seeing my life flash before my eyes in slow motion as Tony was talking. Snapping out of my awake nightmare, I wanted answers to everything before he killed me. It also gave me time to figure out a way to continue living.

"Are you really Tony Buglia or did you take the real one's place at my seminar New Jersey about a year ago?"

"The real Tony didn't want to play ball with my bosses. He might have wandered into the Great Swamp National Wildlife Refuge in New Jersey and drown. Unfortunately, no one will ever know for sure since a body has never been recovered.

"We had a Plan B already prepared and I took his place since I could pass as his twin."

"That's true, Tony, until we started going over the video of that seminar I thought you were one and the same. Fortunately, I have great people who spotted the difference and told me."

"Yeah, but you still couldn't figure out the reason why though." Bragging now, he continued, "We wanted the riverfront so it could be developed into a boardwalk and casino like at Atlantic City."

I started to laugh, I couldn't help myself. "Seriously, you think the fine, upstanding citizens of

Po'thole were going to allow you to put a 'Yankee' business on our nature coast riveria? You're dumber than I thought you were."

He growled. "It was, it is, going to bring in tons of jobs to this area, the poorest county in the entire state of Florida. What makes you think the people wouldn't want this? Jobs, money, a better way of living. Oh, yeah, you have those morons on the city commission who think everything needs to stay the same as it has been for the last one hundred years but they can't seem to understand why the town isn't growing and why no one wants to come here. Who are the idiots, Parker?"

Sad to say, I couldn't really disagree with him. I had said the exact same thing to Tabitha, Celesta, and Shelley, the real holdouts on the city commission. The area definitely needed an infusion of cash and new business. Was a boardwalk and a casino the answer? Heck, who knows but what I did know was that it wasn't worth killing people over. People for all their faults, and we all have them, who meant well but who didn't deserve to die because they voted against a boardwalk and casino.

Trying another tact, I asked, "So, did you kill Bobby Derlicter, Buddy Walker, and Happy Jack Canaday and why? The rumor was you were shaking them, and other business owners, down for fire protection money. Sounds like a New Jersey thing to me."

Tony giggled again. "Yeah, I did. Well, actually, Tommy did it. He didn't much like them anyway 'cas they always acted like they were better than him...or so he said. Who cares what the reason was, he got rid of them."

"But that doesn't make any sense, Tony. You had three people killed who were paying you money under the table. Money that you aren't making now."

"And you own a company, Parker? Get rid of the worms and go for the big fish! Do you really think the only money I make is from shaking down some redneck business owners? That's just to get them under my control.

"Bobby Derlicter had a lot of power and pull in the city. He wasn't on board with the casino coming in. He was fine with the boardwalk because it was family-oriented whereas the casino is more adult-oriented."

Well, score points for Bobby. He did have a heart after all. I had always suspected Bobby had a soft spot for kids; although he didn't have any, due to that unfortunate incident with his daddy back in high school.

"Buddy Walker wanted the largest spot on the boardwalk for his deli and when I told him no he told me he'd tell everyone in town that I was shaking him and others down. He threatened to report me to the state and," Tony gloated, "everyone knows you don't threaten me, including you, Parker!"

I was now sitting up in bed and was pretty sure flinging a pillow at Tony was not going to make him leave me alone. I didn't see anything I could use as a weapon within arm's reach either. The only thing I could do was to keep him talking and hoping that someone would show up, although, since it was pitch black outside, the chance of having visitors wasn't real high.

"Pray tell, Tony," I said as calmly as I could, "when did I ever threaten you? The worse I did was refuse to go out to eat with you."

"You made me look like an idiot in front of my men." He growled.

I laughed, "I don't think you needed much help there. You did that all on your own."

Wrong thing to say to a man with a gun. Before I could react, Tony was around the side of the bed, grabbed my wrists and handcuffed me.

"See how you like being in cuffs."

Sometimes I wish there was an automatic zipper on my mouth but nooo words slide out on their own accord. Do I ever wish I could take them back? Yes, of course, especially right now.

"Don't you realize if you kill me, there will be cuff marks on my wrists?"

"If I kill you? You make me laugh, Parker. I will kill you,

no two ways about it, and the cuffs will come off shortly before that. Even if I leave them on, it will appear that Misty Dawn needed help in subduing you. It's all good, sweetheart. It's all good."

"What about Happy Jack?" I asked. I was doing anything I could think of to distract him from my impending demise.

"What about him? Oh, why did I kill him? That's the easiest one of all. He wouldn't let me use any of his cars whenever I wanted."

I couldn't believe what I was hearing. This man was getting crazier and crazier on his reasons why he killed people.

"What?" Okay, not the most intelligent question I've ever asked but it did serve a purpose.

"Do you have any idea how hard it is to go see a girlfriend in my official car?"

I interrupted him, incredulous, "You mean you killed him because he wouldn't loan you a car to go see Miss Rose D'light?"

"Yes. That dip weed said it would run up too many miles on his precious used cars. What an idiot! Did he really think that the scum that bought his used cars really paid that much attention to the mileage? What an idiot."

"Why barbeque dinners as the last meal and, specifically, why barbeque for Buddy? Everyone knew he didn't touch the stuff." Keep that boy talking as long as possible.

"Because that's all you Southerners seem to eat is barbeque. Made sense to me."

And this explains some of the major differences between Yankees and Southerners and local eating habits versus an outsider coming in.

"Didn't you notice that there's only two barbeque restaurants in all of River County but that there's a ton of fried food places? The barbeque dinners waved flags that it wasn't a local who had killed the guys. Therefore, it couldn't have possibly been Misty Dawn. And you, sir, are not a local." I was bluffing that others might have figured it out also and was hoping that it might throw some doubt in his mind.

He laughed. "Who cares? No one likes Misty Dawn and the Lady Gatorettes. Those women are nuttier than their grannies homemade fruitcakes."

I felt obligated to defend the ladies since they had been so kind and protected me; well, up until this nutcase showing up in my bedroom in the middle of the night. I still had hopes that one or all of them would show up.

"Tony, every one of the Lady Gatorettes has a heart of gold. Okay, so they're a little overly exuberant when they have had too much coffee and sugar but the same thing could be said about anyone."

"A little overly exuberant?" He laughed, "They're crazy during the best of times but when they are hyped up on something...and who knows what they're really taking...they're like monkeys on cocaine."

"Oh, come on, Tony! You know perfectly well they only consume caffeine, sugar, and beer.

They don't do drugs at all. That's not fair!"

"Oh, so now you're their best friend, huh? It figures."

I didn't like the way this conversation was going. I needed to get him back on track by talking about the other murders.

"Tony, why Scooter? Everyone knew he could be bought off. Plus, he was the mayor. Yeah, maybe you would have had to pay him a little more but he's the one guy that could get the casino and the boardwalk pushed through."

"That guy was something else!" Tony exploded. "He was already being paid to let me know what was going on in this area."

"Wait!" I interrupted him. "Scooter was already making money under the table before you came here?"

"Yes. You probably don't know but Celesta and Shelley do, he went to Atlantic City right before I came down here. He told everybody that it was a mayor's convention. It wasn't. My guys already had their eye on Po'thole, called him up and asked if he would like an all-expenses paid trip to Atlantic City. It might have been suggested to him that he would have his choice of escorts to show him around town. He, of course, jumped at the bait.

"While he was there, and we really did give him the VIP treatment, we showed him the plans for the riverfront. In fact, we even took pictures of him looking at the plans and giving a thumbs up. He also had one arm around one of the escort's waist in the photo."

And there was the blackmail angle.

"He assured us everything would go along smoothly. Of course, we gave him a big casino check for one hundred thousand dollars and took his picture with that as well." Tony laughed.

Blackmail angle number two. I wondered at the stupidity of Scooter but knew it was far more likely that it was just greed on his part. He probably never thought anything about a couple of pictures being taken. Photos that could be shown to his wife later on or even shown to Gracie Blanche. He was probably just thinking in terms of more money being funneled down to his Cayman Islands bank account. I wondered if Gracie Blanche knew about that account and if she had siphoned off any of it. Nah, probably not. The only possibility of that happening would be if she donated the money to the First Baptist Church and they built a new wing or building with Scooter's name on it as a major contributor.

"But why kill him?" If nothing else, I could be focused when need be.

"Because that twit couldn't get Tabitha, Celesta, and Shelley in line. We had him on board and we had Johnny 'Ten Fingers' on board. He was a given but he was a shrewd negotiator, only in it for himself. We needed one more vote and we thought Tabitha was the weakest link. I went to talk to her on several occasions and she wasn't receptive to anything."

I smiled, although probably unseen by Tony, "And you discovered that she was anything but a pushover, right? Tabitha was a gracious Southern lady who was a steel magnolia."

"What does that mean?"

I rolled my eyes. "It means she was tough as nails and you couldn't push her around. You also probably didn't know she had called me because of death threats, did you?"

"I did when you showed up at her house. She'd still be alive if she had just taken the money and voted for the riverfront development."

There had to be some serious money behind all of this and

even more serious money to be made by having the riverfront developed.

"Wait, Tony, something isn't making sense. There's been talk of a casino but everyone seems to be more focused on the boardwalk aspect. Why?"

He snorted, "Because that's the first thing that's going to be developed and then we bring in the casino as the boardwalk's almost finished."

"And Celesta and Shelley figured that out, right?" I had my doubts about those two figuring it out to that extent but they were slowing things down.

"I don't think so. I think the only thing those two have figured out is that they want everything to stay the same and no new development anywhere. They don't understand growth. Regardless, they're next on the list."

"Why Murphy?"

He snorted. "I didn't like him."

"And what about Joe D.?" I held my breath. I really hoped I wouldn't hear anything awful about him being on the take.

He laughed, "Joe D. can't keep his pants zipped up. He has nothing to do with anything."

"What about the one hundred thousand dollars?" I thought I got a whiff of doughnuts through the air conditioning vent but couldn't be sure. I hoped against hope that one or all of the Lady Gatorettes had come in through the trap door in the kitchen floor. I also hoped they were not their normal rambunctious selves and making a ton of noise announcing their arrival.

"So, you've killed six people all for the sake of growth. Oh, yeah," I could be sarcastic now because I figured I was just minutes away from dying. "Let's not forget all of the money you're making."

Tony chuckled, "Still can't count, can you, Parker? It's seven deaths and Misty Dawn is going to be blamed for all of them. You're number seven. If you are a praying person, you need to start praying now because at the count of three you're going to meet your maker. One, two..."

I shut my eyes at one and hoped God would take pity on me. I hoped He would let me into heaven where I could meet up with my parents again. I knew they were in heaven because they were good people. Me, well, I tried but...

There was a loud pop sound. I felt wet stuff all over me, vaguely wondering why I could still feel anything. The wet stuff smelled like coffee. God has coffee in heaven! Apparently my sins weren't so great that He wouldn't let me into heaven. I was saved!

I kind of expected to hear the hallelujah chorus and see angels in bright white robes escorting me upwards. I could still hear Tony and then remembered that sound was supposedly the last thing to go in the dying process. Where were my angels? I smelled coffee.

"What the…?" Tony was cussing. Then another gun shot and I felt a body hit the bed.

Chapter 33

Once again I made national news while in Po'thole. I allegedly stopped a serial killer from murdering any more politicians and redneck business owners, although some of the extremist far-right whackos were sending me emails by the thousands congratulating me.

Saffron Woo had secured another huge advance for my next crime book, god knows what it is going to be on since I still had to write this one, and she was beyond giddy with excitement. She had booked me on every national tv show four months from now, totally convinced that I would have a rough draft of the book by then. Yeah, only if I didn't eat, sleep, go out but drank plenty of coffee I might be able to do it. I hated her but that was always subject to change.

Tony Buglia was dead. Johnny "Ten Fingers" had the perfect alibi because he was sitting in the River County jail talking to his attorney and couldn't have possibly killed Tony.

Celesta was home with her ten million cats and talking on the phone to Sophia about protecting the riverfront's environment from future development. Celesta and Sophia frequently had insomnia and often spoke on the phone late at night. She couldn't have killed Tony.

Shelley was home having a sleepover with her grandchildren and they all verified, independently, that she was on the floor in a sleeping bag while they were watching raunchy late night infomercials on tv.

Who knew what the Lady Gatorettes had been up to? No law enforcement personnel wanted that assignment and it was decided, quietly amongst themselves, that it was best just to let sleeping dogs lie.

Me? I was hailed as a hero. The official version is that Tony broke into my house, was hiding in my bedroom, held me at gunpoint when I came through the door, and I somehow managed to throw a large cup of hot coffee on him, thus blinding him temporarily. It was long enough for me to reach my gun behind the vase in the living room and shoot him in the middle of the head in self-defense.

The truth, and it would never see print, was that the Lady Gatorettes had installed an infra-red camera in my bedroom so that it faced the door and had seen everything unfolding. Although they were only about fifty yards away, they had to make a donut run before commencing to save my life.

As Rhonda Jean explained it they were hungry and hadn't eaten anything in a couple of hours. That was their justification on wasting twenty minutes of my life's time. I could have been saved sooner but, then again, Tony would not have told me everything prior to getting shot.

The gals came up through the kitchen trap door and, yes, it was fresh donuts I smelled coming through the air conditioning vents.

Misty Dawn is the one who threw the scalding hot coffee and hit the back of Tony's head, distracting him momentarily from killing me. It was also the coffee that splashed on me when I thought God was taking me to heaven.

When Tony turned around, Misty Dawn shot him in the middle of his head killing him instantly.

The status on the riverfront development? The only three

remaining city commissioners voted to keep the riverfront as it was. No new development would be coming any time soon.

Johnny "Ten Fingers", while never admitting to accepting money from outside influences, did make a very large and generous donation to the Policemen's Benevolent Fund. Celesta and Shelley believe he's turned his life around for the good. Yeah, when pigs fly. I headed back home to Atlanta where I believed I'd be safe from any future Po'thole craziness.

I was wrong.

ABOUT THE AUTHOR

Okay, true confession time. I have a wicked sense of humor. I write both fiction and non-fiction which makes me a hybrid writer or someone who just can't stop writing. Haven't won any major awards to brag about...and, trust me, I would if I could.

I absolutely love readers because without you I'd be eating peanut butter and crackers. Actually, I greatly appreciate you and your support. The best reward I get is when someone tells me they laughed out loud at my books and that it brightened their day.

People are always asking if I'm available for speaking engagements. The short answer is "Yes, of course." In fact, I can even do a Facebook Live Video event for your readers group.

Be sure to sign up for my newsletter Be sure to sign up

for my newsletter at www.SharonEBuck.com to receive notices and new releases before the general public.

ACKNOWLEDGMENTS

Many, many thanks to Allegra Kitchens, Cindy Grooms Marvin, Marsha Davis-Flowers, Pam Minnick, Barbara Smothers, Jack Owen, and Teena Hamilton for your encouragement.

Made in the USA
Coppell, TX
17 December 2025

66210936R00423

LE DRAGON ET LE TIGRE

DAVID PAYNE

LE DRAGON ET LE TIGRE

Confessions d'un taoïste à Wall Street

Roman

Traduit de l'américain
par Brice MATTHIEUSSENT

37, rue du Four
75006 Paris

Le présent ouvrage est le dix-neuvième titre de la collection
« *Les romans étrangers* »
dirigée par Tony Cartano

Si vous souhaitez recevoir notre catalogue et être tenu régulièrement au courant de nos publications, envoyez vos nom et adresse en citant ce livre aux

Presses de la Renaissance
37, rue du Four 75006 Paris

et pour le Canada à

Edipresse
5198, rue Saint-Hubert
Montréal H2J 2Y3

Titre original : *Confessions of a taoist on Wall Street* (publié par Houghton Mifflin Company, Boston, 1984).

© 1984, William David Payne III.
© 1986, Presses de la Renaissance pour la traduction française.

ISBN 2-85616-360-2   H 60-3049-4

*Pour ma mère,
Margaret Leah Rose Payne Long —
En premier acompte d'une dette que je ne
pourrai jamais lui rembourser.*

> Surpassant cet art
> Qui, selon vous, ajoute à la nature, existe un art
> Que la nature façonne.
>
>   Shakespeare, *Le conte d'hiver.*

Première Partie

Tao (la Chine)

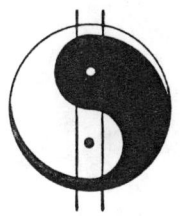

1

Ma première impression de lui est liée à une photographie découverte par un des moines dans la bourre de l'oreiller sur lequel j'étais couché en arrivant chez eux. Sur ce cliché, il semble à peu près du même âge que moi aujourd'hui, peut-être même un peu plus jeune. Vêtu d'une robe chinoise en soie comme d'une veste de smoking recouvrant ses habits civils, un verre ballon dans une main, l'autre glissée nonchalamment dans la poche d'un large pantalon kaki, il est debout à côté de son avion dont le nez peint porte le célèbre emblème de l'AVG — la gueule rouge béante du tigre aux rangs acérés de dents abstraites et ensanglantées. Je remarque aussi qu'il porte des chaussures bicolores. Elle est avec lui. Serrant d'un geste gauche le bras de l'aviateur, ma mère se tient sous l'hélice, dont une pale est figée au-dessus de sa tête comme une épée saisie au moment de sa chute. Habillée à l'occidentale — jupe plissée, chaussures de ville, socquettes blanches roulées au-dessus de la cheville —, elle porte la casquette d'officier de son compagnon rejetée sur la nuque, penchée avec désinvolture. Mais trop gros, le couvre-chef a commencé de glisser vers ses yeux pour masquer son visage — d'autant plus indistinct qu'elle ne regarde pas directement l'objectif, mais à côté, comme distraite par un objet situé un peu en dehors du cadre, une chose qui a échappé à l'appareil photo.

Contrairement aux traits de ma mère, ceux de l'aviateur semblent taillés à coups de serpe. Ses cheveux bruns et raides se dressent sur sa tête, qu'il penche légèrement en regardant l'objectif avec un sourire railleur destiné aux amis restés au pays, au photographe, à moi — un sourire que je n'ai jamais pu élucider, mais qui pourtant (et peut-être précisément pour cette raison) me charme infiniment. L'ambiguïté du personnage tient sans doute moins à son sourire qu'aux lunettes de soleil qui le surmontent et cachent l'expression de ses yeux. C'est le modèle de lunettes portées par les aviateurs et les policiers, équipées de verres en forme de larme vert foncé.

La mélancolie froide, anonyme, de ces lunettes au-dessus du sourire malicieux — l'une d'un masque moderne qui paraît dissimuler quelque immémoriale souffrance humaine ; l'autre, le sourire, en grande partie innocent, peut-être incapable de la souffrance impliquée par le masque — cette juxtaposition m'a toujours frappé comme une impertinence presque monstrueuse... et en même temps merveilleuse. Comment expliquer cela ? Les années passées à le regarder avec la tendresse affamée de l'orphelin ont exacerbé mon désir en une tension aussi extrême qu'exquise. Quand je m'absorbais trop longtemps dans cette photographie, mon imagination cédait à une surabondance d'images qui toujours l'évoquaient, lui. Le rêve a été mon seul recours. Car je n'ai jamais vu mon père. Sauf une fois... peut-être... tout à la fin, quand il fut trop tard, debout sur la galerie de la Bourse de New York. Mais c'est la fin de mon histoire, et non son début.

Çà et là, dans les régions reculées de la Chine postrévolutionnaire, enclave précaire dans le terne univers de notre Grande Muraille du progrès, on trouve encore parfois quelques vestiges de la tradition. Comme l'ancolie pousse entre les briques, la Chine éternelle fleurit dans les fissures qui signalent la ligne de faille de nos temps modernes. Je sais que c'est vrai, car j'ai passé mon enfance à errer parmi les splendides ténèbres de ce passé révolu.

Surnommée depuis des temps immémoriaux « la terre céleste », la province du Szu-ch'uan est une contrée de brumes et de fleurs, une contrée qui touche le ciel. Les légendes abondent dans ces paysages grandioses, où des rochers à pic dominent des abysses si profonds qu'un homme peut y tomber, dit-on, neuf jours d'affilée sans en toucher le fond. La pierre se tord à l'image de bêtes étranges punies par Dieu, figées dans les convulsions de leur vigueur primitive pour quelque péché d'arrogance — révolte matée bien avant que Wu Ting, l'Illustre Ancêtre, n'ait soumis le Pays du Diable et donné aux hommes un gouvernement. Dans la forêt-nuage du Szu-ch'uan, bambous et rhododendrons sont des géants trempés et gluants, hauts de quarante pieds, irrigués par les torrents de montagne qui dégringolent vers les cascades. Tombant sur une hauteur de mille pieds, ces torrents se dispersent en gouttelettes iridescentes avant d'atteindre les bassins inférieurs — toujours habités par leurs anciens seigneurs les dragons, qui bondissent et culbutent, barattent les eaux en écume dans leurs accès de joie diluvienne. Maîtres de leur domaine solitaire, ils se pavanent le soir et acceptent l'hommage des animaux qui viennent y boire, inclinant avec vénération leur tête pour laper l'eau froide et pure, et cligner leurs yeux phosphorescents.

Le Szu-ch'uan a toujours fourni à la Chine, sinon ses meilleurs poètes, du moins ses meilleurs rêveurs — il les a produits et protégés quand la patrie avait tourné vers eux son visage de colère. Là, dans les lieux isolés, si vous faites silence et que vous cultivez l'esprit adéquat, vous entendrez peut-être les trilles surnaturelles d'une flûte taoïste, jouée par quelque ermite ou magicien, l'un de ceux dont il est dit : « Il marche sans peur parmi les animaux, parle leur langage, se nourrit de la rosée de l'air. »

Selon une histoire populaire, ce fut dans cette province du Szu-ch'uan que les dieux se retirèrent — les dieux de tonnerre au faciès courroucé ainsi que les bodhisattvas souriants et les Immortels bienveillants — devant la vertueuse fureur du Président Mao et de ses gardes rouges pendant cette triste et honteuse parenthèse de notre histoire connue sous le nom de

Révolution culturelle. Éloigné de Pékin par mille milles et autant d'années, le Szu-ch'uan a toujours été, et demeure aujourd'hui, une région peu touchée par l'histoire ou le progrès.

Pour expliquer cela, la superstition, bien que séduisante, est superflue ; la géographie suffit : les montagnes et les fleuves. A l'ouest se dresse l'Himalaya, la plus haute chaîne du monde, dont les pics brillent sous une lumière épurée qui n'a jamais réussi, et ne réussira jamais, à faire fondre leur glace bleu-noir. Ce massif montagneux nous isole ; le fleuve également. Car si, dans son cours principal, le Yang-tsê est une grande artère qui unit les terres lointaines de l'extérieur aux cités côtières, il n'est plus navigable dès la frontière de notre province. Rivière tumultueuse, bourbeuse, parsemée de rapides, il fait rage dès qu'il plonge du plateau du Tibet et jusqu'aux gorges de San-hsia, à l'est de Ch'ung-ch'ing, avant de rejoindre Shanghai et la mer de Chine. Au Szu-ch'uan, le fleuve est un fil d'argent qui déçoit, isole ce qu'il devrait relier.

Ce fut là, à cette époque, le long d'un lointain affluent du Yang-tsê, dans le sud-ouest du Szu-ch'uan, à un jet de pierre des champs de pavot du Yunnan, que je grandis. Mais qui suis-je ?

Je m'appelle Sun I (prononcez Soun Ye*). Du moins, c'est ainsi qu'on m'appelle. Mon sobriquet... Quant à mon vrai nom, eh bien pour citer le célèbre aphorisme de Lao-tseu : « Le nom qui peut être nommé n'est pas le vrai Nom. » Cela s'applique on ne peut mieux à mon cas.

Car Sun I est un jeu de mots. Les moines, mes « frères aînés », décidèrent impitoyablement de m'affubler de ce surnom quand j'arrivai chez eux, nourrisson braillard et incrédule. Malheureusement la plaisanterie — dont j'ai tiré davantage de larmes que de rire — a duré.

Je dois m'expliquer. *Sun* et *I* sont les translittérations de deux caractères chinois qui signifient, littéralement, « déclin » *(Sun)* et « montée » *(I)*, ou si l'on préfère « profit et perte ». Comme, à ce moment, les moines ne pouvaient avoir qu'une idée superficielle de mon caractère, mon surnom ne fait certainement pas allusion à quelque ambiguïté de ma personnalité, ou à mes perspectives d'avenir — ce n'est pas une allusion volontaire. D'ailleurs, les moines ne formèrent pas ce nom eux-mêmes, ni par calcul, ni par malice, ni par quelque talent heureux (pour eux) de clairvoyance. L'inspiration occulte les guida. Car *Sun* et *I* désignent aussi les quarante et unième et quarante-deuxième hexagrammes du *Yi king*, le *Livre des mutations*. Voici le verdict de l'oracle quand les moines le consultèrent à mon sujet pour la première fois : *Sun*, ou « Perte », se désintégrant en son contraire, son image renversée, *I*, le « Gain ». (*Sun* est également le nom d'un des huit trigrammes fondamentaux : le « Doux ».)

Avant de poursuivre, laissez-moi dire un mot du *Yi king*, car plus d'une fois son avis s'est révélé prophétique, ou a modifié le cours de mon destin.

Le *Livre des mutations* allie les vertus de la Bible chrétienne à celles de l'almanach ; c'est une œuvre intensément religieuse, voire mystique, et en même temps totalement pragmatique, à l'image de l'esprit chinois dont il est le reflet. Le temps ayant accumulé dans ses pages des couches successives

---

* *Sun* : soleil, en anglais.

de sagesse comme autant de strates géologiques, il peut servir de guide pour le développement spirituel — comme les *Exercices* de Loyola chez les jésuites —, mais aussi bien, un paysan consultera l'oracle pour connaître la date à laquelle planter le riz ou l'orge. Plus cyniquement, le joueur peut l'utiliser pour prédire le résultat d'un jet de dés, bien que dans son cas le résultat soit davantage sujet à caution, car l'unique condition requise par l'oracle est *ling* qui, traduit librement, signifie « pureté de cœur ». Il est dit : « A ceux qui ne sont pas en contact avec le Tao, l'oracle renvoie une réponse inintelligible, car un conseil sensé ne servirait à rien. » Pourtant, cette pureté n'est pas aisément établie : un joueur peut la posséder, un prêtre pas.

La meilleure description du *Yi king* que j'aie jamais entendue fut peut-être donnée par mon maître Chong Fou, qui le compara à un puits dont les briques sont façonnées par des ouvriers humains, mais qui renferme les eaux froides et transparentes du Tao, tirées du pur réservoir de l'Être, dont aucun homme ne peut atteindre le fond.

Le *Yi king* se fonde sur le concept taoïste de la Grande Opposition Primordiale, connue en Occident par le symbole du *T'ai chi* — la Roue de la Vie (parfois nommée Œuf du Chaos) dans laquelle la lumière et les ténèbres, le *yang* et le *yin*, se mêlent comme deux bêtes gigantesques dans un combat mortel ou l'étreinte amoureuse. Toutes choses naissent de cette guerre, de cet amour incessants entre les contraires, qui alternent cycliquement, chacun se régénérant de la désintégration de l'autre qu'il porte en son sein comme un embryon fatal et qu'il nourrit au prix de sa propre existence. Les arts taoïstes, les « cent voies » de la méditation, dont l'étude du *Yi king* ne représente qu'une seule, ont pour but d'unifier ces opposés dans le soi, de reformer la totalité qui existait avant que l'Un, le Tao, n'éclate en une multiplicité d'objets séparés. Une fois soignée la blessure primordiale de la division, l'adepte retourne à la source immobile de l'Être et réussit l'accord avec le monde. Ainsi, en abandonnant les désirs et les ambitions précaires de l'ego, il devient aussi irrésistible qu'une force de la nature, capable de conquérir même la mort.

Pour revenir au *Yi king*, le taoïste utilise des baguettes d'achillée ou des pièces afin de lire — aussi précisément qu'un chimiste mesure des quantités d'éléments de base dans une solution — la composition de son destin. Car le taoïste est le chimiste universel, et le Tao la solution universelle qu'il analyse — la « soupe élémentaire », le plasma hors duquel les « dix mille choses » de la nature furent tirées, et auquel elles finiront par retourner.

Je dois maintenant finir d'expliquer la plaisanterie contenue dans mon nom, car je n'en ai élucidé que le premier niveau.

Hormis un détail de mon apparence, j'aurais pu mener une vie à peu près normale en Chine. En qualité de mâle, je possédais une certaine valeur et l'on aurait pu me vendre à un couple sans enfants pour perpétuer leur lignée. Dans ma situation, les nourrissons de sexe féminin connaissaient un sort plus cruel. Un jour, alors que je cherchais des herbes dans la forêt qui entourait le monastère, je découvris un bébé de sexe féminin allongé près du torrent, comme endormi, mais son mutisme était d'un bleu significatif... Malgré l'avantage que me conférait mon sexe, mon premier contact avec le monde aurait pu avoir la même conséquence fatale sans les moines. Pour cela, je leur pardonne volontiers la petite plaisanterie qu'ils se permirent à mes dépens.

Laissez-moi vous dire que je suis né avec ce qu'en Chine on nomme par euphémisme « une légère difformité de l'organe visuel » : mes yeux avaient « trop de blanc ». C'est ainsi que les Chinois qualifient l'individu à qui manque l'épicanthus dans l'angle interne de l'œil. Voici un passage du *Livre des mutations* concernant le trigramme *Sun* :

> Le Doux... est avance et retraite, indécision, odeur. Parmi les hommes, cela désigne ceux qui ont les cheveux gris, ainsi que ceux qui ont un large front ; *cela désigne ceux qui ont beaucoup de blanc dans l'œil* ; ceux qui sont âpres au gain et qui, au marché, gagnent trois fois leur mise. Enfin, c'est le signe de la véhémence.

Et voilà le coup de poinçon qui m'a laissé meurtri. Mais il y a pire. Les Chinois accablent parfois les Occidentaux de l'épithète dépréciatrice « yeux blancs ». Manquant d'épicanthus, ces derniers possèdent relativement plus de « blanc » que les Orientaux, fait que les Chinois — du moins les plus frustes, les plus provinciaux — ne cessent de railler. Je dois dire qu'on se moqua souvent de moi pour cette raison. Quand j'allais acheter du riz chez les paysans avec Wu, je me battais souvent contre les petits teigneux qui nous suivaient partout, me dévisageaient, reniflaient ma différence comme des bêtes sauvages.

Beaucoup plus tard, après mon arrivée en Amérique, le jeu de mots sur *Sun* prit une tournure inattendue et me ramena vers un élément de ma petite enfance. En Chine, il existe un rituel appelé « donner le signe ». Le nourrisson doit choisir parmi plusieurs objets symboliques placés autour de lui par ses parents, dans mon cas, par les moines. La préférence de l'enfant fournit soi-disant un indice infaillible de son destin d'adulte. Dans mon cas, l'objet fatal fut un petit œuf en pierre dans lequel étaient gravés les traits d'un singe, recroquevillé innocemment en fœtus, mais la tête dressée et « le regard féroce ». C'était le Singe infâme, dont je découvris ensuite que le nom chinois, signifiant « Grand Sage, Égal du Ciel », était transcrit en anglais par *Sun* Wu K'ung !

Pour comprendre la pertinence de mon association avec Singe — en sus du « regard féroce » —, vous devez savoir qu'après être sorti de son œuf de pierre, Singe passa sa jeunesse, comme moi la mienne, à gambader parmi la Montagne des Fruits et des Fleurs, se livrant à mille ébats joyeux dans le style habituel des singes. Pourtant, ainsi que le raconte Wu Ch'eng-en dans son célèbre récit, *Le voyage en Occident*, Singe devint mélancolique en songeant à sa nature mortelle ; il décida de partir vers l'Océan occidental à la recherche d'un sage capable de lui enseigner les Soixante-Douze Transformations. Cela accompli, on le nomma aux plus bas échelons de la Bureaucratie céleste, où il servait l'Empereur de Jade en qualité de laquais. Mais Singe sentait ses talents s'étioler dans les écuries. Ainsi, la veille du Grand Banquet de la Pêche, il se révolta, porta des toasts à sa propre santé au point de vider le plus clair des réserves du ciel. Il poursuivit par une beuverie colossale de trois jours, où il vola des quantités astronomiques d'Élixir Or et Cinabre de Lao-tseu, chaparda les Pêches d'Immortalité et perpétua d'autres forfaits pour lesquels, décidèrent les dieux, le seul châtiment adéquat était la mort — un gril prolongé dans l'alambic alchimique de Lao-tseu. Le seul problème était que Singe, qui avait bu vin et élixir, qui s'était empiffré de Pêches d'Immortalité (sans parler du fait que son corps était en pierre), était devenu invulnérable. Le laquais qui avait fait bombance avait gagné non seulement une immortalité, mais plusieurs, moyennant quoi, lorsqu'on ouvrit l'alambic de Lao-tseu, il en sortit plus guilleret que jamais et sans la moindre blessure, sinon ses yeux définitivement rougis par la fumée. Il reprit aussitôt le sentier de la guerre. En désespoir de cause, il fallut appeler le Bouddha en personne. Singe fut alors emprisonné pendant cinq cents ans sous une montagne de pierre.

Telle fut sa jeunesse. Mais ses vraies aventures ne commencent que plus tard, avec sa libération. Le Bodhisattva de Compassion, Kuan Yin, le laissa sortir à condition qu'il se conduise correctement, devienne le disciple et protecteur d'un moine nommé Tripitaka, triste hère parti en Inde pour retrouver les écritures mahayana. C'est le voyage vers l'ouest auquel le titre du livre de Wu Ch'eng-en fait allusion. Après dix-sept années et d'innombrables aventures plus incroyables les unes que les autres, Singe, en compagnie du larmoyant Tripitaka et d'autres animaux fabuleux, atteint enfin le ciel, trouve les textes convoités et les ramène en Chine. En récompense de leur prouesse et de leur compassion, ils reçurent l'illumination, chacun selon son mérite.

L'histoire de Singe, que j'obligeais inlassablement Wu à me raconter pendant mon enfance, me ravissait tout en m'attristant. J'avais beau adorer Singe, l'idée d'une association aussi étroite me déplaisait. Car bien qu'aimable, il était grossier. Pourtant, j'étais bel et bien lié à lui en vertu du signe que j'avais fourni. La traduction de son nom par Arthur Waley — *Sun* Wu K'ung — constituait la dernière et plus amère incarnation du jeu de mots.

Il était inévitable, je suppose, que mon tempérament versatile et ma tendance aux querelles soient baptisés par les frères « Nature de Singe », terme qui, dans leur argot particulier, suggérait l'entêtement, une imagination débridée, la malice et un cœur inquiet, véhément. Quand il me corrigeait après mes incartades, Wu insistait particulièrement sur cette dernière qualité — la véhémence. Faisant preuve d'une étonnante prémonition, l'oracle ne l'avait-il pas signalée comme un des attributs de mon caractère, au même titre que la forme de mes yeux ?

M'inclinant devant le destin, je supportais et l'insulte et les coups, avant de m'enfuir pour pleurer en silence. Ensuite, Wu, qui était sentimental et foncièrement bon, se sentait bourrelé de remords. Il venait me consoler, me tendait ses grosses mains pleines de friandises. Puis il ajoutait toujours que j'étais trop sensible, trop « doux ». *Sun* n'était-il pas le signe de la douceur ?

Oui, même Wu, mon meilleur ami, m'abreuvait parfois de ses sarcasmes (mais, il est vrai, avec davantage de tendresse et d'humour que les autres). Ce fut lui qui m'apprit qu'entendant mon nom pour la première fois, j'ouvris de si grands yeux que, bien qu'il fût minuit passé et qu'il fît nuit noire, le coq se mit à chanter dans la cour en croyant voir poindre l'aube.

En fait — ainsi que vous l'avez peut-être deviné — ma « difformité » tenait à une seule et unique raison : j'avais un père américain. Pour dire la vérité — et employer une autre de ces circonlocutions polies si exaspérantes et typiques de mon peuple (dues à l'influence pernicieuse du confucianisme et de ses « trois mille trois cents règles » d'étiquette) — je suis un « enfant de la guerre ». En bon anglais, un bâtard.

Mon père se nommait Eddie Love. Pilote, il arriva en Chine en 1941 avec l'AVG, l'*American Volunteer Group*, plus connu sous le nom de Tigres Volants. Je l'appris de bonne heure, car notre abbé Chong Fou eut un jour l'occasion d'offrir à Love l'hospitalité du monastère, dans des circonstances sur lesquelles je reviendrai. Chong Fou me transmit ce qu'il apprit de l'histoire de mon père. C'était peu. Je découvris plus tard que Love était le seul enfant d'un homme qui possédait une des plus grandes fortunes capitalistes d'Amérique. Arthur Love, mon grand-père, renonça à s'occuper activement de ses biens à cause de certaine « indisposition constitutionnelle », pour devenir un dilettante et un mécène vivant en reclus. Cette découverte me poussa à me demander si Eddie Love n'avait pas été une sorte de réfugié en Chine, fuyant le cocon débilitant et privilégié de ses parents, s'il n'avait pas cherché le danger comme un antidote à la présence insipide de son père. Je ne l'ai jamais su de façon certaine... ni cela, ni quoi que ce fût touchant à son caractère. Car mon père était un merveilleux illusionniste, un fantôme. Quand j'ai tenté de m'approcher de lui, de l'attirer vers moi pour l'étreindre, il a toujours mis en scène sa propre disparition, de sorte que mes bras ne se refermaient jamais que sur le vide.

Je connaissais bien sûr quelques faits. Esquisser son portrait à grands traits n'est pas si difficile. Comme les autres pilotes de l'AVG, il avait la réputation d'être courageux, sans entraves, indiscipliné, fantasque. Comme eux, il avait suivi en Chine le général Claire Chennault, par principe, pour l'aventure ou pour l'argent (bien que ceci paraisse improbable), ou simplement pour échapper à la routine du service ordinaire. Il ne s'était pas enrôlé dans une fraternité des plus reluisantes. Pourtant, pendant les sept mois qui ont précédé l'entrée officielle en guerre de l'Amérique, engageant ses troupes dans le théâtre de la Chine, de la Birmanie et de l'Inde, avec une centaine de Curtiss P-40 Tomahawk, les Tigres Volants ont seuls défendu la Chine contre la puissance aérienne japonaise.

Grâce à leurs efforts, la porte de sortie de la Route birmane est restée ouverte, dernière voie d'approvisionnement conservée par les Occidentaux. Kunming et, ultimement, Ch'ung-ch'ing elle-même — la capitale provisoire, où Tchang Kaï-chek et son gouvernement kuomintang s'étaient réfugiés pour opposer leur ultime résistance — dépendaient de cette artère vitale. Eût-elle été coupée, la Chine serait probablement tombée. Que les Tigres Volants aient pu opérer efficacement contre une force aérienne supérieure technologiquement et numériquement, cela est déjà remarquable. Mais qu'ils n'aient pas subi une seule défaite au cours de cinquante batailles aériennes importantes, cela tient du miracle. Voilà pourquoi, avec la RAF pendant la bataille d'Angleterre, on les considère comme la meilleure escadrille d'attaque qui ait jamais existé, pourquoi ils ont connu une sorte d'apothéose virtuelle, entrant dans le royaume de la légende militaire.

L'apothéose de mon père fut pour moi beaucoup plus que « virtuelle ». Enfant, je le considérais littéralement comme un dieu. Dans mes moments de mélancolie, je rêvais souvent qu'un jour il viendrait à mon secours, plongerait du soleil dans son P-40 pour m'emporter vers l'Occident. Alors j'aurais été heureux. C'était un fantasme désespéré, je le sais, mais je rêvais aussi avec véhémence. Rétrospectivement, il me semble aujourd'hui que mon enfance fut incroyablement heureuse, mais que dès qu'il entra dans ma vie j'appris ce qu'est vraiment le désespoir.

2

Le monastère où je grandis s'appelait Ken Kuan, ce qui signifie littéralement « vue » *(kuan)* de « montagne » *(ken)*. Mais pour les taoïstes (friands de ce genre de subtilité) ce nom cache un autre sens. Par extrapolation, *ken* peut vouloir dire « rester immobile », et *kuan* « contemplation ». Cela fait allusion à la forme de méditation connue sous le nom de *tso-wang* : « être assis avec l'esprit vide ».

Des deux points de vue, Ken Kuan portait bien son nom. Il était perché sur une falaise rocheuse des contreforts de l'Himalaya près des sources du Yang-tsê, qui dévale la chaîne du Tanglha ; depuis des temps fort reculés, cette montagne abritait les moines taoïstes qui s'y réfugiaient, abandonnant leur attachement à « la place du marché » du monde souillé, désireux de s'embarquer pour le difficile voyage du retour au Tao — un voyage nommé le Retour à la Source.

Ce but ultime est unique, mais les approches en sont multiples. De même que tous les rayons de la roue convergent vers le moyeu, de même les nombreux types de méditation — les « cent voies » — convergent dans la Voie unique, qui est le Tao. Quatre de ces voies étaient pratiquées à Ken Kuan.

La première était l'étude des textes sacrés, essentiellement le *Yi king*, mais aussi le *Tao-tö king* de Lao-tseu, le *Tchouang-tseu*, le *Lie-tseu* et d'autres œuvres moins importantes. Cette formation était mnémonique et exégétique.

La deuxième était *tso-wang*. Dans certains de mes premiers souvenirs, je joue parmi les moines assis en rang dans le temple, absorbés dans leur « méditation assise ». Sur l'ordre de Chong Fou, on me permettait d'aller et venir à ma guise, à l'unique condition que je fusse absolument silencieux. A la moindre incartade, on appelait Wu et je prenais la poudre d'escampette, oreilles rougies fouettées par le vent. Pourtant, aussi étrange que cela puisse paraître, cet expédient s'avérait rarement nécessaire. Bien que mon attention fût modeste et que je fusse malicieux comme tous les enfants (plus peut-être), je me tenais presque toujours à carreau en leur compagnie. La peur n'y était pas étrangère, je suppose. Mais il y avait autre chose... Souvent, j'observais le visage des frères — certains crispés par l'effort de concentration, perlés de sueur, d'autres calmes et souriants, nimbés de la lumière subtile de l'extase intérieure — et j'essayais de percer le mystère de leur immobilité. Parfois même je mimais leur respiration et leur posture, m'efforçant de me concentrer sur le Passage Mystérieux du Précieux Pouce Carré, situé au milieu du front entre et juste au-dessus des yeux (lieu de la glande pinéale, cet œil rudimentaire) où l'on voit les premières lueurs de l'Ineffable, comme une aurore boréale de l'esprit.

Bien sûr, ma « méditation » n'était pour l'essentiel qu'une simple imitation de ses aînés par un enfant joueur ; mais là encore, il y avait autre chose. Souvent, assis parmi les frères en méditation, surtout en présence de Chong Fou, je ressentais des choses curieuses. Mon corps frémissait, m'avertissait d'une imminence, comme si au plus profond de moi-même une porte s'ouvrait sur un autre monde, laissant passer une bourrasque glacée qui faisait se dresser les poils de mes bras ; ou bien j'étais brusquement submergé par une inexplicable vague de joie qui grossissait, éclatait puis déferlait, pour inonder mon cerveau d'un fluide mystérieux, aussi froid et violent que l'eau de la mer en hiver, puis qui refluait au rythme d'une diastole (tel un cœur mystique se relâchant) pour bientôt m'inonder à nouveau. Les dernières lueurs de ces expériences se prolongeaient pendant quelques heures. Je ne peux attribuer ces sensations qu'aux effluves électriques de la béatitude des moines, que j'étais capable d'accueillir à cause de l'innocence absolue de mon cœur enfantin. Tel fut mon premier avant-goût du profond bien-être apporté par la quiétude — plonger dans le pur bassin du Soi, en sortir revigoré, rafraîchi — et j'avais soif d'y goûter encore.

J'ai souvent pensé que le Tao m'accordait cette consolation à la place de la sécurité que d'autres enfants trouvent auprès du sein maternel, que je n'ai jamais connu. Plus que toute autre, cette pensée d'un manque et d'une absence provoqua les accès de mélancolie dont, enfant, je souffris (et les crises de rage qui suivaient, aussi inéluctables que les nuages noirs engendrent le tonnerre et la foudre). En grandissant, je réfléchis pourtant que j'avais connu des pacificateurs autrement extraordinaires. Ne m'avait-on pas octroyé « la Simplicité à contempler... le Bloc Brut à tenir... le détachement et le peu de désirs » ? Lao-tseu ne les appelait-il pas « les aliments qui viennent du sein de la Mère » ? Car le Tao est une mère plus vaste que les autres, la Grande Mère de tout. Bien que bâtard, elle ne m'avait pas rejeté. A son sein, je bus le doux lait de la vie éternelle, nourriture des dieux et des Sages Immortels. Qui, après tout, aurait pu revendiquer ascendance plus prestigieuse ?

Alors pourquoi étais-je donc tantôt inconsolable, tantôt amer ? Et pourquoi, inlassablement, retournais-je vers cette photographie de mon père au sourire cryptique et aux lunettes noires, tel un ambassadeur d'un autre monde ?

La troisième « voie » était la récitation des *Dix Chants du Chercheur de Bœuf*, familièrement nommés *Les Dix Taureaux*. Cette méthode incluait une part d'exégèse textuelle, comme l'étude des livres sacrés, mais aussi, comme *tso-wang*, certains exercices de yoga, en particulier la « régulation des souffles » indispensable à la vocalisation adéquate des syllabes. Par sa difficulté et sa complexité, cette méthode évoque la formation du chanteur d'opéra occidental.

Ces *Chants* sont si anciens que leur auteur est inconnu, effacement qui correspond sans doute à une nécessité. Dans ces textes, il décrit son simple labeur — chercher un taureau égaré, le retrouver, le ramener chez lui, se reposer à la fin de la journée. Voici le premier :

> Dans le pré du monde, j'écarte les herbes hautes
> pour chercher mon taureau.
> Suivant des fleuves sans nom, perdu dans le labyrinthe
> d'un sentier de montagne bordé d'arbres,
> Mes yeux épuisés se brouillent, mon cœur vacille ;
> car je ne le retrouve pas.
> J'écoute, défait, la stridulation sans âme des cigales
> dans le bois où la lune ne luit pas.

Derrière le sens littéral existe un ensemble d'allusions ésotériques. Ainsi, la cigale symbolise les distractions du monde des sens, le bourdonnement monotone et incessant de la « place du marché » dont le novice ne parvient pas à se libérer. Les débutants qui pratiquent *tso-wang* entendent souvent un tintement régulier, qui n'est pas sans rappeler « la stridulation sans âme » de l'insecte. Tel est le premier seuil à franchir.

La quête du taureau est une métaphore : le taureau désigne le Tao, « plus sombre que tous les mystères,/ La Porte qu'ont franchie toutes les Essences Secrètes ». Et les étapes de la quête — la recherche, la découverte, la domestication, l'usage et enfin la liberté — sont les seuls à passer pour atteindre la réalisation ; mais en fait, il n'y a rien à atteindre, sinon la réalisation de ce qui a toujours été depuis le début, mais à quoi nous étions aveugles à cause de notre attachement au monde des Fausses Apparences, que les bouddhistes nomment « Samsara ». Il est dit que le Samsara est le Nirvâna. Les taoïstes expriment cette idée plus concrètement par le célèbre paradoxe selon lequel « désirer l'illumination revient à chercher un taureau alors qu'on est assis sur son dos ». Les *hsien*, ou Immortels Taoïstes, sont souvent représentés assis sur le dos d'un taureau.

La méditation des *Dix Taureaux* contient une urgence et une émotion particulières. Car les *Chants* conviennent parfaitement à la voix aiguë et limpide d'un jeune garçon (à son ineffable mélancolie). L'adolescence dissipe ce timbre obsédant au moment précis où elle confère la maturité affective indispensable au chanteur désireux de rendre toute la gamme émotionnelle des *Chants*. Dilemme classique : le jeune garçon possède un instrument que seuls ses aînés sauront utiliser avec discernement, apprécier à sa juste valeur. Trouver un individu chez qui les deux talents cohabitent, du moins naturellement, est rare. C'est là un facteur très réel qui a présidé à la création des castrats de cour qui ont infesté la Chine depuis l'époque des Tcheou jusqu'à notre siècle. Nul doute que leur disparition constitue un « grand bond en avant » pour sortir des ténèbres féodales ; néanmoins, les *Chants* et la vie contemplative en général ont tristement dépéri depuis lors. Les aficionados sont toujours à l'affût du « garçon précoce » qui pourra leur rendre justice.

Si je me suis étendu aussi longuement sur ce sujet, la vanité est peut-être à blâmer. Voyez-vous, j'ai un temps été célèbre (« connu » serait sans doute plus juste) pour mon interprétation des *Dix Taureaux*. Jusqu'à ce que ma voix mue — rite de passage qui me troubla profondément (mais je crois que c'est le lieu commun de toutes les adolescences). Souvent, dans les profondeurs résineuses de la forêt, je m'asseyais seul pour chanter. Le soleil qui filtrait entre les branches des pins mouchetait mon visage et mes mains tandis que j'accomplissais ma méditation solitaire, seulement accompagné par le frémissement du vent dans les arbres. Le plaisir engendra la facilité ; la facilité se mua en fierté, la fierté en ostentation. J'exhibai mes talents dans les espaces publics du monastère. La jalousie éclata parmi les moines. En plus des épithètes cinglantes de leur arsenal offensif, ils concoctèrent ceci : « le jeune coquelet ».

Je me rappelle un incident parmi tant d'autres. Un jour, je fredonnais pendant que Wu et moi transportions de l'eau, quand j'entendis quelqu'un chuchoter malicieusement ce nouveau sobriquet derrière mon dos. J'ignore pourquoi je vis rouge cette fois-là, mais j'entrai dans une telle rage que Wu dut renverser un plein seau d'eau sur ma tête pour me calmer. Je ne devais pas avoir beaucoup plus de dix ans. Je me revois debout sur les dalles froides de la cuisine, tremblant tandis qu'il m'essuyait.

« Pourquoi te mets-tu toujours dans ces états ? » me sermonnait-il en me frottant vigoureusement. Il secoua la tête et répondit lui-même à sa question. « Ne dis rien, je sais. Tu es un coléreux. L'oracle ne l'a-t-il pas déclaré ? C'est ton côté *Sun*, ta Nature de Singe. Si tu ne fais pas attention, tu vas t'en mordre les doigts. »

« Qu'est-ce qui te rend si malin ? » le défiai-je en le laissant essuyer la morve de mon nez.

Wu se redressa et me regarda gravement. « Je connais les signes, dit-il en soupirant, trop bien... Je les vois dans tes yeux. »

Il y avait une dernière forme de méditation, le plus complexe et ardu des arts taoïstes — l'alchimie. Comme chez son homologue occidentale, le but de l'alchimie taoïste est la transmutation des éléments de base — spécifiquement le blanc de plomb (mercure) et le cinabre — en or. Les tenants de l'école populaire y voient un processus matériel dont le but est la richesse. Mais pour les vrais initiés, il s'agit d'une métaphore renvoyant à une transformation d'une autre espèce, une transmutation intérieure.

Le blanc de plomb et le cinabre représentent les termes de l'opposition fondamentale : la multiplicité sous sa forme la plus simple. Cette opposition existe non seulement dans le monde, mais en chaque être ; il faut la dépasser pour réaliser l'unité, guérir la blessure mortelle que chaque individu porte en son cœur depuis sa naissance jusqu'au jour où il en meurt. Le blanc de plomb est *yang*, le principe mâle, symbole du sperme ; le cinabre est *yin*, principe femelle, sa pigmentation suggère le sang menstruel. Ces éléments sont réconciliés par la décoction de la Pilule (ou Elixir) Or-Cinabre, qui est aux taoïstes ce que la pierre philosophale est aux mages occidentaux. Sa fabrication adéquate est un gage de vie éternelle.

L'école fondée par Sun Ssu-mo-tseu représente une variante intéressante de ce thème. Pour obtenir la fusion du blanc de plomb et du cinabre, les adeptes de cette alchimie pratiquent un rapport sexuel ininterrompu, mais soumis à une discipline draconienne. L'homme diffère en permanence son éjaculation pour empêcher toute perte de fluide vital *yang*, lequel, contrairement au *yin*, est limité et irremplaçable. Par ce moyen, le réservoir intérieur de la précieuse essence vitale s'emplit goutte à goutte. Nommée yoga du Tigre Blanc/Dragon Vert, cette école faisait horreur à maints taoïstes et s'est éteinte quand les autorités l'ont interdite. Pourtant, qui sait ? Est-il si absurde de penser que, dans quelque temple en ruine au fin fond du royaume, deux anciens adeptes aux visages ratatinés et édentés, mais aux regards alertes et brillants, pratiquent religieusement la copulation rituelle dans l'espoir de sauver leurs âmes immortelles ?

Quoi qu'il en soit, à Ken Kuan ce yoga ne faisait pas partie du curriculum. En fait, la chasteté était la règle de l'ordre — règle non écrite, mais strictement appliquée. Pour autant que je sache, car ma connaissance des rites était de seconde ou troisième main. L'alchimie était seulement pratiquée par les adeptes d'âge mûr, et toujours sous l'œil attentif du maître, Chong Fou (qui, disait-on, avait déjà distillé la liqueur d'immortalité). Car de graves dangers étaient liés à sa pratique. Surtout l'empoisonnement. Certains moines — qui prenaient les choses au pied de la lettre — essayaient de transmuer les parties corruptibles de leur nature en ingérant directement mercure et cinabre, d'abord par petites quantités, pour ensuite augmenter graduellement les doses à mesure de la tolérance de leur corps — réalisant ainsi un mithridatisme alchimique. Comme on l'imagine, cela se révélait désastreux pour le foie, et la mort s'ensuivait généralement. Néanmoins, ses sectateurs (les survivants) soulignaient non sans satisfaction les vertus indéniables de leur technique pour conserver le corps dans la tombe. En tant que méthode d'embaumement, l'empoisonnement par le métal surpasse jusqu'aux arts égyptiens et rivalise avec les fosses de goudron de l'époque mésozoïque.

Mais il existait des dangers d'un autre ordre. Je me rappelle l'histoire d'un moine qui, après une erreur de manipulation, perdit son âme, laquelle s'envola entre les côtes de son corps comme un oiseau-chanteur d'une cage ouverte. Deux jours durant, il l'entendit chanter dans la cime d'un arbre près de sa fenêtre. Puis elle disparut dans les ténèbres de la forêt, et il dépérit avant de mourir de désespoir. D'autres, dont j'entendis parler, furent emprisonnées dans une forme animale pour expier leurs fautes. Certaines tombèrent directement en enfer.

Je dois reconnaître que ces histoires me plaisaient. Wu les égrenait comme une fontaine intarissable. Un jour que je ramassais des *mo-erh* (« oreille de nuage », champignon de souche noir), je découvris un sanctuaire de renarde en ruine caché parmi les feuilles, à flanc de colline. Wu me raconta ensuite l'histoire de la belle anachorète Hu Li, qui se tenait « au seuil de l'illumination » — dernière étape où une concentration absolue est requise — quand des soldats impériaux la sommèrent brutalement de composer l'Élixir pour le fils du Ciel. Afin de se venger de cette irruption, le jour que l'empereur avait choisi pour son apothéose, Hu Li lui ordonna de renvoyer gardes et domestiques, puis lui servit le « Banquet Céleste » qu'elle avait préparé de ses propres mains — banquet dont le mets principal, apporté dans un plat couvert, était la tête encore fumante du fils de l'empereur, un nourrisson aux yeux blancs bouillis. Pour cette énormité, les dieux emprisonnèrent Hu Li dans le corps d'une renarde, où elle séjourne de toute éternité, avec la permission d'assumer forme humaine à certaines saisons ; elle se transforme alors en ravissante jeune fille qui erre la nuit dans la campagne pour séduire puis dévorer les voyageurs trop crédules. Les sanctuaires de renarde, où l'on dépose souvent des offrandes de viande fraîche et de poulets vivants, sont censés apaiser Hu Li et les autres Fées Renardes dont elle est la reine.

Dès ma prime jeunesse, possédé du sombre désir de l'interdit avec lequel les jeunes Occidentaux envisagent le sexe, j'attendis le jour où Chong Fou m'initierait à ces rites mystérieux. Mon plus grand regret fut peut-être qu'en quittant la Chine, je n'avais toujours pas commencé ma formation. Wu disait que Chong Fou ne m'enseignerait jamais rien tant que je n'aurais pas appris à contrôler mon esprit, ajoutant que c'était mon « tempérament de sauvage » qui faisait hésiter le maître. Peut-être avait-il raison, bien que je ne l'eusse jamais pensé à l'époque. J'avais tendance à écarter d'emblée les conseils de Wu, surtout sur ce chapitre, car lui-même n'avait jamais été initié aux mystères.

Comme je l'ai si souvent mentionné, je dois vous parler un peu de Wu, mon maître, employeur, esclave, nourrice et mère substitutive, tyran et protecteur, l'ami formidable de ma jeunesse. Wu était un paysan, que l'amour de la bonne chère et de la boisson avait rendu, dans son âge mûr (où je le trouvai), presque aussi large que haut. Il n'était pas gros, cependant. Son ventre, bien que gigantesque, était aussi dur que celui d'un bouddha de pierre. Il ne tremblait pas sur les terrains accidentés, mais cahotait tout d'une pièce au-dessus des amortisseurs incongrus de ses jambes fuselées. Les dons naturels de Wu pour les arts culinaires lui avaient valu son poste de maître queux dans la cuisine de Ken Kuan. Dès que je fus en âge de travailler, je devins son aide, position qui me plaçait avec lui au plus bas échelon de la hiérarchie sociale.

Je ne l'ai jamais regretté. Le bon naturel de Wu fut une compensation suffisante. Bondissant dans la cuisine, ses bras gesticulant en tous sens pour mettre un peu d'ordre dans un capharnaüm de couteaux, légumes, casseroles, il me racontait ses merveilleuses histoires, brodait sans fin sur des thèmes simples et donnait libre cours à sa créativité. Ce fut une des grandes joies de mon enfance.

Mais la médaille avait son revers. Voyez-vous, il incombait aussi à Wu d'exécuter toutes mesures punitives me concernant. Il était d'une fidélité exemplaire, parfois même inspiré, dans l'exercice de son devoir. Un exemple : Wu avait une barbe plutôt fournie pour un Chinois, qu'il rasait au mieux tous les trois ou quatre jours (à l'exception du toupet qui poussait entre sa lèvre inférieure et son menton, qu'il conservait par vanité). Ainsi, son maxillaire arborait toujours une ombre aussi bleutée que le sol d'une forêt d'arbres à feuilles persistantes. Chaque fois que je réussissais à l'exaspérer jusqu'aux inévitables représailles, il se penchait au-dessus de moi comme pour me confier un secret, puis tel un porc-épic malveillant, frottait le dur chaume de sa barbe contre la tendre peau de ma tête. C'était là rude punition, mais cent fois méritée, j'en suis sûr. Car Wu était toujours juste. Il avait bon cœur ; son côté terrien constituait un parfait antidote à l'univers éthéré des autres moines qui, contrairement à lui, venaient généralement des strates les plus élevées de la société.

Wu n'était pas naturellement religieux, il possédait fort peu sinon rien de la sensibilité tourmentée du dévot. Il ne méditait pas souvent sur les illusions des sens ou la vanité de la richesse et du monde. En fait, à ma connaissance, il ne méditait tout bonnement jamais. En tout cas, je ne l'y ai jamais surpris, à moins qu'on puisse considérer les arts culinaires comme une forme de méditation, auquel cas il devait réellement être fort proche de la béatitude. Car, ainsi que je l'ai signalé, il fréquentait ses fourneaux avec une dévotion exemplaire. Cependant, je suis au regret de dire que tout le monde n'appréciait pas à sa juste valeur le mal qu'il se donnait. En effet, la plupart des moines prenaient Wu pour un glouton et un libertin. Ce qu'il était, j'imagine, du moins selon les critères monastiques, les seuls applicables à son cas.

Wu partait chaque année en vacances pour le Nouvel An. Pendant son absence, les moines affamés le vilipendaient sans pitié, rivalisant de virtuosité dans l'invention de nouvelles formes ingénieuses et perverses d'assassinat verbal. Ils prétendaient qu'il était parti faire la noce pendant une semaine, jouer la nuit aux tables de mah-jong de Ch'ung-ch'ing, louer les services de prostitués (homme, femme ou enfant, raillaient-ils, Wu ne voyait pas la différence) et accomplir avec eux des actes innommables, ajoutant pour faire bonne mesure qu'il ne dessoûlait jamais plus d'une demi-heure. Il n'existait pas la moindre preuve de leurs dires, sinon, bien sûr, celles que la méchanceté invente. (Malgré tout, je vis un jour Wu ramené inconscient dans une charrette à fumier.)

Mais à supposer que ces rumeurs aient eu quelque fondement, aussi mince fût-il, je me suis souvent demandé où Wu trouvait l'argent de ses virées. Car il y avait fort peu d'argent liquide à Ken Kuan. Certains des moines les plus cyniques racontaient à mots couverts que Chong Fou en personne finançait ses orgies, et qui plus est, que cet argent provenait des maigres réserves que nous économisions pour acheter ce que nous ne pouvions ni cultiver ni fabriquer nous-mêmes. Enfant, je ne prêtais nullement foi à ces ragots. Notre abbé encourageant volontairement les débauches d'une de ses ouailles ? Impensable ! Aujourd'hui, je n'en suis plus aussi sûr. La subtilité et la puissance de l'esprit du maître fendaient la sagesse conventionnelle comme la proue d'un navire l'océan amorphe. Tout ce que je puis dire avec certitude, c'est qu'indépendamment des raisons qu'avait Chong Fou de gâter Wu (s'il le gâta jamais), tout cela fut calculé pour rapporter un gros bénéfice sur l'investissement initial (spirituellement parlant, bien entendu). Ce fut peut-être par cette concession qu'il gagna la confiance de Wu. Car il l'avait bel et bien gagnée, par des moyens honnêtes ou tortueux. Dans sa loyauté,

Wu ressemblait à un chien bâtard au grand cœur prêt à se battre à mort pour défendre son maître.

Pourtant, sa foi vacillait parfois. Wu avait un côté irascible. Quand il fallait effectuer des travaux extraordinaires, il grommelait souvent. Pareille occasion se présentait à l'époque du Grand Festival de Printemps où nous veillions toute la nuit comme une équipe de sages-femmes inquiètes pour prier et aider la nature à accoucher de son fardeau incandescent, le soleil. Pendant que les chanteurs se relayaient, Wu et moi nous affairions dans la cuisine sans interruption, profitant de la moindre pause pour dormir un peu. J'allais et venais en courant, je cueillais des herbes — gingembre, ail, piments verts —, je ramenais de l'eau du torrent qui dansait au pied des falaises, plongeait en de courtes cascades dans une succession de vasques d'écume et de roc. En période de crise, Wu m'accompagnait. Notre tâche était particulièrement épuisante puisque nous devions remonter les seaux pleins d'eau le long d'une pente raide aux étroites marches taillées dans la pierre. Wu montait en soufflant et ahanant ; son visage rosissait à travers le chaume bleu qui couvrait ses joues et sa gorge. Il me grondait souvent, car mes seaux avaient invariablement perdu l'essentiel de leur contenu quand nous arrivions au sommet de la pente.

« *Aiya !* s'écriait-il. Les pierres ont-elles soif pour que tu leur donnes autant à boire de notre précieuse eau ? Regarde mes seaux ! Quelle eau ai-je renversée ? »

C'était vrai. Grâce à un don ou une chance extraordinaire, Wu ne semblait jamais perdre une goutte bien qu'il gravît ce traître escalier deux fois plus vite que moi. (J'essayais de limiter les dégâts en montant lentement, choisissant mon itinéraire à l'avance, posant un pied devant l'autre avec un soin calculé.)

« Je ne comprends pas, lui avouai-je. Tu as certainement un truc. Explique-moi ta méthode. »

Wu fit claquer sa langue et secoua la tête d'un air désapprobateur. « Sauvage, dit-il, tu n'as toujours pas compris. C'est précisément ça — l'excès de méthode — qui te leurre, vide quasiment tout ton seau, et obligera peut-être mon pied à caresser ton honorable postérieur. » Sa plaisanterie le fit rugir de rire. « Pourquoi te sens-tu obligé de faire deux voyages quand je n'en fais qu'un ! Tu n'apprendras donc jamais ? Tu es trop scrupuleux. Tu ne dois pas essayer de calculer le moindre de tes pas. Comme si ton cerveau chétif était assez malin pour venir à bout de cette grande montagne !

— Très bien, dis-je sombrement, puisque tu es si malin, comment fais-tu ?

— Comment je fais ? » Il se pencha au-dessus de l'abîme. « Je ferme les yeux et ne pense à rien. Mon esprit est ailleurs. Mes jambes trouvent leur chemin sans moi, même sur les terrains les plus accidentés. »

Peu habitué à une dissertation philosophique aussi longue, il se sentit gêné par mon regard inquisiteur.

« Comment veux-tu que je t'explique la façon dont je m'y prends ? » s'écria-t-il sur la défensive en regardant autour de lui comme si la réponse avait dû se matérialiser dans l'espace.

Alors une idée parut le frapper, et il éclata d'un rire incompréhensible. « Je ne m'en souviens même pas moi-même ! » Puis il s'éloigna en se dandinant, son gros ventre bondissant et rebondissant entre les deux seaux immobiles.

Bien qu'il ne l'ait sans doute jamais su, Wu était à sa façon un homme accompli. Mais à l'époque, j'étais trop jeune pour l'apprécier à sa juste valeur. Après tout, la gastronomie était peut-être pour lui une forme de méditation. Je suis sérieux. Car l'activité à laquelle un homme se voue avec toute la force de son être — lui-même se transformant en satellite de son acte, se soumettant à sa gravité comme à une discipline qui doit l'astreindre à l'ultime et dure orbite de la perfection — cette activité n'est-elle pas une forme de méditation ? Cela est écrit dans mon livre. La méditation est ce qui conduit au Tao, et le Tao, dans l'un de ses innombrables avatars, est aussi nommé « le Parfait ».

Je crois que l'épisode des seaux d'eau prouve que Wu agissait en accord avec le Tao. Il avait appris l'art du *wu-wei* ou de « l'activité sans action » (le mouvement dont le cœur est immobilité), qu'il pratiquait avec une habileté que peu, sinon aucun des moines plus éthérés possédaient. Naturellement, ils le méprisaient, ne voyaient qu'un grossier paysan chargé de la tâche indigne de préparer la nourriture du corps, tandis qu'eux cherchaient à alimenter leur esprit. Dans l'ensemble et sans amertume, Wu partageait leur opinion. Pourtant, je suis convaincu que Chong Fou comprenait en secret et approuvait cette situation. Appliquant ses propres méthodes subtiles, le maître fournissait à son disciple le régime spirituel adéquat, et apprenait à Wu à se laisser porter par les flots invisibles du *yin* et du *yang*.

Cette théorie fut implicitement confirmée par Wu lui-même, qui, dans l'intimité détendue qui suivit l'heureuse conclusion d'un des grands festivals mentionnés plus haut, me raconta une partie de l'histoire de sa vie.

« Wu, es-tu né ici, comme moi ? » lui avais-je demandé avec une naïveté enfantine (encore trop jeune pour connaître la vérité).

Mon gros ami éclata de rire. « Combien de fois un singe sort-il d'un œuf de pierre ? Sans doute pas plus d'une fois tous les mille ans. » Il secoua la tête. « Non, Sun I, Wu fut engendré de façon classique. J'ai grandi au-dehors et suis venu à la Voie sur le tard.

— Pourquoi as-tu choisi cette vie ?

— Choisi ? » Il ricana. « Je ne l'ai pas choisie, c'est *elle* qui m'a choisi. » Les mains de Wu s'immobilisèrent au-dessus du hachoir, puis il les essuya sur le tablier sale qu'il portait autour de la taille. Les autres étaient partis se coucher, et maintenant — récompense spéciale de nos efforts conjugués —, il coupait des navets pour préparer les crêpes sucrées dont je raffolais.

« Qu'as-tu fait avant ? » demandai-je.

Il m'adressa un regard inquisiteur, puis scruta le vide comme s'il essayait de se souvenir.

« Je viens d'un village de fermiers près de Ch'ung-ch'ing, dit-il en recommençant de hacher les navets. Toute ma famille — grands-parents, tantes, oncles et cousins — habitait ce village. Nous cultivions des légumes, nous élevions des poulets pour le marché de la ville.

— Pourquoi es-tu parti ? Tu étais malheureux là-bas ? »

Wu ne leva pas les yeux de son hachoir. « Pas toujours, finit-il par répondre d'une voix sombre. Le travail était dur, mais la vie supportable. Mes parents me dorlotaient même un peu, surtout ma mère, car j'étais son dernier fils, son "bébé", et il y avait peu de chances pour qu'elle en eût un autre. Mais quand je tombai amoureux et voulus me marier, quelque chose changea en elle. Elle se mit à me regarder bizarrement. Notre familiarité cessa du jour au lendemain. Elle se retira, parlant rarement, sauf pour lancer des remarques sarcastiques à propos de ma future épouse. Je ne comprenais pas, car Chaï était une jeune fille simple et modeste, timide même. Et jolie, Sun I. Je l'aimais. Le jour de notre mariage fut le plus heureux de ma vie.

« Quand je la ramenai à la maison de mon père, ma mère afficha aussitôt son hostilité. Impitoyable, elle traitait Chaï comme une domestique, l'obligeait à nettoyer le sol d'un bout à l'autre de la maison, jusqu'aux chambres placées sous la responsabilité d'autres épouses. Et si elle trouvait la moindre trace de poussière, Chaï devait tout recommencer. Ce n'est qu'un exemple parmi tant d'autres. C'était injuste, mais ma mère avait le droit de se conduire ainsi, et Chaï supporta patiemment l'épreuve. Simplement, sa modestie naturelle devint manque d'assurance, mutisme ; son visage se creusa, comme si quelqu'un écrasait son esprit. Mon cœur se brisait, mais je ne pouvais rien faire. Je pensais toujours que ma mère finirait par céder à la pitié.

« Un jour, en revenant des champs, je trouvai Chaï en larmes. Elle refusa d'abord de me regarder, mais quand j'insistai, elle s'effondra et me raconta ce qui s'était passé. Alors je vis sa joue tuméfiée, les bleus qu'elle portait sur le dos et les flancs. Elle avait posé une question considérée comme impertinente par ma mère, qui l'avait rouée de coups avec un bambou. Furieux, j'allai aussitôt voir mon père pour lui demander la permission de déménager. Hors de question, répondit-il. Le temps de la moisson approchait ; mes parents, qui vieillissaient, ne pouvaient se passer de notre aide. "Patience, dit-il. Quand tu auras un fils, elle cédera."

« Nous plaçâmes donc tous nos espoirs dans une naissance. Et bien sûr, le premier hiver, Chaï fut enceinte. J'étais ravi, Chaï semblait reprendre courage. Nous commençâmes à envisager l'avenir sous un jour nouveau. Mon père aussi était content. Quand je lui appris la nouvelle, il quitta un instant son masque austère et sévère, éclata de rire et m'assena une tape sur l'épaule comme à un ami. Puis il me dit d'annoncer l'heureux événement à ma mère.

« Je rougissais de plaisir en arrivant devant elle. Elle me regarda avec curiosité, puis me demanda ce que je voulais. Je lui dis la nouvelle et, à ma grande surprise, elle resta de glace, ses yeux brillant d'une lumière morte. Elle me congédia d'un signe de tête.

« Je n'ai jamais compris cela, Sun I. Peut-être son âge et sa décrépitude... Ses seins ratatinés à force d'avoir allaité tant d'enfants — elle était définitivement sèche. La présence d'une jeune femme éclatante de santé et qui abritait une nouvelle vie lui rappela peut-être sa propre stérilité, sa mortalité, et l'irrita jusqu'à la folie. En tout cas, au lieu de partager notre joie, ma mère redoubla de mépris. Elle obligea Chaï à travailler aussi durement que d'habitude, bien que Chaï commençât à se fatiguer plus vite à cause du bébé. Finalement, en désespoir de cause, j'ai essayé de parler à ma mère, je lui ai demandé de comprendre notre position. De ma vie, je ne l'ai jamais vue aussi furieuse. Elle tremblait, blêmissait. Puis elle se mit à m'injurier, à se frapper la poitrine en criant que si sa façon de s'occuper de la maison ne me plaisait pas, je pouvais aller vivre ailleurs. Comme j'aurais aimé la prendre au mot ! Mais une fois encore mon père me l'interdit. Il me demanda de rester jusqu'à la naissance de l'enfant pour voir si ma mère ne changerait pas d'attitude. Je ne pouvais que lui obéir.

« Un jour d'automne, alors que sa grossesse était presque à terme, Chaï enjamba la clôture du jardin avec un fagot de petit bois, trébucha et tomba. Elle se mit à saigner et entra bientôt en travail. Une de mes tantes entendit ses cris et sortit de la maison en courant. Elle accoucha de son enfant sur place, dans le chaume de la récolte de tournesols, mort-né. On ne put rien faire pour arrêter l'hémorragie. Quand j'arrivai, Chaï aussi était morte. »

Wu se tut ; une profonde humiliation empourprait son visage. Il semblait s'étouffer — littéralement — sur ce morceau de son passé régurgité par la mémoire.

« C'était un garçon », dit-il enfin avec une colère que le temps n'avait pas entamée.

Je pensais qu'il avait fini de parler, quand, après un long silence, il reprit brusquement.

« Après cela, je haïs ma mère avec toute la violence dont j'étais capable. Je savais mon attitude critiquable, mais c'était plus fort que moi. Chaque fois que je la voyais, je voulais saisir son cou ridé entre mes mains pour le tordre comme celui d'un poulet. Un matin, après m'être disputé avec elle, je partis pour les champs et continuai de marcher sans regarder en arrière. Depuis ce jour, je n'ai jamais revu ni elle ni mon père. Je suppose qu'aujourd'hui tous deux sont morts depuis longtemps. »

« C'est à ce moment que tu es venu ici ? » lui demandai-je après un silence respectueux.

Wu secoua la tête. « Non. Je suis ensuite allé en ville. Un temps, j'ai travaillé dans les marchés ; je chargeais et déchargeais les caisses pour les vendeurs. Un jour, je suis tombé sur mon frère, mais il a aussitôt détourné les yeux et feint de ne pas m'avoir vu. Vers cette époque, j'ai rencontré une bande de mauvais garçons, dont certains se droguaient. Ils me firent connaître l'opium. Mon cœur était malade, Petit Sauvage. La drogue coûtait cher. Je me fis piéger. Mon créditeur, le propriétaire de la fumerie, était aussi un requin de l'emprunt, lié aux sociétés secrètes locales. Aucune affaire ne se traitait dans le voisinage sans qu'elles touchent une forte commission. Elles nous laissaient acheter l'opium à crédit jusqu'à ce que nous soyons accrochés, ensuite elles pressaient le citron. Avant peu, ma santé se mit à décliner. Trop épuisé pour travailler, je décidai de jouer pour les rembourser. Mais les sociétés secrètes possédaient aussi les tables de jeu, qu'elles manipulaient. C'est presque drôle, mais à l'époque je soupçonnais déjà la vérité. Quoi qu'il en soit, plus rien n'avait désormais d'importance pour moi. Je ressentais une sorte de joie fatale, Sun I, tu vois ? Comme une vigne vierge, le jeu enserrait mon cœur dans ses vrilles et y régnait en maître tout-puissant. Au-delà même de l'opium, c'est la pire des drogues. Pas seulement pour moi — car mes émules se comptaient par centaines, peut-être par milliers. J'ai appris quelque chose pendant ces longues nuits fiévreuses où je regardais les dés dévorer tous mes biens, et plus encore... »

Aujourd'hui encore je revois les yeux de Wu fixés sur moi quand il me dit cela.

« En tant que peuple, nous paraissons peut-être sceptiques ou léthargiques, mais il y a en nous un élément aventureux, que les dés savent révéler. Nous sommes une race de joueurs, Sun I, n'oublie jamais cela. Je l'ai oublié, et ce fut ma déchéance. » Il hocha la tête.

« Tu vois, au bout d'un moment je compris que je ne pourrais jamais rembourser mes dettes. Ils m'envoyèrent un de leurs "ramasseurs de fonds". Il cogna ma tête contre la table de la cuisine au point que le sang m'aveuglait, tout en me suppliant de me montrer "raisonnable". Je les avais trompés volontairement, disait-il. Ils voulaient que je respecte mes engagements, que je trouve une compensation équitable. Mais la seule chose qui me restait pour les dédommager était ma vie, et je savais qu'ils n'auraient aucun scrupule à me l'enlever. Ainsi, je m'enfuis de nouveau.

« Cette fois, j'étais à moitié fou. Mes nerfs étaient à bout. Je souffrais des symptômes du manque. Je ne sais pourquoi, mais je me rappelai une histoire que j'avais entendue, enfant, à propos d'un sage qui habitait les montagnes, un grand sorcier qui connaissait l'art de la transmutation du plomb en or. Nanti de cette maigre information, je partis à sa recherche en me renseignant sur lui dans les temples où je passais. Le plan que mon cerveau dérangé avait concocté était d'extorquer à ce type, de gré ou de force, son secret alchimique. Une fois que j'aurais maîtrisé ses techniques, je serais retourné en ville pour me venger. Les rôles auraient alors été inversés, je les aurais obligés à ramper devant moi. Tu vois, je n'avais toujours rien compris. Ah ! Quel imbécile j'étais !

« Je mis de nombreux jours pour arriver ici. Quand enfin je fus en vue du monastère, j'étais à bout de forces — décharné (difficile à croire, hein ?), malade, les vêtements en lambeaux, hirsute. On aurait dit un mendiant, pire qu'un mendiant. Pire qu'un lépreux ! Deux jours durant, je restai à la porte en suppliant qu'on me laisse entrer. Les moines me riaient au nez. "Qu'est-ce qu'un épouvantail comme toi pourrait faire avec un aussi grand homme que Chong Fou ?" Finalement, le maître m'entendit hurler et leur dit de me faire entrer.

« Je n'oublierai jamais cette première rencontre. Il m'observa d'un regard si intense que je sentis presque la fibre de mon cœur s'effilocher. Je ne réussis pas à affronter ce regard. En fait, je faillis bien pleurer.

« "Que veux-tu de moi, Regard Fuyant ?" me demanda-t-il en se moquant de ma couardise.

« Je me prosternai trois fois comme on m'avait dit de le faire, puis me lançai dans le discours fleuri que je répétais mentalement depuis des jours, trébuchant fréquemment sur les mots difficiles.

« "Tu veux devenir un grand alchimiste, transmuter le plomb en or, c'est bien ça ?" résuma-t-il quand j'eus terminé.

« "S'il vous plaît, seigneur."
« Il éclata de rire. "Pourquoi t'es-tu mis cela en tête ?"
« J'hésitai, puis bafouillai : "Voyez-vous, seigneur, je suis très sérieusement endetté." Après quoi je souris d'un air penaud.
« Mais Chong Fou ne vit pas le moindre humour. Brusquement, il cessa de rire et m'examina des pieds à la tête. "Du vent ! dit-il enfin. Tu es une vraie plaie."
« Certains moines se mirent à ricaner. Je me jetai aux pieds du maître en protestant à grands cris. "Donnez-moi une chance de faire mes preuves ! Je suis prêt à tout ! Ordonnez, j'obéirai."
« Chong Fou avait presque quitté la pièce quand il s'arrêta et se retourna. Prenant mon courage à deux mains, je le regardai droit dans les yeux. Tel un lutteur qui mesure son adversaire, il me jaugea du regard. Puis un vague sourire apparut sur ses lèvres. "Vraiment tout ?"
« "Oui ! Oui ! m'écriai-je, ravi. Promettez-moi seulement de m'aider."
« Il caressa son menton et plissa les yeux, conscient de me mettre au supplice.
« "S'il vous plaît ! implorai-je. Enseignez-moi."
« "T'enseigner quoi ?" demanda-t-il sévèrement.
« "Eh bien, la Voie, ça va de soi."
« Il secoua la tête. "On ne peut enseigner la Voie."
« "Alors indiquez-moi au moins la bonne direction. Donnez-moi un indice. Je m'occuperai du reste."
« "Tu es tenace, reconnut-il, bien que cela ne joue pas forcément en ta faveur." Il me jeta un coup d'œil appréciateur.
« "Alors ?"
« Soit exaspération ou acquiescement, je ne sais, mais le maître soupira. Interprétant ce signe en ma faveur, je poussai un cri de joie.
« "Très bien donc, concéda-t-il. Dans ton cas, et comme première étape vers ce but exaltant, je suggère un bon dîner." A cet instant, je décelai pour la première fois la nuance de rire qui n'est jamais totalement absente de la voix du maître, la gaieté de ses yeux.
« Il me conduisit dans la cuisine. A la porte, il jeta un coup d'œil circulaire dégoûté. Des piles de tranchoirs en bois et de bols sales envahissaient la pièce, des bataillons de fourmis emportaient les déchets.
« "Il y a plusieurs mois, nous avons eu le grand malheur de perdre notre cuisinier, expliqua-t-il en soupirant. Depuis sa mort, les choses ne sont plus comme avant."
« "Je suis désolé de l'apprendre, dis-je, pour compatir. Que lui est-il arrivé ?"
« "Un os de poulet", répliqua Chong Fou en gonflant ses joues et roulant les yeux vers le ciel pour signifier une fin violente.
« J'aurais dû tenir respectueusement ma langue, mais ne pus me retenir. "Je croyais que vous étiez végétariens."
« Chong Fou acquiesça gravement. "Précisément. On a suggéré qu'il avait eu ce qu'il méritait."
« Bien qu'il eût parlé le plus sérieusement du monde, sa réponse me frappa comme extrêmement drôle. J'éclatai de rire malgré moi. J'étais

certain qu'il serait choqué, et peut-être me jetterait de nouveau sur la route. A ma grande surprise, son rire se joignit au mien.

« "Oui, oui, cela a quelque chose d'amusant finalement, reconnut-il en essuyant ses larmes. Mais entre ; bien que je sois gêné de t'offrir l'hospitalité dans ces conditions, prépare-toi un dîner à ta convenance".

« Je me confondis en remerciements, allumai un feu et mis de l'eau à chauffer pour du riz. Il se trouvait que les poches de mon manteau contenaient quelques morilles et pignons que j'avais trouvés dans la forêt la nuit précédente en cherchant de la nourriture. Je hachai les champignons, puis les mis à frire dans un peu d'huile avec quelques piments du potager.

« Pendant ce temps, Chong Fou était resté sur le seuil, apparemment pour réfléchir. Il avait beau ne pas faire attention à moi, sa présence m'embarrassait. Au bout d'un moment, je remarquai qu'il m'observait comme un épervier. "Je constate que tu as un certain talent pour ce genre de choses", lança-t-il sur un ton faussement anodin. Gêné, je versai le riz avec les légumes et remuai le tout dans l'huile. Alors que j'allais servir, il se frappa brusquement le front et poussa un cri si abrupt que je faillis renverser mon dîner dans le feu. "C'est ça !" Je le regardai, stupéfait. "Je viens de trouver la discipline idéale pour toi !"

« "Comment ça ?"

« Il montra ma main. Je la regardai. Je tenais toujours la casserole. Confus, je relevai les yeux vers son visage. Il hochait la tête avec enthousiasme.

« "Je ne comprends pas", avouai-je, honteux de ma propre stupidité.

« "Tu vas rester ici et devenir notre cuisinier !" Il poussa un cri de joie fort peu monacal, puis sortit en trombe de la pièce.

« Je reconnais qu'au début je ne fus pas très emballé. Mais je désirais apprendre l'alchimie, et si tel était le sacrifice requis, eh bien j'étais prêt à l'accepter ! Du moins tant que je n'aurais pas mieux à faire. Cela changeait du travail dans les champs, et le statut de cuisinier était certainement préférable à celui de vagabond.

« Ainsi le temps passa, et je suis resté. J'allais voir le maître à intervalles réguliers pour lui demander quand il comptait commencer à m'instruire dans les arts secrets.

« "Continue à cuisiner, rétorquait-il. Tu progresses vers ton but."

« Je laissais quelques mois passer avant de renouveler ma demande. "Maître vénéré, disais-je, je suis prêt à recevoir votre enseignement concernant les principes de l'alchimie."

« "Ne t'inquiète donc pas ! me répondait-il. Tu avances à grands pas, tu brûles les étapes. Continue à cuisiner. Tu as trouvé ta vraie vocation."

« Je finis par renoncer et cessai de le supplier. Aujourd'hui, je ne suis pas plus près de transmuter le plomb en or qu'il y a vingt ans. »

Sur cette remarque désenchantée, le récit de Wu atteignit sa conclusion, ou plutôt, devrais-je dire, s'acheva en queue de poisson, mourut ignoblement. Je ressentais de la compassion pour mon ami. A ma grande surprise, il éclata de rire, sans chagrin ni amertume, d'un rire pur et joyeux.

On aurait dit un homme qui venait d'entendre la meilleure plaisanterie de sa vie et goûtait la satisfaction supplémentaire d'avoir lui-même raconté cette plaisanterie, tirée de sa propre expérience et dont il faisait les frais.

A l'époque, je ne compris pas son attitude, qui me parut vaguement stupide, ou pire encore. Mais rétrospectivement, l'histoire de Wu prit pour moi de plus en plus d'importance, au point que j'y vis comme une prophétie — oui, une sorte de prophétie de mon propre destin. Je me suis souvent demandé si c'était pure coïncidence, ou si Wu possédait, peut-être sous forme rudimentaire, la profonde sagesse du sage.

Quelle que soit la réponse à cette question, elle ne saurait diminuer la dette que j'ai envers lui. Dans le paysage rocailleux de mon enfance, lui seul se dresse, unique repère. Exception faite, bien entendu, de Chong Fou. Mais l'influence du maître était plus rare, plus intangible. Comme une épiphanie spectaculaire, il se matérialisa toujours aux moments cruciaux de mon existence. Une heure passée avec Chong Fou ressemblait à un amour de vacances, mais Wu était mon pain quotidien, mon bourreau, ma consolation. D'autres moines m'apprirent à lire et à écrire, à compter les baguettes d'achillée, à chanter, à explorer d'autres champs de la connaissance ; Wu m'apprit ce que je sais de la vie.

Il paraît donc approprié que ce fût Wu qui vînt me trouver un matin pour me dire à voix basse de me préparer à une audience avec Chong Fou. Un inconnu était arrivé, m'annonça-t-il, et le bruit courait qu'il était venu pour me parler.

3

L'événement avait de quoi étonner. Les visiteurs étaient des plus rares à Ken Kuan ; on en voyait presque aussi souvent que des dragons censés habiter le torrent qui coulait au-delà des murs. Et de même que les dragons, on considérait les visiteurs comme des annonciateurs de changement de fortune, parfois pour le bien, mais plus souvent pour le pire. Car les gens nous évitaient par peur de représailles indéterminées de la part des autorités. Cela subvertissait la fonction sociale du monastère et nous empêchait de remplir notre mandat de Compassion pour Toutes les Créatures, qui est le premier et plus grand des Trois Trésors du taoïsme. (Le second est la Frugalité, qui est liée au premier. Volontairement choisie, la Pauvreté est une forme de compassion envers le monde inanimé, un geste de respect et de déférence pour les choses. Le troisième trésor est l'Humilité, ou la Modestie, qui implique de renoncer à exercer un pouvoir actif sur les hommes.)

Revenons à notre isolement. En fait, il avait ses avantages. Comme on dit ici en Amérique : « Qui perd gagne. » (Version chinoise du même proverbe : « La merde fait pousser le maïs. ») Des rapports trop fréquents avec le monde extérieur risquent d'écarter le sage de son vrai but. Il est bien connu, mais rarement compris, que la foire d'empoigne qu'est le monde pousse le cœur humain à l'émeute et à la rébellion. Échappant à cette tentation, nous respections d'autant plus facilement nos restrictions.

Tant et si bien qu'au cours de mes vingt et une années de vie monacale, je pouvais presque compter sur mes doigts les hôtes reçus à Ken Kuan ; et pendant tout ce temps aucun n'était venu me rendre visite. Je trouvais cela parfaitement normal, car qui se serait donné la peine de venir me voir ? Je ne possédais ni nom ni famille — du moins aucune qui se souciât de me reconnaître. La seule exception possible était ma mère. Mais pour une raison quelconque — je ne saurais dire précisément pourquoi — j'avais toujours pensé qu'elle était morte. Je crois que cela tenait à la photographie. Car l'appareil de photo l'avait surprise, il avait révélé sa vulnérabilité, la fragilité de son lien au monde. Mais il y avait davantage... appelons cela intuition. L'univers, même le petit coin paisible que j'avais exploré, paraissait trop âpre pour la femme que j'avais rêvée. Elle y avait sans doute vécu, autrefois, pendant quelques brèves années. Je ne retrouvais nulle part l'éclat qui avait dû être le sien, l'aura impalpable que mon âme, j'en suis sûr, aurait aussitôt reconnue. Non, pour moi elle était morte, sinon dans la réalité, du moins dans la mémoire.

Quant à mon père, à supposer qu'il fût vivant (et le même instinct me disait qu'il vivait), il était très loin, de l'autre côté de l'océan, sur un autre continent. Après toutes ces années, pouvait-ce être lui ? Cette pensée m'emplit de terreur (et de désir !) au point que je fus pris de nausées et de suées.

Pourtant, en plus de la rareté des visites, en plus de l'existence en moi de ce vide émotionnel auquel personne n'avait jamais touché et que, malgré tous mes efforts, je ne pouvais imaginer comblé, la nouvelle annoncée par Wu avait une autre raison de m'exciter. Que je reçoive un visiteur, mon premier visiteur, en ce jour précis de l'année (de ma vie !) semblait trop extraordinaire pour attribuer sa venue à une coïncidence. Car c'était le jour de mon anniversaire : j'avais vingt et un ans. Cela rendait toute l'affaire étrange, comme si cette visite était un cadeau, un précieux fragment d'épave (témoin d'un malheur englouti), que le Tao avait tiré de ses profondeurs insondables pour le déposer à mes pieds en cette occasion. Mais quoi ?

Mes pas laissaient des empreintes humides sur les dalles de schiste de la cour intérieure, que je traversai vers la partie sud du monastère où se trouvait la cellule du maître. Au centre de la cour poussait un vieux pêcher tordu, mais plein de sève, qui portait chaque année « une pêche pour chaque moine », selon l'expression consacrée des frères. Comme je me penchais sous ses branches, je remarquai avec un sentiment proche du chagrin que les fruits avaient déjà succédé aux fleurs. Vertes et menues, les pêches pendaient aux branches noueuses comme des gouttes d'eau le long d'un toit après la pluie.

Plus tôt dans la matinée, j'avais consulté le *Yi king* et reçu une réponse que je ne me rappelais pas avoir rencontrée auparavant : *Chia Jen*, « La Famille ». Cet hexagramme est construit à partir des deux trigrammes fondamentaux, *Sun*, « Le Vent », au-dessus de *Li*, « Le Feu », qui me suggérèrent l'incitation à un acte violent, peut-être destructeur, une conflagration, un incendie attisé par le vent.

Le jugement disait :

> La famille est l'embryon de la société, le sol nourricier où l'exercice des devoirs moraux est facilité par l'affection naturelle, si bien que dans un cercle étroit une base de pratique morale est créée... Ces principes s'appliquent ensuite aux relations humaines en général.

Ce jugement ne me concernait-il pas particulièrement ? Comme j'avais grandi sans l'influence bénéfique des liens familiaux, mes instincts moraux ne manquaient-ils pas de quelque enracinement fondamental ? Bien que discrète, l'allusion était difficilement évitable. Cette interprétation était renforcée par la nature faible du premier trait de l'hexagramme, vieux *yang* se désintégrant en *yin*, la lumière en obscurité. Voici le commentaire :

> Si l'on commence trop tard à introduire l'ordre, la volonté des enfants a déjà contracté de mauvaises habitudes, les humeurs et les passions ayant grandi créent des obstacles et engendrent le remords.

Ce fut donc avec un mauvais pressentiment que je frappai à la porte de Chong Fou.

Sa voix cristalline et affectueuse me répondit : « Entre ! » Je m'inclinai très bas sur le seuil, saluant d'abord le maître, après quoi je me tournai vers le visiteur, que je saluai plus formellement.

C'était un Chinois âgé qui ressemblait étonnamment à Chong Fou sur certains points (tous deux auraient pu suggérer une étude de la différence dans la ressemblance), sinon qu'il portait l'habit élégant mais démodé depuis longtemps du gentilhomme confucéen, ou *chün-tseu*, la classe traditionnelle des bureaucrates et des lettrés. A cette époque, les *chün-tseu* avaient disparu de la société presque aussi complètement que les maîtres taoïstes comme Chong Fou. Dans la Chine traditionnelle, les maîtres étaient les alter ego des *chün-tseu*, mais ils dédaignaient la stricte observance des formes et du rituel pratiquée par les confucéens, pour suivre les injonctions intérieures de la Voie. Le vieux confucéen portait la longue robe de soie et la toque du lettré ; il tenait à la main une canne à pommeau d'ivoire de grandes beauté et ancienneté, dont la laque noire brillait. En contraste, Chong Fou portait la simple robe de bure monacale (bien que sa qualité d'abbé lui eût permis de se vêtir avec élégance). Sous sa toque, le visiteur était scrupuleusement chauve ; les tempes de son crâne rasé luisaient de l'éclat ciré des vieux meubles. Les cheveux argentés de Chong Fou étaient réunis au sommet de sa tête où ils formaient le chignon traditionnel taoïste. Leurs mains étaient semblables, aussi noueuses que les racines d'arbres vénérables qui ont essuyé maintes tempêtes, des mains mouchetées de mélanine, signe de l'âge. Tous deux portaient la moustache et le bouc du mandarin. Tous deux avaient le regard brillant du sage, mais les yeux de Chong Fou luisaient avec une nuance de chaleur, tandis que ceux du visiteur évoquaient le reflet du soleil hivernal sur la glace. (Oui, quel excellent sujet d'étude de la ressemblance dans la différence.)

« Joins-toi à nous, petit frère, me dit Chong Fou en me faisant signe d'approcher. Une vieille connaissance est venue te rendre visite. »

Je regardai l'inconnu. Les traits du vieillard m'étaient certes vaguement familiers, mais je ne parvenais pas à le remettre. La remarque du maître me troubla. « Une vieille connaissance ? »

Les yeux de Chong Fou pétillaient. « As-tu donc oublié ? Enfin, c'était seulement hier ! »

Une fois encore, je dévisageai l'inconnu, qui m'observait aussi intensément que je l'observais. « Je suis désolé, maître, dis-je, mais vous devez faire erreur. Nous ne nous sommes jamais rencontrés. »

Chong Fou rugit de rire. « Jamais, Sun I ? Dis-moi — tu es vraiment sûr ? »

Je commençai à me troubler. Qu'y avait-il dans son visage qui interdît si bizarrement le souvenir ?

Quand le maître s'aperçut de ma perplexité, ses pointes firent place à une tendresse amusée, presque triste. « Sun I, dit-il, voici l'homme qui t'a amené chez nous il y a tant d'années. »

Le visiteur acquiesça : « Bien que ce ne soit pas notre première rencontre, je crois que nous sommes de "vieilles connaissances qui se sont perdues de vue". Je m'appelle Hsiao. Je suis ton oncle. » Ses traits s'éclairèrent brusquement. Ce que j'avais pris pour familiarité se révéla ressemblance. « Ta mère était ma sœur. »

Mon esprit se mit à vaciller comme sous l'effet d'un choc brutal. Mes yeux scrutèrent désespérément la pièce pour voir si elle ne contenait pas quelque légende capable de m'aider à comprendre le code indéchiffrable dans lequel il s'exprimait — « oncle », « sœur », « mère » —, ces mots évidents trouvèrent immédiatement leur place et je fus comme un aveugle congénital à qui un coup de poing révèle l'éclat terrifiant du monde.

« Sun I, poursuivit l'inconnu (mon oncle !), tout ceci doit être très éprouvant pour toi — voir un parent se matérialiser après tant d'années. Peut-être t'en irrites-tu. Mais laisse-moi t'expliquer la raison de ma venue. Contrairement à ce que tu penses peut-être, elle a peu de chose à voir avec ta mère. »

Il hésita, puis se reprit. « Enfin, ce n'est pas tout à fait vrai. En fait, ma venue serait impensable sans ta mère — comment pourrait-il en être autrement ? Mais le lien n'est qu'indirect. C'est à la demande d'un homme nommé Eddie Love que je viens aujourd'hui te voir. Love était ton père. » Il s'attendait apparemment à ce que cette révélation provoque une forte réaction ; quand il découvrit que ce n'était pas le cas, Hsiao en tira la conclusion qui s'imposait. « Tu sais donc... » Le ton de sa voix exprimait un mélange de surprise et de fatalisme. « Voici maintes années, je lui ai fait une promesse, une promesse que je peux seulement tenir aujourd'hui. Il voulait t'offrir un cadeau à l'occasion de ton passage à l'âge adulte.

— Quel cadeau ? demandai-je, partagé entre l'excitation et la terreur.

— Le cadeau le plus important qui soit. Le don de ta propre histoire. »

Retenant mon souffle, je le regardai en écarquillant les yeux. Il me semblait que le destin venait de sortir de l'ombre pour poser sa main sur moi. A cet instant, je compris que, toute ma vie, j'avais attendu sa venue.

« Vous êtes ici pour me dire qui je suis », répondis-je sans même comprendre le sens des mots qui jaillissaient du plus profond de moi-même.

Chong Fou secoua la tête. « Qui pourrait te dire cela, Sun I ? Aucun homme n'a le pouvoir d'accorder pareil savoir à autrui, bien que ce soit le seul qui importe. La découverte de ta vraie nature, de ton Moi Authentique — qu'est-ce que l'"histoire" en comparaison ? Un détail superflu. »

Hsiao cligna froidement des paupières. « Un détail superflu, vraiment. Qu'est-ce qu'un moi sans son histoire, sans son passé? »

Chong Fou sourit. « Il existe un *koan* zen dans lequel le maître exhorte son disciple à lui montrer son Visage Originel d'avant la naissance de ses parents. Si ce Visage Originel, qui est le Moi Authentique dont nous parlons, existe avant la naissance de ses propres parents (soit éternellement, de tout temps), à quoi bon l'histoire ?

— Pourtant, rétorqua Hsiao, Confucius lui-même ne dit-il pas : "Celui qui ne marche pas dans les traces ne saurait espérer trouver son chemin jusqu'à la Chambre Intérieure" ? Vous savez, naturellement, quelles sont ces traces ?

— Bien entendu ! s'écria Chong Fou, feignant un zèle sincère. Celles du Taureau taoïste ! » Reniflant de plaisir, il se tourna vers moi et m'adressa un clin d'œil. « J'ai toujours dit que le vieux maître K'ung, derrière tous ces oripeaux de confucianisme, était un vrai taoïste...

— Absurde ! s'exclama Hsiao en se détournant avec dédain. Ces traces sont celles des ancêtres, Sun I. » Marquant une pause, il changea de tactique. « Je suis un humble lettré. J'ai voué mon existence aux Quatre Travaux.

— Voyons, réfléchit le maître. Ne s'agit-il pas du plagiat forcené, de l'esprit vagabond, du goût immodéré pour les mets épicés, et du penchant pervers pour les petits garçons ?

— Non, Chong Fou, je parle du luth, des échecs, de la littérature et de la peinture. Mais cessons ce "combat de Dharma", attelons-nous à la tâche qui nous occupe. » Mon oncle se tourna vers moi. « A bien y regarder, les paroles de ton maître ne sont pas totalement déplacées. Car en dernière analyse, je peux seulement te transmettre certaines informations — qui étaient tes parents, comment ils se sont connus, ce qui leur est arrivé, pourquoi tu es venu ici... Quant à la valeur de ces informations — si elles sont cruciales pour ta connaissance de toi-même, comme je le maintiens, ou, ainsi qu'il le suggère, "superflues" —, ni lui ni moi ne peuvent en décider. Tu dois choisir toi-même. »

Il scruta mes traits avec une expression de douleur évidente. « Mais avant de trancher, tu dois prendre une autre décision. Ton père m'a demandé de te laisser une porte de sortie : *ne pas savoir*. Prévoyant que tu préférerais peut-être rester dans l'ignorance, il m'a chargé de te raconter cette histoire *seulement si tu désirais l'entendre*. Ce n'est pas une histoire agréable, Sun I. En fin de compte, qui peut en décider ? Il vaudrait peut-être mieux que tu continues à l'ignorer. »

Il se tourna vers Chong Fou, et ils s'inclinèrent gravement l'un vers l'autre, tels deux adversaires tombant d'accord sur une question d'honneur.

Je me tournai moi aussi dans cette direction, cherchant désespérément une aide. Mais malgré une ombre de pitié dans le regard du maître, son visage ne me fournit aucun indice. Comme un vent glacé qui m'aurait traversé, je fus pris d'une haine féroce pour cet homme, Hsiao, qui faisait brusquement irruption dans ma vie pour m'obliger à accepter le fardeau irrévocable de son cadeau.

« Comment pourrais-je refuser ? demandai-je avec amertume. Vous avez déjà détruit ma paix.

— Elle risque d'être détruite bien davantage, Sun I, intervint le maître, prenant la défense de l'adversaire avec qui il venait de croiser le fer. Fais attention. Tu dois réfléchir avec prudence. C'est le sens du devoir qui pousse ton oncle à te parler. Il serait injuste de t'empêcher de choisir. Tu ne dois pas le blâmer. Mais à partir de maintenant, tu es responsable de ce qui se passera. Choisis soigneusement, avec la douceur et la pénétration que te confère ton nom, sans la véhémence impulsive qui est son complément plus obscur, et à laquelle tu as beaucoup trop cédé dans le passé. Aujourd'hui, tu es un homme, et tu dois agir selon. »

Je cherchai désespérément en moi-même quelque chose à quoi me raccrocher, comme le nageur qui cède à la panique tend la main vers une branche basse de la rive tandis que le courant écumant l'emporte. Je ne trouvai rien.

Aussitôt, d'une voix ferme, je dis : « Parlez-moi.

— Ah ! » gémit mon oncle, dont les mains se crispèrent involontairement.

Le maître se leva brusquement pour partir. Il s'inclina devant Hsiao, puis devant moi — deux saluts identiques. Je n'étais pas assez bouleversé pour ne pas saisir les implications de son geste. Elles me terrifièrent. Je me sentis affranchi, dépossédé. Brutalement sevré du passé, je ressemblais à l'oisillon qu'on pousse hors du nid pour qu'il vole ou tombe, sans rien pour m'aider à trouver mes ailes, sinon la prémonition de quelque instinct ignoré.

4

Longtemps, mon oncle et moi restâmes assis, les yeux dans les yeux. Son visage était grave, mais plein de curiosité et peut-être de tristesse. Des signes de sympathie et de vulnérabilité nuançaient son impassibilité, tel un regard humain à travers les fentes d'un masque de bois. Ce qu'il vit sur mon visage, dans mes yeux, je ne saurais l'imaginer — peut-être une sorte de faim, la sombre résolution de souffrir sans fondre en larmes.

« J'ignore ce que tu sais déjà, commença-t-il. C'est une longue histoire, mais je dois te la raconter depuis le début pour ne rien oublier.

« Je crois que je dois d'abord te parler de mon père... mon père respecté... » Entre ces deux expressions, Hsiao hésita légèrement et inclina la tête en signe de vénération. En même temps, son visage se modifia. Je peux m'être trompé (cela dura un instant), mais je crois l'avoir vu grimacer, comme un homme qui avale une potion médicinale — thérapeutique, mais amère. « Car en un sens, il cultiva la terre où poussa cette végétation luxuriante. »

Quand mon oncle souligna le mot « luxuriante », ses lèvres se retroussèrent de nouveau en une expression de léger dégoût, qui évoquait étrangement un sourire. Pourtant le masque conservait sa gravité sereine. Etait-ce de l'ironie ? Je n'aurais su le dire.

« Cet homme — ton grand-père, Sun I — regardait vers l'avenir, c'était un "progressif". Contrairement à moi, il était, comme il disait, "désentravé des préjugés du passé". Non parce qu'il était inculte, mais parce qu'il était ambitieux. Ces deux termes n'ont rien d'irrespectueux, car mon père se vantait de l'un comme de l'autre.

« C'était un entrepreneur "tous azimuts" — pour l'essentiel, il spéculait sur les marchandises —, un représentant de cette nouvelle race qui apparut en Chine pendant les années d'influence étrangère (c'est-à-dire occidentale) après l'arrivée de Sun Yat-sen au pouvoir, qui avait des relations au niveau international (c'est-à-dire occidental) et qui comprenait l'organisation des affaires modernes (oui, occidentales). Ainsi qu'il le disait, il avait troqué le boulier contre le registre à double entrée. (Contrairement à l'opinion courante, Père avait un certain sens de l'humour.) Nous nous sommes battus pendant toute mon enfance, mais quand ta mère est née, il avait déjà amassé une fortune respectable. Car à cette époque, les hommes serviables, à l'esprit vif, pouvaient gagner de l'argent, beaucoup d'argent. Et Père possédait ces deux qualités. Bien qu'il eût un pied dans tous les commerces, la marchandise qui l'enrichit fut l'opium. A côté de sa résidence principale à Ch'ung-ch'ing, il possédait une propriété dans la province du Yunnan, près de Kunming, où il supervisait les semailles et la récolte du pavot. Peu après les premiers bombardements de Ch'ung-ch'ing en 39, il envoya là-bas ma mère et ma sœur pour toute la durée de la guerre. Je les y rejoignis bientôt.

« Notre mère appartenait à une famille d'aristocrates ruinés, mais toujours prestigieux. Pour lui, ce fut une bonne alliance : bien que pauvre, elle lui apporta en dot une denrée dont il avait autrement besoin que d'argent : une légitimité aux yeux du monde. Car ta grand-mère, Sun I, était une grande dame à tous points de vue. Peut-être lui manquait-il seulement une certaine fermeté de caractère — dont elle n'aurait sans doute pas eu besoin en d'autres circonstances, et qu'en tout état de cause mon père étouffa en elle. Éduquée à l'ancienne, soumise mais non servile, elle possédait grâce, charme, esprit — qualités qu'il n'appréciait guère, leur préférant la rude vivacité des paysannes, leur reddition facile. Pour un homme comme lui, le raffinement de notre mère semblait sans doute un peu recherché. Pourtant, elle était l'aboutissement de mille ans d'éducation, de mille ans de loisirs, si frêle et délicate, avec ses pieds bandés, ses "lis d'or", se déplaçant à tout petits pas dans la maison, s'arrêtant régulièrement pour se reposer et s'éventer. Ses semblables ont disparu de la terre. Elle ne comprenait pas le mode de vie moderne, Sun I. Tout cela lui semblait disgracieux, vulgaire, trop pressé. Complètement déroutée par les initiatives commerciales de mon père, elle s'en méfiait instinctivement. Mais, elle n'osait pas interférer, car on lui avait appris à obéir à la volonté de son mari, leçon que renforçait le tempérament de Père. Comme je l'ai dit, il était ambitieux, et ce trait conférait à son caractère une certaine férocité. Il ne supportait pas facilement la contradiction ; et en aucune manière de la part d'un membre de sa famille.

« J'étais l'aîné. Ta mère avait presque vingt ans de moins que moi, et sa naissance fut inattendue. Elle chut des reins fatigués de ma mère "comme une feuille d'automne tombe d'un vieil arbre" — mon père répétait volontiers cette image. D'ailleurs, son nom, Ch'iu-yeh, signifie "Feuille d'Automne". Pour maintes raisons il est approprié, car c'était une enfant vive, enjouée, et pourtant — je ne sais comment définir cela —, on aurait dit la vivacité de la vie sur son déclin, un éclat de la peau qui suggère non la santé débordante, mais la fièvre du corps. Ses moments de ravissement étaient des bonheurs de courte durée. Ensuite, elle se flétrissait, s'étiolait, consumée par quelque feu intérieur. Des malaises s'ensuivaient, maladie indéterminée dont les racines étaient peut-être autant spirituelles que physiques, une sorte de mélancolie, troublante chez un être aussi jeune.

« Vu notre grande différence d'âge, et parce que mon père, dont la fortune augmentait, commençait à mépriser les "attitudes provinciales" de nos voisins, ta mère passa son enfance dans un relatif isolement. Non qu'elle eût été négligée ; le contraire fut vrai. Ils étaient fous d'elle. Quand elle tombait malade, ma mère lui donnait en secret des friandises et des médicaments de luxe — ginseng et nids d'oiseau — prescrits par les anciens aux cheveux blancs, praticiens de la vieille école qui l'avaient soignée dans son enfance. Mon père aussi la gâtait. Elle était sa préférée, son "trésor". Je crois qu'il comprenait sa solitude. Car malgré son ubiquité sociale, la multitude de ses "contacts", il était seul, lui aussi, en butte à la méfiance et à la haine de ses pairs, qui servaient la puissance et non l'homme. Et puis dans une large mesure, Ch'iu-yeh était la créature de sa folie... ou de son génie... son petit prix de consolation humain. Il ne recula devant aucune dépense pour lui acheter les plus beaux jouets, des articles importés d'Europe : boîtes à musique allemandes, bonbons français, poupées blanches en porcelaine autrichienne. Dans cette lutte d'influence menée avec de telles armes, ma mère ne pouvait l'emporter. Père engagea une gouvernante anglaise pour Ch'iu-yeh, qui s'initia de bonne heure à l'anglais, langue qu'elle parla bientôt mieux que son dialecte natal, le szu-ch'uanais.

« Malgré toutes ces attentions, Ch'iu-yeh passait seule le plus clair de son temps, à rêver, j'imagine. Le seul art traditionnel que ma mère réussit à lui transmettre fut la couture. Ch'iu-yeh devint assez douée en broderie, et je crois qu'elle exprima une bonne part de ses fantasmes par ce biais. Mais pour l'essentiel, sa vie affective restait en friche, amorphe. Chaque jour, elle se découvrait de nouveaux enthousiasmes, qu'elle rejetait presque aussitôt, comme des robes portées une fois, puis mises au rebut. Quand elle lisait des romans anglais, elle croyait leurs personnages réels. Son esprit se délectait à la pensée de lieux éloignés — l'Angleterre, mais bien davantage l'Amérique, que sa gouvernante (qui y avait des enfants) lui décrivait en termes grandioses. Ces images exotiques auraient été inoffensives pour une jeune fille occidentale, mais pour une Chinoise elles furent déplacées. Leur temps n'était pas encore venu. Les pieds des femmes étaient toujours bandés. Je crois que cela fragilisa encore son tempérament. Parfois, elle abandonnait son livre pour éclater en sanglots sans raison. Je conseillai la discipline, mais mon père était trop entiché, trop fier des talents de Ch'iu-yeh pour prendre les mesures qui s'imposaient.

« Lorsque Tchang Kaï-chek, en 1937, fit de Ch'ung-ch'ing la capitale de la Chine en état de guerre, ta mère, à peine âgée de seize ans, était trop jeune pour saisir la gravité de la situation. Les jours de marché, quand sa gouvernante l'emmenait en ville, elles passaient des heures à déambuler dans les rues, se mêlant à l'incessant flot d'activité, admirant le flux bigarré de la vie alors que les réfugiés affluaient des régions côtières plus cosmopolites.

« Toutes sortes de richesses se déversaient en ville, car les nantis, craignant la confiscation de leurs biens, fuyaient devant l'avant-garde de l'armée japonaise. Quelques mois après l'arrivée du Généralissime, le prix du terrain doubla, puis tripla. (Mon père devenait chaque jour plus prospère.) Et en même temps, des taudis apparurent, en bambou, fer-blanc, feuilles de bananier, carton — tout ce qu'on pouvait récupérer — assemblés avec de la boue séchée ou des morceaux de ficelle. Le vent les abattait comme châteaux de cartes, la pluie les emportait. Et en une nuit, tel le mildiou, ils étaient de nouveau là. Le plus horrible se dressait sur un terrain vague en bordure de la cité, où quelques centimètres de terre masquaient tant bien que mal cent années de pestilence. Les moustiques se multiplièrent ; les maladies devinrent endémiques — choléra, dysenterie, trachome, et bien sûr syphilis. La seule eau disponible provenait d'un infect fossé qui servait à tous les usages. Les femmes y jetaient les déjections nocturnes de leur famille ; quand les excréments étaient emportés en aval et que l'eau semblait claire, elles lavaient leur seau et l'emplissaient d'eau qu'on buvait. Précaution élémentaire ! Mais parfaitement superflue, car vingt mètres en amont, une autre mère de famille faisait la même chose. C'était une infection. La cité entière empestait ; et mêlée à cette puanteur, on respirait partout l'odeur nauséabonde des pâtés de porc qui mijotaient dans des chaudrons pleins de graisse.

« Les rues de la cité n'étaient que vacarme et clameurs diverses. Les hommes discutaient dans tous les dialectes, les femmes négociaient sur les marchés ouverts, les bébés pleuraient, les poulets caquetaient, les portefaix psalmodiaient leurs mélopées en hissant les marchandises hors des jonques accostées aux rives du Yang-tsê, les dinandiers vantaient leurs articles — cure-dents et petites cuillères, grelots en forme de bouddha, grattoirs, boucles d'oreille et amulettes —, les vendeurs de calicot entrechoquaient des blocs de bois pour attirer le chaland, les cartomanciers frappaient sur des carapaces de tortue comme sur des tamtams et lançaient les baguettes d'achillée. C'était un somptueux capharnaüm, et une grande tentation pour la jeunesse. Mais un son plus étrange encore se mêlait à ces évocations de la Chine éternelle : le bruit des hommes blancs qui parlaient des langues européennes, "les démons aux yeux bleus de l'Océan Occidental", comme on les appelait souvent.

« Cette effervescence féconde bouillonna dans la cité jusqu'en 1939, date des premiers bombardements. En deux ans, la chair voluptueuse du romanesque pourrit et tomba, dénudant les os terribles de la guerre. Après les longs étés d'incessants bombardements, les habitants hagards marchaient dans les rues, amaigris par une angoisse chronique et le manque de sommeil. Une solidarité sinistre existait, celle des damnés privés de tout espoir. Le moral fut à son plus bas après le bombardement de l'hôpital de la Croix-Rouge. Le vent poussa sur toute la ville l'odeur de la chair carbonisée (il n'y a pas odeur plus horrible). Alors qu'ils couraient dans les rues pour s'abriter dans des souterrains, de nombreux habitants entendirent les cris des agonisants bloqués à l'intérieur, ils les entendirent alors même que les flammes rugissaient devant eux, grillant leurs cheveux et leurs sourcils à plusieurs dizaines de mètres de là.

« Heureusement pour elles, bien avant que la situation n'eût empiré, ma mère et ma sœur étaient parties à la campagne près de Kunming, loin du danger — goûtant à une apparente sécurité. »

Le regard de mon oncle effleura mon visage ; une fois encore, il eut ce sourire allusif, déconcertant. « Ce fut là que les Américains entrèrent en scène. Ah, quelle glorieuse épiphanie ! Ce groupe de jeunes et magnifiques aviateurs placés sous les ordres du général Chennault. Epuisés, en mal de n'importe quel espoir, nous les avons accueillis comme des dieux, des sauveurs... même moi, qui aurais dû mieux savoir à quoi m'en tenir. » Il rit.

« Les Américains n'émirent aucune objection à notre dévotion. Eux-mêmes se considéraient comme les envoyés de Dieu. Dans le meilleur des cas, leur attitude envers les Chinois fut toujours hautaine, celle du missionnaire confronté aux païens ignorants. Au pire, ils se montraient tyranniques, capables de frapper les jeunes garçons qui les servaient dans leurs camps, comme d'autres frappent un chien.

« Leurs croyances d'Américains se réduisaient à ceci : une vie propre, une pensée propre, et du "tonus" ! Comme si pareille hygiène — l'eau et le savon — pouvait éliminer les terribles péchés du cœur humain, qui après des siècles de suppuration avaient pourri jusqu'à la moelle de l'organisme et submergé le monde de leur pestilence. Oh, crois-moi, ils n'avaient pas la moindre idée de ce qu'ils côtoyaient — les maux accumulés de l'humanité, dans lesquels *eux aussi* avaient leur part. Les Américains se prenaient pour une race neuve, exempte de la culpabilité collective de l'humanité. Comment auraient-ils pu s'intéresser au passé ? Ils étaient uniquement tournés vers l'avenir. Pourtant, ils auraient dû arriver en Chine comme des suppliants, implorer notre aide pour acquérir la connaissance des vérités humaines, la vraie moralité enseignée par tous nos sages — confucéens *et* taoïstes — qui commence par la compréhension et s'achève par la mise au pas des sombres désirs du cœur.

« Mais les Américains n'avaient pas assez d'estomac pour se laisser mettre au pas, surtout par eux-mêmes. Pour eux, le mot "moralité" était une caractéristique nationale qui dissimulait leur conviction irraisonnée d'entretenir une relation privilégiée avec Dieu. Ils étaient tellement innocents. Mais d'une innocence terrible, comme celle des bêtes fauves, aussi dangereuse pour eux-mêmes que pour autrui. Des prédateurs technologiques, voilà ce qu'ils étaient, si habiles dans l'art de tuer et d'imposer leur volonté par la force, qu'ils croyaient passée de mode l'autre et plus exigeante moralité. Des innombrables tragédies spirituelles de la guerre, la moindre ne fut pas qu'elle parut leur donner raison. Non, Sun I, ce furent eux — pas les Japonais, et encore moins nous-mêmes — ce furent eux les infidèles, les barbares, chaque Américain coulé dans la peau du pionnier cheminant vers l'Ouest, vers les étendues vierges et sauvages de son propre esprit, armé d'un fusil et d'un couteau.

« Je suis amer parce que j'ai passé de nombreuses années à réfléchir à cela. Jadis, je me suis moi aussi entiché de l'Occident. Mais un contact direct avec cet univers m'a fait changer d'avis. Alors que j'étais encore un homme relativement jeune, mon père m'a envoyé dans une école de commerce américaine, pour augmenter mes chances, comme il disait. Ce programme de "peaufinage" alla directement contre mes penchants naturels. Mais mon père était trop absorbé dans ses calculs divers pour s'en apercevoir, ou bien, s'il le remarqua, pour s'en soucier, si obnubilé était-il par la perspective de moderniser ses opérations avec mon aide. Fidèle à mes obligations filiales, j'ai réussi à refréner mes instincts de révolte et à lui obéir. C'est pour moi une victoire dont j'ai toujours été fier. Mais je n'ai pas oublié quel enfer j'ai traversé.

« Au bout de deux années en Amérique, je fus convaincu que je ne pourrais poursuivre mes études qu'au prix de ce qui possède une réelle valeur dans la vie. Autour de moi, je voyais les jeunes gens jeter le lest de leurs principes, retrouver la maigreur et l'instinct de l'animal pour la chasse, la poursuite de la carrière rapide, fuyante, du gain exorbitant. L'argent, ou plutôt le profit, était Dieu en Amérique. Quand je compris cela, j'en fus malade. Le mot "modernisation" devint pour moi synonyme de maladie, et non de panacée. Après un violent combat intérieur, je trouvai la réponse au problème qui me torturait. Je compris que je devais rentrer en Chine, m'excuser auprès de mon père pour la déception que je lui procurais, expliquer mon point de vue et vouer le reste de mon existence aux valeurs confucéennes qui ont soutenu la vie saine et civilisée dont nous jouissions depuis si longtemps. Je croyais qu'il comprendrait. »

Mon oncle se tut. Son visage était injecté de sang. Les veines de son cou saillaient et palpitaient. En cet instant, il ne semblait pas vieux. La conviction fanatique du jeune homme brillait dans ses yeux, retirait tout âge à sa douleur et l'identifiait à la mienne. Pourtant, comme ses paroles suivantes le prouvèrent, Hsiao ne soupçonna pas ma sympathie.

« Tu me prends probablement pour un réactionnaire vieux jeu, un fossile d'une autre époque. » Il fit un effort visible pour sourire et contrôler son émotion. « Dans une certaine mesure, je suppose que c'est le cas. Mais je veux souligner que ce ne fut pas la rudesse des coutumes américaines qui m'offensa. En ce domaine, qui diffère étonnamment d'un peuple à l'autre, il faut avoir l'esprit large. Pourtant, la tolérance est difficile envers une race d'individus qui, des mois durant, ne mangent pas une seule bouchée de riz. A la place, ils consomment des quantités astronomiques de chair de porc et de bétail, qu'ils servent à table dans un état indescriptible : d'énormes tranches à peine grillées à la flamme et dont le sang dégouline encore. Là, ils découpent l'horrible charogne, la dépècent avec des instruments de cuisine — grands couteaux et fourches à trois dents nommées fourchettes. Je n'en ai jamais rencontré un assez habile pour manier une paire de baguettes. Je me sentais plutôt nerveux à ce genre de dîners, comme un marin naufragé participant à un festin de cannibales et qui redouterait de passer à son tour au "barbecue" !

« Mais plus que tout cela, c'était le vide de leur regard qui m'inquiétait. Ils ne tiraient aucun plaisir de la contemplation de ce qui les entourait, leurs pensées se fixaient sur quelque but lointain, qui s'éloignait toujours davantage quand ils s'en approchaient, une chose qu'ils appelaient (avec un indicible pathos) "bonheur". La nature n'a pas le pouvoir de les contenter. » De la main, il montra la fenêtre ouverte. On apercevait au loin les chaînes solennelles du massif montagneux qui s'étageaient vers un ciel de lapis-lazuli. Le vent frais qui soufflait dans la forêt de pins nous apportait l'odeur de la résine. Et du ravin inférieur, à peine audible, montait le rugissement cristallin du torrent qui bondissait sur son lit de galets. Mon oncle soupira. « Ils regardaient ces cadeaux d'un œil ignare, n'y voyant qu'objets à domestiquer, à s'approprier pour leur usage personnel, prêts à torturer jusqu'au dernier fragment de beauté inoffensive et naturelle pour s'assurer un revenu confortable de leurs investissements.

« Mais j'en ai assez dit, et plus que je ne comptais. Retournons au thème central de mon histoire...

« Les Chinois idolâtraient donc les Américains à cause de leurs efforts héroïques contre les Japonais. Ils étaient braves. Indiscutablement. Moi aussi, je m'étonnai de leur courage et de leur résolution. Mais j'étais seul à reconnaître leurs limitations en tant que peuple, leur égoïsme et leur arrogance, leurs conceptions dangereusement simplistes de l'histoire et de la moralité. Au moindre signe de réserve, mon père entrait en rage. Il s'était pris d'affection pour les Américains, "toute idolâtrie mise à part", prétendait-il. Mais à mes yeux, son affection allait beaucoup plus loin.

« Notre maison devint une des retraites préférées des officiers de l'AVG pendant leurs heures de loisir. Ils étaient flattés par la sollicitude de mon père qui rivalisait avec les autres familles en vue pour courtiser les aviateurs américains. Je considérais cela comme une rivalité indigne et ridicule, et je fis part de mon opinion à mon père ; car je sentais que le silence aurait été une déloyauté plus grande encore. Confucius lui-même ne déclare-t-il pas qu'un homme peut faire des reproches à ses parents si la situation le justifie ? Je fus peut-être dur, ou pas assez nuancé. Je sais seulement que mon père se mit en colère. J'étais pour lui une honte et un fardeau alors que j'aurais dû être son bras droit. Me reprochant d'avoir "trahi la cause" (je suppose qu'il voulait dire les Affaires), il me traita de parasite, de fainéant, pire encore. Je fus mortifié, Sun I. Quand il me dit qu'il me jugeait totalement inutile, je le pris au mot et quittai fièrement la maison. Je m'installai à Kunming, louai une mansarde de lettré où je soignai ma douleur en me plongeant dans la lecture des classiques et rêvai sombrement à l'Age d'Or de Yao et de Shun. Pourtant je restais informé de ce qui se passait à la maison par ma mère et les domestiques, qui me prirent en pitié et résistaient instinctivement aux comportements inhabituels qu'ils constataient autour d'eux.

« Les aviateurs américains, fascinés par l'"étrangeté" de notre maison, trouvaient le cadre "charmant" — ce qu'il était certainement, mais sans l'emphase ironique qui accompagnait leurs louanges ambiguës. Il y avait un bassin dans la cour centrale, rempli de cyprins dorés et de feuilles de lotus. Un pont finement sculpté et peint l'enjambait. Autour de ce bassin, la maison s'épanouissait en cercles concentriques semblables à ceux que crée la pierre lancée dans une mare, chacun relié au suivant par une belle porte lunulaire. Malgré la beauté du lieu, les Américains pouffaient discrètement en voyant que nous tirions l'eau d'un puits, que nous possédions un générateur électrique rudimentaire et, honte suprême à leurs yeux, un WC installé dans une cabane. Ni les étagères couvertes de classiques, ni les soieries brodées, ni les inestimables objets laqués que ma mère avait apportés comme sa seule dot — d'une qualité inimaginable en Amérique — ne purent les convaincre qu'ils foulaient un sol civilisé.

« Ta mère avait l'autorisation de participer comme elle l'entendait aux réjouissances destinées à ces hôtes. Afin de prouver ses idées libérales, mon père la dispensa de toute restriction. Ma mère eut beau pleurer et supplier, il persifla les anciennes coutumes qui réglaient la conduite des femmes non mariées. "Préjugés moyenâgeux", raillait-il. Ta mère circulait donc librement parmi les jeunes officiers, à qui elle offrait l'hospitalité de la maison. Elle les interrogeait sur le rôle de la femme en Occident (elle répétait souvent qu'elle se considérait comme une Occidentale, mais née en exil

— commentaire qui ravissait régulièrement nos invités). Quand ils insistaient sur les dangers qu'ils couraient ou sur leur isolement dans notre pays, elle prenait sur elle de les réconforter. Cela devint une sorte de mission pour ta mère. Avec l'arrivée des Américains, elle s'épanouit, et la mélancolie persistante contre laquelle elle avait lutté depuis si longtemps disparut. » Brièvement, mon oncle parut se perdre dans le souvenir, souriant d'un air vague et désenchanté. Puis son visage reprit une expression dure.

« L'un d'eux était un jeune homme répondant au nom d'Eddie Love. D'emblée, il fut pour moi une énigme, bien qu'il m'attirât. Je le rencontrai à la maison de mon père peu avant notre rupture, lors d'un cocktail donné en l'honneur des Américains. J'ai dit "rencontrai", mais ce n'est qu'une façon de parler. Une rencontre implique un échange significatif entre deux êtres comparables, une sorte de reconnaissance mutuelle. Ce n'est pas ce qui se passa entre nous. Je rencontrai Love comme on tombe parfois sur l'un de ces fabuleux animaux dressés qui viennent de l'intérieur des terres ou de l'étranger pour s'exhiber dans nos rues. Peut-être en as-tu vu. Les plus fréquents sont les ours danseurs ou les singes qui accompagnent les joueurs d'orgue de Barbarie. Moi, je parlerais du "tigre danseur" que je vis un jour. Cet animal, capturé et transporté de Birmanie par voie de terre, arpentait d'une seule foulée sa robuste cage de bambou, marchant de long en large, ou plutôt en cercles répétés, sans jamais perdre l'équilibre tandis que sa cage tressautait sur les pierres du chemin. On aurait dit un tourbillon de gaz noir et orange en suspension dans une bouteille hermétiquement close, des énergies primitives désireuses de retourner à une nature d'où on les avait injustement arrachées. En marchant, le tigre tournait de droite et de gauche son énorme et terrible tête pour scruter les passants ; ses yeux verts aux pupilles verticales brillaient d'une fureur étrange, impersonnelle, sans commune mesure avec la haine humaine, une fureur d'une beauté surprenante.

« Le "truc" de son dresseur était d'une bêtise atroce et ressortissait de ces instincts humains enfouis mais indéracinables que sont la cruauté et la violence. Avec mille précautions, il montait sur le toit de la cage, qui était assez élevé, en adressant à la foule un sourire odieux de fausse modestie, puis il s'inclinait avec une humilité feinte et laissait prendre des lambeaux de viande rouge dégoulinante au-dessus de la tête du tigre. L'animal, qu'on avait manifestement affamé et exaspéré au-delà de toute mesure, s'asseyait sur son arrière-train et griffait l'air comme un chat domestique ; parfois, cédant à la rage, il bondissait vers la viande, et sa tête heurtait le plafond de la cage, alors que le dresseur retirait brusquement l'appât, à peine capable de cacher son plaisir. Puis le tigre retombait sur le plancher de la cage où il gisait quelques instants, pantelant. Mais bientôt, il essayait encore, sachant peut-être que c'était sans espoir, mais incapable de résister à son appétit. Ainsi, la "danse" se poursuivait.

« Je ne comprendrai jamais tout à fait pourquoi cette image, avec ses sous-entendus de violence refoulée, est liée pour moi à Eddie Love, mais le fait est que je ne pense jamais à lui sans évoquer ce spectacle. Sous maints rapports, il incarnait le principe opposé, jubilant, libre et ouvert. Mais il y avait autre chose en lui, la marque du danger. Bizarrement, il m'a toujours rappelé l'un des dieux du panthéon grec — un Hermès en smoking, avec des lunettes d'aviateur et ce sourire légèrement canin, une sorte de voleur saltimbanque serrant une rose entre ses dents, qui vous dépouille en vous charmant.

« Mais il y a une explication plus simple : Love aussi était un "tigre", bien que de l'espèce volante plutôt que dansante. A bien y réfléchir, je me demande pourtant s'il ne ressemblait pas davantage au dresseur qu'au tigre. Peut-être Love avait-il un peu des deux. Quand je le vis pour la première fois, il accomplissait des tours de prestidigitation.

« J'arrivai tard à la maison et découvris les invités rassemblés dans la cour près du bassin. Love, en cravate et queue-de-pie, debout au sommet de la courbe du pont, faisait des tours de magie en annonçant son propre numéro d'une authentique voix d'aboyeur.

« "Voici ce soir, pour votre plaisir, mesdames et messieurs (surtout mesdames), quelques numéros inédits de pres-ti-di-gi-ta-tion qu'aucun Chinois n'a jamais contemplés et qui vous feront frémir... — il dessina un cercle enflammé dans l'espace, ses doigts brillaient comme des diamants crachant des flammes colorées — à travers le cerceau de feu ! Numéros directement importés de la Grande Foire Américaine !"

« Il déboutonna les poignets de ses gants blancs, les jeta nonchalamment dans son haut-de-forme noir, qu'il cogna ensuite contre son genou. Deux colombes apeurées s'en échappèrent pour se poser brièvement sur le mur du jardin avant de s'envoler dans le crépuscule. Des applaudissements unanimes s'ensuivirent, et quelques cris émerveillés — dont ceux de ma sœur. Je repérai Ch'iu-yeh assise au pied du pont près de notre mère. Penchée en avant sur sa chaise, les mains crispées sur ses cuisses (comme si elles aussi risquaient à tout moment de s'envoler), ta mère était suspendue au moindre geste de Love avec une intensité que je ne pus m'empêcher de remarquer. Ses joues étaient empourprées, et cette tache de couleur réhaussait sa beauté, la rendait superbe même pour l'œil blasé, émoussé, d'un frère.

« Entre-temps, Love avait ouvert son chapeau du plat de la main pour le poser de guingois au-dessus de son œil, comme l'acteur américain Fred Astaire. Soudain, l'expression d'un étonnement exagéré — yeux écarquillés, lèvres retroussées en un "o" minuscule — envahit son visage. Il souleva son chapeau, explora le sommet de son crâne d'une main délicate, et découvrit (son sourire mima le plaisir innocent de l'enfant) un minuscule œuf moucheté. Il le posa en équilibre sur ses doigts comme dans un coquetier, pivota de la taille, provoquant l'admiration du public. Soit accident, soit volontairement — je n'ai jamais su —, alors qu'il saluait, il laissa tomber l'œuf, dont le jaune vif se répandit sur les planches du pont, entre lesquelles il coula jusqu'aux eaux sombres du bassin. L'espace d'un instant, ton père sembla hésiter, perdre sa belle assurance. Mais comme le public criait de joie, Love se lança aussitôt dans une nouvelle bouffonnerie.

« Totalement ravi par le déroulement de la soirée, mon père se tenait debout un peu à l'écart, un gros cigare aux lèvres. Il avait arrêté l'un des jeunes Américains pour bavarder avec lui dans cet anglais démotique dont il était si fier, lui expliquant sans doute ses projets de développement des "rapports commerciaux" entre l'Est et l'Ouest. Pour moi, lui aussi ressemblait un peu à un magicien, tandis qu'il agitait son barreau de chaise comme une baguette magique, et gratifiait l'assemblée d'un sourire si suave que Dieu lui-même, eût-il été surpris avec cette expression, se serait senti légèrement stupide. Le malheureux soldat qui bénéficiait de tant de largesses tenait manifestement à rester poli, mais aurait sans doute préféré boire un peu plus et apprendre un peu moins. » Je crus déceler une nuance d'affection bourrue dans la voix de Hsiao, quand il évoqua son père, une sorte de contrepoint discret à son chagrin trop évident.

« La plupart des tours de Love appartenaient au répertoire classique, mais l'eussé-je un peu connu, j'aurais sans doute deviné qu'il gardait un atout inédit dans sa manche. Il débordait d'une incroyable fantaisie, à la fois extrêmement séduisante et parfaitement exaspérante. Quelque chose le poussait à des actes qui, sur le moment, étaient superbes, uniques — parfois irritants, peut-être, comme le grain de sable autour duquel l'huître fabrique sa perle. Mais en d'autres occasions, sa fantaisie tombait à plat, engendrait des monstruosités, telles les concrétions grises et difformes qu'on trouve le plus souvent dans ce coquillage. Je l'ignorais à l'époque, mais j'allais assister à une manifestation de cette fantaisie. Réussie ou non, je te laisse en juger.

« Le public applaudissait ton père qui s'acheminait vers son apothéose. Une succession interminable et ahurissante d'objets précieux ou triviaux apparut hors du chapeau haut de forme comme d'une source inépuisable débordant des objets hétéroclites du désir terrestre. D'une main désinvolte, il lança à la foule émerveillée des mouchoirs en soie décorés de luxueuses broderies, puis tira du chapeau des chaussettes et des sous-vêtements sales. Un modèle réduit du P-40, reproduction fidèle jusqu'aux mâchoires de tigre peintes sur le nez, jaillit en pétaradant, exécuta plusieurs loopings vertigineux avant de s'écraser dans les eaux du bassin. Love sortit de son chapeau des fleurs en papier et des drapeaux américains, puis salua l'accident avec tous les honneurs militaires. Il jeta ensuite faveurs et serpentins, bonbons et sucres d'orge. Une chandelle romaine s'éleva dans le ciel pâlissant.

« Enfin, à court de munitions, il releva sa manche, plongea la main dans le chapeau, l'explora en vain, et haussa les épaules, apparemment prêt à renoncer. Il s'éloigna (tous les yeux étaient rivés sur lui), puis hésita, pivota sur les talons. Il chercha une dernière fois, comme pour s'assurer qu'il n'avait rien oublié, et sortit une petite patte couverte de fourrure, après quoi suivit un gros lapin à l'expression sarcastique, qui huma l'air avec méfiance en remuant les oreilles. Cliché inévitable de la plupart des magiciens ordinaires, ce lapin qui suivait la folle succession d'objets acheva le numéro en une sorte d'apothéose hilare, totalement imprévue. Le public explosa de rire. Un spectateur tomba réellement par terre. D'autres avaient les larmes aux yeux.

« Pendant cette catharsis, presque à l'insu de son public, ton père le magicien plongea la main dans son chapeau et en sortit une grenade à main. On entendit un cri étouffé, puis le silence. Souriant, rouge de triomphe, Love dégoupilla la grenade et la lança dans la foule. L'homme qui, un instant plus tôt gisait à terre en proie au fou rire, se recroquevilla sur le ventre et protégea sa tête entre ses bras. Quelque part vers l'arrière, j'entendis une femme pousser un bref hurlement hystérique. La plupart des spectateurs restèrent figés sur place, médusés. Toutes nos terreurs se matérialisaient sous nos yeux, cette menace de mort violente qui nous harcelait depuis si longtemps. Chacun, en son for intérieur, céda à ses peurs secrètes. Alors elle explosa... avec un chuintement ridicule, manifestement destiné à suggérer un pet. Pendant une longue minute, personne ne rit.

« Personne sauf Love. Debout sur le pont, nous dominant de quelques pieds, il lança sa tête en arrière en poussant un hennissement sauvage, tel un étalon qui se cabre et dont la crinière fouette violemment l'air. Il y avait dans ce rire plus que de la fierté ou du triomphe ; il contenait une note que je n'avais jamais entendue, sinon en rêve. Dans mon esprit, je l'associai à la tristesse qui, selon les vieilles femmes, est la gaieté des elfes et des fées, des dieux et des démons — ces étranges créatures dont la puissance excède les imaginations les plus extravagantes des hommes, mais qui sont impuissantes à satisfaire leur désir le plus urgent : mourir. Tandis que j'écoutais son rire, un frisson s'empara de moi, et l'idée se glissa dans mon cerveau qu'il était fou.

« Les autres ne durent pas remarquer ces signes de mauvais augure. Car suivant l'exemple des Américains (qui étaient complètement sous le charme de Love), tous les spectateurs éclatèrent d'un rire tonitruant. Je fus étonné de voir, pour la première fois depuis des mois, des visages heureux autour de moi. Comme une vague, le soulagement avait déferlé sur l'assemblée, emportant tout le monde dans la gaieté délirante inspirée par Love. C'était moins ton père que le monde lui-même qui semblait être devenu fou.

« Et puis cela passa. L'homme qui avait mordu la poussière se releva et brossa la saleté de son habit en souriant. Il paraissait ravi.

« "Ce Love !" s'écria un Américain.

« "Quel type !"

« "Il est cinglé !" (Cela sur le ton de la plus vive admiration.)

« "Quel sens de l'humour !"

« De toute l'assemblée, ta mère fut peut-être la plus emballée par le numéro. Je la vis debout au pied du pont, attendant que Love en descendît. Pour employer une expression américaine, on eût dit qu'elle "mourait d'envie de le connaître". » Mon oncle s'abîma un instant dans une sombre introspection ; quand il reprit son récit, son sourire était devenu urbain et cynique.

« Love descendit avec le lapin perché en équilibre instable sur le bras, tel un faucon ; de sa main libre, il caressait ses oreilles. Quand il remarqua le visage rayonnant de Ch'iu-yeh tourné vers lui, il se figea et la dévisagea avec de grands yeux. La pose avait de quoi impressionner, mais Ch'iu-yeh ne se troubla pas. Je me concentrai sur son visage, car j'y discernais quelque chose que je n'avais jamais vu auparavant. Au-delà de la fierté, par-delà les rougeurs du plaisir, comme un élément plus dense qui supportait les deux, il y avait une vulnérabilité si résolue qu'elle confinait au pouvoir — non, qui *était* le pouvoir.

« Sur le visage de Love se lisaient curiosité et vivacité, ainsi peut-être qu'une trace d'amusement, évidente dans la façon dont ses lèvres ébauchaient un sourire, puis se rétractaient, avant de reprendre leur manège.

« "Qu'en pensez-vous ?" lui demanda-t-il enfin.

« "Je crois que vous êtes un vrai magicien, M. Love", répondit Ch'iu-yeh, un peu timidement mais avec une excitation qui me rappela le tintement nerveux et cristallin des prismes d'un lustre quand une porte s'ouvre quelque part et qu'un courant d'air traverse la maison.

« Extrêmement beau, extrêmement dangereux, Love s'inclina à partir de la taille devant le compliment, sans jamais quitter des yeux le visage de ma sœur.

« Ch'iu-yeh souriait plaisamment. "Mais dites-moi, votre magie est-elle réelle, ou simple dextérité ?"

« Il lui rendit son sourire. "Y a-t-il une différence ?"

« "Bien sûr !"

« Love haussa les épaules avec une froideur maussade. "Je ne fais pas de promesses."

« Surprise par ce brusque changement de ton, Ch'iu-yeh rougit. "En tout cas, votre spectacle m'a plu." Sa voix tremblait un peu.

« "Je vous remercie, répondit-il. J'aime ce numéro. Il est très drôle, tant qu'il dure."

« Les yeux de la jeune Chinoise s'agrandirent de curiosité. "Tant qu'il dure ?"

« "Ensuite, je dois affronter certaines complications — vous savez, des *responsabilités*." Son emphase mimait l'horreur. Elle attendit. "Je veux dire, bien sûr... (il marqua un temps d'arrêt, son humeur changea de nouveau)... que faire de tous ces sacrés lapins ?" Abandonnant toute réticence, il devint suffisant, paillard. "En quelques nuits ils se mettent à pulluler. Ces saletés de bestioles se multiplient comme..." A côté de lui, un de ses camarades éclata de rire. Comme pour prouver ses dires, Love souleva le lapin par la peau du cou. "Pièce à conviction numéro 1 : l'arme du crime", dit-il en grimaçant.

« Les pattes de l'animal ruaient frénétiquement dans le vide. C'était désopilant et pathétique, mais cela frisa le tragique quand le lapin poussa brusquement un cri perçant. La plupart des gens n'ont jamais entendu ce couinement, Sun I, car d'habitude ce n'est qu'au moment de la mort que ces timides créatures rompent leur silence. Je me rappelai mon enfance, quand il me réveillait parfois la nuit ; je savais alors qu'un hibou avait attaqué le clapier et refermé ses serres sur la gorge d'un de ses habitants. Ce cri est d'autant plus glaçant qu'il ressemble à celui d'un enfant humain.

« Sans relâcher sa prise, Love souleva le lapin devant son visage et plongea son regard dans ses yeux stupides dilatés de terreur. "Qu'est-ce qui ne va pas ?" lui demanda-t-il en riant gaiement. Il paraissait ignorer ou mépriser la panique de la bête, mais je ne crois pas qu'il se montrait délibérément cruel.

« "Vous ne le tenez pas comme il faut", le gronda Ch'iu-yeh en saisissant l'arrière-train de l'animal. "Comme *ceci*." Elle prit le lapin dans ses bras, où elle l'installa tel un nouveau-né. "Son petit cœur bat la chamade." Elle lui adressa un regard de reproche. "Il est presque mort de peur." L'animal se calmait contre la jeune fille. "Vous devriez être plus doux", conseilla-t-elle en lui tendant le lapin.

« "Vous vous y prenez très bien, remarqua Love avec un hochement de tête appréciateur. C'est sûrement l'instinct maternel. Peut-être accepteriez-vous de m'en débarrasser ?"

« Ch'iu-yeh hésita. "Vous voulez dire : que je le garde ?"

« Il acquiesça.

« Son regard alla de l'homme à la bête, puis retourna vers Love. "Oh oui ! Je peux vraiment ?"

« "Je vous en prie."

« "Comment appeler ce lapin ou cette..." Elle regarda l'animal avec perplexité.

« Love hésita, puis saisit et leva rapidement la patte arrière de l'animal. Il simula la stupéfaction. "*Lapin*", dit-il en fronçant les sourcils d'un air docte. Le visage de Ch'iu-yeh s'empourpra. "Quant au nom, poursuivit-il en feignant de ne pas remarquer la gêne de la jeune fille, d'habitude je les appelle *Bugs* ou *Junior*, quelque chose dans ce style. Mais dans le cas présent, hum — il s'éclaircit la gorge — un spécimen aussi exceptionnel — un mâle authentique. Un lapin d'une virilité incontestable... Je crois qu'il n'y a pas à hésiter davantage."

« Embarrassée par l'ironie de l'Américain, Ch'iu-yeh le regardait timidement. Sa lèvre inférieure tremblait un peu. "Oui ?"

« "Eh bien, *Peter*, bien sûr !" s'écria-t-il joyeusement.

« Aujourd'hui j'ignore encore si ce fut naïveté de la part de ma sœur, ou brillante repartie. Son visage ne trahit aucun indice. Un temps, elle resta apparemment sans comprendre, puis son regard s'illumina. "*Peter Rabbit ?* demanda-t-elle doucement. Je connais ce conte de fées."

« Love eut l'air d'avoir reçu un coup de poing à l'estomac (plus bas peut-être). Blême, il regarda curieusement Ch'iu-yeh, comme s'il la voyait pour la première fois. Il semblait un peu honteux, mais aussi éprouver comme une tendresse nouvelle et troublée. Alors il s'abandonna à un rire complice. Moi-même, je faillis tomber amoureux de lui, Sun I. »

« Je me suis alors présenté. Love était d'excellente humeur, et nous bavardâmes jovialement pendant qu'à côté de nous, Ch'iu-yeh caressait le lapin avec une attention contrainte. Je l'observais du coin de l'œil, en me souvenant d'une jeune Américaine que j'avais vue jadis dans un parc d'attractions, serrant dans ses bras l'animal empaillé que son ami venait de gagner à un stand. Mais l'animal de Ch'iu-yeh était vivant.

« Love se déclara surpris par ma connaissance de l'anglais, et par celle de Ch'iu-yeh, qui parlait cette langue encore mieux que moi. Il possédait quelques notions de cantonais, acquises auprès de plusieurs cuisiniers et domestiques chinois — très en vogue à une certaine époque dans les classes supérieures de New York. Quand il nous demanda comment nous avions appris sa langue, je lui parlai brièvement de l'enthousiasme de mon père pour la "culture" occidentale — les affaires — et sa décision de m'envoyer étudier en Amérique. A la mention du mot "affaires", je remarquai avec surprise un changement dans l'expression de ton père, comme un nuage masquant brusquement le soleil. A l'époque, bien entendu, je ne soupçonnais pas les profondes résonances personnelles que ce mot évoquait chez lui. Je lui demandai son avis, mais il s'en tira par une pirouette.

« "Les affaires ? dit-il. Ça me rappelle une blague. Qu'y a-t-il de commun entre les affaires et une blanchisserie chinoise ?" Il ne me laissa pas le temps de répondre. "Les deux sont pleines de chemises. Peut-être de chemises amidonnées. Je ne me souviens pas. C'est mon père qui me l'a racontée."

« Peu dupe de la fausse nonchalance de sa réponse, je scrutai son visage. "Et qui est votre père ?"

« Love se détourna aussitôt comme si j'étais brusquement devenu invisible, et reprit sa conversation avec Ch'iu-yeh. Me sentant pour ainsi dire congédié, je m'éloignai de quelques pas et entamai une conversation avec un autre invité. Mais ma curiosité était piquée, d'autant que ton père semblait s'intéresser à Ch'iu-yeh. Je me sentis invinciblement attiré vers eux. Bien que je ne sois pas intervenu dans leur dialogue, je me tins assez près d'eux pour en surprendre quelques bribes.

« "Est-ce un chrysanthème que vous portez au revers de votre habit, M. Love ? lui demanda-t-elle. Je n'en ai jamais vu de cette couleur." Elle rougit, gênée par la simplicité de sa remarque et par l'évidence de son embarras.

« "Appelez-moi Eddie", répondit Love. Il fixa ses yeux avec une expression rêveuse qui évoquait l'ivresse, comme s'il avait complètement oublié la question de ma sœur. Puis il sursauta et baissa les yeux vers sa propre poitrine.

« "Cette chose ?" Il haussa les épaules. "Je ne sais pas. Je suppose que c'en est un. On dirait les fleurs qu'on offre aux filles pour les matches de football." Il lui sourit comme un jeune garçon, à la fois timide et impétueux. "Elle vous plaît ? Elle sent très bon." Tirant à moitié la fleur de son revers, il fit un pas vers Ch'iu-yeh. Elle recula.

« "Les chrysanthèmes ont une odeur amère, dit-elle. Tout le monde le sait."

« "Pas celui-ci."

« Partagée entre le doute et l'admiration, elle le regarda, puis, cédant au visage avenant de Love, lui rendit son sourire. Elle glissa ses doigts avec confiance sous le revers de l'habit, ferma les yeux et se pencha vers la poitrine de l'homme comme pour y poser sa tête pendant une danse, tirant la fleur vers elle.

« Alors que la main de Love plongeait vers la poche de poitrine de son smoking pour y prendre un mouchoir, Love croisa mon regard par hasard et m'adressa un clin d'œil complice. Je fus gêné d'être surpris à espionner si honteusement leur conversation, mais le clin d'œil de l'Américain avait un autre sens.

« Brusquement, Ch'iu-yeh poussa un léger cri et recula en bredouillant et battant des paupières. Stupéfaite, elle leva les yeux vers Love. Je remarquai alors une goutte d'eau qui descendait le long de sa joue, et compris que la fleur était artificielle, un accessoire du sac à malices du magicien, et qu'il l'avait arrosée en appuyant sur une poire. A voir l'expression de ma sœur, on aurait pu confondre la goutte d'eau avec une larme. Elle resta un instant en équilibre sur son menton, puis Love l'essuya avec son mouchoir avant qu'elle n'ait eu le temps de tomber.

« "Vous m'avez joué un tour !" s'écria-t-elle avec pétulance. Elle semblait hésiter entre l'outrage et le désir enfantin de se laisser gagner par le rire.

« Love tapota le visage de Ch'iu-yeh avec son mouchoir en souriant avec sympathie. "Je n'ai jamais promis, dit-il pour la deuxième fois. Et puis je vous devais bien cela pour le lapin."

« La balance pencha. Ta mère rougit, sourit. Love lui rendit son sourire. Je vis alors la reconnaissance briller dans leurs yeux, d'une lumière si vive qu'elle parut illuminer le crépuscule. Ce fut comme un briquet à silex, Sun I ; à cet instant je vis l'étincelle innocente jaillir entre eux avant de se muer en conflagration, sans deviner les ravages ultérieurs de cet incendie. »

Les échos du gong familier se répercutèrent étrangement ; ils convoquaient les moines qui travaillaient dans le jardin à la méditation de l'après-midi dans les recoins obscurs du temple. L'appel sembla dérisoire et incongru dans l'air brûlant de l'été. Par la fenêtre, je jetai un regard impatient aux moines couverts de sueur et de coups de soleil qui traversaient la cour en silence, puis mes yeux se posèrent de nouveau sur le visage de mon oncle.

5

« A partir de cette date, pas un jour ne passa sans que Love n'envoie à Ch'iu-yeh un bouquet de fleurs fraîchement coupées — roses, iris, parfois orchidées, mais le plus souvent des chrysanthèmes. Chaque matin, elles apparaissaient devant sa porte dans un panier plat en osier, douze ou treize fleurs soigneusement enveloppées dans du papier journal. Pendant longtemps, personne ne comprit comment elles arrivaient là ni qui les apportait. Elles apparaissaient "comme par magie". Cela devint prétexte à plaisanterie pour les domestiques, et un sujet d'inquiétude pour ma mère. Mon père, qui passait le plus clair de son temps à Ch'ung-ch'ing, n'apprit jamais leur existence.

« Pourtant, c'était assez innocent. Love ne les apportait pas personnellement ; il avait recruté un allié loyal dans nos rangs, un domestique de la maison de mon père, auquel l'Américain s'était lié d'un étrange attachement. Peut-être devrais-je m'étendre brièvement sur ce sujet, car il éclaire un aspect de son caractère que je n'ai pas encore évoqué.

« Vois-tu, à côté de la folle gaieté qui l'anima le soir où il fit la connaissance de Ch'iu-yeh — ce charme problématique mais évident —, ton père avait une autre facette. D'autres facettes, devrais-je dire. Car malgré sa réputation d'extraverti (de "boute-en-train", disaient les Américains) — une réputation que, selon moi, il cultivait sciemment et non sans dégoût, voire douleur —, je suis convaincu que Love partageait seulement avec autrui quelques miettes de sa vie intérieure, et dissimulait passionnément l'essentiel. Il cachait ainsi ses tendances dépressives, lesquelles étaient à l'origine de ses rapports avec le domestique dont je viens de parler, un jeune homme nommé Chiang Po, l'apprenti de notre jardinier.

« Pour autant que je sache, Chiang Po n'avait que du sang paysan dans les veines, aussi boueux que les eaux du Fleuve Jaune. Cependant, il était de ces rares individus des classes inférieures qui semblent posséder les instincts d'un prince. Bel homme, grand, brun et fluet, il avait ce fin visage grave qu'on trouve seulement parmi les descendants des khans. Chiang Po était d'origine mongole, mais il ne possédait ni la robuste santé ni le physique râblé de ses ancêtres. Il était maigre, délicat, voire frêle. Je pense que sa santé fut compromise par un sérieux accès de fièvre dont, enfant, il souffrit, probablement la scarlatine, car son visage en portait la terrible signature, stigmates dont le seul effet était d'accentuer sa beauté, comme les cicatrices infligées par le temps à l'ivoire ancien. Certains domestiques avançaient une autre explication de sa fragilité ; on chuchotait que Po se droguait, ou s'était drogué, à l'opium. Je ne fis aucun effort pour connaître la vérité. Dans les deux cas, cela ne concerna pas son rapport avec ton père.

« Chiang Po était fier, de la fierté sauvage de sa race, une fierté que sa dépendance semblait hausser à une intensité presque pathologique. Distant, difficile, il parlait seulement quand on lui adressait la parole, répondant alors avec une grande concision. Il semblait repousser toute tentative d'intimité, ou même de civilité, comme une marque de paternalisme. A maintes reprises, mon père avait failli le renvoyer pour insolence, mais chaque fois ma sœur, timidement secondée par ma mère, avait pris sa défense avec une telle fougue qu'il avait renoncé. (Finalement, quand Ch'iu-yeh ne fut plus là pour le défendre, Père mit sa menace à exécution. Beaucoup plus tard.) Selon moi, Ch'iu-yeh agissait seulement par pitié pour la dure existence de Chiang Po. Au contraire, ma mère appréciait beaucoup les services de Po qui, avec un goût sûr, décorait sa table de superbes arrangements floraux qui exprimaient l'élégance nerveuse de son esprit.

« J'entretenais peu de contacts avec Po, mais je l'avais remarqué. Chaque fois que je croisais son regard, des lueurs de colère aussi vives que l'éclair bondissaient vers moi. Je respectais cela en lui. Ce garçon qui semblait vivre un perpétuel état de siège se permettait seulement deux plaisirs : ses fleurs, qu'il soignait avec une dévotion quasiment religieuse, et la musique. Po jouait du *erh-hu*, violon mongol à deux cordes dont le timbre ressemble à s'y méprendre à celui de la voix humaine, surtout dans l'expression de la mélancolie.

« Par-delà toute barrière de classe, de culture, voire de langue (bien que ton père eût rapidement comblé ce fossé), Chiang Po et Love se rapprochèrent chaque jour davantage. L'âme du serviteur ressemblait à une clef dont les encoches correspondaient parfaitement aux gardes de la personnalité de ton père, dont il ouvrit bientôt la serrure. D'autres serviteurs me racontèrent que parfois, quand il était dans une certaine humeur, surtout après sa blessure, Love passait des heures assis sur le pont de la cour de notre maison, balançant ses jambes dans le vide, les yeux baissés vers le sombre miroir du bassin, tandis que derrière lui Chiang Po jouait de son violon avec son archet en crin de cheval et chantait. Cela, Po ne l'aurait fait pour aucun autre. Parfois, il chantait des mélodies joyeuses, pleines de virtuosité ; le *erh-hu* imitait alors le hennissement des chevaux et le rythme de la cavalcade (les Mongols sont les meilleurs cavaliers du monde), mais le plus souvent les chansons étaient tristes — chants de paysannes dont les hommes sont partis guerroyer, qui s'enflaient en éclats de colère suraigus, puis retombaient pour se muer en gémissements —, longues plages monotones évoquant les jours interminables livrés au désespoir. Cette musique touchait ton père, apaisait quelque blessure à la source cachée au plus profond de lui-même, voilée, comme je l'ai dit, dans le secret.

« Sans les bavardages des domestiques, j'aurais peut-être ignoré ces épisodes jusqu'au jour où, par hasard, je tombai sur l'une de ces scènes.

Mais gardons cela pour plus tard. Je dirais ici que ces rumeurs piquèrent la curiosité déjà considérable que je portais à ton père.

« Je recherchais sa présence, et dans une certaine mesure il me rendait ces marques d'intérêt, me consultant avant de se procurer certains articles chinois, surtout des textiles. Un jour, nous visitâmes ensemble les fermes du Szu-ch'uan où l'on fabriquait la soie. Ce voyage reste profondément gravé dans mon souvenir, car il marque l'apogée de mon intimité avec ton père. Je lui avais demandé pourquoi il s'était porté volontaire pour servir en Chine. Il resta silencieux un long moment, puis, avec un étrange sourire, me répondit : "un désir solitaire de volupté". Quand je l'interrogeai à nouveau, il récita un poème du poète irlandais Yeats. Il s'intitule *Un aviateur irlandais prévoit sa mort* :

> Je sais que je rencontrerai mon destin
> Quelque part dans les nuages ;
> Ceux que je combats, je ne hais point,
> Ceux que je protège, n'aime pas davantage ;
> Mon pays est la Croix de Kiltartan,
> Mes compatriotes les pauvres de Kiltartan,
> Aucun dénouement ne les rendra plus malheureux,
> Ou plus heureux qu'avant.
> Nulle loi, nul devoir ne me pousse à lutter,
> Ni hommes publics, ni foules en liesse ;
> Un désir solitaire de volupté
> M'amena dans les nuages à ce tumulte ;
> J'ai tout bien pesé, tout médité,
> Les années à venir m'ont paru trop mince amour,
> Et amour trop mince les années passées,
> Au regard de cette vie, de cette mort.

« "Un désir solitaire de volupté" — je n'ai jamais oublié ce vers.

« Je fus également frappé par le silence de Love au sujet de sa famille. C'était remarquable, surtout par contraste avec l'enthousiasme des autres aviateurs sur ce chapitre. Avec la plaque d'identité, l'étui de photos semblait fourni à tous les soldats par le gouvernement des Etats-Unis. Les Américains le portaient, non pas contre leur cœur comme les Chinois, mais avec leur argent au contact d'une partie également privée (bien que peut-être moins sacrée) de leur anatomie. Là, disponibles à tout moment, se froissaient "les proches et les chers". Les aviateurs consacraient beaucoup de temps à se passer ces photographies, entre eux et à quiconque exprimait le désir de les voir, en déclarant avec une ferveur patriotique, et parfois une sentimentalité pleurnicharde : "J'aimerais tellement être de retour au pays."

« Bizarrement, Love ne semblait pas partager leur enthousiasme unanime. Ses camarades ne savaient comment expliquer ses réticences concernant son foyer et sa famille. Je crois qu'ils craignaient sa réserve et lui en auraient tenu grief s'il n'avait pas rétabli l'équilibre en d'autres domaines — par sa vivacité et son charme, par sa "magie", résultats d'une éducation qu'ils ignoraient et dont, l'eussent-ils connue, ils auraient probablement nié la valeur — mais surtout dans les airs, où l'œil froid et attentif de la Mort nivelait toute différence. Là, où l'on ne pouvait plus mentir, ton père dévoilait son cœur.

« Love était l'un des deux ou trois meilleurs pilotes de son escadrille, les Pandas. Au combat, son style était audacieux, parfois téméraire, mais il possédait les réflexes rapides d'un athlète et s'en tirait indemne à chaque fois. (Sauf une... Pourtant, c'est pure spéculation de ma part, et peut-être présomption, que de lui reprocher son accident. En tout cas, il ne fut jamais cassé, ni même, à ma connaissance, blâmé. Bien au contraire, on le décora.) Mais la valeur de ton père pour son unité ne se limitait pas à ses talents physiques. Il possédait le don de la stratégie, lequel se manifesta d'abord sur des détails techniques avant de s'épanouir en une contribution tactique de première importance. A cause de ce don, Chennault tenta d'affecter Love à des vols de reconnaissance pour lui éviter le moindre risque. Love refusa. Finalement, compte tenu de tous ces facteurs, le silence de ton père concernant sa famille, loin de jouer en sa défaveur, accrut son prestige auprès de ses camarades. Ils respectaient son mutisme comme un point d'honneur, s'interdisaient toute indiscrétion. Ils allèrent même jusqu'à le protéger activement dans la mesure de leurs moyens. » Hsiao se leva et marcha vers la fenêtre, devant laquelle il s'arrêta pour regarder dehors. Quand il reprit, je ne voyais pas son visage, seulement ses mains qu'il serrait et desserrait derrière son dos.

« Ainsi, pendant très longtemps j'ai ignoré comme tout le monde que Love appartenait à l'une des douze plus riches familles d'Amérique, famille fondée par l'un de ces grands industriels du XIXe siècle, qui se dressèrent hors de la boue et du limon primitifs comme de terribles prédateurs pour dévorer leurs adversaires et croître au point de dominer la cime des arbres pour jouir d'une vue panoramique qui s'étendait jusqu'à l'horizon du monde — en seigneurs universels qu'on pouvait presque compter sur les doigts de la main. Les Morgan, Mellon, Carnegie, Rockefeller, Vanderbilt, Du Pont — si les Love étaient moins célèbres que ceux-là, c'était peut-être qu'ils avaient continué à exercer un contrôle direct sur leur empire alors que les autres s'étaient éparpillés comme des vaches sacrées dans les verts pâturages des bonnes œuvres pour les fertiliser. Jusqu'à une date relativement récente, les Love n'avaient pas eu le temps de bâtir de grandes fondations, de construire les bibliothèques, musées et universités qui avaient fait la notoriété des autres. Car telles sont les activités des grandes familles sur le déclin. La culture, l'apprentissage du beau et du bien, sont les derniers signes de la vigueur d'antan. Et la beauté, bien que seule capable de sauver et de rendre la vie supportable, n'est rien de plus que ceci — un splendide parasite qui se nourrit aux dépens du corps. Il ne faut jamais oublier cette terrible vérité.

« Les Love ne risquaient pas d'oublier ce qu'ils n'avaient jamais appris. Ils échappaient depuis longtemps à cette déchéance. Depuis plusieurs générations, le pouvoir se transmettait de père en fils. Le père d'Eddie Love, Arthur Love, fut le premier maillon déficient de la chaîne, forgé non dans le fer ou l'acier, mais dans une substance plus délicate et fragile. A cause de lui, les Love perdirent le contrôle de la grande corporation qu'ils avaient faite (et qui les avait faits).

« Ayant étudié les sciences économiques, je connaissais le scandale qu'Arthur Love avait déclenché à Wall Street (qui, pour ton information, Sun I, est le cerveau attentif du système nerveux financier de l'Occident). Sa déconfiture, ou son apostasie, appelle ça comme tu voudras, défraya la chronique. Pourtant, je ne fis jamais le lien entre ce père et ce fils. Rétrospectivement, tout cela paraît évident, élémentaire ; peut-être l'évidence même du lien m'aveugla-t-elle. Pourquoi ton père devait-il se donner tant de mal pour dissimuler une ascendance dont d'autres, presque tous les autres, se seraient vantés ? Quelle que soit la réponse, il s'avéra que je n'eus pas besoin de la chercher : *elle me trouva.* Comme on dit en Amérique, eût-ce été un serpent, il m'aurait piqué.

« Tout arriva par hasard. Un matin, je parcourais un exemplaire mutilé d'un célèbre magazine américain, le *Time* (diffusé en Birmanie six semaines plus tôt, puis parachuté par un avion-cargo américain), quand mon œil fut attiré par les gros caractères d'un titre imprimé en bandeau sur la couverture :

LOVE IS DEAD
(L'AMOUR EST MORT)

« "Absurde !" pensai-je. La situation de l'humanité avait beau sembler désespérée en ce moment de l'histoire, pareille déclaration métaphysique paraissait néanmoins ridiculement outrée. A la lecture de l'article, je découvris bientôt que le bandeau de la couverture n'annonçait aucun drame planétaire, mais une simple chronique nécrologique. Je dis "simple", mais je réalisai aussitôt que le défunt devait être une personnalité importante — président, magistrat de la Cour suprême, grand général, peut-être même vedette de Hollywood — mais plus probablement un homme très riche, quelque magnat de la haute finance. »

Mon oncle prononça ces derniers mots d'une voix stridente tandis que la grimace sans joie que je connaissais désormais retroussait la commissure de ses lèvres.

« Maintenant, écoute-moi bien, Sun I, car l'histoire qui suit est instructive, c'est l'un des rares exemples de conduite individuelle estimable qui s'est jamais élevé au-dessus de l'ignoble mêlée de la place du marché américain. Art Love — Arthur Edward Love IV, pour être exact, le père d'Eddie — avait été dans sa jeunesse l'un des hommes les plus puissants du monde : président du conseil d'administration, principal actionnaire et directeur général de l'*American Power and Light Corporation*. Il représentait peut-être l'exemple le plus proche de monarchie héréditaire que l'Amérique ait jamais produit. Mais il ne put se maintenir à la tête de son conglomérat. Je ne suis même pas certain qu'il l'ait désiré. C'est là tout le problème.

« Ç'avait été un petit garçon doux et paisible, de nature plutôt fragile, mais précoce, sensible aux "beautés subtiles" de l'art — caractéristiques qui ne convenaient peut-être pas à un futur César de la finance, rôle que son père, A.E. Love III, "Big Ed", avait choisi pour lui en accord avec les traditions familiales. Une éducation sévère, destinée à instiller chez l'enfant quelques rudiments de l'"'instinct du tueur'", eut peu d'effets sur

Arthur Love, sinon qu'il se mit à souffrir de troubles nerveux, et que la douceur et le lyrisme de son tempérament enfantin firent place à une humeur morbide et mélancolique.

« Pourtant, ce fut seulement à la mort de son père — je veux dire de Big Ed —, que l'épilepsie qui devait ravager la vie d'Art Love se déclara dans toute sa violence. La première crise survint lors des funérailles. Cette maladie était d'autant plus inquiétante qu'Arthur était censé remplacer son père. Si, pendant les premiers mois, ses performances ne lui valurent aucune accolade, les observateurs qualifiés lui accordèrent néanmoins son examen de passage. Beaucoup, moi compris, s'étonnèrent de son endurance et de sa solidité. Le laudanum que ses médecins lui administraient l'aida peut-être à conserver son équilibre. Mais le prix de cette cure fut lourd, car Arthur Love s'intoxiqua au laudanum pour le restant de ses jours.

« Son règne, ou son administration, reste gravé dans les mémoires comme une ère silencieuse et funeste. On eût dit que l'odeur de la mort planait sur Wall Street. D'insolites manifestations de pitié apparurent chez des hommes qui en avaient perdu le goût, qui en fait avaient perdu le goût de tout, sinon de la chasse, et du sang. Chez les Love, le sang avait toujours été un élément privilégié, depuis le premier A.E. Love, le terrible patriarche du clan qui avait enlevé la corporation (connue à l'époque sous le nom de *American Gas*), "Jubilee" Jim Fisk, l'impitoyable âme damnée de Jay Gould. L'assassinat de Fisk par un mari outragé — Fisk avait soi-disant séduit sa femme — intervint au moment précis où le premier Love et lui-même se livraient une lutte acharnée pour contrôler l'*American Gas*, et alors que Love semblait avoir épuisé toutes ses munitions. Les ragots allèrent bon train, mais le tribunal se prononça pour le "crime passionnel" et choisit d'en rester là. Je crois que personne ne sut la vérité, personne sauf A.E. Love — qui ne cédait pas facilement aux remords, d'autant que la mort de Fisk lui avait ouvert la voie du saint des saints de la toute-puissance terrestre, dont il avait rêvé toute sa vie. Son arrière-petit-fils était d'une étoffe totalement différente. Comme je l'ai dit, la communauté financière a toujours eu l'intuition que le règne d'Art Love serait bref. Et pourtant la façon dont il se termina... personne ne s'y était attendu.

« Essaie de t'imaginer, Sun I. Entre les mains de son père et de son grand-père, APL avait grossi et s'était diversifié en une douzaine de secteurs, y compris celui de l'armement pendant la première guerre mondiale. A l'époque de l'accession au pouvoir d'Arthur Love, *American Power and Light* était devenu, en terme d'avoirs permanents, la plus grosse entreprise d'Amérique, donc évidemment du monde. » Hsiao sourit d'un air lugubre. « Bien sûr ! Ses performances lui avaient valu une place au soleil du *Dow Jones Industrial Average,* clef de voûte indiscutable du système. Ce fut alors que les investisseurs la baptisèrent "lA PupiLle de l'œil américain". » Hsiao sourit de nouveau.

« Tout cela, Art Love le perdit, ou devrais-je dire : *s'en débarrassa*, lors de cette mémorable assemblée des actionnaires, à la fin de sa première année, quand il annonça au conseil d'administration qu'il "se lavait les mains du sang rituel" — expression qui devint célèbre à Wall Street.

« Imagine-toi, Sun I, devant un auditorium bondé par les nantis et les moins riches — ceux qui avaient troqué leurs modestes économies contre quelques actions, qu'ils conservaient avec une confiance indestructible comme les reliques de la Croix, plus toutes les têtes couronnées de la finance américaine et internationale —, Arthur Love répudia et stigmatisa l'ensemble de la communauté, qualifia ses membres de grands prêtres adonnés aux "messes noires", à la célébration des mystères sacrificiels de l'entreprise privée, qu'il définit comme une nouvelle religion aussi vieille que le péché : l'intérêt personnel. Puis il entreprit de fustiger sa propre famille, allant jusqu'à suggérer que l'anecdote de Wall Street selon laquelle on ne baptisait pas les Love dans l'eau bénite mais dans le sang n'était pas dépourvue de fondement. Les mains de son arrière-grand-père étaient rouges du sang du meurtre, dit-il, et chaque génération, assumant son héritage, avait trempé dans ce péché : "L'injustice des pères éclabousse les enfants, et les enfants des enfants, jusqu'à la troisième et la quatrième génération." Il était le quatrième de la lignée, déclara-t-il ; avec lui la malédiction s'éteindrait. Il refusait de transmettre cette culpabilité à ses propres enfants, priait pour qu'un jour ils lui en fussent reconnaissants. Son arrière-grand-père s'était rendu coupable du meurtre d'un seul homme — c'était déjà assez de sang. Il refusait de participer à l'assassinat d'une civilisation. »

Hsiao hocha la tête. « Oui, la personnalité d'Arthur Love tranchait sur celle des habitués de Wall Street ; il était différent, et selon moi meilleur, quoique moins fort. » Hsiao croisa mon regard. « A la fin de son discours, Love eut une crise d'épilepsie et s'écroula sur scène. Selon certaines rumeurs, alors qu'on le transportait en chaise roulante, bavant et gesticulant, dans l'allée centrale de l'auditorium, plusieurs grands pontes et généraux de Wall Street pleurèrent en public. » Hsiao sourit cyniquement avant d'achever : « J'ignore s'ils plaignaient le prince déchu ou versaient des larmes sur leur propre sort.

« Dans la communauté de la finance, la première réaction fut une tristesse générale. Le lendemain de la chute de Love, on n'échangea aucune action de l'APL, et les courtiers unanimes décidèrent de s'habiller en noir. Mais quand Arthur Love se rétablit et ne reprit pas son poste, l'humeur de Wall Street passa de la tristesse à la perplexité, puis glissa insensiblement vers l'hostilité ouverte. Car il devint de plus en plus évident qu'une ère s'était achevée dans la vie d'Art Love. Il n'avait nullement parlé en l'air. Une fois son état stabilisé par le laudanum, les anciennes prédilections de l'enfance se réaffirmèrent. Après son ascension et sa chute vertigineuses du pinacle de la puissance et de la gloire, il fit retraite en lui-même, devint un timide reclus. Il s'enferma dans sa propriété de famille de Sands Point, à Long Island, où il se transforma en mécène et philanthrope, protégé des vicissitudes et des migraines du monde par un paradis artistique, tel un Adam art nouveau ou le roi fou Louis II de Bavière. Bien que son intention de se dissocier totalement de la corporation restât lettre morte, il n'assista plus jamais aux assemblées des actionnaires, abandonnant à d'autres la gestion de ses intérêts.

« A Wall Street, on suggéra malicieusement que son cerveau avait été privé d'oxygène pendant sa crise et que Love n'était plus "tout à fait de ce monde". Certains firent courir le bruit qu'il se droguait. Pourtant, médecins et psychiatres déclarèrent que le traumatisme avait agi sur les neurones de son cerveau à la manière d'un électrochoc, et réalisé "une cure miracle". D'autres, moins férus de théories ingénieuses, dirent tout simplement qu'il était devenu heureux. » Hsiao acquiesça. « Oui, Sun I, un précédent tout à fait admirable. » Il soupira. « Aujourd'hui, Arthur Love est mort. Oui, je connaissais fort bien toute cette histoire, à l'exception d'un détail crucial. Comme mes yeux parcouraient les colonnes jusqu'au dernier paragraphe de l'article du *Time*, je tombai sur les mots suivants : "M. Love laisse une femme et un fils unique, A.E. Love V (nommé Eddie d'après son grand-père, Big Ed Love). Aux dernières nouvelles, Eddie Love se trouve à Kunming, en Chine, où il sert dans l'AVG sous les ordres du général Chennault."

« Maintenant, Sun I, essaie d'imaginer l'effet que cette découverte eut sur moi. »

6

« Je fus stupéfait d'apprendre la paternité de Love. Que ce jeune homme, à qui ma sœur semblait de plus en plus sérieusement attachée, ait été l'héritier manifeste d'une des plus grandes fortunes d'Amérique (et donc, bien sûr, du monde) me prit totalement au dépourvu et m'emplit de terreur. Auparavant, bien qu'un élément de sa personnalité m'inquiétât, j'éprouvais de l'affection pour lui. Il était l'Occident, il était l'Amérique — éternellement jeune et imprudent, joyeux, charmeur, audacieux et amoral — voleur divin et rieur dérobant les pommes des Hespérides, de l'Arbre de Vie ou de l'*American Power and Light*, comme tu voudras, agissant dans une totale impunité, s'empiffrant et empilant dans son haut-de-forme ce qu'il ne mangeait pas ! On ne pouvait s'empêcher d'admirer, même si finalement on désapprouvait.

« Mais toutes mes réflexions sur ses qualités pâlirent à la lumière de ma découverte. Dans mon esprit il se mit à briller d'une lumière terne, comme un bijou maudit (un isotope radioactif, peut-être, dont le contact est mortel, mais qui possède le pouvoir de sauver le monde). Love était le diapason dont les vibrations s'accordaient à mes obsessions. Dès lors, indépendamment de ses particularités, il fut pour moi le symbole des Love, qui eux-mêmes représentaient la classe d'hommes que je redoutais le plus, et que je redoutais parce que je connaissais leur puissance. »

Hsiao s'était mis à arpenter la pièce. De temps à autre, inconsciemment je crois, il frappait sèchement les dalles avec le fer de sa canne. Je l'observais ; de la palette contradictoire des émotions qu'il m'inspirait, l'anxiété et la pitié l'emportèrent.

« Pourtant, malgré certains pressentiments de mauvais augure, ma première réaction à l'histoire des parents de Love fut la sympathie. Je discernais une ressemblance entre nous — bien que je ne pusse la définir clairement ; tout simplement, peut-être, nous étions lui et moi fils d'un père et, de ce point de vue, échaudés. » Hsiao chercha mon regard ; la légèreté de sa remarque le fit sourire. Mais presque aussitôt, son visage se renfrogna et il reprit ses déambulations.

« Selon les lois de l'étiquette non seulement confucéennes mais universelles, je compris que je devais avant tout présenter mes condoléances à ton père. Je réfléchis que, vu l'état déplorable des communications, j'aurais peut-être même à lui apprendre la nouvelle. C'était là une perspective alarmante, mais que j'étais prêt à affronter. Car il y avait une autre raison pour laquelle je tenais à lui parler : Ch'iu-yeh. La découverte de son héritage avait réveillé mes instincts protecteurs. Cette découverte annihilait pour moi toute possibilité d'une conclusion heureuse à leur liaison.

« Je le cherchai d'abord à sa caserne. Il n'était pas avec les pilotes que je trouvai dans la "salle des mégots", où ils attendaient impatiemment la sonnerie d'alarme *ching-pao* annonçant un raid aérien ; aucun ne put me dire où le trouver. Je fis la tournée des bars de Kunming où les Américains se réunissaient parfois. Sans plus de succès. Finalement, je renonçai.

« Pensif et irrésolu, mes pas me ramenèrent inéluctablement vers notre maison. Quand j'arrivai, ma mère était seule dans la pièce de couture, absorbée par sa broderie. J'étais habitué à ce spectacle, mais ce jour-là il avait quelque chose d'inhabituel. Loin d'être absorbée par son ouvrage, ma mère cousait d'une main distraite. Son travail de couture gisait, négligé, sur ses cuisses, tandis qu'un autre travail occupait ses pensées et que ses lèvres remuaient en silence, méditant quelque énigme ou paradoxe épineux. Ce spectacle libéra en moi un flot de tendresse — voir cette vieille femme, si impuissante, mais qui luttait pourtant avec détermination pour pactiser avec l'existence.

« Quand elle s'aperçut de ma présence dans la pièce, elle me lança un regard implorant et jeta son ouvrage à terre. J'ouvris la bouche pour parler, mais elle ne m'en laissa pas le temps et m'entraîna vers la porte coulissante en papier de riz qui donnait sur le jardin.

« "Écoute", dit-elle en posant un doigt sur mes lèvres.

« Comme venant de très loin, une musique étouffée pénétra dans ma conscience. Retenant mon souffle, je tendis l'oreille. Les accents lugubres d'un violon arrivaient du jardin. Quelqu'un chantait — une voix d'homme, manquant de pratique, mais aussi émouvante que toutes celles que j'ai entendues depuis.

« La chanson m'était vaguement familière. C'était une ballade contemporaine intitulée *Au fil du fleuve*, assez populaire à l'époque. Par son thème et la simplicité de son style, on l'aurait facilement confondue avec une des chansons du *Shih Ching*, qui étaient déjà anciennes du temps de Confucius. Elle racontait l'histoire d'une paysanne dont le mari, mobilisé, a dû partir.

> ... se battre et mourir
> Pour un lopin de terre stérile et inutile
> Le long d'une lointaine frontière
> Alors que ta place était ici.
> Car bien que tu l'aies ignoré,
> J'attends de nouveau un enfant...

« La femme poursuit en se plaignant amèrement des difficultés de la vie sans son mari. Prise d'un violent dépit, elle lui reproche les propositions d'aide d'autres hommes, "nantis, et jeunes gens robustes". Puis elle cède aux lamentations, terminant ainsi :

Mais jamais je ne pourrai aimer un autre homme,
Même si je me remarie. Car tu as laissé
Cette désolation dans ma chair, ce souvenir —
Ton jeune corps agile —
Et mon cœur refuse toute sagesse.

« La musique s'arrêta. Mes yeux étaient pleins de larmes, mais je ne me sentais pas malheureux. Je crus me réveiller après un long sommeil. Ma curiosité s'était mystérieusement dissipée.

« Pourtant, cette sensation ne dura qu'un instant. Revenant à moi, je serrai doucement la main de ma mère (elle aussi s'était figée, comme ensorcelée) et ouvris en grand le panneau de la porte.

« Là, dans la cour, debout au pied du pont, se tenait Chiang Po. Il posait doucement son *erh-hu* contre un poteau. L'archet en crin de cheval pendait dans sa main comme la queue d'un animal accablé. Bien que toujours sous le charme de sa musique, je ne parvenais pas à comprendre ce qu'il faisait là en plein après-midi, jouant des chansons tristes pour les poissons et les oiseaux comme si la seule contrainte à laquelle il acceptait de se plier était son bon vouloir. Alors j'entendis un chuchotement et je compris qu'il n'était pas seul.

« "Ne t'arrête pas, s'il te plaît", demanda une voix funèbre.

« Changeant légèrement de position, je vis qu'il y avait quelqu'un avec Po dans le jardin : Love. Assis sur le pont, il balançait ses jambes au-dessus de l'eau et regardait d'un air absent le sombre miroir du bassin. Ch'iu-yeh était à côté de lui. C'était elle qui avait parlé. Je ne les avais pas vus plus tôt à cause d'une treille qui me les masquait partiellement.

« "Il est ici depuis midi, murmura ma mère ; assis, il regarde dans l'eau en lançant des miettes aux poissons. Ch'iu-yeh a bien essayé de le consoler et de le faire parler, mais il s'est contenté de secouer la tête et de réclamer Po pour qu'il joue. La musique semble apaiser son esprit. Qu'a-t-il, selon toi ? Va lui parler."

« Incapable de bouger, je regardai Love avec un étonnement muet ; il scrutait sombrement son propre reflet dans le bassin. Le calme de l'eau était seulement brisé par les carpes et les cyprins curieux qui émergeaient de leur univers de vase pour l'observer, comme affligés d'une stupéfaction égale à la mienne. Des bulles brisaient la surface quand leurs lèvres charnues articulaient leur monotone o muet, telles des pleureuses professionnelles qu'il rétribuait en miettes de la miche de pain rassis posée sur ses cuisses.

« Je compris qu'il venait d'apprendre la mort de son père le jour même ; aussitôt, je ressentis une sympathie si profonde que mes yeux s'emplirent de larmes.

« "Ressaisis-toi, dit sévèrement ma mère. Tu es son ami. Va le voir."

« Ses remontrances me firent honte et me tirèrent de mon rêve. Je la regardai par-dessus mon épaule, passai la porte, que je tirai derrière moi. A ce bruit, Chiang Po se tourna vers moi avec une expression d'hostilité manifeste. Puis il s'éloigna. Love leva brièvement les yeux, mais mon apparition sembla sans effet sur lui, pour autant qu'il m'ait reconnu. Ses yeux vides parurent me traverser sans me voir — comme ceux d'un drogué, aurais-je pensé si j'avais soupçonné Love de prendre de l'opium. Une seconde après, il retournait à ses sombres occupations. Les yeux de Ch'iu-yeh restèrent fixés sur mon visage pendant que j'approchais.

« Je passais en revue toutes les formules de condoléances que je connaissais. Tels des chevaux boiteux en armure rouillée, les phrases conventionnelles s'entrechoquaient dans mon esprit, plus mortes que vives. Au dernier moment, tout courage m'abandonna.

« "Qu'y a-t-il, Eddie ?" lui demandai-je lamentablement en posant la main sur son épaule.

« Ch'iu-yeh, qui tenait sa main, me regarda d'un air suppliant et me fit signe de partir. Quand je secouai la tête, son regard devint haineux.

« Pendant quelques instants, Love ne dit rien, absorbé par la contemplation du bassin comme s'il essayait de sonder ses profondeurs nuageuses. J'étais presque sûr qu'il n'avait rien entendu, mais il se tourna vers moi. Debout sur le pont derrière lui, je devais avoir le soleil dans le dos, car ton père protégea ses yeux en grimaçant. Alors, comme si une idée venait de le frapper brusquement, la ride soucieuse qui barrait son front disparut, et son visage devint lumineux, presque transparent. Il glissa la main dans la poche de son uniforme, en sortit ses lunettes noires et les mit.

« "Maintenant, je vois de nouveau", murmura-t-il en riant doucement, comme si ces mots possédaient une signification cachée.

« "Eddie, lui dis-je avec une terreur croissante, ça ne va pas ? Dis-moi ce qui ne va pas."

« Love tourna vers moi un visage étonné, comme un animal intelligent incapable de deviner le désir de son maître. "Ce qui ne va pas." Ses traits se tordirent soudain en un sourire forcé qu'il sembla incapable de dominer. On eût dit son visage violé par quelque force extérieure. Ses lèvres se retroussaient sur ses dents comme l'argile façonnée par les mains d'un sculpteur invisible dans la violence de l'inspiration. Puis il se mit à rire, exactement comme à la fin de son numéro de magicien, et la même angoisse me noua la gorge. Mais maintenant je comprenais sa cause — l'accent désespéré de ce rire, son côté forcé, l'absence totale de joie — tout cela m'apparut dans un éclair d'une terrible clarté. Je compris alors que ma première intuition avait été la bonne. Ton père était fou. Avant que je n'aie pu reprendre mes esprits, il se mit à parler.

« "Ça ne va pas ? imita-t-il cruellement. Ça ne va pas ?" Ses yeux balayèrent l'espace, comme si un prodige venait de traverser son univers intérieur. "Tu n'es donc pas au courant ? s'écria-t-il d'une voix aiguë. J'ai été promu !" Cela déclencha un autre éclat de rire dément, cette fois suivi par quelques sanglots.

« "Eddie, repris-je avec tout le calme dont j'étais capable. Eddie..."

« Il m'ignora et se mit à divaguer. Je ne suivais son discours qu'avec beaucoup de difficulté. "Hsiao, me dit-il, as-tu jamais fait un rêve qui soit devenu réel ? Il y a un mois, six semaines, j'ai fait ce genre de rêve. Je volais. Un simple rêve... mais c'était tellement réel. Je sentais le caoutchouc usé de mon masque à oxygène, j'entendais le vent siffler dans les canons. Je me croyais seul dans le ciel jusqu'au moment où j'entendis un deuxième moteur. Je crus d'abord que c'était David, mon ailier, mais j'entendis alors des balles siffler autour de ma tête, ricocher sur le blindage du cockpit. Je décidai de plonger en mettant les gaz à fond, une chute de six mille pieds, comme une pierre, suivie d'un looping et d'une stabilisation. Mais quand je regardai derrière moi, il était encore là. J'essayai tout ce que je savais, sans réussir à me débarrasser de lui. Finalement, en désespoir de cause, je tirai le manche à balai, mis le nez vers le ciel et commençai à grimper. Je mis les gaz pendant une bonne minute. Mon cœur battait dans mes oreilles. A chaque instant, je m'attendais à me retrouver en perte de vitesse, à bousiller mes ailes, à prendre une balle dans le réservoir. Mais quand je réalisai que je n'entendais plus le moteur de l'autre, je regardai derrière moi. Rien que du ciel bleu en dessous de moi. *Ting-hao* — j'avais réussi ! Je poussai un cri de joie.

« "Alors l'avion apparut sous mon aile, tout en bas. Pour la première fois, je le vis bien. Des soleils rouges sur les ailes. Un Zéro. Mais je n'arrivais pas à comprendre pourquoi il était si bas, car les Zéros sont plus légers, plus manœuvrables que nos appareils ; leur vitesse ascensionnelle est plus élevée. Alors, à travers la vitre de l'autre cockpit, j'aperçus le visage du pilote. Il abritait ses yeux avec sa main, il me cherchait, et je compris qu'il m'avait perdu dans l'éclat du ciel. Car je montais droit vers le soleil. Maintenant, il semblait proche, d'une proximité impossible. Sa lumière m'éblouit. Je songeai brusquement que seules mes lunettes noires m'avaient sauvé. Contre le cercle incandescent du soleil, j'étais invisible, totalement blanchi.

« "Quand je regardai de nouveau en bas, je vis que les soleils jumeaux s'étaient miraculeusement enflammés. L'appareil brûlait. Le pilote, qui avait réussi à sortir, tombait en chute libre vers la mer. Mais ce n'était plus le pilote japonais ; c'était mon père. Je distinguais son visage ; il tombait à travers l'espace bleuté vers la courbe de la terre. Il tira sur le cordon de son parachute. Mais quand celui-ci s'ouvrit, seul un écheveau de mouchoirs de magicien se déploya, dessinant une traînée multicolore derrière lui comme la queue d'un cerf-volant. Je voulus le sauver. Mais quand j'essayai, je m'aperçus que les commandes ne répondaient plus et que je montais inexorablement. Une odeur de brûlé envahit le cockpit, comme de cire et de plumes, et quand je regardai devant moi pour la dernière fois, je ne volais plus du tout vers le soleil, mais droit vers le visage de Dieu ; et enfin, ce fut *mon propre corps* que je vis tomber en chute libre vers la terre." La voix de ton père était étouffée, pressante.

« "Qu'est-ce que ça veut dire ? demandai-je. Je ne te comprends pas, Eddie. Tu divagues." Je saisis doucement son bras et tentai de le mettre debout.

« "Non, non, dit-il en se dégageant. J'ai fait ce rêve et il s'est réalisé. Ecoute-moi, Hsiao..." Quand il prononça mon nom, il me regarda droit dans les yeux ; il avait retrouvé son équilibre mental.

« "Tous les jours suivants, je me suis senti inquiet. Il me semblait que mon rêve contenait un élément que je devais comprendre. Et puis j'ai trouvé..."

« Il se tut et je retins mon souffle, persuadé qu'il allait associer ce rêve prémonitoire à la mort de son père, ce qui aurait suggéré un rapport télépathique entre eux. Mais je me trompais.

« "C'était une stratégie de combat, dit Love d'une voix excitée en scrutant mon visage pour voir si je comprenais. Bien sûr ! Une inspiration tactique, un don du ciel ! D'accord, ce n'était pas nouveau. Enfant déjà, j'en avais entendu parler dans les livres sur la première guerre mondiale — Richthofen, les as allemands —, ils appelaient ça « le Hun dans le Soleil ». Chennault l'avait évoqué pour mémoire, ajoutant que cette tactique était dépassée. Mais le système de pré-alarme permettait de la ressusciter. Le premier matin, je n'en parlai à personne sauf à David, car je tenais à l'essayer pour tester son efficacité. Quand nous entendîmes *ching-pao*, notre symphonie de guerre barbare — batterie de cuisine, cloches de vache, clairons, sirènes, gongs — nous rejoignîmes nos appareils au pas de course et décollâmes. Mais au lieu de rester en palier à dix-huit mille pieds pour attendre l'ennemi à son altitude habituelle comme nous le faisions jusque-là, nous grimpâmes plus haut, à vingt-quatre ou vingt-cinq mille pieds, et nous décrivîmes des cercles en gardant le dos au soleil. Entre lui et eux, nous réussissions un authentique tour d'escamotage. Ils ne nous virent même pas. Quand ils arrivèrent, nous piquâmes vers eux à pleins gaz — bon Dieu, un P-40 qui se laisse tomber, moteur à fond, est un truc terrible — deux cents ou trois cents miles à l'heure. Nous les avons ratiboisés, une vraie boucherie, Hsiao. Bouffés tout crus, sang, tripes et cervelle. Ils n'ont jamais compris ce qui leur arrivait — jusqu'au dernier moment, quand il fut trop tard. Dieu de Dieu, c'était tellement beau. Tellement beau..." Je me rappelle avoir pensé que ses yeux étaient ceux du tigre, Sun I, fixés au loin sur le paradis d'une jungle tropicale. Puis son regard revint vers moi.

« "Tu ne vois donc pas ? C'est idéal. D'abord il y a l'avantage naturel de la défense. L'attaquant doit venir jusqu'à toi. Il n'a d'autre choix que de s'engager. Les Japs peuvent nous avoir sur pas mal de plans, mais s'ils veulent bousiller le terrain de Kunming, ils sont bien obligés d'amener leurs bombardiers, pas vrai ? Ainsi, nous savons où ils seront. Ensuite, grâce au système de pré-alarme, nous connaissons leur angle d'attaque probable. Ce qui nous fait gagner un temps précieux. Nous pouvons être prêts et les attendre de pied ferme. Il ne reste plus qu'à maximiser l'avantage que nous donnent tous ces éléments. Voilà ce que le rêve m'a révélé, une tache aveugle (*littéralement !*) que je peux utiliser contre l'ennemi, un camouflage contre lequel il ne peut rien, un tour de passe-passe si rapide qu'aucun œil ne saurait le détecter... Là-dessus, Chennault veut m'accorder une promotion. Plutôt marrant, non ? Une promotion ?"

« L'ironie grotesque de cette idée m'échappa d'abord, jusqu'à ce que j'y réfléchisse dans le contexte de la mort de son père. *Une promotion !*

« Je devrais remarquer, Sun I, que pour une raison quelconque, Love n'accepta jamais cette promotion (de simple chef de vol à vice-commandant de l'escadrille des Pandas). Personne n'a jamais pu me dire pourquoi il l'avait refusée. Peut-être préférait-il tout simplement conserver un profil bas, éviter la position trop visible, et donc vulnérable, d'un grade élevé. Parmi les Tigres Volants, comme ailleurs dans les forces armées, il existait deux hiérarchies qui ne se recouvraient pas toujours : l'une, légitime, fondée sur l'ancienneté et le grade, et une autre, occulte, liée aux qualités personnelles — charisme, intelligence, courage, inventivité. Ton père préférait évidemment la seconde. Love sentit sans doute qu'il avait peu à gagner d'une promotion formelle — sinon des migraines et des responsabilités supplémentaires sans le moindre gain appréciable de pouvoir.

« Mais pour revenir à... Je compris alors que je devais abattre mes cartes, lui révéler ce que, seul peut-être parmi toutes ses connaissances en Chine, je savais.

« "Eddie, lui dis-je en prenant une profonde inspiration, j'ai lu dans un magazine que ton père était mort. Je suis désolé pour toi, vraiment désolé."

« Jamais je n'aurais prévu sa réaction. Dès que j'eus dit ces mots, une transformation inquiétante se produisit chez Love. Il se raidit, son visage se pétrifia. Ses lèvres se crispèrent violemment, puis il rougit comme une femme. Je sentais qu'une émotion terrible le submergeait, qu'il luttait pour la contrôler. Il me dévisagea avec une intensité qui me fit trembler. Mais moi, je voyais seulement la surface brillante de ses lunettes noires qui réfléchissait ma propre image, et rien des yeux qui m'observaient derrière. Longtemps son regard resta posé sur moi, comme pour m'annihiler. Quand il cessa de rougir, son visage devint d'une pâleur étrange, livide. Puis son expression vira à la malice. Je ne l'oublierai jamais. Il me lança un regard méchant. L'ironie et le sacarsme inspirèrent sa question suivante :

« "Tu es sûr de ne pas me confondre avec un autre ?"

« Je secouai tristement la tête. "De quel autre pourrait-il s'agir ?"

« "Toi, Hsiao." Sa réponse était moins une question qu'un verdict. Il éclata d'un rire moqueur. Il se releva, passa devant moi avec un air menaçant puis, d'un pas furieux, franchit la porte et partit dans la rue.

« Ch'iu-yeh le suivit, et moi derrière elle pour lui demander ce qu'il avait voulu dire. Mais quand nous arrivâmes dans la rue, il avait disparu, laissant seulement derrière lui une succession de miettes de pain, comme celles que les enfants du conte occidental lâchent en marchant pour retrouver leur chemin hors de la forêt enchantée jusqu'à la sécurité de la cabane de leurs parents. »

L'austère gravité du visage de mon oncle faillit me faire manquer l'ironie de ses paroles. On eût dit qu'il tentait de me communiquer, par la seule puissance de sa concentration, un niveau du récit que les mots étaient impuissants à transmettre.

« Cet épisode me troubla longtemps, Sun I. La douleur due à la mort de son père était responsable de son état ce jour-là, sur le pont, je n'en doutais pas. En fait, d'après ce que je savais d'Arthur Love, les tendances dépressives de ton père semblaient une preuve patente de sa filiation. Mais pourquoi mes condoléances simples et sincères avaient-elles mis Eddie dans une telle rage ?

« Ma première idée fut d'attribuer sa réaction à la folie. Certaines de ses paroles — surtout ses dernières répliques agressives — relevaient d'un état situé en deçà ou au-delà de la normalité. Mais à mieux y regarder, je trouvai une autre explication. Sa colère tenait-elle au fait que j'avais dévoilé le secret qu'il avait si soigneusement caché à ses amis, et espéré oublier en quittant l'Amérique — le secret de sa paternité, la source de sa plus grande honte ? Je crus alors comprendre son terrible silence alors que les autres aviateurs ressassaient leurs familles. »

Hsiao prit une profonde inspiration, soupira et s'appuya contre le dossier de sa chaise. « Je comprenais tellement bien le problème de Love ! Comme fils, il aimait son père ; en tant qu'homme, il en avait honte. Ce n'était pas sans rappeler, même de loin, ma propre situation. Sa dernière remarque cryptique ne faisait-elle pas allusion à cela ? Il n'était certainement pas naïf au point de croire qu'il pouvait continuer à me cacher sa véritable identité. *Je savais qui il était !* Ayant découvert le père, j'avais découvert le fils.

« Il existait pourtant une différence cruciale entre nous. Love avait frappé aveuglément son père, et à travers lui, son propre héritage, son propre passé... toute son histoire, qu'il avait fuie pour venir se battre en Chine. Il ne comprenait pas que cette rébellion était suicidaire, qu'en mutilant son histoire, il se mutilait lui-même ; qu'en la perdant, il se perdait. La mort d'Art Love rendait irrévocable la décision du fils. Un organe — peut-être son âme elle-même — avait été arraché à ton père, fumant et ensanglanté, laissant une plaie béante qu'il porterait à jamais dans sa chair. Je crois que ce fut cela qui lui fit franchir la frontière de la folie et l'entraîna dans la forêt ensorcelée. Sans espoir de jamais en sortir. Car il avait détruit la seule voie qui ramène à la sécurité du territoire connu : la carte qui est la connaissance du passé.

« Je ne suis pas psychologue, Sun I, mais pour moi l'automutilation psychique de ton père se trouve physiquement confirmée par son accident. Celui-ci eut lieu moins d'une semaine après qu'il apprit la mort d'Art Love, et je ne peux m'empêcher de penser qu'il y eut davantage à l'œuvre que les simples "hasards de la guerre". Je ne crois pas que ce drame fut délibéré ou prémédité, mais je penche en faveur d'une autre hypothèse : un conflit intérieur non résolu depuis trop longtemps, et qui finit par s'objectiver, par se jouer dans le théâtre du monde extérieur.

« Il accomplissait une mission ordinaire de bombardement avec son groupe de quatre appareils. Ils survolaient le fleuve au nord de Kunming, quelque part au-dessus de la frontière du Yunnan et du Szu-ch'uan, non loin de Ken Kuan en fait. Ils venaient d'attaquer plusieurs sampans transporteurs de marchandises quand ils aperçurent un contingent d'avions japonais — bombardiers à long rayon d'action, escortés par dix-huit chasseurs-intercepteurs Zéros, qui rentraient d'une mission au-dessus de Ch'ung-ch'ing. Pris par surprise, numériquement inférieurs, les Américains étaient de plus désavantagés par leur altitude. Car les Japonais volaient au-dessus. Heureusement, ils ne virent pas tout de suite le groupe de Love. Les quatre appareils grimpèrent directement dans la formation de bombardiers avant que les Zéros, qui ne s'attendaient pas à une attaque du sol, ne puissent riposter. Deux bombardiers furent abattus lors de la première passe — l'un par ton père. Ensuite les ennuis commencèrent. David Bateson, l'ailier d'Eddie, me raconta que les Zéros les interceptèrent à vingt-deux mille pieds — six Japs qui plongèrent directement du soleil. Il dégagea à droite, ton père à gauche, et ils piquèrent pour prendre de la vitesse. Bateson me dit qu'il ne comprit jamais ce qui se passa ensuite. Quand il vit de nouveau Love, son appareil incontrôlable tombait en spirale vers le fleuve et laissait derrière lui un sillage de fumée noire. Il vit des flammes danser le long du fuselage, puis les ailes se désintégrèrent. Il scruta le ciel à la recherche d'un parachute, mais il y avait trop de fumée. Il ignora donc si ton père avait eu le temps de quitter son appareil.

« Quand ils revinrent à Kunming, on demanda par radio aux forces terrestres chinoises opérant dans la région, surtout de la guérilla communiste, de rechercher un pilote américain abattu. Au bout d'une semaine sans nouvelles, Love fut considéré comme disparu, vraisemblablement mort.

« Il ne l'était pas pourtant, pas tout à fait. Il n'avait apparemment pas épuisé ses neuf vies. (Mais tiens-en le compte, Sun I. Dans la série d'épisodes quasiment miraculeux qui suivent, il a bien dû en gaspiller une demi-douzaine.) Quoique étourdi et gravement brûlé, il réussit à sortir à temps de son cockpit, grâce à un ultime coup de reins. Quand l'air le fouetta, dit-il ensuite à Bateson, il vit le stabilisateur vertical de son appareil se ruer vers lui comme un aileron de requin. "J'ai fermé les yeux et pissé dans mon froc". Bateson fut pris de fou rire quand il me répéta la remarque de Love. La seconde suivante, son parachute s'ouvrait en secouant son harnais. Ton père, qui descendait sain et sauf, vit un Zéro plonger vers lui. Les Japonais avaient la sale habitude de voler sous les parachutistes ennemis pour leur trancher les jambes, les mutiler sans les tuer. "Le vol au quart de poil" était le summum de la cocasserie dans la bouche de ton père. Une rafale de mitrailleuse mit son parachute en lambeaux. Une balle l'atteignit dans le dos et traversa son abdomen selon un angle bizarre : elle frôla les artères et les organes vitaux, pulvérisant seulement un fragment de vertèbre thoracique — l'apophyse spinale, fragile excroissance osseuse de la colonne vertébrale. Ton père s'évanouit et tomba dans le Yang-tsê d'une hauteur de deux cents pieds. Des hommes de la tribu Lolo qui, sur la berge, avaient observé l'escarmouche et la chute spectaculaire de l'Américain, le repêchèrent.

« Traditionnellement, les Lolos étaient un peuple de chasseurs, mais ils s'étaient reconvertis dans la culture du pavot, *Papaver somniferum*, pour gagner de l'argent et troquer l'opium contre des armes et des articles divers. Bien que primitifs, ils possédaient comme tous les Chinois la fibre du commerce. Love avait des devises chinoises dans son blouson d'aviateur, ainsi qu'un précieux revolver de calibre 44. Les Lolos, qui échangeaient leurs services contre des marchandises, s'approprièrent ces articles et entreprirent de soigner ton père. Ils utilisèrent des herbes pour guérir ses brûlures et lui firent manger de grandes quantités d'opium afin de calmer ses souffrances.

« Love passa deux semaines en convalescence avec eux, les accompagnant à la chasse dès qu'il eut retrouvé ses forces. Par la suite, d'absurdes rumeurs s'élevèrent à propos de cet épisode. Le bruit courut que Love avait été initié dans cette tribu. Des vœux échangés, une coupe de sang partagée — je ne sais quoi. Il finit par partir, accompagné d'un guide. Voyageant de nuit, ils traversèrent les lignes jusqu'à notre camp et arrivèrent à un avant-poste communiste. Pendant cette marche, il découvrit ce monastère, où je crois qu'il passa la nuit. Son retour à Kunming fut quasiment triomphal.

« Comme il était prévisible, Love ne parla pas beaucoup de cet épisode de sa vie, se contentant de plaisanteries du genre de celles que me raconta Bateson. J'en entendis moi-même quelques-unes, qui me troublèrent. Son humour contenait une sorte d'abandon nihiliste. A propos de l'opium, il déclara de but en blanc : "Si j'avais su ce que c'était, je n'en aurais pas mangé. J'ai pris ça naïvement pour du crottin." Il ajouta qu'il soupçonnait les Lolos d'avoir du "sang hébreu" ; car ils avaient réussi à le soigner avec de la "soupe de poulet". "De la soupe de poulet ?" lui demandai-je. "Exactement. Seulement, ils avaient une façon originale de la préparer. Ils décapitaient une poule vivante, renversaient le cou au-dessus d'un bol, puis buvaient le contenu. Ça paraît dégoûtant, je sais, mais avec un peu de Worcestershire, je crois que tu t'y ferais." » Hsiao secoua la tête.

« Bien que l'aventure de ton père l'ait métamorphosé en héros, pour moi, Sun I, elle recelait maintes implications tragiques. Ma position privilégiée me permit de comprendre la culpabilité de Love après la nouvelle de la mort de son père, et comment elle l'avait conduit, inconsciemment, droit dans le viseur du pilote japonais. Si seulement il avait réussi à se réconcilier avec son père, comme je le fis avec le mien, malgré d'innombrables faux départs. J'attribue son échec à la différence de nos milieux sociaux respectifs. Elevé dans une tradition plus sage, plus humaine, j'ai pu dépasser mes antipathies, accorder à mon père le respect et l'obéissance auxquels sa position de chef suprême de la famille lui donnait droit. Le confucianisme m'a permis cela. Peu d'esprits ont pleinement compris que cette vérité réside au cœur de l'enseignement du Maître et illumine tout le reste de sa doctrine — nous devons honorer nos parents *indépendamment de leurs mérites personnels*, car ils sont les récipients sacrés du baume de la continuité sociale. C'est une vérité élevée, difficile. Aux non-initiés ou aux esprits manquant de discernement, elle semblera peut-être repoussante, voire fanatique, une forme de servitude spirituelle, de dévotion aveugle ou hypocrite. Mais c'est un paradoxe moral de grande valeur. Ce qu'est la Chine, ce qu'elle a accompli (une tradition culturelle ininterrompue pendant cinq mille ans n'est pas un mince exploit) est inextricablement lié à ce paradoxe, et au principe social qu'il implique. La piété filiale est le principe qui cimente le monde humain. S'il est oublié ou négligé, comme l'exprime ce poète irlandais que ton père aimait tant : "Les choses tombent ; le centre ne peut pas tenir ; l'anarchie se déchaîne sur le monde." J'ai appris cela fort tard, Sun I. Ma vie n'est pas exemplaire, mais au moins je l'ai compris. Je crains que ton père ne l'ait jamais appris.

« Love était conditionné par les valeurs occidentales — bravade, agressivité, adoration candide de la puissance et de la réussite, indépendamment des moyens employés pour y aboutir — si bien qu'il dut considérer son père comme un raté. Pour moi, Art Love fut l'un des personnages les plus estimables du panthéon de la haute finance américaine, au moins pour cette raison qu'il transcenda ses valeurs égoïstes et superficielles. Mais la haine de ton père fut sans doute décuplée par le dégoût des Américains pour la vieillesse, par cet antagonisme décourageant qui oppose là-bas les générations. Il n'en va pas de même ici en Chine, Sun I. En Amérique, on n'encourage pas les jeunes à glaner humblement l'expérience et le savoir plus vastes de leurs parents ; on les pousse à s'opposer à eux et, si possible, à les dépasser. Les générations sont condamnées à une guerre sans fin. Ce que l'une a bâti, la suivante œuvre pour le raser et construire son nouveau royaume sur les ruines de l'ancien, dresser ses murs de brique dans lesquels sont sertis, comme des fossiles, des fragments calcinés d'os humains. Ce processus ressemble curieusement aux cycles de prospérité et de crise du capitalisme américain. Ce comportement autodestructeur est profondément enraciné dans le tempérament américain, et virtuellement institutionnalisé dans leur gouvernement "démocratique" — où à peine les dirigeants installés, à peine leurs priorités et leurs initiatives définies, l'électorat les remplace par "quelque chose de nouveau et de meilleur" — et jusque dans leur religion, avec sa métaphore de la mort et de la résurrection. Vois-tu, Sun I, c'est cette éternelle insatisfaction de la réalité, de ce qui est, qui produit ce désir inquiet si caractéristique de l'Amérique et des Américains. Voilà pourquoi, tel le phénix, ce pays se détruit continuellement lui-même et tente de renaître de ses cendres. C'est aussi la principale promesse du christianisme. Qu'est-ce donc, sinon un tour de passe-passe ? Cela n'autorise le développement d'aucune tradition telle que nous en connaissons en Chine. Pour moi, Sun I, l'Amérique est l'image précise et glaçante de ce que doit être l'enfer, un labeur semblable à celui de Sisyphe qui roule sa pierre vers le sommet d'une haute montagne pour la voir dégringoler chaque fois qu'il touche au but. Quel pathos, quelle futilité... tragique. » Hsiao poussa un bref soupir de compassion. « Eddie Love était tout à fait ce genre de personnage. »

Le regret sincère qui perçait dans ces phrases ne fit qu'accroître mon respect pour mon oncle. Je le découvrais capable de pitié et de compassion pour ce qu'il détestait. Mais je ne pouvais souscrire à sa haine. D'autant que son intensité semblait passablement partisane. J'étais effrayé, décontenancé. Jamais je n'avais entendu parler de l'Amérique en termes aussi durs — comme d'un « enfer » — mais toujours comme d'un paradis ; je ne pouvais m'empêcher de me demander si une nécessité personnelle ne lui dictait pas des condamnations aussi sévères. Le plus souvent, je l'avais écouté passivement, voire avec crédulité ; mais chaque fois qu'il avait évoqué l'Amérique, son père ou le mien (surtout le mien), chaque fois que cette expression d'amer dégoût, si proche du sourire, avait tordu ses lèvres, j'avais ressenti une gêne — une gêne approfondie en malaise, parfois en douleur, à mesure qu'il approchait de la coda de son monologue. Le portrait de mon père surtout, qui me paraissait presque une charge, me déplaisait. Ses sous-entendus d'autosatisfaction le rendaient suspect à mes yeux. Et puis comment aurais-je pu tirer un trait sur vingt années d'adulation passionnée, même sur la base d'arguments aussi convaincants que ceux de Hsiao ? J'avais écouté avec délices le récit de tous les "faits". Mais les réminiscences de mon oncle avaient seulement fortifié ma conviction que mon père était un être extraordinaire. Pour moi, ces faits contredisaient précisément l'interprétation qu'il en faisait. Pourquoi aller chercher la folie afin d'expliquer les actes de mon père ? Rien de ce qu'il avait accompli ne me semblait particulièrement insensé — excentrique, peut-être, marqué du sceau indélébile de sa signature inimitable — mais nullement insensé. Je doutais surtout de ses allégations touchant au tempérament autodestructeur de mon père, qui aurait causé son accident d'avion. Il était peut-être plus facile pour Hsiao de taxer mon père de déséquilibré que d'affronter la vérité suggérée par Love : à savoir que Hsiao voyait le monde à travers le prisme de ses propres préoccupations, ses propres angoisses de fils. Voilà pourquoi il n'avait pas compris la remarque de mon père : « Tu es sûr de ne pas me confondre avec un autre ?... Toi, Hsiao. » Tout cela me semblait assez évident. Je devinais que les conceptions erronées de Hsiao tenaient davantage à son attitude ambiguë envers son propre père qu'à la prétendue folie du mien.

Ainsi, malgré tout le respect qu'il m'inspirait, je jugeai mon oncle présomptueux. « *Je savais qui il était !* Ayant découvert le père, j'avais découvert le fils. » Je n'étais pas d'accord. Je me rendais peut-être coupable du même péché, j'introduisais peut-être un biais dans mes jugements — un biais aussi profond et indéracinable que mon attitude fondamentale envers le monde —, mais je refusais ses conclusions avec passion, avec *véhémence* !

7

« Alors, Sun I, reprit Hsiao en interrompant ma rêverie, sans vouloir sembler mesquin — car j'aimais sincèrement ton père, je crois que tu en es maintenant convaincu — je me dis que son accident avait résolu mes problèmes. »

Mon regard incrédule, horrifié, lui fit aussitôt préciser sa pensée. « Vis-à-vis de Ch'iu-yeh, naturellement. » Il hocha la tête. « J'avais seulement différé mon entretien avec lui. Ce jour-là, près du bassin, il eût été impoli de sonder les intentions de Love vis-à-vis de ma sœur. Sa douleur, immense, méritait le respect. Ensuite, après son séjour chez les Lolos, la situation se dégrada. Love était le héros du moment ; les admirateurs grouillaient autour de lui. J'hésitai à percer la bulle flatteuse de sa célébrité (bien qu'elle me parût équivoque) avec l'aiguille d'une suspicion peut-être infondée. Rien d'indécent, en tout cas rien d'irrévocable ne s'était produit entre ma sœur et cet homme. Du moins, à ma connaissance.

« En plus de mes difficultés, un refroidissement subtil mais évident modifia nos relations à partir de ce moment — du côté de Love, pour être exact. Je remarquai une raideur nouvelle dans ses manières, derrière laquelle il se protégeait contre le secret que je partageais désormais avec lui. Cela m'attrista, car j'avais beau me méfier de ses intentions envers Ch'iu-yeh, je lui souhaitais du bien. L'homme m'intéressait énormément ; et ses dernières mésaventures, surtout son accident, avec ses implications de détresse psychologique latente, ne firent qu'accroître ma fascination. J'éprouvais pour Love un intérêt quasi scientifique, tel un chercheur observant une des plus rares espèces de la nature, peut-être un monstre. Cependant, au-delà de cet intérêt, j'éprouvais beaucoup de sympathie pour lui, plus que de la sympathie : il s'agissait d'une sorte d'identification. » Hsiao haussa tristement les épaules. « Malgré cela, le fossé se creusa entre nous. Eddie me fut inutile dans ma campagne pour éteindre l'incendie qui s'était allumé entre lui et Ch'iu-yeh. Je dus chercher de l'aide ailleurs.

« Mon allié le plus sûr, mon seul allié, fut ma mère. Vivant à la maison, "derrière les lignes", elle était mieux placée que moi pour suivre les derniers développements de l'affaire. Depuis son retour, me dit-elle, Love passait presque tous ses loisirs sous notre toit avec Ch'iu-yeh. Tout suggérait que la liaison amorcée lors de leur première rencontre s'épanouissait. Le temps dont Love disposait n'y était pas étranger ; car pendant toutes les semaines que dura sa convalescence, il ne vola pas. Ma mère était particulièrement choquée par la permission que Père accorda à Ch'iu-yeh de régler ses propres activités à sa guise. Quand mon père les vit se tenir par la main — spectacle qui aurait mortifié tout autre parent chinois —, il sourit jovialement et opina du chef. Tout cela me bouleversa. Je trouvais que Ch'iu-yeh jouissait de libertés que son éducation ne lui avait permis ni de respecter ni de défendre. Comme ma mère s'était révélée incapable de convaincre mon père des conséquences éventuelles de son libéralisme, elle me supplia de renoncer à ma fierté pour lui parler. Jusque-là, pour des raisons que je suis certain que tu apprécieras, j'avais décidé de ne confier à personne le secret de Love. Mais si le bonheur de Ch'iu-yeh en dépendait, je sentais qu'il valait mieux tout dire à mon père. J'étais persuadé qu'il comprendrait le péril et découragerait cette relation avant qu'elle n'ait eu le temps d'anéantir la vie de ma sœur.

« Mais dans mes calculs, j'avais négligé un facteur essentiel. Ainsi, mes révélations produisirent l'effet diamétralement opposé à celui recherché. Tandis qu'il écoutait mes confidences, mon père devint pensif. Je poursuivis et constatai avec horreur que ses yeux brillaient d'une lueur calculatrice que je connaissais trop bien. Malgré toutes ses faiblesses, je ne m'étais pas attendu à cela. J'ai honte de le dire, même aujourd'hui. Il ne sut pas résister aux perspectives commerciales que lui promettait cette alliance.

« Ainsi, plutôt que de mettre un terme à leur liaison, mon père l'encouragea en cachant soigneusement qu'il connaissait le secret de Love. Comme je le méprisai ! » Hsiao respira profondément. « Mais ensuite, il souffrit, ensuite il pleura des larmes de sang. La seule conséquence positive de toute cette affaire fut son ultime revirement. Car Père désavoua finalement les occidentalismes qu'il avait si aveuglément acceptés comme articles de foi, et qui étaient responsables de toute cette tragédie. Mais son abjuration arriva trop tard.

« Comme j'avais échoué avec lui, il ne me restait plus qu'un seul espoir. Ch'iu-yeh écouta patiemment ce que j'avais à lui dire, mais je voyais que mes paroles avaient pour seul effet d'affermir sa détermination à persévérer afin de l'emporter sur "les malentendus et les persécutions", comme les héroïnes des romans qu'elle avait lus. Dans ses yeux brillaient la joie indicible de son amour et la pitié qu'elle éprouvait pour moi, le malheureux incapable de comprendre le profond mystère dans lequel elle était immergée.

« Ce fut alors que je remarquai pour la première fois la transformation qui s'opérait en elle, et m'émerveillai en silence, me demandant si elle était seulement due à l'émotion qu'elle ressentait, ou s'il y avait autre chose. Elle devint étrangement taciturne, mais sans tristesse. On eût dit qu'un magnifique coucher de soleil l'inondait, répandait sur son âme ses couleurs chaudes, un éclat que je connaissais sans pourtant réussir à le situer, tel un souvenir d'une vie antérieure. Une candeur nouvelle apparut sur son visage, sa voix devint plus grave, altérée, comme si une marée l'entraînait vers les eaux plus profondes de sa féminité, loin de la sécurité du banc de sable où elle avait passé son enfance.

« Ce fut à ce moment qu'elle commença de coudre. Elle fila de la soie brute, la teignit en rouge sang, puis la tissa en soie damassée — un méandre labyrinthique. Quand cela fut achevé (elle travaillait rapidement), elle se retira dans sa chambre et entama les broderies. Elle faisait mystère de son ouvrage, et pourtant nous savions... Car le rouge est la couleur rituelle qu'on porte seulement en deux occasions : le mariage et la naissance. (Tu l'ignores peut-être, Sun I, mais *Fu*, le signe "heureux", est le premier élément du mot "rouge" — jeu de mots profondément enfoui dans notre rituel.) Tu vois, ta mère confectionnait son *p'ao*, la robe de mariée qu'elle comptait porter pour célébrer son union avec Eddie Love.

« Du moins nous le crûmes à l'époque. Et dans une certaine mesure, je le pense toujours. Pourtant, certains signes suggèrent qu'elle savait d'emblée que ce mariage n'aurait jamais lieu. Je me suis souvent demandé si elle ne connaissait pas déjà son état. Dès le début, elle a peut-être voulu te transmettre ce tissu, Sun I. L'explication la plus simple suffit sans doute ; cependant, un détail du vêtement me frappa quand je le vis pour la première fois, beaucoup plus tard, et m'a toujours semblé significatif. Ta mère broda le *Fu* du bonheur en plusieurs endroits, mais le signe *Shou*, qui l'accompagne toujours et signifie "longue vie", est absent. Comme si elle avait deviné qu'elle ne vivrait pas longtemps, même pas assez pour le porter. » La voix de mon oncle se troubla, il cacha son visage derrière sa main. Quand il redressa la tête, il ne me regarda pas, mais tourna les yeux au loin, vers le passé.

« Je ne sais plus combien de temps cette situation dura — deux mois, peut-être trois. Dans ma mémoire, un brouillard s'étend sur cette époque, une impression de légèreté et de dérive. Car à notre insu je crois que nous étions tous contaminés par leur amour, emportés par le rêve. Vers la fin, je me permis même brièvement d'espérer.

« Mais l'inévitable se produisit. Un jour, je lus un avis affiché sur la place du marché. J'aurais dû m'y attendre ; pourtant la nouvelle me prit complètement au dépourvu. Le destin œuvre parfois avec une ruse tellement insidieuse... Son ironie veut que nous aurions dû nous réjouir de la nouvelle. Pourtant, quand je la lus, mon cœur se brisa à cause de Ch'iu-yeh. L'avis annonçait l'entrée en guerre de l'Amérique. L'AVG serait dissous le 4 juillet — jour de l'Indépendance — et remplacé par les forces aériennes régulières. Après avoir résisté si longtemps et farouchement, les Tigres Volants rentraient chez eux, ou étaient libres de le faire. »

« Dès que je lus cet avis, je partis à pied vers la maison de mon père. Ch'iu-yeh devait savoir. En ce début de matinée, la rosée qui avait fixé la poussière du chemin ne s'était pas encore évaporée. Cela aurait pu rendre le trajet agréable, ma mission eût-elle été moins grave. Mais déjà, j'avais endossé le rôle que je tiens aujourd'hui devant toi, celui du messager de mauvais augure — un rôle que j'espère ne plus jamais devoir jouer.

« Quand j'atteignis le sommet de la longue pente qui s'élève des rizières jouxtant la cité, mon cœur battait la chamade. Je fis halte pour reprendre mon souffle et contempler de ce point de vue élevé les formes irrégulières des champs qui dessinaient comme un patchwork aux couleurs de la terre — vert pâle, ocre, jaune d'or — jusqu'à la vaste étendue du lac Tien Chih, dont les eaux boueuses s'agitaient sous une brise qui m'atteignit bientôt. Les paysans travaillaient déjà. Je les voyais, minuscules taches bigarrées, se déplacer à travers les nuances plus sombres du blé d'hiver qui montait jusqu'à leur poitrine, ou accompagner les points blancs plus gros de leurs bœufs, telles les voiles de navires en pleine mer, qui retournaient la terre en friche. Il se dégageait de ce panorama une impression de calme et d'éternité qui apaisa mon cœur, un sentiment de permanence qu'aucune vicissitude, pas même la guerre, ne semblait pouvoir altérer.

« Alors que je laissais la contemplation de l'horizon lointain me réconforter, j'entendis un grondement dans le ciel et, levant les yeux, j'aperçus l'escadrille de Love, les Pandas, qui volaient en formation serrée, comme une bande d'oies migratrices, près du soleil. Mais des oies redoutables, mangeuses d'hommes aux gueules barbares de carnivores, créatures cauchemardesques tout droit sorties du bestiaire de l'enfer. Les paysans aussi avaient interrompu leurs activités pour, la main en visière, regarder la vision qui traversait le ciel. Comme eux, j'étais un paysan bouche bée dans les rizières du Moyen Age tandis que la terrible épiphanie du futur surgissait au-dessus de nos têtes pour nous imposer un autre univers aussi incompréhensible que la magie — incarné par un chasseur américain équipé de mitrailleuses et de bombes incendiaires. Ce fut alors que je compris enfin cette évidence : les Américains qui étaient venus pour nous libérer étaient en fait nos plus grands ennemis. L'inertie humaine de la Chine était trop puissante pour être longtemps dévoyée par un envahisseur japonais ; comme dans le passé, nous finirions par digérer nos ennemis, conquérir les conquérants par l'assimilation. Mais qui aurait pu nous sauver de nos amis ? Car les Américains, peut-être sans même le vouloir, avaient acheté notre complicité dans leur grand projet qui consistait à nous refaire à leur image. Contrairement aux Japonais, ils travaillaient de l'intérieur, minaient les fondations, restructuraient jusqu'au désir. Et ma pauvre sœur se tenait sur le seuil de la nouvelle Loi. »

« Quand j'arrivai, la maison commençait à s'éveiller. Je rencontrai Chiang Po dans le jardin, qui travaillait sous la haie orientale. Il coupait de pâles chrysanthèmes jaunes avec son sécateur brillant en acier inoxydable, puis les posait dans un panier plat en osier. Il leva la tête à mon approche, me lança un regard furieux, puis se remit au travail. Alors, j'eus enfin la réponse à la question qui nous avait tant intrigués. Il était l'émissaire secret de Love. Une sensation proche du dégoût accompagna cette découverte, car je compris que les fleurs que Love envoyait à Ch'iu-yeh venaient de notre propre jardin.

« J'allai directement à la chambre de ta mère, et frappai à la porte. Ne recevant aucune réponse, je pris sur moi d'entrer. Elle reposait sur son lit de plumes, la couverture repoussée, ses épais cheveux noirs dénoués pour la nuit. Ils entouraient son visage comme une calligraphie tracée à l'encre la plus noire sur le tissu blanc du drap, un hiéroglyphe circulaire qui enfermait le message codé de son destin, mais écrit dans une langue pour moi incompréhensible. Pendant quelques minutes, je restai debout à côté du lit. La sueur perlait à la racine de ses cheveux. Ses paupières palpitantes suivaient les mouvements de ses yeux qui parcouraient le paysage intérieur d'un rêve. L'ombre et la lumière jouaient sur son visage ; ses lèvres balbutiaient en silence, comme si elle écoutait quelque vieille chanson familière dont elle fredonnait les paroles.

« Quand je la touchai, elle ouvrit aussitôt les yeux et s'assit. Je saisis sa main. "J'ai quelque chose à te dire", déclarai-je doucement. Elle me regarda sans comprendre, puis une terreur vertigineuse happa son visage. Elle serra ma main de toutes ses forces. Je hochai la tête et, pour dissiper ses inquiétudes, auxquelles elle était sujette depuis l'accident de Love, ajoutai rapidement :

« "Il va bien."

« Elle retomba sur l'oreiller et ferma les yeux. "L'AVG est dissous, lui dis-je. Ils vont rentrer chez eux, Ch'iu-yeh. Il y avait un avis au marché." J'attendis sa réponse, mais elle resta silencieuse. "Tu as entendu ?"

« Comme si elle faisait un effort gigantesque, ta mère ouvrit les yeux et me regarda. Il y avait de la lassitude et de la frustration dans ce regard, et aussi de la pitié. Mais au-delà, une sorte de... comment dire ? Un amusement triste, une distance désenchantée, comme de quelqu'un qui aurait regardé le monde de très haut après l'avoir quitté.

« "Je sais", murmura-t-elle d'une voix qui, par-delà sa fatigue superficielle, exprimait l'envoûtement, et avec le même visage que le soir où elle rencontra Love pour la première fois.

« Je restai bouche bée, n'en croyant pas mes oreilles. "Tu sais !" J'étais ébahi, Sun I, complètement ahuri. "Mais comment ? lui demandai-je quand j'eus retrouvé l'usage de la parole. Comment l'as-tu appris ?"

« Elle secoua la tête. "Peu importe. Je sais. Je l'ai toujours su." Elle scruta mon visage. "Tu ne comprends toujours pas, n'est-ce pas ?"

« "Non ! m'écriai-je. Je ne comprends rien du tout !"

« Ta mère soupira et détourna la tête. D'un geste léger du poignet, comme pour écarter une mouche estivale, elle me congédia. Elle regarda par la fenêtre ouverte, et son expression devint très calme, très distante, telles les montagnes du paysage, et comme elles, très froide. Aujourd'hui, je me demande si elle n'avait pas prévu le dénouement, et tout pardonné à l'avance. »

« Sun I, je ne peux me reprocher mes actes. Mes intentions étaient strictement honorables. » Sa voix hésita. « Mais je comprends aujourd'hui que chacune de mes interventions ne fit qu'aggraver la situation, excitant l'envie de mon père, et m'aliénant d'abord Love, puis Ch'iu-yeh. Oui, après cet incident, elle aussi se mit à m'éviter. De plus en plus impuissant, de plus en plus inquiet, j'envisageais avec désespoir l'enchevêtrement irrévocable des passions.

« Un autre mois s'écoula sans événement notable. Comme un accessoire de notre environnement qui avait toujours été là et le serait toujours, l'AVG ne montra aucun signe de démobilisation.

« La seule évolution visible concernait Ch'iu-yeh. Sa transformation physique suivait son cours inexorable. Je ne sais plus quand je découvris que son évolution n'était pas simplement spirituelle, mais aussi physique, changement attisé par le brusque apport d'hormones pendant que son corps se préparait à l'incroyable et dur mystère de la naissance. Ce fut peut-être cet après-midi-là dans le jardin ; par hasard, je tombai sur eux, alors qu'ils se retrouvaient sans doute pour la dernière fois, bien que tous deux l'ignorassent.

« Il était tard, entre chien et loup, comme la première fois. Ils étaient assis côte à côte près de l'endroit où Love avait jadis fait son numéro. Penché vers elle, sa main effleurant le bras de Ch'iu-yeh, il chuchotait à son oreille. Les yeux de ma sœur étaient clos, sa gorge et ses joues empourprées. Elle souriait timidement, les larmes d'une récente dispute n'avaient pas eu le temps de sécher sur ses joues. Ses deux mains pressaient une fleur contre sa poitrine — un chrysanthème. Un à un, elle arrachait les pétales blancs qu'elle jetait dans le bassin en murmurant des mots que je ne compris pas.

« Je l'observai enlever le dernier pétale, les yeux toujours clos. Tournant la fleur mutilée dans sa main, elle l'explora doucement de ses doigts, comme l'aveugle palpe le visage de ceux qu'il aime. Alors son sourire disparut ; elle pâlit, brisa la tige sans vie. Les pétales lumineux sombraient lentement dans les eaux foncées, saturées de tanin, du bassin, comme des feuilles de thé au fond d'une tasse. Maintenant tout oracle était superflu.

« Brusquement Ch'iu-yeh sanglota, se leva et faillit tomber en se dégageant de l'étreinte de Love. "Ce n'était qu'un jeu", l'entendis-je crier pour la calmer. Elle s'éloigna en courant, sanglotant de plus belle. Quelque chose dans sa course, une lourdeur languide qui métamorphosait ses mouvements en caricatures d'eux-mêmes me fit comprendre qu'elle était enceinte. Sans l'ombre d'un doute ni d'un espoir, je sus.

« Quand elle arriva devant moi, elle m'aperçut et se figea. Je n'ai jamais oublié son expression : on eût dit qu'elle s'éveillait d'un rêve. Une terreur indicible, sans fond, illuminait son regard. Je crois qu'elle avait enfin réalisé qu'il ne l'avait jamais aimée et ne l'aimerait jamais — pas à la façon dont elle avait rêvé et qu'elle réclamait. Je m'approchai pour la consoler, mais elle s'enfuit. J'hésitai, puis la suivis vers la maison. Au moment de franchir le seuil, je me retournai pour regarder Love une dernière fois, mais il avait disparu. »

« Quand mon père ouvrit finalement les yeux — ou plutôt rétrécit assez son champ de vision pour voir les choses sous une lumière réaliste —, l'état de Ch'iu-yeh le mit au désespoir. Cela servit de prétexte à notre réconciliation.

« Un jour, il me fit venir à la maison. Hurlant comme un possédé, se mordant les mains de rage ou pleurnichant comme un enfant, il m'informa du "déshonneur" de Ch'iu-yeh — un mot depuis longtemps absent de son vocabulaire, banni à cause de ses "associations rétrogrades". Love, profitant de sa jeunesse et de son innocence, avec toute la ruse et la fourberie du séducteur confirmé, l'avait dépouillée, assouvissant sa propre lubricité au prix de la dignité de Ch'iu-yeh, s'écria-t-il en peignant le tableau de l'opprobre le plus noir, mais pas nécessairement le plus véridique. Toute la faute lui incombait, poursuivit-il, car son cœur trop confiant attendait des autres le même code d'honneur que celui qu'il respectait. Si seulement il avait pu se douter de la duplicité fondamentale de cette crapule ! (Pour l'occasion, mon père avait oublié l'avertissement que je lui avais donné.) Love venait pourtant d'une si bonne — il voulait dire "riche" — famille ! Qui aurait pu soupçonner pareille infamie ? Et qu'était la richesse sans l'honneur ? Et caetera, et caetera. L'hypocrisie de Love était désormais une affaire entendue, bien que Père n'ait jamais sondé les intentions de l'Américain. Je vis aussitôt quel rôle mon père me réservait. Tous ses espoirs de "sauver la face", comme il disait, reposaient désormais sur moi.

« "Pourtant, quel gendre splendide il aurait fait !" gémit-il enfin, couronnant de cette lamentation une demi-heure d'injures pour la plupart injustifiées.

« Cette comédie me dégoûta. Ma désillusion dissipa la colère que j'avais d'abord ressentie contre Love. Une fois encore, une sympathie spontanée naquit en moi à la pensée du profond chagrin que la folie du père de Love, ou sa folie présumée, devait lui causer, un chagrin encore accru par l'indéracinable piété filiale du fils. Cela me rendait quasiment palpables la douleur et la solitude de ton père, et ce fut seulement en évoquant l'image de Ch'iu-yeh que je pus me rappeler à qui je devais fidélité et obéissance.

« Poussé par le pur devoir et sans le moindre espoir de succès, j'allai à la caserne pour affronter Love. Je constatai avec surprise que l'épreuve de la veille l'avait marqué. Ses yeux avaient perdu leur éclat, de profonds cernes bleutés les entouraient, résultat des nuits d'alerte ou de l'insomnie due à la culpabilité, je ne sais. Il était assis dans la "salle des mégots" de la cabane de garde, où il fumait d'un air apathique en jouant au solitaire. Un éclair passa dans ses yeux quand il me vit, puis la tristesse revint lorsqu'il comprit la raison de ma venue. Son visage se crispa, ses yeux restèrent rivés aux cartes, évitant mon regard.

« "Prends une chaise", me dit-il.

« Vu les circonstances, son hospitalité était blessante. Je restai debout et scrutai silencieusement son visage.

« "Allez, Hsiao, insista-t-il d'une voix lasse. Ne sois pas comme ça."

« Il approcha une chaise pour moi, et j'acceptai de m'asseoir.

« Il continua de battre et rebattre les cartes. "Prends-en une", me dit-il brusquement en me tendant le paquet.

« Je lui adressai un regard de reproche, mais il refusa d'en tenir compte. Je cédai une fois encore et choisis une carte.

« "Tu veux que je te dise ce que c'est ?"

« "Je suppose que, de toute façon, c'est ce que tu vas faire, non ?"

« "Dame de pique", dit-il en ignorant ma réponse.

« Il avait raison. Il reprit la carte, la remit dans le paquet, qu'il battit avant de me le tendre en éventail une deuxième fois. "Prends-en une autre."

« Je ne bronchai pas.

« "Prends-en une autre !" commanda-t-il en agitant les cartes devant mon visage.

« Je m'exécutai. De nouveau, la dame de pique.

« Pour la première fois depuis mon arrivée, Love croisa mon regard. "Elle sort toujours, cette salope", dit-il.

« Puis il rit, exactement comme l'après-midi où il avait stupéfait son public en tirant la grenade à main de son haut-de-forme. Mais son expression était tout sauf amusée — on aurait dit une grimace. Et le son qui sortit de sa gorge ne fut pas l'éclat de rire exubérant que j'attendais, mais une sorte de plainte aiguë que j'associai aussitôt au couinement du lapin que, ce même après-midi, il avait saisi par la peau du cou.

« J'eus envie de vomir. "C'est très malin, Eddie."

« "Non, pas du tout. Le paquet est truqué", réussit-il à éructer entre deux hoquets. Il essuya les larmes de ses yeux et retourna le paquet qu'il étendit sur la table. Il n'y avait que des dames de pique.

« "Je l'ai commandé spécialement, expliqua-t-il, pour mes dames de cœur."

« "Tu es fou", lui dis-je, dégoûté.

« Il haussa les épaules d'un air indifférent.

« Nous nous tûmes. Il continua de se convulser en silence. Retrouvant le contrôle de soi, il essaya autre chose.

« "Tu sais sans doute que nous allons rentrer." Je levai les yeux et soutins son regard. Sa cigarette pendait à la commissure de ses lèvres ; il se pencha en avant pour prendre son portefeuille dans sa poche arrière. "Laisse-moi te montrer quelque chose."

« A ma grande surprise, il sortit une photo. Je songeai alors qu'il était peut-être exactement comme les autres — pire encore... oui, pire. Cette idée me donna un plaisir plus doux que toute revanche.

« "Voici ma fiancée", expliqua-t-il en faisant glisser le cliché vers moi sur la table, comme s'il sortait une autre carte de son jeu.

« La jeune fille avait à peu près le même âge que ma sœur, mais ses cheveux étaient longs et soyeux, aussi jaunes que les épis de maïs, et pas noirs comme ceux de Ch'iu-yeh ; ses yeux étaient aussi bleus et souriants qu'un ciel d'été, et non sombres et pleins de tristesse.

« "Qu'en penses-tu ?" demanda-t-il sans réussir à s'empêcher de sourire.

« Toute haine disparut en moi. Ce "pire encore" dépassait les bornes. A cet instant, ton père semblait la vivante incarnation de ce demi-dieu, jeune et exubérant voleur de pommes, oublieux du désespoir qu'il causait — un bref regret avant de partir vers de nouvelles conquêtes, de nouvelles diversions. Je me sentis gêné par son incroyable naïveté.

« "Elle est très jolie", dis-je sincèrement, douloureusement.

« "N'est-ce pas ?" Il se pencha pour examiner la photo de près, vérifier avec plaisir ce qu'il savait déjà.

« "Mais il vaudrait mieux pour elle oublier qu'elle t'a jamais connu, Eddie", lui dis-je, m'obligeant à reprendre l'initiative.

« Il se raidit sur sa chaise.

« "Elle s'en remettra avec le temps, poursuivis-je. Mais pas Ch'iu-yeh, je le crains."

« "Ne dis pas ça, Hsiao. Ta petite sœur est plus solide que tu ne penses. Quelques larmes et ce sera fini."

« "Si je te comprends bien, rétorquai-je froidement, ton intention est de l'abandonner ?"

« Love soupira et secoua la tête. "Essaie de te mettre à ma place, Hsiao. Tu as vécu en Amérique. Tu sais ce qu'on pense de ce genre d'union, là-bas."

« "L'honneur varie donc tellement selon la latitude ?" demandai-je d'une voix glaçante. J'avais préparé cette réplique de longue date.

« "Ouais, ouais, je connais ça par cœur, esquiva-t-il, mais Hsiao, tu sais aussi bien que moi que ça ne marcherait pas. En Amérique, les mariages mixtes ne sont pas vraiment bien vus. Nous serions rejetés partout."

« "Tu veux dire que les gens penseraient que tu t'es abaissé à épouser une *squaw* ?" Je ne maîtrisais plus ma colère.

« "Ne prends pas les choses comme ça, se défendit-il. Ce n'est pas ce que moi, je pense, mais ce que les autres penseront peut-être."

« "Pourquoi te préoccuper de ce que pensent les autres ?"

« "Je dois vivre avec eux. Pas toi."

« "Alors pourquoi ne pas rester ici, en Chine, puisque tu es si sensible à l'opinion d'autrui ? Ici, je crois que la seule discrimination qu'on te ferait subir jouerait en ta faveur."

« L'air surpris avec lequel il accueilla ma suggestion me prouva qu'il n'avait jamais envisagé sérieusement cette possibilité.

« "Tu pourrais jouer au Grand Chasseur Blanc", ajoutai-je méchamment.

« Il réfléchit avant de répondre. "Non, dit-il en secouant tristement la tête, mais avec conviction, je ne pourrais jamais être heureux ici."

« Je ris amèrement. "Et le bonheur de ma sœur ?"

« Je lui rendis la photographie. "Réfléchis, Eddie. Réfléchis bien. Tu les as trompées toutes les deux. Heureusement, il est toujours en ton pouvoir de réparer la plus grave de ces injustices. Inutile de te dire ce que tu dois faire. Néanmoins, je dirai ceci : si tu rentres dans ton pays, tu blesses cette fille une deuxième fois, et Ch'iu-yeh encore plus profondément. Tout ce que tu as fait est encore pardonnable... Mais ensuite, plus de rédemption."

« Son visage montrait un désespoir si sauvage que je faillis le plaindre. Mais il ne dit rien.

« "Eh bien, Eddie, soupirai-je en me levant pour partir, qui sait ? Malgré toi, tu as peut-être sauvé Ch'iu-yeh du pire — du malheur de vivre avec un homme comme toi."

« Après cela je m'attendais à ne plus jamais revoir Love. J'imaginai qu'après sa démobilisation il prendrait ses jambes à son cou sans s'arrêter pour souffler, jusqu'à ce que la moitié du monde le sépare de sa honte. Ensuite, dans le contexte familier et rassurant de son foyer, il parviendrait à l'oublier progressivement, jusqu'à la réduire à une sorte de mauvais rêve, une plaisanterie douteuse. Il finirait même par y repenser avec fierté comme à un testament de sa virilité et de son charme, une preuve de son pouvoir sur les femmes.

« Mais selon son habitude, il me surprit. Il me fit comprendre une fois encore à quel point je connaissais mal cet homme, ses motifs profonds, ses émotions. Pour moi, Sun I, ton père a toujours évoqué ce haut-de-forme où je le vis plonger la main la première fois que je le rencontrai ; je ne savais jamais ce qui en sortirait — un lapin, ou une grenade à main. »

★

« Juste avant le départ des Américains, Tchang Kaï-chek instaura une fête en leur honneur, la Journée nationale de l'Aviation. Il y eut un défilé dans le centre de la ville, suivi d'une cérémonie où tous furent décorés du Grand Cordon spécial du Ciel Bleu et du Soleil Blanc, la plus haute distinction militaire qu'un étranger pût recevoir. Le Généralissime en uniforme blanc, un lourd sabre cliquetant à sa hanche ceinte de soie noire, avançait sur l'estrade, serrait la main de chaque aviateur et s'inclinait cérémonieusement devant lui. Il tenait sa casquette contre son corps, coincée sous le bras, et pliait la nuque en signe de déférence et de gratitude. Mme Tchang suivait un peu plus loin, un grand sourire décontracté aux lèvres, et bavardait avec les pilotes dans son anglais du Texas tandis qu'elle épinglait les médailles sur leurs poitrines. J'observais la scène, perdu au milieu de la foule. Quand ils arrivèrent à Love, je songeai que le cœur humain est un domaine étrange ; car bien qu'héroïque au combat, l'Américain avait trahi la confiance la plus intime et la plus grave. Qui aurait pu m'expliquer ce paradoxe ? Les dieux se moquent certainement de nous en nous confrontant à de telles énigmes.

« Quand Mme Tchang épingla la récompense sur son torse — à l'endroit précis où il avait piqué le faux chrysanthème qui fut à l'origine de tout —, je surpris le regard de Love. Il rougissait de fierté. Bien qu'un peu hâve, il semblait se remettre facilement de la blessure intérieure que, de toutes mes forces, j'avais tenté de lui infliger. Je fis demi-tour et me frayai un chemin à travers la foule, soudain au bord des larmes.

« Je n'étais pas allé très loin quand je sentis une main se poser sur mon épaule : c'était Love. Il haletait.

« "J'ai dû courir pour te rattraper. Ecoute, Hsiao." Il s'interrompit pour reprendre son souffle. Son visage était congestionné par l'effort et le bonheur irrépressible de celui qui va retrouver sa patrie après une longue absence. Il paraissait extrêmement beau en cet instant, d'une beauté intolérable.

« "Je n'ai rien à te dire", lui lançai-je en sentant mon cœur se glacer. Pourtant, Sun I, je ressentais aussi de la peur ; et je savais que cette peur me concernait, parce que Love, qui aurait dû être mon ennemi, m'importait.

« "Je n'en ai pas pour longtemps, m'apaisa-t-il. Je sais ce que tu penses de moi, Hsiao."

« "Vraiment, Eddie ? m'interrogeai-je en silence. Le sais-tu vraiment ?"

« "Tu es peut-être en droit de penser ça. Je veux juste que tu saches que je suis sincèrement désolé de ce qui s'est passé. Je n'ai jamais voulu que les choses tournent ainsi. Mais j'ai réfléchi et j'ai décidé que rester ici et épouser Ch'iu-yeh serait encore pire. Jamais elle ne me pardonnerait ; et je ne me pardonnerais jamais moi-même. Personne ne serait heureux."

« "Encore le bonheur, rétorquai-je cyniquement. Pourquoi as-tu toujours ce mot à la bouche ? Tu te comportes comme si le bonheur était une sorte de droit fondamental."

« La surprise, le doute, et une étincelle d'ironie destinée à contrer la mienne jouèrent sur ses lèvres, ébauchèrent un sourire. Quand il comprit que je parlais sérieusement, la sincérité et la gravité l'emportèrent.

« "C'est vrai, dit-il avec un beau sourire. Qu'y a-t-il d'autre ?"

« Je fouillai son visage à la recherche de la moindre trace d'impertinence, mais il était absolument sérieux. Je compris alors pour la première fois à quel point il était jeune ; malgré moi, sa dignité et sa candeur m'émurent. Le spectacle d'instincts aussi purs mis au service d'une conception aussi naïve du monde me frappa comme une tragédie impondérable. Distillée jusqu'à son essence, je crois que c'était cette particularité de l'Amérique qui nous exaspérait tant, nous autres — le vieux monde, *les* vieux mondes — et en même temps nous inspirait paradoxalement une vision de rédemption.

« Mais j'étais trop blessé, trop combatif, pour céder à semblables émotions. "C'est vrai, répliquai-je avec mépris. J'avais oublié la Déclaration d'Indépendance. Le bonheur est garanti."

« "Hsiao, dit-il doucement, ignorant ma remarque, il n'y a rien d'autre à faire."

« "Pourquoi m'as-tu arrêté, alors ?" lui lançai-je avec colère et impatience. Tout cela a déjà été réglé. Tu as donc plaisir à répéter cette scène ?"

« Il secoua tristement la tête. "Non. Je suis venu te demander un service."

« Je le regardai, incrédule. Il acquiesça gravement.

« "Que peux-tu bien vouloir me demander ?"

« "Cela concerne l'enfant."

« "L'enfant !" J'étais stupéfait. "En quoi cela te regarde-t-il ?"

« "Je tiens à faire ce que je peux, expliqua-t-il. Je me sens responsable."

« "Tu te sens responsable envers l'enfant, mais pas envers la mère ? Je te prie d'excuser mon esprit obtus, Eddie, mais je ne comprends pas. Explique-toi."

« "Pardonne-moi, Hsiao. L'enfant est innocent ; Ch'iu-yeh a fait un choix."

« Je grimaçai, mais retins ma langue. Un long silence suivit, où je le jaugeai avec férocité.

« "Je t'ai toujours bien aimé, Hsiao", dit-il enfin.

« "Pourquoi cette faveur ?" le coupai-je brutalement.

« Love soupira. "J'ai passé un accord avec l'abbé d'un monastère."

« "Un monastère ! Tu as perdu la tête ? Nous ne sommes pas dans l'Europe catholique du Moyen Age, tu sais."

« "As-tu une meilleure idée ?" Ses yeux étincelants se posèrent sur moi pour la première fois depuis le début de notre conversation.

« A mon grand chagrin, je n'en avais pas.

« "Alors ?"

« Je restai silencieux.

« Love sembla interpréter ma perplexité comme de la rancune. Une trace d'animation apparut sur son visage.

« "En plus, Hsiao — il reprit le ton jovial qu'il avait adopté avant l'aggravation de la situation — c'est vraiment un endroit super." Il sourit.

« "*Super* !" répétai-je en grognant de dégoût, sans en croire mes oreilles.

« "Que connais-tu exactement des monastères chinois, Eddie, si je peux me permettre ?"

« "Eh bien, j'ai séjourné dans l'un d'eux, au Szu-ch'uan, après avoir été abattu. Tu te souviens ?"

« "Première nouvelle."

« "Ça te plairait, Hsiao." Il sourit d'un air rêveur. "L'abbé est un vieux bonhomme extraordinaire, un véritable oiseau rare. En fait, le plus étrange est qu'il m'a rappelé mon…" Ton père s'interrompit brusquement, mais je vis son visage s'assombrir tandis que son esprit suivait le cours de ses pensées.

« "De quelle sorte de monastère s'agit-il ?" demandai-je calmement.

« Il parut s'éveiller de sa rêverie. "Devine", dit-il en souriant.

« "Pour l'amour du ciel, Eddie, ce n'est pas un jeu."

« "Ça tombe sous le sens !" fit-il en ignorant mon reproche. Il me lança un clin d'œil.

« Je jugeai scandaleuse sa légèreté. Mais j'avais appris à entrer dans son jeu. "Bouddhiste, j'imagine."

« "Faux."

« "Taoïste alors."

« Il répondit par un hochement de tête exagéré.

« "Et alors ?" Ses mystères à bon marché me rendaient furieux et impatient.

« "Je tiens à ce qu'il soit éduqué dans la religion de ses ancêtres."

« "Que veux-tu dire ? Il n'y a pas de taoïstes dans notre famille et, autant que je sache, il n'y en a jamais eu."

« "Je ne parle pas de *ta* famille, dit Love, mais *de la mienne*."

« "Que dis-tu ? Tu as des ancêtres taoïstes ?" J'étais parfaitement exaspéré.

« "Bien sûr. Les Love ont toujours adoré le Tao." Il y avait un éclair, une lueur de folie dans son regard. "Bon dieu, nous l'avons quasiment inventé !"

« Je secouai la tête. "Je suis désolé, Eddie, mais je ne comprends plus."

« "Qu'y a-t-il de si incompréhensible ? Réfléchis une seconde, Hsiao. Il sera le dernier taoïste d'une longue lignée de taoïstes. Le même mais différent."

« Une faible lumière vacilla au fond de mon cerveau. "Tu veux dire…"

« Il acquiesça, m'exaspérant toujours par l'effronterie de son sourire. "C'est ça", répondit-il. "Tao — D-O-W (il épela pour éviter tout malentendu) comme dans l'Index industriel Dow Jones."

« "Impossible ! m'écriai-je, indigné. Tu es complètement fou. C'est monstrueux ! Impensable ! As-tu la moindre idée de ce qu'est le Tao (je veux dire T-A-O) ? C'est l'antithèse absolue de la chose adorée par *ta* famille."

« Love haussa les épaules. "C'est l'essence ultime de l'univers, n'est-ce pas ?" Il éclata d'un rire dément.

« "Oui, dis-je, mais…"

« "Voilà ! s'écria-t-il sur un ton sans réplique. Tu as tout compris !" »

« Après cet épisode, Sun I, pouvait-on encore douter de la folie de ton père ? Bien qu'il donnât l'impression fallacieuse d'une sorte de "méthode" déconcertante, et qu'il jouît de longues périodes de lucidité, la suite des initiatives que prit ton père révélait sa folie. Selon l'expression courante, il était fou à lier.

« Ton visage me dit que tu renâcles devant mes conclusions. Mais comment expliquer cela autrement ? Cette nonchalance oblique avec laquelle il prit cette décision, une décision qui décida de ta vie, et dont il avait assumé la responsabilité, assumé *volontairement* la responsabilité — comment la nommer, sinon par le mot de folie ? Choisir l'avenir d'un être, de son propre enfant, sur la base d'un jeu de mots ! Et quel jeu de mots !

« Le plus difficile à expliquer est peut-être le soutien que j'apportai au plan de ton père. Mais je n'avais pas le choix, Sun I. Je ne trouvai pas de meilleure idée. Et puis, comme je l'ai dit, sa folie avait quelque chose de méthodique. A maints égards, ce plan semblait le meilleur pour tout le monde ; pour Ch'iu-yeh, à qui il donnait l'espoir de reprendre une vie normale, et pour toi, mon garçon, parce que franchement il n'y avait rien d'autre à faire. Je devins donc son agent exécutif. Quand il m'expliqua le rôle qu'il voulait que je joue, il était de nouveau étonnamment lucide. Il avait réglé jusqu'au moindre détail comme s'il s'était agi d'une stratégie de combat. Il m'incombait de te livrer sain et sauf au monastère, puis, au bout d'un certain nombre d'années, de revenir pour accomplir ce que j'ai fait aujourd'hui — essayer de te donner une idée de ton histoire. De te donner cela, et autre chose encore... mais l'heure de ce deuxième don n'a pas encore sonné. »

Mon oncle s'interrompit et soupira de lassitude. « Ce qui m'amène à la dernière partie de mon récit, Sun I. Car il reste à raconter l'histoire de ta mère, qui est brève. Et infiniment triste. Chaque fois que je me souviens d'elle, je pense au vers du *Shih Chinq* :

Dans l'arrière-pays vit une biche ;
Parmi les roseaux blancs elle s'attarde... à jamais.
L'approche du printemps faisait palpiter le cœur d'une jeune fille ;
Les promesses d'un beau voyageur causèrent sa perte.

« Ce qu'elle ressentit, les pensées qui l'occupèrent pendant ses mois de réclusion, je peux seulement les conjecturer. Elle ne m'en parla jamais, ni à personne — sauf, peut-être, à Chiang Po, que le départ de Love endeuilla pareillement. Fidèle au rituel désormais morbide, il continua de lui apporter les mêmes chrysanthèmes qu'auparavant, et jusqu'à la fin de la saison. Les fleurs prenaient maintenant un aspect funèbre, qui me terrifia. Je voulus lui épargner la torture de semblables associations. Mais les chrysanthèmes avaient beau l'attrister, elle semblait avoir besoin de leurs visites. Je n'eus pas le cœur d'ordonner à Chiang Po d'interrompre son manège.

« Peut-être parlaient-ils ensemble de Love, je l'ignore. Mais chaque fois que j'évoquais ce sujet, ta mère tournait simplement la tête vers la fenêtre pour contempler les montagnes, comme elle le fit le jour où je crus lui annoncer le départ de Love. Que voyait-elle là-bas ? Sans doute la puissance du massif nimbé de lumière froide, sa grandeur inhumaine.

« Un seul objet concentrait désormais toute son attention. La robe. Jour et nuit, elle s'appliquait à ses broderies. Il y avait une sorte de désespoir fébrile dans sa façon de travailler. Elle semblait craindre de ne pas finir à temps, bien qu'aucun de nous ne comprît la raison de son travail, maintenant que tous ses espoirs s'étaient écroulés. Ce mystère nous était insupportable. Il existait pourtant une explication, la pire : que la douleur soit venue à bout de l'esprit de Ch'iu-yeh. Nous n'en parlions jamais, mais je crois que cette éventualité nous obsédait tous, jusqu'à mon père, qui à partir de cette époque se retira graduellement du monde. Il négligea ses intérêts, mangea peu, se mit à errer la nuit dans la maison en parlant seul. Quelles qu'aient été les préoccupations de Ch'iu-yeh (aujourd'hui encore, je les ignore), il est certain que cette robe exerça une emprise terrible sur son imagination. A la fin, cela devint une obsession. Tous ses troubles cachés, ses douleurs inexprimées passèrent dans cette broderie, et le cruel espoir qui la nourrit la tourmenta jusqu'à la fin. C'est un objet splendide et effrayant (tu le verras, Sun I ; mais pas encore), une tapisserie pleine de symboles et de présages terribles. Quand elle interrompit son ouvrage — deux jours seulement avant d'entrer en travail —, une expression lointaine adoucit son visage et me fit craindre le pire. On aurait dit le regard d'un athlète après la course. Son esprit était en paix, mais c'était la paix de qui aspire à sombrer dans l'inconscience de la mort, du voyageur qui touche au but. »

« Tu es né pendant la nuit de la pleine lune d'août alors que l'été nous brûlait de ses derniers feux. Bien qu'il fît très chaud, je me souviens de traces de fraîcheur, les premières de l'année, qui imprégnaient l'air comme un carillon lointain. On avait ouvert en grand les fenêtres de la chambre de ta mère pour faire entrer cette prémonition de l'automne. La sage-femme âgée maugréa, mais le médecin, un officier américain qu'on avait été chercher à la base sur la demande de mon père, ne s'y opposa pas. Ce fut un accouchement relativement peu compliqué, d'après ce que j'ai appris. Vers la fin cependant, il se passa une chose étrange, que ma mère me raconta ensuite. Alors que Ch'iu-yeh reposait dans son lit, calée entre les oreillers et cherchant son souffle, au milieu d'une puissante contraction elle cria le nom de ton père. A ce moment, la lumière vacilla et une ombre palpita sur le lit. Quand j'entendis les cris stupéfaits des gens présents dans la pièce, je me ruai à l'intérieur, redoutant un malheur. Tous levaient les yeux vers une énorme phalène qui était entrée par la fenêtre ouverte et décrivait des cercles autour de l'ampoule nue. A ce spectacle, je frissonnai de tous mes membres.

« Ta mère gémit alors, et ton pied émergea ; car, né par le siège, tu es arrivé dans le monde comme un nageur qui tâte l'eau avant d'y plonger.

« Je ne suis pas superstitieux, Sun I, mais l'image de cette phalène ne m'a jamais quitté. Elle arriva juste après le cri de Ch'iu-yeh, comme une émanation d'un autre monde, l'émissaire fantomatique d'Eddie Love, son mandataire pour la naissance. Il est pourtant inutile de forcer les faits. Aussi bien, ç'aurait pu être un présage de mauvais augure, car le lendemain de ton accouchement une infection se déclara dans la matrice de ta mère. Le médecin affirma qu'il n'y avait pas lieu de s'inquiéter, qu'il s'agissait d'une complication mineure fort commune. Mais l'infection se propagea de façon incontrôlable dans tout le ventre. Ma sœur agonisa pendant plusieurs jours ; elle délira souvent, car elle refusa la morphine que mon père avait réussi à se procurer — comme pour le punir, ou se punir elle-même, ou simplement la vie, la vie en elle. Quand elle était lucide, elle souffrait beaucoup. Elle sombra enfin dans l'inconscience et mourut quelques heures après.

« Le jeune médecin était désespéré quand il vint nous apprendre sa mort. "Je ne comprends pas, dit-il. Les antibiotiques auraient dû enrayer l'infection."

« J'eus pitié de sa foi naïve. Malgré toute son intelligence et son savoir médical encyclopédique, il ne pouvait comprendre ce simple fait que Ch'iu-yeh avait renoncé... Non, elle n'avait pas renoncé ; ta mère a désiré la mort. Contre cette résolution, toutes ses connaissances médicales, qu'il avait payées si cher, furent inopérantes. Rien n'aurait pu la dissuader. Après ta naissance, Sun I, je crois que ta mère sentit sa tâche terminée. La mort dut être un grand soulagement pour elle. Je l'espère. »

8

Bien que sa voix fût ferme, de grosses larmes roulaient sur les joues de mon oncle quand il conclut.

En revanche, mes yeux étaient secs, et l'étaient restés tout au long de la narration. Celle-ci avait duré plusieurs heures ; Hsiao avait joué avec mes émotions comme d'un instrument, en parcourant toute la gamme, de l'insupportable angoisse de l'attente à la pitié et au désespoir pour finir par une sorte de joie fiévreuse. Ou même de bonheur, comme celui du mendiant pour qui les cieux s'ouvrent, révélant leurs trésors ; car mon histoire me semblait ainsi — une minuscule crèche d'ivoire, un camée figurant le visage d'une femme, un sceau portant une promesse et une obligation, deux émeraudes sombres en forme de larmes aux couleurs du mystère de Love. Tel un mendiant, possédé d'une faim tactile nourrie par l'absence, je palpais et caressais mes joyaux, jaugeant poids et rondeurs, les levant vers le soleil pour compter leurs facettes et leurs pailles. Je me repaissais de ces possessions, moi qui n'avais jamais rien possédé, sans comprendre ni me soucier de ce que le précieux héritage que la vie venait de m'offrir — la bénédiction d'une histoire — était au mieux équivoque, et peut-être une malédiction. Mais je n'avais pas pleuré.

L'excitation avait exacerbé mon imagination, abandonnée dans un état d'apathie post-tumescente, ou plutôt dans une paix triste et clairvoyante où je reconnaissais que quelque chose en moi et dans le monde avait changé, définitivement changé, et que le Sun I qui s'était assis en tailleur aux pieds de son oncle pour écouter une histoire du passé avait disparu, déposé, dépouillé de sa souveraineté, réduit au statut de monarque titulaire et remplacé par un régent que je connaissais à peine. Comme après une transmutation alchimique, une mitose émotionnelle, je m'étais moi-même divisé, et mon « fœtus immortel », mon alter ego, dont l'embryon avait toujours été présent en moi, était né... ou rentré en possession de son propre héritage après d'amères années d'un exil affamé. Mais qui était-il ? Qui étais-je ? Cette question, qui ne s'était jamais posée auparavant, faisait maintenant problème. Je ne savais plus. La connaissance de mon origine et de mon histoire m'avait dépossédé de moi-même.

Plus que jamais, je croyais la réponse liée à mon père. Qui était cet homme, Eddie Love ? Son identité semblait encore plus fuyante que la mienne, mais les deux étaient connectées, si bien qu'en trouvant l'une je trouverais l'autre. Son mystère était mon mystère.

Cette idée m'enchanta. Tandis qu'elle voletait dans mon esprit, je souriais comme un nouveau-né qui contemple les couleurs réfractées de l'arc-en-ciel à travers un prisme placé au-dessus de sa tête.

Mais je retournai peu à peu à mon ancien moi. Cet émerveillement paisible, presque agréable, s'évapora comme une nuée, laissant derrière lui un résidu plus durable, quoique moins plaisant : la peur. Je pris conscience d'une irritation lancinante de mon cœur, comme les grattements inquiets et incessants d'un animal ou d'un insecte dans la charpente d'une maison, qui cherche à en sortir, ou à s'y enfouir. Ce fut pour moi quelque chose de nouveau. Pourtant, je sentis que ces griffes avaient toujours été là, juste en deçà du seuil de la perception.

Perdu dans mes rêveries, je ne remarquai pas que mon oncle Hsiao s'était levé pour aller chercher Chong Fou. Quand je revins à moi, je découvris les deux hommes debout au-dessus de moi qui m'observaient, soucieux et attentifs.

« Où étais-tu parti, petit frère ? » me demanda Chong Fou d'une voix triste et étouffée qui suggérait (comme la brume et un changement de température indiquent la proximité d'un vaste océan insoupçonné) la présence en lui d'un profond réservoir de compassion.

Quand je regardai ses yeux, où la lueur de gaieté était maintenant voilée mais non éteinte, je sus qu'il comprenait ma douleur et souffrait avec moi. Mes propres yeux s'emplirent de larmes. Le doux soulagement que j'avais refusé jusqu'alors m'emporta. Je penchai la tête et pleurai calmement dans les plis de ma soutane.

Quand je cessai de pleurer et que mon cœur fut soulagé, mon oncle reprit doucement la conversation.

« Sun I, dit-il, fidèle au souhait de ton père, je t'ai raconté ces choses en tête à tête. Mais si j'avais eu le choix, j'eusse préféré que ton maître restât avec nous. Pourtant, je comprends la clause requise par Love, car les problèmes personnels tels que ceux-ci exigent délicatesse et circonspection. Partage-les si tu le désires ; c'est ton privilège et non ton obligation. Nous en avons fini, et tu as probablement des questions. J'ai demandé à Chong Fou de se joindre à nous, car ses vues peuvent compléter les miennes, corriger éventuellement certains jugements excessifs. J'espère qu'il corroborera mon point de vue sur la folie de ton père, et qu'il t'aidera à trouver la paix.

— Folie ! répéta le maître avec étonnement. Est-ce donc la conclusion que vous avez tirée ? Love fut certainement difficile à comprendre, du moins au début. Mais fou ? J'ai du mal à le croire.

— Pouvez-vous vous expliquer, maître ? le pressai-je.

— Connaissez-vous l'histoire de la rencontre de Confucius avec Lao-tseu ?

— *Oui* », dit Hsiao d'un air pincé.

Je secouai négativement la tête.

Ignorant Hsiao, le maître se tourna vers moi. « Les choses se passèrent ainsi, Sun I. Vois-tu, Confucius commit une sérieuse erreur. Il interrogea Loa-tseu à propos d'un détail de l'étiquette d'un rituel. Il reçut une rude rebuffade (certaines versions parlent même d'un coup de pied dans le fondement), puis il retourna désespéré vers ses disciples. » Le maître m'adressa un clin d'œil. « Il était si humilié qu'il était presque *fou* lui-même. Heureusement, ou malheureusement — à toi d'en décider —, l'un de ses protégés, un homme subtil à l'œil acéré, put noter avec une plume d'oie les divagations du vieux maître Kong :

> Le ciel a donné aux bêtes sauvages de la forêt des pattes pour s'éloigner de moi en courant ; de même, les poissons des profondeurs ont des nageoires pour fuir ; les oiseaux possèdent leurs ailes pour s'écarter du danger. Pour les ailes, il existe des lacs ; pour les nageoires, des filets ; pour les pattes, des pièges. Mais du dragon — qui sait comment il s'élève vers le ciel dans la brume et les nuages ? Aujourd'hui, j'ai rencontré Lao-tseu, et cet homme est un dragon. »

« Cette anecdote est manifestement apocryphe, interrompit Hsiao, l'œuvre de quelque scribe taoïste malicieux. Les dates rendent hautement improbable pareille rencontre.

— Les dates ? » Chong Fou éclata d'un rire tonitruant. Je crois bien que malgré moi je ris aussi.

« Bon ! » maugréa Hsiao. Il rougit d'embarras.

« Vous devez reconnaître que cela éclaire certaine situation, fit remarquer Chong Fou sur un ton plus conciliant.

— Je ne reconnais rien », répliqua Hsiao.

Le maître haussa les sourcils.

Hsiao renifla deux fois d'un air de dignité offensée, avança le menton, lissa un temps sa robe, puis nous pardonna magnanimement en disant : « Si nous voulons essayer d'aboutir à une conclusion en cette affaire si importante, messieurs, je suggère que nous nous en tenions aux faits.

— Oui, bien sûr, concéda Chong Fou avec diplomatie, vous avez tout à fait raison, les faits... Eh bien, laissez-moi vous raconter l'arrivée de Love telle que je m'en souviens.

« Tard un après-midi, nous entendîmes un bourdonnement dans le ciel qui s'amplifia bientôt en un hurlement strident. Nous sortîmes en courant dans la cour pour voir ce qui se passait. Un avion passa en rase-mottes au-dessus des toits, si bas que le vent de l'hélice aplatit le seigle dans le potager et souleva des tourbillons de poussière sur le chemin. C'était un appareil japonais : ses ailes portaient deux soleils rouge sang. Le crépitement des mitrailleuses me fit d'abord croire que nous étions attaqués. J'essayai frénétiquement de rassembler les moines à l'intérieur. Mais presque aussitôt, un deuxième avion nous survola, identifiable aux mâchoires béantes peintes sur son museau, ou son nez — je ne connais pas la terminologie. Bref, c'était un Américain, qui harcelait le premier appareil, si bien que plusieurs moines se mirent à applaudir. Je trouvai bizarre de fêter divinité aussi féroce, mais je me laissai aller à l'enthousiasme général et frappai moi aussi dans les mains.

« Les avions montèrent, leur taille devint celle de petits oiseaux. La main en visière, nous les regardions, médusés, tourbillonner, piquer et s'esquiver comme pour jouer ou accomplir un rituel nuptial compliqué, deux créatures angéliques dans le silence bleu de l'espace. Alors l'un d'eux explosa — une énorme boule de feu orange — et la seconde suivante une explosion mille fois plus violente que le tonnerre secoua la montagne. La beauté et l'horreur du spectacle me coupèrent le souffle — la grâce trompeuse de la danse, puis la vaporisation d'une vie humaine. Bouche bée, nous vîmes le deuxième appareil chuter derrière les montagnes en traînant derrière lui un panache de fumée noire. Profondément éprouvés après le plaisir profane que nous avions pris au spectacle, nous rentrâmes afin de prier pour que la vie du deuxième pilote fût épargnée.

« Quelques jours passèrent. Nous avions presque oublié cet incident quand, un matin, un petit groupe de Lolos se présentèrent à la porte avec un jeune Américain. Pâle et amaigri, il était épuisé par son voyage, hébété par l'opium dont ils l'avaient nourri pour calmer sa douleur. Il dormit dix-huit heures d'affilée, jusqu'au lendemain à la tombée de la nuit. Il se réveilla régénéré. Je me souviens de lui et de notre entrevue comme si c'était hier. Malgré ses traits hâves, il était grand et très beau selon les critères occidentaux. Son visage était avenant et mobile. Il souriait souvent, et bien. Ses dents étaient très blanches. En plus de son charme physique et malgré sa connaissance approximative du chinois, il appréciait beaucoup la conversation et avait un faible pour les plaisanteries. Il était manifestement bien éduqué. Cependant, il avait une nervosité dans le regard qui sondait constamment la surface des choses à la recherche d'un élément que, je le crains, cette surface ne pouvait lui offrir. Je me rappelle l'avoir comparé à une hirondelle volant de branche en branche sans jamais se poser. Je n'avais jamais vu pareille inquiétude. Même en tenant compte de son état et des circonstances, je ne parvins pas à l'expliquer. Mais il me plaisait, il me plaisait beaucoup, et je ressentais aussi pour lui une certaine pitié. Car en l'écoutant parler et en observant ses mimiques, je soupçonnai que son cœur était le geôlier d'un malheur qui dépassait toute souffrance physique, et je m'interrogeai sur sa cause.

« Il se restaura, nous bavardâmes brièvement, puis je l'emmenai visiter le monastère. Je lui montrai les jardins et les cloîtres, Sun I, puis je l'emmenai au sommet de la tour sud-ouest, qui abrite la clepsydre. Apparemment, Love n'avait jamais vu d'horloge à eau. L'ingénieuse simplicité de son mécanisme — le goutte à goutte de l'eau, les cercles concentriques dans le puits en chêne — durent éveiller un écho dans son esprit, car il resta longtemps à regarder l'eau qui s'égouttait de la citerne supérieure, serpentait le long du mince tuyau, perlait, puis tombait dans la vasque inférieure, comme des larmes. De fait, ces gouttelettes qui font monter imperceptiblement le niveau et se convertissent en minutes et en heures, sont appelées "les larmes du temps".

« Le hasard voulut que six heures sonnèrent alors que nous étions là-haut. » Le maître se tourna vers Hsiao pour expliquer. « Notre clepsydre a un cycle de douze heures. Chaque matin et chaque soir à six heures, le puits est plein. L'eau fait alors basculer un lourd poids relié par une corde au battant de la cloche de la tour. Ainsi les moines sont-ils convoqués à la méditation. Le mouvement du poids ouvre également une écluse au bas du puits, par laquelle l'eau se rue dans une douve circulaire. Puis elle retourne vers la citerne, et le cycle recommence.

— Je vois, dit mon oncle, qui écoutait très attentivement. Dispositif admirable. Au cours de mes recherches, j'ai lu la description d'instruments comparables. Elle doit être très ancienne.

— Oui, acquiesça Chong Fou. On dit qu'elle fonctionne sans interruption depuis trois cents ans. Dans son va-et-vient, elle ressemble aux marées de la mer.

— En plus régulier ! ajouta Hsiao, profondément impressionné.

— Oui, en plus régulier », dit le maître. Il sourit malicieusement. « Aux marées du *yin* et du *yang*, alors : *elles* ne varient jamais. »

Mon oncle se renfrogna.

« En tout cas, poursuivit Chong Fou, Love fut profondément ému par ce spectacle. Quand la cloche sonna et que le puits se vida, sa physionomie se transforma. Sa vivacité s'éteignit comme une bougie. Tout son charme et son enjouement, si manifestes jusqu'alors, s'évanouirent comme s'ils n'avaient jamais existé. Il restait figé près de la clepsydre, sondant les ténèbres du puits vide, dont un limon chevelu couvre les parois. Son visage semblait vide, mais on y discernait une trace de souffrance.

« Quand il s'éveilla enfin de son rêve, il me regarda avec une expression curieuse et me demanda : "Quelle est votre conception de la mort ?" »

Le maître marqua un temps pour nous laisser réfléchir à la portée de cette question. « J'aurais peut-être dû le signaler plus tôt, mais pendant notre promenade Love m'avait interrogé à propos de la vie du monastère — horaires, régime, activités, et ainsi de suite — et sur certaines de nos croyances, mais comme en passant. J'avais porté ces questions au compte de la politesse, d'une volonté de manifester un minimum d'intérêt pour notre mode de vie. Ainsi, j'aurais pu continuer à considérer comme anodine sa dernière question. Mais je ne pense pas que c'était le cas. Quelque chose dans sa façon de la poser, l'urgence de sa voix, l'importance même de la question, empêchèrent cette interprétation.

« Je crois avoir hésité avant de lui répondre, car Love, sans doute gêné ou inquiet de s'être trahi devant moi, se lança dans un aparté humoristique conçu, assez ingénieusement je crois, pour camoufler d'une odeur trompeuse la piste de son émotion. La paume de sa main frappa son front, comme s'il se rappelait brusquement quelque chose. "Attendez une seconde ! s'écria-t-il. Ne répondez pas. Je sais tout. Où avais-je la tête ? L'autre jour, à Kunming, je me suis fait endoctriner par l'un de vos frères... Enfin, je crois qu'il était taoïste. Il avait une carapace de tortue et plusieurs douzaines de baguettes magiques. Il y avait des tambours, des clochettes et des tambourins, de l'encens qui fumait. Sacré bon spectacle. Quand je l'ai interrogé sur mon avenir, il m'a répondu que j'avais été chien lors de ma précédente existence, mais qu'avec un peu de chance je serais dieu dans la prochaine. Je lui donnai un dollar pour sa peine, et ce qui restait de mon cigare, puis je lui dis qu'il avait deviné les termes corrects, mais tête-bêche — j'avais été un dieu, mais je courais le danger mortel de finir au chenil pendant le prochain tour de manège." Ton père rit. "C'est bien ça, non ? demanda-t-il. Comment appelez-vous ce truc ? La transsubstantiation ? Non, ça c'est catholique. La transmigration ! Voilà."

« Je souris d'un air appréciateur à ses bouffonneries. "Je crains que vous n'ayez confondu nos conceptions avec celles des bouddhistes, Eddie. La transmigration est *leur* truc. Nous sommes beaucoup trop simples pour avancer théories aussi farfelues."

« Ton père se calma. "A quoi croyez-vous alors ?"

« "A propos de la mort ?"

« Il acquiesça en se penchant en avant pour écouter avec une attention surprenante de sa part. Je remarquai ses poings serrés, les muscles crispés de son maxillaire.

« "Eh bien, simplement que les choses retournent au Tao", répondis-je.

« A ces mots, Love grimaça comme de douleur et frissonna de tous ses membres. Puis, sans raison, il rejeta sa tête en arrière et se mit à rire, un rire étrange et haut perché qui me glaça le cœur...

— La folie ! » siffla Hsiao comme un corbeau au cri perçant.

Chong Fou l'ignora et poursuivit : « "Eddie, lui dis-je, me comprenez-vous ? Comprenez-vous le sens de *retour* ?" Son expression était à la fois désespérée et rusée. "Oh oui, répondit-il, je comprends. Vous voulez dire extinction." »

« Il n'y eut rien d'autre. Mais, Sun I, ce bref échange me donna un aperçu de l'être le plus intime de ton père. Dans une lumière semblable à celle d'une balise marine, j'entrevis la forme amorphe qui le tenaillait, qui le poursuivait, son dos visqueux émergeant des vagues, son regard mort luisant un instant avant de disparaître à nouveau sous l'eau. Love n'était pas le garçon amusant et futile que j'avais d'abord suspecté ; c'était un homme qui méritait mon respect et ma pitié. J'en acquis la conviction cet après-midi-là, et je demeure convaincu, Sun I, que ton père était de ceux dont le destin particulier est de supporter la pensée de leur mort en cette vie, de sa propre mort et, au-delà, de la Mort elle-même, le sombre sommet glacé qui se dresse au bout du monde.

« Je ne saurais dire quelles souffrances lui conférèrent cette marque. Mais ce signe distinctif passe difficilement inaperçu —, du moins pour moi qui ai vécu dans la pénombre des cloîtres parmi cette triste élite dont la seule distinction tient à l'intensité de son malheur, causé par la pensée permanente de la fin. C'est une dévotion rare qu'ils ont le privilège fatal de célébrer avec passion durant toute leur existence. Eddie Love était l'un d'eux, l'un de nous — j'en suis presque certain. Car cette marque ne saurait passer inaperçue à l'œil exercé.

« Contemplée sous la lumière adéquate, cette conscience est un accomplissement spirituel — un don, plutôt, car elle est le catalyseur qui conduit à renoncer au monde et révèle sa nature transitoire. Néanmoins, je soupçonne que ton père partageait sur ce sujet l'opinion courante, et qu'il aurait de loin préféré renoncer à son don plutôt qu'au monde. En cela, peut-être, résidait sa tragédie personnelle.

« Mon impulsion première fut de le décharger de ce malentendu qui le tourmentait, de lui dire qu'il y avait un espoir : le Retour à la Source.

« "Vous voulez dire la méditation ? me demanda-t-il. La composition de la Pilule ?"

« Je fus surpris qu'il en connût l'existence, et le lui dis.

« Il eut un haussement d'épaules dépréciateur. "Non seulement j'en ai entendu parler, mais j'y ai goûté."

« "Vraiment ?" lui demandai-je, sceptique.

« "En quelque sorte. A cela, ou à son équivalent."

« "Que voulez-vous dire ?"

« Son sourire devint presque espiègle. "L'opium, expliqua-t-il. Les Lolos se sont chargés des présentations."

« Son cynisme me fit reculer. "L'opium est une parodie insidieuse et débilitante de la joie profonde de l'illumination", le tançai-je doctement.

« De nouveau il haussa les épaules. "Peut-être. Mais il a tous les avantages de son homologue et coûte infiniment moins cher à produire. On pourrait même le fabriquer sur une chaîne de montage." De nouveau, il rit de son rire sauvage.

« Je compris alors que dans son état, Love n'aurait pu saisir — ou du moins apprécier — la subtile différence qui séparait le Tao de l'extinction. Je pouvais seulement espérer que ses souffrances agiraient comme une pénitence qui atténuerait ses transgressions et le purifierait. Quelque chose me disait que ton père était de ceux qui doivent trouver leur propre Voie dans le monde, que je ne pouvais rien faire pour l'aider. Car, ainsi que je l'ai déjà dit : "Du dragon — qui sait comment il s'élève vers le ciel dans la brume et les nuages ?" Ton père, Sun I, était un dragon.

« Je ne peux pas te dire grand-chose d'autre. Le matin suivant, il partit pour Ch'ung-ch'ing. Je ne l'ai jamais revu. Ton oncle se fit l'intermédiaire de tous nos rapports ultérieurs... Je ne l'ai jamais revu, mais j'ai souvent pensé à lui... » Le maître sourit. « Chaque fois que je t'ai regardé dans les yeux, Sun I. »

Nous restâmes silencieux un moment, chacun absorbé par ses propres préoccupations. Je fus le premier à parler.

« Qu'est-il devenu, à votre avis ? »

Le maître soupira. « Qui sait ? Pour moi, Love ressemblait à un animal blessé. Un jour, il y a longtemps et par hasard, j'ai traversé ses erres qui avaient croisé le chemin régulier de mon propre destin. Je m'arrêtai pour m'agenouiller dans la poussière et toucher le sang frais qui maculait sa trace, sentir son odeur sur mes mains. Puis mon regard a suivi sa piste jusqu'à ce qu'elle ait disparu dans les ténèbres de la forêt où je n'osai m'aventurer, n'ayant ni le temps, ni le goût, ni le talent de la suivre.

« Je me suis souvent demandé si sa blessure le ferait souffrir jusqu'à sa mort, ou si elle le handicaperait, le ralentirait jusqu'à ce que son infatigable ennemi le rattrape et le poignarde dans le dos. Mais ma plus grande peur était qu'elle le harcèle sans relâche jusqu'à ce que, désespéré, il se déchire de ses propres mains. »

Le maître marcha vers la fenêtre. Dehors, la nuit tombait, enveloppant les vallées d'une lumière diaphane. Mais les pics de l'Himalaya étaient en teu, ils brûlaient d'une flamme rose pâle comme les cierges des vêpres dans la lumière d'église de l'après-midi finissant. Tourné vers eux, le maître reprit la parole.

« Peut-être a-t-il atteint les hautes montagnes où le chasseur ne peut aller, où l'air froid et la lumière du soleil, les neiges éternelles et le vaste panorama des terres inférieures ont apaisé son esprit, lui permettant de guérir et de retrouver son unité. Peut-être a-t-il appris à vivre avec cette douleur dans sa chair, jusqu'à ce qu'elle devienne son amie et sa conseillère, et que dans ses yeux brille cette profonde santé qui est la seule sagesse. »

Pendant qu'il parlait, je fermai les yeux et me concentrai sur le personnage de la photographie. Une douce paix descendit sur mon âme. Quand je les rouvris, je vis mon oncle Hsiao qui secouait la tête avec tristesse. « Je ne crois pas », dit-il.

Je sentis un vide s'ouvrir au centre de mon être, mes battements de cœur résonnèrent dans la cavité de mon corps.

« Vos paroles m'ont permis de mieux comprendre Love, ajouta Hsiao en s'inclinant vers Chong Fou. Vous l'avez sans doute mieux perçu que moi, l'observant sans passion et sans jamais pâtir de son comportement. Votre puissance de compassion est certainement plus développée que la mienne. Mais en un jour, en une heure, que peut-on apprendre d'un homme ? Contrairement à moi, vous ne l'avez pas côtoyé pendant maintes semaines. Vous n'avez pas eu l'occasion de discerner et de peser tout ce qu'il y avait de fruste et d'irréfléchi en lui, de constater qu'il tuait tout ce qui essayait de l'aimer. Voilà pourquoi, Chong Fou, je pense que votre point de vue est biaisé ; et par-delà, que cette chose qui le suivait à la trace, ce que vous appelez "l'adversaire", le Chasseur (que vous, le connaissant si peu, ayez vu, cela m'étonne !) n'était pas la mortalité — mais Love. C'était lui-même. »

Hsiao se tourna vers moi. Son visage était congestionné. « Maintenant je comprends enfin cette image dont le sens m'a échappé pendant si longtemps : le tigre et le dresseur. Tu te souviens ? La réflexion de ton maître m'a donné la solution.

— Que voulez-vous dire ? » demanda Chong Fou.

Hsiao garda ses yeux rivés aux miens tandis qu'il s'expliquait. « Le tigre — c'est la bête fauve de son affection filiale naturelle. Le dresseur est l'amer noyau d'orgueil qui appâtait cette affection et finit par la détruire. Il s'est lui-même infligé sa blessure. Love était le Chasseur qui se traquait lui-même en tant que proie. Tu comprends ? » Dans son excitation, mon oncle lui-même ressemblait à un prédateur. « J'ai failli connaître le même sort. Mais j'ai fini par étreindre mon adversaire, alors que Love a continué la lutte.

— Excusez-moi de vous interrompre, dit Chong Fou, mais puisque vous m'avez demandé de compléter ou contredire votre point de vue, je dois dire que, pour moi, cette insistance sur les rapports de Love avec son père tient simplement à vos préjugés confucéens, à un sens hypertrophié de la piété filiale.

— Vraiment ? répliqua mon oncle avec son triste sourire forcé. De mon côté, j'aurais pu attribuer à vos présupposés *taoïstes* votre insistance sur notre caractère mortel comme facteur déterminant de la personnalité de Love. »

Un silence tendu tomba entre eux. J'essayai de saisir toutes les implications de cette suggestion.

« S'il n'était pas fou, c'était un monstre, lança brusquement Hsiao. Dans les deux cas, il est clair que vous ne devriez pas encourager l'admiration de ce garçon.

— Un monstre ! » Chong Fou était incrédule. « Vous ne pensez sans doute pas que Love était un homme mauvais, que ses actes étaient pervers ?

— Mauvais ? demanda Hsiao. L'irresponsabilité qui détruisit ma sœur dans la fleur de l'âge, qui aboutit à l'abandon d'un enfant innocent — comment qualifier ces choses, sinon de "mauvaises" ? Mais peut-être préférez-vous les mettre au compte de l'inexpérience, ou même d'une "innocence excessive"? » Il eut un rire amer.

« Non, répondit Chong Fou, Love n'était pas innocent. Mais il n'était pas complètement coupable. Je le vois comme un homme victime d'un concours de circonstances dont il ne fut que partiellement responsable.

— A qui incombent-elles donc ? » interrogea Hsiao d'une voix grave et posée.

Le maître inclina la tête. Quand il la releva, des larmes voilaient son regard bien qu'il sourît. « Au monde.

— Vous êtes trop cynique, mon ami, lui reprocha Hsiao, mais doucement, avec affection et respect. C'est la vision pessimiste de l'anachorète et du rêveur. » Il secoua la tête. « Non, Chong Fou, bien que lettré, je suis plus réaliste que vous. Je vis plus près du monde des hommes et des choses, où j'ai appris mes vérités. Quant à vous, je crains que la solitude et l'altitude ne vous aient intoxiqué. L'air raréfié de votre retraite vous tourne la tête. » Il sourit. « Finalement, les gens n'ont pas tort de dire que les taoïstes sont des rêveurs.

— Et les confucéens des hommes de bien dépourvus de tout bon sens », contre-attaqua Chong Fou.

Tous deux rirent doucement.

« Dites-moi, Chong Fou, reprit mon oncle, toujours de bonne humeur mais avec une trace de son ancienne passion, comment expliquer, sinon par la folie, l'impertinence, la bizarrerie monstrueuse avec laquelle il décida du sort de cet enfant ? » Il tendit la main vers moi.

« Vous parlez du jeu de mots, je suppose ?

— Précisément ! Tao et Dow ! » Hsiao me regarda en levant les sourcils comme si moi seul pouvais apprécier l'absurdité de cette juxtaposition.

Le maître haussa les épaules. « Sans autre critère disponible, quelle meilleure décision aurait-il pu prendre ? Il suivit l'impulsion première de sa propre nature inconsciente. Est-ce une preuve de folie ? Je choisis de penser que non. Ce serait plutôt l'essence même de notre mode de vie.

— Voulez-vous dire que Love était un taoïste ? » Hsiao plissa les yeux, comme s'il soupçonnait une plaisanterie qui le dépassait.

« Le Tao est large et profond, dit le maître avec un sourire ambigu.

— Allons bon. Vous m'étonnez, Chong Fou, rétorqua Hsiao. J'aurais pensé que vous auriez de sérieuses objections à associer votre Tao sacré à l'ultime symbole occidental de l'avarice et de l'intérêt personnel. Mais vous ignorez peut-être ce que représente le Dow — l'américain, s'entend ?

— Mon ignorance est grande, dit le maître, mais il me semble que le Dow est une sorte de pouls de l'activité économique en Amérique.

— Exactement ! exulta Hsiao. "Economique".

— En ce sens, poursuivit Chong Fou sans tenir compte de la remarque de l'autre, n'est-il pas analogue au Tao du *Yi king*, qui est également un pouls ?

— En quel sens ? objecta Hsiao avec humeur. Expliquez-vous, je vous prie.

— Eh bien, le propre pouls du monde, qui révèle les battements de cœur de la vie à celui qui écoute — à celui qui prend le temps de maîtriser son langage secret, d'apprendre pour ainsi dire par cœur la musique incessante et régulière de sa diastole et de sa systole, et parfois la fausse note qui signale son trouble, ses murmures et ses fibrillations. »

Mon oncle retroussa les lèvres, savourant l'analogie. « Limpide, reconnut-il, mais malheureusement spécieux. Vous m'avez régalé de plusieurs anecdotes taoïstes, Chong Fou ; je vais vous rendre la pareille. Souvenez-vous des paroles du poète :

> Les hommes d'affaires se vantent de leur habileté,
> Mais en philosophie ils ressemblent à des nouveau-nés.
> Se targuant de leurs pillages réussis,
> Ils oublient de méditer l'ultime destin du corps.
> Que savent-ils du Maître de la Vérité Obscure
> Qui contempla le vaste monde dans une coupe de jade,
> S'affranchit du ciel et de la terre par ses conceptions illuminées,
> Sur le char de la Mutation franchit la Porte de l'Immutabilité ?

« Dites-moi, Chong Fou, n'est-il pas vrai que le grand Tao des sages est la Voie de la transcendance de soi ? Comment concilier cela avec le Dow des Américains, qui est surtout la voie de l'intérêt personnel ?

— "Peut-on dire de ces hommes qu'ils ont atteint la réalisation ? riposta le maître en citant un célèbre *fan-yen*, ou paradoxe, de Tchouang-tseu. Dans ce cas, il en va de même pour nous tous. Ou bien ne peut-on pas dire de ces hommes qu'ils ont atteint la réalisation ? Dans ce cas, ni nous ni aucune chose ne l'a jamais atteinte."

— Balivernes ! ricana Hsiao. "Tao et Dow" — il n'y a pas de sophisme plus honteux. Ils sont inconciliables, de toute éternité, comme les grands contraires fondamentaux dont vous autres taoïstes parlez si souvent, le *yin* et le *yang*. Qui cherche à les concilier, à réduire leur inimitié implacable, cherche à subvertir les lois mêmes de l'univers !

— Votre raisonnement est subtil et séduisant, concéda le maître, mais seulement en apparence. Je crains qu'à un niveau plus profond, au niveau le plus profond, vous soyez complètement dans l'erreur.

— Je vous supplie de me corriger », dit Hsiao avec une ironie académique.

Le maître s'inclina, comme devant une demande fondée. « Connaissez-vous l'histoire de Tchouang-tseu et de Tong-kouo ?

— Ancêtres célestes, pourvu que ce ne soit pas encore une de vos interminables paraboles taoïstes !

— Tong-kouo demanda à Tchouang : "Où est le Tao ?" commença le maître sans se démonter, et Tchouang répondit : "Où n'est-il *pas* ?"
« "Montrez-le-moi", poursuivit l'élève.
« Tchouang montra une fourmi.
« Tong-kouo fut perplexe, mais sa nature têtue le poussa à insister. "Le trouve-t-on aussi bien dans une chose encore plus triviale ?"
« Tchouang montra les herbes.
« "Le grand Tao dans de banales herbes ! s'écria Tong-kouo. Est-ce possible ?"
« Tchouang acquiesça vigoureusement." Le Tao réside même dans cet étron", dit-il en donnant un coup de pied dans un tas de crottin sur le chemin. » Chong Fou adressa un regard serein à mon oncle — il triomphait.

Hsiao ne broncha pas. « Et que devons-nous conclure de cette déclaration sibylline ?

— Tout simplement que le Tao réside en toutes choses, les nobles et les ignobles, et pas moins dans ce qu'on qualifie d'impur que dans ce qu'on qualifie de pur. »

Mon oncle retira un grain de poussière dans son œil, puis renifla. « Je dois reconnaître que je n'ai jamais compris cette sagesse. Je me suis toujours détourné de votre religion pour cette raison précise : elle me paraît irresponsable, voire immorale.

— Navré de vous déplaire, s'excusa le maître, dont les yeux pétillaient d'une joie discrète, pourtant, cela est écrit : "Quand la Voie déclina, la bonté et la moralité s'instaurèrent." » Son regard se posa sur moi. « A toi, Sun I, je déclare : le Tao se trouve sur la "place du marché" aussi bien que dans le temple, et chacun de nous doit suivre son propre chemin là où il le conduit. »

A ces paroles, un barrage céda en moi, un océan se rua dans la brèche. Mes yeux quittèrent son visage — tristesse et compassion derrière son ironie (comme la pointe bleue au centre de la flamme d'une bougie, là où la chaleur est la plus intense) — pour celui de Hsiao, le vieux confucéen au visage semblable à un masque qui portait maintenant une expression de gravité... et autre chose. Etait-ce la défaite ? Mais comment aurait-il pu imaginer une issue différente à cette joute oratoire dont j'étais l'enjeu implicite ? Vingt et une années d'éducation, de confiance et d'affection pesaient sur l'autre plateau de la balance. Malgré la forte impression qu'il m'avait faite, il ne pouvait espérer l'emporter, en un après-midi, sur l'inertie de toute ma formation.

Néanmoins, j'éprouvais pour lui une immense affection, un grand respect. Je sais aujourd'hui qu'en ce jour lointain où, timidement, je remarquai en silence leurs ressemblances et leurs différences, leur ressemblance dans la différence, j'étais en présence de deux grands émissaires du passé qui, attelés ensemble comme de puissants contraires, *yin* et *yang* incarnés, par leur amour et leur guerre avaient rendu notre civilisation immortelle, seule parmi toutes celles de la terre.

Ensuite, le maître appela Wu, qui apporta du thé vert et une corbeille des fruits les plus mûrs du vieux pêcher de la cour. Les deux hommes burent et mangèrent en silence, par déférence pour moi, je crois, et pour la sévère épreuve à laquelle on venait de soumettre mes émotions. Mais je suppose qu'ils furent également heureux de pouvoir se manifester leur estime réciproque d'une façon plus cordiale que par la lutte morale intransigeante et magnanime à laquelle ils s'étaient livrés pendant tout l'après-midi, décidant maintenant d'une trêve pour honorer les humbles rituels d'une hospitalité affectueuse.

Chong Fou prit la plus grosse et la plus prometteuse des pêches de la corbeille, dont il éplucha la peau en une spirale parfaite. Puis il coupa la chair en croissants.

« Pour vous, mon ami. » Il offrit les morceaux de choix à mon oncle.

Il s'adressa à moi avec une politesse plus familière. « En veux-tu un quartier, Sun I ?

— Oui, merci, maître », répondis-je en tendant la main vers lui.

Gardant le morceau qu'il me destinait, il rit doucement. « Réponds d'abord à cette énigme : quelle est la pierre qui porte en elle la vie nouvelle ? »

Sa question me décontenança. Je réfléchis, fronçai les sourcils, mais en vain. « Je ne sais pas.

— Il ne sait pas ! » répéta-t-il, comme étonné. Il regarda Hsiao, puis me dit : « Eh bien, ceci te revient de droit ! » Il me lança adroitement le noyau de pêche à la tête, qu'il heurta avec un bruit mat et creux. Le projectile atterrit ensuite sur mes cuisses.

Je me frottai le crâne en lui adressant un regard féroce.

« Tu ne vas pas me remercier ? me demanda-t-il malicieusement.

— Vous remercier de quoi ? De la bosse que je vais avoir ? »

Le maître regarda Hsiao comme s'il lui demandait de témoigner de mon ingratitude. « Singe n'a jamais su apprécier à leur juste valeur les services rendus. » Puis il se tourna vers moi. « Je ne crois pas que tu réalises ce que tu tiens dans ta main.

— Je crois que si, répondis-je sur un ton sarcastique.

— Qu'est-ce donc ?

— Un noyau, dis-je en haussant les épaules avec mépris.

— Une pierre ! » me corrigea-t-il.

Un vague soupçon traversa mon esprit.

« Exactement, dit-il en hochant la tête. La pierre qui porte en elle la vie nouvelle. Et sais-tu pourquoi on l'appelle ainsi, pourquoi, selon la légende, Tchouang-tseu en choisit un comme pierre tombale ? »

Je secouai la tête négativement.

« Parce que le noyau est l'âme du fruit, à partir duquel il crée son nouveau corps. Voilà pourquoi le pêcher est symbole de vie éternelle pour les taoïstes, et pourquoi le premier abbé de ce monastère en planta un dans la cour, dont nous mangeons le fruit en ce moment.

« C'est là mon dernier souvenir de ton père, Sun I. Je l'avais presque oublié jusqu'à ce que Wu apporte ces fruits. Ce fameux après-midi dont j'ai parlé, après notre promenade, nous aussi avons partagé le thé et les pêches. Je cherchais un moyen d'égayer ton père après sa triste rêverie près de la clepsydre, et je trouvai ceci. Quand je lui lançai le noyau, exactement comme je te l'ai lancé, et que je lui racontai cette histoire, il condescendit à me récompenser d'un sourire... (le maître rayonnait, je ne pus cacher mon plaisir) tout comme toi maintenant. Mais il prit le noyau, le mit dans sa poche et, pour autant que je sache, l'emporta avec lui. »

L'amusement qui avait joué sur les lèvres de mon oncle pendant la première partie de cet échange disparut aussitôt qu'il comprit la teneur des bouffonneries de Chong Fou. Il examina sa tasse de thé d'un air soucieux.

Comme je tenais la mienne en silence et buvais de lentes gorgées du liquide brûlant, je ressentis un plaisir surprenant, comme si on m'avait honoré d'une faveur. Pris par l'ambiance familière et rassurante de la cellule du maître où, enfant, j'avais passé tant d'heures heureuses à jouer avec des jouets simples — un noyau de fruit, une baguette d'achillée —, je sentis l'histoire de mon oncle et toutes ses implications troublantes s'estomper dans une sorte d'irréalité comme si elles ne m'avaient pas concerné. Tout cela ressemblait à une histoire lue dans un livre, une histoire triste, mais de cette tristesse qui nous rafraîchit mystérieusement et nous ravit parce que les douleurs évoquées ne sont pas les nôtres. Et de fait, échapper au sort des protagonistes nous donne quelque motif de nous réjouir du nôtre. De plus, ces histoires, quand elles sont bonnes, nous conduisent en la présence solennelle d'une vérité, dont nous jouissons illicitement, car sans avoir payé le prix fort de la souffrance, moissonnant ses récoltes les plus secrètes, le précieux et incomparable trésor de nos rêves.

Mais alors même que je savourais ce doux répit, des phrases et des images de la narration déferlaient sur moi, accélérant mon pouls. Ces brèves intrusions ressemblaient à de lointains roulements de tonnerre qui font frissonner celui qui somnole dans la chaleur rêveuse d'un long après-midi d'été en espérant qu'elle durera toujours.

Enfin mon oncle posa sa tasse et tendit les bras en se raclant la gorge, signalant ainsi qu'il était prêt à terminer sa mission. Il semblait résigné, comme s'il comprenait que le temps avait joué contre lui. Mais sa dignité restait inentamée : bien qu'il eût perdu cette bataille, la guerre était loin d'être finie. Je vis avec tristesse ses traits se durcir et je retrouvai le masque auquel j'étais maintenant habitué.

« Je suis profondément reconnaissant de votre hospitalité, dit-il poliment en s'inclinant vers Chong Fou, et de votre conversation. Mais le temps presse. Je dois partir avant la nuit pour pouvoir descendre de la montagne. Car la "voie" est traître... (s'autorisant une ultime pique, il employa ironiquement le mot *tao*) et je ne me sentirai pas en sécurité avant d'avoir atteint la grand-route. »

Le maître leva la main pour l'interrompre, mais mon oncle poursuivit. « Inutile d'essayer de me convaincre. Je ne peux rester. Quand j'aurai tenu la dernière partie de ma promesse, je devrai partir. »

Un long moment il scruta mon visage — de nouveau l'homme que je connaissais. Son expression était pleine de doute et d'inquiétude, la question que ses yeux me posaient était tout pour moi. Et avec cette angoisse, un vague regret. Il savait sans doute que le manque de temps et la complexité des problèmes humains l'empêcheraient probablement de connaître la réponse.

Plongeant la main dans les replis de sa robe, il en sortit un paquet enveloppé dans un papier marron et attaché avec une ficelle. « Ouvre-le, il contient un trésor. Rien au monde ne peut y être comparé. C'est la robe, Sun I. Fais-en l'objet de ton étude et de ta dévotion. Voici tout ce que tu sauras jamais d'*elle*, et de cette partie secrète de toi-même qu'elle t'a léguée. Cette broderie, peut-être mieux que je ne l'ai fait aujourd'hui, te permettra de trouver le fil de ton héritage et de ton destin, car cette robe fut tissée au-dessus de toi alors que tu reposais dans l'obscurité de la matrice. Le claquement régulier du métier, le bruit de l'aiguille perçant la soie, le doux crissement du fil qui glisse — peut-être dans quelque recoin secret de ta mémoire résonnent-ils encore, et ils continueront, car tel est l'accord fondamental de ton être. Les piqûres de cet ouvrage plus que toute autre chose, plus même que les chromosomes de tes cellules qui, nous dit-on aujourd'hui, constituent les fils conducteurs de la vie, ont peut-être fait de toi ce que tu es et ce que tu deviendras. Réfléchis et tire tes propres conclusions. Mais souviens-toi : elle est irremplaçable. Garde-la en lieu sûr. Garde-la comme ta vie — elle est peut-être ta vie. »

Quand mon oncle me la tendit, un calme soudain envahit mon esprit. Je regardai le paquet, écoutai le papier crépiter dans mes mains, sentis le vague parfum qu'il exhalait — la senteur d'une fleur broyée puis distillée en essence, qui exprima pour moi, alors et à jamais, l'indicible mélancolie du monde. Car je savais que c'était le parfum de ma mère, la douce odeur de la mort qu'elle respira à son dernier soupir.

Mais je n'eus guère le temps de rêver. Mon oncle me pressa. « Et voici le cadeau de ton père. »

Je regardai sans comprendre la petite bourse noire qu'il me tendit.

« Elle est arrivée d'Amérique voici des années », me dit-il en la posant dans ma paume et refermant mes doigts dessus. « Ce fut son dernier message — si l'on peut appeler cela un message. » Il me dévisagea attentivement. « Mais avant d'ouvrir cette bourse, j'aimerais que tu regardes ceci. » Il me tendit une enveloppe de papier bulle qui portait les cachets d'une poste inconnue.

Je l'ouvris et sortis une couverture du magazine *Time* : on avait arraché le reste. Le visage souriant de mon père, presque aussi grand que nature, me regardait. C'était un dessin, une caricature, une tête énorme sur un corps minuscule. Il semblait plus vieux, plus empâté que sur la photo ; et il portait un costume trois pièces au lieu de l'uniforme dans lequel j'avais l'habitude de le voir. Mais il n'y avait aucun doute possible ; c'était Love.

Il était coincé dans le cockpit d'un avion miniature dont le nez portait les mâchoires de tigre que je connaissais bien, mais qui souriaient d'un air lubrique comme après une obscénité ou une plaisanterie paillarde. Malgré l'intention parodique, l'artiste avait rendu exactement le sourire de mon père. Comme pour dissiper tout malentendu quant à l'identité du personnage, Love portait ses lunettes d'aviateur aux verres en forme de larmes vert foncé, ce symbole d'anonymat qui était devenu son signe distinctif. Mais maintenant, il y avait un reflet dans ces lunettes, un reflet merveilleux, comme d'un autre monde, plus mystérieux que n'importe quel rêve. Rassemblées sur la surface convexe de chaque lentille, et donc redoublées, se dressaient d'immenses structures scintillantes de verre ou d'acier, aussi hautes que l'Himalaya, et les sombres abysses qui les séparaient comme des canyons. C'étaient bien sûr des bâtiments, mais j'y vis d'étranges excroissances minérales, stalagmites piquées de diamants, cristaux de quartz déchiquetés jaillis de la terre lors de bouleversements préhistoriques. On eût dit la Galerie des Miroirs d'une foire monstrueuse, tours réfléchissant des tours réfléchissant des tours, tantôt lisses et rectangulaires, tantôt hérissées de flèches, tels des clochers d'église qui s'élèvent vers le ciel et indiquent le soleil derrière la tête de mon père. Comme pendant une éclipse, la lueur blanche de la couronne solaire nimbait les traits de Love en dessinant une auréole ambiguë.

« Il vole au-dessus des gratte-ciel de Manhattan, m'expliqua Hsiao, au-dessus du quartier de la finance pour être exact : Wall Street, aussi surnommée la Cité d'Emeraude. »

Il y avait une allusion sarcastique dans sa voix, que je remarquai sans la comprendre. « La Cité d'Emeraude, comme dans le conte de fées chinois ? demandai-je. La ville où habite l'Empereur de Tchou ?

— Non, Sun I, seul un empereur déchu habite cette cité d'Emeraude, et le conte de fées est strictement américain. » Son ironie me parut empoisonnée. « Mais c'est une autre histoire, trop longue pour que je te la raconte maintenant. »

J'attendis en espérant qu'il poursuivrait, mais il ne dit rien.

« Que signifient ces mots ? » demandai-je en lui rendant la couverture.

Hsiao scruta mon visage, soupira, puis me lut le gros titre :

« LE HUN DANS LE SOLEIL DE WALL STREET !
L'AMÉRIQUE ET L'*AMERICAIN* (P&L)
ONT UNE NOUVELLE IDOLE
EDDIE LOVE
L'HOMME (D'AFFAIRES) DU JOUR. »

« Qu'est-ce que ça veut dire ? » demandai-je, anxieux.

Hsiao me jaugea du regard. « Je l'ignore. »

— Vous l'ignorez ! » J'étais incrédule. « Vous devez le savoir ! Où avez-vous trouvé ceci ?

— On me l'a envoyé d'Amérique, dit-il, sans adresse d'expéditeur. Quant au sens de cette couverture, Sun I, la vérité est que *je ne veux pas le connaître*. Le jour où j'ai fait cette promesse à ton père — cette promesse qui a pesé sur moi comme un fardeau depuis toutes ces années, et dont je me libère enfin aujourd'hui — j'en fis une autre... à moi-même. Je me suis juré de ne plus jamais avoir le moindre rapport avec Eddie Love. J'ai tenu ces deux promesses.

— Mais c'est élogieux, n'est-ce pas ? lui demandai-je avec véhémence en montrant le magazine. Vous pouvez au moins me dire cela. »

— Apparemment, oui. »

D'un éclat de rire, je me débarrassai de sa voix lugubre. « Vous voyez bien ! Cela règle définitivement le problème. S'il était fou, comme vous le prétendez, comment pourrait-il recevoir un tel hommage du monde ? Regardez ! "L'HOMME D'AFFAIRES DU JOUR". Vous l'avez dit vous-même. »

Alors, pour la dernière fois, les lèvres de mon oncle se retroussèrent en son habituel sourire dégoûté. « Et si le monde qui l'honorait était fou, Sun I ? As-tu pensé à cela ? »

Je le regardai sans voix ; un instant, je jouai avec l'idée que *lui-même* peut-être était fou.

« Tu n'as pas encore ouvert la bourse », intervint calmement Chong Fou. Le ton posé de sa voix fut un immense soulagement, comme un coup d'épingle dans un ballon trop gonflé.

« Non, répondis-je avec reconnaissance, je ne l'ai pas encore ouverte.

— Vas-y. »

Comme en transe, j'obéis et fis sauter la pression. La bourse était si légère que je me demandai si elle était vide ; mais je discernai une forme le long de la couture inférieure. Je glissai mes doigts dans l'étroit orifice, touchai d'abord quelque chose de doux, puis un objet dur. Je sortis une chose que je ne pus identifier. Cela ressemblait à une quenouille, à une brindille couverte d'écorce en feutrine. C'était un moignon ou une souche : un moignon de petite patte, un morceau de fourrure effilochée et de cartilage, une petite excroissance osseuse. Reliée à cela par une fine chaîne d'or, une clef. Une clef suspendue à un porte-bonheur — une patte de lapin. Je l'examinai avec aversion, la chair desséchée, morte, les tendons noircis comme des lacets de cuir, l'os sectionné. J'adressai un regard suppliant au maître, puis à Hsiao.

« Il y a autre chose », dit Hsiao.

Je fouillai de nouveau dans la bourse et en sortis un billet. Ajustant ses lunettes en demi-lunes, Hsiao nous fit l'honneur de traduire :

> Joyeux vingt et un ans !
> D'un Dowiste à un autre,
> Une clef, une chaîne, un porte-bonheur :
> La patte de lapin pour la chance ;
> La chaîne, nécessairement ;
> La clef, une clef majeure
> (Puisse-t-elle t'assister),
> Un rossignol, qui ouvre les sombres
> Secrets du cœur (car cette clef
> Ouvre toutes les portes), et pour la congrégation
> Des croyants (car nous sommes tous de la même foi,
> N'est-ce pas ?) une clef d'église qui
> T'enivrera d'extase, ou
> Te fera entrer dans la Grande Cathédrale du Dow.
>
> Ton père,
Love.

Mon oncle me tendit le message en m'observant par-dessus ses lunettes, le front ridé d'inquiétude. Il plissait les yeux comme un vieux marin face au vent sur un promontoire rocheux, qui cherche dans le tumulte chaotique des éléments le navire dont on redoute le naufrage. Au fond de son regard, une lueur brillait pour moi, qui me proposait l'espoir d'un havre, un port en eau profonde. Mais il dut comprendre qu'il ne pouvait me sauver, que tout espoir était perdu, car à cette même lueur vacillante j'aperçus les larmes que les embruns salés lui arrachaient, et je les vis se figer sur son visage.

Alors il m'embrassa gauchement, férocement. Son masque me vola de nouveau son visage. Aussi rapidement qu'il était entré dans ma vie, il en sortit.

9

Ce même soir, peu après le départ de Hsiao, Wu accourut dans la cellule en tablier sale, pestant et maugréant comme une domestique mal lunée. Il m'envoya aussitôt à la cuisine, où il préparait le repas du soir, car il avait besoin d'aide pour manier les soufflets et hacher les légumes.

Il aurait dû faire appel à un autre novice. Car j'étais trop épuisé pour accomplir mon travail correctement. Deux fois j'éteignis le feu en essayant de le faire prendre. Ensuite, alors que j'aiguisais le couteau à découper, je renversai accidentellement la jarre d'huile, dont le contenu se répandit alentour. Mes mains étaient si glissantes que je réussis à peine à saisir le couteau.

« Qu'est-ce qui t'arrive ? me gronda Wu. Fais un peu attention, bon sang ! »

Ces mots avaient à peine quitté sa bouche que le couteau bondit de la pierre à aiguiser et faillit me sectionner l'index. L'entaille n'était pas trop profonde, mais mon doigt saignait beaucoup. Je réussis même à faire tomber quelques gouttes de sang dans un énorme *ting* de riz cuit que, dans mon agitation, j'avais oublié de couvrir.

« Ma parole, tu le fais exprès ! » s'écria Wu en s'arrachant les cheveux. Il ne restait plus qu'à consacrer puis brûler ce riz, qui aurait suffi à nourrir tout le monastère. Le manger eût été un sacrilège terrible, une violation de tous nos préceptes végétariens, presque un acte de cannibalisme. (Cela n'empêchait pourtant pas les dieux de savourer leur sacrifice.)

En marmonnant des obscénités dans sa barbe, Wu lava et nettoya ma blessure, ses mains potelées pressant la mienne avec la tendresse rude et efficace d'une vieille mère. Quand il eut fini de nouer la bande de gaze autour de mon poignet, il me chassa de la cuisine et m'interdit d'y remettre les pieds avant le lendemain. Je fus trop heureux de lui obéir.

Dans le chaos sauvage de mes impressions et de mes émotions, un objet m'obsédait avec une force particulière : la robe. Elle me fascinait, suscitait toute la passion et l'enthousiasme d'un amant — la tendresse défaillante, la timidité et le désir, le besoin irrésistible de la rencontre et, simultanément, l'angoisse de la découverte. Je ressentais une sorte de respect ; mais nuancé, voire dominé par une chose fort différente. Une partie de moi-même désirait se retirer, jouir de la robe en privé, comme un animal qui se tapit dans l'obscurité de sa tanière pour ronger un os savoureux.

Peut-être étais-je simplement surexcité par les événements de la journée. En tout cas, vaguement étourdi par l'hémorragie et avec un pincement d'attente au creux de l'estomac, j'allai dans le temple, que je savais désert à cette heure, emportant le paquet enveloppé que Hsiao m'avait donné et mon couteau à découper pour trancher la ficelle. Là, j'allumai une lampe à prière afin d'examiner mon cadeau secret, mon nouveau — et premier — bien.

Dans le profond silence du temple, à la lumière de la flamme qui vacillait sur son réservoir d'huile, je m'assis pour réfléchir. Immuables et rassurantes, les dalles de schiste rafraîchissaient mon corps. Je craignais d'ouvrir le cadeau de ma mère. J'entendis un rossignol chanter quelque part dans la nuit : sa musique fournit une excuse agréable à mon inaction.

Je tombai alors dans un état méditatif, une transe excessivement délicieuse, ponctuée de tremblements d'extase nerveuse tels que je n'en avais jamais connu. Mon corps brûlait de fièvre, frissonnait de froid. Le chant de l'oiseau ne semblait venir d'aucune direction particulière, ou bien de toutes les directions de l'espace ; à la fin, je crus qu'il sortait de moi-même.

C'était une tension abstraite, tantôt triste, tantôt nimbée de joie ; pourtant, il ne s'agissait ni de joie ni de détresse dans l'acception habituelle de ces mots. Car malgré sa beauté, la mélodie était aussi froide et dépourvue de sens que la lueur des étoiles... ou plutôt peut-être, contenait un sens trop profond pour que le cœur le saisît. Perdu en moi-même, j'oubliai l'oiseau et faillis croire que c'était mon âme qui chantait en une langue inconnue, à cause de la robe et de ma mère. Je dus retourner à la réalité du temple pour me rassurer. Quand j'ouvris les yeux, je commençai par ne rien voir. Puis, par la fenêtre ouverte qui donnait sur la cour, un léger mouvement, une ombre voletant devant le croissant argenté de la nouvelle lune me prouvèrent mon erreur. L'oiseau venait de se poser sur les branches supérieures du pêcher où il donnait sa sérénade.

J'allai à la fenêtre et me penchai sur son appui pour l'écouter. Dehors, les étoiles scintillaient. Elles pendaient aux branches comme les lumières d'un lustre, tremblant dans les ténèbres cristallines de l'univers. Quand mes yeux furent habitués à l'obscurité, je distinguai les vraies pêches, minuscules globes opaques qui se détachaient contre le ciel du soir bleu foncé — fruits obscurs parmi les fruits de lumière.

Enfin, je sortis le couteau à parer de la manche de ma soutane où je l'avais caché avant de quitter la cuisine. Je tranchai la ficelle autour du paquet, dépliai méticuleusement le papier marron.

Les lourds plis du somptueux tissu dégringolèrent devant moi quand je le levai vers la lumière. A ma grande surprise, une phalène papillonna devant mon visage. Tel un pilleur de tombe pénétrant dans une crypte, j'avais tiré cette momie de son long sommeil nourricier dans le caveau soyeux de la robe. Quand la phalène émergea, un nuage du même parfum qui avait provoqué ma délicieuse tristesse de l'après-midi s'éleva avec elle. Mais tandis que ce parfum m'avait alors semblé affadi, éventé, il s'imposait maintenant jusqu'à l'écœurement.

Cela peut-être me troubla. Peut-être étais-je seulement fatigué. Ou bien ce qui m'angoissa fut la complexité de l'odeur que je découvrais maintenant, et qui en plus du parfum évoquait la poussière et le cèdre. Sans doute la robe avait-elle séjourné pendant des années au fond d'un coffre enfermé dans un grenier ; mais mon esprit forma l'image d'un cercueil. Au moment précis où cette association traversait mon cerveau, je remarquai un bruit sourd et régulier, bourdonnement ou stridulation, comme d'un moteur minuscule. La phalène tournait autour de la flamme de la lampe à prières. Je frissonnai en me rappelant l'allusion de Hsiao à l'ombre papillonnante qui avait traversé la chambre de ma mère le jour de ma naissance. J'essayai d'attraper l'insecte pour l'écraser entre mes ongles, mais avec l'instinct d'un somnambule il m'échappa. Le vrombissement monotone de ses ailes — le bruit d'un avion volant très haut par-dessus une montagne, imaginai-je — se poursuivit alors que je commençais d'examiner la robe. Il tissait un étrange contrepoint au chant du rossignol.

Comme mon oncle Hsiao l'avait annoncé, la robe était couleur rouge sang. Pourtant, ce n'était pas la couleur de la sanguine, celle du sang riche en oxygène que le cœur propulse dans les artères ; dans la pénombre du temple, on eût dit le sang des veines, assombri et souillé par les déchets corporels. (Je devais ensuite découvrir que cette teinte changeait avec la lumière, et selon le tempérament et l'humeur du spectateur.)

Comme je tenais le tissu entre mes mains, mes doigts sentirent le motif frappé dans la soie, ce que Hsiao avait nommé le « méandre labyrinthique ». Mon œil se perdit alors dans le dédale du broché, dans ses passages et ses couloirs obliques. Je découvris qu'il suffisait d'y pénétrer pour ne plus pouvoir en sortir. Les cloisons semblaient se refermer sur mes pas, m'obligeant à aller de l'avant vers le cœur du labyrinthe, jusqu'au sanctuaire de son sens caché.

Sur le panneau central du dos, la lisière noire du monde supportait le bord du soleil en un crépuscule ou une aube écarlate, — impossible de savoir de quelle frontière entre le jour et la nuit il s'agissait. Le seul repère était un arbre mort et noueux, à l'exception d'une branche supérieure feuillue, d'où pendait un fruit unique, vert et indéterminé. Il m'évoqua inévitablement le pêcher de la cour, que l'après-midi même le maître m'avait appris à voir comme un symbole de vie éternelle, et où le rossignol chantait déjà. Inspiré par ces coïncidences ou par un instinct plus profond, je devais toujours interpréter cette image ainsi.

Que signifiait-elle ? Etait-ce une vision d'espoir, ou au contraire infiniment amère, ce fruit vert suspendu aux branches d'un arbre de vie aux trois quarts mort ? Je ne savais pas. Mais il y avait tellement plus... L'œil quittait rapidement cette scène pour passer au chef-d'œuvre conçu par ma mère. Loin au-dessus de la terre, deux bêtes gigantesques tourbillonnaient vertigineusement dans l'air, embrassées, toutes griffes dehors, sans qu'on puisse dire si c'était pour tuer ou copuler. Crocs dénudés, mâchoires béantes, chacune semblait aspirer le souffle vital dans la gueule de l'autre, puis la ressusciter d'un sauvage baiser.

Ces fauves étaient respectivement le Dragon et le Tigre : le premier doté d'yeux comme des émeraudes scintillantes et d'un corps doré semé d'écailles satinées bleu-noir ; le deuxième, le Tigre, d'un blanc pur et terrible, à l'exception de sa gueule dégoulinante du sang qui coulait de la gorge de son adversaire ou de son propre cœur broyé. Les yeux du Tigre étaient bleus, aussi bleus que l'espace, bleus comme aurait dû l'être le ciel.

Le sang qui ruisselait des blessures des monstres convergeait en un seul torrent qui descendait du ciel et lavait l'aube (ou le crépuscule), tombait vers la terre en une pluie amère, une pluie de sang, qui aurait stérilisé la nature tout entière — à l'exception de la pêche verte qui mûrissait miraculeusement sur la branche de l'arbre mort. Qu'était ce fruit ? La dernière boursouflure empoisonnée jaillie des cendres de l'holocauste ? Ou bien le fruit précieux de l'espoir humain, dont la croissance rachetait aux yeux de ma mère la destruction générale ? L'averse de sang me rappela la signification symbolique des bêtes en tant que forces primitives, nuage et vent : l'une tournoyant et se métamorphosant dans les cieux, adoptant à son gré toutes sortes de formes fantastiques, — le Dragon ; l'autre, silencieux, invisible, rapide, comme le Tigre bondissant pour attaquer. Ces deux éléments, qui guerroient ou copulent, engendrent la pluie qui nourrit la terre. Il existe d'ailleurs une expression toujours utilisée en Chine, « le jeu du vent et des nuages », euphémisme désignant le rapport sexuel. Ce motif de la robe m'apprit la légende secrète qui donnait voix aux angoisses de ma mère. Car le Dragon et le Tigre, ainsi que le savent tous les Chinois, symbolisent également l'amour entre l'homme et la femme. Ces bêtes primitives imbriquées dans leur étreinte équivoque et brodées par ma mère figuraient Ch'iu-yeh et Eddie Love.

Ayant reconnu cela, je compris qu'en un sens peu éloigné du littéral ma mère s'était elle-même cousue dans le tissu, et que cette robe était elle, aussi sûrement que si la soie eût été sa peau écorchée, son aiguille celle du tatoueur inséminant une teinture indélébile. Pourtant, j'aurais tellement préféré que cette aiguille lui ait servi comme celle du chirurgien, et son fil pour suturer les plaies de sa vie blessée. Ce vœu futile engendra une observation. Car la robe comportait un détail bizarre. Dans la vie, Love avait détruit ma mère ; mais sur la robe, l'issue du combat entre Dragon et Tigre était indécise, et le resterait. Aucun des deux fauves ne remporterait jamais la victoire.

Mon imagination discerna alors un nouveau motif dans les volutes du méandre : une empreinte digitale ensanglantée. Pour ma mère, le long et patient labeur de la robe devait-il servir à une vengeance à retardement mais implacable ? Voulut-elle faire savoir que la fuite de Love était illusoire, qu'elle ne le laisserait jamais partir, mais le poursuivrait comme une Furie à travers le monde, polluant à jamais tout ce qu'il toucherait ou aimerait ? Cette pensée me fit trembler, mais en même temps me causa une sorte de plaisir vengeur... Peut-être voulait-elle seulement dire qu'une telle guerre ne connaît pas de vainqueur et n'en connaîtra jamais. Par-delà ces interprétations, l'équilibre du combat me prouvait une chose : au fond de son cœur, ma mère n'avait jamais renoncé.

L'image de mon père telle qu'elle apparaissait sur la caricature — visage empâté, lunettes noires peuplées de ces gigantesques cristaux — traversa alors mon esprit et je sentis une brûlure farouche envahir mon cœur — la haine. Cela dura seulement un moment. Car la fascination, l'espoir, l'amour même conspiraient contre la haine, trois fleuves de baume qui se jetaient dans l'océan troublé de mon âme, et dont les eaux pures dissolvaient les sels et les acides intolérables de mon amertume. Mais en cet instant, sous la griffe du ressentiment, je sentis un frémissement ébranler toute la Création. Les fondations solides du monde tremblèrent ; tremblèrent mais ne s'écroulèrent pas.

Alors qu'assis, je rougissais, suais et que mon cœur battait la chamade dès que je pensais à lui — Eddie Love et ce monde lointain reflété dans les verres —, une impulsion irrésistible s'empara de moi ; je levai les yeux. Pour la troisième fois de la soirée, je vis la phalène. Le halo fantomatique des ailes, son bourdonnement incessant comme elle poursuivait sa veillée funèbre autour de la flamme — tout cela me fit frissonner malgré moi.

Je songeai aux femmes qui élèvent les vers à soie dans la vallée. Elles attendent les premières feuilles du mûrier blanc en avril, puis décrochent des murs de leurs entrepôts les papiers roulés qui contiennent les œufs de l'année passée et les glissent dans les plis de leurs robes matelassées pour les couver comme des poules jusqu'à ce qu'ils éclosent. Ensuite, elles les posent sur des plateaux avec des morceaux de feuilles pour qu'ils se nourrissent. Quand les vers sont repus, ils se dressent à la verticale pour éjaculer la soie par leur tête, tissant habilement leur sperme en linceul ; leur corps dessine alors un huit — l'emblème de l'infini. J'avais souvent entendu ces femmes chanter en travaillant. Leur chant était beau et étrange, mais je ne pus me rappeler que quelques bribes décousues... « Le cercueil de satin où meurt le ver à soie est la matrice d'où émerge le bombyx. »

Cet insecte agaçant qui papillonnait maintenant dans le halo de la lampe, telle une planète morte tournant autour du soleil de sa passion révolue, avait peut-être été un ver à soie. Ressuscité du tombeau de son cocon, poussé par la force de la mémoire, il était revenu dans le but ignoble de dévorer ce qu'il avait autrefois créé, ravager la soie pour perpétuer son vrombissement absurde. Je compris alors que ce rituel lugubre, cette veillée mortuaire qu'il célébrait sans la moindre joie, était à lui-même destiné.

Mais plus tristes encore, et plus horribles, les mots qui remontèrent jusqu'à moi hors de l'abîme de la mémoire : « ... Le ver à soie est le père de la mite. »

★

J'ai dit que le Dragon et le Tigre symbolisent l'amour entre les sexes. Cette interprétation est destinée au commun des mortels. Originellement, leur copulation renvoyait à un rituel ésotérique taoïste qui ne ressemblait qu'en apparence à l'amour érotique : le yoga Tigre Blanc/Dragon Vert. Ma mère avait dû s'initier aux mystères de la « culture duelle », par ses lectures ou ses conversations. Car la robe décrivait ce rite trop minutieusement pour qu'il s'agît d'une coïncidence.

Ce que je sais de la technique Tigre Blanc/Dragon Vert, je le dois au maître, qui connaissait toutes les écoles du taoïsme, anciennes et modernes, ainsi que leurs pratiques clandestines. (Je me suis parfois demandé si lui-même, dans sa jeunesse, n'avait pas participé à ces mystères sexuels.)

Ce yoga, lié à l'alchimie, tente de composer la Pilule Or-Cinabre, la fusion du *yin* et du *yang*, à travers un rapport sexuel hautement formalisé, pratiqué à certaines époques de l'année en accord avec les configurations astrales et l'avis de l'oracle. Pour le mâle, le but de cette copulation consiste, tout en maintenant une continence séminale stricte (le cas échéant par un artifice : un anneau de jade qui serre la base du pénis, empêche l'éjaculation et induit « le flux inversé »), à exciter sa partenaire à une série d'orgasmes pour absorber à son propre usage les fluides *yin* qu'elle sécrète alors. Ces fluides, mêlés à son propre sperme, sont aspirés dans le corps et chauffés comme dans un creuset, les poumons faisant office de soufflets, jusqu'à ce qu'ils s'élèvent enfin par les deux canaux parallèles à l'épine dorsale vers le centre *ni-wan* situé au sommet du crâne. Le résidu, qui se condense et s'égoutte vers le bas, permet de composer la Pilule Or-Cinabre.

Cette technique fut évidemment conçue par les mâles pour leur propre usage. Comme leur réserve de fluide *yang* est restreinte et facilement entamée, ils ont besoin de la compléter avec le fluide *yin* que toutes les femmes possèdent en quantité inépuisable. Les femmes n'ont pas grand-chose à gagner de cette pratique (sinon peut-être une activité sexuelle agréable pratiquée dans un but charitable), mais certaines se soumettent volontiers à cet acte sexuel altruiste.

Cette soumission acceptée, cette idée que la femme se laisse utiliser par l'homme qui repousse ainsi l'échéance de la mort, me suggéra de façon poignante l'amour de ma mère pour Eddie Love. Peut-être plus encore que son exploitation, l'idée de son immense *pouvoir* passif, le caractère inépuisable de son essence vitale féminine, attirèrent mon attention. J'eus alors une intuition surprenante.

Selon une variation subtile et insidieuse du yoga Tigre Blanc/Dragon Vert, la femme cherche à subvertir l'intention de l'homme, à l'exciter au point qu'il perd tout contrôle de lui-même, lâche son sperme dans son vagin, lui offrant ainsi son fluide *yang* qui accroît la longévité de la partenaire. Ce fut par ce moyen que Hsi Wang Mu, la Mère Royale du Ciel Occidental, atteignit l'immortalité, épuisant l'existence de mille jeunes gens. Aussi incongru que cela puisse paraître, telle fut la pensée qui traversa mon esprit tandis que je contemplais les broderies de ma mère : histoires de jeunes gens dévoyés de leur propre intérêt, séduits par des femmes puissantes et abusives, des jeunes gens qui s'étaient épuisés à l'amour, éjaculant jusqu'à la dernière giclée de leur sperme vital dans les ténèbres voraces, offrant l'immortalité au lieu de la gagner.

Ces histoires éveillèrent un écho en moi. Pourtant, dans le cas de mes parents, c'était la femme qu'on avait séduite et qui avait tout donné. *Mais était-ce réellement le cas ?* Certains détails m'en firent douter. Certes, je ne pouvais contester la sincérité de Hsiao, mais je savais que sa perception des événements était faussée. Si son portrait de ma mère était véridique, comment expliquer l'égalité des deux grands adversaires de la robe ? Hsiao avait dû juger absurde pareille égalité, au mieux un rêve pathétique, au pire une dangereuse illusion. Mais si elle fut simplement la femme trompée, la victime de Love, que signifiait sa réponse à Hsiao quand mon oncle lui avait appris le départ imminent de Love : « Je sais... Je l'ai toujours su » ?

Je commençai maintenant à soupçonner que Hsiao n'avait pas totalement compris le mystère de ma mère, pas plus qu'il n'avait compris celui de Love. A l'insu de mon oncle, la passion et la perspective de la maternité l'avaient peut-être transformée en femme capable de puiser dans l'expérience ancestrale de la race et de s'en nourrir. Hsiao, de tant d'années son aîné et peu habitué à penser à ma mère autrement qu'à une enfant gâtée, fut peut-être incapable d'appréhender les changements qu'il devina en elle, médita et finit par classer comme purement physiologiques. En tout cas, il était certainement plus rassurant pour lui d'attribuer à ma mère une démence temporaire plutôt que de reconnaître la grande passion de son existence.

Tandis que j'examinais la robe et réfléchissais à la femme qui l'avait brodée, je réalisai que mon oncle avait négligé certaines profondeurs chez ma mère, des trésors cachés de caractère, pleins de complexité, de richesse et d'ambiguïté, comme il en existe toujours chez les êtres que nous aimons et croyons connaître. Mon oncle Hsiao avait laissé beaucoup de choses de côté — malgré lui, parce qu'il les ignorait et n'aurait pu les comprendre. En fait, son récit n'était rien d'autre que sa propre interprétation des événements. Pour reconstruire le squelette décharné des faits bruts, je pouvais lui faire confiance aveuglément. Mais quant au reste — la morphologie générale —, je devais m'en remettre à moi seul pour inventer, ou choisir (selon le cas) mon histoire, moi-même... le monde.

Cette perspective vertigineuse provoqua de nouvelles associations dans la robe. Je détaillai les yeux du Tigre. Ces yeux bleus étaient-ils ceux de mon père, les yeux cachés derrière les verres en forme de larmes vert foncé ? Ma mère avait-elle connu Love, après tout... mieux que Hsiao, mieux que n'importe qui ? Avait-elle découvert ce que dissimulaient les lunettes de soleil, avait-elle contemplé sa nudité, parce qu'elle l'aimait ?

Dans ce cas, j'imagine que chaque fois que les yeux de ma mère rencontraient les siens pour lui offrir sa pitié et son espoir, ils déchiraient le cœur de Love comme des tisons, et une blessure mystérieuse se rouvrait en lui, accompagnée d'une bouffée sulfureuse de chair carbonisée. Car pareil savoir est un pouvoir qui peut détruire aussi bien que sauver. Isolé depuis si longtemps dans l'enfer glacé de son secret, Love considéra peut-être avec une sensibilité maladive le printemps qu'elle lui offrait, respirant la charogne dans la brise tiède, au lieu des senteurs revigorantes de la terre féconde. Alors la peur, plus que la satiété ou l'indifférence, le firent s'enfuir, la peur de la bête sauvage qui redoute d'être capturée. Oui, peut-être ma mère fut-elle le chasseur ; ni notre caractère mortel, ni l'angoisse filiale — mais *elle*. Brusquement, je compris. Elle avait chassé Love hors de sa foi et de son adoration innocentes, les yeux grands ouverts à son ambivalence envers l'existence. Elle avait regardé ses meilleurs et ses pires côtés, et elle les avait acceptés, elle avait tout accepté ; cela fut plus terrible pour mon père que les bêtes noires évoquées par Hsiao et Chong Fou hors de l'obscurité de leur propre cœur afin d'expliquer la nature de mon père.

Je vis aussi que Love s'était lui-même trahi à travers ses propres échappatoires ; car ma mère avait fini par le capturer... Ici même, dans la robe. Capturer, mais sans essayer de le dresser. Ce Tigre n'était pas dressé à danser. Il était libre de s'accoupler et de tuer à son gré. Tel était le dernier message de la robe, adressé à lui mais décrypté par moi : « Tu vois, je désirais seulement t'aimer, pas te posséder. Ceci a été mon amour — un combat que j'aurais provoqué tous les jours, le cœur léger, en sachant que je ne pourrais jamais gagner, sans vouloir gagner (mais pas davantage perdre). Maintenant je suis abandonnée. Que désirais-tu que j'aie retenu ? Quoi de plus précieux que ce que je t'ai offert — le fruit le plus délicat de la vie ? Tu l'as laissé ici sans y goûter, suspendu à l'arbre pour qu'il tombe de lui-même. »

L'allusion de la robe au yoga Tigre Blanc/Dragon Vert éveillait tant d'associations que je mis un certain temps à réaliser que le Dragon de ma mère n'était pas vert, mais jaune. Je ne prétends nullement à l'analyse scientifique : le cœur s'est-il jamais rendu aux arguments importuns de la science ? Le fait est que, loin de réduire à néant mes intuitions, la couleur du Dragon les renforça, ajoutant même une nouvelle dimension à ma compréhension du *p'ao*. Je vis les anneaux concentriques s'écarter encore de l'impact de la pierre, incorporer une zone de sens plus vaste encore, donner au dessin de ma mère une portée qui dépassait la sphère purement personnelle. Comme je les contemplais, le Tigre Blanc et le Dragon Jaune devinrent non seulement mon père et ma mère, mais les races caucasienne et mongoloïde elles-mêmes (plus spécifiquement, les Américains et les Chinois), cultivant un amour équivoque — car toutes choses aiment leur antithèse —, bondissant maladroitement dans les bras de leur partenaire, comme si elles hésitaient entre l'agression et la passion amoureuse. Cette conclusion devint irrésistible quand je songeai que le *Yi king* identifie le Dragon et le Tigre à des points spécifiques du compas : l'est et l'ouest, respectivement.

Ma mère suggérait-elle que sa liaison avec Love était un paradigme, un précédent à la conjugaison qui commençait alors à se dessiner entre l'Est et l'Ouest ? Mais dans ce cas, quel exemple dangereux ! Et pourtant fructueux... dangereusement fructueux... fructueusement dangereux.

La robe me proposa une ultime association, que je dois inclure dans ce catalogue. Elle concerne le zodiaque chinois, dont les signes embrassent toutes les années, et pas simplement les mois, reflétant ainsi, je crois, le rythme absolument différent de la vie orientale, le sens plus sûr de l'immensité du temps qu'a mon peuple. (Plus tard, un mois en Amérique me semblerait une année en Chine.)

Le Tigre et le Dragon sont les habitants les plus puissants du zodiaque chinois. Pour éviter la situation décrite par ma mère dans la robe — leur affrontement —, ces animaux sont sagement séparés par une région intermédiaire, une sorte de zone démilitarisée céleste. Ils s'adressent des regards méfiants et pleins de désir, ils s'épient de part et d'autre du territoire neutre d'une seule année, dont la divinité tutélaire est l'animal le plus faible de ce bestiaire/panthéon : le Lapin. Nuit après nuit, comme pris dans le faisceau d'un projecteur, on le voit galoper dans le ciel au clair de lune, courir pour sauver sa vie, puis plonger dans le trou noir de son terrier pour en émerger timidement à la naissance du mois suivant. (Pour les Orientaux, la pleine lune est un lapin, non une face humaine.) Le Lapin est le réfugié cosmique, chassé de son pays natal par l'agression des deux superpuissances qui s'affrontent sur son terrain.

Ce Lapin me troubla. Il rappelait le lapin que Love avait offert à ma mère lors de leur première rencontre, l'animal craintif dont le couinement, selon mon oncle, ressemble si étrangement aux vagissements d'un nouveau-né humain.

Je mis la robe de côté, car je sentais que j'avais épuisé ses possibilités, et moi-même par la même occasion ; je me levai pour arpenter le sol du temple. Le rossignol n'avait jamais cessé de chanter. Son chant m'attira vers la fenêtre.

Quand je m'assis pour l'écouter, l'histoire de Wu me revint en mémoire, celle du moine dont l'âme blessée s'était enfuie entre les côtes de son corps « comme un oiseau-chanteur hors d'une cage ouverte », pour se poser sur un arbre, pleurer sa douleur et chanter à son maître un long adieu désespéré, puis disparaître à jamais dans la forêt.

A cet instant, la branche frémit comme la corde d'un arc ; l'oiseau cessa de chanter et s'envola dans la nuit. Mon œil suivit la trajectoire de son vol à travers le ciel jusqu'à ce qu'elle eût obscurci le brillant croissant de la lune nouvelle et disparu, comme avalée par sa concavité. A l'endroit exact où il avait pénétré, ou paru pénétrer, je distinguai une décoloration bleutée, une ombre, l'ébauche d'une forme. Je reconnus dans cette tache la patte du Lapin céleste. Elle émergeait de l'astre argenté comme de la doublure en soie perlée d'un haut-de-forme noir.

Et vrillant le silence qui suivit le départ du rossignol, j'entendis le bourdonnement de la mite derrière moi.

10

Quand ce soir-là je finis par m'écrouler sur mon lit, j'étais saturé, *inondé* d'émotions et de possessions nouvelles : amour, terreur, culpabilité, espoir, folie — innombrables contradictions. L'écheveau embrouillé de ma propre histoire reposait à côté de moi comme une planète égarée enfin retrouvée, attirée par la gravitation de mon cœur. Désormais, j'étais comme tout le monde, j'avais un pedigree. J'étais humain ; j'étais mortel. Quant à ce qu'elle impliquait, je ne me serais jamais risqué à aventurer une opinion, tant était récente mon initiation à ces mystères. Eussé-je essayé, je ne serais sans doute arrivé à rien. Car, à dire vrai, cette nuit-là je n'étais pas bon à grand-chose — sinon au délire. Wu me dit ensuite que, lorsque je le croisai dans le cloître alors que j'allais me coucher, en réponse à son salut et ses questions à propos de ma main blessée, je lui adressai seulement une grimace de Singe toqué, marmonnai une stupidité avant de retomber dans un silence têtu et de m'en aller. Quand j'arrivai à ma cellule, je m'effondrai sur ma paillasse et sombrai dans un sommeil sans fond.

Pas assez profond, cependant, pour effacer les rêves. Comme si je n'avais pas eu assez d'émotions pendant cette journée, je fus assailli par le premier épisode d'un rêve récurrent qui malgré sa banalité me bouleversa.

Au début de chaque rêve, je me retrouvais en train de suivre les traces d'un animal, ou d'animaux. Les empreintes étaient parfois celles de sabots, parfois celles de pattes ou de serres. Le paysage changeait à chaque rêve, mais avec une constante : j'entendais toujours, plus ou moins près, le bruit de l'eau courante ; tantôt le bruissement d'un ruisseau ou d'un filet d'eau, tantôt le rugissement d'un torrent tumultueux. A travers les prairies d'altitude aux herbes hautes, étoilées de la gentiane bleue des montagnes, ou dans les forêts-nuages où le soleil brillait comme une grosse et pâle lampe à pétrole qui flottait dans la brume, et où j'entendais les gouttes d'eau crépiter sur les feuilles des rhododendrons ; tantôt sur les champs de neige, ou dans la chaleur étouffante et l'argile visqueux d'une rizière ; tantôt dans les déserts, tantôt dans une plaine interminable, à travers les marais salants d'un estuaire et jusqu'à de lointaines cavernes souterraines, je les suivais, arrivant enfin et toujours à la mer où le bruit de l'eau courante se mêlait au soupir des vagues. Là, sur une plage de sable volcanique, je m'accroupissais à la lisière de l'océan pour examiner les dernières empreintes qu'effaçait la marée montante. Le soleil qui sombrait dans les eaux ressemblait à une larme de sang qui coulait en silence sur la face bleue du ciel. Je me sentais perplexe et frustré d'avoir perdu la trace de mon gibier, mais la mer dont l'immensité s'étendait à perte de vue m'apaisait par son impassibilité monumentale, son absolu manque de détail, de complexité. Ce calme gris, aussi sombre qu'une fin ou un commencement, distrayait mon esprit de sa chasse vaine, me dédommageait.

J'ignore si cela fut lié à la première manifestation de ce rêve, mais le matin qui suivit le départ de Hsiao je m'éveillai en proie à une vague anxiété, et (bizarrement, vu ce que mon oncle m'avait offert, tant spirituellement que matériellement) avec la conviction d'une perte irrémédiable, comme d'un bien dont j'aurais ignoré l'existence avant qu'on me l'eût enlevé. Pour la première fois je fis l'expérience d'un creux et en même temps d'un poids terrible au centre de mon être, sensation qui devait rarement me quitter par la suite, sinon dans le sommeil et, quelque temps, dans la méditation. Je ne savais comment l'expliquer, mais quelque chose avait changé. Je n'étais plus heureux.

Jusqu'à ma méditation en fut touchée. Je cessai de passer aussitôt dans cet état d'intensité apaisante auquel j'étais habitué après tant d'années de pratique. Je vécus une régression et fus dorénavant distrait par un bruit précis. Cela ressemblait un peu à l'eau courante de mon rêve, et davantage au sifflement de la bouilloire juste avant que l'eau ne bouille pour de bon ; mieux encore, je le comparai à une radio qui grésille entre deux stations dans une pièce éloignée de la maison, crache et chuinte ses parasites électrostatiques. Mais pour moi, l'image qui le décrit le mieux est tirée du premier des *Dix Chants du Chercheur de Bœuf* :

> Mes yeux épuisés se brouillent, mon cœur vacille ;
>   car je ne trouve pas le taureau.
> J'écoute, défait, la stridulation sans âme des cigales
>   dans le bois où la lune ne luit pas.

La cigale symbolise l'esprit inquiet, incapable de repos, le cœur passionnément attaché au monde des sens, et qui redoute de s'abandonner, de couler comme une pierre (une plume !) dans le Vide immaculé et brillant. En plus de sa valeur d'onomatopée, l'image a d'autres mérites. Car la stridulation monotone et mécanique des cigales mâles dans la forêt par une nuit d'été, qui chantent le désir de la chair, cette musique obsédante d'un appétit maladif, insatiable, et qu'il faut apaiser ou mortifier — cette image fait pressentir l'enfer charnel de l'homme. La méditation, le retour à la source paisible de l'être, essaie de faire taire cette musique, d'imposer silence à la cigale qui chante toujours « dans le temple du cœur ».

Alors qu'assis sur mon coussin à prière, je tentais de plonger sous la surface tumultueuse de ma conscience pour rejoindre plus bas les courants froids qui couraient en silence, une image de ma jeunesse révolue passa devant mes yeux.

Debout dans le temple, je tenais un balai que j'avais trouvé dans un recoin et que je maniais comme une arme pour tenter de chasser une cigale — une vraie cigale — entrée par la fenêtre ouverte pendant la méditation du matin ; elle poussait l'insolence jusqu'à profaner de ses stridulations le sanctuaire et l'activité solennelle qui s'y déroulait. Quand je l'aperçus, elle disparaissait dans la crypte de Kwan Ti, la sauvage divinité guerrière aux yeux qui louchent et au visage maculé non de poussière, mais par la fumée et les souillures du combat. Scandalisés par cette intrusion sans précédent, les yeux injectés de sang de Kwan Ti semblaient sur le point de jaillir de leurs orbites. J'inspectai la divinité aussi respectueusement que possible pour essayer de chasser l'insecte de sa cachette. Soudain la créature émit un vrombissement perçant et s'envola impudemment sous mon nez. Mes bras décrivirent des moulinets frénétiques pour l'intercepter, mais je réussis seulement à déloger une lampe à prière, qui explosa sur le sol avec le bruit d'un signal d'alarme aérienne *ching-pao*.

Les frères, jusque-là tranquillement assis, oublieux de la tâche que j'effectuais pour eux, ouvrirent les yeux et regardèrent autour d'eux comme des hommes réveillés en sursaut, visités par la prémonition d'un danger. Pétrifié de terreur et de tristesse, je rougis jusqu'à la racine de mes cheveux et restai planté là comme un imbécile, tandis qu'ils évaluaient la situation. Certains secouaient la tête, d'autres acquiesçaient, d'autres encore se penchaient vers leur voisin, cachaient leur bouche derrière leur main pour chuchoter des syllabes sifflantes et venimeuses. Leurs yeux disaient « coupable ».

Wu, qui de la cuisine avait entendu le tumulte et deviné sa cause, apparut sur le seuil avec son gros bambou. Quand il m'aperçut tremblant et pitoyable, il soupira, puis s'avança sombrement vers moi pour accomplir son devoir. A peine m'avait-il saisi par le poignet et fait pivoter pour m'appliquer le bâton, que la voix du maître résonna.

« Amène-le-moi. »

Sa voix n'était ni douce ni sévère ; pourtant, je tremblais de terreur quand Wu me traîna sur le sol.

« Tu vas y avoir droit », dit-il dans sa barbe, mi-méprisant, mi-apitoyé.

Je n'en doutai pas une seconde. Bien que Chong Fou ne m'eût jamais puni, je le redoutais infiniment plus que Wu avec tous ses instruments de torture (et son grand cœur qui fondait aisément). Car je croyais dur comme fer que Chong Fou était un magicien capable d'opérer sur moi une horrible métamorphose. N'avais-je pas entendu dire que les alchimistes avaient toujours besoin du sang frais et pur des enfants — ingrédient essentiel à la composition de la Pilule Or-Cinabre ? Certains moines avaient même été assez cruels pour m'affirmer qu'on m'avait soigné et nourri depuis tant d'années dans ce seul but, comme une dinde de Noël chinoise. Chong Fou allait-il me suspendre par des crochets et des grappins au-dessus de la flamme blafarde du cobalt pour distiller mon essence vitale comme on extrait la sève de l'érable, puis la concentrer dans un alambic et la boire à longs traits goulus comme une coupe d'eau-de-vie, avant d'essuyer sa bouche sur la manche de sa soutane en rotant ? Cela ou un scénario similaire ne me semblait nullement improbable.

« Je croyais que tu voulais t'asseoir avec nous, dit le maître.
— Oui, implorai-je humblement, mais...
— Mais quoi ?
— C'est un petit Sauvage, voilà tout, intervint Wu. C'est son côté *Sun*, sa nature de Singe. Il n'y peut rien. »
Les moines pouffèrent. Chong Fou ne tint pas compte de la remarque.
« J'ai entendu une ci-ci-cigale stridu-du-duler, bafouillai-je. Si fort que je ne ne pouvais pas me con-concentrer. »
Il écarquilla les yeux. « Tu l'as vraiment vue, n'est-ce pas ? »
J'acquiesçai.
« Où ?
— Là ! » Je montrai la crypte. J'aperçus Kwan Ti qui me regardait d'un air menaçant, réalisai aussitôt mon geste sacrilège et tombai vivement à genoux devant la statue pour me prosterner plusieurs fois avec véhémence.
« Et tu as voulu faire taire cet insecte irrespectueux pour nous rendre service ? »
Je hochai la tête.
L'ombre d'un sourire passa sur les lèvres de Chong Fou. « Hmmm. Fort louable. Mais tu n'as pas songé que si tu étais resté immobile, la cigale t'aurait inévitablement révélé ses intentions, et aurait peut-être même fini par s'en aller d'elle-même ? »
Cette hypothèse me parut hautement improbable, mais comme je craignais d'abuser de ma bonne fortune, je restai coi, me contentant de gonfler ma joue avec ma langue et de rouler les yeux vers le plafond.
« Tu en doutes ? demanda Chong Fou en riant. Ta foi dans le Tao est faible, petit frère. Ignores-tu que pour ceux qui comme toi sont affligés d'une âme souvent inquiète, il y a toujours une cigale qui chante dans le temple du cœur ? »
Cette soudaine métaphore dépassait les capacités de mon jeune esprit. J'en déduisis naïvement qu'il suggérait à mots couverts que la cigale était une hallucination.
« Mais c'était une vraie cigale ! m'écriai-je, protestant passionnément contre cette interprétation à la fois humiliante et injuste. Je l'ai vue !
— Naturellement », dit Chong Fou d'une voix apaisante. Il posa la paume de sa main sur mon cœur comme pour le calmer. « Et où est-elle maintenant, à ton avis ? » demanda-t-il à voix basse.
Retenant mon souffle, je tendis l'oreille, mais il n'y avait plus rien... seulement mes battements de cœur. Je soupirai. « Elle est partie. »
Avec un geste si vif qu'il me fit une peur bleue, le maître éloigna sa main de ma soutane et la ferma.
« Ecoute », dit-il en approchant son poing de mon oreille comme s'il renfermait quelque chose.
A ma grande surprise, l'espace confiné de sa main émettait un lointain sifflement, un chuintement qui n'était pas sans rappeler le rugissement de la mer contenu dans les volutes spiralées d'un coquillage, auquel sa main âgée ressemblait en effet.
Je n'eus pas le temps de réfléchir à ce mystère, car Chong Fou éclata de rire. Il ouvrit la main, une cigale s'en échappa, s'envola et sortit du temple par la fenêtre.

★

    Ce matin-là, comme j'étais assis dans le temple, distrait de ma méditation par ces réminiscences, je songeai que le tour de magie du maître s'était gravé dans mon esprit d'enfant. Car après cet épisode, j'avais littéralement adoré Chong Fou et décidé de marcher sur ses traces, réfléchissant avec un sérieux exemplaire au moindre de ses gestes et à toutes ses paroles comme à ceux d'un oracle qui aurait détenu la clef de la sagesse. Tel fut le processus de mon éducation : sans coercition, mais par la douceur ou la terreur, planter dans le cœur du disciple les graines de l'espoir et de l'émerveillement, lui offrir une lampée de cette eau mystérieuse et limpide qui seule peut étancher la soif intolérable des désirs terrestres.
    Au bout de trois années d'efforts soutenus, j'avais enfin franchi le seuil pour entrer dans le silence. Mais à l'époque, ma concentration était trop imparfaite pour maintenir longtemps cet état. Au bout de cinq ans de perfectionnement, je n'étais jamais distrait plus d'une fois par semaine. A dix-neuf ans, je pouvais entrer à volonté dans une transe profonde et y rester presque indéfiniment. J'avais enfin appris à imiter l'action de l'eau qui s'infiltre à travers le sol apparemment imperméable des apparences pour rejoindre le froid et pur réservoir du Tao.
    Deux années s'étaient écoulées depuis, et je pensais sincèrement ne plus jamais être ennuyé par la cigale dans le temple du cœur. Ce matin-là, dans le temple, je fus donc bouleversé quand cette musique douloureuse que je connaissais si bien résonna dans mon cœur. Je décidai de consulter l'oracle.
    Je tombai sur l'hexagramme *Su*, le cinquième du *Livre des Mutations*, « L'Attente, la Nutrition ». *Su* est constitué du trigramme *K'an*, ☵, « L'Insondable », au-dessus de *K'ien*, ☰, « Le Créateur ». L'image de *K'an* est l'eau, son attribut le danger. L'image de *K'ien* est le ciel, son attribut la force.
    Voici le commentaire :

> Tous les êtres ont besoin de la nourriture d'en haut. Mais les aliments sont administrés en leur temps, qu'il faut attendre. L'hexagramme montre les nuages dans le ciel, répandant la pluie qui réjouit tout ce qui croît et pourvoit l'homme de nourriture et de boisson. Cette pluie viendra à son heure. On ne peut la contraindre à venir ; il faut l'attendre. L'idée de l'attente est encore renforcée par les propriétés de chacun des trigrammes : au-dedans, force ; devant, danger. Face au danger, la force ne se précipite pas mais sait attendre, tandis que la faiblesse tombe dans l'agitation et n'a pas la patience d'attendre.

    L'allusion au « danger » me fit dresser l'oreille. J'ignorais ce dont il s'agissait précisément, mais le mot fit résonner un diapason en moi. Un frisson prémonitoire me glaça, intensifié par ce que je lus dans le jugement, où il était écrit : « Il est avantageux de traverser les grandes eaux. » Je savais parfaitement que « traverser les grandes eaux » était une métaphore qui renvoyait à n'importe quelle décision. Mais la signification littérale de cette expression se fixa dans mon esprit, et une image de mon rêve apparut

brusquement devant mes yeux : je me vis accroupi sur le sable, comme dans une attitude de déférence, le regard tourné vers l'horizon marin, alors que le soleil sombrait dans l'océan où il s'éteignait.
Le commentaire relatif à *Su* se poursuivait ainsi :

> Le consultant a devant lui un danger à surmonter. La faiblesse et l'impatience sont impuissantes. Seul l'homme fort assumera son destin, car il peut tenir bon jusqu'à la fin grâce à son assurance intérieure. Cette force se révèle dans une sincérité inflexible. C'est seulement quand nous avons le courage de regarder les choses telles qu'elles sont, sans la moindre illusion ni duperie, qu'il se dégage des événements une lumière qui nous permet de reconnaître la voie du succès.

Le premier trait, ou trait inférieur de l'oracle, était « ferme », un neuf. Je passai aux applications des traits et lus :

Neuf au commencement signifie :
Attente dans le pré.
Il est avantageux de demeurer dans ce qui dure...

> Le danger est encore loin. On attend encore sur le sol uni. Les conditions sont encore simples, mais on ressent l'imminence d'un événement. Il faut continuer à mener une vie régulière aussi longtemps que possible.

Bien que les allusions répétées au danger m'aient un peu inquiété, et peut-être aussi légèrement excité, j'étais bien décidé à ne pas courir de risque inutile. Je suivrais l'avis de l'oracle et continuerais à « mener une vie régulière aussi longtemps que possible ». Ce fut dans cet état d'esprit que, ce même après-midi, j'écoutai les paroles du maître concernant la retraite annuelle qui allait bientôt commencer, ma première depuis ma majorité. Elle prendrait un sens particulier pour moi, car à la fin des six jours de solitude et de jeûne, je prononcerais mes vœux et recevrais l'ultime initiation à l'ordre.
« Fragments d'épaves flottant sur l'océan de la vie, voués à la désintégration et à la métamorphose — bouchons à la dérive, morceaux de varech lacérés et déracinés, bois flottant qui finit par couler, commença le maître, voilà quelques images de nous-mêmes. Mais nous avons pourtant un rôle à jouer, nous sommes indispensables au schéma général. Car notre but est d'enrichir la solution du Tao et d'assurer l'avenir. La perte d'un seul grain de sable annoncerait la fin du monde. Le Tao lui-même serait aspiré dans le vide qui s'ensuivrait.
« Pourtant, cela est inconcevable ; car le Tao est aussi le vide. Il ne saurait y avoir ni perte ni destruction, seulement le Retour, le voyage de retour au Tao, que vous accomplirez durant cette retraite. Partez le cœur léger, progressez avec diligence. Apprenez à vous connaître et à vous accepter, ainsi que votre place dans l'ordre global. C'est la seule voie qui conduit à l'harmonie que, tôt ou tard, si vous persévérez, vous accomplirez.

Tout le reste est souffrance, futilité — un combat voué à l'échec pour circonvenir la Voie de la Vie, qu'on ne peut circonvenir. Chacun de nous doit voyager sur cette route et affronter ses terreurs. Il n'y a pas d'autre Voie.

« Cherchez-la donc résolument, chacun à sa façon, selon sa voie privée. Il n'existe aucune directive supplémentaire, car on ne trouve pas deux chemins semblables ; mais à l'horizon tous convergent vers un unique point de fuite pour disparaître dans les ténèbres que nous appelons la mort. Alors peut-être, de ce point de vue supérieur, nous discernerons le tout et nous comprendrons. Mais jusque-là, chacun doit œuvrer obscurément à l'écart des autres. »

Une étrange sensation me submergea quand je me rappelai l'exhortation du maître. La « voie privée » dont il parlait évoquait « la voie du succès » mentionnée dans l'hexagramme *Su*. « C'est seulement quand nous avons le courage de regarder les choses telles qu'elles sont, sans la moindre illusion ni duperie, qu'il se dégage des événements une lumière qui nous permet de reconnaître la voie du succès. » Déconcertant de penser qu'il s'agissait peut-être de la « voie privée » des créatures mortelles, dont le faisceau convergeait vers l'« horizon » dont parlait le maître.

Cette nuit-là, je rêvai encore d'empreintes de pas, je m'accroupis encore sur la plage pour regarder l'immensité de l'océan, écouter le rythme mélancolique des vagues.

Le premier jour de la retraite, je consultai de nouveau l'oracle. A ma grande surprise, il m'orienta encore vers *Su*. Le trait ferme s'était élevé d'un cran, à la deuxième place.

> Neuf à la deuxième place signifie :
> Attente sur le sable...

> Le danger s'approche peu à peu. Le sable est près de la rive du fleuve, et l'eau signifie danger... Celui qui reste calme parviendra à ce qu'à la fin tout aille bien pour lui.

La récurrence du rêve et du reflet de ses images dans l'oracle me convainquit qu'il s'agissait de bien plus que d'une coïncidence, que j'assistais aux prémices d'une nouvelle phase de mon existence, comme si j'essayais vainement de déchiffrer les caractères à peine lisibles d'un vieux parchemin à l'encre passée qui énonçait mon destin. L'idée que je devais à tout prix comprendre le sens de mon rêve s'imposa à moi. Je tentai de me calmer, ainsi que l'oracle le conseillait, mais je fus inquiet toute la journée. J'essayai de méditer, mais la stridulation de la cigale s'était amplifiée.

Le troisième jour fut sans surprise, implacable. Avec l'insistance morbide d'un mendiant errant qui porte son horrible message comme une lanterne à travers le monde, son texte enluminé, un crâne humain en guise de *memento mori*, l'oracle me renvoya une fois de plus à *Su*. « Le danger »,

« l'attente », une « reconnaissance » imminente — comme auparavant. Mais le trait ferme s'était élevé d'un autre cran :

> Neuf à la troisième place signifie :
> L'attente dans la vase
> Provoque l'arrivée de l'ennemi.

« L'attente dans la vase » — expression appropriée. Car ce jour-là un pan de moi-même céda, comme les planches d'un vieux pont que j'aurais emprunté chaque jour de ma vie, sans imaginer une seconde qu'il pût pourrir — non, qu'il *pourrissait* — alors que je foulais son tablier. Il céda, et je replongeai dans la nature fétide, la fange primordiale, la crasse et la beauté auxquelles j'avais échappé et dont je me croyais définitivement préservé... J'en étais sorti, j'y retournais — après le répit voulu par mon destin, après ma jeunesse, ce bref séjour dans le sanctuaire immaculé du Tao —, j'y retournais.

Ce jour-là, malgré ma résolution de bannir toute pensée du monde, mon esprit se tournait irrésistiblement vers mes parents. Je me souvins des mots prononcés par Hsiao à propos de ma mère — « Dans l'arrière-pays vit une biche ; parmi les roseaux blancs elle s'attarde... à jamais » — et je fondis en larmes. Mes sanglots passèrent aussi vite qu'une ondée, mais sans soulager mon cœur. Au contraire, ils le laissèrent plus lourd, lourd d'une douleur impalpable, qui n'était pas seulement de la douleur, mais renfermait des graines d'amertume et de haine. Une fois de plus, le visage de mon père parut se matérialiser devant moi, pavillon flottant en haut du grand mât du navire qui venait de pénétrer dans le port tranquille de mon existence. Son sourire était la grimace facétieuse de Jolly Roger ; ses lunettes, les orbites creuses d'un crâne... mais tellement tristes les verres incurvés vers le bas, de la tristesse figée d'un masque, ou du clown, qui peint le domino de la souffrance sur sa propre peine, et rit. Il y avait de la beauté et du mystère sur ce visage, un secret que je devais percer. Ma mère, malgré l'énigme de la robe, n'était pas aussi étrange. La conviction d'une cause commune, d'une humanité partagée, me rendait intelligible son destin. Mais Love, je ne pouvais le comprendre.

Pourtant, je ne désirais rien de plus au monde. Je l'avais trop aimé pour renoncer, aimé d'un amour aussi fort, d'une foi primitive aussi résolue que mon amour du Tao. Les révélations de Hsiao — que je ne pouvais qu'accepter — ne modifièrent en rien mon sentiment. En fait, dans un subtil clair-obscur, le jeu d'ombres esquissé par Hsiao pour peindre mon père fit seulement ressortir les couleurs et les traits essentiels, accentua les turbulences du portrait — le *yin* embrassant, définissant, complétant le *yang*. Et ce *yin* n'était pas maléfique, pas davantage que la nuit qui suit incessamment le jour dans le flux et le reflux du temps, qui participe du cycle de la nature dans l'univers changeant et inchangé. Peut-être mon père était-il aussi peu coupable que la nuit... Mais je ne pouvais plus croire à cela. La haine avait fait irruption dans toute sa violence et cohabitait maladroitement avec l'amour, tels deux énormes navires qui luttaient bord à bord à l'embouchure du port, convoitaient l'unique mouillage et attendaient le changement de marées.

Qui était cet homme ? Je devais l'apprendre. Etait-il fou, comme Hsiao le prétendait ? Ou bien était-il le dragon de Chong Fou, une « ébauche » d'Immortel, un boddhisattva à l'état brut ? Peut-être le membre d'une espèce totalement différente — unique, sans précédent — une espèce que même leur expérience ne les avait pas préparés à identifier : poisson magique, léviathan somnolant depuis cent millions d'années au fond de l'océan, créature mutante encore visqueuse du liquide amniotique de la création, trop neuve pour apparaître dans les classifications existantes, et qui avait ouvert une brèche dans leurs filets, les déchirant comme de la gaze... une créature qu'ils avaient aperçue sans pouvoir la capturer ni la retenir, qui avait replongé dans la mer, et qu'on avait vue pour la dernière fois en route vers l'Ouest, vers l'Amérique et le Nouveau Monde.

Mais si Chong Fou et Hsiao ne savaient que penser de lui, quel espoir me restait-il de découvrir sa nature ? Comment Love aurait-il pu entrer dans le schéma général de ce que je connaissais ? A quel accident ou hasard (ou à quelle loi inconnue) devait-il son existence ? Etait-il une aberration de la nature, ou existait-il d'autres êtres qui lui ressemblaient — toute une civilisation peut-être, constituée de ses semblables, qui adoraient un dieu barbare, un dieu dont le nom était... quoi ? Comment appelaient-ils leur divinité sauvage, quel nom chuchotaient-ils dans leurs prières ?

Comme pour répondre à cette question, le jeu de mots crucial me revint en mémoire, et dans un éclair éblouissant toutes mes interrogations, tous mes doutes et mes peurs se fondirent dans ce mot unique, cette syllabe qui était à la fois question et réponse, ce schibboleth que je répétais mécaniquement, convaincu qu'il constituait la clef de tout, *la clef* « qui ouvre les sombres secrets du cœur... une clef d'église... qui pourra te faire entrer dans la Grande Cathédrale... » Oui ! Le mot ! « Dow ». « L'autre », le Dow américain, le Dow de mon père, « le même mais différent ». Quelle était cette entité mystérieuse ? Je n'en avais pas la moindre idée. Mais ce jeu de mots me fascinait comme un charme magique. Quel rapport avait-il avec le Tao que je connaissais ? En quel lieu son flot tumultueux et écumant refluait-il dans l'océan paisible du Tao ? Car il devait refluer. Tout remontait vers la Source. Il le devait.

Je serrai la bride de mon imagination et m'arrêtai de justesse au bord d'un précipice vertigineux. Ce fut une réaction saine, mais qui ne me sauva pas. Car la graine du doute avait été plantée, beaucoup plus tôt peut-être... glissée dans le tendre sillon de mes fontanelles alors que je reposais dans la matrice de ma mère. L'instant précis de cette insémination importe peu. Le fait crucial était que la machine s'était mise en branle, la question avait été posée, et le voyage entamé, qui devait me conduire ici. Je pense parfois que tout ce qui arriva ensuite fut pure nécessité.

Après une nuit d'insomnie passée à arpenter ma cellule en écoutant les cigales striduler leur prophétie implacable dans les ténèbres, je me tournai à nouveau vers l'oracle, mais cette fois avec le pressentiment de la fatalité, comme un coupable qui attend le verdict du tribunal — un verdict que son cœur connaît déjà. Pour la quatrième fois, *Su* :

Six à la quatrième place signifie :
Attente dans le sang.
Sors du trou.

La situation est extrêmement dangereuse. Elle est maintenant de la plus grande gravité — une question de vie ou de mort... On ne peut ni avancer ni reculer. Toute retraite est coupée, comme si l'on était dans un trou. Il n'est alors que de tenir bon et de laisser le destin suivre son cours.

Je repris mes pérégrinations inquiètes. Incapable de méditer, je ne tenais pas en place. Le monde palpitait comme un essaim bourdonnant. La moitié du temps de retraite s'était déjà écoulé, et mon cœur, loin de s'abandonner, loin de trouver le calme et la pureté du miroir qu'aucune image ne souille, s'inquiétait et battait la campagne chaque jour davantage. Les reflets qui usurpaient la surface du miroir, loin de se dissiper, devenaient plus précis, comme tracés au laser — la blancheur du soleil concentrée par des prismes ou une loupe gravait de façon indélébile l'image de mon père dans son tain. Incapable de méditer, j'eus recours à un expédient : réciter le Grand Vœu, et le réciter encore pour empêcher mes pensées de suivre leur cours abrupt et despotique :

Le Tao engendra l'Un ;
L'Un engendra successivement deux choses,
Trois choses, puis dix mille.
Moi, pèlerin en cette vie, exilé
Décidé à rentrer chez moi,
A retourner à la Source,
Je choisis de ces dix mille choses, ces
Trois Trésors pour me soutenir
Dans ma faiblesse pendant la première étape du voyage —
Humilité, Frugalité, Compassion —
Mais quand je serai plus fort
Et qu'ils deviendront superflus — un handicap
Dans ma quête — je renoncerai aussi
A eux, réduisant le nombre
De mes besoins, de mes bagages, à deux,
Yin et *Yang*,
Termes de la Grande Opposition Primordiale,
Qu'en moi-même, par un effort sans réserve,
J'espère réconcilier dans l'Un,
Restaurant ainsi l'Unité, l'Harmonie, la Voie
Qui est et était, retournant ainsi
A mon ultime destination

TAO

Mère de toutes les existences
Que nous voyons autour de nous,
Spectacle kaléidoscopique des Apparences :

TAO

L'Un de cette multiplicité
Foisonnante, lui-même
Immuable et donnant
Naissance à tous les changements.

Voici ma foi :
La Réalité est Une,
Et le Tao est la Réalité.
Je la déclare
Entière et véridique
Sous peine de perdition.

Ainsi :

Je renonce au monde à jamais
Afin de l'améliorer.
Je renonce à moi-même
Afin de me trouver.
Puissé-je ne pas me détourner de cette résolution
Avant que l'enfer ne soulage les damnés
Et que mon âme ne se transforme en cendres.

Les mots couraient dans mon esprit comme l'eau sur les pierres. Sans cesse je me surprenais à penser à lui, comme l'aiguille d'une boussole irrésistiblement attirée par le nord. Je me ressaisissais alors et reprenais ma pieuse litanie en espérant que le vœu parviendrait à me libérer de la gravité de l'amour, à m'affranchir de la puissance de son charme.

Mais ce fut le vœu lui-même qui eut raison de moi. En une seconde, nettement, efficacement, une partie de moi-même se brisa ou fut amputée, comme par une chirurgie perfide, — mon cœur, mon foie, un de mes organes vitaux, tranché puis jeté au rebut. Sous anesthésie locale, j'étais éveillé et je l'aperçus à côté de moi sans passion. Plus tard seulement, quand j'eus deviné le changement qui s'était produit en moi, je pus évaluer l'étendue de ma perte.

Je sais précisément le moment où cela se produisit :

Voici ma foi :
La Réalité est Une,
Et le Tao est la Réalité.

Alors que je récitais ces mots, je fus aveuglé par une clarté hallucinante qui modifia à jamais les traits familiers de mon univers ; brusquement, les paroles du vœu se transformèrent en cendres sur mes lèvres. Je compris que je n'y croyais pas, ou du moins n'en étais plus certain. Je doutai. Je sus alors que je ne prononcerais jamais mes vœux. Le faire sans la foi eût signé ma damnation. Pourtant, j'étais damné dans les deux cas, perdu dans les deux cas.

La reconnaissance dont l'oracle avait parlé s'était produite. Je comprenais que ma foi avait été entamée, peut-être irrémédiablement, par le récit de mon oncle et ses allusions à un autre monde, un autre ordre d'expérience étranger au mien, irréconciliable avec le mien. Voilà ce qui m'avait tenaillé, avait miné mes certitudes durant ces jours de retraite — le caractère irréconciliable de ce monde, le monde que j'avais vu reflété dans les lunettes de mon père, un monde d'un exotisme impossible, scintillant, beau, pernicieux, un lieu de magie, de folie, de pouvoir, de richesses et de désir, où toutes les certitudes se renversaient, où le déshonneur n'était pas incompatible avec le plus grand courage et où la voie de l'intérêt personnel ne conduisait pas à la destruction, mais à des sommets vertigineux d'extase et de pouvoir où tous les rêves devenaient vrais ! Pourquoi cette vision me fascinait-elle tout en me terrifiant ? Une partie de moi-même (le « nouveau » Sun I ?), une essence volatile transmise par les gènes de mon père, désirait-elle, avec l'instinct sûr de l'oiseau migrateur, retourner vers cette Source, *sa* source — non le Tao, mais le *Dow* ? L'« ancien » Sun I méprisait ce désir qu'il jugeait hérétique et blasphématoire, la trahison de sa foi.

Mais était-ce vraiment le cas ? Ce jeu de mots était-il un monstrueux canular de la nature, deux têtes sur une seule paire d'épaules, ou bien reflétait-il une identité réelle entre les deux visions ? Étaient-elles finalement une seule et même chose ? Si ce qu'on m'avait appris était vrai, il le fallait : « La Réalité est Une, et le Tao est la Réalité. » Sur la vérité de cette proposition, je misais mon avenir, et au-delà, le salut de mon âme. Et si je me trompais ? J'allais m'unir indissolublement, risquant ainsi l'enfer, à une foi que je voyais tournée en dérision par le sourire espiègle de mon père, fragmentée à l'infini par les reflets éblouissants, insidieux et multipliés des gratte-ciel de Manhattan !

J'étais à la croisée des chemins, mais les deux voies qui s'offraient à moi menaient à la perdition. Soit je renonçais à la foi de mon enfance et je perdais tout ce que j'avais jamais possédé ou connu, soit je m'y accrochais sans plus y croire, auquel cas je me damnais. Les images de mon enfance me submergèrent comme des livres de comptes remplis de dettes écrasantes, chacune signée de mon nom, seule caution qu'on m'eût jamais réclamée (mon nom, cette monnaie qu'aucune loi ne reconnaissait, cette devise courante aujourd'hui totalement dévaluée). J'étais plein de désespoir et de ressentiment.

Brusquement, j'eus peur de l'enfer. Je pensai à Yen Lo-Wang, le Sombre Seigneur de la Mort, lisant la liste de mes péchés et de mes vertus aux scribes et autres bureaucrates affairés de l'enfer — ma vie : une page blanche portant un seul caractère noir, une souillure, le péché de mon apostasie, de ma trahison — puis me remettant entre les mains des licteurs démoniaques qui se querellaient et se disputaient mon cœur palpitant comme des vautours un quartier de viande, et jetaient mon cadavre sanglant dans un profond bassin d'excréments où il pourrirait pour l'éternité dans un grouillement d'énormes vers roses.

Pourtant, entre deux accès de désespoir, une paix semblable à la mort m'envahissait. J'étais celui qui assiste à sa propre agonie pendant l'holocauste final. L'énorme nuage déroulait ses lentes volutes sous mes yeux, s'épanouissait pétale par pétale, tel un vaste lotus noir s'ouvrant silencieusement au cœur de l'espace. « Même au milieu du danger, il y a des moments de répit. » *Su* — le trait ferme à la cinquième place.

Toute la journée du lendemain, jusqu'à ce que ma cellule commençât à s'assombrir, m'annonçant le crépuscule, je restai allongé sur les pierres froides et regardai le mur sans rien voir, sans bouger ni penser. Enfin, je me sentis un peu revivre. Je me levai, puisai une louche d'eau, dont je bus une gorgée, et lavai mon visage. Je sentis une bouffée d'espoir. Bien qu'incapable de prononcer mes vœux pour l'instant, avec le temps je pourrais peut-être... si je consacrais toutes mes journées à la méditation et m'immergeais totalement dans la Voie. C'était certes un échec, mais sans doute pas insurmontable. La vie m'accorderait peut-être une deuxième chance.

Au dehors les cigales stridulaient inlassablement dans les ténèbres. Cette nuit-là, je fis de nouveau le même rêve. Mais cette fois avec une variation. Alors que j'observais la surface grise de la mer, je fus saisi d'une prémonition. Je me retournai pour regarder le terrain que je venais de parcourir et, l'espace d'un instant, j'eus l'impression incongrue que les empreintes me suivaient, comme si une bête invisible était sur *mes* traces, l'avait toujours été. Elles se rapprochaient de moi, écrasaient le sable ; terrifié, je fis volte-face et pénétrai dans l'eau. Celle-ci me montait à la taille quand je compris ce qui se passait. Je pivotai aussitôt en hurlant, alors qu'une vague gigantesque déferlait sur moi et m'engloutissait.

Peu après, je me levai machinalement, pris la boîte en cyprès qui renfermait mes baguettes, l'ouvris et les sortis. Alors, pour la dernière fois, je sondai mon destin. Telle une voix montant la gamme jusqu'au contre-ut, le trait ferme s'était élevé d'un cran par jour dans l'hexagramme *Su*. Il ne pouvait aller plus haut :

> Six en haut signifie :
> On tombe dans le trou...

L'attente est terminée ; le danger ne se laisse plus écarter. On tombe dans le trou et il faut se résoudre à l'inévitable. Tout semble alors avoir été vain. Mais c'est précisément dans cette détresse que survient un tournant imprévu. Sans que l'on ait agi personnellement, il se produit une intervention extérieure, dont on peut d'abord se demander ce qu'elle signifie : est-elle délivrance ou destruction ?

Je fermai le livre, me levai et, violant le protocole de la retraite, quittai ma cellule. Sans savoir pourquoi ni ce que j'allais dire, j'allai instinctivement voir le maître.

Chong Fou était assis sur un tapis à prière au fond de sa cellule, jambes pliées en tailleur dans la position du lotus, les mains fermées et les paumes levées, son pouce gauche coincé dans sa main droite. Je croyais qu'il n'avait pas remarqué mon arrivée, mais sans ouvrir les yeux il dit doucement : « Bienvenue, Sun I. Je t'attendais. »

Ses yeux s'ouvrirent lentement. Quand ses iris s'agrandirent, je vis l'éternité refluer devant moi, de plus en plus loin, comme un paysage aperçu à travers le mauvais côté d'un télescope, qui paraît s'éloigner jusqu'à prendre la dimension d'une tête d'épingle. Ses pupilles ressemblaient aux minuscules taches aveugles qui flottent au cœur du kaléidoscope, sereines et pourtant entourées d'un spectacle changeant et fébrile. La lumière de l'autre monde quitta graduellement son visage. Il était pâle, sa peau presque translucide, son souffle à peine perceptible ; il me regardait avec une impassibilité où l'on ne sentait nulle trace de familiarité ni d'émotion... bien que loin, très loin, brillât une étincelle, un souvenir, de pitié.

« Alors », murmura-t-il ; à ce mot, les vannes de ma souffrance s'ouvrirent. Je pris mon visage dans mes mains, et pleurai.

« Ne pleure pas, Sun I », dit-il, mais sa voix trembla ; quand je le regardai, je vis qu'il avait les larmes aux yeux.

Alors je perdis tout espoir. « C'est fini, fini », me lamentai-je doucement pour moi-même, pour lui, pour personne.

Le maître soupira. « Pauvre Singe. Maintenant tu commences à comprendre les difficultés de la Voie. C'est ardu, Sun I. Mais fini ? Qu'est-ce qui est fini ?

— Maître, je vous ai trahi.

— Comment m'as-tu trahi ? »

Je lui racontai tout : les empreintes qui, chaque nuit, me ramenaient au bord du sombre océan gris dans lequel le soleil sombrait comme une larme de sang. Je lui parlai de l'oracle, de son étonnante répétition du signe du danger, de la cigale et de ma méditation distraite, je lui parlai enfin de ma foi anéantie, de mon doute, de mon intuition d'une vérité fugitive et monstrueuse incompatible avec le Tao — les dix mille et une choses, égales et contemporaines du Tao, mais séparées —, des miettes de pain que mon père avait laissées derrière lui, et qui ne ramenaient pas à la Source, mais à un domaine inconnu et inhospitalier dont je ne connaissais rien, sinon le nom : Dow.

« Ah, fit-il. Nous y voilà donc. » Il se tut pour réfléchir ; on n'entendit plus dans la cellule que le bruit étouffé de mes geignements.

« Cesse de pleurer maintenant, dit-il enfin. Tes larmes ne changeront rien à ton destin. Tu ferais mieux de l'accepter. » Il secoua la tête. « Peut-être tout cela est-il pour le mieux.

— Comment pouvez-vous dire une chose pareille ? protestai-je. Je vous ai trahi, je me suis couvert de honte, j'ai perdu ma foi. Et vous me demandez pourquoi je dis que tout est fini ? » Je pleurai amèrement.

« Pour ce qui est de ta dette envers moi, répondit-il, et les autres, tu nous as remboursés depuis longtemps. Tu nous as librement donné ta jeunesse et ta joie, tes enthousiasmes innocents, ta douceur, ta véhémence, ta vie — toutes choses qui furent du levain pour notre pain fatigué. Les autres accusations sont plus graves. Mais je ne peux ni te juger, ni t'absoudre. A toi seul d'en décider. Tu dois obéir aux jugements de ton cœur... Mais dis-moi, est-il possible que la Voie ait disparu si complètement de ton cœur, qu'en quelques jours tu aies jugé comme faux ce que tu avais tenu pour vrai pendant vingt années de ta vie ? »

Je pesai sa question et ne répondis pas immédiatement.

« Tout au fond, je crois toujours au Tao, dis-je enfin. Mais j'ai eu la vision d'une autre réalité en laquelle il me semble que je crois aussi. Selon le Grand

Vœu, le monde est Un. Si le Tao est partiel, alors le Tao est faux. Si ce que j'ai vu est réel, alors le Tao doit être une illusion.

— Ah, dit-il. Maintenant je commence à comprendre. Tu n'as pas rejeté la foi définitivement, tu as seulement commencé à douter. Le doute n'est pas incompatible avec la conviction, malgré les apparences. C'est l'élément *yin*, la foi est le *yang*. Le doute est le filet obscur grâce auquel nous pêchons la foi. Mais le doute et la foi ne sont que des étapes sur le chemin de la certitude qui émane, non de la foi, mais de l'expérience directe de l'unité de la nature et du monde, cette vérité que "la Réalité est Une, et le Tao est la Réalité". A dire vrai, Sun I, ce que tu as perdu ne t'a jamais réellement appartenu. Ta foi fut empruntée à nous tous, car tu étais trop jeune pour en payer toi-même le prix. Mais aujourd'hui, ton heure a sonné. Si tu veux la retrouver, tu dois la mériter.

— Apprenez-moi comment ! »

Il secoua tristement la tête. « J'aimerais le pouvoir. Mais comme je l'ai déjà dit, il existe certains types de connaissances — les vérités les plus hautes — qu'aucun homme ne peut transmettre à un autre.

— Que dois-je faire ? »

Chong Fou scruta longuement mes yeux. « Je crois que tu le sais déjà. »

Je le regardai sans comprendre. « Que voulez-vous dire ?

— Tu dois quitter le monastère. »

Je sentis comme un coup de poignard. Mes lèvres se mirent à trembler. Cela me blessa davantage que tout le reste. « Mais pourquoi ? Il est mon foyer. Je n'ai pas d'autre endroit. Après toutes ces années, est-il juste de me chasser aussi cruellement ? N'avez-vous pas dit que tous les moines apprécient mes qualités ? N'ai-je pas travaillé dur et joyeusement ? Je vous promets de travailler deux fois plus à l'avenir. Mais laissez-moi rester ! Ne me chassez pas ! » Bouleversé par la douleur et le chagrin, je suppliai sans réserve ni dignité.

« Reprends-toi, m'ordonna le maître. Quelle idée ! Comme s'il était question de "te chasser" ! Es-tu un sac d'ordures ou un seau d'eau sale pour que tu envisages qu'on se débarrasse de toi ? Tu es libre de rester. Tu en as autant le droit que les autres. Mais ne t'y trompe pas, Sun I. Le monastère n'est pas ton foyer, et pas davantage le mien ou celui des frères. Ken Kuan est une étape sur la Voie. Tu as été heureux ici, mais quelque chose a changé pour toi et ce ne sera plus jamais comme avant. Tu peux rester, mais rappelle-toi qu'on reste parfois trop longtemps dans le sanctuaire confortable de ses rêves ; comme le fœtus qui somnole dans la matrice de sa mère et refuse de naître, certains êtres ne dépassent jamais le stade infantile. Ils risquent même d'empoisonner le puits de la mémoire. Ce faisant, ils perdent tout. Parfois, c'est seulement en renonçant à une chose que nous pouvons la conserver. »

« C'est juste », songeai-je en cédant à la triste extase de l'humiliation. Et je demandai : « Où vais-je aller ? »

— Je crois que tu connais aussi la réponse à cette question. »

J'attendis.

« Tu ne vois donc pas, Sun I ? Tu as eu un aperçu de ton destin : il te conduit au-delà de ces portes, vers le monde. Mais ne tarde pas, sinon la piste va refroidir. »

Ces mots éveillèrent une association en moi. Les paroles de l'oracle me revinrent en mémoire : « C'est seulement quand nous avons le courage de regarder les choses telles qu'elles sont, sans la moindre illusion ni duperie, qu'il se dégage des événements une lumière qui nous permet de reconnaître la voie du succès. »

« Observe les signes, dit le maître. Tu dois suivre les traces de pas de ton rêve.

— Mais où ? demandai-je. Où mènent-elles ?

— Qui pourrait le dire ? Si nous le savions... » Il retroussa les lèvres en haussant les épaules.

Je lui adressai un regard implorant.

« Le but final est un mystère que toi seul peux percer à jour.

— Peut-être, rétorquai-je avec amertume. Mais comment ?

— Le secret est enfoui en toi. Cherche donc en toi. *Observe les signes.* Les indices sont dans ton rêve et dans l'oracle. Où aboutissent les traces de pas ? Toujours à cette même plage, au sable sur lequel tu attends, les yeux fixés sur l'immensité de l'océan. Comme tu l'as toi-même deviné, il s'agit des "grandes eaux" que, selon l'oracle, tu dois traverser.

— Mais est-ce une vraie mer, ou une étape de mon développement intérieur ? Vous avez dit que la réponse était enfermée dans mon cœur. Dans ce cas, à quoi bon retourner sur la place du marché, m'exposer à la contagion du désir et de l'avidité, si la réponse est en moi et que la méditation peut m'aider à la trouver ?

— Sois semblable au lotus, dit le maître, qui pousse dans la boue et conserve néanmoins sa pureté. Prends avec toi tes trois Trésors, la frugalité, l'humilité et la compassion — tu n'auras besoin de rien d'autre. »

Inspiré par le désespoir, je m'obstinai à résister. « Mais Lao-tseu lui-même dit :

Sans franchir sa porte,
On connaît le monde entier.
Sans regarder par sa fenêtre,
On voit la voie du ciel.
Plus on va loin
Moins on connaît.
Le sage connaît sans voyager,
Définit sans voir,
Accomplit sans agir. »

Le maître éclata de rire. « Quel dommage qu'il n'y ait pas davantage de sages ! Malheureusement pour le reste d'entre nous, la voie est souvent beaucoup plus tortueuse. Il n'existe pas de règles immuables, aucun dogme sur lequel se reposer. Souviens-toi, Lao-tseu a également dit — pour commenter ses propres sentences — "Celui qui parle ne sait pas ; celui qui sait ne parle pas." Et aussi : "Pour rester entier, laisse-toi plier !" et "Plus tu le nettoies, plus il devient sale".

« La Voie ressemble à l'eau, Sun I, pas à la pierre. Comme l'eau,

Elle coule sans interruption et se contente de remplir tous les trous sur son passage ; elle ne recule devant aucun passage dangereux, ni aucun plongeon ; rien ne saurait lui faire perdre sa nature essentielle... Ainsi, quand on est sincère face aux difficultés, le cœur peut comprendre le sens de la situation. Et dès que nous avons acquis la maîtrise d'un problème, l'action que nous entreprendrons réussira d'elle-même. Dans le danger, il importe seulement de mener à bien tout ce qui doit être fait et d'aller de l'avant sans tergiverser.

« "C'est seulement quand nous avons le courage de regarder les choses telles qu'elles sont..." » dit le maître. Il sourit et brusquement, je pris une profonde inspiration et m'obligeai à suivre son initiative terrifiante.

« Que signifie l'eau dans mon rêve ? demandai-je.

— Tu l'as dit toi-même, c'est l'océan.

— Mais... »

Il me coupa la parole. « Dis-moi : le soleil se couchait ? Cela ne t'évoque rien ? »

Je réfléchis un instant. « L'Ouest ? »

Le maître acquiesça et je sentis de nouveau sur ma nuque le picotement d'une révélation imminente.

« Mais l'animal ?

— Ça ! s'écria-t-il. Je m'étonne que tu n'aies pas encore fait le rapprochement.

— Vous voulez dire que vous savez ? »

Il sourit mystérieusement, pencha la tête en arrière et se mit à chanter. Sa voix limpide et haut perchée envahit la cellule :

« Sous les saules qui longent le fleuve, je trouve les traces.
Il y a maintenant des traces de pas partout, même sous l'herbe violette.
Elles se dirigent vers les montagnes lointaines ; ma voie est claire,
Aussi évidente que mon nez au milieu du visage alors que j'éclate de rire à la face du ciel. »

L'extase de la révélation inonda mon cœur. Je reconnus soudain la présence qui rôdait si près de moi dans la pénombre nocturne, que je pressentais sans la reconnaître. Le chant s'intitulait « La découverte des empreintes », deuxième de la série des *Dix Taureaux* !

« Si je comprends l'enseignement, j'aperçois les empreintes du Taureau, dit le maître, citant le commentaire.

— Est-ce possible ? Cette bête que j'ai suivie pendant tant de nuits à travers les paysages sauvages de mes rêves, pour finir par réaliser qu'*elle* me suivait, est donc le Taureau ?

— N'as-tu pas parlé des sabots ? »

Le frisson glacé du doute passa dans mon dos. « Mais parfois c'étaient des pattes ou des serres.

— La voie du doute est identique à la voie de la vérité, dit-il. Les deux font retourner à la même destination. »

Je le regardai bouche bée, comme le jour où il avait extrait la cigale de mon cœur.

« Tu commences à comprendre », me dit-il.

Un éclat de rire joyeux jaillit de mon cœur. Je sentis les premières lueurs de l'aube poindre en moi, promesse de chaleur et de réconfort pour le voyageur trempé jusqu'aux os qui tremble de froid dans la nuit.

« Maître, dis-je, si seulement cela pouvait être vrai.

— Crois, et ce sera la vérité. » Il m'adressa un clin d'œil. « Comme tu le vois, Sun I, rien n'est terminé. Je devrais plutôt dire que tu as à peine commencé. "Sans avoir encore franchi la porte, j'ai pourtant repéré le chemin." Tu n'as pas échoué, Sun I, tu ne nous as pas trahis. Tu as trouvé la Voie, ta "voie privée" qui ramène à la Source, au Tao.

— Et elle conduit vers l'Ouest, murmurai-je avec terreur, vers le Dow.

— Absolument ! acquiesça le maître en riant. Ce rôle a été écrit pour toi, et tu l'as répété toute ta vie. Car tu vas reprendre le rôle de Singe dans son voyage vers l'Occident. Mais cette fois, tu dois également incarner Tripitaka, parti retrouver les textes sacrés de la révélation. »

Je souris, pas tant de la plaisanterie du maître que de ce qui se passait en moi. Tel un rayon de soleil perçant les nuées au milieu de la tempête, une impression d'émerveillement, de reconnaissance, avait envahi mon cœur. Je sus brusquement que tout cela était vrai, que j'avais entrevu mon destin, le joyau dans le lotus qui attendait depuis le commencement du monde que je me dresse pour le réclamer. Et la vague conviction d'un doute indéfinissable, qui ne m'avait jamais quitté depuis ma naissance, disparut, s'évanouit en un instant, s'évaporant comme la rosée froide dans la lumière de ce nouveau matin.

« Il existait autrefois une tradition de pèlerinages religieux dans notre ordre, dit Chong Fou. Car il y a toujours eu des hommes à qui — caprice du sort ou du caractère — les "cent voies" ne suffisaient pas, des hommes qui ne pouvaient voyager dans les chariots éprouvés qui suivaient les sentiers battus. Pour eux, le voyage intérieur aboutissait au monde. Ton père, me semble-t-il, était de ceux-là. Ce que je vis chez le père, je ne pus m'empêcher de le chercher chez le fils. J'ai toujours pensé qu'un jour toi aussi nous quitterais pour suivre ton chemin dans le monde. Ce jour est arrivé. Les cent voies sont ardues, Sun I. Elles requièrent des risques et des sacrifices. Mais celle-ci est la plus difficile. Dans les cent voies, il y a au moins le réconfort d'une communauté d'esprits capables de partager leurs enthousiasmes, leurs doutes, et ainsi de se soutenir mutuellement. Et puis le monastère offre relativement peu de tentations. La voie qui conduit dans le monde est une voie solitaire et dangereuse. Les gens ne comprendront pas ta passion, ou s'ils la comprennent ils craindront ses implications pour leur vie, et ainsi te mépriseront. D'autre part, le risque est plus grand. Car la place du marché regorge de passions dangereuses qui imprègnent l'air, aussi invisibles et virulentes que les germes de la peste. Il est difficile d'échapper à la contagion. De ceux qui partent, quelques-uns reviennent, mais la plupart trouvent le monde trop succulent, trop beau et riche, et y succombent. Mais il ne faut pas les condamner. Car ces hommes sont inextricablement pris dans le Tao. Selon le *Tao-tö king* :

... l'homme cherche sans passion
Le cœur de la vie
Ou passionnément
Cherche sa surface,
Mais cœur et surface
Sont essentiellement identiques,
Les mots ne les opposent
Que pour exprimer l'apparence.
Si un nom est requis, la surprise les nomme tous les deux :
De surprise en surprise
L'existence s'ouvre.

« Voilà pourquoi il est dit : "Le Tao est aussi sur la place du marché." »
« Une distinction est pourtant nécessaire. Etre *dans* le Tao n'est pas être *avec* le Tao. Certains consacrent toute leur existence à nager contre le courant ; ils sont dans le courant, mais pas avec lui — à leurs risques et périls. Le Tao est trop fort, trop puissant ; ils finissent par se noyer. Ne sois pas comme eux. Fais de ton voyage, non l'abandon de tes principes, mais leur affirmation, non une occasion de dépravation, mais la grande épreuve de ta sincérité, de la pureté de ton cœur. Car seul l'homme qui conserve son intégrité, fidèle à lui-même et à ses convictions face aux séductions de tous ordres, sait que ces convictions ont un fondement véridique et durable dans son âme. Pour lui, le voyage dans le monde n'est pas une déchéance, mais un sacrement. »

Après cela, nous restâmes silencieux. Je me sentais heureux, mais d'un calme terrible. L'angoisse avait engourdi mon esprit. Le nouveau moi que j'avais senti émerger pendant le récit de mon oncle passait lentement de la matrice au monde, clignant des yeux dans la lumière, ignorant s'il devait sourire ou vagir. Le soleil avait réussi à percer les nuages au zénith d'un ciel venteux. Un instant, il brilla dans toute sa splendeur, puis les cumulus le masquèrent de nouveau. Le soleil était la révélation ; les nuages, le doute. Des frissons glacés alternaient avec la sensation délicieuse du chaud soleil sur mon cou et mes joues, tandis que je restais assis dans le printemps vert et sauvage de la révélation de Chong Fou, parmi des fleurs inconnues qui sortaient du sol boueux et détrempé.

Je redoutais de prendre la décision de partir, de m'engager irrévocablement dans une voie aussi désespérée. Mais apparemment, tous les signes s'accordaient à la désigner comme ma voie. Je désirais cependant recueillir une ultime preuve.

« Maître, dis-je, j'aimerais consulter les *Mutations*.
— Tu veux t'en remettre à sa décision ? »
J'acquiesçai. « Mais... »
Chong Fou me regarda d'un air interrogateur. « Mais ?
— Pourriez-vous le consulter à ma place ? Votre maîtrise est tellement plus grande que la mienne, et votre *ling*. Vous obtiendrez peut-être une réponse plus parlante.
— Je constate que les mœurs des diseurs de bonne aventure ont pénétré jusqu'ici, remarqua Chong Fou avec une nuance de reproche. Est-ce là ce

qu'on t'a enseigné, Sun I ? Nous allons donc devoir procéder à une purge, comme les communistes ! » Il reprit son sérieux. « Nous pouvons en effet aider les novices à interpréter l'oracle. Mais nous ne devons jamais manier les baguettes à la place d'autrui. Elles doivent entrer en contact avec l'individu qui pose la question. Le toucher est d'une importance primordiale. Chacun a sa façon de tenir les baguettes, gentiment, fermement, avec des mains moites d'anxiété, ou qui restent de glace. Ces choses ne sont ni arbitraires, ni insignifiantes ; elles sont la fleur de la personnalité humaine, et à travers elles les baguettes ont le pouvoir de retrouver le chemin des racines de la fleur. A tout moment, ce que nous faisons est le produit de toute notre histoire. Tous nos actes, même les questions que nous posons, forgent un nouveau maillon de la chaîne. Et ces maillons forment une séquence si vaste qu'elle dépasse rapidement la sphère du conscient ; mais la chaîne existe, on peut retrouver sa trace en utilisant un type de savoir plus puissant, une intuition scientifique qui se fonde sur le *Yi king*. Ainsi, tout importe dans la manipulation des baguettes — et si nous voulons nous approcher de l'oracle, nous devons procéder personnellement, et non par procuration. Personne ne devrait avoir l'audace de prendre la mesure du destin d'autrui. »

Il me passa ensuite les baguettes. Il m'ordonna de fermer les yeux et de formuler très précisément ma question, puis de frotter mes doigts contre les tiges d'achillée pour que ma vie s'écoule dans le bois, l'anime et l'imprègne.

« Dois-je me conformer aux signes et suivre mon rêve vers l'Occident, vers l'Amérique, demandai-je, ou bien rester et chercher à calmer les passions éveillées par ces découvertes, à travers la méditation et la vie monacale ? »

Je regardai Chong Fou, qui me fit signe de commencer. D'abord, je divisai grossièrement les quarante-neuf baguettes en deux tas. Je pris une baguette sur la pile de droite et la plaçai entre le petit doigt et l'annulaire de ma main gauche. Prenant le tas de gauche dans ma main gauche, je comptai des paquets de quatre jusqu'à ce qu'il en restât quatre seulement — que je plaçai entre l'annulaire et le majeur de ma main gauche. Passant au tas de droite, je le divisai de même en paquets de quatre jusqu'à ce qu'il en restât quatre seulement, que je plaçai entre le majeur et l'index gauches. J'additionnai le nombre de baguettes réunies dans cette main, et en trouvai neuf. Pour ce premier calcul, on ne tient généralement pas compte de la baguette unique (coincée entre le petit doigt et l'annulaire), de sorte que mon total définitif était huit. Il me donna le trait inférieur de l'hexagramme : *yin*. Puis je répétai cinq fois de suite cette procédure, qui aboutit à l'hexagramme suivant : ☲☶. Ken, ☶, « Montagne », en dessous de Li, ☲, « Feu », avec un trait « ferme », un neuf, en haut.

Une étincelle s'alluma dans les yeux de Chong Fou quand il vit cela.

« L'oracle t'a parlé très clairement, Sun I, dit-il. Regarde : en bas la Montagne reste en place, alors qu'au-dessus le Feu bondit et refuse de s'apaiser. Tu as tiré *Liu*, Sun I, le signe du Voyageur. »

Je sentis un pincement au ventre, comme si un événement merveilleux et inexplicable venait de se produire.

« Qu'il en soit ainsi », dis-je en mon for intérieur.

Pourtant, alors que je m'habituais à la perspective du Voyageur, le visage du maître s'assombrit. « Regarde de plus près, Sun I, dit-il. Le dernier trait que tu as tiré est un trait ferme, vieux *yang* se désintégrant en *yin*. "Neuf en haut signifie : Le nid de l'oiseau brûle", dit-il, récitant de mémoire.

« D'abord le voyageur rit,
Puis il doit se lamenter et gémir.
Il perd étourdiment la vache.
Malheur. »

Je sentis une nausée m'envahir.

Le visage du maître était grave et inquisiteur. « Rappelle-toi, Sun I, ces présages annoncent ce qui peut être, pas forcément ce qui doit inévitablement arriver. Le nid brûlé symbolise la destruction de son propre foyer, l'endroit où l'on se retire pour se reposer et se protéger. Cela désigne aussi la perte de son sanctuaire spirituel. Semblable malheur résulte d'un défaut de conception du nid. C'est une grande infortune, mais qu'on peut rectifier — ou sinon rectifier, du moins compenser. Mais le Voyageur ne doit surtout pas céder à la légèreté ou à la véhémence, car s'il perd le contrôle de lui-même et de ses désirs, il est perdu. Il rira peut-être quelque temps, mais au bout du compte il pleurera.

— Et la vache ? demandai-je. Cela signifie-t-il que je ne trouverai jamais le Taureau ?

— Pas nécessairement, répondit-il. La vache et le Taureau sont le *yin* et le *yang* du Tao unique, les mêmes mais différents. Elle est sa contrepartie féminine, la terre sous son ciel, acceptant et absorbant passivement ce que lui, dans son exigence, crée et fournit agressivement. Si le Taureau est puissant, tempétueux, la vache est douce et docile. Elle représente l'Humilité, la Modestie, le troisième des Trois Trésors, le pouvoir de subir les revers avec la souplesse du roseau, sans se raidir, se gonfler d'orgueil et de colère, au risque d'être brisé. Néanmoins, elle demeure stérile sans l'étincelle céleste qu'il porte en son corps et qui le pousse à une rage extatique, que seule la vache peut apaiser. Voilà pourquoi, quand le Taureau entre en fureur, l'éleveur place la vache dans l'étable à côté de lui. Car sa fierté courroucée risque de l'entraîner trop loin ; il aspire à un ciel que, sous forme humaine, il entreverra peut-être mais ne connaîtra jamais, et perdant contact avec la terre il risque de se blesser ou de blesser autrui. Non, on peut perdre sa vache et pourtant trouver le Taureau, mais ce serait une découverte sinistre. Dans l'élevage comme dans la vie intérieure, les deux sont indispensables à la conception et à la maturation du bonheur. »

Pendant que j'écoutais ses paroles, mon malaise s'accentua.

« Ce présage est de mauvais augure, dit Chong Fou. Mais je suggère que tu y voies un avertissement, et non une prophétie. L'oracle a manifestement fait allusion à ton voyage. Ne perd pas courage. Regarde — il y a encore autre chose. Suis l'évolution des traits fermes ; vois-tu le nouvel hexagramme qui se dessine ? »

Comme je redoutais d'autres mauvais présages, je ne parvins pas à me concentrer. Je remarquai alors une lueur d'espoir sur le visage de Chong

Fou. J'examinai la nouvelle configuration des coups de pinceau sur la feuille de papier qu'il tenait, et, oui, le nouvel hexagramme né de la métamorphose des traits était *Hsieh*, « la Délivrance ».

Ce fut ainsi que le jour du Grand Festival, dans le tumulte frénétique de la fête — roulement de tonnerre des timbales, fracas des cymbales, beuglement des clarinettes, réverbérations du gong, tous instruments rassemblés dans la cour principale du monastère —, je m'éclipsai sans être remarqué des autres moines. Le maître, qui semblait un peu guindé et mal à l'aise dans son habit de cérémonie, comme un jeune Américain engoncé dans son costume du dimanche, pourtant conscient de sa propre fatuité et ravi de la situation, m'accompagna à la porte de derrière avec Wu qui, malgré tous ses efforts, ne réussissait pas à cacher sa tristesse. J'avais placé mes quelques possessions dans un sac que je portais en bandoulière : une couverture, une paire de sandales de rechange en fibre végétale, un bol à aumônes, mon *Yi king* et mes baguettes d'achillée, une petite provision de riz, et soigneusement pliée au fond du sac, la robe de ma mère, dans laquelle j'avais cousu la clef, la lettre, les photos et la bourse —, mes trésors.

Le maître était joyeux, son visage détendu, ses yeux gais et brillants comme ceux d'un enfant. Je le sentais d'humeur affectueuse et malicieuse.

« *Hai* ! s'écria-t-il. Je t'envie, Sun I. Comparé à ceci — d'un léger signe de tête, il désigna la cacophonie qui montait de la cour —, le monde doit paraître un havre de paix, une retraite contemplative ! » Il rit joyeusement. « Ton cœur est-il léger comme une plume ?

— Maître, dis-je, c'est aujourd'hui la fête de la vie ; je sens pourtant qu'une partie de moi est en train de mourir. » Debout sur le seuil, je pris une fois encore mon visage entre mes mains et pleurai.

« La fête de la vie, certes, dit Chong Fou d'une voix douce, et de la renaissance de l'année. Mais pour renaître, Sun I, nous devons d'abord mourir.

— J'ai peur.

— Tant mieux ! Cela prouve que tu n'es pas complètement privé de bon sens ! Ne lutte pas contre cette peur. Elle sert un but. Laisse ton cœur fondre et s'épancher. Souviens-toi des mots du *Yi king*. Grave-les dans ta mémoire :

> L'eau donne l'exemple de la conduite à suivre en pareilles circonstances. Elle coule sans interruption et se contente de remplir tous les trous sur son passage ; elle ne recule devant aucun passage dangereux, ni aucun plongeon ; rien ne saurait lui faire perdre sa nature essentielle. Dans tous les cas, elle reste fidèle à elle-même.

« Mais je ne connais même pas le chemin, protestai-je.

— Suis le fleuve », dit Wu, qui leva les yeux pour la première fois.

Chong Fou acquiesça. « Exactement, Sun I. Souviens-toi de ton rêve. Ne t'éloigne jamais de l'eau courante au point de ne plus l'entendre. Suis le fleuve, il te conduira à la mer. »

Je réfléchis en silence à ces conseils.

« Je dois retourner auprès des moines avant qu'ils ne remarquent mon absence, dit le maître qui interrompit ma rêverie. Mais auparavant, la tradition veut qu'on donne un cadeau au pèlerin avant son départ, quelque chose qui l'aidera dans ses pérégrinations. »

Des plis volumineux de son habit, il sortit alors un bâton. « Tiens ! » s'écria-t-il en me le lançant. Je dus me ressaisir en un éclair pour éviter de recevoir le bâton sur la mâchoire.

« Qu'est-ce qu'un voyageur sans un bâton ? dit-il en riant. J'ai taillé celui-ci de mes propres mains dans un regain de mûrier blanc sauvage que j'ai trouvé dans les bosquets voisins du monastère. Aucun bois n'est plus dur et plus souple. Voilà pourquoi le sage conseillle d'"attacher ses espoirs au mûrier". A l'exception de son embout de fer, il est simple et sans ornementation. Laisse-le ainsi. Il représente le "Bloc Brut" de ta nature primitive, non souillée par l'éducation ou une quelconque amélioration. »

Je m'inclinai avec reconnaissance devant lui. Quand je me redressai, Wu se posta devant moi en silence, fit glisser de son épaule la lanière d'une outre à vin, et la passa à la mienne.

« Là, s'écria le maître. Que ce bâton te serve à atteindre ton but élevé, et cette outre à vin ton désir véritable ! Maintenant, si ton cœur abrite un doute ou un regret, parle, car le moment est venu de nous séparer. »

Je pris une profonde inspiration. « Je suis résolu, dis-je. Je regrette seulement deux choses.

— Lesquelles ?

— D'abord, de ne plus avoir la moindre chance d'être initié aux rites de l'alchimie ; ensuite, de vous perdre à jamais, de ne plus jamais vous revoir.

— Ne plus jamais se revoir ! répéta-t-il comme étonné. Notre destination n'est-elle pas la même ? Sois exact au rendez-vous et nous serons réunis — tu peux en être certain ! Quant à l'alchimie, tu peux en parler à ton grand ami éploré ici présent. Wu te le dira aussi bien que moi : la véritable alchimie se produit seulement dans l'alambic du cœur du sage. »

Il posa alors sa vieille main noueuse sur mon buste, légèrement, avec modestie, comme il l'avait fait voilà si longtemps, et je sentis une énergie éternellement jeune s'écouler en moi. Puis, brusquement, il fit volte-face et retourna au festival d'un pas vif, en riant gaiement ; il soulevait son habit afin qu'il ne traîne pas sur le sol et marchait comiquement, telle une vieille femme relevant ses jupes pour courir entre les flaques d'eau.

Wu restait planté là, l'air gêné, en traînant les pieds ; la tête baissée, il évitait mon regard. Je marchai jusqu'à lui et jetai les bras autour de son cou. Le chaume de sa barbe piqua ma joue comme tant de fois déjà, mais aujourd'hui ses larmes tièdes mouillèrent mon visage.

« Dépêche-toi ! dit-il en me repoussant sans ménagement. A ce train-là, le soleil va se coucher avant que tu ne sois parti. »

Je le regardai puis fondis moi aussi en sanglots.

« Petit Sauvage ! » gémit-il piteusement.

Alors, comme deux crétins, nous avons geint et vagi de concert, accompagnés par le tumulte de la musique du festival. Le côté comique de la situation nous frappa simultanément, et tout aussi brusquement nous éclatâmes de rire.

« Pauvre Singe, tu n'as pas une chance de t'en tirer dans le vaste monde. »

Essuyant mes larmes sur la manche de ma soutane, je reniflai et répondis dignement : « Je suis un homme maintenant, Wu.

— A quoi bon ? se lamenta-t-il. Cela veut seulement dire que tu auras deux fois plus de vices qu'avant, deux fois plus de prétextes pour t'écarter de la voie. » Il me jaugea d'un regard sinistre. « Tu seras une proie facile pour les prostituées et les voleurs.

— Mais que pourraient-ils me voler ? protestai-je. Je n'ai pas d'argent.

— Ah ! J'ai dit la même chose autrefois, gémit-il. Mieux vaut être riche. Car ainsi, on peut les acheter avec des espèces sonnantes et trébuchantes. Quand ils s'apercevront de ta pauvreté, il t'arrivera ce qui m'est arrivé. A défaut d'autre chose, ils te voleront ton cœur. »

Je voulus rire, mais sa voix était si lugubre que ma gaieté naissante fit long feu. Pourtant, je refusais de le quitter sur une note aussi triste.

« Je crois que tu te trompes à propos des femmes ! » le contredis-je avec un clin d'œil que je voulais joyeux.

Wu posa ses deux mains sur mes épaules et scruta longuement mes yeux. « Oui, tu as peut-être raison, reconnut-il en pouffant malgré lui. Avec ce visage, je doute que tu coures beaucoup de risques de ce côté. » Presque aussitôt, il revint à la charge. « Mais je t'avertis, méfie-toi des dés ! Toutes ces années, je l'ai vu sur ton visage et dans ton caractère. Le jeu causera ta perte si tu n'y prends garde. »

Je ne pus m'empêcher de rire en entendant une dernière fois son éternelle et poussiéreuse mise en garde. Bien que je n'eusse jamais manifesté le moindre désir de tenter ma chance au jeu, Wu ne manquait jamais une occasion de m'admonester à ce sujet.

« Et toi Wu, plaisantai-je, évite l'alcool de riz, et cesse d'attribuer à autrui des vices qui sont tout bonnement les tiens. »

Wu secoua la tête. « Tu es trop malin pour ne pas en souffrir, Sun I. Un jour, tu te souviendras de mes paroles. Prends seulement garde que ce ne soit pas trop tard. »

Ainsi, avec cette vision d'humour et d'apocalypse pour m'égayer, je partis. J'ajustai mon barda sur mes épaules, puis franchis la porte d'un pas décidé, plantant fermement mon bâton à chaque enjambée. A mesure que je descendais le sentier escarpé, la cacophonie du carnaval s'éloignait peu à peu, dominée par le rugissement du torrent dont les eaux tumultueuses se précipitaient au bas des falaises, pleines d'écume et de folie, vers la destination inimaginable de l'océan.

LE LIEN

1

Que dire de ma longue migration vers la mer ? Je passai la fin de ce premier été à rejoindre Shanghai, un voyage qui en d'autres circonstances aurait seulement duré quelques semaines, voire quelques jours. Pourtant, je n'ai jamais regretté le temps que j'y ai consacré. Profondeurs bleues du ciel d'été, lents cumulus pommelés, la Voie lactée, la rosée du matin qui scintille sur les brins d'herbe, chariots et chars à bœufs, la poussière de la route, le fleuve, tantôt impétueux, adolescent, criard, qui se baratte en grumeaux livides, tantôt résigné comme un vieillard, argent bruni dans les courbes, mais toujours en quête d'ailleurs, toujours insatisfait — mes jours et mes nuits se fondaient en une splendeur composée de semblables impressions. Ma liberté s'accompagna d'une nouvelle vision, d'une transformation physique. Je crus quitter une photographie sépia pour un univers tridimensionnel et coloré, ou bien chausser une paire de lunettes pour la première fois après des années de vision partielle, remplacer la pâle aquarelle de la myopie ignorée par une définition nouvelle du monde. L'air lui-même devint acéré, l'espace et la profondeur reculèrent, laissant derrière eux un vide rugissant dans lequel je m'engageais en tremblant de peur et de plaisir. Etrangement, ce fut seulement en le quittant que je connus mon pays natal, que j'embrassai ses diversités étonnantes et son identité plus étonnante encore. Ces journées furent comme un seul jour, une longue extase de retrouvailles et de départs.

A certains moments, pourtant, le côté vivant et immédiat du paysage se dissipait et je ressentais une impression de déjà vu. Comme lors d'une double exposition, des scènes vaguement remémorées se superposaient à l'univers visible. Je devais alors me frotter les yeux pour m'assurer que j'étais éveillé, car je croyais voir devant moi le paysage de mon rêve. Un jour, je fis cette expérience au crépuscule, debout au sommet d'une haute crête dominant une gorge où se déroulait le ruban noir du fleuve qui chutait verticalement sur deux cents pieds dans une lueur éblouissante, tels des massifs hallucinants de rhododendrons filmés en accéléré, épuisant des années d'existence en quelques secondes, diffusant un tonnerre assourdi et une brume diaphane d'eau vaporisée vers les hauteurs du canyon ; et un autre jour, à midi, alors que je me reposais sur la berge à l'ombre d'un arbre en me curant les dents avec une tige d'herbe. Un bœuf sortit des arbres sur la rive opposée du fleuve et avança lourdement pour se désaltérer. Repliant ses pattes avant, il se laissa tomber de tout son poids dans l'argile visqueuse, regarda impassiblement l'eau couler devant lui et but calmement ; ses yeux violet foncé n'avaient pas de blanc, sinon aux coins, et encore étaient-ils plutôt jaunes mouchetés de rouge comme des œufs en gestation — des yeux si profonds, si patients, tels deux trous noirs absorbant indifféremment le fleuve, les arbres, le paysage tout entier, jusqu'à ce que l'histoire, le monde lui-même aient disparu en eux pour devenir une simple inflexion de leur vaste savoir qui incluait tout, et rien. Un instant, il me regarda alors que je mâchais mon brin d'herbe, et m'absorba aussi dans son iris violet comme dans l'un de ses sept estomacs qui étaient peut-être les royaumes de toute existence. Puis le bœuf fit pivoter sa tête massive pour observer les arbres ; le soleil se posa sur un fil d'argent qui dégouttait de sa gueule et brilla brusquement comme un rayon de la toile d'araignée primordiale. J'avais banni ces visions de mon sommeil, mais je découvrais qu'elles s'incarnaient désormais sous le soleil et que mon rêve était devenu le monde.

Bien que chaque heure apportât une nouvelle merveille à l'être depuis si longtemps reclus, naïf et inexpérimenté que j'étais, je crains qu'un récit exhaustif ne s'avère une chronique fastidieuse. Ainsi, dans la mesure du possible, je veux épargner au lecteur la reconstitution monotone de mon voyage, la liste des noms de lieux, les traités relatifs au commerce et à l'agriculture locaux, les digressions botaniques et ornithologiques — tout ce terrible bric-à-brac si prisé des voyageurs professionnels, si ennuyeux pour le commun des mortels. De plus, mes tribulations pendant ce parcours continental sortent du cadre strict de mon récit, qui ne reprend qu'avec mon arrivée à New York. A cette époque, j'ai cependant vécu une expérience que je ne saurais passer sous silence. Car si mon départ de Ken Kuan fut une sorte de naissance — mon accouchement, mon expulsion hors de la matrice de l'enfance — alors cet événement marque le rude baptême de mon entrée dans la vie.

Depuis des jours je voyageais vers la province méridionale du Yunnan, dans la région de l'opium et le long d'un cours d'eau qui alimentait les affluents supérieurs du Yang-tsê, un torrent écumant enflé par les eaux de fonte du glacier. Je n'apercevais aucun signe d'habitation humaine, sinon de temps à autre l'efflorescence des pétales blancs ou pourpres du pavot sur les pentes escarpées, où d'obscures tribus cultivaient le *Papaver somniferum* pour les seigneurs de l'opium de Birmanie et de Thaïlande. Parfois les fleurs étaient fanées, et du bulbe immature entaillé d'un couteau suintait un latex blanc qui virait au brun et durcissait au soleil. C'était une terre sauvage et tourmentée, jonchée de blocs de roc, hachurée de cascades qui dévalaient des versants boisés et plongeaient dans la rivière. L'air palpitait d'un tonnerre assourdi, comme un roulement de tambour lointain. Je m'asseyais parfois pour regarder l'eau jusqu'à ce que mes yeux se brouillent et que je discerne une faible musique fantomatique dans le bruissement de la rivière, un son à l'intérieur d'un son, comme de voix chantant une mélodie presque compréhensible en contrepoint du tumulte des eaux, un chœur triste, une lamentation universelle. Wu m'avait dit un jour que c'étaient les voix des noyés de la rivière qui réclamaient leur enterrement, des hommes et des femmes enrôlés de force au service du dieu pour que leurs larmes accroissent le flux des eaux.

Dans ce paysage erratique, des îlots luxuriants dus au dépôt de terres fertiles transportées par le vent alternaient avec des champs de pierres nues, des terrains érodés, stériles. Cette région était d'une beauté inhumaine, étrange : parois de canyons veinées de rouille, cendres et pierres ambrées, profonds lacs d'ombres et vastes pans de ciel éblouissant, d'un bleu inaccessible. La rivière avait parfois fendu des montagnes entières. On voyait alors les strates de sédiments comprimés, comme sur un arbre coupé les cercles concentriques des ans, chacune signalant un âge géologique ; et dans ce décor statique, le présent éternel du fleuve, lame d'argent qui disséquait le cadavre de la terre pour une autopsie impitoyable, s'enfonçant toujours plus profond dans le passé tout en coulant vers l'avenir.

Pendant ma progression dans ces étendues sauvages, je m'étais presque exclusivement susténté de ma petite provision de riz avec laquelle j'avais quitté le monastère. Quand j'atteignis le confluent du Yang-tsê, que les habitants du lieu nomment le Fleuve au Sable d'Or, j'avais marché pendant deux jours sans manger. Là, les eaux laiteuses, couleur caramel, de l'affluent se mêlaient au cours plus sombre du grand fleuve qui entamait déjà sa métamorphose chromatique pour s'approcher de la teinte de l'océan ; j'arrivai en fin d'après-midi près d'un village au bord du fleuve — un groupe de huttes, certaines construites en bois et boue sur la pente boisée qui aboutissait à la rive, d'autres plus près de l'eau bâties en bambou sur pilotis au-dessus de la bande blanche d'une plage sablonneuse. L'une d'elles était recouverte d'un toit en tôle ondulée, sans doute un signe de richesse parmi tant de chaume, d'autant que j'entendis bientôt un transistor brailler à l'intérieur. Sur le porche de cette maison une femme, accompagnée d'une petite fille accrochée à ses jupes, mettait du linge à sécher avec des gestes lents et approximatifs. Elle portait un sarong jaune en soie brodée qui semblait incongru, inapproprié à la banalité de la tâche qu'elle accomplissait. De temps à autre, la femme et la petite fille allaient vers la balustrade pour observer la scène qui se déroulait à leurs pieds sur la plage.

Hissée parmi plusieurs embarcations primitives qui ressemblaient à des canoës et sur lesquelles un filet séchait, une jonque à fond plat et poupe haute, voiles lattées et coque de bois noir, prenait des allures fantastiques dues à sa taille pourtant modeste, car le bateau était juste assez grand pour recevoir une petite cabine de fortune à l'arrière. Des personnages allaient et venaient comme des fourmis sur le sable, chargés d'énormes ballots, que d'autres soulevaient de leur dos pour les faire disparaître dans la soute. Debout à la proue, un homme corpulent que je pris pour le capitaine du navire agitait les bras comme un sémaphore déréglé et aboyait des ordres d'une voix que la radio ne parvenait pas à couvrir.

Je fis une brève halte sur le surplomb d'où j'observais ce spectacle, puis sortis de mon sac mon bol à aumônes et commençai à descendre la pente.

A mesure que j'approchais, je m'intéressai de plus en plus au bourdonnement fébrile et à tous ces visages qui, malgré leur saleté ou leurs rides, me paraissaient uniques et fascinants après mon long séjour au monastère.

En passant devant la cabane au toit de tôle ondulée, je lançai un coup d'œil furtif à la femme qui me regarda sans la moindre pudeur et m'adressa un sourire qui me parut lascif. J'attribuai aussitôt cette interprétation à ma propre nature pécheresse et détournai les yeux. Elle m'appela à voix basse, avec un signe du menton ; mais je me rappelai le conseil de Wu et pressai le pas en faisant la sourde oreille.

A ma grande déception, mon apparition parmi mes semblables ne leur inspira pas l'enthousiasme que j'éprouvais. Comme je plantais mon bâton et sautais du petit rebord rocheux dans le sable, un silence de mort tomba sur la plage, seulement interrompu par le faseillement nerveux des voiles dans les bourrasques qui s'engouffraient par la gorge. Les coolies se raidirent sous leurs ballots, m'observèrent furtivement dans l'ombre de leurs chapeaux de paille pointus. L'homme imposant et laid debout à la proue abaissa son poing massif qui scandait jusqu'alors la manœuvre et me dévisagea en plissant les paupières ; ses yeux avaient la couleur du limon du fleuve. Je remarquai un revolver coincé dans sa ceinture. Les hommes qui discutaient sur la grève me jetèrent des regards méfiants par-dessus l'épaule ; ils répondirent en grognant et crachant au large sourire amical que je leur adressai, puis m'oublièrent pour reprendre leur conférence, comme s'ils avaient déjà décidé que je ne méritais pas leur attention. Profondément décontenancé par cet accueil, je restai à l'écart, indécis.

« *Psst* », entendis-je encore. Levant la tête, j'aperçus la femme qui me regardait avec un sourire rusé en me faisant signe d'approcher.

A défaut de mieux, je fis quelques pas vers elle et m'inclinai respectueusement en contrebas de la plate-forme.

« C'est la première fois que je te vois, dit-elle en feignant une nonchalance à travers laquelle l'impatience perçait comme une lame de couteau. Tu es beau garçon — bien élevé, par-dessus le marché ! Qu'as-tu à vendre ? » Elle se pencha sur la balustrade pour exhiber la fente sombre de ses seins. « De l'opium ? Où est-il ? Dans les collines ? Combien ? Confie-toi à moi, je t'aiderai. »

Incapable de répondre, je rougis et me tournai vers la petite fille, qui lui ressemblait, mais comme les contraires se ressemblent — à l'envers : l'incarnation de l'innocence perdue de sa mère, peut-être. C'était une enfant splendide, propre et paisible, aux grands yeux lumineux. Pourtant son regard me déconcerta davantage que celui de la femme. Je détournai les yeux.

« Bon, garde ça pour toi, reprit la mère avec irritation. Comme tu voudras. Les hommes..., se lamenta-t-elle. Tu dois parler à mon mari. Le connais-tu ? Il est là-bas, le vieux renard. » Elle désigna l'endroit de la plage où les conciliabules frénétiques battaient leur plein autour d'un homme mince et âgé que distinguaient non seulement le raffinement relatif de son vêtement, mais aussi les rides de son visage, un Chinois de l'ethnie Haw parmi les physionomies plus lourdes d'autres tribus. Il courait çà et là d'un air soucieux, désespéré, discutait avec divers personnages d'une voix agaçante et haut perchée, une sorte de gémissement perçant et obséquieux. Je le regardai procéder à l'inventaire, peser des marchandises, effectuer quelques calculs rapides sur un boulier, puis d'une bourse qu'il portait à la ceinture sortir de petites sommes qu'il donnait à contrecœur et en grimaçant de douleur. Un jeune assistant l'accompagnait, réplique exacte du vieux Chinois, mais qui semblait âgé de dix ans. Ce jeune protégé assistait à la transaction d'un air impassible, sans broncher ni ciller. Sa tâche consistait à porter le boulier et la balance, à les présenter sur demande avec des démonstrations de piété exagérées, tels les accessoires sacrés de la Grande Messe du commerce que le vieillard et lui-même — grand-prêtre et acolyte respectivement — célébraient au fin fond de l'univers.

« Votre fils ? » demandai-je à la femme.

Elle acquiesça, puis se redressa en gonflant la poitrine. « Nous achetons », dit-elle d'un air suffisant.

Des monceaux de marchandises exotiques jonchaient la plage, matières brutes d'espèces diverses provenant des recoins les plus reculés des montagnes et destinées à être vendues à des prix exorbitants en aval du fleuve. La femme me fit comprendre qu'on formait ici deux convois, l'un terrestre destiné à la Birmanie, l'autre qui devait descendre le fleuve vers Ch'ung-ch'ing et, au-delà, Shanghai et la côte. Le convoi de Birmanie consistait en un seul produit : l'opium. Les marchandises à destination de Shanghai étaient plus variées. La femme bavardait sans discontinuer, les énumérait pour mon édification — la moitié de ses paroles se perdaient dans le rugissement du fleuve. Il y avait des caisses d'œufs d'oiseaux soigneusement enveloppés dans des feuilles, certains mouchetés, fragiles et minuscules, d'autres de la taille d'une tête de bébé, grotesques et repoussants ; des paquets de peaux de toutes couleurs et textures, parfois pas plus grandes que la paume de la main, couvertes d'une douce fourrure duveteuse qui servirait à fabriquer les pinceaux de calligraphie. Il y avait des paniers de plantes, des racines en forme de testicules, des mousses qui poussaient seulement à l'ombre de certaines falaises. Il y avait des blocs de jade brut et des perles de rivière, des sacs pleins d'ailes cassantes de chauves-souris séchées au soleil, capturées dans des cavernes souterraines, ainsi que des chauves-souris vivantes enfermées dans des cages où elles somnolaient en bruissant au soleil, accrochées tête en bas sur des barreaux, enveloppées de leur linceul noir, qui criaient et chiaient quand on les dérangeait. Il y avait de l'huile d'abrasin, des ramies, de la soie, du tabac, du thé et des plantes médicinales.

Mais le plus étonnant était le *pai hsiung*, le panda géant muselé qui arpentait lourdement sa cage posée sur le plateau d'un fruste chariot aux roues de bois grossier, dont le joug traînait dans le sable. L'animal s'immobilisait de temps à autre pour darder entre les barreaux un regard féroce et mélancolique de ses yeux couleur du miel sombre de montagne quand il jaillit d'une ruche brisée. La puissance de sa concentration me convainquit presque qu'il mémorisait le visage des hommes présents pour se venger le moment venu. Cela aussi me bouleversa.

Son regard s'attachait avec une intensité particulière à quelqu'un que je n'aurais peut-être pas remarqué si la bête ne me l'avait, pour ainsi dire, désigné. Il était assis à l'arrière du chariot, le dos tourné à la foule, curieusement indifférent à l'agitation fébrile de la plage. Son apathie, cependant nuancée par une sorte de tension contenue, comme un dur noyau métallique, contrastait tant avec la gesticulation passionnée des autres qu'elle lui conférait un mystère encore renforcé par le visage invisible. Il portait un uniforme militaire en piteux état que je ne situai pas : il n'était pas communiste, je l'eusse alors reconnu. A côté de lui, un fusil mitrailleur était posé contre le chariot à côté d'un sabre courbe japonais, incongru et semblable à ceux des officiers de l'armée impériale japonaise pendant la deuxième guerre mondiale, fière relique de l'héritage des samouraï. Le seul autre trait distinctif de l'individu était une cicatrice livide qui montait verticalement dans ses cheveux coupés à un demi-centimètre du crâne. Cette ligne blême rejoignait le sommet de sa tête, puis, telle une route disparaissant à l'horizon, se perdait dans le paysage inconnu de son visage. Je remarquai aussi une volute de fumée blanc laiteux au-dessus de son épaule, qui montait d'une petite pipe dont il vidait périodiquement le contenu en la tapotant contre un montant du chariot pour que le vent répande les cendres sur le sable.

« Qui est-ce ? demandai-je à la femme en regardant son visage.

— Tsin, répondit-elle, le soldat... Enfin, autrefois il était soldat — aujourd'hui mercenaire pour les seigneurs de l'opium de Birmanie, même s'il travaille aussi pour nous sur ce coup. » Elle se tut, comme si elle n'avait plus rien à dire.

Mon regard la poussa à continuer. Elle haussa les épaules. « Je ne sais pas grand-chose de lui. Seulement ce que j'ai entendu. On raconte qu'il fut l'un des favoris du Généralissime pendant la guerre. Mais on raconte tellement de choses — et tellement de mensonges. Il lui est arrivé quelque chose. Je ne sais pas quoi au juste. Je crois que personne ne le sait vraiment. En tout cas, personne d'ici. J'ai entendu dire qu'il avait assassiné quelqu'un — mais la moitié de ces hommes ont assassiné quelqu'un, ou voudraient le faire croire aux autres. En tout cas, il tomba en disgrâce, fut cassé et dut se réfugier dans cet endroit perdu, qu'il quitta quand les communistes prirent la région en cinquante. Il s'enfuit de l'autre côté de la frontière, vers les Etats de Shan, avec les derniers soldats de l'Armée nationaliste qui se reconvertirent dans le convoyage des caravanes le long de la nouvelle route de Birmanie — je parle du trafic de l'opium. Tsin est une exception. Il est le seul à se risquer au-delà de la frontière, au Yunnan, pour en ramener l'op. Le Kuomintang le réceptionne de l'autre côté. C'est un boulot dangereux, mais très bien payé. Il fait le voyage une fois l'an, au moment de la récolte, avec quelques Lolos qu'il embauche. De ce côté-ci, quand il attend la récolte, il chasse pour mon mari afin de rentabiliser l'aller comme le retour. Intelligent, Tsin... Bien que fumeur, on peut lui faire confiance — ce n'est pas comme ces coolies qui se vautrent dans la boue. Juste un peu d'opium par-ci par-là mélangé à son tabac. C'est la seule chose dont on soit vraiment sûr, le seul indice. Le bruit court qu'il a commencé de fumer après sa disgrâce. » Elle secoua la tête. « Nous ne pouvons faire confiance qu'à lui pour certaines tâches. L'ours, par exemple. Tu le vois, là-bas ? Il est destiné à un zoo en Amérique. Les gens vont payer de l'argent pour voir sa misère. Tu te rends compte ? Quelle idée bizarre... Les gens sont prêts à payer pour n'importe quoi, du moment que c'est difficile à obtenir. Cet animal est plus précieux que toutes les marchandises de Shanghai réunies. Tsin a dit à mon mari qu'après avoir trouvé sa trace, il a mis neuf jours à repérer sa tanière. Ils sont tellement discrets et rusés, ces animaux, rien à voir avec les gentils ours en peluche qu'on fait d'eux. Regarde sa taille. Ces pattes ! Il peut tuer un homme, et le dévorer. On parle de pousses de bambou, mais tu crois qu'il ferait le difficile devant un bon quartier de chair humaine ? Surtout un grand mâle comme celui-là ! Crois-moi, si j'en rencontrais un dans la forêt, je ne m'arrêterais pas pour le caresser.

« Mais Tsin est parfait pour ce genre de travail. Tous les autres prétendaient que c'était impossible. Tu sais comment il s'y est pris ? Opium et viande rouge. Très malin. Et puis il ne faut pas essayer de lui chercher noise. Tu vois ce sabre ? Il ne s'en sépare jamais. C'est cette arme qui est responsable de la cicatrice sur sa tête. Du moins, c'est ce qu'on prétend. Il l'a pris à un officier japonais pendant la retraite de Shanghai. Il paraît que cet officier dirigeait la poursuite. Son enthousiasme guerrier le sépara de ses propres troupes. Tsin était à l'arrière-garde pour protéger la retraite de l'armée chinoise, mais il s'attarda si bien que lui aussi fut coupé de ses troupes. Les deux hommes se rencontrèrent donc en terrain neutre, entre les armées, tous deux épuisés et à court de munitions à cause de la bataille. Ils luttèrent pendant des heures, bien après le crépuscule, sabre contre sabre, puis au corps à corps, et ce fut Tsin qui l'emporta. Alors que l'officier japonais blessé à mort reposait sur le dos, il offrit à Tsin son sabre qui était resté dans sa famille depuis le Moyen Age, transmis de père en fils. C'est une belle histoire, tu ne trouves pas ? Même si, comme le reste, elle n'est qu'une rumeur... Que te dire d'autre ? Personne ne le connaît intimement. J'ignore ce qui le motive profondément. D'ailleurs je ne veux pas le savoir. Un type comme lui, qui vit seul et sans femme comme un animal sauvage, qui ne connaît personne et que personne ne connaît — il y a sûrement quelque chose qui cloche chez lui. Tout ce que je peux dire avec certitude, c'est qu'il est différent des autres. Il n'y a pas de bassesse en lui. Pas de douceur non plus, peut-être. Mais pas de bassesse. »

Cet homme, Tsin, était accompagné par un molosse de race indéterminée, assis sur son arrière-train musculeux entre le soldat et la foule, comme pour soulager son maître du fardeau de la vigilance. Sa couleur, son impassibilité absolue donnaient l'impression d'une bête taillée dans un bloc compact de granite. Il ne bougeait jamais, sinon pour battre des paupières — ou plutôt fermer un seul œil, car l'autre orbite contenait une sphère de verre laiteux, dont l'aspect mort et le total manque d'expression me glacèrent le sang. Une fois pourtant, au bruit du soldat qui tapotait sa pipe contre le montant du chariot, je vis l'épaisse queue battre deux fois le sable avec éloquence, et le molosse de pierre tourna la tête pour regarder son maître. L'espace d'un instant, son œil mort lui-même brilla d'un amour muet et sauvage. Ce signe d'affection passa inaperçu du soldat qui continua de fumer en silence.

A mesure que la femme parlait et que j'observais la scène, celle-ci prenait sens dans mon esprit. Je conclus que ce capharnaüm de marchandises exotiques, rassemblées par une troupe également bizarre d'aventuriers et de mercenaires, aboutirait entre les mains de lointains citadins claquemurés à Shanghai ou Pékin, qui, ainsi qu'on me l'avait appris, désiraient avec un appétit inconscient et atavique les fragments d'une nature qu'ils avaient détruite autour d'eux. Mais ils n'étaient plus capables de digérer cette nature, du moins pas complètement, pas brute, si bien qu'ils consommaient seulement ses produits les plus recherchés : animaux dans les zoos, plantes préparées en proportions médicinales par des apothicaires — aphrodisiaques et cordials, fortifiants, émétiques, diurétiques, laxatifs —, une nature prémastiquée, fermentée, filtrée, tamisée, sublimée, raffinée... bref, dénaturée.

Telle était la fonction de cette bande de gaillards aux allures de pirates qui s'agitaient sur la plage : distiller la vie pour d'autres, entreprise risquée mais fructueuse. Et sur leurs visages ignorants, dangereux, je distinguai les linéaments de philosophes grossiers, initiés à une intimité privilégiée avec la nature. Qui étaient-ils sinon les « taoïstes naturels » dont Chong Fou parlait si souvent, ceux qui comprenaient directement la Voie, par l'expérience vécue et sans le bagage encombrant des idées ?

La figure du capitaine se détachait nettement du lot, présence haute en couleur dans cette assemblée aussi pittoresque que picaresque. Après mon arrivée, il reprit ses braillements, criant ses ordres d'une voix de stentor, couvrant d'insultes et de sarcasmes tous les coolies qu'il apercevait. Ses mots ressemblaient à des fouets : les hommes grimaçaient et sursautaient sous leurs coups. Certains, évidemment intimidés par sa présence, marmonnaient des paroles de rancœur, l'observaient craintivement du coin de l'œil comme une bête blessée qui se prépare à charger. L'homme traversait une crise de rage aiguë. Jamais je n'avais vu visage aussi féroce — ses yeux jetaient des éclairs, les veines saillaient sur son cou. Sa colère évoquait l'abandon à une ivresse tumultueuse, une extase belliqueuse — peut-être une humeur emportée, irréfléchie. Je n'aurais su dire si cette exaltation frisant l'apoplexie était une caractéristique permanente de l'individu, ou si une circonstance précise avait motivé sa colère. De temps à autre, il me dévisageait avec une familiarité déconcertante. Il y avait de la curiosité et de la méchanceté dans son expression, et bien qu'il me sourît, je sentais qu'il cherchait un moyen pour me faire ramper.

« Et celui-là ? demandai-je à la femme.

— C'est le propriétaire et le capitaine de la jonque, dit-elle. Il emmène nos marchandises jusqu'à Ch'ung-ch'ing. Gare à lui, me prévint-elle à voix basse. A première vue, lui et Tsin paraissent opposés, mais ils se ressemblent sous maints rapports. C'est le seul capitaine qui ose faire remonter un navire aussi loin en amont, même pendant les crues de printemps. Il est emporté, il n'est pas bon — un homme dangereux, violent. Méfie-toi de lui. » Bien que son portrait ne fût pas flatteur, elle parlait avec prudence et respect, d'une voix plaintive, admirative, qui me suggéra davantage qu'un rapport banal, comme si elle connaissait intimement cet homme, et en souffrait.

« Que voulez-vous dire ? demandai-je.

— Je sais de quoi je parle », répondit-elle sobrement avec un sourire amer.

Là-dessus, comme pour lui donner la réplique, le capitaine (qui n'avait pu nous entendre, car nous nous tenions loin de lui et avions parlé à voix basse) me lança un regard ravi et cria au marchand : « Ta femme a trouvé un nouveau partenaire ! »

Le vieillard, absorbé dans une transaction, sursauta et porta la main à son oreille. « Plaît-il ? »

Il était apparemment à moitié sourd, car son fils tira sur sa robe et le fit pivoter vers le capitaine. Quand il comprit d'où venait l'apostrophe, le marchand s'inclina et grimaça un sourire déférent, exhibant des dents noircies et gâtées

« Je n'ai pas entendu, capitaine ! s'écria-t-il d'une voix zélée, comme s'il s'agissait d'une bonne plaisanterie qu'on lui destinait. Qu'avez-vous dit ? »

Le capitaine ne se donna pas la peine de répondre et se contenta de tendre la main vers nous. Quand le marchand nous vit, son sourire forcé se brisa en mille fragments qui restèrent un instant suspendus à ses lèvres comme des perles tremblant sur un fil. Malgré sa sénilité, il rougit. Il leva un bras décharné, agita le poing.

« Combien de fois faut-il te répéter de rester dans la maison ! » hurla-t-il d'une voix d'eunuque.

La femme plissa les yeux avec une expression de froid mépris. « Vous m'avez dit cela, mon mari ? Je ne me rappelle pas. En tout cas, vous ne devriez pas vous énerver ; vous savez que vous avez le cœur fragile. Le manque d'exercice l'a fait se ratatiner à la taille d'un foie de poulet. Et si vous mouriez ? Qu'adviendrait-il de moi ? Nous serions tellement tristes : plus personne ne nous donnerait d'argent.

— Salope, zézaya-t-il haineusement, vautour, vipère, catin...

— Ah ! ah ! rugit le capitaine. Tu as raison, vieux. Tu as hérité toute une ménagerie avec elle. Je t'ai toujours dit que tu avais fait une bonne affaire cette fois-là. Elle mérite jusqu'au dernier sou que tu as payé pour l'acheter. D'ailleurs, combien était-ce ? Voyons... Je devrais m'en souvenir, mais j'ai oublié. Toi, tu te rappelles, n'est-ce pas, marchand ? Tu n'oublies jamais une somme. »

Le marchand se tourna vers lui et sourit avec une haine impuissante. « Inutile de ressasser cette vieille histoire. Elle a perdu tout son piment. Et puis grâce à vous, nous l'avons tous entendue une bonne douzaine de fois.

— Ah ! ah ! rit encore le capitaine en me regardant. Pas tout le monde... Ça ne me paraît pas si vieux. Seulement quinze ans. Ta femme a un peu changé depuis — elle est mieux habillée. » Il hocha la tête pour appuyer ses dires, puis, jouant l'acheteur potentiel, déclara froidement : « Mais plus aussi jeune. » Le capitaine fit mine de retirer son chapeau et de s'incliner vers elle, politesse que contredisait son sourire ironique. « Ravi de vous rencontrer, madame ! Vous vous souvenez de moi ? »

La femme releva le menton et lui offrit son profil en guise de réponse.

« Regardez comme elle est fière ! s'écria le capitaine. Regardez comme elle se pavane et fait la coquette ! Tu faisais pas tant la fière à l'époque ! On s'est bien connus quand je t'ai trouvée dans ce bordel à soldats de Ch'ung-ch'ing. » Le vice assombrit ses traits, puis fit place à un sourire malicieux. « Mais une fois putain, toujours putain — voilà ce que je pense. Pas vrai, marchand ? »

Le visage du vieillard s'empourpra de honte et de fureur, mais il contraignit ses lèvres à sourire et répondit avec une rage contenue : « Le capitaine plaisante. Quelles qu'aient été les mœurs de ma femme, elle s'est amendée. »

Le capitaine rit de plus belle. « Tu connais peut-être les affaires, mais pas les femmes. Regarde-la, sa coiffure, ses vêtements, les yeux doux qu'elle fait à ce garçon. Elle en meurt d'envie, je peux te le dire. Pas avec un vieux tas d'os et de graisse comme toi, mais avec de la chair fraîche, de la viande rouge, du sang neuf. Tu ferais bien de la surveiller cette nuit, sinon demain matin tu te réveilleras cocu. » Sur la plage, les hommes commençaient à rire. « Elle fait peut-être la mijaurée, mais malgré tous ses chichis, je peux te dire qu'elle ne demande que ça. D'ailleurs, je suis bien placé pour le savoir. Ah ! ah ! Ce serait pas la première fois, hein salope ? » Il saisit son entrejambe de façon suggestive ; son regard croisa le mien. « Mais je ne t'ai pas encore parlé de ce voyage, la fois où je l'ai ramenée de Ch'ung-ch'ing. Ce devait être — bah, la deuxième ou troisième affaire que nous traitions ensemble.

— S'il vous plaît ! » implora le marchand en posant les mains sur les épaules de son fils. « Le garçon. »

Le capitaine poursuivit comme si de rien n'était, s'adressant tantôt au marchand, tantôt à la foule. « Quand je suis parti d'ici avec la marchandise, il m'a demandé de lui chercher une femme. Inutile qu'elle soit belle, me dit-il, pourvu qu'elle ait les reins solides. Ah ! ah ! Cela m'a fait tellement rire ! Il m'a grassement payé pour cette mission, et d'avance. Une de tes rares erreurs de jugement, marchand. Tu étais sans doute un peu nerveux. J'ai gagné une bonne somme dans l'affaire. On pouvait acheter une femme pour trois fois rien à l'époque, et j'ai choisi la marchandise la moins chère de la ville. Pourtant elle était solide, ainsi qu'il l'avait demandé, et pas vraiment laide, si l'on n'y regardait pas de trop près. Tout était au bon endroit. Je sais de quoi je parle, j'ai vérifié avant de livrer la marchandise, et aussi après ! »

Il se tourna vers le marchand. « Mais ce n'était peut-être pas exactement le modèle que tu désirais ? Ah ! ah ! Tu ne t'attendais pas à avoir autant de fil à retordre, pas vrai ? Moi non plus d'ailleurs. Car ce fut seulement à bord du bateau que je compris à quelle tigresse j'avais affaire. Dès que nous eûmes levé l'ancre, elle se colla à moi comme une sangsue. A la fin de la première journée, il ne me restait plus un poil sur la queue. Puis elle se repentit. Toute la nuit, elle pleura et tenta de m'arracher les yeux. J'ai dû la ligoter au mât et la bâillonner avant de pouvoir fermer l'œil. Ça l'a guérie. Je l'ai laissée là toute la nuit, et le lendemain matin elle était douce comme un agneau. Pendant le reste du voyage, elle m'a obéi au doigt et à l'œil. Mais quel voyage ! Elle était jeune à l'époque, ne l'oubliez pas. Ses seins étaient fermes et ronds. Rien à voir avec la vieille peau qu'elle est devenue. T'a-t-elle jamais raconté comment je l'ai baisée ici même sur la plage la nuit précédant ton mariage ? » Il cracha dans le sable, sans doute pour commémorer le lieu de son exploit. « Elle a couiné et grogné comme une truie, et pleuré pour que je remette ça. Elle me suppliait de la reprendre avec moi. Mais je suis pas complètement idiot. Et puis les affaires sont les affaires, pas vrai, le vieux ? Nous avions conclu un marché. Ah ! ah ! »

Son humeur changea de nouveau. « Excuse-moi, marchand, mais tu ferais bien de la garder sous les verrous cette nuit — et la petite aussi. J'en connais plusieurs ici présents qui ne cracheraient pas dessus. Ils en ont assez de baiser des brebis, des chèvres de montagne — il regarda Tsin —, des ours, l'arrière-train de leurs camarades, n'importe quel trou où planter leur poireau. Hein, les amis ? »

Il y eut quelques ricanements. Certains se renfrognèrent. Tsin ne broncha pas.

« Tu connais le vieux dicton : quand une miche est entamée, qu'est-ce qu'une tranche de plus ou de moins ? Moi-même, j'aimerais assez la troncher, histoire de voir si elle tient toujours la forme. Ah ! ah ! »

La femme cracha puis, tirant brusquement la fillette derrière elle, rentra furieuse dans la maison. Je tentai de m'éclipser aussi discrètement que possible, mais le capitaine cria : « Où vas-tu, joli minois ? Viens donc un peu nous distraire. Qu'as-tu à vendre ? A moins que tu sois venu nous aider à charger ? Ça vaut un repas, tu sais.

— Je suis prêtre, dis-je avec une dignité exagérée et un filet de voix à peine audible.

— *Quoi ?* cria-t-il.

— Prêtre », répétai-je en rougissant d'embarras.

Il me regarda avec incrédulité, comme s'il attendait la réplique suivante, puis lança sa tête en arrière en poussant un hennissement. Quand son hilarité fut apaisée, il se remit à hurler des ordres et m'ignora comme si j'étais devenu invisible.

C'était déjà pénible de se tortiller sur l'hameçon de ses questions sournoises, mais ce fut presque pire de me sentir mis sur la touche, laissé à moi-même. Brusquement, je devins une sorte de bête curieuse ; ceux qui n'avaient pas encore daigné remarquer mon existence m'observaient maintenant sans la moindre gêne, parfois avec méfiance ou hostilité. Je retrouvai un peu de courage en songeant que, si les espoirs que j'avais placés en eux s'avéraient illusoires, je pouvais néanmoins compter sur la générosité proverbiale des voleurs. Car si ces hommes n'étaient pas les sages rustiques que j'avais escomptés, alors c'étaient certainement des criminels.

D'emblée, le succès de mon entreprise parut compromis. Les premiers candidats que j'approchai me repoussèrent avec force gestes d'exorcisme, grimaces, sifflements. J'aurais pu y voir un présage de mauvais augure et battre discrètement en retraite, mon amour-propre égratigné mais presque intact. Pourtant l'instinct du joueur malchanceux me poussa à insister.

Comme je passais de l'un à l'autre, un gros homme chauve m'adressa un clin d'œil et des signes de tête pour que j'approche. Encouragé, j'avançai vers lui, m'arrêtai à quelques pas, m'inclinai respectueusement et tendis mon bol.

« Une aumône pour un pauvre prêtre », lui dis-je selon la formule rituelle.

J'entendis alors un raclement de gorge suivi d'un sifflement bref et sec. Etonné, je levai les yeux et découvris une morve visqueuse et verdâtre qui flottait comme une huître dans mon bol. Le gros homme me sourit avec un cynisme incroyable, ses yeux réduits à deux fentes obscures par les poches de graisse qui les entouraient, comme les rebords d'une bourse quand on en tire le cordon.

Je sentis le sang se ruer vers mon visage. Mes mains tremblèrent de rage. Le sourire de l'obèse disparut brusquement, remplacé par une expression de ruse froide. Je vis sa main se poser sur la poignée d'une dague coincée dans sa ceinture en cuir. Tous les yeux étaient fixés sur nous. Mon adversaire grinçait des dents en attendant la rixe. Je réussis à me maîtriser, pivotai sur les talons et rejoignis le bord du fleuve où je m'agenouillai pour laver mon bol dans le courant rapide. « Humilité, chuchotai-je sauvagement, compassion. »

Ma dérobade provoqua les spectateurs présents sur la plage. Je fus sifflé, moqué, bafoué. Bombant le torse comme un crapaud, l'obèse m'apostropha : « Hé, poule mouillée, tu as oublié de me remercier ! »

Je feignis de n'avoir rien entendu et traversai la foule d'un air lugubre. Pris d'une inspiration subite (peut-être parce qu'il était le seul à ne pas me manifester d'hostilité), je m'avançai derrière le soldat. Je m'arrêtai à quelques pas du chariot, puis m'adressai à Tsin.

Il parut d'abord ne pas m'entendre. Puis, quand je répétai ma demande, il se retourna lentement pour me regarder. Ce que je vis me glaça d'horreur. La cicatrice redescendait sur son front en une ligne déchiquetée, comme un éclair qui aurait fendu son sourcil et frappé le cratère mort de son œil. Car *exactement comme l'orbite du chien*, celle de son maître contenait une bille de verre laiteux dont la couleur évoquait les gaz et les cendres qui s'élèvent des entrailles d'un volcan tropical, ou les vapeurs de la glace artificielle qu'on utilise sur scène pour certains effets spéciaux. Mais contrairement à l'œil de l'animal, celui de l'homme semblait partiellement vivant, car il brillait d'une lueur sulfureuse, comme une boule de cristal ou une lune morte réfléchissant les rayons du soleil. Ce spectacle diabolique — le globe opalescent de verre translucide flottant dans un visage blême, cadavérique — glaça mon sang dans mes veines.

« Que veux-tu ? » demanda-t-il d'une voix rauque, presque un chuchotement, mais dont la douceur me surprit.

« Je n'ai rien mangé depuis deux jours, dis-je. Si vous pouviez me donner quelque chose... »

Le soldat se retourna et, à ma grande frayeur, saisit son sabre. Mais il le reposa aussitôt et plongea la main dans un sac. Il en sortit deux gâteaux de riz qu'il me lança vivement l'un après l'autre, puis me tourna le dos et se remit à fumer.

Son geste m'émut profondément. Je me prosternai dans le sable, me perdis en remerciements. Il n'y prêta pas davantage attention que tout à l'heure aux battements de queue affectueux de son molosse.

Je glissai un gâteau dans mon barda, m'assis et commençai de manger l'autre à petites bouchées, mâchant lentement pour savourer son goût.

Comme je mangeais, le marchand qui poursuivait ses pérégrinations frénétiques s'approcha de moi et me foudroya du regard. Levant les yeux par hasard, je m'efforçai de ne pas me laisser démonter.

« Une aumône ! » m'écriai-je stupidement en souriant et tendant mon bol à deux mains.

« Tu n'auras pas d'aumône ici, petit morveux ! répliqua-t-il d'une voix éraillée. Nous ne croyons ni à la charité, ni à la religion. L'autorité du *gouvernement* ne s'exerce même pas aussi loin en amont du fleuve. » Il rit de sa propre plaisanterie.

Puis il me dévisagea brièvement en caressant son bouc. « Prêtre, hein ? Comment savoir que tu ne mens pas ? Quelle magie pratiques-tu ? Sais-tu prédire l'avenir, provoquer la pluie, faire monter l'eau du fleuve ? Si oui, nous pourrons peut-être négocier un petit contrat. » Il me sourit en plissant les yeux.

« Ces pratiques ne sont pas dignes de l'adepte authentique, répondis-je froidement, machinalement.

— Heng ! gronda-t-il en grimaçant. Tu vois donc les choses ainsi ! Tu veux manger pour rien. C'est toujours la même ritournelle avec les prêtres. Mais quand on est incapable de rendre un service en échange... »

Une voix sonore interrompit notre conversation. « C'est encore ce prêtre qui fait le malin ? hurla le capitaine. Gare à lui ! »

Posant la main sur le plat-bord de la jonque, il lança son corps de l'autre côté et atterrit dans le sable. Il remonta la ceinture de son pantalon, ajusta son revolver et s'avança crânement vers nous. Il ferma l'un de ses yeux couleur de boue pour m'examiner des pieds à la tête, puis cracha dans le sable.

« Tu veux manger ? »

J'acquiesçai.

« Alors transporte ces ballots comme tout le monde.

— Je n'ai pas peur de travailler », répondis-je avec nervosité.

D'un mouvement de tête, il appela un coolie plié en deux sous une balle de chanvre. Pendant que l'homme arrivait, il continua de me scruter. « Pourquoi n'as-tu pas le crâne rasé, si tu es prêtre ?

— Je suis taoïste, et non bouddhiste.

— Un taoïste ! Moi qui les croyais tous morts et enterrés. Il en reste donc... »

D'un coup de reins, le coolie se dégagea de son fardeau qui tomba à mes pieds.

« Mets-le sur tes épaules », dit le capitaine.

Je me débarrassai de mon barda, pliai les jambes et m'efforçai de soulever la balle. Le chanvre était plus lourd que je ne pensais, mais je réussis à le charger sur mon dos. Une seconde, je vacillai et faillis tomber.

« Ici on n'a pas besoin de mendiants ni de bellâtres, pour faire les yeux doux aux femmes. Compris, le prêtre ? Chez nous, si un homme veut manger, il travaille — ainsi que l'a dit l'Oncle Mao. Nous sommes de bons communistes. Nous vivons dans un Etat prolétaire, tu te souviens ? Mais peut-être n'es-tu pas un homme... Paraît que, dans le temps, on les leur coupait. »

J'entendis quelques rires gras dans la foule. La sueur qui ruisselait sur mon front m'aveuglait. J'essayai de lever les yeux, mais aperçus seulement des chevilles et des mollets. Soudain, je le sentis m'agripper violemment par-derrière.

« Voyons ça de plus près. Que portes-tu sous toutes ces frusques ? » Il se colla étroitement contre moi. Profitant du fait que j'étais plié en deux, il me saisit aux hanches et entama une série de mouvements obscènes qui provoquèrent l'hilarité des spectateurs. Un barrage céda en moi. Je me redressai au prix d'un violent effort. La balle de chanvre percuta la poitrine de l'homme et l'obligea à reculer. Je laissai tomber mon fardeau, pivotai sur mes talons pour lui faire face, poings serrés.

Un seul regard au visage du capitaine suffit à me terrifier. Je découvris sur ses traits une expression de bonheur monstrueux qui court-circuita ma colère. Le blanc de ses yeux avait viré au rosâtre, comme sous l'effet de la boisson ; les iris avaient presque disparu, dilués par le flot d'adrénaline. Ses pupilles ressemblaient à deux tunnels où s'engouffrait l'obscurité de la préhistoire, une obscurité qui ne connaissait ni humanité ni sentiment moral. Il y avait un cauchemar dans ses yeux — mon cauchemar, mon rêve — et sa beauté me suffoqua, bien qu'elle menaçât de me détruire, de détruire le monde en une gigantesque conflagration instantanée.

J'essayai d'arrêter son poing quand il jaillit, mais il franchit la barrière dérisoire de mes bras comme un écran de papier. Sa main frappa mon visage comme un météorite percute la surface de la terre. Il y eut une explosion, un éclair éblouissant ; l'impact m'envoya lourdement à terre. L'univers tourbillonna, puis je perdis conscience.

Quand je rouvris les yeux, je regardais droit dans le soleil, qui commençait à se coucher. J'avais un goût amer, cuivré dans la bouche ; je crachai dans ma main et un morceau de dent brisée jaillit avec le sang rouge sombre. Je me rappelle avoir pensé que le coucher de soleil s'écoulait par ma bouche.

Le capitaine se dressait près de mes pieds, jambes écartées, poings sur les hanches, la tête baissée vers moi. « Debout », commanda-t-il.

Comme je ne bougeais pas, il s'avança au-dessus de moi et se courba pour saisir le devant de ma robe. Sa main tordit le tissu et me hissa. J'aperçus alors le soldat debout derrière nous. Sa silhouette mince masqua un instant le soleil, jetant sur nous une ombre longue. Son sabre était dégainé ; d'un geste précis et silencieux, il le glissa entre le visage de mon adversaire et le mien, pressant la pointe contre le front du capitaine, juste entre les yeux.

« *Aiya !* cria-t-il en me lâchant.

— Laisse-le tranquille », murmura Tsin de sa voix rauque ; d'une légère pression de la lame, il obligea l'autre à se redresser centimètre par centimètre.

La poitrine du capitaine se soulevait rapidement, de colère, de peur ou de surprise.

« Tsin, dit-il d'une voix sourde que l'émotion faisait trembler, je ne te cherche pas querelle.

— Tant mieux pour toi, répondit le soldat. Dans ce cas, tu laisseras ce garçon tranquille.

— Pourquoi le défendre ? Qu'est-il pour toi ?

— C'est mon affaire », répliqua sèchement Tsin en rengainant son sabre d'un geste vif et précis. Il fixa un instant le visage du capitaine, puis se retourna pour partir.

« Espèce de sale drogué », siffla le capitaine. Comme le soldat ne répondait pas, il s'enhardit. « Pour qui te prends-tu ? Je vais t'apprendre à te mêler de tes oignons. » Sa main s'approcha de son revolver, soit pour faire feu, soit simplement pour intimider, je ne saurais dire.

« Attention ! » m'écriai-je.

Mais le soldat avait déjà pivoté, et dégainé en se retournant. Il regardait droit devant lui avec une concentration hallucinée. Son dos était raidi, son attitude hiératique. Un rai de lumière croisa la lame d'acier et l'embrasa comme le filament d'une ampoule électrique. Se dressant sur la pointe des pieds, il brandit un instant son sabre au-dessus de sa tête et parallèlement au sol, tenant fermement à deux mains la longue poignée cannelée, la pointe dirigée vers l'avant, le tranchant vers le ciel, son coude gauche coincé contre le plexus solaire. Il fit un deuxième pas rapide, sa jambe droite décrivit un arc de cercle dans le sable, puis passa devant le corps. Dans le même temps, il amena l'arme devant son visage, lame perpendiculaire au sol, tranchant dirigé vers l'avant. Dans le troisième mouvement, ses poignets s'élancèrent de côté, le sabre pointa vers la gauche, lame toujours parallèle à la terre, mais décalée de la trajectoire du corps. Ce faisant, il ramena sa jambe gauche et s'avança vers sa cible, mais sans se redresser, pliant plutôt les genoux vers le sol. Bien que chaque pose eût été précisément marquée avec l'élégance sévère de la danse, leur enchaînement dura le temps d'une profonde inspiration suivie d'une expiration. Le soldat accroupi se retrouva à moins d'un mètre du capitaine, qui venait à peine d'extraire son revolver de sa ceinture et se mettait en position de tir.

Je ne saurais dire exactement ce qui se passa ensuite. Le soldat mania son sabre si vite qu'il disparut littéralement. J'entendis le sifflement de l'acier qui fend l'air, puis un claquement sec, comme du métal contre le métal. Le revolver tomba dans le sable avec un bruit mat, et près de lui, sectionnées aussi nettement que par une paire de ciseaux, les dernières phalanges de l'annulaire et du petit doigt de la main droite du capitaine.

Le visage du gros homme s'empourpra comme sous le coup de la honte. Il hésita, sembla essayer de comprendre ce qui venait de se passer, de décider quoi faire. Alors il cria. Il tomba à genoux en serrant sa main blessée, la pressa contre son ventre. Puis il courba la tête et se balança lentement d'avant en arrière.

Avec la même rapidité qu'auparavant, Tsin harponna le revolver tombé dans le sable, enfilant l'extrémité de sa lame dans le pontet comme dans le chas d'une aiguille. Il releva brusquement le sabre et lança l'arme à feu au-dessus de sa tête. La pression de la lame sur la détente déclencha un coup de feu. Le revolver décrivit une longue courbe au-dessus du fleuve puis disparut dans l'eau avec un bruit d'éclaboussures lointain.

Le capitaine redressa la tête, exhiba un visage blême de dépit et de haine, mais Tsin appuya aussitôt son pied nu sur le cou et enfonça dans le sable le visage de son adversaire.

Partagé entre l'horreur et l'incrédulité, je vis le soldat brandir de nouveau son sabre dans la première position — pointe dirigée vers l'avant, tranchant vers le ciel, coude gauche fermement coincé contre le plexus solaire. Il poussa un cri perçant et se prépara à abattre son arme.

« Non ! protesta le marchand en se jetant de tout son long sur le condamné. Tsin ! Epargne-le ! »

Le soldat hésita, mais son regard ne perdit rien de sa fixité. Il haletait. Une grosse veine bleue saillait sur son front à côté de la cicatrice qui était devenue aussi blanche que le givre.

« Il a le sang chaud, c'est un crétin, mais sans lui nous sommes ruinés, plaida le marchand. Lui seul peut transporter la marchandise à travers les rapides.

— Je travaille avec la Birmanie. Que veux-tu que cela me fasse ? » demanda Tsin sans baisser son sabre, alors que ses muscles se détendaient légèrement.

« L'ours ! s'écria le marchand. Nous devons le livrer à Shanghai ; il est sans valeur tant que les Américains ne l'ont pas réceptionné. Pense au temps que tu as mis à le capturer. Tout cela pour rien ! »

Le soldat se tourna vers le vieillard qui se prosternait devant lui, levait des mains implorantes, cillait et grimaçait de terreur. « Etrange que ce soit toi qui me demandes sa grâce, lâcha-t-il sombrement.

— Je n'ai pas de rancune envers lui, dit le marchand. Oublie cela ! Il y a des décisions plus importantes. Nous devons mener à bien cette affaire.

— "Les affaires", dit le soldat avec mépris. Si je l'épargne aujourd'hui, je devrai être sur mes gardes nuit et jour. » Il fronça les sourcils, mais baissa son arme. « Pourtant je te dois cela, marchand. Puisque tu t'es interposé entre lui et le sabre — même si je sais pertinemment que le seul profit motive ton courage — je lui ferai grâce... cette fois-ci. » Il retira son pied de la nuque du capitaine, qu'il envoya rouler dans le sable, puis rengaina son arme avec dédain. « Remercie ton bienfaiteur, capitaine, dit-il. Et écoute-moi bien. Si jamais je dois à nouveau dégainer ce sabre à cause de toi, tu ne vivras pas assez longtemps pour voir cette lame rentrer dans son fourreau. J'en fais le serment. »

Sur ce, le soldat me regarda pour la première fois. Son visage qui avait repris des couleurs semblait rajeuni. Son œil de verre réfléchissait les lueurs rouges du couchant.

« Suis-moi », dit-il avant de s'éloigner d'un pas décidé.

Le marchand l'accompagna avec maintes courbettes et remerciements. « Mille mercis, mon ami ! Emmène ce jeune homme et prends du bon temps. Détendez-vous ! Nous nous occuperons du chargement de l'ours en ton absence. » Tsin continuait de marcher sans daigner répondre. Quand il passa près du chariot, il se pencha pour fixer une chaîne au collier du molosse. « Reste là », lui dit-il. A cet ordre, l'animal se raidit et frémit comme la corde d'un arc, montrant peut-être qu'il allait redoubler de vigilance.

Le soldat dépassa le chariot et s'engagea sur le sentier qui montait vers les huttes. Ignorant ce qu'il désirait de moi, rempli de terreur, redoutant de provoquer moi-même sa colère, je le suivais à distance, les yeux fixés sur sa cicatrice comme sur un signe géodésique, un méridien qui me permettrait peut-être de m'orienter dans l'univers cauchemardesque où j'étais tombé.

Quand nous fûmes un peu éloignés, le soldat s'arrêta. A mon grand étonnement, il rit et rougit comme une jeune fille. « Pourquoi restes-tu en arrière ? s'écria-t-il.

— Je... je..., bafouillai-je.
— Evidemment, tu désapprouves ma conduite ! Tu es un pacifiste. En te sauvant la vie, j'ai enfreint tes règles morales. » Il rit. « Essaie de faire preuve de compassion. »

Coupant court à son ironie, j'inclinai gravement la tête. « Je vous dois la vie. »

Il haussa les épaules, fronça les sourcils. « Je t'ai peut-être rendu le plus mauvais service qui soit. »

Il m'observa. « Comment t'appelles-tu ?
— Sun I.
— Eh bien, Sun I, viens donc bavarder avec moi, dit-il avec enthousiasme. Je vois bien que tu as peu d'expérience du monde. Tu ne serais pas en sécurité là-bas, sur la plage. Ces hommes ne feraient qu'une bouchée de toi. Mais je veillerai sur toi. Qui sait ? Nous deviendrons peut-être amis. En tout cas, nous pouvons tuer quelques heures ensemble en partageant une pipe.
— Merci, répondis-je en déglutissant avec difficulté, mais je ne fume pas. »

Il rit — un rire bref et tranchant —, puis son visage redevint grave. « Tu es mon débiteur, répliqua-t-il d'une voix péremptoire, et c'est moi qui t'invite. »

Quand je l'eus rejoint, nous poursuivîmes en silence vers l'une des bâtisses de pierre. Malgré l'absence de tout indice, je pressentais que c'était notre destination, car contrairement aux autres maisons du village, un mince filet de fumée s'échappait de son toit et témoignait d'un feu — incongru vu l'époque de l'année et la chaleur de l'air. De plus, alors que nous approchions, je remarquai une odeur qui s'échappait du lieu, une douceur équivoque et particulière, comme de fleurs sauvages mêlées de crottin. Assis dehors dans la poussière, le dos appuyé au mur de pierres, je vis un homme émacié, spectral, qui semblait atteint d'une maladie indéterminée. Ses mains inertes reposaient à ses côtés, paumes tournées vers le ciel ; sa tête pendait sur son cou comme un fruit mûr trop lourd pour la tige. Quand nous passâmes devant lui, il tordit le cou sans lever la tête et nous adressa un bref regard vitreux. Presque aussitôt, sa tête retomba contre sa poitrine et il sombra de nouveau dans l'apathie.

« Est-il malade ? » demandai-je.

Tsin me regarda avec incrédulité, puis éclata d'un rire rauque. « Malade ? Au contraire. Il est au comble du bonheur ! »

Nous franchîmes le seuil et pénétrâmes dans une pièce faiblement éclairée. Mes yeux mirent un certain temps à s'accoutumer à la pénombre ; puis, à la lumière du modeste feu de charbon de bois qui rougeoyait au creux d'une pierre posée au milieu de la pièce et d'une forêt de lampes à pétrole essaimées comme une constellation d'étoiles dans les ténèbres, je commençai à distinguer le lieu et ses occupants. Partout des hommes étaient assis ou allongés sur le sol ou sur les bat-flanc de bois fixés aux murs, certains reposant leur tête sur des oreillers de porcelaine lisse et blanche. Un vieillard ratatiné dont les seins pendaient comme ceux d'une femme chauffait attentivement dans la flamme d'une lampe un petit fragment d'une matière noire qui ressemblait à de la poix, et qu'il considérait avec la fixité de l'affamé devant un repas. La boulette était enfilée au bout d'une longue aiguille, que l'homme tourna lentement et régulièrement jusqu'à ce qu'elle se mît à grésiller et se muer en une pâte visqueuse qui fumait légèrement. Il la plaça ensuite dans le fourneau d'une pipe aussi longue et massive qu'un hautbois, glissa doucement l'embout entre les lèvres de l'homme allongé à côté de lui, puis alla servir quelqu'un d'autre. Certains clients s'étaient recroquevillés en fœtus, comme s'ils dormaient, mais leurs yeux grands ouverts avaient la même expression vitreuse que ceux de l'homme aperçu dehors. Les occupants des niveaux supérieurs étaient presque invisibles, dilués comme des fantômes dans la fumée laiteuse qui stagnait près du plafond. Personne ne parlait ; personne ne riait ni ne souriait. Tous fumaient en silence, oublieux de leurs voisins, du lieu, peut-être d'eux-mêmes. Hormis le craquement intermittent d'une allumette, le bruissement du charbon de bois dans l'âtre ou un bref soupir, on n'entendait rien.

« Tu es taoïste, m'as-tu dit ? » demanda Tsin.

J'acquiesçai d'un hochement de tête.

Il sourit et désigna la pièce d'un large mouvement de son sabre. « Bienvenue à la Source, au royaume de l'abondance. Tu contemples ici *wu-wei* sous sa forme la plus achevée. » Cette fois, son rire fut perçant, vaguement démoniaque.

« Ce sont des drogués, lui dis-je gravement pour lui reprocher son irrévérence. Le plaisir de l'opium est une parodie insidieuse et ultimement débilitante de la joie profonde de l'illumination, ajoutai-je en répétant le maître comme un perroquet.

— Peut-être, dit-il, mais je ne suis pas différent d'eux.

— Comment est-ce possible ? »

Il sourit. « Tu penses à ce qui s'est passé sur la plage ? » Il hocha la tête. « Cela prouve simplement ton inexpérience. L'opium n'induit pas nécessairement un état de torpeur — seulement chez ceux dont l'âme est déjà engourdie. L'opium rend chacun plus proche de soi. C'est là son mystère. Mais tu as raison — "ultimement débilitante". Car au bout du compte, tous se ressemblent. » D'un geste du menton, il désigna l'homme allongé sur le sol à nos pieds. « Je sais qu'un jour je finirai comme lui. Sinon aujourd'hui, alors demain. Et sinon demain, dans dix ans. Le plus tôt sera le mieux en ce qui me concerne. » Il rit et m'invita à m'asseoir.

Il continua de parler en préparant une pipe. « Bien que tu ne dises rien, tu te demandes pourquoi je ris, pourquoi je parais aussi content. » Il s'arrêta pour me lancer un regard de défi. « C'est le goût du sang, Sun I. Il a sur moi un effet tonique. »

J'ignorai s'il avait dit cela pour me choquer, mais je fus atterré. Mon expression le fit rire. « Ce fut jadis ma raison de vivre, ce pourquoi je devins soldat. Le destin en est responsable. Aussi loin que je me souvienne, rien d'autre ne m'a intéressé — ni la gloire, ni l'argent, ni le pouvoir tel que le monde l'entend. Il existe une seule et unique forme de pouvoir absolu pour un homme : prendre la vie. Donner la vie est aussi un pouvoir, mais c'est le privilège des femmes, ou leur fardeau. L'âme ne connaît ses plus profondes passions que dans ces deux activités.

« Adolescent, je chassais le cerf dans la forêt avec un arc et des flèches. Je me rappelle encore ma première mise à mort, comment l'univers entier — le passé, le futur — pâlit quand je me dressai devant ma proie et bandai mon arc. Mes battements de cœur emplissaient mes oreilles, ma bouche était sèche, mais mon bras immobile. Je vis l'œil liquide briller de panique quand il m'aperçut, et alors je connus pour la première fois l'intimité, plus profonde que toute autre, qui lie le chasseur à sa proie. Je décochai ma flèche, l'entendis frapper la poitrine avec un bruit soyeux, puis le craquement des os brisés quand elle s'enfonça vers le cœur. Une fine écume de sang monta aux lèvres de la bête. Elle leva la tête vers le ciel avec une grâce de danseur, ouvrit sa gueule pour pousser un dernier cri — appel muet, prière ou imprécation, je ne sais — peut-être pour boire le bleu frais du ciel et apaiser la brûlure de son cœur. Je n'ai jamais réussi à exprimer ce que je vis alors, l'irruption brutale de la vie, la panique élémentaire — ce qu'on aperçoit au fond des yeux d'une femme quand les digues cèdent, qu'on s'enfonce en elle pour la dernière fois et que l'orgasme la submerge. La même chose, mais en plus intense.

« Puis le cerf tomba sur le flanc ; ses pattes frissonnaient, les nuages énormes filaient au-dessus de lui, le ciel bleu du monde se reflétait dans ses yeux ouverts. L'instant suivant, tout s'éteignit, ses yeux s'obscurcirent et se voilèrent. J'étais seul au cœur de la forêt dans la chaleur ; les bruits des oiseaux et des insectes s'interrompirent, le monde entier retenait son souffle comme par respect. Puis je sentis de nouveau la brise jouer sur mes joues, la morsure impatiente reprit possession de mon ventre, bien que moins insistante. Je soulevai la charogne encore chaude sur mon épaule et l'emportai pour la dépecer. Ah, Sun I, après cela rien ne fut jamais pareil. Je connaissais désormais ma vocation, mon but : devenir un prêtre comme toi — il me sourit —, célébrer le grand mystère de la mort. »

Absorbé par ses paroles, Tsin avait posé la pipe à côté de lui. « Mais la chasse n'est qu'un pâle substitut de la chose elle-même, un exercice préparatoire. Il y a si peu de risques que cela finit par devenir presque mécanique. Les spécialistes de mon art savent que l'intensité de l'expérience est directement proportionnelle au risque. Seule la recherche d'un adversaire de force égale permet d'aborder les aspects les plus secrets du mystère. Ce qui veut dire tuer des hommes. Non pas le meurtre accompli sournoisement et par surprise, forme la plus dégradante de déshonneur et de lâcheté, mais la guerre. Voilà pourquoi ce grand sacrement fut donné au monde : afin que l'homme parvienne à se connaître dans son essence immuable. Toutes les platitudes de la politique — justice, souveraineté, légitime défense — ne sont que des excuses inventées par ceux qui n'ont pas le cran d'affronter la vérité (ou qui pensent que la majorité d'entre nous sommes trop couards pour cela) : la bataille est la plus haute expression de l'aspiration humaine, la raison ultime de notre existence, qui nous fait dépasser nos limites pour accéder à la divinité ; nous tuons non pas à cause d'une regrettable nécessité, mais pour nous resourcer et augmenter notre force, parce que notre esprit s'en repaît, parce que nous ne vivons réellement que dans l'instant où nous enlevons la vie. Le reste du temps, nous subissons en somnambules cette sombre morsure d'impatience. Si tu crois que je plaisante ou que je divague, interroge donc n'importe qui a goûté à cela, connu la joie sauvage du duel avec un ennemi dans la bataille. Tu remarqueras que chez tous, aussi différents soient-ils, le passage des années aura effacé maints souvenirs, mais pas celui-là. Malgré la terreur qu'il a peut-être connue, ou le remords d'avoir dû agir contre ses convictions, cette expérience sera nécessairement liée à une beauté déchirante que, malgré tous ses efforts, il ne pourra jamais oublier. Car elle est incommensurable avec les autres plaisirs ou vérités de la vie — même l'amour des femmes. Etrange que tout savoir soit irrévocablement lié à la destruction. Mais c'est ainsi.

« J'ai vécu relativement longtemps, du moins pour un membre de ma profession, et tout ce que je sais, la somme de mon expérience, se résume à ceci : un homme naît, goûte peut-être — s'il a de la chance — quelques brèves années de bonheur illusoire dans les bras de sa mère, et puis un jour, mystérieusement, une morsure s'empare de son cœur. Il s'éveille à cette dure réalité que tout est transitoire, que tout ce qu'il aime et connaît lui échappe sans cesse. A l'ombre de cette vérité, il remplit ses jours de ternes devoirs, invente un stratagème pour tuer le temps jusqu'à sa mort, et seulement alors, l'espace d'un instant aussi bref qu'un battement de paupières, au seuil du néant éternel, il entrevoit peut-être la vérité — à savoir que son existence est dépourvue de sens et qu'il aurait mieux fait de ne pas naître. Je porte ce savoir en moi depuis mon enfance. Il est la source ultime de la morsure dont je t'ai parlé. Et il existe une seule méthode pour l'apaiser. Les seuls moments de ma vie où je me suis senti soulagé de ce vide furent au plus fort de la bataille, quand j'ai regardé mon adversaire dans les yeux et que je l'ai tué sans haine. Pourquoi en est-il ainsi ? A toi de me le dire, car je l'ignore.

« Mais comment pourrais-tu me comprendre ? Que connais-tu de l'extase du combat ? Ecoute-moi, Sun I. Une part de nous-mêmes répond à l'appel du feu dévastateur qui ravage les villages, aux gémissements des femmes, aux meuglements terrifiés du bétail, aux craquements et aux sifflements du bois qui brûle, à la chaleur insupportable du chaume qui s'enflamme, grille les sourcils, dessèche les lèvres, noircit la peau, à l'odeur de la chair carbonisée. C'est un sentiment de réalité et de présence qui nous dispense des dieux. Il sature et rassasie, convainc l'esprit de l'existence d'une vérité absolue. Les consolations de la religion, le sens de la vie, les incertitudes de l'avenir — tous ces problèmes et ces dilemmes nous apparaissent alors sous leur vrai jour, spécieux, et ils s'évanouissent. L'insatisfaction qui tenaille notre ventre disparaît elle aussi. Nous cessons d'être divisés avec nous-mêmes. La réalité trouve son apothéose quand, dans la mêlée, nous affrontons un seul adversaire. C'est une chose étrange. As-tu déjà vu des chiens se battre ? Les hommes ne sont pas foncièrement différents. Eux aussi se dévisagent avant de bondir, sondent l'âme de l'ennemi avec un mélange de respect et de défi, comme pour apposer leur signature au combat. Des volumes de savoir non écrits s'échangent alors dans cet instant éternel, le plus beau de toute vie. Tu te dresses devant ton opposant sans rien lui cacher, débordant de vitalité mais aussi prêt à mourir... Pareille vulnérabilité est plus profonde que l'amour. Cet affrontement constitue la seule intuition que nous aurons jamais de l'éternité, car une telle faveur est seulement accordée à ceux qui sont prêts à la payer de leur vie.

« Le premier homme que j'ai tué — je me rappelle son visage avec une parfaite netteté, mieux que celui de mon père ou de ma femme. Cela se passait pendant la chute de Shanghai. Je l'ai surpris dans une ruelle. Je n'oublierai jamais la tristesse, la surprise et la détermination sauvage de son regard. Il était beau, entier, transfiguré ; ç'aurait pu être un Immortel, et sais-tu ? Il m'a souri, sans ironie, sans triomphe ni résignation, mû par une joie spontanée, il me semble. Oui, de la joie. Je lui ai rendu son sourire. J'étais pour lui ce qu'il était pour moi, même quand nous avons levé nos armes pour faire feu. J'ai eu la chance d'être un peu plus rapide. J'ai visé, appuyé sur la détente. Alors pour la première fois, d'une voix que je reconnus à peine comme la mienne, j'entendis monter de ma gorge le cri aigu, spontané, du triomphe primitif (inséparablement mêlé de souffrance), tandis que son corps criblé de balles titubait puis tombait. Le souffle coupé, je marchai jusqu'à lui pour scruter son visage, et je vis les nuages blancs flotter sur la mer noire de ses pupilles, les mêmes nuages que dans les yeux du cerf, comme des pétales sur un puits recouvert d'une fine pellicule de glace. Sa vie s'écoulait sur les pavés. Alors que je suivais chaque phase de la découverte dans ses yeux mourants, il perdit conscience, emporta les ultimes révélations par-delà la frontière de ce pays inconnu où je ne pouvais le suivre, me laissant plein de regret, partagé entre une terreur et un émerveillement tels que je n'en avais jamais connu, simplement parce que j'étais encore là, vivant. Le mystère et la beauté indicibles du monde me frappèrent alors de plein fouet. Jamais, je crois, je ne me suis autant approché de la religion, même par le plus noir des péchés.

« Cette sensation se prolongea jusqu'au lendemain. Je m'éveillai comme après un soir de beuverie, tous les muscles courbatus, les nerfs tendus, l'esprit engourdi, le corps brisé par le combat. C'est une douleur étrange, lancinante, Sun I, comme une migraine, mais qui frapperait aussi l'esprit ; elle jette une lumière particulière sur tout, révèle sur le visage des hommes la beauté époustouflante de leur mort future, une beauté que la bataille, plus que toute autre chose, souligne. Cette douleur me fit pleinement comprendre que pour moi le combat est la seule réalité, et qu'en fin de compte la cause, le prétexte importe peu — seule compte la chose elle-même. »

Le soldat, qui avait parlé dans une sorte d'état second, hésita. Une ombre traversa son visage. « Un homme que j'aimais et pour qui j'ai tué me dit un jour que je le dégoûtais, qu'il me méprisait, que mes services lui étaient odieux, que j'avais commis un péché monstrueux, irréparable. Je me sentis trahi et feignis de ne pas le comprendre. Quelles paroles étaient-ce là dans la bouche d'un grand guerrier ? Mais une partie de moi-même entrevit alors ce qu'il voulait dire, et comprit qu'il avait raison. Pourtant, ma vie ne s'en trouva pas bouleversée. La damnation me paraissait un prix modique à payer pour la douceur d'une telle extase.

« La damnation, Sun I, est bel et bien le prix que j'ai payé. Mais quand un homme a connu le goût du sang, il ne peut plus l'oublier. Pourtant, j'ai à moitié réussi, troquant une drogue contre une autre, la plus puissante contre une obsession moindre. » Il saisit la pipe, puis se rassit et me regarda avec attention. « Tu sais, tu me rappelles un ennemi que j'ai affronté dans une bataille, un jeune communiste, un garçon de ton âge. Alors que j'allais porter le coup de grâce, la digne gravité de son expression me fit comprendre que, même s'il vivait cent autres années, il ne connaîtrait plus jamais l'extase qu'il avait atteinte sous mon sabre. Et je lui ai tranché la tête, je l'ai cueilli comme une fleur avant qu'elle ne se flétrisse sur sa tige. J'étais la colère de Dieu, Sun I, l'ange de beauté et de miséricorde. Je l'ai amené à ce lieu ultime où tout est clair, puis affranchi de l'horrible maladie de la vie... »

La voix de Tsin se brisa, un sanglot à demi étouffé monta de sa gorge quand il prononça ces derniers mots. Il plaça le fourneau au-dessus de la flamme et bientôt l'opium se mit à grésiller en sifflant. Quand il porta l'embout de la pipe à ses lèvres, la lueur rougeâtre du charbon de bois incendia son œil de verre. Mais dans son autre œil, le vivant, une étincelle d'angoisse ou de colère apparut, mince vestige de volonté consciente, fragile radeau sur la mer de sa pupille noire.

Il inhala une première bouffée, qu'il retint dans ses poumons, continuant de parler entre ses dents serrées. « Mais tout cela est du passé maintenant. » Il y avait des larmes dans ses yeux, puis... le vide. Une déferlante engloutit le radeau dans le néant quand il exhala.

Un quart d'heure plus tard, toute la beauté que j'avais vue sur le visage de Tsin avait disparu. Il était redevenu le personnage pâle, cadavérique, aperçu sur le chariot. On eût dit qu'un dieu impitoyable s'était glissé dans son corps pour lui accorder un sursis de vitalité surnaturelle dont l'éclat sauvage avait consumé jusqu'aux sources de son être. Cette horrible et pitoyable transformation éveilla en moi un profond ressentiment contre la vie qui l'avait amené à une telle déchéance. Car bien que son apologie de l'« extase du combat » m'eût dégoûté, j'avais discerné sur son visage une expression de réelle passion, maintenant disparue et remplacée par quelque chose d'incroyablement pathétique, presque obscène. L'opium calmait la fureur de son cœur, mais je me demandai si le remède n'était pas pire que la maladie. Le cas échéant, j'aurais nié avec véhémence que la passion qu'il avait mise dans ses mots fût une preuve de leur véracité. Son idée était indéfendable. Pourtant, je ne pouvais l'écarter à la légère, d'autant que l'homme était d'une authenticité incontestable. Du moins comprenais-je parfaitement ce qu'il désignait par « la morsure d'impatience qui tiraille le ventre ». De quoi pouvait-il s'agir, sinon des cigales dans le temple du cœur ?

Il me tendit la pipe et je la pris. Non pour la raison que vous pourriez imaginer. Car son expression ne contenait plus ni menace ni violence, rien qui me forçât la main, seulement un appel muet et discret à la solidarité où je discernais un désir d'abandon, comme un pacte fraternel... mais je n'aurais su dire sur quelles bases il avait été signé.

Je serrai la tige mince entre mes lèvres comme l'embouchure d'un instrument à vent, puis aspirai jusqu'à ce que la pastille noire grésille. La première bouffée me fit tousser violemment. J'en inhalai une seconde avec plus de précautions. Le front plissé par l'effort de concentration, j'attendis que la magie me transfigure. Mais il ne se passait rien. J'inhalai de nouveau. Toujours rien. Je commençais à me demander si l'efficacité de cette drogue ne relevait pas du mythe, ou si je lui étais réfractaire, ou encore si je m'y prenais mal, quand un nuage de chaleur et de douceur inonda soudain mon cerveau. On eût dit qu'un magicien avait lancé sa cape sur moi ; dans un panache de fumée multicolore, avec le bruit sec d'une bouteille de champagne qu'on débouche, un génie minuscule se matérialisa, vert et musclé, avec des boucles d'oreilles et des bracelets de cuivre aux bras, un chignon sur son crâne à demi rasé et des yeux noirs qui brillaient de malice. Ce diablotin au visage éminemment sympathique exécutait les tours les plus extraordinaires. Je m'entichai aussitôt de lui — de ses oreilles pointues, de ses allures de farfadet facétieux.

« Je suis ton serviteur », dit-il en s'inclinant respectueusement devant moi ; puis il métamorphosa le monde en un organisme vivant qui palpitait et luisait faiblement. Je chevauchai la houle des continents, mon oreille perçut le tumulte du magma liquide qui courait sous la croûte terrestre comme le sang dans mes veines.

Mais ses tours de magie fatiguèrent mon génie. Il devint pâle et irritable ; je découvris bientôt qu'il avait besoin d'une constante stimulation, d'une alimentation régulière pour empêcher son humeur de virer à l'aigre. Il s'allongeait alors et se mettait à trembler en fixant sur moi de grands yeux implorants. Davantage pour l'apaiser que pour me faire plaisir, j'aspirais donc une autre bouffée, qui le requinquait aussitôt, lui rendait tout son allant et le faisait jurer, avec beaucoup de sincérité et de chaleur, de mieux me servir désormais. Ce manège se répéta un nombre incalculable de fois. J'en vins à redouter l'épuisement inévitable de ses forces. J'observais d'un œil consterné le contenu de la pipe en me demandant ce que je ferais quand il serait réduit en cendres. L'expression absente des autres fumeurs allongés dans la pièce prenait maintenant tout son sens. Je lisais clairement en leur âme, j'y découvrais une sorte de pitié, mais statique, sans la force ni même la volonté de corriger ce qu'elle déplorait. A chaque nouvelle bouffée, le sursaut d'énergie de mon gnome décroissait, jusqu'à ce qu'il sombre dans un état comateux, saisi de tremblements et des convulsions de l'agonie. Je compris alors avec un frisson que la situation s'était modifiée — inversée pour être exact : j'étais devenu son serviteur. Une vague de panique monta de mon ventre comme une bulle chauffée à blanc puis, éclatant sur mes lèvres en une ultime parodie de plaisir innocent, se métamorphosa en papillon, en monarque, qu'avec une joie enfantine je voulus attraper. Mais dans ma main, le papillon devint la phalène, le *Bombyx mori* aux pattes velues et aux yeux à facettes miroitantes. Je perdis alors conscience et sombrai dans un rêve.

Je servais le thé et des pêches au grand chien de pierre, dans la vaisselle rituelle du monastère. Assis à l'écart, digne et silencieux, l'ours attendait sa part. La petite fille tissait une guirlande de fleurs de pavot pour le cou de l'ours ; le chien portait déjà la sienne. Quand je versai le thé en maintenant le couvercle fermé, le chien me regarda d'un air bizarre, la tête penchée sur le côté. Je baissai les yeux pour essayer de comprendre le sens de son regard. Par le bec de la théière, ce n'était pas du thé qui coulait, mais un jet épais de sang fumant et visqueux. Reculant d'horreur et de dégoût, je faillis lâcher la théière. L'animal remarqua mon désarroi, et d'une voix humaine m'adressa quelques mots d'apaisement qui clarifièrent aussitôt la situation et soulagèrent ma terreur — des mots que je fus incapable de me rappeler ensuite. Puis il inclina sa tête massive et se mit à laper le contenu de sa tasse.

Je fus réveillé en sursaut par des aboiements frénétiques. Je ne sus tout d'abord s'ils venaient de l'extérieur ou si mon esprit les avait produits. Quand j'ouvris les yeux, j'eus l'impression de remonter des grandes profondeurs océaniques, de quitter enfin les ténèbres oppressantes pour retrouver la lumière et un air respirable. Je m'assis et regardai autour de moi, vaguement reposé par le sommeil, mais loin d'être lucide. Rien n'avait changé. Les drogués, toujours allongés, contemplaient de leur regard vitreux l'horizon doré que je venais de quitter. Mais il faisait maintenant nuit noire, et le soldat avait disparu. Son absence me remplit d'abord d'inquiétude, puis je réfléchis qu'il était probablement sorti pour surveiller le chargement de l'ours.

Un grand silence bruissant s'étendait sur le monde, où je reposais, aux aguets. Les aboiements que j'avais entendus, ou cru entendre, avaient cessé, si bien que je dus les porter au compte de mon imagination. Mais les coups de tonnerre intermittents qui se déchaînaient loin au-dessus du fleuve et se répercutaient en échos lugubres entre les murailles du canyon étaient bien réels, tout comme les stridulations métalliques des cigales qui montaient dans les ténèbres. De temps à autre, un éclair de chaleur emplissait le ciel de lueurs blafardes qui découpaient les montagnes en ombres chinoises. Soudain, dominant le vacarme des autres bruits, le cri plaintif et suraigu d'un oiseau de nuit éclata dans les collines. Son chant m'était inconnu, mais pas complètement... il évoquait un bruit familier, un bruit plus ancien que la mémoire, presque un appel au secours, mais quand le mal est fait et que rien ne peut le réparer.

Je ne saurais dire exactement pourquoi, peut-être était-ce l'effet de la drogue, mais dans cette immobilité écrasée de chaleur, le cri de l'oiseau, le bruissement des cigales et les roulements du tonnerre m'emplirent d'un étrange pressentiment. Je me sentis inquiet, curieux. Je me levai, étendis mes bras courbatus, puis, ramassant mes affaires, tâchai de rejoindre la porte et sortis, dirigeant vaguement mes pas vers la plage.

Je retrouvai sur la colline la plate-forme où, quelques heures plus tôt, j'avais observé la scène pour la première fois ; je baissai de nouveau les yeux. Un essaim de lumières se déplaçaient sur la grève comme des vers luisants aperçus de loin dans une prairie d'altitude à travers la brume argentée du crépuscule — torches portées par des mains invisibles.

Quand je descendis sur la plage, je discernai la rumeur de voix nombreuses, qui murmuraient avec excitation. Sur ce fond sonore, les cris de l'oiseau s'étaient élevés en un crescendo où je reconnus bientôt une origine indubitablement humaine. Je remarquai que la cage de l'ours était exactement au même endroit qu'à mon arrivée, et cela m'étonna, car j'avais entendu le marchand promettre de la faire charger. Plus étrange encore, à la lumière de la pleine lune qui jetait son sillage argenté sur le fleuve, je vis que la porte était ouverte. Chaque rafale de vent qui s'engouffrait dans la gorge la faisait grincer sur ses gonds. Cela, et les lamentations de l'oiseau me suggérèrent un souvenir imprécis, agaçant car englouti dans l'oubli. Troublé, je regardai par-dessus mon épaule en continuant de marcher, et trébuchai sur quelque chose. Je retrouvai mon équilibre et, au clair de lune, aperçus une énorme forme sombre allongée dans le sable. Je crus d'abord qu'il s'agissait du panda, mais en m'approchant je reconnus le molosse. Allongé sur la plage, il paraissait presque endormi. Pourtant ses yeux étaient ouverts, le globe de verre brillait d'une lumière spectrale sous la lune, à laquelle il ressemblait. L'espace d'un instant, je crus que le chien, désireux de continuer à monter la garde, dormait littéralement « les yeux ouverts ». Mais en l'examinant de plus près, je remarquai que sa tête baignait dans une mare, une sorte de vaste tache humide dans le sable couvert d'une pellicule liquide. Je m'agenouillai en tremblant à côté de l'énorme bête. Avec une horreur fascinée, je trempai un doigt dans la flaque, puis le portai à mes lèvres. Doux et visqueux, je reconnus le goût du sang. M'approchant encore, je vis une plaie béante au-dessus de l'oreille, et l'éclat terne du crâne. L'os était fendu jusqu'au cerveau. Je me souvins de mon rêve, m'allongeai dans le sable et vomis.

Quand mes spasmes se furent calmés, je me relevai et me précipitai au centre de la plage. « Que s'est-il passé ? m'écriai-je. Où est Tsin ? »

Les porteurs de torches qui jusqu'alors ne m'avaient pas vu ou pas daigné me remarquer, interrompirent leur manège et s'immobilisèrent pour m'observer tandis que leurs chuchotements mouraient sur leurs lèvres. Un étrange silence tomba. Le vent fouettait la flamme des torches, les cigales stridulaient, l'eau se précipitait dans la gorge rocheuse ; mais personne ne me répondait. Ce fut comme un rêve où tous les protagonistes sauf moi savaient ce qui se passait, et mus par la peur, la méchanceté ou un mutisme insurmontable, refusaient de me renseigner.

Exaspéré, je me détournai pour regarder la grande ombre muette du navire qui se détachait sur la transparence cristalline de la nuit. Mon œil se posa sur un cercle pâle qui vacillait au-dessus du pont comme un cierge fantomatique. Je m'approchai et reconnus les traits de la femme au sarong qui arpentait le pont d'un air hébété en se tordant les mains. Ses cheveux étaient hirsutes, ses yeux brillaient d'un éclat sauvage au clair de lune ; elle marchait et gémissait selon un rythme obsédant qui semblait plus vieux que le monde, poussait des cris qui me calmèrent, quand bien même ils témoignaient d'une horrible tragédie. Je reconnus alors la source des ululements bizarres que j'avais pris pour ceux d'un oiseau de nuit particulier à la région ; et cédant à leur appel spectral, je me dirigeai vers eux.

Quand elle entendit le bruit de mes pas sur la passerelle, elle pivota brusquement et leva des mains crispées comme des serres devant son visage, qu'elle détourna légèrement afin d'esquiver une attaque.

« Qui est-ce ? siffla-t-elle d'une voix rauque et stridente qui signifiait la menace aussi bien que la peur.

— Sun I, dis-je, le prêtre. »

Elle abaissa ses mains et me dévisagea dans les ténèbres en plissant les yeux. Rassurée quant à mon identité, elle s'approcha et saisit mes poignets.

Ses yeux s'agrandirent. J'y lus le même émerveillement qui m'avait frappé dans ceux de la fillette, mais la terreur et non l'innocence en était la cause. La proximité de la femme me permit de remarquer que son sarong était taché, maculé. Etait-ce du sang ?

Elle me regarda en silence avec une expression implorante qui me bouleversa. Car bien qu'il fût évident qu'une tragédie venait de se dérouler, je n'avais pas la moindre idée de ce dont il s'agissait ni de ce que je pouvais faire.

« Qu'y a-t-il ? demandai-je. Dites-moi ce qui est arrivé. »

Un tremblement incontrôlable s'empara de ses lèvres, ses traits se tordirent comme si elle allait pleurer. Elle essaya de parler, mais aucun son ne sortit de sa bouche. Le spasme décrut brièvement, puis redoubla de violence. Elle se mit à haleter. Elle finit par s'y abandonner et sanglota hystériquement. Tombant à genoux, elle enfouit son visage dans mon vêtement.

« Qu'y a-t-il ? Qu'est-ce qui ne va pas ? » lui demandais-je sans arrêt, de plus en plus inquiet. Elle continuait de pleurer sans répondre à ma question. Puis sa crise de larmes s'arrêta aussi brusquement qu'elle avait commencé. La femme leva vers moi des yeux limpides, tourmentés.

« Viens avec moi », dit-elle de la voix extasiée d'une prophétesse sur le point de révéler un mystère. Me tirant à deux mains, elle m'emmena vers le plat-bord du navire qui faisait face au fleuve.

« Je l'ai entendue tomber là dans l'eau, comme une pierre, poursuivit-elle de sa voix inquiétante, en désignant un point indistinct dans le flux puissant. Il y a eu un trou noir dans le fleuve quand elle est tombée, puis des millions d'éclats scintillants, comme une vitre brisée.

— Quoi ? lui demandai-je en la tournant doucement vers moi pour l'arracher au spectacle horrible qui l'obsédait. Qu'est-ce qui est tombé ? »

Elle grimaça de nouveau, mais réussit à contrôler ses larmes. Me prenant par la main, elle me fit traverser le pont vers la poupe où se dressait la cabine de fortune.

« Où m'emmenez-vous ? lui demandai-je, inquiet à l'idée du capitaine.

— Tu as peur ? » répondit-elle d'un ton sarcastique.

Arrivé sur le seuil, je refusai d'aller plus avant.

La femme lâcha ma main et se planta en face de moi. « Tu m'as demandé ce qui s'était passé. Va donc voir toi-même. » Elle leva le bras pour désigner la pénombre de la cabine.

J'entrai avec précautions, autant poussé par la curiosité que par la honte et le sens de l'honneur. A la lueur fuligineuse d'une petite lampe à pétrole fixée au mur par une cheville, je distinguai une table de marin où s'entassait le traditionnel bric-à-brac : piles de cartes nautiques, inventaires griffonnés, une boussole, une pierre à encre et son encrier, des pinceaux, un boulier. Tout autour, j'aperçus des piles de marchandises, des rouleaux de cordages, une multitude d'objets hétéroclites qu'on avait entassés là par manque de place dans la cale. Partiellement caché par l'une de ces piles, un lit de camp était installé le long du mur opposé à la porte de la cabine. De l'endroit où j'étais, je n'en voyais pas la tête, mais à l'autre extrémité les jambes nues d'un homme dépassaient d'un mur de peaux. Elles étaient largement écartées, l'une allongée sur le lit, l'autre pendait mais sans que le pied ne touchât le sol. Le corps affichait un certain relâchement, une torpeur qui surprenaient même chez un dormeur. Mon pouls accéléra. Je me retournai vers la femme avec un regard interrogateur.

Elle ne broncha pas. Pétrifiée, elle regardait fixement les jambes nues. Ses sourcils étaient froncés, son visage crispé. Une fois encore, elle leva lentement le bras et désigna le lit.

« Va voir », dit-elle.

A ces mots, une excitation malsaine s'empara de mon bas-ventre, le pressentiment d'un désastre.

Je lui adressai un regard suppliant, mais elle resta impassible. Je ne pouvais me dérober à l'injonction de son bras. Je pris une profonde inspiration, me raidis par avance contre ce que j'allais découvrir, puis m'obligeai à traverser la cabine.

Contournant le mur de marchandises, je pénétrai dans son ombre. D'abord, Dieu merci, le spectacle du lit me fut épargné. Puis mes yeux s'habituèrent à l'obscurité, et je vis le corps du capitaine allongé nu dans les draps tachés et froissés. Seulement le corps. L'homme avait été décapité — sa tête n'était visible nulle part. Les épaules et le cou tranché baignaient dans une flaque de sang tiède, le moignon bleuâtre de la colonne vertébrale dépassait d'un fouillis de veines et d'artères dans lesquelles le sang avait commencé de coaguler en caillots grumeleux qui se couvraient de marbrures au contact de l'air vicié. Alors que je regardais le cadavre, l'esprit ébranlé par-delà l'horreur, le dégoût ou toute autre émotion, la voix de la femme s'éleva derrière moi avec la même intonation de pythie.

« J'étais déjà couchée. Le vieux ronflait à côté de moi entre ses dents pourries. J'entendis alors un sifflement à l'extérieur de la maison. Je ne voulais pas le rejoindre. Je jure que je ne voulais pas. Mais quelque chose céda en moi, et je ne pus m'en empêcher. Je me mis à pleurer. Comme une somnambule, je sortis du lit et commençai de m'habiller. Soudain, je fus heureuse et me moquai du reste.

« Il était soûl quand je le rejoignis. En descendant la colline, il voulut agacer le chien. Le molosse grognait et bondissait vers lui en tirant sur sa chaîne. Tu sais ce qu'il a fait ? Il lui a tiré dessus en riant. Mais l'animal n'est pas mort tout de suite. Il grinçait des dents, luttait contre sa chaîne pour se hisser vers nous. Le capitaine ramassa une bûche qui traînait et fendit le crâne de la bête. Plusieurs fois il abattit la bûche sur sa tête. Finalement, l'animal cessa de bouger. Rassasié de violence, le capitaine se releva en titubant. Ses lèvres étaient couvertes d'écume. Il but une gorgée à sa bouteille, s'essuya la bouche sur la manche de sa veste, et cracha. Tout en me poussant devant lui vers la jonque, il ouvrit la porte de la cage du panda avec la bûche trempée de sang dont il venait d'assommer le molosse, puis l'utilisa comme un aiguillon pour obliger le panda à sortir de sa cage. Quand la bête en émergea, elle se dressa sur ses pattes arrière et fit mine de l'attaquer, mais elle se laissa retomber lourdement avant de s'éloigner en écrasant les fourrés. Reprenant une autre lampée, il rit de plaisir, puis m'entraîna sur la passerelle.

« J'avais peur. "Que va faire Tsin quand il s'en apercevra ?" demandai-je. Il éclata de rire et me répondit qu'il tuerait aussi Tsin.

« Nous étions allongés ici, lui en moi, quand la porte grinça.

« "Qu'est-ce que c'est ?" lui demandai-je anxieusement en me raidissant.

« "Le vent, soupira-t-il. Rien du tout." La flamme de la lampe vacilla.

« Il se mit à me besogner en grognant comme font les hommes. Alors, au moment précis où il commençait de jouir, Tsin fut sur nous comme un ouragan. Saisissant ses cheveux par-derrière, Tsin le hissa en l'air tandis que son sperme giclait sur mon ventre. Le soldat, qui souriait en dénudant les dents, chuchota à l'oreille de mon amant quelques mots qui m'échappèrent. J'entendis la lame taillader la chair, puis avec un bruit sourd s'enfoncer dans les muscles compacts et sectionner la colonne vertébrale. Le corps retomba sur moi, le sang jaillit du cou comme d'une fontaine. Tsin brandit la tête en la tenant par les cheveux. Ses yeux vivaient encore, dit-elle en éclatant d'un rire hystérique. Je les vis rouler de terreur et d'incrédulité alors même que le soldat achevait de séparer la tête du tronc. »

Elle se tut, s'approcha de moi, posa légèrement la main sur mon bras, puis chuchota à mon oreille.

« Regarde, sa queue, dit-elle en tendant le bras avec une expression étonnée qui semblait innocente, mais était d'une incroyable obscénité, il bande encore. » Puis elle la toucha doucement comme pour s'en assurer.

A ce spectacle — sa tendresse pour le corps mutilé qu'elle caressait comme une chose vivante, un minuscule animal craintif qu'elle redoutait de blesser ou d'effaroucher —, un sanglot brûlant monta de ma gorge. L'abandonnant au chevet du mort, je sortis de la cabine en courant, renversant tout sur mon passage. Un acide corrosif attaquait mon cerveau, détruisait ma raison. La folie se rua en moi comme un liquide chaud et suffocant, comme le sang ; je courus sans but, tel un homme dont les vêtements ont pris feu et qui cherche à fuir la morsure des flammes, trop éperdu pour comprendre qu'elles l'accompagnent et qu'il les attise par sa course. Je tombai de la passerelle et atterris dans le sable avec un bruit sourd. La chute me coupa le souffle. Une minute, je restai allongé, hébété de douleur, puis je retrouvai mes esprits. Alors la question essentielle, que j'avais oubliée dans ce tumulte obscène, me revint en mémoire : où était Tsin ?

Quand je levai la tête, je vis le marchand hagard sortir de la maison et descendre sur la plage en se frottant les yeux. La petite fille était déjà là, peut-être depuis longtemps, inaperçue de moi ou des autres ; tranquillement assise dans le sable, elle observait tout ce qui se passait avec des yeux calmes et graves. Le marchand courut vers elle et la souleva par les épaules en la secouant violemment. « Où est ta mère ? »

L'enfant se raidit et se mit à pleurer en silence.

« Où est-elle ? » hurla-t-il, furieux de la passivité de la fillette.

Elle continua de pleurer doucement sans répondre à la question du vieillard. Dégoûté, il la laissa tomber comme une poupée de son, puis se dirigea vers le groupe d'hommes le plus proche afin de les interroger.

Je traversai en courant la plage éclairée, puis me campai devant elle en attendant qu'elle prenne conscience de ma présence. Elle ramassait des poignées de sable qu'elle laissait couler par le trou de son petit poing fermé, comme à travers un sablier. Ses épaules étaient secouées de sanglots silencieux. Quand elle remarqua mes pieds, elle leva son visage vers moi et, s'essuyant les yeux sur sa manche, tenta d'arrêter de pleurer. Elle eut un hoquet, renifla, puis attendit que je parle.

Je restais sans voix, incapable de poser ma question. Peut-être était-ce la folie de cette nuit, peut-être une folie plus profonde encore, mais je réalisai que je connaissais cette enfant, que je l'avais toujours connue, que mon sort était inséparablement lié au sien. Je reconnus son expression avec la certitude absolue qu'on éprouve seulement devant le miroir ou en touchant les os de son propre visage. Malgré sa jeunesse, elle possédait la présence morale des vieillards proches de la mort, comme si elle avait maintes fois gagné et perdu bien plus que le cœur ne peut endurer, et cependant survécu, purifiée par la souffrance. Elle s'était affranchie de tous les éléments purement, bassement personnels pour ressembler à un os dans le désert, blanchi par le soleil des siècles, son innocence têtue devenant l'unique qualité, la seule essence minérale de sa personnalité que le temps n'avait pas gommée, mais accentuée, lui accordant ainsi la vertu du grand âge tout en préservant son extrême jeunesse. Deux minuscules pleines lunes flottaient dans la nuit d'encre de ses pupilles comme deux hosties posées sur un plateau d'oubli. Je laissai ce sacrement pénétrer mon cœur, et malgré toute cette folie, je fus submergé d'une paix plus profonde que celle que j'avais connue au cours de mes années de méditation solitaire au monastère. La frénésie et l'horreur, l'initiation aux rites sanglants de la violence que j'avais vécue cet après-midi-là — cela et le reste disparut de ma conscience, chassé par une béatitude bienfaisante qui m'envahit et que je désignai du nom de Tao. Peut-être était-ce le Tao. Loin de ternir ce souvenir, les années en ont accru l'éclat au point de lui accorder la puissance d'un talisman. Quand le charme se dissipa, je pus enfin parler.

« Où est-il allé ? » lui demandai-je doucement. La fillette leva le bras comme l'avait fait sa mère, et me désigna une trouée dans la forêt.

Quand j'atteignis la limite de la plage, je me retournai afin de lui dire quelque chose, mais ne trouvai plus mes mots. Constatant mon embarras, elle leva la main pour me congédier ou me dire adieu, pour me signifier que les mots étaient inutiles, que tout était clair entre nous. Sa main ouverte resta brièvement figée en l'air comme une fragile fleur nocturne au bout de la tige de son bras gracile, et je compris que je ne la reverrais jamais, que mon destin m'imposerait de la chercher toujours et d'errer sans jamais trouver la paix. Avec cette certitude gravée de façon indélébile dans mon cœur, je m'engageai dans la forêt, consumé par un remords inconsolable.

Je trébuchai dans la nuit en suivant un pinceau de lune blafard qui me guidait entre les arbres. La forêt m'avala en quelques minutes. Tous les dix mètres je criais le nom du soldat et m'arrêtais pour écouter, mais en vain. Mes mots se perdaient dans le vent qui avait forci, agitait la cime des arbres, faisait bruisser les feuilles, craquer les branches. A mesure que je m'enfonçais dans les ténèbres, le sentier s'estompait, puis finit par disparaître complètement. Il me restait pourtant la lune pour me guider, et le bruit du fleuve que j'entendais encore malgré son éloignement. Mais la lune qui plongeait vers l'ouest se coucherait bientôt derrière les sommets de l'Himalaya qui semblaient tendre vers elle des bras avides, comme un enfant monstrueux qui tente d'arracher un pendentif du cou de sa mère. Et même avant qu'elle ne fût couchée, l'énorme masse nuageuse qui montait à l'occident menaçait de l'obscurcir. Des filaments et des lambeaux de nimbus passaient devant elle comme des cavaliers ailés. Des gouttes de pluie se mirent à tomber, d'abord quelques-unes, mais presque assez grosses pour remplir une tasse à thé. L'arborescence d'un éclair zébra les montagnes, suivie d'un coup de tonnerre ; je crus que le monde vacillait sur ses bases. Je me forçais à aller de l'avant en ignorant ces présages sinistres. Il se mit bientôt à pleuvoir à verse. La lune disparut derrière un nuage. Le vent fouetta la cime des arbres. Des torrents de pluie diluvienne tombaient autour de moi, criblaient le sol. Dans le vacarme de l'orage, je n'entendais plus le fleuve. Je fus ainsi privé de mon dernier repère. Quelque temps, je m'obstinai à patauger dans la boue et me perdis pour de bon. Je déclarai finalement forfait devant la puissance des éléments et m'accroupis misérablement sous un surplomb rocheux ; recroquevillé sur moi-même, en proie à un violent tremblement qui me faisait claquer des dents, j'attendis que l'orage se calme alors qu'il semblait au contraire redoubler de violence. Epuisé, perdu, découragé, émotionnellement anéanti — bref, à bout de forces —, je finis par m'allonger sur la terre humide tandis que des gouttes d'eau glacée dégoulinaient du rocher sur mon visage, et je sombrai dans un sommeil de mort.

A mon réveil, l'aube pointait. La pluie avait cessé. J'étais trempé jusqu'aux os, glacé, courbatu ; je tremblais de tous mes membres. Peut-être était-ce l'effet de la fièvre, mais je me sentais malgré tout purifié, comme si j'étais mort et ressuscité, réincarné non sous forme humaine, mais dans une essence minérale transparente, mes organes métamorphosés en un verre brun qui s'embuait chaque fois que je respirais. Comme l'or ramassé dans l'eau claire d'un torrent, la lumière limpide de l'aube inondait la forêt, brillait sur les gouttes de rosée qui perlaient les grandes feuilles vert foncé des plantes grimpantes, coulaient comme de la résine sur les aiguilles des pins, remplissaient les fleurs qui poussaient çà et là dans la mousse. A mon immense plaisir, mon oreille perçut le bruit cristallin relativement proche de l'eau courante. Je m'assis et découvris que mes pas m'avaient mené près d'un ruisseau qui finirait sans doute par me ramener au cours d'eau principal. Poussant sur sa berge dans le profond secret des bois, plus belle que tout ce que j'avais jamais vu, j'aperçus une fleur pourpre, presque noire, qui évoquait un croisement entre le pavot et l'oiseau de paradis. Des gouttes d'eau tremblaient sur ses pétales, glissaient parfois et tombaient en laissant une trace scintillante sur la surface diaprée. Une beauté hallucinante nimbait toutes choses. Je m'enivrai de la douceur rafraîchissante de cette matinée, en rassasiai mon esprit.

Je dus m'endormir, car lorsque je me réveillai pour la deuxième fois, je sentis sur mon visage la chaleur du soleil. Une lueur rose inondait mes paupières closes. Je m'abandonnai longtemps à cette douce lumière matinale sans ouvrir les yeux, jusqu'au moment où une ombre traversa mon visage. Imaginant qu'un nuage masquait le soleil, je me dis que je devais en profiter pour secouer mon indolence et me préparai à me lever. J'ouvris les yeux en soupirant. Alors je vis le panda géant dressé au-dessus de moi ; ses yeux fauves brillaient d'une vie souterraine semblable au magma incandescent du centre de la terre, fournaises plus brûlantes que tout ce que j'avais jamais vu, et qui pouvaient me réduire instantanément en cendres. Le souffle coupé, je faillis hurler, mais réussis à refouler mon cri au fond de ma gorge. Son museau humide palpitait à une dizaine de centimètres de mon visage. Les narines noires se dilataient et se contractaient chaque fois qu'il me reniflait. Je sentis qu'il éprouvait la même peur, la même excitation que moi. Je me rappelai alors les paroles de Tsin à propos de l'étrange intimité qui lie le chasseur à sa proie, du sentiment d'hyperréalité qui s'empare de l'être sur le point de mourir. Je compris ce qu'il avait voulu dire ; l'énorme bête dressée au-dessus de moi plongeait son regard intolérable dans mon âme, et je crus contempler le disque du soleil au zénith.

L'ours fut le premier à détourner les yeux. Levant son museau, il huma le vent, comme distrait par une odeur désagréable, une chose qu'il redoutait, haïssait peut-être. Pendant ce temps, mon esprit cherchait désespérément un stratagème pour fuir. Je pouvais crier, le frapper de mon bâton avant de prendre les jambes à mon cou. Mais quand le panda baissa de nouveau la tête, il pantelait et je lus dans ses yeux un féroce désir de justice comme dans ceux du Dieu de colère. Il ouvrit sa gueule rouge, un filet de salive dégoulina de sa langue et s'écrasa au milieu de mon front. Je pris une profonde inspiration, fermai les yeux, me détendis et m'abandonnai à mon sort — j'ouvris largement mon cœur à la mort. J'essayai d'imaginer ce qui allait se passer, si la bête écraserait ma poitrine sous sa patte, ou si je sentirais son haleine brûlante sur mon visage, puis l'intérieur visqueux de sa gueule se refermer autour de ma tête tandis que ses crocs s'enfonceraient dans mes os et broieraient ma boîte crânienne. Finalement, cela importait peu. Je restais aussi immobile qu'une jeune fille qui attend nerveusement la sensation du viol alors que son amant la pénètre. La dernière chose à laquelle je pensai fut la petite fille — son regard grave, tranquille...

Quand je rouvris les yeux, le panda s'éloignait en balançant son arrière-train massif. Il descendit au bord du ruisseau, but de l'eau, s'assit, jeta un regard derrière lui, se laissa tomber comme un arbre qu'on abat, puis se releva. A mon grand étonnement, il jouait avec moi, il me faisait presque des avances. Il se pencha pour arracher la splendide fleur noire ; tout en la mâchant, il se retourna et me lança un regard où je lus de la timidité. Puis il se remit à quatre pattes, traversa le ruisseau avec précaution. Sur la rive opposée, il s'arrêta pour humer encore l'air ; il avait complètement oublié mon existence. Accélérant le pas, il disparut dans les fourrés.

Je ramassai fébrilement mes affaires, puis errai sur la rive du ruisseau, bouleversé par l'étrangeté de l'existence. Ken Kuan me semblait éloigné de plusieurs années, un vague souvenir d'une autre vie, avant que le monde ne se fût révélé dans toute sa splendeur terrifiante. Le monastère ressemblait à un royaume imaginaire, un domaine féerique bâti parmi les neiges éternelles, où la pure lumière du ciel brille à jamais, où la détresse ne saurait entrer — comme une de ces retraites qu'on dressait jadis contre la peste, parfaitement isolée du monde et de sa contagion. Pourtant, malgré toutes ces précautions, peu à peu, par quelque minuscule et imperceptible pore ou fissure, la vie s'était glissée à l'intérieur pour déposer dans mon cœur le virus tenace de son infection, notre caractère mortel.

Tel un jeune prédateur qui, lors de sa première chasse, repère une odeur dans le vent, son gibier prédestiné, s'arrête et se fige, dresse l'oreille, dilate ses narines sans même savoir pourquoi — car seul l'instinct et non la mémoire lui permet de reconnaître sa proie —, je perçus l'odeur qui m'avait tant suffoqué le jour où Hsiao m'avait raconté son histoire et communiqué l'excitation lancinante de l'attente. Je compris brusquement la nature de cette odeur. C'était celle de la vie. Mon cœur fut inondé du même bonheur sauvage que j'avais vu sur le visage du soldat quand il avait ri en rougissant et parlé de l'extase incomparable qui accompagne le coup de grâce.

Je m'assis pour contempler l'eau du ruisseau et penser à Tsin, cet homme problématique, damné malgré sa grâce, sauvé dans sa damnation. Cette pensée en amena une autre, indissociable de la première : celle d'Eddie Love, mon père. J'eusse été fort en mal de spécifier ce qu'il avait à voir avec Tsin ; mais ils étaient liés. Je le savais d'instinct, infailliblement, comme un animal. L'odeur s'était amplifiée. Je m'étais engagé sur le chemin qui était le mien.

Je laissai mes yeux se brouiller dans le tumulte blanc des eaux et sombrai dans un rêve sonore. Une fois encore, j'entendis les lamentations dominer faiblement le vacarme du torrent. Mais il y avait maintenant une voix nouvelle dans le chœur des morts de la rivière, une voix profonde et virile qui gémissait pitoyablement de terreur. Je plaignis le sort du capitaine, m'étonnai de l'ironie horrible de sa mort — perdre sa tête. Je songeai au grand chien de pierre, au panda ; au marchand et à son épouse. Mais je songeai surtout à la petite fille. Le souvenir de son visage me faisait toujours frissonner, accélérait le rythme de mon sang. Comment, par quel mystère du cœur avais-je compris cela — qu'elle était ma proie désignée, la vie incarnée ? N'était-ce qu'une illusion ? Ne l'apercevais-je pas déjà dans le sillage de mon existence avec Wu et Hsiao, Chong Fou et tous les êtres qui m'avaient ému d'une façon ou d'une autre, êtres à jamais disparus, engloutis dans le passé ? Mais je devais maintenant repartir, reprendre ma route en direction de la mer.

Je retrouvai le cours d'eau principal. Pendant tout le premier jour, je ne rencontrai âme qui vive, et pas davantage le matin du lendemain. Mais dans l'après-midi, alors que je longeais un bras d'eau dormante, j'entendis soudain des rires et des cris. Je ne vis d'abord rien. Puis, à ma grande surprise, la jonque à coque noire émergea d'une courbe en glissant silencieusement vers moi, comme en rêve. Je distinguai les visages d'une demi-douzaine d'hommes que j'avais aperçus sur la plage. Même de la berge, il était évident qu'ils étaient ivres morts.

Quand ils m'aperçurent debout sur la rive, la main en visière, ils se turent comme auparavant sur la plage. Ensuite, d'un commun accord, eût-on dit, ils se mirent à m'adresser des grands signes en criant.

« Hé ! Rejoins-nous ! Plonge ! » hurlaient-ils. Ils mimaient les gestes de la nage, collaient l'une contre l'autre les paumes de leurs mains comme pour plonger, gonflaient les joues, se pinçaient le nez, nageaient dans l'air.

Pris d'une joie incompréhensible, j'arrachai mes sandales, les fourrai dans mon barda, courus vers l'eau et plongeai sous leurs applaudissements. J'atteignis le milieu de la rivière au moment précis où la jonque passait. Ils se penchèrent par-dessus le plat-bord et me repêchèrent, dégoulinant et à bout de souffle.

« Bien joué ! s'écrièrent-ils en me tapant dans le dos. Excellent prêtre ! »

L'un d'eux adressa un clin d'œil à ses compagnons et dit pour me taquiner : « Tu as certainement été poisson dans ton incarnation précédente.

— Ou singe, lança un autre en roulant des yeux et avec des mimiques qui les firent se tordre de rire.

— Crétin ! s'écria un troisième. Il est taoïste, pas bouddhiste ! » Alors j'éclatai moi-même de rire.

Je m'aperçus avec surprise et une légère angoisse que l'obèse tenait la barre. Je commençai par me méfier de lui, mais il semblait avoir complètement oublié notre altercation. Il m'accueillit comme un vieil ami et m'expliqua la situation. Quand le marchand avait découvert la mort du capitaine, il s'était arraché les cheveux en gémissant pendant quelques minutes, maudissant le sort et battant sa femme. Puis il s'était un peu calmé. Une fois le corps enterré, il se mit à comptabiliser son manque à gagner en homme d'affaires efficace, et envisagea diverses solutions afin de minimiser ses pertes. Il finit par opter pour cet expédient. Il recruta plusieurs volontaires expérimentés capables d'entreprendre le voyage à la place du capitaine et leur ordonna de transporter la marchandise jusqu'aux rapides. S'il y avait assez d'eau, ils devaient continuer jusqu'à Ch'ung-ch'ing ; sinon, diriger la jonque vers l'avant-poste le plus proche. Là, ils s'arrangeraient pour faire transporter les marchandises par voie de terre, ou les vendraient aux enchères. Comme il avait dû leur offrir un pourcentage pour les inciter à entreprendre ce dangereux voyage, tous désiraient affronter les rapides, car les denrées de la cale se vendraient cinq fois plus cher à Ch'ung-ch'ing que dans un petit comptoir perdu en amont du fleuve. Ils ressemblaient davantage à des enfants en vacances qu'à des marins sur le point de franchir des rapides comptant parmi les plus dangereux du monde.

Je naviguai avec eux tout l'après-midi. Nous nous amarrâmes à la tombée de la nuit, bûmes et mangeâmes ensemble. Je leur racontai même une partie de mon histoire. Nous repartîmes le lendemain matin à l'aube. Nous naviguions depuis deux heures quand, au détour d'une courbe, nous vîmes un petit campement. L'un des hommes d'équipage me dit que nous étions maintenant à moins d'une heure des rapides, et que, si je désirais les quitter, je devais le faire sur-le-champ, car le fleuve serpentait ensuite entre les murailles d'un canyon. J'avais décidé plus tôt de lier mon sort au leur. Je l'aurais peut-être fait si une chose sur la rive n'avait attiré mon attention et modifié instantanément ma décision.

« Regardez ! s'écria l'obèse en tendant la main. Ils l'ont trouvée ! »

Là, empalée sur un pieu de bois vert haut de quatre ou cinq mètres, la tête du capitaine regardait le fleuve.

« Mon Dieu ! fis-je. Qui a permis ce sacrilège ? Pourquoi l'exhibent-ils ainsi ?

— C'est la coutume du fleuve, expliqua-t-il sombrement. Pour celui ou ceux qui la cherchent. »

Cela me stupéfia, me révolta ; mais ce qui apparut quand nous approchâmes fut pire encore. Les autres le remarquèrent au même instant que moi. Leur fureur se déchaîna sur le bateau.

« Pourquoi ? » demandai-je en courant de l'un à l'autre. Tous secouaient la tête. Je finis par interroger l'obèse.

« Tsin », me dit-il. Et là-dessus, je sautai à l'eau.

« Au revoir ! leur criai-je en nageant dans le courant. Au revoir ! »

Ils m'adressèrent des signes d'adieu et lancèrent mon barda dans le fleuve. Je nageai pour le récupérer puis touchai la berge un peu en aval. Je regardai la jonque noire disparaître au-delà d'une courbe, puis me dirigeai vers le spectacle monstrueux. La tête de l'homme était couverte de mouches, putrescente, fétide, presque méconnaissable. Mais ce fut l'autre qui m'attira. Car, empalée sur un pieu vert, mâchoire pendante, sa langue rouge recouvrant à moitié les crocs aiguisés, je vis la tête du panda, que le profil du capitaine m'avait d'abord cachée. Les yeux révulsés étaient couverts d'une taie chassieuse. Je pleurai de rage.

Au bout d'un moment, je me mis à la recherche de Tsin, sans espérer vraiment le trouver, sans vouloir vraiment le trouver. L'odeur de la vie que j'avais si brièvement respirée était désormais associée à celle de la mort, à l'infecte puanteur de la destruction gratuite, telles des fleurs sauvages mêlées au crottin.

Comme le petit génie dans son nuage de douceur écœurante, Tsin se manifesta avec la senteur de l'opium. Car ici aussi, comme partout en Chine où les autorités ne peuvent appliquer la prohibition, on trouvait une fumerie, différente au-dehors mais identique à l'intérieur — les mêmes visages aveugles contemplaient sans âme la lumière éblouissante, le mystère exquis de la désintégration due à l'alcaloïde. Je découvris le soldat recroquevillé sur le sol comme un fœtus, les yeux rivés au mur, sa tête reposant sur un oreiller de porcelaine comme celle d'un cadavre sur une pierre tombale. Le sabre, qui avait glissé de sa main, gisait à terre. Je touchai son épaule, la secouai. Il me regarda, mais sans paraître me reconnaître. Je vis seulement mon propre visage, reflété dans son œil de verre.

2

Entre ma dernière rencontre avec Tsin et le jour où j'atteignis le delta du Yang-tsê au-dessus de Shanghai, de nombreuses semaines s'écoulèrent. J'étais encore loin en amont de Ch'ung-ch'ing et à plusieurs centaines de milles du port de I-ch'ang, où j'embarquai enfin sur une barge de riz pour le reste du voyage, acceptant de renoncer à mon salaire en accord avec mon vœu de pauvreté, travaillant seulement pour payer mon voyage et mon séjour à bord (pratique qui me permettrait ensuite de rejoindre les quais de New York City). Comme je n'ai pas le temps de décrire tous les lieux traversés au cours de ma descente vers la mer, j'évoquerai mon itinéraire en notant les transformations graduelles que j'ai observées dans le tempérament du fleuve qui, comme le Tao lui-même, est « toujours changeant, toujours identique ».

Le Yang-tsê « émerge mystérieusement des nuages ». Ainsi s'exprime le voyageur Yan Bin au VIe siècle avant J.-C., et cela est encore vrai aujourd'hui. Sa source, tout en haut des monts Tanglha, personne ne l'a vue. Pourtant, aussi loin en aval que Ken Kuan, situé sur l'un des innombrables affluents, le fleuve anonyme qui ne figure sur aucune carte demeure dans son état premier, vierge de tout limon, clair, froid et pur. Ici, dans son premier avatar, le fleuve est un enfant qui se rue avec une joie torrentielle dans de profonds défilés à travers un paysage fantastique de pins et d'arcs-en-ciel que les rayons de lumière extraient de ses brouillards prismatiques. Infatigable, débordant d'énergie, il coule avec une extase sauvage, insouciant de sa propre mort. Mais peu à peu, par une métamorphose imperceptible, cette passion se modère quand le fleuve approche de l'adolescence. Sa vie est désormais plus profonde, ternie par divers limons. Bien que toujours fougueux, ses accès de colère sont moins fréquents qu'auparavant et précèdent une contemplation paisible, son sens des responsabilités se développant en proportion de sa culpabilité, du fardeau de son passé. Ainsi le Yang-tsê franchit-il les gorges de San-hsia à la frontière du Hupeh et du Szu-ch'uan, taillées dans le schiste et le grès rouge brique, où en compagnie de la Min et de la Chia-ling qui arrivent du nord, il se dissipe en une dernière et folle débauche, l'ultime caprice de sa jeunesse.

Au-delà, le fleuve entre dans la force de l'âge. De grands navires qui sillonnent les océans font leur apparition ; leur étrave déchire sa surface lisse, arrachant des copeaux, des flocons blancs et des échardes liquides qui se fondent presque aussitôt dans le magma poli. Enfin, rassasié par l'excès de ses plaisirs, léthargique, presque épuisé, le Yang-tsê aborde sa vieillesse. Gonflé par l'abondance de ses expériences, large et profond, saturé des sédiments de ses vies multiples, le cours du fleuve devient quasiment immobile, sauf çà et là quand sa surface paisible est troublée d'un tourbillon subit, indice d'un courant plus rapide qui le travaille en profondeur et l'attire inexorablement vers son rendez-vous avec la mer. A travers de riches terres cultivées, des rizières d'un vert éclatant qui s'étendent sur ses rives aussi loin que porte le regard, sans une colline ni un arbre pour arrêter la vue, le fleuve s'écoule, maintenant sujet aux crues et autres troubles gériatriques, aux dysfonctions de la sénilité, mais laisse malgré tout derrière lui de riches alluvions, sa dette envers la terre. Enfin, à son embouchure avec la mer, le delta du Yang-tsê est si large — quinze milles — que personne ne saurait l'embrasser d'un seul coup d'œil.

Je n'oublierai jamais le sentiment d'achèvement et de regret qui me submergea quand je respirai pour la première fois l'odeur de l'océan, la puanteur douceâtre et salée de la procréation et de la corruption. Nous naviguions le long d'une bande d'écume dans les remous de la marée où grouillaient crabes, poissons et crevettes ; les taches blanches des mouettes au repos mouchetaient l'eau noire. Des vendeurs téméraires dirigeaient leur sampan droit sur la coque de notre bateau, nous proposaient fruits frais et canard rôti, feux d'artifice et œufs de mille ans, puis se laissaient dériver dans le lent sillage de la barge en continuant de vanter leurs marchandises à grands cris. L'océan se dressait devant nous ; personne ne s'esclaffa, personne ne se frotta les yeux, mais tous hochèrent simplement la tête, comme si une longue attente aboutissait enfin au résultat escompté, sans apporter de surprise inespérée mais sans non plus décevoir ; car même si nous menons une existence confinée au milieu des terres, nous connaissons tous la mer par avance, ainsi que le Tao.

Perché sur un mât de charge, j'aperçus la ligne des brisants où le flot noir du fleuve rencontrait les eaux gris vert de la mer de Chine et, après un bref combat, succombait à sa douce euthanasie. Quel spectacle ! Au confluent des deux masses liquides, au-delà du seuil magique, l'être majestueux disparaissait avec tous ses secrets, tous ses péchés, ses souvenirs et ses passions insatisfaites. Quand on avait connu la véhémence de sa jeunesse, sa vie tumultueuse puis assagie, comment prophétiser une mort aussi douce ? Il y a là un mystère qui demande à être éclairci... Mais je me suis déjà trop étendu sur ce sujet.

De Shanghai, je longeai la côte à bord d'un autre cargo qui m'emmena à Hsia-men, également appelé Amoy. Là, par une nuit sans lune, je me glissai dans la mer en remorquant mon barda arrimé à une planche de bois. Je m'engageai dans ces eaux âprement contestées, parcourus à la nage les deux milles du détroit de Formose qui sépare le continent de l'île nationaliste de Quemoy, progressant lentement vers le rivage que j'apercevais au loin : l'île libre de Taiwan, l'autre Chine !

Je demeurai sur cette petite île le temps de me reposer. Au bout de quelques jours, j'embarquai à bord d'un vapeur à destination de Manille, regardai la côte s'estomper vers l'horizon, vers le passé — ma dernière vision de ma terre natale, de mon enfance, un trait sombre entre ciel et mer, comme un coup de pinceau sur un caractère inachevé.

Manille. Ce fut là que je connus mon premier Américain, mon ami Scottie, qui me prit sous son aile. Je voyageai avec lui pendant plus d'un an, travaillai sur des navires de toutes tailles et apparences, fréquentai tous les ports d'Indonésie et de Malaisie, m'aventurant même une fois ou deux jusqu'à Bangkok et Saigon, ainsi qu'on l'appelait à l'époque. Ce fut Scottie qui m'apprit l'anglais.

Bien que je l'eusse fréquenté quotidiennement pendant plusieurs mois, je n'ai jamais eu le sentiment de bien le connaître. Fort, corpulent, frisant la cinquantaine, il avait un visage profondément buriné, ridé comme une vieille pièce de cuir, qui exhibait aussi les ravages de l'alcool — un fin réseau de veines sur chaque joue et une tache rouge au bout du nez qui donnait l'impression qu'il venait de le plonger dans un verre de vin.

Le rhum pourtant, et non le vin, était le vice ou le plaisir de Scottie, ainsi qu'il le qualifiait alternativement. « Ecoute-moi, Sun I, disait-il souvent. Un coup de rhum au petit déjeuner et une lampée du même cru avant d'aller se coucher — rien de tel pour donner le moral, garder la forme et chasser la déprime, sacrebleu ! » Tout le temps que je le connus, Scottie appliqua ce régime à la lettre.

Scottie possédait le rude courage des marins, leur passion pour les virées, leur talent pour le blasphème inspiré — bref, toutes les qualités de la profession. Pourtant, il y avait autre chose chez Scottie — une curiosité toujours en éveil, une vague inquiétude, parfois une réflexion profonde —, signes d'une activité intellectuelle qui surprenait chez un homme comme lui, d'une sensibilité et d'une subtilité sous-jacentes que l'habitude du silence et de la dissimulation avaient étouffées. Je n'appris jamais ce qui le tenaillait. Bien que généralement loquace, il parlait peu de son passé. Une fois seulement, alors que je lui racontais l'histoire de ma mère, il laissa échapper quelque chose à propos de la sienne.

« Ma vieille mère a renoncé à la vie à l'âge de vingt-cinq ans, dit-il. Un jour, elle a mis un tablier de ménagère et ne l'a plus jamais quitté. Elle errait du matin au soir dans la maison en récitant de la poésie. Emily Dickinson. » Ce souvenir le fit rire. « Je me rappelle pas grand-chose de ma vieille. Juste ses mains — ridées à cause de la lessive, on aurait presque dit des serres — et cette foutue poésie. Elle déclamait si souvent ces saloperies qu'elle réussit même à m'en fourrer dans le crâne. » La tristesse nuançait la rancœur de ses paroles. « La seule poésie que j'ai jamais aimée commençait par : "Ma vie s'est dressée — un Revolver Chargé." »

L'insatisfaction générale de Scottie se manifestait par la boisson, mais se lisait encore plus clairement dans ses éternelles jérémiades relatives à son expatriation. Il n'avait pas remis les pieds aux États-Unis depuis plus de vingt ans. Je ne me souviens pas de la durée exacte de son exil, mais *lui* la connaissait parfaitement et répétait ce nombre avec un orgueil pervers.

« Ça fait combien maintenant, Scottie ? » le taquinaient les marins. Il regardait alors sa montre et répondait par un nombre d'années, de mois, de semaines, jours, heures et minutes, avec un sourire semblable au reflet du soleil sur une lame de couteau.

A bord d'un bateau, chaque soir après le repas et avant de rejoindre sa couchette, il avait l'habitude de cocher la date sur le calendrier, puis d'ajouter une barre aux milliers qui la précédaient par groupes de cinq dans le registre noir qu'il appelait son agenda et qu'il conservait avec un soin aussi méticuleux qu'un avare son livre de comptes. Cela fait, il buvait une bonne lampée de rhum à la bouteille, grognait de contentement, retirait ses chaussures sans les délacer, puis se laissait tomber sur son sac de couchage.

Les qualités intellectuelles de Scottie se manifestaient surtout par son intimité avec les phénomènes célestes, les étoiles en particulier. La seule fois où je le vis presque joyeux, nous étions de quart de nuit au large de la côte de Java ; après quelques coups de rhum, il se mit brusquement à tournoyer sur le pont comme un derviche séduit par une matelote de marin, le doigt pointé sur les constellations de tous les quartiers du ciel, et dévida cinquante ou soixante noms en quelques minutes, qu'il récita comme une litanie, une incantation. Alerté par ce tumulte, le capitaine passa la tête hors de la timonerie et nous ordonna de mettre une sourdine.

Scottie connaissait non seulement le nom des constellations, mais la mythologie qui s'y rattachait. Pendant les longues heures de veille dans ces lointaines mers équatoriales, il m'a souvent distrait avec les histoires fabuleuses des dieux et des déesses de la Grèce antique, généreusement assaisonnées de ses commentaires pimentés, son côté « ricain » équivoque et vantard, comme il disait. Ce fut l'une des techniques qu'il utilisa pour m'apprendre l'anglais, et quand ma compréhension de cette langue s'améliora, j'en vins à apprécier ses histoires autant que j'avais aimé celles de Wu. Pourtant, au-delà de la simple distraction, quelques-unes me touchèrent profondément. L'une d'elles me hante toujours.

« Regarde, Sun I ! Voici Orion, le bâtard de Poséidon, me dit-il une nuit. Il a l'air un peu sonné pour l'instant, vautré sur l'horizon, mais il vient juste de sortir du lit dans le palais de son paternel où il dort toute la sainte journée. Son cerveau est plein de toiles d'araignée. Laisse-lui encore quelques minutes ! Attends un peu qu'il monte de quelques degrés, et tu vas voir ce que tu vas voir. Sacrebleu, ça ne s'oublie pas facilement ! Il n'y a pas spectacle plus époustouflant dans tous les cieux qu'Orion en chasse avec ses chiens déchaînés autour de lui. »

Il poursuivit en me racontant comment le Grand Chasseur, « qui aimait la bonne chair, dans les deux sens du terme », tomba amoureux d'une mortelle, Mérope, et fut aveuglé par son père, Œnopion.

« Orion se retrouva dans un sacré pétrin, Sun I. Il poussait des hauts cris, comme l'une des innombrables bêtes qu'il avait trucidées, le sang ruisselait de ses orbites ; il rejoignit en titubant la côte d'Ionie, qu'il descendit jusqu'à la hauteur de Lemnos. Il entendait sur l'île le marteau d'un cyclope résonner contre l'enclume tandis qu'il forgeait la foudre de Zeus. Héphaïstos, le forgeron en chef, eut pitié d'Orion et lui délégua le cyclope Kédalion pour le guider. Kédalion prit momentanément congé de sa forge, donna une bonne épée à l'aveugle en guise de canne, puis partit avec Orion en pèlerinage au temple d'Apollon, le dieu de la lumière. Là, Orion fixa son regard laiteux sur le soleil, qui aveugle celui qui voit, mais rend la vue à l'aveugle ; et comme les autres, le Chasseur recouvra la vue. Ravi, il se mit à sauter comme un cabri, à hurler sa joie à la face du ciel, sans même prendre le temps de remercier son bienfaiteur. Kédalion leva une main débonnaire pour réclamer son épée, mais finit par laisser tomber en haussant les épaules, car c'était un domestique habitué aux caprices de ses patrons. Apollon, au contraire, n'oublia jamais cette impolitesse. »

Scottie me raconta alors comment Apollon convainquit sa sœur Artémis, la déesse de la chasse, qui aimait Orion, de tuer son amoureux pendant qu'il nageait en pleine mer, et comment, effondrée de douleur, elle fit monter le Chasseur dans le ciel et le métamorphosa en constellation.

« Tu vois les trois étoiles brillantes qui forment une ligne inclinée ? poursuivit-il. C'est la ceinture d'Orion. Juste en dessous il y a une tache de lumière — son épée, celle que lui donna Kédalion. Ou plutôt son fourreau ; car, comme tu vois, il brandit son épée au-dessus de sa tête, serrée dans son poing. Les trois étoiles de la ceinture pointent vers Sirius, l'Etoile du Chien. Elle se trouve dans la constellation de Canis Major — le Grand Chien ; c'est l'étoile la plus brillante du ciel. Canis Major est le fidèle chien d'Orion. »

Quand Scottie me montra l'œil brillant et vitreux du Grand Chien qui scintillait près de l'horizon, l'impression floue de déjà-vu qui avait agacé mon esprit pendant tout son récit se précisa enfin. A cause de Tsin, l'histoire du chasseur aveuglé, avec ses accessoires (l'épée et le chien), qui finit par succomber à sa passion de la chasse, prit pour moi une résonance nouvelle. J'ignore si je peux expliquer cela, mais on eût dit que l'épreuve que j'avais si récemment traversée — « le rude baptême de mon entrée dans la vie », comme je l'ai nommée ailleurs —, ne tenait pas à une rencontre fortuite, particulière à ma trajectoire, mais entrait dans une trame plus large, conçue voici fort longtemps et jouée maintes fois peut-être sur le globe terrestre et en de nombreuses langues, jusqu'à ce que les Grecs lui accordent la valeur éternelle du mythe, et avec le génie altier de leur race lèvent les yeux vers le ciel pour la découvrir déjà présente, écrite dans les étoiles.

Mais c'était loin d'être tout. Ces résonances se répercutaient au-delà de Tsin dans une direction que je ne pouvais encore soupçonner, non seulement vers la Chine et le passé, mais vers New York, l'avenir.

Scottie reprit son exposé.

« Maintenant, Sun I, regarde un peu plus haut dans le ciel. » Il tendit le bras. « Cette étoile brillante est Aldébaran, dans les cornes de Taurus. On dirait qu'Orion est menacé de ce côté-là, qu'il risque de se faire "empaler sur les cornes d'un dilemme", si tu vois ce que je veux dire.

« Je peux t'apprendre tout ce que tu as besoin de savoir sur Orion, Sun I. Mais ce taureau est une énigme. J'ai discuté son cas avec les autorités du monde entier ; personne ne semble connaître sa véritable identité. Après tout, Taurus signifie simplement "taureau", et rien de plus. C'est un peu mince comme point de départ. On m'a raconté qu'il symbolise l'animal dont Zeus a endossé la forme pour séduire Europe, la princesse phénicienne, et l'emmener en Crète. "Le rapt d'Europe", comme on dit dans la littérature. Je suppose qu'on pourrait étayer cette interprétation, mais à mon avis elle ne fait pas le poids.

« D'autres prétendent qu'il s'agit du taureau blanc pour lequel Pasiphaé avait le béguin ; bien que cette version soit plus scabreuse, je crois qu'elle ne manque pas de jugeote. Tu connais l'histoire ? Non, bien sûr que non. Eh bien, je vais te résumer ça en quelques mots. Pasiphaé était la reine de Crète, l'épouse de Minos. Comme je l'ai dit, elle se prit d'un amour monstrueux pour cet animal qu'elle voyait paître et fulminer dans les pâturages de son époux. En salope astucieuse et madrée qu'elle était, elle s'arrangea pour que Dédale, le Grand Artificier, construise une vache de bronze où elle pénétra et qu'elle fit amener dans le pâturage. Le taureau l'observa d'abord d'un œil méfiant, la renifla sous toutes les coutures puis, décidant que tout était en ordre, la monta et fit ce qu'il devait faire, au grand plaisir de Pasiphaé, et, j'imagine, à son inconfort plus grand encore. (Je ne voudrais pas m'attarder sur ces détails anatomiques, Sun I, mais un taureau adulte a un organe long comme ton bras !) Le vieux truc du cheval de Troie, tu vois. Les Grecs ont eu recours à ce genre d'expédient plus d'une fois. Mais dans le cas présent et selon toute apparence, ce fut le cheval sans les Troyens, car Pasiphaé se retrouva enceinte et donna naissance au Minotaure. Ce qui me ramène à mon sujet.

« Le Minotaure était un monstre hideux, mi-homme mi-bête. Certains prétendent qu'il avait le corps d'un taureau et la tête d'un homme, d'autres l'inverse — en tout cas le résultat n'était pas particulièrement réussi. Par-dessus le marché, il avait sale caractère ; sanguin, vindicatif, il aimait la chair humaine. Bien que Minos, faisant preuve d'une clémence inhabituelle chez les Grecs, ait pardonné à sa femme, il ne put se résoudre à faire du Minotaure son successeur. Il préféra demander à Dédale de construire le célèbre Labyrinthe, où il enferma le monstre en lui offrant de temps en temps un jeune homme ou une jeune fille en pâture pour calmer son appétit et l'empêcher de mettre son royaume sens dessus dessous. D'ailleurs, la Crète ne s'en portait pas plus mal, car les Athéniens subissaient à l'époque le joug de Minos qui, en impérialiste patenté, leur imposait de nourrir le monstre. Horrible, non ? Chaque année, un navire quittait Athènes avec sept jeunes gens et autant de jeunes filles, puis voguait vers la Crète avec des voiles noires. Cela dura jusqu'au jour où Thésée, le fils du roi, enragé par cette humiliation, résolut de délivrer son pays au risque de sa vie. Ainsi, malgré les protestations d'Egée, il s'embarqua l'année suivante avec treize autres condamnés.

« Or les Dieux aimaient Thésée — formule d'une sublime concision par laquelle les Grecs signifiaient tout bonnement que Thésée avait du pot. Dès qu'il débarque en Crète, Ariane, la fille de Minos et de Pasiphaé, tombe amoureuse de lui et décide de l'aider à tuer le Minotaure. Je ne veux pas pinailler, car je reconnais que cela ajoute une dimension amoureuse à notre affaire, mais je trouve le détail un peu gratuit, compte tenu de la position d'Ariane. Dis-toi, Sun I, que le Minotaure était son demi-frère — une sorte de honte, de bavure, pour ne pas dire plus. A mon avis, elle aurait aidé Thésée même sans l'aimer. Enfin, peu importe...

« Ariane lui donna un glaive et une bobine de fil qu'il dévida derrière lui en s'enfonçant dans le Labyrinthe afin de pouvoir retrouver son chemin. Personne ne sait précisément ce qui arriva ensuite à Thésée. Tu peux visualiser la scène jusqu'à un certain point — un quartier de lune dans le ciel, le sable qui crisse doucement sous ses pieds nus, la lueur rouge des torches qui vacille sur les murs de pierre, ses battements de cœur terrifiés quand il respire la première bouffée d'air croupi, l'odeur de merde et de sang, quand il entend les halètements rauques au cœur du Labyrinthe... Pour la suite, l'imagination est impuissante. Lorsqu'il retrouva ses compagnons, ceux-ci ne firent jamais la moindre allusion à l'incident qu'ils traitèrent comme une sorte de blessure de guerre. Et Thésée ne livra pas la moindre information sur le sujet. Peut-être est-ce mieux ainsi.

« En tout cas, il réussit — de cela nous sommes certains. Il tua le monstre, brisa le cœur de la jeune fille, et pour couronner le tout, succéda à son père sur le trône d'Athènes. Car soit qu'il ait voulu rentrer en quatrième vitesse, ou qu'il n'avait plus toute sa tête à lui après l'histoire de la Crète, Thésée oublia d'amener les voiles noires pour en hisser des blanches, ainsi qu'il l'avait promis à son père en cas de victoire. Debout sur une falaise en dehors de la ville, le vieil Egée avait guetté tous les jours ; quand il vit le navire revenir avec "les voiles funestes", il pensa que tout était perdu, poussa un gémissement, porta la main à son cœur, s'effondra dans les bras de ses serviteurs et passa l'arme à gauche. Certains de ses détracteurs ont suggéré que Thésée avait oublié de changer le jeu de voiles "accidentellement exprès", si tu vois ce que je veux dire... De fait, la douleur due à la mort de son père fut certainement mitigée par son accession au pouvoir. Mais ce ne sont là que spéculations gratuites, ragots irresponsables, et selon moi pures calomnies.

« En tout cas, Sun I, si l'on avait pu transporter Orion dans le ciel et le ressusciter après sa mort, pourquoi pas le Minotaure ? Voilà du moins ma théorie pour élucider l'identité du taureau. » Scottie se tut, releva l'arrière de son chapeau de ciré, et se gratta la nuque. « Bien sûr, si le Taureau céleste est le Minotaure, alors Orion doit être Thésée — ce qui complique salement notre enquête ! Bon sang de bonsoir ! Tu me suis ? Cette vacherie de taureau (excuse-moi !) n'a pas fini de nous donner du fil à retordre ! »

Peut-être, lecteur, imagines-tu ce qui traversa mon esprit, moi qui avais jadis connu la célébrité (notoriété convient sans doute mieux) pour mon interprétation vocale des *Dix Taureaux* ! Oui, dans les cornes de Taurus je vis non le Minotaure, ni son père, pas même le taureau blanc qui enleva Europe — bien que cette option me plût particulièrement, car après tout ce taureau avait au moins le mérite d'être l'incarnation de Zeus, le père des dieux —, non, plutôt que ceux-là, je vis le Taureau du taoïsme, ce symbole fondamental de l'illumination pour ma religion, dont les traces de pas m'avaient poussé à entreprendre ce pèlerinage incertain vers des régions sauvages et exotiques ! Je compris avec une joie soudaine que je l'avais enfin trouvé, ou du moins brièvement aperçu ! Je peux difficilement décrire l'excitation qui s'empara de moi. Je dirais simplement que mon bonheur fut nuancé d'un pressentiment sinistre. Car dans l'histoire de Scottie, le

Taureau était lié à un ensemble d'associations inédites et troublantes. Il y avait certes sa nature ambiguë, mais surtout un tragique retournement de situation : en effet, le Chasseur — Orion, Tsin ou un autre — ne désirait pas domestiquer le Taureau, le soumettre à un labeur ordonné comme le paisible bouvier de la parabole, mais, sacrilège innommable, il brandissait son épée pour le tuer !

Je ne confiai bien sûr rien de mes pensées à Scottie, qui, après avoir bu une longue rasade à la bouteille, reprit son monologue.

« Le Taureau n'est pas le seul problème que le vieux Orion a sur les bras, Sun I. » Il s'essuya la bouche sur sa manche, puis tendit la main. « Làhaut, un peu plus au nord, tu vois ce groupe d'étoiles ?

— Oui, répondis-je. En Chine, on l'appelle la Louche.

— Exactement. Bonne description. En anglais, c'est la Casserole. Ces étoiles se trouvent dans la constellation Ursa Major, la Grande Ourse. »

Je dressai l'oreille.

« Il semblerait que l'Ourse aussi ait de mauvaises intentions envers le Chasseur, et ce non sans raisons. Regarde comme cette bête est enchaînée à l'étoile polaire et cruellement harcelée chaque nuit. Elle peut seulement tirer sur sa chaîne, rugir de colère, faire les cent pas autour de Polaris, lancer des coups de patte aux chiens d'Orion qui l'attaquent par surprise toutes griffes dehors, et avant qu'elle n'ait pu réagir, battent en retraite au-delà de l'Equateur céleste et se réfugient dans l'hémisphère sud. C'est un jeu cruel et méprisable, Sun I, où jusqu'à maintenant Orion a eu la partie belle. Mais cette chaîne ne tiendra pas le coup éternellement. Sacrebleu, un jour cette Ourse va réussir à se libérer et à semer la panique parmi les constellations.

« Personne ne voit les mêmes choses dans les étoiles, Sun I. D'ailleurs, certains ne voient rien, car ils n'ont jamais pris le temps de les regarder. Et parmi ceux qui les connaissent, tu en trouveras toujours un ou deux pour contester mes interprétations. Mais personne ne me fera démordre de ce que je vais te dire. Lève les yeux une minute. J'aimerais que tu me dises comment se présente Orion : de face, de dos ou de profil ? Ne t'inquiète pas, les experts ne s'intéressent jamais à ce genre de détail. Alors, le Chasseur fait-il face au Taureau, comme le soutiendraient sans doute les spécialistes, avec son chien *derrière* lui ? Je sais bien que c'était un géant et qu'il avait de longues jambes, mais franchement — crois-tu qu'il courait plus vite que ses chiens ? Ou alors fait-il face de l'autre côté, vers l'Ourse (son épée est levée dans cette direction) que ses chiens harcèlent ? Problème difficile, Sun I. Mais pour moi le vieil Orion, soit par bravade ou négligence, ou bien les deux, s'est laissé piéger dans une situation pour le moins délicate — coincé entre le marteau et l'enclume, comme on dit —, harcelé par des bêtes féroces : l'Ourse derrière lui et le Taureau devant ! Ou vice versa, selon l'interprétation choisie. » Emporté par son improvisation, Scottie éclata d'un rire ravi. « Ho ho ! Par tous les minarets de Constantinople ! Regarde un peu Orion ! Ouvre grands les yeux, Sun I. Regarde-le se tourner tantôt d'un côté, tantôt de l'autre, pour parer les attaques de ses deux adversaires ! »

Scottie était maintenant complètement ivre, « rond comme une barrique de rhum », disait-il, ou « raide comme un manche à balai ». Notre quart de veille étant presque fini, la leçon touchait de toute façon à son terme. Je l'ai dit, les références au Chasseur, au Taureau et à l'Ourse évoquaient de façon quasi surnaturelle mon expérience. Quand nous descendîmes dans le ventre du navire pour rejoindre nos couchettes, j'étais dans un état d'excitation que je n'avais jamais connu, sauf le jour où Hsiao s'était présenté à Ken Kuan afin de me raconter l'histoire de mes parents.

Mais une fois encore, je dois « suivre l'exemple judicieux de l'eau », aller de l'avant comme le fleuve.

Après une année de va-et-vient entre tous les ports de la mer de Chine avec mon ami Scottie, nous nous embarquâmes sur un cargo qui transportait du teck par le détroit de Malacca puis la mer d'Andaman avant de faire escale à Rangoon, où plus de vingt ans auparavant le paquebot hollandais *Jaegersfontaine* avait débarqué le premier contingent de l'AVG, des hommes qui voyageaient incognito en se faisant passer pour missionnaires, étudiants, chasseurs de fauves, hommes d'affaires, explorateurs, et autres couvertures délicieusement absurdes sans doute inventées par un fonctionnaire des douanes à l'imagination hollywoodienne. Je sentis mon cœur se serrer de sympathie et de pitié en pensant à ces jeunes gens — mon père parmi eux — aux chemises hawaïennes bigarrées, l'appareil photo autour du cou, bronzés après les semaines passées en chaise longue sur le pont à boire des limonades fraîches servies par des garçons en livrée, à poser pour les photos des amis, jouer aux cartes, écrire des lettres aux parents, plaisanter (« Ah certes, mon cher, je compte diantrement rapporter de Birmanie un trophée de tigre du Bengale ! » cela prononcé d'une voix distinguée en ajustant un monocle imaginaire), comme si tout cela était une énorme farce. Puis silencieux, accoudés ensemble au bastingage du pont supérieur de l'élégant paquebot hollandais, ils avaient dû contempler d'un œil grave la saleté de Rangoon, respirer la première bouffée d'air fétide, l'« omniprésente puanteur de l'Asie », après les jeux, les plaisanteries, les vantardises, prendre la mesure de la distance incalculable qu'ils avaient parcourue, et de la réalité écrasante, irréductible, de l'Orient. Ils avaient sans doute compris qu'à leur réveil les melons d'eau pourris ne seraient pas transformés en carrosses, ni les rats en valets de pied, qu'ils ne pourraient dissiper l'enfer terrifiant où ils allaient bientôt pénétrer, et pas davantage le chasser avec le geste nonchalant du metteur en scène d'Hollywood qui réclame le décor suivant, compris enfin qu'ils devraient passer de l'autre côté de cette frontière effrayante, traverser « le rideau de feu », s'ils voulaient retrouver ce qu'ils connaissaient.

A Rangoon, Scottie et moi eûmes du mal à trouver un embarquement. Tous les emplois qu'on nous proposa étaient locaux, mais comme je parlais maintenant assez couramment l'anglais, j'étais prêt à continuer mon voyage, soit par le canal de Suez, la Méditerranée, les colonnes d'Hercule et l'Atlantique-Nord, soit par « la route qui longe le cul du monde » comme l'appelait Scottie, celle qui contournait l'Inde puis l'Afrique. Une semaine s'écoula, dix jours. Enfin, un matin, on nous avertit qu'un navire grec, le *Telemachos*, à destination de New York via Colombo et Capetown chargeait au port. Nous partîmes aussitôt examiner le bateau.

Notre première impression fut décevante. Debout sur le quai, mains glissées dans les poches arrière de nos jeans, tête penchée, nous observâmes une coque striée de rouille et les hommes qui travaillaient sur le pont, sous les grues. Ils dirigeaient de grosses caisses en bois au-dessus de l'écoutille centrale du cargo, puis les faisaient descendre dans la cale. Scottie formula ce jugement lapidaire : « Un vrai fer à repasser, Sun I. Je serais pas étonné qu'ils transportent de la contrebande. »

Un examen plus approfondi nous permit de découvrir que la barre de pont d'un des deux canots de sauvetage était brisée et que les gilets de sauvetage du bord étaient de véritables loques. Nous n'aperçûmes pas le moindre extincteur, la salle des machines était noire de graisse et si glissante qu'on risquait de se rompre le cou en la traversant ; quant au mât de charge et au pont supérieur, ils étaient couverts de la suie que vomissait la cheminée. Le pire était peut-être qu'on avait réaménagé l'avant-bec pour y entreposer des marchandises, et relégué les cabines des marins dans un entrepont humide, exigu et qui puait l'eau de cale.

« Je voudrais pas faire cent mètres dans cette baignoire, déclara Scottie, et encore moins la moitié du tour du monde.

— Je te comprends », dis-je.

Il scruta mon visage. « Toi, tu vas embarquer, n'est-ce pas ? »

Je haussai les épaules. Il semblait vulnérable, peiné. « Je ne peux pas m'éterniser ici », me justifiai-je.

Il hocha la tête. « Faut trouver un moyen de décaniller, hein ? » Scottie baissa la tête pour réfléchir, s'éloigna de quelques pas, pivota sur ses talons, revint.

« Et puis zut, dit-il avec un sourire penaud, je t'accompagne ! » Il fit claquer sa main sur sa cuisse pour appuyer sa décision, et ajouta : « Sacrebleu ! »

Nous signâmes donc notre engagement, installâmes nos affaires à bord, avant de rejoindre nos places sur le pont avec les autres membres de l'équipage.

Personne ne semblait connaître la nature de notre cargaison, ni même avoir la moindre curiosité pour elle. Quand nous interrogions quelqu'un, on nous retournait toujours la même réponse : « misc. » (pour « miscellanées »), sur un ton qui suggérait que nos interlocuteurs considéraient cela comme une marchandise bien définie. Le capitaine lui-même, un Anglais, nous en apprit à peine davantage, ajoutant seulement que nous transportions entre autres de nombreux objets de culte sauvés (« raflés », commenta Scottie avec cynisme) dans un temple bouddhiste du Tibet, et à destination du Metropolitan Museum de New York.

Voilà ce que nous savions quand nous sortîmes du delta de l'Irrawaddy dans le golfe de Martaban et mîmes le cap vers le sud, vers Sri Lanka. Plus tard, Scottie et moi procédâmes à une petite enquête qui aboutit à certaines découvertes méritant d'être rapportées ici.

Nous étions à quelques jours de Colombo, à la latitude du cap de Bonne-Espérance (30° sud), mais encore à l'est de celui-ci. Après une croisière paisible dans les eaux tropicales de l'océan Indien, nous nous retrouvâmes presque du jour au lendemain au cœur de l'hiver. Ce fut horrible. La mer était déchaînée ; des vagues de douze mètres déferlaient sur le navire, l'eau pénétrait par les dalots. Le vieux bateau tanguait et roulait, se cabrait pour gravir la montagne liquide, puis tremblait sur sa quille, vibrait comme une cloche et retombait dans le creux de la lame. On ne voyait rien au-dessus de nous — ni le soleil pendant la journée, ni la lune ou les étoiles la nuit — seulement un voile grisâtre de nuages bas. Une couche de glace couvrait le pont, alimentée par une bruine incessante — pluie glacée entrecoupée de grésil, mais le plus souvent de la neige fondue qui contenait des fragments de glace déchiquetés.

Pour ajouter à nos soucis, une partie de la cargaison s'était détachée dans la cale. Nuit après nuit, allongés sur nos couchettes où nous essayions de trouver le sommeil, nous entendions un vacarme incessant de glissements et de chocs, comme si quelque chose tentait de se libérer et cognait violemment contre les cloisons. Une nuit, après un coup de roulis particulièrement fort, nous entendîmes un fracas assourdissant.

« Sacrebleu ! rugit Scottie en sautant de sa couchette. Je vais découvrir l'origine de tout ce boucan, quitte à me rompre les os ! »

Enfilant son ciré et ses bottes, il saisit un épissoir et se dirigea vers l'échelle.

« Attends-moi ! murmurai-je en me hâtant de mettre une veste. Je t'accompagne. »

Quelques minutes après, nous descendions une échelle métallique dans une cale complètement obscure. Une fois arrivés au fond, Scottie gratta une allumette. Il jeta un coup d'œil circulaire en la tenant au creux de sa main.

« Tu es là, Sun I ? chuchota-t-il. Fait tellement noir que je trouverais même pas ma queue pour pisser ! Où est cette foutue ampoule électrique ? »

Je la trouvai et l'allumai.

« Merde alors ! jura-t-il. Voilà ce que j'appelle une loupiote fichtrement faiblarde dans une cale fichtrement sombre ! »

C'était vrai. L'ampoule formait un pâle halo jaunâtre jusqu'à deux ou trois mètres, puis capitulait devant les ténèbres. Une longue rallonge nous permit cependant de l'emporter avec nous entre les hautes piles de caisses en bois. Au fond de la cale, près de la cloison qui nous séparait de l'entrepont, il y avait un grand espace vide où nous découvrîmes ce que nous cherchions. Deux énormes caisses avaient rompu leurs chaînes et s'étaient renversées. La première était complètement fracassée. Dégageant les morceaux de planches, nous aperçûmes une grande idole à la peau dorée, qui tenait une épée et dont la face reposait contre les tôles du plancher. Sa tête baignait dans un halo de neige poudreuse qui s'était apparemment glissée dans la cale pendant les brefs instants où nous avions ouvert l'écoutille. A l'aide d'un palan, nous la redressâmes sans trop de mal. Quand je brandis l'ampoule devant elle, je reconnus Manjusri, le boddhisattva de la Sagesse Transcendante. Car il tenait le lotus dans sa main gauche — le Livre du Savoir reposait sur la fleur — et dans sa dextre le glaive enflammé avec lequel il tranchait le Nœud de l'Illusion. Le dieu avait souffert dans sa chute. Son nez avait totalement disparu de son visage, et au milieu de son front le troisième œil — qui, contrairement aux deux autres yeux presque fermés, était grand ouvert, fixé sur l'autre monde — s'était fendu. Alors que j'examinais Manjusri, le navire tangua violemment.

« Bon sang de bois ! » rugit Scottie en basculant en arrière. La baladeuse vacilla, son filament vira à l'orange pâle, puis s'éteignit définitivement. J'entendis la deuxième caisse glisser lourdement avec un bruit sourd et fis un bond de côté. Un objet dur et froid érafla mes côtes en déchirant mes vêtements. Quand je fus précipité contre la cloison, un choc métallique assourdissant se répercuta dans toute la cale.

En tâtonnant, je découvris sur ma gauche ce que je pris pour un gigantesque pieu de métal qui clouait ma veste à la cloison. A ma droite, un deuxième pieu saillait des planches de la caisse transpercée.

« Sun I, mon trésor, tu es mort ? chuchota Scottie d'une voix anxieuse.

— Ça va, répondis-je en me dégageant, mais non sans abandonner derrière moi un pan de vêtement. Et toi ?

— Oh, quelques douzaines de bras et de jambes cassés. Mais laisse-moi le temps de reprendre mon souffle, je serai bientôt frais comme un gardon. »

Il frotta une allumette. « Où es-tu ? demanda-t-il.

— Par ici. Apporte-moi les allumettes.

— Merde alors, Sun I. Vise un peu ça — il y a plus de neige qu'avant sur le sol. Nous avons pourtant fermé l'écoutille derrière nous, n'est-ce pas ? Elle ne peut quand même pas arriver jusqu'ici par la manche d'aération, tu ne crois pas ? »

Je ne voyais pas de quoi il parlait.

« Sacrebleu ! » s'écria-t-il soudain. Je vis sa main lâcher l'allumette, qui tomba sans s'éteindre et s'immobilisa sur le sol. Elle jeta une pâle lueur circulaire sur la fine poudre blanche de la neige et continua de brûler.

« Nom de Dieu de bordel de merde ! » jurait Scottie en bondissant d'un pied sur l'autre dans les ténèbres. « La prochaine fois que j'essaie de foutre le feu à mes vêtements, rappelle-moi qu'il existe des façons plus expéditives de s'envoyer dans l'au-delà !

— Scottie, dis-je en écoutant ses jurons d'une oreille distraite, regarde ça.

— Quoi donc, petit trésor ?

— L'allumette. »

Scottie interrompit ses simagrées pour regarder avec moi l'allumette dont la flamme faiblissait. Elle tremblota quelques secondes, puis s'éteignit.

« J'ai la berlue ou quoi ? » s'écria Scottie. Il frotta une autre allumette, qu'il laissa tomber à côté de la précédente. « Voyons ça de plus près ! »

Fait inexplicable, la neige ne fondait pas autour de l'allumette !

« Que mon rhum se change en eau si je sais ce que ça signifie ! dit Scottie. Une neige qui ne fond pas — on aura tout vu ! »

Je désirais cependant satisfaire ma curiosité première. « Les allumettes, Scottie. » Il en frotta une, puis me tendit la boîte en poursuivant son examen.

Je grattai une allumette ; quand la flamme s'éleva, une odeur de soufre monta vers mes narines. Parmi les ombres obliques créées par la flamme vacillante, je vis ce qui ressemblait à *deux énormes cornes* de bronze qui dépassaient lugubrement de la caisse brisée ! Je lâchai l'allumette en poussant un cri. « Scottie !

— Sacripan, que... souffla-t-il en s'approchant de moi. Tu ne crois tout de même pas qu'ils ont ligoté le diable avant de l'enfermer dans cette caisse, hein ?

— Je vais l'ouvrir.

— Avant, je crois que tu ferais bien de jeter un coup d'œil par ici », dit-il d'une voix sombre.

Nous nous agenouillâmes à l'endroit qu'il venait d'examiner. Je scrutai l'intérieur de la caisse défoncée ; la faible lueur me permit seulement de discerner une énorme main noire qui tenait ce que je pris d'abord pour un tambour, mais qui se révéla finalement un sablier aussi gros que mon buste. De son verre fendu, un mince filet de sable immaculé filtrait sur le sol et grossissait une petite pyramide parfaitement blanche.

« Voilà donc ce que c'est », dis-je, soulagé d'avoir éclairci ce mystère.

Sans un mot, Scottie passa sur sa langue le bout de son index et de son majeur, puis les posa sur la pyramide, dont le cône parfait s'écroula.

« Sors ta langue », dit-il.

Surpris par la gravité de son expression, je m'exécutai. Il passa ses deux doigts sur ma langue, et je perçus un goût acide, sulfureux, que ma salive dissipa, puis le goût faiblement salé des doigts de mon ami. Le goût initial était d'autant plus déplaisant qu'il me rappelait quelque chose.

« C'est de l'héroïne », dit Scottie.

Le circuit se ferma aussitôt dans ma mémoire, le courant circula. Bien que moins terrestre, cette saveur rappelait faiblement mais immanquablement celle de l'opium — écho fantomatique, désincarné, comme d'une vérité ou d'un mensonge perçu à un niveau d'abstraction plus élevé.

Scottie se releva et se campa devant la statue dorée du dieu. Frottant une autre allumette, il la tint en l'air et observa attentivement son visage. « Viens ici, dit-il, regarde ça. »

De l'iris fêlé au milieu du front de Manjusri, un filet presque imperceptible s'écoulait d'un seul tenant jusqu'à l'arête du nez brisé qui le divisait en deux flux symétriques, lesquels descendaient de chaque côté du visage doré jusqu'à la commissure des lèvres. La poudre scintillait à la lueur de l'allumette comme des grains de poussière dans un rai de soleil, puis tombait sur le sol. Comme j'observais le visage du dieu dans un silence pétrifié, il me vint à l'esprit qu'il pleurait, que de l'œil de la Sagesse Transcendante au milieu de son front, des larmes chimiques s'écoulaient, des larmes de poudre.

« Cette saleté est pleine d'héroïne ! » remarqua Scottie.

Le claquement métallique de l'écoutille qu'on soulevait résonna soudain au-dessus de nos têtes. Un puissant pinceau de lumière troua l'obscurité. Scottie et moi nous cachâmes derrière une caisse.

« Y a quelqu'un en bas ? interrogea la voix du capitaine. Vous feriez mieux de sortir ! » Il attendit une réponse. Puis, d'une voix assourdie, nous l'entendîmes parler au second. « Probablement une caisse qui s'est détachée. Occupe-t'en demain matin. Et fixe-moi cette bâche, nom de Dieu !

— Maintenant, capitaine ? répondit le second.
— Qui m'a foutu une bande d'empotés pareils ? Et puis tant pis. Ça peut attendre demain. »

L'écoutille fut refermée avec un claquement sec. Nous attendîmes quelques minutes avant de gravir l'échelle et nous glisser jusqu'à notre cabine. Nous ne sûmes pas si le capitaine nous avait vus. En tout cas, il n'en parla jamais. Mais pendant tout le reste du voyage, un homme armé monta la garde près de la cale. Je ne découvris jamais ce que contenait la deuxième caisse — du moins pas avant plusieurs années, et par hasard. Mais j'avais déjà largement de quoi alimenter mes réflexions et mes inquiétudes. Car nous naviguions vers l'Amérique avec une cargaison compromettante sous nos pieds. Ce fut pour moi une ironie cruelle qu'après mon long pèlerinage, je dusse atteindre ma destination en compagnie de marchandises de contrebande !

★

Un matin, juste avant l'aube, Scottie me tira de ma couchette.
« Qu'y a-t-il ? demandai-je d'une voix endormie.
— Habille-toi et monte sur le pont », dit-il en escaladant l'échelle avant que je ne puisse l'interroger davantage.

Je lui obéis en somnolant, et arrivai sur le pont où il m'attendait. Un brouillard que l'aube rendait opalescent recouvrait la mer ; il n'était pas épais, mais réduisait la visibilité à une centaine de mètres et conférait au paysage un caractère irréel, comme une scène de rêve. Je bâillai, me frottai les yeux, regardai autour de moi d'un air hébété. « Où sommes-nous ?
— Voici les rives de la mer Jaune, répondit-il avec un sourire énigmatique.
— Allez... » lui dis-je, légèrement agacé.

Il poursuivit :

« Voici — la terre — qu'inonde le Soleil Couchant —
Voici — les Rives de la mer Jaune —
Où il se lève — où il se rue —
Voici — le Mystère de l'Occident !

— La mer Jaune ? » L'espace d'un instant, je crus rêver ; et dans mon rêve j'étais rentré en Chine. Alors une forme émergea brusquement du brouillard et parut planer vers nous.

« La voilà ! » dit Scottie.

A quatre-vingts mètres environ, flottant dans les nuées, je vis un ange gigantesque et féroce — peut-être une Furie — dont la lumière ambiguë de l'aube empêchait de discerner l'expression, qu'elle fût de bienvenue ou de courroux. Je ne devinai même pas son sexe. Pourtant, malgré le flou fantomatique de ses formes, certains traits m'apparurent clairement : sa patine verdâtre, les traces de corrosion dues au manque d'entretien et à la violence des éléments. Sa tête était ceinte de ce qui ressemblait à une couronne d'épines, mais dont les piquants pointaient vers l'extérieur. Comme Manjusri, sa main droite brandissait très haut un glaive enflammé, et sa main gauche tenait un livre. Mais le glaive semblait brisé ; quand notre navire s'approcha de la statue, je m'aperçus que ce n'était pas un glaive, mais une torche. Les yeux de l'ange, aveugles et vides, étaient tournés vers la mer ; tandis que la lumière montait à l'est, jetant des ombres noires dans les orbites, je songeai au Chasseur, « qui fixe son regard laiteux sur le soleil » afin de recouvrer la vue. Cette image en suscita une autre — celle d'Eddie Love et de ses lunettes noires.

« Bienvenue en Amérique ! s'écria Scottie en interrompant ma rêverie. C'est la statue de la Liberté ! Qu'en dis-tu ? »

Comme je ne répondais pas, mais continuais de regarder l'apparition en silence, perdu dans mes pensées, Scottie en profita pour me faire part des siennes.

« Voilà plus de vingt ans que je n'ai pas revu cette vieille branche, dit-il en secouant la tête et faisant claquer sa langue. Ce spectacle est censé te réchauffer le cœur, te faire monter les larmes aux yeux, mais sacrebleu ! elle me glace le sang ! Regarde-moi un peu cette salope ! J'espère ne plus jamais voir effigie aussi glacée, aussi écrasante, Sun I. Lis donc les mots écrits sur son flanc...

> Donnez-moi vos pauvres et vos déshérités,
> Vos masses compactes aspirant à la liberté,
> Le rebut malmené de vos rivages grouillants.
> Envoyez-moi les sans-patrie ballottés par la tempête,
> Je lève ma torche près de la porte d'or.

« Telle est du moins la version officielle. Tous les gamins américains l'apprennent par cœur à l'école. Mais ne sois pas assez stupide, Sun I, pour croire que cela fait référence à toi. Car il faut lire entre les lignes : "Toi qui arrives ici, abandonne tout espoir." »

Bien que plus tranchées, les impressions de Scottie n'étaient pas si éloignées des miennes, que j'attribuai d'abord à l'effet de la brume et de mon réveil brutal ; mais par la suite je devais souvent m'interroger avec une curiosité avide sur l'expression de la grande Muse de la Liberté. Et quoique le temps ait fini par émousser mon sentiment premier, l'impression mélancolique d'un présage de malheur ne me quitta jamais complètement.

Deuxième Partie

Dow (New York)

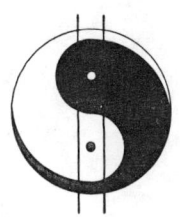

1

Quand le soleil se leva, la brume s'évapora presque instantanément. L'effet en fut magique, comme d'un voile qui se déchire. Manhattan s'éveilla sous mes yeux. Je vis la langue de terre effilée s'avancer dans la baie comme un coin, entre l'Est River et l'Hudson qui naît dans les Adirondacks, puis traverse Tarrytown, Sleepy Hollow, Spuyten Duyvil, cette riche campagne tirée du néant sauvage par les Hollandais qui exorcisèrent les esprits primitifs et humanisèrent le paysage par leur labeur ; puis le fleuve traverse Palisades, coule sous le pont George-Washington, posé comme un collier de perles scintillantes sur la gorge d'une femme colossale qui dans la lumière ambrée de l'aube rejoint son foyer marin après une nuit de réjouissances. Plus loin (plus près), les cheminées de Hoboken, blafardes en ce début de matinée éclaboussé de soleil, crachaient leurs fumées bleues, blanches ou orange, et des flammes qui me rappelèrent le phénomène électrique connu des marins sous le nom de feu de Saint-Elme, que j'avais vu pour la première fois au large de la côte africaine — aigrette blanc-bleuâtre qui monte et descend mystérieusement dans le gréement, ballon d'hélium rempli d'un feu spectral. Alors que l'île de Manhattan émergeait du brouillard, je me retrouvai brusquement sous ces latitudes lointaines du bout du monde : la langue de terre qui s'effilait à Battery devint une version miniature du cap de Bonne-Espérance, et les deux grands fleuves qui mêlaient leurs eaux les océans des hémisphères occidental et oriental. Cette illusion fut encore accentuée par le miroitement de la cité enchantée qui se dressait sous mes yeux ; les énormes tours de verre et d'acier bondissaient vers le ciel avec une beauté cruelle, tels les icebergs que j'avais vus près du pôle, d'une blancheur éblouissante en surface, virant à l'indigo dans la masse, et noirs au plus profond de la glace, vestiges de la banquise, fastueux palais qu'aucun soleil d'été ne pourrait liquéfier et qui scintillaient orgueilleusement en cette aube du mois d'août... La Cité d'Emeraude — je comprenais maintenant l'expression de Hsiao, je commençais à la comprendre. Car New York ressemblait à une cité taillée par Dieu sous une loupe de joaillier.

Autour des flèches étincelantes de Wall Street et du centre ville, j'aperçus une frénésie croissante : Manhattan s'éveillait, la vie bouillonnait de nouveau. J'entendais le bourdonnement lointain de la circulation, les coups de klaxon de l'autre côté de la baie, le claquement saccadé d'un marteau-piqueur, que la distance et l'eau amortissaient en un bruit quasiment éthéré. Je voyais le flot incessant des taxis jaunes sur FDR Drive, je les entendais bondir et rebondir sur les nids-de-poule, les suspensions grinçaient sur les interstices du macadam. Sur le pont de Brooklyn j'entendais le grondement du métro aérien qui se dirigeait vers Flatbush Avenue, puis Coney Island. Je voyais les banlieusards traverser le pont de Manhattan en venant de Queens. Je voyais les câbles du pont de Brooklyn briller au soleil comme les filaments argentés d'une toile d'araignée. Et tout cela fit naître en moi une nostalgie pour un paysage que je n'avais jamais contemplé, une nostalgie qu'expliquait en partie l'analogie avec le cap de Bonne-Espérance, mais pas complètement. Etait-elle due au reflet des lunettes noires de mon père sur le dessin que Hsiao m'avait donné ? Je sais seulement que je ressentis comme une étrange dislocation lorsque Scottie m'apprit que *Manahatta*, en algonquin, signifie « Terre Céleste » exactement comme *Szu-ch'uan* !

Alors que nous passions devant Ellis Island en approchant de Battery, le navire obliqua à tribord vers l'East River, à travers le chenal connu sous le nom de Porte de l'Enfer. Accoudés au bastingage, nous regardions le spectacle en silence, jusqu'à ce que Scottie prenne la parole.

« Sun I, mon trésor, je sais que tu attends ce moment depuis longtemps et que tu meurs d'envie de poser le pied sur cette terre. Mais bon Dieu, tu sais aussi bien que moi ce que nous transportons. Il y a une chance pour que nous passions la douane sans encombre. Qui sait ? On a fort bien pu graisser quelques pattes en haut lieu. Dans ce cas, tu pourras t'esquiver en douce pendant que nous déchargerons, te perdre dans les dédales de la cité, trouver une planque où les fonctionnaires de l'immigration ne viendront pas te dénicher. Ce ne serait pas la première fois que ce plan marcherait. D'un autre côté, si les douaniers passent le bateau au peigne fin et qu'ils trouvent la chnouf, ce qui est à la portée de n'importe quel crétin nanti d'une paire de mirettes, alors le rafiot sera confisqué et tu pourras dire adieu à l'Amérique. Tu n'auras pas la moindre chance de t'en tirer. On te collera illico presto sur une vieille coque de noix à destination de la Chine... après tout ce que tu as enduré pour arriver jusqu'ici ! Rien que d'y penser, j'ai envie de pleurer ou de tuer quelqu'un ! N'attends aucune pitié de ces salopards. Tant qu'ils font leur boulot de bureaucrates et que tout baigne, ils se contrefoutent de ce qui se passe. Quand tu seras rentré chez toi, les Rouges pourront te rôtir vivant ou enfoncer leurs aiguilles d'acupuncture dans tes paupières — au choix. » Après cette envolée, Scottie prit une profonde inspiration et descendit un peu des sommets de sa juste colère. « Bref, Sun I, sans plus gâcher ma salive, j'ai envisagé ta situation sous toutes les coutures ; le meilleur conseil que je puisse te donner est de prendre le taureau par les cornes et de piquer une tête.

— Tu veux dire...

— Plonge ! s'écria-t-il. Et sauve qui peut, comme on dit dans la marine ! Après tout, tu sais nager. D'accord, l'eau n'est pas idéale pour prendre un bain. Elle semble noirâtre et huileuse, elle pue un peu, mais elle n'est pas plus infecte que l'eau de fond de cale où nous avons mariné dans ce foutu entrepont ! Sacrebleu, Sun I, si ce fer à repasser est le *Telemachos*, alors

Ulysse a vraiment dû garder des cochons ! Puisque tu as survécu à un mois de navigation sur cette latrine flottante, ce n'est pas un quart d'heure dans l'East River qui va te tuer. Simplement, évite d'en boire ; le pire qui puisse t'arriver est d'attraper la gale. Alors courage ! File chercher ton précieux paquet. Je suis bien placé pour savoir que tu le tiens prêt depuis le jour où nous avons embarqué.

— Mais Scottie, dis-je, et toi ?

— Ne t'inquiète donc pas pour moi, trésor. Que veux-tu qu'ils me fassent ? Je ne suis qu'un banal marin. J'ai trouvé du boulot sur cette baignoire ; si elle transporte de la drogue, ce n'est pas ma faute. Le pire qui puisse m'arriver, c'est qu'ils me renvoient à Manille franco de port, ce que je considérerais comme une faveur. Pour tout t'avouer, je ruminais l'idée de retrouver le plancher des vaches, mais la vue de cette foutue statue m'a fait changer d'avis. Voilà vingt ans — il regarda sa montre —, deux mois, douze heures et vingt-deux minutes, que je n'ai pas mis le pied aux Etats-Unis, et m'est avis que je vais encore attendre vingt ans avant de voir de quoi il retourne. Maintenant file ! »

Je plongeai par l'écoutille, laissant glisser les montants de l'échelle entre mes mains comme un pompier descend le long de son poteau, puis saisis mon barda et me hâtai de remonter. Bien que fort excité à l'idée de toucher au but et tout aussi inquiet du déroulement de la dernière épreuve, je sentis une sorte de déchirement quand je regardai Scottie.

« Voilà, mon trésor, dit-il. Nous y sommes. Si tu n'y vois pas d'inconvénient, nous nous dispenserons des adieux. J'en ai trop vécu et je n'ai jamais remarqué qu'ils facilitent les choses, pas davantage qu'ils hâtent les retrouvailles ou soient de la moindre utilité. J'ai donc renoncé à cette habitude. Tu as été un bon camarade de bord. Mais si je devais choisir entre toi et la bouteille, je choisirais le rhum. Nous avons passé un ou deux quarts inoubliables, tu ne m'as jamais demandé de te prêter de l'argent, si bien que l'un dans l'autre je crois que tu vas me manquer. Je te souhaite donc bon vent. » Là-dessus, il me sourit, me tendit sa grosse patte, puis m'attira doucement vers le bastingage.

« La surface de l'eau est assez éloignée, dit-il en se penchant. Mais n'y pense pas. Je te lancerai ton paquet quand je verrai ta tête. »

Je baissai les yeux vers l'eau noirâtre. « Je ne suis pas sûr de pouvoir », dis-je en déglutissant avec difficulté.

Scottie soupira. « C'est ce que je craignais. Okay, trésor. Je vais te faciliter les choses. Contente-toi d'obéir à Scottie. Inspire profondément et détends-toi. » Je fis ce qu'il me demandait. « Maintenant ferme les yeux et compte très lentement jusqu'à trois. Un... deux... TROIS ! »

Il me saisit alors par-derrière et me jeta, gigotant et me débattant comme un chat, par-dessus bord. Je réussis à pousser un bref hurlement de protestation, mais quand je vis l'eau sombre se ruer vers moi, j'eus la présence d'esprit de fermer la bouche avant de percuter la surface. Tout le chagrin, le ressentiment, la peine, l'attente ou l'excitation que j'aurais pu ressentir se dissipèrent instantanément quand l'eau fouetta mon corps et l'absorba. Avec l'énergie du désespoir, je me débattis pour remonter à la surface. Je commençai à reprendre mes esprits en soufflant et crachant quand mon barda atterrit lourdement sur ma tête et me renvoya sous l'eau. Mes efforts pour rester à flot m'empêchaient de remarquer les divers déchets qui flottaient autour de moi ou la brûlure de ma peau. Je réussis cependant à lancer un dernier regard à Scottie qui, penché au bastingage, m'encourageait, alternait flatteries et injures en une litanie d'expressions sans doute pittoresques et dignes de lui, mais où je distinguai seulement quelques « sacrebleu » et autres « trésor ». Pour témoigner de l'intérêt passionné qu'il portait à mon cas, il avait retiré son chapeau et l'agitait comme un étendard dans la bataille en m'exhortant à des efforts redoublés. Quand il me vit hors de danger, il le remit aussitôt, après avoir passé ses doigts dans ses cheveux clairsemés comme s'il eût redouté un progrès de sa calvitie. Puis il s'éloigna du bastingage et disparut pour de bon. Je recrachai une gorgée d'eau putride, puis m'élançai vers le pilier ouest du pont de Brooklyn en nageant le crawl américain.

★

En me hissant à quatre pattes sur la rive, je ressentis un picotement étrange sur et sous la peau, qui n'était pas entièrement dû à l'épuisement ni à la joie qui me submergea lorsque mes paumes et mes pieds touchèrent pour la première fois le sol américain — un sol jonché, soit dit en passant, de tessons de bouteille, capsules, canettes de bière et quelques préservatifs usagés —, mais, me semble-t-il, à une chimie différente. Il se trouva que je touchai terre à une centaine de mètres au nord du marché aux poissons de Fulton Street, près d'un parking miteux niché sous les poutrelles du métro aérien. L'ombre du FDR Drive plongeait l'endroit dans une obscurité permanente.

Ma progression vers le rivage avait été observée à mon insu par les employés du parking, deux jeunes Italiens que je vis en levant les yeux ; chacun avait posé un pied sur la rambarde saturée de créosote qui délimitait le périmètre de leur juridiction et empêchait les voitures de tomber dans la mer. Chacun avait posé un coude sur le genou levé et tenait en main une liasse de dollars froissés.

« Hé, Tony, qu'est-ce que c'est à ton avis ? demanda l'un. Une poiscaille ?

— Non, répondit son ami. Sûrement un immigré de Brooklyn. Tu sais bien qu'on les laisse plus passer sur le pont. Faut qu'ils aient un visa.

— Hé, hé. Elle est pas mauvaise, celle-là, Tony. Je te parie cinq dollars. »

Les deux jeunes gens portaient un blue-jean retroussé aux chevilles, une chemise collante en acétate ouverte jusqu'au plexus solaire, qui dévoilait une poitrine velue et de minces chaînes d'argent auxquelles des crucifix étaient fixés. Tous deux avaient une moustache noire soigneusement taillée et une abondante chevelure coiffée en brosse ; tous deux abordaient une brioche naissante. Ils se ressemblaient de façon remarquable.

« Qu'est-ce qui t'arrive, mec ? m'apostropha numéro un, T'as raté ton train, ou quoi ? »

Tony rit, puis, feignant de prendre ma défense, dit à son acolyte :

« Hééé ! Un peu de respect, s'il te plaît. Il s'entraîne peut-être pour les Jeux Olympiques. En tout cas, c'est sûrement le premier type à traverser la passe de Brooklyn.

— "La passe de Brooklyn" — hé hé, tu me tues, Tony. Tu crois tout de même pas qu'il fait ça tous les matins, non. »

Tony haussa les épaules. « Qui sait ? Ces RO sont capables de tout — tu sais bien, les Rusés Orientaux. »

Ils échangèrent un regard lourd de sous-entendus.

Pendant leur conversation, j'avais continué à ramper à quatre pattes en les observant comme un animal traqué, tandis que l'eau dégoulinait de mon visage dans les immondices. Bien que leur attitude ne fût ni amicale ni hostile et qu'ils vissent dans mon apparition une simple distraction dans la monotonie de leur routine matinale, une occasion de plaisanter, j'étais conscient de l'illégalité de ma situation et désireux de ne pas me faire remarquer, surtout par une quelconque autorité. J'attendis en silence la fin de leur manège, espérant qu'ils s'éloigneraient bientôt, me laisseraient le temps de souffler et de décider ce que je devais entreprendre.

« Mec ! reprocha numéro un. Tu sais donc pas que cette flotte est pleine de saloperies et de merde ? » Il se tourna vers Tony. « T'as déjà vu mon oncle, Joey ?

— Ouais, et alors ?

— Il m'a dit que, si un jour je voulais faire disparaître un type, j'avais qu'à le lâcher dans le fleuve. Il fondrait comme un cube de glace.

— Ouais, dit Tony. Comme dans le Magicien d'Oz.

— La BD ?

— Non, crétin, le bouquin.

— Hééé, Tony, v'là que tu t'prends pour un lettré, maintenant ? »

Tony le regarda avec mépris. « Tu te rappelles pas le seau d'eau que Dorothy jette sur la Sorcière Maléfique ?

— Eh ben ?

— Eh ben il était plein d'eau de l'East River. »

Tous deux rirent.

« Il dit pas grand-chose pour plaider sa cause, hein ? » lança numéro un. Ils attendirent, comme si j'allais répondre. Au bout de quelques instants, il saisit le bras de son ami.

« Allez, viens, Tony, dit-il. Ce type est un enfoiré.

— Ouais, mec, un vrai zigoto.

— "Un zigoto" ! Vraiment Tony, où vas-tu chercher des mots pareils ?

— Putain de trou du cul de Chinetoque... »

Leurs voix s'éloignèrent. Je pris une profonde inspiration et m'allongeai sur le dos en poussant un soupir de soulagement. Au-dessus de ma tête, un ciel d'été sans nuage occupait l'espace, le même ciel que j'avais connu en Chine, mais avec une teinte jaune grisâtre et une vibration de l'air que j'attribuai à la pollution. Je l'avais abandonné derrière moi, et il m'avait une fois encore retrouvé. C'était la seule chose que je reconnaissais.

Je me répétais sans arrêt : « C'est le même univers. C'est le même univers... »

Toutes proportions gardées, je ressentais un peu ce qu'avait dû éprouver

Christophe Colomb en débarquant pour la première fois au Nouveau Monde, alors qu'il s'attendait à être accueilli par les émissaires du Fils du Ciel, vêtus de soie et portés en palanquins, et qu'il découvrit quelques sauvages hirsutes et à moitié nus, couverts de plumes et de peaux de bête.

Pourtant, malgré l'étrangeté de tout de qui m'entourait, je me souvins des mots de Chong Fou : « Le Tao se trouve aussi sur la place du marché. »

« Il faut qu'il en soit ainsi, me dis-je. Le Tao doit aussi expliquer tout ceci. »

Cette pensée calma mon esprit. Pour la première fois depuis des semaines, je me détendis complètement et relâchai mon attention. Je me sentis lavé par les tâches et la douce monotonie de la vie en mer, le travail et le sommeil, le soleil et la mer... Je me sentis bronzé, reposé, en paix. J'eus soudain la certitude que ce Nouveau Monde que j'avais enfin atteint et à quel prix (car n'avais-je pas tout sacrifié ?), tout comme celui d'où je venais, se dressait sur les fondations insondables du Tao et obéissait à ses lois. Je pris une longue inspiration, pliai mes jambes en lotus, et, face au soleil matinal qui se levait maintenant au-dessus de Brooklyn, pratiquai *tso-wang* pour la première fois depuis longtemps. Puis je réunis mes affaires, escaladai la berge et m'élançai sans peur, presque joyeusement, vers l'immense domaine sauvage créé par l'homme, l'Amérique.

Poussé par le hasard ou l'irrésistible instinct des origines qui oblige le saumon à quitter l'océan pour remonter les torrents jusqu'à la frayère ancestrale, je me dirigeai vers le sud en errant avec une nonchalance tranquille à travers le spectacle coloré du marché aux poissons de Fulton Street, semblable au fleuve qui serpente paresseusement, peu pressé d'atteindre sa destination et peut-être même inconscient de tendre vers un but. Le jour commençait à blanchir et miroiter dans la chaleur d'août ; il n'avait pas encore viré à la moiteur rance du milieu de journée. Une délicieuse fraîcheur océane entourait le bâtiment blanc du marché et les étals grillagés à l'intérieur, la saine puanteur de la pleine mer mêlée de glace et de saumure. La chaleur matinale était restée aux portes du marché.

Pénétrant dans son périmètre magique, je ressentis l'excitation vivifiante de la fraîcheur d'avant l'aube, comme lorsqu'on ouvre la porte d'un réfrigérateur. Les tonnes de glace exhalaient un souffle frais qui sentait vaguement le poisson. Des tuyaux d'arrosage abandonnés inondaient le sol de ciment. Des hommes allaient et venaient en bottes noires ou orange montant jusqu'au genou, vêtus de cirés qui luisaient d'humidité. D'énormes camions aux remorques de tôle scintillante chargeaient ou déchargeaient derrière les étals. Plusieurs manœuvres faisaient la queue avec des diables, qui bavardant, qui regardant en silence l'intérieur caverneux de la remorque réfrigérée où deux débardeurs corpulents et barbus, affublés de casquettes et de manteaux jaunes maculés de graisse noire, chargeaient de grosses caisses en bois pleines de poissons sur les diables des convoyeurs.

En me promenant entre les étalages, je lus les noms des poissons griffonnés au crayon noir et sous forme abrégée sur les couvercles râpeux des caisses de bois clair — « merl. », « mor. », « lot. », « had. », « maque. » — et les noms des chalutiers qui les avaient pêchés — le *Deborah Bay*, le *Vicki*, l'*Ironsides*, le *Mystic Light* de Chatham. Certains bateaux avaient des ports d'attache aux noms étranges — Galilee, Rhode Island, Kill Devil Hills, N.C.

Plus loin, j'aperçus un restaurateur vêtu de blanc immaculé des pieds à la tête, mal rasé, vaguement endormi mais alerte, qui fronçait gravement les sourcils en plongeant la main dans une caisse ouverte ; il en sortit un bar, jaugea du pouce la fermeté de la chair, tandis que son œil exercé brillait d'une gourmandise infiniment subtile. Je vis des carrelets vert foncé, aussi gros que des feuilles de bananier ou des éventails d'osier tressé, couchés sur des lits de glace pilée blanche comme leur propre chair cuite, et qui contractaient leurs mornes mâchoires carrées de boxeurs : des flétans, qu'on aurait facilement confondus avec les précédents, n'eût été leur petite bouche en forme de téton ; des carpes vivantes qui tournaient paresseusement dans un bassin ; des crabes à carapace molle enveloppés d'algues ; des bigorneaux, des moules, des couteaux, longs et fins comme des doigts de femme ; et enfin un saumon rose doré dont l'aspect semblait impliquer une étincelle de conscience, une insatisfaction angoissée qu'on croyait discerner dans son œil. Sans m'attarder sur rien de particulier, j'observai tout avec une attention patiente ; puis je ressortis dans la rue.

Je vis aussitôt un vieux Chinois en haillons, dont les doigts serraient le grillage d'un étal tandis qu'il regardait les allées et venues à l'intérieur. Ses vêtements en loques et son air résigné faillirent me convaincre qu'il s'agissait d'un moine errant. Mais il y avait de la faim, de la cupidité dans sa résignation, et rien de l'expression éthérée, apaisée, qu'on attend chez le prêtre. Je compris que c'était un mendiant. Quand il remarqua que je m'intéressais à lui, il me dévisagea avec une intensité étonnée.

« Une pièce pour une tasse de café ? me demanda-t-il en anglais, tendant machinalement une main jaune et ridée.

— Désolé, répondis-je dans la langue de notre pays natal, je n'ai pas d'argent.

— Tu viens d'arriver », dit-il en chinois, comme si ses soupçons se trouvaient confirmés.

J'acquiesçai.

« Où vas-tu ? »

Je haussai les épaules. « J'aimerais bien le savoir.

— Cherches-tu quelque chose de particulier ? »

Pour une raison que je ne saurais expliquer, je pensai qu'il me comprendrait peut-être et répondis : « Le Tao.

— Le Tao », répéta-t-il en s'attardant sur les voyelles comme pour en savourer l'essence rare et délicate. Il fouilla mon visage, plein de méfiance et de doute, puis éclata brusquement d'un rire dément, un rire brisé par une atroce quinte de toux. Il allongea son bras décharné et tendit un index noueux vers le sud.

« Tu es sur la bonne voie, m'informa-t-il en retournant à l'anglais. C'est juste un peu plus bas. »

Puis il s'éloigna en titubant dans la direction opposée, riant toujours de son rire dément.

★

Ah, lecteur, imagine mon excitation et mon émotion quand, tournant au coin de la rue, je m'engageai dans Wall Street pour la première fois ! Ce long ravin ombreux s'étendait devant moi comme le lit d'un fleuve préhistorique creusé entre les murailles d'un canyon. Alors que, près de l'East River, je découvrais tous ces lourds bâtiments de style Beaux-Arts couverts par la patine du temps et de la respectabilité, et — spectacle plus étonnant encore — les constructions modernes de verre et d'acier, l'inexplicable nostalgie, l'impression de déjà-vu que j'avais ressenties en découvrant la cité, me submergèrent de nouveau. La faille sinistre dans laquelle je marchais me rappela-t-elle le paysage près de Ken Kuan, comme dans quelque étrange toile cubiste ? Car si les bâtiments parodiaient l'aspect éternel des montagnes, alors la rue elle-même était le flux du fleuve. Bien que « préhistorique » en un sens, Wall Street était loin d'être désert. Certes, aucune eau ne coulait entre ses berges, mais un flot tumultueux d'humanité envahissait son lit.

Comme je m'engageais dans la foule matinale, j'attirai l'attention d'une jeune secrétaire qui se rendait à son travail en mangeant un beignet à la confiture. Elle avait des seins plantureux qui tressautaient au rythme de la marche et une façon de balancer ses hanches qui, bien qu'un peu voyante et inélégante, voire vulgaire, provoqua mon admiration. Je dus lui adresser un regard suppliant, ou sembler particulièrement désespéré, car elle m'arrêta pour me jauger.

« Le Dow ? » lui demandai-je avec un haussement d'épaules et un sourire penaud, en espérant qu'elle me comprendrait.

L'extrémité rose de sa langue lécha un peu de confiture sur sa lèvre supérieure, puis elle m'adressa un signe de tête comme pour désigner quelque chose derrière elle. « C'est par là, au coin de Wall et de Broadway », dit-elle, après quoi elle repartit vers son bureau.

Je me retrouvai bientôt à l'entrée de la Bourse de New York qui donnait sur Wall Street. Je tentai de me glisser dans le flot des gens qui franchissaient la porte, mais fus arrêté par un grand garde noir qui posa sur moi un bref regard fatigué et tendit son gros bras noir pour m'empêcher d'aller plus loin.

« Où est votre badge ? demanda-t-il.
— Badge ? couinai-je.
— L'entrée des visiteurs est au coin de la rue », dit-il.

Quand je la trouvai enfin, je tombai sur les arrières d'un groupe de touristes japonais avec lesquels un œil non averti aurait pu m'accorder une vague ressemblance, même si je ne possédais pas l'emblème distinctif de leur fraternité pécuniaire : l'appareil de photo et ses accessoires aussi indispensables qu'encombrants, grâce auxquels avec une discipline et une efficacité admirables ils se photographiaient mutuellement devant les portes de la Bourse, en souriant joyeusement comme les heureux propriétaires d'une nouvelle maison.

Vaguement stupéfait par toutes ces nouveautés, je regardais le voyant lumineux clignoter sur le panneau de l'ascenseur — 1, 2, 3 — quand brusquement, comme par magie, les portes s'ouvrirent et nous sortîmes dans une pièce tendue de rouge : le Centre de Réception des Visiteurs, plus élégant et luxueux que tout ce que j'avais jamais vu.

Une jeune femme qui s'exprimait en un langage ardu, hautement technique, nous entraîna derrière elle. Elle désigna un long et mince tableau électronique bleu foncé sur lequel s'affichaient une série de symboles lumineux verts — lettres et chiffres mélangés en configurations bizarres. Sous le tableau se trouvaient plusieurs machines dotées de claviers, devant lesquels des personnes d'aspect fort divers appuyaient sur des boutons, puis attendaient que des hiéroglyphes numériques apparaissent sur les écrans. Ils notaient parfois un nombre sur le bloc de papier froissé qu'ils tenaient en main.

« Voici les Quotrons, les machines de cotation électroniques, expliqua la jeune fille. Il suffit que vous formiez les trois lettres qui symbolisent votre action, et la machine vous indique sa cotation, avec la baisse ou la hausse quotidienne ou annuelle, sa valeur lors de la dernière séance, et ainsi de suite. L'un de vous possède-t-il une action dont il voudrait vérifier la valeur ? » Avec un sourire encourageant, elle regarda son groupe en battant des paupières et ouvrant des yeux où brillait un zèle aseptisé.

Personne ne broncha. Les Japonais, qui semblaient submergés d'une modestie féodale, dansaient d'un pied sur l'autre dans un silence gêné. Un jeune homme finit par parler. « Toyota ? » demanda-t-il timidement, en souriant et s'inclinant devant la guide.

Tous les visages se tournèrent vers la jeune fille, qui rougit fortement. Certains des membres les plus malicieux du groupe se mirent à glousser, puis, comme saisis par la contagion, tous les autres ricanèrent discrètement.

« Essayons Mitsubishi ? demanda un jeune Japonais en poursuivant la plaisanterie.

— Non, dit-elle froidement, je crains que ces entreprises ne soient pas cotées en bourse. » Entraînés par leur guide vexée, les Japonais repartirent rapidement. Je me faufilai parmi les derniers du groupe.

On nous conduisit sur la Galerie des Visiteurs qui surplombait la grande salle de la Bourse. J'attendais depuis longtemps ce moment, lecteur, en essayant d'imaginer ce que je découvrirais. Malgré cela, je fus profondément étonné, profondément ému. C'est une des impressions que j'emporterai dans ma tombe. Mais seule l'émotion est encore fraîche et nette ; le spectacle lui-même s'est estompé dans mon souvenir, rendu indistinct par son énormité même. Je me rappelle seulement un vaste bouillonnement d'énergie, comme des vagues de chaleur dans le désert, contemplées du promontoire de la Galerie, une mer tumultueuse qui s'étendait aussi loin que le regard. Je pressentais que je descendrais de ma montagne pour traverser ce désert, que je devrais le faire. Mais je manquais d'associations pour comprendre ce que je voyais ; j'en avais une seule, si profonde et si dérisoire que j'hésite à la mentionner. Un désert, certes, mais seulement aujourd'hui, rétrospectivement. En cet instant, ce fut pour moi une prairie, l'immense prairie palpitante de l'Ouest américain, sa version abstraite et claquemurée, mais où ne manquait aucun des personnages colorés que mon imagination baptisait cowboys, Indiens, troupes de cavalerie galopant pour secourir les chariots assiégés. Je vis même les chevaux et les bisons. Créatures de rêve, mais pourtant si réelles. La frontière sauvage du capitalisme... Quand je me revois après toutes ces années, si différent de ce que j'étais alors, je peux me permettre le luxe de la pitié. Une pitié pure, aussi pure que s'il s'agissait d'autrui.

Le voilà donc, me dis-je — le Dow, « l'autre », le Dow américain. Cela ressemblait au microcosme de tout l'univers humain. Que ne contenait-il pas ? Alors que j'écarquillais les yeux, l'idée traversa mon esprit que même Eddie Love était peut-être en bas — en train comme les autres de conclure une transaction, de faire une offre, de signer un contrat. En cet instant même, il jetait peut-être un coup d'œil distrait vers la Galerie et m'observait sans se douter de mon identité, mais en ressentant une émotion incompréhensible. De toutes mes forces je scrutais la foule, je cherchais, espérant presque découvrir un homme en lunettes d'aviateur aux verres en forme de larmes vert foncé. Et quand je réalisai la futilité de mes efforts, je cherchai quelqu'un d'autre — un vieux Chinois ridé mais au regard toujours brillant, quelqu'un qui ressemblât à Chong Fou, qui avait goûté à la paix délicieuse du Tao, appris à se contenter de « riz grossier, de l'eau froide du puits, d'un coude plié en guise d'oreiller »... mais je ne le trouvai pas davantage.

« Le Dow... Que ne contenait-il pas ? » Cette pensée m'obsédait comme le refrain d'une chanson, mais son sens se transforma. Coupant court à mon émerveillement, l'ancien doute refit surface. Contenait-il le Tao ? Où était le Tao *en tout cela* ? Était-il même quelque part ? Je ressentis un vertige terrible, puis les paroles du vœu surgirent :

TAO

Mère de toutes les existences
Que nous voyons autour de nous,
Spectacle kaléidoscopique des apparences,

TAO

L'Un de cette multiplicité
Foisonnante, lui-même
Immuable et donnant
Naissance à tous les changements.

Mais maintenant ces paroles réconfortaient au lieu de troubler. Debout sur la galerie de la Bourse de New York, je fermai les yeux pour murmurer les mots du vœu que j'avais répété chaque jour depuis mon enfance, et auquel j'avais à jamais renoncé :

Voici ma foi :
La Réalité est Une
Et le Tao est la Réalité.
Je la déclare entière et véridique
Sous peine de perdition.

Ainsi :
Je renonce au monde à jamais
Afin de l'améliorer.
Je renonce à moi-même
Afin de me trouver.
Puissé-je ne pas me détourner de cette résolution
Avant que l'enfer ne soulage les damnés
Et que mon âme ne se transforme en cendres.

Puis je jurai de rester fidèle à ce serment. Retrouvant le chemin de mes origines, je fis le vœu de ne jamais les oublier ni les trahir, mais de chercher le Tao même ici, même au cœur du labyrinthe.

Maintenant seul dans la pénombre du couloir — les touristes japonais avaient depuis longtemps pris leurs photos et poursuivi leur visite —, je me préparai moi aussi à partir. Pourtant je ne pus résister à un dernier regard au vaste panorama. Le sol de la grande salle était couvert de feuilles de papier — rose, jaune, bleu ciel —, comme des pétales de fleur ou les confetti qu'on jette au Nouvel An (le plus nouveau, en effet, que j'eusse jamais connu), comme de la paille répandue sur le sol de ce grand sanctuaire du commerce. Je remarquai que la foule se déplaçait en cercle, dessinait une sorte de tourbillon. « Qu'est-ce que ça veut dire ? Où vont-ils ? » me demandai-je. Ce mouvement circulaire suggérait maintes choses, mais ne révélait rien. Pourtant je perçus la rumeur qui montait de la grande salle, semblable au rugissement de l'océan qui assaille les continents, aux cris de la foule dans un stade en plein air — clameur sauvage et primitive mêlée de douleur et de jubilation, de larmes et de rire, applaudissement, récrimination, espoir et dépit —, je perçus l'ample rumeur de la vie, celle des humains qui fêtent et pleurent leur condition, mais se dirigent vers un but que personne ne connaît.

Abasourdi et las, les yeux brûlants et les oreilles sifflantes, je sortis dans la chaleur moite sous le ciel éblouissant qui écrasait la cité. Je marchai tête baissée, les yeux fixés sur mes pieds, et heurtai plusieurs personnes dans la rue, dont certaines réagirent avec colère, et d'autres me demandèrent si j'avais besoin d'aide. Brusquement, je débouchai sur Broadway à l'heure de pointe de midi. La grande artère grouillait de gens qui marchaient vers la station de Lexington Avenue à Chase Manhattan Plaza, hélaient des taxis, commandaient Coca-Cola et parts de pizza, s'engouffraient dans les bars à air conditionné dont les enseignes au néon orange vantaient la bière glacée.

Je remarquais vaguement ce qui se passait autour de moi, mais mon esprit était obnubilé par autre chose. Quand, émergeant de ma rêverie, je levai les yeux pour la première fois, je découvris la silhouette massive et crénelée de Trinity Church, ses clochetons noircis, sa lourde grille en fer forgé, les arabesques dentelées de ses décorations gothiques, son cimetière plein d'herbe verte, curieusement vivant parmi les étendues grises de la pierre. A cause de sa position surélevée en haut de la légère pente de Wall Street, l'église aurait pu passer pour l'origine, la Source, « tout en haut des monts

Tanglha », de ce grand Yang-tsê de la finance. (En ce cas, on aurait pu affirmer à juste titre que le Retour à la Source, au Dow, était un bref voyage, mais malgré tout difficile.) L'église de Trinity, qui régnait sur le Quartier de la Finance et incarnait son âme, sa conscience, était loin d'être immaculée : elle semblait n'avoir pas été nettoyée depuis le Grand Incendie, d'où, tel le phénix, elle s'était dressée, carbonisée par son long et stoïque ministère, chancelant au bord de ce qu'un esprit facétieux aurait appelé les Régions Infernales. L'église ressemblait davantage à une huître fumée, ou à l'un de ces œufs de mille ans qu'on voit dans les épiceries de Chinatown, qu'à une âme. Pourtant, c'était peut-être la chose la plus proche d'une âme que Wall Street pouvait concocter.

Quittant la chaleur étouffante et la cohue frénétique de Broadway à midi, je m'aventurai dans l'espace frais et ombreux de l'église qui, à ma grande surprise et en un contraste frappant avec le tumulte extérieur, était totalement vide — une vaste caverne plongée dans la pénombre. Je clignai des yeux en pénétrant dans le narthex et admirai le sol de la nef couvert de mosaïques. Je dépassai des rangées de bancs en bois, dont la plupart portaient des plaques d'argent gravé. Les coussins de prière en velours lie-de-vin étaient lustrés, usés par endroits. Devant la chaire sculptée, je remarquai une magnifique bible reliée en cuir de Russie, ouverte sur le lutrin sous une petite lampe dorée ; un ruban de soie pourpre marquait la page. J'atteignis enfin l'autel simple et massif, couvert d'une sorte de nappe décorée d'arabesques florales brodées dans le tissu. On avait appliqué sur cette nappe deux lettres grecques entrecroisées, χ et ρ. (Un khi-rho, comme je devais l'apprendre plus tard). Au centre de l'autel, comme pour un banquet, se dressait un vase de lis des champs aux pétales immaculés. Un peu à droite, un reliquaire encastré dans le mur contenait des objets dont l'apparence d'ustensiles de cuisine renforçait cette impression de banquet : un petit plat en or avec un motif ciselé sur son pourtour, un calice, une boîte en argent qui aurait pu renfermer des bonbons ou peut-être des cigarettes qu'on distribuerait après le festin. Mais où était la nourriture ? Et qui allait manger ? Le garçon doré suspendu à la croix derrière l'autel paraissait pris de faiblesse, comme s'il avait perdu l'appétit, et personne ne semblait arriver. J'aurais volontiers accepté de manger le cas échéant, mais contrairement aux innombrables temples que j'avais visités en Asie, où l'on vous offrait toujours au moins une tasse de thé, ici dans ce sanctuaire chrétien l'hospitalité semblait plus qu'improbable.

Tandis que je ruminais ces pensées innocentes, une transformation surprenante métamorphosa l'église. Une éclaircie s'était produite dans le ciel nuageux, permettant aux rayons du soleil d'atteindre la cité, ou bien l'astre avait commencé de décliner vers l'ouest et atteint la position fixée par l'architecte et le maître-verrier, mais une lumière soudaine embrasa les fenêtres supérieures de la claire-voie. Une pluie d'or filtrée par les vitraux inonda l'église, et je découvris l'un des spectacles les plus magnifiques que j'aie jamais vus. Je m'assis sur un banc et levai la tête pour examiner un aspect de l'église qui m'avait échappé jusqu'alors.

Je crus tourner les pages d'un somptueux livre enluminé écrit en une langue inconnue, mais où les images me permettaient d'entrevoir un récit dont le sens m'échappait. Je vis un vieillard à barbe blanche, au visage angoissé, ruisselant de larmes, tourné vers le ciel, un couteau de boucher brandi au-dessus de sa tête pour frapper. Un jeune garçon était ligoté devant lui, les yeux pleins d'incrédulité et d'horreur, les avant-bras levés en un geste de défense ou de protestation pitoyablement entravé par la corde. Derrière eux, un bélier blanc piétinait furieusement les fourrés dont il ne parvenait pas à dégager ses cornes.

Il y avait une scène nocturne décrivant un groupe d'hommes ivres qui dansaient sur le sable blanc du désert autour d'un feu de camp. Des femmes nues renversaient la tête et riaient avec mépris, peur, excitation, tandis que des hommes lubriques les maintenaient sur leurs genoux et serraient les poignets des femmes entre leurs mains musclées. Des étoiles éblouissantes brillaient dans le ciel. Parmi elles, un homme vêtu d'une longue tunique sacerdotale poussait les autres à la révolte en brandissant une figurine au-dessus de sa tête — un veau d'or — et en défiant les cieux. Dans un coin de la scène, debout dans les ombres tremblotantes, un vieillard habillé en blanc prenait son visage entre ses mains tandis que des fragments de pierre gisaient à ses pieds.

Je vis un garçon aux joues couvertes d'un léger duvet, entouré de nombreux patriarches à barbe grise, robes noires, chapeaux bizarres, dotés d'yeux plissés et calculateurs. Dans sa main gauche, il tenait une pièce de monnaie où l'on discernait le profil d'un militaire à la mâchoire carrée, aux cheveux coupés court, au long nez aquilin, et dont les oreilles retenaient une couronne de lauriers. L'autre main du jeune homme, vide, pointait vers le ciel.

Le panneau suivant montrait le même jeune homme au bord d'un précipice. Les genoux serrés au creux de ses bras, il regardait gravement le panorama qui s'offrait à lui — champs de blé, armées en marche, vaisseaux aux voiles blanches sur la mer bleue —, et qu'un homme plus âgé au visage glaçant lui décrivait avec un large geste du bras, comme pour lui dire : « Tout cela pourrait t'appartenir. »

C'étaient de splendides panneaux isolés, mais il y en avait d'autres, deux triptyques surtout, où l'on voyait les mêmes personnages dans des poses ou des situations différentes, ce qui suggérait une sorte de séquence narrative. Dans le premier, deux amants heureux, lui riant, elle réservée, se regardaient avec une ardeur innocente, tous deux nus dans un berceau de verdure. Il y avait des fleurs dans l'herbe ; autour du jeune couple, des animaux paisibles somnolaient au soleil, la tête posée sur leurs pattes. La scène était charmante, à un détail près. A l'arrière-plan, bizarrement décalé et vaguement inquiétant à cause d'un effet de perspective inhabituel, se dressait un arbre qui attira mon attention, car il ressemblait à celui qu'avait brodé ma mère sur la robe. Comme l'autre, cet arbre se réduisait à un squelette décharné : mais il n'était pas totalement stérile. De sa branche la plus basse, un seul fruit pendait, vert et indéterminé. Cet arbre occupait le centre du deuxième panneau ; un serpent paré de bijoux et dont la peau opalescente contrastait avec l'écorce noire était enroulé autour du tronc. Sa langue bifide sortait de sa gueule, il observait avec une subtilité menaçante la scène qui se déroulait dans l'herbe en dessous de l'arbre. La femme, effrayée et plus pâle qu'auparavant, tendait le fruit marqué de l'empreinte de ses dents à l'homme qui allongeait le bras pour le saisir. Sur le troisième panneau, tout avait changé. Un ange courroucé tout de blanc vêtu brandissait un glaive enflammé au-dessus de sa tête (comme la statue dans la baie de New York) et chassait devant lui les amants désespérés vers un univers flétri, non plus vert mais d'un gris noirâtre et couvert de ronces. Ils pleuraient en fuyant, agitaient les bras, ou plutôt un seul bras, car l'autre servait à cacher leur sexe. Ils joignaient piteusement les genoux, comme si même en courant ils faisaient l'impossible pour dissimuler leurs parties honteuses. Sous le triptyque, écrits dans une langue que j'ignorais, je lus ces mots gravés dans la pierre : « *Memento homo quod cinis es et in cinerem reverteris.* »

Sur le premier panneau de la deuxième séquence (dans l'abside, au-dessus de l'autel, peut-être l'endroit le plus visible de toute l'église), mon regard tomba enfin sur une chose que je reconnus — quelqu'un plutôt, un pâle homme barbu aux yeux las et aux lèvres serrées. C'était Jésus ; même au Szu-ch'uan j'avais fait connaissance avec ce visage émacié, douloureux, grâce aux peintures naïves fournies par les missionnaires. Je reconnus l'homme, mais pas la scène. Car il se tenait devant une table couverte d'une nappe blanche comme l'autel. Pourtant cette table supportait un modeste festin : une miche de pain entamée, une carafe de vin rouge. Plusieurs hommes d'âges et types divers entouraient Jésus — l'un robuste, le teint florissant, encore jeune, un autre, un adolescent pâle et sensible, éthéré. Pourtant, aussi différents fussent-ils, tous étaient assis *derrière* la table et regardaient leur hôte avec des expressions qui couvraient toute la gamme des émotions. Isolé sur le côté, tournant le dos au spectateur, un homme accroupi à la barbe fournie contemplait, non Jésus, mais le croûton qu'il tenait dans sa main blanche. Les yeux de l'homme, dont on voyait le profil, étaient exorbités, son visage tordu d'un horrible rictus. Sous ce panneau, gravé dans le mur, était écrit : « *Hoc est corpus meum.* »

Dans la seconde scène du triptyque, trois croix se détachaient contre le ciel au sommet d'une colline nue, un homme cloué sur chaque. La Crucifixion — ma modeste connaissance des légendes chrétiennes allait jusque-là. Sur l'épaule de l'homme crucifié à la droite du Christ, un ange minuscule était perché ; sur l'épaule de son vis-à-vis, un diable noir aux dents pointues et aux yeux rouges pleins de méchanceté ; deux cornes dépassaient du front du démon qui avait des pattes de bouc aux sabots fourchus. Jésus était au centre ; un soldat casqué tendait vers lui une éponge piquée au bout d'une lance. Les yeux du Christ, deux croissants blancs, étaient levés vers le ciel, vers le disque noir du soleil au zénith obscurci par une éclipse totale. Au pied de la croix, trois soldats jouaient aux dés dans la poussière. Deux baissaient les yeux d'un air déçu, tandis que le troisième sautait de joie et tendait le bras vers l'enjeu, un vêtement rouge sang, une sorte de robe. Sous la scène était écrit : « *Eloi, Eloi, lama sabachthani ?* »

Le troisième et dernier panneau décrivait un sépulcre creusé à flanc de colline, dont l'énorme pierre était soulevée ; un ange était assis dessus, apparemment invisible des deux hommes debout de chaque côté de la tombe, mains posées sur le rebord de pierre comme s'ils venaient d'examiner l'intérieur ; ils se dévisageaient avec des expressions stupéfaites. En dessous d'eux, sur une route qui longeait le bas de la colline, une femme éplorée retirait ses mains de son visage mouillé de larmes pour regarder avec inquiétude un étranger debout sur la route devant elle. Était-ce le Christ ? Je le supposai ; mais son aspect était étonnant. Sa chair luisait d'une opalescence blafarde, comme du poisson avarié ; et bien qu'il sourît à la femme avec douceur et amour, il levait sa paume blessée en un geste évident d'interdiction, la blessure rouge du clou bien en évidence. « *Noli me tangere* », disait l'inscription.

Quand j'eus examiné ces vitraux à loisir, je sortis dans le cimetière. Assis sur un banc de pierre, je remarquai de nouveau un sifflement dans mes oreilles, comme le son d'un verre en cristal dont un doigt mouillé frotte le rebord. Tous mes sens se tendirent vers ce crissement à la limite du spectre auditif. Par la grille en fer forgé, je regardai les hordes multicolores qui pressaient le pas dans la rue et je sentis l'émotion m'étreindre — un extrême plaisir inexplicablement mêlé de tristesse et de regret. Un oiseau moqueur chantait derrière moi dans les branches d'un saule pleureur. J'écoutai son chant, si différent de celui du rossignol ; je regardai les fleurs sauvages qui poussaient parmi les tombes, remarquai la lumière dorée, implacable, qui blanchissait les brins d'herbe soyeuse oscillant dans le vent. Alors que mon œil rassasié examinait toutes ces richesses, il se posa sur une stèle noircie par le temps, pierre tombale de quelque vieux puritain. La tombe s'était fissurée sous la poussée de la terre qui avait dressé la dalle en un angle bizarre. Le nom en était désormais illisible, mais l'on distinguait encore le visage du mort gravé dans la pierre, le sourire immonde de la bouche sans lèvres, et les mots suivants : « Homme, souviens-toi, tu es poussière, et tu retourneras à la poussière. » Alors je découvris la réponse à la question qui m'avait tourmenté quand je me tenais sur la Galerie de la Bourse. Où ces multitudes se dirigeaient-elles si joyeusement, vers quel but ?

« Ici, chuchotaient les tombes. Ici. »

2

Les ombres commençaient à s'allonger quand je ressortis dans la rue. Sans destination précise, perdu dans le tumulte de la cité, je m'en remis à mon instinct et choisis une direction au hasard. Remontant Broadway, je me surpris à suivre deux têtes menues couvertes de cheveux noirs qui émergeaient périodiquement de l'océan mouvant des passants, comme les oiseaux de mer que j'avais observés du pont du *Telemachos*. Ces têtes appartenaient à deux jeunes Chinois qui jouaient au football avec une boîte vide de Coca-Cola, couraient et se faufilaient adroitement dans la foule, troublaient de leurs zigzags exubérants, imprévisibles, le flot régulier de la circulation piétonne, et poussaient des cris d'oiseaux ravis qui contrastaient étrangement avec le vacarme général de l'avenue. Une fois, à cause d'un mauvais calcul, ils perdirent le contrôle de leur « ballon ». La boîte rouge et blanche s'immobilisa devant un homme d'affaires en costume bleu nuit à fines rayures qui marchait d'un pas rapide en portant un attaché-case en cuir. Brusquement distrait de ses pensées, il regarda l'objet avec curiosité, abandonna toute gravité et la renvoya aux gamins d'un coup de pied précis et fougueux, lui-même redevenant l'espace d'un instant un jeune adolescent. Ils n'eurent pas autant de chance la deuxième fois. Un homme en apparence pas radicalement différent du premier trouva sa progression pareillement entravée, examina la boîte vide avec férocité et l'écrasa rageusement du talon. Les garçons se figèrent au milieu de la rue pour regarder leur bourreau avec une expression désolée, comme s'il les avait eux-mêmes écrasés. Mais ils se reprirent vite et s'écrièrent : « *Fang pi*, espèce de trou du cul ! » L'homme se retourna et agita son poing avec colère. Les gamins excités autant qu'effrayés éclatèrent de rire et s'enfuirent dans la direction opposée en abandonnant sur le champ de bataille la dépouille dérisoire.

Je les suivis sans prendre la peine d'observer les avenues ou les rues traversées, et quelques minutes plus tard je remarquai que le quartier grouillait de Chinois. Comme par une métamorphose magique, j'étais à Chinatown ! Les costumes trois-pièces et autres attaché-cases, les visages blancs des Occidentaux, tous les signes du Dow disparurent, et tel un alevin rejeté à la mer par un pêcheur attendri, je retrouvai mon élément naturel, des scènes presque familières. Quelle surprise de voir tous ces bâtiments typiquement occidentaux — carrés, fonctionnels, utilitaires — animés de l'intérieur par le flux bigarré de la vie chinoise, ce chaos impénitent, foisonnant, haut en couleur ! J'entendais la rumeur de voix innombrables, dont la plupart s'exprimaient en cantonais (bien que le parlant avec hésitation, je le comprenais presque aussi bien que mon propre dialecte), les femmes marchandaient devant les étalages couverts de poissons, de ciboulette, de gingembre. Les enseignes de tous les bâtiments portaient des caractères chinois ; je souris de plaisir en passant devant une cabine téléphonique au toit incurvé en forme de pagode, comme un temple chinois. Des rangées d'épiceries bien achalandées et de boulangeries chinoises dénotaient une communauté prospère. Les vitrines regorgeaient d'articles qui auraient fait le bonheur de n'importe quel Chinois ; bouteilles de sauce à l'huître, de vinaigre de riz ou de sauce spéciale (« Nourriture pour gourmets ») fabriquées par la *Koon Chun Sauce Factory* de Hong Kong. Il y avait des flacons de sirop, des prunes, des dattes, des ananas, des poires « Nid d'Hirondelle », des jus d'arbouse et de grenadine ; de l'extrait de ginseng, de l'ambre couvert de sucre, des dattes de Pékin ; il y avait des sardines séchées, des seiches fumées ; des haricots noirs, des haricots pour la soupe de tortue ; des tortues vivantes dans une caisse ; de grandes jarres vernies remplies d'œufs de mille ans encore couverts de la boue où ils avaient baigné pendant deux mois seulement (le jaune avait viré au vert bouteille, le blanc à un bleu translucide) ; il y avait de la *Pearl River Bridge Double-Black Soy Sauce*, « recommandée à tous les foyers et restaurants pour la friture, la cuisine à la vapeur, les viandes braisées, afin de relever la soupe et les aliments cuits auxquels il suffit d'ajouter une goutte de cette sauce pour obtenir un plat délicieux » ; il y avait des mets luxueux — nid d'oiseau, aileron de requin, tête de canard, lèvres de poisson, chauve-souris (« Rat Céleste »), lézard, serpent ; il y avait de l'*Imported Girl Brand Florida Water*, sorte d'Aqua-Velva chinoise... bref, tout ce que le cœur pouvait désirer, ou l'argent acheter. Mais sur ce dernier point, je ne pus que maudire une fois encore ma pauvreté, et la mélancolie nuança désormais le plaisir de mon inventaire.

Alors que, vaguement découragé, je descendais une étroite ruelle et que mon estomac grondait, une porte battante s'ouvrit brusquement sous mon nez, laissant échapper une bouffée de vapeur épicée. Dans ce nuage savoureux, comme un petit *genius loci* jaune — authentique dieu des fourneaux —, un homme d'âge mûr vêtu d'une grande toque de chef, d'un tablier sale et d'un T-shirt sans manches taché de sueur, apparut devant moi, prêt à catapulter sur la voie publique et votre serviteur un seau plein d'ordures. Heureusement, il m'aperçut et se figea in extremis, m'épargnant ainsi une couche de saleté supplémentaire sur mes guenilles crasseuses. Le malheureux sembla mortifié d'avoir failli m'offenser. Il sourit et s'inclina, répétant sans arrêt en anglais : « Excusez je vous prie ! Excusez je vous prie ! » Bien que mince et assez petit, doté d'une expression timide où je ne vis pas tant le résultat de notre éducation qu'un trait permanent de sa personnalité, il y avait en lui quelque chose de gai et de chaleureux, surtout dans ses yeux dont l'un était cerné d'ecchymoses. Me rappelant le vieil adage chinois à propos d'« une rencontre inopinée dans la rue », je joignis les paumes de mes mains et m'inclinai très bas à la façon des prêtres.

« Honoré monsieur, je suis étranger ici, seul, sans ami ni personne pour me guider, commençai-je en me lançant dans une série de clichés laborieux auxquels me réduisait mon ignorance du cantonais. Si ma situation n'était pas aussi désespérée, je ne m'adresserais pas à vous, que je ne connais pas, je ne m'aventurerais pas à abuser de votre hospitalité. Pourtant, dans les circonstances présentes, j'espérais que vous pourriez me recommander un endroit peu coûteux où me loger et retrouver mes esprits, et peut-être me procurer un repas. »

Ma plaidoirie alambiquée le laissa bouche bée, comme si j'étais un spécimen tombé d'une autre planète, ou plus simplement le dernier représentant d'une époque révolue. Puis il domina sa surprise et sourit. « Vous êtes originaire du Szu-ch'uan, me répondit-il dans mon propre dialecte. Prêtre ? »

Je m'inclinai de nouveau pour acquiescer. « Taoïste, précisai-je afin d'éviter tout malentendu.

— Ah, dit-il. Un homme éduqué. Je suis honoré.

— L'honneur est pour moi, répliquai-je.

— Non, non, protesta-t-il.

— Si, si, insistai-je.

— En tout cas, cette rencontre est inespérée, dit-il. Le destin l'a voulu ainsi. Car nous sommes de la même province. Bien que j'habite ici depuis de nombreuses années, moi aussi je suis né au Pays Céleste. Près de Cheng-tu. »

Après tous les bouleversements de la journée, la pensée du pays natal me fit monter les larmes aux yeux. Troublé, je m'inclinai profondément une fois encore en cachant mon visage. Mon interlocuteur fit preuve de tact et d'indulgence, me laissa le temps de retrouver le contrôle de moi-même avant de poursuivre.

« Vous êtes arrivé récemment ?

— Est-ce tellement évident ? » demandai-je en reniflant et m'essuyant les yeux.

Il sourit avec bienveillance en hochant la tête.

« Aujourd'hui même », dis-je.

Il haussa les sourcils.

Un filet de fumée filtra alors par la porte. Le cuisinier huma l'air, puis écarquilla les yeux comme s'il pressentait une catastrophe.

« Excusez je vous prie ! » s'écria-t-il en retournant à l'anglais dans sa confusion, et il fila ventre à terre vers ses fourneaux. Il repassa brièvement la tête par la porte battante pour me dire : « Attendez ici. »

J'entendis des cris de récrimination et d'excuse dans un szu-ch'uanais rapide, haletant, puis un grand sifflement de vapeur, comme un fer chauffé au rouge plongé dans un bac d'eau froide. Une rafale d'ordres suivirent.

La porte s'ouvrit enfin. A ma grande surprise, ce ne fut pas mon nouvel ami qui apparut, mais un garçon de mon âge, vêtu comme le chef hormis la toque, et dont les traits exprimaient le dépit et la culpabilité, comme s'il venait de se faire houspiller et qu'il le méritait. Il passa la tête et m'adressa un regard morne.

« Maintenant il est occupé, dit-il. Il m'a demandé de vous donner ceci. »

Par la porte, il me tendit une serviette en papier qui contenait du *dim sum* brûlant dont la graisse avait par endroits transpercé la cellulose.

« Et ceci », ajouta-t-il en me donnant un morceau de papier. Puis il disparut derrière la porte ballante qui pivota sous mon nez quand je m'avançai pour protester et le rappeler.

Je poussai un soupir et baissai les yeux vers les mots griffonnés en caractères rapides et mal formés sur un ticket vert de serveur :

Pour le jeune dragon affamé
Qui est sorti de la brume
Et que nous avons rencontré devant cette porte,
Acceptez ceci, s'il vous plaît.
                                    Ha-p'i Lo
P.S. Pour le logement adressez-vous à
Mme Chin, 17 Mulberry Street.

Je fus touché par les efforts de cet homme pauvre et manifestement peu éduqué pour improviser des vers à la manière des anciens ivrognes taoïstes, Li Po et les Sept Sages du Bosquet de Bambou. Je voulus le remercier, mais craignis de le déranger encore. Je fourrai dans ma bouche l'un de ses beignets croustillants et brûlants, mordis la pâte frite et atteignis le cœur onctueux en me jurant de revenir le remercier, puis je repartis de bien meilleure humeur et me mis en quête de l'adresse indiquée.

Après avoir arrêté plusieurs personnes dans la rue pour les interroger, je trouvai ce que je cherchais. De la rue, j'observai le bâtiment avant d'y entrer. On eût dit un tombeau, tant ses briques étaient noires de suie. L'immeuble, qui donnait de la bande, paraissait dans un état de décomposition organique avancée et s'effondrait de l'intérieur comme un vieil invalide dont les os s'effritent. Le seul élément à peu près convaincant du bâtiment était l'escalier d'incendie, une lourde armature en fer datant de Mathusalem et couverte d'innombrables couches de peinture rouge vif censées créer une illusion de sécurité. Une faible ampoule jaunâtre brillait dans le vestibule au sol carrelé d'un damier noir et blanc disposé en tourbillon géométrique. Au-delà, à travers le panneau de verre biseauté de la porte, j'aperçus un étroit escalier qui montait brusquement vers une région enténébrée.

Je poussai sur la porte en déglutissant avec difficulté. J'avoue que je fus presque soulagé de la trouver verrouillée. J'allais tenter ma chance ailleurs quand je remarquai un bouton lumineux orange sur le chambranle. Approchant mon visage, j'avisai une plaque au-dessus du bouton : « Appuyez pour entrer. »

J'hésitai, puis enfonçai courageusement le bouton en redoutant quelque surprise désagréable. Rien ne se produisit. Tel un chiot curieux poussant de la patte une tortue sur la route, je m'enhardis et appuyai de plus en plus fort. À la troisième tentative, je faillis ricaner ; mais le piaulement nasillard qui sortit du mur m'envoya valser au bas des marches, la queue entre les jambes.

Secoué, je remontai timidement le perron en tenant la rambarde. La porte était ouverte. Sur la pointe des pieds je traversai une entrée obscure. A droite et à gauche, des verrous cliquetèrent, des portes s'entrebâillèrent tandis qu'on laissait les chaînes en place. Des yeux sombres examinèrent le couloir par les minces fentes. Je m'approchai d'une porte pour demander mon chemin, mais elle claqua aussitôt sous mon nez, puis j'entendis un fracas de chaînes et de verrous. Au bout du couloir, sous une autre ampoule jaunâtre, je découvris une porte blindée munie d'un étrange bouton de verre à facettes. Un panneau défraîchi rédigé en anglais et chinois était fixé sur sa partie supérieure par quatre clous de cuivre terni. L'impression et la calligraphie dénotaient un travail de professionnel, mais exécuté en un style vieillot, précieux. L'ensemble était entouré d'une frise d'étoiles et de croissants de lune :

MME CHIN
GÉRANTE & OCCULTISTE
DIPLÔMÉE DE L'UNIVERSITÉ

CARTOMANCIENNE :
Consultations de *Yi king*
Radiesthésie
Chiromancie
Feng-shui
Phrénologie
Aruspice
& etc.
Service à la demande

MÉDECINE DOUCE
CHIROPRAXIE
CONSEIL CONJUGAL
POTIONS D'AMOUR
HOMÉOPATHIE
(extraction de dents)
CHAMBRES A LOUER   MONT-DE-PIÉTÉ
LA MAISON NE FAIT PAS DE CRÉDIT ! ! !
Renseignez-vous à l'intérieur

Courageusement, j'appuyai sur la sonnette. Au bout d'un moment j'entendis un meuble pesant qu'on faisait glisser sur le plancher, puis des pas pressés. On ouvrit le verrou. La porte s'entrebâilla.

« Qui est-ce ? » demanda en chinois une voix stridente qui évoquait un hermaphrodite pointilleux quant à sa diction, suffisant, efféminé à défaut d'être féminin.

« On m'a dit que je pourrais peut-être trouver une chambre à louer, répondis-je.

— Aiyi ! Tantine ! Il y a quelqu'un qui veut te voir », appela-t-il par-dessus son épaule.

J'entendis japper et gratter au bas de la porte.

« Couché ! » siffla le jeune homme. Un autre jappement s'ensuivit, puis un bruit de pattes paniquées, comme un patineur qui tente de retrouver son équilibre sur la glace, ou de petites griffes qui se plantent dans un plancher de bois. « Odieux animal !

— Attendez ici », m'intima-t-on d'une voix péremptoire. La porte claqua devant mon visage. Je fis le pied de grue pendant plusieurs minutes avant d'entendre la chaîne de sécurité qu'on retirait. « Entrez », m'ordonna-t-on. La lourde porte pivota sur ses gonds.

Je découvris un jeune homme à la pâleur extraordinaire — hormis deux taches colorées sur les pommettes — et aux lèvres si rouges que je suspectai un maquillage. Il était vêtu avec une élégance théâtrale, quoique vieillotte, une excentricité pesante : une veste de lin blanche aux épaules rembourrées ; une fleur noire en daim, un chrysanthème, piquée à son revers ; un foulard de soie jaune — trèfles à quatre feuilles bleu nuit agrémentés de pois rouge sang ; des bretelles ; un pantalon à pli ; des bottines noires en cuir souple qui se fermaient à l'intérieur de la cheville. Ses cheveux noirs de jais étaient tirés en arrière et couverts de gomina. Son parfum me rappela l'odeur du clou de girofle. Il me dévisagea avec une expression dédaigneuse qui frisait l'hostilité. Ses superbes yeux sombres étaient brillants et magnétiques comme ceux d'un serpent, pleins d'une exquise sensibilité et d'une haine tout aussi exquise.

Se retournant, il écarta cérémonieusement le pan d'une lourde draperie, une soie damassée bleu-verdâtre aux bords décorés de glands qui pendait du linteau d'une double porte. Il la poussa de son bras, sourit avec une courtoisie hypocrite, puis d'un signe de tête presque imperceptible m'invita à franchir la tenture. Je le frôlai d'assez près pour sentir son haleine chaude sur mon oreille, et entrai. La draperie retomba derrière moi. Ses pas s'éloignèrent. Une porte s'ouvrit, se referma. On me laissait seul.

Tous les rideaux étaient tirés. Autour de l'un d'eux, comme un rectangle découpé dans du papier noir, un mince liséré de lumière filtrait par la fenêtre, si brillant qu'il en devenait incolore. Hormis cela, l'éclairage était entièrement artificiel : un lampadaire en cuivre dont l'abat-jour de soie blanche avait pris la teinte du vieux parchemin ; un bougeoir d'argent terni posé au centre d'un mandala de dentelle sur un lourd buffet de sombre acajou sculpté (la flamme blanche et dorée flottait dans la cire comme une lune gibbeuse sur l'eau). Une senteur âcre imprégnait l'air, une douceur équivoque et particulière, comme de fleurs sauvages mêlées de crottin. Brusquement saisi de nausées, je m'effondrai dans un fauteuil.

La pièce était remplie d'un lourd mobilier sombre, où l'on remarquait surtout une armoire fermée, une ottomane recouverte de velours lie-de-vin et un fauteuil d'amour dont chaque pied griffu enserrait une boule de bois. Il y avait des tissus partout — des mètres de chintz ancien cachaient les tables, des tapisseries décoraient les murs. Une *tanka* tibétaine représentait le labyrinthe d'un mandala circulaire — une gigantesque toile au centre de laquelle un dieu noir attendait avec des yeux déments injectés de sang, mille bras et le plus subtil des sourires. Il portait au front une tiare faite d'un croissant de lune, ou bien de cornes. Mais il y avait surtout une multitude de nappes et napperons, écharpes décoratives et têtières en fine dentelle jaunissante qui enveloppaient toutes choses comme une toile d'araignée. Et vraiment, la pièce ressemblait à l'antre d'une araignée décrépite, où les innombrables bibelots et objets — poupées thaï, le Pa Hsien ou les Huit Immortels, confections françaises en vertugadin, perroquets de porcelaine peinte — étaient comme des dépouilles d'insectes suspendues dans la toile, fragments anéantis de vie ailée, bourdonnante, qui attendaient le retour de l'araignée.

Alors que je sombrais en me débattant dans cette imagerie répugnante, je fus ramené à la réalité par l'horrible sensation d'une pression froide et humide contre ma jambe. Je bondis sur mes pieds comme un chat hors de l'eau. Quand je me retournai, mon cœur battait la chamade. Cherchant mon souffle, prêt à défendre ma vie le cas échéant, je scrutai le plancher obscur sous le meuble en m'attendant à découvrir une créature rampante, semi-végétale, qui en voulait à ma vie.

Au lieu de quoi j'aperçus un chiot tout blanc à l'exception de deux oreilles noires et souples, quatre pattes solides, et un museau humide et granuleux — celui-là même qui m'avait donné cette sensation désagréable. Assis sur son arrière-train, il dodelinait de la tête et dressait à demi ses oreilles en me regardant d'un air perplexe. Sans raison apparente, il se mit à geindre en remuant sa queue, laquelle frappa le sol avec la régularité d'un métronome.

« Viens ici, *mon trésor !* » m'écriai-je en imitant Scottie malgré moi, tant mon soulagement était grand. Je m'accroupis, frappai dans mes mains, essayai même de siffler — *Ffuuit ! Ffuuit !* — mais sans résultat.

Le chien, qui semblait aussi désemparé et désorienté que moi, me pardonna ma gaucherie. Il se dressa tant bien que mal sur ses pattes flageolantes et s'approcha de moi d'un air pataud. Notre rencontre fut mémorable et fort agréable. Je le caressai ; il battit de la queue — nos manifestations de tendresse se renforçant mutuellement. Léchant ma main et la trouvant apparemment à son goût, il alla jusqu'à la mordre vigoureusement, familiarités auxquelles je dus mettre un terme, non que je les trouvasse déplacées, mais parce que ses dents minuscules, bien qu'à peine sorties des gencives, piquaient ma peau comme autant d'aiguilles.

Alors que je me pliais de bon cœur à ce jeu innocent, je remarquai un mouvement à la périphérie de mon champ visuel. Une ombre passa devant la bougie. Quelque chose se crispa en moi. Quand je levai les yeux, je vis un être vêtu de noir : une vieille femme debout dans l'ombre, qui observait. J'ignorais depuis combien de temps elle était là. Je ne l'avais pas entendue entrer. Elle portait le chong-sam traditionnel de soie noire, sans la moindre broderie mais de la meilleure qualité, avec un motif de svastikas. Une petite broche, un croissant de lune argenté incrusté de nacre, était piquée sur sa poitrine vaste et généreuse, impressionnante chez une femme de son âge, tout comme sa taille, qu'elle avait conservée menue — ruines d'une femme qui avait peut-être été séduisante. A côté du bijou, un lourd anneau de clefs était suspendu entre ses seins par un fil de nylon transparent. Elle le caressait pensivement en m'observant, et le mouvement de ses doigts produisait un faible cliquetis mécanique, comme les perles d'un boulier ou la navette d'un métier à tisser. Ses doigts déformés par l'arthrose exhibaient des bagues enchâssées de pierres semi-précieuses : pierre de lune, topaze, lapis, perle, cornaline, et une grosse émeraude.

Elle s'avança dans le halo de la bougie où je pus enfin distinguer ses traits. Son visage jaune, aussi ridé qu'une vieille garniture de cuir, pendait sur ses os en vagues liquides. Ses cheveux, qu'elle avait remontés en un chignon négligé, étaient aussi rêches que du crin de cheval, presque uniformément gris, bien qu'encore striés de quelques fils noirs. Mais le plus remarquable était les yeux, deux fentes étroites dépourvues de cils. L'étincelle d'un feu pâle y brillait encore comme une luciole, souvenir de quelque lointaine nuit d'été préservé dans l'ambre sombre de la chassie. Le blanc de l'œil n'était pas blanc, mais couleur ivoire, terni par le temps.

Pendant que je la regardais, elle pencha légèrement la tête vers son épaule gauche, geste presque timide par lequel elle reconnaissait ma présence ; puis elle sourit d'un air écœurant : ses yeux disparurent dans les replis de la chair molle, ses lèvres se retroussèrent sur des dents tachées, gâtées, et une couronne en or.

« Je suis Mme Chin, dit-elle.

— Et moi Sun I, répliquai-je d'une voix mal assurée.

— Sun I... hmmm..., murmura-t-elle. Un nom inhabituel...

— Je viens pour une chambre, dis-je rapidement, afin d'éviter toute intimité avec cette créature.

— Il y en a une de libre.

— Combien ? »

Elle sourit. « Chaque chose en son temps. Nous devons d'abord faire connaissance. Votre patronyme ?

— Je suis prêtre.

— Ah. Vous avez donc grandi dans un monastère. » Son regard me jaugea. « Je m'en serais doutée. »

Je lui lançai un coup d'œil acéré. « Comment cela ?

— Quelque chose dans votre visage — les yeux, je crois. » Elle sourit.

Je rougis en changeant de position. Très mal à l'aise, comme si elle connaissait, ou pouvait facilement deviner mes secrets les plus intimes, je tentai une retraite discrète, quitte à me déprécier. « Je crains de vous faire perdre votre temps, Mme Chin. J'ai lu sur votre porte que vous ne faisiez pas de crédit. »

Elle battit des paupières. « Pas de crédit. Et alors ?

— Eh bien, je dois être franc avec vous. Je n'ai pas d'argent pour l'instant. Je comptais sur votre patience jusqu'à ce que j'aie trouvé du travail.

— Ne nous laissons pas arrêter par cette broutille, répliqua-t-elle avec une amabilité surprenante. Nous devons d'abord parler avant de nous engager. Qui sait, vous possédez peut-être une chose aussi précieuse que l'argent... plus précieuse peut-être. Je sais que vous avez un faible pour les animaux, observa-t-elle en changeant de sujet. Trait admirable, et ô combien révélateur.

— Qui résisterait à ces yeux ? » répliquai-je en levant le menton du chiot pour les examiner. J'ébouriffai ses oreilles. « J'aimerais en avoir un comme celui-ci. Où l'avez-vous trouvé ?

— Nous les choisissons à la fourrière », dit-elle.

Je le retournai sur le dos, grattai son ventre. « Comment s'appelle-t-il ?

— Son nom ? » Elle rit. « Oh, nous les gardons rarement assez longtemps pour leur donner un nom. »

Étonné, je levai les yeux. « Il y en a d'autres ?

— Il y en avait. »

Je croisai son regard, qui ne m'apprit rien.

« Fan-ku ! cria-t-elle brusquement en tournant la tête. Fan-ku ! Cesse donc d'écouter derrière la tenture et viens chercher cet animal. »

Le jeune homme entra ; ses joues étaient cramoisies de honte sous la poudre, mais il réussit à conserver un sang-froid absolu.

« Tu as appelé, Aiyi ? demanda-t-il en feignant l'indifférence.

— Où étais-tu ?

— Dans la chambre, répondit-il froidement.

— En train de vernir tes ongles de pied, je suppose, insinua-t-elle, bien que rayonnant de fierté devant le jeune homme. Ou de te caresser ? »

Les yeux de Fan-ku s'assombrirent comme du velours frotté à rebrousse-poil, mais il ne mordit pas à l'hameçon.

Mme Chin se renfrogna. « Emporte ce chien », dit-elle d'un ton cassant.

Il me foudroya du regard, puis saisit brusquement le chiot par la peau du cou.

« Ar-r-r ! fit l'animal.

— La ferme ! siffla l'autre en l'étouffant à moitié tandis qu'il s'éloignait vers la porte.

— Attends ! » dit-elle.

Très lentement, avec un plaisir pervers, elle contourna l'ottomane pour aller s'asseoir dans le fauteuil d'amour. Quand elle fut installée, elle leva les yeux vers le jeune homme avec le même sourire immonde qu'elle m'avait adressé, mais rehaussé d'une expression de cruauté affamée. Elle leva légèrement le menton et dit d'une voix mielleuse : « Embrasse Aiyi avant de partir. » Sans le regarder, elle sourit dans le vide, figée dans une attente suffisante.

Fan-ku se raidit ; ses épaules tremblèrent, ses yeux s'écarquillèrent légèrement, le blanc devint visible tout autour de l'iris. Lentement, comme hypnotisé, il s'avança vers elle. L'espace d'un instant, il regarda haineusement la joue offerte. Je redoutai une issue violente à l'épreuve de force déclenchée par Mme Chin. Mais Fan-ku finit par se pencher pour embrasser la chair flasque, après quoi il fit volte-face et sortit en trombe de la pièce.

Comme une statue miraculeusement animée par ce baiser, Mme Chin s'épanouit après ce témoignage de servilité. Elle m'observa avec une expression pleine de ruse et de défi que je trouvai parfaitement insondable et ne désirai surtout pas approfondir. « Quel joli garçon, dit-elle, et tellement fier... »

A défaut d'autre chose, j'optai pour la platitude : « Votre neveu habite avec vous ?

— Neveu ? » Elle me regarda d'un air étonné, comme si elle ne comprenait pas ma question. Puis elle sourit. « Vous vous méprenez, Sun I — "tantine" n'est qu'un gage de son affection. Nous ne sommes pas parents... » Elle baissa la voix « ... bien que cette perspective serait loin

de lui déplaire. Je suis veuve, voyez-vous, je l'ai été plusieurs fois. » Elle badinait. « Je m'habille en noir en signe de deuil perpétuel. » Lascivement, elle fit glisser sa main sur son sein droit jusqu'à la hanche. « Je n'ai pas d'enfants, pas de famille — sinon moi-même.
— Excusez-moi », dis-je.
Elle rit. « Vos excuses sont superflues. M'occuper de moi me suffit amplement ; je n'ai pas besoin d'autrui. Je peux vous assurer que je ne m'ennuie pas une seconde. »
Décontenancé par le ton enjoué de sa voix, je restai silencieux et m'interrogeai sur la nature exacte de leurs rapports.
« Tss, tss, siffla-t-elle en souriant, comme si elle devinait mes pensées. Tu es très innocent, Sun I. » Levant sa main fermée, elle remua un doigt crochu pour me faire signe d'approcher. « Viens ici. »
Je m'installai de l'autre côté de la table, dont je serrai le plateau comme une ancre qui m'éviterait de dériver vers des eaux plus dangereuses.
« Plus près », murmura-t-elle.
Incapable de résister, j'approchai, me penchai toujours davantage au-dessus d'elle, les yeux rivés à son visage avec une horreur fascinée, comme un lapin hypnotisé par un serpent.
« Tu vois, Sun I », chuchota-t-elle, son visage si près du mien que je sentis son haleine comme une toile d'araignée sur ma joue, respirai l'odeur ténue de la corruption, poussière et naphtaline mêlées en un parfum douceâtre, écœurant, « je suis une douairière ». Elle s'appesantit sur le mot avec une séduction menaçante.
« Vous êtes riche ? »
Quand elle sourit, sa dent en or brilla de façon obscène dans sa bouche. « Comme Crésus. »
Je repris contrôle de moi-même, reculai et me levai.
« Ne t'enfuis pas, mon joli, susurra-t-elle. Je ne vais pas te manger. Viens donc t'asseoir à côté de moi. Je vais te lire les lignes de la main.
— Je suis ici pour une chambre, répondis-je froidement. En tant que prêtre taoïste, je sais utiliser le *Yi king*. Je n'ai pas besoin de diseuse de bonne aventure.
— Fais plaisir à une vieille femme, me cajola-t-elle. Tu apprendras peut-être quelque chose que tu ignores. »
Je me dirigeai vers un fauteuil à contrecœur.
« Pas là-bas », dit-elle. Elle tapota le coussin de velours du fauteuil d'amour. « Ici. »
Quand je m'assis, elle escamota prestement le napperon de dentelle et découvrit une table octogonale en bois noir lustré. Au centre se trouvait l'Œuf du Chaos, et à chaque angle, incrustés de marqueterie d'ivoire, les huit trigrammes. Je faisais face à *Sun*.
Je fus d'abord étonné, désagréablement. Puis je songeai qu'elle connaissait mon nom et avait peut-être fait pivoter la table. D'autre part, une coïncidence n'était pas à exclure. Je fouillai son visage à la recherche d'un indice. Son sourire ne m'apprit rien. Mais je remarquai que la douairière, ainsi qu'elle s'était elle-même appelée, était assise devant les trois lignes brisées de *K'un*, le trigramme de la Terre ou de la Mère.

Prenant ma paume entre ses mains froides et moites, elle l'examina attentivement, comme si sa surface était transparente, un bassin opaque dont elle tentait de sonder le fond.

« "Sun I", chuchota-t-elle. Dans ton nom, le Gain et la Perte sont mêlés. Sur ta paume également. » Elle scruta mon visage.

Je me tortillais nerveusement sur le fauteuil. « Que voulez-vous dire ?

— Tu es arrivé ici récemment », poursuivit-elle en ignorant ma question. Puis elle baissa de nouveau les yeux. « Après un long voyage où tu as pris beaucoup de risques. Des sacrifices personnels ont été faits...

— Des mois de dur labeur en mer ont rendu mes mains calleuses, concédai-je. Inutile d'être chiromancienne pour me dire cela. »

Elle me regarda. Un savoir fatal luisait au fond de ses yeux ; indubitable et millénaire, il me fit douter des intentions de Mme Chin, que jusque-là je croyais mauvaises. Elle ignora l'affront implicite et poursuivit : « Des sacrifices personnels ont été faits... mais ils ne sont rien comparés à ce qui va suivre. » Son sourire était presque satisfait. « Tu es venu ici pour chercher quelque chose, je me trompe ?

— Peut-être, répondis-je, mais aucun don n'est nécessaire pour deviner cela. Pourquoi donc aurais-je entrepris un voyage aussi difficile ?

— Quelque chose ou *quelqu'un* », précisa-t-elle avec un sourire énigmatique mais triomphant.

Au fond de moi-même une porte s'ouvrit, un courant d'air froid hérissa les poils de mes bras. « Exact, concédai-je calmement. Mais qui ? Ou quoi ?

— Difficile à dire, répondit-elle avec une moue crispée. Ta paume est très inhabituelle. Vois comme la ligne du destin est nettement marquée pendant un certain nombre d'années, puis se divise en deux lignes, l'une obliquant vers le haut, l'autre vers le bas. Cela signifie une nature divisée ; une part de toi-même aspire au royaume de l'esprit, l'autre est attirée vers le bas, vers le monde matériel. Ta quête comme ton nom est ambiguë — le Gain et la Perte, la matière et l'esprit. Je peux seulement te dire que tu es venu chercher les deux univers, mais que tu trouveras seulement l'un d'eux. Car le prix de l'un est la perte de l'autre.

— Je trouve tout cela un peu vague, Mme Chin, dis-je en reprenant confiance. Cela pourrait s'appliquer à n'importe qui.

— Je vais donc être plus précise, dit-elle. Tu es venu chercher quelqu'un, mais tu ne trouveras qu'une idée ou une croyance ; ou alors, cherchant une idée, tu ne trouveras que la personne... seulement *l'homme*. Car c'est bien d'un homme qu'il s'agit, n'est-ce pas ? »

L'effet de surprise dû à sa spécification du genre fut émoussé par sa question, que j'interprétai comme un doute. « Est-ce vraiment à *moi* de vous le dire ? répliquai-je avec une ironie joyeuse. N'est-ce pas aussi écrit sur ma paume ? »

Elle croisa mon regard et se tut.

« Tout cela est bien énigmatique, Mme Chin, continuai-je. Vos prédictions me dépassent peut-être, mais je dois vous avouer qu'elles ne m'ont rien appris. »

Elle haussa les épaules. Ses yeux s'éteignirent. « Que souhaites-tu entendre ? Si tu me résistes, je ne peux rien t'apprendre. » Sa voix maintenant mécanique semblait se parodier elle-même. « Tu deviendras très riche. Tu tomberas amoureux.

— Ne vous moquez pas de moi, Mme Chin », dis-je.

Je vis alors sur son visage quelque chose que je croyais connaître. « La vie est faite de semblables banalités, rétorqua-t-elle. Elle n'en est pas moins terrible ou mystérieuse. »

L'âge et une immense lassitude — voilà ce que je reconnaissais sur ses traits, dans ses paroles, ainsi qu'une amertume profondément ancrée qui croissait chaque année comme le cancer se nourrit des cellules saines de l'organisme avant d'usurper finalement toutes les facultés de la vie. Il ne restait plus que cela, une énorme tumeur maligne et incurable qui se nourrissait d'elle-même. Sa vie s'était réduite à une seule fonction : ressentir de la douleur, et sa contrepartie vicieuse — en infliger à autrui. Telle était la souffrance secrète de l'araignée ; et le soulagement était devenu synonyme de mort, la sienne propre ou celle de la mouche. Je vis tout cela sur le visage de Mme Chin, que malgré ma répulsion je trouvai poignant. J'eus pitié d'elle. Ce fut ma première erreur.

« Continuez, s'il vous plaît, dis-je calmement en lui tendant ma main que j'avais fermée.

— Non, siffla-t-elle en la repoussant avec irritation. Vous avez détruit ma concentration. » Elle se leva, puis traversa la pièce.

Son ton offensé fit son effet. « S'il vous plaît, Mme Chin, insistai-je, persuadé qu'elle n'attendait que mes prières pour changer d'avis.

— Je vous ai donné tous ces conseils gratuitement, répliqua-t-elle. Si vous voulez en savoir plus, vous devez payer.

— Avec quoi ? demandai-je. Je vous ai déjà dit que je n'avais pas d'argent. »

Pressentant ma capitulation imminente, elle feignit de « remarquer » mon barda posé sur l'ottomane. « Et moi, je vous ai déjà dit que vous possédiez peut-être quelque chose d'aussi intéressant que l'argent. » Du menton elle désigna mon sac. « Qu'y a-t-il là-dedans ?

— Seulement des effets personnels, répondis-je. Rien qui puisse vous intéresser. Regardez de nouveau ma paume, s'il vous plaît. »

Elle contourna l'ottomane. « J'ai vu tout ce que j'avais à voir sur ta paume. Les objets personnels en apprennent parfois autant. » Avec un sourire gourmand, elle saisit la cordelette de mon sac entre le pouce et l'index. « Puis-je ? »

Pris d'une vague nausée, j'hésitai stupidement ; elle en profita pour continuer.

« Mme Chin !

— Ne t'inquiète pas, dit-elle d'une voix rassurante. Tu peux me faire confiance. »

Je me sentis paralysé, livré pieds et poings liés à son effronterie.

« Fan-ku ! appela-t-elle. Apporte-moi mes lunettes ! »

Presque avant qu'elle n'eût fini de parler, il entra avec les lunettes.

« Tu écoutais encore, mon chéri ? » interrogea-t-elle cauteleusement en les mettant.

Cette fois, lui aussi sourit. Il se campa derrière le fauteuil de sa « tante », puis, tel un oiseau de proie, fixa mon sac avec une patience tendue, affamée.

Impuissant, je regardais Mme Chin passer au peigne fin mes possessions les plus intimes avec une gloutonnerie raffinée. Je compris alors pourquoi l'insecte tombe dans les rets de l'araignée. Ce n'est ni stupidité ni erreur de sa part, et pas davantage la fourberie de l'araignée. Seulement, elle l'appâte d'une vérité — elle lui permet d'entrevoir brièvement sa solitude secrète, le rituel stérile d'une existence qu'elle est condamnée à mener éternellement et sans joie — alors, croyant adoucir cette souffrance, l'insecte se prend dans la toile, puis est dévoré.

Le pillage méthodique s'interrompit brutalement. Elle sortit du sac la photo de mon père, l'approcha de la bougie, cambra les reins en fronçant les sourcils, puis poussa ses lunettes vers la pointe de son nez.

Une excitation malsaine fit frémir mon ventre.

« Voici l'homme que tu es venu chercher, dit-elle sans me regarder.

— Vous le connaissez ? » demandai-je en m'avançant sur le fauteuil d'amour, pris d'un soudain espoir.

Elle tint la photo au-dessus de son épaule pour que Fan-ku l'examine, puis elle croisa mon regard. « Comment s'appelle-t-il ?

— Eddie Love, répondis-je d'une voix tremblante qui trahissait mon émotion.

— Ton père ? » demanda-t-elle en guettant ma réaction.

Je ne dis rien.

« Un Américain..., réfléchit-elle. Maintenant je commence à comprendre.

— Mais le connaissez-vous ? »

Son air mystérieux qui m'avait tant fait espérer s'évanouit, remplacé par un sourire figé.

« Malheureusement non, répondit-elle. Il était soldat ? Quel bel homme avec cet uniforme ! Tu lui ressembles. Joli garçon...

— Réussirai-je à le trouver, Mme Chin ? » implorai-je, maintenant désireux de croire à ses dons extralucides, prêt à croire tout ce qui pourrait m'aider à retrouver mon père.

Elle m'observa attentivement par-dessus ses lunettes. « A ta place, dit-elle, je me demanderais plutôt si je désire vraiment le retrouver.

— Que voulez-vous dire ? » Sa réponse m'avait ébranlé.

« Je t'ai dit tout ce que tu as besoin de savoir. »

Nos regards s'affrontèrent, puis son attention se reporta vers le contenu de mon sac, d'où elle sortit la robe pliée en un rectangle de la taille d'un petit livre.

« Tiens-la en l'air », ordonna-t-elle à Fan-ku.

Saisissant délicatement deux angles du tissu, il le déroula d'un léger mouvement du poignet.

Mme Chin poussa un cri de surprise et porta la main à sa poitrine. Elle se mit à tripoter ses clefs machinalement. La pièce était totalement silencieuse à l'exception du léger tintement métallique, qu'on aurait pu prendre pour le bruit des pensées de Mme Chin.

« Tourne-la », intima-t-elle.

Avec l'élégance dédaigneuse d'un matador, Fan-ku lui présenta le panneau postérieur, le soleil, l'arbre stérile, le fruit, les deux bêtes gigantesques qui tourbillonnaient au-dessus du monde.

Moi aussi, je me laissai fasciner. Je la revoyais pour la première fois depuis un certain temps et réalisai que le souvenir photographique que j'en gardais avait pâli. Sa beauté me parut inédite, incommensurable avec celle que je me rappelais. J'avais mémorisé chaque nuance, chaque méandre du labyrinthe, presque chaque fil ; mais tous ces détails me stupéfièrent à nouveau. L'ensemble paraissait modifié, plus saisissant, purifié, comme si la robe avait subi une distillation supplémentaire et que ses qualités se fussent affinées au point de lui faire franchir le seuil magique qui sépare de l'immatériel, de la pure essence, de la pensée, de l'éther.

Mon incrédulité s'accrut encore quand je réussis à m'arracher à ce spectacle doux-amer. Mme Chin, assise au même endroit qu'auparavant, le visage impassible, les yeux rétrécis, ronronnant comme une chatte... pleurait. Deux larmes s'étaient arrêtées sur ses joues, deux petites gouttes de mercure scintillant qui cheminaient sur le désert parcheminé de son visage.

Je fus ému. « Mme Chin, dis-je, vous pleurez.

— Tu sembles surpris, fit-elle. Que penses-tu de moi ? Suis-je si vieille et hideuse que je n'aie pas le droit de verser une larme ? Quelle femme pourrait voir ceci sans pleurer ? »

Incapable de répondre, je restai silencieux.

« Fan-ku, apporte la pipe. » Elle se tourna vers moi. « Je n'ai jamais vu un travail de cette qualité. Pourtant, je collectionne — pour moi et d'autres. »

Il apporta un plateau avec une lampe, une soucoupe d'opium noir pâteux, une pipe au fourneau d'argent ciselé. Il détacha une boulette, qu'il modela entre ses doigts, puis la piqua au bout de l'aiguille et la tint dans la flamme.

« Veux-tu te joindre à nous ? » demanda-t-elle en me tendant la pipe pleine.

J'agitai la main pour refuser.

Nous restâmes silencieux pendant qu'ils fumaient ; deux fois ils remplirent le fourneau. Quand ils eurent terminé, Mme Chin se leva et traversa la pièce vers l'armoire. Louchant vers ses clefs, elle en choisit une, un minuscule rossignol, puis se pencha pour l'introduire dans la serrure. Elle se redressa et fit pivoter la porte du meuble. « Viens voir », dit-elle en m'invitant d'un lent geste du bras à la rejoindre.

A l'intérieur, je découvris d'innombrables trésors : soieries damassées, gazes, florentines, robes de toutes couleurs, allant des nuances les plus pâles de gris et de rose au noir et au rouge en passant par des pourpres profonds, des mauves et des indigo, un arc-en-ciel de teintures éclatantes, chacune étonnante et étrange, comme réalisée pour un unique vêtement.

« Ceci est japonais, dit-elle avec une fierté presque dédaigneuse en passant un ongle effilé sur un vêtement somptueux. Une célèbre courtisane de Tokyo l'a porté, à l'époque où la ville s'appelait Edo. » Sa voix s'égrenait selon un rythme incantatoire, comme si elle récitait de la poésie ou accomplissait un rituel qu'elle avait maintes fois célébré et maîtrisait parfaitement. Fan-ku nous avait rejoints sur la pointe des pieds et regardait à côté de moi. La passion morbide avait quitté son visage, qui semblait presque doux. Ses traits maquillés exprimaient la terreur naïve de l'enfant confronté à un festin attendu depuis si longtemps que ses rêves en ont fait une obsession magique, presque sainte.

« Ceci appartenait à l'abbé d'un monastère, poursuivait-elle en montrant un autre vêtement. On raconte qu'il le porta sur son lit de mort, et que la dernière nuit les moines épuisés qui le veillaient s'endormirent. Quand ils se réveillèrent le lendemain matin, le corps avait disparu et ils trouvèrent seulement ceci dans la literie. »

Elle toucha une troisième parure. « Celle-ci vient de la cour de Mandchourie. Elle fut portée par une jeune aristocrate, une favorite de l'Impératrice Douairière Tzu Hsi. Malgré son rang, elle tomba amoureuse d'un domestique du palais, un garçon d'extraction plébéienne. Ils furent découverts. Lui fut exécuté à cause de sa prétention ; elle, enfermée pour l'empêcher de porter atteinte à ses jours. Mais elle refusa de boire et de manger, se suicida passivement. Remarque le phénix à l'œil affligé.

« Ce sont mes plus belles pièces, continua-t-elle. Mais aujourd'hui, en découvrant cela, j'ai perdu tout amour pour elles. »

La majesté qu'elle affichait m'impressionna, m'effraya presque. Pourtant je la vis disparaître brusquement. Ses traits se durcirent. « Je veux cette robe, me dit-elle en saisissant la broderie de ma mère. Dis-moi ton prix. »

Je me raidis, la toisai calmement. « Elle n'est pas à vendre.

— Allez, allez, coassa-t-elle en se ratatinant sous mes yeux. Je ne vais pas te voler. Je sais reconnaître la beauté. Chin paie au juste prix, et en dollars. J'ai des clients qui seraient prêts à tuer pour cela. » Elle sourit d'un air énigmatique. « Moi-même... ah ah ! Mais toute plaisanterie mise à part, que représente cette robe pour toi ? Tu es trop jeune pour l'apprécier. Je ne veux pas t'insulter, mais entre tes mains, elle est "comme un diamant dans un sac de riz". Et puis tu as la jeunesse pour toi. Tout t'est encore possible, alors que pour moi la palette des plaisirs se réduit d'heure en heure, se rétrécit comme la pupille de l'œil. La chose elle-même, la vie, est désormais trop éblouissante pour mes yeux fatigués. Je dois la contempler en sous-main, à petites doses médicinales, à travers ceci... ou cela. » Elle désigna d'abord la robe, puis Fan-ku. « Laisse-moi l'acheter au moins par charité. Je ne pinaillerai pas sur le prix.

— Elle appartenait à ma mère, Mme Chin, répondis-je. Certaines choses ne peuvent être achetées ni vendues.

— Tss, tss, tss, dit-elle. Laisse de côté les bons sentiments. Chaque chose a son prix pour qui sait attendre. Sinon aujourd'hui, alors demain. Tout est affaire de temps, de circonstances.

— Si cela est vrai, c'est une vérité mondaine. »

Elle eut un sourire cynique. « Tu en connais d'autres ?

— Je suis prêtre », dis-je.

D'un haussement d'épaules, elle balaya mon objection. « Et moi une vieille femme. »

Je secouai la tête en commençant de remballer mes affaires. « Je suis désolé, Mme Chin. Je crains de vous avoir fait perdre votre temps, et d'avoir perdu le mien par la même occasion.

— Et la chambre ? demanda-t-elle.

— Comme je vous l'ai dit, je n'ai pas d'argent.

— Et comme *moi* je te l'ai dit, tu possèdes peut-être quelque chose d'aussi intéressant. J'avais raison. » Son sourire immonde envahit de nouveau son visage ridé.

« Vous ne comptez pas échanger ceci contre une chambre ? lui demandai-je un peu cruellement.

— Non, non, fit-elle pour m'apaiser, bien sûr que non. Il suffirait que tu le laisses en dépôt. Je te le rendrai dès que tu pourras me payer. »

Je la regardai avec méfiance ; j'hésitais.

« Allez, allez, me cajola-t-elle, je fais une exception pour toi ; fais-en une pour moi. J'ai confiance en toi — aie confiance en moi. De toute façon, ajouta-t-elle, quel autre choix as-tu ? Il se fait tard. Où irais-tu ? Qui d'autre t'accepterait, alors que tu es sans le sou et que personne ne te connaît ? Ne sois pas stupide. Ravale ton orgueil et laisse-moi t'aider. »

Je l'observai en essayant de sonder ses intentions. Une lueur d'angoisse brillait dans ses yeux, comme chez l'araignée effarée qui voit la mouche se débattre contre le dernier fil qui la retient, presque libre...

« Viens, dit-elle, je t'emmène en haut. »

Et pour une raison que je ne saurais complètement expliquer, je me résolus à la suivre, ou plutôt je me laissai emmener.

« Je vous accompagne ? interrogea Fan-ku.

— Je traite une affaire, répliqua-t-elle sèchement. Reste ici. »

Elle retira les diverses chaînes, ouvrit les verrous puis la porte, et clopina dans le couloir. Je suivis sa silhouette voûtée.

L'ascension fut interminable. Elle montait marche par marche, posant son pied avec mille précautions, puis, agrippée à la rampe, ramenait laborieusement l'autre à côté du premier. J'avais pitié d'elle, mais elle refusa vigoureusement mon aide.

« Il y a un ascenseur, siffla-t-elle d'une voix asthmatique, mais il est provisoirement en panne. » Quand je vis la cage condamnée par des planches, je songeai qu'il était hors de service depuis longtemps, peut-être des années.

L'épreuve épuisante de l'escalier me fit comprendre pour la première fois de la journée à quel point j'étais fatigué. Quand nous atteignîmes le palier supérieur, je dormais à moitié.

« Voici le dernier étage », dit-elle enfin.

Je scrutai le couloir. « Où est la porte de ma chambre ?

— Pas ici, répondit-elle.

— Pas ici ?

— Non. Il y a encore un escalier qui mène au toit. Je t'offre la garçonnière.

— La garçonnière ? »

Elle fronça les sourcils. « Enfin, la cabane. »

Nous commençâmes la dernière étape de l'ascension. Au-dessus de la porte métallique cabossée qui ouvrait sur mon nouveau domaine, je vis une pancarte *Exit*.

« Nous y voilà », annonça-t-elle.

Elle choisit une clef autour de son cou, l'inséra dans la serrure, puis appuya sa vieille épaule décharnée contre la porte, et s'arc-bouta tel un marin. Je dus l'aider. La porte céda brusquement, nous précipitant, la douairière et moi, sur le toit. Une bande de pigeons stupéfaits s'envolèrent en roucoulant, comme une poignée de ternes confettis, puis se posèrent un peu plus loin. Le toit était couvert de gravillon étendu sur du bitume. Il crissa sous nos pieds quand nous nous dirigeâmes vers mon nouveau foyer, une petite cabane de guingois coincée entre un ciel d'encre et la cage d'ascenseur. Une kyrielle de conduits de cheminée coudés, asymétriques, surmontés d'étranges chapeaux, jaillissaient du toit à des angles incongrus. Je respirai les odeurs de cuisine d'une bonne douzaine de chambres ; des voix désincarnées montaient par la cage d'ascenseur : quelqu'un chantait, un bruit de vaisselle, une femme houspillait son mari, les vagissements d'un nouveau-né. L'immeuble en touchait plusieurs autres réunis autour d'un puits sombre qui tenait lieu de cour. Baissant les yeux, je distinguai des monceaux d'ordures, des assiettes brisées, des réfrigérateurs défoncés, des meubles en mille morceaux, des coussins tachés, éventrés — le royaume dérisoire du rebut. De l'autre côté, le fleuve ; le grand pont scintillait dans le ciel. Au-delà, Brooklyn.

« Belle vue, dis-je, charmé.

— Une vue magnifique ! » corrigea-t-elle.

D'autres pigeons s'envolèrent quand nous entrâmes dans la cabane. Le sol était couvert de leurs excréments.

« Ça a besoin d'un peu de nettoyage, reconnut-elle.

— Je ferai peut-être pousser des légumes, supputai-je.

— J'aime ta façon de voir les choses. En tout cas, c'est très clair et très aéré. » Elle fronça les sourcils en avisant une vitre brisée. « Il n'y a pas d'eau chaude, mais la plomberie est en bon état. Les toilettes sont là. » Elle me montra un infect WC à la turque à l'autre bout de la pièce. « Le matelas est compris dans la location. » Elle donna un léger coup de pied dans un rectangle de mousse posé à même le sol et couvert de guano.

« Combien ?

— Soixante-quinze dollars par semaine, répondit-elle en toussant dans sa main.

— *Combien ?* » redemandai-je, non parce que le loyer me semblait déraisonnable — que connaissais-je aux loyers ? —, mais parce que j'avais mal entendu.

« Disons cinquante. Mais pas un *cent* de moins.

— Ça me paraît correct. Je prends. »

Elle hocha la tête. « C'est une affaire. Tu seras bien ici. » Elle se retourna pour partir.

« Qu'est-ce que c'est que ça ? » Je montrai quelques effets épars dans un coin : une veste de blue-jean délavée sans manches, un morceau de tube noir, une seringue en plastique, la cellophane froissée d'un paquet de cigarettes qui contenait encore un léger résidu de poudre blanche, un morceau de miroir brisé, une lame de rasoir rouillée.

« Tout ça appartenait au précédent locataire », répondit-elle en se hâtant de réunir ces objets. Elle s'avança vers la cage d'ascenseur et fit mine de les jeter.

« Attendez ! dis-je. Et s'il veut les récupérer ?

— Je ne crois pas qu'il risque de revenir, dit-elle avec une ironie ambiguë. Enfin, comme tu voudras. » Un sourire sarcastique retroussa ses lèvres quand elle remit les objets en place. « Après tout, tu sauras peut-être quoi en faire. Voici tes clefs — j'avais oublié. Cette fois, au revoir. »

Je m'inclinai, prêt à me retirer.

« Sun I... » fit-elle.

Je me retournai.

La douairière affichait la même expression que lorsqu'elle avait demandé à Fan-ku de venir l'embrasser. Un instant, je craignis qu'elle me demandât la même chose.

« Viens me voir, dit-elle, souvent ! »

Je souris et fermai la porte.

« Quel joli garçon ! » l'entendis-je marmonner tandis que ses pas s'éloignaient sur le gravier.

3

Je brisai la croûte de guano avec un manche de balai cassé, la poussai sur la terrasse, puis disposai tendrement mes quelques biens dans la chambre. J'admirai une fois encore la vue, soupirai de satisfaction, retournai le matelas en mousse et sombrai aussitôt dans un sommeil voluptueux. Il devait être minuit ou presque quand je me réveillai (mon horloge biologique était encore réglée sur le rythme du bateau et celui des quarts). J'avais oublié où j'étais. En l'absence du bourdonnement apaisant des moteurs, de la bauge du navire caressé par les vagues languides des tropiques ou malmené par les déferlantes de la pointe de l'Afrique — le sifflement étouffé du vent de l'autre côté de la cloison, le bouillonnement et les éclaboussures des embruns —, je me sentis un instant désorienté. A la place de ces bruits familiers, presque rassurants, j'en découvris d'autres que je ne connaissais pas : le gloussement ridicule des pigeons roucoulants, le chuintement liquide des voitures dans les rues (qui n'était pas sans rappeler celui des vagues), les coups de klaxon intermittents, plus ou moins éloignés, le rire grêle et assourdi d'une femme dans la rue, quelqu'un jouant un vieux disque rayé de l'Opéra de Pékin — une femme chantait d'une voix stridente une mélodie qui parlait de dynasties oubliées et de la mort de l'amour. Ces sons étaient comme de minuscules bateaux en papier qui flottaient sur la mer immense du silence, le profond silence vibrant de la nuit où j'entendis pour la première fois l'accord fondamental de la cité, le murmure subliminal de tous les générateurs et condenseurs — conditionneurs d'air, réfrigérateurs, ventilateurs —, de toutes ces machines qui fonctionnaient sans bruit : et plus ténu encore, le métabolisme des habitants endormis, la combustion organique du sommeil, tout cela amalgamé dans cette vaste rumeur élémentaire.

J'écoutai les yeux fermés, jusqu'à ce que ce bruit me trouble, s'enfle en un rugissement auquel je ne pouvais échapper. Il évoquait une vie pour moi insituable. Brusquement, je m'éveillai complètement, tous les sens aux aguets. Je me levai et sortis. Contemplée du toit, la cité me sembla encore plus étrangère malgré sa beauté, une parente éloignée des immenses galaxies lointaines qui tourbillonnaient dans la nuit et dont Scottie m'avait parlé. Je décidai d'aller marcher pour calmer ma nervosité.

Quand j'arrivai dans le vestibule du rez-de-chaussée, une clef tourna dans la serrure de la porte de l'immeuble et quelqu'un entra. A ma grande surprise, c'était Ha-p'i, le chef cuisinier ; il portait encore son tablier sale noué à la taille, mais il avait mis une veste légère — beaucoup trop grande pour lui — et retiré sa toque blanche, changements vestimentaires qui le faisaient paraître encore plus frêle qu'auparavant.

« M. Ha-p'i ! » m'écriai-je.

Le son de ma voix le fit grimacer. Sans même regarder mon visage, il courba l'échine, rasa le mur en accélérant le pas.

« Attendez ! » Je posai la main sur son épaule.

Il tomba par terre en hurlant de terreur, se recroquevilla, cacha son visage entre ses mains. « S'il vous plaît ne me faites pas de mal, implora-t-il en un chuchotement frénétique, je sais que je suis en retard, mais j'ai eu des frais imprévus cette semaine. Je vous promets que cela ne se reproduira pas. Je vous donnerai tout ce que je vous dois vendredi.

— M. Ha-p'i, dis-je doucement pour essayer de le calmer. Vous faites erreur. Je suis le prêtre que vous avez rencontré cet après-midi, et si gentiment aidé. Vous vous rappelez ? »

Il écarta timidement les bras pour lever la tête, me regarda en louchant dans la lumière incertaine. Quand il me reconnut, le soulagement se peignit sur ses traits, aussitôt suivi d'un horrible dépit. « Oh merde, lâcha-t-il, le jeune dragon. »

Bondissant sur ses pieds, il se mit à s'incliner en s'excusant copieusement ; malgré la lumière fuligineuse du vestibule je vis qu'il rougissait. « Excusez, je vous prie ! Excusez, je vous prie ! s'écriait-il piteusement. Je vous ai confondu avec un autre. Maintenant vous savez tout. J'ai perdu la face pour de bon !

— Je ne comprends pas ce que vous dites, répondis-je pour soulager sa gêne. Je suis votre débiteur...

— Débiteur ! gémit-il.

— ... car vous m'avez fait rencontrer Mme Chin, et nous sommes parvenus à un accord pour une chambre. » Je m'inclinai profondément. « Vous êtes mon bienfaiteur.

— Non, non, objecta-t-il.

— Si, si », insistai-je.

Il se calma un peu. « Vous exagérez, dit-il en me retournant ma courbette, cette fois avec plus de dignité et de réserve. Je suis toujours heureux d'aider à ma façon insignifiante. » Il marqua un temps d'arrêt, puis ajouta avec un rien de terreur : « Vous avez trouvé l'appartement que vous cherchiez ? »

J'acquiesçai fièrement.

Comme il s'était relevé, je remarquai qu'il tenait un objet sous son bras, qu'il dissimulait tant bien que mal. Examinant la chose de plus près, je découvris une patte de poulet qui dépassait comiquement du papier journal. Quand il s'aperçut de mon intérêt, je sentis poindre chez lui une nouvelle crise de gêne.

« Et les beignets, me hâtai-je d'ajouter pour lui couper l'herbe sous le pied. Je n'en ai jamais mangé d'aussi bons depuis que j'ai quitté le Szu-ch'uan, et rarement au Pays Céleste ! »

Il rougit de plaisir et entama le pas de deux traditionnel de la modestie et de la dénégation. « Vous ne devez pas flatter un vieil idiot, dit-il. Il risquerait de vous croire.
— Je ne vous flatte pas, rétorquai-je.
— Si, vous me flattez, insista-t-il.
— Non, non.
— Si, si. »
Après quelques courbettes et protestations supplémentaires, l'équilibre fut suffisamment rétabli pour que nous puissions entamer une conversation digne de ce nom.
« Mme Chin m'a donné la garçonnière, l'informai-je fièrement.
— Garçonnière ?
— Sur le toit, expliquai-je.
— Ah, dit-il, la cabane. » Cette fois, je crois qu'il rougit de ma situation. Il se reprit aussitôt et ajouta : « Perchoir idéal pour un jeune dragon ! »
Sa remarque n'était pas dépourvue d'espièglerie, me sembla-t-il. Les rôles étaient inversés ; ce fut mon tour d'être gêné, même si j'ignorais pourquoi. Se montrait-il subtilement condescendant parce que je n'avais pas d'argent ? Mais je me repris rapidement en me souvenant que la Pauvreté était l'un de mes Trois Trésors.
Je m'obligeai à sourire. Nous dansions d'un pied sur l'autre sans savoir quoi nous dire ; je songeai brusquement qu'il rentrait à peine de son travail, qu'il avait été debout toute la journée. « Pardonnez-moi ! dis-je. Où ai-je la tête ? Vous devez être fatigué. Je ne veux pas vous retenir davantage.
— Excusez, répliqua-t-il. Je ne pourrai pas dormir tout de suite. Je suis trop nerveux. Si je ne savais pas mon hospitalité trop modeste pour un jeune homme cultivé comme vous, je vous inviterais volontiers à partager une petite coupe de vin avec moi avant de me retirer. »
Je sentis son invitation sincère et compris qu'un refus de ma part l'eût conforté dans son excessive modestie — j'acceptai donc. Derrière lui, je montai l'escalier jusqu'au troisième étage et le suivis au fond du couloir. Il glissa sa clef dans une serrure, puis se pencha vers moi pour chuchoter : « Nous ne devons pas faire de bruit. Ma femme et ma fille dorment. »
Nous entrâmes dans la cuisine sur la pointe des pieds et nous jetâmes tête baissée sur une corde à linge tendue à travers la pièce.
« Excusez je vous prie ! » dit Lo en repoussant chaussettes, mouchoirs, slips, soutien-gorge et caleçons. On avait laissé une veilleuse allumée au-dessus de l'évier, qui éclairait son émail blanc d'une propreté méticuleuse mais terne, peut-être entamé par des récurages trop fréquents et scrupuleux. Le sol aussi — un damier de linoléum rose et ivoire moucheté comme des œufs de pigeon — bien que luisant d'encaustique, paraissait usé par le zèle domestique. Tout était d'une nuance jaunâtre, comme si un nuage couleur d'urine devait stagner dans l'appartement tant que Lo y vivrait.
« Bienvenue dans la maison d'un pauvre homme, dit-il en détachant précipitamment la corde à linge.
— Je suis honoré, répondis-je en m'inclinant.
— Tout l'honneur est pour moi.
— Non, non.

— Si, si. »

Il m'invita à m'asseoir devant une table de métal installée contre un mur ; sa surface était un tourbillon brillant de Formica gris perle ceint d'une bande d'aluminium ; les pieds, des tubes creux de la même substance, reposaient sur des cales de caoutchouc noir. Trois chaises assorties à la table et tendues de tissu rouge entouraient celle-ci ; une quatrième était repoussée dans l'espace exigu qui séparait le réfrigérateur du mur. L'ensemble donnait une impression agréable de capharnaüm ordonné.

Bien que cette cuisine ressemblât peu à celle où j'avais grandi à Ken Kuan, les odeurs que j'y perçus — l'arôme fumé de l'huile de sésame, le gingembre piquant, l'ail, le chou froid et son parfum amer, presque fruste — déclenchèrent un délicieux flot de nostalgie. Des chapelets de piments pendaient du plafond, ficelés comme Wu m'avait appris à le faire !

« Ah, ces odeurs ! m'exclamai-je en reniflant l'air. C'est comme si je rentrais chez moi.

— Considérez que vous êtes ici chez vous ! » Ha-p'i tourna vers moi un visage rayonnant. « Vous avez l'instinct d'un cuisinier », dit-il en se tapotant le nez.

Je ris. « Rien d'étonnant ! J'ai quasiment été élevé dans la cuisine du monastère.

— Vraiment ? Cuisinier par-dessus le marché ! Le jeune dragon a de multiples talents !

— Je ne saurais prétendre au titre de cuisinier, objectai-je. On ne me permit jamais de faire plus que laver les ustensiles, allumer le feu, hacher les légumes. C'était pour moi une grande occasion quand Wu me laissait m'occuper du riz ! »

J'avais voulu plaisanter ; mais Lo plissa les yeux et hocha gravement la tête. « Les anciennes méthodes sont les meilleures. Les jeunes d'aujourd'hui sont trop impatients. Ils refusent la discipline. Ils veulent tout de suite s'attaquer aux grandes choses. "Débuter au sommet", voilà la philosophie de mon fils. » Il soupira en secouant la tête. « Je ne sais pas, il a peut-être raison. En tout cas, Wo s'en tire très bien. » Lo prit une expression dégoûtée qui contrastait avec l'éloge de son fils. « Comme vous, il a son propre appartement ! » Il me regarda d'un air implorant, comme désireux que je confirme son enthousiasme. « Pourtant, quand il était avec moi, je n'ai jamais pu en tirer grand-chose. Ma femme prétend que je le rudoyais. Mais il geignait et regimbait comme une vieille femme. Je craignais qu'il n'arrive jamais à rien dans la vie... Comme ce jeune gars que j'ai maintenant — toute la sensibilité et l'enthousiasme d'une carpe ! Il faut toujours être derrière lui, mais il est fier et arrogant ! Au bout de deux semaines, il se prend pour un grand chef cuisinier ! Maintenant il refuse de laver les poêles. Cela offense sa dignité. » Le ricanement de Lo imita celui de son aide. « Il veut cuisiner ! Que puis-je faire ? Wo a peut-être raison. Une tâche aussi humble est peut-être "rasante", comme il dit, et les jeunes ont besoin d'"émulation, d'excitation, de responsabilités". Même si tous les grands chefs ont fait leur apprentissage ainsi que vous l'avez décrit, s'initiant à leur profession à dix ans, comme moi, sans avoir le droit de casser un œuf avant quinze ans ! Au moins, cela inculque le respect indispensable de l'art.

Attendre si longtemps pour casser un œuf en fait un sacrement ; c'est ainsi qu'on devient le prêtre et l'artiste de sa profession. Bah, je crois que les temps ont changé. J'ai voulu essayer les nouvelles méthodes. Ce garçon veut cuisiner : je ne vais pas entraver son génie !

« Et qu'arrive-t-il ? Un vrai désastre ! Deux fois cette semaine il a gâché mon meilleur plat — La Copulation Délicieuse des Dragons Bondissants ! Une tragédie ! J'en aurais pleuré ! Et maintenant, *maintenant*, après ce fiasco, il se déclare prêt à s'initier au porc ! Les Fesses Ondoyantes de la Belle Femme, il veut s'y frotter ! Vous connaissez ce plat ? Une pure merveille ! » Il embrassa l'extrémité de ses doigts. « Mais pardonnez à un vieil homme. Je suis trop bavard !... Le vin ! »

Dans le placard au-dessus de l'évier, il prit aussitôt une bouteille, qu'il caressa tendrement entre ses mains. Une lueur brumeuse brillait au fond de ses yeux.

« Voilà plus de trois ans que je garde cette bouteille de vieux Kao Liang, dit-il. Ce soir, nous allons trinquer ensemble. »

Je fus flatté, quoiqu'un peu inquiet de boire de l'alcool.

« J'ai si rarement l'honneur de boire en compagnie d'un homme cultivé, poursuivit-il, d'un homme qui a *cultivé le goût*. Après tout, les anciens rites de la convivialité furent inventés par vos prédécesseurs. »

Je déglutis avec peine en me demandant si je pourrais répondre à son attente. Il faisait allusion à l'extravagant concept populaire des « taoïstes ivrognes », entretenu par Li Po et les poètes dilettantes des T'ang. J'allais lui avouer que je ne connaissais pas davantage le vin que « Les Fesses Ondoyantes de la Belle Femme », quand il fit sauter le bouchon de la bouteille et tourna vers moi un visage radieux.

« Zut, pensai-je, trop tard. Oh et puis tant pis... »

Souriant nerveusement, je le vis transvaser son contenu dans un pichet de porcelaine qu'il fit chauffer au bain-marie sur la cuisinière. Puis il sortit deux tasses du placard — de minuscules objets en porcelaine gris-bleu décorés des caractères *Fu* et *Shou* — et les posa sur la table à nos places respectives. Quand le vin fut prêt, il remplit chaque tasse.

« Aux fermiers de l'anecdote, à qui le vin révèle la compréhension et l'estime mutuelles », dit-il, faisant allusion à une célèbre histoire chinoise. Il leva sa tasse vers moi avec un large sourire. Puis son visage se crispa sous le coup de la concentration, comme le plongeur sur la falaise regarde les vagues et le roc avant de s'élancer. « *Kan pei !* » s'écria-t-il selon l'expression rituelle qui signifie « cul sec ». Sur ce, il vida sa tasse d'un coup.

Désireux de ne pas me trahir, je suivis son exemple et comptai sur ma nature de Singe pour l'imiter parfaitement. Je faillis tomber à la renverse avec ma chaise.

Mon estomac se contracta de douleur quand le liquide descendit. Il me fit une douce violence. Sous une apparence sirupeuse, je découvris pillage, rapt, meurtre sanglant. Les larmes me montèrent aux yeux ; je cherchai mon souffle.

Lo s'appuya contre le dossier de sa chaise, leva un peu la tête, ferma les yeux et soupira : « Ah, les subtilités du vin. » Avec un doux sourire, il saisit le pichet, remplit de nouveau nos tasses, puis me regarda rêveusement en battant des paupières comme s'il attendait quelque chose.

Je cherchai désespérément une formule pour un toast. « À... » La sobriété, la tempérance, la modération — ces mots pervers me venaient spontanément à l'esprit. « À la tradition, trouvai-je enfin sans beaucoup de conviction.

— *Kan pei !* » s'écria-t-il chaleureusement.

Cette fois, la violence de l'alcool rencontra moins de résistance et eut un effet mitigé sur mon organisme : une fois le choc initial passé, une chaleur agréable diffusa de mes intestins traumatisés et chatouilla l'extrémité de mes doigts.

« *Sui pien !* » annonça-t-il après ce deuxième toast. « Comme il vous plaira ! » Cela annonçait la fin des toasts obligatoires. Nous bûmes donc « à loisir », moi caressant ma tasse le plus longtemps possible entre deux gorgées, lui ralentissant à peine son allure. Bizarrement, sa taille semblait augmenter à mesure qu'il buvait, ou bien c'était moi qui rétrécissais !

« Il est relativement rare de rencontrer un compatriote du Szu-ch'uan, dit-il, surtout un homme aussi accompli que vous. Comme vous l'avez sans doute remarqué, l'immense majorité des Chinois qui vivent ici sont cantonais. La plupart nous considèrent comme une tribu de barbares hirsutes qui courent les montagnes et mangent de la viande crue. » Il rit avant de poursuivre sur un ton de fierté blessée. « Je suis chef cuisinier. Depuis l'âge de quinze ans, j'ai consacré ma vie à l'acquisition de ce que nous appelons "le goût authentique". » (Il utilisa l'expression *zhen wer*.) « S'agit-il d'un désir barbare ? Je ne vous dis pas cela par orgueil, mais seulement pour minimiser mes défauts, qui sont incommensurables.

— Maintenant, c'est *vous* qui exagérez, dis-je en rotant, pour ce qui est de vos défauts. »

Il secoua sombrement la tête. « Hélas non. » Il leva les yeux, croisa mon regard. « Je vous dois une explication pour ce qui s'est passé dans le vestibule.

— Ce n'est pas nécessaire, lui assurai-je. Et puis, qu'y a-t-il à expliquer ? Vous m'avez pris pour un agresseur.

— Vous êtes bien bon de m'accorder autant de crédit, dit-il, mais la vérité est autre. » Il m'adressa un regard sinistre, secoua la tête. « Oui, Sun I, nous avons bu ensemble ; cela oblige à la franchise. De plus, ajouta-t-il avec un sourire penaud avant de roter, comme dit le proverbe, "le vin délie les langues". »

Public captif, je croisai les mains et acquiesçai.

Son prologue fut un soupir. « Je me demande parfois comment tout cela est arrivé — ou plutôt, comment j'en suis arrivé là. Quand j'ai débarqué à New York, je n'étais pas très ambitieux. Une seule passion me possédait, comme un prêtre, comme vous, mon ami. Je n'avais personne à charge, je désirais seulement perfectionner mon art. Quant à l'argent, j'en possédais plus que je n'avais jamais rêvé, autant que je voulais. J'en avais même en trop, dont j'économisais une partie et dépensais l'autre en des amusements que je considérais comme innocents. Oui, je jouais. Mais à l'époque c'était une distraction, pas un vice. Je contrôlais parfaitement mon existence, que je jugeais assez bonne.

« Le mariage changea tout cela. S'il vous plaît, ne vous méprenez pas.

Ma femme et mes enfants — voilà mes seules consolations, mon seul bien dans la vie. Mais en essayant de subvenir à leurs besoins, peu à peu — même aujourd'hui je ne comprends pas très bien ce qui s'est passé —, j'ai senti le gouvernail m'échapper. Ma femme vient d'un autre milieu. Elle m'a épousé par amour, alors qu'elle aurait pu trouver un bien meilleur parti. Elle était habituée à un certain style de vie que je me sentis obligé, non, que je *voulus* lui maintenir. Parce que je l'aimais, je visai haut en espérant bien faire. Avec mes modestes économies, je versai un acompte pour acheter un restaurant et contractai un emprunt pour payer mes traites. Sun I, je suis heureux à la cuisine. Dans mon élément. Je fais mon travail avec un plaisir tranquille, je m'occupe des petits détails. Une carpe fraîche à l'œil limpide et à la chair élastique, un canard rôti correctement découpé — le premier coup de couteau incise la peau dorée croustillante, le fumet onctueux s'élève de la viande tendre —, la préparation des sauces, réussir l'exacte proportion de *xiang* avec l'ail et les piments dans un plat épicé, ou de *nong* dans une cassolette mijotée à feu doux (je reproduis les termes chinois intraduisibles de Lo), de *xien* avec les crevettes ou les légumes à peine saisis dans la poêle pour leur faire rendre leur fraîcheur et leurs essences naturelles... autant de choses que je comprends instinctivement et qui me rendent heureux. Je ne recule pas devant l'effort. J'essaie sans cesse de me surpasser. Comme un grand calligraphe, je sais qu'un seul trait peut gâcher l'ensemble, ou exprimer les joies et les tristesses d'une vie. Je n'ai pas peur. Je prends des risques. Dans la cuisine, je suis un artiste, un commandant. Je sais qui je suis et ce qui doit être. Je ne connais ni le doute ni l'hésitation. Mais quand j'en sors, quand j'enlève ma toque blanche et que je quitte mon modeste royaume, je pénètre en territoire hostile. Je perds toute confiance en moi. Je me recroqueville, j'attends l'insulte. Pourquoi, je l'ignore. Mais c'est ainsi — comme vous l'avez vous-même constaté dans le vestibule.

« Même dans la salle de restaurant, au-delà des portes de la cuisine, je me sens mal à l'aise. Tel fut mon calvaire, Sun I : les dix mille frustrations et migraines liées à la direction d'une affaire complexe — je ne comprenais goutte à tous ces tracas qui m'agaçaient profondément. Affronter le banquier, le blanchisseur, les menuisiers, plombiers, électriciens, grossistes, remplacer un four défectueux, payer les factures — je trouvais tout cela déplaisant, exaspérant. Je voulais me retirer dans la cuisine où je me sentais libre. Mais même là, ma béatitude fut empoisonnée. Car vois-tu, en tant que cuisinier mon cœur me conseillait une chose, et en tant que propriétaire une autre. Le cuisinier que je suis savait qu'un œuf supplémentaire conférerait au plat la consistance et la saveur voulues ; mais le propriétaire savait que l'amidon était beaucoup moins cher et convenait à la rigueur. La clientèle commença par affluer. Les gens disaient que la nourriture était bonne, et nos prix étaient les plus bas de la rue. En tant que cuisinier, je fus flatté ; en tant que propriétaire, je fis mes comptes et m'aperçus que notre marge bénéficiaire n'était pas assez élevée, que nous perdions même parfois de l'argent. Je dus augmenter mes prix. Quand les clients revinrent, ils constatèrent le changement et se sentirent floués, comme si j'avais essayé de les appâter pour mieux les plumer. Ils désertèrent mon restaurant ; pire, ils bavardèrent. Ma renommée en pâtit. Les affaires aussi. Je dus rogner sur les dépenses — baisser le chauffage, économiser davantage sur les ingrédients. Et nous devînmes rapidement un restaurant comme les autres : mêmes prix, même nourriture... à cette seule exception que les gens connaissaient davantage les autres. Tant et si bien qu'en l'absence d'un autre critère, ils retournèrent où ils avaient déjà été. Nous n'avons même pas eu de deuxième chance.

« Je ne pouvais pas honorer mes traites. Je me mis à boire, à négliger mon affaire. Certains soirs, je jouais. L'excitation du jeu me faisait oublier le reste. Mais contrairement à l'époque où je vivais seul, je ne pouvais me payer le luxe de perdre l'argent que je jouais. Et je perdais plus souvent que je ne gagnais. Mes créanciers s'énervaient. Pour ne pas couler complètement, je dus emprunter de l'argent à des sources illégales — qui me prêtèrent, à dix pour cent par semaine. Ah, Sun I, j'aurais dû comprendre que j'étais fichu. Mais non. Peu à peu, de combine en déclaration de dette, je me retrouvai prisonnier de cet écheveau financier dont, même aujourd'hui, je ne peux me libérer. J'étais aveugle. Un soir où j'avais trop bu, je me mis à gagner. Je m'exaltai, je crus que je ne pouvais pas perdre. Des idées délirantes s'emparèrent de moi. Je sentis que ma chance tournait enfin. Je méritais un répit. La vie me le devait. C'était *mon droit* ! Tout semblait possible. En espérant gagner gros et rembourser d'un coup tous mes créanciers, je misai le restaurant. » Il hésita, son visage s'effondra — jamais je n'ai vu expression aussi pitoyable.

« Ah, Sun I, je crois encore que le jeu était truqué. » Il secoua la tête. « Mais peu importe. La nouvelle se répandit comme une traînée de poudre. Le lendemain matin, tous mes créanciers réclamèrent leur dû. Et je n'avais rien — même plus le restaurant — pour les rembourser. J'étais en faillite. Les banquiers prirent ce qu'ils purent en faisant jouer les autorités. Les autres firent preuve de moins d'aménité. Ils m'emmenèrent dans un bâtiment en ruine au bord du fleuve, me firent monter sur une chaise, placèrent un nœud coulant autour de mon cou, m'ordonnèrent de faire ma prière. Puis ils me poussèrent dans le vide. Je vis le sol se ruer vers moi, pensai à ma femme et à mes enfants en attendant le choc de la corde. Mais elle ne se tendit pas, la mort me rata. Une exécution simulée. Ils me dirent en riant qu'ils ne comptaient pas me laisser m'en tirer aussi facilement. C'était la méthode italienne. Les hommes d'affaires et les voyous chinois sont plus subtils, moins dogmatiques, même s'ils ont aussi un faible pour les effets théâtraux. J'avais plus de valeur pour eux vivant que mort. Ils m'accordèrent un sursis. Je leur donne maintenant la moitié de ce que je gagne... en échange de ma vie.

— Depuis combien de temps ?

— J'ai récemment commencé de payer le fils d'un des hommes auprès de qui j'avais contracté mon premier emprunt.

— Mais c'est intolérable ! m'indignai-je. Qui sont ces gens ?

— Ne me le demandez pas. » Il me rendit mon regard, puis hocha la tête. « Oui, ça a été difficile. Mais j'ai au moins ma famille. Ma femme m'a prouvé son amour. Elle a renoncé à tout pour moi, elle a vendu ses parures de jeune fille, qui constituaient sa dot ; elle a même pris des travaux de couture pour m'aider à joindre les deux bouts. Et tout cela sans le moindre reproche. Sans ces revers de fortune, je n'aurais jamais connu l'étendue de son amour. Et puis bizarrement, quand j'eus perdu tous ces biens, je redevins heureux. J'ai ma cuisine, je sais le rôle que je dois y jouer. Je me considère comme chanceux. Malgré tout, nos enfants sont restés à l'écart du drame. Mes erreurs ne les ont pas éclaboussés. Ils ignorent tout de ce que je viens de vous dire. Tous ont quitté Chinatown pour faire leur vie ailleurs, tous sauf la benjamine, Yin-mi, qui commence à voler de ses propres ailes. Wo a un bon travail et possède son propre appartement. Li, l'aînée, est indépendante depuis l'âge de dix-huit ans. Elle est entrée à l'université grâce à une bourse et s'est accrochée jusqu'à la licence. Maintenant elle étudie l'anthropologie à Columbia. Dans deux ans, elle aura son doctorat. »

Le visage de Lo était emprunt d'une sorte de douceur, qui n'était pas seulement due à l'ivresse. Il semblait rasséréné, détaché. Le vin avait résolu son problème. Il avait trouvé l'oubli et la paix grâce à l'alcool et aux confidences. Il semblait presque reconnaissant. J'éprouvai pour lui de la pitié, mais aussi une certaine admiration.

« Je me suis trop attardé sur mon histoire, dit-il en relevant la tête, d'une voix légèrement pâteuse. Et vous, mon jeune ami ? Racontez-moi la vôtre. »

Comme je ne voulais pas me faire prier après la confiance qu'il venait de me témoigner, je m'ouvris à lui et parlai sincèrement de moi-même. Quand j'abordai l'épisode de la Bourse, je sentis Lo s'agiter. Seule la courtoisie l'empêcha de m'interrompre, mais je remarquai qu'il mourait d'envie de s'exprimer. Plusieurs fois, je marquai un temps d'arrêt pour le laisser parler, mais il resta coi, redoubla de politesse, insista pour que je finisse d'abord.

Interloqué par son attitude, je me hâtai d'achever mon récit puis, d'un regard, lui signifiai que j'en avais terminé.

« C'est le destin qui nous a fait nous rencontrer, Sun I ! s'écria-t-il d'une voix excitée en approchant de moi son visage empourpré. D'ailleurs, je vous l'ai déjà dit. Vous n'allez pas croire la merveilleuse coïncidence dont je vais vous parler ! Mon fils, Wo, que vous rencontrerez — il a son propre appartement. » (L'ébriété le poussa à répéter ce détail avec enthousiasme, comme s'il s'agissait d'une révélation.) « Wo travaille à la Bourse de New York ! Peut-être connaît-il votre père. Ils sont peut-être collègues ! »

J'étais stupéfait. « Qu'y fait-il ?

— Oh, je ne connais rien à tout ça, répondit Lo avec modestie. Je sais seulement qu'il occupe un poste important, très important. J'ai investi de l'argent sur ses conseils. » Il fronça les sourcils. « Mais peu importe... »

J'imaginai un homme élégant, suave et impassible qui évoluait parmi une nuée de subordonnés empressés, zélés, et répondait à leurs requêtes par un battement de paupières ou un hochement de tête.

« Vous devez le rencontrer le plus tôt possible ! poursuivit Lo. Je suis sûr que vous deviendrez bons amis. Chaque samedi, la famille au grand complet se réunit pour le déjeuner — une occasion unique ! — tous les oncles et tantes, tout le monde. Wo est devenu la vedette de ces déjeuners, on le respecte à cause de ses excellents conseils d'investissement. Chacun vient le consulter. Venez déjeuner avec nous si vous êtes libre. » Il exultait.

« Sun I ! Le destin n'a-t-il pas admirablement organisé notre rencontre, manifesté toute la subtilité esthétique et le bon goût d'un grand chef préparant son meilleur plat ?
— La Copulation Délicieuse des Dragons Bondissants ! » m'écriai-je, moi-même un peu éméché. Nous portâmes un toast enthousiaste.
Une inspiration délirante s'empara de moi. « Pensez-vous qu'il pourrait me trouver du travail ? » Mon cerveau entrevit dix mille choses.
Lo m'adressa un regard surpris. « Vous, un prêtre, accepter ce genre de travail ? » Il semblait scandalisé.
« Pourquoi pas ? Je dois faire quelque cnose.
— Vous devez faire quelque chose..., répéta-t-il d'une voix perplexe. Vous avez certainement de l'argent ? »
Je secouai la tête.
« Fauché ? »
J'acquiesçai.
« Mais vous possédez votre propre appartement ! protesta-t-il comme si ma situation financière méritait discussion. Je ne veux pas me montrer indiscret, mais combien avez-vous payé pour cela ?
— Rien, répondis-je.
— Rien ? Impossible ! Depuis quand Mme Chin fait-elle crédit ?
— Vous vous rappelez la robe dont je vous ai parlé ? Je l'ai laissée en gage. »
Une violente inquiétude bouleversa le visage de Lo. « Oh merde.
— Qu'est-ce qui ne va pas ? » demandai-je, consterné.
Il fixa sur moi un regard vitreux qui ne me voyait pas, un regard tourné vers la boule de cristal qui, dans son esprit, lui montrait l'avenir et le passé — son passé, mon avenir. Il grimaça de douleur.
Je touchai doucement son coude. « Lo, vous vous sentez bien ? »
Il fut saisi d'un bref tremblement, puis revint à lui. « Vous devez la récupérer. » Il saisit inconsciemment ma main.
« Je vais le faire, lui assurai-je. Dès que j'aurai l'argent.
— Non ! s'écria-t-il. Dès que possible, maintenant, tout de suite !
— Mais comment ? » Sa véhémence me déconcertait. « Avec quoi ?
— De combien avez-vous besoin ?
— Cinquante dollars », lui dis-je.
Il me regarda, en proie à une indécision torturante, comme pris dans un dilemme insoluble.
« Je vais vous les prêter, dit-il enfin en poussant un profond soupir.
— Mais vos propres dettes !
— Ne m'en parlez pas ! gémit-il en cachant son visage dans ses mains.
— Lo, dis-je, comprenez-moi, je vous remercie de votre proposition, mais cela est-il vraiment indispensable ? Elle ne va tout de même pas me rouler ?
— Vous rouler ! s'écria-t-il. Cher enfant, là n'est pas la question ! Le chat *roule-t-il* la souris ? L'araignée *roule-t-elle* la mouche, sa proie désignée ? Pas une seconde ! Le meurtre est la fonction du prédateur, la seule chose qu'il connaisse. C'est son obligation, sa *moralité*.
— Mais quel rapport avec Mme Chin ? »
Son visage s'assombrit. « Je ne suis pas un homme éduqué comme vous,

Sun I. J'ignore les mystères de la divination et "les trois mille trois cents règles" de l'étiquette rituelle. Mais l'expérience m'a appris quelque chose. J'ai grappillé quelques fragments et lambeaux de sagesse tout au long de ma dure existence dans le monde réel. Ce que j'ai appris, je l'ai appris à mes dépens. Nous avons bu ensemble. J'ai été franc avec vous. Alors croyez-moi sur parole : récupérez cette robe. »

Mon exaltation vira brusquement à l'angoisse. Plein de doutes, incapable de penser clairement, je baissai les yeux vers la table. Le tourbillon amorphe du Formica se mit en rotation, refléta parfaitement le chaos de mon esprit. Je me sentais hébété, anesthésié par l'alcool.

« Attendez ici », dit Lo en s'écartant de la table. Il trébucha sur sa chaise qui tomba bruyamment. Il grimaça. « *Chuut.* » Bêtement, il posa un doigt sur sa bouche en titubant vers le couloir. Je l'entendis heurter un mur, puis un autre. « *Chuut* », dit-il à chaque fois. Je posai ma tête sur la table. Il y eut un moment de silence, puis un choc assourdi suivi d'un crépitement feutré — des pièces de monnaie tombaient sur un tapis.

« Oh merde », chuchota-t-il.

J'entendis le claquement d'un verrou qu'on ouvrait, un bruit de porte.

« Papa ? » fit une voix de jeune fille. Tout se figea. Puis des bruits de pas dans le couloir.

Quand je levai la tête, je découvris une jeune fille de seize ans, peut-être dix-sept, debout dans l'encadrement de la porte, les yeux fixés sur moi... ou plutôt je discernai vaguement une forme spectrale qui tremblotait et oscillait dans les vapeurs de l'alcool. Son expression était alerte mais dépourvue de peur, voire un peu curieuse. Elle battit des paupières, mais resta immobile, manifestant un sang-froid naturel, aussi pur que chez un animal.

Elle avait de courts cheveux noirs coupés à la garçonne, ébouriffés de sommeil ; elle portait un pyjama blanc d'enfant trop petit pour elle, qui remontait sur ses avant-bras et ses chevilles, comprimait des seins peu volumineux mais bien développés. Ils gonflaient le tissu avec une douce indolence, ses mamelons pointaient. Ses hanches étaient aussi étroites que celles d'un garçon, elle avait de longues jambes fuselées et des omoplates saillantes. Elle paraissait hésiter entre deux âges, deux états, gauche et féminine tout à la fois, comme un insecte qui vient de sortir du cocon, doté de la mémoire physique, des instincts exigus de la chrysalide, et du corps tout neuf du papillon, de ses ailes somptueuses mais encore maladroites.

« Qui êtes-vous ? demanda-t-elle.

— Je...

— Yin-mi ! » intervint Lo en un murmure implorant, exaspéré. Les yeux de la jeune fille restaient fixés sur mon visage. « Que fais-tu debout ? Retourne au lit. »

Elle le regarda. « Pourquoi ce bruit ?

— Pour rien !

— On aurait dit la boîte à couture de maman.

— Pourquoi poses-tu des questions dont tu connais la réponse ?

— Tu prenais de l'argent.

— Va te coucher, Yin-mi ! Tu n'es pas encore trop âgée pour les fessées.

— Lui as-tu demandé la permission ? »

Lo se tourna vers elle avec une expression menaçante, des yeux étincelants. Elle le regarda calmement, sans trahir la moindre peur. Ses yeux à elle étaient sombres, profonds, transparents. Les observant, je pensai à la mer nocturne où j'avais plongé au large de l'île de Quemoy pour nager vers ma liberté.

J'y discernai pourtant autre chose. Tandis qu'elle se tenait devant son père, résolue à ne pas céder, je sentis une perplexité, un trouble nouveaux, une émotion qu'elle maîtrisait mal. Sous mes yeux, elle s'avança vers Lo et posa légèrement ses mains sur ses épaules en le dévisageant gravement. « Tu as bu, n'est-ce pas ? » Sa voix était parfaitement calme.

Lo ne dit rien.

Elle se mit sur la pointe des pieds et embrassa silencieusement sa joue. Avant de disparaître dans le couloir, elle s'arrêta brièvement pour me lancer un dernier regard par-dessus l'épaule, mais assez longtemps pour que je puisse y lire douleur et suspicion. Ce regard me brûla, déchira mon cœur comme un tison.

Après mon départ, Lo s'affaissa comme une chambre à air crevée, soupira comme l'air qui s'en échappe. « Tenez, dit-il en plaçant dans ma main une liasse pliée de billets écornés. Apportez ça à Mme Chin à la première heure. »

Diverses pensées et émotions contradictoires se bousculèrent dans mon cerveau quand je regardai les dollars défraîchis, les premiers que je touchais. Le coup d'œil de la jeune fille, mon vœu de pauvreté — tout cela déclencha en moi une violente culpabilité. La vue de l'argent m'emplit de dégoût, me révolta. Pourtant mes yeux ne parvenaient pas à s'en détacher : le fin réseau vert des lignes ondoyantes qui entouraient Washington, tel un Sphinx à la fois grave et sybarite ; au dos, cette étrange pyramide, l'œil humain dans la plaine stérile et l'inscription « *Novus Ordo Seculorum* ». Ces images me touchèrent autant que celles des vitraux de l'église de Trinity. Mais ce fut la répulsion qui l'emporta.

« Lo, je vous prie de ne pas le prendre mal, mais je ne peux accepter cet argent. Mon vœu me l'interdit.

— Comment allez-vous faire ? On ne peut pas survivre ici sans argent. Et ne venez-vous pas de m'interroger pour un travail ? A la Bourse de New York encore ! »

Mon esprit embrumé par l'alcool n'avait pas relevé cette contradiction. Je la méditai. « C'est vrai, admis-je, mais là-bas je placerai mon travail au service d'un but plus élevé, l'argent ne sera qu'accessoire, un mal nécessaire, inévitable. D'ailleurs, je pourrais peut-être trouver un arrangement. Jusqu'ici j'ai vécu d'aumônes ; pourquoi ne pas continuer ?

— Balivernes ! s'écria-t-il. Très louable, mais parfaitement utopique. Vos nobles idéaux ne tiendront pas une semaine. Le code ici en vigueur, Sun I, n'a rien à voir avec celui du monastère, mais il n'est pas moins strict. Si vous voulez vous en tirer, vous devez vous habituer rapidement à la rude discipline du monde réel. »

Mes résolutions vacillèrent. J'hésitai. « Cependant..., commençai-je piteusement sans savoir quoi objecter.

— Allez, allez — laissez votre fierté de côté. Faites-moi confiance, Sun I, vos scrupules sont déplacés. Peut-être êtes-vous gêné parce que cet argent appartient à ma femme ? Ecoutez, mon garçon, je la connais. Elle ne m'en tiendra pas rigueur. Bien au contraire ! Mais elle serait très malheureuse d'apprendre que vous avez dilapidé votre héritage pour la cabane de la terrasse. Et si le remboursement vous tracasse, chassez également ce souci !

— Oui, cela aussi m'inquiète. » Je saisis immédiatement la perche qu'il me tendait. « Comment vous rembourser ?

— J'attendais cette question. » Il eut un sourire déconcertant. « J'ai une idée qui, à mon avis, sera avantageuse pour nous deux. Excusez je vous prie mes arrière-pensées, mais voici : pourquoi ne pas venir travailler avec moi au restaurant jusqu'à dimanche — jusqu'à ce que Wo vous procure une position plus convenable, si je puis dire. Ce sera un plaisir pour moi, et samedi prochain vous aurez largement gagné de quoi rembourser Mme Ha-p'i. Vous pourrez prendre tous vos repas là-bas, même gagner un peu d'argent de poche ! Une combinaison fantastique, si je puis me permettre ! Mieux, cela me permettrait de me débarrasser de l'autre andouille ! Qu'en dites-vous ?

— Eh bien... » L'alcool et la culpabilité avaient entamé mon pouvoir de décision.

« Allez, m'encouragea-t-il, n'hésitez pas. L'orgueil ne convient pas à un prêtre. Et puis quel autre choix avez-vous ? »

Il avait raison. Je soupirai, haussai les épaules pour lui signifier mon accord.

« Fantastique ! dit-il en bondissant de sa chaise. Vous pouvez me rejoindre là-bas demain dès que vous aurez réglé le petit problème qui vous concerne. Soyez ferme avec elle. Vous saurez retrouver le restaurant ? »

J'acquiesçai.

« Que diriez-vous de boire une dernière tasse pour fêter notre collaboration ! » Il tendit le bras vers le placard.

« Je crains de devoir partir.

— Oh, fit-il d'une voix dépitée, je vois. » Il me regarda tristement, puis son visage s'illumina. « Nous devons recommencer souvent ! Votre compagnie m'a fait un bien considérable ! A partir d'aujourd'hui vous faites partie de la famille, comme mon propre fils ! »

Je fus ému par sa gentillesse, dont je me sentais profondément indigne. « Merci », dis-je, trop soûl pour manifester la moindre éloquence.

Sur le seuil, nous fûmes tous les deux gênés. Coupant court aux salamalecs, il me tendit la main alors que je m'inclinais. Nous rougîmes. Puis, pour se racheter de son impolitesse, il s'inclina alors que j'avançais la main. Nous réussîmes enfin à coordonner nos efforts, compensant nos échecs précédents par une courbette suivie d'une poignée de mains suivie d'une ultime courbette. Je parvins ensuite à battre en retraite sur le palier.

« Bonsoir, lui dis-je, et merci pour tout.

— Bonsoir ! » me répondit-il avec enthousiasme en maintenant la porte ouverte.

Je titubai vers la cage d'escalier. Je réussis tant bien que mal à négocier le virage de la rampe et commençai à monter ; quand je me retournai une dernière fois, Lo était toujours devant sa porte, le visage rayonnant d'affection paternelle.

Je me tournai et me retournai dans mon lit, abruti par l'alcool, désirant le doux oubli de l'inconscience, mais incapable d'y céder ; mon cerveau anesthésié subissait néanmoins la vibration lancinante de la fraise du dentiste que je sentais tarauder le nerf, sensation certes douloureuse mais jamais insupportable, et dont la permanence tenait ma conscience en éveil, loin du seuil magique de la dissolution dans le sommeil. J'étais inquiet, comme souillé. Cet argent me tourmentait. Je le cachai sous le matelas. De temps à autre, l'image de la fille de Lo (il l'avait appelée Yin-mi) apparaissait devant mes yeux comme une vision du paradis aperçue dans les brumes trompeuses de l'alcool. Cela aussi finit pas disparaître et j'écoutai abjectement les bruits qui montaient par la cage d'ascenseur — le Puits des Soupirs. Tout en bas, comme du cœur du monde, le grincement rythmé d'un sommier et les gémissements indéchiffrables d'une femme montaient vers moi ; sa voix ne ressemblait à rien de ce que je connaissais. Je n'avais jamais entendu ces halètements qui m'étaient pourtant familiers. Ils m'apaisèrent bizarrement, comme la main qui balance le berceau initie aux premiers émois de la sexualité. Je dérivai bientôt dans cette cadence. Le bruit se fondit dans le murmure environnant et le sommeil se dressa devant moi comme une vague : un mur d'eau noire scintillante surmonté d'une frange d'écume qui virait à l'émeraude dans les rayons du soleil. Quand la lame déferla, j'entendis le cri étouffé de la femme flotter tel un oiseau de mer sur le rugissement de l'océan, un cri doux et désespéré. Je songeai alors que la vibration fondamentale de la cité, sa rumeur élémentaire, ressemblait au bourdonnement que j'avais entendu le jour même dans la grande salle de la Bourse.

Mais il y avait autre chose, un son plus profond, plus élémentaire encore, dont les autres n'étaient que les échos perçus à des distances croissantes et avec une résolution décroissante. Qu'était-ce ? Avant de pouvoir le découvrir, je sombrai dans le sommeil.

4

Quand je me réveillai le lendemain matin, mes yeux étaient poisseux, enduits d'une croûte jaune. Je dus les ouvrir avec mes doigts en songeant que j'avais pleuré dans mon sommeil. Je les frottai avec l'articulation de mes index pour soulager ma démangeaison. Lorsque je les rouvris, je vis de minuscules comètes blanchâtres voleter à la périphérie de mon champ visuel, puis remarquai que le soleil atteignait déjà le niveau des toits. L'air s'embrasait. J'avais trop dormi !

Je me débarbouillai à l'eau froide couleur de rouille du robinet, pris mes clefs et fermai ma porte. En tournant la clef dans la serrure, je me rappelai l'argent et mon désagréable rendez-vous avec Mme Chin. Cette seule pensée me donna la nausée. Je me creusai la tête pour trouver un prétexte plausible, une excuse, une raison de reporter cette corvée : j'étais déjà en retard ; cela pouvait attendre demain... mais non, je me rappelai le visage consterné, paniqué, de Lo, et ce que je risquais de perdre. Je poussai un profond soupir et retournai à ma chambre chercher l'argent.

Fan-ku m'examina d'un air mauvais par la porte entrebâillée, puis déclara que la douairière n'était pas chez elle. Nos regards s'affrontaient en silence quand dans l'autre pièce s'éleva le chuchotement monotone d'une incantation.

« D'accord, murmura-t-il avec sa mauvaise humeur habituelle en ouvrant la porte. Mais elle a un client, elle ne peut pas vous recevoir maintenant. »

Quand je lui dis que j'avais l'argent, il tendit la main en frottant son pouce contre ses doigts, un geste que je n'avais jamais vu, mais que je n'eus aucune peine à comprendre. « Donnez, je le lui transmettrai. » Son sourire était une version moins réussie, quoique prometteuse, de celui de la douairière.

A cet instant, un piaulement déchirant vrilla le silence. J'entendis un choc étouffé, une cavalcade ; le bas des deux pans de la tenture s'ouvrit brusquement et le chiot apparut, museau au ras du sol, yeux exorbités, pattes battant l'air frénétiquement, corps en équilibre précaire ; l'animal fonçait droit devant lui. Quand il m'aperçut, il aboya plusieurs fois avec désespoir et se jeta dans mes bras, car je m'étais baissé pour l'accueillir. Pris d'une affection paniquée, il lécha mon visage, enfouit son museau froid dans mon cou.

Une main couverte de bijoux écarta alors la tenture et Mme Chin apparut ; elle portait une étrange tiare en plumes de paon, tenait une serviette blanche ainsi qu'une paire de ciseaux en acier inoxydable. Je considérai la scène avec stupéfaction et un léger malaise. La douairière me toisa sévèrement. « Prends le chien, Fan-ku », dit-elle, les yeux rivés sur moi, pas sur lui.

Je ne voulais pas abandonner mon ami, mais je n'avais aucun droit sur lui, aucune raison de le garder. Le chiot me lança un coup d'œil sinistre, accusateur, quand le jeune Chinois s'en empara et l'étouffa à moitié au creux de son coude. Lorsqu'il repoussa la tenture, à la lumière de l'unique bougie posée sur la table où la veille la douairière m'avait lu les lignes de la main, j'aperçus en contrejour la tête et les épaules d'un homme. Mon cœur s'arrêta. Il se passait trop de choses. Je voulus partir.

« Où as-tu trouvé ça ? demanda la douairière avec humeur en avisant la liasse de billets que je tenais en main. Tu t'es prostitué ! »

Je rougis, m'empêtrai dans ma réplique. « J'avais oublié. Je possède cet argent depuis mon arrivée en Amérique.

— Tu mens, ricana-t-elle. Reviens plus tard. Je suis occupée. Je n'ai pas le temps de te recevoir. »

Fan-ku revint et se campa à côté d'elle.

« *Tout de suite !* dis-je,... s'il vous plaît. »

Elle haussa les sourcils sous le coup de la surprise et de l'outrage, puis, plissant les yeux, tenta de me faire fléchir. Je ne bronchai pas.

Son sourire odieux déforma ses traits. « Comme tu voudras. Va la chercher ! aboya-t-elle à Fan-ku sans cesser de sourire. Quelqu'un t'a parlé derrière mon dos. Qui ? »

Je baissai les yeux.

« Je suis dure en affaires, mais pas malhonnête, dit-elle d'un ton vertueux. C'est vrai, je veux cette robe, mais je n'aurais pas été jusqu'à la voler. J'avais espéré que nous deviendrions amis, je vois maintenant que cela est compromis. Dommage... Quel joli garçon ! » Elle se renfrogna. « Tout ça est ta faute. »

Fan-ku arriva avec la robe.

« Rends-lui son bien ! Je m'en souviendrai », dit-elle en reculant vers la tenture ; elle m'adressa le sourire que je trouvais infiniment plus glaçant que le regard fixe dont elle avait essayé de m'intimider un peu plus tôt. Son visage disparut brusquement derrière les pans de la draperie. J'entendis les marmonnements reprendre dans la pièce.

La robe serrée contre moi, je ressortis dans le couloir. La sueur dégoulinait sur mon front. J'étais content de l'avoir récupérée ; pourtant, à bien y réfléchir, je craignais de m'être montré injuste envers Mme Chin. Et si les mises en garde de Lo n'avaient été qu'inquiétudes paranoïaques dues à la boisson ? Même dans le cas contraire, comment justifier tous ces efforts, cette avidité, ces passions hideuses provoquées par un simple bien matériel ? Pour la première fois, mon expérience confirmait une vérité abstraite apprise au monastère : la possession d'un bien matériel est une gêne pour l'esprit ; mais paradoxalement, l'inhumanité de ce dogme me frappa aussitôt — cela aussi gagné par ma propre expérience. Ce qui m'avait paru limpide irréfutable, dans l'atmosphère raréfiée de Ken Kuan l'était infiniment moins ici, où j'avais quelque chose à perdre.

A cet instant précis, un couinement strident, hallucinant, déchira le silence ; il provenait de l'appartement — du chiot. Mes cheveux se hérissèrent sur ma nuque. Pivotant sur mes talons, je fis face à la porte anonyme avec la sensation d'un horrible écœurement. Que se passait-il dans l'appartement ? Je levai le poing pour redemander à entrer, mais me ravisai, déglutis difficilement et m'éloignai de cette porte le plus vite possible.

Lo occupait la position suprême de Maître Queux *Number One* au *Palais de la Joie de Luck Fat* dans une ruelle miteuse de Chinatown. Le restaurant servait une cuisine raffinée dans une atmosphère élégante, vaguement décadente, voire macabre. On se serait cru dans une catacombe : une série de boyaux tortueux aboutissaient à de petites cellules où se régalaient les clients, une majorité de gros hommes d'affaires chinois en costume et cravate de polyester, parfois accompagnés de bruyantes jeunes femmes au regard dur, dont le maquillage outrancier semblait avoir pour seul but de dissimuler leur éventuelle beauté. Ces hommes qui mangeaient voracement tenaient leur assiette près de leur bouche afin d'engloutir des mets savoureux et s'interrompaient seulement pour faire descendre la nourriture avec du Courvoisier qu'ils buvaient sec dans de grands verres, aussi impunément que s'il se fût agi d'un thé clair.

Lo abattait un travail considérable avec fort peu d'aide. Dès que je quittai la ruelle pour pénétrer dans son royaume, je constatai qu'il ne m'avait pas menti la veille au soir en déclarant que sa personnalité se modifiait dans la cuisine. Il n'était ni bourru ni désagréable, mais, contrairement à Wu, pas davantage détendu ni jovial. Il ne pouvait se payer ce luxe tant il était débordé. Tête baissée, absorbé dans quelque profond rythme intérieur, il allait de l'avant. Deux marmitons travaillaient sous ses ordres. Ils connaissaient leur travail. Leur cadence commença par m'intimider, mais quand je les eus bien observés, je pris le train en marche. J'essayais de me souvenir de tout, si bien que lorsque je les avais vus préparer un plat, je trouvais moyen de faciliter leur tâche la fois suivante, sortant les ramequins avant qu'ils ne les réclament, huilant la poêle, anticipant leurs gestes. Ils me récompensaient de grognements et de hochements de tête approbateurs, ou bien, si mes initiatives avortaient, ils me chassaient devant eux comme un poulet terrifié talonné par l'arbitre implacable de son destin, le fermier. Le premier jour, je commis des erreurs stupides, mais le deuxième je commençai à prendre le tour de main. Le troisième, j'étais devenu membre à part entière de l'équipe. Lo m'avait surnommé « L'Assistant Dragon Numéro Un ».

Malgré le peu de temps que je passai avec eux, je me perdis une fois ou deux dans mes souvenirs, hypnotisé par des tâches qui m'étaient familières depuis l'enfance. Quand je levais les yeux, je m'attendais à découvrir Wu. Et quand je ne le voyais pas, je jetais un regard perplexe sur ce lieu inconnu — « le voyage de mille milles » s'effaçait de ma mémoire, je régressais vers l'adolescence. Alors la réalité me heurtait de plein fouet, et avec un soupir je retournais au présent.

Le troisième jour, un vendredi, fut mon dernier. Le déjeuner de famille devait avoir lieu le lendemain.

★

Nettoyé et coiffé, vêtu de ma plus belle robe (la seule passable qui me restât), je me présentai ponctuellement à midi à l'appartement des Ha-p'i. Une femme potelée d'âge mûr, en vêtements traditionnels, vint m'ouvrir. Le visage empourpré, elle essuya ses mains sur un torchon, s'inclina légèrement et m'adressa un regard inquisiteur mais absent, comme si mille autres choses occupaient son esprit. Pourtant, quand elle me sourit — pur réflexe de politesse, sans doute —, je découvris une simplicité, une modestie, une timidité et une gaieté telles que je me sentis personnellement reconnu et l'objet de toutes ses attentions. Elle me plut aussitôt. Malgré ses traits un peu empâtés et son double menton, son visage était aussi limpide que celui de Yin-mi — je devinai alors que cette femme était sa mère. Chez l'aînée, cette nudité de l'expression semblait le signe d'une profonde modestie, d'un bien précieux. Mais chez la fille, il y avait tout cela, et plus encore.

« Mme Ha-p'i ? » demandai-je.

Elle acquiesça.

« Je suis une connaissance de votre mari. Je m'appelle Sun I.

— Sun I ! dit-elle. Bien sûr ! Pardonnez-moi, s'il vous plaît. Entrez ! »

Un peu troublée, elle ouvrit la porte en rougissant. Nous nous inclinâmes l'un devant l'autre.

« Qui est-ce ? s'écria Lo dans l'autre pièce.

— Le jeune dragon », répondit-elle.

Je rougis à mon tour.

Elle rayonnait, dansait d'un pied sur l'autre.

Dans un coin de la cuisine, une jeune femme habillée à l'occidentale était absorbée dans une conversation avec un Américain. Le jeune homme m'observa par-dessus l'épaule de sa compagne, et son regard s'attarda sur moi d'une façon presque gênante. Quand elle s'aperçut que l'attention de son ami fléchissait, elle se retourna brièvement, me remarqua, puis se remit à parler. Bizarrement, ce regard rapide, superficiel, me décontenança davantage que l'examen prolongé du jeune homme.

Elle portait une robe de soie noire fendue le long d'une jambe, imprimée en quinconce de paons couleur émeraude et turquoise qui faisaient la roue en exhibant une myriade d'yeux iridescents. Longue et moulante, elle suggérait un corps souple, félin — vaguement provocant, mais doté de l'innocence absolue (de l'amoralité, plutôt) de la chatte. La jeune femme portait aussi des pendentifs où la faux nacrée d'un croissant de lune tenait une pleine lune d'argent bruni dans une étreinte implicite, telle l'immensité immergée d'un iceberg sous sa calotte éblouissante de soleil. Je n'avais jamais vu personne qui ressemblât à cette femme. Je l'examinai peut-être un peu plus longtemps que ne l'exigeait la politesse.

Mme Ha-p'i le remarqua et se hâta de nous présenter. « Sun I, voici quelqu'un que j'aimerais vous faire connaître », dit-elle, davantage pour attirer leur attention que la mienne.

La jeune femme se retourna.

« Notre fille aînée, Li, et son... — elle hésita un instant, rougit — "ami", Peter. »

Peter me salua et serra ma main avec une douce et longue pression, sans rien dire mais en me jaugeant d'un air bizarrement réservé, presque sarcastique — ainsi, Mme Chin la veille quand elle avait scruté Fan-ku comme on examine un plat appétissant. Son regard lui servit à prolonger la poignée de mains ; mal à l'aise, je dus presque me dégager.

Mais plus encore que le comportement incompréhensible de son compagnon, la jeune femme me troublait — ses yeux surtout, qui ne ressemblaient pas à ceux de sa mère ou de sa sœur, qui ne ressemblaient à rien, sinon aux yeux du panda, couleur du miel sombre de montagne quand il jaillit d'une ruche brisée. Je sentis mon estomac se contracter quand je croisai pour la première fois leur regard ; et ensuite, dans la mesure du possible, j'évitai de les voir. Si les yeux de Yin-mi, brièvement aperçus, évoquaient la clarté et la franchise, comme le soleil au zénith révèle l'immensité de la mer, ceux de sa sœur étaient pleins de ténèbres. Je soupçonnais un feu qui couve, une lumière diaphane, ambiguë ; elle me fit penser à un être voluptueux après une nuit de rites secrets, un être qui ne serait pas complètement présent, mais s'attarderait parmi les ombres de quelque souper aux chandelles et trouverait le monde bien pâle comparé au souvenir de sa sublime expérience, transigerait avec lui par indulgence, n'ayant besoin de rien de ce qu'il peut offrir.

Couple étrange... Je n'étais pas vraiment sûr qu'ils me plaisaient. Aucun des deux. Ils me semblaient une version rajeunie de Mme Chin et Fan-ku.

Nous parlâmes de choses et d'autres. Elle dit étudier l'archéologie, ajouta qu'elle se passionnait aussi pour l'ethnologie, puis proposa en passant que nous nous retrouvions un jour pour évoquer mes expériences en Chine. J'acceptai sans enthousiasme, moitié parce que je voulais être aimable avec la fille de mes hôtes, moitié parce que le ton de sa voix suggérait que cette rencontre n'aurait jamais lieu.

« Peut-être pourrais-je vous payer de retour », ajouta-t-elle avec une pointe de provocation amusée. Sans raison, je rougis jusqu'aux oreilles.

Elle rit. « Je veux dire, vous raconter des contes de fées par exemple, des contes occidentaux — ce serait une sorte d'échange.

— Oh, je pourrais lui raconter de plus jolis contes de fées que toi », intervint Peter.

Elle fronça les sourcils. Puis ils s'excusèrent, prétextant un « vernissage » au Village. Quand ils franchirent la porte, je surpris les yeux de Li qui me fixaient attentivement. Je frissonnai. De nouveau, cette contraction de l'estomac. J'avais décidé qu'elle ne me plaisait pas, mais mon ventre se crispa davantage quand ils partirent.

Ah oui... ai-je parlé de sa beauté ? Il n'est peut-être pas insignifiant que j'aie oublié, ou gardé pour la fin, ce qui me parut le plus important. Mais cette beauté stupéfiante, je ne l'admis d'abord qu'à contrecœur. Car sa perfection avait la froideur distante de la lune, quelque chose qui me repoussait tout en m'attirant.

Lo ne se montrait toujours pas. Comme à mon arrivée, Mme Ha-p'i et moi nous retrouvâmes seuls sans savoir quoi nous dire ; je me rappelai brusquement ce que j'avais dans la poche et que je destinais à mon hôtesse. L'argent ! Je l'avais presque oublié.

« Pardonnez mon étourderie, Mme Ha-p'i, la suppliai-je. Cela ne signifie pas que je n'apprécie pas votre générosité. Bien au contraire. » Je plongeai la main dans ma poche.

« Ma générosité ! » Elle rougit, porta machinalement la main à sa poitrine. « Que voulez-vous dire ? »

Par-dessus son épaule, je vis Lo émerger du couloir. Comprenant aussitôt la situation, il se mit à m'adresser des signes frénétiques, secoua la tête en tous sens, écrasa son index contre ses lèvres.

J'avais déjà sorti la liasse. En voyant les mimiques de Lo, j'hésitai à la donner à sa femme. Mais il était trop tard. Elle me regarda avec une simplicité consternée. « Pourquoi cet argent ? »

J'adressai à Lo un coup d'œil suppliant. « Je suis désolé, m'excusai-je en haussant les épaules et grimaçant un sourire lamentable. Je croyais.. »

Elle se retourna vers son mari. « Lo ? »

Il semblait à la torture. La tête basse, le visage cramoisi d'humiliation, il attendait.

« De quoi s'agit-il ? demanda-t-elle avec inquiétude en saisissant la main de son mari. Lo... ? »

— J'aurais dû t'en parler, répondit-il d'une voix pitoyable. Mais il s'agissait de la robe de mariée de sa mère. Il l'avait confiée à Mme Chin.

— Mme Chin ! » s'écria-t-elle.

Une cousine enceinte, l'épouse d'un des invités, qui avait suivi Lo dans la cuisine pour remplir son verre au robinet, semblait pétrifiée de stupeur tandis qu'à son insu, l'eau coulait sur sa main.

Lo attira sa femme à l'écart pour lui parler à voix basse.

Je restai figé sur place pendant qu'ils discutaient avec animation.

La jeune femme reprit contrôle d'elle-même et commença de rincer systématiquement tous les verres entassés dans l'évier en tendant l'oreille, me sembla-t-il, pour ne pas manquer un mot de la conversation.

Pendant que Lo parlait, Mme Ha-p'i tournait parfois la tête vers moi ou baissait les yeux sur la liasse de billets que je tenais toujours stupidement à la main sans savoir quoi en faire. Après une minute environ, Lo se tut. Mme Ha-p'i tourna lentement son visage vers son mari qui baissait la tête comme un petit garçon prêt au châtiment, mais qui espère encore le pardon. La tendresse maternelle éclaira les traits de la femme qui se pencha pour embrasser doucement la partie chauve du crâne. Lo soupira, leva les yeux avec reconnaissance.

Mme Ha-p'i avança vers moi en me tendant la main, rayonnante et confuse.

« Je suis désolé... » commençai-je.

Elle caressa spontanément ma joue, geste qui m'aurait choqué si je n'avais été profondément ému. « Non, ne vous excusez pas, dit-elle. Je suis contente. »

Par-dessus son épaule, je vis Lo s'essuyer le front avec son mouchoir. Croisant mon regard, il m'adressa un clin d'œil malicieux qui me renversa.

« Venez, dit-il en s'interposant entre nous. Nous avons fait une belle frayeur au jeune dragon. Il n'a pas l'habitude des intrigues mesquines de la vie domestique, car il a passé toute sa jeunesse à caracoler parmi les nuages. Nous ne devons pas le monopoliser. Il est ici pour voir Wo et discuter d'affaires importantes. Il faut les présenter immédiatement ! »

Il saisit mon bras et nous nous engageâmes tous trois dans le couloir. La jeune femme enceinte se hâta d'essuyer ses mains sur un torchon et trottina derrière nous.

Dans le couloir, j'entendis le brouhaha de la conversation qui se déroulait dans l'autre pièce.

« Vous avez réussi à la récupérer ? me demanda Mme Ha-p'i, désireuse de connaître le fin mot de l'histoire. Je parle de la robe.

— Oh, oui, répondis-je. Cela s'est relativement bien passé. Mme Chin n'a pas semblé ravie de me voir, mais après quelques sarcasmes, elle s'est montrée presque aimable. Cela m'a surpris. Après les avertissements de Lo, je m'attendais à des difficultés.

— Vous avez de la chance, dit-elle, avec dans la voix une trace de rancœur incongrue. Cette femme est dénuée de tout scrupule.

— Oui, acquiesça la femme enceinte en un chuchotement empressé. Certains prétendent même qu'elle est en cheville avec la Triade.

— La Triade ? » demandai-je en me tournant vers elle alors que nous entrions dans le salon.

Le bourdonnement de la conversation s'interrompit. Quand je levai les yeux, je vis la moitié des invités me regarder. Il y avait peut-être douze ou quinze personnes, tous Chinois, tous vêtus à l'occidentale, à l'unique exception d'une vieille femme. Leur âge s'échelonnait entre celui de l'aïeule aux cheveux blancs, assise à gauche dans un élégant fauteuil de cerisier chinois — le seul beau meuble de la pièce —, et celui de Yin-mi, installée à côté d'elle au bord d'une chaise à dos droit où elle suivait poliment la conversation de la femme âgée. Le buste droit, assise dans une pose merveilleuse de naturel, elle tenait délicatement sur ses genoux serrés une tasse de thé et sa soucoupe. Elle portait un corsage blanc flottant à col rond et un ruban noir noué en cravate, une jupe sombre, de longues chaussettes blanches et des chaussures en cuir. Remarquant le silence, elle aussi interrompit ses activités pour m'observer avec curiosité en battant des paupières. Je compris brusquement ce que son visage avait de si extraordinaire et troublant : elle ressemblait étonnamment à la fillette que j'avais vue dans le village en amont du fleuve où j'avais rencontré Tsin ! Mon pouls accéléra.

« La Triade, répéta en anglais une voix dure et nasillarde. Ne me dites pas que vous croyez encore à cette vieille scie ? »

Les murmures reprirent dans la pièce.

« D'accord, elle a bien sûr existé à une certaine époque — elle existe peut-être encore d'ailleurs, mais ce n'est plus qu'un symbole. Elle a aujourd'hui autant d'influence à Chinatown que le Ku Klux Klan. Les Italiens les ont mis au chômage depuis longtemps. »

J'avais profité de cette diversion pour reprendre contenance et pivoter vers l'orateur : le jeune homme rondouillard vautré sur le canapé au bout du salon ressemblait de façon déconcertante au Bouddha, du moins pour la corpulence. A peu près de mon âge, il portait une chemise synthétique hawaïenne d'un grenat brillant avec des éclaboussures jaune et orange électrique pour éblouir encore davantage l'œil. Son ventre tendait le tissu qui s'arrêtait à quelques centimètres au-dessus de son jean, exhibant ainsi une bande de graisse livide et quelques poils noirs de même épaisseur et texture que ceux qui ornaient sa lèvre supérieure en une imitation dérisoire de moustache. Une épaisse mèche noire de cheveux hirsutes masquait à demi son œil droit. Il me dévisagea sans la moindre expression, puis d'un coup de tête releva la mèche rebelle et passa la main dans ses cheveux pour stabiliser leur édifice précaire.

« Mais Wo... » objecta quelqu'un.

Wo !

« ... et le trafic de drogues — l'héroïne et l'opium qui envahissent les rues de Chinatown ? »

« Oui, renchérit un autre, et le jeu ? »

C'était donc Wo ? Mon attente fut totalement frustrée. J'essayai de combler le hiatus entre l'homme que j'avais imaginé et la réalité ; ce fut avec beaucoup de difficulté que j'écoutai la suite de la conversation.

Wo haussa les épaules d'un air suffisant. « Tout cela est du ressort de la Cosa Nostra », trancha-t-il nonchalamment, ex cathedra, en repoussant sa mèche noire d'un coup de tête. Le coin de sa lèvre duveteuse se releva en un sourire blasé. « Financée, naturellement, par une multinationale quelconque. »

Les invités échangèrent des regards appréciateurs. Aucun n'osa élever d'autre objection, car la référence aux « multinationales » ajoutait une dernière touche à l'infaillibilité de sa bulle papale.

Sur ce, il se tourna vers son public — tous les hommes présents dans la pièce, agglutinés autour du canapé, jouaient du coude pour s'approcher de lui, telle une assemblée de courtisans empressés — et reprit la conversation que j'avais manifestement interrompue. Les invités, qui posaient leurs questions en anglais, trahissaient leur plus ou moins bonne connaissance de la grammaire. Wo ne manquait pas une occasion d'émailler ses réponses de noms impressionnants — National Semi, Con Ed, Standard Cal, Schlumberger, IBM, et un sigle que je reconnus avec un pincement d'excitation, APL —, que les autres accueillaient par de petits cris de plaisir ou de gratitude. Un homme prenait même des notes. Wo lâchait ces noms avec toute la superbe et la nonchalance d'un monarque dispensant ses largesses à ses sujets ; et vraiment, tandis qu'il se pavanait, les bras étendus sur le dossier du canapé, son pied potelé (chaussé de tennis montants noirs) coincé sous son séant pour que personne n'ose s'asseoir à côté de lui, Wo n'était pas sans évoquer un jeune prince débraillé accordant une audience à un parterre admiratif.

« C'est Wo ! chuchota Lo à mon oreille comme si je pouvais encore l'ignorer. Venez, je vais vous présenter. »

Saisissant la manche de ma robe, il se fraya un chemin dans la foule qui ne s'écartait qu'à contrecœur.

Il se raclait la gorge. « Excusez je vous prie », disait-il, adoptant ce qui semblait le langage diplomatique officiel en présence de la couronne.

Wo leva la main pour intimer le silence à son interlocuteur, puis regarda son père. « Salut, p'pa, dit-il. On discute en ce moment de trucs vachement importants, tu saisis ? Qu'est-ce qui y a ?

— Excusez je vous prie, répéta Lo avec déférence. Il y a ici quelqu'un que je voudrais te faire connaître. » Il m'attira à ses côtés en présence de Sa Majesté.

« Voici Sun I. » Il recula d'un pas pour que je formule ma requête.

J'ignorais si je devais recourir à un titre quelconque pour m'adresser à Wo — peut-être Votre Ampleur. Je finis par opter pour une attitude moins formelle et m'inclinai très bas. « Votre père m'a beaucoup parlé de vous », dis-je en chinois, employant notre langue maternelle d'abord parce que je m'y sentais plus à l'aise, mais aussi peut-être avec un zeste de perversité simiesque. « Je suis très heureux de vous rencontrer.

— Je cause pas cette merde, répliqua froidement Wo en anglais.

— Wo ! » s'écria Mme Ha-p'i, scandalisée.

Il haussa les épaules, repoussa la mèche qui tombait sur son œil droit. Puis, avec un soupir de lassitude, il s'extirpa lentement du canapé. Quand il fut debout, il me tendit la main, serra la mienne mollement, sans enthousiasme, en me dévisageant avec un intérêt mitigé. « Drôle de tenue que vous portez là », dit-il en frottant ses ongles contre ma robe.

Je pris cela pour un compliment et répondis sincèrement : « Vous aussi.

— Ah ouais ? Elle vous plaît ? Je l'ai payée trente tickets. » Il remonta sa mèche une fois encore, et je songeai brusquement que ce geste, loin d'être purement utilitaire, exprimait l'autosatisfaction, la suffisance. « Vous êtes celui qui bosse dans le Dow, hein ?

— C'est un taoïste ! » interrompit Lo pour m'aider, sur un ton qui soulignait la singularité et l'importance de ma condition.

« Un Dowiste ! s'écria Wo d'une voix de fausset en éclatant de rire. Ouah, p'pa, t'es vraiment génial quand tu parles anglais !

— Excusez je vous prie, dit Lo en rougissant de honte.

— Un *prêtre* taoïste », intervint une voix. Tout le monde se retourna.

Assise dans la même position qu'auparavant, Yin-mi tenait toujours sa tasse de thé sur ses genoux, mais une lueur brillait maintenant dans ses yeux et ses joues étaient roses.

Mon cœur s'emballa. Qu'elle se fût donné le mal d'enregistrer et de citer un détail aussi dérisoire me remplit d'un immense bonheur.

« Ça y est, j'ai pigé, répondit Wo. Taoïste comme la religion. » Il retroussa les lèvres, opina du chef. « C'est *cool*. » Releva sa mèche. « Vous savez prédire l'avenir et tout le bordel ? »

J'inclinai la tête avec gêne.

« Hé, tu pourrais peut-être employer ce truc pour prévoir les fluctuations... » Il réfléchit. « Non, trancha-t-il, tous ces tours de passe-passe religieux sont des foutaises. »

Je me raidis.

« Je vais te dire ce qui est vraiment super magique : l'IBM 360. »

Il y eut des grognements approbateurs dans l'assistance.

« Bon, euh... *Sonny* — tu t'appelles bien *Sonny** ?
— Sun I, rectifiai-je non sans agacement.
— Ouais, *Sonny*, comme je disais, que puis-je faire pour toi ? »
Lo profita de cette ouverture pour nous pousser sur le canapé l'un à côté de l'autre. « Vous parlez », dit-il en s'attaquant à la tâche ingrate qui consistait à maintenir les courtisans à l'écart. Pendant que nous attendions que le brouhaha décroisse, j'observai attentivement le visage de Yin-mi qui parlait avec la vieille dame ; elle l'aida bientôt à se lever, se rassit, souffla sur son thé et en but une gorgée.
« Hé, *Sonny*, m'apostropha Wo avec ennui, tu vas rester assis à bayer aux corneilles, ou tu veux qu'on cause ?
— Excusez-moi, dis-je. Je sais que vous devez être très occupé. Votre père m'a parlé de votre importante position à la Bourse de New York. »
Wo repoussa sa mèche avec une véhémence et une majesté inhabituelles. « Ouais, et alors ?
— J'espérais que vous pourriez m'aider. » Je baissai les yeux modestement. « Je voudrais me familiariser avec le Dow.
— Je croyais que t'étais déjà taoïste, remarqua-t-il avec un sourire facétieux.
— Je parle du Dow américain.
— Le Dow Jones, ajouta-t-il doctement. Ecoute voir, *Sonny*, va falloir séparer nettement les deux choses si tu veux causer avec moi. Il y a une petite différence, tu sais.
— Superficiellement peut-être, répliquai-je, poussé à la rébellion par sa condescendance. Mais à un niveau plus profond, les deux sont une seule et même chose.
— Ah ouais ? Je suis pas philosophe, mais j'avale pas facilement les couleuvres. Tu veux bien expliquer ça, ou alors on fait comme si t'avais rien dit ? »
Ouvrant la bouche pour répondre, je remarquai que Yin-mi avait levé les yeux de sa tasse qu'elle tenait à quelques centimètres de ses lèvres en me regardant avec attention. J'ai alors comparé la gravité lumineuse de son visage à une gorgée d'eau pure après la liqueur lourde, presque obscène que j'avais devinée sur les traits de sa sœur. Loin de détourner les yeux, elle continua de m'examiner avec intérêt, comme si elle attendait ma réponse. Gêné, je baissai les miens.
« Le Tao est la Source, dis-je calmement en choisissant mes mots avec soin, comme si je plaidais ma cause au tribunal devant un jury exigeant.
— La source de quoi ? demanda-t-il. Du Mississippi ?
— De tout, répliquai-je. Le Tao est la matrice de l'existence, le creuset sans forme où naissent les dix mille formes et où elles retournent enfin, comme dans une tombe.
— Ouah ! s'écria Wo en agitant une main molle. Balance pas toute la sauce d'un coup, fiston ! Sinon faudra que je réclame un sac en papier à l'hôtesse de l'air. »

---

* Jeu de mots hélas intraduisible : *sonny* signifie fiston *(NdT)*.

Je ne saisis pas parfaitement sa raillerie, mais sentis qu'il se moquait de moi. Je me troublai.

« Laisse-le finir, Wo. »

Nous tournâmes tous deux la tête, lui avec irritation, moi avec gratitude.

« La ferme, Yin-mi.

— Continuez », m'encouragea-t-elle d'un murmure qui ignorait l'insulte. Ses joues étaient de plus en plus rouges.

« Ouais, d'accord, concéda Wo. La suite. Je vois toujours pas le tableau. A quoi ça ressemble ?

— Le Tao ne ressemble à rien, répondis-je, non pas à lui, mais à elle. C'est une absence, le vide brillant qui réside au cœur de l'existence. Il est apaisement, harmonie, émancipation du soi. »

Elle rougit, mais continua de m'écouter. Une lumière jouait dans son regard.

« Ça a pas l'air folichon, commenta Wo. Comme je disais, de simples tours de passe-passe totalement irréels. En tout cas, pas de doute, ça n'a strictement rien à voir avec le Dow — l'autre, *mon* Dow Ça c'est du concret ! Tout ton baratin en jette, mais c'est trop théorique : ça tient pas le coup à l'expérience. Le Dow est exactement l'inverse — pas "l'émancipation *du* soi" — il prononça mon expression avec une emphase moqueuse — mais l'émancipation *de* soi — tu connais ? *Number One*. Moi le premier. Chacun pour soi, tous les coups sont permis, pas de quartier et Dieu pour tous. Le chien mange le chien. Le chat mange la souris. Le chien mange le chat. L'homme mange le chien. Et chacun se démerde comme il peut, tu vois ce que je veux dire ? Voilà pour *mon* Dow. Et si tu crois que c'est pas réel, va donc y faire un tour. » Il releva sa mèche. « A moins d'un kilomètre d'ici, tu peux le vérifier avec tes cinq sens si ça te chante ; coupes-en une tranche avec un couteau et étale-la sur un bout de pain. Si tu me montres ton Tao à toi et que je le voie comme ça, alors je me convertirai peut-être. Pour l'instant je préfère investir mon fric dans ce que je connais.

— Ce spectacle est stupéfiant de vitalité, je ne le nie pas. » Je soupirai en me creusant la tête pour trouver une réfutation appropriée. « Mais à cause de son évidence même, le monde phénoménal est toujours aisément retenu par le tamis grossier des sens. La facilité avec laquelle on appréhende une chose ne prouve pas sa réalité. En fait, les illusions sont infiniment plus simples à saisir que les vérités. Votre Dow est une de ces illusions ; il a la réalité d'une ombre. Le Tao est le corps qui jette cette ombre. Il jette les ombres des "dix mille choses" — le Dow n'en est qu'une parmi tant d'autres.

— Ouais, mais je le vois pas, ton Tao, *Sonny*. Une ombre possède au moins la même forme que la chose qui la provoque, pas vrai ? Je veux dire, il y a une ressemblance évidente entre les deux, non ? Mais le Tao et le Dow ! Ils sont complètement opposés, à ce qu'il me semble. Je veux dire, t'as déjà vu un poulet avec une ombre d'hippopotame, ou un camion Mack avec une ombre de call-girl ?

— Essayez de raisonner ainsi, dis-je, puisant mon courage, voire mon inspiration dans l'attention concentrée de Yin-mi. Imaginez un torrent de montagne, tumultueux, impétueux, qui dégringole le long d'un versant abrupt... (Elle acquiesça.) Maintenant, suivez son cours mentalement. Quand il arrive en bas de la montagne, la pente s'adoucit ; il ralentit, s'élargit, creuse un lit plus profond. Ensuite, après un voyage de mille milles, ce fleuve, qui était autrefois un torrent écumant sur un versant lointain, se jette dans la mer, toute rage épuisée, absorbé comme un détail insignifiant par la masse immense, apaisé aussi doucement qu'un enfant coléreux par le sein de sa mère. Ce torrent de montagne capricieux — voilà votre Dow. L'océan est mon Tao. » Yin-mi applaudit gaiement. J'étais moi-même assez satisfait de ma métaphore. Elle me venait à l'esprit pour la première fois et je la tirais de mon expérience.

« Ça présente pas mal, dit Wo. Mais je suis toujours pas convaincu. C'est bien beau, les images, mais la poésie est une chose, la logique une autre. Je veux des preuves. Dis-moi donc où les deux choses se rencontrent. Pour reprendre ta métaphore, montre-moi le... comment ça s'appelle ?... tu sais bien, le... — il regarda Yin-mi en faisant claquer ses doigts — ... l'endroit où le fleuve se jette dans l'océan ?

— Le delta, chuchota Yin-mi, à moi.

— Ouais, le delta, dit-il. Où il est ? »

Je commençai à répondre, mais toute inspiration m'avait quitté. Je ressemblais à l'élève qui le jour de l'examen passe fébrilement en revue les informations qu'il a mémorisées, sans rien trouver pour répondre à la question du professeur.

Je voulus improviser une réponse spécieuse en espérant sauver ma mise, mais paralysé par la gravité pleine d'espoir de Yin-mi, échouai lamentablement. « Je ne sais pas, dis-je. Je n'ai pas encore trouvé cet endroit.

— Ah ah, c'est bien ce que je pensais, répondit-il, soulagé.

— C'est peut-être ce que vous êtes venu chercher ? » suggéra timidement Yin-mi, d'une voix qui tremblait un peu.

Je ne répondis pas ; c'était inutile. Un pacte nous liait désormais ; une question silencieuse et une réponse tacite ; des conditions posées et acceptées. Elle me dévoilait toute la profondeur de son être. Je n'avais jamais lu autant de choses sur un visage.

« Tiens tiens ? fit Wo d'un air surpris, amusé, légèrement sarcastique. Vous avez fait connaissance, on dirait ? »

Le charme fut rompu. Yin-mi baissa les yeux vers sa tasse de thé.

« Comme je disais, fiston, poursuivit-il, le delta... Tu admettras que c'est la foi qui te fait croire à son existence. Pour moi, c'est OK. J'crois que la religion, c'est justement ça, mais je risquerais pas mon fric là-dessus. Tu choisis ta religion, moi la mienne... Mais comment en sommes-nous arrivés là ? Tu me disais que tu voulais te familiariser avec le Dow, c'est ça ? »

J'acquiesçai.

« Ecoute, faut juste que je te pose une question. Si le Dow est tellement irréel et fumeux, et l'autre si formidable, pourquoi te faire chier ? On dirait bien qu'il y a une contradiction quelque part. Me dis rien... » Il me sourit malicieusement, avec un air de complicité dans une affaire louche. « Tu as quelques billets que tu aimerais investir, vrai ou faux ?

— Cela irait contre mon vœu de pauvreté, l'informai-je froidement.

— Sans blague ! » Il semblait ébahi. « Faire du fric va contre tes principes, hein ? Elle est pas mauvaise, celle-là !

— Je désire simplement étudier le Dow en tant qu'observateur désintéressé, expliquai-je. Observer sans participer. »

— Baigner dedans, mais sans te mouiller, hein ? »

J'acquiesçai. « Et puis, ajoutai-je, je n'ai pas d'argent à investir.

— Je t'aime bien, mec, vraiment. Mais que crois-tu que je puisse faire pour toi ?

— Eh bien, compte tenu de votre haute position, j'espérais que vous pourriez me trouver un emploi. »

Wo frémit comme si ma réponse l'avait pris au dépourvu, caressé à rebrousse-poil. « Un emploi, hein ? Je savais bien que tout ce fatras philosophique cachait quelque chose. » Il réfléchit. « Ecoute, *Sonny*, si je voulais, je pourrais probablement te faire bosser là-bas comme saute-ruisseau ou grouillot, mais suis mon conseil, trouve autre chose. Un mec religieux comme toi... vraiment je comprends pas. Incruste-toi au restaurant. Tu seras plus heureux avec Lo. P'pa prétend que tu as un vrai talent pour la cuisine. Et puis, à la Bourse on te traiterait comme un esclave, tu serais exploité.

— Je m'en moque, le coupai-je. L'argent n'est pas mon but. J'en veux seulement assez pour vivre.

— Je sais pas...

— Ecoutez, Wo, dis-je en désespoir de cause, abattant mon dernier atout. Il y a une chose dont je ne vous ai pas parlé. En plus du delta (j'adressai à Yin-mi un coup d'œil reconnaissant), mon intérêt pour le Dow tient à une autre raison. J'ai fait tout ce chemin jusqu'en Amérique pour tenter de retrouver mon père. Vous êtes mon seul espoir.

— Ton père ? » Il haussa les sourcils. « Voilà pas autre chose... J'ai comme l'impression qu'après toute la philosophie et les métaphores, on entre enfin dans le vif du sujet. » Une ombre de perplexité traversa son visage. « Mais je vois pas le rapport avec un boulot que je pourrais te trouver.

— Mon père est lié au Dow, répondis-je. C'est ma seule piste. Je ne sais pas où le chercher ailleurs.

— Dis donc, tu espères tomber dessus par hasard, ou quoi ?

— Peut-être, répondis-je. Je ne sais vraiment pas. C'est une intuition.

— Une intuition ? C'est la méthode taoïste ? Je veux pas me moquer de toi ni rien, tu comprends, mais tout ça serait pas un peu démodé ? Je veux dire, nous vivons au XXe siècle, pas vrai ? Tu as déjà entendu parler des annuaires téléphoniques ?

— Annuaire téléphonique ?

— Ouais. Y a donc pas d'annuaires en Chine ?

— Pas au monastère, répondis-je.

— Ah ouais, vive la nature et à bas les capotes anglaises, hein ? C'est quand même plus sympa de vivre ici. » A côté du canapé, sur une table basse, un téléphone était posé sur l'annuaire de Manhattan. « Exerce un peu tes doigts », dit-il en le tirant. Il cligna de l'œil, puis repoussa la mèche rebelle. « Allez d'accord, donne-le-moi.

— Quoi ?

— Le nom, le nom.
— Oh, fis-je, Love.
Il lécha son index, se mit à feuilleter. « Law... Lee... Lie... Low... Zut, trop loin. Le voilà — Love. Les initiales ?
— A.E. ou Eddie.
— Eddie Love. » Il retroussa les lèvres. « Eddie Love... Où donc ai-je entendu ce nom ? Hé, c'était pas... — Il fit claquer ses doigts — ce type d'APL — celui qui s'est emparé de l'affaire. Le gros scandale et tout ?
— Il s'agit de son arrière-arrière-grand-père, rectifiai-je.
— Non ? C'est si vieux que ça ? »
J'acquiesçai.
Il me dévisagea brièvement, puis haussa les épaules. « T'es mieux placé que moi pour le savoir. L'histoire est pas mon fort. Tout ce que je sais, c'est que ça s'est passé avant mon époque. » Il sembla réaliser brusquement les implications de son rapprochement. « Tu plaisantes ou quoi ? Ce type, ou son arrière-petit-fils, peu importe — l'un des *Love* est ton père ? »
J'acquiesçai encore.
« Allez..., fit-il d'une voix légèrement menaçante. C'est une plaisanterie ? Je te le conseille pas ; si c'en est une, je vais vraiment me fâcher.
— Ce n'est pas une plaisanterie », l'assurai-je.
Il regarda dans le vide comme s'il entrevoyait une perspective mirobolante. « Ouaaooh ! dit-il en étirant démesurément les syllabes. Pas mal. Pas mal du tout. Tu comptes porter plainte ?
— Wo ! » protesta Yin-mi.
Je pense que mon visage vira au cramoisi.
« OK, OK, dit-il, conciliant. Je n'ai donc pas à me mêler de ça ? Désolé. Oublie ma question.
— Et le nom ? lui rappela Yin-mi.
— Exact : A.E. Love. » Il se concentra sur la page. « Il y a un A.C Love... Un D.C. Love... mais pas de A.E. Love.
— Cherchez à Eddie, proposai-je.
— Non, pas de Eddie non plus. Il y a un E.E. Love (on dirait une star du porno, pas vrai ?) Un E. Love tout simple, ça t'irait ? Il y a un E. Love On essaie ?
— Oui ! »
Il coinça le récepteur sous son menton et composa le numéro. « Allô ? Je voudrais parler à M. Love. » Il m'adressa un clin d'œil. « Allô ? Allô ? Eddie Love ? *Elijah !* Quel drôle de nom... Soyez donc pas susceptible... Ah ouais ? Toi aussi, bouseux, dans une fosse à purin ! » Il raccrocha violemment.
« Désolé, dit-il. Pas de chance. Mais il est peut-être sur la liste rouge. »
Il téléphona aux renseignements. « Y a-t-il un A.E. ou Eddie Love sur la liste rouge ? Ouais, comme ça se prononce. Vérifiez les derniers abonnés, voulez-vous ? Quoi ? Je sais bien que vous ne pouvez pas me donner cette information. Est-ce que je vous ai demandé son numéro ? Je veux simplement savoir si ce nom figure sur la liste rouge. Vous pouvez bien me dire ça, non ? Quoi ? il n'y a pas de Love. Pas de Eddie non plus. OK, chérie, passe un bon week-end. Salut. »

Wo reposa le combiné, releva sa mèche, puis haussa les épaules avec une moue fataliste. « Pas trace de ton gars, dit-il, du moins selon les renseignements de New York. » Il fronça les sourcils : il réfléchissait. « Un type de son envergure habite peut-être en banlieue. Probablement à Westchester ou Hamptons, ou dans le Connecticut. Si on veut tout vérifier, on en a pour la journée. J'aimerais t'aider, *Sonny*, sincèrement. Mais... » Il tourna ses paumes vers le plafond avec un sourire gêné.

« Je pourrais vous aider, proposa Yin-mi.
— Vraiment ?
— Ouais, dit Wo, bonne idée. Prenez donc le téléphone et branchez-le dans la chambre des parents, d'ac ? Ici, nous devons régler des affaires importantes. Essayez d'abord les agglomérations dont je vous ai parlé, puis les villes desservies par le train. Vous aurez peut-être de la chance. » Il se baissa pour débrancher le téléphone, enroula plusieurs fois le fil autour du combiné, puis me le lança. « A plus tard.
— Et mon emploi ? demandai-je.
— T'as de la suite dans les idées, pas vrai ? Ecoute, fiston, laisse tomber. Je te jure que c'est pas une bonne idée.
— S'il vous plaît », dis-je d'une voix calme, suppliante.

Il serra les lèvres en une grimace qui ne présageait rien de bon.

« Wo ! C'est un ami de papa, insista Yin-mi. Pourquoi hésites-tu ? Sa demande est tellement modeste.
— Ah ouais ? Tu crois peut-être que tout le monde fait mes quatre volontés là-bas, hein ? »

Certains courtisans, qui depuis quelque temps s'étaient approchés le plus discrètement possible, échangèrent des regards stupéfaits, que Wo remarqua.

« Non que ce me soit impossible, comprends-moi bien, si je le voulais.
— Alors pourquoi refuses-tu ? » demanda-t-elle simplement.

Tous les invités observaient Wo, qui sentit sa marge de manœuvre se réduire, comme si on mettait sa légitimité à l'épreuve. Serrant et desserrant les poings, il haletait un peu, foudroyait Yin-mi du regard.

Elle réagissait à son irritation avec la même expression que je lui avais vue l'autre soir devant Lo — sans peur ni haine, mais avec une sincérité cristalline qui renfermait, tel un précieux trésor dans une vitrine de musée, une question pleine de candeur, un noyau de vulnérabilité absolue qui réclamait une réponse tout aussi sincère.

« D'accord, d'accord, capitula Wo avec un soupir agacé. Lundi matin, neuf heures moins le quart, retrouve-moi à Trinity Church. »

Un murmure d'adoration parcourut la foule.

« Merci ! » m'écriai-je, comblé.

Wo lança sa mèche en arrière comme un grand personnage. « Ça va, ça va, dit-il. Mais pas de courbette, hein ? Je supporte pas ces conneries.
— Je vous serai éternellement reconnaissant, Wo, dis-je, sans doute avec extravagance, mais absolument sincère.
— Ouais, répondit-il presque à regret, j'espère bien... » Il gloussa. « Mais t'inquiète pas, faudra que tu me renvoies l'ascenseur.
— Tout ce que vous voudrez ! » promis-je.

Je me repentis aussitôt des doutes que j'avais conçus en le voyant pour la première fois. Je suis convaincu que, m'eût-il tendu sa main potelée, je l'aurais embrassée comme celle d'un empereur.

Par bonheur, l'occasion ne se présenta pas. Il cessa de nous regarder pour nous signifier que l'audience était terminée, attira l'attention d'un des courtisans empressés qui piaffaient en coulisse, et d'un ahurissant mouvement de tête lui fit comprendre qu'il pouvait approcher. Alors il se laissa lourdement tomber sur le canapé parmi les coussins. En moins d'une seconde, la horde fondit sur nous ; les sujets bannis étaient rappelés de leur exil par un monarque versatile dont les caprices suscitaient gratitude, amour et admiration. Par-dessus le tourbillon compact, je cherchai Yin-mi.

« Au secours ! Fuyez ! » s'écria-t-elle en riant et tendant le bras au-dessus de la foule. Surpris et charmé par sa gaieté enjouée — une facette de sa personnalité que j'ignorais —, je saisis sa main. Mais ce fut elle qui me guida. Sa paume était fraîche et menue, ses doigts exerçaient sur les miens une pression décidée. Dans un chaos de corps comprimés les uns contre les autres, nous avançâmes centimètre par centimètre. Je m'en remis à elle, m'abandonnant volontiers à la douce et brève extase de la dérive sous la conduite de Yin-mi. Je me sentais autant en sécurité que le jeune enfant qui s'endort entre les bras de sa mère et goûte à un bonheur inconscient, irresponsable. D'une ultime poussée, nous fûmes chassés à l'autre bout de la pièce vers les ténèbres extérieures. Quand elle lâcha ma main, un léger désespoir s'ouvrit en moi.

Mais le visage en feu, un peu essoufflée, elle se retourna pour me sourire : ma blessure guérit aussitôt et je fus largement dédommagé.

5

La chambre à coucher des Ha-p'i était un capharnaüm exigu. On pouvait seulement s'asseoir sur le lit qui s'étendait comme une plaine affaissée dont les marches semblaient menacées par le chaos — un chaos toutefois aussi bien agencé que dans la cuisine, comme si la confusion procédait d'un ordre sous-jacent. Les draps étaient de la même couleur que les tennis de Scottie, un gris cireux qui témoignait d'innombrables lavages. En revanche, le fil du motif brodé à la tête du lit, un entrelacs de *Fu* et de *Shou*, était sans doute aussi rouge et vif que le jour de leur mariage. Je compris que c'était l'œuvre de Mme Ha-p'i à cause de la pelote à aiguilles — un Chinois souriant aux yeux plissés et au gros ventre — posée sur un oreiller sous une lampe de chevet. Le bonhomme était lardé d'épingles et d'aiguilles à broder dont le chas portait d'innombrables fils multicolores, comme les rubans chatoyants fixés aux banderilles du picador. Pourtant, le Chinois souriait. Ce martyr bon enfant me rappela Wo, lui aussi soumis à une sorte de malédiction vaudoue. Je dus m'exhorter à l'Humilité pour me convaincre que cette association était sans doute gratuite, inspirée par ma jalousie de la position enviable de Wo. Du même côté du lit, posé sur un carton à chapeau, se trouvait un superbe coupon de soie noire avec une frange de houppes, qui ressemblait à un châle. Une partie de la pièce de soie était tendue sur un tambour à broder. Dans le cercle de bois brut, Mme Ha-p'i avait commencé un chrysanthème — une tige d'un vert éclatant surmontée du poudroiement doré d'une fleur somptueuse semblable à un nuage. Je ressentis un pincement de nostalgie douce-amère — la robe, ma mère, Love... le faux chrysanthème qui avait tout déclenché...

« C'est beau, n'est-ce pas ? dit Yin-mi en remarquant mon intérêt pour la fleur. Ma mère brode pour une de ses amies, Mme Chen, qui possède une boutique d'antiquités sur Mott Street et prend les broderies en dépôt. »

Je savais mon désir futile, mais je voulais qu'elle comprenne mon émotion, la peine qui me nouait la gorge. Pourtant je ne pus me décider à parler.

« A quoi pensez-vous ? » demanda-t-elle doucement.

Je ris amèrement. « A plus que je ne saurais dire.

— C'est la robe de votre mère, n'est-ce pas ? »

Je fus surpris. « Comment le savez-vous ? Vous semblez lire dans mes pensées.

— Mon père, répondit-elle simplement.
— Il vous a parlé de la robe, de l'argent ? Mais il n'a rien dit à votre mère. Pourquoi ?
— Je l'ai interrogé, dit-elle avec une franchise qui me fit rougir et baisser les yeux. Cela vous gêne ?
— Non, répliquai-je. Enfin, oui... Je ne sais pas. »
Elle rit, d'un rire aussi limpide que son regard.
« Aujourd'hui, en arrivant, je crois avoir commis une bourde stupide, dis-je. J'ai fait mine de rendre l'argent, mais ta mère n'a rien compris à mon geste. J'ai eu l'impression d'être un imbécile, pire, un criminel. Ton père a dû s'expliquer. Je crains de l'avoir mis dans de beaux draps.
— Ce n'est pas grave, me rassura-t-elle. Il a l'habitude. Il vit de cette façon.
— Comment cela ? demandai-je, un peu étonné. De quelle façon ?
— Toujours au bord d'un précipice quelconque, plein de bonnes intentions, prêt à aider — lui-même ou autrui — mais d'habitude les choses empirent après son intervention.
— Pourtant il m'a aidé. »
Elle sourit. « Je sais. Il vous apprécie. Vous *admire*.
— Je ne vois pas pourquoi, répondis-je, gêné.
— Il vous considère comme un homme éduqué. »
Je ris. « Oh, ça *!* Il s'est mis en tête que j'étais un connaisseur. Je ne comprends pas. Rien ne saurait être plus éloigné de la vérité. »
Elle vacilla un peu, ferma les yeux, dodelina de la tête. « Ah... les subtilités du vin », soupira-t-elle. L'imitation était parfaite.
« Exactement ! » m'écriai-je, ravi.
Nous éclatâmes de rire.
« J'avais honte de lui avouer mon ignorance, admis-je.
— C'est sans importance. Il s'en doute certainement. Il désirait seulement boire et parler avec quelqu'un. Il est trop seul, il ne connaît que le travail.
— Oui, acquiesçai-je en gloussant. Je peux en témoigner. »
Elle me regarda gravement. « Je crois que mon père retrouve en vous sa propre jeunesse. Il admire vos rêves, vos idéaux. Surtout votre liberté. Il ne peut plus se payer le luxe de rêver. La vie lui a retiré cette consolation. Voilà pourquoi il boit. C'est son seul plaisir. Il a tout sacrifié pour nous.
— Tu l'aimes beaucoup, n'est-ce pas ? » lui demandai-je sur un ton radouci.
Elle hocha la tête. « Et je l'admire. »
Je décelai dans sa remarque une pointe de blâme ou de défi... une comparaison implicite qui, bien qu'inconsciente, tournait à mon désavantage.
« Je me demande ce que ta mère a pensé ? » dis-je, comprenant aussitôt que cette question ne m'intéressait pas, que je recherchais, un peu sournoisement peut-être, l'approbation de Yin-mi.
« Elle est très sensible, dit-elle. Complimente-la pour sa cuisine. Surveille mon père : il est passé maître en ce domaine. Il suffit qu'il dise à ma mère que son canard laqué à elle ou son potage aux nids d'hirondelle est meilleur que celui qu'il prépare, pour qu'elle fonde littéralement. Elle rougit, lui tape

sur le bras, le cajole, le dorlote et accepte immédiatement toutes ses propositions. Il utilise ce stratagème depuis des années. » Elle sourit. « Il n'a pas l'air comme ça, mais sous son apparence polie, il tient un peu du coquin. »

Je me rappelai son clin d'œil.

« Yin-mi, dis-je, l'autre nuit dans la cuisine...

— Oui ?

— Qu'as-tu pensé ?

— Pensé ? »

J'acquiesçai.

« J'ai pensé que mon père fauchait l'argent que maman gagnait avec ses broderies, répondit-elle. Et j'avais raison. » Elle rit.

« Non, dis-je, je voulais dire... de moi ? »

Son rire, qui dorait ses yeux comme le soleil la surface d'un lac, s'évanouit, englouti par des profondeurs graves et tranquilles.

« Juste avant de sortir de la cuisine, dis-je. Tu t'es retournée pour me regarder.

— Je me souviens, dit-elle.

— Tu avais cette expression... »

Elle cligna des yeux.

« J'ai cru que tu me méprisais. »

Elle parut surprise, sa voix s'adoucit : « Je ne savais que penser.

— Tu le sais maintenant ? demandai-je, incapable de maîtriser le tremblement de ma voix.

— Je ne suis pas certaine, dit-elle. Oui, je crois que je sais. Un peu. »

Cette modeste concession provoqua une joie disproportionnée. Je sentis mon cœur s'envoler comme un ballon dans un ciel bleu sans nuage. J'essayai de le ramener à la raison, mais en vain.

Yin-mi pencha la tête et me dévisagea avec curiosité. Ses traits évoquaient un horizon illimité, la plénitude solennelle qu'on découvre en mer. Trouvant la réponse à sa question, ou peut-être, plus vraisemblablement repoussant celle-ci à plus tard, elle finit par détourner les yeux.

« Je crois qu'il y a des annuaires dans ce tiroir, dit-elle en montrant une commode. Je ne suis pas sûre qu'ils soient récents, mais autant les consulter. Occupe-t'en pendant que je téléphone. »

Elle suivit les conseils de Wo, commença par Hamptons, puis le comté de Westchester. En l'absence de toute réponse positive, elle entreprit d'appeler systématiquement les villes desservies par la ligne de l'Hudson. Pendant ce temps, j'explorai les vieux annuaires. Il y en avait une douzaine, quelques-uns du New Jersey, la plupart de diverses localités de Long Island. Ces listes interminables m'impressionnèrent. Chaque volume promettait une révélation imminente et me tourmentait. Mon espoir insufflait la vie, l'intérêt, voire du suspense aux mornes pages remplies de caractères identiques... jusqu'à l'inévitable déception. Les fascicules devenaient alors de sinistres inventaires, des rames oppressantes de noms abstraits, absurdes.

Je quémandai le secours de Yin-mi. Coinçant le récepteur entre son menton et sa clavicule, elle haussa les épaules. « Toujours rien, murmura-t-elle. Je vais essayer la ligne de New Haven. »

Je me penchai sur un autre volume. Nouvelle déception. Il m'en resta bientôt un seul : celui de Port Washington. Je regardai sa couverture avec indifférence, l'ouvris en soupirant. Une chose retint alors mon attention. Je retournai aux pages de garde. Parmi les bureaux centraux énumérés en petits caractères, je découvris un nom que je reconnus : Sands Point. Brusquement, je me rappelai : le domaine de la famille Love. Hsiao l'avait mentionné. Mon pouls accéléra.

Remarquant mon excitation, Yin-mi plaqua la main contre le pavillon du récepteur qu'elle posa sur ses cuisses. « Qu'y a-t-il ?

— Je l'ai peut-être trouvé, lui dis-je en feuilletant l'annuaire. Je me suis rappelé quelque chose... Une seconde. Loman... Lord... Losey... Love... Love... Le voilà ! A.E. Love IV, Douze Lighthouse Road.

— OK, calme-toi, me conseilla-t-elle, aussi excitée que moi. Donne-moi le numéro.

— Trois-six-neuf..., dis-je.

— Trois... six... neuf, répéta-t-elle en composant les chiffres sur le cadran qui cliquetait, puis chuintait en revenant en arrière.

— Deux-trois-deux-sept.

— Deux... trois... deux... sept. » Elle colla le récepteur à son oreille. « Ça sonne », chuchota-t-elle. Elle me le tendit.

Je le regardai d'un air absent, puis observai Yin-mi. Elle m'encouragea d'un signe de tête. Soudain, je compris : *j'avais trouvé — c'était la connexion* — les spires de cet ombilic noir allaient me relier à lui. Dans quelques secondes, à l'autre bout du fil, il décrocherait, le circuit se fermerait, les impulsions électriques traverseraient les aimants, sa voix allait courir le long des torsades de cuivre pour atteindre les fils vivants de mes nerfs, entrer dans ma vie. Saisi d'une violente extase, mon cœur s'emballa. Puis la terreur émergea des limbes de la conscience, une panique innommable, irraisonnée.

« Sun I, dit-elle, le téléphone. »

Je le saisis. Un maelström silencieux se rua dans mon oreille interne à travers le disque troué du récepteur, un néant qui appelait une réponse, un océan vide et bourdonnant qui réclamait l'éclair frémissant de la vie.

J'entendis un déclic, des parasites, puis une voix féminine.

« Le numéro demandé, trois-six-neuf-deux-trois-deux-sept, n'est plus attribué. Je vous prie de consulter l'annuaire ou votre documentation, ou de contacter une opératrice. Ceci est un enregistrement. » Clic. Bruit blanc. La stridulation des cigales.

Je replaçai lentement le récepteur sur le poste

Yin-mi me regardait en silence.

« La ligne a été coupée, dis-je, dégoûté.

— Laisse-moi essayer encore. » Elle décrocha. « Je me suis peut-être trompée de numéro. »

Je restai prostré, apathique. Elle écouta la sonnerie en examinant le plafond. Son visage se tendit brusquement. Puis il prit une expression désolée. Elle raccrocha en soupirant. « Je suis navrée. »

Tournant l'annuaire vers elle, elle explora la colonne. « A.E. Love IV », murmura-t-elle pensivement, le doigt immobile sur la page. Puis elle ferma le volume.

« Attends une seconde, dis-je en reprenant espoir à mesure que je me rappelais plus précisément les paroles de Hsiao. Mon père était le cinquième. Nous venons d'appeler son propre père, Arthur Love.
— Tu sais quoi ? répliqua-t-elle en montrant le volume. Cet annuaire a plus de dix ans. Ils ont peut-être changé le numéro. Essayons les renseignements de Port Washington. »
Mais il n'y avait plus la moindre mention de A.E. Love, ni IV, ni V. Ce nom semblait avoir été effacé du rôle de l'humanité.
« Ne te décourage pas, dit Yin-mi. Il a peut-être déménagé. Il y a encore plein d'endroits que nous n'avons pas essayés. »
Elle s'obstina courageusement pendant dix autres minutes ; je l'observais résigné, presque indifférent.
« Ne sois pas triste, dit-elle enfin en soupirant malgré elle. Allez, reposons-nous un peu. Emmène-moi sur le toit. Tu ne m'as pas encore montré où tu vivais. »
Soumis, je la laissai me guider une fois encore. Nous croisâmes sa mère dans la cuisine.
« Où allez-vous ? demanda-t-elle, surprise. Le déjeuner est presque prêt.
— Nous mangerons plus tard, dit Yin-mi. D'accord ? Nous montons sur le toit. »
Mme Ha-p'i nous regarda d'un air étonné, mais céda quand elle remarqua mon abattement. « Bon. Mais ne restez pas trop longtemps. »

★

De l'obscurité confinée de l'immeuble froid et humide, nous sortîmes au soleil, à l'air libre. Je crus sentir une légère brise, mais c'était seulement l'effet du passage de l'intérieur à l'extérieur. L'air était humide, d'une luminosité éblouissante. Ma fidèle cohorte de pigeons, habituée à mes pérégrinations, ne se dérangea même pas à notre arrivée, et nous dûmes les chasser dans un concert de roucoulements outragés.
« Tu les as apprivoisés, remarqua Yin-mi avec innocence, comme impressionnée.
— Ou vice-versa », répliquai-je d'un air las.
Elle rit, puis m'observa gravement, non sans pitié. « Ne perds pas courage, murmura-t-elle.
— A quel propos ? demandai-je un peu méchamment. Pour les pigeons ? Je me suis résigné à leur présence.
— Tu sais bien que je ne parle pas d'eux, mais de ton père. »
Je haussai les épaules. « Je ne me décourage pas. Je n'ai jamais cru le trouver de cette façon. »
Elle attendit une explication.
Une autre bulle remonta du puits de la mémoire. « Je dois suivre l'impulsion première de ma nature inconsciente, dis-je en me rappelant les paroles du maître à Hsiao. Car c'est l'essence de notre Voie.
— Tu as une grande foi, dit-elle. J'admire cela. »
Je ne répondis pas, car de nouveau j'avais surpris par hasard la facette de son être qui ressemblait à la petite fille. Une étincelle bleue dansait dans ses pupilles que je ne pouvais quitter des yeux.

« Pourquoi me regardes-tu ainsi ? » Sa franchise était comme une seconde nature, sans peur, spontanée. Malgré elle, je me sentais intimidé, un peu.

« Il me semble que nous sommes de vieilles connaissances qui se sont perdues de vue », dis-je en souriant intérieurement de voir la remarque de Hsiao se présenter d'elle-même à mon esprit. Je ris pensivement en me rappelant.

« De vieilles connaissances qui se sont perdues de vue ?

— Sans arrêt aujourd'hui, ces échos déconcertants du passé, pensai-je à haute voix. Il me semble avoir déjà vécu tout cela. J'ai toujours eu cette impression depuis mon arrivée à New York, mais jamais autant qu'en ce moment. Pourquoi ? »

Elle attendit.

« Le jour où j'ai quitté le monastère, la dernière directive de mon maître fut de suivre le fleuve. "Il te conduira à la mer", dit-il.

— Au delta, commenta-t-elle avec un léger sourire.

— Oui, dis-je en lui rendant son sourire. Voilà à quoi je pensais, au voyage, quand cette métaphore m'est venue à l'esprit — le torrent de montagne qui dévale la pente, puis se jette enfin, toute rage épuisée, dans l'océan calme et étale, en un dernier acte totalement dépourvu de violence ou de passion, un acquiescement : le Dow dans le Tao. Bizarre que je n'y aie pas pensé plus tôt. C'était déjà là, en moi ; il aura fallu ma discussion avec Wo pour que je le découvre. Mais je ne crois pas que ce fut grâce à lui, plutôt à cause d'une chose que j'ai aperçue dans tes yeux et qui m'était familière. "De vieilles connaissances qui se sont perdues de vue." Nous nous sommes peut-être déjà rencontrés, Yin-mi, il y a très, très longtemps. »

Son visage avait pris des couleurs ; ses épaules tremblaient un peu, comme si elle essayait de reprendre son souffle. Mais elle ne détourna pas les yeux et je trouvai le courage de poursuivre.

« Je dois être plus précis. Pendant mon voyage, alors que j'étais encore loin en amont du fleuve, je suis entré dans un village. Il y avait beaucoup de gens réunis là — marchands, chasseurs, voleurs, des types humains dont j'ignorais l'existence — et parmi eux, le plus étrange de tous, un nommé Tsin. Il était soldat, mercenaire plutôt. Tsin m'a sauvé la vie... et pris celle d'un autre. »

Je lui racontai toute l'histoire ; évoquai le soldat et le capitaine, l'opium, l'extase du combat, l'apothéose du meurtre et du cadavre mutilé que j'avais découvert dans les draps froissés, sanglants.

Elle m'écouta attentivement, patiemment. Mais à mesure que mon récit progressait, elle s'enflamma. Fascinée par mes paroles, elle s'y abandonna comme à un charme, à un magicien — à moi. Et par contrecoup, je devins inspiré, exhumai de nouvelles et délicieuses associations qui m'avaient échappé jusqu'alors, tels des fruits gisant dans l'herbe haute au fond d'un pré. Je me sentis merveilleusement soulagé, libéré, semblable au fleuve enflé qui s'écoulait vers la mer, vers elle. Pour Yin-mi, je décrivis avec une minutie particulière le moment où je me réveillai dans la forêt et découvris le panda dressé devant moi avec, dans les yeux, « un féroce désir de justice comme dans ceux du Dieu de colère ». Je lui parlai ensuite de la fillette, du regard d'adieu qu'elle m'avait adressé et que j'avais porté dans mon cœur en quittant ce lointain avant-poste barbare pour traverser le monde, franchir le cap de Bonne-Espérance, vers l'Amérique et, enfin, New York. « Tu pourrais être sa sœur jumelle, dis-je, ou bien elle-même dans quelques années. »

J'observai ses réactions.

« "De vieilles connaissances qui se sont perdues de vue", murmura-t-elle doucement. Maintenant je crois comprendre. » Elle sourit, mais craintivement. Je décelai dans son sourire la même perplexité troublée que j'avais remarquée l'autre soir dans la cuisine, comme une réticence qu'elle cachait difficilement.

« Qu'y a-t-il ? demandai-je. Qu'est-ce qui te gêne ? »

Elle secoua la tête. « Rien. En fait, je suis très contente que tu m'aies confié cela.

— Tu sembles tellement sérieuse.

— Je suis émue, dit-elle. C'est tout. Ton histoire est si étrange, si terrible. Tu étais tellement animé, presque excité en parlant. Cela m'attriste. »

Ses traits se crispèrent comme si elle choisissait soigneusement ses mots. Sa gravité ingénue, ses remarques simples et sincères me touchèrent et se chargèrent brusquement d'un grand poids.

« Surtout le passage relatif au soldat, continua-t-elle sans tenir compte de mon regard scrutateur. Tu semblais si exalté. Toute cette violence, cette soif de sang — tu étais fasciné. Pourquoi, Sun I ?

— Fasciné ! protestai-je. *Horrifié*, tu veux dire. »

Ses sourcils se froncèrent sous le coup de la concentration. « Pourtant, tu as insisté avec tellement de plaisir sur toutes ces atrocités qu'elles en paraissent presque belles. » Je grimaçai. « Mais je te crois, Sun I. Derrière tes mots, je sentais ton horreur. Je ne crois pas que c'était mon imagination. » Elle affirma cela comme on pose une question.

Je secouai la tête, incapable d'y répondre.

« Pourquoi m'as-tu confié tout ça ? »

J'interprétai son changement de ton comme un signe de protestation ou d'impatience. « Je ne sais pas, répliquai-je, échaudé.

— Pourquoi ai-je le sentiment que tu m'as donné une responsabilité ?

— Je ne voulais pas me décharger sur toi, m'excusai-je. Seulement t'expliquer.

— Je sais, dit-elle. Tout va bien. Je suis contente. »

Elle toucha ma main et, contre toute attente, me sourit. Je fus tellement surpris que je ne sus comment réagir. Quelque chose me submergea, qui aurait pu passer pour du bonheur ou du désespoir, mais qui n'était ni l'un ni l'autre, une pure tonalité affective sans contenu.

« A quoi penses-tu ? » demanda-t-elle. Elle rit de mon désarroi. « Dis quelque chose ! »

J'en fus incapable, car complètement perdu dans la contemplation de son visage que le rire bouleversa comme un kaléidoscope qui adopte une nouvelle configuration. Je remarquai qu'une de ses dents était légèrement de biais, et cette imperfection — si ridicule, si dérisoire, si *factuelle* — faillit me faire rire et pleurer en même temps. Sa lèvre se releva comme un rideau, révélant un liséré rose de gencive au-dessus des dents ; un reflet minuscule scintilla sur la nacre de la salive, et je fus stupéfait. Sous les yeux, la peau diaphane au grain serré ressemblait au pétale d'une orchidée violette, trop lisse et fragile pour être vraiment de chair ; comme dans la transition entre deux états, on eût dit qu'elle évoluait vers la pure spiritualité de l'œil. Dans l'iris gauche, couleur d'acajou, je discernai une infime paillette d'or au-dessus de la pupille, légèrement décentrée, comme une inclusion dans une pierre semi-précieuse, le défaut qui en décuple la valeur. Ses cils, son front, la ligne vermillon de sa lèvre, tout m'apparut avec la netteté saisissante de la mer ou d'un gouffre au clair de lune. Quand sa gaieté reflua, elle essuya du dos de sa main gauche une trace d'humidité au coin de l'œil, et dans le même mouvement enroula une mèche de cheveux noirs autour de son oreille. Je suivis des yeux ce petit geste inconscient et devins moi-même flexible, cheveu dans la mèche. Plus étonnant encore, l'âme de Yin-mi, son essence, brillait dans tous ces détails physiques et, comme le soleil à travers les vitraux de l'église, leur insufflait la chaleur et la vie. Cette expérience était incommensurable avec tout ce que je connaissais ; elle me fit comprendre que je n'avais jamais réellement *vu* un être humain, ni connu la moindre intimité jusqu'alors. Cette évidence ne devait pas durer, sa propre intensité le consuma. Mais, le peu que j'avais vécu ne suffit pas à me souffler le nom de ce que j'éprouvais. Dans le cas contraire, ma Frugalité et tout ce qu'elle impliquait eussent empêché ce nom d'atteindre ma conscience.

« Crois-tu à la réincarnation ? »

Sa question correspondait tout à fait à mes pensées. Elle découlait évidemment de notre dialogue, mais elle me frappa comme une coïncidence singulière. Etranger à moi-même, incapable de la moindre décision, je laissai une autre phrase éclore passivement sur mes lèvres : « Nous sommes beaucoup trop simples pour avancer des théories aussi farfelues. » Une impulsion incontrôlable s'empara de moi ; je lançai ma tête en arrière, éclatai de rire. J'entendis l'hystérie sous-jacente à mon rire, mais comme celle d'un autre. Elle m'intéressait, mais sans m'émouvoir.

Yin-mi m'adressa un regard inquiet, interrogateur.

« Ce n'est pas une idée taoïste, lui dis-je en m'obligeant à reprendre le contrôle de moi-même, pourtant... » Je secouai la tête, décontenancé.

« Le père Riley nous a parlé de la réincarnation aux CJT, dit-elle.

— Le père Riley ? demandai-je. CJT ? »

Elle rougit. « Le père Riley est notre pasteur. CJT signifie : Conférences pour les Jeunes de Trinity.

— L'église de Trinity ? »

Elle acquiesça.

« J'y suis allé ! »

Elle rit. « Moi aussi ! Plusieurs fois. En fait, je suis membre de la congrégation.

— Tu es chrétienne ? » J'étais surpris.

Elle rougit. « J'essaie. Je suis du culte épiscopalien.

— "Episcopalien", répétai-je en soupesant ce mot bizarre.

— On dirait une ère géologique, non ? remarqua-t-elle. C'est du moins ce que je pensais — le silurien, le précambrien, le crétacé, l'épiscopalien...

— Est-ce une secte ? demandai-je.

— Confession serait plus exact, répliqua-t-elle avec une gravité amusée.
— Comme c'est étrange !
— Quoi donc ? demanda-t-elle.
— Que tu sois chrétienne !
— Pourquoi étrange ?
— Tu es *chinoise* !

— Chinoise et *américaine*, rectifia-t-elle. Souviens-toi que tu es aux États-Unis, Sun I. Regarde les toits là-bas. Cette flèche. C'est le clocher d'une église — l'église de la Transfiguration sur Mott Street. De rite catholique romain. Cette ville est pleine d'églises, presque toutes chrétiennes. Il n'y a pas de temples taoïstes ici. C'est *toi* l'étranger, tu es peut-être le seul taoïste de toute la ville de New York, une minorité réduite à un seul membre. » Elle sourit. « A l'exception bien sûr de l'autre espèce, celle de Wall Street. Mais ils ne sont pas religieux. La Bourse de New York n'est pas une église. » L'idée parut l'amuser.

« En quoi les églises diffèrent-elles des autres immeubles ? » Son assurance m'avait un peu agacé, mais je lui posai cette question avec davantage de sincérité que de perversité.

Elle me regarda d'un air perplexe. « Je n'en sais rien, répondit-elle d'un ton adouci. Mais dans la Bible, le Christ chasse les marchands du temple.

— S'il avait été taoïste, il leur aurait fait une place, conjecturai-je. Ou bien il aurait transformé en église leur maison de comptes. »

Elle se demanda s'il fallait me prendre au sérieux ou non, puis choisit de rire. « Quelle drôle d'idée ! Je crois que je ne devrais pas rire. C'est sûrement un blasphème. » Elle rit pourtant.

« Mais comment a-t-il pu les chasser ? » Cela me tracassait.

« On ne t'a jamais dit qu'il était plus facile à un chameau de passer par le chas d'une aiguille qu'à un riche d'entrer dans le royaume de Dieu ?

— Et pourquoi donc ? rétorquai-je. Dieu n'a-t-il pas aussi créé les riches et leurs activités ? Sur quelles bases pourrait-il les répudier ?

— Cela me semble évident.

— Pas à moi.

— Leurs activités souillaient sa maison, expliqua-t-elle. Ils ne respectaient pas les commandements. »

Je hochai la tête, peu convaincu. « C'est donc ça la Voie chrétienne ?

— Peut-être, dit-elle. Je ne vois pas très bien ce que tu veux dire.

— Votre Dieu exclut ; le Tao embrasse, pontifiai-je avec un mélange de fierté et d'amertume.

— Il embrasse même ce qui est mauvais ? Mais à quoi sert-il alors ?

— C'est là tout le problème, non ? »

Elle secoua la tête. « Je ne comprends pas.

— Tu te souviens du delta ? »

Un léger trouble apparut sur son visage. « Tu devrais peut-être en parler avec le père Riley, je ne suis pas sûre de pouvoir répondre à ta question.

— Tu y as peut-être déjà répondu », dis-je.

Elle m'observa avec perplexité. « Je peux te demander quelque chose ?

— Bien sûr.

— Quand tu parles du "Tao", que veux-tu dire exactement ? J'ai bien une idée, mais je n'en suis pas sûre. Est-ce comme le ciel ? »

Je souris malgré moi. « Pas exactement. Mais quelque chose comme ça.
— Alors tu crois que tout le monde devrait aller au ciel, les pécheurs comme les autres ?
— Je ne crois pas au ciel comme à un lieu où nous allons, répondis-je. Le ciel est un lieu qui existe seulement dans notre esprit.
— Un lieu imaginaire ?
— Non. Juste un lieu intérieur. »
Le regard de Yin-mi était grave et vulnérable. « Moi aussi, je crois à cela, dit-elle d'une voix douce.
— Quant aux péchés et aux mérites, poursuivis-je — la sentant sur le point de capituler, j'adoptai inconsciemment le ton du prêche —, ils nous apparaissent comme tels à cause de nos préjugés, de notre vision faussée. Finalement, ils sont relatifs, illusoires.
— Tu le penses vraiment ? » demanda-t-elle d'une voix tremblante qui me toucha. Je voulus répondre affirmativement, mais sa fragilité et sa confiance me firent hésiter, retenir la réponse toute faite que j'avais au bout de la langue. « Eh bien, ce qui est vrai pour le sage l'est souvent moins pour le commun des mortels. »

Par un accord tacite dont notre silence témoignait, nous décidâmes de mettre un terme à notre controverse.

« Je crois que tu devrais rencontrer le père Riley, dit-elle. Il t'expliquera beaucoup mieux que moi tout ce qui touche à la religion chrétienne. Et puis il connaît aussi la philosophie orientale. La première fois que je l'ai entendu, à mon lycée, il parlait justement de cela. Il a évoqué le Zen et l'hindouisme, mais également cité le taoïsme. A l'université, avant d'entrer au séminaire, il a suivi un cours de religion comparée ; il disait que les similitudes entre les Sutras, les Védas et les Saintes Ecritures étaient très frappantes.

— Oui, concédai-je, mais c'est presque un truisme que de dire que toutes les religions sont essentiellement identiques, que la réalisation qu'elles promettent est la même, non ?

— Je ne crois pas qu'il serait d'accord avec toi, objecta-t-elle. Car il affirmait que le christianisme était différent, qu'il avait apporté une nouveauté qui avait bouleversé l'histoire et la conscience. Il disait que le christianisme avait dépassé ses propres origines judaïques, et avec elles les religions primitives.

— Et quelle est cette grande révélation ? demandai-je ironiquement.
— L'amour, répondit-elle simplement.
— L'amour ! » J'étais incrédule. « Ce n'est pas vraiment une idée nouvelle, tu sais, Yin-mi. Après tout, la compassion est l'un des Trois Trésors du taoïsme, et elle tient aussi une grande place dans le bouddhisme. J'aimerais savoir comment les chrétiens s'y prennent pour revendiquer la paternité de ce concept.

— Il faut que tu lui demandes, dit-elle. Je suis incapable de retrouver ses arguments. » Après un silence, elle ajouta : « Rencontre-le.
— Peut-être, répondis-je sans m'engager.
— Un soir, tu devrais m'accompagner à une séance des CJT. »
Je réfléchis.
« Pourquoi pas ce soir ? » Elle s'illumina. « Je sais qu'il te plairait. Il est merveilleusement cultivé, intelligent, sensible, et bon. Viens.

— Pas ce soir », répliquai-je avec une réticence que je ne comprenais pas totalement. Je voulais faire plaisir à Yin-mi, mais je me sentais tiraillé, irrité par son admiration. « Une autre fois peut-être. »

Elle sembla déçue.

« Ne te vexe pas. J'aimerais prendre le temps d'y réfléchir.

— Ça va, je comprends.

— Je t'accompagnerai une autre fois.

— Promis ?

— Promis. »

Elle sourit joyeusement ; je considérai ma modeste concession largement récompensée.

« Mais dis-moi, Yin-mi, repris-je en revenant sur un point que je n'avais pas compris, comment es-tu devenue épiscopale ?

— Episcopalienne, rectifia-t-elle. Eh bien c'est très simple. L'église est à quelques blocs seulement de la maison. Chinatown appartient à la paroisse de Trinity. Avec d'autres ecclésiastiques, le père Riley apparaît parfois en public pour expliquer l'église et sa religion aux membres de la communauté qui risqueraient de ne jamais en entendre parler. Tu sais, l'Eglise épiscopalienne est traditionnellement un bastion du conservatisme WASP.

— WASP ? demandai-je.

— Protestant, blanc et anglo-saxon*. Briser la glace avec les minorités n'est pas facile. Le père Riley veut bouleverser tout cela, rendre l'Eglise à l'ensemble de la communauté, et non plus la cantonner à Wall Street. Il dérange beaucoup de gens qui ne se gênent pas pour le dénigrer. Mais c'est une personnalité progressiste, il refuse de transiger. Lui-même attribue son obstination à son sang irlandais.

« Je l'ai entendu pour la première fois à mon lycée. Je te l'ai déjà dit. A la maison, je n'avais jamais eu le moindre contact avec la religion, ni ressenti son besoin. Pour moi, les Chinois ne sont pas vraiment religieux au sens occidental du terme. Chez eux, c'est davantage une activité sociale ; mais je crois que lorsqu'ils s'y intéressent, ils atteignent les sommets. » Elle sourit. « Ou du moins les extrêmes. Je me sentis attirée, un peu comme si une porte venait de s'ouvrir et que j'entrais dans une pièce inexplorée de mon esprit. Là, je découvris maints objets bizarres et merveilleux couverts de poussière et de toiles d'araignée, dont je ne connaissais pas l'usage. Peut-être n'en avaient-ils aucun, mais je savais que cela ne diminuerait pas leur importance, les rendrait au contraire deux fois plus précieux. Comment dire ? Lors de cette première conférence, je suppose que j'ai jeté mon premier coup d'œil dans cette chambre. Depuis ce jour, je l'explore peu à peu. Il me reste beaucoup à découvrir. Peut-être ne peut-on même pas tout connaître — qui sait ?

« Mais je suis reconnaissante au père Riley de ce premier aperçu. C'est un orateur extraordinaire, très charismatique. Ce jour-là, ses paroles m'ont bouleversée, comme les tiennes aujourd'hui. » Elle sourit ; je rougis. « Malgré sa proximité, je n'étais jamais entrée dans l'église. Bizarre, non ? Eh bien, après l'avoir entendu, j'ai décidé d'y aller. J'ai remis plusieurs fois

---

* *White Anglo-Saxon Protestant (NdT).*

ma visite, et puis un samedi j'ai pris mon courage à deux mains. Il n y avait presque personne à l'intérieur. Jamais je n'avais rêvé d'une beauté aussi stupéfiante. Je m'assis discrètement sur un banc au fond de la nef. Longtemps je regardai la voûte — si haute — et les vitraux. Puis une femme entra, assez grosse, d'âge mûr, avec des hauts talons et une de ces jupes tuyau de poêle qui donne l'impression qu'on a les genoux attachés en marchant. Elle portait une étole de renard, ou peut-être en belette, qui mordait sa propre queue autour du cou de la femme, et des gants de cuir noir fixés au poignet par un bouton de perle — le tout d'excellente qualité, très élégant, je m'en souviens parfaitement — et puis un chapeau démodé dont la voilette était baissée. Elle se signa, fit une génuflexion, puis s'agenouilla devant un banc proche du mien et entreprit de retirer ses gants. Ses mains tremblaient beaucoup. C'était terrible. Je fus presque choquée de voir des mains hideuses émerger de ces gants de luxe — des mains d'un blanc cireux moucheté de taches brunes couleur tabac qui trahissaient un mélanome, et striées de grosses veines bleuâtres. Elle ne m'avait pas plu quand je l'avais aperçue, mais j'eus soudain pitié d'elle, du tremblement de ses mains, des efforts qu'elle faisait pour retirer le bouton des gants. Moins gênée, je lui aurais peut-être proposé mon aide. Elle réussit enfin à enlever son autre gant. Très discrètement, presque timidement, elle remonta sa voilette et me regarda droit dans les yeux. J'eus honte d'être surprise à l'observer, mais il n'y avait pas de reproche sur son visage. Elle avait des yeux si tristes, si doux, Sun I. Il y eut comme une rencontre entre nous. Je lui souris, elle me rendit mon sourire en hochant la tête comme ça. » Yin-mi répéta le geste de la femme. « Puis elle se détourna pour prier, posa les coudes sur le banc de devant, serra les mains presque convulsivement. Je l'observai un instant, mais finis par détourner les yeux avec un sentiment de culpabilité. Cet incident me frappa. Vaguement inquiète, j'envisageais de me lever pour partir quand je fus prise d'une impulsion subite et m'agenouillai sur le prie-dieu. Comme elle, je serrai les mains devant moi. Je ne me suis jamais sentie aussi embarrassée de ma vie ; mes joues étaient en feu. Je suppliais le Ciel pour qu'elle ne regarde pas de mon côté. Cela passa. Je ne récitais aucune prière, mais peu à peu le calme s'instaura dans mon esprit, une sorte de fourmillement glacé, comme si un vent froid soufflait autour de moi. J'eus la chair de poule, mes yeux s'emplirent de larmes, je fondis en sanglots. Pourquoi, je l'ignore. Je n'avais jamais rien vécu de semblable. Cela dura quelques minutes seulement ; ensuite, je me sentis stupide et déprimée, mais en même temps plus forte, régénérée. Tu comprends ce que je veux dire ?

— Je crois, répondis-je. Un peu. »

Elle sourit. « Cela a changé avec le temps. Mon émotion est moins forte, mais plus enrichissante. Je ne peux la comparer qu'à la natation.

— La natation ? »

Elle opina du chef. « Il se passe une chose similaire quand on nage longtemps. Tu avances, tu comptes les brasses et brusquement tu perds conscience du temps. Bien sûr, tu ne t'en aperçois qu'après, quand tu te réveilles et que tu nages toujours aussi régulièrement, mais l'espace d'un instant, tu es parti ailleurs... Je ne sais comment dire... comme si tu sortais de ton corps. C'est effrayant, mais merveilleux aussi. » Son front se plissa sous l'effet de la concentration et avec une simplicité qui provoqua ma tendresse. « J'ai eu le sentiment d'un événement surnaturel, presque d'un miracle. Quand j'ai relevé la tête, la femme était partie, ce qui m'a attristée, car j'aurais voulu qu'elle fût là pour partager mon expérience, au moins par un regard. Je me suis levée ; avant de sortir, j'ai pris quelques brochures. De retour à la maison, j'ai rempli la carte postale et l'ai glissée dans une boîte à lettres.

« La semaine suivante, j'ai reçu un coup de téléphone d'un des assistants du père Riley. » Elle rit. « Ma mère a cru que c'était un garçon du lycée qui m'appelait pour un rendez-vous. Quand elle m'a dit que quelqu'un voulait me parler, elle s'est mise à gesticuler silencieusement, à me donner des conseils inaudibles. Elle fut déçue quand je lui annonçai qui m'avait appelée. Je ne suis même pas sûre qu'elle m'ait crue. » Yin-mi sourit. « En tout cas, je me rendis à un cours d'initiation du dimanche matin. Puis on m'invita aux conférences du CJT. Après quelques semaines, j'ai décidé de me convertir et j'ai suivi la retraite de confirmation. J'ai été baptisée au printemps dernier. Voilà toute l'histoire. Rien de plus banal, non ? Pas de trompettes, pas d'archange ni de lumière aveuglante... Une histoire parmi tant d'autres. Tu es probablement fatigué de m'écouter. »

Elle rit — se moquant d'elle-même, de moi, de beaucoup de choses. Son visage était nimbé d'une lumière douce que je trouvai belle mais vaguement agaçante. Je restai muet.

Elle attendit d'abord une réaction semblable à celle que mon récit avait provoquée chez elle, puis avec un trouble presque blessé, comme si ma réticence la peinait. J'eus honte. Ses commentaires avaient été si généreux. si chaleureux. Mais je ne savais que dire.

« Je crois que nous devrions descendre déjeuner », reprit-elle au bout d'un moment. La déception et la gêne qu'on sentait dans sa voix me bouleversèrent, mais un scrupule m'interdit d'y remédier.

« Je n'ai pas faim, dis-je dans un accès d'introversion blessant, que je méprisai aussitôt mais fus incapable de réfréner.

— Mais ma mère va se vexer, protesta-t-elle. Elle compte particulièrement sur ta présence.

— Excuse-moi, rétorquai-je. Dis-lui que je ne me sens pas bien.

— Qu'y a-t-il, Sun I ? implora-t-elle. Pourquoi as-tu changé d'avis ? Ai-je dit quelque chose... ?

— Je suis fatigué, voilà tout », répondis-je sans mentir vraiment mais en accordant un poids exagéré à une circonstance mineure.

Elle me regarda d'un air soucieux. « Tu viendras quand même avec moi au CJT ?

— J'ai promis, non ? » dis-je, incapable de dominer mon irritation.

Elle me sourit néanmoins. La modestie et la sincérité de son expression ne firent qu'augmenter mon agacement.

« Au revoir, Sun I. »

Je tendis la main d'un air maussade.

Elle la saisit, puis, à ma grande surprise, s'approcha de mon visage pour embrasser légèrement ma joue. « Sun I, murmura-t-elle à mon oreille, moi aussi j'ai l'impression de te connaître depuis longtemps. » Ensuite, elle se hâta de sortir. Bourrelé de remords, je la regardai partir, le cœur en déroute.

6

Très ému et fort excité, je faisais les cent pas aux abords du portail en fer forgé de Trinity, scrutais la longue queue des taxis jaunes qui, l'un après l'autre, quittaient le flot de la circulation, se rangeaient contre le trottoir et, tels des fourgons à bestiaux, dégorgeaient leur élégante cargaison de bétail rutilant en costume mille raies. A chaque nouvel arrivant, je trottinais vers la portière jaune qui s'immobilisait et jetais un coup d'œil anxieux par la vitre latérale dans l'espoir de découvrir la mèche noire de mon mentor tant attendu, Wo. Mon comportement n'était guère apprécié des chauffeurs de taxi ni de leurs clients. Je commençais à céder au découragement quand, dominant le brouhaha des hommes et des voitures, la voix de Wo s'éleva comme un Angélus nasillard.

« Hé, *Sonny* ! Ça gaze ? »

Ce fut pour moi une musique céleste. Ravi, je parcourus la file des taxis au pas de course en examinant toutes les banquettes arrière ; mais à ma grande stupéfaction, la voix semblait venir d'ailleurs.

« Par ici ! »

Je me retournai vers le trottoir. Et là, ne sortant ni d'un taxi ni d'une limousine comme je m'y étais attendu, mais noyé dans le flot grisâtre et anonyme qui émergeait, oui, de la bouche de métro, j'aperçus Wo ! *Deux ex machina*, sans aucun doute ; mais avec la mauvaise machine ! Une deuxième fois, mon attente fut totalement déçue. Pire encore, il ne portait même pas de costume trois pièces, mais la même chemise hawaïenne que j'avais vue l'avant-veille, agrémentée d'un ornement supplémentaire — une tache de moutarde sur la poche gauche qui semblait avoir transporté un hot-dog. Le spectacle chamarré de ses acolytes dégingandés — tous portaient des chemises hawaïennes, imitaient servilement le style de leur maître — n'apaisa aucunement mes inquiétudes, car je n'aurais jamais imaginé pareil assortiment de jeunes boiteux hirsutes aux sourires niais et aux dents saillantes. On eût dit les employés en déroute d'un cirque de bienfaisance. Je fus d'abord stupéfait, puis mortifié, puis profondément impressionné. Je me convainquis que leur laisser-aller vestimentaire était plus admirable que le plus élégant costume-cravate. Quel merveilleux mépris des conventions sociales ! C'était positivement d'inspiration taoïste ! Digne de Tchouang-tseu en personne ! La compassion, la grandeur d'âme impliquées par la décision de Wo de s'associer à ces malheureux... ah, quel être sublime ! Après tout, l'étonnante ressemblance de Wo avec le Bouddha n'était peut-être pas fortuite ; elle dépassait certainement le cadre mesquin de la seule corpulence. J'eus honte de l'avoir jugé si vite à son apparence et me reprochai une erreur que je n'aurais jamais commise autrefois.

« Allez faire un tour, les mecs », intima Wo à ses compagnons ; il était tellement sûr de son autorité qu'il ne se retourna même pas pour vérifier qu'on lui obéissait. Il repoussa sa mèche et saisit mon bras avec un large sourire un peu figé.

« Alors *Sonny*, dit-il, c'est le grand jour ! Hé hé hé ! Prêt à faire la carpette et à lécher les culs ? »

J'opinai du chef avec enthousiasme.

« Mais rappelle-toi bien, dit-il sur le ton de l'avertissement, je te promets rien. »

Je me décomposai.

« Enfin je crois pas qu'il y aura de problème. »

Je repris courage. « Merci, Wo. Vous ne savez pas combien c'est important pour moi. J'aimerais tellement pouvoir vous rendre un service en échange.

— Je suis content que tu abordes le sujet, dit-il avec désinvolture. Il se trouve qu'il y a quelque chose...

— Quoi donc ? répliquai-je, comblé. Tout ce que vous voudrez. Que dois-je faire ? »

Quand il me regarda, toute son assurance avait disparu, remplacée par une expression inquiète, presque traquée.

« Tu verras bien », dit-il avec un sourire énigmatique et sans joie.

Nous arrivâmes alors à l'entrée de la Bourse que je n'avais pu franchir quelques jours plus tôt. Le même bras du même garde noir m'interdit le passage jusqu'à ce que Wo s'avance pour l'amadouer.

« Ça baigne, George, dit-il en lançant sa mèche en arrière. Il est avec moi. »

George nous regarda d'un air méfiant, puis avec un haussement d'épaules nous laissa passer sur la bonne foi de Wo. Je fus pétrifié par cette manifestation d'« influence » et, pour tout dire, rassuré. Nous franchîmes la porte côte à côte, aussi comprimés que l'eau dans un goulet d'étranglement par la pression de la foule derrière nous.

A l'intérieur, le comportement de Wo changea du tout au tout. Sa vantardise débraillée qui m'avait impressionné au point de me sembler presque admirable, fit long feu et il devint nerveux, agité. Il adressait des sourires confus, déférents (où je vis les premiers signes de sa ressemblance avec son père) à des hommes mûrs qui portaient de somptueux costumes et lui retournaient un rictus froid ou ne daignaient même pas le remarquer. Sa main étroitement serrée autour de mon coude, il me guida à travers la foule vers les ascenseurs, puis au seizième étage, où il me laissa devant le bureau d'une secrétaire préposée à l'embauche, à qui il marmonna quelques phrases incantatoires comme un magicien de pacotille désirant accomplir quelque tour et douloureusement conscient de son manque de talent. Il me jeta un sourire d'excuse, plongea dans la foule et disparut. « J'arrive dans une seconde », l'entendis-je dire alors que la secrétaire levait les yeux avec une expression de surprise qui fut loin de me plaire.

« Qu'est-ce qui se passe ? demanda-t-elle en regardant autour d'elle comme une bête fauve affamée. C'est vous qui avez dit ça ? » Elle ferma un œil pour me lorgner.

Je secouai la tête. « Non, c'est M. Ha-p'i, répondis-je en montrant derrière moi l'endroit où Wo venait de disparaître.

— Monsieur *qui* ?

— Ha-p'i, répétai-je en détachant les syllabes.

— Eh bien il peut aller se rhabiller jusqu'à neuf heures, dit-elle, et vous aussi ! »

Son indifférence au nom de Wo éveilla chez moi une méfiance tardive, bien qu'encore mitigée.

L'employée, une femme d'âge indéterminé (entre vingt-cinq et quarante ans), avait des cheveux blonds oxygénés et arborait un maquillage outrancier totalement dépourvu de goût. Mais son trait le plus remarquable était ses sourcils qui se rejoignaient au-dessus du nez comme les fils d'araignée dans la mire d'un bombardier et lui donnaient un aspect fort menaçant. Avant cette interruption, elle avait été très occupée à limer ses ongles, tâche qu'elle reprit aussitôt, apportant tous ses soins à la remise en état d'une cuticule endommagée. Je me raclai la gorge pour attirer de nouveau son attention.

Elle me foudroya alors du regard en limant avec une vigueur redoublée, métamorphosant ainsi un geste neutre, anodin, en comportement subtilement agressif. D'un geste sauvage de sa lime en carton et avec force mouvements de tête et haussements d'épaules, elle attira mon attention vers l'horloge. « Je commence pas à travailler avant neuf heures », m'informa-t-elle.

Il était neuf heures moins deux.

A cet instant précis, un jeune homme se rua vers le bureau, le visage congestionné, l'attaché-case malmené comme une masse d'arme, les pans de sa veste flottant derrière lui. « Sally, appelle-moi le service du personnel ! cria-t-il d'un ton péremptoire en passant ventre à terre devant le bureau. *Tout de suite !* »

Lâchant dans sa panique tous ses instruments de manucure, elle décrocha le téléphone et composa un numéro aussi vite que le lui permirent ses ongles si récemment pomponnés ; elle en cassa un contre le cadran. « Merde ! » siffla-t-elle furieusement en glissant prestement son doigt dans sa bouche. Pendant qu'elle attendait qu'on lui répondît, elle croisa mon regard, sa peau s'empourpra sous le fond de teint et elle me décocha un coup d'œil venimeux, comme pour dire : « Vous n'avez pas honte ! » Puis elle prononça quelques paroles précipitées dans le récepteur, enfonça une touche et raccrocha violemment.

« *Alors*, dit-elle, menaçante, que puis-je faire pour vous ? » Son regard disait : *contre* vous.

— Mon bienfaiteur, M. Ha-p'i... je marquai un temps d'arrêt pour qu'elle enregistre le nom... m'a suggéré de me présenter ici pour un emploi.

— Monsieur *qui* ? répéta-t-elle d'une voix irritée. Peu importe. J'ai compris. » Elle se mit à brasser des papiers. « Messager, je suppose ? »

Je la regardai sans comprendre. « Messager ? »

Elle jeta les papiers sur son bureau en grognant de rage, puis m'adressa un regard assassin. « Oui, messager. Vous savez, grouillot, saute-ruisseau, écureuil.

— Ecureuil, dis-je, moitié par naïveté, moitié pour l'irriter, c'est un animal ?

— "C'est un animal", imita-t-elle en minaudant. Charmant. Vraiment charmant. Oui, c'est un animal — ça a quatre pattes et ça vit sur Wall Street, tout comme les haussiers et les baissiers, également nommés taureaux et ours. Mais l'écureuil reste dans son trou et garde un profil bas. Vous croyez que ça collera ? Ou comptiez-vous postuler pour le poste de président de la Bourse ? » Elle me sourit avec une suffisance vindicative.

« Messager me convient tout à fait », répondis-je, peu désireux de mettre de l'huile sur le feu.

Soulagée d'avoir humilié le témoin de sa propre humiliation, elle s'adoucit légèrement et aborda les problèmes pratiques. « OK, dit-elle, vous connaissez la procédure, n'est-ce pas ? »

Je secouai la tête.

« Bon, c'est vraiment très simple. Vous remplissez un formulaire ici même. Votre candidature reste dans un fichier pendant six mois. Puis vous serez convoqué quand votre tour viendra. S'il ne se passe rien, vous pourrez poser une nouvelle candidature. D'accord ?

— Vous voulez dire que je ne commence pas à travailler aujourd'hui ?

— Aujourd'hui ! » Elle n'en croyait pas ses oreilles. « Sincèrement, j'en doute ! J'ai vu des petits gars poser leur candidature trois, quatre fois de suite avant de travailler. Vous êtes bien pressé. » Un voyant se mit à clignoter sur son téléphone. « Une minute. » Elle décrocha. « Oui, monsieur ? Très bien. Une pénurie ? Trois places ? Oui monsieur, il y en a un ici même. Mais ne devrais-je pas convoquer les gens inscrits sur la liste ? Oui monsieur ! Je l'envoie immédiatement en bas ! » Elle raccrocha et me dévisagea avec méfiance. « Vous saviez qu'on manquerait de personnel ce matin, pas vrai ? Quel est le nom de votre contact, déjà ?

— M. Ha-p'i. »

Elle haussa les épaules. « Vous avez de la chance.

— Vous voulez dire... ?

— Z'êtes embauché. »

Je me sentis submergé de bonheur. La cote de Wo, qui avait singulièrement baissé pendant cette entrevue, remonta aussitôt et fila vers les étoiles.

« Déjà travaillé à la Bourse ? demanda-t-elle. Non, bien sûr que non. Eh bien remplissez ces formulaires ; je vais demander à quelqu'un de vous montrer le circuit. » Elle plongea la main dans un carton derrière son bureau et me tendit une blouse bleu pâle amidonnée qui sortait de chez le teinturier, pliée en carré et dont le col portait un numéro. « Essayez donc ça. »

Je glissai mes bras dans les manches, la boutonnai, roulai les épaules. « Je crois que c'est un peu grand. »

Elle ricana. « Taille unique. »

Haussant la mire de ses sourcils, elle jeta un coup d'œil derrière moi qui visait une autre personne. « Oh, vous là-bas, le jeunot — oui, *vous* ! Venez voir ici. »

Je me retournai timidement vers sa nouvelle victime, peiné d'avoir gâché malgré moi la matinée d'un innocent.

« J'ai du boulot pour vous. Emmenez-le avec vous et apprenez-lui les ficelles du métier. »

Figé au milieu de la pièce, rouge comme une tomate, la bouche crispée en un rire penaud au-dessus d'une blouse bleu pâle, exactement semblable à celle qu'on venait de me donner, mais d'où dépassait le col de sa chemise hawaïenne, je découvris... oui, Wo ! Je n'en crus pas mes yeux.

« Wo ! » m'écriai-je, stupéfait.

Il lança sèchement sa mèche en arrière, puis haussa les épaules. « T'attendais peut-être Henry Fonda ? Je t'avais dit que je revenais, non ? »

La secrétaire nous considéra avec méfiance.

« Mais...

— Allez, dit-il. Faut qu'on aille pointer. »

En marchant, Wo ne regardait ni à droite ni à gauche, mais rougissait extraordinairement, exhibant des nuances inédites de vermillon et de violacé. Je trottinai en crabe à ses côtés en le dévisageant stupidement.

Nous nous arrêtâmes bientôt pour parler. De près, Wo me parut un peu répugnant. « Je t'ai bien eu, pas vrai ? se vanta-t-il faiblement.

— Alors tout ça est une plaisanterie ? » lui demandai-je, perplexe.

Il retroussa les lèvres en secouant la tête. « Certainement pas.

— Alors tu es un écureuil, dis-je avec étonnement, *exactement comme moi !*

— Hé, pas de sarcasmes, hein ? répondit-il d'une voix brusque. Ouais, je suis messager. Et alors ?

— Mais ta famille — tu leur as dit...

— Je leur ai jamais menti, me coupa-t-il vivement.

— Pas ouvertement.

— Ecoute, *Sonny*, je sais que t'es prêtre et tout, mais épargne-moi ton homélie, d'accord ? Qui es-tu pour juger ? Tu m'as demandé de te trouver du boulot, je te l'ai trouvé, oui ou non ?

— Oui, dis-je, et je t'en remercie.

— Tu as bien dit que tu me rendrais la monnaie de ma pièce, hein ? » J'acquiesçai.

« Alors voilà...

— Quoi ? demandai-je.

— Motus et bouche cousue.

— Mais Wo, protestai-je, ils investissent leur argent durement gagné en suivant tes conseils. » Songeant à son père, j'ajoutai : « Un argent qu'ils ne peuvent pas se permettre de perdre.

— Hé, t'emballe pas, répondit-il en retrouvant son assurance pateline. C'est pas parce que je suis un péon dans la hiérarchie que je connais pas le marché. Je prends mes infos au sommet. Bon dieu, je fais un meilleur score que la plupart des pros, au moins sur le papier. Et dès que j'aurai un petit capital à faire tourner — mec, je prends mes cliques et mes claques ! Non, écoute voir, l'embrouille de la semaine dernière était due à un carouillage imprévisible. J'ai prévenu papa que c'était risqué. Faut être gonflé pour miser mille tickets. » Il haussa les épaules en riant.

« D'un autre côté, fiston — il adopta un ton plus humble — si le vieux savait, ça le tuerait. Juste au moment où on commence à se démerder un peu, tu vois ? J'veux dire, tu t'imagines pas la galère de bosser pour lui dans ce restau ! Je faisais jamais rien comme y fallait, enfin d'après lui. Un véritable esclavage, vieux ! Et il a suffi que tu te pointes pour être bombardé Assistant Dragon Numéro Un. Ça m'a vraiment cassé les couilles. Mais parlons d'autre chose. Il est enfin heureux depuis que je me suis tiré et que j'ai trouvé ce boulot. Il entrave que dalle à ce que je fais, mais au moins il me prend plus pour un raté. Quand je lui ai dit que j'avais un appart, il a été scié. Il n'y est jamais venu, évidemment. J'habite l'East Village — un taudis pour dire les choses comme elles sont. Et alors ? Il croit que je m'en sors. Pourquoi lui enlever ses illusions ? Tu piges ? »

Je hochai la tête.

« Motus et bouche cousue ?

— D'accord », dis-je à contrecœur, déchiré entre la pitié et l'indignation, songeant aussi aux sentiments des autres membres de sa famille, qui m'inspiraient davantage d'affection que lui, surtout en ce moment.

Il poussa un soupir de soulagement et sa face se fendit d'un large sourire presque joyeux. « En plus, dit-il, j'ai toutes les chances de devenir rapporteur. » Ses ongles frottèrent le revers de sa blouse, il m'adressa un clin d'œil. « Veston noir et tout le tintouin. Allez, magne-toi, on va être en retard. »

Ces révélations me laissèrent dans un état vaguement nauséeux. Mon entreprise se plaçait d'emblée sous des auspices pour le moins ambigus. Wo semblait l'exemple typique de l'individu dans le Tao (ou le *Dow !*), mais qui ne vivait pas avec le Tao, car il nageait à contre-courant. J'eus sincèrement pitié de lui, mais je ne pouvais pas faire grand-chose, sinon fuir son exemple et tirer la leçon de ses échecs.

Non, mes débuts furent tout sauf glorieux. D'autant que je me découvris moins de talents pour le métier de messager que pour celui d'aide-cuisinier aux côtés de Lo. C'était prévisible, j'imagine. Mais les circonstances semblèrent conspirer contre moi. J'eus la malchance de tomber sur le même courtier plusieurs fois pendant cette première matinée et de commettre une bourde à chaque rencontre. Parmi les hordes aryennes d'hommes brusques, compétents et impeccablement habillés qui paradaient au parquet en attendant la séance dont l'ouverture serait annoncée par une sonnerie, cet individu était une bizarrerie, un membre d'une autre espèce peut-être menacée. En fait, c'était presque le cas, car cet homme — « Aaron Kahn », annonçait l'étiquette épinglée à son revers, « Négociant au parquet » — était juif. Mais en cette matinée, je remarquai à peine cette singularité, car j'en étais encore au stade où tous les visages blancs se ressemblaient plus ou moins ; et sur les Juifs, ces créatures fabuleuses, mes connaissances étaient fort approximatives, dépourvues de toute base scientifique, seulement dérivées de la mythologie. Oui, Kahn fut mon premier Juif.

Son aspect était légèrement lugubre : un visage lourd aux bajoues flasques, des poches sous les yeux, comme un raton laveur ou un panda, deux cataplasmes bleuâtres de noceur. Il arborait un visage de morse abattu, d'amateur de bonne chère déprimé. Ses cheveux clairsemés bouclaient sur sa nuque, presque jusque sur son col. Ils dégageaient pourtant la courbe majestueuse du front, une calotte monumentale et digne comme une vieille montagne ou l'œuvre d'un grand maître dissimulée sous une peinture moderne et maladroite. Kahn exhibait son tempérament dépressif sans fausse pudeur ; on eût dit qu'il s'y était installé avec le même confort que d'autres réussissent à trouver sous le cilice, qu'il en avait presque fait un ami. Je ne sais comment expliquer cela, mais son apparence sinistre n'excluait pas une sorte de pose qui frisait la parodie, un éclat sarcastique du regard qui la contredisait et lui accordait même un charme équivoque.

Il reniflait beaucoup. Son nez était rouge ; ses yeux larmoyants. Il les tamponnait de temps à autre avec son mouchoir, qu'il tirait, non de sa poche de poitrine — l'endroit unanimement choisi et approuvé par ses collègues Wasp —, mais de la poche latérale de sa veste, hermétiquement cousue et purement décorative chez les autres. Celle-ci contenait d'ailleurs tout un bric-à-brac, dont un atomiseur de Dristan, qu'il débouchait à intervalles réguliers pour en insérer l'embout dans ses narines, me donnant ainsi l'occasion de remarquer qu'il portait aux poignets des bracelets de cuivre — pour se protéger de l'hygroma, ainsi que je le découvris plus tard. Contrairement aux apparences, cet homme ne se laissait pas aller, ou du moins se négligeait-il avec raffinement. Ses vêtements étaient du meilleur tissu et d'excellente coupe, bien qu'il les portât peut-être une fois de trop sans les faire nettoyer ni repasser, si bien qu'ils dégageaient une odeur légèrement rance, presque rassurante dans ces déserts d'asepsie parfumée, surtout pour mon odorat asiatique. Il arborait l'élégance fripée d'un corsage porté deux fois, d'abord au déjeuner de mariage puis pour la cérémonie, à des fins d'économie. Ainsi qu'il me l'annonça ensuite de sa façon inimitable, Kahn incarnait le type même de l'« anal expulsif » — concept que je ne peux pas davantage expliquer que « Nature de Singe ». On comprend immédiatement ou jamais. En tout cas, nous étions évidemment faits l'un pour l'autre.

Quand je le vis pour la première fois, il mangeait des bonbons qu'il tirait d'un sac en papier serré dans sa main gauche. Le sac était fermé par un ruban rose ; sur une étiquette couleur argent bruni, on lisait les mots « *Bonwit Teller* » écrits en caractères romains brillants. Sa main plongeait dans un trou percé au flanc du sac, puis expédiait les friandises dans sa bouche comme du pop-corn, tandis que son visage inexpressif ne trahissait aucune émotion, en tout cas aucun plaisir. A une distance presque insondable, on lisait sur ses traits une très vague anxiété et, légèrement plus près de la surface, du regret. L'observant, je fus frappé par ses mains fort délicates dotées d'excroissances soyeuses de poils noirs qu'on eût dit peignés, contrairement aux rares cheveux qui couvraient son crâne. Des sparadraps protégeaient presque toutes les extrémités de ses doigts ; et ses ongles, lorsqu'ils étaient visibles, semblaient avoir subi l'érosion d'un rognage obstiné.

« Que regardes-tu, Confucius ? railla-t-il quand il remarqua que je l'observais. Ta mère t'a donc pas appris la politesse ? Ou est-ce que tu ne manges pas à ta faim ? »

Il ne s'était pas attendu à ce que je fusse aussi mortifié et vexé par sa pique ; aussi, pris de remords, il s'approcha de moi comme pour me faire une confidence et chuchota à mon oreille : « C'est plus fort que moi », aveu agréable énoncé avec une humilité et une sincérité manifestes, dans le meilleur style « mea culpa ». Je voulus lui pardonner — et l'eusse certainement fait, si une nuance indéfinissable de son attitude ne m'avait convaincu qu'elle tenait de la farce.

« Tiens, prends un bonbon », dit-il en me tendant le paquet tout en en catapultant un dans sa bouche, utilisant l'ongle de son pouce en guise d'engin balistique, comme aux billes.

« Non ? » Il haussa les épaules. « Tant mieux ! J'allais me retrouver à sec ! » ajouta-t-il, l'œil brillant de convoitise. Il glissa le paquet dans sa poche et m'examina attentivement. « Tu sais, petit, tu me rappelles quelqu'un — mais impossible de retrouver qui. » Il attendait ma réaction ; quand il comprit qu'il n'en obtiendrait pas, il haussa les épaules et s'éloigna en reniflant avec indifférence, à moins que ce ne fût de dérision. Il disparut au coin d'un bureau de négoce, se noya dans la foule.

La cloche sonna peu après et la séance commença. Je fus aussitôt englouti dans l'océan tumultueux que j'avais seulement contemplé d'en haut. Mon impression d'une perspective illimitée, l'étrange nostalgie ressentie en découvrant le parquet, tout cela s'estompa à mesure que je m'absorbais dans ma tâche. Mes efforts pour rester à flot me laissaient peu de temps à consacrer aux théories.

Une fois encore, comme à l'époque où j'aidais Wu à la cuisine de Ken Kuan, je me retrouvai au bas de la hiérarchie sociale. Le messager figure en effet au dernier échelon du personnel de la Bourse. Il doit satisfaire tous les caprices de ses supérieurs : rapporteurs, téléphonistes, coursiers, spécialistes (bien que ces derniers daignent rarement descendre de leur pinacle pour utiliser leurs services, ou même remarquer leur existence). Sommairement apostrophé par un maître ombrageux et tonitruant, le messager de deuxième classe est censé comprendre sa mission à demi-mot, grâce à un simple geste — une feuille de papier frénétiquement agitée sous son nez, une contraction convulsive de la tête et des épaules serrées contre le récepteur d'un téléphone (laissant ainsi les mains libres de griffonner des ordres ou de caresser une tasse de café tiède). Se ruant dans la brèche comme de la chair à canon, il doit se dispenser des pourquoi et des comment. Il prend ses jambes à son cou, poussé par le sens du devoir et comme chargé d'une haute mission, même s'il ignore tout à fait la nature de celle-ci. Une fois hors de vue, il fait des pieds et des mains pour deviner les intentions de son employeur du moment, invente d'étranges rituels magiques pour apaiser à distance le courtier et s'immuniser lui-même contre sa Colère Divine. D'habitude, ces rites s'avèrent inefficaces, un pur gâchis d'énergie nerveuse, car il continue de se faire houspiller à la moindre occasion.

Telle fut du moins ma propre expérience en cette première matinée. Peut-être fut-elle un peu particulière, car je reconnais volontiers que je n'étais pas le candidat idéal pour franchir ce seuil vénérable et sillonner le parquet, poussé par ces alizés que la langue anglaise nomme justement « vents du commerce ». Je fis malgré tout des progrès. Peu à peu, on finit par développer une sorte de sixième sens, de perception extrasensorielle fiscale qui permet, à partir des indices les plus ténus, de déduire les intentions insondables des courtiers. Cela prend parfois des jours, voire des semaines ! Ce premier matin, comme je l'ai dit, je fus désemparé.

Mon approche du problème était totalement erronée, voyez-vous. Ce n'était certes pas entièrement ma faute, car ma formation ne m'avantageait guère. J'étais handicapé par un sens hypertrophié de l'étiquette. Hélé par un courtier qui brandissait fébrilement une feuille de papier devant son visage comme s'il s'agissait de la formule perdue de la transmutation alchimique de Sun Mo Tseu, j'étais incapable de réfréner une profonde révérence. Quand je me redressais, un autre messager avait déjà transporté le papier à la cabine téléphonique ou au télétype le plus proche. Le courtier, voyant son numéro affiché sur le tableau d'annonces, réfléchisssait probablement déjà à un nouvel ordre, non sans m'avoir auparavant foudroyé d'un regard assassin qui me damnait sans rémission et me vouait aux régions infernales les plus reculées, réservées à ces âmes perdues que les terriens classent comme « totalement irrécupérables ». Ces rencontres me désarçonnaient, m'inquiétaient, me désolaient. Elles se produisirent deux fois avec Kahn, une fois en début de séance, l'autre vers midi. La première fois, il marmonna simplement quelque chose entre ses dents, puis se tourna vers un autre messager ; mais la deuxième fois, il se figea, l'œil menaçant, et me dévisagea avec une pitié exaspérée. Submergé de honte et de chagrin, je faillis fondre en larmes.

« Tu veux un conseil d'ami, petit ? me lança-t-il.

— Maître ! m'écriai-je malgré moi en tombant à genoux.

— Ça alors ! » dit-il, surpris. Jetant des coups d'œil inquiets à droite et à gauche, comme s'il redoutait qu'on nous vît, il se pencha pour saisir mon coude.

« Debout ! Debout ! gronda-t-il. Bon Dieu, petit ! D'où viens-tu, du Kansas ?

— De Chine, répondis-je.

— De Chine ! C'est encore pire ! Tu n'es pas un de ces *boat people*, au moins ? Ecoute, petit, j'ignore les us et coutumes de ton pays, mais je peux te dire qu'ici ça ne se fait pas. Première leçon pour vivre à Manhattan : ne jamais s'excuser — *en aucune occasion. Surtout* si tu es dans ton tort. C'est le suprême faux pas. Vu ? »

J'acquiesçai.

« Tu sais quel est ton problème ? Tu es trop poli. D'accord, les bonnes manières sont louables, mais dans ton cas elles te coupent l'herbe sous le pied, si j'ose dire. Comme disait mon oncle, l'Ashkénase fou — sans qui je ne serais pas ce que je suis : "Pas de gloire sans couilles." Alors s'il te plaît — un peu plus de *chutzpah* et un peu moins de Salamalecs Orientaux. Sinon ta carrière sera brève. » Il passa un doigt en travers de sa gorge. « ... Un seul jour.

— Aidez-moi à corriger mes défauts, le suppliai-je humblement alors que des larmes de gratitude envahissaient mes yeux. Apprenez-moi ce *hu... hu... hutspa*.

— On dit : *chu... chu... chutzpah*, me corrigea-t-il. OK, n'en fais pas tout un plat. S'il y a une chose que je ne supporte pas, c'est bien le *schmaltz*. Il figure à égalité avec le *gefilte fisch* sur la liste de mes Suprêmes Aversions. » Il m'observait avec une sympathie morose. « Tiens, prends donc un bonbon. Ça va te calmer. » Sa main plongea dans sa poche et fouilla. « Non, prends plutôt un de ceux-ci. Je vais en manquer. Faudra que je passe chez Bonwit's en rentrant chez moi. » Il me tendit un long objet mince enveloppé de papier brillant. « Je n'aime pas ceux-là », m'informa-t-il gravement en montrant son cadeau — une barre de chocolat 100 000 $. « Mais ils me dépannent en cas de besoin. Ecoute, petit, reprit-il, je te donne encore une chance. » Il sortit de sa poche son portefeuille, dont il tira un billet de vingt dollars. « Si tu allais nous chercher à déjeuner ? Monte-moi ça dans mon bureau, le deux cent dix un. Et, ah, petit... je compte sur toi pour la monnaie...

— Qu'aimeriez-vous manger ? » demandai-je timidement ; je n'avais aucune idée des mesures à prendre pour apaiser un appétit comme le sien et j'étais terrifié à l'idée de provoquer sa colère.

« Oy ! s'écria-t-il, exaspéré. Un peu d'initiative, que diable ! Utilise ton imagination ! »

Je m'inclinai machinalement, m'arrêtai au milieu de ma salutation et retrouvai la position verticale. Il soupira, retourna vers le parquet, puis pivota brusquement sur ses talons pour me lancer : « Mais pas de hamburgers ni de boulettes italiennes ! »

J'appelai Lo d'une cabine publique : « Lo mon avenir dépend de vous ! m'écriai-je hors d'haleine. Vous devez m'aider !

— De quoi s'agit-il ? me répondit-il d'une voix perçante, contaminée par ma panique. Vous avez besoin d'argent ?

— Non ! m'écriai-je. *De nourriture !*

— De nourriture ? » Il rit. « Pas de problème. Laissez-moi faire. Pour combien ?

— Deux, dis-je, mais...

— Excusez je vous prie, venez chercher dans quinze minutes. »

J'eusse voulu lui faire sentir l'extrême importance de sa mission, la délicatesse de jugement dont il devait faire preuve, mais c'était trop tard. Plein d'appréhension, je poussai la porte, sortis dans la rue grouillante et trottinai vers Chinatown comme un conducteur de *rickshaw*.

Devant le restaurant, sous l'enseigne P LAIS DE LA OIE DE LUCK FA, semblable à un sourire au néon auquel auraient manqué plusieurs dents, se dressait une grande pancarte que je n'avais jamais remarquée, une sorte d'affiche à deux pans qui invitait les piétons venant dans les deux sens à la spécialité du lundi, la BUVETTE DIM SUM !!!

La salle, bien que plus sombre qu'un magasin de pompes funèbres, et à peu près aussi gaie, résonnait pourtant du fracas des plats et des assiettes, ainsi que des bruits des clients — grognements, rires, cris — issus des grottes secrètes et répercutés dans les couloirs sinueux de ces catacombes chinoises.

Lo apparut, avec dans son sillage le jeune freluquet qui avait été réélu par défaut, et les deux marmitons, tous portant des sacs blancs en papier.

« Je vous supplie de pardonner mes exigences, dis-je en m'inclinant profondément.

— Excusez je vous prie ! objecta-t-il en m'adressant une révérence plus profonde encore. Aucune exigence ! Le jeune dragon fait partie de la famille.

— Merci, dis-je avec reconnaissance en adressant un signe de tête à chacun. Vous êtes apparemment très occupés aujourd'hui.

— Putain, et comment ! jura le jeune freluquet. on s'croirait au zoo ! »

Les trois autres lui lancèrent un regard sévère, silencieux, désapprobateur, qui le fit rentrer dans sa coquille.

Lo opina gravement du chef. « Très.

— Il y a aussi des plats à emporter ! dis-je en montrant les sacs en papier. L'un de ceux-ci est-il pour moi ?

Ils se regardèrent, puis éclatèrent de rire. « Tous, dit Lo.

— Tous ? demandai-je, incrédule. Mais, Lo, je n'ai que vingt dollars.

Il secoua la tête. « Pas de problème. Frais de la maison.

— Je ne peux pas !

— Vous devez !

— Non non !

— Si si !

— Mais comment vais-je transporter tout ça ? »

Il tendit le doigt vers la porte. A travers le verre teinté, je vis un taxi qui attendait. Il eut un sourire espiègle.

« Mais... mais... »

Il agita les mains. « Trêve objections. Nous devons retourner travailler. »

Ils entreprirent alors de déposer leurs paquets entre mes bras.

« Voici les tranches de méduse, les nouilles froides au sésame... » Il décrivait les plats avec éloquence, excité par sa propre générosité. « Voici le canard confit, le chou brûlant épicé, les œufs de mille ans, les rognons hachés sauce piquante... et en guise de plat principal, ah ! (il embrassa le bout de ses doigts) scrupuleusement préparé selon la recette historique du grand Ho Ha de la dynastie Tang : La Sublime Translation de la Grande Ourse au Ciel !

— Lo... », dis-je en interrompant sa rhapsodie d'un chuchotement timide — j'hésitai à briser son enthousiasme, mais m'y sentis néanmoins contraint —, « qu'est-ce, exactement, que "La Sublime Translation de la Grande Ourse au Ciel" ? »

Il me regarda en se demandant s'il avait bien entendu. « Le jeune dragon, qui a consacré tant d'années à acquérir le "goût authentique", un parangon parmi ses pairs, ignore La Sublime Translation de la Grande Ourse au Ciel, le plus célèbre chef-d'œuvre du plus grand cuisinier de tous les temps ? » Il semblait scandalisé. Secouant la tête, il commenta sa question d'un léger soupir, comme s'il se lamentait sur la dégradation de la vie moderne et sur une époque où même les jeunes les plus doués pouvaient atteindre l'âge adulte dans un état d'ignorance aussi déplorable, de quasi-barbarie. « Un bouillon de pattes d'ourse », dit-il d'une voix sinistre.

Son visage s'éclaira brusquement quand il se rappela le vin. « Une bouteille de vieux Mao T'ai, me glissa-t-il à l'oreille avec une gourmandise et une mine de conspirateur. Vous apprécierez au moins cela. »

Je souris et le remerciai nerveusement.

« Et en guise de dessert, reprit-il, retrouvant toute sa verve pour le bouquet final, votre plat préféré !

— Lo ! protestai-je, vous n'avez pas... »

Si — des crêpes au navet parfumé, fourrées aux crevettes et assaisonnées de sauce d'huître !

« Un banquet digne du Fils du Ciel ! » m'écriai-je, partagé entre stupéfaction et gratitude.

« Bah, protesta-t-il modestement. Le dragon exagère. » Il bomba néanmoins le torse.

« Maintenant, partez ! s'écria-t-il en me poussant vers la porte. Hâtez-vous avant que ça ne refroidisse ! »

Chargé de mes précieuses marchandises, qui se réorganisaient à mesure que j'approchais de ma destination — les sacs du dessus tombaient par terre, je les ramassais, puis les glissais sous la pile, et ainsi de suite selon une progression arithmétique assez semblable à la rotation des cultures —, j'arrivai enfin au bureau 2101, en sueur et hors d'haleine. Le nom qui figurait sur la porte me fit arrêter. Car, au lieu de Kahn, je découvris « Ahasvérus ». Je demeurai ainsi dans le couloir, indécis.

« Entre ! Entre ! beugla-t-il d'une voix impatiente en poussant la porte de l'intérieur. Qu'est-ce qui t'a pris tout ce temps ? J'attends depuis trente secondes. »

Je titubai dans le bureau en semant mes sacs de droite et de gauche.

« Il y a de la monnaie ! Il la compta. Dix-huit dollars ! Incroyable ! Au fait, qu'as-tu acheté ? Des galettes d'avoine ? » Il plissa les yeux et me regarda en hochant la tête. « Pas mal, petit. Comment t'appelles-tu ?

— Sun I, répondis-je.

— Je dois au moins t'accorder ça, *Sonny*, dit-il, confirmant ainsi au-delà de tout espoir de rédemption le nom de baptême forgé par Wo — ma nouvelle identité dowiste — tu es peut-être un peu lent, mais pour ce qui est d'exécuter les ordres et de ramener à déjeuner, fonction la plus importante du grouillot, à toi le pompon. Je t'accorde un satisfecit, du moins rapport à la quantité et au prix. Espérons seulement que c'est mangeable — il tendit la main vers le sac le plus proche —, car ce pourrait être le début d'une longue et fructueuse association.

— M. Kahn, puis-je vous poser une question ? »

Il leva la tête, cligna des yeux ; la moitié de son avant-bras avait déjà disparu dans un sac. « Bien sûr, petit, vas-y.

— Ahasvérus, est-ce votre nom de famille ? »

Il gloussa. « Non, non, petit, c'est une blague. C'était un célèbre parent à moi — mon oncle. »

Bien que peu satisfait de sa réponse, je n'eus pas le temps de l'interroger plus avant.

« Bon Dieu ! Qu'est-ce que c'est que ça ? » Il sortit un morceau de méduse, le renifla d'un air méfiant, puis le tendit à bout de bras. Il m'adressa alors le regard vide du morse, tenant délicatement la tranche de méduse entre le pouce et l'index, comme avec des pincettes. « Antipasto chinois ?

— Méduse aux condiments, répliquai-je.

— Hmm... pas mal. On dirait un bout de poisson.

— Exactement ! m'écriai-je avec enthousiasme. Goûtez-en un morceau ! »

Il grimaça de dégoût. « Je ne peux même pas manger de *ketchup*, petit, répondit-il d'une voix lugubre. Jésus Marie, la crème anglaise me donne envie de gerber. Je n'y peux rien. Constitution fragile, vois-tu, due au bouillon de poule que j'ai ingurgité pendant toute ma jeunesse. Mon éducation juive. J'ai essayé de m'en affranchir, mais... (il soupira en haussant les épaules avec fatalisme) on n'échappe pas à ses origines. C'est le destin. La gravité du sang, vois-tu.

— Allez-y, insistai-je.

— Va me chercher un verre d'eau, dit-il en me tendant un gobelet plastique, juste au cas où. Dans le couloir. »

A mon retour, je le découvris avec stupéfaction qui piochait dans les sacs, la main leste et les joues gonflées. « Ch'est fameux », réussit-il à articuler.

J'entrepris de l'aider : j'ouvrais les sacs, décrivais leur contenu, glissais sa serviette dans son col de chemise. Il expédia rapidement les amuse-gueule et attaqua le plat de résistance. Il tamponna alors ses lèvres avec une serviette en papier, eut une moue satisfaite, puis se frotta les mains.

« Qu'y a-t-il là-dedans ? demanda-t-il d'une voix excitée. Non, ne me dis rien : mousse de fruits grillés marinés dans la sanie, j'ai gagné ? »

Son trait d'esprit m'échappa comme un missile mal guidé. « Je ne connais pas ce plat, répondis-je innocemment. Mais si les ingrédients en sont disponibles, je suis certain que mon ami Lo pourrait vous le préparer.

— Laisse tomber, dit-il en se mouchant bruyamment.

— En tout cas, poursuivis-je, cette création particulière se nomme Sublime Translation de la Grande Ourse au Ciel.

— Traduction ?

— Non, rectifiai-je, Translation.

— *Traduction*, répéta-t-il.

— Ah, fis-je, bouillon de pattes d'ourse.

— Bon ! éructa-t-il en mâchant vigoureusement. Un peu coriace, mais savoureux.

— Ce plat tire son nom de la constellation Ursa Major, expliquai-je en me rappelant les cours de Scottie et espérant qu'un peu de sauce intellectuelle aiguiserait son appétit.

— Remarquable ! dit-il. Ce bouillon d'ourse détrône tous les couillons de la bourse ! »

De sa baguette, il désigna alors un sac fermé. « Et ça ?

— Le vin ! m'écriai-je. Je l'avais complètement oublié !

— Du vin par-dessus le marché ! dit-il. De mieux en mieux ! »

Je sortis la bouteille et vis qu'un billet y était fixé.

« C'est quoi, l'addition ? demanda-t-il.

— Pour les connaisseurs, expliquait la calligraphie grossière de Lo, le plus subtil des vins. Buvez à longues goulées ! » Je souris et mes yeux s'embuèrent de gratitude. Je lus à haute voix.

« Sers-m'en un peu », dit Kahn en jetant son eau dans une plante verte. Je versai.

Il huma son bouquet. « Hmm... intéressant. » Levant le gobelet vers ses lèvres, il en but une gorgée. « Seigneur ! s'écria-t-il en recrachant le vin sur son bureau. On dirait du gin frelaté !

— Il a le goût acquis, rétorquai-je avec dignité.

— Ho ho, minauda-t-il. Quel raffinement, mon cher ! Alors, et les rouleaux de printemps ? réclama-t-il ensuite en s'adossant à sa chaise.

— Je crains que...

— Je plaisantais, petit. Bon Dieu, ne sois pas si indécrottablement sérieux ! Un peu de *chutzpah*, que diable !

— *Hu... hu...*

— *Chut*zpah, dit-il. Persévère, ça va venir. Maintenant, fiston, parle-moi un peu de toi. Mais sois bref et concis, nous n'avons pas de temps à schmoozer. Quand es-tu arrivé, la semaine dernière ? »

J'acquiesçai.

« Bon sang, tu es sérieux ? »

Je clignai des yeux sans mot dire.

Il secoua la tête. « Qu'est-ce qui t'amène à New York ? Ne me dis rien — les bagels, hein ?

— Je... je...

— Cesse donc de bafouiller, petit. Un peu plus de...

— *Hutzpah !* » ajoutai-je vivement.

Il opina du chef d'un air approbateur. « Ça vient.

— Je désire comprendre le fonctionnement du Dow », dis-je pour répondre à sa question.

Kahn grimaça un sourire. « Comme nous tous. Quoi d'autre ? Tu veux gagner un million en vitesse, puis faire venir Mama et Papa-san sur le *Queen Elizabeth Deux*, c'est ça ? Cabines de luxe pour tous les cochons et poulets ?

— Ma mère est morte, répondis-je avec dignité. Et je n'ai jamais connu mon père.

— Désolé, petit, dit-il. Je voulais pas te vexer. Je cause, je cause, et puis... — il haussa les épaules — c'est plus fort que moi. Alors, que comptes-tu faire de tout ce pèze putatif ?

— Pèze ? interrogeai-je.

— Argent.

— Gagner de l'argent ne m'intéresse pas, répondis-je.

— Ça alors ! fit-il. Gagner de l'argent ne l'intéresse pas ! Je croyais que tu avais dit que tu voulais comprendre le Dow ?

— Oui, répliquai-je. Mais pas dans un but de gains personnels. La richesse à laquelle j'aspire est d'un autre ordre.

— Je crois repérer un idéaliste, me coupa-t-il sèchement.

— Idéaliste ? demandai-je. S'agit-il d'une secte comme les épiscopaliens ?

— En quelque sorte, fit-il.

— Je ne suis pas chrétien.

— Moi non plus, petit.

— Je suis taoïste.
— Et moi juif, dit-il machinalement pour avoir le dernier mot. Ouah ! Quoi ? Bon Dieu de bonsoir ! s'écria-t-il soudain, comme s'il comprenait enfin le sens de ma dernière réplique. Un *taoïste* ? Comme le taoïsme *chinois* ?
— Vous connaissez le taoïsme ? lui demandai-je, surpris.
— Petit, protesta-t-il. Regarde-moi dans le blanc des yeux ! Ai-je vraiment l'air d'un schmo total ? Regarde ce parchemin. » Il tapota le verre d'un document encadré et accroché au mur derrière son bureau. « Tu vois ça ? Université Columbia. Licence ès lettres. Et la maîtrise en prime ! Le même Kahn que tu contemples aujourd'hui si abattu — ou exalté, tout dépend du point de vue — fut autrefois un membre à part entière de la communauté académique. Bien que mon terrain de prédilection fût la "lutte et rature", il m'est arrivé de faire des incursions derrière les lignes dans le département des religions comparées. Je *sais* ce qu'est le taoïsme ! En revanche, ce que j'ignore, c'est ce qu'un taoïste tel que tu prétends l'être vient faire sur le parquet de la Bourse de New York.
— Mais je vous l'ai dit, répondis-je. Je désire comprendre le fonctionnement du Dow.
— Epelle-moi un peu ça.
— D-o-w.
— Bon Dieu ! s'écria-t-il. C'est bien ce que je pensais — un jeu de mots ! » Il retroussa les lèvres et se mit à réfléchir. « Hmm... je crois que ça me plaît. Oui, nous tenons là un excellent slogan publicitaire — une accroche du tonnerre de Dieu, comme aurait pu dire feu Mark Twain : le Tao dans le Dow. Qu'en penses-tu ? Nous pourrions peut-être le fourguer au service des Relations Publiques de la Bourse, histoire d'humaniser leur image de marque. Cinquante-cinquante. D'accord ? »
Je secouai la tête.
« Hé, ne sois pas trop gourmand, protesta-t-il. D'accord, l'idée vient de toi. Mais sans moi tu ne saurais pas quoi en faire. J'ai des relations dans le milieu, petit. Il fut un temps où j'étais moi-même dans la publicité. Phase Deux de ma carrière. Vois-tu, j'avais tout misé sur l'université, quand... ah, zut, inutile de parler de ça. Disons simplement que j'ai manqué de fonds. Ce pauvre Kahn, un malheureux nourrisson impitoyablement sevré du mamelon institutionnel, puis jeté sans préavis dans le froid monde réel... Attention, petit, ne laisse jamais personne te raconter ce genre de bobard : le monde n'est ni aussi froid ni aussi réel qu'on aimerait te le faire croire. Bref, j'ai tenté ma chance dans une agence de pub, d'où je fus arraché par la peau du cou, façon de parler, par les bons soins de mon oncle Ahasvérus, le Juif Errant, dont j'ai largement hérité la propension au vagabondage.
— *Le* Juif Errant ? demandai-je, les yeux écarquillés de stupeur.
— Enfin..., tergiversa-t-il, *un* Juif Errant. En tout cas, il m'a légué son fauteuil à la Bourse. Phase Trois — ou Quatre, plutôt, la Trois étant celle où je travaillais au service de Dieu et de la patrie pour le BIG. Mais c'est une autre histoire.
— Vous êtes donc devenu courtier ? demandai-je innocemment.
— Petit, je t'en prie ! » protesta-t-il en se redressant avec une fierté

dédaigneuse. Du pouce, il me montra son badge. « Je suis négociant au parquet, et non un vulgaire esclave de la commission. Je travaille à mon compte, en toute indépendance. Comparé à moi, le courtier est un simple plébéien. » Il soupira, retrouva des proportions moins impressionnantes. « Bien sûr, les temps sont durs. J'en suis parfois réduit à exécuter les ordres dont les garçons de course ne peuvent se charger. Je n'aime pas m'abaisser à cela, évidemment. Mais la survie l'emporte sur la dignité, pas vrai ? Tu vois, les négociants au parquet sont une espèce menacée. En fait, je suis l'un des derniers survivants d'une race en voie de disparition, un loup solitaire, pour ainsi dire. Autrefois, quand mon oncle Ahasvérus était dans la fleur de l'âge, les choses étaient différentes. Un négociant au parquet pouvait gagner correctement sa vie en pinaillant sur des quarts ou des huitièmes de dollar. Et puis il pouvait tricher. Terminé, tout ça ! Cette époque merveilleuse est bel et bien révolue. On nous a systématiquement chassés, exterminés. Mon propre cas est encore plus dramatique. Vois-tu, mon oncle Ahasvérus a eu beau me rendre riche d'un seul coup, il a négligé de me fournir la condition sine qua non sans laquelle la possession d'un fauteuil devient autant un atout qu'un inconvénient — je veux dire : l'argent. Car qu'est-ce qu'un fauteuil sans argent ? Que suis-je censé faire, m'asseoir dedans ? Ce n'est même pas confortable ! Un de ces sinistres accessoires proto-américains sans coussins, sans accoudoirs ni rien. Pas un Juif qui se respecte n'accepterait de mourir là-dedans. Mon sort, vois-tu, ressemble beaucoup à celui de la vieille aristocratie sudiste. Je suis un pauvre de la terre — un pauvre du fauteuil, si tu préfères. Bien que mon capital non capitonné s'élève à près d'un quart de million de dollars, je dois faire des pieds et des mains pour trouver de l'argent frais, du moins dernièrement. Quasiment réduit à schnorrer, petit ! C'est humiliant ! Mes amis changent de trottoir dès qu'ils me voient. Par-dessus le marché, ils veulent ma peau !

— Qui donc ? demandai-je, inquiet.

— Tu sais bien, les goyim, le BEV — *tout le monde*. Comment veux-tu t'en tirer avec tous ces règlements et les charges qui augmentent — les frais généraux, taxes de virement, impôts sur les transferts — ils me bouffent littéralement tout cru. Et puis j'ai perdu ma paix intérieure. Sans parler de mon équanimité ! Tu vois ces valises sous mes yeux ? Je n'en dors plus la nuit. Elles n'ont pas toujours été là, tu peux me croire. Bon Dieu, j'étais un type potable avant d'entrer dans les affaires. Ne souris pas ! Je parle sérieusement. Je levais un bout de fesse chaque fois que l'envie m'en prenait. Maintenant je perds mes cheveux, et ça fait belle lurette que je n'ai plus d'appétit. Non, vraiment, petit, je me barre en couilles. Voilà ce qu'ont fait de moi sept ans de déveine. Je ne sais pas combien de temps encore je vais tenir le coup. Je suis sérieux ! En tout cas, il me reste probablement quelques mois seulement à vivre. »

Je ne pus réprimer un sourire, qu'il remarqua ; il changea alors son fusil d'épaule.

« Tu te poses donc la question qui s'impose : pourquoi ne revend-il pas son fauteuil pour trouver un boulot qui lui convienne mieux ? Oui, moi-même je me le suis souvent demandé. Serais-je un esclave de l'éthique protestante du travail ? Que non, petit, Kahn n'est pas protestant ! Bien sûr, les Juifs ont concocté leur propre version endémique de cette délicieuse institution. Cela s'appelle la culpabilité. Dans son cas et pour résumer la chose, fiston, Kahn souffre d'un amour masochiste de la bouche qui le mord. C'est l'appel du monde sauvage, vois-tu. Je ne peux pas y résister. Je n'ai jamais pu.

« Bon Dieu, petit, j'ai seulement besoin d'un répit, tu comprends ? Comme un exemplaire du *Wall Street Journal* de mercredi une heure avant l'ouverture de la séance du jeudi. Hé, hé ! Non que je me soucie immodérément de l'argent, tu me suis. Je ne suis pas un matérialiste. Je veux seulement montrer à tous ces Wasp qu'un Juif aussi en a dans la culotte. » Il saisit son entrejambe de façon suggestive. « C'est le principe de la chose qui m'intéresse. Hé, hé ! Tu piges ? Principal ? Intérêt ? Comment t'expliquer ça, petit ? Je te l'ai dit, c'est l'appel du monde sauvage. Le marché est la dernière frontière, un monde sauvage créé par la civilisation. La lutte classique pour la survie. J'aime ça — c'est plus fort que moi. J'ai toujours aimé ça. Voilà donc mon histoire, du moins dans sa version expurgée. » Il plissa les yeux et me dévisagea pensivement. « Alors comme ça tu veux entrer dans le Dow ? Et un taoïste encore ! Je pourrais peut-être te mettre le pied à l'étrier...

— Vraiment ? » J'étais fou de joie. « C'est là le plus ardent de mes désirs : devenir le disciple de l'étudiant chevronné du Dow que vous êtes !

— Une seconde, m'interrompit-il. Qu'est-ce que c'est que cette histoire de disciple ? Laisse-moi te rappeler une fois encore que le protocole en vigueur ici n'a rien à voir avec ça. Nous ne sommes pas en Chine.

— Mais vous allez m'apprendre ? demandai-je, plein d'espoir. Montrez-moi au moins par où commencer !

— Ce que tu veux apprendre ne saurait être enseigné, répondit-il, et cette phrase m'en rappela une autre, à moitié oubliée. L'expérience est la seule façon. Bien sûr, au début, je te surveillerai pour que tu ne commettes pas de bourde grossière dans tes investissements.

— Investissements ?

— Oui, dit-il. Il est bien question de ça, non ?

— Mais je vous ai déjà expliqué que je ne voulais pas gagner d'argent.

— Tu veux comprendre le Dow, oui ou non ?

— Evidemment, répliquai-je, mais... »

Il secoua la tête. « Petit, dit-il d'une voix solennelle, hiératique, il n'y a qu'une seule façon de procéder. Si tu veux comprendre le Dow, tu dois jouer le jeu.

— Mais c'est impossible ! m'écriai-je, horrifié. Cela irait contre mes principes. Je désire seulement un savoir objectif. Je veux observer sans participer.

— Ah ah, dit-il, la mentalité universitaire — je la repère à un kilomètre. Tu es partisan de la méthode hygiénique, hein ? Je ne te la recommande pas, petit. Tu risques d'être déçu. » Il s'interrompit, comme pour me donner l'occasion de me rétracter. « Enfin, chacun mène sa barque comme il l'entend. Si tu as décidé de tenter ta chance par la face Nord, je verrai ce que je peux faire pour toi — à condition que tu continues à me fournir le déjeuner. Marché conclu ?

— Oh oui, acquiesçai-je. Absolument ! Merci !
— D'accord, d'accord, pas de schmaltz, hein ? »
Je joignis les mains contre ma poitrine et inclinai la tête.
« Maintenant, je déclare cette schmooze levée ! On se retrouvera au parquet ! Et souviens-toi, petit...
— Je sais, m'écriai-je aussitôt. *Chut*zpah ! »

7

Au cours des une ou deux premières semaines, je dînai tous les soirs chez les Ha-p'i. D'habitude, nous étions seulement trois, Yin-mi, sa mère et moi, Lo étant retenu par son travail jusqu'à une heure tardive. Dès le début, je me sentis détendu en présence de Yin-mi ; un sentiment de paix m'envahissait, à l'origine parfaitement mystérieuse, presque comme s'il eût émané d'elle un effluve de calme, une incandescence que son âme irradiait indifféremment alentour, aussi prodigue que le soleil, nous accordant ainsi, dans une mesure moindre, ces mêmes qualités d'équilibre et de calme intérieur qu'elle possédait au plus haut point et qu'avec le temps je reconnus comme le noyau même de sa personnalité. Paradoxalement, cette impression même de paix, dont l'intensité et la profondeur étaient incommensurables avec toute cause que j'aurais pu alléguer, me troublait profondément. C'était pourtant un trouble délicieux, un serrement de cœur qui avivait le cours de mon sang. Je le sentais tressaillir en moi comme une faible décharge électrique, un frémissement d'excitation nerveuse. Bien que le redoutant, je le regrettais quand il me quittait, c'est-à-dire quand elle s'en allait.

Mme Ha-p'i constituait une gêne plus mondaine et tolérable. Plusieurs jours durant, elle ne relâcha jamais son attention, courant en tous sens, souriant pour un rien, remplissant ma tasse après chaque gorgée, me proposant des choses dont je n'avais nul besoin. Ses incessantes marques de politesse me plongeaient dans l'angoisse, me rendaient aussi sensible qu'un cheval ombrageux. Je faisais front comme je pouvais, car je n'avais guère le choix, et puis je comprenais que son attitude était dictée par une authentique sollicitude à mon égard. L'énergie qu'elle manifesta au cours des premiers jours fut vraiment admirable, bien qu'à peine supportable pour l'autre camp, où je me trouvais malgré moi. Elle était infatigable, implacable. Je frisais le désespoir. La maladie semblait chronique et son issue fatale — sinon pour elle, du moins pour moi. Au bout d'un moment, cependant, elle montra quelques signes de faiblesse. La réalité reprit peu à peu le dessus. Les menues efflorescences d'une vulnérabilité charmante commencèrent à poindre dans les fentes et les fissures qui émaillaient le mur compact de sa politesse. Je fus aux anges. Je songeai seulement alors (ou plutôt, devrais-je dire, ma supposition fut alors confirmée) que son comportement avait quelque chose de sournois, que tout ce cérémonial compliqué était motivé, non par l'amour, mais par le devoir, parce que l'étiquette le requérait, et que ce n'était nullement la manifestation d'une affection spontanée. Quand apparurent les premiers signes de relâchement, je poussai en mon for intérieur un soupir de soulagement, et maudis Confucius de nous enchaîner ainsi à des institutions aussi compliquées et perverties.

Je n'oublierai jamais son premier faux pas. Elle avait préparé le dîner pour nous, penchée au-dessus de la cuisinière, une cuillère en bois à la main, regardant la colonne de vapeur qui montait d'une casserole où un carrelet mijotait dans une sauce à l'ail et au gingembre ; elle attendait l'instant fatidique. A des signes imperceptibles à l'œil non exercé, le poisson révélait qu'il était prêt au sacrifice. (Lo, qui m'expliquait un jour la préparation de ce plat, me déclara solennellement que le carrelet lui adressait « un clin d'œil » quand il était cuit à point. Il refusa de s'expliquer. Plusieurs fois, alors que je travaillais au restaurant, il m'avait surpris penché au-dessus de la casserole dans la vapeur, épiant le clin d'œil du poisson, tandis que l'animal dardait vers moi son regard mort et triomphant, car vide de tout signe. Mais un jour, je fus presque certain de le voir. Lo m'informa alors en termes péremptoires que je m'étais trompé. Apparemment, le clin d'œil « authentique » est un phénomène trop bref et subtil pour être remarqué par qui ne possède pas le vrai *zhen wer*.) Toujours est-il que Mme Ha-p'i — qui connaissait bien son affaire — courut porter notre poisson sur la table. Avec un craquement humide, la cuillère s'enfonça dans l'épine dorsale molle, d'où s'écoula un peu de délicieuse moelle brûlante. Arrosant nos portions de jus de cuisson, elle courait en tous sens pour servir les plats accessoires et les condiments pendant que Yin-mi et moi restions assis, impuissants. Quand enfin elle eut terminé, elle se laissa lourdement tomber sur sa chaise et poussa un énorme soupir de lassitude. Son visage était rouge et luisant. Avec le torchon du four, elle essuya la sueur qui perlait à son front, puis le lança négligemment par-dessus son épaule en direction de l'évier.

« Sun I, passe-moi donc le sel. » Les mots bénis avaient réussi à franchir les barbelés de la censure, tel un pigeon voyageur franchissant les murailles avec un rameau d'olivier dans le bec.

Je fus tellement abasourdi que je faillis rater cette occasion inespérée. Mais Yin-mi me donna un léger coup de pied sous la table, et je me levai aussitôt pour aller chercher le sel. Quand je me rassis, Mme Ha-p'i avait pris conscience de son manquement. Elle leva vers nous des yeux chagrinés et découvrit deux jeunes gens qui souriaient malicieusement. Je lui présentai alors le sel avec une politesse exagérée, et Yin-mi éclata de rire. Mme Ha-p'i rougit, hésita, puis se joignit à notre bonne humeur. L'incident ne suscita aucun commentaire. Ensuite, malgré de brèves rechutes, elle s'amenda et adopta ce qui me paraît être son style caractéristique, que je peux seulement décrire comme l'omnipotence d'une mère désorientée. Je fus rapidement assimilé ; dès lors, je connus pour la première fois les consolations pesantes de la vie domestique, et devins un membre à part entière de la famille. Je découvris alors un bonheur tel que je n'en avais jamais connu auparavant et, pensai-je à l'époque, plus grand.

Parfois, après le dîner, Yin-mi et moi montions sur le toit ; nous restions assis, jambes pendantes, parlant de tout et de rien, regardant les passants dans la rue, jetant des miettes aux pigeons, écoutant le puits des soupirs (d'où monta un soir le bruit troublant que j'avais déjà entendu, la berceuse primordiale du sexe). Ainsi profitions-nous des longs et vaporeux crépuscules d'été en contemplant l'énorme soleil rouge qui descendait vers le fleuve couleur de fumée, disparaissait enfin derrière les sombres collines de Palisades dans les terres sauvages du Jersey. Nous étions sous l'empire d'une chose que ni elle ni moi ne comprenions — ou du moins imparfaitement. C'était sans importance, car nous avions tout le temps devant nous. Nous nous contentions de cette intimité paresseuse et prolongée, de cette lente dérive vers... une émotion qui était peut-être de l'amour. A cette époque, je l'eusse pourtant nié avec véhémence (en produisant des arguments idéologiques, le cas échéant), mais cette pensée ne me vint jamais à l'esprit. Il suffisait de suivre le cours du fleuve ; le temps importait peu.

Je poursuivais les épisodes de mon récit, de cette version chinoise des *Mille et Une Nuits*. Et Yin-mi était ma Schéhérazade, du moins pour la patience. Elle supporta ma narration, m'encouragea même à rêver ses développements ultérieurs — si généreuse, pleine de chaleur et de sympathie (mais aussi capable de désapprobation).

La seule ombre au tableau était ma réticence forcée concernant Wo. Les rares fois où Yin-mi s'enquit de son frère, je trouvai presque insupportables sa franchise et la grande solennité de son regard. Chaque fois, je fus sur le point de trahir ma promesse, mais réussis à me retenir à temps, à conserver le secret de Wo qui, à ma grande honte, était aussi devenu le mien. J'improvisais une échappatoire, Yin-mi n'insistait pas. Je la sentais pourtant insatisfaite. La perplexité et le trouble vague que je lisais sur son visage me désolaient davantage que le reste.

Si Yin-mi me laissait les coudées franches, il n'en allait pas de même avec sa mère. Sans tenir le moindre compte de ma gêne, Mme Ha-p'i me harcelait constamment à propos de son fils, sans doute convaincue à juste titre que c'était là la chose la plus naturelle du monde et qu'elle-même était dans son bon droit. Je la plaignais, son souci touchait chez moi une corde sensible et m'obligeait à mentir ou à éviter habilement la vérité sans recourir au mensonge.

Pour cela et d'autres raisons, Wo et moi nous évitions délibérément à la Bourse, car notre complicité dans le péché gâtait l'estime que chacun eût pu avoir pour l'autre. Cette stratégie commune, adoptée d'un accord tacite, s'avéra efficace sur notre lieu de travail. Mais sur le terrain du 17, Mulberry Street, elle ne donna pas d'aussi bons résultats. Peu à peu, le poids du secret introduisit une gêne subtile dans mes rapports avec ma famille adoptive, une tension infime mais sensible, comme la cigale qui avait jadis troublé ma méditation dans le temple — et cette cigale se nommait la conscience. Je fréquentais toujours l'appartement des Ha-p'i, mais beaucoup moins assidûment que par le passé.

Alors que dans ma vie privée je traversais une phase d'isolement, devenant, selon l'expression de Kahn, une sorte de « loup solitaire », l'inverse était vrai de mes activités professionnelles. Du jour de notre première conversation autour de ce mémorable déjeuner, je me mis à suivre Kahn dans la grande salle comme un chien de salon ou un disciple enthousiaste (mais en manifestant aussi peu de schmaltz que possible). Aaron Kahn — mon nouveau maître !

Et quel maître désagréable il était ! Du moins voulait-il se faire passer pour tel. Il raillait constamment mes « Salamalecs Orientaux », m'exhortait à davantage de *chutzpah*, le cri de guerre des combattants ashkénazes, ainsi qu'il me l'apprit. Ce concept difficile demeura pour moi à peu près incompréhensible jusqu'au jour où une intuition éblouissante me révéla qu'il s'agissait de la contrepartie yiddish du mot chinois signifiant « véhémence », la qualité que le *Yi king* assigne au trigramme *Sun*. Moyennant quoi salamalecs orientaux, qui m'avait semblé presque aussi abscons, s'appariait naturellement à « douceur ». Comme le lecteur s'en souvient certainement, ces polarités — douceur et véhémence — constituent le *yin* et le *yang* du trigramme *Sun* qui figure dans mon nom. Tel fut le fondement du jeu de mots malheureux qui, ainsi que je l'ai dit, s'attache à mes pas depuis ma naissance. Pauvre nom ! Plus malmené que jamais depuis sa récente « amélioration » par les soins de Wo et de Kahn, qui avaient pris la liberté de le traduire du chinois en anglais — de taoïste en dowiste, pour ainsi dire — avec ce résultat : *Sonny* !

La lumière de cette découverte (le sens de *chutzpah*) tremblotait comme la flamme ténue d'une bougie dans les ténèbres générales de mon esprit. Le répit fut passager. Car songez aux implications de ma découverte ! Toute ma vie, on m'avait conseillé d'agir « avec la douceur et la pénétration impliquées par ton nom, et non la véhémence impulsive qui est sa contrepartie sombre et à laquelle tu as trop souvent donné libre cours dans le passé », pour reprendre les paroles du maître. Ayant à cœur mon intérêt, Chong Fou et Wu m'avaient inlassablement répété de mortifier ma Nature de Singe et de m'attacher aux qualités de mon caractère. Véhémence : *chutzpah* ; douceur : Salamalecs Orientaux — vous commencez sans doute à comprendre mon dilemme. Alors que mes anciens mentors avaient cherché à étouffer la première pour développer la seconde, mon nouveau maître, Kahn, me poussait à l'attitude inverse. La flamme de la bougie s'éteignit rapidement. Fondu au noir !

Cependant, bien que l'opinion de Kahn pesât lourd dans la balance, elle ne faisait pas le poids contre vingt années de formation intensive. J'étais certes déchiré, écartelé, mais je ne pouvais remettre en cause les fondements même de mon être ; d'ailleurs, je n'avais nullement l'intention de m'écarter des principes de mon éducation. Je serais d'abord taoïste, ensuite dowiste. (Mais tout le problème était là, n'est-ce pas ? Je voulais être les deux. Mieux, je voulais que les deux choses se confondent. Il le fallait. « La Réalité est Une, et le Tao est la Réalité. » Cela incluait le Dow, nécessairement ; en d'autres termes, le delta.) Et puis, je ne crois pas que j'aurais pu changer, l'eussé-je voulu. Si, au cours de toutes ces longues années passées au monastère, la véhémence, ou ma Nature de Singe, avait été une maladie chronique et incurable, maintenant que je la désirais, je ne la trouvais plus nulle part. J'étais devenu aussi docile qu'un lapin ! Les effets de la cure étaient peut-être à retardement ; peut-être agissait-elle seulement maintenant ? Il semblait bien que toute trace de *chutzpah* eût été éliminée de ma personnalité.

Pourtant, bien que Kahn se plaignît constamment de mes « SO » (Salamalecs Orientaux) et sous-entendît que ma présence lui pesait, ses jérémiades se révélèrent bientôt une preuve de son affection. Ah, Kahn ! Je crois qu'il était secrètement ravi et flatté, car lui-même était tellement solitaire. Néanmoins, il maintenait obstinément une distance entre nous, allant un jour jusqu'à déclarer d'une voix exaspérée qu'il songeait à me remettre aux bons soins de l'Organisation mondiale d'assistance, la section des Nations unies qui s'occupe des réfugiés.

Ce n'est pas pur hasard si je parle des Nations unies. Car, appliquant à la lettre mon intention d'observer sans participer, n'évoquais-je pas l'observateur neutre confronté à cette grande bataille qui commence chaque jour ponctuellement dans la grande salle de la Bourse de New York à dix heures du matin et fait rage jusqu'à quatre heures de l'après-midi, heure à laquelle la sonnerie de clôture (que je ne pus jamais totalement dissocier du gong de la clepsydre de Ken Kuan) annonce la fin de la séance ? Alors les combattants se retirent en des lieux plus hospitaliers, dans l'atmosphère fraîche et enfumée de clubs et de bars où ils discutent des derniers développements de la campagne. Les plus grands jeux stratégiques du monde : chaque homme, un général ; et toutes les pertes sur le papier ! L'authentique Elysée des guerriers capitalistes, où toutes les armées vaincues retournent se battre dès le lendemain matin — du moins la première bouffée enivrante que je humai en ces lieux m'en donna-t-elle le sentiment.

Kahn était une sorte de Mosby juif* : un feu follet, un démon qui se matérialisait brusquement là où on l'attendait le moins, qui arrêtait les trains (le Burlington Northern un jour, le Canadian Pacific le lendemain), dévalisait les banques (Chemical, Chase Manhattan), faisait le mort au moment crucial quand le marché vacillait, bluffait, se déguisait (parfois en lui-même, feignant de négocier pour son propre compte alors qu'il travaillait pour un autre, mercenaire temporaire, livrant seulement le nom de son commanditaire après la conclusion de l'affaire — après la tuerie). Je m'attachais obstinément à ses pas à travers les tranchées, devant les redoutes et les fortifications en demi-lune des dix-huit postes, au parquet et au garage, parmi ses relations choisies. Ainsi, au poste numéro deux...

« Combien, la *Steel* ? » lançait-il de sa voix de ténor nasillard, tel un Pavarotti s'échauffant avant son plus grand rôle, l'amoureux courtisant sa belle, transfiguré par la joie de sa profession.

« Cinquante-huit un quart, rétorquait le spécialiste, un baryton revêche (le méchant, le père méfiant).

— Cinquante-huit et un huitième, pour cent actions », proposait Kahn. Silence sinistre ; la tension monte.

Alors, brusquement, dans les coulisses, l'angélus limpide du soprano, comme un vibraphone de cristal frappé par des maillets d'argent, s'élève au-dessus de la foule et annonce : « Je prends ! »

---

* John Singleton Mosby (1833-1916) : colonel de cavalerie des Confédérés *(NdT)*.

Orchestre, *tutti* ! La salle en délire applaudit à tout rompre. Le spécialiste, enfin consentant, annonce les bans.

Les amants éperdus de bonheur se jurent fidélité éternelle dans un bref duo lyrique où ils expriment leur extase, sans oublier de mentionner, selon la coutume qui régit ces rituels d'alliance, leurs noms, numéros et les firmes qu'ils représentent. Kahn, s'il ne travaille pas pour son propre compte, « laisse tomber » à ce moment, tel un Paolo devant sa Francesca, soupirant piteusement et regrettant de s'être décarcassé pour autrui.

Dans l'univers mystérieux de la Bourse, semblables « alliances » ne sont pas uniques. Il y a ainsi les arcanes de l'article 72 qui stipule en substance que, lorsque deux offres sont enregistrées simultanément, chacune égalant ou dépassant le nombre d'actions proposées au prix affiché, les enchérisseurs rivaux tirent à pile ou face et le gagnant remporte la totalité des actions. Comme Kahn aimait ce genre de match ! Je me rappelle le premier auquel j'assistai, qui eut cette conséquence imprévue que l'affrontement cimenta notre relation. Pour cette petite scène, le spécialiste, dans le rôle du croupier, contemple le parterre d'un œil indifférent, impassible, puis tend à Kahn son *penny* spécial, qu'il a tiré de la poche de poitrine de sa veste.

« Alors, William, t'as peur de perdre ta monnaie ? » raille Kahn, commettant ainsi une bourde grossière. Les autres courtiers échangent des regards stupéfaits, le spécialiste dévisage le butor par-dessus ses lunettes en demi-lune, sans daigner répondre.

Kahn s'en moque. Plein de lui-même, possédé par son démon, comme il disait parfois, il affiche joyeusement sa cupidité, la jette au visage des autres comme un défi. Bien que rougissant pour lui, je ne peux m'empêcher d'admirer son exubérance, ses mauvaises manières. Quelle *chutzpah* ! Quel *mensch* !

« Viens voir ici, petit Abraham », roucoule-t-il à la pièce de monnaie. Il la frotte entre ses paumes pour la « chauffer », il se met à psalmodier : « Père des douze tribus d'Israël, Aaron, le fils d'Ida et de Moe, fait appel à toi. Si tu es toujours quelque part là-haut avec ton bâton de berger et que tu nous surveilles comme tu es censé le faire, regarde un instant ta progéniture sans foi ni loi, et aie pitié d'elle. Mets l'ennemi en déroute ! Aide-moi à multiplier mon bétail, mes biens mobiliers et immobiliers, sans parler de mon capital ! Je jure de renoncer à mes manières shegetz et d'épouser une gentille petite Juive comme Ida l'avait... Qu'est-ce que c'est ? » Il tend l'oreille, feint d'écouter. « Très bien, c'est donc un schmeer ! Qu'est-ce que le népotisme pour un Juif ? Pas vrai, les gars ? » Avec un sourire féroce, il dévisage les courtiers de la foule, qui conservent un silence glacé. En pareils instants, le sens de l'humour de Kahn prend une tournure bizarrement autodestructrice, presque fanatique. Une aura de tragédie l'entoure alors, et sans qu'il me l'ait jamais avoué, je sais que c'est plus fort que lui. Ce genre de scène contribue à son ostracisme, lequel alimente à son tour son désespoir chronique.

« Viens ici, petit, appelle-t-il par-dessus son épaule en continuant de frotter la pièce. Souffle dessus. » Il tend ses paumes, pressées l'une contre l'autre en une attitude de prière, vers mes lèvres. « L'oncle Ahasvérus possédait un phylactère. Mais ils sont passés de mode. J'ai besoin d'un porte-bonheur, petit, d'un trèfle à quatre feuilles. C'est peut-être toi. »

Sur ce, il lance la pièce en l'air, beaucoup plus haut que nécessaire, si bien qu'elle disparaît presque dans la voûte de cathédrale de la Bourse.

« Pile ! » s'écrie l'autre courtier alors que la pièce atteint l'apogée de sa trajectoire et commence à redescendre avant de rebondir sur le sol et de rouler, obligeant la foule à s'écarter ; puis elle pivote un instant sur la tranche, hésite, tombe : face.

Je ressens alors un frison d'excitation que je réprime aussitôt. Me tournant vers Kahn, que je m'attends à voir sauter de joie, je le découvre encore plus impassible que moi, les yeux rivés à la pièce, le regard vide, pensif. Il pivote vers moi, en tripotant le bracelet de cuivre qu'il porte au poignet.

« Et voilà, dit-il. Faut qu'on reste ensemble, petit. Tu es mon fer à cheval, ma patte de lapin. » Je l'observe répéter obsessionnellement son geste machinal, en songeant que dans l'entrepôt de sa personnalité extraordinaire, parmi les innombrables articles de l'inventaire, mon ami à l'éducation raffinée possède aussi quelques traces de superstition.

Mais cette scène m'apprit bien autre chose sur Kahn. Quand elle fut terminée, il était dégoûté. Il me renvoya sèchement, se retira en lui-même. En fin d'après-midi, quand il s'adoucit enfin et me permit de l'approcher, je découvris un homme que je reconnus à peine. Beaucoup plus jeune d'aspect, plus droit, il arborait une dignité inhabituelle, une expression de souffrance transcendée, comme s'il avait lutté et vaincu. Ses yeux d'ordinaire larmoyants étaient secs et brillaient d'une lumière positivement spirituelle, son visage semblait transfiguré, presque beau. Une noblesse secrète était remontée du plus profond de son âme. Kahn était devenu un prince.

Je n'ai jamais parfaitement compris les raisons de cette métamorphose remarquable, et les quelques éclaircissements que j'obtins n'arrivèrent que plus tard. Un soir dans un bar, après plusieurs verres, il laissa tomber son masque de réserve pour m'accorder une preuve indubitable d'affection.

« Suis-moi, petit, m'ordonna-t-il d'une voix un peu pâteuse, allons faire un tour aux gogues. » Bien que prêtre et novice, je reconnus dans cette invite l'un des plus hauts témoignages de camaraderie masculine (Ah, Wu, que n'ai-je appris grâce à toi ?).

Kahn enlaça mes épaules pour assurer son équilibre tout en m'honorant d'un signe tangible de son amitié. Nous essuyâmes quelques regards incendiaires, mais étions au-dessus de semblables mesquineries, ou au-delà.

Dans les toilettes carrelées, devant les miroirs, sous les tubes fluorescents, tenant nos schlongs respectifs, nous soulageâmes nos vessies dans les urinoirs scintillants, baissant de temps à autre les yeux pour nous assurer que tout se déroulait normalement, nous adressant des sourires rayonnants d'affection silencieuse, clignant des yeux, ne ressentant nul besoin de parler.

D'un signe de tête, Kahn me montra un graffiti sur le mur.

To do is to be (Faire, c'est être) — Sartre
To be is to do (Etre, c'est faire) — Camus
Scoobie doobie doo — Sinatra

« Etre, c'est souffrir, petit, dit-il sans sourire, quand tu es juif.

Aaron Kahn », ajouta-t-il sombrement, comme pour s'attribuer la citation.

Mais revenons à la grande salle de la Bourse... A la conclusion d'une affaire, Kahn me tendait un billet où étaient inscrits son nom et matricule, ainsi qu'une brève description de la transaction ; je filais alors aux cabines téléphoniques pour transmettre l'information, via la maison de courtage, au client lui-même. A mon retour, j'observais la matérialisation magique des symboles sur le ruban électronique qui coulait comme un ruisseau bleuâtre rapide et silencieux, un ruisseau rempli de petits poissons verts phosphorescents, numériques et alphabétiques. J'étais à chaque fois bouleversé de voir les informations ainsi transférées, puis, à la vitesse de la lumière, diffusées sur des écrans similaires dans toutes les maisons de courtage d'Amérique. C'était comme si j'avais contribué, par mes modestes fonctions, à l'établissement des Moyennes, au flux et au reflux du Dow.

Mais comme on dit dans le milieu de la Bourse, quand on a exécuté un ordre, on n'a plus grand-chose à apprendre de cette technique. Bien que profitant immensément des leçons de Kahn au parquet, à mesure que le temps passait et que je comprenais davantage les opérations boursières, je réalisai peu à peu que, dans ma quête pour élucider les mystères du Dow, je ne pouvais en rester là.

« Maître..., dis-je un jour à Kahn.

— Bon sang de bonsoir ! Cesse un peu de déconner avec tes "maître", vu ? explosa-t-il. Je ne suis pas ton maître, petit. Tu n'es pas un esclave. On est en Amérique, réveille-toi. Ni esclaves, ni maîtres. Conduis-toi en mensch ! »

Après lui avoir laissé le temps de se calmer, je poursuivis avec déférence. « Mais dans ce grand mystère et cet art insondable qu'est le Dow, il doit exister des maîtres renommés... euh, des sages, me repris-je quand j'eus essuyé un regard meurtrier, qui ont pénétré jusqu'au cœur de la vérité et ainsi peuvent offrir leurs lumières aux autres dans leur quête, tout comme il y en a en Chine dans les grandes religions ?

— Ecoute, petit, dit-il en me prenant à part, ne te vexe pas — je dis ça pour ton bien —, mais faudrait que tu changes un peu de langage. On croirait entendre l'oracle de Delphes ! Pour l'amour du Ciel, redescends sur terre ! Quant à ta demande, il se trouve que j'ai goupillé un truc à ce sujet. J'ai une petite surprise pour toi. Tu es pris cet après-midi à deux heures ?

— Je travaille, comme vous le savez.

— J'ai réglé le problème avec ton superviseur, dit-il en souriant. Tu vas chez le médecin.

— Chez le médecin ?

— Le sorcier ! m'informa-t-il en s'amusant de ma perplexité.

— Mais je ne suis pas malade, protestai-je.

— Jésus Marie, ne sois pas si prosaïque, petit ! C'est une métaphore. Je parle du sorcier *économique*, celui qui prétend expliquer les fluctuations du marché. En d'autres termes, un stratège de l'investissement. A vrai dire, question sorcellerie, ce type n'appartient pas vraiment à l'avant-garde. Ernie Powers figure, pour ainsi dire, à l'avant-garde de l'arrière-garde, ou de la vieille garde ainsi que ses zélateurs préfèrent se considérer. Il est le plus éminent tenant encore vivant, peut-être le seul tenant encore vivant, de

l'école de la Valeur Intrinsèque — que nous pourrions qualifier de philosophie antédiluvienne ou préhistorique du marché — doublé d'un Fondamentaliste pur et dur. Si tu veux t'initier aux lois du marché, autant commencer par le commencement. Et E. Powers est sans conteste le commencement, un fossile vivant, l'incarnation du Boursicoteur Prudent, espèce jadis célèbre à Wall Street, mais aujourd'hui quasiment éteinte, une sorte d'Homme de Pékin fiduciaire, si tu préfères. Cela devrait te suffire pour le situer. En tout cas, E.P. est président du conseil d'administration et principal directeur d'une petite société de management, Powers and Burden, qui s'occupe exclusivement d'une clientèle triée sur le volet, une sorte d'aristocratie du fric. J'ai tiré quelques ficelles et réussi à te faire admettre cet après-midi à l'assemblée des actionnaires. Tu vas donc entendre le baratin de ce bon vieil Ernie.
— Merci, maî... Kahn, dis-je
— Pas de quoi, petit. Encore une chose...
— Oui ?
— Mets la pédale douce sur les Salamalecs Orientaux. Pas de courbettes, hein ? Tout le monde n'est pas aussi tolérant que moi. Si tu commences ton cirque, ces gars-là n'hésiteront pas à appeler les flics. Je ne plaisante pas. »

Je lui promis, avec beaucoup de déférence, de me conformer scrupuleusement à ses directives, puis battis en retraite aussi rapidement que possible.

Il s'avéra que la ficelle qu'il avait tirée était passablement usée. Quand j'arrivai, je découvris une veste blanche et un nœud papillon noir qui m'étaient destinés, puis on me fit entrer subrepticement, avec les employés et les autres extras chargés de servir les hors-d'œuvre, dans la salle où les actionnaires étaient réunis.

Ernest Power, senior, était un grand vieillard élégant doté d'un toupet de cheveux blancs comme neige, fins comme du duvet, et de joues qui ressemblaient à deux pommes bien astiquées. Digne et affable, il affichait l'expression cassante, intransigeante, de qui est convaincu de détenir la vérité. Bref, il jouait au grand ponte, sinon au tyran. Il semblait laisser les autres poursuivre leurs stratégies personnelles, fussent-elles erronées, pour cette seule raison que leurs errements l'amusaient et le faisaient rire comme un vieux renard qui se gausse de l'impénitente folie humaine. Il entra dans la salle sans tambour ni trompette, tel un patriarche participant à une petite réunion de famille. Il s'arrêta fréquemment en chemin pour bavarder, serrer une main ici ou là, s'informer d'un mari cloué au lit par la goutte, d'un petit-fils qui étudiait le droit à Harvard. Il s'arrêta pour prendre un toast au foie gras sur le plateau que je portais, puis s'écria gaiement : « Comment, il n'y a pas de pâtés impériaux ? »

Après quelques remarques préliminaires, on lut les minutes et le rapport financier annuel, sans doute préparés par quelque comptable libéral, et dont plusieurs exemplaires circulaient, protégés par un étui de cuir, comme une Bible ou le menu d'un restaurant de luxe. Powers le commenta, insista sur certains points, puis invita les convives à lui poser des questions.

Aucune main ne se leva. Tout le monde était parfaitement content, parfaitement confiant, tel un troupeau de moutons devant son berger. Powers réclama un canapé. Alors que je trottais le long du mur, quelqu'un se leva dans le fond. « Confiez-nous votre secret, M. Powers : comment expliquez-vous votre réussite depuis tant d'années ? » La question était posée sur un ton légèrement malicieux.

Une étincelle s'alluma dans les yeux bleu foncé de l'auguste vieillard, qui évoquaient la couleur de l'océan et témoignaient sans doute d'un tempérament aussi versatile. Il se mit debout, m'abandonnant sous le podium, le cou tordu, comme si j'eusse levé les yeux vers un monument imposant et battu par les vents.

« Élémentaire, mon garçon, répondit-il. S'en tenir à des principes fondamentaux. Garder la tête froide et une solide position financière. Et si cela est encore trop compliqué, alors gardons la tête froide et oublions tout le reste. »

Des gloussements ravis éclatèrent dans le public composé d'hommes et de femmes qui lui ressemblaient beaucoup, mais seulement comme des alliages ressemblent à un métal pur.

« Autre chose encore. » Son visage devint sévère. « Ne jamais spéculer !

— Qu'entendez-vous par "spéculation", M. Powers ? Je croyais que nous vous payions pour faire cela à notre place ? » renchérit le même interlocuteur, qui prenait de l'assurance et parlait maintenant avec davantage d'aplomb. Moi-même et les autres extras exceptés, c'était la personne la plus jeune de la salle, ce qui ne l'empêchait pas d'avoir dépassé la cinquantaine depuis belle lurette. Pourtant, c'était un jeunot, et peut-être pour souligner sa verdeur, il semblait déterminé à prendre le parti des forces du progrès, à se faire pour ainsi dire l'avocat du diable dans un procès de famille.

« Jeune homme, les honoraires que nous percevons justifient que nous investissions votre argent, mais sans jamais spéculer, rétorqua Powers.

— Quelle est la différence ? »

Une ombre traversa le visage de Powers ; puis, se maîtrisant, il sourit avec une expression de suave condescendance, comme pour manifester son indulgence envers une brebis égarée du troupeau. « Contrairement à l'investissement, la spéculation ne se fonde pas sur la Valeur Intrinsèque, pontifia-t-il.

— Pouvez-vous développer ? »

Un brouhaha d'impatience agita le public.

« La Valeur Intrinsèque ? beugla Powers avec désespoir. Voulez-vous dire que vous ignorez le fondement de la théorie financière, la clef de voûte de l'investissement sain ?

— Non, M. Powers, je ne l'ignore pas, reprit l'impertinent. Mais simplement, j'aimerais l'entendre exposée par la voix de son maître, si je peux me permettre. »

Powers manifesta son plaisir en éructant un rire haché, qui n'était pas sans rappeler un aboiement. Puis il se campa sur le podium comme une armée d'occupation qui s'installe en vue d'un long séjour. « Tout cela est vraiment très simple, dit-il, comme toutes les grandes idées. Selon la théorie de la Valeur Intrinsèque, la cote d'une valeur mesurée par les Moyennes, mais aussi bien dans le cas d'une compagnie donnée, reflète intimement les conditions économiques. Cela paraît évident, n'est-ce pas ? Il y a pourtant une kyrielle de foutriquets — si, si, je vous assure — qui prétendent que cette cote est entièrement soumise au hasard, ou qu'elle obéit peut-être à une loi, mais qu'on ne découvrira jamais celle-ci par un examen rationnel. Nous ne sommes pas d'accord. Nous pensons qu'il y a une raison, et qu'on peut expliciter cette raison. Une comparaison : le marché est un engrenage dans le moteur de l'Amérique. Ses dents sont reliées au rouage plus imposant de l'économie, et l'ensemble fonctionne rationnellement comme une machine, même si les rapports d'engrenages sont difficiles à calculer. » Powers se renfrogna. « Certains sceptiques en sont à se demander dans quel sens l'énergie motrice est transmise — de l'économie au marché, ou vice versa. C'est là pure fumisterie, un enfant le comprendrait aussitôt. On ne fait pas couler une rivière avec la roue d'un moulin. Oui, à long terme, le Dow reflète la santé de l'économie. Économie prospère : marché en hausse, conjoncture "taureau" ; économie en crise : marché en baisse, conjoncture "ours". Le Dow anticipe parfois la tendance de quelques semaines ou mois. Mais selon le même raisonnement, les fluctuations d'une action reflètent la santé et la viabilité financières de la compagnie qui l'émet. Plus la compagnie est solide — c'est-à-dire, plus forte sa Valeur Intrinsèque —, plus l'action est cotée, et à long terme, plus son prix est élevé. L'investisseur compétent peut juger de cette viabilité en étudiant soigneusement son bilan, le bénéfice par action étant le facteur d'estimation essentiel, même s'il est loin d'être le seul. Il faut aussi examiner les dividendes, l'actif et le passif, la dette à long terme, la qualité du management, l'état du marché, ainsi qu'une myriade d'autres facteurs. Et tous ces éléments doivent à leur tour être examinés dans le contexte du macrocosme : taux d'intérêt, inflation, déficit fédéral, balance du commerce, PNB, indices à la construction, production industrielle, grèves, et ainsi de suite, sans parler de l'environnement *politique* — guerres, élections, coups d'État. Mais que tous ces arbres ne nous cachent pas la forêt ! Personnellement, je suis un adepte inconditionnel du PB : le Rapport Prix / Bénéfices — ce qu'une action coûte divisé par ce qu'elle rapporte ; et plus c'est bas, mieux ça vaut. Le PB est un indicateur fiable par la Valeur Intrinsèque (dans la mesure où il n'est pas trop faussé par ces farfelus de "comptables créatifs" qui pullulent et brouillent les cartes).

« Mais aucun système n'est infaillible. C'est pourquoi les investisseurs intelligents ont besoin de conseillers professionnels comme nous. "La dernière ligne et celle d'au-dessus" — telle est notre devise. Une autre raison qui rend nos services irremplaçables est que, même si à long terme la Valeur Intrinsèque tire son épingle du jeu, à court terme toutes sortes d'aléas la malmènent. La peur et la cupidité, les némésis jumelles du marché, affolent l'investisseur imprudent de leur regard de gorgone... Oui, qu'y a-t-il ?

— Regard de gorgone ?

— Vous savez parfaitement à quoi je fais allusion. Elles le poussent à spéculer, à miser son argent sur des valeurs illusoires. L'homme qui choisit cette voie court à sa perte. Il connaîtra peut-être quelques succès à court terme, voire un triomphe ou deux, mais au bout du compte peu prospèrent de cette façon, qu'ils soient ours ou taureaux. Voilà pourquoi il est essentiel de garder la tête froide. Le spéculateur est un joueur. Il joue son va-tout sur un coup de dés. C'est la stratégie du désespoir, la première étape d'un processus irréversible de désintégration morale qui provoque nécessairement la ruine financière. A l'inverse, l'investisseur ne joue jamais — et nous sommes tous des investisseurs dans cette salle, j'ose le dire, même vous, jeune homme, malgré la feinte pugnacité que vous manifestez... Sinon, vous ne seriez pas ici. L'investisseur ne laisse rien au hasard. Son but est de *conserver son capital* et de le voir *fructifier*. La Valeur Intrinsèque est la clef de cette démarche. Si, comme nous le maintenons contre vents et marées, il y a une raison et que cette raison se nomme Valeur Intrinsèque, alors étayer cette certitude d'un capital n'est pas spéculer, mais investir sur une valeur sûre. Tel est le but de notre programme. Sur le marché boursier et à long terme, comme l'action de l'eau sur la pierre, l'éphémère passe et disparaît, ce qui est solide résiste et prospère. Appelez cela Qualité, Réalité, Vérité, comme vous voudrez — autant de noms pour une seule chose : la Valeur Intrinsèque.

— Mais à long terme, nous serons tous morts, M. Powers, intervint sombrement la mouche du coche.

— Ta ta ta, persifla Powers. Je crois que Keynes décocha ce trait d'esprit quelques dizaines d'années avant vous. »

L'impertinent rougit.

« Écoutez, jeune homme, poursuivit Powers, Maynard Keynes était beaucoup trop malin et subtil pour ne pas être nocif. Quand il voulut affiner le socialisme, il transforma Karl Marx lui-même en avorton universitaire. Sa politique est directement responsable de l'état déplorable où se trouve aujourd'hui notre pays, sans parler de la Grande-Bretagne. Jeune homme, quand on mange, il faut payer. » Il marqua un temps pour laisser à l'assistance le loisir de méditer cette profonde vérité, profitant lui-même de cette pause pour avaler un canapé. « Toute cause produit un effet, et cet effet est directement lié à la cause qui l'a créé — cela est inéluctable, même si à première vue le lien n'est pas évident. Nous récoltons exactement ce que nous avons semé. Tôt ou tard, d'une façon ou d'une autre, on reçoit la monnaie de sa pièce. Je crois que les Orientaux appellent cela le Karma. En d'autres termes, il n'y a pas de création ex nihilo. Le monde n'est pas arbitraire. La raison existe et on peut l'expliciter. Si vous me demandez pourquoi tant de gens passent à côté de cette raison, je vous répondrai ceci : ils se laissent aveugler par leurs émotions. Vous vous rappelez ce que j'ai dit au début ? Il faut garder la tête froide.

— N'oubliez pas une solide position financière », lança quelqu'un. Quelques rires s'ensuivirent.

« Oui, cela aussi, acquiesça Powers. Mais en fin de compte, c'est la clarté des idées qui importe. Là dehors, dans la jungle de la Bourse, le chaos règne. La Valeur Intrinsèque est difficile à reconnaître, à discerner du mensonge, du vacarme, de la foire d'empoigne. Mais elle est là, croyez-moi. Quel monde serait le nôtre si elle n'existait pas ? Dites-le-moi, jeune homme. Pouvez-vous imaginer un monde sans Valeur Intrinsèque, un monde où n'existerait aucune raison rationnelle susceptible d'expliquer pourquoi les choses sont ce qu'elles sont ?

— Je ne crois pas, M. Powers, répondit-il, refroidi.
— Faites un effort. Je crois que vous pouvez en imaginer un. »
Le type réfléchit un peu, puis suggéra timidement : « Faites-vous allusion au Tiers-Monde, M. Powers ?
— Non.
— Je ne vois pas...
— Mais si, nous connaissons tous le monde auquel je fais allusion — un monde privé de la rédemption de la Valeur Intrinsèque —, c'est du moins ce qu'on dit, et j'espère sincèrement qu'aucun de nous n'aura jamais l'occasion de le visiter.
— Vous voulez parler du bloc communiste, M. Powers, n'est-ce pas ?
— Vous brûlez, si j'ose dire. Non, jeune homme, je parle de l'enfer. Le seul lieu où la justice divine de la cause et de l'effet soit suspendue, où tout soit arbitraire, où règne le despotisme du pur (c'est-à-dire de l'impur) hasard. Oui, mon jeune ami, un univers privé de sens. Parfaitement arbitraire. C'est cela, l'enfer. Vous comprenez donc que la Valeur Intrinsèque est bien davantage qu'une simple théorie financière, bien davantage qu'une simple conception du monde. »
L'assistance se leva alors pour lui faire une ovation.
« Pouvez-vous nous expliquer comment vous avez réussi à garder la tête froide pendant toutes ces années ? demanda humblement le pécheur converti.
— Non, mon garçon, il n'existe aucune recette pour cela, contrairement aux allégations de Billy Graham. Billy est un petit futé, il a de bonnes intentions et des principes sains. Son seul problème est qu'il manque d'humour. Pour revenir à votre question, je suis toujours prêt à discuter affaires ; mais ma religion ne concerne que moi. »

Cette expérience me stimula, même si j'en sortis abasourdi. Les idées nouvelles qui bouillonnaient dans mon cerveau me plongeaient dans une confusion presque agréable. Une bonne part de l'homélie de Powers m'était passée au-dessus de la tête, « comme l'eau du Huang Ho sur les plumes du canard de Pékin », selon l'image frappante de Kahn lorsqu'il sonda ensuite mes impressions et déplora l'indigence de mon compte rendu. Une chose demeurait néanmoins gravée dans ma mémoire. Une phrase inoubliable : « Il y a une raison et on peut l'expliciter ». Je trouvais cela profondément rassurant. Cela avait pour moi une valeur quasiment magique, comme certaines phrases de la liturgie taoïste : « La Réalité est Une, et le Tao est la Réalité. » Kahn déclara que je m'entichais de cette phrase parce qu'elle apportait de l'eau au moulin de mes préjugés religieux, le taoïsme étant par essence téléologique. Je le remis promptement à sa place, car, du moins dans ce domaine, j'avais davantage de connaissances que lui. Le taoïsme n'entretenait aucun préjugé, l'informai-je catégoriquement. Il dévissa le bouchon de son atomiseur de poche, aspira une longue giclée de Dristan, puis se moucha bruyamment. Certes, sa réponse était passablement ambiguë, mais elle me satisfit.

Il y avait à l'évidence d'étonnantes similitudes entre le taoïsme et la théorie de Powers. Plus je réfléchissais au concept de Valeur Intrinsèque, plus il me semblait familier. Je remarquai alors une analogie proprement stupéfiante. Quelle est, me demandai-je, cette essence qui sous-tend la réalité quotidienne et qu'il faut découvrir coûte que coûte, extraire du vacarme et du capharnaüm — des distractions bigarrées de la place du marché ? C'est le Tao, répondis-je,

> L'Un de cette multiplicité
> Foisonnante, lui-même
> Immuable et donnant
> Naissance à tous les changements...

sur la place du marché du monde illusoire. Mais sur cet autre « marché », n'était-ce pas la Valeur Intrinsèque ? (Étrange, aussi, que le terme taoïste désignant le monde profane soit justement le même que le nom de l'arène où se jouait quotidiennement la destinée du Dow, le marché. Encore une coïncidence, comme le jeu de mots Dow et Tao ? Je trouvai cela bizarre...)

Ces conjectures avaient beau mobiliser mon attention, elles furent bientôt oubliées au profit d'une autre, une considération apparemment mineure, à peine abordée lors de la conférence. Elle prit pourtant entièrement possession de mon esprit. Car je brûlais de découvrir le sens de l'allusion cryptique que Powers avait faite aux « ours et taureaux ». Pour la deuxième fois, j'entendais quelqu'un évoquer ce bestiaire incongru dans un contexte similaire. Ces animaux avaient-ils une valeur symbolique dans la mythologie séculière de la Bourse ? Le matin de mon embauche, la timidité m'avait empêché d'interroger le secrétaire à ce propos, mais j'étais maintenant bien décidé à élucider cette question. Par chance, la réunion des actionnaires de Powers and Burden se termina à temps pour que je pusse retourner à la Bourse avant la clôture de la séance. Je trouvai Kahn dans la Salle des Courtiers.

« Kahn ! criai-je sur le seuil de la pièce en courant vers lui. Qu'est-ce que les taureaux et les ours ? »

Tout le monde se retourna pour me dévisager. Puis la salle entière éclata de rire.

Je me plantai devant lui, ahanant comme un cheval après une course.

« Bon Dieu, petit ! s'écria-t-il. Calme-toi un peu, veux-tu !

— Je dois savoir ! hurlai-je.

— D'accord ! Tu vas savoir ! Rien de plus simple, pas de quoi te mettre dans un pareil état. Un ours est un type qui spécule en anticipant une baisse des valeurs — un pessimiste, autrement dit. Il fait son beurre sur le scepticisme et la méfiance, la pénurie et l'achat d'options de vente. De même, un marché d'ours est un marché où les valeurs baissent. La sale passe, la crise. Le taureau est l'exact contraire — un optimiste, celui qui achète en anticipant une hausse. Un marché de taureau à long terme est le rêve de tous les investisseurs, ours exceptés (ils grognent et hibernent). C'est un peu comme le *yin* et le *yang*, petit. Le taureau est *yang* ; l'ours est *yin*. Ensemble, ils font tourner le monde, monter et descendre le Dow. Vu ?

— Mais alors, avançai-je timidement, on pourrait presque dire que le taureau est le symbole *dowiste* de l'illumination ?

— Ouais, plus ou moins », concéda-t-il.

Je m'éloignai comme un somnambule. Derrière moi, j'entendis Kahn me lancer : « Hé, petit — on dirait que tu es en train de résoudre ton problème de SO. Ce n'est pas encore tout à fait de la *chutzpah*. Il te manque le dosage adéquat de style et de finesse, mais tu es sur la bonne voie. Simplement, ne file pas à l'extrême inverse, okay ? »

Je sortis dans l'après-midi brûlant ; mes jambes m'entraînèrent malgré moi contre le flot des passants, en direction de l'East River. J'étais ahuri, hébété, seulement conscient de la tonalité fondamentale de la cité. Quand je quittai les ombres de Nassau Street pour la chaude lumière dorée du soleil, humant ma première bouffée d'air salin et pollué, mon esprit parut se vider d'un coup. Bien que légèrement ivre, je percevais avec une acuité rare la texture sensuelle du monde environnant. Le soleil jetait des veines argentées sur le fleuve dont la couleur bleue me surprit. Ses rayons obliques traçaient des brillances mouvantes le long des vagues qui remontaient vers Brooklyn, sous un brouillard diaphane et rosé. Des pigeons roucoulaient de contentement au-dessus des rues. L'ordure elle-même révélait des beautés ambiguës.

Comme je marchais, un refrain s'emparait parfois de mon esprit :

> Un rossignol chante dans un bosquet de saules au bord de la rivière.
> Le soleil est doux, une faible brise caresse les branches qui oscillent,
>   dévoilant la face argentée des feuilles.

Qu'était cette chanson ? Elle voletait dans mon esprit, chaque fois plus insistante. Et si familière ! Pourtant, malgré tous mes efforts, je ne parvenais pas à la situer, ni à retrouver la suite du poème. Je vis un avion argenté décoller des pistes lointaines de La Guardia. Il décrivit un lent arc de cercle au-dessus de Manhattan, ses ailes scintillant dans la lumière, passa juste au-dessus de ma tête, puis disparut dans le soleil. Brusquement, un barrage céda au plus profond de moi-même, et les mots se bousculèrent :

> Vois le Taureau, il ne peut se cacher !
> Cet énorme poitrail, cette narine frémissante, cette courbe sèche
>   de la corne massive,
> Quel poète leur rendra justice ?

Oui, c'était le troisième chant des *Dix Taureaux !* Un fragment du commentaire me revint aussitôt en mémoire : « Il aiguise son oreille dans la cacophonie des bruits communs, et soudain la claire musique de la Source émerge ! » Oui, les bruits communs : le gloussement des pigeons, les mots de la conférence de Powers, le coup de tonnerre d'un avion à réaction qui franchit le mur du son. Quelle importance ? « Le Tao réside implicitement dans les choses les plus triviales, comme le sel dans l'eau de l'océan, comme le liant dans la peinture. Il est le plasma neutre dans lequel les éléments vitaux de la Nature sont en suspension. » Je me rappelai brusquement mon rêve : l'apparition des empreintes de pas qui s'éloignaient devant moi, le fantôme fuyant de mon destin dont j'avais identifié la trace avec l'aide du maître, mais que, jusqu'à cet instant, je n'avais jamais regardé en face. Oui, cela m'était enfin accordé — mon « Premier Aperçu du Taureau », symbole d'illumination non seulement pour les taoïstes, mais aussi pour les dowistes !

8

Bien que toujours aussi éloigné de mon père — dont je n'avais pas encore parlé à Kahn à cause d'une absurde appréhension après ma vaine recherche téléphonique, déception que je ne confiais à personne et à laquelle j'évitais même de penser —, du moins progressais-je vers mon autre but que je sentais relié au premier, la compréhension du marché. Enfin ! Le parallèle découvert entre le Tao et la Valeur Intrinsèque n'était-il pas prometteur, la preuve, même ténue et sujette à caution, d'un lien entre Tao et Dow (le delta, selon l'expression clairvoyante de Yin-mi) ? J'en étais convaincu.

Après E.P. et la Valeur Intrinsèque, Kahn déclara que j'avais impérativement et sans délai besoin d'un antidote pour « m'empêcher, dit-il de m'ossifier dans la fatuité ». Le programme de la cure commençait par une confrontation avec l'école de l'Analyse Technique, dont les praticiens sont connus sous le nom de Chartistes à cause de leur prédilection pour, et de leur utilisation massive de graphes comme outils prospectifs destinés à prédire les fluctuations des prix et des volumes. Pour la sagesse conventionnelle de Wall Street, l'Analyse Technique représente l'antithèse stratégique, voire, en un sens, métaphysique, du Fondamentalisme fiduciaire à la Ernie Powers.

Peu après la réunion de Powers and Burden, Kahn m'informa que le Congrès international des Chartistes se tenait en ville et organisait une convention dans un hôtel de l'Upper West Side. Bien que Kahn se définît lui-même comme un iconoclaste dédaignant toutes les approches « purement théoriques » ou « dogmatiques » de la stratégie de l'investissement — ce qu'il appelait les « méthodes hygiéniques » —, il me proposa de m'accompagner pour ma deuxième expédition, car le bruit courait que Clyde Newman Jr., le gourou montant de l'Analyse Technique, indépendamment de sa perspicacité analytique, « faisait un numéro du tonnerre de Dieu ».

« Au moins, nous allons bien rigoler, dit Kahn, qui ajouta : Il est originaire de Topeka, Kansas. C'est suffisant pour que j'y coure. »

Ce matin-là, un vendredi, Kahn appela l'hôtel de son bureau et apprit que la convention se déroulait comme une sorte de séminaire permanent, avec des conférenciers qui se succédaient sans interruption sur le podium, de dix heures du matin jusque tard dans la nuit. Newman devait prendre la parole à six heures.

« Nous irons en taxi après la clôture, annonça Kahn. Je te l'offre. »

Quand la sonnerie résonna, je bouillais d'impatience. Je courus dans la rue, hélai un taxi dont le chauffeur dut faire un écart pour m'éviter. Kahn qui me suivait en soufflant comme un asthmatique, faisait semblant de boiter, laissait tomber son attaché-case, son parapluie ou son imperméable, se baissait pour le ramasser, s'immobilisait au milieu de la chaussée afin d'essuyer la sueur qui ruisselait sur son front ou bien effectuer quelques mystérieuses manipulations de chiropraxie au niveau de ses reins avant de repartir.

Il s'engouffra enfin dans le taxi, s'effondra sur le siège arrière où il étala ses membres, ahanant comme une baleine échouée, et dit au chauffeur : « Bonwit Teller. »

Je le regardai avec surprise.

« Je dois m'arrêter en chemin pour me réapprovisionner. Ça te dérange ? me demanda-t-il d'une voix irritée.

— Vous voulez dire, les bonbons ? » rétorquai-je non sans une légère ironie.

Sentant ma déception et mon impatience, il ajouta sur un ton plus conciliant : « Nous en aurons peut-être besoin. »

Malgré le détour, le taxi nous déposa devant l'hôtel avec une demi-heure d'avance. Un orateur parlait devant une salle presque vide. Les rares personnes présentes étaient éparpillées dans le plus grand désordre ; certains chuchotaient, d'autres écoutaient, un ou deux prenaient des notes, quelques-uns somnolaient à la périphérie, le chapeau de gala légèrement incliné, le visage non rasé tombant par saccades vers la poitrine. Quand ils se réveillaient en sursaut, ces noceurs impénitents jetaient quelques regards désorientés alentour, puis de nouveau piquaient lentement du nez.

Comme nous nous asseyions, nous assistâmes à la relève de la garde : un nouveau conférencier arriva, petit homme en costume sombre aux mains fébriles et au visage convaincu.

Il brassa ses papiers, souffla dans le micro. « Non, je ne suis pas Clyde Newman », dit-il avec un sourire timide, comme pour plaisanter.

Silence de mort.

« M. Newman prendra la parole dès que j'aurai terminé, ajouta-t-il, le visage enfoui dans ses notes. Je ne serai pas long, je vous le promets. » Quelque part dans le fond de l'auditorium, le nasillement strident d'un mirliton. « J'aimerais vous parler aujourd'hui de la théorie du Dow..., commença-t-il.

— Bon Dieu ! songeai-je. La théorie du *Dow* ! »

Du coup, toute la salle se réveilla. Sifflements et bruits divers. Des avions en papier filèrent au-dessus de nos têtes.

Le conférencier se racla la gorge. « ... et de son rapport à l'Analyse Technique. »

Kahn secoua mon bras. « Allez viens, petit, murmura-t-il. Cette salade est préhistorique. Inutile d'écouter ces radoteurs de deuxième zone. Allons faire le tour du pâté de maisons en attendant la vedette.

— Non, Kahn ! dis-je. Je veux écouter ça.
— Ah, la jeunesse », soupira-t-il. Il croisa les bras, ferma les yeux et s'allongea dans son fauteuil, faisant ostensiblement la sieste.

Malgré tous mes préjugés favorables, cette conférence fut en effet d'un ennui mortel. Néanmoins, l'orateur dit une ou deux choses qui retinrent mon attention. Par exemple ceci : Charles Dow et William Hamilton, son bras droit du *Wall Street Journal*, soutenaient que le mouvement du Dow ressemble au flux et au reflux de l'océan. Le mouvement primaire — l'inertie à long terme d'un marché ours ou d'un marché taureau — est la marée, à l'intérieur de laquelle les mouvements secondaires — les réactions aux tendances ours ou taureau qui corrigent les excès de la tendance fondamentale sans en inverser le sens —, correspondent aux vagues. Quant aux fluctuations journalières, ce sont les rides de l'océan. Dow et Hamilton considéraient ces dernières comme insignifiantes. Dow s'était particulièrement attaché aux renversements de tendance à long terme, ce que le conférencier nommait le point de vue de la Moyenne Flottante des Deux Cents Jours. Je voulus demander à Kahn ce que cela signifiait, mais il dormait comme un loir.

« Il a perdu de vue les arbres à cause de la forêt, conclut sobrement l'orateur. Il ressemblait à l'homme préhistorique qui découvre la roue mais s'en sert uniquement pour jouer à la toupie. Si bien qu'il nous échut d'accoupler la roue à l'essieu du chariot. Dow reste pourtant le père de notre tribu et mérite notre reconnaissance. »

Quelques cris s'élevèrent dans le public, que le conférencier prit pour un encouragement — à tort, comme il s'en aperçut aussitôt.

« Mais je pense que nous devons surtout à Dow le concept de décompte.
— Dehors ! » cria quelqu'un dans le fond.

Les gens entraient dans l'auditorium.

« Nous voulons Newman ! »

Une lame de fond s'éleva alors — « New-man ! New-man ! » — menaçant d'emporter l'orateur comme une ride dérisoire balayée par un mouvement primaire.

A ce moment, Newman en personne sortit des coulisses, un homme impeccable au visage de faucon, vêtu d'un costume bleu ciel couvert de paillettes dans le dos et sur les revers, d'une ceinture et de chaussures blanches, qui le faisaient ressembler à une vedette de *country music* sans guitare. Souriant, il leva les mains au-dessus de sa tête pour intimer le silence (mais aussi, sans doute, saluer ses admirateurs), et posa sur le public un regard affligé d'un léger strabisme qui lui donnait un air vaguement fanatique.

« Nous allons parler du décompte, mon frère, épargnez-vous donc ce mal, dit Newman en s'immisçant entre l'orateur et le lutrin.
— Dans ce cas, je crois que j'ai terminé », concéda le petit homme. Il réunit ses notes d'une main tremblante, puis s'écarta, à la grande jubilation du public. J'eus pitié de lui.

Kahn, qui s'était réveillé, se pencha vers moi pour chuchoter à mon oreille : « Le père de Newman était évangéliste dans une secte obscure du Middlewest dont j'ai oublié le nom. Enfin, tu vois le genre, un de ces groupes qui font scission à cause d'une querelle doctrinale quelconque. Selon l'article que j'ai lu, ils croyaient dur comme fer que le jus de raisin se transsubstantiait en vin, ils prônaient les vertus du travail et niaient le caractère inné du mal chez les élus. Je te dis ça parce que Clyde Junior a grandi sous la houlette de la religion et s'est forgé une solide réputation de prosélytisme. C'est plus fort que lui, j'imagine, il a l'évangélisme dans la peau.

— Qu'est-ce que l'évangélisme ? demandai-je.

— L'évangélisme ? » Kahn s'adossa dans son fauteuil pour réfléchir. « L'évangélisme est une institution américaine qui combine admirablement les talents nationaux du commerce et de la vertu. »

Prenant alors la parole, Newman passa d'abord en revue ses contributions dans le domaine de la « cartographie créative », puis cita plusieurs « formations » nouvelles que, selon lui, les spécialistes de la décimale devaient absolument ajouter à leur liste standard. En sus de Tête et Épaules, Double Toit, Rectangle, Carreau, Losange, V Renversé, Drapeau, Étendard, Coquille Saint-Jacques, Intervalle d'Exhaustion, Intervalle d'Inertie, Ile Renversée, Ligne de Tendance, Spirale, Tourniquet et Maximum Complexe — le nanan, le pain quotidien du Technicien —, Newman évoqua quelques configurations plus ésotériques qu'il avait découvertes et baptisées à sa façon bien caractéristique. Il y avait la Croix du Calvaire, dont il était particulièrement friand. La Croix Latine, dit-il, indiquait trop de passion dans le marché, avec tous les risques d'excès spéculatifs que cela impliquait. La Croix Archiépiscopale traduisait une action concertée du puissant cartel des évêques anglicans, sous la direction du Très Révérend et Très Honorable Archevêque de Canterbury ; les Croix Grecque et de Jérusalem indiquaient un intérêt ethnique pour le marché de la part de ces communautés. La Chi-Rho annonçait une ruée sur les produits pharmaceutiques. La Croix Tau était particulièrement taureau. Il y avait enfin la Croix de Malte qui, clamait-il, prédisait l'arrivée d'éléments peu scrupuleux et manipulateurs sur le marché (sombre allusion à la Cosa Nostra).

« Qu'en dis-tu, petit ? murmura Kahn en se penchant vers moi. Je commence à discerner un motif parmi tous ces motifs. »

De fait, bien que Newman se vantât d'être « objectif comme un homme de science », ses découvertes découlaient manifestement de ses préoccupations personnelles. Les « formations » de Newman portaient la signature de son dieu, il nous les décrivait comme un Daniel irascible devant une assemblée frileuse de Balthazar terrifiés.

Newman demanda alors s'il y avait des questions. Quelqu'un se leva et l'interrogea sur le rapport qui liait telle formation à certains effets boursiers.

« Dites-moi si je vous comprends bien, mon ami, commença Newman. Vous me demandez en fait "la raison" ultime ? »

Dans la salle, quelques Techniciens chevronnés ricanèrent.

L'homme opina en toute innocence.

« Laissez-moi répondre à votre question par une autre question », continua Newman. Il marqua un temps, puis tonna : « Croyez-vous en Dieu ? » Et tout en beuglant, il frappa du plat de la main la pile de ses notes et se pencha vers le lutrin, son strabisme brillant de fureur, comme s'il allait incontinent dévorer son interlocuteur.

Celui-ci lança des regards paniqués autour de lui, tel le naufragé sur le point de se noyer qui cherche désespérément une main pour le hisser hors de l'eau. Ses voisins s'agitaient nerveusement sur leurs sièges en évitant ses yeux. Les mirlitons, pressentant le désastre, se taisaient.

« Eh bien... euh, je crois que oui, admit-il à contrecœur, en l'absence de toute autre échappatoire.

— A la bonne heure ! s'écria Newman en assenant un autre coup de poing sur ses notes, puis il se redressa. Maintenant, j'aimerais vous demander si vous comprenez toujours les desseins du Tout-Puissant, en toute circonstance de la vie quotidienne — disons, la mort soudaine d'une épouse bien-aimée, ou un jeune enfant arraché à votre affection dans la fleur de l'âge ? »

La question toucha manifestement une corde sensible chez le malheureux. Baissant les yeux, il renifla et répondit d'une voix contrite qui semblait prête à se briser en sanglots. « Non, je ne comprends pas ce genre de chose. J'avoue que parfois j'ai le sentiment qu'Il est cruel, ou même... peut-être... qu'Il n'existe pas.

— Mais vous avez la foi ? »

L'homme hésita, toussa dans sa main. « Oui, concéda-t-il sans conviction.

— Dieu soit loué ! » enchaîna Newman d'une voix de stentor, mais il se reprit aussitôt et poursuivit ses devoirs socratiques.

« Et n'est-il pas vrai, mon frère, que même si les voies du Seigneur sont impénétrables, tout au fond de votre cœur vous connaissez votre devoir, vous savez ce que vous êtes appelé à faire pour traverser les difficultés de la vie et porter votre croix quotidienne ?

— Oui, dit l'autre.

— Alléluia ! s'écria Newman. Maintenant, comprenez-vous ? »

— Franchement, non, répondit l'homme. Je ne comprends pas.

— Eh bien ce n'est pas grave, mon frère, dit Newman. Ne vous découragez pas. Je vais vous aider à voir la lumière. Qu'ai-je fait jusqu'ici, commença-t-il, sinon comparer l'attitude du Vrai Croyant envers son Dieu et celle de l'Analyste Technique confronté au marché ou, plus exactement, au Dow ? Le Croyant, même s'il ne comprend pas toujours les voies du Seigneur, qui peuvent lui paraître dures et absurdes, voire totalement machiavéliques, a *malgré tout* le sentiment qu'*il y a...* — sa voix s'éleva d'un ton pour souligner ses derniers mots — ... un but qui est effectivement réalisé, que le Seigneur *a* une bonne raison de faire ce qu'Il fait, et que toutes nos actions et souffrances, quand bien même elles nous sembleraient cruelles ou triviales de notre misérable point de vue, sont décidées par Lui pour notre bien ultime, et entrent dans le Plan Global grâce auquel notre Sauveur Jésus-Christ, le Divin Architecte, bâtira un jour sa Jérusalem céleste sur cette terre périssable ! Pas un moineau ne tombe, mes frères, sans que notre Père céleste ne le voie et n'approuve !

« Par l'étude des textes sacrés de la foi chrétienne, le Nouveau Testament en particulier, le Croyant, suivant l'exemple de Jésus et de ses disciples, trouve sa place dans le Plan, même s'il ne comprend pas complètement sa nature. De la même façon, le Technicien, bien qu'il ne prétende jamais comprendre pourquoi le Dow se comporte de telle ou telle manière — c'est-à-dire, la *raison* — peut néanmoins, grâce à l'application scrupuleuse des textes de sa religion — les graphiques —, extrapoler des règles de conduite qui le prépareront à l'avenir. Tout est une question de foi, mes frères. Nous sommes peut-être incapables de pénétrer le sublime mystère du Dow, ou l'esprit de Dieu, mais cela est-il si important ? L'étude des graphiques nous permet de pressentir son but ultime et de distiller une "morale pratique fiduciaire" capable de nous enrichir.

— Louons le Seigneur ! hurla quelqu'un.

— Amen, mon frère », répondit Newman.

Puis il redonna la parole au public. Un jeune homme âgé de dix-sept ou dix-huit ans tout au plus et doté d'une pomme d'Adam palpitante qui montait et descendait au fil de ses mots comme une balle de ping-pong au sommet d'un jet d'eau, leva la main. « Je crois vous comprendre, M. Newman, commença-t-il. Pourtant je ne vois pas comment vous pouvez écarter aussi catégoriquement les facteurs fondamentaux. Prétendez-vous qu'en regardant les fluctuations journalières d'une action donnée sur un papier millimétré, vous en concluez la santé financière de la compagnie concernée ?

— Ah, fit Newman, qui sourit et joignit les mains en une attitude pieuse. Je vois que nous avons un Thomas parmi nous. Jeune homme, dit-il, se penchant une fois encore par-dessus le podium, la "santé financière de la compagnie concernée" — soit, cette prétendue "Valeur Intrinsèque" — est totalement superflue. L'investisseur n'a même pas besoin de connaître le *nom* d'une compagnie pour décider d'acheter ou non ses actions, bien que cette information soit certes utile quand il s'agit de transmettre votre ordre à votre courtier. » Il se rembrunit. « Il a seulement besoin de ses graphes et de l'Analyse Technique.

« Ah ah ! Difficile à avaler — je le vois à votre expression. Vous regimbez. Fils, c'est là le Gethsémani de tous les Chartistes, le test suprême de la foi. Je suis très content que tu aies posé cette question, car cela m'amène à une considération que mon très éminent prédécesseur sur ce podium a ébauchée aujourd'hui. Voyez-vous, tous les Techniciens orthodoxes croient fermement que le Dow lui-même, l'Index Mère, nous épargne le lassant examen des innombrables détails dont se soucient les Fondamentalistes, détails trop nombreux pour être tous étudiés, puis intégrés avec le coefficient adéquat dans l'équation générale par un organe aussi inefficace et faillible que le cerveau humain, lequel, tout compte fait et malgré les prouesses dont il est parfois capable, est sujet à la corruption inhérente à toute chair. Et pourtant, grâce à la miséricorde de Notre Seigneur, qui dans son infinie compassion a donné à l'homme le Dow, ce fardeau intolérable ne pèse pas sur nos épaules. Fils, *tout est décompté dans le Dow*. Mais au cas où tu n'aurais pas encore entendu ce mot, écoute bien. "Le décompte" est le noyau même de notre foi... Eh bien, qu'y a-t-il ? » demanda-t-il avec irritation.

Son « très éminent prédécesseur », sans doute encouragé par le qualificatif flatteur, piaffait d'impatience sur son fauteuil, brandissait ses notes en l'air, apparemment fort désireux de participer au débat. « J'ai ici une citation de William Hamilton qui, je crois, répond parfaitement à la question posée, dit-il d'une voix excitée. Puis-je la lire ? »

Newman semblait sur le point de refuser quand un arpège strident monta du clan des mirlitons, *fortissimo e appassionato* ; jetant un regard féroce dans cette direction, il adressa un hochement de tête à son prédécesseur, qu'il infligea en guise de punition à ses zélateurs récalcitrants.

« Hamilton écrit, commença le petit homme, "La faiblesse de toute autre méthode" de stratégie d'investissement "tient au fait qu'on incorpore à tort des éléments superflus. Il devrait pourtant être évident que les Moyennes prennent déjà en compte tous ces éléments", sous-entendu : fondamentaux, "exactement comme un baromètre considère tout ce qui affecte le temps. Le mouvement des prix représente la prévision globale des événements futurs. Le marché représente tout ce que tous les gens savent, espèrent, croient, anticipent" et, si j'ose dire, "les espoirs et les peurs de l'humanité, la cupidité, l'ambition, les actes de Dieu, l'invention, les tensions et les crises financières, la météorologie, les découvertes, la mode, ainsi qu'une myriade d'autres facteurs qu'on ne saurait énumérer sans omission... et tout ce savoir est distillé jusqu'au verdict de la Bourse."

— Voilà qui est fort bien dit, reprit Newman. Merci. Tu vois, fils, le Dow absorbe et reflète absolument tout, des bilans d'entreprise jusqu'aux bulletins de santé du président. C'est une mesure globale des innombrables facteurs qui définissent l'état financier du pays. Un baromètre — c'est le mot, et non seulement de l'Amérique financière, mais de la nation tout entière. Oui, fils, le Dow est le pouls de l'Amérique. Tu es encore sceptique, je le vois. Tu vas dire que j'exagère, que je me suis contredit, que je suis plus Fondamentaliste que les Fondamentalistes, qui même dans leur arrogance la plus outrée et la moins circonscrite, ne réclameraient pas pour le Dow semblable universalité, convaincus — peut-être comme toi — qu'un indicateur financier doit restreindre son champ d'application au domaine de la finance. Rappelle-toi pourtant ceci : tout est décompté. *Tout.* Le Dow, comme Dieu, est omniscient. Telle est notre foi. Je ne prétends pas comprendre pourquoi il en est ainsi, mais me limite à cette simple constatation empirique...

« Ce qui m'amène au principal objet de ma conférence d'aujourd'hui. Mes frères, j'ai choisi cette occasion pour vous présenter un nouvel et merveilleux indicateur, qui, à mon humble avis, s'avérera d'un intérêt considérable pour vous-mêmes et vos enfants, ainsi que pour les générations ultérieures. Je l'ai baptisé Oscillateur Newman de Fréquentation des Églises. Mes frères, nous avons tous entendu dire que les périodes de crise — récession, dépression, guerre, famine, peste et *tutti quanti* — sont des périodes de vaches grasses, des périodes *taureau*, pour la religion. Nombre d'entre vous ont peut-être accepté ce dogme comme une évidence, et moi le premier pendant de nombreuses années. Mais maintenant j'ai vu la lumière. Frères, n'est-il pas clair que ce vieil axiome est blasphématoire, une souillure pour le nom de notre Sauveur Jésus-Christ ? D'ailleurs, qui s'est vraiment donné le mal d'examiner les données d'un œil objectif et dénué de passion ? Personne, je pense, jusqu'au jour où j'ai humblement entrepris cette tâche pour la plus grande glorification du Seigneur. Car aujourd'hui, après des mois d'études et de recherches, notre équipe a abouti à cette conclusion infiniment gratifiante qu'il existe une corrélation *positive* entre la fréquentation des églises de ce pays et la fermeté du *Dow Jones Industrial Average*. En étudiant les données des vingt dernières années, j'ai découvert un parallèle marqué, indubitable, entre l'OMBE — Occupation Maximale des Bancs d'Église — et les phases taureau de la Bourse. Inversement, en période de déclin religieux, quand une fraction statistiquement signifiante de la population s'est détournée du sourire radieux de notre Sauveur, la force du marché — mesurée non seulement par le Dow, mais par d'autres indices, dont la vente à court terme (qui montre une corrélation inverse avec l'OMBE) — a été entamée.

« Mais pour nous 'autres investisseurs, quelle importance cela a-t-il ? Frères, je vous dis et vous répète que la religion est un bon placement. Jésus-Christ lui-même est taureau pour l'Amérique ! Nous devons donc nous repentir avec diligence. Chaque soldat du Seigneur doit mettre sa maison en ordre et faire l'impossible pour convertir les païens, exhorter ses frères et ses sœurs récalcitrants à rentrer dans le giron avant qu'il ne soit trop tard, non seulement pour le bien de la brebis égarée, mais pour que vous et moi palpions des dividendes supplémentaires !

— Louons le Seigneur ! s'écria le public.

— Je vous le dis, mes frères, certains d'entre vous ont peut-être douté de ce que j'annonçais dans la Lettre Boursière "Bonne Nouvelle" de Newman, à savoir que dans un avenir très proche le Dow atteindrait un niveau que même les taureaux les plus furieux de notre profession n'osent rêver. Seigneur Tout-Puissant ! Pouvez-vous imaginer, mes frères, la croissance mirifique de notre index révéré si Jésus-Christ accomplissait sa promesse de revenir sur terre à la fin du millénaire, *ainsi que cela a été prophétisé*, non seulement par moi, mais par d'autres personnes respectables sous tous rapports et possédant un CV blanc comme neige ? Oui, mes frères, j'ai vu les indicateurs ! Ce jour béni ne saurait tarder ! Repentez-vous ! Soyez prêts, car il vient comme un voleur dans la nuit. Si je pouvais vous dire ce que mes yeux ont aperçu pour un avenir assez proche, quand j'ai scruté le couloir du temps ! Frères, j'ai le don de la prophétie, celui des langues inconnues, et je veux témoigner ! J'entrevois un jour meilleur où les efforts des fidèles seront récompensés, non pas de ces trésors que la mite et la rouille corrompent mais — doux miracle ! — d'un bien que l'inflation ne saurait dévaluer ! Quand mon regard scrute le sombre couloir du temps et que je tends l'oreille, je vois des anges étincelants danser au parquet de la Bourse, j'entends de joyeux hosannas, louanges et remerciements, se répercuter sous la voûte bénie à la place des pleurs et des grincements de dents qui résonnent aujourd'hui dans cet antre de l'iniquité, Sodome et Gomorrhe, cet enfer terrestre ! »

Les mirlitons braillèrent comme des trompettes en furie. Toute l'assistance, en proie à une violente agitation, gémissait, pleurait, se tordait sur les sièges. Certains s'écroulèrent même dans les travées, l'écume à la bouche, les yeux révulsés. Une force irrationnelle électrisait la foule. contaminant aussi Kahn et moi-même

« Nous ferions peut-être mieux de filer, chuchota Kahn avec une expression exagérément soucieuse, avant qu'ils ne décident de nous "sauver". Car nous sommes tous deux des païens ici. En ce qui me concerne, j'ai échappé au baptême jusqu'à maintenant, et je compte persévérer dans cette voie le plus longtemps possible. Et puis, ajouta-t-il avec une grimace, je ne sais pas nager. »

Passablement ahuri, je le laissai m'entraîner vers la sortie.

9

« Bon Dieu, je boirais volontiers un verre ! Et toi, petit ?... Petit ? »
J'étais encore légèrement hébété.
« Quoi, tu as faim ? hasarda Kahn.
— Un peu, répondis-je.
— Alors suis-moi, nous allons casser la croûte. Paraît qu'il y a un nouveau restaurant français sur Columbus Avenue. Je t'invite à dîner. »
Je le remerciai en marmonnant, sincère mais absent, car j'essayais de trouver un sens quelconque au volcanisme verbal de Newman. Je suivis Kahn servilement, machinalement.
Le maître d'hôtel ne remarqua pas tout de suite notre présence. A travers un paravent ajouré qui séparait l'entrée de la salle proprement dite, nous l'aperçûmes près de la porte de la cuisine, bavardant avec un groupe de serveurs. Jamais je n'avais vu cadre aussi élégant. Un grand lustre en cristal pendait au centre de la pièce, des bougies blanches fichées sur des bougeoirs de cuivre décoraient les tables et jetaient comme une pluie d'or sur les prismes du cristal supérieur. Le lustre s'irisait aussi d'éclats verts dus à une petite oasis de fougères et de bambous qui poussaient à la verticale de celui-ci. Sur une pierre noire, lisse et moussue, un voile translucide d'eau fraîche coulait régulièrement, puis se métamorphosait en ruisselet qui traversait le jardin intérieur sur un lit de fin sable blanc.
Quand il nous aperçut, le maître d'hôtel fronça les sourcils, s'interrompit au milieu de sa phrase et se hâta de rejoindre son poste.
Son froncement me fit soudain comprendre que nous n'avions pas fière allure, loin de là. Kahn avait depuis longtemps tombé sa veste, qu'il tenait sur son bras. Il avait aussi remonté ses manches jusqu'au coude, ouvert son col de chemise et baissé son nœud de cravate jusqu'au deuxième bouton. Quant à moi, je n'étais pas vraiment élégant, avec mes tennis et ma chemise bleue.
« *Messieurs** ? » dit l'homme avec un léger hochement de tête plein de déférence et de hauteur. Il nous dévisageait sans enthousiasme.
« Une table pour deux, dit Kahn.
— *Monsieur* a réservé ?

---

* En français dans le texte.

— Réservé ! s'écria Kahn, incrédule. Et pourquoi donc ? » Il tendit le bras au-dessus de l'épaule de l'autre. « Regardez — j'aperçois d'ici deux, trois, quatre, *cinq* tables libres. »

Le maître d'hôtel fit claquer sa langue avec regret. « Je crains qu'elles ne soient toutes réservées, monsieur.

— Je n'apprécie guère votre humour », répliqua sèchement Kahn.

Comme un instituteur ou un chef d'orchestre, le maître d'hôtel leva son stylo en or pour tapoter une petite pancarte posée sur le comptoir : « Sur réservation uniquement. »

« Très bien, nous allons donc réserver », dit Kahn en se tournant vers moi avec un haussement d'épaules.

Le maître d'hôtel s'inclina, puis passa derrière le comptoir en sautillant comme un moineau. « Pour quelle heure, monsieur ? demanda-t-il en ouvrant un registre.

— Quelle heure est-il ? » demanda Kahn.

L'employé leva son avant-bras, puis, d'un doigt, écarta adroitement sa manche. « Sept heures quarante-cinq, monsieur.

— Okay, fit Kahn, je réserve pour sept heures quarante-six. Je file aux gogues faire un brin de toilette. » Il m'adressa un clin d'œil.

« *Oh la la, monsieur** ! se lamenta l'autre en fermant brusquement son registre. Nous n'avons pas de table avant onze heures ! » Il fit claquer sa langue d'un air faussement contrit.

« Dites donc, c'est un club privé ou quoi ? aboya Kahn avec irritation.

Le maître d'hôtel se raidit. « Nous nous réservons le droit de refuser les clients indésirables, monsieur.

— Ouais, surtout les Chinetoques et les Youpins, pas vrai ? » Il se tourna vers moi. « Viens, petit. J'connais un endroit près d'ici où ils seront ravis de prendre notre argent. »

Une fois dehors, je m'aperçus que Kahn connaissait mal les environs, si bien que nous finîmes par échouer dans un pub irlandais d'Amsterdam Avenue. L'endroit était crasseux et mal éclairé, le sol couvert de sciure ; cela sentait le rance et l'urine ; quelques vieux accessoires de pêche à la truite décoraient les murs couverts d'une patine acajou poussiéreuse.

« C'est quand même mieux, non ? dit Kahn sans conviction. Un peu de couleur locale... »

S'essuyant les mains sur son tablier maculé, un jeune homme d'environ vingt-cinq ans quitta l'extrémité opposée du bar, où il regardait un match de boxe à la télévision avec un compagnon plus âgé ; il s'avança lentement vers nous. Il portait un survêtement aux manches bleues remontées sur les bras et des chaussures de course à pied. Il marchait en chaloupant comme un marin, si bien que son épaisse tignasse rousse se gonflait et s'aplatissait à chaque enjambée.

« 'soir, messieurs », dit-il avec un accent irlandais à couper au couteau. Il essuya la table avec un torchon. « Quesse voulez boire ?

— Que nous proposes-tu, fiston ? demanda Kahn.

— Meilleure bière de New Yo-ork, répliqua-t-il. La vraie de vraie. Mon

---

* En français dans le texte.

oncle Mick, là-bas (il désigna le quartier de viande affalé devant la télévision, hypnotisé par les deux Noirs qui se battaient et dont les grognements étouffés traversaient le bar jusqu'à nous), c'est un vrai artisse. Y met six minutes à remplir la chope. Y a d'la crème au-d'ssus, mais la bière est si épaisse qu'y faut presque un couteau et une fourchette pour en v'nir à bout. Un vrai repas. Et sacrément bon. J'ai jamais vu un type aussi fort, même à Belfast, où c'que j'vivais. »

Kahn ne sembla pas impressionné. « Je suppose que vous faites fermenter vous-mêmes le houblon ? » lança-t-il en reniflant légèrement.

Le garçon passa à côté de l'allusion olfactive. « J'irais pas jusque-là, grogna-t-il. Mais c'est la meilleure bière qu'j'ai jamais bue.

— Donne-moi un Dry Sack, commanda Kahn.

— Un Dry Sack, répéta-t-il en griffonnant sur un calepin crasseux.

— Avec de la glace.

— Glace. » Il rajouta une arabesque nerveuse sur son calepin, qu'il poignarda ensuite d'un point.

« Et du lait », ajouta Kahn.

Le garçon lui jeta un regard perplexe. « *Du lait ?* »

Kahn eut un sourire penaud, puis sa main caressa son ventre. « Dyspepsie, tu comprends ? expliqua-t-il.

— Dur ! répliqua le garçon. Vous voudriez pas un Pepto-Bismol ? Ça fait un pansement gastrique.

— Très drôle, dit Kahn d'un air lugubre.

— Et votre ami ?

— J'ai toujours faim, dis-je à Kahn.

— Navré, petit, j'avais oublié. » Il se tourna vers le serveur. « Qu'y a-t-il à grignoter ?

— Grignoter ?

— Oui, dans le genre amuse-gueule ?

— Eh bien, dit-il, Oncle Mick fait de bons sandwiches à l'oignon. »

Kahn grimaça. « Apporte-nous simplement des biscuits salés.

— Et comme boisson ?

« Je ne sais pas, dis-je. Je...

— Sers-lui aussi un Dry Sack, coupa Kahn. Ça va te plaire, petit. C'est aussi doux que le truc chinois que tu bois parfois.

— Avec du lait ? demanda le serveur. Ou sans ?

— Sans », répliqua Kahn en plissant les yeux.

Le garçon fit mine de s'éloigner.

« Et n'oublie pas les biscuits salés, lui lança Kahn, qui ajouta à voix basse : Crétin... "Y faut presque un couteau et une fourchette pour en v'nir à bout", imita-t-il. Quel cinéma ! Que dirais-tu, petit, si je me laissais pousser la barbe et les nattes, si j'accrochais un porte-monnaie à ma ceinture et que je me balade comme Shylock en éructant des aphorismes yiddish avec un accent bien gras et en braillant de temps en temps une vieille chanson juive... » Il jeta un regard noir en direction du serveur. « Crétin. Tu as remarqué son expression ? Belfast... Je parie qu'il fait partie de l'IRA. Sur la brèche à New York avec Oncle Mick. » Il prononça cette dernière phrase sur un ton sarcastique, comme le titre d'un vieux film.

« Qu'y a-t-il, Kahn ? » demandai-je, surpris par sa véhémence inhabituelle.

Il soupira et s'avachit sur sa banquette en frottant ses tempes. « Mes sinus, petit. Ils m'en font voir de toutes les couleurs. Avec cette poussière... ils vont finir par avoir ma peau. Une douleur lancinante, continuelle, juste derrière les yeux. »

Le serveur revint avec nos boissons et un panier contenant plusieurs *Captain's Wafers* posés sur une serviette en papier.

« Vous avez de l'aspirine ? demanda Kahn.
— J'vais voir, répondit l'autre.
— L'chayim », lança Kahn en levant son verre. Il but une longue gorgée, puis soupira.

« Kan pei ! rétorquai-je. C'est bon. Comment s'appelle ce vin, déjà ?
— Dry Sack.
— Hmmm. » Je léchai ma lèvre supérieure. « Délicieux ! »

Le garçon revint et posa un cachet d'aspirine sur la table, près du coude de Kahn.

« Seulement un ? demanda-t-il, incrédule. J'en ai au moins besoin de trois. Je souffre, ajouta-t-il avec un regard douloureux.
— Faudra payer, dit le serveur.
— Combien ? demanda Kahn qui se redressa aussitôt, sur le qui-vive.
— Vingt-cinq cents pièce.
— Cinq pour un dollar », proposa Kahn.

Le serveur sortit un flacon de sous son tablier. Kahn s'avachit de nouveau pour atteindre le fond de sa poche de pantalon, d'où il tira un billet froissé, qu'il lissa sur la table, puis poussa vers le serveur, en gardant la main posée dessus comme un presse-papier vigilant.

Le jeune homme fit tomber les comprimés l'un après l'autre, referma le bouchon et tendit la main en direction de l'argent.

« Hé, il y en a seulement quatre ! protesta Kahn, qui ramena aussitôt le billet vers lui.
— J'vous en ai d'jà donné un, fit le serveur. Ça fait cinq.
— Je pensais que le premier était aux frais de la maison, se plaignit Kahn.
— Vous pensez trop, dit le serveur avec un sombre sourire.
— Seigneur, petit, qu'est-ce que c'est que ce type ?
— Le Seigneur a rien à faire dans tout ça, maugréa le serveur.
— Écoutez, argumenta Kahn. Cinq comprimés ne me servent à rien. J'ai besoin de six. Trois maintenant, et trois plus tard.
— Vingt-cinq cents. »

Éxaspéré, Kahn soupira et tira de sa poche une autre pièce, qu'il envoya rouler sur la table.

Le serveur l'attrapa adroitement alors qu'elle tombait par terre. Retirant le bouchon du flacon, il en sortit un autre comprimé, qu'il lança sur la table avant de s'éloigner.

« Prends donc un biscuit », dit Kahn, qui poussa le panier vers moi. Il renversa la tête pour catapulter les aspirines dans sa bouche l'une après l'autre entre deux gorgées de vin.

Je mordis dans un biscuit, mais ma mâchoire s'immobilisa à mi-chemin et je reposai ledit biscuit sur la table. Il était rance et mou.

« Allez, petit, mange, dit-il. Je croyais que tu avais faim. » Il en prit un, mordit un morceau, qu'il recracha presque aussitôt dans la sciure.

Le serveur regardait dans le vague. D'un signe de tête, Kahn attira son attention.

« Une aut' tournée, messieurs ? »

Kahn leva les yeux vers lui, haussa les épaules et tendit ses paumes vers le plafond en un geste de capitulation ironique, mi accusation, mi appel. « C'est quoi, des matzos ? demanda-t-il. Voilà cinq sacs. » Il sortit un billet de cinq dollars. « Traverse la rue si c'est indispensable, mais pour l'amour du Christ, apporte-nous des vrais gâteaux salés ! »

Le jeune homme prit l'argent et revint deux minutes plus tard.

« Merci bien, dit Kahn avec une courtoisie exagérée. Sholem. Sholem aleichem. Si maintenant tu nous servais une autre tournée, notre bonheur serait complet.

« Alors, petit, poursuivit-il en déchirant le carton de la boîte de biscuits, qu'as-tu pensé de Newman ? Une vraie bête de scène, hein ?

— Fascinant, répondis-je en buvant une autre gorgée de Dry Sack, dont j'appréciais de plus en plus le goût, mais...

— Mais ? »

Je soupirai. « Mais sa conférence m'a encore embrouillé les idées.

— Tant mieux, dit-il. Excellent. Faut toucher le fond avant de commencer à voir la lumière...

— Ce qui me chiffonne, c'est qu'elles semblent totalement irréconciliables, poursuivis-je en pensant à haute voix.

— Quoi donc ?

— La Valeur Intrinsèque et l'Analyse Technique.

— Ah bon ? Dernière nouvelle..., rétorqua-t-il cyniquement.

— Powers affirme que l'investisseur astucieux doit passer le bilan au peigne fin — les ventes, les dividendes, l'actif, le passif... "la dernière ligne et celle d'au-dessus", alors que pour Newman on n'a même pas besoin de connaître le nom d'une compagnie pour savoir s'il faut ou non acheter ses actions. Seuls les graphiques importent.

— Attention, petit, m'avertit Kahn, ils envisagent le problème sous des angles très différents. Les Fondamentalistes s'intéressent au long terme, à la croissance et aux revenus réguliers. A l'inverse, les Techniciens sont avant tout des négociants désireux de réaliser des profits rapides en jouant sur les fluctuations journalières. Ils ne nient pas catégoriquement l'importance des facteurs fondamentaux, ils soutiennent seulement que ces facteurs sont triviaux. Car leur impact sur les fluctuations journalières a déjà été décompté. C'est autre chose qui tient le devant de la scène. Ils ne disent rien sur la nature de cette chose — cet éther fantomatique et quasiment divin qui se manifeste dans les oscillations récurrentes de leurs graphes, un mystère séduisant, mais parfaitement hermétique.

— "Quand on le cherche, il n'y a rien de solide à voir ; quand on l'écoute, il n'y a aucun son audible. Mais quand on l'utilise, il est inépuisable", récitai-je d'un air songeur.

— Absolument, petit, dit Kahn qui paraissait penser à autre chose, c'est tout à fait ça.
— Il s'agit d'une citation, l'informai-je, tirée du *Tao-tö king*. C'est du Tao qu'il est question.
— Hmm, fit Kahn en buvant une gorgée de vin. On dirait vraiment le Dow. Coïncidence intéressante.
— A mon avis, il s'agit de bien davantage », répliquai-je, puis je lui servis le plat que je mijotais depuis un certain temps : « Je crois que l'Analyse Technique et le taoïsme partagent des points de vue tout à fait similaires.
— Par exemple ?
— Eh bien, dans sa conférence sur la Valeur Intrinsèque, Ernie Powers a résumé sa position en une phrase : "Il y a une raison, et on peut l'expliciter." J'y pensais pendant que nous marchions ; il me semble qu'on peut résumer en une autre phrase la position de Newman.
— Ah ouais ? Alors, quelle est la *Weltanschauung* de l'Analyse Technique ?
— "Il y a une raison, mais nous ne la connaîtrons jamais" », répondis-je.
Il retroussa les lèvres en hochant la tête. « Okay, je t'accorde ça... Il faut néanmoins ajouter : nous ne la connaîtrons peut-être jamais, mais nous pouvons *l'utiliser*.
— Exact, acquiesçai-je.
— Autrement dit, ils sont ontologiquement d'accord, dans la mesure où cette entité existe, reprit-il, mais épistémologiquement leurs positions sont irréconciliables.
— Je ne suis pas certain de vous comprendre, dis-je, — mais cette affirmation ressemble étrangement à celle qui sous-tend le *Yi king*. »
Il me fit signe de poursuivre.
« Bien que le Tao, comme le Dow, soit supposé inaccessible à l'intellect, on peut le sonder grâce au *Livre des Mutations*, exactement comme le Dow grâce aux graphiques — et, une fois sondé, l'utiliser. Si j'ai bien compris, toute la philosophie de l'Analyse Technique pourrait grosso modo se résumer à cette citation du *Tao-tö king* :

> ... en étudiant la Voie telle qu'elle fut,
> On peut appréhender les choses telles qu'elles sont.
> Car comprendre ce qui fut au Commencement,
> Cela se nomme l'essence de la Voie. »

Je me tus afin de laisser Kahn intervenir. Mais peut-être à cause des effets lénifiants de l'alcool, il resta pour une fois passif, s'en remettant à mes initiatives.
« L'idée de "décompte" entre parfaitement dans ce schéma, continuai-je. Si le *Yi king* permet de prédire l'avenir, c'est qu'il se fonde sur un concept similaire de décompte, mais à une échelle incomparablement plus vaste.
— Allez, me raconte pas que tu crois à cette fumisterie comme quoi le *Yi king* permettrait de prédire l'avenir, railla Kahn, qui reprenait du poil de la bête. J'ai toujours cru que le *Livre des Mutations* était une sorte de guide spirituel. On ne peut pas prédire l'avenir avec ce bouquin, n'est-ce pas ?

— Mais si, répondis-je avec entrain. Je peux en témoigner.
— Sans blague ? Tu plaisantes ! Tu y crois vraiment ? »
Je hochai la tête.
Il s'affaissa sur sa banquette, le regard vitreux et sceptique.
« Exactement comme le Dow est "omniscient", poursuivis-je, c'est-à-dire qu'il reflète un ensemble de paramètres qui dépassent le cadre étroit de la finance, le *Yi king* englobe tout, la totalité de l'histoire du monde. »
Sans doute à cause de l'inhabituelle réceptivité de Kahn, ou de l'exaltation de la découverte, ou encore de mon épuisement nerveux après cette longue journée riche en péripéties diverses — tous ces facteurs se renforçaient probablement —, tandis que j'exposais ma théorie à Kahn, je devins inspiré. Comme Newman, je me sentais disposé à prophétiser. De cette manière fortuite dont les images se bousculent en pareille occasion, je songeai à certaines paroles de Scottie à propos des étoiles. Il avait dit que tous les actes de la création produisaient un effet, une énergie sujette aux métamorphoses, mais indestructible. Comme la lumière d'étoiles éloignées de milliards d'années-lumière, mais qui n'en atteint pas moins notre planète après un voyage aussi considérable, les événements de l'histoire persistent à se faire sentir comme des vibrations, des ondes de choc qui voyagent, non à travers l'espace, mais dans le temps et jusqu'au moment présent. Le *Yi king* ressemble à un instrument psychique infiniment sensible à cette énergie résiduelle, dont il accomplit une sorte de spectroscopie en la réduisant à ses composants élémentaires, si bien qu'il révèle les secrets cachés du passé et de l'avenir. Et tout comme le taoïste se met en accord avec le Tao par l'intermédiaire du *Yi king*, le dowiste — le Technicien — entre en résonance avec le Dow grâce à l'étude des graphiques, qui lui servent de baguettes divinatoires. » Je marquai un arrêt. « Alors ?
— Alors quoi ? demanda Kahn.
— Pensez-vous qu'il s'agisse d'une simple coïncidence ? »
Il haussa les épaules. « Plutôt d'une sorte de synchronicité à grande échelle, quasiment au niveau historique. La roue a été inventée plus d'une fois, non ?
— Qu'est-ce que la synchronicité ? demandai-je.
— La synchronicité ? Ça désigne simplement deux événements ou deux idées qui semblent reliés comme la cause et l'effet, que seule la causalité pourrait expliquer, alors qu'on peut démontrer qu'ils sont indépendants. Une "connexion mystique", si tu veux.
— Oui, connexion mystique, répétai-je, reprenant aussitôt l'expression à mon compte.
— Mais finalement, tout cela nous mène à quoi ?
— Vous ne croyez pas que c'est la preuve d'un delta, lui demandai-je, d'un confluent entre le Dow et le Tao ?
— Je sais pas, petit. Certes, l'image est frappante. Mais pour moi, le delta, comme tu l'appelles, ne doit pas être un pur lieu mental. Il faut que tu le découvres dans le monde réel. Sinon il comptera pour rien. »
Sa réponse me fit réfléchir. Quand je relevai les yeux, je m'aperçus que Kahn fouillait mon visage. Les coudes posés sur la table, il tripotait machinalement ses bracelets de cuivre et me dévisageait avec une expression

quasiment prédatrice qui m'interloqua. Voyant ma surprise, il m'adressa un sourire qui me fit frissonner.

« Tu veux savoir ce qui m'intéresse vraiment dans ce que tu as dit ? » me demanda-t-il. Il se pencha vers moi au-dessus de la table. Stupéfait, je reculai instinctivement sur ma banquette, son visage si proche du mien que je respirais son haleine sucrée, les relents d'alcool mêlé de salive.

« Tu affirmes qu'on peut utiliser le *Yi king* pour prédire l'avenir, chuchota-t-il d'une voix sourde que l'émotion faisait trembler. A ton avis, pourrait-on s'en servir pour choisir des actions ? »

Quand il vit mon expression scandalisée, il reprit contrôle de lui-même, abandonna sa posture de fauve en arrêt, se redressa. « Je te demande ça par curiosité, bien sûr.

— Je crois », répondis-je, pas totalement rassuré. Je me raclai la gorge. « Oui, on pourrait s'en servir... à condition de l'utiliser avec l'esprit adéquat, avec suffisamment de *ling*.

— Qu'est-ce que *ling* ? demanda-t-il.

— La pureté de cœur. »

Kahn grimaça, visiblement échaudé.

« Quant à savoir si l'on *devrait* l'utiliser, poursuivis-je, c'est une autre paire de manches. A mon avis, se servir du *Yi king* à des fins de profit personnel serait un sacrilège. Cela trahirait l'esprit du Tao. Celui qui recourrait à de telles pratiques s'infligerait très certainement un préjudice spirituel irréparable, il perdrait le *ling* qu'il possédait et cesserait donc de pouvoir commander à l'oracle. Il est écrit : "A ceux qui ne sont pas en contact avec le Tao, l'oracle ne retourne aucune réponse intelligible, car celle-ci ne servirait de rien."

— Une justice poétique, hein ? dit Kahn.

— Exactement. »

Kahn parut s'effondrer intérieurement. Avec un profond soupir, il s'avachit sur sa banquette, ses yeux s'éteignirent. « T'as raison, petit, dit-il. A cent pour cent. J'admire tes principes. Ne m'en veux pas de t'avoir posé ces questions — c'était plus fort que moi.

— Bien sûr que non ! » rétorquai-je, rassuré par sa contrition ; la confession de sa faiblesse augmenta même mon estime pour lui.

« Merci, petit, dit-il avec dans la voix un léger tremblement. C'est très important pour moi. Tu sais, pendant ta tirade, j'ai pensé... tu me rappelles quelqu'un. » Il scruta sombrement mon visage.

Mon estomac se contracta. Frissonnant d'excitation, j'ouvris la bouche pour murmurer le schibboleth, le nom secret que je portais dans mon cœur comme une braise de feu qui, attisée par la plus légère brise, menaçait de m'incendier.

« Tu sais qui ? » demanda-t-il.

Je secouai la tête, étouffé par l'émotion, incapable d'articuler un mot.

« Moi-même », dit-il.

Je le regardai dans les yeux.

« Parfaitement, déclara-t-il, moi. Tu parais surpris. Je te comprends. Je ne veux pas dire tel que je suis aujourd'hui, mais tel que je fus autrefois, quand je suis venu ici pour la première fois — frais émoulu de l'université, avec toutes mes idées et mes principes, le même enthousiasme juvénile que toi. Et comme toi, j'étais puceau. J'avais encore ma cerise, moralement parlant, une Napoléon, pas une marasquin... La dernière fois que je l'ai regardée, on aurait dit une olive ratatinée plantée sur une fourchette. Mais au début, disons pendant ma première année, tout cela me sembla neuf et passionnant, un spectacle digne de l'époque élizabéthaine (je pensais encore avec des références littéraires), plein de pompe et de fastes, un spectacle puissant, irrévérent, fantasque, immoral, vulgaire, mais débordant de vie — aux antipodes de l'université. Des images, des impressions, des idées aussi audacieuses que celles que tu viens de formuler tourbillonnaient dans ma tête. » Son visage se rembrunit. « Tu as vu tout cela dans la conférence de Newman, alors que pour moi c'était du simple schlock. Je suis peut-être plus sage, mais je t'envie, petit. Sincèrement. On dit qu'il n'y a rien de plus excitant que la frénésie du commerce, je sais pas mais j'y crois. Pourtant elle finit peut-être par te rendre amer. En t'écoutant, j'ai pensé que je n'avais plus d'idées. Ça m'attriste. J'ai perdu tout ça quelque part en chemin. Ne perds pas les tiennes, petit.

« Pour un type qui place la schmaltz juste à côté du gefilte fisch sur la Liste de ses Suprêmes Aversions, je me lamente beaucoup, hein, petit ? » Il vida un quart de son verre d'un coup.

Pris de pitié, je voulus court-circuiter son autocritique avant qu'elle n'atteignît des proportions trop démesurées, et lui adressai la question que j'avais désiré lui poser un peu plus tôt. « Que voulait dire l'"éminent prédécesseur" de Newman avec sa Moyenne Flottante des Deux Cents Jours ? »

Les yeux baissés, Kahn semblait absorbé dans la contemplation des glaçons qu'il faisait tinter au fond de son verre comme des icebergs dans une mer polaire. « Hein ? fit-il, distrait. Ah oui. La Moyenne Flottante des Deux Cents Jours. C'est un indicateur de tendance, fils. Plus ou moins.

— Un indicateur de tendance ?

— Une façon de repérer une direction générale qui sous-tend les oscillations du Dow. Si tu te contentes d'observer les fluctuations journalières d'une action donnée, ou même du Dow, tu auras du mal à discerner un mouvement général à long terme. La courbe monte et descend comme l'électrocardiogramme d'une chienne en chaleur. Mais il y a malgré tout une tendance, une direction globale. C'est le fil d'Ariane qui te permet de te repérer dans le labyrinthe des flux à court terme. Pour cela, il suffit de lisser les hauts et les bas des cotations de clôture journalières, pendant disons deux semaines, puis de relier les points ainsi obtenus pour tracer une ligne droite qui monte ou descend selon une pente variable. Recommence pendant deux cents jours ouvrables, et tu trouveras la Moyenne Flottante des Deux Cents Jours. Elle permet de visualiser une direction invisible, de découvrir l'unité dans la multiplicité.

— Pourquoi deux cents jours ? demandai-je.

— Je l'ignore. Mais cela fait environ neuf mois de jours de travail. A moins, tu risquerais de confondre une réaction secondaire avec une tendance primaire, comme disait l'"éminent prédécesseur". En fait, tu pourrais rallonger la sauce *ad libitum*. Une Moyenne Flottante des Deux Cents

Semaines, et, pourquoi pas bon Dieu, des Deux Cents Ans ? »
Brusquement, il se figea.

« Kahn ? lui dis-je, inquiet.

— Chut ! Chut ! m'intima-t-il en agitant frénétiquement la main pour réclamer le silence. Ne bouge pas. Ne respire pas. Je crois que ça vient. Um... umh..., grogna-t-il. Ça y est, je la sens. Oui... oui... Une vraie ! Une authentique, une indiscutable *idée* !

— Qu'est-ce que vous dites ?

— Écoute, petit, Newman a bien affirmé que le marché, le Dow, était une sorte de baromètre qui reflétait la météo de la nation, englobait toutes les passions et les ambitions de la population ? »

J'acquiesçai sans enthousiasme.

« Eh bien, selon lui, la somme totale de toutes ces impulsions disparates égale — ou du moins est liée — au Dow, à sa Moyenne Flottante des Deux Cents Jours. D'où sa conception du Dow comme signe vital majeur de la nation, distillat de l'Amérique elle-même, manifestation de l'essence de notre culture (ou de son absence). Cette Moyenne à Deux Cents Jours nous fournit un aperçu de la tendance globale — appelons-la Sens Ultime. Le Sens Ultime est l'unité qui sous-tend la multiplicité vertigineuse du Dow et de notre vie nationale, économique, sociale, politique, intellectuelle, religieuse, etc., l'ensemble étant décompté dans le Dow Jones. Une fois que tu as clairement compris la nature et la direction du Sens Ultime, tu peux l'utiliser, du moins en théorie, indépendamment du flux et du reflux des paniques et des spéculations ponctuelles. Certes, le Sens change, mais très lentement, car son inertie est énorme, aussi énorme que l'Amérique elle-même. Seul un effort gigantesque pourrait provoquer une modification sensible de sa direction. Notre vie nationale oscille fébrilement autour de la moyenne impavide du Sens Ultime, comme les fluctuations journalières autour d'une immense Moyenne Flottante des Deux Cents Jours. Mais le Sens Ultime est plus proche d'une Moyenne Flottante des Deux Cents Ans, laquelle exprime l'inertie historique de ce pays — le Sens Ultime de l'Amérique ! Songes-y, petit ! Les conséquences sont proprement hallucinantes. Des Moyennes Flottantes sur des durées de plus en plus longues ! Au-delà de la Moyenne Flottante des Deux Siècles pour l'Amérique, une Moyenne Flottante des Deux Mille Ans, qui exprimerait l'inertie historique cumulée de l'homme occidental depuis la naissance du Christ. Et cette Moyenne Flottante des Deux Millénaires, une minuscule goutte d'eau dans la Moyenne Flottante des Deux Millions d'Années pour la race humaine : laquelle s'intègre à son tour à la Moyenne Flottante des Deux Milliards d'Années pour la vie sur terre ! »

Sapant lui-même son enthousiasme, il ajouta ironiquement : « Kahn devient profond malgré lui. » Il sourit. « Qu'en dis-tu, petit ? Je ne suis peut-être pas aussi irrécupérable qu'on le pensait. Le vieux Kahn a peut-être encore quelque chose entre les oreilles ? »

Sentant que ses questions relevaient de la pure rhétorique, je ne bronchai pas.

« Pas vrai, petit ? insista-t-il.

— Bien sûr », répliquai-je.

Il soupira en secouant la tête. Le bref météore de l'exaltation spéculative disparut derrière l'horizon, et Kahn retomba dans sa dépression coutumière. « Je n'en suis pas si certain », gémit-il, et je compris alors qu'il avait seulement quémandé mon approbation pour le plaisir de se contredire lui-même.

« Garçon ! s'écria-t-il. Deux Dry Sack ! »

10

Son exaltation légèrement tapageuse me fit comprendre que Kahn était sur la voie de l'ébriété, ce dont je ne m'inquiétai pas vraiment, peut-être parce que j'approchais moi-même rapidement de cet état.
« Je me demande parfois ce que je fais ici, se lamenta-t-il.
— Qu'à cela ne tienne, allons ailleurs, proposai-je.
— Pas dans ce bar, plouc, rétorqua-t-il sèchement, je parle de la Bourse.
— Ah, fis-je en prenant un air sérieux.
— J'avais parfois des illuminations. Je me réveillais en sursaut, persuadé d'être de retour dans ma turne de Columbia, en pleine forme après une petite sieste. Les visages des courtiers et des négociants se brouillaient, leurs voix se fondaient en un rugissement semblable au... au crissement de millions d'ailes d'insectes, un nuage de sauterelles africaines, ou alors... — son visage s'éclaira, comme si Kahn se souvenait — ... oh oui, la radiation fondamentale qu'ils ont découverte aux laboratoires Bell. Jamais entendu parler de ça ? Mi-température, mi-bruit de fond, d'après ce que j'ai compris, irradiant tout l'univers — trois degrés Kelvin, je crois —, un lointain écho du Big-Bang piégé à Wall Street, antidote parfaitement approprié à tant de cupidité et de vanité, une sorte de memento mori (apprécié par tous les étudiants en littérature) pour nous rappeler ce qui nous attend au bout du chemin (la même chose qu'au début). Bref, un éclair de terreur existentielle. Tu vois ce que je veux dire, petit ?
— Absolument pas, avouai-je.
— Procédons autrement, dit-il. Tu connais le rêve du papillon de Tchouang-tseu ? »
J'acquiesçai.
« Eh bien, arrête-moi si je me trompe, mais après son rêve il s'est réveillé sans pouvoir décider s'il était un homme qui s'était rêvé papillon, ou un papillon qui se rêvait homme. C'est bien ça ?
— Tout à fait, dis-je.
— Bon. Mon cas est parfaitement similaire : je ne savais pas (et parfois je ne sais toujours pas) si j'étais un cochon de capitaliste qui se prenait pour un intellectuel, ou un intellectuel qui se prenait pour un cochon de capitaliste.
— Je vois, dis-je.

— Excuse-moi, poursuivit-il, mais j'aimerais te poser une colle. Dans vingt ou trente ans, quand tu auras mon âge, où crois-tu que tu seras ?
— A Ken Kuan », répondis-je sans hésiter.

Il hocha la tête. « Si tu m'avais posé cette question il y a trente ans, alors que je trimais dans ma turne, je t'aurais répondu la même chose — l'université au lieu du monastère. Pour moi, ce sont de simples variations sur un thème unique. Si tu m'avais dit que je trafiquerais bientôt des actions au parquet de la Bourse de New York, je t'aurais ri au nez. Je ne me serais même pas vexé, tellement ça m'aurait semblé grotesque. Prends mes paroles pour ce qu'elles valent, petit ; je ne suis pas le genre de type à pontifier ou à déblatérer sur la sagesse de l'expérience, mais tu ne trouves pas que les choses évoluent parfois bizarrement ? » Il soupira, but une longue rasade, agita les glaçons dans son verre comme s'ils allaient lui révéler un souvenir oublié.

« En deuxième année de fac, j'ai vécu une merveilleuse histoire d'amour avec la littérature anglaise, surtout la période élizabéthaine. Shakespeare... » Ses traits s'éclairèrent d'un sourire spontané, presque enfantin, que je ne lui avais jamais vu. « *Henri IV*, première partie. Tête Brûlée, Hal, le "chevalier obèse", Sir John Falstaff, paillard impénitent — Dieu que j'aimais cette pièce ! Peut-être pas la plus somptueuse qu'il ait écrite, pas aussi profonde que *Lear* ou *Hamlet*, mais il n'y a rien de plus hilarant ! Et merde, rien de plus triste. Et débordant de compassion — le vieux roublard n'a jamais rien pondu d'aussi tendre. Il y roule la race humaine dans une drôle de farine — "ce bagage d'humeurs, cette huche verrouillée de bestialité, ce paquet gonflé d'hypocrisie, cet énorme baril de xérès, ce sac à boyaux tout plein, ce bœuf gras rôti avec la farce dans son ventre, ce vice vénérable, cette iniquité grise, ce père ruffian, cette vanité surannée" — bref, Falstaff. Et il lui pardonne, ainsi qu'à nous et au reste... mieux, il l'aime. Difficile de connaître le monde comme lui et de l'aimer malgré tout, non par pitié, mais avec humour. Ce seul fait explique peut-être sa stature de géant : il pouvait regarder la réalité en face sans vaciller ni mourir, ni broncher, ni regimber, ni virer à l'aigre, falsifier, maquiller, biaiser, simplement la voir telle qu'elle est, et rire du fond du cœur, rire d'elle, avec elle, à cause d'elle — et puis surtout l'aimer. Rien de plus banal en apparence, sauf que personne n'a jamais été capable de refaire ça, du moins d'en laisser une trace écrite. Sans doute pour ça qu'il semble insondable — parce que le fond de ses pièces, son fond, son fondement était celui de l'univers, le cul du monde. Et voilà pourquoi les échos de son rire nous font encore frissonner, comme le Big-Bang. Trois degrés Kelvin. » Peut-être pour excuser sa logorrhée, il m'adressa un sourire penaud. « Navré, petit. On dirait que j'ai bu un coup de trop.

— Ne vous excusez pas, répondis-je. J'aime vous écouter... Mais, qui était Shakespeare ? »

Il grogna. « Peu importe. Je mérite tout ça, petit, je *te* mérite. C'est sûrement une sorte de pénitence pour des crimes commis dans une vie antérieure. Ce que j'essaie de t'expliquer, du moins de te faire sentir, c'est que toute ma formation littéraire avant la licence était merveilleusement indépendante de ma vie personnelle — et me plaisait peut-être précisément pour cette raison. Quand j'ai lu *Le marchand de Venise*, je me suis identifié à Jessica, la fille de Shylock. Elle se sent prisonnière d'un héritage barbare et répugnant, elle meurt d'envie de se faire enlever par Lorenzo et les chrétiens. Ah, "cette qualité de pitié" ! s'écria-t-il en secouant ses bajoues et pointant l'index en l'air comme Jimmy Durante. Une seule différence nous séparait, elle et moi : après quatre ans passés à Mont-Nébo et quatre autres à Columbia, j'avais réussi mon assimilation. Je me considérais comme déraciné, désinfecté, "guéri", ou tout autre mot à ta convenance. Bref, un authentique shegetz. Tu vois, petit, je ne suis pas né génial. J'ai dû y arriver à la sueur de mon front. A l'époque, je ne comprenais rien à la gravité du sang.

— Qu'est-ce que c'est ? lui demandai-je.

— Je vais t'expliquer : fais passer un Wasp à la moulinette de l'éducation libérale occidentale ; tu auras beau ajouter gousses d'ail et poignées d'épices, le résultat sera toujours une bonne potée yankee ; fume un Juif, tu obtiendras immanquablement un filet de poisson ratatiné. Inutile de t'apitoyer, personne n'y peut rien. C'est ça la gravité du sang. Un "Juif assimilé" ressemble à un poivrot qui a cessé de boire, petit. Il reste alcoolique et mortifie simplement son désir d'alcool. Même chose avec le Chinois ou le nègre. Tu peux l'éduquer, arrondir ses angles, passer une couche de peinture blanche sur ses mauvaises manières, mais impossible d'éliminer la noirceur de son cœur. Ça te paraît raciste ? Ça ne l'est pas. Le monde serait peut-être plus paisible et plus harmonieux, mais à mon avis il deviendrait sacrément plus emmerdant si chaque Juif était une Jessica et chaque nègre un Oncle Tom. Et si c'est le mot "nègre" qui te gêne, alors laisse-moi te dire que l'homme noir n'a pas le monopole de l'indignation vertueuse. Le jour où le mot "juif" sera débarrassé de toutes ses connotations péjoratives, alors nous serons tous de gentils petits youpins et d'adorables nègres, heureux comme la vermine dans un sommier, et toutes ces épithètes injurieuses se métamorphoseront en termes affectueux. Mais en attendant ce jour, je parlerai de nègres, et on pourra bien me traiter de youpin.

« En tout cas, voilà peut-être pourquoi, en année de licence, j'ai bifurqué vers la littérature américaine, premier pas dans la quête de mon identité, la couche de sucre autour de la pilule amère de mon indéracinable judéité. Si j'avais dû l'avaler d'un coup, je crois que je me serais étouffé. J'ai appris à devenir juif en apprenant l'Amérique. J'ai fini par écrire une thèse sur Mark Twain. Pas grand-chose à voir avec la renaissance juive, diras-tu, sauf qu'il parle une fois de lui-même comme du "Sholom Aleichem américain". » Il sourit encore.

« Bien sûr, j'ai traversé ma "phase juive" quand j'étais adolescent. Phase Un de l'existence d'Aaron Kahn. Mais je crois que je l'ai abandonnée avec mon yarmulke après ma bar mitzvah. Entre cela et l'université — la Phase Trois —, s'intercale mon premier contact avec la Bourse. Oncle Schmuel, également connu sous le nom de Hanaël, entre en scène. T'en ai-je déjà parlé ?

— Vous m'avez dit avoir hérité votre fauteuil d'un oncle, répondis-je, mais je croyais qu'il s'appelait Ahasvérus, et non Schmuel ou Ha-machin.

— Schmuel, Hanaël, Ahasvérus..., un seul et même personnage. Ce que je t'ai servi, petit, n'était qu'un résumé digne et docte de la Vie de Kahn. Tu ignores encore les plaisirs somptueux de la version non expurgée. » Il grimaça un sourire. « Mes premiers souvenirs de l'Oncle Schmuel (je ne l'ai jamais appelé Hanaël ; pour autant que je sache, seule ma mère utilisait ce nom) remontent à l'époque où nous habitions Flatbush Avenue ; une fois l'an, il venait déjeuner chez nous, dans notre appartement situé au-dessus du mont de piété de mon père, traînant en remorque une bombe sexuelle aussi blonde qu'imbécile qui minaudait dans l'étole de vison qu'il lui avait offerte et qu'elle gardait sur les épaules pendant tout l'après-midi. Elle restait assise comme un filet de poisson fumé pendant que nous schmoozions et mangions, refusant tous les plats traditionnels en reniflant dédaigneusement et relevant le nez comme si toute notre succulente cuisine choquait son odorat — le piroshki de ma mère aussi, ce qui était le plus impardonnable des péchés, une véritable gifle —, elle restait donc là avec son vison, sans rien dire, souriant d'un sourire dur et figé, les genoux serrés comme dans un étau, semblable à l'un des lévriers de César avec son foulard à carreaux, "Noli me tangere" quasiment écrit sur son front. Ma mère frisait l'apoplexie. Moe lui jetait des regards furtifs, timides, charmeurs, inquiets, tout en jouant aux cartes avec Oncle Schmuel, lequel passait un sacré bon moment, oubliait les tensions sociales — que dis-je, la *guerre raciale* — qui opposaient les femmes, se retournait de temps à autre pour caresser sa shiksa sous le menton avec le plaisir reconnaissant et un peu luxurieux de l'âge mûr, en disant : "Elle est pas chouette, Moe ? Vise un peu sa silhouette ! Et puis, un appétit d'oiseau, un vrai colibri !" Les deux hommes tapaient le carton au milieu du nuage de fumée des cigares que mon oncle achetait à Manhattan ; ils buvaient du scotch de contrebande, jouaient au gin rummy pour dix cents le point, Schmuel misait à la place de papa, parce qu'il pensait que celui-ci était fauché comme les blés, puis, passant outre les protestations de papa, il épongeait toutes ses dettes après le dernier *Hollywood* et laissait de l'argent sur la table en guise de pourboire. Je sentais que c'était parfois aussi pénible pour Moe que pour ma mère. Mais il adorait Schmuel.

« Ils étaient demi-frères de la même mère, une femme originaire d'une famille de musiciens de Varsovie, très sophistiquée, très cosmopolite, bien que peu fortunée. Elle tomba amoureuse d'un jeune noble hongrois, un baron, je crois, qui séjournait à Varsovie pour "se cultiver" — le premier Hanaël. Selon Schmuel, il devait être assez fringant et sans doute plutôt noceur. Elle se jeta à sa tête, il s'enticha d'elle, brièvement...

« Quand sa famille découvrit qu'elle était enceinte, elle la déshérita. L'affaire se serait mal terminée si mon grand-père n'était tombé follement amoureux d'elle. Agé de quarante ou cinquante ans, il était considérablement plus vieux qu'elle. Il avait déjà fait fortune dans le prêt sur gage. Il s'installa avec elle, donna même son propre nom à Schmuel et l'éleva comme son fils. Mais ma grand-mère, peut-être par amertume (on la comprend), insista pour l'appeler Hanaël et lui fit apprendre le français. Mon grand-père n'en continua pas moins de l'appeler joyeusement Schmuel. Ils se parlaient en yiddish. Bizarrement, mais pas tant que ça, quand il apprit l'anglais — surtout par des amis qui pratiquaient le yiddish —, Oncle

Schmuel s'exprima avec un fort accent d'Europe de l'Est. C'était incroyable de l'entendre placer une expression française avec une intonation et un accent parfaits, comme du saumon fumé servi avec de la mayonnaise.

« Quand il eut dix-huit ans, Schmuel conçut une passion dévorante pour les arts militaires et voulut devenir hussard — ambition difficilement réalisable, vu l'antisémitisme notoire des Polonais. Mais son père — son vrai père, le premier, Hanaël — qui ne s'était pas trop décarcassé pour lui jusque-là, fut pris de remords et tira quelques ficelles. Schmuel reçut son brevet d'officier, non pas, bien sûr, en tant que Schmuel, mais sous le nom d'Hanaël. Cela peina sans doute mon grand-père (dont le seul engagement politique connu était une vague prédilection pour le pacifisme), mais je ne crois pas qu'il eut trop de mal à surmonter sa déception. Jeune homme, Schmuel ne semblait pas vraiment juif — j'ai vu des photos —, plutôt slave ou bohémien. Certainement à cause du sang hongrois de son père. Par la suite, les os et les cartilages de son visage se révoltèrent, accomplirent une sorte de réalignement tectonique. Les premiers souvenirs de papa évoquent un élégant officier en uniforme, le shako coincé sous le bras, dressé de toute sa taille dans le salon avec ses bottes de cheval montant jusqu'aux genoux, ses moustaches gominées, son bras enlaçant la taille de ma grand-mère rougissante et ravie ; mon grand-père, le pacifiste, reste un peu en retrait et sur ses gardes, détrôné par son beau-fils qui n'appréciait peut-être pas à sa juste valeur tout ce que son père adoptif avait fait pour lui (mais la gratitude et la tendresse ne sont pas nécessairement les qualités premières qu'on attend d'un Ahasvérus).

« Alors la guerre éclata, la première guerre mondiale. Schmuel fut blessé quelques mois après le début des hostilités. J'ignore comment cela s'est passé, mais je me plais à l'imaginer chargeant sabre au clair, filant comme une flèche devant le soleil, les sabots de son cheval tonnant sur le sol, fonçant droit vers une batterie ennemie. Pour la gloire de Dieu et de la Pologne ! Fauché comme un épi de blé. Schmuel vint en convalescence à la maison. Par bonheur, il avait seulement reçu un peu de mitraille dans l'épaule. Mon père lui servait le petit déjeuner avec le journal du matin. Schmuel racontait parfois une anecdote sur la guerre, caressait brièvement la tête de mon père et lui donnait quelques *grosz* pour qu'il s'achète du réglisse.

« Il passa quelques mois à la maison ; du jour où il retourna à la guerre, papa n'entendit plus jamais parler de lui... Jusqu'à ce fameux après-midi où ils se retrouvèrent par hasard sur Delancey Street à New York, lorsque papa le vit acheter un œillet pour sa boutonnière à une fleuriste ambulante. Schmuel ne le reconnut pas, contrairement à mon père. Il était déjà en route vers la fortune, il avait acheté son fauteuil à la Bourse. Quant à ce qui s'était passé entre-temps... ? Il existe une seule trace de cette époque : une photo d'Oncle Schmuel habillé en chasseur, chapeau de feutre, manteau en peau de mouton, bottes de cavalerie et, bizarrement, une boucle d'oreille. Un fusil niché au creux du coude, une cartouchière barrant son torse, il est accroupi dans la neige et adresse un sourire chaleureux à l'appareil photo. Sa main droite maintient ouverte la gueule d'un loup adulte, dont il retrousse la babine supérieure pour dénuder ses crocs. Les yeux du loup sont révulsés, l'un brille d'un éclat étrange. Cette photo m'a toujours hanté. L'appel du monde sauvage — je crois que j'ai ça dans le sang.

« A l'époque en question, néanmoins — je parle des déjeuners annuels à Flatbush Avenue —, Schmuel n'était encore que l'oncle fortuné à la shiksa, un hôte que je haïssais à cause de ma mère et tolérais à cause de mon père. J'avoue que je me laissais amadouer par les délicieux bonbons qu'il me rapportait des antres secrets de New York, les premiers auxquels j'aie jamais goûté. Oui, l'Oncle Schmuel, alias Ahasvérus, joua un rôle fondamental dans l'épanouissement de mes vices, développant jusqu'au péché mignon de la gourmandise, ce premier et véniel écart qu'on peut cependant considérer comme le Péché Originel de Kahn. Mais ce que je retiens surtout de ces premiers souvenirs, davantage que l'Oncle Schmuel, ce sont toutes ces shiksas, ces secrétaires pimbêches trop bien habillées, trop fardées, toutes ces petites mijaurées aux fesses serrées et à la bouche en cul de poule. Une nouvelle chaque année, mais toujours la même.

« Vois-tu, je piétinais encore dans la Phase Un, "Piété Juive Exacerbée", un bourgeonnement bref mais vigoureux, une recrudescence d'identité raciale. Aucun de mes parents n'était particulièrement bigot, mais il était hors de question que je coupe à ma bar mitzvah. Pas de bar mitzvah, pas de mensch ! Cette perspective ne m'enchantait guère ; ce fut donc avec une résignation découragée que j'attendais ma "b.m.", ainsi que Moishe Lipshitz, qui habitait le même pâté de maisons et devait avoir treize ans deux semaines plus tôt que moi, baptisa l'événement avec mon plein accord, car malgré notre âge, nous nous prenions tous deux pour des cyniques endurcis. » Kahn rit en hochant la tête. « Dans cet état d'esprit, je croyais dur comme fer que les religieux ne parviendraient jamais à m'embobiner. Mais j'ai eu droit au lavage de cerveau... Non, ce fut mieux que ça. Vois-tu, j'avais compté sans Herschel Liebowicz, notre rabbin. Herschel était un pur et dur, un jeune type très beau, athlétique, un mètre quatre-vingt-dix, une tignasse bouclée. Il possédait du charisme. Il y avait quelque chose sur son visage, une sorte de lueur chaleureuse et humaine, et même un peu plus. Comme s'il écoutait en permanence une vibration de l'air inaudible pour les autres. Il avait trouvé le grand truc, ça se voyait sur son visage, et il transmettait ça comme de l'électricité à tous ceux qui le côtoyaient. C'était un superbe Juif, un David, le rejeton d'un de ces sombres guerriers aux muscles déliés et aux yeux rieurs qui écumaient les déserts de Palestine en pagne et sandales, brandissant leurs lances et instillant la peur dans le cœur des Gentils, avant la Diaspora, quand nous étions encore le peuple élu de Dieu... » La voix de Kahn se brisa. Il sortit son atomiseur de Dristan pour enrayer la douleur, inhala bruyamment, puis soupira en s'essuyant les yeux. « On dit qu'après la guerre, Herschel est parti s'installer en Israël avec toute sa famille. J'en aurais pleuré. C'est le genre de type qui te marque pour la vie et dont tu vérifies périodiquement l'adresse, tu vois ce que je veux dire ? Comme s'il portait le flambeau pour nous tous. » Sa voix trembla de nouveau. « Excuse-moi, petit. C'est plus fort que moi. » Il aspira une longue goulée d'air.

« Bref, pendant la période d'endoctrinement, où j'apprenais à lire, ou du moins à répéter comme un perroquet les passages essentiels de la Torah, je tombai complètement sous son charme. Mon noviciat, bien que succinct, fut très intense. Chaque fois qu'il s'approchait de moi, mon cœur battait la chamade. Cet état de grâce se prolongea pendant la durée des cours, ce qui me fait penser rétrospectivement qu'il s'agissait davantage de magnétisme animal de sa part que de conviction religieuse de la mienne. Le culte du héros plutôt que la religion. Mais pendant toute la retraite, je fus sérieux comme un pape, si j'ose dire. Il n'y pas de quoi rire. (Il rit.) J'étais devenu un inconditionnel de la vertu, une putain de zélote, petit ! La piété ? J'étais si pieux qu'on m'avait surnommé "Siddhartha". Je plaisante pas, petit.

« J'avais une tante, la sœur de ma mère. Un jour, je reviens de la synagogue, et je la trouve à l'appartement. Ma mère est sortie faire une course. Dès qu'elle aperçoit mon yarmulke, elle m'adresse un regard malicieux et dit : "Je vois que tu as pris le voile." Bon Dieu, elle aurait mieux fait de se taire ! Je lui ai sacrément fait payer sa désinvolture ! Je me suis lancé dans un long sermon où je reprochais aux Juifs leur dépravation, gémissais sur la grandeur perdue des tribus, les exhortais à se regrouper pour retrouver la gloire d'Israël — une authentique jérémiade. Quand j'eus terminé, ma tante était pétrifiée de stupeur, bouche bée, comme si elle venait de se faire attaquer dans la rue. Un peu plus tard, après le retour de ma mère, je l'entendis lui dire par la porte de la cuisine : "Mais qu'a donc ton Aaron ? On dirait le buisson ardent — il brûle et ne se consume pas !" Cela pour te donner une idée de mon fanatisme de l'époque : je ne badinais pas... Jamais le moindre rire ni l'ombre d'un sourire. C'était une affaire sérieuse. Pas question de déconner. Moishe Lipshitz attrapa aussi le virus, il ne fut pas aussi atteint que moi, mais il se payait de bonnes poussées de fièvre ; parfois, aux pires moments, il était saisi de logorrhée et devait courir vers le public le plus proche. On aurait dit un couple de Vieux Marins juifs, petit. Deux illuminés dans le même pâté de maisons — une sacrée épine au pied de la communauté. »

Kahn subit alors une crise d'éternuements asthmatiques. « Où en étais-je ? Ah oui, le buisson ardent. Il régnait dans la famille une sorte de certitude implicite — graine insidieusement semée par ma mère, plante soigneusement arrosée par icelle : je deviendrais un savant. A propos, petit, sais-tu ce qu'est un génie ? »

Je secouai la tête.

« Un gosse moyen doté de parents juifs. Dans mes rares moments de lucidité, j'étais néanmoins assez sage pour regimber. Mais les opérations clandestines d'Ida étaient trop sophistiquées. Je n'avais pas une chance sur mille de m'en tirer. Je croyais sincèrement que je pourrais faire ce que je voudrais — tu sais, monter à la grande échelle, jouer au guichet pour les Brooklyn Dodgers. Sous l'influence d'Herschel, la graine plantée par ma mère trouva un nouvel engrais. Et quel engrais ! Un jour, je suis rentré de la synagogue à la maison pour annoncer à la cantonade et sur un ton sentencieux que j'allais consacrer mon existence aux études talmudiques. Herschel, qui m'encourageait prudemment, se mit à m'apprendre l'hébreu. Après la cérémonie de la bar mitzvah, il me prit à part pour m'offrir un splendide exemplaire de la Torah relié en cuir avec un fin ruban pour marquer ma page. Chaque fois que j'y pense, j'ai envie de pleurer comme une madeleine. Il affirma qu'avec un peu d'obstination, je parviendrais un jour à comprendre ses "austères beautés". Ses austères beautés... » Kahn secoua la tête. « Petit, la contamination du monde fut trop forte pour moi. Je succombai. Et puis il y avait Ahasvérus.

« Un jour — avant ma bar mitzvah — mon père m'a emmené déjeuner en ville. Après le repas, nous sommes passés à la Bourse. C'était ma première virée. Il m'a emmené sur la galerie. La fureur et le capharnaüm, le gigantisme de la salle me laissèrent pantois. Alors que nous sommes là-haut, papa aperçoit oncle Schmuel et l'apostrophe en yiddish en hurlant comme un dément. Un silence de mort s'abat sur la foule. Tout le monde lève les yeux vers nous. J'aurais voulu rentrer sous terre, petit. Vraiment. Mais l'Oncle Schmuel s'illumine alors comme un sapin de Noël (je devrais peut-être dire un menorah). Il nous fait signe de descendre, et papa m'entraîne derrière lui à travers la foule, les yeux rivés aux craquelures du parquet. Écoute bien, petit. C'est à cet instant que Kahn aperçoit pour la première fois l'Ashkénaze fou. Dans la grande salle de la Bourse, Oncle Schmuel était dans son élément, comme une mouche sur un tas de merde. Il cessait d'être Schmuel pour devenir Ahasvérus ! Bon Dieu, il se comportait comme si toute la Bourse lui appartenait. Quelle *chutzpah* ! Quel *mensch* ! Je le dévisageais, incrédule, en me demandant s'il s'agissait vraiment du même homme. Il semblait avoir grandi de vingt centimètres, rajeuni de dix ans. Un halo extatique nimbait son visage, comme une version séculière — sans doute devrais-je dire profane — de l'aura sacrée d'Herschel Liebowicz. Toutes mes croyances vacillent. Un goy en costume fantaisie arrive alors vers lui, ils se serrent la main. Ils schmoozent quelques minutes ; le type offre un cigare à Oncle Schmuel, l'allume. Puis Oncle Schmuel se tourne vers nous.

« "Jesse, dit-il, je te présente mon frère Moe et son fils Aaron à la veille de sa bar mitzvah. Allez, serrez la main de Jessie Livermore, le Grand Ours."

« Jessie Livermore ! Tu te rends compte, petit ? A l'époque, évidemment, je ne le connaissais ni d'Ève ni d'Adam. Mais bon Dieu ! Je serre la main du type et il m'offre un cigare. J'ai douze ans et il m'offre un cigare ! J'aurais dû le garder ! Ah, petit, les géants foulaient encore la terre à cette époque. Ce devait être pendant l'été vingt-huit, un peu plus d'un an avant le krach. Le marché était florissant. Tout le monde, absolument *tout le monde* faisait son beurre en écoutant Eddie Cantor chanter *Making Whoopie* à la radio. Mon oncle disait que ce fut l'année où même les schlemiels se sentirent pousser des ailes. Jusqu'à papa qui fut contaminé par la fièvre ambiante et investit de l'argent sur les conseils d'Oncle Schmuel. Il acheta des RCA à quatre-vingt-cinq dollars. Quand ses actions furent cotées cent dollars, il devint nerveux. Pauvre papa ! Il n'était pas exactement un schlemiel, certainement pas un schlimazel, mais peut-être un peu nebbish. Allons bon, qu'est-ce qui t'arrive ?

— Excusez-moi, dis-je, mais qu'est-ce qu'un slm... ?

— On prononce *schlem-*, petit, schlemiel. Disons qu'un schlemiel est le type qui renverse la soupe chaude sur le veston du schlimazel, et que le nebbish est le gars qui s'excuse et doit essuyer ledit veston. C'est du moins la définition classique. Mon oncle disait qu'un schlimazel est un schlemiel qui n'a pas entendu les nouvelles. Je suis peut-être un schlemiel, petit, mais pas un schlimazel. Voilà ce que moi, je dis. Et tu peux me croire sur parole.

« Ses RCA, papa les a vendues à cent cinq en ayant le sentiment d'être un millionnaire. Un an après, elles avaient grimpé à quatre cent vingt ! Tu te rends compte, petit, *quatre cent vingt !* C'était l'âge d'or. Cet après-midi-là, alors qu'il serrait la main de mon oncle et offrait généreusement ses cigares, je parie que le vieux Livermore commençait à lâcher du lest, à larguer quelques actions par-ci par-là. Il fut probablement l'un des seuls types qui ne perdit pas sa chemise et sa cravate lors du Jeudi Noir (le Jeudi Schwarz, comme disait mon oncle). Bon Dieu, il a même profité de l'effondrement des cours. D'ailleurs, on ne lui a jamais pardonné d'avoir gagné du fric sur le dos des autres. Quoi qu'il en soit, ce n'est pas Livermore qui a causé leur ruine. Ces trous de cul en sont eux-mêmes responsables. Il a joué le jeu, et l'a mieux joué que les autres. Il était peut-être Wasp, mais l'Oncle Schmuel disait toujours qu'il était juif au fond de son cœur. Le seul type qui ait jamais gagné un million de dollars en misant sur le désespoir d'autrui. Merde, petit, encore plus juif que les Juifs. Le Grand Ours ! Tu parles d'une constellation ! Si je devais choisir un héros à la Bourse — Ahasvérus mis à part —, il serait celui-là.

« Cette première rencontre avec Oncle Schmuel dans la grande salle de la Bourse fut pour moi une révélation. Ce type était un mensch. Bien sûr, j'étais encore sous la coupe d'Herschel, mais la graine était semée.

« Assez bizarrement, ma bar mitzvah elle-même marque le passage crucial entre la Phase Un et la Phase Deux, autrement dit : de la Piétié juive à la Fièvre d'Ahasvérus. Aussi étrange que cela puisse paraître, à dater de ce jour, je m'éloignai de Herschel pour entrer toujours davantage dans l'orbite de mon oncle. Ce ne fut pas la cérémonie elle-même qui provoqua ce changement. Elle fut aussi émouvante, solennelle et grandiose que je l'avais espéré. Je parle de la fête qui suivit.

« Mon père et celui de Moishe Lipshitz mirent leur argent en commun pour louer une salle de danse pendant l'après-midi et engager un orchestre de ménestrels locaux dirigés par Freddie "Freeloader" Epstein, qui jouait du Wurlitzer et assumait les fonctions d'animateur du quartier. Voyons, en plus de l'organiste, il y avait un type à l'accordéon, un autre au glockenspiel, un virtuose neurasthénique du violon, qui, peina pendant tout l'après-midi et joua même les polkas avec un vibrato mélancolique. Il y avait une clarinette, un type avec un tambour sur un podium, qui brisa une de ses baguettes et joua ensuite avec une seule baguette et un balai. Ouais, un vrai orchestre de bric et de broc, mais tous les musiciens étaient juifs et jouaient donc avec émotion à défaut d'harmoniser leur partition avec celles de leurs voisins. Bref, leur enthousiasme compensait largement leur manque de métier. La douzaine de bouteilles de cidre que papa avait laissées fermenter au grenier contribua d'ailleurs à réchauffer l'atmosphère. Ce fut une fête tout ce qu'il y a de plus correct. Rien de spectaculaire, une réunion parfaitement respectable.

« Mais avec l'arrivée de l'Oncle Schmuel, les choses prirent une autre tournure : le moteur s'emballa, le passé sombra dans la banalité. "Oy vay !" s'écrie alors ma mère. Je la regarde, elle tient sa mâchoire comme si elle souffre d'une rage de dents, ses yeux écarquillés sont tournés vers la porte. Mon regard suit le sien, et *ecce homo* ! Ahasvérus fait son entrée comme une sorte de Gatsby juif, de Messie mondain ! Je te jure, petit, tu n'as jamais vu pareille chutzpah. Rappelle-toi, nous sommes en 1928. Ahasvérus est dans la fleur de l'âge, il a cinquante-cinq ans, et toujours sa prestance militaire, les épaules larges et la taille fine. Son costume est impeccable, la vraie classe. Il a rejeté ses cheveux gominés en arrière. On dirait Valentino dans le *Le Sheik*. A son bras, la shiksa de rigueur. Sauf qu'aujourd'hui c'est une minette dans le vent — mise en plis, collier de perles, chaussettes, jupe courte, fume-cigarette, tube de rouge à lèvres — la panoplie au grand complet. Toutes les matrones juives qui prospèrent dans la baleine de corset sont à deux doigts d'en perdre leur dentier. Un musicien joue une fausse note, la musique sombre progressivement dans l'inanité. Oncle Schmuel avance en se pavanant et bombe le torse. A son bras sa shiksa trottine en roulant des hanches ; elle se penche vers son oreille pour chuchoter quelque chose, éclate d'un rire nerveux haut perché sans remarquer, ou feignant de ne pas remarquer que tout le monde a les yeux rivés sur elle. Schmuel s'arrête au milieu de la piste de danse pour regarder à droite et à gauche avec un large sourire, puis il sort un cigare et l'allume. "Hoy, Moe ! appelle-t-il en levant légèrement la tête. Fiens par ici." Papa, avec une expression de timidité étonnée, lâche la main de ma mère, laquelle est sur le point de glisser de sa chaise, et s'exécute.

« "Je feux te présenter Delores, dit-il avec son accent yiddish à couper au couteau, ma fiancée jazz. Le drésor dans zon écrin de sadin. *Voilà mon frère, chérie*.*"

« "Grrrand fou, va ! couine la minette. Toi et ton flan-céééé." Elle tend à papa la main au fume-cigarette (qui, soit dit en passant, ne contient aucune cigarette), puis exécute machinalement une petite révérence.

« Je vois ma mère se mordre le poing. "Oy gevalt ! gémit-elle. Dire que j'aurai vécu pour voir ça !"

« A cet instant précis, Freddie Epstein fait preuve d'une remarquable présence d'esprit et entonne les premières mesures de *Making Whoopie* sur son Wurlitzer ; l'orchestre enchaîne courageusement.

« "Oh yeah ! s'écrie Delores, qui claque aussitôt des doigts. Viens Schmooey, dit-elle en tirant sur son bras. Je veux t'apprendre le Black Bottom."

« "Danse donc avec le gamin, dit-il en la poussant vers moi. Fiens, Moe. Che feux te mondrer quelque chose. *Il y a une surprise en bas.*" Il fait claquer ses doigts. "*Vite, vite** !"

« Ils se dirigent vers la porte et la shiksa me prend par la main. "Viens, mon biquet", susurre-t-elle avec un petit sourire espiègle. J'ai une boule dans la gorge et une autre dans ma poche de pantalon, mais Dieu merci les Ritals du marché aux poissons (où je travaille — une brillante idée de mon père) m'ont appris une demi-douzaine de pas, assez pour m'en tirer en cas d'urgence. Me voilà donc en train de me trémousser avec cette Lulu le jour de ma bar mitzvah. J'essaie de ne pas regarder, mais c'est plus fort

---

* En français dans le texte.

que moi : oui, elle ne porte vraiment rien en dessous. Je veux dire, je les vois tressauter, les loches de Lulu et tout le tintouin ! J'attrape presque un torticolis à essayer de suivre leur rythme ! Elle sait parfaitement que je les dévore des yeux, et ça la fait glousser. Oh, doux Jésus ! Elle a aussi ce long collier de perles, et chaque fois que son buste pivote, il met les perles sur orbite, lesquelles me giflent au passage. Alors Delores se défonce pour de bon ; sa jupe remonte et j'aperçois le slip qu'elle porte en dessous, le petit truc mousseux qui moule son cul, et puis ses cuisses dénudées jusqu'aux genoux !

« Quand elle me dit : "Tu t'en tires bien", je deviens un derviche, je la fais tourbillonner à toute vitesse, elle se cambre en arrière en me lançant au visage des éclats de rire nerveux, elle s'abandonne à mon rythme, me provoque à accélérer encore. Petit, je comprends brusquement le sens profond de la bar mitzvah. Du fin fond de mon cœur, je bénis Oncle Schmuel, désormais Ahasvérus à jamais, qui m'a offert ce cadeau.

« La suite est quasiment incroyable ! La chanson s'achève. Je reste planté devant ma Lulu, cramoisi et hors d'haleine. La shiksa aussi est un peu essoufflée. Elle est excitée, elle a le visage en feu. Perdant soudain son aplomb, elle cherche anxieusement Oncle Schmuel des yeux.

« Quand il arrive, elle court se réfugier dans ses bras.

« "Alors, il sait danser ?" lui demande-t-il.

« Elle glousse de plaisir et m'adresse son sourire espiègle. "C'est un bon, Schmooey, dit-elle, il danse le Black Bottom comme un pro. D'ailleurs, il pourrait t'apprendre une chose ou deux."

« "Ah, si ch'avais sa jeunesse !" dit-il. Puis il me lance un clin d'œil avec un geste du menton vers Delores. "Qu'en dis-tu, fiston, ça te plaît ?"

« Je ne sais plus où me mettre. Il sort un cigare de sa poche de poitrine et me l'offre en chuchotant à mon oreille : "Quel tuchis, Aaron ! *Quel cul** ! Tu la feux, elle est à doi."

« Petit, je frise la crise cardiaque. Par bonheur, il n'est pas indispensable de la violer sur-le-champ. Un coup de cymbales et un roulement de tambour annoncent la suite des festivités. Oncle Schmuel frappe dans ses mains, la porte s'ouvre violemment, et une demi-douzaine de petits shvarzers en livrée entrent dans la salle en portant... Dieu de Dieu, ce qu'ils portent ! Deux douzaines de bouteilles de pétillant, le vrai de vrai, importé directement de France et sans étiquettes ! Des quantités similaires de gin de première bourre, rien à voir avec ces saletés industrielles frelatées. Cela pour les invités ordinaires. Pour la famille — soit lui-même et papa —, un demi-gallon d'authentique scotch acheté au prix fort à la flotte du rhum mouillée à trente milles au large des côtes, et distribué par les vedettes rapides de la Cosa Nostra. Inutile de te dire que l'Oncle d'Amérique a prévu tous les accessoires indispensables. Un gros nègre luisant arrive de la rue, chargé de deux blocs de glace bleutée de vingt-cinq kilos, sans la moindre paille ni bulle, qu'il tient avec des tenailles, un dans chaque main ; il titube comme un type constipé, la sueur dégouline sur son visage, les blocs de glace transpirent aussi, lisses comme du verre. Il les dépose dans une grande bassine émaillée

---

* En français dans le texte.

apportée pour l'occasion ; essuie son front avec son avant-bras, pousse un énorme soupir, puis sort un pic à glace de sa poche arrière et martèle doucement le bloc avec un maillet en bois jusqu'à ce qu'une minuscule fissure blanche apparaisse dans la masse bleue sous la pointe d'acier. Il recommence trois ou quatre fois l'opération dans le même plan, puis assène un léger coup de maillet, et brusquement le glacier se fend parfaitement en deux ! Ah, petit, un événement banal, rien d'extraordinaire vraiment. En temps ordinaire, je n'aurais rien remarqué, mais aujourd'hui cela me paraît miraculeux. Je ressens le besoin d'applaudir. Nous offrons au nègre une longue ovation et un généreux pourboire !

« L'alcool commence à couler à flots, puis arrivent les cadeaux ! Quelques semaines auparavant, papa m'a pris à part pour me dire : "Oncle Schmuel voudrait t'offrir quelque chose de spécial. Qu'en dis-tu ?" Tu sais ce que j'ai répondu, petit ? L'édition complète du Talmud en soixante-trois volumes ! "Euh, tu n'as pas une autre idée ?" me demande mon père. Mais non, je m'obstine, lui dis que j'ai bien réfléchi, que je n'en démordrai pas : le Talmud en soixante-trois volumes ! Papa hausse les épaules, me dit qu'il va voir ce qu'il peut faire. Et comment crois-tu qu'Ahasvérus interpole ma requête ? Qu'apporte-t-il au freluquet pour sa bar mitzvah ?

« Après nous avoir laissé le temps de nous rafraîchir le gosier au champagne (lui-même se versant de larges rasades de scotch), Schmuel demande à l'orchestre de s'interrompre, puis sort tranquillement quelque chose de sa poche. "Donne-moi ta main, Aaron", dit-il, le regard un peu embué en prévision de ma surprise. Je m'exécute et il me glisse quelque chose au doigt. Je me demande ce que c'est, un diamant ? Non, trop léger. Je l'approche de mes yeux : c'est vert, en papier, comme les petites bagues que nous fabriquons à l'école avec des billets d'un dollar, pliés et repliés pour que le chiffre apparaisse à la place du sceau. Oncle Schmuel se moquerait-il de moi ? Je regarde de plus près. Après le un, il y a un zéro... et un autre... et un autre... un billet de mille dollars ! J'en reste pantois. Pour moi, un billet de cinq dollars est synonyme de richesse ; un billet de dix, une fortune colossale ; un billet de cent, une dangereuse utopie, un délire vertigineux qui tient du mythe et de la ploutocratie ; mais un billet de mille ! *Mille dollars !* Petit, ce genre de miracle n'existait qu'au Monopoly ! Je jette mes bras autour de son cou. "Paie-toi ton Talmut chi tu feux, Aaron, dit-il en reniflant, lui-même un peu dépassé par sa propre générosité. Che n'ai pas eu le cœur de te l'offrir moi-même. Pas le chour de ta bar mitzvah !" Et il m'embrasse sur les lèvres...

« Yo ! s'écrie Kahn à l'adresse du serveur. Apporte-nous une autre tournée de la même chose !

« Après cela, Oncle Schmuel s'est enivré et a entonné l'hymne national polonais avec papa. Ahasvérus réclame une polonaise et tend le bras vers ma mère (originaire d'Ukraine). "Enlève tes sales pattes de là, espèce de porc !" couine-t-elle en appelant mon père à la rescousse. Mais l'orchestre a déjà entamé une polka ! La fête dégénère alors en beuverie. La shiksa, maintenant totalement écœurée par la frénésie environnante, prend une pose plus typique de son rôle ; elle s'appuie contre le mur, croise les bras sur sa poitrine comme pour en interdire l'accès et toise Ahasvérus comme Michel dut toiser David quand il se dévêtit pour danser devant l'Arche d'Alliance, en short, ou plutôt en pagne — peu importe — mais "le méprisant du fond du cœur". Brusquement, je ne la désire plus. Je déborde d'amour et de pitié pour mon oncle. Je le cherche et le trouve penché au-dessus d'une gamine de mon âge, dont la mère terrifiée se dresse derrière sa progéniture et serre ses épaules avec un sauvage instinct maternel.

« "Il a une schlong longue comme ça", murmure mon oncle à la gamine, en parlant de moi, je présume. Du plat de la main, il se tranche le coude. "Ne me demande surtout pas comment je l'ai appris. Je le sais, voilà tout. C'est de famille, tu comprends ? Ne rate pas une occasion pareille !" Pour Ida, c'est la goutte d'eau qui fait déborder le vase. Furieuse, elle me traîne jusqu'à la porte en me tenant par l'oreille et m'interdit formellement de fréquenter Ahasvérus. Naturellement, cette prohibition ("p" minuscule), comme la majuscule, ne fit qu'accroître les délices de la transgression. Pour Ahasvérus et moi, ce n'était qu'un début. La salle tanguait lentement autour de moi, tournoyait comme un manège, alors qu'Ida me traînait à travers la piste de danse vers la sortie. La dernière chose que je vis fut Herschel Liebowicz debout dans l'encadrement de la porte, son talith plié dans une main, et dans l'autre mon exemplaire de la Torah, que j'avais complètement oublié. Il me le tend avec un beau sourire grave, puis lève la main pour me dire au revoir. Son regard est très triste, comme s'il comprenait que c'est la fin. Oh, nous nous sommes revus. J'ai assisté à quelques cours d'hébreu. Mais notre séparation symbolique eut lieu ce jour-là. Une gravitation plus puissante m'entraînait loin de lui, et il le savait. Quand nous arrivâmes dans la rue, j'avais les larmes aux yeux. Sans dire un mot, ma mère me ramena à la maison, où elle prit la peine de réchauffer un bol de bouillon de poule qu'elle m'obligea à boire avant de m'expédier au lit à six heures du soir — le jeune bar mitzvah était devenu un homme. »

« Après cela et pendant au moins un an, Ahasvérus et moi fûmes comme cul et chemise. Tout le restant de l'été, chaque après-midi à trois heures quand j'avais terminé mon travail au marché aux poissons, je courais à la Bourse et restais avec Oncle Schmuel jusqu'à la fin de la séance. Je baignais dans l'euphorie la plus totale. Quand je foulais le sol du parquet, je croyais avoir franchi un cercle magique et vivre dans un monde enchanté. Tous les courtiers paraissaient ivres de prospérité, gonflés comme des tiques, peut-être vaguement obscènes. Je tenais pour acquis qu'il en avait toujours été ainsi, que les choses ne changeraient jamais, dans les siècles des siècles. Vraiment, petit, c'était l'Age d'Or. Le marché n'avait jamais été aussi florissant, et ne le redeviendrait jamais. L'euphorie régnait partout. Quand j'y repense aujourd'hui, ma mémoire évoque une grande salle baignée d'une lumière surnaturelle. Je suppose que cela m'a marqué de façon indélébile et inconsciente. Car à l'époque, c'était à peine davantage qu'un décor, l'arrière-fond musical sur lequel Ahasvérus, mon joueur de flûte de Hamelin, modulait son solo. J'appris bien sûr à lire les annonces du tableau, à gérer quelques valeurs — les RCA de mon père, par exemple — mais ce fut plus pour me gagner les faveurs et l'approbation d'Ahasvérus que par un authentique intérêt de ma part. Les chiffres sont trop abstraits pour émouvoir un enfant de cet âge. Et puis je n'avais rien investi de ma poche. » Il m'adressa un regard lourd de sous-entendus. « Je n'avais pas contracté la maladie. Comme je l'ai dit, cela dura environ un an, jusqu'à la chute, ou le krach, appelle ça comme tu veux. Pendant cette période, à mon insu et à celui de ma mère, Ahasvérus proposa à papa d'ouvrir un compte pour financer mes études. Malgré tous ses défauts, papa avait sa fierté. Il refusa d'abord d'en entendre parler. Mais Schmuel lui demanda un jour pourquoi lui-même devrait se priver de ce plaisir. Dans sa position, cet argent ne lui coûterait aucun sacrifice. Qu'allait-il faire de toute sa fortune, la léguer au gouvernement après sa mort ? Il tenait à l'investir dans une cause utile. Et j'étais presque devenu son fils, ajouta-t-il.

« Papa finit par céder. A l'automne suivant, on m'inscrivit au Mont-Nebo, une école privée huppée de Manhattan pour Juifs fortunés, surtout des rejetons de familles allemandes émigrées en Amérique avant la Guerre civile. Ils regardaient de haut les Ashkénazes qui, comme mes parents, comme moi, venaient d'Europe centrale ou d'Europe de l'Est, et étaient arrivés plus tard, vers le début du siècle. Pour eux, j'étais un "youpin". » Kahn eut un rire amer. « Eh oui, petit. Mon séjour au Mont-Nebo m'a appris une ou deux choses sur la discrimination, en particulier ceci : les antisémites les plus virulents sont les Juifs eux-mêmes. Mais ce n'est pas moi qui leur jetterais la première pierre. Car, pour dire la vérité, je me mis à adopter leurs attitudes. Au Mont-Nebo, je me joignis de mon propre chef à l'élite libérale juive, à l'aristocratie des assimilés — bref, je devins un shegetz. Ce fut évidemment un processus graduel, je mis un certain temps à réussir cette turpitude. D'ailleurs, ce ne fut qu'à Columbia que je parachevai mon œuvre. Mais j'avais déjà entamé ma métamorphose en assimmulatto, un simulacre, un simulateur, une simulation — bref, en Jessica. L'ironie burlesque de l'affaire étant, bien sûr, que mon oncle, l'Ashkénaze fou, finançait toute l'opération. Son or servait à la mirifique transmutation du petit Aaron en oie blanche. Et avec quel résultat ? Je devins aussi snob que la shiksa, je méprisai Schmuel en mon for intérieur. Je jouais Jessica avec son Shylock, je crachais sur son argent vulgaire et ses façons vulgaires. Je suis pourtant à moitié excusable, car je n'ai jamais su qu'Ahasvérus payait la note, et quand je l'appris ce fut trop tard pour le remercier. Mais soyons honnêtes : je me demande si j'aurais réagi différemment si je l'avais su.

« Mon éducation consista en un lent et subtil éloignement de Schmuel au profit du vaste courant de la culture américaine (telle que je la percevais), un mouvement primaire, si tu veux. Cette distance eut des causes plus immédiates, tel le krach de 29. L'été était terminé ; j'avais interrompu mes pèlerinages à Wall Street, chaque après-midi. J'étais à l'école le jour où c'est arrivé — le 24 octobre, le Jeudi Noir. Papa m'a dit qu'il avait toujours ignoré combien Schmuel avait perdu, d'abord parce qu'il n'avait jamais su combien il avait possédé. Mais, petit, l'épreuve se grava sur son visage. Une année auparavant, pendant l'été enchanté de 28, il avait (je suppute) cinquante-cinq ans et paraissait dix ans de moins. A l'été 1930, on aurait dit un poivrot de soixante-dix ans. Je ne blague pas. Cette fois-là, Ahasvérus ne retomba pas sur ses pieds. Une fois ou deux, pendant les congés scolaires, je suis allé le voir à la Bourse comme au bon vieux temps. Le changement me stupéfia — chez l'homme, dans le lieu. On eût dit un magasin de pompes funèbres où Ahasvérus aurait joué le rôle du cadavre. Il était fébrile, oubliait souvent de se raser, son haleine empestait presque toujours l'alcool. J'en sortis déprimé. Je le fréquentai de moins en moins. Et un beau jour, papa m'annonce qu'il est à l'hôpital. Je lui demande si je peux aller le voir, il me dit que non. Je ne vois donc pas Oncle Schmuel pendant presque un an. Chaque fois que j'interroge papa sur sa maladie, mon père est évasif. "Épuisement", dit-il. Je n'ai jamais appris la vérité, mais je crois qu'il a eu une dépression nerveuse.

« Pourtant, Ahasvérus avait du ressort. Mais il avait sans doute utilisé huit de ses neuf vies. Quand les affaires reprirent en 34, il était de retour dans la grande salle, où il se démenait comme le beau diable qu'il avait toujours été. Je suis sûr qu'il fit des pieds et des mains pour remonter la pente, mais, vois-tu, il y avait quelque chose de cassé en lui. Il ne retrouva jamais complètement sa verve d'antan, et pas davantage sa fortune. Oh, il redevint modérément riche, mais jamais comme au bon vieux temps.

« La distance qui nous séparait s'était considérablement agrandie. J'étais en première année à Columbia, et je considérais l'époque où j'emballais du poisson avant de m'accrocher aux basques financières d'Ahasvérus avec une condescendance désenchantée, comme "un épisode de ma jeunesse". Je me souvenais de lui avec plaisir, mais sa stature s'était ratatinée dans mon esprit. Pour moi, jeune intellectuel juif cultivé promis à une brillante carrière universitaire, il devint de plus en plus un atavisme incongru, l'incarnation vulgaire et légèrement comique du vieux boursicoteur, un personnage totalement déplacé aux temps modernes. Certes, nous restions en contact. Il me téléphonait parfois pour me proposer de déjeuner avec lui, et si je n'avais rien de mieux à faire — dissertations à rédiger, filles à draguer —, j'acceptais. Mais l'ancienne magie avait disparu. Jadis, il avait toujours été celui qui donnait, et moi le bénéficiaire de sa générosité. Maintenant, il était évident qu'il désirait quelque chose de moi. J'étais pour lui le talisman émotionnel avec lequel il essayait pathétiquement de recréer son ancienne personnalité. Il voulait guérir sa fierté blessée au contact de l'adoration que je lui avais autrefois si libéralement dispensée. Et parce qu'il en avait désespérément besoin, je ne pouvais la lui donner. Ces déjeuners étaient tristes pour lui comme pour moi. Ils me firent douter de ma mémoire. Je me convainquis que mes souvenirs l'avaient démesurément grandi, si bien que je sombrai dans l'excès inverse et rapetissai ses paroles et ses actes. Ainsi, d'un commun accord, nous espaçâmes nos déjeuners. Je n'oublierai jamais ce qu'il m'a dit la dernière fois que nous nous sommes retrouvés : "Je suis peut-être un schlemiel, Aaron, mais je ne suis pas un schlimazel." La portée de cettre phrase ne me frappa que beaucoup plus tard. Peut-être ne voulais-je pas comprendre.

« Ahasvérus est mort deux ans plus tard. *Thanksgiving* 1941. J'étais en année de licence. Il était descendu en Floride avec mes parents. Deux semaines de soleil et de distractions dans la fabuleuse Miami. Papa me téléphone pour m'annoncer qu'il vient d'avoir une attaque. Écoute bien, petit. Au lit ! Mais ne va pas imaginer qu'il dormait... Oui, la femme est une tapineuse, pas exactement un parangon de délicatesse. Elle déclare à papa qu'elle a été flattée par l'évanouissement de son client. Elle croit qu'il jouit, mais il se met à virer au bleu. Alors elle hurle, et le privé du boxon crochète la serrure. "Pour un vieux, c'était un amant merveilleux", renchérit la catin en guise d'oraison funèbre. Sincères souvenirs. Papa en a pleuré. Mais au moment du coup de téléphone, Ahasvérus n'a pas encore passé l'arme à gauche. Le médecin a pourtant lâché le morceau : le cas est désespéré. Pourtant, avec Ahasvérus, qui sait ? Il a les yeux ouverts, un peu vitreux, mais ouverts, me dit papa. On n'est pas sûr qu'il reconnaisse les gens, ni même qu'il soit conscient. Mais nous avons pensé que tu voudrais peut-être venir."

« Je suis à mille milles de Miami. La fin du semestre approche. Et ce n'est pas n'importe quel semestre. Je louche vers l'énorme pile de bouquins que je dois potasser avant mes oraux, qui ont lieu dans dix jours. Le moment ne saurait être plus mal choisi. "Papa, je dis, s'il ne vous reconnaît même pas..."

« "Nous n'en sommes pas sûrs", objecte-t-il aussitôt.

« "Oh la la, je fais, quelle panade."

« "Calme-toi, Aaron, dit-il. Nous ne voulons pas t'influencer. C'est à toi de décider."

« Je prends ma décision : je reste à New York (ça m'a vraiment fendu le cœur).

« Le lendemain de mon examen — que je réussis, non pas exactement haut la main, mais pas non plus ras du cul, si tu vois ce que je veux dire —, je reçois un télégramme : Ahasvérus est mort. Je bourre une valise et saute dans un taxi qui m'emmène à l'aéroport. Je prends l'avion pour la première fois de ma vie. Un DC 3 d'*Eastern Airlines*. Avec les escales et tout le bordel, il met la journée et la moitié de la nuit à rejoindre Miami. Papa est bon à ramasser à la petite cuiller, Sonny. Pleure toutes les larmes de son corps. Nous restons ensemble dans la chambre d'hôtel, à boire du scotch jusqu'au matin. Il me raconte toute la schmeer — l'argent, le compte ouvert pour financer mon éducation, tout. J'en suis malade. Malade comme un chien. Je me sens écrasé de culpabilité, anéanti jusqu'à la fin de mes jours. Pour couronner le tout, papa me raconte que Schmuel a retrouvé sa lucidité juste avant la fin et qu'il m'a réclamé. Le vieux aurait peut-être pu m'épargner ça, tu ne trouves pas ? Mais non, fallait qu'il m'enfonce carrément ! Qu'il me foute dans la mouise et m'écrase du talon ! Merde alors ! » s'écria Kahn méchamment, et du bras il envoya valser son verre par terre. « Apporte-m'en un autre », ordonna-t-il au serveur.

« Et voilà, petit. New York City, quelques jours plus tard. La lecture du testament. Le compte en banque est à sec. Je ne peux plus retourner en fac. Même papa dit qu'il l'ignorait. Tout a disparu. Tout, sauf le fauteuil. Le putain de fauteuil. Qu'Ahasvérus, comme de bien entendu, me lègue. Et le comble — en stipulant qu'il ne pourra pas être vendu avant mon trentième anniversaire. Tu te rends compte ? Il a même payé ses créances. Sacré Ahasvérus !

« Petit, pendant une bonne semaine, je n'ai plus été moi-même. Je suis resté cloîtré dans cet appartement de la cent quinzième rue à piquer des crises, lancer des objets contre les murs, pleurer comme un veau et parfois dormir quinze heures d'affilée. La rage, le remords, l'apitoiement, la culpabilité — je passais de l'un à l'autre. Et ils me sont passés dessus. Je buvais du whisky, prenais des douches froides, buvais du café noir, mangeais des bonbons, par paquets entiers, par caisses ! Quand je retrouvais ma lucidité, j'essayais de décider quoi faire de ma vie. Le suicide me semblait la seule alternative rationnelle pour mettre fin à ma souffrance. Mais que veux-tu, je suis trop irrationnel pour passer à l'acte. Et puis je ne supporte pas la souffrance. » Il haussa les épaules en m'adressant un sourire d'excuse. « Figure-toi que le destin vole alors à mon secours. 7 décembre 1941, les Japonais bombardent Pearl Harbor. Bah, je n'ai rien à perdre, je m'engage donc dans l'armée et coupe les ponts derrière moi. De toute façon, je n'y serais pas plus mal qu'ailleurs. Je remplis donc mes formulaires, d'accord ? et passe la visite médicale. Devine quoi ? Réformé pour cause de pieds plats. Moi qui m'inquiétais seulement de mon poids ! C'est quand même humiliant !

« Alors, pour ne pas prolonger un suspens intolérable, disons que Kahn passe les quatre années suivantes à manger des bonbons dès qu'il en a l'occasion, ce qui n'est pas si fréquent, et à calculer des statistiques de production pour le BIG — Bureau d'Information de la Guerre, pour ton information, petit — ce qui, soit dit en passant, explique que je ne t'aie pas accompagné à la conférence d'E. Powers sur la Valeur Intrinsèque : je ne supporte plus ce genre de baratin. La peur du fusil (la peur du beurre, aussi). J'ai accumulé assez de données fondamentales pour le restant de mes jours. Et pour d'innombrables vies ultérieures. Évidemment, tous les trente-six du mois, à cause de ma "formation littéraire", on me laissait rédiger un communiqué de presse pour les beaux yeux d'Elmer — Davis, je veux dire. Bref, je me la coulais douce. J'avais tout le temps de réfléchir. Et plus de temps encore pour ne pas réfléchir. Quand je me suis un peu calmé, j'ai pensé que je reprendrais le collier pour faire un doctorat après la guerre. J'éprouvais parfois quelques doutes quand je me rappelais ma performance aux oraux ; je me demandais si j'avais vraiment pour vocation d'ébaubir la communauté académique. Mais c'étaient seulement des aberrations passagères. A l'époque, l'université était mon foyer. Qu'aurais-je pu faire d'autre ? Ah, ah, ah ! Mais n'anticipons pas !

« Bon, nous finissons par lâcher le petit joujou d'Oppenheimer sur les Japonais, lesquels commencent à piger le tableau. Faut pas déconner avec Bwana. Dieu est avec lui. Jésus Marie ! Nous roulons donc les tapis du BIG, fermons les portes à clef, et chacun rentre chez soi, retour au monde réel. Quant à moi, je me retrouve sur le pavé, juvénile épave juive qui doit encore subir pendant deux ans le diktat d'Ahasvérus avant de pouvoir vendre son sacré fauteuil. Je demande à mon vieux s'il peut payer mon inscription en fac, il me répond qu'il n'a pas les moyens. "Et puis, ajoute-t-il, tu as vingt-huit ans. Il serait temps que tu penses à rentabiliser tes études. Trouve-toi un boulot pendant deux ans. Économise. Si, après ça, tu veux toujours retourner en fac, libre à toi." Que répondre à ça, petit ?

Je trouve un emploi dans une agence de publicité : je pisse de la copie pour Pepsi-Cola et autres causes exaltantes. Mes anciens copains de Columbia sont atterrés et *tout à fait* compatissants. En fait, ça ne va pas trop mal. Kahn n'a pas lieu de se plaindre. Il se pique même de poésie. Ah, petit, quelle déchéance allait être la mienne !

« Les deux années fatidiques s'écoulent donc. Je n'ai pas mis les pieds en fac depuis six ans. Je suis devenu un peu suffisant, j'ai pris de l'embonpoint. Je suis rouillé. Écoute, petit. Voilà le plus triste. J'ai mes deux ans d'économies, d'accord ? Assez de fric pour tenir jusqu'à la vente du fauteuil, laquelle doit me permettre de passer mon doctorat sans trop de soucis d'argent. Voire confortablement. Comme un pacha, même ! Devine ce que je fais de mon pécule, petit ? Je l'investis en Bourse. Pepsi-Cola. Exactement. J'avais pissé tellement de copie pour cette boîte que j'ai fini par me vendre à elle. Ne me demande surtout pas comment j'ai pu en arriver là, je l'ignore toujours. Ç'a été plus fort que moi, je suppose.

« Que dire de la suite ? » Il secoua la tête. « Le marché est la dernière frontière, un monde sauvage créé par la civilisation. Dans ce pays, c'est le dernier endroit où la lutte pour la survie se poursuit comme à l'époque mésozoïque. Tous les grands prédateurs se baladent encore en liberté, et usent librement de leurs privilèges de vénerie et de meurtre. Comprends bien, petit, c'est ainsi que je voyais Ahasvérus. Et c'est ainsi que je me vois. L'appel du monde sauvage. Et le négociant au parquet est le roi de la jungle de notre univers, l'incarnation la plus pure de ce type. Nous sommes pourtant une espèce menacée. A coups d'ordonnances et de décrets, on essaie de nous éliminer. Malgré toutes leurs parlotes sur la libre entreprise, l'intérêt personnel que nous défendons est de nature si pure et si extrême que la plupart des hommes ou même des hommes d'affaires ne peuvent envisager froidement notre position sans sourciller. C'est pourtant le test ultime du système de la libre entreprise, la *reductio*, non pas *ad absurdum*, mais *ad essentiam*, sans laquelle tout l'édifice s'écroule.

« Ce que je t'ai dit ce soir te prouve sans doute que je n'ai jamais pu me réconcilier totalement avec ce rôle. C'est pourtant une activité à laquelle j'aspire, une partie de moi-même. Mais une autre aspiration, aussi intense et contradictoire, me pousse dans la direction diamétralement opposée. Alors ? Intellectuel ou cochon de capitaliste ? » Il haussa les épaules. « Je crains parfois que la guerre qui les oppose ne m'empêche de vraiment devenir l'un ou l'autre. Voilà ce que j'admirais — non, adorais — chez des hommes comme mon oncle ou Jessie Livermore : la rage brûlait en eux à l'état pur. Une violence sauvage immaculée. Toutes considérations morales mises à part, petit, c'est un spectacle inoubliable à voir, un organisme si totalement en harmonie avec lui-même, si unique et dénué de culpabilité. Mon ambivalence est peut-être un stade ultérieur de l'évolution, qui peut en juger ? Je sais seulement que cette chose que l'intellect rejette peut t'amener en un lieu où l'intellect ne va jamais, où toutes les discussions froides et pondérées ressemblent à un radotage pédant. En ce lieu, toutes les règles sont transgressées. La rationalité ressemble à la mécanique de Newton : idéale pour décrire le monde ordinaire, mais confronte-la aux extrêmes, aux univers infiniment grand ou infiniment petit, et elle vole en éclats ; ce qui prouve d'ailleurs son caractère globalement spécieux. Je songe parfois que toute moralité, toute loi est une simple mécanique newtonienne contredite par la relativité des états modifiés de la conscience.

— L'extase du combat, murmurai-je, brusquement ramené en arrière par les spéculations de Kahn.

— C'est ça, petit, dit-il, comme s'il comprenait. Pour le fric. »

Nous restâmes un instant silencieux, tous les deux caressant nos verres, tous deux ivres morts mais totalement lucides. De temps à autre, Kahn ou moi soupirions. Qu'y avait-il à ajouter ?

Il leva enfin les yeux. « Et voilà, petit, toute la megillah. Tout est vrai, jusqu'au moindre mot. » Il grimaça un sourire. « ... au moins un mot sur deux. Alors, dis quelque chose. Quel est ton verdict ?

— Je ne sais que dire, répondis-je. Je suis épuisé. »

Kahn soupira. « Je te pardonne, petit. C'est une sacrée dose à assimiler en une seule séance. Pour ma part, cependant, la version non expurgée de la Vie de Kahn se réduit à un unique jugement moral, succinct et substantiel, une sorte de conception du monde comparable à celles des Fondamentalistes et des Techniciens, la *Weltanschauung* de Kahn : "Je suis peut-être un schlemiel, mais je ne suis pas un schlimazel." Est-ce trop demander ? » Cette fois, je sentis que sa question n'était pas purement rhétorique.

Je secouai la tête. « Je ne crois pas. »

Il soupira. « Merci, petit. J'apprécie. J'aurais peut-être dû annoncer la couleur dès le début, et ainsi nous épargner les rigueurs de l'histoire ? »

Nous rîmes tous les deux.

« Dernier verre ! » s'écria le serveur.

Mais nous avions assez bu — plus qu'assez. Quand nous poussâmes la porte du bar pour sortir dans la rue, nous nous figeâmes, le souffle coupé. L'aube new-yorkaise était rouge sang, démente, pleine d'une beauté funèbre qui évoquait des lendemains de guerre ou de famine, une grande cité incendiée à l'est, consumée par l'holocauste. Des volutes de vapeur opalescente s'élevaient des caniveaux dans l'air humide, comme pour signaler une récente tuerie. Il y avait aussi de larges flaques d'eau sur les trottoirs, que l'aube faisait rosir comme du sang dilué. Quand j'avançai sous la conflagration blafarde du ciel, mon regard fut attiré par la succession des feux de croisement de la quatre-vingt-sixième rue, nodules discrets de lumière irréelle, tels des rubis dans un brasier, qui luisaient sans dégager de chaleur ; et tandis que je les regardais en retenant mon souffle, l'un après l'autre ils passèrent au vert.

11

J'ouvris les yeux et regardai autour de moi. Le sang battait dans ma tête, je me sentais nauséeux. Je ne savais quel jour on était. La lumière suggérait le crépuscule. J'étais du moins dans ma chambre. On frappait toujours à la porte.

« D'accord, d'accord bon Dieu ! criai-je. J'arrive. Qui est-ce ? »

Assis sur mon matelas, j'aperçus l'extrémité du nez de Lo écrasée contre la vitre de ma fenêtre.

« Excusez je vous prie ! dit-il d'une voix fébrile en entamant sa petite danse propitiatoire dès que j'eus ouvert la porte. Je ne pensais pas vous trouver endormi à cette heure.

— Quelle heure est-il ? demandai-je d'une voix pâteuse.

— Presque six heures ! Avez-vous oublié ? Vous deviez déjeuner avec nous.

— Nous sommes donc samedi ? » m'écriai-je en reprenant mes esprits. Mon Dieu — Yin-mi ! Brusquement, je me rappelai. J'avais promis de l'accompagner ce soir aux CJT. Lo m'observait attentivement. « Le jeune dragon a peut-être bu trop de vin ? »

Je gémis. « Lo, avez-vous une aspirine ? Non, trois aspirines, ajoutai-je aussitôt. Je souffre. »

Il secoua la tête. « Excusez je vous prie. L'aspirine est parfaitement inutile dans votre cas. Croyez-moi, j'en sais quelque chose. » Il m'adressa son sourire espiègle.

« Aidez-moi, Lo », me lamentai-je en serrant mes tempes entre mes mains.

Il retroussa les lèvres. « En pareille situation, une seule solution, pontifia-t-il. Et certains affirment que le remède est pire que la maladie. »

« Je m'en moque ! m'écriai-je. Quelle est cette solution ?

— Boire un autre verre d'alcool ! »

Je poussai un gémissement plaintif et courus aux toilettes.

« Surtout, ne pas vous en aller ! dit-il en me tapant sur l'épaule alors que j'étais plié en deux au-dessus de la cuvette. Je reviens tout de suite ! »

De fait, il revint quelques instants plus tard, avec une bouteille. Pris de sueurs froides, j'étais allongé sur mon matelas, osant à peine respirer de peur de compromettre le précaire équilibre gastrique que mes haut-le-cœur avaient réussi à instaurer.

« La première gorgée est la plus désagréable, m'informa-t-il en emplissant nos coupes respectives. Mais croyez-moi, vous vous sentirez ensuite frais comme gardon. »

Malgré ma faiblesse, j'étais assez lucide pour remarquer, non sans déplaisir, qu'il était inhabituellement loquace.

« Je crois pas que je pourrai. » Je reculai en grimaçant quand il tendit la coupe vers mes lèvres. La seule odeur du vin faillit me faire vomir.

« J'appréhendais cela, remarqua-t-il en fronçant les sourcils. Le jeune dragon doit suivre mes instructions, sinon... — il secoua tristement la tête — pas d'espoir. »

Je lui adressai un regard blessé, inquisiteur, puis acquiesçai avec un soupir résigné.

« Okay, ouvrez votre bouche... », m'encouragea-t-il.

J'obéis.

« Et fermez les yeux... »

Je n'en eus pas besoin ; ils étaient déjà clos.

« Feriez mieux de vous pincer le nez, ajouta-t-il prosaïquement, juste au cas où... Et voilà la surprise ! Kan pei ! »

Quand je repris conscience, ce fut comme si j'étais mort pendant quelques instants avant de ressusciter sur la table d'opération.

Assis sur une chaise à côté de mon lit, Lo regardait sa montre. « Vous êtes resté évanoui pendant trente secondes. Je crois que c'est un record. Comment vous sentez-vous ? »

Je me frottai les tempes. « Pas trop mal », répondis-je. Je me concentrai sur mon estomac : pas de problème non plus de ce côté. « Pas mal du tout, en fait. » Je me dressai dans mon lit. « Je me sens en pleine forme. Buvons un autre verre ! »

Il m'envoya des coups d'œil ravis en versant le vin.

« A... la solution ! proposai-je.

— Kan pei ! s'écria-t-il.

— Ah, les subtilités du vin », dis-je.

Lo éclata de rire. « Voilà trop longtemps que je n'ai pas eu le plaisir de boire avec le jeune dragon.

— Tout le plaisir est pour moi, le contredis-je avec une petite révérence.

— Non, non, protesta-t-il.

— Si, si », insistai-je.

Nous rîmes tous les deux.

« Ah, Sun I, vous nous manquez terriblement au restaurant. » Il prit une mine défaite. « Rien n'est plus pareil depuis le départ de l'Assistant Dragon Numéro Un.

— Comment va le jeune freluquet ? Travaille-t-il toujours avec vous ?

— Hélas. » Lo haussa les épaules. « Que pourrais-je dire ? Le freluquet poursuit sa déplorable carrière, laissant un sillage de désolation partout où il passe, détruisant tout ce qu'il touche, cassant, gâchant, ruinant nos efforts conjugués. Nous sommes tous d'accord : votre bref séjour chez *Luck Fat* fut comme un Age d'Or. » Il me regarda timidement. « Vous ne songeriez pas à revenir parmi nous, par hasard ?

— Ah, Lo, vous êtes trop gentil. Votre proposition me fait tellement plaisir. » Je poussai un soupir. « Mais ce que vous me demandez est impossible, du moins pour l'instant. Je commence seulement à progresser dans ma quête. Jusqu'ici, je n'ai fait qu'égratigner la surface du Dow. J'ai tellement à apprendre, et puis je ne peux pas revenir en arrière.

— Je vois, dit-il, déçu. Enfin, si jamais vous changez d'avis... »

Je lui souris et nous vidâmes nos coupes en silence.

Lo tendit la main vers la bouteille.

« Non non, dis-je en posant ma main sur ma coupe.

— Si, si, insista-t-il. Nous devons aiguiser notre perception avec une autre tournée, puis discuter. Nous avons négligé cela la dernière fois. Dans notre insouciance, nous avons non seulement renoncé au plus grand plaisir du connaisseur, mais insulté le vin lui-même. Ce soir, nous devons expier nos péchés. »

Je déglutis avec difficulté en prenant la coupe qu'il me tendait.

« Alors, qu'en pensez-vous ? demanda-t-il gravement, après m'avoir laissé le temps de réfléchir.

— Lo — je posai ma coupe sur la table et inclinai la tête —, je vous ai trompé en vous laissant croire que j'étais un connaisseur. A dire vrai, en ce qui concerne les subtilités du vin, je suis un parfait néophyte.

— Votre modestie vous honore, rétorqua-t-il, mais vous ne devez pas vous sentir gêné de ma présence. Après tout, nous avons bu ensemble ; cela oblige à la franchise. Allez, allez. Votre opinion sincère. »

Mon regard implorant resta sans effet. « Eh bien, hasardai-je, il soutient la comparaison avec certain cru auquel j'ai récemment goûté — la nuit dernière, pour tout vous dire. »

Il se redressa, l'œil brillant d'intérêt. « Quel est le nom de ce cru ? »

Je me raclai la gorge. « Dry Sack, réussis-je à articuler.

— Dry Sack. » Il hocha la tête avec une moue dubitative. « Je n'ai jamais entendu parler de ce cru. Il doit être très rare.

— Si vous ne le connaissez pas... » Avec un haussement d'épaules, je le laissai tirer ses propres conclusions. « Et votre opinion ? »

Il retroussa les lèvres en une moue dépréciatrice. « Bah, ce n'est pas un grand cru, certainement pas un Dry Sack ! Même si vous avez la bonté de les comparer. Même pas aussi savoureux qu'un Kao Liang. Personnellement, je le trouve un peu paresseux, vaguement léthargique au palais. » Il chercha mon approbation.

« Oui, un peu sirupeux, il me semble.

— Mais pas trop sucré ? ajouta-t-il vivement.

— Oh, non ! m'écriai-je avec inquiétude, regrettant aussitôt mon intrépidité stupide. Nullement trop sucré. Je voulais seulement dire, un peu... épais ? » hasardai-je avec précaution.

Lo prit une profonde inspiration, puis, lentement, opina du chef. « Oui, exactement. Un peu "épais", un tout petit peu apathique, comme si l'esprit l'avait abandonné. Mais pas vraiment loin du but ? » relança-t-il avec une candeur touchante, presque enfantine.

« Non, certainement pas ! acquiesçai-je.

— Pas vraiment... médiocre ?

— Parfaitement buvable, lui assurai-je.

— Absolument, n'est-ce pas ? dit-il, satisfait. Vraiment, c'est un vin de sang royal, mais peut-être pas de très haut lignage. Ce n'est pas le prince impérial, mais l'un de ses frères cadets, à qui le destin a accordé d'immenses talents sans la chance de les développer, et qui ainsi les a dilapidés sans résultat. Un vin de grand malheur, de tragédie, peut-être. »

Il me regarda avec solennité ; je compris alors qu'en toute inconscience mon ami parlait de lui-même.

« Un vin noble, sincèrement, dis-je calmement.

— Il y a tellement longtemps que je n'ai pas apprécié la compagnie d'un homme qui comprenne réellement les subtilités. » Ses yeux s'embuèrent de larmes. « Je peux boire avec vous, Sun I. Vous êtes un homme cultivé.

— Vous exagérez, protestai-je.

— Non, non.

— Si, si.

— Mais il est l'heure de partir, me rappela-t-il. Nous sommes déjà en retard. Yin-mi va s'inquiéter. »

« Ouvre, femme, c'est moi, appela-t-il. J'amène un visiteur. »

Nous entendîmes les verrous cliqueter fébrilement.

« Oh, Sun I ! s'écria Mme Ha-p'i, dont le visage s'illumina aussitôt. Entrez donc. Où étiez-vous ? Nous nous sommes inquiétés !

— Je ne me suis pas réveillé, marmonnai-je avec un laconisme coupable.

— Mais nous ne vous avons pas vu depuis une semaine ! protesta-t-elle. Vous êtes devenu un parfait étranger.

— Je t'en prie, femme, intervint Lo avec une feinte rudesse. Si tu piailles et que tu t'esclaffes ainsi, tu vas l'effrayer pour de bon. Tu ne sais donc pas que les dragons sont des créatures farouches, même si leur colère est terrible ?

— Mais que mange-t-il ? dit-elle.

— Comment veux-tu que je le sache ? » Il haussa les épaules. « C'est un dragon, n'est-ce pas ? Peut-être se nourrit-il d'air ! » Il lui adressa une œillade discrète ; elle leva l'extrémité de ses doigts vers ses lèvres comme pour contenir un rire d'oiseau.

Pour la première fois, je perçus l'humour et le léger reproche contenus dans la comparaison de Lo. Je ris d'un air entendu. « Je ne suis pas aussi éthéré que vous le suggérez, Lo. En tout cas, mon ascétisme n'est certainement pas assez développé pour résister à la perspective d'un des excellents repas de Mme Ha-p'i ! »

Elle rougit, rayonna et se troubla, au comble de la félicité. Lo la saisit par la taille, l'attira vers lui, en profita pour caresser son postérieur d'une main affectueuse.

« Lo ! Notre invité ! s'écria-t-elle, scandalisée. A quoi penses-tu ? »

— Tu n'imagines tout de même pas que Sun I va se formaliser ? rétorqua-t-il. Crois-tu vraiment que, dans ses pérégrinations, le jeune dragon n'a jamais été initié au "jeu du vent et des nuages" ? Allez, femme. Bien que jeune dragon, c'est aussi un jeune homme. » Il m'adressa un clin d'œil complice.

« Tu ne vois donc pas que tes paroles le blessent ! » s'indigna Mme Ha-p'i, en assenant une tape sur l'épaule de son mari.

Ma culpabilité, ou mon innocence, devait se lire sur mon visage. Lo parut sincèrement surpris.

Elle regarda attentivement son mari. « Tu as bu, n'est-ce pas ? »

La bouche en cul de poule, il tint son pouce et son index à un centimètre l'un de l'autre pour indiquer un petit verre.

« Que se passe-t-il ? demanda Yin-mi en émergeant du couloir. Tu as raison, maman, mets-les dehors ! Est-ce qu'ils se liguent contre toi ? Chasse-les tous les deux ! Vous devriez avoir honte — une pauvre femme sans défense ! » Lo et moi subîmes aussitôt la contagion de son rire cristallin. Mme Ha-p'i hésita, tergiversa, puis nous imita. La crise potentielle était évitée de justesse.

« En tout cas, vous semblez tous les deux bien joyeux, poursuivit Yin-mi, presque aussi malicieuse que son père.

— Nous sommes d'humeur royale ! renchérit Lo en me lançant une œillade.

— Ils ont bu », dit Mme Ha-p'i sur le ton du reproche mais avec un sourire indulgent.

Une ride se creusa au front de Yin-mi. « Tu veux dire papa, corrigea-t-elle, certainement pas Sun I ? »

Son visage exprimait la même candeur et la même curiosité que ce premier soir où elle s'était campée sur le seuil de la cuisine pour m'observer, voire une légère trace d'amusement, et ces trois émotions indépendantes se fondaient dans la grande solennité qui était le motif central et la caractéristique de son être.

Je dus baisser les yeux.

Mais au lieu de me reprocher mon écart, à ma grande surprise elle éclata de rire en songeant à l'absurdité de sa question — *moi*, boire ? « Allez. » Elle saisit gaiement mon bras. « Nous allons être en retard si nous ne nous dépêchons pas.

— Tiens, prends donc cette ombrelle, dit Mme Ha-p'i. La météo annonce des averses et peut-être un orage en fin de soirée. »

Les rues étaient pleines d'enfants qui faisaient de la bicyclette ou jouaient au base-ball, de voisins qui prenaient le frais sur leur perron ou bavardaient sur les escaliers d'incendie. Des couples âgés se promenaient bras dessus, bras dessous dans les rues ombreuses. Ils s'arrêtaient et souriaient en nous voyant, s'inclinaient légèrement en un salut qui nous incluait, ou du moins nous invitait, dans le mystère de leurs visages heureux, le secret millénaire de la continuité humaine, de la fidélité et de l'amour conjugal, ce que le taoïsme nomme « l'esclavage volontaire à la Roue ». Malgré l'ambiguïté de pareille assimilation vu ma position, j'étais touché et reconnaissant. Je me sentais flatté, voire excité. D'une timide pression de la main, Yin-mi se serrait contre mon bras, me faisant presque espérer (je ne pouvais pourtant espérer cela, je n'en avais pas le droit) qu'elle ressentait une émotion comparable. Nous poursuivions notre marche en silence.

« On dirait que j'ai encore causé des ennuis à ton père », remarquai-je au bout d'un moment.

Elle scruta mon visage avec une expression amusée, au bord du rire. « Vous aviez l'air tellement contents de vous, tous les deux, dit-elle, ajoutant aussitôt : Mais il se débrouille très bien seul pour se mettre dans le pétrin. » Elle dit cela avec un soupçon de malice qui me rappela de nouveau Lo, mais son regard était très tendre, presque triste, comme si elle comprenait notre incartade et la pardonnait.

Peut-être aurais-je dû manifester ma gratitude, mais une partie de moi-même — appelons-la Nature de Singe (excitée par le vin) — refusait d'être pardonnée et reprochait à Yin-mi sa présomption. Pour la deuxième fois, je sentis mon cœur se révolter. Cet embrasement passager aurait sans doute fait long feu, n'eût-elle accompagné de ces mots son regard solennel : « Vraiment, tu ne devrais pas le pousser à boire, tu sais.

— Le pousser, *lui* ! éclatai-je.

— Il travaille tellement dur, expliqua-t-elle calmement, et contrairement à toi il ne possède aucun sanctuaire spirituel où se réfugier quand le plaisir s'est évaporé et qu'il se retrouve honteux et malade ; il n'a rien pour tempérer son désir ou atténuer les effets néfastes.

— De quoi parles-tu ? » demandai-je en feignant de ne pas comprendre. Elle était grave. « Tu le sais très bien.

— De l'ivresse ? dis-je.

— Oui, si tu veux, "de l'ivresse", ou plus précisément de ce que tu m'as un jour décrit comme "les mystères exquis de la désintégration".

— C'était à propos de l'opium, objectai-je.

— Cela revient au même, dit-elle tristement mais fermement, c'est aussi mauvais. »

Je fus frappé par la profondeur de sa remarque, et me rappelai brusquement ma première rencontre avec Mme Chin. Bizarrement, les paroles de Yin-mi me plurent, suscitèrent mon admiration sans pourtant diminuer mon ressentiment. « Même si, comme tu le prétends, il ne possède aucun sanctuaire où se réfugier, poursuivis-je, il a sa "solution". Laquelle, précisément, "revient au même"...

— Quelle solution ? » demanda-t-elle innocemment.

J'hésitai avant de répondre. Je sentais en elle cette fragilité et cette confiance qui, plusieurs fois déjà, avaient éveillé ma compassion alors que j'étais sur le point de céder à une impulsion violente. Elles m'émurent de nouveau, aussi profondément qu'avant, mais je m'accrochai à mon ressentiment. Selon l'expression favorite de Kahn, ce fut plus fort que moi. « Boire un autre verre ! » répondis-je en affectant la légèreté, alors que j'étais en proie à la nausée et à l'abattement, suivis aussitôt d'une immense apathie, d'une lassitude qui me rappela les douloureuses descentes d'opium, quand le sang a consumé jusqu'à la dernière particule du puissant stimulant et qu'il ne charrie plus que sa fange.

Elle continua de m'observer en silence, avec cette grande solennité plus terrible que le pire des reproches. Sous ma torpeur, je sentis poindre la honte et la culpabilité — d'abord dirigées contre moi, puis, balayant toutes les barrières, englobant aussi Yin-mi. J'essayai de dégager mon bras, mais elle refusa. Quelque chose se déchaîna dans mon cœur. Sans réfléchir, par un pur réflexe, je levai la main libre comme pour la frapper, bien que je n'en eusse pas vraiment l'intention.

« Je vais te frapper, dis-je d'une voix rauque, si tu ne me lâches pas. »
Elle secoua la tête sans sourciller. « Pas question, répondit-elle. Surtout quand tu es comme ça.
— Comme quoi ? » Une deuxième fois, je tentai de me dégager, mais avec moins d'énergie, découvrant en moi-même le désir de ne pas être lâché, et dans le même temps la peur qu'elle pût le faire.
« Ivre, dit-elle.
— Je ne suis pas ivre ! criai-je.
— Tu es éméché alors, et idiot ! » cria-t-elle aussi fort que moi, peinée de devoir élever la voix.
Ravi de sa réponse, j'éclatai de rire.
Elle fondit en larmes.
Saisi d'une tendresse douce et douloureuse, je la regardai pleurer. « Yinmi, dis-je enfin d'une voix calme, toute colère dissipée, excuse-moi. Tu as raison. Je suis un idiot. »
Ses yeux brillèrent de joie à travers ses larmes. « Chut, fit-elle en pressant son index contre mes lèvres. Tu ne dois jamais dire ça, ni le penser. C'est mon privilège. » Elle rit en reniflant. « Donne-moi ton mouchoir. » J'obéis passivement. Elle tamponna ses yeux, puis se moucha bruyamment. « Là, dit-elle en me le rendant. Maintenant, nous sommes quittes. » Elle rit joyeusement ; creusé par cette rapide inversion des émotions, son visage rayonna comme sous le coup d'un violent effort physique.
Une fois encore, l'imperceptible couture du tissu de la réalité se déchira, et sur son visage je découvris maints secrets palpitants et scintillants. Ses traits se brouillèrent ; chaque détail, magnifié, épuisa mon œil et devint un monde. Dans ses yeux, sur sa chair et ses cheveux, je vis la beauté élémentaire de la matière incréée tourbillonner sans fin, se transmuer avec une volupté bouleversante et subtilement obscène qui impliquait la ruine, la putréfaction inhérente à toute vie. Et aussi rapidement qu'elle s'était déchirée, la couture se referma, et la jeune fille redevint elle-même, Yinmi, celle que je connaissais. Ma nausée s'allégea de toute culpabilité, se mua en pitié, en tendresse, en cette même émotion que j'avais ressentie le premier jour à New York, assis sur un banc du cimetière de Trinity, alors qu'à travers les barreaux de la grille en fer forgé je regardais la foule qui grouillait dans la rue, et que les tombes me révélaient leur secret.
« Qu'y a-t-il ? demanda-t-elle d'une voix qui tremblait. Tu n'es plus fâché contre moi, n'est-ce pas ? »
Je secouai la tête.
« Pourquoi me regardes-tu ainsi ?
— Je ne sais pas.
— Tu pleures ! dit-elle avec surprise.
— Vraiment ? » Je pressai mes cils entre mes doigts.
« Tu ne sais pas pourquoi, dit-elle calmement.
— Et toi ? » lui demandai-je.
Elle sourit. « Si, je crois que je sais. Un peu. Je crois que je le sais depuis le début, depuis le premier soir. »
Je l'interrogeai du regard.
Sans me donner la clef du mystère, elle reprit mon bras en souriant et nous repartîmes.

★

« Maintenant, reste ici, m'ordonna-t-elle en me dirigeant vers un banc dans le fond de l'église. Il y a une messe spéciale ce soir. Je dois chanter dans le chœur. Je viendrai te chercher quand ce sera fini. »

Puis elle disparut dans la sacristie.

Une fois encore je me retrouvais seul à Trinity. Après notre dispute, je goûtai avec soulagement le calme de l'édifice. Il y avait quelque chose d'apaisant dans le crépuscule perpétuel de l'église, l'immensité et la profondeur de l'espace empli de sombres nuées impalpables qui dissolvaient les angles saillants et les embrasures en une solution homogène. La rumeur qui régnait dans l'église était liquide, semblable au murmure silencieux d'un coquillage qui évoque le va-et-vient d'un lointain océan. Et vraiment, avec ses clochers et ses arcs gothiques, Trinity ressemblait à une immense conque renversée dans laquelle, telles les créatures sans défense des grands fonds, les membres de la congrégation et moi-même nous étions temporairement réfugiés. L'écho majestueux de sa cavité acoustique évoquait l'harmonique subtile du flux et du reflux des eaux primordiales, le Tao. L'église devint l'incarnation physique d'un état méditatif que j'avais autrefois connu aussi facilement que je venais ce soir d'entrer dans cet édifice, mais que, depuis la visite de Hsiao et mon départ de Ken Kuan, je trouvais de plus en plus difficile de recréer. Cette association en suscita une autre : l'église et ses ténèbres splendides semblaient imiter l'expression des yeux de Yin-mi.

Levant le regard vers les claires-voies et les vitraux, je fus déçu de les découvrir muets et inexpressifs, comme de vastes plans d'eau obscurs sous la lune, miroitant parfois brièvement du reflet des bougies qui brûlaient dans la nef. Pour compenser cette perte, une impression d'imminence que je n'avais pas remarquée la première fois régnait dans l'église, tel un orage sur le point d'éclater. Et comme à l'intérieur d'un cumulus, l'atmosphère semblait grésiller d'un feu électrique invisible, à croire que quelque intelligence divine y méditait et menaçait de se révéler en une terrible épiphanie. Ignorant presque tout du Dieu chrétien, j'appréhendais cette éventualité, m'interrogeais sur son déroulement. Allait-il se manifester sous une forme bénigne, illuminer de son sourire le monde qu'il avait créé, ou bien exhiber les crocs et les yeux exorbités, injectés de sang, d'un Mahakala ?

Avec un étonnement et un plaisir presque sensuel, j'observai les accessoires de la messe, dont les fonctions m'avaient paru si mystérieuses la première fois, et dont j'ignorais toujours l'usage : le chandelier à sept branches qui éclairait l'autel au-dessus du linge immaculé. « XP » — que signifiaient ces initiales ? L'emblème alchimique de quelque breuvage magique accordant la vie éternelle ? Je remarquai le ciboire d'argent où, invisibles, les hosties non consacrées attendaient le geste rituel du prêtre, la patène sur laquelle il en bénirait et briserait une, le calice pour le vin.

Sans bruit, le chœur et les célébrants rejoignirent le vestibule. L'organiste entonna quelques accords graves et tonnants avant le cantique, puis la procession commença. Ils marchaient deux par deux, vêtus de noir, le recueil de cantiques ouvert entre leurs mains. Un jeune homme, qui portait le crucifix, passa devant mon banc. Le cuivre scintillait à la lumière vacillante des bougies, le garçon triste au corps svelte, efféminé, et au visage marqué qui alliait la force et la faiblesse de l'homme et de la femme, de la jeunesse et de la vieillesse, était suspendu par les clous cruels qui transperçaient ses pieds et ses mains, sous l'écriteau INRI.

Quand elle passa près de moi, Yin-mi me sourit timidement. Elle saisit le recueil de cantiques dans sa main gauche pour m'adresser un signe rapide derrière sa couverture, un petit salut discret et syncopé. Riley fermait la procession, seul, les mains serrées derrière le dos sur un livre. Il souriait, le regard dans le vague, comme absorbé par une spéculation qui venait de se révéler à lui. Je le reconnus aussitôt d'après la description de Yin-mi.

Bien qu'approchant la quarantaine, il semblait beaucoup plus jeune ; il était grand et large d'épaules, mais d'une maigreur presque cadavérique. Il avait un vaste front et de pâles yeux gris-bleu dont le regard semblait particulièrement abstrait, mais qui, ainsi que je l'appris ensuite, pouvaient très vite devenir étonnamment perçants. Ses cheveux roux séparés par une raie formaient une sorte de vague sur un côté de sa tête. Son teint était agréable, extrêmement blanc ; sa peau translucide, mouchetée de taches de rousseur sous les yeux, qui lui accordaient du charme et une certaine fragilité. La délicatesse de son teint n'expliquait pas entièrement l'aura qui nimbait son visage ; je la reconnus aisément : le rayonnement éthéré, légèrement maladif, de l'homme habitué au jeûne. Je l'avais souvent remarqué chez les frères à Ken Kuan. Mais alors que chez ces derniers il suggérait l'intériorité et la sérénité, l'aura de Riley évoquait une extase, un débordement, un corps musical qui résonnait comme un diapason à la fréquence de l'âme, laquelle vibrait dans une tonalité trop élevée pour que la matière pût y résister. Son regard possédait une intensité difficilement soutenable, comme celui des yeux de l'ours, et que l'intelligence rendait seulement plus accessible, moins effrayante. Quand il me remarqua en passant devant moi, cette intensité parut littéralement me brûler ; elle suggérait une certitude et une conviction que j'avais ignorées jusque-là.

Il n'était pas beau : malgré le baume de ses taches de rousseur, ses traits exprimaient une concentration désagréable qui écartait cette possibilité. L'homme dégageait pourtant une impression de mélancolie fatale, comme « un signe extérieur et visible de grâce intérieure et spirituelle », et de l'instant où je le vis, avant même que nous parlions, je pressentis sa sincérité et sa grandeur ; je compris pourquoi Yin-mi lui accordait toute sa confiance, pourquoi, en fait, elle l'aimait. Ainsi, dans mon état de lucidité enivrée et la confusion de mes autres émotions, je ressentis un pincement de jalousie à cause d'elle — une jalousie tout à fait insconciente.

Lénifiant, un peu soporifique, le service progressait autour de moi comme un fleuve, un grand spectacle d'images oniriques qui baignaient et enveloppaient ma conscience, m'attiraient vers quelque consommation inimaginable. Bercé jusqu'à un état de voluptueuse passivité par les fastes somptueux qui se déroulaient sous mes yeux, j'observais l'entrelacs du rituel qu'on tissait devant l'autel, sans rien comprendre, sans même éprouver le besoin de comprendre. Vers le milieu du service, je remarquai avec un léger agacement que l'huissier debout dans la nef latérale devant moi m'adressait un regard insistant de douce exhortation. La main posée sur le dossier du banc (il portait une grosse chevalière d'or qui crissait légèrement contre le bois, comme s'il eût frappé à la porte de ma conscience), il me fixait en hochant la tête. Bien que peu désireux d'être dérangé dans mon agréable torpeur — préférant ici comme à la Bourse observer sans participer, mais tenant aussi à respecter non seulement l'esprit, mais, dans la mesure du possible, la lettre de toutes les religions —, je décidai que je ne courrais pas grand risque à me soumettre à leurs réquisits. Je me levai donc et suivis les autres vers l'abside. Je constatai avec plaisir que ma menue concession mettait Yin-mi aux anges. Car lorsque je passai devant elle en allant vers l'autel, je la vis du coin de l'œil m'adresser un signe de la main, geste peut-être un peu voyant, mais qui prouvait sans nul doute qu'elle était ravie de mon initiative qu'elle ne m'avait pas suggérée. A mon tour, je lui adressai un petit signe de la main.

Avec le talent immémorial de Singe pour l'imitation improvisée et un sentiment de vague stupidité (mais pour ainsi dire en mission professionnelle), j'observais les autres s'agenouiller devant le crucifix, puis s'aligner le long de la rambarde de l'autel. Les genoux posés sur un coussin de velours rouge sang lustré par les rotules d'innombrables fidèles, je les imitai quand ils appuyèrent leurs coudes sur la balustrade de cuivre brillant, la main droite serrée dans la gauche, et qu'ils inclinèrent la tête. J'avais certes déjà vu des chrétiens en prière, mais cette position des mains fut pour moi une découverte. Je réfléchissais à la signification possible de ce *mudra* chrétien, quand il me fut soudain expliqué, de façon *palpable*. En effet, surpris par une légère pression sur la paume de ma main, j'entendis les mots « faites ceci en mémoire de moi » ; j'ouvris aussitôt les yeux et vis Riley passer le long de la balustrade, au-dessus de moi. Il s'arrêtait brièvement devant chaque communiant, déposait quelque chose dans sa main, murmurait ces mêmes paroles incantatoires d'une voix émue dont le timbre s'accordait parfaitement à la pénombre de l'église. J'examinai ma main quand il m'eut dépassé et découvris une gaufre blanche mince comme une feuille de papier et estampée d'une croix. La voix de Riley était devenue un bourdonnement apaisant et inarticulé. En mémoire de qui ? me demandai-je. Je n'eus pas le temps de poursuivre mes réflexions, car je remarquai que mes voisins tiraient la langue dans la main, puis la rétractaient en même temps que le petit disque de pain (sans mâcher, sans le moindre mouvement des maxillaires — mon œil de Singe prit bien garde à cela), et le laissaient se dissoudre en savourant son goût sans accélérer le processus par la mastication. Personnellement, je trouvai ma gaufre plutôt fade ; je me rappelai mon expérience de la nuit précédente dans le bar irlandais avec Kahn, mais pas un instant ne songeai à mépriser l'hospitalité bienveillante de ces croyants.

Quand ce petit gâteau chrétien anémié se fut dissous, je vis Riley retourner au début de la rangée, cette fois avec la coupe. Chaque fois que son rebord touchait les lèvres d'un fidèle, il l'essuyait avec une serviette blanche et la tournait légèrement avant de faire boire le suivant. De nouveau, j'entendis les mots « en mémoire de moi ». Quand il me tendit la coupe, j'eus de nouveau une agréable impression de passivité. Je me rappelai que Wu me berçait quand j'avais la fièvre, assis sur une chaise à côté de mon lit d'enfant, me nourrissant de ses propres mains, me donnant des bonbons et des breuvages calmants avant d'essuyer mes lèvres avec un linge propre. Ce souvenir plaisant s'agrémenta d'une autre association, une coïncidence qui m'amusa et me ravit. Quand je goûtai le vin, je le reconnus immédiatement. Aucun doute possible, c'était du Dry Sack !

Malgré la distance avec laquelle je participai à ce rituel, je fus étrangement ému quand il s'acheva. Cette unique gorgée suffit peut-être à réactiver mon ébriété, car je sentis un doux feu liquide embraser non seulement ma tête, mais mon cœur. Je me relevai tant bien que mal et, les jambes flageolantes, regagnai ma place comme les autres. Je remarquai non sans soulagement qu'eux aussi semblaient un peu éméchés. Leurs visages suggéraient la quiétude et l'accomplissement. Je songeai brusquement à Lo, regrettai qu'il ne fût pas à mes côtés. Un connaisseur tel que lui n'aurait pas manqué d'apprécier les subtilités de pareil cru. Retournant vers mon banc, je fus pris d'une soudaine envie de rire et de courir jusqu'au bout de la travée. Mais je réussis à me maîtriser, rejoignis ma place et, imitant toujours les autres, m'agenouillai et joignis les mains.

Mon hilarité enfin reflua peu à peu, remplacée par un sentiment de paix et de gratitude qui semblait sourdre du plus profond de mon être. Depuis quelque temps, je l'ai déjà dit, la méditation ne me satisfaisait plus, me devenait même inaccessible. Mais sur ce banc de Trinity, je connus alors un état plus limpide et intense que je n'en avais jamais vécu. Dans le temple du cœur, les cigales se turent pour faire place à une musique feutrée, comme le bruit de la neige tombant sur l'océan, laquelle faiblit à son tour jusqu'au soupir étouffé d'une conque, puis, magiquement, rien... le silence parfait du vide. Il y avait si longtemps que je n'avais pas entendu ce silence ! Pour la première fois depuis de nombreux mois, mon âme se sentit libérée. Comme l'eau de pluie qui s'amasse dans une dépression calcaire, puis s'infiltre dans les capillarités du roc, je me confiai à la force de gravité, au Tao, pour qu'il me ramène à la nappe souterraine. Je coulai lentement et sans résistance, soumis à cette force inexorable qui érode les continents. Une impression de joie et de profond renouvellement m'envahit. Je me sentis nettoyé, souple, régénéré. Des larmes fraîches ruisselèrent sur mes joues.

Debout dans l'abside à gauche de l'autel, je vis un jeune garçon d'une douzaine d'années dont le frêle visage trahissait une santé fragile et qui faisait des efforts touchants pour conserver sa gravité. Il lisait un texte, levait de temps à autre les yeux vers l'assistance qui écoutait le timbre pur de sa voix de soprano (je songeai à ma propre enfance, à ma pratique des *Chants*). Pour la première fois depuis le début du rituel, je me concentrai vraiment et j'entendis ces mots :

> « Quand je parlerais les langues des hommes et des anges, si je n'ai pas l'amour, je ne suis qu'un airain qui résonne, ou une cymbale qui retentit.
>
> « Quand j'aurais le don de prophétie, et quand je connaîtrais tous les mystères et toute la science, quand j'aurais une foi totale, à transporter les montagnes, si je n'ai pas l'amour, je ne suis rien.

« Quand je distribuerais tous mes biens pour l'entretien des pauvres, quand je livrerais mon corps au feu, si je n'ai pas l'amour, cela ne m'avance à rien.

« L'amour est patient ; l'amour est dévoué ; l'amour n'est pas envieux ; il n'est pas infatué ni hautain.

« Il ne fait rien de malséant, il ne cherche pas son intérêt, il ne s'emporte pas, il ne tient pas compte du mal.

« Il ne prend pas plaisir à l'injustice, mais trouve sa joie dans la vérité ;

« Il excuse tout, il croit tout, il espère tout, il endure tout.

« L'amour ne renonce jamais. Les prophéties disparaîtront ; le don des langues cessera ; le don de connaissance disparaîtra.

« Notre science est imparfaite, nos prophéties sont imparfaites.

« Mais quand sera venue la perfection, alors disparaîtra ce qui est imparfait.

« Quand j'étais enfant, je parlais comme un enfant, je pensais comme un enfant, je raisonnais comme un enfant. En devenant homme, j'ai éliminé tout ce qu'il y avait de puéril.

« Aujourd'hui, nous voyons comme dans un miroir, confusément ; alors nous verrons face à face. Aujourd'hui, je ne connais que partiellement ; alors, je connaîtrai comme je suis connu.

« Actuellement, trois choses demeurent : la foi, l'espérance, l'amour ; mais la plus grande des trois, c'est l'amour. »

Avec quelle attention fascinée, voire terrifiée, j'écoutai ! Ce passage était aussi émouvant et puissant que n'importe quel texte du *Yi king*. Jamais des mots ne m'avaient paru aussi beaux, ni atteint des régions aussi profondes de mon esprit. Je ne parvenais pas à me l'expliquer. Bien que ce passage fût parfaitement limpide et son sens général aussi peu ambigu que la clarté du jour, il me stupéfiait, comme si ces mots eussent tissé un voile scintillant et frémissant qui masquait une forme dont j'entrevoyais pourtant quelques fragments. « Aujourd'hui, je ne connais que partiellement ; alors, je connaîtrai comme je suis connu. » Et surtout ceci : « Aujourd'hui, nous voyons comme dans un miroir, confusément ; alors nous verrons face à face. » Quelle splendide et impondérable épiphanie annonçaient donc ces mots ?

A la fin du service religieux, après le départ du chœur, je demeurai assis sur mon banc, l'esprit en proie à la perplexité, à mille conjectures. Je sentis brusquement une autre présence et découvris Yin-mi debout devant moi, qui observait mon visage avec grand sérieux, comme elle avait scruté celui de son père le premier soir dans la cuisine, le même pli de concentration barrant son front. Elle était très pâle. Au bout de quelques secondes seulement, je remarquai qu'elle pleurait en silence. Interprétant à tort ses larmes selon mon humeur, je fus submergé de joie, plus que jamais convaincu qu'une sympathie lucide et intime nous liait et qu'elle partageait mes émotions. Je ne ressentis nul besoin de parler ; je touchai seulement sa main.

A ma grande surprise, elle frissonna et la retira aussitôt.

« Qu'y a-t-il ?

— Sun I, dit-elle d'une voix tremblante, réalises-tu ce que tu as fait ? »
Sa gravité m'inquiéta. « Que veux-tu dire ?
— Tu as communié.
— Ça ne te fait pas plaisir ? lui demandai-je.
— Plaisir ! Tu n'as donc pas remarqué que je te faisais signe de t'éloigner de l'autel ?
— Je ne comprends pas, dis-je, implorant. Je me suis contenté d'imiter les autres. Ai-je commis une erreur ? Je te jure que je ne l'ai pas mâchée.
— Les autres sont des chrétiens, précisa-t-elle. Tu n'es même pas baptisé. Tu n'as pas droit à ce sacrement. »
Je la regardai stupidement ; l'extase sereine de ma méditation vola en éclats. Je me sentis humilié, je voulus me venger. « Dis donc, c'est un club privé ou quoi ? lâchai-je, reprenant avec amertume l'apostrophe de Kahn.
— Ça n'est pas drôle, dit-elle sévèrement. Essaie de comprendre : ceux qui ne sont pas baptisés n'ont pas le droit de communier... C'est même sans doute un péché mortel, ajouta-t-elle après une brève hésitation. Oui, j'en suis presque sûre.
— Péché mortel ?
— Un péché pour lequel il n'y a pas de rédemption, pas de pardon.
— Allez..., rétorquai-je avec scepticisme en riant jaune pour essayer de lui soutirer un sourire. Ce ne peut être aussi grave que ça. Pour tout te dire, cela m'a assez plu ! »
Elle fondit en larmes. « Oh, Sun I, comment peux-tu plaisanter avec la damnation et la mort de ton âme ?
— La damnation ? répétai-je. La mort de mon âme ?
— Viens avec moi, décida-t-elle brusquement saisissant ma main.
— Où allons-nous ? lui demandai-je avec insouciance, partagé entre l'amusement et la colère, mais surtout ravi de me laisser conduire et de sentir la pression de sa main.
— Nous allons voir le père Riley. »

Il était seul dans la sacristie, debout devant une table sur laquelle on avait remisé les accessoires du culte. Quand nous franchîmes la porte, il retirait un linge blanc de la patène. Je me rappelle ce détail parce qu'alors qu'il saisissait le tissu entre le pouce et l'index, je songeai à un magicien sur le point d'accomplir un tour, plongeant la main dans les plis de son mouchoir pour en sortir une colombe. Lorsqu'il entendit la porte s'ouvrir, il remit le linge en place et se retourna pour nous accueillir.

« Ah, ton ami taoïste, dit-il en souriant avant de me tendre la main. Je voulais faire ta connaissance. Yin-mi m'a dit que tu m'évitais par peur de te laisser convertir ! » Remarquant alors l'inquiétude et la fébrilité de mon amie, il redevint grave. « Qu'y a-t-il, Yin-mi ? »
Elle lui adressa un regard implorant, ses lèvres tremblaient légèrement. Je compris alors l'étendue de la confiance, du respect et de l'affection qu'elle lui accordait — une intimité d'où j'étais exclu et qui me menaçait vaguement. Je sentis une douleur aiguë et irraisonnée, panique et rébellion mêlées.

« C'est ma faute », dit-elle en courbant la tête, retrouvant inconsciemment le rythme immémorial de la confession.

Il saisit sa main comme pour la consoler. « Qu'as-tu fait ?

— J'ai oublié de prévenir Sun I à propos de la communion... Il a communié. » Une ombre traversa le visage de Riley. « Il n'est même pas baptisé », poursuivit-elle ; elle fondit de nouveau en larmes et ajouta, non sans exaltation : « C'est un péché mortel !

— Calme-toi, dit-il avec une douce autorité tranquille. Ne te mets donc pas martel en tête. Un péché mortel ! » A ma grande stupéfaction, il sourit comme si cette idée l'amusait.

Yin-mi cessa de pleurer. « Ce n'en est pas un ? » dit-elle en reniflant.

Le front de Riley se plissa sous la concentration. « Eh bien, je dirais qu'il s'agit d'une question théologique assez épineuse. Mais je me demanderais d'abord comment on peut parler de péché mortel à propos de Sun I. La damnation me paraît absurde, pour le moins redondante, dans le cas d'un taoïste, tu ne crois pas ?

— Que voulez-vous dire ? demanda-t-elle.

— Simplement qu'en qualité de "païen et infidèle" (il prononça ces mots avec une emphase ironique), Sun I est déjà condamné. » Il m'adressa un clin d'œil comme pour réclamer mon indulgence ; je compris alors qu'il plaisantait, qu'il tentait simplement de détendre l'atmosphère.

Mais je n'étais pas d'humeur à plaisanter. « Ce n'est pas possible, le défiai-je.

— Oh, que si, rétorqua-t-il avec une brusquerie glaçante. C'est la vérité. Mais, continua-t-il en essayant de changer de sujet, n'est-ce pas une excellente entrée en matière ?

— Vous voulez dire que tous ceux qui ne sont pas chrétiens sont automatiquement condamnés à l'enfer ? insistai-je.

— Quelque chose comme ça, répliqua-t-il. Les catholiques romains nomment cela "les limbes". Mais soucieux de démocratie, nous ne faisons plus la différence depuis un certain temps.

— Vous ne le pensez pas vraiment ? demandai-je en imitant l'ironie de sa voix.

— Si, dit-il, brusquement sincère. Même si cela est très mal vu dans les salons. La plupart des gens préfèrent éviter les corollaires désagréables de la foi. Ils aimeraient remiser ce genre de dogme dans les oubliettes de l'Histoire, avec le chevalet, les vis et autres accessoires de l'Inquisition. Mais la foi aussi a ses rigueurs. Si j'accepte la grande prémisse, je dois accepter toutes ses conséquences. Le Christ a dit : "Je suis la voie, la vérité et la vie ; aucun homme ne trouve mon Père sans m'avoir suivi." C'est une dure vérité. Peut-être n'est-elle pas à mon goût. Mais je l'accepte.

— Elle est méprisable, rétorquai-je. Je ne crois pas que j'aime votre foi. »

Il eut un sourire sans joie. « Parfois, je ne suis pas certain de l'aimer, moi non plus. Mais là n'est pas la question. Le salut est trop important pour qu'on le réduise à une simple affaire de goût.

— Jésus a donc condamné Lao-tseu et le Bouddha aux flammes de l'enfer, dis-je ironiquement.

— Sans nul doute, bien que j'imagine qu'on a certainement donné à ces sages une chambre de luxe — l'Élysée, par exemple. » Il me regarda d'un air narquois.

« Comment osez-vous parler aussi légèrement ? lui reprochai-je. La damnation de la moitié de l'humanité est un problème religieux pour d'autres que vous, pour *moi* par exemple !

— J'essaie de te convertir, dit-il avec son sourire ambigu qui mêlait mystérieusement la sincérité et l'ironie.

— Dans ces conditions, je n'ai pas à m'inquiéter de mes autres infractions, dis-je. Cette affaire de Communion devient une simple bagatelle.

— Je n'irais pas jusque-là, objecta-t-il, même si ton ignorance t'excuse en partie. Je suppose que tu n'as pas péché à dessein ? »

Rendu encore plus furieux par sa proposition de pardon à peine voilée, je refusai d'entrer dans son jeu. « Je dois vous dire que votre assurance à propos du salut et votre exclusion des autres voies ne me plaisent pas du tout. Pourquoi vous croyez-vous le seul à détenir la vérité ?

— Je n'aime pas me montrer dogmatique, Sun I, mais je dois te renvoyer aux articles de la foi. Numéro dix-sept : "Qu'ils soient maudits, ceux qui croient que chacun sera sauvé par la Loi ou la secte qu'il fréquente. Car les Saintes Écritures nous exhortent à suivre uniquement le Nom de Jésus-Christ si nous voulons être sauvés."

— Et qui s'arroge le droit de pontifier ainsi ? demandai-je sur un ton mordant.

— La Convention de l'Église protestante épiscopale d'Amérique.

— Pourquoi devrais-je me ranger à leur avis ?

— Eh bien, si leur autorité ne te suffit pas, laisse-moi me réclamer d'une autre. Tu me demandes pourquoi je crois ? » La conviction brillait dans son regard. « A cause de ceci. » Il posa la main sur son cœur exactement comme l'avait fait Kahn. Il désignait, bien sûr, l'intuition, la connaissance du cœur.

Je fus surpris et, bizarrement, ému. J'avais beau me défier de son magnétisme, Riley m'attirait. Je commençai à comprendre la colère et l'indignation de Hsiao devant cette arrogante certitude occidentale ; je me demandai si elle n'était pas liée à cette austère intransigeance chrétienne : « Aucun homme ne trouve mon Père sans m'avoir suivi. » Quelle différence avec le taoïsme et le bouddhisme, qui reconnaissent la valeur de toutes les voies, considèrent leur but comme unique, et qui sont infiniment plus généreux, plus riches d'ambiguïtés. Pourtant, malgré son assurance inébranlable, Riley n'affichait aucune arrogance ; je devais lui accorder cela. Sa conviction me troublait plus que tout le reste, le rendait dangereux à mes yeux.

« Mais qu'a donc de si particulier votre petit rituel pour que vous le protégiez avec une telle jalousie ? » demandai-je.

Riley haussa les sourcils. « Tu veux dire que tu ne comprends pas le sens de la messe ?

— Vous parlez du Dry Sack et des biscuits salés ? dis-je méchamment.

— Viens voir ici », me commanda-t-il sèchement en s'approchant de la table devant laquelle il se tenait quand nous étions entrés dans la sacristie. Il souleva le linge et saisit une hostie. « Tu vois ça ? » Me retournant la main, il la posa sur ma paume.

Obéissant à une impulsion perverse, je remis l'hostie dans le ciboire. « Qu'est-ce que c'est, des matzos ? »

Riley se renfrogna et reprit la petite galette ronde. Il l'éleva au niveau de son front, la brisa en disant de cette voix envoûtante que j'avais déjà entendue : « Prenez et mangez ; ceci est mon corps, qui est brisé pour vous : faites ceci en mémoire de moi. » Il ferma les yeux et la plaça sur sa langue.

Levant le calice à deux mains, il poursuivit : « Ceci est mon sang, qui est répandu pour vous et pour maints autres, pour la rémission de vos péchés. » Il se retourna, me regarda droit dans les yeux d'un air accusateur et menaçant.

« Charmant symbolisme », commentai-je avec une malice que je ne ressentais pas vraiment.

Il secoua la tête. « Cela n'a rien de symbolique, Sun I. »

La lumière se fit dans mon esprit. « Vous voulez dire... »

Il acquiesça. « Tu aurais dû mieux écouter. J'ai dit : "Doux Seigneur, faites qu'en mangeant la chair de Ton fils bien-aimé, et en buvant son sang, nous puissions laver nos corps souillés grâce à son corps, et nos âmes grâce à son sang très précieux, et que nous puissions à jamais demeurer en lui, et lui en nous." »

— Mais c'est du cannibalisme ! m'écriai-je, révolté.

— Ne sois pas trivial, me tança-t-il. C'est beaucoup plus profond que cela. »

Je tournai mon visage stupéfait vers Yin-mi en espérant qu'elle me soutiendrait, puis, regardai de nouveau Riley. Ils me rendirent mon regard sans ciller, avec fermeté, conviction, et une sorte de curiosité, comme si mes réactions les intéressaient. J'étais muet de stupeur, aussi pétrifié que le voyageur sur un sentier de montagne qui, sentant une légère secousse sous ses pieds, un lointain grondement semblable au tonnerre, se fige et tend l'oreille en une attitude vigilante de curiosité dénuée d'inquiétude, à quelques secondes de sa fin, alors que trois cents mètres plus haut l'avalanche descend sur lui, rapide, silencieuse et implacable. Tsin se matérialisa alors devant moi, tel que je l'avais vu en cet instant terrible où il avait levé les yeux de la pipe qu'il préparait, le visage empourpré par l'adrénaline, la victoire, l'« extase du combat », les braises rougeoyantes du feu se reflétant dans son œil de verre : « C'est le goût du sang, Sun I. Il a sur moi un effet tonique. » Cette apparition me frappa d'un tel effroi que sa signification m'échappa presque complètement. Je voyais bel et bien Tsin flotter à un pied au-dessus du sol, la lueur rouge de son œil qui me harcelait et me raillait. Comme je le regardais bouche bée, en proie à l'hébétude et à la stupéfaction, une suite de phrases traversèrent mon esprit, sans lien apparent : « ... faites ceci en mémoire de moi... » En mémoire de qui ? « Aujourd'hui, nous voyons comme dans un miroir, confusément ; alors nous verrons face à face... » et ceci : « ... si je n'ai pas l'amour, je ne suis rien. »

« Si je n'ai pas l'amour » — l'éclat blafard de l'œil du soldat explosa brusquement en une myriade d'étoiles, une supernova, une conflagration qui consuma l'univers tout entier et me laissa hagard, temporairement aveugle. Quand je recouvrai la vue, le reflet avait rétréci aux dimensions d'un ongle qui flottait comme un minuscule croissant de lune sur la mer d'un verre de lunette en forme de larme vert foncé. L'espace d'un instant, le visage de mon père plana devant moi, la tête penchée sur le côté, son sourire énigmatique, impertinent, presque monstrueux, et, en même temps, merveilleux ! « Faites ceci en mémoire de moi... » Alors il se dissipa et les ténèbres m'engloutirent.

12

« Qu'est-ce que ça signifie, à ton avis ? » entendis-je Riley demander à Yin-mi en un murmure inquiet. Ouvrant les yeux, je les vis indistinctement, comme dans un miroir embué, ou sous l'eau, deux silhouettes floues qui m'encadraient.

« Je ne sais pas très bien, répondit-elle sur le même ton. Regardez, il a repris conscience.

— Que signifie quoi ? » demandai-je en me redressant dans le fauteuil où ils m'avaient installé ; l'aberration visuelle se dissipa rapidement, telle la brume qui s'évapore au soleil, laissant seulement une vague brûlure et une sensibilité inhabituelle à la lumière.

« Comment te sens-tu ? me demanda tendrement Yin-mi en serrant ma main.

— Je ne sais pas — bien, je crois. Que signifie *quoi* ? » répétai-je.

Elle adressa un regard peiné, interrogateur, à Riley, qui tourna les yeux vers moi. « Tu t'es évanoui pendant quelques secondes, dit-il. Tu as déliré. Tu répétais sans cesse la même phrase. Nous avons essayé de la comprendre.

— Quelle phrase ? »

Il plissa les yeux. « "Un festin princier pour un Dowiste." »

L'esprit en déroute, je battis plusieurs fois des paupières. Un silence de mort tomba sur la pièce.

« A quoi penses-tu ? demanda Yin-mi. Tu souris tellement bizarrement.

— Un festin princier pour un Dowiste », répétai-je en m'attardant sur chaque syllabe, ravi des sonorités de la phrase. Alors j'éclatai de rire.

« Sun I, dit Riley d'une voix préoccupée qui me surprit et me flatta, tu es sûr de te sentir bien ? Je ne veux pas t'inquiéter, mais ce qui vient de t'arriver ressemble à une crise. Il n'y a jamais eu d'épileptiques dans ta famille ? »

Cette remarque, que je jugeai calomnieuse, me rendit toute ma lucidité. « Certainement pas, répondis-je. Une simple réaction au vin, un point c'est tout. Je n'ai pas l'habitude de boire.

— Une simple gorgée de vin ne suffit pas à expliquer ton évanouissement, fit-il remarquer avec raison.

— Lui et mon père ont bu avant que nous ne venions ici, intervint Yin-mi.

— Absolument, confirmai-je. Et puis je crois que vous sous-estimez l'efficacité de votre sacrement. Après tout, le vin de communion n'est pas un cru ordinaire, ainsi que vous me l'avez aimablement fait remarquer. C'est en fait un élixir très puissant ! Comment échapper à l'ivresse en buvant pareil vin ? »

Riley se tourna vers Yin-mi avec une ébauche de sourire. « On dirait qu'il reprend du poil de la bête, commenta-t-il malicieusement. D'accord, Sun I, ce n'est pas moi qui nierai la vérité de ce que tu viens de dire, même si ton ironie est un peu facile. Pourtant, l'efficacité du sacrement se limite d'ordinaire au niveau spirituel, métaphysique.

— Allons bon ! m'écriai-je. Il y a quelques minutes, vous me disiez qu'il n'avait rien de symbolique, et maintenant vous me racontez que, tout compte fait, il s'agit seulement d'une métaphore.

— Tu as raison, Sun I, reconnut Riley. C'est plus qu'une métaphore. Nous croyons vraiment que le Christ est présent dans le calice, mystiquement présent et non pas littéralement ni physiquement. Nous ne croyons pas à l'idée catholique de la transsubstantiation.

— Que voulez-vous dire ? demandai-je d'une voix acerbe.

— Je t'expliquerai une autre fois.

— Pourquoi pas maintenant ? » le défiai-je.

Il sourit avec indulgence. « Excuse-moi, Sun I, mais je ne peux pas discuter théologie avec un taoïste soûl. Tu m'obliges à souligner le fait que tu es toujours ivre — littéralement, et aussi peut-être métaphysiquement. » Son sourire devint encore plus condescendant et paternel, plus gai aussi. « Allons boire une tasse de café en bas. Cela devrait nous permettre d'éclaircir la situation.

— Je ne bois pas de café, répliquai-je sèchement.

— Ah, encore un sacrement occidental que tu désapprouves ! poursuivit-il avec entrain. Pourtant, si tu n'y vois pas d'inconvénient, Yin-mi et moi le prendrons. Tu devrais nous imiter, ajouta-t-il. Le café t'aidera peut-être à retrouver ta lucidité.

— Je ne suis pas ivre, rétorquai-je sombrement.

— Allons allons, fit-il avec condescendance, il n'y a pas de honte à ça. Après tout, je suis prêtre, non ? Et j'ai du sang irlandais ! Ton état n'a rien de nouveau pour moi.

— Ne jouez pas au paternaliste, dis-je. Vous préférez éviter ma question.

— Très astucieux, dit-il en ouvrant la porte de la sacristie. Cela s'appelle une "retraite stratégique", un truc que j'ai appris au séminaire. Les Anglicans sont passés maîtres dans cet art. » Il me fit un clin d'œil. « Mais ne t'inquiète pas, tu ne perds rien pour attendre. »

Une atmosphère de fête, de carnaval, régnait au sous-sol de l'église où avaient lieu les réunions des CJT. Des « sessions impromptues » se déroulaient dans plusieurs pièces et il y avait aussi une tombola ; le jeune garçon qui avait lu l'épître, maintenant en habits laïques, faisait tourner le tambour du bingo et annonçait les numéros inscrits sur les balles de ping-pong sortantes ; à la guitare électrique et au saxophone, deux adolescents (accompagnés à l'épinette par une paroissienne échevelée dont ils ne semblaient guère apprécier ni même remarquer la contribution) jouaient du jazz « progressif » et claudiquant devant un groupe de jeunes filles assises pieds nus sur le plancher, les bras serrés autour des genoux, le menton posé sur les rotules, qui se balançaient au rythme de la musique, pour autant qu'on pût en discerner un. On avait aménagé un bar improvisé. De toutes ces distractions, cette dernière me parut la plus séduisante.

« Je peux t'offrir quelque chose ? » me demanda Riley.

Je lui souris malicieusement. « Je prendrai un Dry Sack avec...

— Ne me dis pas la suite, me coupa-t-il en levant la main. Avec des glaçons et un zeste de venin. » Il rit. « Malheureusement, nous ne buvons pas d'alcool ici, Sun I. Si tu veux monter à l'étage où l'on te servira tous les cocktails que tu pourras payer, libre à toi, mais il faut que tu sois membre à part entière de la communauté. » Il m'adressa un clin d'œil. « Raison de plus pour te convertir. Maintenant, je dois vous laisser pour aller saluer mes ouailles. Occupe-toi bien de lui, Yin-mi — nous ne voudrions pas perdre un épiscopalien en puissance.

— Tu lui plais », chuchota-t-elle dès qu'il se fut éloigné.

Je me renfrognai. « Je ne suis pas sûr qu'il me plaise.

— Tu as tout fait pour, rétorqua-t-elle, avant d'ajouter : mais je crois que tu l'aimes bien.

— Qu'est-ce qui te fait croire que je lui plais ? demandai-je en ignorant sa remarque.

— Ça se voit. Tu le défies. J'aimerais seulement que tu sois un tout petit peu moins agressif.

— Moi, agressif ! m'écriai-je, exaspéré. Et lui alors ? »

Elle éclata d'un rire ravi. « Je vais chercher un Coca. Veux-tu quelque chose ?

— Seulement qu'on me laisse tranquille, répondis-je avec humeur.

— Tu ferais mieux d'être gentil avec moi, me taquina-t-elle, sinon je pourrais te prendre au mot ! » Elle rit encore.

Je la regardai s'éloigner. Plusieurs fois, elle s'arrêta pour parler à des amis, toucher leurs mains, échanger de chastes baisers affectueux, éclater de ce rire spontané que j'aimais tant. Je sentis mon cœur se serrer, partagé entre la tendresse et le ressentiment. Et la culpabilité. Que faisais-je donc, me demandai-je, dans une église chrétienne ? Certes, j'y avais suivi Yin-mi. Pourtant je ne voulais surtout pas m'attacher à cette fille. L'amitié, la compassion désintéressée faisaient partie de mon sacerdoce. Mais si elle attendait autre chose — davantage — de moi ? Inévitablement, un jour viendrait où je retournerais au monastère. Mon passage dans son univers tenait à une seule raison et serait bref. Quand ce jour arriverait, je ne voudrais pas la blesser. Voilà ce que je me disais. Pourtant, dans mon cœur, je savais que je craignais surtout pour moi-même. Je m'étais déjà aventuré si loin dans ce monde, me semblait-il, et à chaque pas le terrain devenait plus glissant. J'étais terrifié à l'idée de descendre si loin que je ne pourrais plus jamais retourner en arrière. La boisson, par exemple — quelle honte ! A quels excès elle m'avait poussé. Et pourtant, c'était plus fort que moi, ou plutôt, je semblais l'apprécier avec un peu trop d'enthousiasme.

Au bar, Riley s'approcha d'elle, lui dit quelque chose. Tous deux se retournèrent vers moi en riant.

Je me rebiffai, me retirai davantage en moi-même. Je ruminai de sombres pensées, tirai des plans sur la comète.

« Le père Riley m'a chargé de te donner ça, avec les compliments de la maison, dit-elle en me tendant un gobelet en carton.

— Qu'est-ce que c'est ? demandai-je en reniflant avec méfiance le liquide rouge sang avant d'y tremper mes lèvres.

— Une Vierge Mary, dit-elle en riant.

— Une Vierge Mary ?

— Une Bloody Mary sans alcool. »

Je m'inclinai en direction de Riley, qui me regardait à travers la pièce. Il leva son Pepsi comme pour porter un toast.

« Je n'en veux pas, dis-je. J'ai eu assez de vos sacrements pour la journée. Je n'ai pas besoin qu'on me serve les mystères menstruels*. »

Yin-mi rougit. « C'est du jus de tomate, précisa-t-elle aussitôt.

— M'en fous. J'en veux pas.

— Tu es vraiment difficile, me reprocha-t-elle. Pourquoi es-tu toujours sur la défensive ? Tu te comportes comme si le père Riley allait te passer au fil de son épée si tu refusais de te convertir.

— J'ai davantage peur d'être brûlé vif, rétorquai-je. Ce serait pas la première fois.

— Tu as déjà été brûlé ? » Elle rit. « Détends-toi. Ceci est une fête, et non une séance de l'Inquisition.

— D'après ce que j'ai vu, les chrétiens ne font pas toujours la différence entre les deux. Mon oncle Hsiao m'a dit un jour que, lorsqu'il déjeunait avec des Occidentaux, il se sentait comme un marin naufragé invité à un festin de cannibales, et qui redoute à tout moment de passer, lui aussi, à la casserole. Je n'aimerais pas découvrir brusquement que vous me dévisagez avec des yeux affamés. »

Elle eut un sourire étrange, plissant les yeux comme si j'étais très loin d'elle. « Je ne t'ai jamais vu comme ça, aussi...

— Véhément ? demandai-je innocemment.

— Oui, véhément. Et amer. On dirait presque quelqu'un d'autre. »

Ses mots me firent sourire. « Oh non, c'est bien moi, une facette indélogeable de ma nature. Je n'y peux rien, ajoutai-je, plus par défi que pour m'excuser.

— Tu devrais peut-être éviter de boire, me conseilla-t-elle.

— Peut-être, raillai-je, mais c'est tellement drôle.

— Content de voir que vous vous amusez, dit Riley en s'approchant de nous. Moi-même, j'ai eu une pensée réconfortante. » Il se tourna vers Yin-mi. « N'est-il pas délicieux, et rassurant, qu'un observateur indépendant confirme la puissance de nos mystères, leur donne une assise quasiment scientifique ? » Puis vers moi : « Ton expérience de ce soir constitue certainement un argument plus éloquent et contraignant que tous ceux que je pourrais avancer, tu ne crois pas ?

---

* Dans *Bloody Mary*, *bloody* signifie ensanglanté *(NdT)*.

— Non, dis-je. Même si j'admets la puissance de votre sacrement, le problème de sa moralité reste en suspens.

— Ah ! fit-il. Je vois que tu as profité de la pause pour fourbir tes arguments. » Il rit. « Eh bien allons-y. A toi l'honneur. Quelles objections morales fais-tu au sacrement de la communion ?

— C'est du cannibalisme, dis-je. Pur et simple. Vous ne pouvez pas le nier, et pas davantage m'accuser de trivialité. Manger la chair et boire le sang — quel genre de divinité invoque donc ce mystère ? Un dieu que je n'aimerais pas rencontrer dans un couloir sombre, et encore moins adorer ! Il me fait penser aux goules et aux vampires !

— Tu oublies que c'est Dieu lui-même qui donne son corps et son sang très précieux pour sauver l'humanité.

— D'accord ! concédai-je. Voilà qui est bien dit. Ce sont ses adorateurs qui le dévorent. Vous faites de votre Dieu une victime.

— Ce que tu dis avec mépris est profond à ton insu, Sun I.

— Eh bien, je retire la métaphore, rétorquai-je. Votre Dieu innocent se laisser cannibaliser par ses zélateurs. C'est donc les chrétiens qui sont des goules et des vampires.

— Pourquoi es-tu si amer ? demanda-t-il.

— Ne m'avez-vous pas condamné à l'enfer ? »

Il acquiesça. « Oui, mais aussi invité à la résurrection.

— Je ne crois ni à votre enfer ni à votre résurrection, dis-je. Ni à votre Dieu patelin et souffreteux.

— Tu ne le connais pas. Notre "Dieu patelin et souffreteux", comme tu l'appelles, qui s'est fait crucifier pour la rédemption de nos péchés — et a montré un courage plus grand encore...

— "Vos" péchés, corrigeai-je.

— Non, *nos* péchés — les péchés du monde. Tu es inclu dans le rachat général, si tu veux bien accepter Son sacrifice dans ton cœur. C'est là le Dieu doux, aimant, le Dieu du Nouveau Testament, Jésus, le Fils. Mais il y a aussi Dieu le Père, Jéhovah, le Dieu de l'Ancien Testament. Et tu fais bien de le craindre, car il est terrible quand on le provoque, c'est le Dieu de colère.

— Je me doutais bien qu'il y avait une entourloupe. Sacré tour de cochon...

— Il n'a aucune patience avec les cyniques, je peux te l'assurer ! »

Je fus indiciblement ravi de le faire enfin sortir de ses gonds.

« Mais Sun I, reprit-il plus calmement, si je ne me trompe, le taoïsme et le bouddhisme aussi ont leurs divinités terrifiantes : les horribles dieux de la libération qui tentent d'effrayer l'adepte pour lui faire franchir le précipice vers l'illumination — Kwan Ti, Mahakala, Yamantaka. De façon très approximative, je dirais que le Dieu de l'Ancien Testament a une fonction similaire.

— A cette différence près : nos dieux sont psychologiques, métaphoriques, si vous voulez. Ils symbolisent les pouvoirs secrets du cœur. Le paradis repose en nous, ainsi que tous les dieux, dis-je en regardant Yin-mi, et l'enfer aussi. Voilà pourquoi je ne crains pas vos anathèmes.

— C'est une belle idée, dit-il. Moi-même, je l'ai assez souvent méditée

— Vous semblez pensif, remarquai-je. Peut-être est-ce moi qui finirai par vous convertir ? »

Il secoua la tête en souriant. « Peut-être, mais je ne le crois pas. Malgré toute ta persuasion, Sun I, je ne pense pas que tu fasses le poids avec mon propre Méphistophélès intérieur. J'ai flirté avec cette idée, mais l'ai abandonnée. Ta "voie" ne me satisfait pas.

— Pourquoi donc ?

— Parce qu'elle est insuffisante, elle laisse trop de choses de côté.

— Que laisse-t-elle de côté, père Riley ?

— Le monde, dit-il, le monde tel qu'il est.

— Que voulez-vous dire ? Les taoïstes vivent aussi dans le monde. Regardez-moi.

— Oui, mais selon vos enseignements, le monde est un rêve, une illusion, tous nos actes et nos souffrances sont aussi illusoires, et nous-mêmes rien d'autre que le résultat d'une "vision faussée". Pour moi, les êtres humains ont une évidence élémentaire, irréfutable, qui précède toute métaphysique et la fonde. Ils se définissent par leurs actions et leurs souffrances — peut-être surtout par leurs souffrances...

— Etre, c'est souffrir, citai-je cyniquement en me rappelant Kahn.

— Quelque chose comme ça, dit-il. Mais vous niez la réalité de la souffrance, et ainsi vous retirez à la vie toute dignité et toute passion. Si le monde extérieur n'existe pas, alors nos souffrances aussi sont illusoires. Et je ne peux accepter cela. Je vois trop de souffrances chaque jour. Elles ont une évidence brute, brutale même, qu'aucune métaphysique n'aura jamais — du moins pour moi.

— Mais vous vous trompez, dis-je. Le problème n'est pas de savoir si la souffrance est réelle ou non, seulement de comprendre qu'elle est superflue et que chacun se l'inflige malgré lui.

— Je ne crois pas à cela. Cela contredit mon intuition fondamentale du monde. Mais laissons la métaphysique ; une seule chose m'a vraiment convaincu de l'inadéquation du point de vue oriental : en niant le monde extérieur et la réalité de la souffrance, vous nous privez du même coup de la seule consolation que nous ayons.

— Laquelle ?

— L'amour, dit-il, "si je n'ai pas l'amour, je ne suis rien" — tu te souviens de l'épître ? (Je remarquai que Yin-mi rougit.) Sans monde extérieur, sans autre, il ne saurait y avoir d'amour. Et il ne saurait y avoir d'amour sans souffrance.

— Vous oubliez, objectai-je, que la Compassion est l'un des Trois Trésors du taoïsme.

— Ce n'est pas la même chose, rétorqua-t-il.

— De quoi parlons-nous, alors ? »

Il soutint mon regard. « Vivre dans le monde tel qu'il est. L'amour est dans le monde et souffre. La compassion est un regard désabusé qu'on jette par-dessus son épaule quand on a déjà quitté le monde. Elle est au-delà de la souffrance, immunisée contre elle et, pour cette raison même, un peu anémiée et méprisable, sans importance en fin de compte.

— Pourquoi doit-on toujours souffrir ? demandai-je.

— Si tu l'ignores, je ne peux pas te l'apprendre.

— Peut-être parce que l'attachement à ce monde — à ses demi-vérités, son caractère transitoire et contradictoire — satisfait le besoin de nous blesser nous-mêmes, suggérai-je. Désireux d'un lieu situé au-delà des vanités et de l'éphémère, incapables d'en trouver un, nous nous punissons et rajoutons ainsi aux punitions du monde. »

Riley devint triste. « Cela est très profond, Sun I, bien que partiellement vrai — une explication dangereuse surtout pour celui qui la formule. Mais ne comprends-tu pas que nous devons d'abord être brisés ? C'est pour cela que le Christ a dit : "Celui qui voudra sauver sa vie la perdra ; et celui qui voudra la perdre pour moi la trouvera." »

Riley était ému ; et son émotion me toucha, bien que je ne fusse pas convaincu. « Vous êtes très persuasif, concédai-je, et manifestement sincère. Je respecte cela. Mais vous avez laissé quelque chose de côté. L'amour n'est pas la seule consolation. Il y a aussi la paix intérieure, les "joies de la voie". Le Retour à la Source propose de riches récompenses à ceux qui ont la force d'affronter ses rigueurs, son austérité — et au bout du chemin, la plus grande de toutes les joies, l'illumination.

— Ah oui, la "paix qui dépasse l'entendement" dans sa version chinoise, dit-il, retrouvant son ironie. Je ne marche pas dans la combine.

— Je ne vous oblige pas à "marcher dans la combine", répliquai-je avec indignation. Je n'essaie pas de vous convertir. Je respecte vos croyances, du moins la plupart. Pourquoi ne pas me rendre la politesse ?

— C'est vrai, je me sens contraint d'essayer de te convertir, même si je plaisante parfois à ce sujet. "Il y aura plus de joie au Ciel pour un seul pécheur repenti que pour quatre-vingt-dix-neuf justes qui n'ont pas besoin de repentir."

— Vous me considérez donc comme un pécheur ? demandai-je d'une voix moqueuse.

— Bien sûr ! Un charmant pécheur — et parfaitement récupérable, qui plus est. Mais je reconnais que mes motifs ne sont pas entièrement désintéressés. Ta conversion ferait bon effet dans ma comptabilité céleste. Car pour l'instant, je crois que mon compte est plutôt débiteur. »

Je ris. « Votre foi est trop exigeante.

— Tout amour est exigeant ! » répliqua-t-il.

Je me sentis rougir, mais résistai à son charme. « Que d'exigence et de passion ! Que d'extase ! J'ai du mal à comprendre une religion qui décrit son état le plus saint et son accomplissement spirituel comme une ébriété. Votre plus grand mystère se révèle dans une coupe de vin. Le sacrement du taoïsme — pour autant qu'il y en ait un — révélerait son plus grand secret dans une gorgée d'eau froide et limpide tirée du puits primordial. Ma formation m'a appris que l'extase déforme plus qu'elle ne révèle. L'extase est une forme de besoin, et le besoin falsifie. Ne sommes-nous pas plus près de la vérité en ces moments de tranquillité, quand notre concentration se fixe sur nous-mêmes et que notre jugement n'est pas faussé par la passion, par le désir ?

— Ce que tu appelles tranquillité est pour moi une résignation désespérée. Même si pareil apaisement est possible, je me demande s'il en vaut la peine, s'il ne nous fait pas renoncer à l'essentiel.

— A quoi donc ?

— A l'amour, Sun I. J'en reviens toujours à cela. "Il excuse tout, il croit tout, il espère tout, il endure tout. L'amour ne renonce jamais."

— Jamais, vraiment ? répondis-je, méditant un instant la portée de cette phrase. Je me demande. Je me demande aussi si l'amour n'est pas cruel.

— Si, bien sûr, aimer c'est souffrir, mais... — il me regarda attentivement — tu dis cela d'une façon si bizarre. A quoi penses-tu au juste ? »

Je fixai Yin-mi en souriant tristement. « A rien, mon père, dis-je, à rien. »

Notre joute verbale se poursuivit tard dans la soirée, longtemps après que les derniers invités des CJT se furent éloignés dans la nuit. Nous avons sillonné en tous sens ces mêmes territoires frayés lors de ces premières escarmouches, abordant pourtant un sujet inédit que je signalerai brièvement à cause de son intérêt.

Comme la conversation prenait un tour plus intime, Riley m'interrogea sur les raisons de ma venue à New York et de mon travail à la Bourse, une décision qu'il ne comprit pas (je ne lui avais rien dit de mon père) jusqu'à ce que je lui eusse parlé du delta.

Quand je lui expliquai l'image, il serra ses mains l'une contre l'autre, son regard se perdit dans le vague.

« Maintenant je commence à comprendre. C'est passionnant, Sun I... Mais sais-tu, je crois qu'il existe un parallèle chrétien.

— Ah bon ? répondis-je.

Il se balança en avant sur sa chaise et fouilla mon visage. « Oui. Ta tentative de chercher le Tao dans le Dow — ou, à l'inverse, et peut-être plus précisément, de localiser le Dow sur la carte de la réalité conçue par les philosophes-cartographes taoïstes — ressemble tout à fait aux efforts chrétiens pour réconcilier l'existence du mal dans le monde avec un créateur absolument bon. Ce problème irritant est la poussière autour de laquelle des générations d'apologues ont sécrété la perle de la théologie chrétienne. Je suppose que toutes les religions naissent d'une douleur similaire, taoïsme inclus. Bien que vous ne formuliez pas le problème en termes de bien et de mal, vous devez néanmoins vous demander pourquoi le Tao s'est dégradé dans "les dix mille choses", pourquoi son harmonie originelle s'est ainsi fragmentée, pour engendrer le chaos du monde illusoire, la "place du marché", donnant ainsi à l'homme la tâche de Retourner à la Source. Car si le Tao était si parfait et harmonieux, pourquoi s'est-il désintégré ? Que s'est-il passé ? Comment l'avons-nous perdu ? Je ne sais pas si les taoïstes répondent à cette question, dit-il comme si je pouvais éclairer sa lanterne.

— Le Tao ne s'est pas désintégré, lui assurai-je. Il n'a jamais été perdu. Il est immanent en nous.

— Ah, "immanent"... dit-il. Mais c'est une échappatoire. Même s'il existe ici et maintenant et qu'il en a toujours été ainsi, pourquoi ne le percevons-nous pas ? Comment expliquer nos errements — voilà où le bât blesse. Nous appelons cela la Chute.

— Alors, quelle est la réponse chrétienne ?

— Il y en a plusieurs, dont certaines assez ingénieuses. Ainsi, celle formulée dans l'Exultet : *"O certe necessarium Adae peccatum... O felix culpa."*

— Qu'est-ce que ça veut dire ?
— "Ô péché d'Adam vraiment nécessaire... Ô chute heureuse".
— Pourquoi heureuse ?
— En apportant le péché et la mort dans le monde, la Chute a aussi apporté la possiblité de la rédemption.
— N'aurait-il pas mieux valu laisser les choses dans leur état premier ?
— Peut-être, d'un point de vue d'économie rationnelle. Mais nous devons considérer ces choses avec l'œil de l'artiste. Sans la Chute, sans l'apparition de la multiplicité, il n'y aurait pas eu d'amour. L'amour est la force de gravité qui peut réunir tous ces fragments éclatés dans un monde déchu. L'amour est l'effort du médecin pour se guérir lui-même. Quand nous nous aimons, nous participons à la réintégration mystique du corps de Dieu. A quoi tu peux bien sûr rétorquer que tout aurait été infiniment plus simple si Dieu ne s'était pas blessé, s'il avait conservé son intégrité. C'est là le cœur du problème. Le processus de la réintégration — l'amour — devient plus important que le but lui-même. Voilà la révélation chrétienne, la lumière nouvelle que le Christ a donnée au monde : la Chute était non seulement nécessaire, mais un bien. Car ce que nous avons perdu — l'intégrité — est largement compensé par ce que nous avons gagné — l'amour. L'amour est la plus grande des qualités spirituelles, et en un sens le christianisme l'a inventé. Il requiert l'incomplétude et, de ce fait, est inaccessible à vous autres taoïstes. Cela me paraît l'échec des religions orientales : elles essaient de retourner en arrière, elles répudient le salut qui nous est offert dans le monde tel qu'il est, le monde déchu. Comme une autruche qui enfouit sa tête dans le sable, le taoïste refuse de voir la grâce qui nous est proposée ici et maintenant, et que cette grâce dépasse la consolation utérine de l'état que nous avons perdu ; il refuse de voir que le plus grand bien procède de la plus grande tragédie, c'est-à-dire la division originelle, la Chute. C'est cela le miracle, vois-tu — "L'amour a bâti sa demeure sur le lieu de l'excrément", comme dit Yeats. Nous devons être brisés pour retrouver notre intégrité par l'amour. »

Je lui exprimai mon désaccord en termes vigoureux, étayant ma position d'arguments qui me parurent irréfutables. Hormis ce point, nous n'abordâmes aucun autre sujet digne d'être mentionné ; Yin-mi profita néanmoins d'un silence pour évoquer la robe de ma mère, qu'elle décrivit à Riley en termes hyperboliques. Quand il me dit qu'il aimerait beaucoup la voir, j'acceptai non sans réticence car je soupçonnai fortement que cette proposition participait de leur conspiration pour me convertir. Riley eut alors une idée. Pourquoi ne pas l'apporter à une réunion des CJT et en parler brièvement, évoquer sa construction, son symbolisme, utiliser la robe comme une sorte de tremplin pour raconter ma propre histoire — « j'ai grandi dans un monastère taoïste au fin fond de la Chine occidentale », « une évasion risquée vers la mer », etc. ? Je suspectai alors secrètement que, malgré sa solide formation, Riley était un peu trop fasciné par le mystère oriental et qu'il perdait la tête. Il voulut faire imprimer des affichettes qui annonceraient ma « prestation » dans tout le quartier de Wall Street. Ses airs protecteurs m'agacèrent légèrement, mais je fus malgré tout flatté. Ainsi, après avoir feuilleté le calendrier de l'église et fixé une date suffisamment lointaine « pour que la nouvelle puisse se répandre », Riley me convainquit d'accepter.

« Eh bien, Sun I, je suis ravi de t'avoir enfin rencontré et que nous ayons eu cette petite discussion, dit-il en nous raccompagnant, Yin-mi et moi, sur le trottoir. Tout est réglé pour la conférence ?

— Je crois, répondis-je.

— Bien. Nous nous reverrons donc à cette occasion, sinon avant. Oui, avant, j'y tiens ! Sens-toi libre de passer quand tu veux. Simplement... — ajouta-t-il avec un regard désapprobateur — ne blague plus avec la communion. » Il rit. « Attends que nous t'ayons converti. Ensuite, tu pourras lâcher la bride à ta soif de Sacrement. C'est un banquet ininterrompu, "nourriture à volonté" pour le prix du couvert et jusqu'à la fin des temps !

— Le prix à payer est trop élevé, dis-je en m'autorisant l'ombre d'un sourire.

— Pas du tout ! s'écria-t-il. Pense à tout ce qu'on te donne : un véritable festin de sept plats ! Cinq sacrements partiels en guise de hors-d'œuvre, plus deux plats de résistance. Et pour le dessert, l'espoir du paradis !

— Et pensez à tout ce que je perds, rétorquai-je.

— Que perds-tu ?

— "Le Mystère", dis-je en citant le premier chapitre du *Tao-tö king*. Ou plutôt, "ce qui est plus sombre que tout Mystère, la Porte de toutes les Essences Secrètes". » Je secouai la tête. « Non, je préfère mon humble souper à votre festin : le riz grossier, l'eau froide du puits, le creux d'un coude en guise d'oreiller... et ce qui accompagne cela — un cœur apaisé.

— Et l'amour, Sun I ? demanda-t-il gravement en regardant aussi Yin-mi. Qu'en fais-tu ? »

Je rougis, mais soutins son regard. « "Seul celui qui se débarrasse à jamais du désir verra les Essences Secrètes ; celui qui ne s'est jamais débarrassé du désir ne verra que les Résultats."

— "Qu'un homme voie sans passion le cœur de la vie, répliqua-t-il, ou qu'il voie passionnément sa surface, le cœur et la surface sont essentiellement identiques, les mots seuls les font paraître différents afin d'exprimer l'apparence." »

Profondément impressionné, je restai silencieux. Car Riley venait de réciter une traduction contradictoire du même passage du *Tao-tö king* que je venais de citer.

Il saisit la main de Yin-mi et lui dit bonsoir, puis la mienne, qu'il serra d'une douce pression intime qui me gêna un peu. « Ce sera la dernière parole que je t'adresserai ce soir, Sun I, dit-il. Que fais-tu de l'amour ? Et puis ceci, ajouta-t-il en glissant dans ma main un petit exemplaire du Livre de Prières. Je tiens à ce que tu l'aies. Regarde-le quand tu auras un moment. » Il haussa les épaules. « Qui sait ? »

Quand nous le quittâmes, il resta sur le seuil pour nous voir franchir le portail en fer forgé et rejoindre Broadway. Toute trace de malice avait disparu de son visage ; j'aperçus seulement le reflet d'un lampadaire dans son œil, un scintillement qui, l'espace d'un instant, me rappela la lueur dans l'œil du soldat, le Chasseur.

13

A cette heure et en accord avec les prévisions de Mme Ha-p'i, le ciel s'était obscurci et couvert. D'énormes cumulus semblables à des monuments de cendre bleuâtre s'étaient massés au-dessus de la mer et cinglaient vers nous en apportant une bouffée iodée de l'Atlantique Nord. L'air avait fraîchi, les voix portaient étrangement loin. Je crus entendre les cris des débardeurs de Brooklyn et les éclats de voix des équipages sur les pétroliers qui approchaient du port. Entre les roulements de tonnerre intermittents, je remarquai le crépitement doux et secret de la pluie sur le trottoir, je l'entendis avant de la sentir sur moi, respirai aussi son odeur — l'âcre senteur de la vapeur mêlée d'asphalte qui montait de la rue, presque avec un soupir de soulagement. Ouvrant l'ombrelle de sa mère, Yin-mi m'invita d'un geste sous son orbe protecteur, et nous poursuivîmes dans le même silence intime et légèrement interdit. Elle tenait timidement mon bras ; bien que sa proximité me réconfortât, elle me troublait aussi. Je ne pouvais m'y abandonner sans réserve, elle me menaçait sans que je susse pourquoi. Cela m'avait déjà inquiété ; peut-être cette proximité était-elle à l'origine de ma « mystérieuse rancœur ». Mais cette impression n'avait jamais été aussi forte que ce soir, pendant ma conversation avec Riley. Notre discussion avait aiguisé ma perception ; ce que cette intimité menaçait en moi était beaucoup plus essentiel que toute considération philosophique : elle ébranlait le sentiment même de son intégrité, au sens le plus profond du terme, le noyau même de mon être. Je refusais de me laisser troubler par les sophismes persuasifs de Riley, mais cette douce pression sur mon bras, cette intimité silencieuse étaient infiniment plus menaçantes... « Et que fais-tu de l'amour ? »

Alors que nous passions sous le pont de Brooklyn, la foudre frappa le pilier le plus proche. Un instant, le fleuve tout entier s'illumina d'une fluorescence blafarde, l'eau sombre bouillonna dans cette lumière fantomatique. Quand il toucha le pilier et fut absorbé par les poutrelles d'acier, l'éclair ressemblait à une ligne brisée tracée à la craie sur un tableau noir ; toute l'énergie électrique fut aspirée par les câbles, puis canalisée à travers le chaos des eaux jusqu'aux sombres régions chthoniennes sous le fleuve, où elle se dissipa et s'enfouit.

Alors il se mit à pleuvoir. Nous restâmes à l'abri du pont pour regarder

l'orage, intimidés et admiratifs. Au bout de quelques minutes, Yin-mi parla : « On dirait que la pluie ne va pas s'arrêter de sitôt. Ma mère va s'inquiéter. Si on courait jusqu'à la maison ? » Ses yeux brillaient de défi.
 « Je ne sais pas, répondis-je d'une voix hésitante. Ce n'est pas tout près.
 — Allez, dit-elle, le premier à la maison ! » Elle souriait comme je ne l'avais jamais vue sourire, avec une audace impertinente, un rire provocateur et narquois. J'étais partagé entre la surprise et un vague sentiment d'humiliation. Alors elle s'élança sous la pluie battante. « Le dernier arrivé est un œuf pourri ! s'écria-t-elle. Un œuf de mille ans pourri ! »
 Quand j'entendis son rire, je m'élançai à mon tour. La pluie glacée me coupa le souffle. Je fus instantanément trempé jusqu'aux os. Mes orteils se crispaient dans mes chaussettes mouillées ; je croyais courir avec des semelles de plomb. Comme je remontais une buse d'écoulement, je tombai de tout mon long dans l'eau. Ma chute ne fit qu'augmenter mon hilarité. Je me relevai sur les coudes et me mis à barboter et gigoter comme un poisson joyeux qui s'ébat dans une mer chaude et peu profonde. Ruant des quatre fers, hurlant de joie, je perdis tout sens de la réalité. Puis j'entendis son rire moqueur devant moi, et je repartis. Quand je distinguai son corsage blanc à travers les diamants brisés de la pluie, un désespoir subit m'étreignit. Je pris mes jambes à mon cou, mais au bout d'une centaine de mètres crus que mon cœur allait éclater ; un instinct me convainquit pourtant de l'insignifiance de ma douleur. Je la rattrapais régulièrement, jusqu'au moment où, à ma grande surprise, elle bifurqua dans une rue que j'ignorais. Je m'arrêtai au coin et scrutai un cul-de-sac désert. Personne. Où était-elle passée ? Mon cœur battait la chamade ; brusquement je ressentis la nécessité de m'accroupir pour renifler les pierres. L'absurdité de cette idée me fit rire comme un imbécile. Poursuivant mon examen, je découvris plusieurs ruelles que Yin-mi avait pu emprunter. Je savais parfaitement que, si je me trompais, je la perdais et perdais tout court. J'allais retourner sur mes pas vers l'artère principale dans l'espoir de la battre de vitesse, quand je remarquai l'ombrelle brisée qui gisait au croisement d'une ruelle, le papier blanc qui ressemblait à un pétale arraché par l'orage. Sa trace, un indice volontairement laissé derrière elle. Sans même m'arrêter pour ramasser l'ombrelle, je m'engageai dans le labyrinthe.
 A vingt ou trente mètres de l'entrée, la ruelle obliquait brusquement vers la gauche, si bien que je perdis de vue la rue. Dans l'obscurité environnante, je ralentis et progressai avec davantage de précautions. Il me suffisait d'étendre les bras pour toucher les deux murs couverts d'une couche épaisse et visqueuse de suie sale, fraîche et vaguement moussue. Hormis l'éclat fantomatique des nuages que j'apercevais par une étroite fente au-dessus de ma tête, il n'y avait pas de lumière. D'abord je me fiai presque uniquement au toucher. Les squelettes inaccessibles des escaliers d'incendie se détachaient en ombres chinoises contre la bande opalescente du ciel. Le crépitement de la pluie était plus faible ici ; j'entendais devant moi le gargouillement de l'eau qui chutait dans un égout invisible. Malgré l'obscurité, les filets d'eau qui ruisselaient sur les façades des bâtiments luisaient d'un éclat argenté, comme des filons phosphorescents dans une grotte humide. De temps à autre, de pâles ordures filaient près de mes pieds,

emportées par le ruisseau qui coulait d'un côté de la venelle. Les odeurs aussi suggéraient un monde souterrain, la pluie et l'asphalte sentaient les cendres, je respirais l'obscène fécondité des ordures. Quelque chose fila à deux ou trois mètres devant moi. Je me figeai et scrutai les ténèbres. Puis cela se retourna et la lumière se refléta dans ses yeux — un rat. Il me dévisagea avec un regard presque intelligent plein d'une ruse immémoriale, puis retomba à quatre pattes et s'enfuit.

Cette apparition dissipa complètement mon hilarité, la remplaça par un pressentiment de malheur qui glaça mon excitation sans l'annuler. Une image traversa alors mon esprit, et mon cœur cessa de battre pendant quelques secondes ; l'ombrelle brisée gisant sur le trottoir suggérait une autre interprétation. Et si ce n'était pas un indice volontairement placé sur mon chemin ? S'il s'était passé quelque chose ? Il y avait peut-être eu quelqu'un dans la ruelle quand elle s'y était engagée. Et si... ? Ma terreur fut si forte que je faillis vomir ; mon appréhension atteignit une intensité intolérable. Je marchai plus vite. A mesure que mes yeux s'habituaient à la pénombre, je distinguais d'autres rats. Ils étaient partout, chassés des égouts par l'orage. La venelle serpentait sans cesse, de nouveaux embranchements s'offraient à mes pas tous les trois ou quatre mètres, et je finis par me perdre complètement. Je me désespérai, tel un homme plongé dans une eau si opaque qu'il ne distingue même pas ses propres bulles et ne sait où nager pour retrouver l'air et la lumière. De plus en plus convaincu de m'être fourvoyé, je voulais retourner sur mes pas. Mais je n'étais pas davantage certain de pouvoir retrouver l'entrée du labyrinthe que de m'y orienter.

Je contournai alors un mur, et une étendue grise s'ouvrit devant moi — non pas la lumière, mais le soupçon d'un espace ouvert. Je pénétrai dans un étrange terrain vague entouré de tous côtés par les murs de bâtiments élevés, une sorte de cour intérieure couverte d'objets au rebut : meubles brisés, réfrigérateurs broyés comme des épaves d'automobiles accidentées, leur émail blanc brillant d'un éclat lugubre, énormes sacs poubelles verts dont le contenu se répandait sur le sol. Je reconnus aussitôt le modeste royaume perdu des objets abandonnés que j'avais souvent contemplé de ma terrasse. Du toit, je n'avais jamais vu la venelle qui aboutissait à la courette, et encore moins un itinéraire pour rejoindre la rue. Il devait pourtant en exister un. J'entrepris de longer les murs en les tâtant de la main. Quelques secondes avant de l'atteindre, j'aperçus un rectangle plus sombre dans la pierre. Je pénétrai dans l'ouverture et aperçus enfin le halo d'un réverbère. Je me mis à courir. Je trébuchai, m'égratignai les mains, me relevai. Je retrouvai alors un paysage familier ; plié en deux, mes mains couvertes de sang posées sur mes genoux douloureux, je m'arrêtai pour reprendre mon souffle. Je fus tellement soulagé que j'en oubliai Yin-mi. Quand je repensai à elle, je me redressai pour regarder autour de moi, et à cet instant précis quelque chose me saisit par-derrière. Je bondis dans la rue en hurlant. J'entendis alors son rire moqueur et excité tandis qu'elle montait les marches quatre à quatre vers le vestibule. Elle ferma la porte derrière elle, me regarda brièvement derrière la vitre avant de disparaître. Je restai un instant hébété, puis la rage la plus violente que j'aie jamais connue s'empara de moi. Je gravis les marches en courant. La porte était fermée à clef. Je la secouai plusieurs fois avec une sauvagerie imbécile avant de me rappeler que j'avais la clef. Je l'enfilai dans la serrure ; en la tournant, j'aperçus mon reflet dans la vitre, un visage gonflé de sang, cramoisi, les veines saillant sur mon cou, mes pupilles dilatées au point d'absorber presque totalement l'iris.

Elle était appuyée contre la porte intérieure, les mains soutenant ses reins, un genou levé, le pied posé à plat contre le panneau. Son genou légèrement rentré suggérait la féminité et une pudeur instinctive. Ses cheveux trempés brillaient d'un noir intense. Ses yeux pétillaient, toute son attitude exprimait le triomphe ainsi qu'une timide capitulation — la plaisanterie était terminée, ou du moins il ne tenait qu'à moi qu'elle le fût. Mais mon attention se fixa surtout sur ses seins, parfaitement visibles à travers le corsage mouillé, et ses mamelons érigés à cause du froid. Elle ne faisait rien pour les cacher. Je remarquai qu'elle aussi haletait légèrement. Je bondis sur elle sans avoir la moindre idée de ce que je faisais. J'enlaçai sa taille et la soulevai en serrant de toutes mes forces, la regardant droit dans les yeux. Elle rit de plaisir et d'excitation. Je sentis le sang se ruer dans mes veines comme je serrai davantage. Au bout d'un moment, son rire disparut. La douleur la fit un peu grimacer, puis, avec une sorte de tristesse attendrie, elle se pencha languissamment vers mon visage et m'embrassa sur les lèvres, m'embrassa avec sa langue. Stupéfait, je la lâchai. Elle retomba avec souplesse sur ses pieds et recula de quelques pas en fixant sur moi un regard curieux, vulnérable. Les yeux rivés aux siens, je n'étais conscient que d'une chose — le goût de sa bouche, adouci presque insupportablement par la saveur prolongée du vin.

« Pourquoi as-tu fait ça ? lui demandai-je d'une voix tremblante.

— Je ne sais pas, dit-elle. Dois-je fournir une raison ? »

Brusquement je me mis à pleurer. Je portai mes mains à mon visage, m'abandonnai à une crise de larmes déchirante.

« Ne pleure pas, murmura-t-elle en revenant vers moi pour enlacer mes épaules. Ne pleure pas, Sun I. » Je sentis la douce pression de son corps qui se coulait de tout son long contre le mien, ses vêtements froids, humides, et puis la chaleur de sa nudité qui irradiait à travers le tissu, me brûlait presque.

Je levai vers elle mon visage crispé de sanglots.

« Chut, fit-elle. Tout va bien. Tu as froid. Viens, je vais te préparer du thé et te donner une couverture chaude. »

Je capitulai et la laissai une fois encore prendre en main la situation.

« Regardez-moi ça ! s'écria Mme Ha-p'i qui jeta sa broderie à terre et se leva de son fauteuil. Vous êtes tous les deux trempés jusqu'aux os ! » Le soulagement et la sympathie lisibles dans sa voix se nuançaient d'une critique implicite. « Yin-mi, va te changer immédiatement », ordonna-t-elle sur un ton sans réplique. Confondue, la tête rentrée dans les épaules, Yin-mi marmonna un timide « Oui, m'man », avant de disparaître dans le couloir.

« Sun I, suis-moi », me commanda-t-elle. J'obéis moi aussi ;

instantanément, nous devînmes deux enfants déférents. Mme Ha-p'i m'emmena jusqu'à la chambre d'amis. « Wo a laissé quelques affaires ici quand il a emménagé dans son appartement, dit-elle, plus pour elle-même qu'à moi. Voyons... » Elle ouvrit le placard et, d'une main nerveuse, passa les cintres en revue. Elle me lança par-dessus son épaule une chemise hawaïenne imprimée jaune et orange. « Et un pantalon. » Elle se retourna en me présentant un bermuda en madras.

« Inutile qu'ils aillent ensemble, non ? demanda-t-elle avec humeur en découvrant la sombre révolte qui s'affichait sur mon visage.

— Non, madame, dis-je. C'est parfait.

— Bien. Va te changer dans la salle de bain. Prends donc aussi ça, dit-elle en me lançant une ceinture. Wo est solidement bâti, et tu es plutôt... mince. » Elle prononça ce dernier mot avec une emphase que je trouvai insultante.

« Mince ? » songeai-je en silence en examinant mon corps. Je ne m'étais jamais considéré comme particulièrement mince, mais j'étais si intimidé et sous l'empire de tels SO que je pus seulement souscrire à son jugement. Si Wo l'obèse pouvait passer pour « solidement bâti », alors je tenais sans doute du fil de fer.

Comme j'étais dans la salle de bain, toutes les lumières s'éteignirent dans l'immeuble. Quand j'en sortis, Mme Ha-p'i avait déjà allumé des bougies. Je retournai au salon et remarquai que Yin-mi n'était toujours pas revenue. La brusque et impitoyable efficacité maternelle qui avait animé Mme Ha-p'i s'adoucit quand elle m'aperçut, si timide, confondu et fragile, comme emmailloté et phagocyté dans cette vulgaire exhibition criarde d'acétate belliqueuse. Son indignation s'apaisa. J'avais redouté son rire, mais ce furent la tendresse et la pitié qui apparurent sur ses traits. Elle retira sa boîte à couture de la chaise à côté d'elle, en tapota le tissu rose passé pour m'inviter à m'asseoir. Quand je lui obéis, ma déférence inconsciente dut être si profonde qu'elle éveilla sans doute un souvenir dans son esprit, car d'un geste affectueux plein de sollicitude maternelle, elle écarta doucement les épis de mon front. Puis elle poussa un profond soupir et retourna à sa broderie.

« Alors, Yin-mi et toi avez-vous passé un bon moment ? demanda-t-elle.

— Oui, m'dame », dis-je.

Elle me regarda bizarrement. Je ne sais plus où je croyais être, mais j'étais réduit à un total infantilisme, régressant si loin en moi-même que j'avais perdu l'usage de la parole. Il me semble qu'elle le comprit. Elle approcha la broderie de son visage, puis fouilla dans son panier à la recherche d'une bobine de fil. Tout en travaillant, elle m'observait de temps à autre par-dessus ses lunettes en demi-lune.

Quand Yin-mi entra finalement sans bruit, ses cheveux secs ébouriffés par la serviette, en pantalon de pyjama et chemise à col rond bleu foncé, sa mère quitta un instant son aiguille des yeux pour la regarder. « Sun I a peut-être envie d'une tasse de thé, ma chérie. Tu devrais aller faire chauffer de l'eau. » A ces mots, Yin-mi fit demi-tour et ressortit en silence, comme sous hypnose.

Mme Ha-p'i m'observa. Je rougis. Un sourire étrange apparut sur ses lèvres et dès lors elle se concentra sur son ouvrage, travailla de ses doigts rapides et habiles, enfin absorbée et donnant presque l'impression d'avoir oublié ma présence. Malgré son mutisme, je n'éprouvais aucun malaise, mais me sentais inclus et accepté dans l'atmosphère paisible qu'elle irradiait, dans ce halo domestique défraîchi mais confortable. Je me mis à observer de plus en plus fixement les mouvements compliqués de ses doigts. Ses mains fatiguées étaient sillonnées d'un réseau de grosses veines bleues dont la beauté me bouleversa. Elles luisaient d'un éclat presque trop réel. Une fois encore, la couture imperceptible du monde s'ouvrit et se referma, me donnant un aperçu vertigineux de la vie intime de sa main : le sang plein d'oxygène battait dans les artères de son poignet, puis refluait dans les grosses veines sur le dos de sa main ; les souples tissus des muscles striés se dilataient et se contractaient quand ses doigts remuaient ; les tendons, les os, les ligaments...

Je me fondis dans ce spectacle magique. A la fois apaisant et mélancolique, il évoquait de façon poignante un souvenir enfoui, ma douleur secrète. Je remarquai enfin que le rythme de ses doigts avait nettement ralenti, que son attention se portait ailleurs. Elle scrutait mon visage avec cette profonde gravité que j'avais déjà remarquée chez Yin-mi. L'espace d'un instant, je crus voir la fille me regarder derrière le visage de la mère, comme si cette femme mûre était une statue inachevée qui, réduite à son essence élémentaire par le ciseau du sculpteur, révélerait précisément Yin-mi.

« Tu pensais à ta mère, n'est-ce pas ? » dit-elle avec émotion.

Bien que je n'en eusse pas pris conscience plus tôt, je compris qu'elle avait raison. Sa clairvoyance m'étonna. Pendant une seconde d'intimité suspendue, le caractère formel de notre rapport s'évanouit. Puis, presque d'un commun accord, nous retrouvâmes notre distance habituelle ; elle reprit sa broderie et j'allai à la porte attendre le retour de Yin-mi.

Quand elle parla, ce fut sur un ton plus ordinaire. « Tu sembles rêveur et préoccupé ce soir, Sun I, hasarda-t-elle. Tu as des problèmes, mon chéri ? L'argent, peut-être ? » Elle soupira. « Tu sais combien nous sommes pauvres, mais si nous pouvons t'aider... » Elle sourit. Je fus touché.

« Ou bien..., ajouta-t-elle avec désinvolture, haussant les sourcils en achevant une maille, pourquoi ne pas en parler à Wo ? Il pourra peut-être faire quelque chose pour toi. » Je faillis me laisser prendre à son ton anodin, mais mon œil exercé remarqua sa manœuvre. Je détectai la ruse maternelle implicite, qui suivait son cours inflexible. J'attendis, soupirai, et comme de bien entendu... « Dis-moi, Sun I reprit-elle d'une voix sincère et implorante en écartant son ouvrage, est-il heureux ? »

La brève intimité que nous venions de partager, bien qu'évanouie, dirigeait encore puissamment mes émotions. Une fois encore, je faillis trébucher, trahir ma résolution de protéger Wo. Je songeai qu'il eût certainement été soulagé de se débarrasser de ce fardeau ; mais je ne pus.

« Je le vois rarement, dis-je en examinant mes mains, mais pour autant que je sache, il est heureux. »

Pendant un long et désagréable moment, je sentis son regard fouiller mon visage. Puis elle soupira et reprit son ouvrage. « Oui, dit-elle d'une voix lasse, comme se récitant une litanie à laquelle elle ne croyait guère, je sais qu'il se débrouille bien. Il a son propre appartement maintenant. Mais parfois je m'inquiète. » Sa voix venait de se briser, je vis qu'elle pleurait. Mon cœur se déchira.

Elle renifla en m'adressant un sourire d'excuse à travers ses larmes. « Pardonne-moi, Sun I. Les mères sont parfois terriblement ennuyeuses, non ? »

D'une voix calme, mais qui tremblait un peu, je répondis : « Je ne crois pas, Mme Ha-p'i. »

Elle se mordit la lèvre, puis tendit le bras pour toucher ma joue. « Mon pauvre garçon ! »

Yin-mi émergea du couloir avec un plateau supportant une petite théière brune et trois tasses de porcelaine qui tintaient sur leurs soucoupes. « Où est papa ? » demanda-t-elle sans remarquer le geste de sa mère.

Mme Ha-p'i soupira, puis entreprit de réunir les objets posés sur sa robe. « Il dort depuis des heures, ma chérie. Il est allé se coucher juste après votre départ. Il était très fatigué.

— Tu veux dire ivre, rectifia Yin-mi avec une ironie lugubre.

— Ne sois pas irrespectueuse. » Sa mère la rabroua, mais avec une patience dépourvue de colère. « Tu sais combien ton père travaille dur.

— Oui, je sais, répondit vivement Yin-Mi. Mais il était ivre. »

Aucune des deux ne parla. Il régnait entre elles une tension que je n'avais jamais sentie.

« Veux-tu du thé ? demanda enfin Yin-mi, froidement mais avec une nuance de remords rancunier.

— Non merci, ma chérie, répondit sa mère. Tu sais que je n'en bois jamais le soir. J'ai déjà bien assez de mal à dormir. » Se tournant vers moi, elle m'adressa son sourire de mère désorientée, puis ajouta : « Bonsoir, Sun I. Je suis si contente que tu sois venu nous voir. Viens plus souvent, je t'en prie. Quand tu veux... Oh ! » s'écria-t-elle en partant d'un rire nerveux, retrouvant brusquement son masque de politesse guindée. « J'avais oublié. Je n'étais pas censée parler de ça. Enfin, tant pis. Lo dort. Tu ne lui diras rien, n'est-ce pas ? »

Je souris en secouant la tête. « Non, promis-je, et je vous promets de revenir bientôt. » Je lui tendis ma main.

Elle s'appuya dessus pour se pencher et embrasser Yin-mi sur la joue. « Ne te couche pas trop tard, chérie. »

Vautrée dans son fauteuil, les bras pliés sur la poitrine en une attitude défensive, Yin-mi réagit passivement et se contenta de lever le menton pour recevoir le baiser de sa mère.

Mme Ha-p'i la regarda, soupira une fois encore, puis s'éloigna silencieusement sur ses chaussons de soie, entra dans sa chambre et referma la porte derrière elle.

Après son départ, Yin-mi se détendit. J'étais déconcerté, un peu vexé. Elle versa du thé brûlant dans ma tasse et me la tendit. « Quoi ? demanda-t-elle en remarquant mon expression.

— Rien, dis-je. Je pensais seulement que tu avais manqué de respect envers ta mère.

— Oh, Sun I ! protesta-t-elle d'une voix exaspérée en laissant tomber

bruyamment sa soucoupe sur le plateau. Tu ne sais même pas de quoi je parle. Et ma mère refuse d'ouvrir les yeux.
— Sur quoi ?
— Sur la vérité.
— A savoir ?
— A savoir que mon père est un alcoolique. »
Je la regardai avec incrédulité.
« Oh, allez. Tu t'en es sûrement aperçu ? » Elle eut un rire amer. « Non, c'est sans doute trop étranger à ton expérience. Ce genre de chose n'arrivait pas au monastère, je suppose ? » Elle secoua la tête. « Parfois, ça me déprime tellement de vivre ici. Je ne supporte plus de les voir vieillir, se voûter, gâcher leur vie à force de mesquineries, de peurs et de soucis d'argent. Pourquoi se battent-ils ? Pour survivre ? » Elle rit avec dérision.
Ses paroles me surprirent. « Je ne suis absolument pas d'accord, rétorquai-je. Les voir tous les deux ce soir m'a fait plus que jamais comprendre à quel point ils sont remarquables. Quels trésors n'ont-ils pas amassés pendant toutes ces années d'épreuves et d'affection partagées ! »
L'étonnement de Yin-mi vira à l'aigre. « Tu te débrouilles toujours pour retourner comme une crêpe les arguments de ton interlocuteur, n'est-ce pas ? »
Je souris avec complaisance. « C'est un vieux truc que j'ai appris au monastère, me vantai-je en singeant Riley. Les taoïstes sont célèbres pour cela.
— Ta sagesse est bien prématurée, Sun I, rétorqua-t-elle avec mépris. C'est celle que l'érudit tire de ses lectures, sans le moindre risque et à peu de frais. Tu l'as apprise avec ton esprit, mais sans tes mains ni tes pieds, et sans ton cœur. »
Je levai la main pour protester.
« Laisse-moi finir. Quand je regarde mes parents, je vois la médiocrité, l'indignité, la souffrance sans espoir — le genre de souffrance qui épuise et finit par écraser. Oui, mon père est un alcoolique, car la souffrance a touché les centres vitaux de son esprit, les a flétris. Mais vois-tu, je le respecte plus que toi. Pourquoi ? Parce qu'au moins il a vécu. Tu transportes ta philosophie avec toi comme une carapace qui te protège du monde, mais elle t'emprisonne aussi à l'intérieur de toi-même — comme un préservatif entre toi et la réalité. Oh, bien sûr, je sais que tu as souffert, mais pas de la même façon. Pour toi, tout est un jeu. Tes souffrances sont du cinéma, elles sont sans conséquences durables. Des souffrances comme les tiennes seraient un luxe pour mon père. Tu t'arranges toujours pour les métamorphoser en croissance spirituelle — tu pratiques l'art du jardinier qui avec son sécateur taille une plante pour qu'elle s'épanouisse, mais ne touche jamais au nerf secret de sa vie.

« Le monde réel est une forêt, Sun I, pas un jardin. C'est la vie et la mort qui se jouent et se risquent, pour de vrai. Ta philosophie te rend aveugle à cette évidence. Tu n'es impliqué dans aucune réalité, tu n'as rien aimé. Pour toi, tout cela est une illusion déplorable, digne de compassion mais surtout pas d'engagement. L'admiration que tu exprimes pour mes parents est empoisonnée par l'ozone que tu ramènes de la stratosphère de ta condescendance. Ils ne sont rien de plus pour toi que des cobayes de laboratoire. Mais je te le répète, je les respecte davantage que toi et toute ta philosophie. Parce que tu n'as jamais aimé quelque chose comme mon père a aimé, au point d'endurer toutes les souffrances du monde pour la conserver, et jusqu'à la mort de ton propre esprit. »

Cette brusque tirade diffamante provoquée par ma remarque anodine me décontenança complètement, et ce d'autant que j'ignorais sa cause réelle. J'aurais pu me sentir blessé, mortifié, mais j'étais trop stupéfait. Et puis l'expression de Yin-mi mobilisait toute mon attention. Je ne l'avais jamais vue ainsi ; ses beaux yeux disaient une horrible douleur, comme deux grandes blessures qui réclamaient un dédommagement que je ne parvenais pas à comprendre.

« Tu as raison, dis-je enfin d'une voix apaisante pour essayer de la consoler sans paraître paternaliste. Mais chacun de nous fait son choix ; ton père a choisi sa vie, moi la mienne. Qui dira lequel a raison, ou même si nous n'avons pas tort tous les deux ?

— C'est exactement ça ! s'écria-t-elle. Tu as tellement perdu contact avec le monde réel que tu y crois vraiment — "chacun de nous fait son choix". Conneries ! Ma mère et mon père n'ont jamais pu se payer le luxe d'un tel choix. Ils ont pris ce qu'on leur donnait et ont façonné leur vie avec. Dans le meilleur style scolastique, tu demandes : "Qui dira lequel a raison ?" Mais je te jure que, même si mon père est un coolie et un poivrot, je le respecte plus que toi parce qu'il a eu le courage d'aimer de tout son cœur et de se sacrifier, alors que toi, avec toute ta précieuse philosophie, tu as toujours eu une soupape de sécurité, une échappatoire. »

Elle pleurait, presque hystériquement. Bien que piqué au vif, je m'inquiétai davantage pour elle que pour moi. Jamais je ne l'avais vue dans cet état. Ses accusations étaient pourtant trop douloureuses pour que je ne me défende pas.

« Je me trompe peut-être, répondis-je d'une voix calme et neutre, mais il me semble que nous sommes tous libres de choisir notre vie. Si nous ne le sommes plus, c'est qu'à un moment nous avons renoncé à cette liberté en échange d'autre chose. Cela aussi est un choix. En Chine, les monastères étaient ouverts à tous. Ton père aurait pu devenir moine. Mais il a choisi de partir pour l'Amérique, de se marier et de fonder une famille. C'est sa "voie", et elle me paraît bonne. Bien sûr, il est privé des consolations du détachement, tu as raison sur ce point. Mais il a une compagne pour l'aider à surmonter les épreuves de la vie, un amour aussi solide que les fondations du monde. Cela aussi est une consolation. Et tu comprends sans doute que c'est une consolation dont je suis privé, moi — et tous ceux qui choisissent la voie monastique.

— Mais pourquoi, Sun I ? Pourquoi dois-tu te priver de cette consolation ? » demanda-t-elle, la tendresse et la pitié se mêlant maintenant à sa colère.

Je compris enfin ; cette découverte fut agréable, mais aussi torturante comme le fumet d'un banquet auquel je ne serais jamais convié. « Tu voudrais que j'abandonne ma philosophie, que je renonce à ma quête, à tout ce que tu dénigres, à tout ce que j'aime...

— Oh non, Sun I ! me coupa-t-elle en posant un doigt sur mes lèvres. Ne pense surtout pas ça. Ta recherche m'est précieuse. J'aime ta philosophie, ta foi honnête, ta pureté de cœur, ton innocence et ton courage...
— Mais...
— Chut, murmura-t-elle. Tu ne vois donc pas ? Ce que je dis importe peu. J'aime tout cela parce que je t'aime. »

Elle saisit mes mains et m'attira facilement contre elle, tourna doucement ma tête, la posa sur son épaule et caressa mes cheveux. « Depuis le premier soir, chuchota-t-elle. Tu croyais que je te méprisais... » J'entendais le sourire de sa voix, l'entendais sans le voir. « Mais tu te trompais. Je voulais simplement être sûre. »

Je ressentis une telle lassitude, un tel désir d'inconscience, une telle envie de me fondre en elle — une lassitude que je portais peut-être en moi depuis des années sans même la connaître. Mais j'ouvris les yeux et la repoussai tendrement à bout de bras. « Tu ne dois pas m'aimer, Yin-mi, lui dis-je doucement, pas de cette façon. Car je ne pourrai jamais t'aimer ainsi. Ne me demande pas le joyau secret de ma vie, car je l'ai déjà promis.
— Comment ça, promis ? A qui ?
— A ma religion. Te donner ce que j'ai déjà promis serait un parjure impardonnable.
— Tu te trompes, Sun I, dit-elle. Je te demande seulement ton cœur. De ton âme, je te laisse libre de faire ce que tu veux, ou ce que tu dois. Je n'ai jamais songé à te voler ton joyau secret. Je me contenterai d'une aumône plus modeste.
— Mais comment les séparer ? » demandai-je en perdant contenance.

Elle sourit en clignant des yeux. « Je sais qu'ils sont séparés.
— Oh, Yin-mi, dis-je d'une voix fatiguée, si je pouvais aimer de cette façon, je ne voudrais personne d'autre que toi. Je te le jure. Mais essaie de comprendre, mon destin me lie à un autre chemin.
— Tu es si jeune, dit-elle. Comment peux-tu connaître ton destin ? » Ses yeux exprimaient une tendre soumission, mais aussi une assurance dont je n'avais jamais vu la pareille, sinon peut-être dans le regard du maître. Pourtant, l'assurance de Chong Fou incluait une nuance de gaieté, un élément auquel on pouvait se raccrocher pour ne pas couler, alors que celle de Yin-mi englobait tout comme un immense océan, où je me sentis sombrer. Pris d'une panique soudaine, je me raidis et marchai vers la fenêtre.

Elle ne me suivit pas. Au bout d'un moment, j'entendis les tasses et les soucoupes tinter lorsqu'elle retira le plateau. Ce bruit me parut aussi feutré et rassurant que le crépitement de la pluie après les sinistres roulements de tonnerre. L'électricité n'était toujours pas revenue.

Je regardai dehors. La lune éclairait les poutrelles des escaliers d'incendie en dessous de moi. Ce spectacle me rappela le panorama de Ken Kuan, la vue plongeante dans le ravin où le torrent argenté bondissait parmi les rochers, son vacarme vigoureux qui se dispersait, se raréfiait, se muait en un murmure insinuant à mesure qu'on s'en éloignait. Tout proche et pourtant lointain. Cette opposition évoquait une bataille observée par les soldats dans les tranchées — l'éclair livide des obus qui explosent au-dessus de leurs têtes —, et la même scène vue de loin par des spectateurs inquiets debout sur les murs de cités bien défendues, à qui elle paraît simplement triste et de mauvais augure, comme un coucher de soleil hivernal qui jette une lumière mourante sur les champs stériles, étreint leurs cœurs du désir poignant de l'été. « ... Un préservatif entre toi et la réalité... » « Aujourd'hui, nous voyons comme dans un miroir, confusément... » « Tu n'as jamais aimé comme mon père a aimé, au point d'endurer toutes les souffrances du monde, et jusqu'à la mort de ton propre esprit... » « Et l'amour, Sun I ? » Les voix de cette soirée refluaient vers moi pour me hanter comme le chœur des morts de la rivière. Mais plus obsédants encore, l'étreinte équivoque de Yin-mi et le goût de sa bouche. Pour une raison mystérieuse, des images de guerre continuaient à défiler devant mes yeux ; elles jaillissaient comme le magma à travers une fissure qu'un glissement de plaques tectoniques avait ouverte dans mon cœur, là où jadis la terre n'avait jamais tremblé. Je me vis en objecteur de conscience chargé de monter la garde sur les remparts ; je baissais les yeux vers les colonnes de fantassins qui se déployaient tout en bas dans les rues, certains garçons pas plus âgés que moi et tout aussi terrifiés à l'idée de mourir. Je souris amèrement. Mais où était l'ennemi ? Qui était-il ? Peut-être rien de plus que ce que Riley avait nommé « vivre dans le monde tel qu'il est ». Comme les soldats passaient sous une arcade, le regard de l'un d'eux croisa le mien, et sur ses traits juvéniles, tirés par la peur et la résolution, d'une beauté farouche trop intense pour son âge, je vis une sagesse amère et un reproche silencieux qui fouillaient les recoins les plus secrets de mon esprit. J'avais vu ce même regard dans les yeux de Yin-mi.

Jamais auparavant, du moins à un niveau aussi viscéral, je n'avais conçu le moindre doute quant à la validité de la Voie que j'avais apprise sous la tutelle de mes mentors taoïstes. Pour moi, libérer son cœur de l'influence pernicieuse de la passion, affranchir son esprit du désir plutôt que le souiller des eaux boueuses d'aspirations refoulées, constituait l'idéal à atteindre — la voie du renoncement était supérieure à celle de l'acquisition. Mon cœur en était toujours convaincu. Mais ce soir, autre chose avait imprimé sa marque sur moi. Pourquoi ressentais-je ce doute, cette honte, comme si l'on m'eût accusé de lâcheté ? Peut-être parce que je refusais de livrer cette vieille bataille avec les armes habituelles, préférant rentrer en moi-même, convaincu que la guerre pouvait seulement aggraver les hostilités et se perpétuer. Pourtant, le regard de ceux qui vont affronter un péril mortel est un terrible reproche pour qui reste sur les murailles. Et ce regard ne peuplait-il pas tous leurs yeux — ceux de Yin-mi, de Lo, de sa mère, et jusqu'à ceux de Riley ? Peut-être l'eussé-je supporté, si ce soir je n'avais ressenti la secousse sismique du doute. Comme une Atlantide mentale qui remonte du fond de l'océan dans une tempête tumultueuse d'écume et de vapeur, tout un continent émotionnel inconnu se dressa devant moi, un hémisphère essentiel et surprenant, un Nouveau Monde découvert dans un cadran où les cartographes mandarins avaient échoué à le localiser. Des forêts et des montagnes fertiles, des pâturages fréquentés par les cerfs et les bisons, d'immenses bassins fluviaux qui aboutissaient à des mers intérieures, des champs de céréales florissants remplaçaient maintenant les océans amorphes et monotones, l'eau salée du Tao qui dissolvait tout. Ce continent était l'amour, et ses vastes panoramas, sa fécondité monstrueuse, l'étrangeté des animaux qui y paissaient et y chassaient me firent perdre toute échelle, me réduisirent à rien sous la gigantesque coupole de ces cieux. Je désirais l'ancienne sécurité du monde que j'avais connu : le grand jardin entretenu par des moines dévoués, où ne poussaient ni séquoïas ni pins Douglas, mais ces arbres *p'en-tsai* qui croissent pendant des générations sans jamais grandir au-dessus de la taille d'un homme ; un lieu où tous les rochers sont soigneusement disposés dans un but symbolique et esthétique, où ils ne sont jamais dangereux, jamais sujets au moindre glissement de terrain ; où les rivières canalisées gargouillent avec une musique toujours identique, où des rossignols, et non des aigles, occupent les arbres pour chanter. Je désirais un jardin, pas une forêt — surtout pas ce monde sauvage. Je fus submergé de terreur en contemplant ce Nouveau Monde, ses délices et ses dangers, car il me fit entrevoir une autre Voie, un *tao* d'amour, l'égal et le complément du *tao* de la quiescence, qui, ensemble, constituaient la dichotomie irréductible du monde, opposés et irréconciliables tant que durerait l'univers. Pourtant, comment cela pouvait-il être, si « La Réalité est Une, et le Tao est la Réalité » ? C'était impossible. Soit ce nouveau continent étincelant était une illusion, soit... Pouvais-je même formuler l'autre terme de l'alternative ? Le Tao était une illusion. Car si le Tao est seulement partiel, alors le Tao est faux. Riley avait-il raison de dire que le Tao n'accordait aucune place à l'amour, ou bien existait-il quelque inimaginable... « delta », oui, delta, où ce torrent bouillonnant se jetait lui aussi dans l'océan mystique ? Mieux, était-il possible, ou même concevable, que le delta où l'amour se consumait pour rejoindre la paix intérieure fût identique à celui où le Dow se jetait dans le Tao ? Je songeai alors que, jusqu'à mon arrivée en Amérique, le Tao que j'avais connu et révéré sans qu'il ne m'en coutât beaucoup avait seulement été une version émasculée, un échantillon de laboratoire, une fleur de serre. J'avais connu la lumière sans les ténèbres. Et elles se dressaient maintenant comme une mer bouillonnante autour de moi ; j'étais échoué sur la grève d'où j'observais l'orage monter en me demandant s'il épargnerait le lopin de terre que je considérais comme mien.

En proie à ces pensées troublantes, je sentis brusquement la présence de Yin-mi derrière moi.

« Tu es là ? lui demandai-je sans me retourner.

— Oui, dit-elle doucement.

— As-tu parfois peur, Yin-mi ?

— Qu'y a-t-il à redouter ? répondit-elle avec un léger tremblement dans la voix.

— Je ne sais pas, dis-je. Quelque chose au fond de notre cœur. »

Nous restâmes tous deux silencieux, puis je l'entendis pleurer. Je me retournai.

« Pourquoi pleurer ? demandai-je en m'approchant d'elle et posant légèrement ma main sur son épaule.

— Je ne sais pas, sanglota-t-elle en souriant à travers ses larmes, quelque chose au fond de mon cœur. »

Elle saisit ma main et la pressa contre sa joue en fermant les yeux. J'entendis de nouveau le cor du chasseur résonner au loin, les aboiements énervés de la meute, je sentis mon cœur prêt à céder ; mais de nouveau, je résistai.

Un bourdonnement sourd se mit à grésiller dans l'air. Les ampoules luirent d'une faible lumière brune. Le bourdonnement s'amplifia et la pièce s'emplit soudain d'une incandescence blafarde, peu naturelle après l'obscurité apaisante, comme les projecteurs de la science impitoyablement braqués sur les régions les plus intimes du cœur.

Je vis le bleu pâle de l'orchidée sous les paupières de Yin-mi irritées par les larmes. Elle semblait blessée, sa peau était blanche, comme poudrée. Pourtant elle ne m'avait jamais paru aussi séduisante. Je me sentais nu et honteux. Je retirai vivement ma main.

« Bon, dis-je d'un air faussement dégagé, l'électricité est revenue. Je me demande quelle heure il est. Tard, je suis sûr. Je crois que je vais rentrer.

— Je pourrais préparer le lit dans la chambre de Wo, proposa-t-elle. Pourquoi ne restes-tu pas ? Oui, reste, s'il te plaît.

— Je ne peux pas, Yin-mi », dis-je, presque implorant.

Je regardai une dernière fois ses yeux aussi calmes que ceux de la fillette sur la grève, puis je m'enfuis devant elle.

« Au revoir, lui lançai-je en ouvrant la porte, sans me retourner.

— Quand reviendras-tu ? » me demanda-t-elle alors que le pêne claquait dans la gâche. Je m'éloignai comme si je n'avais pas entendu.

14

La « version non expurgée » de la Vie de Kahn, ma communion illicite à Trinity, la poursuite effrénée sous la pluie, la déclaration d'amour de Yin-mi — j'étais stupéfait, et terrifié, par la profusion, la fécondité, la confusion du « monde réel » et de la vie de mes amis, de la mienne aussi je suppose (culpabilité par association), même si je résistais à cette conclusion, persistant à me considérer comme un observateur et non un participant, convaincu qu'une telle objectivité était possible et justifiée. Je dus aussi inclure la répulsion dans la palette émotionnelle de ce week-end. J'étais plein de nostalgie pour le monastère, la simplicité, les plaisirs chastes des moines, et j'aspirais à me perdre dans la méditation. Mais j'étais incapable de me concentrer, de me dissoudre. Les cigales dans le temple du cœur stridulaient plus fort que jamais. Des pensées troublantes se bousculaient dans mon esprit : la question de Riley, « Et l'amour, Sun I ? » ; l'apparition de Tsin ; la vision des seins de Yin-mi, tels des boutons non éclos qu'on renonce à cueillir ; le goût de sa bouche. Et flottant au-dessus de tout cela, comme le chat du Cheshire, le sourire mystérieux et légèrement sarcastique de mon père, allié à cette phrase de la liturgie, « Faites ceci en mémoire de moi ». Ces images remontèrent à ma conscience, accompagnées de bouffées brûlantes d'une honte quasiment physique. *Tso-wang* fut impraticable. Même le sommeil me fuyait. Dès que je fermais les yeux, la litanie des voix obsédantes s'emparait de mon esprit, flottant sur le même courant d'air que la rumeur du Puits des Soupirs, pour se fondre dans le murmure élémentaire de la cité. Lundi matin, j'arrivai à la Bourse épuisé, nauséeux, le cœur serré de désespoir. Je désirais tant retrouver le lieu immaculé et brillant qui, je le savais, était toujours en moi, mais dont j'avais perdu le chemin. Peut-être liée à mon manque de sommeil, je ressentais aussi une étrange brûlure aux yeux, que j'avais remarquée pour la première fois après mon évanouissement à l'église. Cette douleur n'avait pas diminué pendant le week-end.

Pour couronner le tout, j'étais intellectuellement surmené par mes efforts infructueux pour réconcilier les deux stratégies financières incompatibles auxquelles Kahn m'avait introduit. Les informations relatives à la Valeur Intrinsèque et à l'Analyse Technique se bousculaient dans mon cerveau sans m'avoir encore payé le moindre dividende en termes de savoir objectif —

en fait, elles n'avaient fait qu'accroître ma confusion. Impitoyable, Kahn m'exhorta à une autre expédition le matin même.

Il avait téléphoné aux Ha-p'i dimanche soir pour me demander de le retrouver au petit drugstore de Pearl Street où nous allions parfois, avant l'ouverture de la séance, prendre nos ablutions — comme aurait dit Scottie —, lui son café, moi mon thé du matin. « Je te réserve une grande surprise », disait son message ; il me mit sur des charbons ardents, comme Kahn le faisait si souvent. Pourtant j'étais content de pouvoir lui parler en tête à tête. Car les événements des deux derniers jours avaient rendu intolérable mon incertitude à propos de mon père. Si quelqu'un pouvait me renseigner sur l'histoire ultérieure d'Eddie Love, ce devait être Kahn. Car qui connaissait plus intimement l'aspect humain de Wall Street, la vie secrète des grandes corporations et des hommes qui les dirigeaient ? Parmi tous ses titres de gloire, Kahn pouvait se vanter d'être un répertoire ambulant des scandales de la Bourse. Et j'étais enfin prêt à surmonter la peur de ce que j'allais découvrir.

Alors que, installé dans mon compartiment du drugstore, je m'exhortais à la chutzpah et au courage au-dessus de ma tasse de thé fumant, Kahn entra en trombe et me prit par surprise.

« Viens, petit, m'intima-t-il d'une voix pressante en saisissant mon bras pour m'entraîner vers la sortie. Pas de temps à perdre. Si tu te grouilles, tu pourras attraper celui de huit heures quarante-deux.

— Celui de huit heures quarante-deux ?
— Oui, tu vas à New Haven.
— New Haven ! Où est-ce ?
— Dans le Connecticut.
— Où est le Connecticut ?
— Le long de la voie, espèce de schmo. Comment veux-tu que je le sache ? Consulte ton atlas !
— Mais pourquoi vais-je là-bas ?
— Tu as rendez-vous avec le Dr J. — Julius Everstat — un vieux copain ; on était ensemble au Mont-Nebo et au BIG. C'est un mathématicien de Yale, il a bossé sur l'application des techniques statistiques à l'étude du marché. Je tiens à ce que tu aies au moins une teinture de l'approche académique de l'analyse du marché. Et puis, il a une histoire intéressante à te raconter.
— Mais pourquoi New Haven ?
— J'aurais volontiers goupillé quelque chose un peu plus près de chez nous, à Columbia ou à la NYU, mais il se trouve qu'à Manhattan l'intello ne s'épanouit pas dans sa forme la plus pure et virulente, probablement parce qu'ici on ne peut pas assurer l'environnement parfaitement aseptisé indispensable à sa croissance — trop de parasites, dans tous les sens du terme.
— Mais j'ai besoin de vous parler.
— Voilà bien ton problème, petit : trop de parlote, pas assez d'action.
— Mais c'est important !
— Important ! Qu'y a-t-il de plus important que ton éducation ? Faut que t'en veuilles, petit. Souviens-toi du vieil adage de l'Ashkénaze fou : "Pas de gloire sans couilles".

— Kahn ! m'écriai-je d'une voix exaspérée en secouant ses bras pour le faire taire.

— D'accord, cent fois d'accord — nous parlerons ! Mais *après* ton retour, okay ? Maintenant, bouge-toi le tuchis, pour l'amour du Christ ! J'ai prévenu le gars, il vient te chercher à la gare. C'est quand même un peu fort ! Écoute-moi : je te fais une fleur, et je dois te supplier de l'accepter ? Tiens, prends ça. » Il me fourra quelque chose dans la main.

« Qu'est-ce que c'est ? demandai-je.

— Un billet, répondit-il. Exactement, je t'ai même acheté ton billet. Tu vois quel chic type je suis ? Tu ne mérites pas un tel ami. Et ça — son adresse et son numéro de téléphone. Juste au cas où il oublierait le rendez-vous. Julius est un garçon charmant, mais terriblement distrait. Maintenant vas-y ! File ! » Sur ces mots, il me projeta littéralement dans l'entrée de la station de Lexington Avenue, où je pris le métro pour Grand Central.

Le train de New Haven émergea du tunnel de la gare au voisinage de Harlem, puis longea Park Avenue vers la cent-vingt-quatrième rue. L'avenue ne ressemblait nullement à ce qu'elle était dans le centre ville. Des immeubles calcinés ou noircis par les flammes longeaient la voie, un pot de géraniums décorait parfois un escalier d'incendie, une corde à linge exhibait des vêtements dont les couleurs criardes servaient sans doute à se prémunir contre la saleté déprimante du décor. Ce fut ensuite un paysage lunaire de tours, l'Élysée du logement social, une utopie où les enfants jouaient non pas parmi les asphodèles ni même dans l'herbe, mais sur l'asphalte. Le paysage s'aéra graduellement. Son échelle devint plus humaine, plus intime. Magasins serrés les uns contre les autres dans les ruelles de villes sans nom, églises blanches surmontées de clochers, usines délabrées, murs de pierre noire le long des voies. Puis ce furent les forêts et la mer. Quand le train dépassa un marais salant où les ajoncs commençaient à jaunir, je fus surpris et ravi de découvrir des millions de papillons blancs et orange qui voletaient dans l'air. Bien que l'été déclinât seulement depuis quelques jours, un pressentiment de l'automne imprégnait l'air, une certaine clarté dans les lointains et, malgré la chaleur, une trace de fraîcheur, comme lorsqu'on respire au-dessus d'un verre de glace pilée. D'énormes cumulus filaient vers l'horizon, tels des clippers cinglant toutes voiles dehors au-dessus de l'Atlantique vers Cathay.

Les craintes de Kahn s'avérèrent justifiées. Julius n'était pas là. Les impératifs et les responsabilités de l'existence mondaine étaient apparemment trop contraignants pour lui, ou trop triviaux pour son attention exclusivement monopolisée par l'étude des hautes mathématiques. Par-dessus le marché, le numéro de téléphone que Kahn m'avait donné était sans doute celui de l'appartement de Julius, car personne ne répondit à mon appel. J'avais heureusement l'adresse de son bureau, si bien qu'avec un soupir je partis à pied en demandant mon chemin. Je souris aujourd'hui en songeant que mon initiation au Chemin Aléatoire débuta fort prosaïquement dans la rue avec l'action de mes jambes — consolation qu'hélas je ne pus alors apprécier à sa juste valeur.

Quand j'arrivai enfin au bureau d'Everstat, la porte était ouverte. Je découvris le savant profondément concentré, penché au-desus d'une table couverte de listings d'ordinateur vert pâle dont les extrémités s'enroulaient comme de vieux parchemins ; celui qu'il examinait était maintenu par une règle à calcul, une tasse à thé et un bloc-notes cubique. L'expression méditative de son visage, ses grognements intermittents, les caresses qu'il prodiguait à sa barbe, où il tissait machinalement de minuscules mèches pointues avant de les démêler, tout cela me plut. Peut-être avais-je trouvé un authentique mage occidental, l'homme qui pourrait enfin mettre un terme à la confusion qui me bouleversait.

Quand je frappai, il leva lentement vers moi son regard de myope. « Oui ? demanda-t-il poliment, mais sans enthousiasme.

— Dr Everstat ?

— Bon, qu'y a-t-il ? rétorqua-t-il sèchement en louchant vers sa montre. Bon Dieu ! Je suis en retard ! » Quand il bondit de sa chaise, je remarquai sur son blue-jean le pli impeccable du nettoyage à sec. Son T-shirt portait cette inscription : « Les statisticiens sont un meilleur pari. » Il donnait l'impression d'un homme habillé par sa mère et sa petite amie, tant ces détails vestimentaires contrastaient avec ses traits émaciés dus sans doute à des années de pensée solitaire.

« Excusez-moi. » Il passa devant moi pour sortir dans le couloir. « J'ai un rendez-vous très important. Je devais retrouver quelqu'un à la gare il y a vingt minutes. Il est sûrement rentré chez lui. » Il se figea, le regard dans le vague. « Je me demande quelles sont les probabilités pour qu'il soit resté... » Il hésita comme s'il calculait mentalement, puis, se secouant, repartit.

« Dr Everstat ! » criai-je derrière lui.

Il s'arrêta, fit volte-face. « Quoi ? » hurla-t-il avec colère. La compréhension illumina alors son visage. Il leva lentement l'index vers moi. « Vous ? »

J'acquiesçai.

Il se frappa le front avec sa paume en riant. « Bien sûr ! J'aurais dû m'en douter tout de suite à cause de votre... ah... vos particularités physiognomoniques.

— Vous voulez dire que je ressemble à un Chinois ? extrapolai-je en souriant.

— Exactement ! » s'écria-t-il en saisissant ma main, manifestement soulagé de me voir réagir avec humour à son allusion raciale. « Alors, tu es Sun I. » Il prononça correctement mon nom, à la chinoise, ce qui m'impressionna favorablement. « Mon ami Aaron — comment va ce vieux sagouin... ?

— Plus sagouin que jamais. »

Il sourit. « ... m'a dit que tu étudiais le marché et que tu aimerais voir comment nous travaillons ici. »

Je hochai la tête. « J'essaie de me faire une idée valable du Dow à partir de toutes les écoles d'analyse du marché.

— Nous allons te faire gagner du temps et t'épargner quelques efforts superflus, répondit-il fièrement. Il n'existe aucune autre "école" d'analyse du marché. La nôtre est la seule qui mérite ce titre. Certes, il y a des "approches", mais elles ressemblent aux religions primitives. Leurs gourous ne valent pas mieux que les sorciers qui invoquent les divinités animistes ; ils s'en remettent à leurs dérisoires petits fétiches intellectuels pour se protéger contre un pouvoir qu'ils ne comprennent pas.

— Votre méthode est donc différente ? »

Il haussa les épaules avec assurance. « Ils croient à la foi, à l'espoir, à l'amour, à tous les accessoires démodés de la religion. A l'inverse, notre méthode est scientifique. Au lieu de fétiches et de gris-gris, nous sommes épaulés par tout l'arsenal de la haute technologie de l'ère spatiale. »

Sa confiance m'impressionna. « Avec tout ce matériel, vous avez certainement réussi des prouesses dans votre propre carrière d'investisseur. Où sont vos préférences en ce moment ? » demandai-je sans penser à mal.

Crois-moi, lecteur, je ne me serais jamais douté qu'une question aussi innocente — mais qui terrifie les spécialistes du marché comme une question sur le temps les météorologues — plongerait dans une telle confusion cet expert renommé. Everstat rougit, ouvrit la bouche pour parler, se ravisa, perdit contenance, regarda ses chaussures, puis réussit à bafouiller : « Ah... eh bien... vois-tu, Sun I, bien que m'intéressant de près à la Bourse, je... enfin... je n'investis jamais d'argent. » Il sourit d'un air penaud, puis, se reprenant, poursuivit d'une voix plus assurée : « Non, mon étude est strictement désintéressée. C'est indispensable quand on cherche la vérité, non ? L'intérêt personnel est une forme fatale de cécité dans un domaine où la lucidité est essentielle.

— Vos recherches n'ont donc aucune application pratique ?

— Si, dans la mesure où nous conseillons certains investisseurs, expliqua-t-il. Nous leur ouvrons les yeux sur la propagande des Fondamentalistes et des Techniciens, et tous les autres faux prophètes.

— Pourquoi faux prophètes ? l'interrompis-je.

— Parce que leurs conseils sont motivés par l'intérêt personnel, répondit-il. Car presque jusqu'au dernier, ce sont des courtiers qui palpent de grosses commissions quand ils peuvent convaincre leurs clients de vendre ou d'acheter. Non, bien que nos adversaires prétendent que c'est notre talon d'Achille, voire que cela disqualifie notre point de vue, la vérité est objectivement notre plus grand atout. Parce que nous n'investissons jamais nous-mêmes, nos conclusions ne sont faussées par aucun facteur humain.

— Ah ! soupirai-je en éprouvant une indicible joie. Vous observez sans participer.

— C'est à peu près ça », concéda-t-il.

J'eus envie de le prendre dans mes bras pour une accolade fraternelle. « C'est merveilleux ! Enfin un homme qui répond aux aspirations de mon cœur ! Dr Everstat, si seulement vous pouviez me montrer comment vous et vos collègues avez gagné cette profonde connaissance du Dow sans compromettre votre objectivité ni encourir le moindre risque, cela aurait une valeur inestimable pour mes propres recherches.

— Je suis toujours content de rendre service », minauda-t-il, évidemment flatté par mon enthousiasme ; puis il ajouta sur un ton plus équivoque : « Mais je ne te promets pas que mes explications iront dans le sens de ce que tu désires entendre. » Il me fit signe de passer devant lui. « Par ici. Je vais te faire visiter la boutique. »

Par d'antiques et sombres couloirs sinueux, Everstat me précéda jusqu'à un escalier de pierre plongé dans la pénombre, qui s'enfonçait en tournant dans l'une des innombrables tours du bâtiment. Comme nous descendions avec précautions, j'eus l'étrange impression, malgré la race d'Everstat, de pénétrer dans le labyrinthe de l'esprit anglo-saxon, une région de ténèbres fabuleuses, remplie de personnages grotesques et de saints occupés à mortifier leur chair.

Imaginez ma surprise quand Everstat glissa une clef dans la serrure d'une massive porte de chêne sculptée de gargouilles grimaçantes et d'augustes évêques, et que je découvris, non pas un donjon plein d'instruments de torture ni un autel païen souillé du sang d'un sacrifice humain, mais une salle d'un blanc éblouissant, éclairée par des rangées de tubes fluorescents (il n'y avait aucune fenêtre, nous étions à plusieurs mètres sous terre), où d'innombrables ordinateurs scintillants émettaient toute une gamme de bourdonnements de fréquences variées — aux antipodes du choral anglican auquel je m'étais attendu, une sorte de quartet électronique pour barbier ! Car des hommes en blouse blanche consultaient des listings ou entraient des données sur les terminaux installés contre les murs.

Everstat soupira ; une lueur de satisfaction et de paix intérieure apparut sur son visage quand nous franchîmes le seuil pour entrer dans ce petit paradis, ou plutôt cette matrice de haute technologie. Il m'observa avec une magnanimité quasiment divine, d'un air supérieur mais indulgent, comme s'il prenait en pitié mon ignorance et le difficile voyage que je devrais entreprendre pour parvenir à la sagesse transcendante qu'il avait lui-même atteinte. Nous avançâmes dans une allée ; le claquement discret d'une bobine magnétique qui s'arrêtait ou démarrait ponctuait le bourdonnement électronique des machines.

« Tout est là, mon ami, dit-il avec un large geste du bras. Sais-tu que tu as de la chance d'entrer ici ? Ce sanctuaire est strictement interdit aux profanes. » Il rit. « Mais sérieusement, Sun I, quand tu passes cette porte... (il la montra du doigt, mais elle avait disparu derrière une rangée d'ordinateurs), tu pénètres réellement dans le futur. Ceci est le nec plus ultra. Le hardware, que tu vois, et le software, que tu ne vois pas, mais qui est ici comme l'âme dans le corps, vont révolutionner le monde entier, et pas seulement la stratégie de l'investissement. Mais il faut évidemment un certain temps pour que tout cela "descende" jusqu'à l'homme de la rue — surtout celui de Wall Street. » Il me fit un clin d'œil. « Je dois dire que les hordes capitalistes ont une fâcheuse propension au sarcasme. Mais quelle grande découverte fut aussitôt appréciée à sa juste valeur ? Darwin a encore ses détracteurs. Pourtant, comme l'évolution, le Chemin Aléatoire détrônera tous ses concurrents. Crois-moi sur parole, Wall Street devra tôt ou tard s'y plier. »

Saisi d'un effroi silencieux, je l'écoutai discourir sur les grands bouleversements à venir. Je me mis à douter en comparant les outils dont il disposait pour accumuler des informations avec ceux que mes maîtres chinois m'avaient donnés. Comment pourrions-nous jamais rivaliser avec des magiciens aussi fabuleux ? Comparé à cet arsenal éblouissant, qu'étaient un exemplaire écorné du *Yi king* et une poignée de baguettes d'achillée ? Autant opposer des archers à une armée moderne équipée d'artillerie lourde ou d'armes nucléaires.

« Pouvez-vous m'expliquer, Dr Everstat, comment ces machines vous ont aidé à pénétrer l'essence secrète du Dow ?

— "Essence secrète", pouffa-t-il. On dirait une conspiration pour violer une vierge ou briser le septième sceau. »

Je rougis.

« Pourtant, ce genre de métaphore n'est pas entièrement déplacé, poursuivit-il d'une voix grave, lui-même gêné. Je veux dire, l'"essence secrète". Le Dow a toujours été l'un des phénomènes les plus mystérieux du paysage américain ; on pourrait dire, comme de la Joconde, que son sourire implique une énigme. "Quel est mon truc ?" semble-t-elle demander, et les hommes sont aussitôt séduits. Mais dès qu'ils acceptent le combat qu'elle leur propose, elle dévore, tel le Sphinx, ceux qui ne la satisfont pas, cette Grande Veuve Noire Américaine qui rumine au centre de sa toile et consomme ses partenaires dans les affres de son appétit insatiable. Combien sont entrés dans le labyrinthe et en sont ressortis, Sun I ? Combien ont trouvé la réponse ? Fort peu. Peut-être aucun... Jusqu'à maintenant. Excuse la trivialité de l'expression, mais nous l'avons baisée. Nous avons résolu l'énigme. » Son sourire d'oracle fit place à un froncement de sourcils. « Malheureusement, il se trouve que cette vieille salope n'est pas un coup bien fameux. Comme on dit, les prémisses sont toujours plus agréables que l'acte lui-même.

— Que voulez-vous dire ? demandai-je.

— Je dois retourner en arrière pour te répondre. Selon la sagesse conventionnelle, la théorie du Chemin Aléatoire appliquée à la fluctuation des prix du marché dérive de considérations purement logiques, d'un syllogisme très beau et très élégant. Voici : *Si* les hommes désirent maximiser rationnellement leur profit, et *si* les investisseurs (acheteurs et vendeurs) sont des hommes ; *alors* les fluctuations des prix du marché sont un chemin aléatoire.

— Mais qu'est... ? (J'allais dire : « Qu'est-ce qu'un chemin aléatoire ? » quand il leva la main.)

— Ne m'interromps pas, dit-il. Tout te sera révélé en temps voulu. Tu dois comprendre que cela n'est que le squelette du raisonnement. Mais peut-être ta question conteste-t-elle l'évidence de ces prémisses ? Je reconnais que, moi aussi, j'ai parfois douté de la rationalité du marché. Car il est difficile de nier que des forces psychologiques obscures et perverses — le comportement grégaire, par exemple — sont parfois à l'œuvre. »

Je le regardai avec des yeux ronds, car cela me paraissait évident. D'ailleurs, les habitués de Wall Street en faisaient une donnée trop banale pour qu'il fût même besoin d'en parler.

Everstat poursuivit comme si de rien n'était. « Je crois qu'en pinaillant, on pourrait même s'interroger sur la prémisse mineure : les courtiers de Wall Street sont des hommes. Car leur comportement a parfois des relents de bestialité. Mais en ce qui concerne la prémisse majeure, après ma « sombre nuit de l'âme », j'ai renoncé à l'hérésie ; car, même si un ou deux masochistes veulent perdre leur argent et investissent selon, leur nombre est statistiquement insignifiant en comparaison de la population des investisseurs. Et puis ce genre de phénomène est non quantifiable. » Il prononça ce dernier mot avec une emphase dédaigneuse, comme l'adjectif le plus péjoratif qui fût.

« Mais tout cela, bien que pertinent, m'éloigne de mon sujet. La sagesse conventionnelle — l'idée d'une conclusion univoque logiquement déduite de prémisses évidentes — est très flatteuse pour notre foi en l'altruisme et un comportement rationnel, mais il faut bien dire que c'est une façade plaquée sur la réalité, une façade grecque, équilibrée, ensoleillée, radieuse, rajoutée à un édifice d'un tout autre style, disons une demeure baroque pleine de passages secrets, de recoins et d'alcôves bizarres, un décor plus approprié pour le complot et la trahison. » Il baissa la voix. « Peu de gens connaissent l'histoire que je vais te raconter, Sun I, et moins encore la croient. Néanmoins, je peux garantir son authenticité, car j'y ai joué un certain rôle. En fait, autant te le dire tout de suite, j'ai consacré plus d'un an de ma vie au projet qui aboutit à l'application du Chemin Aléatoire à l'analyse du marché, une recherche qui ne m'a valu ni récompense ni reconnaissance d'aucune sorte. Si je suis amer, c'est donc à juste titre. Mais d'autres ont aussi été lésés, et ma blessure est une simple égratignure, comparée à celle d'un camarade ; d'autant que je peux venger mon affront, alors que mon ami n'en a plus la possibilité.

« J'ai rencontré Michael Schwartz alors que nous étions lycéens au Mont-Nebo — un pâle garçon timide affligé d'un grave problème d'élocution, profondément perturbé, mais aussi extrêmement doué. En fait, Michael était un génie. Jamais je n'ai rencontré mathématicien aussi doué ; mieux, il adorait ça et il savait travailler. Pour lui, les choses étaient des nombres, si bien que, contrairement à moi, il a bientôt abandonné les mathématiques pures (qu'il considérait comme une simple variante élégante du jeu d'échecs une sorte de jeu des perles de verre), pour un champ plus concret — mais la physique théorique est-elle vraiment plus concrète ? Michael était un chercheur quasiment religieux. Son obsession permanente était de distiller l'expérience grâce aux mathématiques. Il m'a dit un jour avoir l'ambition de déduire le jardin du monde vivant dans toute sa splendeur luxuriante à partir de la graine sèche, brune et ingrate de l'équation mathématique. Culotté, non ? Mais n'est-ce pas notre ambition à tous, la quête de l'éternité dans le temps, de l'infini dans le fini, du Nirvana dans le Samsara ?

« A Princeton, il s'est mis à travailler sur la théorie du champ unifié. Il avait trouvé ce qui lui convenait — une tentative de déduire le monde à partir d'une unique loi immuable, de forcer la multiplicité des phénomènes naturels à travers le goulot des équations. Je le vis rarement pendant toutes ces années. Nos chemins se sont séparés. Mais quand nous nous rencontrions, il paraissait plus heureux que je ne l'avais jamais vu, même si sa douleur secrète le taraudait toujours. Enfin, j'étais content pour lui. Je pensais qu'au moins il était en sécurité.

« Voilà pourquoi la nouvelle de son suicide me bouleversa tant. Ce fut une surprise totale. Cela paraissait si absurde, un tel gâchis — du moins au début. Car ensuite, quand j'y réfléchis, sa décision m'apparut comme l'une des plus pures et des plus lucides que je connaisse.

« Je ne suis pas compétent pour t'expliquer l'affaire en détail, car je connais à peine mieux la physique que toi, j'imagine. Je sais seulement que ses recherches étaient liées au problème de la symétrie en miroir des particules élémentaires, laquelle était tenue pour une propriété fondamentale de la nature. L'élégance et la simplicité mathématique de cette théorie avaient dû le séduire. Mais quand il l'approfondit, il rencontra des exceptions déconcertantes, qu'il essaya de ramener dans le droit chemin de la loi de départ. Je ne connais pas bien le scénario, je sais seulement que tout fut déclenché par la publication des expériences de Mme Wu sur la désintégration radioactive bêta, qui faisait voler en éclats la notion de symétrie et ouvrait la perspective vertigineuse d'une asymétrie fondamentale de la nature. Michael lut cet article très soigneusement, sans passion, il fit quelques calculs, puis rentra chez lui, sortit un revolver d'un tiroir et se tira une balle dans la tête. » Everstat se tut.

« Tu ne seras peut-être pas d'accord avec moi, Sun I, mais j'imagine mal une mort plus noble. Voilà de la passion intellectuelle ! Michael vivait son idée, et quand elle l'a lâché, il s'est tué. Mais, diras-tu, quel rapport entre la vie (et la mort) de Michael, et toi ? Tu connais maintenant l'expression "Chemin Aléatoire". Eh bien, c'est le nœud du problème. La mère de Michael savait que j'étais aussi mathématicien (elle ne réalisait pas que nos champs d'étude étaient fort éloignés) ; elle me demanda d'examiner les papiers de son fils pour voir s'ils contenaient quelque chose de valable. Bien sûr, j'acceptai, même si cela empiétait sur mon temps de travail. » Il regarda sa montre, fronça les sourcils. « Il y avait de quoi faire. Michael notait ses idées sur des calepins, une sorte de version mathématique des carnets de Léonard de Vinci. Mon ami avait une immense curiosité. La plupart des calepins contenaient de simples esquisses, des brouillons audacieux, absurdes, parfois pleins d'humour. Mais il s'était attaché à développer une idée en particulier. Il en avait même rempli plusieurs carnets. Il s'agissait de la mise au point d'un modèle mathématique pour les fluctuations des prix de la Bourse ; plus précisément, mon ami voulait définir la loi centrale à laquelle ces fluctuations obéissaient.

« Ce dut être pour lui une simple récréation, un passe-temps distrayant. D'ailleurs, il n'aurait jamais pu tester son modèle, car ses équations étaient insolubles pour n'importe quel cerveau humain, non pour des raisons théoriques, mais pratiques : extrêmement complexes, elles contenaient littéralement des centaines de variables et, comme l'informatique était encore balbutiante, leur résolution aurait pris des années de travail. Pourtant, je ne crois pas que Michael ait jamais réalisé qu'on pouvait les résoudre avec des machines performantes. Mais je le savais. Le vrai problème était de rédiger le programme destiné à tester son modèle. J'estimai ce travail à un an, peut-être davantage. Ces équations m'intéressaient, mais j'hésitais à prendre le risque de perdre un an pour déboucher sur un échec. De plus, j'étais déjà débordé de travail.

« J'écrivis donc une brève lettre à un journal spécialisé pour avertir ses lecteurs de l'existence de ces équations monstreuses et les proposer à quiconque voudrait plancher dessus, à condition qu'il eût les compétences nécessaires. Je reçus quelques réponses vaseuses d'étudiants à la recherche d'un sujet de thèse original ; j'allais remiser les carnets de mon ami au grenier quand je reçus un coup de fil d'un type... peu importe son nom et celui de son patron. Disons simplement qu'il travaillait comme statisticien pour une grosse boîte. Je devais être incroyablement naïf à l'époque, Sun I ; j'avais bien sûr réfléchi aux conséquences de ces équations, mais intellectuellement, abstraitement, pas en terme de pouvoir — jusqu'à ce que je parle à ce type. "Avez-vous la moindre idée du lièvre que vous avez levé ? me demanda-t-il. Si ces équations sont correctes, elles entraîneront une révolution économique. Un marché parfaitement prévisible ! Vous comprenez ce que ça signifie ? Cela équivaudrait à posséder la page financière du journal de mardi avant l'ouverture de la séance du lundi. En un seul jour, vous pourriez devenir l'homme le plus riche du monde, à condition d'avoir assez de capital à investir. C'est d'ailleurs un de mes arguments pour que vous me laissiez participer au projet, le deuxième étant une équipe de recherche aussi nombreuse que vous voudrez pour vous soulager de votre travail et accélérer le processus. Songez-y — je vous offre tout ce que vous voulez ! Nous en aurons pour quelques jours, peut-être une ou deux semaines. La vitesse et le secret sont essentiels. Le marché ne résisterait pas longtemps à ce genre d'opérations, surtout si la rumeur s'en répandait. Cela risquerait de provoquer un krach en comparaison duquel la Grande Dépression ferait figure de période prospère, me dit-il. Vous pourriez mettre le pays à genoux. Vous êtes peut-être assis sur une véritable bombe atomique économique. Et nous vous proposons de devenir l'Oppenheimer de votre Projet Manhattan !" Essaie, Sun I, d'imaginer les pensées qui se sont bousculées dans ma tête ! J'ai raccroché, je suis rentré chez moi, j'ai passé plusieurs jours à réfléchir. Et puis je lui ai téléphoné pour refuser sa proposition. Le lendemain, j'ai demandé un congé et je me suis mis au travail sur le programme.

« Mais ne te méprends pas, Sun I ; ce n'est pas l'intérêt personnel qui a dicté ma décision. En fait, la perspective de posséder un tel pouvoir et de l'exercer me terrifiait. » Il pointa un doigt vers le plafond. « Mais posséder ce pouvoir, et *le refuser*... ah ! Cela serait sublime. Bon, je me suis donc attelé à la tâche. Mon travail consistait surtout à suivre les grandes lignes du projet de Michael. Bon nombre de chercheurs de ma connaissance auraient pu le réaliser. Mais il y avait tellement d'équations ! Michael était pour ainsi dire l'architecte, et moi le menuisier qui concrétisait son rêve. Mon Méphistophélès appointé par la grosse boîte persista à tenter de me séduire — il me proposa des sommes considérables —, mais quand je lui eus résisté une fois avec succès, ou plutôt résisté à moi-même, ses attaques cessèrent de me terrifier et devinrent une sorte de routine un peu pitoyable.

« Je travaillais depuis quelques mois, j'avais bien avancé. C'était l'été. Ce soir-là, j'étais au bureau. Il faisait une chaleur étouffante. J'avais mis en marche mon petit ventilateur rotatif ; il soufflait derrière moi. J'avais tombé la chemise. Il devait être sept ou huit heures du soir. Il faisait encore jour. J'ai décidé de faire une pause, de descendre m'acheter un Coca et un hamburger chez l'épicier italien au coin de la rue. Je bois toujours du thé en travaillant. J'en bois jour et nuit. Sans arrêt, obsessionnellement. J'ai bien essayé d'arrêter, mais j'ai craqué à chaque fois. Et puis ça ne me fait même plus d'effet. Je dors comme une souche après une demi-douzaine de théières.

« Il se trouve que je possède une tasse à thé spéciale. Elle est là-haut dans mon bureau. Tu l'as peut-être vue ? Un cadeau de ma mère. Je la pose à droite sur un napperon pour ne pas marquer le bois. Chaque fois que je quitte mon bureau, je l'utilise comme presse-papier sur mes feuilles. Je la pose d'une certaine façon — l'anse à droite, parallèle au bord de ma table. Un geste purement machinal. Je n'y pense même pas. Ce jour-là, je n'y aurais pas pensé non plus, si je n'avais remarqué un détail insolite. A mon retour, la porte était fermée à clef, comme je l'avais laissée. Je m'assis à ma table, allongeai mes jambes dessus pour manger mon hamburger que je sortis de son emballage ; je mordais dedans quand mon regard fut brusquement attiré par un truc inhabituel. L'anse de ma tasse avait pivoté — pas de beaucoup, il est vrai, juste de quelques degrés, mais assez pour que je m'en aperçoive. Je pose mon hamburger pour regarder ça de plus près, et sur mes feuilles je découvre deux cercles concentriques dus au fond de ma tasse ! De plus, le carnet de Michael est ouvert à une autre page. D'accord, mon ventilateur pouvait en être responsable. Mais les taches de thé circulaires ? Non. Quand j'examine attentivement ma table, rien n'est plus à sa place. Mes stylos sont bizarrement rangés, mes papiers de travers. Tu vas peut-être penser que j'ai imaginé tout ça. C'est ce que je me suis dit. Mais il s'est ensuite passé une chose troublante, Sun I : à dater de ce jour, Méphistophélès a cessé de me téléphoner. Parfaitement. Il a sans doute compris que ses efforts seraient restés infructueux, objecteras-tu ? Peut-être. Mais peut-être aussi n'avait-il plus besoin de moi, car il avait pillé tous mes documents !

« Cet incident me surprit, me rendit prudent, mais je poursuivis mon travail ; simplement, je cachais les carnets de Michael chaque fois que je quittais mon bureau. Bon, sautons quelques mois. Le programme me prit plus de temps que prévu. Presque dix-huit mois. Quand je touchai au but, je me sentis brusquement excité. Un matin, j'allai tester le programme achevé. Je voyais les visages habituels, les professeurs buvaient leur café en bavardant, échangeaient leurs dernières idées, un ami se penchait par-dessus l'épaule d'un autre pour regarder un listing, il posait une question, suggérait une solution. Le train-train ordinaire. Mais pas pour moi. Je me comportais comme d'habitude, mais mon cerveau était en ébullition. Je pensais sans arrêt à Oppenheimer — au jour où ils ont testé la bombe, à Enrico Fermi qui pariait sur la destruction de New Mexico. L'explosion, la joie, l'ahurissement, enfin la terreur, Oppenheimer songant à cette phrase de la *Bhagavad Gita* : "Je suis devenu la Mort, le destructeur des mondes." Mes émotions n'étaient pas foncièrement différentes, Sun I. Ma nervosité m'empêcha presque de frapper les ordres de commande au téléype. Quand j'eus réussi à injecter le programme dans la bécane, je me suis préparé une tasse de thé et j'ai attendu le verdict. Je voulais savoir si mon système d'équation collait... »

Everstat se tut et regarda dans le vague.

« Alors ? demandai-je. Ça a marché ?
— Hum ? répondit-il rêveusement.
— *Ça a marché ?* »
Il plissa les paupières. « Oh oui, Sun I, les équations collaient.
— Alors, quelle fut la réponse ? m'écriai-je, exaspéré.
— La réponse ? » Il sourit comme un crétin.
« *Oui, quelle fut la réponse ?*
— Il n'y a pas de réponse, rétorqua-t-il.
— Je croyais que les équations étaient correctes ! »
Il opina du chef. « Elles l'étaient, Sun I. La réponse est qu'il n'y a pas de réponse.
— Mais c'est impossible, dis-je. Qu'est-ce que ça veut dire ?
— Ça veut dire que les cotes des valeurs fluctuent essentiellement au hasard. C'est l'une de ces étranges aberrations de la nature qui échappent aux lois ordinaires — comme les trous noirs des astrophysiciens —, où l'on constate une asymétrie fondamentale entre la cause et l'effet. Les statisticiens ont baptisé ce genre de phénomène Chemin Aléatoire. »
Je le regardai d'un air ahuri, commençant à saisir le sens de ses paroles. « Vous voulez dire qu'il n'y a pas de raison ultime ? »
Il acquiesça. « On peut formuler cela ainsi.
— Mais c'est absurde ! protestai-je. Comment expliquez-vous le succès notoire de certains professionnels spécialisés dans le choix des valeurs ? »
Il haussa les épaules. « La chance, Sun I. En fait, le spécialiste le plus chevronné n'est pas d'un iota plus avancé que le premier néophyte venu. Et le "système" le plus sophistiqué présenté par les soi-disant experts est aussi valable que la technique classique consistant à lancer des fléchettes sur les colonnes financières de ton quotidien préféré. Les professionnels sagaces comme ton mentor Aaron — il m'est très cher, ne te méprends pas — ressemblent à des types plantés devant une radio coincée entre deux stations, et qui écoutent la friture des parasites en essayant coûte que coûte de se convaincre que ce qu'ils entendent est de la musique.

« Mais laisse-moi finir mon histoire. Moins de deux semaines après ma découverte, je feuillette le dernier *Statistical Forum*, et que vois-je ? Un article sur "Le Dow comme Chemin Aléatoire". Pas la moindre mention de mon programme ou des équations de Michael, évidemment. Le tout extrêmement logique, extrêmement simple et élégant. Voici : une transaction boursière implique deux parties, un acheteur et un vendeur, tous deux des animaux rationnels maximisateurs de profits. Bon. Ils ont accès aux mêmes informations concernant les valeurs qu'ils se proposent respectivement de vendre et d'acheter. La transaction a lieu à un prix que tous deux considèrent comme équitable, sinon ils la refuseraient. Eh bien, si tout cela est vrai et si un homme se sent poussé à acheter et l'autre à vendre, alors aucune loi logique, systématique, ne peut rendre compte de la fluctuation des prix. Les cotes des valeurs fluctuent au hasard. Impeccable, très élégant, irréfutable même ! »

Everstat continua de parler, mais je ne l'écoutai plus. Sa rancœur, réelle ou imaginaire, était intéressante, mais seul me préoccupait le Chemin Aléatoire. Si ce qu'il avait dit était vrai, sa théorie me coupait l'herbe sous le pied : comment continuer à chercher la force secrète qui se cachait derrière les transformations du Dow, l'unité dans la multiplicité ? Car s'il avait raison, cette force n'existait pas ! Lecteur, j'eus l'impression qu'il avait pour de bon lâché la bombe, une bombe métaphysique, et *sur moi* !

Je me souviens à peine de mon départ. Il me proposa de me raccompagner à la gare, mais je refusai et sortis d'un pas vacillant. Tout le long du chemin, je reçus en plein visage le soleil de l'après-midi, sa lumière intense, aveuglante. Ce fut pour moi un grand soulagement de remonter dans le train, de retrouver le verre fumé des fenêtres, l'air conditionné dont la fraîcheur apaisa la douleur de mes yeux et celle de mon esprit. Si j'avais été déprimé dans la matinée, je l'étais maintenant doublement. Tout le temps du trajet jusqu'à New York, je songeai à mes progrès dans l'apprentissage du Dow. Le delta semblait reculer devant moi. Je me sentais, non pas descendre le courant vers la mer du savoir et de l'illumination, la paix, l'accomplissement, la libération, mais au contraire le remonter vers les rapides, vers la confusion, le tumulte, une violence décuplée. En fait, le terme même de « progrès » me parut dérisoire. Car jusqu'à maintenant, mon éducation ne régressait-elle pas régulièrement de la certitude au nihilisme, de l'espoir au désespoir ?

D'abord Powers. « Il y a une raison et on peut l'expliciter. » Pour lui, l'idée de l'homme en tant qu'animal rationnel et maximisateur de profit (« garder la tête froide ») n'était pas une hypothèse d'école, mais un idéal auquel il appliquait sa discipline.

Ensuite Newman. « Il y a une raison, mais nous ne pourrons jamais la connaître ; pourtant, nous pouvons l'utiliser. » La position intermédiaire.

Et enfin, Everstat. « Il n'y a pas de raison. Le Dow est un Chemin Aléatoire. » Était-ce le verdict ultime, le sommet du savoir ? Je refusai cette idée. Car n'impliquait-elle pas un enlisement progressif dans le bourbier du cynisme et de la lâcheté intellectuelle, non seulement au sujet du Dow, mais aussi de l'univers lui-même et de la place de l'homme dans le monde ? Car en dernière analyse, qu'étaient ces stratégies financières sinon des conceptions du monde ? Les degrés de l'échelle aboutissaient cependant au plus bas registre du désespoir.

Était-ce donc la « sagesse » que j'avais espéré recevoir des mains de ces « sages » du marché, qu'on appelait ici des « pros » ? Je me révoltai à l'idée que le système d'Everstat, le Chemin Aléatoire, représentait le nec plus ultra de la science du Dow. Pourtant, ma rencontre avait tellement bien commencé ! Car de tous les sages, lui seul était parti d'une position extrêmement proche de la mienne, lui seul chérissait son objectivité, observait sans participer. Que me restait-il ?

15

Kahn s'adossa à la balustrade de la galerie, et la mitose grouillante du parquet devint l'immense toile de fond floue sur laquelle ses traits se détachaient. Son visage exprimait la gravité et la sympathie pendant qu'il écoutait la litanie de mes doutes et de mes contradictions. Il demeurait étrangement tranquille, silencieux. Et même quand mon flot de paroles se fut tari, il continua de me regarder sans mot dire, un éclair farouche dans l'œil, à la fois sarcasme et exhortation.

« Alors, petit, fit-il enfin, tu as essayé toutes les méthodes hygiéniques, et elles ne donnent rien. Les fétiches de tous les sorciers se sont révélés inefficaces, de dérisoires bricolages de paille et de plumes. Toi qui voulais un charme magique capable de maîtriser la vie ! » Il eut un rire de pitié méprisante. « A quoi se résume donc ton "initiation" au marché ? Tous les experts ont leur système définitif et infaillible, mais tous sont différents, tous contradictoires. Et maintenant tu viens me demander mon propre talisman. Je ne suis pas sûr de pouvoir t'en donner un, petit. Laisse-moi te poser une question. T'attendais-tu vraiment à ce que quelqu'un te fournisse "la réponse", une formule que tu pourrais noter sur un bout de papier, apprendre par cœur et appliquer joyeusement jusqu'à la fin des temps ? Comme ce serait facile ! Et banal. Regarde un peu en bas, petit, dit-il en désignant du menton la grande salle, mais sans me quitter des yeux. La frénésie, l'espoir, le désespoir, l'immense humanité de cette foire d'empoigne, *toute cette vie* — croyais-tu vraiment pouvoir condenser cela en une paraphrase, un *digest* à digérer pendant un semestre et dont l'étude te fournirait la clef du mystère ? Non, petit. Seule est disponible la version non expurgée du Dow. Et je ne suis pas sûr qu'une vie suffise pour se familiariser avec elle. Le Dow est une énigme, petit, une religion, et comme pour toute initiation, celle-ci a son prix. "Dans ce pays, chacun doit payer tout ce qu'il obtient" — j'ai oublié qui a dit ça.

— Mais que pourrais-je donner de plus ! protestai-je. N'ai-je pas déjà tout sacrifié, quitté ma patrie et traversé la moitié du monde pour ceci ? »

Il secoua la tête. « Cela ne suffit pas. Tu as quitté ta patrie, c'est vrai. Mais tu as emporté tes certitudes avec toi. » Il rit. « Tu ressembles à un escargot qui transporte sa maison partout. Oh, je les vois bien maintenant, tes cornes et ta coquille. Elles t'ont ralenti, petit. Tu as parcouru un bout du chemin, mais le plus dur reste à faire. Tu as maintenant atteint une sorte de *nec plus ultra* dans tes pérégrinations. Te voilà aux colonnes d'Hercule, mais au-delà... qui sait ce que tu risques de découvrir ? La cataracte occidentale, la fin du monde ? Personne ne peut répondre à cette question, Sonny. Personne ne peut te dire ce que tu trouveras de l'autre côté. Le risque est total. Mais si tu veux entreprendre ce voyage, tu dois lâcher tout ton lest, retrouver la nudité essentielle du guerrier.

— Je ne suis pas sûr de comprendre, Kahn, dis-je. Que sont donc ce lest dont vous parlez, et cette coquille que je transporterais partout avec moi ?

— Le petit autel portatif que tu abrites au fond de ton cœur, petit, ton Shangri-la spirituel.

— Ne vous moquez pas de moi, Aaron.

— C'est plus fort que moi, dit-il. Et puis, petit, je me moque gentiment, je suis sincère.

— C'est vrai, concédai-je.

— Tes maîtres t'ont appris à valoriser, à rechercher la certitude — afin d'échapper aux ravages du temps —, de la chercher dans un lieu paisible et brillant qui est en toi, un endroit où la méditation te conduit, que tu nommes Tao.

— Oui, reconnus-je. C'est ce qu'ils m'ont appris, et j'y crois.

— Alors que fais-tu ici ? dit-il, en haussant la voix. Si leur réponse te satisfait, pourquoi as-tu quitté le monastère ?

— Je me le demande parfois, répondis-je d'une voix abattue. J'ai cru que ma voie me poussait ici, vers le marché, vers le Dow, mais maintenant je n'en suis plus si certain. Peut-être était-ce seulement une illusion ? Peut-être aurais-je dû rester là-bas, m'obstiner dans la voie que je connaissais, cultiver ce lieu dont vous venez de parler. »

Kahn plissa les yeux avec une expression incrédule. « Et renoncer à la vie ? » Sa question me transperça comme une flèche qui atteint son but. « Voilà ma question, poursuivit-il. Personnellement, si mes certitudes et ma vie deviennent inconciliables, alors je choisis la vie. Je préfère me jeter à l'eau et vivre plutôt que barboter dans l'asepsie feutrée dont ta Voie fait sa plus grande promesse. Choisir cette certitude sécurisante reviendrait à une lobotomie, une castration morale, une sorte de mort. D'ailleurs, la seule certitude est peut-être la mort.

— Ainsi, le Dow — votre Dow — serait la vie ? demandai-je avec une ironie blessée.

— Exactement, petit, dit-il. La vie telle qu'elle est, confuse, tumultueuse, périlleuse (nous courons des dangers mortels ici), peut-être corrompue mais truculente, haute en couleur et débordant de vitalité. Le monde tel qu'il est. » Il hocha la tête en désignant le parquet d'un large geste du bras, comme pour me dire : « Tout ceci pourrait être à toi. » « Hors du limon et de la fange de la vie élémentaire, la réponse doit émerger. Baisse les yeux vers ce bouillon de culture. Si la réponse n'est pas là, alors elle n'existe pas. Point à la ligne.

— Et que dois-je faire pour trouver cette réponse ?

— Tu dois renoncer à ton innocence, dit-il, perdre ta virginité morale.

— Pourquoi la perdre ? rétorquai-je, choqué.

— Pour la donner à la vie. Le petit autel portatif de ton cœur que tu as briqué si amoureusement pendant toutes ces années, lavé à grands seaux d'eau limpide de ton puits, récuré à quatre pattes, épousseté, astiqué pour qu'il reste immaculé — eh bien tu dois maintenant le souiller d'un sacrifice sanglant. A quoi croyais-tu donc qu'il servait ? C'est toi l'agneau pascal, Sonny. Tu dois jouer Abraham et Isaac, te poignarder sur ton autel. Quand tu l'auras souillé, aucun produit d'entretien ne lui rendra son brillant d'origine. La tache restera, mais au moins tu pourras commencer de vivre.

— Dites-moi ce que signifie tout cela, le suppliai-je.

— Ce que ça signifie ? » Il me considéra avec une grave sympathie. « Pour comprendre le Dow, tu dois investir, petit — une partie de toi-même. Il n'y a pas d'autre solution. C'est le prix de l'initiation. Tu dois jouer le jeu. Voilà ce que j'exige de toi et l'ultimatum que je te pose. »

Le tumulte de la grande salle monta vers moi comme le grondement de fondations qui s'écroulent, de dynasties balayées par une révolution, de mondes bouleversés. « Et mon vœu ? demandai-je d'une voix vacillante.

— C'est le sacrifice que tu dois faire.

— Vous réalisez que vous me demander de me damner ? »

Il sourit gravement. « Exact, Sonny, c'est la damnation, la damnation à vie, le grand saut dans le monde tel qu'il est.

— Et le Retour à la Source ? »

Il rit en renversant la tête. « Ceci est la Source, Sonny, tu la côtoies tous les jours.

— Pour vous, le Dow est peut-être la Source, concédai-je. Mais le delta, où les deux se fondent ? Où est-il ? Car ils doivent se rejoindre, Aaron. Vous comprenez certainement cela. "La Réalité est Une, et le Tao est la Réalité."

— Ça sonne bien, Sonny, mais je suis pas sûr d'y croire. Et si la Réalité n'est pas — "une" ? Et s'il n'y a pas de delta ?

— Le delta *doit* exister, dis-je. Si le Tao est seulement partiel, alors le Tao est faux.

— C'est peut-être le cas. Tu dois envisager cette possibilité. Cela est peut-être tout ce qui existe.

— Vous vous trompez ! le contredis-je. Je connais le lieu du Tao.

— Oh, je ne doute pas que tu connaisses ce lieu, dénigra-t-il, ni qu'il existe un état psychologique correspondant à ce vide intérieur dont tu nous rebats les oreilles. Trop de jeûne, trop de silence, trop de méditations inconfortables, la "régulation du souffle", la continence sexuelle — toute la panoplie de la mortification — pas étonnant que cela induise des états de conscience intéressants et assez rares. Mais ces états sont peut-être seulement des aberrations, qui sait ? Et dans cette hypothèse, quelle tragédie de les confondre avec le nanan de l'existence. Quel gâchis.

— Je vous en prie, Kahn taisez-vous, l'implorai-je. Si vous continuez, je vais vous haïr.

— Okay, petit. De toute façon, j'ai fini. » Il fixa distraitement le bout de ses chaussures en fronçant les sourcils. Puis il me dévisagea. « Tu n'as pas l'air très en forme, dit-il. Allons faire un tour, d'accord ? Il nous reste une demi-heure. »

Je lui adressai un regard dénué de toute expression.

— Viens », dit-il doucement avec un mouvement du menton qui me rassura, me réconforta. Il saisit mon coude et je le laissai me guider.

Quand nous sortîmes du bâtiment et nous frayâmes un chemin instinctivement, soumis à quelque gravité élémentaire qui nous entraîna vers le fleuve, j'étais en proie à un immense découragement. L'« ultimatum » de Kahn m'irritait comme un morceau de cartilage indigeste ; je ressentais la nécessité d'aller de l'avant dans ma recherche du sens du Dow et, simultanément, l'impossibilité absolue de le faire au prix fixé par Kahn. Comment relever le défi qu'il m'avait lancé ?

« A supposer que vous ayez raison, dis-je après un long silence en réfléchissant à haute voix — je ne dis pas que vous avez raison, je me contente de suivre votre hypothèse —, comment pratiquement pourrais-je investir ? Je n'ai pas d'argent.

— Bonne question, dit-il en opinant du chef et retroussant sa lèvre inférieure sur la supérieure. L'argent pose un problème. Et puis, avec ton salaire, tu n'as pas une chance d'obtenir le moindre crédit.

— Exactement, acquiesçai-je avec soulagement. Vous voyez donc que, même dans cette hypothèse, mon cas est désespéré...

— Pas si vite, objecta-t-il. C'est très malin, mais je ne te permettrai pas de te vautrer aussi honteusement dans tes indécrottables SO. » Il réfléchit. « Je suppose que les moines n'accumulent pas beaucoup de biens personnels au cours de leur carrière, hein ? Des antiquités, babioles, colifichets, bibelots, symboles taoïstes, de préférence en or ou en argent ? »

Je lui lançai un regard perçant. « Pourquoi me posez-vous cette question ? »

Il haussa les épaules. « Oh, comme ça. Je me demandais simplement si tu ne possédais pas un objet que tu aurais pu vendre. »

Je lui retournai son haussement d'épaules. « Non, je ne vois pas... » Alors je me figeai sur place en éprouvant un vertige grandissant, mon découragement vira brusquement à la panique.

« Petit ? Que t'arrive-t-il, petit ? Aurais-je fait mouche ?

— La robe de ma mère, chuchotai-je, non pas tant pour lui-même que pour moi.

— Elle est belle ?

— Belle ! protestai-je. Elle est irremplaçable ! »

La bouche en cul de poule, il hocha la tête. « Voilà peut-être ce qu'il nous faut. »

Je le dévisageai avec horreur. « Jamais ! m'écriai-je. Ce serait une trahison bien pire que de renoncer à mon vœu.

— Eh bien tu pourrais te contenter de la mettre en gage, suggéra-t-il avec tact.

— Non ! m'écriai-je. Cent fois non ! Je ne m'en séparerai pour rien au monde !

— D'accord, d'accord, calme-toi, petit. Seigneur ! Mais quelle alternative proposes-tu ? Soit la robe au mont de piété, soit le jet de l'éponge et ton adieu au Dow. Tu déclares donc forfait ? » Il secoua la tête en poussant un soupir exaspéré. « Parfois, je me pose des questions sur toi, petit. Bien sûr, j'admire tes principes et tout, mais franchement je me demande si tu vas t'en tirer ici. Tu n'es peut-être pas fait pour vivre dans ce monde.

— Peut-être pas, répondis-je sans pouvoir maîtriser le tremblement de ma voix, intimement blessé par un jugement que, taoïste, j'aurais pu interpréter comme un grand compliment. Je ferais peut-être mieux de retourner en Chine.

— Peut-être, dit-il. Je suis navré, petit, mais c'est comme ça. J'ai fait tout ce que j'ai pu. Maintenant, à toi de jouer. » Il me jaugea d'un air lugubre. « Mais accorde-moi une faveur, okay ? Ne rejette pas ma proposition d'emblée. Donne-toi quelques jours de réflexion avant de prendre ta décision. Songe aussi à cet aspect des choses : te séparer de cette robe n'est pas forcément un sacrilège. On peut aussi bien y voir le sacrifice d'un bien matériel — d'un *lien* — en vue d'obtenir un savoir plus élevé.

— C'est un sophisme, dis-je.

— Vraiment ? Je n'en suis pas certain. Rumine tout ça pendant quelques jours. Si tu te débrouilles pour me ramener cinq cents, ou même mieux, mille dollars, je connais une petite combine où je pourrais te mouiller. Si tout se passe comme je m'y attends, tu pourras récupérer ta robe à la fin du mois, dans six semaines maximum, avec un petit bénéfice en prime qui te permettra de réinvestir si le cœur t'en dit. Qu'en penses-tu ?

— Je pourrais la récupérer ? demandai-je.

— Bien sûr ! dit-il. A condition que tout marche comme prévu, et je crois que ce sera le cas.

— Vous êtes sûr de votre coup ?

— Ne recommence pas », me rabroua-t-il. Puis il m'adressa un regard malicieux. « Petit, tu veux des certitudes ? Fais donc un travail honnête. Dans ce monde, la rédemption est toujours une affaire risquée. Excuse le truisme. Tiens, nous sommes arrivés. »

Presque à mon insu, nous venions de rejoindre le front de mer.

« Ah, soupira Kahn avant d'inhaler une longue bouffée d'air marin. J'adore cette odeur. J'aimerais la mettre en bouteille, l'emmener au boulot comme un flacon de sels — sels au pluriel. Quand l'air empeste l'abstraction et la "puanteur du mensonge", j'en respirerais une bouffée pour me rappeler le vrai sens de ce que nous faisons là-bas.

— Et quel est ce "vrai sens" ? » demandai-je non sans agressivité, car je lui en voulais de son insouciante fantaisie.

Nous avions atteint un point de vue où nous voyions simultanément le fleuve et, légèrement au nord, le marché aux poissons de Fulton Street. Kahn fit encore quelques pas, puis posa sa chaussure sur le muret en ciment, le regard perdu vers Brooklyn. Telle une pièce de monnaie nouvellement frappée, le soleil d'août jetait des éclairs dorés sur les vagues hachées qui semblaient presque bleues.

« Tu sais, je pense mieux en regardant Brooklyn », marmonna-t-il comme s'il n'avait pas entendu ma question. Il se tourna vers moi. « J'ai parfois eu envie de tout plaquer, de revenir ici pour retrouver un boulot sur les quais, un boulot simple et honnête, relié de façon tangible aux besoins fondamentaux de l'homme. Ici, quand tu as les bras plongés jusqu'au coude dans une caisse de poissons, tu ne t'interroges pas sur le sens de tes actes ou la moralité de ton travail. C'est immédiat et sans ambiguïté : tu sers de la nourriture sur les tables de l'Amérique, tu contribues à la vie collective. Ce genre de boulot a une réalité tonifiante qui satisfait un désir de l'âme. En comparaison, Wall Street peut sembler tellement vain, un monde de papier illusoire qui ne contribue en rien au bien-être du pays, de la race ou de l'humanité, contrairement aux gens simples qui fournissent la nourriture à la nation. »

Il soupira. « Je croyais alors que l'énorme machine économique de ce pays, qui commence et s'achève à Wall Street — car tous les chemins y mènent, comme à Rome — était un dispositif stupide, quasiment malhonnête, destiné à multiplier les maillons de la chaîne économique qui relie le producteur au consommateur, les centaines d'intermédiaires qui se glissent entre le pêcheur et la ménagère qui achète sa morue ou son carrelet et le ramène chez elle pour le dîner, diminuant le juste profit que le premier devrait tirer de son labeur, grevant aussi le budget de la seconde qui, à son corps défendant, contribue à graisser toutes ces sales pattes et ces rouages superflus. Cela me semblait injuste, artificiel, vaguement obscène. Je crois qu'à l'époque, j'étais moi-même une sorte de taoïste — ou plutôt de socialiste. » Il sourit. « Pourtant les choses ne sont pas aussi simples. La machine économique n'est pas seulement parasite ; elle fournit une contribution originale : un marché. Sans marchés, les rapports entre producteurs et consommateurs seraient sérieusement compromis, peut-être impossibles. La complexité entraîne la division du travail. Au-delà de la production doit exister un réseau de distribution. D'où le marché et la naissance du commerce.

« Vois-tu, la libre entreprise incite même à l'effort communautaire et à la responsabilité sociale, bien qu'au service de l'intérêt personnel. L'offre et la demande — il était lancé — engagées dans leur dialogue silencieux, éternel. Tu définis ton besoin, ton vœu, ton désir, aussi frivole ou louable soit-il, tu l'enfonces dans la prise adéquate, et le système t'alimente comme en électricité, gentiment, sans douleur et sans poser de questions. Ce marché de Fulton Street... (il haussa les épaules en faisant la moue) n'est qu'une modeste prise de cent vingt volts. Mais le Dow, petit, le Dow est le cœur du réacteur nucléaire. Sans cette fission — qui, je l'admets, comporte des risques de destruction —, tout s'arrêterait, la vie collective cesserait. Et puis, comment la vie elle-même est-elle née ? De la fange et du limon, excités par les dangereuses radiations du soleil. Qu'est-ce que le soleil, la source de la vie elle-même, sinon un gigantesque et perpétuel holocauste nucléaire qui incendie l'espace et nous consumera peut-être un jour ? Elimine le risque, le danger, et tu retournes *illico presto* au silence de la matière inanimée — l'entropie, petit, la deuxième loi de la thermodynamique. Le Dow est le soleil de notre vie économique, Sonny. Malgré sa toxicité, son énergie inépuisable irradie toute la vie de la nation, permet la naissance et l'épanouissement de cette flore incroyablement luxuriante et variée. Le capitalisme, le système de la libre concurrence, c'est ça. En soumettant tout à la discipline de la Bourse, qui récompense et punit, le Dow repousse les limites à l'intérieur desquelles le consommateur exerce son droit fondamental de libre choix. Et afin d'accomplir cela, le système doit prendre le risque d'une excessive complexité. Voilà le schéma fondamental : la liberté ne saurait exister sans la complexité ; mais par sa nature même, la complexité entraîne, doit entraîner une possibilité de décadence.

« Y a-t-il une alternative ? Le socialisme ? Mais le socialisme laisse à peine filtrer assez de lumière pour que la vie ne périclite pas. Bien que produisant, du moins en théorie, une récolte plus rationnelle et homogène, il entrave la fécondité de la nature. La nature, petit, voilà la clef. Les taoïstes sont calés sur la nature, pas vrai ? Les Dowistes aussi. Le capitalisme essaie de laisser la nature réaliser sa propre homéostasie dans la sphère économique.

« Je sais que je m'égare, mais tout ceci est lié au marché, donc à ta décision, Sonny. Tu m'as demandé le sens du Dow ; je viens de te répondre. Je comprends que la perspective d'investir te terrifie. On t'a appris que l'attachement est la racine de tout mal. Tu dois te dire : je cherche à me libérer du monde matériel ; n'est-ce pas le comble de la folie que de chercher cette libération en me plongeant dans le monde matériel ? Mais c'est bien là le paradoxe. Tu te rappelles ce que j'ai dit ? Hors du limon et de la fange de la vie élémentaire, la réponse doit émerger. Il va falloir que tu te salisses les mains, petit. Voilà pourquoi ta tentative d'observer sans participer ne t'a conduit nulle part. Qu'est-ce que l'illumination sinon un distillat de la liberté dont je t'ai parlé ? Libération. Liberté. Voilà le secret, s'il y a un secret. La liberté ne saurait exister sans le mal, ou du moins sans la possibilité du mal. Car ils naissent de la même racine. Cherchant dans la libération le bien ultime de la vie, tu dois risquer son ultime négation dans le mal.

« Et Wall Street est l'épreuve terminale. Le vrai sens de l'investissement n'a rien à voir avec l'argent, mais avec soi. Wall Street est le grand tripot flottant de l'âme, et pour payer tes jetons tu dois sacrifier une parcelle de ton cœur. »

J'observais le fleuve ; les irisations du soleil sur les rides du courant étaient éblouissantes, presque douloureuses. Je n'avais pas suivi tous les méandres du monologue de Kahn, mais ce que j'en avais saisi indiquait une foi désespérée, et pourtant, me sembla-t-il, une foi noble et digne d'admiration. Ce qu'il avait dit — cela se résumait pour moi à une phrase unique et terrible, son ultimatum : « Pour connaître le Dow, tu dois investir » — me rappela les paroles que le maître m'avait adressées voilà si longtemps : « Le Tao est aussi sur la place du marché », et tout cela ressemble à des fleurs sauvages qui envahissent la tombe de la vérité. Sur l'autre plateau de la balance, il y avait l'avertissement de mon oncle Hsiao, l'oracle de la sagesse conventionnelle : « Tao et Dow — il n'y a pas de sophisme plus honteux. Ils sont inconciliables, de toute éternité, comme les grands contraires fondamentaux... Qui cherche à les concilier, à réduire leur inimitié implacable, cherche à subvertir les lois mêmes de l'univers ! » Laquelle de ces deux positions était la vraie ? Je ne pouvais plus tergiverser, je devais choisir. Etrangement, cette perspective ne m'emplissait pas tant de terreur que de tristesse.

« Qu'y a-t-il, petit ? demanda Kahn en interrompant ma rêverie. Tu te frottes sans arrêt les yeux. C'est la poussière ou un moucheron ?

— Non, simplement le reflet du soleil sur l'eau, dis-je. La lumière me blesse les yeux.

— Ne regarde pas le fleuve alors, me conseilla-t-il. Viens. Allons boire un verre au drugstore. Je te paie un Coca. »

J'acquiesçai. Nous tournâmes le dos au fleuve et repartîmes vers la ville.

La vitrine de notre repaire habituel de Pearl Street était en verre fumé, et l'intérieur plongé dans une fraîche pénombre où le conditionneur d'air murmurait (il formait une grande flaque d'eau sur le ciment du trottoir). La lumière artificielle apaisa la douleur de mes yeux, ainsi que mon esprit. Nous nous installâmes au comptoir pour commander deux Cocas que nous bûmes lentement, sans mot dire, nous tournant tantôt un peu à gauche, tantôt un peu à droite, jusqu'à ce que la glace noire eût retrouvé sa blancheur originelle et que nos pailles sucent bruyamment l'air glacé au fond de nos gobelets. Puis nous nous levâmes pour partir. Devant la caisse, je plongeai la main dans ma poche, mais Kahn fronça les sourcils.

« C'est ma tournée, petit », dit-il en posant sa main sur la mienne pour arrêter mon geste.

Je le laissai donc payer. Derrière la longue rangée des étagères remplies de médicaments, visible à partir des épaules, le pharmacien en blouse blanche travaillait dans son domaine privé. Debout sur une plate-forme, à trois marches au-dessus du sol du magasin, il évoquait un prêtre ou un alchimiste ; la concentration détendue de son visage exprimait un profond contentement, il se balançait doucement d'avant en arrière en travaillant à une tâche mystérieuse, peut-être la composition d'une potion rare dans son mortier. Je parcourus d'un regard apathique l'enfilade de ses casiers, mais mon attention s'éveilla quand j'aperçus quelque chose sur le comptoir, quasiment sous mon nez, un objet que j'avais côtoyé des dizaines de fois sans jamais le remarquer. Il s'agissait du présentoir hexagonal des lunettes Ray-Ban. Je me mis à le faire pivoter, découvrant le reflet fragmenté de mon visage dans les miroirs d'essayage. Ma distraction me stupéfia, car ce fut seulement quand j'aperçus la vraie paire que je fis l'association — les lunettes d'aviateur aux verres en forme de larmes vert foncé. Mon pouls accéléra aussitôt. Cédant à une impulsion subite comme si je m'abandonnais à quelque délicieuse perversité, je tendis la main pour les prendre, dépliai les branches de métal souple doré, les levai, les mis, plaçai le demi-cercle métallique derrière mes oreilles et regardai les miroirs du présentoir qui tournait encore. Comme en un film saccadé, je vis l'étrange sourire se répandre sur mes lèvres, un sourire que j'étais bien incapable de déchiffrer.

« Viens, petit », me dit Kahn, interrompant la cérémonie. Dans un des miroirs, je le vis compter sa monnaie et s'éloigner de la caisse. Alors il m'aperçut et sursauta. Nos yeux se rencontrèrent, bien qu'il ne pût voir les miens à cause de l'opacité verte des verres.

« Jésus ! » dit-il.

Je me plantai en face de lui. « Qu'y a-t-il ? »

Il continua à me dévisager, puis secoua lentement la tête comme pour se réveiller. « Rien, petit, je viens de comprendre quelque chose. Je t'ai déjà dit que tu me rappelais quelqu'un, tu te souviens ? Je viens de retrouver qui. »

Mon estomac se contracta. « Qui ?

— Tu ne peux pas le connaître, dit-il d'un air désabusé, un certain Love.

— Eddie Love ? précisai-je d'une voix tremblante, hachée.

— Ouais, tu as entendu parler de lui ? Il n'est pas de ton époque, pourtant. Mais avec ces lunettes, je te jure qu'on dirait Love tout craché. »

Mes genoux se dérobèrent sous moi, je m'accrochai à son bras en avançant mon visage à quelques centimètres du sien, incapable de parler.

« Bon Dieu, petit ! Qu'est-ce qui te prend ? Lâche-moi donc, s'écriat-il en essayant de dégager son bras.

— Kahn, lui dis-je en un murmure rauque, Love est mon père.

— Ton père ! » Kahn laissa tomber toute sa monnaie. Les pièces rebondirent et roulèrent dans le magasin. Il les regarda, puis leva les yeux vers moi. « Tu perds la tête ou quoi ?

— C'est ce que j'essayais de vous dire, poursuivis-je.

— Quand ça ?

— L'autre matin, avant que vous ne m'expédiiez à New Haven. »
Kahn semblait frappé de stupeur.

« Vous le connaissez ? lui demandai-je fébrilement.

— Quoi ? répondit-il avec un regard vide.

— *Vous le connaissez ?*

— Le connaître ! » Il me dévisagea stupidement. « Je l'ai connu — enfin je savais qui il était. Bien sûr. Comme tout le monde.

— Que voulez-vous dire ? lui demandai-je.

— Petit, dit-il avec une expression inquiète en posant doucement la main sur mon poignet, asseyons-nous une minute.

— Vous l'avez connu ? implorai-je alors qu'il me poussait vers une banquette.

— Ne mettons pas la charrue avant les bœufs. » Il se glissa en face de moi. « Bon, pour commencer, qu'est-ce qui te fait croire qu'Eddie Love est — était... Oh, Seigneur !... ton père ? Comment est-ce possible ? Love était américain ; tu es chinois.

— L'AVG, expliquai-je. Il a passé sept mois en Chine.

— Nom de Dieu ! C'est vrai, marmonna-t-il pour lui-même, légèrement étonné. Les Tigres Volants.

— Là-bas, il a rencontré ma mère... » Et commençant par le début, je lui racontai toute l'histoire d'une voix saccadée, bouleversée.

A mesure que la trame des détails et des faits se resserrait, devenait plus imperméable au doute, son étonnement s'accrut et son visage pâlit. A la fin de mon récit, il semblait presque malade.

« Tu as fini ? C'est tout ce que tu sais ? me demanda-t-il quand je me tus.

— Tout ce que je sais ! protestai-je. Je crois que je sais tout.

— Tout ? Mais tu ne sais rien ! C'est juste le début de l'histoire, son retour de Chine.

— Que voulez-vous dire ? Que s'est-il passé ensuite ?

— Bon Dieu ! Laisse-moi remettre un peu d'ordre dans mes souvenirs. Ils sont revenus, voyons, fin quarante-deux ? Oui, c'est ça. Après la dissolution de l'AVG ou plutôt son incorporation au vingt-troisième bataillon, le nouveau commandant, un certain Bissell, refusa aux pilotes la permission de trente jours qu'ils demandaient, et tenta de les obliger à signer un nouveau tour de service qui débutait sur-le-champ, en les menaçant de les faire mobiliser dès qu'ils poseraient le pied aux Etats-Unis. Pas exactement la tactique la plus intelligente avec un groupe comme celui-là, des vétérans endurcis habitués à n'en faire qu'à leur tête et qui entretenaient un rapport quasiment paternel avec leur commandant, Chennault — lequel, soit dit en passant, se fit baiser dans l'affaire. Ce chantage à peine déguisé les mit en rage, ce que personnellement je comprends parfaitement. La plupart des Tigres Volants annoncèrent carrément à Bissell où il pouvait se coller leur ordre de mobilisation et refusèrent leur intégration au vingt-troisième bataillon. Quand ils rentrèrent au pays, ils eurent droit à un véritable triomphe. Tout le monde les connaissait. Les premiers, ils avaient réellement damé le pion aux Japs, prouvé que c'était possible, qu'ils n'étaient pas invincibles. Je crois qu'il y eut même un défilé avec majorettes et tout le tintouin. Je suivais tout ça d'assez près au bureau des informations du BIG. Ils étaient reçus à toutes les réceptions et autres soirées mondaines. Je me rappelle que le nom de Love apparut plusieurs fois dans la rubrique des célébrités. J'ignorais qui il était à l'époque, juste un nom parmi d'autres, tu vois. Ensuite ils se dispersèrent, chacun partit de son côté et l'on n'entendit plus parler d'eux.

« Quand ton père refit surface, il volait en solo. Et ça a fait des vagues. » Kahn s'interrompit. « La métaphore est déplacée, petit, excuse-moi. J'ai appris ça par un article d'une page intérieure du *New York Times*. Ton père, qui s'ennuyait à mourir chez lui, essaya de reprendre du service, mais l'armée refusa sa candidature pour raisons médicales, une blessure au dos, je crois. Alors que fait-il ? Il s'achète un putain de P-40, un appareil d'entraînement, le fait réviser, retaper, peint les mâchoires de tigre et tout le bordel, puis il se met à faire le mariole aux commandes. On pouvait le voir tous les jours de la semaine au-dessus de la plage de Coney Island. Il faisait sensation. Une campagne de presse s'ensuivit pour stigmatiser sa frivolité, l'exercice irresponsable de son privilège "alors que nos gars se battent et meurent pour la patrie", le baratin habituel. Bien sûr, il avait été au feu, et parmi les premiers, mais les journalistes ont la fâcheuse habitude de laisser tomber ce genre de détail. Je crois que la plupart des gens le prenaient pour un cinglé, ou pour un type si excentrique que cela revenait au même. A l'époque, mon diagnostic n'était pas foncièrement différent. Sa notoriété — de mauvais aloi — aurait pu démoraliser n'importe quel type ayant vécu ce qu'avait vécu ton père, ou du moins l'agacer.

— Pourquoi "aurait pu" ? l'interrompis-je.

— Je veux dire, s'il ne l'avait pas prévue, répondit mystérieusement Kahn, voire provoquée.

— Provoquée ?

— Oui, comme une magouille de publiciste, une tactique de diversion.

C'est une de mes théories préférées. Tu sais que ton père avait un faible pour la prestidigitation et les tours de magie, n'est-ce pas ? Eh bien, je crois que d'une main Love agitait le hochet de son excentricité sous leurs yeux pendant que, de l'autre, il leur faisait les poches.

— Les poches de qui ?

— De la direction de l'*American Power and Light.* » Il marqua une pause. « Tu connais l'histoire des Love et d'APL ? »

J'acquiesçai.

« Comment toute la famille avait perdu le contrôle exécutif de la corporation du temps de son père ?

— Oui, oui, Arthur Love, dis-je avec impatience. Je connais tout ça.

— Eh bien personne — et surtout pas les membres du conseil d'administration d'APL — ne croyait qu'Eddie Love s'intéressait de près ou de loin aux affaires. On le considérait comme un simple playboy millionnaire et excentrique, taillé sur le même modèle qu'Arthur Love et doté de vices légèrement différents. A la mort de son père, il avait néanmoins hérité un beau paquet d'actions, maintenues temporairement en dépôt —, en fait le plus gros portefeuille d'actions immobilisées. Figure-toi que pendant qu'il faisait l'andouille avec son P-40 et s'arrangeait pour devenir l'Ennemi Public Numéro Un dans tous les clubs de femmes de Long Island, il achetait des actions en secret, grossissant son trésor par des achats effectués dans tout le pays à partir de comptes numérotés. Très malin, formidablement malin. Il avait vraiment un faible pour l'attaque par surprise. Fin 1943, il s'est pointé à l'assemblée des actionnaires pour la première fois de sa vie. Personne ne le connaissait.

« Bon, ils ont lu les minutes, réglé divers problèmes avant de procéder à l'élection du conseil d'administration pour l'année à venir. Maintenant, il faut que tu comprennes que depuis l'époque d'Art Love, les Love avaient toujours mis leurs bulletins de vote à la disposition de la direction. Cela allait pour ainsi dire de soi. Eddie Love venait juste d'avoir trente ans, l'âge spécifié auquel il devait s'occuper personnellement de son portefeuille d'actions. La direction d'APL ne s'attendait nullement à ce qui se passa, convaincue que le "bloc Love" voterait, comme d'habitude, dans son sens. Mais Eddie Love ne l'entendait pas ainsi.

« Essaie de visualiser la scène. Ce jeune type en lunettes noires se lève dans le fond de l'auditorium et demande à ce qu'on l'autorise à proposer plusieurs candidats de son choix. Bon. Ils commencent par se moquer de sa naïveté ; quand il insiste, ils se raclent la gorge, toussent dans leur main, finissent par refuser sèchement sa demande. Alors il *exige* qu'ils examinent sa requête de plus près, et les directeurs menacent de l'expulser. Brusquement, il abat son jeu : il sort toutes les procurations, elles lui suffisent pour contrôler le vote. Les directeurs sont fous de rage. Tu dois savoir que les prises de contrôle par surprise étaient relativement rares à l'époque. De plus, on ne s'en méfiait pas comme aujourd'hui. Les directeurs furent pris complètement au dépourvu. Pour te résumer la suite, Love nomma son propre conseil. Parmi les nouveaux directeurs figurait l'un de ses anciens potes de l'AVG qui, comme Love, ne savait pas quoi faire après son retour de Chine, était prêt à explorer un nouveau domaine, bref à tenter sa chance dans les affaires. C'était David Bateson, son ancien ailier de l'escadrille. Lors de la réunion des nouveaux administrateurs qui eut lieu immédiatement après, ton père se fit officiellement introniser président-directeur général, puis il rentra chez lui ; en un seul après-midi, il était devenu président du conseil d'administration et PDG d'*American Power and Light*, la corporation la plus puissante de tous les Etats-Unis ! Pas mal pour une journée de boulot, hein ? Wall Street fut stupéfait ; les vieux requins de la Bourse réagirent par l'indignation, le ravissement ou l'hébétude du boxeur KO. Rien de comparable ne s'était jamais produit jusqu'alors, Sonny. La semaine suivante, ton vieux décrochait la couverture de *Time* : "L'homme du jour". "Le Hun dans le Soleil de Wall Street", titrait le magazine. L'article était signé Hackless, chroniqueur pigiste et apologiste attitré des Love.

« Ton père ne se reposa pas sur ses lauriers pour autant. Une fois l'affaire bien en main, il bouleversa toutes ses structures. APL avait considérablement diversifié ses activités depuis sa fondation, mais Love accéléra encore le processus. Sous sa direction, je crois qu'on peut dire qu'APL devint le premier "conglomérat", bien que ce terme ne fût forgé que beaucoup plus tard. A cette époque, ils travaillaient énormément avec des contrats de munitions gouvernementaux, mais ton père — en pleine guerre, n'oublie pas ça — décida de s'attaquer à un marché entièrement nouveau. Devine lequel ? » Il sourit.

« Kahn !

— L'industrie pharmaceutique. Exactement. Quelle audace ! Et par-dessus le marché, il rafle toute la galette ! En quelques mois, il devient le maître et seigneur d'une marchandise particulièrement importante, peut-être la plus grosse part du gâteau : la morphine. APL décroche un contrat du gouvernement pour fournir les forces armées, non seulement des Etats-Unis, mais de tous les pays alliés. Je ne voudrais pas paraître morbide, mais as-tu une idée de la demande formidable d'anesthésiant pendant une guerre mondiale ? Love réussit à produire une came de meilleure qualité et moins chère que tous ses concurrents du marché. Il devient intouchable. Personne ne sait comment il s'y prend. A dire vrai, personne ne s'y intéresse vraiment. Je veux dire, tu n'exiges pas de lire la notice qui accompagne l'ampoule quand tu perds ton sang et que tu souffres, pas vrai ? Que tu sois un être humain *ou* un pays. Ce fut là son coup de génie. Dès lors, il grimpa, toujours plus haut. A la fin de la guerre, ton père était l'un des magnats les plus puissants de Wall Street, l'un des plus riches aussi. Je me rappelle avoir entendu dire que son nom avait figuré sur la liste des dix hommes les plus riches du monde, et quasiment en tête du peloton.

« En même temps, son comportement dans le privé devint de plus en plus excentrique. Le bruit courait qu'il buvait. Les chroniqueurs mondains s'en donnaient à cœur joie dans leurs colonnes. Apparemment, il passait de femme en femme. Sans jamais se marier. On avait raison de parler de son excentricité. Je peux moi-même en témoigner, car j'en ai personnellement fait les frais — ce dont je me serais d'ailleurs volontiers passé.

« Dans le temps, on pouvait monter sur le toit de l'immeuble de la Bourse. Peu de gens le savaient, mais quelques négociants déjeunaient parfois sur cette plate-forme quand le temps le permettait. Ce que je vais te raconter est arrivé peu après le début de ma carrière à Wall Street. Un midi, je monte là-haut en compagnie d'un ami du parquet. Nous nous installons avec nos sacs en papier. Soudain, nous entendons un bruit bizarre, pas très fort au début, comme venant de très loin, mais s'amplifiant à chaque seconde. "Qu'est-ce que c'est ? je demande en m'essuyant la bouche avec une serviette en papier. Tu entends quelque chose ?" "Non, j'entends rien", me répond mon copain. Je regarde autour de moi, dans le ciel — rien. Mais le bruit ne cesse de croître au point de devenir assourdissant. Tout le monde se met à paniquer. Brusquement, une immense ombre ailée balaie le toit, comme un gigantesque oiseau de proie, un ptérodactyle ou un engin du même calibre, et un avion émerge soudain du disque aveuglant du soleil, il pique sur nous en hurlant, moteurs lancés à plein régime. Nous lâchons nos sandwiches pour nous aplatir sur la plate-forme. J'ai pensé à un kamikaze égaré qui n'avait jamais appris la capitulation du Japon et dont un alizé pervers nous faisait cadeau. Au dernier moment, le pilote tire sur son manche à balai et le zinc passe en rase-mottes au-dessus de nous, si près que le gravillon s'envole dans les remous de l'air, nous sentons la chaleur du moteur, respirons les gaz d'échappement. La tête toujours protégée par mes bras, je lève un œil, aperçois les mâchoires de tigre et devine aussitôt qui c'est. Quand il a exécuté une deuxième passe, je l'ai vu — ses lunettes d'aviateur, exactement comme les tiennes, petit —, il nous regardait par-dessus son épaule, la tête renversée, la bouche ouverte comme s'il se tordait de rire et qu'il prenait le pied de sa vie.

« Il nous survole deux fois encore, puis paraît se lasser et s'éloigne en plongeant. Quand nous voyons cet énorme avion disparaître sous la ligne des toits, nous bondissons sur nos pieds et nous précipitons au bord de la plate-forme pour regarder en bas. Petit, ton vieux volait tout au fond du ravin de Wall Street en direction du fleuve. Les murailles des gratte-ciel étaient si proches que les extrémités de ses ailes les frôlaient. D'ailleurs au bout de la rue, il dut incliner légèrement son appareil pour passer. Au fond du canyon, les femmes couraient se mettre à l'abri en hurlant, les hommes restaient plantés sur place, la tête en l'air et la main en visière. Un type pousse un cri scandalisé, mais quelques autres plus audacieux se mettent à applaudir en hurlant de joie. Le gardien court en tous sens en essayant de se rappeler l'emplacement des batteries anti-aériennes, qui de toute façon n'existaient déjà plus à l'époque. Love exécute alors un looping et revient ; cette fois il mitraille la foule, non pas avec des balles, mais avec de petits parachutes en soie multicolores — prune, rose, émeraude, indigo. La plupart de ces fanfreluches bigarrées atterrissent dans la rue. Mais quelques-unes remontent vers le ciel, portées par un courant aérien ascendant. Un parachute atterrit près de nous sur le toit. Nous nous battons pour l'avoir. Devine ce qui était fixé au parachute ? Un paquet de gaufrettes estampillées d'une phrase porte-bonheur, petit. Comme je te le dis. Et toutes portaient le même message. "Amor vincit omnia", soit : "Love (l'amour) conquiert tout". » Kahn secoua la tête. « Tu parles d'une chutzpah ! Peut-être était-il un chouïa meshuga, mais quelles couilles ! Dans l'après-midi, en simple hommage à sa cascade magique, je crois, APL gagne deux points et demi

411

« Mais il réservait ses excentricités à la vie privée et dirigeait la corporation de main de maître. Cinq ans après son accession au pouvoir suprême d'APL, ton père avait atteint les sommets et s'était envolé dans le ciel, petit. Pour décrocher la lune. Personne à Wall Street ne pouvait lui tenir tête. La Bourse n'avait jamais vu un type de cette envergure — si j'ose dire —, une telle maîtrise depuis les barons brigands de la fin du XIXe siècle. En fait, il incarnait le même personnage : le Commodore Vanderbilt tirant des coups de canon sur le pont avant de son yacht, le *Corsair*, au mât duquel il avait fait hisser le crâne et les tibias croisés. Je me rappelle l'article publié à l'époque par Hackless, où il le comparait à Alexandre le Grand : à court d'univers à conquérir.

« Oui, je crois que le scandale éclata en 1950. Quand les communistes pénétrèrent en Chine occidentale et au Tibet pour renforcer leurs positions révolutionnaires, à leur immense surprise, dans... je crois que c'était la province du Yunnan. N'est-ce pas là qu'on cultive toujours le pavot ? Oui, c'est ça. Je m'en souviens parce que c'est l'endroit où il s'est crashé après son escarmouche, la fois où il a été blessé. Bref, au fin fond de la jungle, dans cette lointaine région inaccessible seulement habitée par quelques tribus primitives, ils ont découvert un petit complexe agro-industriel, une sorte de "district autonome" qui se consacrait exclusivement à la culture intensive, à la récolte et au raffinage industriel des divers sous-produits du *Papaver somniferum*, affectueusement connu sous le nom de pavot d'ornement. Des centaines d'employés — fermiers, ouvriers, chimistes — produisaient leur propre nourriture. Ils avaient même un petit auditorium où l'on passait des films occidentaux. L'idée avait, semble-t-il, germé dans l'esprit de Love pendant son séjour dans la région. Il fit même quelques expériences préliminaires, mais ne concrétisa réellement son projet qu'après son accession au pouvoir.

« Je me souviens d'un dessin humoristique publié à côté de l'éditorial du *New York Times* vers cette époque : une patrouille de soldats communistes se fraie un chemin dans un champ de pavot. Son chef, un croisement entre Tchang Kaï-chek et le lapin de garenne, bâille en retirant son fusil de son épaule. "Cinq minutes de repos, les gars, dit la légende. Je crois que je vais m'allonger là pour piquer un roupillon." On distingue au loin les gratte-ciel d'une cité fantastique, qui ressemblent étrangement à ceux de Wall Street. Les grands manitous de l'*establishment* financier ont probablement senti qu'il y avait de l'eau dans le gaz. Mais personne ne s'était attendu à une surprise de cette envergure, à un scandale aussi ahurissant. Sans payer le moindre impôt (sinon sous forme de gros pots-de-vin au Kuomintang qui trempait dans l'affaire jusqu'au cou), en utilisant les terrains gouvernementaux et les réserves inépuisables de main-d'œuvre bon marché, protégé par une organisation paramilitaire sophistiquée recrutée parmi les rangs de l'armée nationaliste, et financé par *American Power and Light*, Love avait créé un véritable État dans l'État, un paradis industriel exclusivement consacré à la production de la morphine. Les pinailleurs patentés s'en seraient peut-être battu l'œil, si l'on n'avait découvert, en démantelant les laboratoires, que ceux-ci fabriquaient non seulement de la morphine de qualité supérieure, mais aussi de l'opium et de l'héroïne. Et en immenses quantités. Il y avait aussi, semble-t-il, quelques mystérieux Siciliens dans le coup. Les officiers de l'organisation paramilitaire apprirent avant les autres que le pot-aux-roses était découvert, et s'enfuirent avec quelques soldats au-delà de la frontière, dans les États de Shan. Les seigneurs de la guerre qui y règnent aujourd'hui sont les derniers survivants de cette armée de l'opium.

« Le scandale contribua à déboulonner Tchang Kaï-chek, qui jura jusqu'à la fin avoir tout ignoré de ce paradis de la drogue. Peut-être disait-il la vérité : car le Kuomintang était alors si corrompu que l'idée d'exercer un contrôle quelconque sur ses activités était devenue pure utopie. Ce scandale contribua aussi à geler les relations entre les Etats-Unis et la Chine pendant les années cinquante. Oh, petit, ç'a été un tollé. Je me rappelle le jour où la nouvelle fut annoncée à la radio. McCarthy ne perdit pas une seconde pour le faire comparaître devant sa Commission aux Activités anti-américaines, désireux de le dévorer tout cru en tant qu'"exécuteur" du régime de Tchang, comme il essaya ensuite d'avoir la tête de Dean Acheson et du général Marshall. Love fut aussi inculpé d'une demi-douzaine de chefs d'accusation, dont fort peu sinon aucun auraient tenu le coup devant un tribunal, car il avait pris soin d'effacer toute trace derrière lui. Je crois qu'il préféra pourtant éviter l'épreuve d'une comparution en justice.

« Les média arrivèrent à la propriété de Love à Sands Point une heure environ avant le FBI. Typique. Les paparazzi grouillaient comme des mouches. Ce fut certainement l'un des premiers "événements médiatiques". A l'époque, ton père vivait seul avec son domestique chinois. Il leur parla très calmement, très civilement, les installa autour du bassin de son petit jardin chinois, parmi les rochers sculptés, les arbres *pen-t'sai* qu'il avait fait planter, leur expliqua-t-il, depuis son retour de Chine. La scène était filmée, d'accord ? Malgré la parfaite impassibilité de son visage, on le sent légèrement à côté de ses pompes, car il ne cesse de leur parler de fruits. "Ils viennent juste d'être cueillis", insiste-t-il, et il leur montre l'arbre, explique qu'il s'agit d'une variété rarissime qu'il a personnellement fait importer de Chine. Il semble obsédé par cet arbre.

— Des fruits ? demandai-je. Quel genre de fruits ?

— Je ne sais pas — quelle importance ? me répond-il, agacé par mon interruption. Litchis, kumquats — non, non, maintenant que j'y pense, c'étaient des pêches. Je m'en souviens parfaitement. Bref, il portait une robe de chambre chinoise en soie au-dessus de ses vêtements ordinaires, et ses lunettes de soleil. Après les boissons de rigueur, il sort une déclaration et la lit devant les caméras : il assume l'entière responsabilité du trafic de drogue, disculpe tous les autres directeurs qui, dit-il, l'ont toujours ignoré, il décortique toute l'affaire, comment l'idée lui est venue après son accident d'avion, etc. Tout ça est filmé, tu te rappelles ? Brusquement, croissant dans le fond des coulisses, on entend un hurlement perçant, suraigu : les sirènes. Love lève la tête, tel un animal qui hume le vent en dressant l'oreille. Puis il s'excuse poliment, traverse la pelouse d'un pas lent et légèrement claudiquant, rejoint son avion dont le moteur chauffe déjà. Les voitures de police négocient la courbe de l'allée sur les chapeaux de roue, les pneus dérapent, le gravier gicle, elles montent sur la pelouse, les flics ont sorti le buste par la fenêtre et brandissent leurs flingues comme au bon vieux temps d'Al Capone. Love saute sur l'aile de son P-40, grimpe dans le cockpit, tire la verrière du pilote au-dessus de sa tête et au moment précis où les voitures s'arrêtent en chassant de la queue et creusant de profondes ornières dans le gazon, l'avion s'éloigne, fait demi-tour et décolle au-dessus des flics qui mordent la poussière pour ne pas se faire décapiter.

« Petit, il leur a servi une chorégraphie aérienne digne de Mozart, une succession de loopings, de tonneaux, d'Immelmanns, des acrobaties en tout genre. Dans le film, tu vois les agents du FBI pétrifiés, la main en visière, bouche bée, le revolver pendant au bout du bras, comme des gamins au cirque. Il exécute un tonneau surprise, puis un demi-tonneau pour se retrouver à l'envers. Le moteur a quelques ratés, puis s'arrête, et Love passe comme un grand oiseau silencieux au-dessus de la foule médusée, pendu au bout de son harnais, tel un polichinelle hilare, levant les yeux vers les flics, les baissant vers les nuages. Il a repoussé la verrière du cockpit, si bien que le vent fouette son visage et l'on dirait un chien qui passe la tête par la fenêtre d'une voiture roulant à tombeau ouvert. Dément, complètement dément — et magnifique. L'un des caméramen m'a dit qu'il n'avait jamais rien vu d'aussi époustouflant : Love retenu là-haut par les sangles de son siège et qui les regarde à l'envers, étrange et ridicule. Le silence était tel, dit-il, qu'on entendait le chuintement du vent dans les canons ouverts du P-40 et le rire cristallin de Love. Alors, sans prévenir, il exécute un demi-tonneau pour retrouver la position normale, fait redémarrer son moteur, plonge à plein régime vers les flics et ouvre le feu. On retrouva ensuite le papier rouge déchiqueté des pétards sur toute la pelouse — une des plus célèbres plaisanteries de ton père. Mais cette fois les flics se défendent ; ils ripostent en se mettant à l'abri, certains avec des armes semi-automatiques. Quelques balles durent faire mouche. A la dernière seconde, Love redresse son appareil, remonte au ras de la cime des arbres, puis exécute un Immelmann — demi-looping et demi-tonneau, gagnant simultanément de l'altitude et changeant de cap —, puis il grimpe en chandelle et disparaît dans le soleil. Dans le dernier plan du film, on distingue deux minuscules serpentins de fumée noire qui semblent attachés aux ailes comme des laisses destinées à le retenir à la terre, des laisses sur le point de se briser.

— Alors, et ensuite ? implorai-je, malade d'excitation. S'il vous plaît, Kahn, ne me torturez pas. Il s'en est tiré, oui ou non ? »

Il me dévisagea avec sympathie, mais je lus un mauvais présage dans son regard. « Oui, p'tit, en tout cas il s'est tiré, dit-il doucement. Vu pour la dernière fois par un flic à moto sur le pont Verrazano — on aurait dit un météore dans le ciel de midi, l'appareil traînait dans son sillage deux langues de feu qui partaient des ailes, comme des flagelles ; des giclées d'huile noire ont éclaboussé l'asphalte du pont. Les baigneurs de la plage de Coney Island ont dit avoir aperçu un éclair blanc au loin en mer, entendu la détonation et pensé que les Russes avaient lâché la bombe sur New York. La carcasse calcinée, éventrée, du fuselage s'échoua sur une partie désertique de la plage près de Far Rockaway, mais les courants déposèrent des morceaux de l'avion jusqu'à Block Island au nord et Cap May, dans le New Jersey, au sud.

Pendant tout l'été, les gens les ramassèrent comme on collectionne les reliques, tu vois ?

— Et Love ? » demandai-je, au bord des larmes.

Kahn secoua la tête. « Navré, petit. »

Je m'effondrai. La caissière nous regarda.

« Il réussit apparemment à quitter son appareil avant l'explosion, car le lendemain un parachute s'échoua à Coney Island. On le découvrit près du rivage, secoué et ballotté par les vagues comme une énorme méduse ou un mouchoir de magicien. Mais le plus étrange était qu'il était vide : personne — pas de corps — dans le harnais. Il l'a, semble-t-il, enlevé pour essayer de nager vers la terre, mais il n'a pas réussi. Les gardes-côtes et la police locale organisèrent des recherches massives. Mais l'avion s'était abîmé à une dizaine de milles en mer. » Kahn soupira. « On n'a jamais retrouvé le corps. Le lendemain, le *Times* titrait : "Love est mort". Suivait une nécro signée Ernest Hackless.

« Quelque temps, les journalistes se demandèrent si le scénario n'avait pas été monté de toutes pièces, comme l'abdication de son père des années auparavant, si Love n'avait pas lancé ses poursuivants sur une fausse piste afin de s'enfuir tranquillement à Rio, La Havane, ou peut-être retourner en Chine, changer d'identité et commencer une nouvelle vie. D'autres déclarèrent qu'il n'était jamais parti, qu'il avait subi une opération de chirurgie esthétique, qu'il travaillait toujours à Wall Street où, incognito, il tirait les ficelles d'American Power and Light. Mais sa blessure et les circonstances de l'accident font qu'il y a très peu de chances pour qu'il s'en soit tiré. Un véritable mythe entoura désormais sa personne, comme toujours, j'imagine, avec ces types qui montent si vite et si haut, loin au-dessus de nous tous, puis disparaissent sans laisser de trace. Comme dit Whitman : "Il est inégalable dans cet ultime demi-sourire, et celui qui assistera à l'apothéose de son départ en sera encouragé ou terrifié pendant maintes années." Moi-même, petit, j'appartiens sans doute à l'un de ces deux camps, mais je ne sais pas lequel. » Kahn renifla, puis aspira une bouffée de Dristan. « C'était un Ahasvérus, petit, un Livermore — bien qu'il fût un homme d'affaires et non un négociant. Je l'entends comme un compliment. Sa sortie de scène ne fut peut-être pas du meilleur goût, mais je l'ai toujours admirée. On peut raconter beaucoup de choses sur ton vieux, mais personne ne niera qu'il savait s'éclipser au bon moment.

— Oui, sanglotai-je avec amertume, il a toujours su disparaître au bon moment.

— C'était le meilleur. Ah, petit, laisse tomber, dit-il tandis que je pleurais de plus belle. Tout ça est de la vieille histoire.

— Pas pour moi, répondis-je, pas pour moi. »

Kahn reconnut que j'avais raison, puis attendit avec une sympathie silencieuse que la source de mes larmes se tarît. Alors il saisit doucement mon bras. « Viens, petit. Sortons d'ici. »

Comme il m'ouvrait la porte, la caissière nous appela. « Hé ! Mes lunettes ! Vous les achetez, oui ou non ? C'est pas un cadeau de la maison.

— Excusez-nous, lui dit Kahn. Donne, petit, je vais les remettre sur le présentoir. » Il me les retira doucement, puis fit demi-tour

Une impulsion bizarre, véhémente, s'empara alors de moi et je saisis le coude de Kahn. « Donnez-les moi, Aaron », dis-je. Je pris mon portefeuille pendant qu'il me regardait, comptai les billets un à un devant la caissière, remis les Ray-Ban sur mon nez, puis poussai la porte et sortis devant mon mentor dans la lumière vive de la rue. Levant les yeux, je m'aperçus que je pouvais regarder le soleil en face.

16

Le choc que je ressentis à la nouvelle de la mort de mon père me fit temporairement oublier toute autre considération, et jusqu'à l'ultimatum de Kahn. Qu'il ait disparu, se fût noyé sans l'ombre d'un doute — mon esprit enregistra aussitôt ce fait, mais mon cœur refusa de l'accepter. S'il en était ainsi, alors cela changeait tout. Mais de quelle façon ? J'eusse été incapable de le dire. En fait, j'étais incapable d'aligner deux idées, seulement rempli d'une vague impression de fatalité, comme si c'était la fin. Mon entreprise tout entière avait échoué ; avec l'interruption obligée des recherches concernant mon père, j'essuyai aussi l'échec de mon enquête sur le sens du Dow, de ma quête du delta, du Tao dans le Dow. Je m'obligeai à accomplir mes devoirs à la Bourse, mais sans conviction, par pur acquis de conscience. La pitié de Kahn ne me gênait pas, toujours présente, une lueur dans son regard que je supportais à peine malgré le filtre des verres en forme de larmes vert foncé.

Je voulais parler à Yin-mi, je voulais que le baume secret et solennel de sa simple présence apaise ma peine et mon amertume. Mais je ressentais une étrange réticence. Dans mon abattement, je devinais que tout avait également changé sur ce front, que je l'avais perdue alors même qu'elle me révélait son amour. Je ne parvenais pas à lui pardonner cela, ma poursuite sous la pluie, notre étreinte équivoque. Deux fois j'allai à leur appartement pour lui parler, deux fois je fis demi-tour devant la porte sans frapper.

Un jour enfin, Kahn me prit à part. « Petit, tu ne peux pas continuer comme ça. Il faut que tu surmontes la nouvelle et que tu vives. J'ai une suggestion à te proposer. J'ignore si cela t'aidera, mais pourquoi ne pas aller jeter un coup d'œil là-bas ?

— Où donc ? demandai-je.

— A Sands Point, l'ancienne propriété des Love. Je me suis renseigné : personne n'y habite plus, sauf le gardien, le vieux Chinois qui travaillait pour Love. Il acceptera peut-être de t'ouvrir la maison et de te laisser fouiner. Ça te fera sans doute du bien, ça calmera ton esprit. »

J'ignore pourquoi, mais son idée me plut — elle me plut davantage que n'importe quoi depuis des jours. Je décidai de la mettre à exécution.

★

Quand le train s'arrêta en gare de Port Washington, j'aperçus un taxi De Luxe garé contre le trottoir, un gros scarabée noir et luisant datant d'une époque révolue. Le chauffeur, un Italien relativement jeune à la paupière tombante et dont le regard hésitait entre le vide et la franchise, était appuyé contre le capot de la voiture, jambes croisées et mains dans les poches.

« Où vous allez ? demanda-t-il.

— Vous connaissez la propriété des Love à Sands Point ?

— La vieille baraque sur la Route du Phare ? Bien sûr. Montez. »

Quand il démarra, je remarquai qu'il m'observait dans le rétroviseur. « Pourquoi que vous allez là-bas ? me demanda-t-il avec une familiarité impensable chez un chauffeur de taxi de Manhattan, et, de mon point de vue, parfaitement déplacée. Z'êtes un copain de Bozo ?

— Bozo ?

— Ouais, Bozo, Bo, le vieux Chinois qui habite le cottage. Je sais pas si c'est son vrai nom, mais c'est comme ça que, nous, on l'appelait.

— C'est sans doute le gardien, pensai-je à haute voix. Non, je ne le connais pas.

— A vot'place, je ferais gaffe. Il a une case en moins, si vous voyez c'que j'veux dire. Pour dire les choses carrément, c'est un putain de barjot. Et puis je crois pas qu'il parle bien anglais.

— Vous le connaissez donc ? » demandai-je.

Il gloussa. « Façon de parler. Quand j'étais à l'école, on allait souvent là-bas le vendredi soir faire la bringue.

— Faire la bringue ?

— Ouais, vous savez, lancer des rouleaux de papier toilette dans les arbres, balancer des boules puantes dans le bassin, jeter quelques œufs et des bombes à eau sur la porte d'entrée — rien de bien méchant. Mais le vieux n'avait pas le sens de l'humour. Il a pris la mouche, comme si la baraque lui appartenait. Il s'est mis à se défendre contre nous, à poser des pièges et tout le bordel. Surtout, il creusait des fosses, comme s'il avait voulu capturer un tigre. Recouvertes de branchages et de feuilles. Benny Fanoli, il a passé toute une nuit au fond d'un de ces trous avec une cheville brisée. Après ça, c'est devenu un sacré champ de bataille. Mais aujourd'hui, les jeunes l'embêtent plus trop ; et puis maintenant je plains ce vieux toqué. Vous dites que vous êtes un ami à lui ?

— Non, répétai-je. Je ne le connais pas.

— Qu'allez-vous faire là-bas alors ? demanda-t-il. Vous songeriez pas à acheter la baraque, par hasard ?

— Elle est à vendre ?

— Ouais, depuis des années. Mais croyez-moi, c'est un vrai taudis. Même dans le temps, elle se barrait en couilles. Elle a dû être belle il y a longtemps, mais on l'a laissée péricliter, tomber en ruine. Et puis ça doit pas être donné. Probablement plusieurs millions de dollars. Rien que le terrain. Pile sur le détroit, à côté de toutes ces villas luxueuses. Vous avez l'argent ? »

Je ris.

« Ouais, moi non plus — enfin, ça vaut le coup d'œil... Bon, nous y sommes. Voici l'allée. Je vous conduirais bien au bout, mais comme vous voyez... » La route était barrée par une chaîne à laquelle était fixée une pancarte « Propriété Privée ».

« Mèrci, je vais continuer à pied.
— Okay, dit-il. Au revoir. Saluez Bozo de ma part. »
Me laissant sur le bas-côté, il démarra et fit demi-tour. L'allée, couverte d'un rare gravier et creusée d'ornières, disparaissait dans ce qui ressemblait à un bois touffu. J'enjambai la chaîne et m'engageai sur le gravier ; à travers l'épais feuillage, j'apercevais de temps à autre de somptueuses villas. Sous la voûte des arbres, l'air était sombre, frais et très humide. Tout était silencieux ; on entendait seulement le gazouillis des oiseaux, le bruit intermittent du vent dans les frondaisons. Le sol inégal et les nids-de-poule de l'allée évoquaient davantage un lit de rivière à sec qu'une route ; à mesure que j'avançais, il me devenait infiniment plus facile de croire que je me dirigeais vers le cœur d'une forêt sauvage que vers une grande maison. Je marchais depuis quelque temps déjà quand je discernai la rumeur lointaine et assourdie des vagues, dont le murmure semblait répondre aux arbres, et, incrusté en elle comme un glas appelant les fidèles aux obsèques, le tintement métallique d'une bouée qui se balançait sur la houle au-delà du banc de sable.

Après un virage, le bois s'interrompait brusquement au bord d'une pelouse. J'arrivai devant une allée circulaire dont l'épais gravier mêlé de coquillages brisés semblait avoir été récemment ratissé. Le disque de gazon central était ombragé par un chêne splendide et solitaire, haut d'une trentaine de mètres, dont les branches noueuses et l'épais feuillage s'étendaient sur une distance considérable. La grande pelouse descendait ensuite en pente douce vers la mer, dont un muret de pierre la séparait. Au-delà, les eaux couleur pétrole du détroit de Long Island brillaient avec une sérénité vide. Plus loin encore, par-delà le détroit, une bande de terre boisée semblait flotter dans l'air bleuté. A ma droite, la pelouse montait légèrement vers un tertre planté de pins et de sapins, mais sur la gauche la pente plus forte aboutissait à la maison entourée de massifs de fleurs en terrasses et sise sur un promontoire qui surplombait la mer et les rochers.

Je fus agréablement surpris, car je m'étais attendu à une bâtisse monumentale, pompeuse. La maison possédait une étrange élégance vieillotte. Sans doute construite au début de l'époque coloniale, elle en avait les lignes excentriques mais plaisantes, la fantaisie capricieuse, comme si plusieurs propriétaires aux goûts légèrement différents l'avaient repensée, modifiée, et qu'elle eût survécu à leurs ajouts au point d'élaborer un langage et une logique personnels. Peut-être sa cohérence se manifestait-elle surtout dans son magnifique toit massif aux lourdes tuiles turquoise imbriquées, brisées çà et là par les avancées asymétriques des mansardes. Pour quelle raison — peut-être son bleu plus foncé qui se détachait contre le ciel —, elle me fit penser à un château de conte de fées.

La maison proprement dite était dans un état de délabrement avancé : plusieurs volets manquaient, des fenêtres étaient brisées (les vitres étaient en verre artisanal, irrégulier), la peinture blanche qui s'écaillait par endroits avait viré à une teinte gris-bleuâtre qui me rappela les tennis de Scottie. L'effet original n'avait pourtant pas complètement disparu ; on eût dit une belle femme qui, avec l'âge, se serait négligée. Devant l'entrée principale, les potiches qui bordaient les dalles de schiste contenaient de somptueux géraniums couleur saumon, telles des torches éclairant en plein jour le chemin d'un banquet ambigu. En contraste avec la présence saisissante de la pelouse, la maison évoquait une région brumeuse de la mémoire, une chose malade, nécrosée mais précieuse, une part de gâteau d'anniversaire enveloppée dans une serviette, puis remisée au grenier dans une malle obscure où elle s'émiettait, finissait par tomber en poussière.

Je ne vis personne en approchant, mais entendis le claquement métallique d'un outil de jardinage, une pelle ou une houe qui frappait la terre meuble selon un rythme régulier. Une voix chantait en chinois — une voix masculine, limpide et poignante, un peu éraillée dans les aigus, mais merveilleusement expressive. Elle venait de l'autre côté de la maison. Suivant la musique, je m'engageai dans une allée bordée de hautes haies de buis anglais soigneusement taillé, qui débouchait aussitôt sur une longue pelouse étroite derrière la maison. Cette pelouse s'élevait à un mètre du sol pour rejoindre une terrasse par une volée de cinq marches en schiste. A une cinquantaine de mètres, à ma droite, la pelouse aboutissait à une piscine vide sans plongeoir, entourée de chaises longues dont on avait retiré les coussins. Au-delà, à travers la mince rangée d'arbres qui bordaient le promontoire, on apercevait le détroit. A gauche et en s'éloignant de la maison, les deux haies se rapprochaient l'une de l'autre en formant un ovale, mais sans se rejoindre, car elles redevenaient parallèles au dernier moment pour former un étroit couloir donnant sur de sombres verdures. Dans ce berceau ovale se dressait une statue de marbre blanc : une Vénus Anadyomède debout dans la modeste vasque d'une coquille Saint-Jacques en fer, vêtue à partir de la taille, faisait sa toilette, son regard vide exprimant un désenchantement teinté de férocité. Elle rappelait la Statue de la Liberté, qui invitait tout en prohibant.

Alors que je l'observais, le chant, qui s'était interrompu, reprit. Je me retournai vers la piscine. Sur une terrasse plus élevée se trouvait un luxuriant jardin potager où poussaient du blé et des tomates, de hauts massifs de petits pois, des melons et des cantaloups. La voix venait de là. Un homme, qui s'était agenouillé, se releva et recommença de bêcher, le visage caché par le large bord d'un chapeau de paille pointu. Il était grand et mince ; malgré ses épaules tombantes, ses gestes étaient très gracieux, presque élégants. Je marchai vers lui sur la pelouse, gravis les marches et restai à l'observer en silence parmi les épis de maïs, m'interrogeant sur une étrange sensation de déjà-vu. Quand il remarqua ma présence, il s'immobilisa, puis leva les yeux en abandonnant sa houe fichée en terre. L'hostilité s'inscrivit sur ses traits. Puis il plissa les yeux pour mieux voir, sursauta, et sa bouche s'ouvrit en une exclamation muette. Grimaçant de douleur, il porta la main à son cœur, recula en titubant sans prendre garde aux plantes qu'il piétinait, trébucha finalement avec un léger cri dans un plant de choux, et tomba à la renverse, poings crispés vers le ciel.

Stupéfait et consterné, je courus jusqu'à lui, m'agenouillai à côté de son corps. Livide, les yeux révulsés, les paupières frémissant comme dans le sommeil paradoxal, il était inconscient. Un fin liséré d'écume ourlait ses lèvres. Craignant qu'il n'ait eu une crise cardiaque ou une insolation, j'ouvris son col, posai sa tête sur mes cuisses et entrepris d'éventer son visage.

Malgré mon inquiétude, je ne pus m'empêcher d'être fasciné par ses traits. Sa beauté fragile, ses pommettes saillantes, les fines cicatrices de son visage qui accentuaient seulement sa beauté comme... comme... Qu'était-ce ? J'avais l'image sur le bout de la langue. Elle me revint brusquement en mémoire : « comme les cicatrices infligées par le temps à l'ivoire ancien ». Oui. Je me figeai. Mon Dieu — était-ce ? Bozo, Bo... Po. *Chiang* Po ? Hsiao n'avait-il pas affirmé qu'il s'était enfui après la mort de ma mère ? Et où aurait-il pu aller, ce serviteur qui adulait mon père ? Oui, c'était lui ! Sans aucun doute possible ! Mon cœur s'emballa quand ce fragment vivant du passé — que, si récemment, j'avais cru irrémédiablement perdu — remonta du puits de l'oubli pour reposer contre moi, un visage serré entre mes mains. Je passai plusieurs minutes dans cette position, puis le sang afflua de nouveau à son visage. Ses paupières frémirent.

« Chiang Po », murmurai-je, anxieux de savoir si sa réaction corroborerait ma supposition.

Il ouvrit les yeux. Malgré la lumière éblouissante, ses pupilles étaient immensément dilatées. Son regard se fixait derrière moi, comme si j'eusse été transparent. Un sourire étrange errait sur ses lèvres. Son expression était celle de l'extase, mais je l'attribuai seulement au malaise dont il venait d'être la victime.

« Je me demandais si vous alliez ouvrir les yeux ou non », dis-je avec cette pointe de blâme malicieux qu'on s'autorise avec les invalides.

Il continua de regarder. Puis ses yeux me virent. « J'avais peur, répondit-il, peur de découvrir que ce n'était qu'un rêve et que vous étiez parti. »

Décontenancé, je lui souris, car je ne voulais surtout pas le contredire.

Alors que nous nous regardions dans les yeux — ou plutôt, que je regardais les siens, car je portais mes lunettes de soleil —, son visage s'illumina d'une sorte de béatitude, celle de l'animal loyal et reconnaissant qui observe l'homme qui le nourrit et le soigne. Les yeux de Chiang Po s'emplirent de larmes. Il tendit la main vers la mienne, la saisit, la pressa contre ses lèvres. « Maître... » dit-il.

Je reculai malgré moi, comme si marchant pieds nus dans un agréable jardin j'avais rencontré un monstre difforme et rampant. Son erreur ne me parut que trop évidente après mon expérience avec Kahn. Il me prenait pour mon père ! Mais même en tenant compte de la ressemblance, tant d'années s'étaient écoulées depuis sa mort ! Aussitôt, le diagnostic du chauffeur de taxi, que j'avais cru exagéré, me vint à l'esprit, et je me demandai si vraiment Chiang Po n'était pas fou.

Par bonheur, il ne remarqua pas ma réaction. Il poussa un profond soupir en fermant les yeux. Son étreinte se relâcha. « Vous êtes revenu », dit-il. Il y avait de la joie dans sa voix, mais aussi une douleur insondable.

« Vous vous trompez, dis-je doucement en m'efforçant de maîtriser mon dégoût. Je ne suis pas l'homme pour qui vous me prenez. »

Il eut une moue de reproche, de ravissement plein d'indulgence. « Vraiment ? répondit-il. Aurais-je attendu si longtemps pour ne pas vous reconnaître ? »

A la lumière feutrée de sa certitude, comme prisonnier de la douce condescendance de son sourire, je sentis mes amarres se détacher et dus faire appel à toute mon énergie pour ne pas me laisser engloutir dans ses pupilles dilatées, dans sa démence.

« On a prétendu que vous étiez mort, poursuivit-il. Mais j'ai toujours su que vous reviendriez, comme vous êtes revenu en Chine après l'accident, alors que nous vous considérions comme perdu. » Il bougea, essaya de se relever.

« Restez allongé, lui dis-je. Vous n'avez pas encore récupéré.

— Non, protesta-t-il en se débattant. Ce n'est pas convenable. » Il s'assit. « Vous devez venir voir la maison. Rien n'a changé. Tout est resté dans l'état où vous l'avez laissé.

— Po ! implorai-je.

— Venez, me pressa-t-il avec le sourire éthéré du souvenir. Nous allons traverser le jardin. Vous allez voir. Rien n'a changé. »

Quelque chose dans son regard lointain et le geste mécanique avec lequel il m'invita à le suivre me convainquit d'être entré de plain-pied dans un rêve éveillé, que Po était le maître de cérémonies qui me guidait dans une visite fantastique maintes fois répétée pendant les années précédentes, mais qu'il n'avait jamais eu l'occasion d'effectuer pour de bon. Je me levai et le suivis au bas des marches, à travers la pelouse, devant la Vénus, dans l'étroit couloir des haies qui aboutissait à un paysage où mon impression d'irréalité s'approfondit. Car ce paysage, je l'avais souvent visité en imagination. Il s'agissait du jardin de la maison de ma mère.

Mes yeux découvrirent tout ce que Hsiao avait décrit : le sombre bassin avec ses flottilles éparses de lotus et de jacinthes d'eau, les pans dégagés de sa surface claire-obscure où se reflétaient les saules et le ciel, l'eau enjambée par l'arche du pont de bois minutieusement peint et sculpté. Les galets et les coquillages brisés de l'allée crissèrent sous nos pas quand, allant vers le bord du bassin, nous passâmes devant d'étranges rochers, des amas de mousse, des arbustes taillés en forme de bêtes hallucinantes et innombrables, un massif d'arbres fruitiers nains et difformes, dont l'un, légèrement à l'écart des autres, était un peu plus grand.

Quand nous approchâmes de cet arbre, Po se tourna vers moi. « Vous vous souvenez de lui ? » Son visage exprimait une connivence, une complicité parfaitement énigmatique.

Je regardai l'homme, puis l'arbre. Il ressemblait étonnamment au pêcher de la cour de Ken Kuan, bien qu'une simple pousse, un rameau, comparé à son vénérable aîné, et cependant lui aussi scarifié et noueux comme un vieillard (mieux : comme l'arbre représenté sur la robe de ma mère). On avait installé un banc de pierre près de ses racines.

« Il a beaucoup grandi, c'est vrai, depuis la dernière fois que vous l'avez vu, mais il est resté chétif et nain. Comme nous le pensions, l'espèce se développe mal sous ce climat trop extrême et changeant. Chaque hiver, je dois l'envelopper à partir du sol pour protéger ses racines contre le gel et les vents de l'océan. Malgré mes efforts, la récolte printanière est au mieux équivoque — une demi-douzaine de fruits chaque année. Néanmoins, j'ai consciencieusement planté les noyaux et soigné les pousses avec amour, selon votre désir, si bien qu'aujourd'hui nous commençons enfin à avoir une sorte de verger, pas très robuste certes, mais qui possède une beauté particulière. Comme la sienne, je crois.

— Celle de qui ? »

Il m'adressa un regard étonné. « La beauté de Ch'iu-yeh, pardi.. Venez », dit-il avec un sourire triste en m'invitant à le précéder sur le pont.

Parce que mes pas résonnaient sur les planches, je posai doucement mes pieds sur le bois, comme à l'église. Quand je redescendis de l'autre côté, je cessai d'entendre Chiang Po derrière moi. Me retournant, je vis qu'il s'était arrêté en haut du pont. Les mains posées sur la balustrade, il observait son reflet dans l'eau avec une expression rêveuse, absente, désenchantée.

« Qu'y a-t-il, Po ? » lui demandai-je en le rejoignant pour poser mon reflet à côté du sien.

Les yeux rivés au bassin, il leva les mains, effleura doucement son visage, lissa les fines pattes d'oie sur ses tempes. Quand il se tourna vers moi, je vis des larmes dans ses yeux. « J'ai vieilli, dit-il, mais vous... » Il tendit le bras et passa l'extrémité de ses doigts sur mes joues comme pour confirmer son impression, peut-être seulement pour s'assurer de ma réalité. « Votre visage n'a absolument pas vieilli. » Il n'y avait aucune trace de ressentiment dans sa voix ; au contraire, il paraissait rayonner de fierté en me regardant. « Mais comment pourriez-vous vieillir ? » Il se tut, puis, d'une voix grave et tendue me demanda : « Vous avez découvert le secret, n'est-ce pas ?

— Le secret ?

— Ce dont vous rêviez sans cesse, répondit-il, même si vous en parliez seulement pour rire. La vie éternelle. »

L'ironie involontaire de sa remarque faillit me faire fondre en larmes.

« Chiang Po... » suppliai-je.

Il descendait déjà de l'autre côté du pont en se tenant à la balustrade et secouant la tête. « Comme tout cela est étrange », soupira-t-il, pris d'une immense fatigue.

Sortant du jardin, nous contournâmes la maison par où j'étais arrivé, puis rejoignîmes l'entrée principale. De la poche arrière de son pantalon, Chiang Po sortit un trousseau de clefs, qu'il manipula pendant que j'attendais sur le perron. Au-dessus de la porte, de part et d'autre du chambranle, deux lanternes de verre et de cuivre étaient repliées dans de petites niches comme des serviettes empesées de restaurant. Les embruns salés avaient obscurci le verre et couvert le cuivre de vert-de-gris. Posée sur un des panneaux, une grosse phalène brune aux ailes mouchetées de noir semblait dormir. Je levai la main pour la faire s'envoler, mais elle tomba en poussière entre mes doigts.

La porte s'ouvrit en grinçant. Une désagréable odeur moisie s'échappa de l'intérieur, semblable à celle de la laine mouillée ; mais l'air était sec, intensément sec, et rappelait l'atmosphère dessiquée d'une boutique d'empailleur ainsi que le parfum du sherry dans l'haleine des vieilles femmes, ces relents de naphtaline et d'eaux de Cologne éventées, de thés, de tisanes, de couvertures tricotées au crochet, une odeur que la désaffection, la préservation et non l'âge rendaient déplaisante.

Nous entrâmes dans un long couloir qui occupait toute la largeur de la maison ; à gauche, un escalier menait au premier étage. Par les étroites fenêtres qui jouxtaient la porte à l'autre extrémité de la pièce, j'aperçus la terrasse, la pelouse, le jardin potager. Le plafond bas était strié de poutres souvent fendues, gauchies ou irrégulières, qui exhibaient les caprices de l'herminette du menuisier ainsi que les déformations dues au temps. Quand elle s'ouvrit, la porte buta contre un porte-parapluies en cuivre rempli de curieuses cannes de marche et d'ombrelles dont le tissu avait pourri au contact des baleines. Il contenait aussi un sabre ornemental dans un fourreau extrêmement vieux et corrodé. Tout exhibait une patine ambrée, comme l'éclat mat d'un parquet ciré depuis longtemps. Le sol était couvert de superbes vieux tapis chinois de couleur cramoisie, élimés par endroits, mais que les ravages du temps et la fragilité de la trame rendaient d'autant plus précieux. Le seul meuble que je remarquai était un vaste divan installé contre le mur de droite, une « pâmoison » victorienne aux bras sculptés en volutes, à la forme tarabiscotée et imposante, couverte de satin rouge sang dont la couleur avait passé. Au-dessus, une scène orientale était peinte à fresque sur le mur : un immense cerisier pleureur perdait quelques pétales au premier plan et encadrait languidement un pavillon bâti sur les rives d'un lac, lequel se détachait sur un fond de montagnes — bien que d'exécution sans doute antérieure, la scène n'était pas sans rappeler le jardin que je venais de traverser. Je me demandai si, avant Eddie Love, un membre de la famille s'était intéressé aux chinoiseries, et je pensai aussitôt à Arthur Love. Mon impression se renforça quand je découvris une kyrielle de bibelots et d'antiquités chinoises, surtout des porcelaines, des lampes, des vases en cloisonné, mais aussi un choix magnifique de bols et de jarres bleu et blanc K'ang Hsi qui semblaient illuminer les ténèbres d'une vieille étagère d'angle.

Quand nous nous engageâmes dans ce couloir, j'aperçus à gauche par une double porte vitrée une salle à manger dont le lustre de cristal imparfaitement enturbanné évoquait une diva ivre aux bijoux en désordre, puis un buffet et une table pareillement protégés d'un tissu blanc. Alors que nous arrivions presque à hauteur de la porte suivante, nous obliquâmes brusquement à droite pour entrer dans une pièce au plafond tout aussi bas, où je remarquai une cheminée de marbre et un piano à queue, de nombreux meubles couverts de housses et une rangée de portraits sombres sur les murs. J'eusse beaucoup aimé les voir, mais Po désirait m'emmener dans la pièce suivante. C'était une bibliothèque — et quelle bibliothèque ! De forme elliptique, longue d'au moins trente mètres, elle occupait quasiment toute l'aile de la maison ; on avait coffré le plafond extraordinairement haut avant de le décorer de médaillons en stuc. Les murs étaient couverts de livres reliés en cuir, aux titres estampés à la feuille d'or. Ici (et ici seulement) l'odeur du cuir était puissante et délicieuse, comme le bouquet d'un vieux bordeaux. Il y avait une table de jeu au plateau carré de cuir vert, une énorme mappemonde, une profusion de sofas moelleux et de fauteuils délibérément disposés afin d'éviter toute intimité, deux escabeaux bas qui permettaient d'accéder aux volumes des étages supérieurs, un bar, un phonographe (une console massive, le Dumont Balladier). Quand Po ouvrit une porte au bout de la pièce, le chuintement des vagues emplit nos oreilles, nous respirâmes une puissante bouffée d'air marin.

Immobile dans la pénombre, Chiang Po m'observait avec un plaisir évident explorer les lieux. Après un moment, quand j'eus assouvi ma curiosité et que je fus disposé à poursuivre mon étrange visite, je me tournai vers lui.

« Alors, dit-il en souriant, êtes-vous prêt maintenant ?
— Prêt à quoi ? demandai-je.
— A monter. »

Je le regardai sans mot dire, m'efforçant de ne pas trahir mon ignorance quant aux espoirs qu'il semblait concevoir.

« Venez », dit-il.

Nous retournâmes sur nos pas jusqu'à l'entrée, puis gravîmes l'escalier vers le premier étage. En haut, nous passâmes devant plusieurs portes fermées, sans doute des chambres, avant d'aboutir à un ensemble de cabines d'essayage et de cabinets aux murs couverts de miroirs biseautés qui évoquaient le Palais des Miroirs d'une foire.

« Attendez ici, dit Po. Je vais allumer les lumières. »

Je le regardai disparaître derrière un mur, puis le suivis avec précaution dans cet espace peuplé de miroirs. Pénétrant dans une allée, je me voyais simultanément en sortir à l'autre bout, et mon image multipliée à l'infini avancer devant moi. J'avais beau en un sens arriver dès que je partais, cette simultanéité engendrait un effet, non de vitesse, mais de retard temporel, car il me semblait marcher sur place, comme sur un tapis roulant, sous le regard impitoyable de mes innombrables sosies. Alors que je cherchais Po à un tournant, je heurtai stupidement une surface froide et dure de verre étamé, puis, rebondissant pour ainsi dire, je partis confiant dans une autre direction, pour rebondir de nouveau. Plus prudent, je m'arrêtai et pivotai lentement sur moi-même pour essayer de retrouver mon chemin ; je fus alors entouré par le cercle étonnant de mes reflets qui semblaient se moquer vaguement de ma perplexité et me défier de sortir du dédale. La troisième fois où je me heurtai à moi-même, je réagis par un accès de colère qui me fut aussitôt renvoyé avec la parfaite symétrie du Karma. Secouant furieusement la porte du cabinet, je réussis à l'ouvrir, créant ainsi une sombre déchirure dans l'illusion. A l'intérieur, je découvris un smoking noir ainsi qu'une chemise empesée et froissée. Au-dessus, posé sur une étagère, un haut-de-forme noir. Soudain les lumières s'allumèrent, je me retournai et vis Chiang Po derrière moi.

« Il est toujours là, dit-il, comme pour se justifier. Je n'ai touché à rien. »

Le corridor aboutissait enfin à un autre escalier, étroit, raide et spiralé, qui se terminait sur un petit palier devant une unique porte fermée à clef, sans autre signe distinctif que son bouton de verre à facettes qui me rappela celui de la porte de Mme Chin. Chiang Po tripota son trousseau, choisit un rossignol qu'il glissa dans la serrure. Quand la porte s'ouvrit, un flot de lumière nous submergea brusquement, explosant de l'intérieur comme après une forte compression ; un courant d'air frais, iodé, nous enveloppa et souleva mes cheveux, avec un sifflement semblable à l'air qui pénètre dans une boîte de balles de tennis ou s'échappe d'une tombe égyptienne.

Ouvrant des yeux stupéfaits, j'entrai dans la pièce la plus merveilleuse que j'aie jamais vue. Les murs, qui formaient les côtés d'un triangle isocèle et s'incurvaient vers la poutre faîtière, étaient couverts d'un papier vert foncé moucheté d'innombrables points blancs, comme des flocons de neige qui tourbillonnaient dans le halo d'un lampadaire, ou, mieux, la poussière d'étoiles de la Voie lactée dans le ciel bleu-noir de minuit. C'était d'ailleurs ce qu'ils figuraient ; le plafond représentait une carte du ciel, un Zodiaque démesurément agrandi sur fond vert. Mes yeux errèrent parmi ces étendues sauvages et scintillantes, je repérai les constellations que Scottie m'avait montrées pour la première fois : Orion, Canis Major, le Taureau, Ursa Major, la Grande Ourse enchaînée à son pieu — elles étaient toutes là ! Avec quelle émotion je scrutai ce ciel nocturne alors même que la lumière du jour entrait à flots par les mansardes ! Bien que déconcertant, ce spectacle avait quelque chose de magique, d'irréel, d'enivrant. Dans une simultanéité semblable à celle du Palais des Miroirs, le jour et la nuit paraissaient respecter une trêve sur ce papier vert, et le temps se figer. L'écoulement des années semblait d'ailleurs avoir épargné ce lieu. Une impression de fraîcheur et d'éclat immuable planait sur la pièce comme un charme. Quel contraste avec l'atmosphère sombre et funèbre des autres pièces ! Comme pour corroborer mon sentiment, l'imposante pendule ancienne qui se dressait à l'autre bout de la pièce s'était arrêtée, les deux aiguilles unanimes indiquant midi, tels des tournesols érigés ou des flèches visant le soleil peint sur un panneau pivotant, à jamais figé au zénith de sa trajectoire. Un vase contenant des chrysanthèmes jaune pâle était posé sur une table protégée d'un napperon. Je devinai facilement qui les avait mis là, mais ce fut comme si dans cette atmosphère diaphane et salutaire ils n'avaient pas bougé depuis le jour où mon père avait disparu, sans se flétrir ni se faner. Mon regard se dirigea vers la mansarde, par laquelle j'aperçus la pelouse et beaucoup plus loin, pointant au-dessus d'un nuage de verdure, l'aiguille blanche d'un clocher qui brillait au soleil. Je ressentis un brusque bonheur, une extase légère, comme grisé par le bouquet de quelque puissant vin qu'on aurait autrefois savouré en ces lieux, le breuvage de la vie éternelle. Oui, dans cette atmosphère de jeunesse, d'immortalité et de joie, je faillis croire que mon père avait réellement composé puis absorbé ce breuvage, qu'il n'était pas mort, mais qu'on l'avait transféré, enlevé au ciel — l'une de ces constellations qui brillaient maintenant au-dessus de moi dans ce ciel émeraude.

J'eus alors une conscience plus vive que jamais de sa présence. C'était sa chambre, il l'avait marquée de son empreinte inimitable. Les objets que j'y vis m'étonnèrent. Mon père avait vécu là tous les âges de sa vie, conservé les souvenirs les plus chers de chacun, disposés en un archipel fortuit dont les îles reliaient la jeunesse à la maturité. Cette chambre évoquait autant un club pour hommes qu'une nurserie. Dans un coin se trouvaient les accessoires de sa carrière de magicien : paquets de cartes truquées, pièces de monnaie aux deux faces identiques ; l'écheveau des mouchoirs noués et multicolores ; le haut-de-forme noir à la doublure de soie gris perle et au double fond ; une malle entourée de chaînes et de cadenas, ses cordes et sabres magiques — tout le matériel classique. Mais il y avait un objet que je n'avais jamais vu : une grande boîte noire laquée qui n'était pas sans rappeler un cercueil, mais en moins long et plus profond, d'où dépassaient à une extrémité la tête d'un mannequin sans visage en perruque noire, et à l'autre des chevilles et une paire de chaussons rouges aux talons carrés et aux boucles de verre si brillantes qu'on eût dit des rubis. Au milieu, une scie à larges dents se tenait en équilibre dans une rainure, interrompant momentanément son ignoble besogne — « couper la dame en deux ». Non loin se trouvait un vaste théâtre de marionnettes, presque aussi grand que moi, dont on avait laissé ouvert le rideau de scène en velours vert foncé, ce qui permettait d'apercevoir les coulisses où Polichinelle et sa femme, abandonnés par les marionnettistes, s'étaient endormis dans les bras l'un de l'autre, front contre front, leurs corps désarticulés soudés en une étreinte anguleuse. Le long de la poutre faîtière du toit où les deux murs se rejoignaient, courant sur toute la longueur de la chambre, un cerf-volant représentait un dragon chinois à la gueule féroce de papier peint et au corps cousu d'une multitude de bandes de soie colorées. Des fils de longueurs variées suspendaient le monstre qui semblait ainsi onduler et se tordre en volant, effet encore renforcé par le courant d'air dont j'ignorais toujours l'origine. Escorte traversant le cosmos, mais peut-être attaquant le dragon, une douzaine de maquettes d'avions — biplan Sopwith Camel, Fokker, Spad — non pas en plastique, mais en balsa et en tissu pour les ailes, peints avec une habileté et une minutie stupéfiantes, pendaient aussi du firmament. Il y avait également un dirigeable et une montgolfière. Sur une étagère, je vis les biographies d'Eddie Rickenbacker et du baron von Richthofen ; *Vol de nuit*, de Saint-Exupéry et, séparé par un Sopwith Camel, *Le petit prince*, du même auteur, à côté du *Prince* de Machiavel. Il y avait d'autres livres, *Le retour d'Houdini du royaume de la mort*, les *Confessions d'un opiomane anglais* par De Quincey, les *Poèmes* de Samuel Taylor Coleridge ; et enfin, sur une desserte, à la place d'honneur en quelque sorte, et à portée de la main, un exemplaire usagé du *Magicien d'Oz* de L. Frank Baum. Parcourant l'introduction d'un œil distrait, je tombai sur cette phrase : « J'aimerais proposer un conte de fées modernisé, où demeureraient l'émerveillement et la joie, mais dont les migraines et les cauchemars seraient bannis. » Cela s'appliquait idéalement à l'esprit de la pièce elle-même !

Je passai lentement en revue des armées de soldats de plomb alignés sur le champ de bataille, des chevaliers en armure qui chevauchaient de fringants coursiers caparaçonnés et s'enfonçaient vaillamment dans les rangs des grenadiers napoléoniens. Je passai devant un volcan de papier mâché sans doute réalisé à l'école ; juché à un angle précaire sur ses pentes calcinées, un brontosaure en plastique cherchait une herbe inexistante et levait les yeux juste à temps pour voir un tyrannosaure, dont le sourire semblait grandir aux dépens de ses pattes antérieures, charger à partir de la savane pour le dévorer. A l'ombre d'un palmier, un tricératops observait placidement la scène en mâchant une touffe verte de bandes de papier lacéré. Il y avait des pièces de Meccano et des accessoires du petit chimiste, alambics, tubes à essais, une échelle de Jacob électrique — tout le bric-à-brac indispensable du jeune savant fou.

Après tous ces objets, il était étrangement glaçant de découvrir l'arc de chasse — une tige incurvée de bois poli à la poignée sculptée, à côté d'un carquois de flèches dangereusement effilées — accroché au mur sous une tête de cerf, un six-cors sur le qui-vive, narines dilatées, une lueur inquiète avivant le noir de ses yeux de verre. M'approchant de l'extrémité de la pièce, je trouvai son uniforme avec les insignes de l'AVG, un Tigre Volant en haut de forme bondissant du soleil, posé sur un porte-vêtements de bois, impeccablement repassé et comme prêt à l'usage, ses chaussures noires cirées de GI rangées dessous. Tout près, sur une table, dans une boîte à cigares Dutch Masters, posé sur un drapeau chinois plié, je trouvai un écrin couvert de velours qui contenait sa médaille et, cliquetant à côté, une balle de sept millimètres émoussée qui, décidai-je, était certainement celle que mon père ou un de ses camarades avait extraite du siège en cuir de son P-40 après qu'elle eut traversé tout son corps en détruisant seulement l'apophyse spinale, cette « fragile excroissance osseuse de la colonne vertébrale ». A côté, je fis une découverte qui me peina, mais ne m'étonna guère : une pipe à opium au fourneau d'argent ciselé. Et avec tous ces trophées, une mèche de cheveux noirs noués par un fil de soie rouge sang, qui me déchira le cœur. Assis sur la commode, ses yeux de boutons me regardant avec une cruelle raillerie, se trouvait le panda en peluche. Près de lui, j'aperçus deux photos de Love — dont une que je connaissais. C'était le tirage original : Love à côté de son avion en lunettes de soleil, pantalon kaki, robe chinoise et chaussures bicolores. Mais il manquait quelque chose, ou plutôt quelqu'un : ma mère. Une paire de ciseaux l'avait soigneusement découpée, la bannissant ainsi facilement de sa vie. Pourtant l'opération n'avait pas complètement réussi ; car émergeant du rebord découpé de la photo, la main blanche et fantomatique de Ch'iu-yeh serrait le bras de mon père au-dessus du coude comme si elle refusait de le lâcher et que, de l'autre monde, elle se vengeât. L'effet était saisissant. L'autre cliché montrait Love petit garçon, debout à côté de la piscine en costume marin, brandissant un biplan au-dessus de son épaule, la tête penchée pour regarder l'appareil de photo, grimaçant à cause du soleil, et la main en visière. La photo était poignante et troublante. Le bonheur du garçon semblait une simple pose, une simulation, comme si son bras eût été fatigué et qu'un souffleur debout derrière le photographe l'eût encouragé, voire exhorté à conserver son attitude de jeu « spontané ».

C'était tout. Il n'y avait rien après la Chine — à croire que sa vie s'était arrêtée là. Mon euphorie originelle me quitta. Quelque chose me blessait et m'échappait, cette froideur fascinante que Hsiao avait décelée dans son rire, non pas de la cruauté ni de la méchanceté, simplement de la froideur. Et vraiment je crus l'entendre résonner partout autour de moi, ce rire. Bizarrement, la chambre me rappelait Ken Kuan, lointaine, monacale, bien que j'eusse été en mal de justifier mon impression. Ainsi, dénuée de tout ascétisme, elle évoquait davantage un palais consacré aux plaisirs de ce monde. Mais on eût dit que la vie n'y avait pas pénétré, bannie par le même charme magique qui excluait le temps. Pendant que j'examinais les objets réunis dans la chambre, ceux de l'enfant et ceux de l'homme, je songeai que l'enfant, loin d'avoir été écrasé sous le poids des ans, avait survécu dans l'homme. Love avait miraculeusement préservé sa jeunesse dans son cœur, comme un fœtus vivant dans un bocal utiliserait ses ouïes prénatales pour respirer le milieu toxique du formol. Mais à quel prix ? Quand j'examinai à nouveau la deuxième photo, j'eus l'impression que toute sa vie durant on l'avait figé dans cette attitude. Je fus pris d'une soudaine pitié pour mon père. La solution du mystère était peut-être facile : un cas de développement interrompu. Quoi de plus banal ? Et pourtant il avait été courageux, il avait inspiré la dévotion. Il avait goûté à la gloire du monde et à sa tristesse, il avait péché. Pour toutes ces raisons et parce que je portais sa blessure dans mon cœur, je ne pouvais le réduire à un adolescent qui n'eût jamais grandi, un enfant prodige qui eût refusé le fardeau de la maturité, — de même que les allégations de Hsiao n'avaient pu venir à bout du culte que je lui vouais. Où était la vérité ? Etait-il possible que tout le temps, derrière l'écran de ses lunettes noires, son regard comme celui du moine se retournât vers lui-même, fixé sur le soleil d'une révélation secrète, ses yeux éblouis par l'éclat insoutenable de sa vision intérieure ? Ou bien son cœur avait-il toujours été froid et vide, et mon père un invalide aux yeux trop fragiles pour la lumière du jour ? Ses lunettes signalaient-elles le désir d'une plus grande liberté, ou une dérisoire tentative de protection ? Cachait-il quelque chose en lui, ou bien se protégeait-il ? Et comment jamais le savoir ? Un grand silence occupait le centre de sa vie ; je me demandais si je devais, si même je pourrais le briser ou le faire résonner. Love avait échappé au monde ainsi qu'à moi-même. Son ambiguïté était sans appel. Elle prouvait d'ailleurs son génie. La seule chose à faire était peut-être de renoncer à le comprendre, comme Hsiao, de reconnaître ma défaite et de retourner à mon point de départ. Pourtant, c'était impossible. Car, ne le connaissant pas, je savais que je ne me connaîtrais jamais.

Alors que cette pensée déprimante occupait mon esprit, on frappa à la porte. Chiang Po entra, fit une profonde révérence, puis s'approcha de moi. Il scruta silencieusement mon visage, et ses yeux devinrent tristes.

« L'humeur vous est venue ? » demanda-t-il, mais c'était moins une question qu'une constatation. Poussant un profond soupir, il me prit par le coude comme un invalide et m'emmena sans résistance vers le lit. Il retourna les oreillers, les frappa du plat de la main, puis les installa contre la tête-de-lit. Ensuite, il me guida doucement sur le lit, releva mes jambes, enleva mes chaussures. Je le vis traverser la chambre jusqu'à un petit écritoire, tourner la clef du tiroir, en sortir une boîte. Il approcha une petite chaise à mon chevet, posa la boîte dessus et l'ouvrit. Un parfum âcre et doux s'en échappa aussitôt, comme des fleurs sauvages mêlées de crottin. Il détacha un fragment de pâte noire, qu'il malaxa entre son pouce et ses doigts. Puis, allumant une petite lampe, il ficha la boulette sur l'aiguille, la fit grésiller au-dessus de la flamme, la plaça enfin dans le fourneau d'argent ciselé de la pipe que j'avais déjà vue, dont il inséra obligeamment l'embout entre mes lèvres. Fasciné par le rituel, j'inhalai et retins la fumée dans mes poumons. Chiang Po prit ensuite une bouffée, puis traversa la pièce jusqu'à la desserte et saisit le volume posé dessus. Il revint vers moi pour le placer entre mes mains, fit une révérence et se retira, me laissant seul.

Quand j'ouvris la couverture du *Magicien d'Oz*, les pages se séparèrent d'elles-mêmes, comme si la reliure avait conservé le souvenir des goûts de son ancien propriétaire. Je me mis à lire :

Ils cheminaient en écoutant le chant des oiseaux multicolores et regardant les fleurs magnifiques qui poussaient maintenant si dru qu'elles formaient un tapis sur la terre. Il y avait de grosses fleurs jaunes, blanches, bleues et pourpres, et puis de grands massifs de pavots écarlates dont le coloris éclatant blessait presque les yeux de Dorothy.
« Quelle beauté ! s'écria-t-elle en respirant l'âcre parfum des fleurs.
— C'est vrai, renchérit l'Epouvantail. Quand j'aurai un cerveau, je l'apprécierai davantage.
— Si seulement j'avais un cœur, comme je les aimerais, ajouta le Bûcheron de Fer-Blanc.
— J'ai toujours adoré les fleurs, dit le Lion ; elles semblent si vulnérables, si frêles. Mais dans la forêt aucune n'est aussi brillante que celles-ci. »
Ils rencontrèrent ensuite de plus en plus de gros pavots écarlates, de moins en moins des autres fleurs ; et bientôt ils marchèrent au milieu d'un immense champ de pavots. Il est bien connu que, lorsqu'on réunit un grand nombre de ces fleurs, leur odeur est si puissante que quiconque la respire s'endort ; et si l'on n'emporte pas le dormeur loin du parfum de ces fleurs, alors il dort éternellement. Mais Dorothy ignorait cela, et elle ne pouvait échapper aux brillantes fleurs rouges qui étaient maintenant partout ; ainsi, ses paupières s'alourdirent bientôt, elle sentit qu'elle devait s'asseoir pour se reposer et dormir.

Tandis que je lisais ce passage, je sentis mes propres yeux sur le point de se fermer.

« Qu'allons-nous faire ? demanda le Bûcheron de Fer-Blanc.
— Si nous la laissons ici, elle va mourir, dit le Lion. Le parfum de ces fleurs nous tue tous. Moi-même, je parviens à peine à garder les yeux ouverts. »

Malgré mon intérêt, j'étais incapable de concentrer mon regard sur la page. Mes yeux sautaient de ligne en ligne, se fixant parfois sur un passage.

« Prends tes jambes à ton cou, dit l'Epouvantail au Lion, et quitte ce champ mortel le plus vite possible. Nous allons porter la fillette ; mais si jamais tu t'endors, nous ne pourrons pas te transporter à cause de ton poids. »
Le Lion s'ébroua donc, bondit et démarra de toute sa vitesse. Quelques secondes après, il avait disparu.
« Faisons une chaise avec nos mains, et portons-la », dit l'Epouvantail...
Ils marchèrent longtemps, mais il semblait que le grand tapis de fleurs mortelles ne finirait jamais. Ils suivirent la courbe du fleuve, et brusquement trouvèrent leur ami le Lion, qui dormait comme une souche parmi les pavots. Les fleurs avaient été trop fortes pour l'énorme bête, qui avait succombé et s'était écroulée non loin de la fin du champ de pavots, que remplaçait devant eux le vert tendre de l'herbe.

« Nous ne pouvons rien faire pour lui, dit le Bûcheron de Fer-Blanc avec tristesse ; car il est beaucoup trop lourd à porter. Nous devons l'abandonner ici où il dormira éternellement, et peut-être rêvera-t-il qu'il a enfin trouvé le courage de se lever. »

De grosses larmes se mirent à couler sans raison sur mes joues, car je n'avais jamais lu ce livre et pouvais seulement me faire une idée très vague de son intrigue. Retirant mes lunettes, je me retournai sur les oreillers et m'abandonnai à ma peine. Je m'endormis.

Je me réveillai en sursaut, convaincu qu'il y avait quelqu'un dans la chambre. Mais je ne vis personne. Mes yeux finirent par se fixer sur un rideau qui ondulait devant la fenêtre d'une mansarde. Une petite cage d'oiseau dorée, que je n'avais pas encore remarquée, était accrochée au plafond de ce recoin. Elle oscillait doucement au bout de sa chaîne dans le courant d'air qui la faisait pivoter dans un sens, puis dans l'autre. Quittant mon lit, j'allai l'examiner de plus près. La minuscule porte entrebâillée créait l'illusion d'une récente occupation, comme si l'oiseau venait à peine de s'échapper. Je découvris ensuite que le mystérieux courant d'air que j'avais déjà senti venait d'une vitre brisée. Ouvrant la fenêtre en grand, je vis le soleil de l'après-midi scintiller sur les vagues du détroit. Pendant que je regardais leurs variations infinies, un petit avion doré apparut au-dessus de l'océan. Le bruit des moteurs s'estompa rapidement ; il devint un petit point noir qui finit par disparaître.

Quand je quittai la fenêtre, je découvris Chiang Po qui m'observait sur le seuil. Il tenait un plateau qui contenait de la nourriture et des rafraîchissements, mais malgré ma faim je les remarquai à peine. Car l'expression étrange de son visage retint toute mon attention.

« Po ? » m'enquis-je doucement.

Il rougissait jusqu'à la racine des cheveux. « Qui es-tu ? » me demanda-t-il d'une voix cinglante.

Levant la main, je voulus toucher mes lunettes et me rappelai brusquement que je les avais retirées avant de m'endormir.

« Po..., commençai-je aussi calmement que possible, laisse-moi m'expliquer.

— *Bâtard*, siffla-t-il, tu as brisé mon cœur.

— Tu ne comprends pas, protestai-je tout en me glissant avec précaution vers le lit pour prendre mes chaussures et mes lunettes.

— Je comprends très bien, rétorqua-t-il en s'avançant vers moi. Tu m'as trompé.

— Involontairement, arguai-je.

— Dehors ! » explosa-t-il, et son visage devint aussi livide que tout à l'heure dans le jardin.

Craignant pour sa sécurité comme pour la mienne, je passai devant lui sur le palier. Au milieu de l'escalier, je me retournai et vis son regard dément traversé d'éclairs de colère, ses mains qui tremblaient, les larmes qui ruisselaient sur ses joues.

« Pardonne-moi, Po. »

Il leva le bras et d'un geste péremptoire me montra la porte inférieure.
« Va-t'en, commanda-t-il. Et ne reviens pas. *Bâtard !* »

17

Après ce voyage, mon abattement atteignit son point le plus bas, ou plutôt son maximum sur l'échelle du désespoir. Etre arrivé si près du but, avoir senti sa présence de façon si palpable, et pourtant savoir qu'il était à jamais hors d'atteinte — ce tourment était sans merci et profondément déprimant. Je crois qu'il mina ma confiance en la vie, et peut-être jusqu'à mon équilibre mental. Ma santé se détériora. A la Bourse, je pris un congé de maladie d'une semaine, grâce à Kahn qui joua magnifiquement le rôle de mon protecteur. Pendant cette période, je quittai rarement ma chambre, et même, à vrai dire, mon lit. Je ne mangeai presque rien. J'étais trop déprimé pour penser à la nourriture. Je ne m'habillais même plus. Je ne me lavais pas le visage ni ne me rasais. Je dormais parfois des heures d'affilée. Éveillé, je restais longtemps à regarder mon image derrière mes lunettes de soleil dans le morceau de miroir abandonné par le précédent occupant de la chambre, — cérémonial névrotique qui s'épanouit démesurément en s'enracinant dans mon désespoir, et m'apaisa curieusement, comme si cette pitoyable imposture pouvait me dédommager de l'avoir perdu pour toujours, lui que je n'avais jamais connu. Au fond de mon cœur, je crois que j'attendais quelque chose, un signe, une lueur quelconque à laquelle je me préparais inconsciemment. J'ignorais totalement d'où elle viendrait, quelle forme elle prendrait, mais j'attendais, et je regardais.

Dans mes rares intervalles de lucidité, il me semblait que mes choix s'étaient réduits à deux, bien que « choix » soit sans doute un mot inexact ; car à mille lieues d'un libre mouvement de l'esprit, j'étais confronté aux deux cornes d'un dilemme et invité à m'empaler sur l'une ou l'autre : gager la robe ou bien partir. Bien que ces deux voies impliquent une compromission irréparable, je penchais en faveur de la seconde. En effet, il me semblait plus honorable, ou plutôt moins déshonorant, de renoncer à une quête conçue dans un moment d'orgueil et probablement vaine — la recherche du delta —, faisant en quelque sorte la part du feu et retournant en Orient, que de trahir la mémoire de ma mère. Et pourtant, si je renonçais à l'idée du delta, qu'allais-je retrouver ? Car si le Dow et le Tao étaient des entités séparées, alors la Réalité était multiple et le Tao un mensonge. Et j'aurais grandi sous le couvert d'une illusion. Il était absurde de retourner vers un mode de vie discrédité. « Le nid de l'oiseau brûle. » La prophétie s'était bel et bien réalisée. Pourtant même cela semblait préférable à la mise en gage de la robe. Bien que je n'eusse pas « prouvé » avec certitude que le delta était un mirage, la mort de mon père lui retirait toute importance. Ma passion, mon obsession s'étaient émoussées. Le sens du Dow cessa de m'exciter, de m'inspirer. Je devins indifférent. Sans lui, le Dow était étranger, un paysage aussi froid et inhospitalier que la face cachée de la lune, privé de la lumière vivifiante de sa vie et de son mystère.

Réfléchissant à cette transformation, je compris que ma quête du sens du Dow et ma tentative pour le réconcilier avec le Tao avaient été une enquête pour le retrouver, *lui*, une tentative pour réconcilier son mystère avec ma Voie, pour le classifier, à la façon de Linné, parmi les phénomènes naturels, la flore et la faune dont ma conception du monde m'avait appris la possibilité, et que je m'attendais donc à rencontrer un jour ou l'autre. Par ignorance, caprice ou instinct précoce de ma part, Eddie Love avait été le Dow pour moi, son incarnation et sa personnification ; avec sa disparition, le Dow devenait un symbole creux, une ruine, un temple abandonné des dieux. Eût-il été vivant, je m'y serais peut-être résolu — à gager la robe —, mais avec la nouvelle de sa mort, à quoi bon ? Raison de plus pour chérir, ne pas risquer de perdre inconsidérément le seul bien que mes parents m'avaient légué.

Pendant plusieurs jours, je me perdis dans une sorte d'absence aboulique. Un matin, j'entendis frapper à ma porte.

« Je peux entrer ? » demanda Yin-mi en passant la tête dans l'entrebâillement de la porte.

J'avais heureusement fait mon lit ; j'étais torse nu, hirsute et non rasé, attablé devant une tasse de thé froid infusé la veille. Je tournai sombrement la tête pour la regarder, puis repris ma position sans répondre à sa question.

« Sun I, hasarda-t-elle avec une timide inquiétude.

— Quoi ? répliquai-je d'une voix bourrue.

— Tu n'as pas l'air bien. Tu es malade ?

— Je vais très bien. »

Elle s'assit sur une chaise à côté de moi, observa mon visage d'un air préoccupé tandis que j'évitais son regard. Elle portait une tenue de plage, sandales et robe d'été en coton blanc ; elle tenait un sac de toile.

« Le père Riley aimerait savoir si la conférence tient toujours, dit-elle timidement.

— La conférence ! murmurai-je, me souvenant brusquement de son existence.

— C'est demain soir.

— Merde ! marmonnai-je.

— Tu avais oublié... ?

— A vrai dire... » Je haussai les épaules en manière d'excuse, la laissant achever d'elle-même.

« Tu vas la faire ? Tu ne vas pas le décevoir ? »

Touché par son ton suppliant, je la regardai brièvement. « Je crois que je n'ai pas vraiment le choix, non ? » répondis-je avec un sourire mauvais.

Elle parut soulagée. « Ce sera peut-être amusant.

— Oui.

— Tu as vu les affiches ?
— Quelles affiches ?
— Il y en a dans tout le centre ville, m'apprit-elle en plongeant la main dans son sac. J'en ai moi-même collé quelques-unes mardi après-midi.
— Je ne suis pas sorti.
— Tiens. » Avec un léger sourire, elle en déroula une sur la table.
Je la regardai en fronçant les sourcils. « Où ont-ils pris cette photo ?
— Un habitué des CJT avait son Instamatic, tu ne l'as pas vu ? On te reconnaît bien, non ? »
Je fouillai son visage afin de savoir si sa remarque contenait une quelconque ironie.
« Pour le père Riley, tu ressembles à un lion dans une fosse de chrétiens affamés », me dit-elle en riant joyeusement. Quand elle vit mon air renfrogné, elle s'obligea à reprendre son sérieux. Son amusement perçait malgré tout, pétillait dans ses yeux. Je ne pus lui en tenir rigueur, car je savais que l'affection, et non la bassesse, tempérait ses légères moqueries. Pourtant je m'interrogeai, car bien que décelant une subtile altération de son être après ce qui s'était passé lors de notre précédente rencontre, je sentis qu'elle l'avait assimilé, accepté, et qu'il ne restait ni blessure ni regret. Son courage, sa souplesse, sa gaieté résolue et irrépressible, tout cela m'impressionnait, me terrifiait même un peu. Je l'admirai plus que jamais, je m'étonnai de mon désir de la revoir. Car sa présence eut un effet tonique sur moi. Cinq minutes après son arrivée, je me sentis passablement mieux que tous les jours derniers, même si rien, je crois, n'aurait pu me rendre la détermination et le courage de persévérer dans une entreprise qui me paraissait maintenant dérisoire.
L'affiche était typique du genre, écrite à la main dans un style sensationnel, puis ronéotée : « Un Aperçu *Exceptionnel* de la Vie dans un Monastère Taoïste *Secret* en Chine par quelqu'un qui y a *Réellement Vécu* (!) et s'Est Enfui afin de *Témoigner* !!! (Avec la Présentation d'Objets Rares et de Grande Valeur — dont une Robe de Cérémonie... & etc.) Vous êtes tous cordialement invités. » Ma photo — on eût juré que je venais de décapiter un poulet vivant avec les dents — était reproduite dans l'angle supérieur gauche.
« Premier pas vers la gloire et la fortune », commenta-t-elle d'une voix enjouée.
A son sourire pincé, je répondis par une moue dégoûtée.
« Il m'a aussi demandé de te montrer autre chose. » Sa main fouilla dans son sac ; ne trouvant pas ce qu'elle y cherchait, Yin-mi le coinça entre ses genoux et regarda dedans. « Tss, fit-elle, déçue. J'ai emmené mes notes, mais j'ai oublié le livre. » Elle s'adossa à sa chaise, allongea ses jambes pour réfléchir. « Au fait, dit-elle en se redressant, tu en as un exemplaire.
— Un exemplaire de quoi ?
— Du livre de prières. »
Je désignai mon étagère de fabrication artisanale, un cageot de fruits retourné, avec des briques en guise de presse-livres. Elle trouva le volume et se pencha pour examiner le livre voisin. « Qu'est-ce que c'est ?
— Le *Yi king*. »

Elle le prit, puis son doigt traça un sillon sur la légère couche de poussière accumulée sur la couverture. « On dirait qu'il n'a pas servi depuis un certain temps », commenta-t-elle.

Sa remarque anodine me piqua au vif.

« J'ai toujours voulu apprendre à m'en servir, dit-elle. Li me l'a offert pour mon anniversaire, mais en anglais. Et puis je n'ai jamais très bien compris à quoi servent les baguettes.

— Ce n'est pas difficile, rétorquai-je. Mais autant commencer avec les pièces. Leur maniement est plus simple, quoique les résultats soient plus grossiers.

— Est-ce important ?

— Tout est important. »

Son regard m'adressa un appel touchant. « Tu pourrais peut-être m'apprendre ? »

Je haussai les épaules. « Oui. Pourquoi pas ?

— Tu n'as pas l'air très enthousiaste, fit-elle remarquer en plissant le front. Tu ne désires donc pas me convertir ?

— Ce n'est pas ma priorité numéro un.

— Vous autres taoïstes êtes vraiment paresseux. Le père Riley est mille fois plus consciencieux que vous. La preuve — elle retourna s'asseoir —, il m'a demandé de te montrer ceci. » Elle se mit à feuilleter le livre de prières. « C'est dans les Articles de la Religion ; numéro vingt-huit, je crois. Oui, voilà. Il m'a dit que cela t'aiderait peut-être à comprendre la signification de la messe et répondrait sans doute à ta question.

— Quelle question ?

— Tu ne te souviens pas ?

— J'ai posé des tas de questions. Je ne sais pas à laquelle tu fais allusion. »

Elle lut sur son bloc-notes. « "Si vous niez le caractère physique de ce rituel, que vous reste-t-il ?" J'ai noté ce qu'il m'a demandé de te dire, expliqua-t-elle en montrant son bloc. Tu te souviens maintenant ?

— Oui, dis-je. Alors ?

— Je peux te le lire ?

— Vas-y.

— "La Communion est non seulement un signe de l'amour que les Chrétiens devraient se manifester ; mais surtout c'est le sacrement de notre rédemption par la mort du Christ : le Pain que nous brisons est participation au Corps du Christ ; de même, la Coupe de Vin est participation au Sang du Christ.

« "La transsubstantiation (le changement de substance du pain et du vin) lors de la communion, ne peut être prouvée par les Saintes Écritures ; elle détruit d'ailleurs la nature du Sacrement... — Retiens ça, dit-elle en me regardant sous ses sourcils levés — et a donné lieu à maintes superstitions.

« "Le Corps du Christ est offert, pris et absorbé lors de la communion, uniquement sur le mode céleste et spirituel. Et le moyen qui permet de prendre et d'absorber le Corps du Christ est la Foi." »

Fermant le livre, elle m'observa brièvement, puis feuilleta son bloc-notes. « Le père Riley m'a dit de bien souligner la différence entre le sacrement et la transsubstantiation. Sur ce point, les catholiques romains font preuve de vulgarité. Lui-même considère la thèse des épiscopaliens comme plus subtile, plus évoluée. La transsubstantiation est vulgaire parce qu'elle suppose le besoin d'un mélange entre les mondes visible et invisible, et soutient que le Christ est littéralement présent dans le pain et le vin. Mais le vrai miracle et l'efficacité du sacrement ne consistent pas en quelque transmutation magique des éléments en sang et chair réels, mais plutôt en l'alchimie plus subtile que la foi opère dans le cœur du croyant. Le Christ est présent sous forme mystique dans le calice. Voilà la signification du sacrement.

— Quelle expression as-tu employée ? demandai-je, l'esprit soudain en éveil.

— Quand ? rétorqua-t-elle. "Le Christ est présent sous forme mystique... ?"

— Non, avant.

— "Le vrai miracle et l'efficacité du sacrement ne consistent pas en quelque transmutation magique des éléments..."

— C'est ça.

— "... en sang et chair réels, mais plutôt en l'alchimie plus subtile que la foi opère dans le cœur du croyant". » Étonnée, elle scruta mon visage. « Quoi ?

— Cette phrase me rappelle une chose que le maître m'a dite autrefois, l'une de ses dernières paroles avant mon départ : "La véritable alchimie se produit seulement dans l'alambic du cœur du sage".

— Alors tu comprends ? »

J'acquiesçai. « Je crois. "Le corps du Christ est offert, pris et absorbé lors de la communion..." Quelle est la suite déjà ?

— "... uniquement sur le mode céleste et spirituel. Et le moyen qui permet de prendre et d'absorber le corps du Christ est la Foi".

— La Foi. » Je m'égarai dans des spéculations imprécises.

— A quoi penses-tu ?

— Hmm ? répondis-je en interrompant ma rêverie. Je ne sais pas très bien. »

Je n'aurais pu préciser, car je ne parvenais pas à mettre le doigt sur l'idée que notre dialogue avait fait naître dans mon esprit. Je percevais ce que je peux seulement appeler une vague perplexité, une turbulence imperceptible sous la surface de ma conscience. Je ressentais une légère irritation, peut-être celle de l'huître confrontée au corps étranger ; j'enregistrais passivement le travail souterrain d'une chaîne d'associations qui mobilisaient mon inconscient, le faisaient sécréter le précieux liquide amniotique autour de l'intrus, transformaient peu à peu celui-ci en une perle lumineuse au sein des ténèbres (à moins qu'il ne devînt l'un de ces monstres difformes qu'on trouve plus communément dans ce coquillage). Je sentais seulement que cela était lié à la foi.

« Alors, dis-je enfin en montrant du menton ses vêtements et son sac, où vas-tu ? »

Elle baissa les yeux sur sa robe comme si elle-même eût oublié qu'elle la portait et qu'elle dût se rafraîchir la mémoire. « Eh bien, je pensais prendre le train de Coney Island, commença-t-elle d'une voix hésitante, presque en s'excusant. C'est sans doute la dernière fois que je pourrais y aller avant la rentrée scolaire. Maman m'a dit qu'elle était d'accord, mais... — elle m'adressa un regard timide et suppliant — elle ne veut pas que j'y aille seule.

— Coney Island..., répétai-je rêveusement en me rappelant l'histoire de l'accident.

— Qu'y a-t-il ? demanda-t-elle dès qu'elle remarqua ma soudaine mélancolie. Tu es déjà allé là-bas ? »

Je secouai la tête avec un sourire triste.

Elle m'adressa un regard perplexe, puis m'expliqua d'une voix grave, sans me quitter des yeux : « C'est à Brooklyn, tout au bout, près de l'océan. »
J'acquiesçai.

« Il y a un parc d'attractions, avec des stands de foire, des manèges et une immense Roue Ferris. Tu es déjà monté sur une grande roue ? »

Je secouai la tête. « Une Roue Ferris ? Qu'est-ce que c'est ?

— Une immense roue qui tourne, avec des nacelles où l'on t'enferme. Tu montes si haut dans le ciel que tu vois à des kilomètres alentour — les bateaux et les voiliers, et par beau temps jusqu'aux gratte-ciel de Manhattan. De là-haut, la cité ressemble à un jouet que tu pourrais prendre dans ta main, à une plaquette de circuit électronique. Il y a aussi une plage et une promenade. Aujourd'hui, il ne devrait pas y avoir trop de monde. » Elle se tut. « Accompagne-moi, proposa-t-elle soudain avec une timide nuance de défi, comme si elle savait à l'avance que je refuserais. Qu'as-tu d'autre à faire ? »

Bien que tenté, j'hésitai.

« Allez ! insista-t-elle. Je te promets de ne pas t'attaquer. »

Je ris. « Je devrais peut-être accepter », dis-je en pensant à mon père, curieux de voir l'endroit où tout s'était terminé. Cette proximité physique me rapprocherait peut-être de mon propre terminus spirituel, songeai-je ; peut-être allais-je enfin trouver ce que je cherchais.

« Bien sûr que tu devrais ! poursuivit-elle. Ça te ferait du bien de sortir.

— Tu as probablement raison. Et puis — mon dilemme me revint à l'esprit — c'est peut-être la dernière fois.

— La dernière fois ? » demanda-t-elle avec un regard de nouveau inquiet.

Je secouai la tête. « Peu importe. Je viens.

— Bon ! s'écria-t-elle. Maman nous prépare à déjeuner. »

Je ris d'un air entendu. « Tu savais donc que j'accepterais avant même de me le demander ? »

Avec un sourire modeste, elle haussa joyeusement les épaules.

« Descends. Je me rase, je me change et je te retrouve en bas.

— A tout de suite », dit-elle en se levant. Sur le chemin de la porte, elle fit un crochet par l'étagère et, montrant mon exemplaire des *Mutations*, me jeta par-dessus l'épaule un regard interrogateur. « Je peux l'emmener ? Là-bas, tu auras peut-être le temps de m'apprendre à m'en servir.

— Bien sûr, répondis-je. Prends-le. »

Elle le glissa vivement au fond de son sac, puis sortit d'un pas allègre.

★

Nous marchâmes jusqu'au pont pour prendre le train. Quand nous traversâmes le fleuve, je le regardai rêveusement ; des mouettes tournoyaient au-dessus de l'eau, le ciel avait cette limpidité cristalline qui annonce la fin de l'été. A mi-distance, j'aperçus la Statue de la Liberté qui fixait sombrement la pleine mer, et le pont Verrazano qui dessinait un terne arc-en-ciel sur l'horizon. Le rythme lancinant du train réveilla mon humeur morose, mais sans plus me faire souffrir. Je me sentais anesthésié.

Yin-mi m'observait en silence. Nos yeux se croisaient parfois ; je m'efforçais alors de sourire, puis détournai le regard en constatant l'anxiété et l'inquiétude du sien. Elle parla enfin : « Tu es si bizarre aujourd'hui. Il s'est passé quelque chose, n'est-ce pas ?

— Oui, reconnus-je calmement. Il s'est passé quelque chose.

— Tu as retrouvé ton père ? » L'appréhension faisait trembler sa voix.

J'acquiesçai en remarquant sa clairvoyance, qui ne me surprit pas vraiment. « Oui, je l'ai retrouvé... et perdu.

— Il n'est pas... ?

— Si », l'interrompis-je, comme pour éviter d'entendre le mot.

Le désespoir, la pitié qui apparurent sur son visage me bouleversèrent. « Oh, Sun I, je suis désolée », dit-elle. Puis elle se mit à pleurer.

« Je sais. » Très ému, je saisis sa main. « Merci. »

Longtemps, nous restâmes silencieux, moi regardant par la fenêtre du train, elle calmement assise à côté de moi. Puis, brièvement, d'une voix neutre, je lui dis ce que j'avais appris.

« Que vas-tu faire maintenant ? » me demanda-t-elle quand j'eus terminé.

« Je ne sais pas. Peut-être retourner en Chine. Je n'ai plus aucune raison de rester maintenant. » Je cherchai son regard. « N'est-ce pas ? »

Elle demeura silencieuse.

« Si je reste, je devrai gager la robe de ma mère, poursuivis-je.

— Pourquoi ? Tu as besoin d'argent ?

— Non, pas vraiment, mais je suis coincé, je n'avance pas.

— Je ne crois pas que tu devrais faire ça. »

Je me tournai brusquement vers elle. « Alors tu penses que je dois partir ? »

Elle secoua la tête. « Non, je ne le pense pas non plus. Mais quoi qu'il arrive, tu ne dois pas gager la robe de ta mère. » Elle dit cela sur un ton péremptoire, totalement convaincu. Je m'étais attendu de sa part à une telle certitude morale, à cette sincérité.

« Mais il n'y a pas de troisième solution. Si je ne gage pas la robe, je dois partir. C'est aussi simple que ça », insistai-je, soudain poussé à la controverse bien que son point de vue corroborât le mien.

« Pourquoi te limiter à une alternative aussi draconienne ?

— Parce que, pour justifier la prolongation de mon absence loin du monastère, je dois continuer à explorer le Dow, et je ne peux le faire sans investir. Kahn m'en a convaincu. Pour investir, je dois avoir des fonds. Et la robe est le seul objet de valeur que je possède.

— Je croyais qu'investir était contraire à tes vœux. »

Son visage était grave.

« C'est vrai », dis-je en me détournant. Je ne dis rien jusqu'à l'arrêt du train à Coney Island, le terminus.

Nous émergeâmes du métro aérien dans le dédale des buvettes et des échoppes de souvenirs installées sous les arches de la voie, puis remontâmes la rue en passant devant les baraques foraines des diseuses de bonne aventure dont les surnoms s'étalaient en lettres cursives sur des palmes fluorescentes, devant des pizzerias, des bars à coquillages, diverses officines. J'aperçus au loin le vaste squelette blanc des montagnes russes, et, plus près, surplombant le parc d'attractions et illuminée en plein jour, la Grande Roue. Elle semblait planer dans l'espace comme un immense cerceau de feu magique ; dans mon abattement, elle me parut un emblème adéquat de la Roue de la Vie elle-même, entraînée par un moteur, métallique et tapageuse, dotée d'un cœur vide, traçant de gigantesques zéros dans le ciel. Ces zéros me narguaient, ainsi que l'inanité pitoyable d'une Voie discréditée. Aucun tigre magique ne bondirait dans ce cerceau de fer, songeai-je. Pas maintenant. Il était trop tard. C'était fini.

Obliquant pour entrer dans le parc, nous longeâmes les attractions : le jet de l'anneau, les fléchettes, le tir à la carabine, la pêche miraculeuse. Les rangées d'animaux en peluche bleus et roses, leurs yeux écarquillés et leurs sourires de gaieté fébrile sous-entendaient une complicité honteuse dans quelque secret compromettant, une attitude que les aboyeurs imitaient de leur mieux, mais pour ainsi dire une octave plus bas, incapables de soutenir pareille exaltation. Affligés d'un cœur simplement humain, ils semblaient épuisés, prêts à renoncer, tout comme moi. Nous entendîmes des éclats de rire excités en provenance des chambres de la Maison Hantée — un lieu morne, grotesque, même pas effrayant — où des squelettes désarticulés montés sur fils et ressorts bondissaient vers les enfants qui hurlaient dans leurs wagonnets. Nous passâmes devant la Tanière de l'Homme-Loup, la Femme à Barbe ; un rabatteur criait : « Venez donc voir Ma-THIEU-sa-lem, le nourrisson le plus vieux du monde, l'adulte le plus jeune de la Terre. Agé de cinq ans selon son certificat de naissance (présenté à l'intérieur pour votre information), affligé d'un mal rarissime et incurable — le GÉ-rontisme — il exhibe les traits ridés et ratatinés d'un vieillard centenaire. Venez le voir radoter dans le berceau de sa sénescence JUUU-vénile... » Sa voix se noya bientôt dans la cacophonie générale.

Après ce défilé clinquant, nous atteignîmes enfin la promenade qui surplombait la plage. La clameur de la foire s'atténua derrière nous, la brise qui soufflait du large chassa les odeurs de frites et d'huile de moteur. L'Atlantique, aussi paisible qu'un étang, était d'une propreté surprenante, son étendue bleu-vert foncé frangée d'un liséré d'écume qui le séparait du sable jaune. La plage quasiment déserte semblait gardée par des rangées de poubelles et de grands panneaux municipaux où, avec une intelligence positivement juridique, s'étalait la liste des activités prohibées : « Il est interdit de Cracher, Forniquer, Se Mettre Nu, Déféquer, Uriner, Avoir un

Comportement Obscène, Boire de l'Alcool, Jouer, Bousculer ou Duper Quiconque, Tout Tapage Nocturne est Egalement Proscrit » (un esprit facétieux avait intercalé la syllabe « pi » après le « Ta » de Tapage, avec pour résultat de proscrire « Tout Tapinage Nocturne »). Une série de jetées en pierre perpendiculaires à la plage s'avançaient assez loin dans la mer. Quelques estivants les empruntaient dans un sens ou dans l'autre, qui marchaient à pas prudents et assuraient leur équilibre en étendant les bras comme des funambules.

Yin-mi alla se changer dans une cabine pendant que je descendais les marches de ciment vers le sable. Retroussant mon pantalon, je m'aventurai au bord de l'eau et me dirigeai vaguement vers les rochers. Une humeur élégiaque s'empara bientôt de moi. Cédant à une lubie morbide, je me mis à chercher des fragments calcinés de l'avion de mon père que la mer aurait rejetés sur la plage ou ensablés près des jetées, comme des doublons d'or semés au fond de l'eau. J'avançai jusqu'à l'extrême limite des brise-lames, où le vacarme du parc d'attractions devenait inaudible, remplacé par le patient lapement de l'eau sur les rochers et le murmure du courant, puis je m'assis, pris mes genoux entre mes bras et rivai mon regard à l'horizon ininterrompu, au ciel si vaste, bleu et vide. De temps à autre, sans raison précise, la phrase de Riley me revenait en mémoire : « L'alchimie plus subtile que la foi opère dans le cœur du croyant. » Pourquoi m'avait-elle frappé ? Était-ce seulement la coïncidence de sa ressemblance avec la remarque de Chong Fou ? Du côté du brise-lames protégé du vent, l'eau était parfaitement lisse ; quand je regardai sa surface, je découvris une fois encore le reflet de mon visage et les lunettes noires. Alors que, menton posé sur les genoux, j'étais perdu dans sa contemplation, un deuxième visage apparut dans le miroir ; je sentis une main effleurer mon épaule.

« Bonjour, Narcisse, dit Yin-mi dont je vis le sourire s'épanouir à la surface de l'eau.

— Qui est Narcisse ? demandai-je.

— Un Grec qui tomba amoureux de son reflet dans l'eau d'un bassin. Quand il plongea pour l'embrasser, il se noya. »

Je réfléchis sans quitter mon image des yeux. « Son reflet l'angoissait peut-être plus qu'il ne lui plaisait, suggérai-je à voix basse. Il a peut-être plongé, non pour l'embrasser, mais pour détruire ce visage qui se moquait de lui, et il a fini par se détruire lui-même. »

Elle se pencha par-dessus mon épaule et regarda avec moi. « Tu vois donc une chose menaçante, sarcastique ?

— Je ne sais pas, répondis-je. Et toi, que vois-tu ?

— Quelqu'un qui essaie de conserver son innocence.

— Peut-on vivre en restant innocent ?

— Oui, murmura-t-elle, je le crois. Tu dois avoir la foi.

— Je n'en suis pas sûr », dis-je ; puis je me levai pour interrompre notre intimité. « Et puis, qu'est-ce que la foi ? »

En marchant le long de la plage, nous aperçûmes au loin deux enfants, un petit garçon et une fillette de quatre ou cinq ans qui travaillaient d'arrache-pied avec des pelles et des seaux en plastique. Debout dans le trou qu'ils creusaient, ils avaient presque du sable jusqu'aux aisselles. A intervalles réguliers, nous les perdions de vue, puis ils refaisaient surface, montant et descendant comme les pistons d'un gros moteur à deux temps. Des gerbes et des giclées de sable jaillissaient de leurs pelles. Un peu plus haut sur la plage, leur mère — chapeau de paille, lunettes de soleil et maillot de bain — lisait sur une chaise longue sous un parasol rayé. De temps à autre, elle jetait un coup d'œil inquiet au-dessus de son magazine pour s'assurer que tout allait bien. Les deux enfants venaient de disparaître au fond de leur trou quand une vague particulièrement audacieuse monta rapidement sur le sable et inonda leur trou. A leurs cris et leurs hurlements d'abord causés par la surprise puis mêlés d'éclats de rire ravis, leur mère se leva d'un bond comme un colosse, puis accourut sur de lourdes cuisses tremblotantes. Ils émergèrent de leur trou en gloussant, puis se mirent à courir presque sur place avec des gestes frénétiques et se jetèrent quasiment dans nos jambes. Nous nous penchâmes en riant pour les écarter de nos genoux ; à notre immense surprise ils se figèrent soudain, puis échangèrent un regard écarquillé de stupéfaction.

« Kitty ! » s'écria le petit garçon d'une voix sourde, bouleversée.

Elle nous regardait en mordant sa lèvre inférieure.

Leur mère les rejoignit alors et tomba à genoux, hors d'haleine. La fillette se réfugia aussitôt dans ses bras. « Ça va ? » demanda anxieusement la femme en repoussant sa fille à bout de bras afin de l'examiner. « Pour l'amour du ciel, ne me faites pas des peurs pareilles ! » Elle posa la main sur sa poitrine et soupira.

La fillette hochait timidement la tête, ses yeux toujours rivés à nos visages.

« Maman ! Maman ! » s'écria son frère en escaladant la femme de l'autre côté avec une véhémence extatique. « C'est vrai ! C'est vrai ! Regarde ! » Il pointait sur nous un index jubilant.

« Ne montre pas du doigt, Johnny, le gronda-t-elle en enlaçant son bras pour maîtriser le membre récalcitrant. Ce n'est pas poli.

— Mais c'est vrai ! protesta-t-il en se débattant.

— Calme-toi, mon trésor ! dit-elle, partagée entre la cajolerie et la réprimande. Qu'est-ce qui est vrai ?

— Ils sont chinois. Nous avons réussi ! »

Je commençai à comprendre leur méprise. La mère devint cramoisie. « Chut, Johnny ! le gronda-t-elle. Ils sont aussi américains que nous. » Resserrant sa prise sur le garçonnet, elle nous adressa un regard navré. « Excusez-le. Je lui ai dit que, s'il creusait assez profond, il finirait par ressortir en Chine. Pas une seconde je n'ai pensé qu'il me croirait. »

Yin-mi éclata de rire.

La femme eut un sourire reconnaissant. « Franchement, quelle imagination ! » Elle le regarda avec une fierté exaspérée.

Quant à moi, je le dévisageai comme un prodige.

Elle saisit sa progéniture par la main et l'entraîna. « Viens, chuchota-t-elle rudement au petit garçon qui ne parvenait pas à détacher son regard de nos visages.

— Mais c'est vrai ! » s'écriait-il d'une voix plaintive. Quand ils remontèrent vers le parasol et la chaise longue, il continua de se retourner dès qu'il le pouvait ; la conviction féroce qu'on lisait dans ses yeux ne diminuait pas.

« *Voilà* la foi ! » dit Yin-mi en riant, comme nous nous éloignions.

Je la regardai avec une expression hébétée, profondément troublé par sa remarque et l'incident proprement dit. Les secousses sismiques que Yin-mi avait provoquées plus tôt dans la matinée avec le passage du livre de Prières gagnèrent en intensité sur l'échelle de Richter de mon inconscient.

Nous achetâmes des Cocas à la buvette la plus proche avant de nous installer sur un banc de bois à l'ombre de la tour rouillée du Saut en Parachute, attraction supprimée des années plus tôt à cause d'une série d'accidents. Nous déballâmes notre pique-nique face à la mer.

« Tu ne manges rien, remarqua Yin-mi au bout d'un moment. Qu'y a-t-il ? Tu sembles préoccupé.

— Je ne sais pas, répondis-je. Toute la matinée, j'ai eu l'étrange impression qu'on essayait de me parler. »

Elle posa son sandwich. « Que veux-tu dire ?

— Comme si une présence invisible planait juste derrière le voile de la réalité en chuchotant quelque chose à mon oreille, mais d'une voix trop faible pour que je distingue les mots, ou dans un langage que je ne comprends pas, comme un oracle.

— De quoi s'agit-il ? demanda-t-elle. Tu as une idée ?

— Voilà l'endroit où il est mort, dis-je en évitant sa question, les yeux tournés vers l'horizon vide. Là-bas.

— Tu crois que c'est lui — ton père ?

— Impossible. Il est mort. »

Elle réfléchit. « L'oracle pourrait peut-être t'aider », suggéra-t-elle.

Je haussai les épaules.

« Pourquoi ne pas essayer ?

— J'y ai pensé, dis-je.

— Pourquoi ne l'as-tu pas fait, alors ? Tu as peur de sa réponse ? »

Je secouai la tête. « Son verdict pourrait seulement me soulager. »

Comme pour me défier, elle fouilla dans son sac et en sortit le *Yi king*. « Tiens. » Elle me le tendit avec une moue d'encouragement.

« Nous avons oublié les baguettes, objectai-je.

— Nous avons des pièces, non ?

— Je t'ai déjà dit que les pièces ne conviennent pas.

— Tu cherches une excuse, n'est-ce pas ? s'enquit-elle doucement mais fermement. C'est sans importance, du moment que tu es sincère. » Elle sortit trois pièces de son porte-monnaie et les plaça dans ma main. Je les acceptai en soupirant.

Je lui expliquai les diverses étapes de la consultation. Celle-ci était beaucoup plus rapide avec les pièces, mais je ne pus m'empêcher de penser qu'elles compromettaient le résultat du rituel. L'hexagramme qui sortit fut *Sui*, le dix-septième, intitulé « la Suite », avec deux traits faibles à la deuxième et troisième place, tous deux des six : *yin*, ou les ténèbres, sur le point de se métamorphoser en *yang*, la lumière. Le jugement était le suivant :

> La Suite obtient une sublime réussite.
> La persévérance est avantageuse. Pas de blâme.

« La Suite », méditai-je en silence. La suite de quoi ? Ou à la suite de qui ? Car il y avait deux routes ; l'une ramenait en arrière, l'autre entraînait vers l'inconnu. Laquelle choisir ?

J'examinai le détail du texte à la recherche d'un indice :

Ce n'est qu'en suivant que l'on en vient à commander.

Cela ne fit qu'augmenter ma perplexité. Je poursuivis ma lecture par la description des traits. Je trouvai ceci :

Six à la deuxième place signifie :
Si l'on s'attache au petit garçon,
On perd l'homme fort.

Mon estomac se contracta. Je lus le commentaire suivant :

Six à la troisième place signifie :
Si l'on s'attache à l'homme fort,
On perd le petit garçon.
En suivant on trouve ce que l'on cherche.
Il est avantageux de demeurer persévérant.

« "Si l'on s'attache au petit garçon, on perd l'homme fort", répéta songeusement Yin-mi.

— "Si l'on s'attache à l'homme fort, on perd le petit garçon", contre-attaquai-je aussitôt.

— Qu'est-ce que ça veut dire à ton avis ? me demanda-t-elle.

— Je ne sais pas. L'oracle conseille deux démarches contradictoires.

— Ou bien il souligne les implications des deux en te laissant libre de choisir.

— Oh, je n'ai pas besoin qu'on me précise mon choix, rétorquai-je avec un rire amer.

— Si tu connais les termes de ton choix et leurs conséquences, demanda-t-elle, pourquoi ne te décides-tu pas ?

— Parce que je veux les deux choses. »

Elle rit, pensant apparemment que je plaisantais.

« Je suis sérieux », précisai-je ; mon expression butée la fit se rembrunir. « Est-ce trop demander, après tout, poursuivis-je, que l'enfant soit préservé en l'homme, qu'il soit chéri et ainsi épargné, que les deux coexistent dans un seul cœur humain ?

— Je ne sais pas, répondit-elle avec un doux sourire. Cela me paraît beaucoup. La vie ne permet peut-être pas ce genre de compromis. »

Je pesai en silence les mots de Yin-mi.

« Tu sais, l'année dernière en cours d'anglais, nous avons lu un essai, dit-elle. Je ne me rappelle ni le titre ni le nom de l'auteur, mais il parlait de l'Amérique. Il disait que ce pays ressemblait à un serpent au temps de la mue, et qu'il devait rejeter la peau morte de son passé européen. Il disait que rien n'est plus naturel à une créature vivante que de se débarrasser de son ancienne peau pour aborder le stade suivant — rien n'est plus naturel, mais rien n'est plus difficile. Parce que franchir ce seuil est très douloureux, presque une mort. En fait, c'est une sorte de mort. Parfois, le serpent reste amoureux des beaux motifs de son ancien corps et refuse de l'abandonner ; alors il tombe malade et pourrit dans son ancienne peau. Elle devient sa tombe.

— Que veux-tu dire ? »

Elle secoua la tête. « Ce sont les paroles d'un autre ; je ne peux pas choisir à ta place. Je m'en suis souvenue et je viens de te les répéter, voilà tout.

— La robe est peut-être l'ancienne peau que je dois abandonner, hasardai-je.

— Peut-être, répondit-elle. Mais c'est plus profond. »

Nous nous regardâmes en silence.

« Dis-moi, Sun I, me demanda-t-elle enfin, lequel est... *était* ton père — l'homme fort ou le petit garçon ?

— C'est bien là le problème, je crois qu'il était les deux. Il n'a jamais sacrifié son innocence pour devenir un homme. Il n'a jamais eu à choisir.

— Ou bien il a refusé.

— Oui, répondis-je avec enthousiasme, je crois qu'il est resté les deux ; il a refusé le dilemme qui consiste à se faire empaler sur une corne ou sur l'autre... Mais il est mort, ajoutai-je en soupirant.

— Je me demande... » réfléchit-elle, le regard dans le vide.

Je l'observai attentivement. « Quoi donc ? S'il est mort ? Je te l'ai déjà dit, l'avion s'est abîmé à dix milles des côtes.

— Pas ça, dit-elle. Physiquement, oui, il est bien sûr mort. Mais dans un autre sens, peut-être vit-il toujours ?

— Comment cela ?

— En toi, répondit-elle. Tu m'as dit qu'il cherchait l'immortalité. Peut-être l'a-t-il trouvée dans ta mémoire, dans ton cœur. »

Sa réflexion me toucha, mais plus à cause de la gratitude que j'éprouvai pour les efforts de Yin-mi que par sa justesse ou son utilité. « Mon cœur me semble si fragile et mortel, répondis-je avec un sourire las. Il n'est pas à la hauteur. »

Elle tendit la main pour effleurer ma joue, comme avait fait sa mère.

« Mais peut-être l'immortalité est-elle seulement cela », hasardai-je, en cherchant une porte de sortie là où je savais qu'il n'y en avait pas ; « assurer la survie du petit garçon dans l'adulte. En ce sens, il a peut-être réussi. »

Nous échangeâmes un sourire triste, affectueux. Elle commençait à ramasser ce que nous n'avions pas mangé.

« Je sais quoi ! dit-elle avec un brusque entrain. Je vais t'emmener sur la Grande Roue ! Un ou deux tours vont te rendre ta gaieté. »

Je la regardai sans expression.

« Oui, affirma-t-elle d'une voix décidée en bondissant sur ses pieds avant de prendre ma main. Tu vas venir avec moi. Je veux m'amuser et tu feras ce que je te dis. Maintenant, *en avant.* »

Je me levai de mauvaise grâce et la laissai m'entraîner, opposant une résistance passive à ses efforts.

Nous achetâmes nos billets à une petite cabane, puis les donnâmes à un employé impassible au bandeau rouge et au T-shirt maculé de graisse. Il tira sur un levier et la Grande Roue s'immobilisa avec un à-coup pendant que les nacelles tremblaient comme des boules accrochées à un sapin de

Noël. Levant la barre de protection, il nous fit signe de monter, puis la verrouilla derrière nous. Je penchai la tête en arrière pour regarder à travers les superstructures géométriques de cette gigantesque toile d'araignée métallique dont les dimensions me donnaient déjà le vertige. Le démarrage fut si brutal qu'avec un hoquet je saisis la barre à deux mains. Nous nous arrêtâmes aussitôt pour embarquer un deuxième couple ; la nacelle se balança d'avant en arrière en grinçant sur son axe.

« Tout va bien », me rassura Yin-mi qui caressait ma main.

Je la regardai d'un œil farouche, déjà terrifié à l'idée de notre prochain déplacement. Alors nous nous élançâmes, aspirés vers le haut comme par les serres d'un gigantesque oiseau de proie, en un mouvement rapide mais qui semblait ralenti par l'énorme circonférence du cercle que nous décrivions, et cette lenteur devenait une torture exquise, une interminable agonie. Nous atteignîmes l'apogée de notre trajectoire, puis commençâmes à descendre. L'angoisse barattait mon estomac. Je n'osais pas regarder en bas, je gardais les yeux fixés droit devant moi. Le ciel était réconfortant, car son bleu indifférencié n'indiquait aucun changement d'altitude.

« Ferme la bouche, chuchota Yin-mi en se penchant vers moi. Tu risques d'avaler un pigeon.

— Un pigeon ! protestai-je sans oser tourner la tête. Depuis quand les pigeons volent-ils si haut ? Un aigle plutôt ! »

Son rire subit un étrange effet Doppler alors que nous filions vers le sol. « Oh ! s'écria-t-elle. Regarde en bas ! »

Comme un crétin, sans réfléchir davantage, je lui obéis. « Ô, mon Dieu, dis-je d'une voix faible, nous allons mourir. » J'eus l'impression vertigineuse de tomber à la renverse, je fus pris de nausées, de palpitations, mes pupilles se dilatèrent — bref, la panique.

« Tu n'as pas l'air bien », dit-elle alors que nous nous élancions pour notre deuxième tour.

Incapable de détourner du champ de bataille ne fût-ce qu'une infime fraction de mes forces psychiques, je ne lui répondis pas, ne la regardai même pas.

« Essaie un truc, suggéra-t-elle. Ferme les yeux, inspire profondément et compte jusqu'à dix. Il a toujours marché pour moi. »

Lui obéissant sur-le-champ, j'entrelardai de prières ferventes l'égrènement des nombres. La technique sembla réussir, car lorsque je rouvris les yeux, je crus que nous ne bougions plus, bien que le vent fouettât toujours mon visage. A mon immense stupéfaction, j'aperçus une mouette si proche que j'aurais presque pu la toucher ; elle battait lentement des ailes, semblait voler en parfaite harmonie avec nous et, ainsi, apparemment immobile. Je trouvai cela merveilleux. Je regardai l'oiseau, il me rendit mon regard. Je crois qu'il me sourit. Je donnai un coup de coude à Yin-mi pour le lui montrer avec un sourire d'extase imbécile, car j'avais temporairement oublié mon malaise. En guise de réponse, Yin-mi me fit signe de regarder en bas, et la profondeur de ma vanité béa sous mes pieds. Nous ne bougions plus. La machine s'était arrêtée, sans aucun doute en panne ; elle nous laissait échoués là-haut (peut-être à jamais !) au zénith de la trajectoire de la Grande Roue ! De nouveau, j'eus du mal à respirer, mes palpitations reprirent. La panique menaçait

de revenir en force. « Nous allons mourir pour de bon ! » pensai-je.
　Je me mis brusquement à hurler de rire, mon angoisse miraculeusement transmuée en hilarité. Je sentis l'excitation du total abandon, un vertige précaire mais délicieux. Je vis les baigneurs s'agiter comme de minuscules microbes sur le sable jaune et, plus loin, l'eau qui virait de l'émeraude au bleu, puis au noir. Les déferlantes ressemblaient à des rognures d'ongle jetées sur une table de marbre noir. Au-delà, la courbe solennelle du monde scindait l'espace avec une grandeur languide, indifférente. J'étais comme l'astronaute inexpérimenté qui, libéré de l'habitacle sécurisant de ses préjugés, s'aventure dans l'espace, s'enivre d'apesanteur, se grise tant de l'ineffable beauté du vide qu'il oublie ses dangers et refuse de rentrer, préférant s'abandonner corps et âme à une orgie de visions d'extase.
　Alors cela arriva. Tandis que nous étions perchés sur notre aire mobile au zénith du monde, un grondement sourd se fit entendre, comme un tonnerre lointain mais régulier qui s'amplifiait sans cesse, ne provenant d'aucune source précise mais de toutes les directions, nous enveloppait de son bruit continu.
　« Qu'est-ce que c'est ? » demandai-je à Yin-mi en me tournant vers elle.
　Elle haussa les épaules puis baissa les yeux vers le sol entre ses genoux. « Que regardent-ils donc ? »
　À nos pieds, tout s'était interrompu. Le parc d'attractions semblait figé, tous les gens pétrifiés levaient la tête.
　Le bruit devenait de plus en plus fort.
　Une main solitaire se dressa au-dessus de la foule, puis une autre, et une autre, qui déclenchèrent une réaction en chaîne, un jaillissement exponentiel de mains, jusqu'à ce que tous les groupes innombrables et unanimes pointent la main vers le ciel.
　« Sun I, dit-elle, la gorge nouée par une honte atavique, je crois que c'est nous qu'ils montrent du doigt. »
　Mais j'avais à peine conscience d'eux, ou d'elle, tant je scrutai intensément le ciel, en proie à un sombre pressentiment alors que le bruit s'amplifiait toujours, tel un soldat sur les remparts qui attend l'aube et la bataille. Le grondement devint assourdissant.
　Alors je le vis. « Regarde ! m'écriai-je en tendant le bras et bondissant contre la barre de sécurité afin de me lever.
　— Assieds-toi ! » hurla Yin-mi en saisissant ma ceinture pour me tirer en arrière.
　La nacelle se balança violemment, comme un navire pris de travers dans une mer déchaînée.
　« Regarde ! m'écriai-je encore, avec une véhémence accrue. Tu ne le vois pas ?
　— Quoi ? » Elle grimaça à cause du soleil, leva la main vers son front. « Je ne vois rien. »
　Elle ne portait pas de lunettes noires ; moi si. Protégé de la lueur éblouissante, je le vis parfaitement émerger du disque solaire — un avion, un Piper argenté, comme ceux qu'on voit souvent en été, remorquant une banderole publicitaire au-dessus des plages grouillantes de monde. Je fus d'abord incapable d'en lire les lettres. Alors l'avion passa en rugissant au-

dessus de nous, si près que j'entendis la banderole claquer dans les remous d'air. Une à une, je déchiffrai les lettres rouge sang hautes de trois mètres :

L-O-V-E (L'AMOUR) N-E R-E-N-O-N-C-E J-A-M-A-I-S

suivi de l'inscription « CEC » — Communauté des Églises Chrétiennes, ainsi que je l'appris ensuite.

Non, cela n'avait rien d'étrange. Aujourd'hui, je peux l'affirmer sans l'ombre d'un doute. Mais à l'époque, je fus cruellement tenté de penser autrement. Je ne sais si je peux expliquer cela, lecteur, mais un déclic se produisit en moi quand je vis cet avion. Appelez cela synchronicité, « connexion mystique », comme vous voudrez, mais le nœud se défit instantanément dans mon esprit. Je me rappelai le passage de l'Épître aux Corinthiens : « Il excuse tout, il croit tout, il espère tout, il endure tout. L'amour ne renonce jamais. » Cela engendra une marée d'associations, qu'il couronnait et parachevait. Je me souvins de la phrase de Riley — « l'alchimie plus subtile que la foi opère dans le cœur du croyant » — et compris pourquoi elle avait touché en moi une corde sensible. A son tour, cette pensée en évoqua une autre, l'image du petit garçon creusant son trou dans le sable, convaincu, comme tous les enfants américains qui ont jamais joué au bord de la mer avec une pelle et un seau, qu'en creusant assez profond dans le sol commun de l'expérience pour traverser le socle granitique de la réalité elle-même, il finirait par émerger dans un monde enchanté nommé la Chine, Shangri-la, le Royaume de l'Imagination, une contrée inédite et exotique, dangereuse et fascinante, peuplée de mandarins et de démons, où les désirs étaient des ordres et où tous les rêves se réalisaient. Il incarnait une image de moi-même — ou plutôt de ce que j'avais été, de ce que j'avais perdu. Moi aussi, j'avais cru autrefois que je pourrais m'agenouiller à Wall Street et, scrutant une dalle, un morceau de trottoir, voire la pierre angulaire de la Bourse de New York, commencer à creuser de mes mains nues la terre assoiffée de lumière, pour déboucher enfin comme une taupe dans la cour de Ken Kuan sous les branches du pêcher ; cru qu'en m'appliquant avec diligence à sonder la matière résistante du Dow avec le diamant de ma foi, comme le criminel qui égratigne les murs de sa cellule avec sa cuiller ou son pic à glace, je retrouverais enfin la liberté sous le vaste ciel bleu de la Chine, dans le paradis immaculé du Tao. Mais la foi avait cédé la première, pulvérisée par la substance adamantine de mon père. Il l'avait ébranlée, et sa mort, loin de me libérer du désir de percer à jour son mystère, avait donné à ma foi le coup de grâce (comme si la preuve de l'inexistence de l'enfer et de Satan dût ébranler la foi qu'on avait en Dieu !) Ô, lecteur, je ne prétends pas comprendre cela, mais j'insiste en ma qualité de témoin et je te demande de me croire : « Le cœur est une région sauvage. »

Un déclic se fit quand je vis cette banderole. Je trouvai ce que je cherchais : le signe. La dernière pièce du puzzle se mit en place, et je compris que Yin-mi avait raison. Il était vivant — peut-être pas au sens où elle me l'avait dit, mais plus profondément. Tel était le message de l'avion : « Love ne Renonce Jamais. » Il avait bel et bien trouvé l'immortalité, non pas physiquement (c'eût été une transsubstantiation vulgaire, pour reprendre l'expression de Riley), pas davantage dans mon cœur, mais en un autre sens plus authentique, et que je connaissais depuis le début. Mais ce savoir avait quitté ma conscience, s'était perdu. Love vivait dans le Dow, je pouvais le retrouver à travers l'Indice, de même que j'avais retrouvé ma mère dans sa robe. Le commentaire qu'avait fait Riley du passage du livre de prières fournissait la clef de l'énigme : « Le vrai miracle et l'efficacité du sacrement ne consistent pas en quelque transmutation magique des éléments en sang et chair réels, mais plutôt en l'alchimie plus subtile que la foi opère dans le cœur du croyant. »

Je compris alors la nature de son immortalité. Il s'incarnait dans le Dow comme le Christ dans le pain et le vin ; le moyen par lequel je pouvais le retrouver était la foi. Une autre intuition me vint alors à l'esprit : s'il avait été le Dow, s'il avait incorporé son énergie séminale et son essence, alors, réciproquement, le Dow était lui ! Tel était le miracle, réalisai-je soudain, que je devais célébrer par le sacrement de ma quête. A cet instant, la foi revint, et avec elle l'espoir. Je me sentis régénéré. Mon travail lent et douloureux atteignit son terme et accoucha de cet être mental, le petit garçon de ma foi retrouvée — mon père. Et mon cœur avait seulement besoin de cette foi pour persévérer. « Il excuse tout, il croit tout, il espère tout, il endure tout... » LOVE NE RENONCE JAMAIS.

Comme je lisais cette phrase dans le ciel de midi, la révélation explosa dans mon cerveau, inonda le monde de lumière. Tel l'éclair aperçu par le soldat dans le canon du fusil ennemi avant que la balle ne le frappe, je vis mon destin et compris qu'il eût été futile d'y résister. Un frisson de peur glaça mon cœur, puis je ressentis un grand soulagement comme si l'on avait retiré un lourd fardeau de mes épaules et que je flottais en apesanteur dans l'espace. Une gaieté irréfléchie jaillit en moi comme l'eau froide et limpide d'un puits artésien à la source mystérieuse, et j'éclatai de rire — un rire que je ne me connaissais pas ; le son de ma propre voix me surprit, audacieuse et profonde, comme si elle montait d'une région inconnue au fond de mon cœur. Et je compris que depuis le début j'avais seulement désiré cela.

Troisième Partie

Le Tao dans le Dow

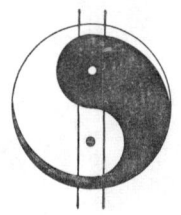

1

Aussitôt après notre retour, je sortis la robe, l'enveloppai dans un papier et descendis chez Mme Chin. Maintenant que j'avais choisi, je devais agir rapidement. Je savais que, si j'hésitais ou même osais y réfléchir, ma résolution m'abandonnerait. Une partie de moi-même comprenait que mon acte nuirait aux projets de Riley et de Yin-mi, mais je ne pouvais m'offrir le luxe d'y penser. Car je dus rassembler toute ma volonté pour simplement tirer les conséquences pratiques de mon choix. Bizarrement, malgré le côté désespéré de ma résolution, j'agis quasiment dans un état second, comme un somnambule, observant mes gestes fébriles avec une froideur fataliste.

Devant l'appartement de Mme Chin, des éclats de rire incontinents flottèrent jusqu'à moi, assourdis par la porte : le rire de la douairière.

« N'y touche pas ! Si tu recommences, je le coupe, l'entendis-je menacer mystérieusement d'une voix câline. Tu es vraiment un vilain garçon, Fan-ku !

— Donnez-moi un peu d'argent, tantine, et je serai encore plus vilain ». susurra-t-il.

De nouveau ce rire inextinguible.

Réunissant tout mon courage, je frappai.

« Chuuut », siffla-t-elle. Un silence pesant tomba dans l'appartement. « Va voir qui c'est. »

La porte s'entrebâilla. Fan-ku me dévisagea par la fente. « Que veux-tu ?

— J'ai besoin de parler à Mme Chin.

— C'est le prêtre, dit-il par-dessus son épaule.

— Dis-lui que nous sommes occupés. Va-t'en ! s'écria-t-elle.

— C'est à propos de la robe », dis-je, évitant moi aussi l'intermédiaire.

Nouveau silence.

« Fais-le entrer, commanda-t-elle.

— Aiyi ! » protesta Fan-ku.

La porte se referma ; une violente querelle s'ensuivit, des murmures stridents, venimeux, que je ne compris pas. Puis la chaîne coulissa sur sa glissière et la porte s'ouvrit.

« Entre », siffla-t-il en me crachant presque le mot au visage. Il avait retiré ses chaussures ; son regard vitreux se posa sur moi. Ses cheveux gominés étaient hirsutes, sa chemise entrouverte sortait de son pantalon. Une tache de rouge à lèvres maculait une de ses joues, juste sous l'oreille.

Un pan de la tenture était fixé au chambranle de la porte par une ceinture à glands. Dans la pièce du fond, j'aperçus une partie du fauteuil d'amour et la table noire octogonale. Une bouteille de brandy était posée dessus, ainsi qu'un verre à moitié plein, que la main de Mme Chin, aux ongles pointus et aux doigts bagués, caressait délicatement ou faisait tinter d'une pichenette distraite.

« Entre », m'ordonna-t-elle de l'angle invisible où elle était assise.

Je dus faire un grand effort pour garder contenance.

La douairière était vautrée à demi nue sur le fauteuil d'amour, le précieux *p'ao* en soie de la courtisane Hsu Tzi — le phénix à l'œil morose — lâchement drapé sur ses épaules nues, par-dessus une combinaison jaune sale dont les broderies de poitrine, exécutées à la machine, figuraient un motif floral qui ressemblait étrangement à des vers grouillant dans la cage thoracique d'un cadavre en décomposition. De son chignon à moitié défait sur sa nuque pendaient de ternes mèches de cheveux sales. Son rouge à lèvres débordait autour de sa bouche, ses yeux étaient vitreux, bouffis. On eût dit deux cuvettes de WC qui se remplissaient lentement, non d'eau, mais de chassie. Entre les fentes des paupières, deux étincelles brillaient comme des allumettes fiévreuses.

« Ne reste pas bouche bée comme un crétin, me railla-t-elle d'une voix méprisante, un peu vexée mais amusée. Un jour, à Shanghai, j'ai vu un paysan descendre d'une charrette de fumier avec ce visage. »

Fan-ku éclata d'un rire gras.

« La ferme, lui dit-elle. Viens ici. »

Il avança vers elle.

« Penche-toi. » Elle prit un mouchoir, le tordit, en plaça l'extrémité dans sa bouche pour l'humecter de salive. Puis, d'une main brusque, elle essuya le rouge à lèvres sur la joue du garçon. « Maintenant, va-t'en. Et ferme la tenture !

— Alors », dit-elle en avisant le paquet que je tenais à la main ; puis elle me jaugea d'un regard impertinent, opina lentement, cyniquement, du chef. « Je te l'avais dit, non ? » Elle se versa avidement une rasade qu'elle but aussitôt en fermant les yeux et frissonnant imperceptiblement. « Chaque chose a son prix pour qui sait attendre. »

Je la regardais avec un reproche muet ; ne disposant d'aucune arme pour me défendre, je provoquais son mépris.

« Laisse-moi la voir. »

Je posai le paquet sur la table ; elle le déballa, tint la robe devant son visage. Le liquide bilieux disparut de ses yeux ; elle devint solennelle, presque majestueuse. « Oui, soupira-t-elle, elle est belle. Je t'en donnerai un bon prix.

— Je ne veux pas la vendre, Mme Chin. »

Le regard qu'elle m'adressa trahissait la surprise, la déception.

« Je désire seulement emprunter, déposer la robe en tant que garantie.

— Tu veux dire la *gager*, ricana-t-elle, ajoutant aussitôt, tu apprends un drôle de jargon avec tes amis.

— "Gager" alors, concédai-je, si vous préférez. »

Elle se versa une autre rasade et contempla sombrement son verre. « Je n'aime pas ça. Tu m'as déjà blessée en insinuant que j'étais malhonnête Pourquoi me faire confiance aujourd'hui ?

— Ce n'était pas que je me méfiais...

— Peu importe, coupa-t-elle. Je vais te dire pourquoi. Parce que tu as besoin de liquide.

— Oui, admis-je, j'ai besoin d'argent. »

Elle ricana. « Les rôles ont changé, n'est-ce pas, Sun I ? Maintenant tu viens me voir. Mais dis-moi une chose : pourquoi devrais-je t'aider ?

— Je ne vous demande pas de m'aider, Mme Chin. Je vous propose une transaction. Je paierai.

— "Payer", dit-elle avec mépris. Que veux-tu que je fasse de ton argent minable, Sun I ? Je n'en ai pas besoin, je suis riche — je suis une douairière. Non, c'est ça que je veux. » Son menton désigna la robe.

« Et puis, poursuivit-elle sans me laisser la chance de changer mon fusil d'épaule ou de la contredire, les prêts sur gage sont trop compliqués. Je n'en fais plus que rarement. Dans le temps, les gens venaient sans arrêt me voir avec leur précieux "héritage", un morceau de jade ou un bout de soie. Je leur donnais de l'argent liquide dont ils devaient me payer les intérêts. Mes taux étaient élevés, je ne te le cache pas. Je n'ai jamais fait crédit sans garantie. De toute façon, c'était un service que je leur rendais, et je fixais des échéances. Un délai draconien, Sun I. Ma patience a des limites. Et puis, je suis une vieille femme, je ne peux attendre éternellement. Mais attention, tout était clairement posé dès le départ. Pas d'entourloupe. Une authentique "transaction", selon ta charmante expression. Et ils étaient d'accord. Alors, le dernier jour, une femme arrive chez moi en pleurant toutes les larmes de son corps, elle se tord les mains, me supplie à genoux de lui accorder un délai supplémentaire "pour l'honneur de sa famille". "Comment pourrai-je jamais regarder ma fille en face si je me sépare de sa dot ?" m'implore-t-elle. Pourquoi me demander ça à moi, hein, Sun I ? Je m'en moque comme de l'an quarante, pas vrai ? Les affaires sont les affaires. Un contrat est un contrat. Bah, fit-elle avec une moue dégoûtée. je transigeais quand les sommes étaient importantes. Mais maintenant pourquoi devrais-je continuer ? Je peux me passer de tous ces tracas. » Elle scruta mon visage pour apprécier l'effet de sa tirade. « Je vais pourtant te confier quelque chose, dit-elle. Malgré l'insulte, tu me plais toujours. Je pourrais peut-être faire une exception pour toi. » Elle eut un sourire écœurant. « Voici ma proposition. J'accepte de te prêter de l'argent, une somme généreuse. Mais je veux que tu me rendes la pareille.

— Comment cela ? demandai-je.

— Tu dois m'accorder une bonne chance d'obtenir ce que je désire. Nous allons fixer une échéance.

— Laquelle ? »

Elle haussa les épaules. « Disons deux mois, dix semaines ? »

Je calculai rapidement. Un mois — Kahn avait bien parlé d'un mois ? « Très bien, acceptai-je en m'accordant le plus long délai possible, dix semaines. Mais... à quel taux d'intérêt ?

— Oh, le taux habituel.

— C'est-à-dire ?

— Dix pour cent.

— Dix pour cent par an ou par semestre ? » demandai-je en essayant de faire le malin.

Elle rit. « Dix pour cent par semaine, mon chou.

— Dix pour cent par semaine ! protestai-je. Mais c'est de l'escroquerie ! »

Elle haussa les épaules en grimaçant. « Ce sont les termes habituels. S'ils ne te conviennent pas, essaie ailleurs. Va voir les Juifs, demande-leur combien ils te proposent pour cette robe. » Elle ricana. « C'est un article assez spécial ; n'importe qui n'est pas capable d'en apprécier la valeur. Et puis je te propose des espèces sonnantes et trébuchantes.

— Combien ?

— Disons cinq cents dollars.

— Cinq cents ! Elle en vaut des milliers.

— Hum... mille, peut-être, concéda-t-elle à contrecœur. Mais rappelle-toi que tu as intérêt à ne pas être trop gourmand. Plus je te prête, plus tes intérêts seront élevés.

— Disons mille cinq cents.

— D'accord, laisse-moi jusqu'à la semaine prochaine.

— J'ai besoin de cet argent immédiatement.

— Pour qui me prends-tu donc, la banque ? rétorqua-t-elle aggressivement. C'est impossible, pas à aussi bref délai. Je ne garde jamais autant d'argent chez moi.

— Très bien, consentis-je, exaspéré. Mille.

— Marché conclu ! » s'écria-t-elle en se frottant les mains comme un avare, comme une mouche. « Dix pour cent par semaine pendant dix semaines, payables tous les vendredis avec ton loyer.

— Ne pourrions-nous pas convenir d'un seul paiement qui accompagnerait le remboursement du prêt ? »

Elle fronça les sourcils. « Tu n'es pas en mesure de m'imposer tes conditions. »

Je déglutis difficilement. « Sinon je ne marche pas. »

Elle me regarda attentivement, puis brusquement rit. « Tiens, tiens, tu aurais donc des tripes après tout ? Je suis ravie de le constater. Je commençais à en douter. » Elle se rembrunit soudain et ajouta d'une voix menaçante : « Tu es dur, je le serai aussi. Si tu dépasses l'échéance... »

Je secouai la tête. « Je ne la dépasserai pas.

— Si jamais tu ne peux pas me rembourser, reprit-elle, tu dois me promettre qu'il n'y aura ni pleurs ni récriminations. »

J'acquiesçai.

« Alors nous sommes d'accord.

— Oui.

— Attends-moi ici, je vais chercher l'argent. Fan-ku ! » appela-t-elle en tripotant ses clefs qu'elle gardait au chaud près de son cœur.

Il apparut sur le seuil.

« Tiens compagnie à Sun I pendant mon absence. » Elle lui adressa un regard appuyé.

Il s'assit sur l'ottomane et me toisa avec un air de défi. Le sourire poli que je lui adressai réussit seulement à exacerber son mépris ombrageux. Gêné, je rougis et baissai les yeux.

Au bout de quelques minutes, je songeai que mon ami et compagnon d'infortune, le jeune chiot, demeurait invisible, que sa vitalité et sa bonne humeur, même bridées, étaient spectaculairement absentes de ce décor sinistre, déprimant. « Fan-ku, hasardai-je en espérant briser la glace, où est le chien ? »

Il me regarda avec des yeux écarquillés, manifestement surpris de ma témérité. « Le chien ? » Il resta perplexe, puis son visage s'illumina. « Oh, tu parles du petit avec les oreilles ? » Levant les mains, il les fit pendre de chaque côté de son visage dans une brève pantomime fort exacte.

« Oui, répondis-je avec un rire de connivence, celui-là.

— Il est parti, m'informa-t-il laconiquement avant de retrouver son attitude hautaine.

— Parti ? demandai-je. Où ? »

Silencieux, il évita mon regard. Puis une heureuse inspiration sembla le frapper. Il gloussa doucement. « Parti vers un foyer meilleur, dit-il.

— Un foyer meilleur ? »

Il éclata de rire. « Ne t'en fais pas. Nous avons déjà un remplaçant. Tu veux le voir ? » Il se leva, puis alla vers la porte et s'arrêta sur le seuil. « Ne touche à rien », m'ordonna-t-il avec un regard méfiant.

Quand il revint, il tenait dans ses bras une petite créature tremblante à l'épaisse fourrure duveteuse et noire, aux oreilles et au museau pointus, aux immenses yeux tristes qui semblaient lancer un timide appel au secours.

Fan-ku caressa le chien ; il me souriait en serrant les dents, m'observait avec une effronterie incompréhensible. « Alors ? dit-il. Qu'en penses-tu ?

— Il est très mignon, répondis-je.

— Oui, n'est-ce pas ? renchérit-il. Beaucoup plus mignon que l'autre. »

Loyal envers mon premier ami, je refusai d'acquiescer.

« Assez malin, aussi », ajouta-t-il.

Je regardais le petit paquet de fourrure tremblante, partagé entre la pitié et le scepticisme.

« Il sait faire des tours, m'informa-t-il.

— Quel genre de tours ? »

Il haussa les épaules avec une moue affectée. « Oh, prédire l'avenir par exemple. »

Je lui adressai un regard franchement moqueur.

« Tu ne me crois pas ? »

A ce moment, Mme Chin revint de la pièce du fond.

« Aiyi, l'appela-t-il d'une voix enjouée, le prêtre ne croit pas que nos chiens prédisent l'avenir. »

Elle sourit brièvement à Fan-ku, plissa les yeux, puis se tourna vers moi. « C'est la vérité, Sun I, bien qu'en général ils ne soient bons que pour une seule séance. »

Fan-ku pouffa ; elle le chassa d'un mouvement de tête excédé.

« Bon, mon cher, commença-t-elle d'une voix solennelle, voici pour toi. » Elle me tendit un sac de papier marron plié en deux, fermé d'un élastique rouge. « Plus d'argent que tu n'en as jamais vu en une seule fois, plus peut-être que tu n'en verras jamais. »

Je l'examinai d'un air absent, vaguement conscient de l'immense contraste entre mon présent engourdissement et la profonde émotion que j'avais ressentie l'autre jour en manipulant l'emballage de la robe de ma mère, en écoutant le papier crépiter entre mes mains, en respirant son parfum triste, équivoque — disparité rendue plus poignante encore par le fait qu'en un sens, du moins selon les règles du monde réel, ceci prétendait être son équivalent, ou « quelque chose d'approchant ». Je me demandai si l'avenir donnerait raison au monde réel.

« Tu ne veux pas le compter ? s'informa-t-elle.

— Comment ? » dis-je, interrompu dans mes réflexions. J'hésitai, puis refusai. « Je vous fais confiance, Mme Chin. »

Elle émit un ricanement incrédule. « Tu es un étrange garçon, Sun I, dit-elle, rêveur et sans cesse ailleurs. Tu es arrivé ici comme un somnambule. Laisse-moi te donner un conseil. Il est temps que tu te réveilles, mon chou. Ce monde-ci n'a rien à voir avec ton précieux monastère dans les montagnes du Szu-ch'uan. Tu ne t'en es pas trop mal tiré jusqu'ici. Tu étais maigre. Aujourd'hui tu prends du poids. Peut-être pas beaucoup, mais suffisamment. Les loups vont repérer l'odeur de la chair fraîche et te suivre à la trace. Prends garde. Tu ferais bien de redescendre sur terre, sinon les autres ne feront qu'une bouchée de toi.

— Merci du conseil, répliquai-je sombrement en me retournant pour partir.

— Attends. »

Je vis qu'elle me tendait quelque chose, une bande de papier.

« Qu'est-ce que c'est ? demandai-je.

— Ton reçu. »

★

Une fois retourné dans ma chambre, je fus la proie du remords. Des bouffées de honte incendièrent mon corps avec la régularité d'un pouls. Incapable de supporter ma solitude, je descendis chez les Ha-p'i pour avouer mon erreur à Yin-min, prêt à accepter ses réprimandes — les désirant peut-être —, mais espérant secrètement son absolution.

Rétrospectivement, ce qui arriva me semble incroyablement juste ou malheureux — même aujourd'hui, je ne sais quel terme choisir —, comme la conclusion qui, avec une logique implacable, découla des prémisses de ma démarche. Yin-mi n'était pas là. En fait, personne ne répondit. Mais la porte mal fermée s'ouvrit quand je frappai, et j'entendis quelqu'un parler, une voix que je ne reconnus pas aussitôt mais que j'avais déjà entendue. Vérifiant le numéro pour m'assurer que je ne m'étais pas trompé d'appartement, j'ouvris la porte avec précaution et jetai un coup d'œil à l'intérieur. Il n'y avait personne. Cependant, au bout du couloir, je vis une jeune femme debout de profil qui tenait le récepteur du téléphone entre sa joue et son épaule, et parlait à voix basse. Quand elle pencha la tête, la masse luisante de ses cheveux noirs tomba en un sombre torrent presque jusqu'à sa taille. Li.

Mon pouls accéléra inexplicablement.

Elle avait posé son avant-bras gauche contre son ventre et tenait son coude droit dans la paume de sa main ; tandis qu'elle parlait, son index tortillait une chaîne d'argent battu aussi fine qu'une toile d'araignée.

Comme je l'observais à la dérobée (position que je voulus abandonner mais sans jamais pouvoir m'y résoudre), je sentis l'excitation de l'interdit provoquer une brusque bouffée d'adrénaline, un raccourcissement de mon souffle.

« Je ne te juge pas, disait-elle. Accepter cela en théorie ne veut pas dire que je veuille coucher avec, non ? Quoi ? "Ethnocentrique" ? » Elle rit. « C'est très spirituel, Peter. Je crois que ton charme augmente à mesure que tes positions sont menacées. C'est pour cela que tu es si dangereux. "Irrésistible" ? Ne sois pas vaniteux — tu aggraves ton cas. Et c'est un luxe que tu ne peux vraiment pas te payer. Une menace ? Si tu veux. Quoi ? Va te faire voir, Peter ! Ne me refais jamais ça ! » Elle raccrocha violemment le récepteur et regarda droit devant elle. « Salaud ! » siffla-t-elle soudain d'une voix basse et glacée. Puis son buste parut s'effondrer, elle se pencha en avant comme une marionnette désarticulée en saisissant ses coudes entre ses mains. Quand elle se retourna, des larmes de fureur débordaient au coin de ses yeux clos. Son expression de souffrance fit bondir mon cœur dans ma gorge.

J'avais presque oublié à quel point elle était belle : ses pommettes hautes, ce flot de cheveux lustrés, ses dents blanches régulières, et surtout ses yeux crépusculaires, couleur de miel comme ceux du panda, et comme les siens, embrasés de passion. J'eus honte de le reconnaître, mais elle était sans conteste plus belle que Yin-mi, d'une beauté plus mûre aussi. Je sais seulement que la vue de ses seins qui ondulaient librement sous la soie me bouleversa (à l'inverse de ceux de Yin-mi, dont la fragilité et le doux renflement adolescent refrénaient l'appétit, comme des boutons non éclos qu'on renonce à cueillir). Un frisson d'excitation physique tel que je n'en avais jamais connu traversa mon corps ; une flambée de sexualité refoulée perça à travers la dure croûte de ma chasteté. Je m'en souviens encore parfaitement — le brusque halètement, la légère faiblesse aux genoux, cette première très pure brûlure d'Éros dans le sang, une sensation que je désavouai avec véhémence, mais uniquement par conviction intellectuelle, sans le remords viscéral que j'avais éprouvé en reconnaissant mon désir pour Yin-mi.

Quand elle m'aperçut, elle ne trahit ni surprise ni agacement. Elle me jaugea avec un intérêt clinique, puis soudain, à ma grande stupéfaction, sourit — une légère inflexion de la commissure des lèvres, un sourire dans lequel je sentis, à la place de ce qui y manquait et qu'on aurait pu attendre, une nuance de provocation maîtrisée. Cette transition instantanée, de la détresse à la séduction, me stupéfia. C'était presque sinistre.

Après m'avoir examiné pendant quelques secondes, elle fit volte-face et entra dans le salon. La froide audace de cet abandon (je ne pouvais lui en vouloir, car j'étais l'intrus), son manque total de curiosité quant à ce que je venais faire à l'appartement, me choquèrent avec la violence d'une gifle. En même temps, je fus piqué au vif. De nouveau la délicieuse morsure de l'excitation fit accélérer mon pouls. Je la suivis instinctivement sans même prendre le temps de réfléchir.

Elle était debout devant la fenêtre où j'avais observé les escaliers d'incendie le soir de la panne d'électricité. Comme auparavant, elle tenait son coude droit dans la paume de sa main gauche et tortillait sa chaîne d'or. Longtemps elle resta silencieuse. J'ignorais même si elle avait remarqué ma présence. Puis elle parla.

« Tu es amoureux d'elle ? » demanda-t-elle.

Le sang se rua vers mon visage, mais Li ne se retourna même pas pour constater ma déconfiture.

« De qui ? » demandai-je, m'obligeant à la circonspection.

Elle me lança un regard aigu et sourit avec un air de reproche. « De ma petite sœur, bien sûr. N'est-ce pas elle que tu es venu chercher ?

— Nous sommes amis.

— Ce n'est pas ce que je t'ai demandé.

— Elle m'importe, concédai-je.

— Mais l'aimes-tu ?

— Je suis prêtre, dis-je. Je suis tenu à certains vœux... » Je m'arrêtai au milieu de ma phrase. Quand je me rappelai d'où je sortais et ce que je venais de faire, j'eus une sorte de vertige, puis ressentis un chagrin si puissant que je faillis fondre en sanglots.

Elle me regarda bizarrement, non sans un certain amusement. « Des vœux ? Tu y es vraiment tenu ? » Elle rit. « Je devrais peut-être essayer ça. » Quittant la fenêtre, elle s'assit à côté sur le canapé et pour la première fois m'accorda toute son attention. « J'ai essayé de te voir. Je crois que tu m'évitais. » Une lueur de malice brillait dans ses yeux.

« Vous éviter ? » répétai-je machinalement en me raidissant, ébloui par sa proximité, par cet aveu d'intimité juste après ses marques de réserve et de froideur. Cela me flatta, me décontenança.

« Oui, répondit-elle, n'étions-nous pas convenus de nous revoir pour bavarder ? » Son regard quitta mon visage ; son sourire pâlit. « Peter a bien failli te faire signe, mais je l'ai retenu. Il te trouve terriblement séduisant. Il est très sensible à la mystique et au charme orientaux. » Elle me dévisagea. « Pourtant tes yeux ne sont pas chinois... Mais il a raison, tu n'es pas mal. »

Cette appréciation me ravit et me terrifia, car elle la formula avec une froideur clinique qui aurait parfaitement pu s'appliquer à un cobaye de laboratoire dont elle eût trouvé pitoyables les efforts et les souffrances, mais sans que ceux-ci suscitent sa sympathie. Une inflexion subtile de sa voix me donna cette impression, mais j'ai pu me tromper. Je ressentis pourtant un frisson de désespoir car je perçus l'immense distance, l'abîme qui nous séparait et me blessait, bien que je n'eusse aucune raison de penser qu'il pût en être autrement.

« J'aimerais en apprendre davantage sur ta vie, dit-elle.

— Ma vie ? » Je repensai à notre première conversation.

« Pour vos études d'ethno- ... J'ai oublié le mot.

— Ethnologie. Tu sais ce que c'est ?

— Pas vraiment.

— C'est l'étude des peuplades et des cultures primitives, expliqua-t-elle. Des systèmes et des valeurs disparus ou en voie de disparition, des langues mortes, des religions oubliées (ses yeux brillaient avec une précision chirurgicale) comme la tienne.

— Ma religion n'est pas oubliée », protestai-je férocement.

Elle sourit plus doucement. « Pas pour toi. C'est pour cela que tu m'intéresses.

— Vous avez l'intention de m'étudier ? » demandai-je avec un rire nerveux.

Elle sourit sans répondre.

« Pourquoi vous intéressez-vous à ces choses ? » poursuivis-je.

Elle haussa les épaules. « Pourquoi pas ? Qui sait quels secrets elles détiennent ? Un fragment sémantique piégé dans la grammaire d'une langue morte comme une bulle brillante dans la glace. Un coup de pic et elle explose en emplissant l'air de son parfum, une bouffée de l'odeur du monde il y a mille ou cent mille ans, quand il était encore jeune.

— Ce genre de découverte doit être très rare.

— Très, concéda-t-elle. Mais mon temps n'est pas si précieux. » Je crus remarquer une ombre désenchantée sur son visage.

« Vous devez être passionnée », dis-je.

Elle haussa les épaules. « Ou morte d'ennui. J'ai peut-être seulement besoin de stimulations mystérieuses. » Son expression morose s'accentua, mais elle souriait toujours avec un lointain amusement, comme si elle me défiait de déceler dans ses paroles la part de sincérité et de mensonge.

« Ce n'est pas très galant d'écouter mes conversations téléphoniques, me reprocha-t-elle d'un air enjoué. Tu as tout entendu ?

— Très peu de chose, lui assurai-je.

— De toute façon, je ne crois pas que tu aurais pu comprendre », dit-elle en fronçant les sourcils. Je me sentis blessé, mais réalisai qu'elle avait raison. « A moins que je ne me trompe ? » Son regard, qui m'avait quitté, se posa de nouveau sur moi.

Je secouai la tête.

« Cela t'intéresse ? » me demanda-t-elle avec une malice soudaine.

Je rougis.

« C'était Peter — tu t'en es sans doute aperçu. Tu as aussi probablement compris que nous sommes amants... parfois. Je devais le retrouver ici ce soir. Nous devions aller voir une pièce de théâtre au Village. Je l'ai appelé voici quelques minutes pour savoir s'il avait déjà quitté son appartement, et il m'a dit qu'il n'y allait pas — ou plutôt, si, qu'il y allait, mais pas avec moi. Il m'a dit qu'il s'était passé quelque chose. J'ai tout de suite compris. *Le salaud.* Quelque chose entre ses jambes. L'un de ses petits amis de Yale a débarqué en ville comme un cheveu sur la soupe, et il m'a plantée là. »

Je me rappelai l'expression douloureuse de son visage et j'osai la regarder. « Je suis désolé.

— Pourquoi donc ? Et puis tu connais seulement une partie de l'histoire. Peter est bisexuel. Tu sais ce que ça veut dire ? Il fait ça indifféremment avec les petits garçons et les petites filles. Joli, non ? » Elle attendit mon commentaire. « Alors ? Tu pourrais au moins être choqué. Je suis déçue. Ce genre de pratique est-il si fréquent parmi les ordres taoïstes ?

— Je ne sais que dire. »

Elle demeura silencieuse ; l'exaspération que je lus dans ses yeux menaçait de me condamner aussi à quelque pogrom global, systématique, dont je ne comprenais pas le motif.

« Il doit être stupide », hasardai-je d'une voix tremblante.

La tête penchée, elle m'observa avec une expression étonnée. « Pourquoi ? »

Je déglutis et me jetai à l'eau. « Parce qu'il risque de vous déplaire.

— Suis-je si spéciale ? lança-t-elle avec un nouvel entrain.

— Vous êtes belle », dis-je gravement, avec une honnêteté scrupuleuse.

Elle rougit et ouvrit de grands yeux. « Tu le penses vraiment ? »

Le visage en feu, je détournai les yeux.

Elle effleura ma main, une étincelle magique d'électricité sexuelle relia nos deux pôles, glaciale et brûlante tout à la fois. Je frissonnai.

« Je ne sais que faire. » Elle reprit ses doléances, mais d'une voix adoucie, plus lointaine. « Sexuellement, je ne peux pas être jalouse d'un autre homme. » Elle se leva et marcha vers la fenêtre, m'excluant de son attention aussi vite qu'elle me l'avait accordée. « Mais ça n'empêche que je me sens dans la peau d'une furie freudienne assoiffée de sang qui désire le castrer, l'amputer de la moitié de sa nature. La jalousie est déraisonnable, dit-il, puisque ses liaisons ne me menacent pas. Et c'est vrai, il est monogame — si je ne tiens pas compte de ses petits amis. Je ne veux pas jouer le rôle de la police des mœurs ni censurer son désir. Mais le fait est que je l'accepte mal. Je ne connaîtrai jamais l'autre moitié de son existence, une gigantesque lacune dans laquelle il disparaît parfois pendant des jours, où je ne peux pas le suivre, où il refuse de m'emmener. La face cachée de la lune. Parfois, j'ai le sentiment de le connaître à peine.

— Mais...

— Mais quoi ? » fit-elle en me lançant un bref regard furieux, comme si je l'avais obligée à se rappeler ma présence. « Pourquoi continuer à le fréquenter ? » Elle s'interrompit, me dévisagea pour voir si elle avait deviné ma question. Lisant un aveu dans mes yeux, elle sourit et parut s'éloigner. « Tu obéis à tes vœux, dit-elle cruellement. Tu ne comprendrais pas.

— Peut-être que si », objectai-je, incapable de maîtriser le tremblement blessé de ma voix.

Elle m'observa en silence, comme pour mettre ma sincérité à l'épreuve. « Très bien, dit-elle. J'aime son ambiguïté. Elle me séduit tout en me répugnant. Car elle naît de sa profonde assurance. Je n'ai jamais connu quelqu'un aussi sûr de lui. Peter possède un secret qu'il refuse de livrer, même par amour. C'est une merveilleuse preuve d'intégrité, si tu me comprends, quelque chose de très beau, de très pur. La plupart des hommes meurent d'envie de s'abandonner ; en une femme, ils cherchent un maître, quelqu'un capable d'absoudre leurs péchés. (L'image de Yin-mi apparut devant mes yeux.) Mais Peter chérit les siens. Ce n'est pas un dogme chez lui, mais quelque chose de totalement inconscient, innocent, une sorte de magnifique liberté animale. Il refuse d'obéir à la loi — à ma loi, à toute loi. C'est la personne la plus libre que j'aie jamais connue, sans doute parce qu'il a la force d'accepter les souffrances dues à sa double nature.

— Il compte beaucoup pour vous », dis-je d'une voix tendue.

Une tendresse douloureuse apparut sur son visage ; elle sourit avec lassitude et reconnaissance. « Je me suis peut-être trompée, dit-elle. Tu peux sans doute comprendre. Oui, je crois que tu comprends. »

Elle s'assit, posa de nouveau sa main sur la mienne, mais cette fois ne la retira pas. L'ombre du désespoir traversa son visage. « Je suis triste ce soir, Sun I. Je ne veux pas rester seule. Accompagne-moi au théâtre. »

La pièce, jouée dans un théâtre expérimental miteux du Village, se réduisit pour moi à un chaos de sons et de couleurs. Assis en silence, j'essayais de sonder mon humeur et mes émotions ; je regardais de temps à autre la femme installée à côté de moi, je me demandais qui elle était, quelle étrange et fatale gravité nous avait réunis sur la même orbite pour un soir, où tout cela nous amènerait. Perplexe, stupéfait, j'observais les pensées et les émotions impalpables miroiter sur ses traits à mesure que la pièce l'emportait sur son erre, ou bien l'abandonnait sur quelque rivage stérile et décevait son attente. Quand je la quittais des yeux, sa réalité s'effritait, devenait équivoque. Alors je la regardais encore, et mes yeux s'émerveillaient de sa présence. Je ne savais plus qui elle était, cela m'importait d'ailleurs peu. Le cercle magique du théâtre se déployait bien au-delà de la scène pour nous englober comme dans un liquide amniotique tiède et irréel. Je crus respirer la lourde atmosphère des rêves, baigner dans un univers crépusculaire et sous-marin, discerner la lueur poudreuse des rais de soleil réfractés à travers les prismes scintillants des cristaux de sel en suspension. Je m'abandonnai complètement à une dérive émerveillée. Le passé sombra dans l'insignifiance. Il me sembla avoir ouvert une porte en moi et pénétré dans un univers différent, ou bien voir le même avec des yeux différents, des yeux sensibles à une longueur d'onde inédite, à quelque lumière raréfiée située en dehors du spectre visible, qui métamorphosait tous les objets quotidiens et en révélait maints autres dont je n'avais jamais rêvé. Rien ne me poussait à juger moralement mon humeur ni mes inclinations. Je me sentais ensorcelé ou drogué, comme dans un rêve d'opium, et tout cela calma ma conscience douloureusement à vif après mon entrevue avec Mme Chin. Le crépuscule de ses yeux sous-entendait un crépuscule dans sa vie — un crépuscule moral. Pour elle, seul comptait le plaisir immédiat, sensuel comme le brusque afflux du sang dans un membre engourdi ou un bref vertige haletant, inquiétant mais pas entièrement déplaisant ; et il y avait aussi cette ombre de désespoir, le désespoir de ne jamais toucher son être profond. Pourtant même cela s'entourait d'une magie sensuelle, d'une sorte de langueur qui atténuait son côté poignant.

J'ignore ce qui m'arriva (ce qui m'était arrivé, plutôt, car j'avais déjà le sentiment d'un fait accompli, d'un tournant irrévocable), mais dès l'instant où la porte s'ouvrit et que je la vis, je perdis le contrôle de moi-même et ne sus plus ce dont j'étais capable. Plus important peut-être, j'oubliai ce dont je me croyais incapable. Sans doute une membrane essentielle de ma personnalité s'était-elle rompue, libérant un flot de ténèbres dont je n'avais jamais soupçonné l'existence. Je me suis souvent demandé quelle part les circonstances — ma récente expédition chez Mme Chin — avaient joué dans cette réaction singulière et sans doute excessive. Notre rencontre fut-elle pure coïncidence, ou bien un effet du destin, une conséquence de cette profonde loi psychologique qui veut que tout ce que nous ne réussissons pas à réconcilier en nous-mêmes, à faire ou à endurer jusqu'au bout, s'incarne immanquablement sous la forme masquée du destin ? Li découlait-elle de mon apostasie, ma réceptivité exceptionnelle à sa présence en était-elle le corollaire ? J'ignore encore les réponses à ces questions. Quand j'y repense, je ressens ce frisson de terreur exaltée, et tout disparaît brusquement autour de moi. L'ancrage de mes certitudes les plus profondes se brisa, je dérivai sur une mer inconnue qui s'étendait d'un horizon à l'autre, je me demandai si ma vie antérieure sur le rivage avait été un rêve, je crus qu'il n'y avait pas de rivage, pas la moindre terre, seulement la mer, cette immense mer qui était elle.

Cela devenait encore plus étrange à la lumière de ce que je venais de vivre à Coney Island, cette rémission spontanée de ma foi chancelante, la nouvelle consécration des buts de mon pèlerinage, la quête du delta, du Tao dans le Dow. La mise en gage de la robe n'avait apparemment pas compromis cette foi ; mieux, comment sinon aurais-je pu la conserver intacte ? Pourtant, ma démarche était pour le moins ambiguë. Aucune justification ne pouvait transformer ma visite à Mme Chin en un acte moral. C'était au mieux un expédient, une concession à la nécessité. Mais l'espoir d'aboutir dans ma quête était justement lié à ce genre d'ambiguïté. L'image du lotus poussant dans la boue, que Chong Fou m'avait expliquée, me revint en mémoire, et pour la première fois peut-être je compris réellement le sens du paradoxe : « Pour rester entier, sois tordu » — pour la première fois aussi je ressentis la sombre joie du nageur, courageux et confiant malgré le péril, désespérément à la dérive dans la vie.

De la pièce, *Le conte d'hiver*, je ne me rappelle presque rien : une jeune fille cueillant des fleurs, une statue prenant vie. La langue en était trop dense et complexe, ma distraction trop définitive. Mais un passage retint toute mon attention, non tant à cause de l'intérêt de la mise en scène proprement dite que des associations personnelles qui s'y greffèrent. Un homme débarquait d'un navire, comme moi-même il n'y avait pas si longtemps, tenant un enfant emmailloté dans ses bras ; puis il errait dans ce qui ressemblait à un désert. Jetant des regards furtifs qui disaient le désespoir ou la culpabilité, il posait l'enfant sur le sol après maintes hésitations ; il soupirait, faisait le signe de croix d'abord sur le nouveau-né, puis sur lui-même. L'enfant poussait un hurlement. L'homme s'éloignait ensuite en ne cessant de se retourner, désespéré par les cris pitoyables. Comme il ne regardait pas là où ses pas le dirigeaient, il ne vit pas ce que le public découvrit — un ours énorme qui observait son approche. Quand l'homme n'est plus qu'à quelques mètres de lui, l'ours se dresse sur ses pattes arrière, et l'homme se jette contre son poitrail. Les yeux écarquillés de surprise, l'homme tend le bras derrière lui et pince involontairement le museau de l'animal, qui émet un grondement irrité. L'homme pivote alors sur ses talons, découvre la bête qui le toise et lui rend son regard. Brisant l'effet dramatique, l'homme lance alors un clin d'œil complice au public qui, à ma grande confusion, éclate de rire. (J'étais possédé d'une sorte de transe terrifiée.) Ensuite, comble d'effronterie, il entraîne l'ours dans une valse, le temps de quelques mesures. Quand il marche sur sa patte, l'animal pousse un rugissement assourdissant, se laisse tomber à quatre pattes et le poursuit jusque dans les coulisses. Un cri à glacer le sang signale le dénouement de leur rencontre.

Tout cela, bien sûr, me suggéra ma propre rencontre à l'aube avec le panda géant après l'après-midi et la soirée dramatiques sur les rives du Fleuve au Sable d'Or, cela me la rappela en enrichissant (ou brouillant) cette association par des allusions à une constellation d'images liées à un passé plus récent — celles de l'homme fort et du petit garçon, tirées du *Yi king*. Malgré le sens littéral de la pièce, dont je ne compris quasiment rien, mon symbolisme personnel vit l'homme fort porter l'enfant de sa propre innocence à travers le désert du monde et, après de grandes angoisses, y renoncer, l'abandonner à son sort et aux éléments. Selon ce scénario, que je projetai par naïveté et par besoin, l'apparition de l'ours était une conséquence directe de l'apostasie de l'homme, et son agonie un effet évident de la justice cosmique. Était-ce pure ignorance ou la conséquence d'un déséquilibre croissant, mais le fait est que je découvris cette pantomime de ma propre vie psychique incarnée dans le monde extérieur. Quoi qu'il en fût, j'y vis un présage. Je m'identifiai au personnage qui, ainsi que je l'appris ensuite, se nommait Antigone : je considérai la mise en gage de la robe comme la trahison de l'enfant qui était en moi, et me demandai si les conclusions de nos deux aventures seraient similaires, si je devais me préparer à une nouvelle rencontre avec l'ours, mais cette fois avec un dénouement différent — non pas un panda géant au goût éthéré pour les fleurs sauvages, mais un grizzly américain assoiffé de sang.

2

Il faisait frais et lourd quand nous sortîmes du théâtre. Bien que la nuit fût tombée depuis longtemps, un nuage opalescent luisait au-dessus de la ville en reflétant ses lumières. Autour de lui, le ciel était resté bleu, comme si le crépuscule se fût attardé au-delà de son heure.

« Il fait beau ce soir », dit Li en étendant les bras. Elle respira une longue bouffée d'air, puis décrivit un cercle lent. « Il n'y en aura plus beaucoup comme celui-ci. » Elle s'arrêta devant moi, l'air préoccupé. « Que dirais-tu d'une expédition ?

— Une expédition ?

— Oui, poursuivit-elle. Une sorte d'enquête ethnologique sur le terrain. » Elle sourit pour elle-même.

« Où ça ?

— Dans l'Upper West Side, bien sûr. Nous sommes vendredi soir. Le délire a envahi les rues. Et comme j'habite là-bas, je serai un cicérone idéal. »

La pièce semblait l'avoir mise de bonne humeur. Charmé par son exubérance soudaine, j'acceptai aussitôt.

« Nous allons prendre le métro, décida-t-elle. Combien d'argent as-tu ? »

Vu que j'avais laissé mon butin sous le matelas de ma chambre, je réussis seulement à trouver deux billets froissés et quelques pièces au fond de ma poche.

« Tss tss, fit-elle avec une feinte désapprobation. Mon pauvre garçon, tu n'as donc pas encore appris qu'un joli minois n'est pas tout dans la vie ? Ou bien manques-tu d'expérience avec les filles ? En tout cas, tu risques de découvrir que je suis un peu plus exigeante que ma petite sœur. » Elle rit. (Malgré son enjouement, je sentais une pointe de sérieux dans sa voix.) « Mais ce soir, c'est sans importance. Fidèles à l'esprit de l'époque, nous ferons semblant de fêter les Saturnales, le monde à l'envers et l'inversion des rôles — mignons petits évêques fessant leurs aînés chauves... (son regard abandonna brièvement le mien, se refroidit), échangeant de tendres caresses avec des acolytes du même sexe ; dames de la cour payant fort cher le privilège de séduire les mendiants. » Ses yeux revinrent vers les miens, qui trahirent sans doute ma blessure d'amour-propre, car j'avais vu une allusion personnelle dans son dernier exemple, comme elle en avait sans doute glissé une malgré elle dans le premier. « Non, Sun I, m'assura-t-elle en secouant la tête et glissant son bras dans le mien, je ne veux pas parler de toi et moi. C'était simplement une image. » Nous partîmes en direction du métro.

Elle s'arrêta brusquement pour se planter devant moi. « Mais à minuit tout est fini — je t'en avertis. » Le ton de sa voix était ambigu, espiègle, joueur, mais aussi d'une gravité à peine masquée par la malice. « Je deviendrai une horrible sorcière et tu devras retourner au fond de ton puits. Le charme sera rompu, je retrouverai le vrai prince, le prince de conte de fées. » Elle me sourit sans joie. « Et plus jamais ce charme ne fonctionnera. Comprends-le bien. Tu as entendu ? »

J'acquiesçai.

Elle fit une moue dubitative. « Je ne suis pas sûre que tu comprennes, dit-elle, pas sûre que tu puisses. » Ses yeux couleur de miel continuèrent à me sonder, puis elle les détourna avec un soupir. « Mais peu importe. Viens, je crois que j'entends le métro. »

L'Upper West Side. Apparemment, Kahn et moi n'avions pas passé assez de temps au nord de la ville pour nous en faire une bonne idée. Li fut une meilleure guide. Quand nous émergeâmes du métro au coin de Broadway et de la Quatre-vingt-seizième rue, une musique latine assourdissante sortait du Casino Havana, où de sombres silhouettes enlacées passaient devant les fenêtres à l'étage, brièvement illuminées par les éclairs blafards des arcs-en-ciel de néon qui allumaient aussi des reflets multicolores dans la rue. Juste en dessous, une vitrine exhibait des statues religieuses, des saints de porcelaine peinte aux traits castillans, des peaux livides comme l'écume, des regards pieusement levés vers le ciel, mais avec une nuance de fier dédain. Dans ce groupe figé, deux yeux menaçants étaient baissés sous un front plissé par une sombre fureur didactique. Comme sur le vitrail de Trinity qui représentait le Christ, le bras était plié au coude, l'index pointé vers le ciel. Mais sur ce bras levé, un plaisantin avait posé une paire de castagnettes, qui pendaient au bout de leur cordon avec une ironie muette, avec l'effronterie inconsciente de la moule. Un Noir barbu, bizarrement vêtu d'un manteau trop grand pour lui, traînait le long de la rambarde de la station et buvait de furieuses rasades d'une bouteille dissimulée dans un sac en papier, en jurant et crachant aux pieds des passants. Un jeune Chicano à la démarche chaloupée et aux vêtements élégants, mais dont les yeux étaient cernés de poches bleuâtres, me bouscula — par hasard, pensai-je, jusqu'à ce qu'il chuchotât en toussant dans sa main pour éviter mon regard : « Fumette, fumette, cocaïne. » N'obtenant pas de réponse, il pivota sur ses talons et disparut dans la foule.

Ces premières rencontres donnent le ton de notre promenade. Car toutes les formes que nous vîmes avaient quelque chose de fugitif, d'insubstantiel. Passant devant une pizzeria, je remarquai un jeune Noir qui agitait deux montres-bracelets derrière le comptoir graisseux, les proposait contre une tranche de pizza, tandis que le propriétaire debout dans la vitrine donnant sur la rue ne lui accordait aucune attention et versait calmement une sauce rouge liquide en une spirale progressive sur le disque pâle de la pâte. Ses bras recouverts d'un épais duvet de poils noirs, comme ceux d'un animal, étaient enduits jusqu'aux coudes d'une fine pellicule de farine qui semblait bleuâtre, vaguement morte. Secouant sombrement la tête pour décliner la proposition, il évoquait un Rhadamanthe souterrain refusant d'accéder à une supplique. Devant une échoppe ambulante, un colosse noir brandissait ses poings vers le ciel en hurlant une rage inarticulée, tel un ours aux abois, tandis que des Américains bon ton aux visages récurés et terrifiés rasaient les murs comme des spectres bien élevés. Et dominant ce tohu-bohu, d'abord charmant mais devenant rapidement insupportable, puis aussi affolant qu'une forme de torture psychologique, l'angélus du glacier, *Rico Freeze*, son interminable et monotone ritournelle, aussi répétitive qu'un disque rayé.

« Ici, c'est toujours Mardi gras », dit Li en souriant pour elle-même comme si ses yeux contemplaient un paysage intérieur. « Et le lendemain, toujours Carême. Mais un carême sans carrosse. » Elle m'adressa un coup d'œil scrutateur, comme pour savoir si son jeu de mots avait fait mouche, d'ailleurs peut-être indifférente à son effet. Inspirant une profonde goulée d'air fétide et d'odeurs mêlées, elle tourna lentement la tête de gauche à droite. « Salô, dit-elle. Les cent jours de Sodome. » Sans comprendre ses paroles, je sentis son désespoir d'animal pris au piège, sa protestation, son courage mystérieux, sa vague résignation, une exquise faillite. « Je ne vais pas m'éterniser ici », chuchota-t-elle presque sauvagement, comme une promesse. Puis elle me sourit. Dans ses yeux je découvris l'ombre de la même douleur que j'avais aperçue dans ceux de Yin-mi après notre poursuite effrénée sous la pluie et que je l'eus repoussée, — une souffrance mieux trempée chez Li que chez la cadette.

« Viens, me pressa-t-elle. J'ai changé d'avis. Tout ça est trop déprimant. Je ne veux plus me promener. Allons chez moi. »

Quand nous pénétrâmes dans la cour intérieure de son immeuble, une cacophonie de musiques dissonantes assaillit nos oreilles : violonistes faisant leurs gammes, riffs de saxophones, une voix de soprano se lamentait devant une des fenêtres des étages supérieurs, s'accrochant comme un chat irascible à un registre suraigu où elle n'aurait jamais dû s'aventurer.

« La musique des sphères, commenta Li, et des pierres et des prières ; bateleurs, arnaqueurs et baladins — le chœur des Muses masturbatrices — Juifs et Druides, Rosicruciens — le paradigme du capharnaüm cosmique, une symphonie de virtuoses privés de chef d'orchestre. Bienvenue dans l'Upper West Side, le Purgatoire des Arts.

« Buenas noches, Ramon », dit-elle au gardien qui vitupérait dans la cabine publique de l'entrée en un espagnol véhément, tout en peignant ses cheveux gominés ramenés en arrière, avant de lisser sa coiffure d'une paume délicate. Posant son peigne sur le récepteur, il eut un sourire crispé et reconnaissant. « Je n'ai pas vu ta moto dehors, dit-elle. Que fais-tu ici ce soir ? »

Ramon haussa les épaules en souriant, puis reprit sa conversation téléphonique.

« D'habitude il travaille de jour, expliqua-t-elle tandis que nous marchions vers l'ascenseur. Ramon a une Harley Mille deux cent cinquante qu'il gare

dans la cour. Tous les jours vers trois heures et demie, ses copains au chômage se rassemblent pour le grand événement : il sort, met le moteur en marche et l'emballe pendant une bonne demi-heure avant de partir vaquer à ses occupations, "por éliminar il carbon dou motor", comme il dit.
— Vous ne semblez pas très heureuse ici », fis-je remarquer.
Elle éclata d'un rire bruyant. « Ah bon ?
— Si l'endroit ne vous plaît pas, pourquoi restez-vous ?
— Mon pauvre garçon, dit-elle. Comme tu comprends peu de chose.
— Vous dites toujours ça. Laissez-moi donc une chance. »
Elle haussa les épaules. « Où pourrais-je aller ? Dans le Lower East Side ? A Chinatown ? En ce qui me concerne, je n'ai pas le choix. Mais tu peux être sûr d'une chose : je ne retournerai jamais à Mulberry Street. Plutôt mourir — ou m'exiler dans le Kansas. Non, plutôt mourir.
— Le Kansas ?
— Le monde réel, si tu veux, expliqua-t-elle. New York est la Cité d'Émeraude. Tu ne savais pas ? » Elle s'interrompit, puis changea de sujet. « Mais tu as tort sur un point. Ce n'est pas parce que je me plains que je n'aime pas ce quartier. J'imagine que tu n'es pas à New York depuis assez longtemps pour avoir remarqué ceci ; les New-Yorkais adorent se vautrer dans leur dégradation. C'est une sorte de rituel commun qu'une longue pratique a sacralisé, comme certaines tribus primitives qui veillent à ne jamais se montrer trop satisfaites de ce qu'elles font ou acquièrent, de peur d'exciter l'envie des dieux. Ce rituel varie selon l'ethnie — Juifs ou Italiens, Chinois ou Pakistanais —, les formules et les fioritures diffèrent, comme les sortilèges, c'est un art qu'on distille à partir de son environnement, mais qui demande aussi passion et imagination, et récompense l'habile praticien d'un gros paquet de valeurs d'échange. Une enquête ethnologique sur le terrain, tu te souviens ? Toi avoir compris ? » Elle sourit, s'arrêta devant une porte et sortit sa clef. « Mais entre donc, dit-elle. Je vous en prie, après vous ! Je te promets de ne pas me moquer de toi et d'être gentille, au moins jusqu'à minuit. »

Quand elle ouvrit la porte, j'entendis une cavalcade feutrée dans l'obscurité. Elle alluma la lumière dans la cuisine, et nous découvrîmes une chatte à l'air dément, debout sur la table de la cuisine, qui fixait sur nous un regard sauvage, son poil gris hérissé sur son cou et son dos arqué. Elle sifflait et crachait comme si elle allait bondir, mais brusquement elle parut changer d'avis et sauta de côté dans la pièce voisine, pattes tendues devant et derrière elle comme si elle planait en apesanteur.
« Qu'est-ce que c'est ? demandai-je en quittant le mur contre lequel j'avais reculé.
— Une chatte, répondit Li d'une voix détendue. C'est Jo. Ne fais pas attention à elle. Elle est un peu cinglée.
— On dirait, marmonnai-je en inspirant profondément tandis que mon cœur retrouvait son rythme normal.
— Veux-tu un verre de vin ? me proposa-t-elle en ouvrant le réfrigérateur. Ou tes vœux t'interdisent-ils l'alcool ?

— Encore un connaisseur ! la taquinai-je gentiment. Seulement si tu me dispenses de l'obligation de discuter les mérites de ton vin. Ton père m'a déjà humilié plus d'une fois sur ce sujet.

— C'est du gallo, dit-elle avec un sourire en acceptant mon tutoiement. Je t'en dispense à condition que tu cesses de faire de l'humour noir. Entre, je t'apporte un verre. »

Très simple et nue, la pièce principale de son appartement évoquait une rocaille japonaise. Le parquet verni était superbement lustré, une lampe de bureau laquée en noir jetait un pâle reflet sur l'érable, comme un soleil brouillé posé sur une mer de bois blond. Quelques plantes étaient disposées avec goût : un asparagus dans un pot suspendu au plafond laissait pendre ses vrilles presque jusqu'au sol, un gigantesque philodendron était planté dans une potiche de faïence marron décorée de dragons dorés. La pièce était étrangement vide, surtout pour une Chinoise. Elle ne semblait pourtant ni négligée, ni inachevée, ni impersonnelle ; il s'en dégageait plutôt l'impression d'une forte présence, mais d'une présence qui s'exprimait par le retrait et le miroitement, un lustre impalpable, précis et parfaitement mûri, comme tout ce qui concernait Li. Cette extrême simplicité, l'éclat du parquet, sa nudité qui faisait résonner chaque pas accordaient à l'ensemble une clarté cristalline, comme une journée d'automne artificiellement recréée en intérieur, et dont la douceur masquait les premiers frimas de l'hiver.

Une faible musique jouait quelque part, une mélodie plaintive, décousue, immédiatement reconnaissable par-dessus la cacophonie entendue dans la cour, mais comme elle sans but apparent. Il s'agissait pourtant d'une gratuité différente : ici, le désordre n'aspirait pas à faire sens, il était apaisant, confortable.

« Ça te plaît ? demanda Li, qui entra et me tendit un verre de vin.

— Qu'est-ce que c'est ?

— Une harpe éolienne.

— Une quoi ?

— Une harpe actionnée par le vent. » Elle but une gorgée de vin, posa son verre, puis ouvrit la fenêtre. Le bruit s'amplifia.

« Éole est le dieu du vent dans la mythologie grecque. »

M'approchant derrière elle, j'aperçus un instrument fixé au rebord de la fenêtre, un châssis de bois muni de cordes tendues à chacune de ses extrémités.

« C'est un cadeau de Peter, reprit-elle. Il m'a dit que cet instrument me ressemblait.

— Pourquoi ? demandai-je. Parce qu'il est sauvage ? »

Son regard devint opaque et lointain. « Non, répondit-elle. Parce qu'il est sans âme. »

Elle se détourna brusquement et partit dans la cuisine. « Je vais préparer quelque chose à manger, m'informa-t-elle sans se retourner. Tu peux t'occuper tout seul, n'est-ce pas ? T'enivrer, fouiller dans mes affaires, tout ce que tu voudras. Simplement, je te demande de ne pas entrer dans ma chambre ; je n'ai pas eu le temps de faire le ménage et tout est en désordre. »

Mon deuxième examen de la pièce me fit découvrir un objet que je n'avais pas remarqué. Posée devant la fenêtre sur un bloc de bois verni noir qui lui servait de piédestal, je vis une figurine d'ivoire haute d'une quinzaine de centimètres, évidemment féminine, qui étrangement ne faisait pas face à la pièce, mais lui tournait le dos comme pour scruter les ténèbres extérieures. Sa silhouette dessinait un S renversé aux courbes douces, la hanche rejetée vers la gauche, le buste souple langoureusement cambré. Une longue main gracile aux ongles sculptés avec une exquise précision reposait contre son flanc. L'autre, levée vers la gorge, maintenait fermé le châle dont elle dissimulait pudiquement ses cheveux et son visage. Cédant à la curiosité, je fis tourner la statuette sans la lever et découvris le profil d'une renarde qui souriait sous le capuchon, les lèvres légèrement disjointes en un rictus de ruse et de malice, les dents sculptées avec la même minutie que les ongles des mains.

Soudain le bruit feutré de pattes tambourinant sur le parquet me fit sursauter, et Jo bondit hors du rectangle noir de la porte de la chambre, traversa la pièce comme une flèche, rebondit sur plusieurs murs. Un deuxième animal était sur ses talons, un chat en tous points différent d'elle. C'était un mâle au poil brillant et noir, un bel animal musclé, gros comme un chat de l'île de Man. La seule imperfection que je remarquai chez lui tenait à l'aspect de sa patte avant droite. Non qu'elle fût exactement déformée, mais elle était de moitié trop grosse pour lui, telle une greffe d'un cousin plus imposant de la famille *Pantera*. Ses yeux aussi étaient étranges, mais plus une fantaisie ornementale qu'un défaut, bleus comme ceux des Siamois, mais légèrement plus foncés, scintillants comme deux pierres précieuses ou la lumière qu'on voit parfois dans les yeux des aveugles.

Je crus d'abord qu'ils jouaient, jusqu'à ce que, bondissant de tout son poids, il la plaquât férocement, se servant d'elle pour amortir l'impact de son corps contre un mur. La chatte cracha et se débattit en miaulant vaillamment, mais quand il l'eut immobilisée en se jetant sur elle de travers, elle se fit plus conciliante et s'abandonna, clouée au sol, le souffle court. Il maintint de ses pattes arrière ses épaules à elle, ajusta son poids, se lécha les babines et pencha la tête comme pour la dévorer en commençant par le ventre. La face de la chatte soumise était vraiment hideuse — écrasée contre le parquet comme un visage humain contre une vitre, les yeux exorbités, le cœur battant frénétiquement contre sa maigre cage thoracique couverte d'un poil rare. Après quelques succions de pure forme à un mamelon sec, les lutteurs se séparèrent et un grand bruit de friture provenant de la cuisine, accompagné d'une explosion de parfums, attira mon attention dans cette direction.

Debout devant un poêlon de fonte noire, Li remuait son contenu avec une spatule en bois. Sur la table, un bol en terre cuite contenait des fragments de choux-fleur, des petits pois frais et une poignée de quartiers de mandarine. « Viens voir, invita-t-elle. Tu aimes la cuisine indienne ?

— Je ne sais pas, dis-je. Je crois que je n'y ai jamais goûté.

— C'est du ghee, expliqua-t-elle en continuant de remuer le liquide frémissant, du beurre clarifié. »

Elle déboucha un petit flacon de verre étiqueté « curcuma » posé sur une étagère en bois au-dessus de la cuisinière, prit une pincée de poudre couleur rouille et la jeta dans la solution bouillonnante, translucide. Une autre explosion technicolor diffusa une senteur âcre dans la cuisine. Sous mes yeux, elle saupoudra successivement des pincées d'épices ocre, grise, rouge brique, et chacune produisit une subtile altération de l'odeur dont la complexité croissait à mesure. Li ressemblait à un alchimiste composant son mélange au-dessus d'une flamme bleue ; et moi à quelque marin passant sous le vent des Iles aux Épices, rêvant à des séjours de félicité, humant les bocaux ouverts : cumin, graines de moutarde, poivre blanc, cardamome, fenugrec, clou de girofle. Plongeant un doigt pour y goûter, je découvris que la moindre trace faisait perler la sueur à mon front ; et incrustés sous mes ongles, je trouvai les témoignages d'une terre que j'eusse grattée — l'argile rouge, le lœss, des sols indélébiles. En cet instant et plus encore ensuite, la préparation de ce curry fort et amer me parut la juste expression culinaire de la personnalité de Li, un mets suscitant une soif si puissante qu'elle transformait en poussière jusqu'à la moelle de mes os et troublait la raison. Li étanchait pourtant la soif qu'elle créait artificiellement, car elle me servit un doux *lassis*, du yaourt, de l'eau de rose, du miel et de la glace pilée mélangés dans un shaker.

Pour le dessert, elle prépara un pamplemousse à la cannelle et au sherry. Ce fut peut-être un peu trop sophistiqué pour mes goûts simples. Je picorai en essayant de paraître ravi malgré mon manque d'appétit.

« Tu n'aimes pas ça ? demanda-t-elle.

— Oh si ! mentis-je. C'est délicieux. »

Elle me lança un regard enjoué. « Je sais ce qui te plairait, dit-elle, mi-vexée, mi-amusée. Un bol de riz avec un peu de sauce aux haricots noirs. »

La honte me fit baisser la tête. Elle avait mis dans le mille.

« Ou quelques crêpes au navet arrosées de sauce d'huître.

— C'est mon plat préféré ! » m'écriai-je, stupéfait.

Elle me lança un clin d'œil. « Je lis dans les pensées.

— Est-ce donc une spécialité de toutes les femmes de ta famille ?

— Bien sûr ! Nous sommes toutes des sorcières. Ma mère est la Bonne Sorcière du Sud qui garde un profil bas et règne sur les farfadets. Yin-mi est Glinda, la sorcière à voix de tamias qui arrive dans une bulle de savon. Et moi, je suis la Sorcière Maléfique de l'Ouest — ou du moins je le deviendrai... (elle regarda sa montre) dans une heure et demie. Si tu ne pars pas avant, je te transformerai en Nabot. » Elle rit. « Mais sérieusement, tu ne te fatigues pas de la "nourriture spirituelle"? Dès que j'approche à moins d'un kilomètre de Chinatown, j'ai des suées, des nausées, des bouffées de fièvre — une sorte de réaction pavlovienne. Il suffit que je pense à la cuisine chinoise pour perdre l'appétit.

— Pourtant ton père — et ta mère — sont de vrais cordons bleus ! protestai-je.

— C'est vrai, admit-elle. Ils n'ont mangé que ça, parlé que de ça et pensé qu'à ça pendant toute leur vie, toute ma vie. Cette seule constatation me rend malade. Je préfère avoir faim plutôt que de manger du *dim sum* ou du *moo goo gai pan*. La jeune Chinoise décrète un moratoire sur les plats à emporter, à paltil de maintenant et jusqu'à dolénavant. » Elle s'inclina, leva ses paumes jointes au-dessus de sa tête. « Excusez je vous prie, melci beaucoup ! »

Bien qu'un peu choqué par cette parodie caustique de son père, je ne pus m'empêcher de sourire. Je sentais qu'elle était éméchée ; moi aussi, d'ailleurs.

« Allez, Sun I, portons un toast. » Elle remplit son verre et fit tinter sa petite cuiller contre lui.

« A quoi allons-nous boire ?

— Tu ne t'attends quand même pas à ce que je te sorte, que je te nourrisse et que, par-dessus le marché, je te souffle à quoi nous allons boire, me gronda-t-elle en continuant de faire tinter son verre. Il faut que tu te décides à prendre l'initiative, et le plus tôt sera le mieux. Car minuit approche. » L'alcool animait son visage, ses yeux brillants se fixaient sur moi avec un mélange d'amusement et de provocation.

« Très bien, concédai-je. A toi. » Je levai mon verre.

Cela ne lui convint pas. Elle baissa la tête, la secoua comme une enfant boudeuse sans cesser d'agiter la cuiller contre le verre. « A moi quoi ?

— A ta cuisine ! proposai-je, charmé par sa colère simulée.

— Hou ! Mauvais ! Ça ne me plaît pas. Essaie encore.

— Très bien, dis-je doucement, la bouche un peu sèche. A ta beauté.

— Hourrah ! s'écria-t-elle gaiement. Je savais que tu y arriverais ! » Quand elle remarqua ma sincérité, elle cessa brusquement son jeu. Mon humeur la contamina. Avec un sourire tendre, elle leva son verre, puis, hésitant, le reposa. « Tu penses vraiment que je suis belle ? »

Touché, j'acquiesçai.

« Viens ici, dit-elle, comme si maintenant elle aussi était légèrement essoufflée. Trinquons. »

Alors que j'étais debout au-dessus d'elle, elle m'adressa un regard presque implorant. « Il est stupide, n'est-ce pas ? »

Je ressentis un frisson délicieusement douloureux quand je compris que, même avec moi, elle pensait à Peter. Mais j'acquiesçai encore. « Oui. »

Elle essaya de se lever, vacilla, se raccrocha à moi. Dans cette position précaire, une main posée sur mon épaule, l'autre serrant son verre de vin contre ma poitrine, elle me dévisagea curieusement, comme si elle me voyait pour la première fois. Elle regarda pensivement ses doigts dans mes cheveux. « Merci », dit-elle, les yeux vaguement brumeux.

Puis elle changea encore d'attitude, elle heurta mon verre avec la violence de l'ébriété, ferma les yeux, but une longue gorgée. Glissant ses deux bras derrière ma tête, ses coudes nonchalamment posés sur mes épaules, tenant toujours son verre, elle rit silencieusement. Puis son visage se détendit complètement et elle m'embrassa sur les lèvres — un baiser léger, mais chaud, humide, prolongé. Je l'observais intensément sans répondre à sa bouche, mais sans lui résister non plus.

Quand elle éloigna son visage, elle resta longtemps sans ouvrir les yeux, les lèvres légèrement écartées sur ses dents en un lointain sourire intérieur. « J'aurais dû faire cela plus tôt », dit-elle. Puis elle me regarda.

Nous restâmes longtemps ainsi à nous observer, ses mains toujours posées sur mes épaules, sans faire le moindre geste pour nous séparer. Je tremblais un peu, je me sentais faible, énervé ; une sensation purement physique, un frémissement nerveux des jambes et des bras. Mais le centre de mon être était étrangement calme. Après un moment, elle se pencha vers moi et m'embrassa encore, cette fois plus profondément, avec sa langue. Derrière le bouquet du vin, je discernai un faible et délicieux arrière-goût de lait suri, sa signature personnelle.

« Assez belle pour te faire rompre tes vœux ? » murmura-t-elle à mon oreille en syllabes tactiles, caressantes.

Le frémissement s'accentua, devint presque un tremblement.

Elle rit par-dessus mon épaule, s'abandonna contre moi. « Ou bien les moines de ton monastère se prémunissent-ils contre cette éventualité ? »

Je ne compris pas sa question avant de sentir sa main s'insinuer entre mes jambes.

Mon sexe durcit brusquement, je reculai violemment.

« Ouh la la ! dit-elle. Mais non, tout est bel et bien là. »

Profondément blessé, choqué en fait, je la regardai avec dépit.

Elle écarquilla les yeux, arrondit la bouche pour imiter mon expression scandalisée. Mais quand elle constata que ma peine n'était nullement feinte, elle s'adoucit. « Ne le prends pas mal », implora-t-elle doucement en passant le dos de sa main sur mon visage.

Ma contrariété disparut, ma faiblesse revint, avivée et comme énervée par le souvenir de cette blessure d'amour-propre, une blessure difficilement pardonnée. « Pauvre garçon, dit-elle avec tristesse et sympathie, viens avec moi. » Me prenant par la main, elle m'emmena vers la chambre à coucher.

« Tu es vraiment vierge ? » demanda-t-elle d'une voix neutre par-dessus son épaule, en faisant glisser la fermeture Éclair de sa robe, mais sans se tourner complètement vers le lit où j'étais assis. Elle la laissa tomber autour de ses pieds, enjamba le cercle du tissu, puis croisa les bras devant elle et fit passer sa combinaison au-dessus de sa tête. Alors elle pivota et les globes blancs et pleins de ses seins oscillèrent doucement comme deux navires à l'ancre — et pour la première fois je vis une femme dans sa nudité. Son corps était svelte et compact comme celui d'un animal. Le visage un peu rouge, elle rayonnait d'une timidité parfaitement maîtrisée et de la fierté d'être si belle. « Tu es terrifié ! » s'écria-t-elle avec un rire surpris, mais sans méchanceté, avec une tendresse presque maternelle que je n'avais jamais entendue dans sa voix. Elle retroussa les lèvres en une moue de pitié, tomba à genoux devant moi, saisit mes deux mains. « Tout va bien », m'encouragea-t-elle doucement, mais elle ne put dissimuler entièrement l'excitation amusée due à ce qui devait être pour elle l'extrême nouveauté de la situation. « Crois-moi — il ne te manque rien. J'ai vérifié. » Elle sourit ; puis, me voyant toujours aussi tendu, redevint sérieuse. « Détends-toi, me dit-elle d'une voix caressante. Rien ne presse. Nous avons le temps. Nous allons parler. D'accord ? Raconte-moi une histoire.

— Li... » Je tournai vers elle un visage poignant. « Je ne...

— Chu-ut. » Elle posa son index sur mes lèvres. « Détends-toi. Raconte-moi une histoire.

— Je ne connais pas d'histoire, répondis-je faiblement d'une voix abattue, en baissant les yeux.

— Parle-moi de toi, alors, proposa-t-elle. C'est l'histoire que j'ai vraiment envie d'entendre. »

Je la regardai d'un air hésitant.

Elle hocha la tête. « Allez, vas-y », m'encouragea-t-elle. Elle remonta les oreillers contre le mur, s'allongea langoureusement derrière moi, m'épargnant ainsi le tourment délicieux de sa nudité, maintint cependant un contact physique avec moi, d'une main qu'elle posa d'abord légèrement sur mon épaule avant de la faire descendre doucement le long de mon dos et de passer un doigt nonchalant entre ma ceinture et ma peau. En même temps, elle allongea sa jambe au bord du lit, la glissa contre mon bras et mon épaule, insinuant son pied sous ma cuisse comme pour le garder au chaud. Bien que complètement spontanés, instinctifs même, ces gestes instaurèrent entre nous une intimité tactile et naïve qui dissipa une bonne part de mes craintes.

Après quelques faux départs qui me nouèrent la gorge et aboutirent à des excuses gênées, j'entamai mon récit. A cette époque déjà, c'était devenu comme un rituel qui, une fois commencé, courait sur son erre. J'abordai toutes les phases de mon existence, esquissant à chaque fois à grands traits le cadre et l'arrière-fond du développement — Ken Kuan, la visite de mon oncle, mon départ, ma descente « au fil du fleuve » —, puis je passai aux étapes plus récentes de ma quête, l'ultimatum de Kahn, la mise en gage de la robe. Quand Li m'interrogea sur la raison profonde de mon départ hors de Chine, je lui répondis en insistant sur le « delta ». Un amer sentiment de trahison crispa un instant mon cœur quand l'image de Yin-mi se matérialisa devant mes yeux — le premier cadeau qu'elle m'offrit —, dont je révélais le secret comme une banalité, à sa sœur, à Li. Je rougis en pensant à elle. Mais alors que son image avait été si présente quelques heures plus tôt, je voyais maintenant Yin-mi à travers un brouillard dense, comme un visage tourné vers moi sur une photographie sépia dans un vieux cadre chamarré en argent terni par l'oxydation. Quel élément l'avait donc obscurci ? Je savais seulement que mon sentiment ressemblait à un requiem, et que Li en était la cause. A la fin de ma narration, j'étais pourtant devenu presque bavard. Je me sentais inspiré, les mots me venaient naturellement, mon exaltation engourdissait toute impression de danger ou de trahison.

Li n'avait pas modifié sa posture allongée, mais elle était devenue distante, songeuse. Elle mordillait l'ongle de son pouce avec un air concentré, lançait son pied au bord du lit et le laissait lentement retomber.

Quand elle s'aperçut que je l'observais, elle interrompit son manège, émergea de ses rêveries, se secoua comme un animal s'ébroue.

« A quoi pensais-tu ? demandai-je.

— Hmm ? Oh, je pensais au delta, et à la pièce. Tu te rappelles ces vers : "Surpassant cet art qui, selon vous, ajoute à la nature, existe un art que la nature façonne"? Pendant que tu parlais, ils me sont venus à l'esprit en rapport avec Peter, et avec toi. Je crois qu'il existe une analogie entre vos deux situations. Vous êtes tous les deux attirés, peut-être possédés par une impulsion difficilement conciliable avec vos convictions — pour toi, c'est le Dow ; pour lui, son ambivalence sexuelle ("cet art qui ajoute à la nature"). Mais il a accepté sa propre dualité, presque en accord avec

Shakespeare qui croit que l'art lui-même *est* la nature. Toi, tu essaies de réconcilier tes contradictions, tu veux gommer l'ambivalence de ton cœur, assassiner l'un de tes moi ou bien l'éliminer comme spécieux. Le delta..., répéta-t-elle en riant doucement pour elle-même. Pauvre garçon, viens ici. » Elle me tendit la main en souriant. Elle se dressa sur un bras parmi les oreillers, en prit un pour moi, qu'elle installa à côté du sien. « Allonge-toi près de moi. »

Je me soumis aux pressions de ses mains, à sa volonté.

« C'est bien, chuchota-t-elle. Maintenant ferme les yeux. Détends-toi. J'ai une idée. »

Elle roula vers moi, posa doucement sa jambe sur la mienne avec une provocation qui me parut presque timide, comme si elle se retenait d'une intrusion plus intime et se contentait de me faire sentir le seul poids de sa jambe. Elle déboutonna ma chemise en commençant par les boutons du haut.

Quand elle eut terminé, elle ouvrit les deux pans, puis se pencha pour caresser mon ventre avec sa joue et ses cheveux, comme une chatte quémandant l'attention ; sa langue décrivit des cercles lents autour de mon mamelon, puis elle le lécha pour qu'il s'érige. Sa langue était râpeuse comme du papier de verre... Ou peut-être mes sens étaient-ils extraordinairement aiguisés : je ressentis un plaisir délicieux, presque insupportable, proche de la torture. Je serrais et desserrais les poings, mon corps s'arquait sous ses caresses.

Elle m'abandonna soudain, s'allongea sur moi en posant les mains sur la couverture, ramena ses jambes près de son corps. « Tu aimes ça », dit-elle, amusée.

Je retombai en haletant puis levai les yeux vers elle, lui en voulant un peu de son pouvoir, et plus encore qu'elle eût interrompu son exercice.

« Tu n'es pas censé regarder.

— Pourquoi pas ? J'aime regarder, dis-je par défi, de plus en plus bouleversé de désir.

— Ferme les yeux, ordonna-t-elle sur un ton péremptoire. Bon. Maintenant... » Elle s'allongea sur le lit. « Je vais te montrer quelque chose — non, n'ouvre pas les yeux. » Deux doigts frais posés sur mes paupières m'en empêchèrent. « Te faire sentir quelque chose, plutôt. Donne-moi ta main. » Elle s'en empara, étendit ma paume sous la sienne. Puis elle la guida doucement le long de son visage, sur son cou, sa clavicule et son sein, où elle la laissa un instant immobile (son mamelon était érigé), avant de la faire glisser sur la peau soyeuse de son flanc, la courbure de sa hanche, et enfin son mont de Vénus où mes doigts étonnés découvrirent une autre texture.

« Sens cela, chuchota-t-elle langoureusement, en tournant la tête sur l'oreiller pour approcher sa bouche de mon oreille. Ce tertre boisé, couvert de fourrure. » Maintenant sa paume sur la mienne, ses doigts sur mes doigts, elle exerça une légère pression, enfonça lentement le majeur en elle. « Un lit de rivière à sec, décrivit-elle, entre deux collines boisées — "au fil du fleuve". » Son rire chuchoté me fit ouvrir les yeux. Sa tête était renversée, sa gorge offerte comme pour le sacrifice. Ses yeux étaient fermés, un trait blanc incurvé luisait entre les paupières. Une lumière surnaturelle irradiait son visage, et tandis que fasciné j'observais son expression d'extase, je sentis la tendresse se mêler à mon appétit douloureux.

« Je t'emmène en prospection, murmura-t-elle en souriant, à la recherche de l'eau — ton doigt est la baguette du sourcier, la racine de mandragore. Tu descends dans le ravin en sondant doucement mais fermement. » Sa main me guida et m'apprit. « Arrête-toi. Là. Tu sens ? La terre humide sous les buissons et les fourrés. Tu dois creuser, et soudain... ah ! » s'écria-t-elle faiblement en perdant le fil de ses indications, le visage crispé comme de douleur ou de concentration. Je crus lui avoir fait mal, mais elle rit de nouveau. « ... remontant de la nappe profonde en bouillonnant... de l'eau ! Tu l'as trouvée. » Elle ouvrit les yeux, et sans transition plongea son regard dans le mien en souriant. « Voilà le delta, aimable sourcier, dit-elle en appuyant fortement sur ma main, le seul qui importe. Voilà le confluent, le lieu de notre rencontre, à toi et à moi... de notre... rencontre. »

L'émerveillement et le pouvoir brillaient dans ses yeux, ainsi qu'un puissant plaisir.

« Alors, dit-elle, vas-tu rompre tes vœux pour moi ? »

Je laissai mon regard s'attarder quelques instants sur elle, non par hésitation, mais parce que je voulais prolonger ce miracle, savourer sa beauté, m'enivrer de bonheur et du sentiment de la fatalité. « Je les ai déjà rompus », répondis-je.

Et c'était la vérité.

3

« Voilà ce que j'appelle un sourire béat, remarqua Li d'une voix amusée. On dirait un petit garçon rassasié de sucreries. Si j'avais un seau d'eau à portée de la main, je le renverserais sur toi pour le simple plaisir de te voir te dissoudre sous mes yeux. » Elle secoua la tête. « Ça ne va pas, Sun I, pas du tout. C'est *moi* qui suis censée me dissoudre, pas toi.

— Je suis très heureux », répondis-je fièrement en tournant vers elle un visage rayonnant et vulnérable.

Elle rit. « Et moi, je veux une cigarette. » Pivotant sur ses fesses, elle lança ses jambes par-dessus le lit et tendit la main vers le tiroir de la table de chevet.

« Je ne savais pas que tu fumais, dis-je, vaguement déçu par cette découverte.

— Je ne fume pas, répondit-elle en fouillant, d'habitude. » Trouvant enfin ce qu'elle cherchait, elle ferma le tiroir d'un geste sec et revint sur le lit où elle écarta ses cheveux avec un mouvement de tête qui me rappela étrangement Wo. Elle gratta une allumette en laissant pendre sa cigarette à la commissure de ses lèvres. « Seulement après l'amour », dit-elle en me défiant du regard avant d'allumer sa cigarette.

Elle aspira une profonde bouffée, la retint dans ses poumons, puis exhala en soupirant ; d'un bref signe de tête, elle me montra le tiroir. « Il y a plusieurs cartouches là-dedans. » Son visage resta parfaitement inexpressif, puis elle pouffa.

Quand je saisis sa plaisanterie, elle ne me fit pas rire.

« Oh, je t'en prie, s'irrita-t-elle, tu ne vas pas bouder et me faire la tête, n'est-ce pas ? J'espère bien que non ; les Saturnales sont terminées.

— Que veux-tu dire ?

— Prends une cigarette, dit-elle sans répondre.

— Je ne fume pas.

— Allez, essaie. Tu as déjà péché, autant boire la coupe jusqu'à Li. Et puis, sinon, ton expérience risque d'être incomplète. Tu peux me croire sur parole. J'en sais quelque chose, non ? »

Je fus inquiété par son changement de ton — une gaieté agressive, brusque. Je m'obligeais à un sourire de complaisance en sentant combien j'étais devenu étranger à moi-même. Brusquement Li m'effraya. Elle semblait puissante, incapable de contrôler son propre pouvoir, ce qui rendait ma position doublement précaire, car je m'accrochais et me fiais à *elle*.

« Très bien », dis-je avec un sourire nerveux et un haussement d'épaules en prenant la cigarette qu'elle me tendait entre mon index et mon majeur. Je m'interrogeai en silence sur la gaucherie voulue de ce geste qui ignorait le pouce — le rituel tacite des fumeurs.

Li observa avec amusement mes tâtonnements. « Tu te compliques la vie, sais-tu ? »

Je levai les yeux ; adossée à l'oreiller, les bras croisés sur l'estomac, elle s'était retirée en elle-même.

J'aspirai la fumée en prenant soin de ne pas trop tirer sur la cigarette, puis levai le menton comme je l'avais vue faire, et la laissai lentement sortir entre mes lèvres arrondies.

« C'est bon, n'est-ce pas ? Sa voix était alanguie, somnolente.
— C'est plus doux que l'opium, remarquai-je en pensant à haute voix.
— Tu as fumé de l'opium ? demanda-t-elle, stupéfaite.
— Deux fois. » Je pris une autre bouffée.

Elle fit claquer sa langue. « Tu es un garçon étrange, Sun I. Plein de surprises. » Elle tendit la main et fit jouer ses doigts comme des ciseaux pour me réclamer la cigarette.

« C'est ma Nature de Singe », expliquai-je en lui donnant ce qu'elle réclamait.

Elle aspira une bouffée. « C'est bon », dit-elle en me la rendant.

Brusquement, je me sentis de nouveau en sécurité. La distance qui nous séparait se mua en une intimité que toute conversation aurait menacée.

Quand la cigarette fut presque consumée jusqu'au filtre, je me penchai au-dessus de Li pour l'éteindre dans le cendrier posé sur la table de chevet. Je remarquai seulement alors qu'il contenait plusieurs mégots. Je n'avais pas surmonté la peine due à cette découverte quand Li bougea.

« Écoute. » Elle leva son index droit et tourna la tête comme pour regarder quelque chose par-dessus son épaule.

« Je n'entends rien, répliquai-je avec une légère irritation qu'elle ne releva pas, en regagnant mon côté du lit.
— Justement, murmura-t-elle avec un soulagement fasciné. Tout est calme. Merveilleusement calme. »

Nous écoutâmes tous deux.

Li finit par soupirer. « Ce silence me fait du bien. Parfois, tard la nuit, on entend seulement l'écho de la circulation qui monte de la cour, un long sifflement feutré qui rappelle le bruit des vagues dans une conque. » Elle sourit. « Le profond soupir de l'océan, un bruit qui ressemble au silence. Le silence », chuchota-t-elle.

Alors le vent se leva et je perçus le grondement sourd des brisants, celui que j'avais entendu pour la première fois au large de la côte chinoise tandis que je faisais route vers le port de Shanghai. La harpe éolienne parut s'emballer.

« "Les bourrasques soudaines du Pays des Fées" », dit-elle sans changer de position, bras croisés sur le ventre, les yeux clos, la tête renversée sur l'oreiller. « Le Pays des Fées. Voilà où j'aimerais aller. Voilà ma destination. Je me meurs, Sun I... je me meurs. Emmène-moi là-bas.

— Je t'y emmènerai », promis-je aussitôt avec extravagance.

Elle sourit, puis tourna la tête sur l'oreiller pour m'observer. « Vraiment, mon doux garçon ? Comment m'emmèneras-tu là-bas ? Sur un tapis volant tissé de bonnes intentions ? Ou bien possèdes-tu une paire d'escarpins magiques ?

— Oui, c'est ça, lui dis-je sans même comprendre sa question. Je vais en trouver une paire. »

Elle rit. « Moi, je sais où tu aimerais m'emmener. Dans ton monastère en Chine. » Une vague pitié traversa son visage, et elle baissa la voix. « Mais telle n'est pas ma conception du Pays des Fées, mon doux enfant. Je crains de ne pas faire une nonne idéale. J'aime trop le péché. » Son sourire contredisait ses paroles ; je la crus pourtant et ne répondis rien.

« Et puis, poursuivit-elle, tu ne peux pas y retourner. Tu as rompu tes vœux. "Plus jamais", dit-elle avec une intonation lugubre. Je t'ai fait rompre tes vœux. Tu dois me haïr à cause de cela.

— Je ne te hais pas, protestai-je tendrement.

— Ça viendra. »

Je secouai la tête. « Je ne pourrai jamais te haïr, Li. Jamais. Je...

— Chuut, dit-elle en posant doucement un doigt sur mes lèvres. Ne dis rien. Sinon, je pourrais bien te haïr. »

Elle se laissa retomber sur son oreiller en soupirant. « Non, déclara-t-elle. Un seul homme peut m'emmener là-bas — mon prince charmant. » Elle eut un sourire sans joie.

« Je pourrais devenir ce prince, insistai-je.

— Oui, tu le pourrais. Tu le deviendras. Mais le prince d'une autre, mon doux garçon. Pas *mon* prince. »

Une sirène vrilla la nuit, mais Li ne réagit pas. J'endurai seul sa stridence, jusqu'à ce qu'elle devînt trop énorme, absorbant toute chose au point de se transformer en un cri jaillissant du centre même de mon être, toute l'angoisse de l'univers condensée en un unique hurlement hystérique et implacable.

« Qu'est-ce que c'est ?

— Je ne supporterai pas beaucoup plus longtemps cet endroit », répondit-elle d'une voix basse, à peine audible, comme se parlant à elle-même. Dans la pénombre de la chambre, je vis des larmes mouiller ses cils et perler au coin de ses yeux. « Nom de Dieu de nom de Dieu, chantonna-t-elle de cette même voix neutre, je ne crois pas que je vais supporter ça longtemps. » Elle se tourna vers moi avec une lassitude exaspérée. « Elles durent parfois pendant deux jours sans s'arrêter.

— Qu'est-ce que c'est ? répétai-je plus doucement.

— Un antivol de voiture. Une nuit, l'hiver dernier, une sirène semblable s'est déclenchée à quatre heures du matin. Elle hurlait toujours quand je suis sortie prendre le bus pour aller à mes cours. Et l'après-midi, quand je suis rentrée. Ce sont les batteries Durplus, dit-elle en riant étourdiment. Ils devraient faire une publicité sur ce thème : "La batterie Durplus de la compagnie Sears a provoqué davantage de suicides que ses deux principaux concurrents réunis. Ne vous contentez pas de moins. Achetez la meilleure. Achetez Sears. C'est proprement sidérant." Quand elle s'est arrêtée — la voiture n'était plus qu'une épave, des gamins avaient brisé le pare-brise et les fenêtres à coups de briques, défoncé les pare-chocs, piqué les enjoliveurs —, j'ai encore entendu cette sirène dans ma tête pendant des jours et des jours. Elle s'est littéralement incrustée en moi. Les cellules de mon cerveau l'ont mémorisée et la répétaient comme un mantra absurde, un bourdonnement cosmique — l'envers flippant de l'Harmonie Primordiale des Taoïstes. » Elle rit encore. « Le plus horrible, c'est qu'au bout d'un moment on en vient à la désirer comme une drogue sécurisante. »

Le hurlement s'arrêta brusquement.

« Merci mon Dieu, soupira-t-elle. Ô, merci mille fois doux Jésus, merci ! »

Je remarquai alors le chat noir au coin du lit ; il avait bondi à mon insu et s'était figé là, aussi immobile qu'une apparition surnaturelle dont les yeux froids et brillants nous auraient observés avec un calme parfait. Il remua soudain la tête pour lécher vigoureusement la fourrure de son épaule, puis allongea voluptueusement ses pattes avant en bâillant et léchant ses babines. Il se redressa comme un danseur après un grand écart, ramena ses pattes vers son corps, puis s'ébroua avec une brève violence en dressant sa queue vers le plafond.

« Elle t'a réveillé ? » fit Li avec un sourire attendri en bougeant pour la première fois depuis quelques minutes.

Le chat miaula plaintivement, puis enjamba adroitement mon pied pour traverser la couverture vers sa maîtresse.

« Mon pauvre poussin », le cajola-t-elle en tendant la main vers lui.

Le chat fit le dos rond et se coula sous la paume en levant la tête vers Li.

« Il est beau, remarquai-je. Viens par ici, minou. » Je fis claquer ma langue, puis mon pouce contre mes doigts. « Minou, minou.

— Il méprise les flatteries, m'informa-t-elle en riant. C'est un aristocrate, un sang bleu. » Elle le fit rouler sur le ventre, puis le caressa. La bête serra le poignet de Li entre ses pattes aux griffes rétractées, rejeta la tête en arrière avec des ronronnements de plaisir.

« On dirait un petit moteur », plaisantai-je.

Elle se pencha au-dessus de lui, le masqua de ses cheveux et se mit elle aussi à ronronner, reproduisant le son — un lent soupir râpeux et guttural — avec une exactitude si étonnante que je frissonnai.

« Que fais-tu ? » demandai-je, vaguement effrayé par son manège et sa concentration.

Elle lança ses cheveux en arrière. « Nous parlons.

— Tu comprends son langage ?

— Bien sûr, affirma-t-elle. Je suis non seulement siamoise, mais aussi ethnologue. » Elle rit avant de reprendre sa conversation féline.

« Comment s'appelle-t-il ?

— Eddie, me répondit-elle en poursuivant son jeu.

— Eddie ! répétai-je en ressentant un choc désagréable. Pourquoi Eddie ?

— Eddie-pe, expliqua-t-elle. Eddie-pe et Jo. Ils forment un couple.

— Mais Joe est un nom de garçon ? Pourquoi as-tu appelé ta chatte ainsi ?

— C'est une abréviation de Jocaste. Jocaste et Œdipe. » Elle m'adressa son sourire amusé, légèrement moqueur. « Tu ne comprends pas ?

— Qu'y a-t-il à comprendre ?
— Œdipe et Jocaste. »
Sa réponse n'éclaira guère ma lanterne. Je la regardai avec perplexité. « C'est la mère et le fils. Tu ne connais donc pas l'histoire d'Œdipe ? » Je secouai la tête négativement. « Raconte-la-moi.
— Tu aimes les histoires, on dirait ? »
J'acquiesçai avec un sourire timide et ravi, car je la sentais sur le point de céder.
Elle soupira. « Très bien, je te raconte celle-là. Mais à une condition
— D'accord.
— Tu ne veux pas connaître ma condition ?
— Si. Alors ? »
Elle rit. « Je ne sais pas encore. Je te la dirai en temps voulu.
— Cela ressemble vraiment à un marché de dupes », protestai-je.
Elle haussa les épaules. « C'est à prendre ou à laisser. A toi de choisir.
— Très bien, opinai-je. J'accepte.
— Bon. Cela se passait en Grèce il y a très longtemps, commença-t-elle. Nous sommes à Thèbes, une ville de Béotie, province qui doit sa célébrité à ses habitations troglodytes et au goût de ses habitants — une majorité de gardiens de cochons — pour le désastre. Œdipe a déclenché un mécanisme diabolique, puis a transmis le mauvais œil à ses fils Étéocle et Polynice, qui furent presque aussi malchanceux que lui et firent l'impossible pour ravager leur cité. Le peu qu'ils laissèrent debout fut ensuite rasé quelque temps plus tard par Alexandre lors de sa campagne de Grèce. Mais c'est une autre histoire.

« Œdipe... Je dois d'abord te parler de son père ; sinon, tu ne comprendrais rien. Il s'appelait Laïos, c'était le roi de Thèbes. A la naissance de son fils, Laïos consulta pieusement l'oracle de Delphes et apprit avec horreur que le nouveau-né lui ravirait son trône et le tuerait si on le laissait grandir. »

Comme elle parlait, une phrase me revint en mémoire : « Si l'on s'attache au petit garçon, on perd l'homme fort » — le verdict de *mon* « oracle ». Je n'eus pas le temps de réfléchir à cette coïncidence, car Li poursuivit sans s'arrêter.

« Incapable de le tuer de ses propres mains, Laïos remit le nourrisson à l'un des gardiens de cochons susmentionnés avec l'ordre de le supprimer.
— Comme dans la pièce ? »
Elle acquiesça. « Oui, comme dans la pièce. Et comme dans la pièce, Laïos eut la malchance de tomber sur un fermier dont le cœur n'était pas totalement sec. Il ne put se résoudre à assassiner froidement le nouveau-né ; après un long combat intérieur, poussé par son sens du devoir et de l'honneur, il décida de pendre le nourrisson par un pied à une branche d'arbre et de l'abandonner à son sort. Quand on le trouva et le détacha, son pied était si enflé qu'on l'appela Gros Pied — Oedi-pous. C'est là l'origine de son nom, pas vrai, Eddie ? » Elle caressa la tête du chat.

« Fin de l'acte un. Suit une ellipse. La caméra pivote. Sur l'écran apparaît un carton : "De nombreuses années plus tard..." Nous sommes sur la route de Delphes. Œdipe a grandi. Il rencontre Laïos par hasard ; aucun ne reconnaît l'autre. La route est étroite. Laïos est pressé. Il est en retard pour un important rendez-vous avec la sibylle. En sa qualité de roi habitué à être obéi, il ordonne à Œdipe de lui céder le passage. Œdipe, qui a lui-même hérité un peu de la fougue royale et qui malgré son milieu n'est pas porté à la modestie, refuse d'obéir. Une confrontation classique s'ensuit. Laïos, bien sûr, entre en rage, dégaine son épée, et pour une raison que je n'ai jamais élucidée, tue le cheval d'Œdipe. Qu'est-ce que ce cheval vient faire dans l'histoire ? Peut-être visait-il Œdipe et a-t-il manqué son coup ? Bref, Œdipe voit rouge et l'occit — il tue Laïos, son propre père, sans se douter une seconde qu'il commet un parricide.

« Deuxième ellipse. Entre le Sphinx. Tu as entendu parler de lui ? Il s'agit d'un monstre particulièrement diabolique, dans la plus pure tradition misogyne, doté d'un corps de lion et d'une tête de femme. Il-elle hantait les routes autour de Thèbes, terrorisait les voyageurs avec une énigme. Pas très impressionnant, comparé aux formes modernes de terrorisme ? Mais si tu ne savais pas répondre à son énigme, il te dévorait — voilà qui rajoute un peu de sel, non ? Voici l'énigme en question : "Quel animal marche à quatre pattes le matin, à deux le midi, et à trois le soir ?"

— L'homme ! répondis-je.

— Je croyais que tu ignorais cette histoire ?

— Je l'ignore, rétorquai-je. Mais c'est une vieille devinette chinoise.

— Tu plaisantes. » Elle cilla. « Bon, il se trouve qu'Œdipe répondit comme tu viens de le faire. Le Sphinx en fut si contrit qu'il se jeta aussitôt de son rocher dans l'abîme. Pour remercier leur sauveur, les Thébains firent d'Œdipe leur roi et lui offrirent en prime l'ancienne reine, la veuve de Laïos. Exactement, Jocaste, sa propre mère. Plutôt piquant, non ? Il faut bien sûr ajouter à leur décharge que tous deux ignoraient l'énormité de leur forfait. Mais les dieux étaient au parfum et décidèrent qu'on ne pouvait laisser impunie pareille abomination. C'était inadmissible, du moins parmi les mortels. Cela équivalait à usurper *leur* prérogative... Ils firent donc s'abattre sur Thèbes la pestilence et la famine, toute la gamme des désastres naturels. Œdipe, qui tenait sans doute de son père une superstition atavique, se tourna vers l'oracle pour découvrir le responsable de ces catastrophes, et fut stupéfait d'entendre son nom. Alors il apprit tout, la double transgression des tabous — le parricide et l'inceste, baiseur de sa mère, assassin de son père. La vérité rendit Jocaste folle ; elle se pendit. Quant à Œdipe, fou de douleur, il se creva les yeux.

— Il se creva les yeux ! »

Elle acquiesça. « Exactement. » Puis Li bâilla en tapotant sa bouche avec le dos de sa main. « Alors ? Mon histoire t'a plu ?

— Si elle m'a plu ! m'écriai-je. Elle est horrible, atroce ! » Puis j'ajoutai après quelques secondes : « Pourtant oui, en un sens, elle m'a plu. »

Elle rit. « Tu es un étrange garçon, Sun I. A quoi penses-tu ? Je vois un drôle de regard dans tes yeux si peu orientaux.

— Je pensais à mon père. »

Elle me dévisagea en silence, puis sourit. « Tu aimes peut-être trop les histoires.

— Je les ai toujours aimées, répliquai-je. C'est plus fort que moi.

— Je ne te le reprocherai pas — c'est aussi l'une de mes faiblesses. Mais prends garde, elles ont la sale habitude de se réaliser. »

Je secouai tristement la tête. « C'est au moins un souci que je n'ai pas. Mon père est mort.

— Oh, je vois. Je suis désolée.

— Moi aussi, dis-je avec un sourire désenchanté.

— Tu te souviens de ce que je t'ai dit ? me demanda-t-elle en changeant de sujet. Dans ce pays, tout le monde doit payer tout ce qu'il obtient. Je t'ai donné quelque chose, maintenant à toi de me rendre la monnaie de ma pièce. A ton tour de te soumettre à ma volonté.

— D'accord, mais que veux-tu ?

— Mes désirs sont des ordres, d'accord ? »

J'acquiesçai.

« Bon. Tu semblais si content pendant que je te racontais mon histoire que j'en ai été jalouse ; je veux une histoire. Une courte, ajouta-t-elle, avant que tu t'en ailles.

— Mais je t'en ai déjà raconté une, protestai-je.

— Je sais, concéda-t-elle. Mais ça ne compte pas. Ton histoire était vraie. Je veux autre chose.

— Quoi donc ? Toutes les histoires que je connais sont tirées de la vie.

— Un conte pour s'endormir, précisa-t-elle alors, quelque chose de baroque et de chinois.

— Un conte de fées », hasardai-je.

Elle sourit. « Exactement. Je t'ai raconté un mythe occidental ; raconte-moi un mythe chinois. Une sorte d'échange culturel. » Elle s'allongea sur les oreillers en soupirant. « Nous pourrions peut-être ainsi développer nos rapports — nos rapports *culturels*, s'entend. Jouer à tu-me-montres-la-tienne et je-te-montrerai-la-mienne. » Elle rit et bâilla encore. « Excuse-moi. Je deviens irritable. Dépêche-toi avant que je ne m'endorme sur toi. »

Je me rappelai brusquement le netsuke dans la pièce de devant. « Hu Li...

— Comment ? » demanda-t-elle d'une voix endormie.

Je lui répétai alors l'histoire que Wu m'avait racontée et dont l'héroïne était une belle anachorète. J'évoquai ses longues veilles solitaires en quête de l'illumination, l'interruption et la revanche monstrueuse qu'elle prit contre le responsable de sa déception, le banquet servi à l'empereur, avec son propre fils en guise de plat de résistance, tel un cochon rôti servi avec une pomme dans la gueule.

« Au moins, elle lui a épargné les tourments du complexe d'Œdipe », commenta Li en serrant les couvertures contre son menton. Les yeux mi-clos, elle souriait. « Laïos aurait dû faire appel à ses services pour le sale boulot. Rien de tout cela ne serait jamais arrivé, il nous aurait épargné bien des souffrances.

— Mais l'empereur aimait son fils, fis-je remarquer.

— Certes, reconnut-elle. Cela renverse le point de vue occidental, n'est-ce pas ? »

J'opinai du chef.

« Mais qu'est-il arrivé à cette fille ?

— Son âme fut emprisonnée dans le corps d'une renarde, lui dis-je.

— Une renarde ? » Li fut soudain attentive.

J'acquiesçai. « On dit qu'elle hante les routes de la Chine pendant la nuit, et que, déguisée en belle femme, elle séduit les jeunes imprudents qu'elle dévore — un peu comme le Sphinx.

— Tu as vu le netsuke dans l'autre pièce ?
— Oui. Où l'as-tu trouvé ?
— C'est un cadeau, répondit-elle d'une voix tendue.
— Je fouillai son visage. « De Peter ? »

Elle sourit et ferma les yeux.

« Je suppose que cela aussi le fait penser à toi ? »

Elle haussa les épaules. « Je suis peut-être l'une de tes Fées Renardes, Sun I — as-tu pensé à ça ? »

Je secouai la tête. « Si tu en étais une, tu ne me le dirais pas.

— Et pourquoi pas ? » Elle m'adressa un regard amusé et provocateur. « Ce serait sans doute la façon la plus astucieuse d'endormir tes soupçons.

— En tout cas, je ne verrais certainement aucun inconvénient à ce que tu me dévores. »

Elle rit. « Méfie-toi, je pourrais bien te prendre au mot. »

De temps à autre dans son sommeil, Li poussait de petits cris plaintifs, lointains, aussi aigus et douloureux que le registre supérieur de la harpe. Je caressais ses cheveux pour la calmer, mais elle secouait la tête, se détournait comme si ma main brûlait sa chair. Il était étrange de la voir errer dans ce paysage invisible, perdue en un rêve où toute sa beauté et sa subtilité s'avéraient impuissantes contre les formes obscures qui se dressaient devant elle.

Incapable de dormir, j'entendis des cloches sonner trois fois dans une tour éloignée. Le vent qui se levait périodiquement transformait le murmure de la harpe en une violente agitation, en une musique déchirante comme un chant funèbre, le désespoir pitoyable d'une chose incapable de formuler sa douleur, ou peut-être d'un dieu dont le langage me restait obscur. Je songeai brusquement que la harpe éolienne ressemblait au *Livre des Mutations*. Comme les baguettes d'achillée, ses cordes paraissaient un instrument conçu par l'ingéniosité humaine, assez sensible pour frémir aux subtiles vibrations galvaniques du Tao. Sa musique, son motif toujours changeant étaient la mélodie incompréhensible de la vie elle-même — incompréhensible, mais peut-être pas dénuée de sens — qui m'avait amené ici ce soir.

Li avait dit qu'elle ressemblait à la harpe, sans âme. Mais la musique que j'entendais était-elle vraiment sans âme, une succession arbitraire de notes et de timbres, ou bien la harpe émettait-elle des vibrations trop subtiles pour être décelées par nos sens grossiers ? J'eusse aisément cru qu'avec son exquise sensibilité, son amoralité dénuée de toute culpabilité, elle ressemblait profondément à un diapason invisible qui vibrait selon les harmoniques de la vie, émettait une note que je n'étais pas habitué à entendre.

Alors que je reposais dans cette douce torpeur irréelle, elle poussa un cri et se dressa sur le lit, haletante. « Qui est là ? demanda-t-elle d'une voix terrifiée. Peter ?

— Ce n'est que moi, dis-je. Sun I. N'aie pas peur. »

Écoutant à peine ma réponse, elle se leva précipitamment pour aller dans la salle de bain. Elle alluma la lumière, ferma la porte derrière elle. J'entendis l'eau couler.

Immobile sur le lit, j'écoutai le bruit de la douche. Comme Li s'attardait, je m'assoupis progressivement. Dans l'agréable entre-deux de la veille et du sommeil, je sentis confusément le lit s'enfoncer sous son poids quand elle revint. Avec un sourire satisfait, mais sans ouvrir les yeux, je m'endormis.

J'ignore depuis combien de temps je m'étais assoupi et ce qui me réveilla, mais quand mes yeux s'ouvrirent, la chambre était plongée dans une quasi-obscurité, à l'exception de la faible lueur des étoiles qui tombait par les fenêtres, et du reflet des lumières de la ville sur les nuages. L'espace d'un instant, je ne sus plus où j'étais, je me demandai si je ne dormais pas dans mon lit à Mulberry Street. Alors, pris d'une violente bouffée de tendresse paniquée, je me souvins de Li. Je tournai la tête vers elle. A côté de moi sur l'oreiller, ses yeux ouverts m'observaient dans les ténèbres. Dans le halo de lumière réfléchie, ils luisaient avec l'incandescence particulière aux yeux des animaux. Soudain, j'entendis un bruit de chasse d'eau, puis, avec un hoquet terrifié, la cavalcade assourdie des pattes d'un chat sur le parquet. Je remarquai qu'il y avait encore de la lumière sous la porte de la salle de bain. Elle s'ouvrit bientôt et Li apparut, enveloppée d'une serviette, ses cheveux ramenés sur sa tête en un vague chignon.

« Tu sais quelle heure il est ? me demanda-t-elle d'une voix cassante. Plus de trois heures du matin, répondit-elle aussitôt. Tu as dépassé le délai dont nous étions convenus. Tu dois partir.

— Mais pourquoi ? » Je m'assis dans le lit. « Quelle différence... ?

— Je t'en prie, ne rends pas les choses plus difficiles qu'elles ne le sont. Je n'ai aucune envie de jouer le rôle de la Sorcière Maléfique. Je t'avais prévenu ; et tu étais d'accord.

— Mais c'était avant ! Je croyais que tu plaisantais.

— Eh bien je ne plaisantais pas. » Une étincelle de pitié brillait dans son regard. Mais elle ressemblait au filament scintillant du croissant de lune que j'avais vu sur ses boucles d'oreilles, et sous ce fragile reflet, froide et pesante, je sentis la masse glacée de sa décision et de son intransigeance.

Stupéfait par la monstruosité arbitraire de son ordre, je sentis mon cœur se briser dans ma poitrine en milliers d'échardes torturantes, comme un cœur de verre, mais je me levai lentement pour enfiler mes vêtements. Quand nous atteignîmes la porte de la cuisine et qu'elle m'eut accompagné jusque dans le couloir, je pleurais.

« Mon pauvre garçon, murmura-t-elle, ne pleure pas pour moi. Ça n'en vaut pas la peine.

— Je suis amoureux de toi, dis-je en sanglotant entre mes mains.

— Ne m'aime pas, me conseilla-t-elle d'une voix triste qui se voulait consolante. Je ne suis pas assez bonne pour toi. Aime ma petite sœur. Vous vous ressemblez. C'est une sorcière bénéfique.

— Mais c'est toi que j'aime, pas elle, répondis-je sauvagement entre deux sanglots.

— Chut, dit-elle en posant un doigt contre mes lèvres. Je ne te ferais aucun bien, Sun I. Tu serais trop délicieux pour moi ; je te dévorerais, je te volerais tes escarpins magiques.

— Tu peux bien me les prendre ! m'écriai-je. Et le reste avec. »

Elle sourit avec une condescendance désabusée. « Mais tu ne les connais même pas, tu ignores la nature de leurs pouvoirs.

— Que sont-ils alors ? »

Elle posa sa main sur mon cœur. « Voilà ce qui t'a amené ici ; et si tu ne les perds pas, ils te ramèneront chez toi, dans le Kansas, dans le monde réel. Garde-les précieusement, Sun I ; ne les donne pas à n'importe qui. Pas à moi, à personne sauf à elle. Tu peux faire confiance à Yin-mi.

— Mais ce n'est pas elle que je désire, répétai-je. C'est toi. Je veux te les offrir.

— Ah, aimable garçon, murmura-t-elle. Tu ne comprends donc pas mon secret ? Je n'en veux pas vraiment. Les escarpins magiques ne servent qu'aux aller simple à destination du Kansas. Moi, je veux aller au Pays des Fées, et tu ne peux pas m'emmener là-bas. »

J'ouvris la bouche pour parler, mais de nouveau elle posa un doigt sur mes lèvres. Elle me retint un instant sous son regard, puis recula et me ferma la porte au nez.

4

Le lendemain matin, un dimanche, je fus réveillé par un coup frappé à ma porte.

« Sun I ? » s'enquit une voix douce et timide.

Je me retournai en grognant tandis que mon cœur s'emballait. C'était Yin-mi.

« Je ne voulais pas te réveiller, s'excusa-t-elle en passant la tête dans l'entrebâillement de la porte. Je ne savais pas que tu dormais encore. Je désirais seulement savoir si ce soir nous pourrions aller ensemble à la conférence. Si je passais te chercher vers six heures et demie ? Tu auras sans doute besoin d'aide pour porter tes affaires ? »

La tête enfouie sous les couvertures, j'étais parfaitement réveillé, en proie à une terreur qui me fit marmonner quelques paroles aussi vagues qu'embrouillées.

« Bon, dit-elle, les interprétant comme un acquiescement. Je te laisse dormir. Tu en as probablement besoin. A tout à l'heure ! » La porte se ferma et je me détendis un peu. Puis elle se rouvrit brusquement. « J'attends impatiemment ta conférence ! s'écria-t-elle avec excitation en guise de post-scriptum. Et je ne suis pas la seule ! » Puis elle s'éclipsa.

J'avais la bouche pâteuse à cause du vin, mais ce n'était rien en comparaison de ma déconfiture morale. La soirée de la veille me semblait irréelle comme un rêve ou un cauchemar, un délicieux et terrifiant cauchemar. Et il y avait Li. Son souvenir ressemblait à une étoile errante, au grand trou noir d'un soleil implosé qui avait pénétré dans mon système solaire émotionnel et m'attirait violemment dans ses profondeurs. Sa présence était tellement immense, si lourde dans mon cœur, qu'il n'y avait presque place pour rien d'autre.

Ma première impulsion — la plus saine — fut de courir après Yin-mi pour lui dire de tout annuler pendant qu'il en était encore temps. Si le mal d'amour et le désespoir n'avaient pas tant entamé ma volonté, j'aurais sans doute trouvé le courage de la prévenir ainsi que Riley. Mais je ne pus me résoudre à lui faire face. Je craignais la clairvoyance de son esprit, je redoutais qu'elle devine que ma trahison avait outrepassé la simple mise en gage de la robe, qu'elle allait infiniment plus loin.

Ainsi, après m'être habillé et avoir mis mes lunettes de soleil, je sortis furtivement de l'immeuble comme un voleur, passai à pas de loup devant la porte des Ha-p'i, résolu à me réfugier dans l'anonymat des rues.

J'errai toute la journée en des lieux inconnus, perdu dans un engourdissement physique et mental que vrillait parfois mon désespoir amoureux comme un coup de clairon ou l'appel mélancolique d'un cor de chasse dans l'air automnal. Car ce jour-là me parut le premier de l'automne. Vers midi, après avoir sans doute parcouru des kilomètres, une suture céda dans mon esprit, une gravité émotionnelle inexplicable mais inéluctable m'attira vers l'Upper West Side, hantant mon cœur comme le fantôme d'une âme morte parcourt une maison abandonnée, le site d'un bonheur remémoré dont on n'a accepté ni pardonné la perte.

Vers six heures et demie, l'heure convenue de mon rendez-vous avec Yin-mi, j'entrai dans un bar et cherchai le numéro de téléphone de Li dans un annuaire, puis je l'appelai de la cabine. Mes mains devinrent moites quand j'entendis la sonnerie à l'autre bout de la ligne. Alors que je renonçais, elle décrocha. Sa voix était indistincte, brouillée. J'entendis de la musique, un rire en arrière-fond sonore.

« Li ?

— Qui est-ce ? demanda-t-elle sèchement.

— C'est moi, répondis-je. Sun I.

— *Qui ?* répéta-t-elle. Parlez plus fort, je vous entends très mal. »

J'hésitai une seconde de trop. « Encore un cinglé », l'entendis-je dire avant le déclic signalant qu'elle avait raccroché.

Quand je tentai de l'appeler une deuxième fois, la ligne était occupée.

Pendant toute l'heure qui précéda la tombée de la nuit, je décrivis des cercles concentriques de plus en plus serrés autour de son immeuble, poussé à cette trajectoire pitoyable et désespérée non tant par la hardiesse que par la fascination. Sous le couvert de la nuit tombante, mes instincts reprirent le dessus. De l'autre côté de la rue, j'examinai l'immeuble comme un cambrioleur prépare son coup. A travers les doubles portes vitrées de l'entrée, je voyais Ramon à son poste habituel devant la cabine téléphonique, où il vitupérait violemment son interlocuteur invisible en passant de temps à autre son peigne dans sa chevelure noire gominée. Prenant mon courage à deux mains, je m'aventurai au coin de l'immeuble, puis dans la cour proprement dite où je me figeai pour compter les rectangles éclairés des fenêtres en essayant de décider laquelle était la sienne. Une silhouette apparaissait parfois, qui faisait accélérer mon pouls.

Alors que j'observais ainsi la façade, une main serra brusquement mon bras juste au-dessus du coude. Ramon me dévisagea avec un sourire éclatant à défaut d'être tout à fait amical. « Qu'est-ce qui t'arrive, mec ?

— Je regardais seulement... »

Il ferma les yeux d'un air entendu. « Ouais ouais, je sais. Mais elle veut pas té voir, mec. Pigé ? Tu férais mieux dé té casser avant que j'appelle les flics. Comprendé ? »

Je hochai la tête et fis mine de partir.

« Pét-être ta queue, elle est pas assez grosse por elle », se moqua-t-il alors que je battais honteusement en retraite.

J'entrai dans le premier magasin de spiritueux que je trouvai, achetai une pinte de Dry Sack, puis errai vers l'est au-delà des avenues — Amsterdam, Columbus, Central Park West — jusque dans le parc où je m'assis sur un banc vert, ouvris mon sac en papier et débouchai ma bouteille. J'avais déjà bu plusieurs rasades quand un clochard noir d'âge mûr et nanti d'une canne, arriva en clopinant sur l'allée asphaltée, s'immobilisa devant moi et se mit à m'observer. Je bus une autre rasade comme s'il n'était pas là.

« Vas-y doucement, mon frère, conseilla-t-il. La nuit va êt' longue. » Il attendit ma réaction. N'en obtenant aucune, il me demanda : « J'peux m'asseoir ? »

Interprétant mon silence comme un acquiescement, il s'installa à côté de moi, la canne entre les genoux. Je tournai brièvement la tête pour le regarder. Un spécimen typique de l'espèce, pensai-je : casquette en tricot, barbe poivre et sel, yeux injectés de sang, manteau élimé, déchiré.

« On dirait qu't'as du vague-à-l'âme, reprit-il. Y a sûrement une femme là-d'sous. » Il secoua la tête d'un air pessimiste. « Hum, hum, c'est bien t'jours la même chose, s'pas ? Chicano, Chinois, Indien ou Négro — tous dans la même galère — z'attrapent tous la même maladie. L'cafard, v'là la maladie, et c'est les femmes les responsables. J'connais point Hong Kong, mon frère, mais j'vais t'montrer comment qu'on chante ça à Santee, en Ca'oline du Sud. » Il s'arrêta pour se racler la gorge, cracha et tendit la main vers moi sans me regarder. « Laisse-moi d'abord boire un coup, si ça t'fait rien. »

Je lui passai la bouteille. Il mit le goulot contre ses lèvres, renversa la tête, but une longue gorgée, puis s'essuya la bouche sur la manche de son manteau. Il tendit la bouteille à bout de bras en louchant comme pour lire l'étiquette à travers le sac en papier. « C'est quoi ?

— Dry Sack, répondis-je.

— Mouah. Ça vaut pas le Thunderbird, mais y s'laisse boire. » Me la rendant, il se mit à chanter d'une voix tremblante, râpeuse, de baryton qui n'était pas désagréable :

« J'demande au Seigneur, envoie-moi un ange,
Oui j'demande au Seigneur qu'y m'envoie un ange.
Et le Seigneur dit : j'peux pas t'envoyer d'ange, Murphy,
Mais j't'envoie Thelma Brown. »

Il rit et se frappa la cuisse. « Ouais, nom de Dieu, j'connais pas Hong Kong, mais v'la comment qu'on chante à Santee. » Il m'observa encore. « Tu m'as l'air d'traverser une sale passe, mon frère. Faut qu'tu r'montes la pente. Bon Dieu ! Pourquoi qu'tu t'en fais ? T'es jeune. T'as la santé. Tu vas trouver une aut' gonzesse. Tiens bon, fiston, j'ai connu ça, moi aussi, et pire encore. Maintenant, j'suis passé d'l'aut' côté. » Il secoua la tête. « Y m'reste pus d'espoir. Et y a pas d'médicament pour guérir mon mal. Une gonzesse m'a coulé. R'garde ça. » Il se pencha en avant sur le banc. « Tu sais c'que c'est ? Rhumatismes artitculaires. J'peux pus m'pencher. A force de dormir en plein air. Ma gonzesse m'a flanqué à la po'te de chez moi. Tu vois mon lacet, mon frère ? Y peut rester dénoué pendant une semaine, tant que j'peux pas m'pencher. Faut qu'j'attente l'été. Montre un peu de charité chrétienne. Donne-moi enco' un coup de pinard, et puis noue mon lacet pour moi. Je t'le d'mande, mon frère. S'il te plaît. »

Ému par son apparente sincérité et son appel pitoyable, je me penchai vers sa chaussure.

Alors il me frappa — pour couronner ma soirée en quelque sorte. Son bagou aurait dû me mettre la puce à l'oreille, je suppose, mais j'étais trop innocent, et puis le spectacle d'un compagnon d'infortune réclamant mon aide m'avait ému. Je crois que sa canne était plombée, car lorsque je me réveillai, en plus d'une terrible migraine, j'avais une bosse sur la tempe, de la taille d'un œuf. Une croûte de sang coagulé s'était formée dans mes cheveux. Plusieurs heures devaient s'être écoulées. J'étais allongé à plat ventre dans l'herbe à côté du banc. La rosée froide était tombée sur moi. Je la voyais scintiller sur l'herbe à la lueur d'un réverbère.

Il avait pris le peu d'argent que j'avais sur moi et aimablement dédaigné mon porte-feuille vide. La bouteille manquait aussi, ce qui était plus grave. Je me consolai en me félicitant d'avoir laissé sous mon matelas le plus gros de ma fortune nouvelle. Je me sentis brusquement inquiet pour sa sécurité, mais ce souci fut bientôt englouti sous la masse de mes autres tracas et tribulations. Titubant sur des jambes cotonneuses, je m'éloignai en zigzaguant, non pas vers la sécurité des rues éclairées, mais en m'enfonçant plus avant dans le parc pour aboutir enfin sur le tertre du réservoir. Je me sentais un peu ivre, peut-être fiévreux. Claquant des dents, les doigts serrés autour des maillons de la chaîne, je regardai par-delà le bassin la maison de pierre qui abritait la pompe et, au sud-est, le cœur de la ville. La nuit était d'une clarté presque surnaturelle. Au-dessus de ma tête, je vis la courbe de la Voie Lactée semblable à un andain découpé dans les champs de ténèbres par une faux scintillante. L'eau était si tranquille que je distinguai le reflet palpitant des étoiles, comme des glaçons qui se heurtent dans quelque sombre cocktail ; et sur l'autre rive du réservoir, silhouettes noires se détachant contre le ciel, les gratte-ciel du centre ville — Chrysler, Pan Am, l'aiguille spectrale de l'Empire State — immenses carcinomes mouchetés d'étoiles. Ce fut sans doute la première fois que la puissante magie de la cité me frappa, me toucha vraiment comme une baguette magique, au point que je me demandai si je pourrais jamais rentrer chez moi.

Je retournai sur mes pas, puis m'allongeai dans une dépression du terrain, protégé du regard des rares passants par un rempart de rochers. Là, je me rendormis, cette fois naturellement, et fus bientôt recouvert par la rosée si froide.

Je passai mon dimanche à retarder l'inévitable retour aux responsabilités et aux récriminations ; mes pérégrinations furent passablement plus courtes que la veille et je marchai d'un pas apathique, déprimé, car j'avais épuisé presque toutes mes réserves d'énergie nerveuse. De temps à autre, je m'inquiétai pour l'argent que j'avais abandonné dans ma chambre. La nuit était tombée depuis longtemps quand je regagnai Mulberry Street, montant sur la terrasse par l'escalier d'incendie pour échapper momentanément à toute embuscade morale.

On avait punaisé un billet sur la porte de ma chambre ; je ne le lus pas avant d'être entré et d'avoir vérifié que l'argent était toujours là. Poussant un soupir de soulagement, je retrouvai mes esprits et, avec un curieux retard, fus submergé de dégoût par mon comportement des deux derniers jours. Je m'interrogeai sur moi-même. Que m'arrivait-il ? Sans même essayer de répondre, je déchirai l'enveloppe en soupirant. C'était un mot de Yin-mi :

Cher Sun I,
Si je ne t'ai pas vu avant, je te supplie de me faire signe dès ton retour. Je suis très inquiète. Le Père Riley et moi t'avons attendu toute la nuit dernière. Nous avons contacté la police, les hôpitaux — partout. Je suis sûre qu'il t'est arrivé une chose terrible ; sinon tu nous aurais donné de tes nouvelles. J'espère tant me tromper. Ç'a été un fiasco à l'église ; nous avons frisé l'émeute. Mais c'est sans importance, pourvu que tu sois sain et sauf. Si tu es blessé ou que tu as des ennuis, laisse-moi essayer de t'aider, s'il te plaît. Peu importe de quoi il s'agit. En tout cas, viens me voir dès que tu auras lu ceci. A n'importe quelle heure. *Je t'en prie.*

Baisers,
Yin-mi.

Refoulant un sanglot dans ma gorge, je froissai la feuille de papier et la lançai vers les ordures. Dans mon état, je ne pouvais me résoudre à une confrontation avec Yin-mi. Pareille épreuve m'aurait achevé, car je me sentais déjà fissuré, parcouru d'une crevasse fine comme un cheveu qui courait des hémisphères de mon cerveau à mes testicules en passant par les ventricules de mon cœur partagé.

Pris de rêves paranoïaques, je me réveillai plusieurs fois trempé de sueur et retins mon souffle pour écouter d'hypothétiques bruits de pas sur le gravier du toit. Chaque fois, je vérifiais fébrilement que l'argent était toujours sous mon matelas, je me levais pour m'assurer que la porte était bien fermée à clef et verrouillée. Plusieurs fois pendant la nuit, je comptais et recomptais les billets pour me calmer, puis me jurais de consacrer le premier dollar de ma nouvelle fortune à l'achat d'une chaîne de sécurité. Le soulagement, voire un étrange bonheur m'envahissaient après ces mauvais rêves quand je glissais la main sous le matelas et caressais le sac en papier. Sa présence me rassurait comme une amulette, un talisman.

Ensuite je retrouvais ma lucidité et réalisais que cet argent était la seule chose susceptible d'intéresser un cambrioleur. Avec un vif déplaisir, je me rappelai une citation : « Les richesses amassées provoquent les voleurs. » Où avais-je lu cela ? Mais oui, évidemment, le *Tao-tö king*. Comment avais-je pu l'oublier ?

A l'aube seulement ces rêves et ces fantasmes se dissipèrent. Je compris pour la première fois la terreur élémentaire des animaux et pourquoi ils chantent avec un tel abandon au lever du soleil. Bien qu'encore plus fatigué que la veille, je fus heureux de me lever. Dans l'espoir de sortir discrètement, je commençai aussitôt de m'habiller, enfilant mon pantalon et ma chemise, puis nouant ma cravate devant le miroir.

Le ciel, qui pâlissait à peine au-dessus des toits, métamorphosait gratte-ciel et immeubles en sombres masses noires, quand Yin-mi apparut. Sans prendre la peine de frapper, elle ouvrit brusquement la porte. J'aperçus son visage dans le miroir.

« Dieu merci », dit-elle d'une voix soulagée autant qu'épuisée. Elle s'effondra sur une chaise, enfouit son visage entre ses mains et fondit en larmes.

Surpris par l'intensité de son émotion, honteux et touché, je me tournai vers elle.

Elle leva vers moi des yeux noyés mais extatiques. « Je me suis tellement inquiétée. Tu n'as pas vu mon mot ?

— Si, je l'ai lu, répondis-je.
— Tu aurais dû me réveiller. Je te le demandais.
— Excuse-moi, dis-je simplement.
— Ça ne fait rien. Je suppose que tu n'as pas voulu déranger. »

Je me vis rougir dans le miroir et me remis à nouer ma cravate.

« Alors ? » s'enquit-elle enfin avec une nuance d'impatience qui me surprit.

Avant que je n'aie pu répondre, elle était debout à mes côtés. « Que s'est-il passé ? » m'interrogea-t-elle avec angoisse en touchant ma blessure à la tête. « Hou-ou. » Elle grimaça, inspira l'air entre ses dents. « Tu es blessé.

— Ce n'est rien, lui dis-je.
— Comment est-ce arrivé ?
— Je me suis fait attaquer.
— J'en étais sûre. Je savais qu'il t'était arrivé quelque chose », dit-elle d'une voix triomphale et vindicative. « Où étais-tu ?
— Dans l'Upper West Side, répondis-je. Dans le parc.
— Ça va maintenant ?
— Mais oui.
— Tu es sûr ?
— Absolument.
— Merci, Seigneur. J'ai dit au Père Riley que tu ne nous ferais pas attendre pour rien, que tu étais sans doute blessé, dans l'incapacité de nous prévenir. As-tu vu un médecin ?
— Ce n'est pas si grave que ça.
— Le cuir chevelu est fendu. » Elle effleura ma plaie. « Ça fait mal ? Laisse-moi la nettoyer ; ta blessure est sale. » Elle mouilla une serviette sous le robinet. Puis, debout sur la pointe des pieds, elle se mit à frotter doucement. « Raconte-moi ce qui s'est passé, me demanda-t-elle doucement, absorbée par le va-et-vient de sa main, sans tenter de croiser mon regard. Et puis... nous pourrons peut-être remettre la conférence à la semaine prochaine, dit-elle d'une voix distraite, comme si elle pensait tout haut.
— Il n'y aura pas de conférence, dis-je en immobilisant sa main.
— Que veux-tu dire ? demanda-t-elle, perplexe, en dégageant doucement son bras. Pourquoi ?
— Parce que je n'ai plus la robe. »

La détresse apparut sur son visage, puis elle haussa les sourcils en commençant à comprendre. « Oh non, murmura-t-elle, on ne te l'a pas volée ? »

L'espace d'un instant, je fus tenté de mentir, mais une fois encore quelque chose dans l'expression de Yin-mi m'en empêcha. Je secouai la tête. « Non.
— Alors que s'est-il passé ? » Elle devint fébrile. « Je ne comprends pas. Qu'est-il arrivé à la robe ? Que faisais-tu dans l'Upper West Side ?
— Je suis allé m'y promener après l'avoir gagée, dis-je en me tournant de nouveau vers le miroir pour fermer mon bouton de col et faire coulisser mon nœud de cravate.
— Tu l'as gagée ! »
Je hochai la tête. « Vendredi après-midi, à notre retour.
— Mais tu ne m'as rien dit. Et quand je suis passée samedi, tu... » Elle se tut, devinant la vérité. Dans le miroir, mon visage était pâle, éteint, funèbre, presque cadavérique. Yin-mi me dévisagea bouche bée. Puis son regard devint aussi profond que ma trahison. Je saisis mon modeste fardeau — le sac en papier —, écartai doucement Yin-mi de mon chemin en marmonnant une excuse lamentable, puis sortis. Je descendis l'escalier quatre à quatre jusqu'à la rue en sachant que je ne pourrais plus jamais supporter la grande solennité de son regard, ni l'oublier.

Je ne réfléchis pas à notre rencontre en marchant vers mon travail. Le désespoir et l'engourdissement avaient pris possession de moi. Mes pensées suivirent le même cours que la veille au soir, comme si rien ne les avait interrompues. Je m'inquiétais un peu à l'idée d'être seul dans les rues. Après l'agression de la veille, cela paraissait le comble de la folie : en risquer une autre, voire une mort brutale, pour... quoi ? Un sac en papier ? Je me rassurai cependant en me convainquant que personne n'aurait pu se douter que je détenais une grosse somme d'argent. Hormis un léger renflement de ma poche, d'ailleurs soigneusement dissimulé sous ma veste, rien ne transparaissait sur ma physionomie. Mais ne me trompais-je pas ? Je devins nerveux. Mon regard n'était-il pas excessivement dégagé, ma démarche ne trahissait-elle pas une inquiétude nouvelle que le voleur expérimenté savait repérer dans une foule de passants anonymes ? Se pouvait-il que mon trésor fût « décompté » sur mon visage ?

« Absurde ! me dis-je en jetant des regards inquiets de droite et de gauche. Pure paranoïa. » Et pourtant, ces angoisses n'étaient-elles pas partiellement justifiées ? Car je sentais qu'un changement, peut-être minime mais indubitable, s'était produit en moi. L'enseignement que j'avais reçu en Chine ne disait-il pas que le moindre changement dans une partie — et peu importait sa subtilité — finissait toujours par se transmettre au tout ? N'était-il pas indiscutable que le visage d'un homme reflétait son état mental ? Cette conviction déclencha en moi une révélation mineure. Je commençai de comprendre l'inscrutabilité, l'absence d'expression qui animent, ou plutôt figent les visages qui circulent sans cesse sur Wall Street, de Trinity jusqu'au fleuve. C'était l'attitude défensive de l'âme, un biais pour s'anesthésier et supporter les harcèlements de l'état de siège permanent. Ces hommes et ces femmes étaient obsédés par la peur de perdre ce qu'ils avaient consacré leur vie à amasser ; ils surveillaient leurs richesses avec une telle férocité que la joie des plaisirs simples avait quitté leurs yeux et que leurs visages, comme ceux des caméléons, prenaient la couleur des murailles du canyon financier de Wall Street.

Pour des raisons de convenance personnelle, je décidai de singer leurs manières pendant la journée, d'endosser le masque de la peur typique de Wall Street : l'œil vitreux, triste et humide, les épaules tombantes. Accélérant le pas, je regardai tantôt droit devant moi, tantôt à mes pieds, j'adoptai une démarche raide, j'évitai les yeux des passants, je foulai ces sentiers battus avec une expression alternativement lugubre et vide, comme les milliers d'êtres anonymes que je voyais quotidiennement franchir le tourniquet du métro, produits homogènes d'une seule et unique chaîne de montage. Mais pour moi, ce n'était qu'un déguisement temporaire, un masque endossé pour la journée afin de tromper les voleurs, d'égarer mes éventuels agresseurs. En dessous, mes valeurs, mon mépris pour cette Babylone, ma pitié et ma compassion pour mes semblables restaient intacts.

Et pourtant... cela aussi était le Tao, me rappelai-je. Je désespérai de jamais mettre au jour le cœur inimaginable de cet horrible paradoxe.

En tout cas, je trouvai mon rôle dangereusement facile à jouer. Car n'avais-je pas déjà adopté inconsciemment l'article le plus important de la panoplie ? Je parle, bien sûr, des lunettes de soleil : « Si tu ne portes pas de lunettes, la lumière somptueuse et éblouissante de la Cité d'Émeraude t'aveuglera. Même ceux qui habitent cette Cité doivent porter des lunettes nuit et jour. » Cette phrase du *Magicien d'Oz*, dont j'avais acheté un exemplaire à mon retour de Sands Point, obsédait mon esprit et renforçait ma conviction.

Quand j'atteignis Trinity, ma démarche avait perdu toute élasticité. Je me sentais déjà épuisé et terrifié à l'idée de la journée qui m'attendait. Je rencontrai Wo dans l'entrée de la Bourse. Je ne l'avais pas vu depuis un certain temps.

« On dirait que tu commences à accuser le coup, remarqua-t-il en me voyant. Finis les bonds de cabri et les déclarations enthousiastes ? »

Ses paroles déclenchèrent mon hostilité. Son amalgame me déplut souverainement ; à mon corps défendant, il semblait m'assimiler à la triste et cynique fraternité des bons à rien et autres traîne-savates dont il était le président et le héraut désabusé. Je dus rougir d'embarras et d'amertume avant de me maîtriser. Ensuite, haussant les épaules avec indifférence, je m'éloignai sans un mot.

De nouveau seul, je me repus secrètement de savoir que je m'étais définitivement placé hors de l'atteinte mesquine de ses calomnies, et ce grâce au contenu de ma poche. Je fus alors la proie d'un sentiment contraire ; j'eus honte de m'enorgueillir de posséder une chose qui, cinq minutes plus tôt, m'avait occasionné tant de sueurs froides. Je me promis solennellement de ne jamais oublier que j'agissais dans le seul but de la connaissance pure, et non par lucre, et à l'avenir de ne jamais perdre de vue, fût-ce un instant, cette distinction cruciale.

Malgré ma résolution et tous mes efforts, tandis que je traversais les couloirs de la Bourse, je me sentis submergé d'une suffisance nouvelle et grisante en regardant mes collègues. Ce fut plus fort que moi. L'idée pernicieuse s'insinua malgré moi dans mon esprit : je les avais en quelque sorte dépassés, nous n'appartenions plus à la même classe. Cette conviction ne s'accompagna d'aucune rancune ; je ressentis au contraire une compassion accrue pour les messagers, j'applaudis leurs efforts dans la compétition sociale. Pourtant, je me demandais en secret combien parmi eux possédaient les qualités requises pour s'élever au-dessus de leur position, une position dont l'indignité ne m'était jamais apparue aussi évidente. Mais je m'étais maintenant hissé hors de leur atteinte pour m'intégrer au monde de la finance. A quoi tenait ma différence ? Je possédais des actions, ou presque. Maintenant j'avais une part du gâteau, je participais à l'avenir de l'Amérique. Du moins en avais-je les moyens.

Quand je trouvai Kahn, je me déchargeai sur lui de tous les soucis, de tous les espoirs et les peurs que la simple et passagère possession de tant d'argent liquide avait éveillés en moi. Enlaçant paternellement mes épaules, il m'entraîna à l'écart de l'activité tapageuse du parquet, puis me consola en ces termes : « Tu vois, petit ? Ça a déjà commencé. » Il opina vigoureusement du chef avec une mine satisfaite.

« Quoi donc ? demandai-je, désarçonné par son ellipse.

— Une seule nuit d'insomnie t'en a plus appris sur le Dow que toutes les semaines que tu as passées ici à observer le match sur la touche, assister à des conférences, poser des questions... Voilà les fameux "soucis dus aux responsabilités". » Son expression de sympathie intransigeante me rappela le regard de Tsin quand il m'avait observé prendre l'embout de la pipe entre mes lèvres et aspirer ma première bouffée d'opium. Il y avait une nouvelle intimité entre nous, un sentiment de fraternité approfondie. Malgré toute la fierté que j'en tirai, je me sentis un peu mal à l'aise ; car cela ressemblait vaguement à l'amitié désespérée, cynique, qui naît parmi les hors-la-loi et les hommes déchus.

« Ceci est la réalité, Sonny, dit-il, et tu viens d'en acquérir un morceau.

— La réalité ? demandai-je. Je n'en suis pas si sûr. Souvenez-vous que ceci est seulement temporaire. »

Il sourit en secouant la tête. « Tu vas découvrir qu'il est beaucoup plus facile d'y entrer que d'en sortir.

— J'investis mon argent, Kahn, l'informai-je, pas mon cœur.

— *Facilis descensus averno*, dit-il, tandis que son regard, loin de m'observer, me traversait.

— Est-ce yiddish ? »

Il sourit. « Presque. C'est du latin.

— Et qu'est-ce que ça veut dire ?

— "Il est facile de descendre en enfer, traduisit-il. Nuit et jour, les portes de Dis restent ouvertes ; mais retrouver notre chemin et remonter vers l'air supérieur, voilà le labeur, voilà la tâche." »

Nos regards se croisèrent.

« Bon ! » dit-il enfin d'une voix tonnante et joyeuse qui signalait un changement de sujet, une saute d'humeur. « Maintenant il s'agit de parler *affaires*, non ? » Il me prit par le bras avec des airs de conspirateur et m'entraîna vers le parquet. « Je crois avoir trouvé la combine idéale ! »

5

« Allons-y, petit, je vais te mettre au parfum », commença Kahn tandis que nous attaquions notre déjeuner. Il succomba alors à une crise d'hilarité imprévue et recracha la moitié d'un éclair. « Désolé, petit, mais comme je vais te l'expliquer, c'est une affaire qui pue. » Il me tendit une serviette en papier. « "Mettre au parfum." C'est pas mal. Il faudra que j'en parle à Norm.
— Que voulez-vous dire ? demandai-je non sans agacement en essuyant des morceaux de pâtisserie sur ma veste.
— Tu vas comprendre à mesure que je t'expliquerai, dit-il. C'est une combine à laquelle je travaille depuis plus d'un an. Je ne t'en ai pas parlé parce qu'elle en est encore à une phase fort délicate, strictement top secret. J'ai un ami du Mont-Nebo, Norman Murdfeld. Il est négociant à la Chambre de Commerce de Chicago. Spécialisé dans le maïs. Vu sa connaissance du circuit, il a pu mettre son grain de sel dans une ravissante petite opération manigancée par un certain Hiram Cox. Hiram est un culterreux, mais on s'en bat l'œil, pas vrai ? Comme Hiram manquait un peu de liquidités, il a proposé une part des actions à Norm, lequel m'a aussitôt rencardé. J'ai sauté sur l'occasion, bien que ça m'ait coûté la peau des fesses. Mon fauteuil et l'immeuble que je possède sont hypothéqués, mais nous sommes à la veille de rembourser nos dettes. Et si je ne me goure pas, notre opération donnera à la progression de Pepsi-Cola des allures de pet de lapin. Je suis sérieux, petit. Ce sera peut-être le coup de maître de ma carrière. Si tout se passe bien, je vais pouvoir fermer boutique pour faire le tour du monde, monter une écurie à Palm Beach ou Boca Raton. Et comme je t'aime bien, petit, je vais te mettre dans le coup.
— De quoi s'agit-il ?
— Une seconde, pour l'amour du ciel ! Ne sois donc pas si impatient ! me rabroua-t-il. Tout te sera révélé en temps voulu. » Il s'adossa confortablement dans son fauteuil tournant pour jouir de son avantage à son aise et engloutir quelques éclairs supplémentaires. Puis il lécha lentement ses doigts, qu'il faisait sortir un à un de sa bouche arrondie en cul de poule avec un geste guilleret et un bruit de succion rappelant un baiser mouillé. « Tu n'en veux pas un ? susurra-t-il avec une politesse perverse.
— Kahn ! le menaçai-je.

— D'accord, concéda-t-il en se penchant brusquement en avant pour planter ses coudes sur le bureau. Voilà de quoi il s'agit : leasing à long terme sur équipement agricole lourd. » Il s'interrompit pour me donner le temps d'applaudir.

Je lui adressai un regard inexpressif.

« Tu sais bien, les tracteurs, les moissonneuses-batteuses, ce genre de matériel, expliqua-t-il. Tu ne vois pas ? Le leasing est pourtant un adorable petit concept. Personne n'y a pensé. Avant c'était toujours : vous achetez, c'est à vous, migraines comprises. Notre idée est avantageuse pour les deux parties : pour le fermier, parce qu'il n'a pas de lourd investissement initial, que les traites sont nettement moins importantes que la normale, et surtout parce qu'il n'a pas à se soucier de l'entretien des machines ; avantageuse pour la compagnie, car nous avons découvert qu'il nous suffisait de créer un service après-leasing efficace pour que le fermier paie notre matériel à notre place, si bien qu'au bout d'une location-vente de six à huit ans, nous avons des tracteurs à moitié neufs, et sans lever le petit doigt, des tracteurs prêts à repartir pour un autre leasing — et dès lors, chaque dollar qui tombe est pur bénéfice. En clair, des tracteurs gratuits.

— Comment s'appelle la compagnie ? »

Il pouffa. « C'est là le coup de génie. Tu es prêt ? Jane Doe. »

Je lui lançai le même regard inexpressif.

« Bon Dieu, petit ! Réveille-toi ! John Deere, tu ne piges pas ? Le leader de l'industrie ? C'est une idée de génie, non ? Pense aux possibilités publicitaires ! "Une alternative plus séduisante." "La meilleure moitié de l'industrie." Imagine ça. » Il tendit ses paumes vers moi comme un magicien, ouvrit un rideau imaginaire, esquissa un cadre entre nos têtes. « Un joli petit champ de maïs apparaît sur ton écran de télé, avec une jolie petite fermière : salopette, nattes tressées, casquettes de base-ball, tout le tintouin. Les mains serrées dans le dos, elle frotte ses orteils dans la poussière avec un air gêné, embarrassé. La caméra s'approche, elle se met à parler : "Bonjour l'Amérique. Je lui envoie une lettre de rupture, à mon Cher John. A partir d'aujourd'hui, c'est chacun pour soi." Brusquement, elle lève les yeux et sourit, mi-fille de ferme, mi-femme fatale. "Les pires choses ont une fin, vous savez", dit-elle. Puis elle jette sa casquette en l'air, secoue ses cheveux, enlève sa salopette pour révéler un bikini à paillettes. "Je suis libérée ! beugle-t-elle. Je n'ai plus que des clopinettes à payer !" » Il se tut, attendant mon avis. « Qu'en dis-tu ? C'est de la poésie hermétique ou quoi ?

— Je ne sais pas, Kahn, tergiversai-je. Ça me paraît intéressant, mais...

— D'accord, d'accord, concéda-t-il de mauvaise grâce, vexé par mon manque d'enthousiasme, tu n'as pas encore entendu le meilleur. Jusqu'ici, Doe se négocie sur le comptoir. Elle s'en sort bien d'ailleurs. Mais nous sommes tous d'accord — "nous", c'est-à-dire Norm, Hiram, moi, plus quelques autres, notre petit cartel d'initiés : nous avons besoin d'un marché plus large. Nous allons donc postuler pour la Bourse.

— Postuler ?

— Oui. Introduire Doe à la Bourse de New York. En d'autres termes, entrer dans le club huppé des têtes de série.

— Ce doit être difficile ? »

Il fit tourner sa main tendue vers moi. « Cosi cosi.

— Avons-nous une chance de réussir ?

— A notre avis, c'est dans la poche, dit-il. Nous avons déjà fait tout le travail d'approche. C'est à ce stade de l'opération que je suis intervenu. Norm et moi avons passé un temps fou à préparer un dossier en béton — tu sais, les plans comptables et tutti quanti —, de quoi épater les gars chargés d'examiner les candidatures d'introduction en Bourse. Jane Doe répond sans problème aux critères de capital et de profit net requis par la Bourse. Mais nous n'avions pas de holdings suffisamment diversifiés, pas assez d'actions détenues par un grand nombre d'actionnaires. Nous avons donc conclu un accord avec les gars du Bureau d'Introduction en Bourse : ils nous laissent entrer dans leur petit cénacle, et nous proposons au public un grand nombre d'actions — un demi-million à dix dollars pièce. Les gars ont marché comme un seul homme, gobé le morceau sans sourciller. Le reste est pure formalité. Il nous reste à présenter notre demande au Bureau des Gouverneurs. Je tiens d'un copain qu'ils vont examiner notre candidature jeudi prochain. La semaine prochaine, notre nom devrait apparaître en lettres lumineuses avec ceux de tous les grands garçons (et filles), la dernière, la plus incroyable trouvaille de l'Amérique ! Ceux qui n'auront pas encore entendu parler de nous feront bien de dresser l'oreille, et vite ! Si nous pouvons créer une dynamique juste après l'offre publique, notre fortune est assurée. Nous risquons de nous retrouver avec une pagaille bien juteuse sur les bras.

— Et si vous ne pouvez pas — créer une dynamique ?

— Ah ! » Il vrilla un index vers le plafond, s'enfonça dans son fauteuil. « Voilà une bonne question, à laquelle nous avons déjà réfléchi. Elle a une réponse ! » Il bondit de nouveau en avant, fixa sur moi un regard perçant. « Maintenant ouvre grand tes oreilles, petit, parce que c'est la partie la plus futée de l'affaire, et la plus secrète. Vois-tu, en qualité de membre du cartel, je peux te révéler que Jane Doe couve d'un œil concupiscent une petite compagnie nommée Sui Generis, qui n'a l'air de rien mais qui est en fait un vrai bijou. Sui possède une série d'usines qui fabriquent de la nourriture pour animaux et des engrais, les deux produits sous le label Sui. Je peux t'annoncer en exclusivité que, depuis trois semaines, nous sommes en négociations top secret avec le fondateur et propriétaire de ladite compagnie, un certain Olaf Tryggvesson. Il n'y a pas à tortiller : Olaf est un infect fils de pute, mais c'est aussi un génie à sa façon. Il a eu une idée, et l'a joliment rentabilisée. Mais il est trop stupide et borné pour comprendre que son idée va beaucoup plus loin que le bricolage local qu'il a mis sur pied. Il est trop con et conservateur. Norm m'a dit qu'il s'est pointé à la réunion en camion Ford, avec une salopette de travail, une barbe de trois jours, qu'il a passé le plus clair de son temps à se curer les dents, chiquer du tabac et cracher son jus dans un gobelet plastique. Il avait du purin sur les bottes, qu'il a refusé d'essuyer "pour raisons morales", soulignant que "la merde a fait fait d'lui c'qu'il était". Touchant, tu ne trouves pas ?

« Mais laisse-moi te dire ce qu'il possède au fin fond de son trou et que nous désirons si fort. Tu vois, il achète le maïs au fermier, puis il le convertit en aliments pour animaux, qu'il revend au fermier, avec bénéfice, pour qu'il nourrisse ses cochons. Ensuite, quand ledit aliment a été pour ainsi dire reconstitué une deuxième fois, il l'achète sous forme de purin pour une bouchée de pain, lequel purin il convertit en engrais grâce à un procédé breveté que Bunge essaie de lui piquer depuis des années. Olaf l'a inventé lui-même. Je ne prétends pas comprendre toutes les subtilités du procédé, je sais seulement qu'il s'agit grosso modo d'une machine destinée à faciliter la conversion des excréments animaux. Elle s'appelle la Dynamo Fécale, ou, plus familièrement, Pompe à Purin. Voilà pourquoi j'ai ri tout à l'heure en t'annonçant que j'allais te mettre au parfum. Vois-tu, l'invention de ce bon vieil Olaf consiste littéralement à convertir la merde en fric. En saisis-tu toutes les conséquences ?

— Je ne crois pas, hésitai-je. Vous pourriez peut-être éclairer ma lanterne.

— Notre bonhomme vend aux fermiers des aliments fort chers, qu'il rachète des clopinettes sous forme de purin. Chimiquement c'est quasiment la même chose, mais le prix de la marchandise a chuté vertigineusement à cause d'une petite "dépréciation" du produit. Tu me Sui ? Il gagne sur les deux tableaux ! » Kahn s'enflammait. « C'est la bonne affaire garantie ! Olaf vend ses aliments, il attend que le prix dégringole, et il rachète bon marché le purin. "Acheter à bas prix, vendre cher" — telle pourrait être sa devise. En revanche, dans ce genre de tractation boursière, on ne sait jamais si le Dow va monter ou descendre. La valeur que tu t'attendais à voir descendre grimpe et tu te retrouves Gros-Jean comme devant. Olaf n'a jamais ce genre de problème. Son affaire bénéficie de la garantie or, d'une sorte d'assurance purin. Ses informations sont infaillibles, en provenance directe de Dieu le Père. Elles sont liées au cycle de la nature lui-même. En tant que taoïste, tu devrais piger ça, petit. Olaf sait qu'indépendamment de toutes les tuiles qui peuvent s'abattre sur lui (sur nous) dans ce monde imprévisible et sournois, les aliments perdent imperturbablement de leur valeur après avoir traversé les intestins d'un cochon. Raisonnement classique, logique irréprochable. A grande échelle, cela pourrait révolutionner l'agriculture dans la ceinture du maïs. Seulement voilà : ce bon vieil Olaf commence à avoir le vertige quand il pense à des nombres de plus de cinq chiffres et à des lieux situés en dehors des limites de son comté. Et puis il n'a plus vingt ans. Il est prêt à vendre son affaire et à prendre sa retraite avec un revenu confortable, pour élever des génisses de concours, des porcs de comices agricoles — tout ce que tu voudras — pendant ses loisirs. Il a déjà passé un accord de principe avec le cartel pour lui vendre une part de Sui. Mais il n'est pas né de la dernière pluie, le salopard. Tu connais l'une de ses conditions ? Il exige d'être partiellement payé en actions de Jane Doe. Ah, il sait reconnaître une bonne affaire... Enfin, tout est quasiment réglé. Olaf dit qu'il veut rester au courant des décisions de nous autres, "cheunes plan-pecs". Mais dès qu'il verra la couleur d'un chèque certifié, m'est avis qu'il lâchera du lest et se mettra à table.

« Maintenant, voilà le scénario, petit. Une valeur nouvelle et bon marché, associée à une idée excitante, fait son apparition à la Bourse. Le public est sceptique. Les gens hésitent, renâclent. Mais elle se met à bouger. De gros paquets d'actions sont échangés. » Kahn sourit. (Je me rappelle parfaitement ce sourire.) « Jane Doe commence à se trémousser, si tu vois ce que je veux dire. Alors la nouvelle tombe d'une fusion imminente. "Avec qui ?" demande le peuple. "Sui Generis", répond ingénument quelqu'un (moi). "Qu'est-ce que c'est que ce nom à la gomme ?" insiste le peuple. "Bunge essaie de l'acheter depuis des années. Voyez-vous, Sui Generis possède un procédé secret..." Bunge ? Procédé secret ? Alors la psychologie prend le relais. Jane Doe grimpe dans la liste des plus forts pourcentages d'activité du *Wall Street Journal*, puis dans la liste des valeurs les plus actives. Le grand public a la puce à l'oreille. Les pékins de province commencent à mordre à l'hameçon, les Techniciens relèvent quelques secousses sismiques dans leurs Oscillateurs d'Activité. Quand notre chérie est cotée quinze dollars, même les vieux brontosaures comme Merrill Lynch dressent leur lourde tête somnolente pour humer l'air, dans lequel flotte une forte odeur de purin. Les grands manitous désignent un spécialiste pour enquêter sur la compagnie et publier un rapport. Probablement Melvin Piper. A qui s'adresse-t-il ? Tu as deviné, à ton fidèle serviteur. "Hé, Aaron, tu as entendu parler de cette compagnie Jane Doe ?" "Qui ? Moi ?" je demande. Alors je lui fais un topo, je le mets au parfum du purin, le tout servi sur une truelle. "Ça va grimper à quarante, je lui dis, peut-être cinquante." "Sainte merde !" s'écrie-t-il en sortant de mon bureau comme un boulet de canon. La semaine suivante, notre chère enfant figure en bonne place dans la *Lettre Boursière* de Merrill Lynch. Avec l'appréciation A A A. "Excellentes chances de croissance. Peu ou pas de risques." Vingt millions d'investisseurs, de Trifouillis-les-Oies, Maine, à San Luis Opisbo trouvent la missive dans leur boîte à lettres, et le téléphone se met à sonner. Les messagers de la maison ne sont pas assez nombreux pour exécuter les ordres. "Hé, Aaron, tu pourrais pas me donner un petit coup de main, s'il te plaît ?" "Naturellement ! je dis. Toujours prêt à rendre service à un ami." Je me mets alors à exécuter des ordres sur ma propre valeur ! Et voilà le travail, petit. Nous avons décroché la lune. C'est impeccable, imparable. Tes mille dollars représentent cent actions. Si tout va bien, tu devrais récupérer trois mille dollars sans problème, peut-être quatre ou cinq mille. Pas mal pour un débutant, non ? Alors qu'en dis-tu ? Tu marches ? »

J'entendis à peine sa question, tant j'étais fasciné par le spectacle de son visage rubicond, radieux, rayonnant de joie. Tandis qu'il me révélait son plan de bataille, je ne l'avais jamais vu aussi heureux. Et je songeais seulement à ce qu'il m'avait dit quelques jours plus tôt : Wall Street est le test suprême de la personnalité.

« Kahn, répondis-je enfin, vous savez que j'ai confiance en vous. Sans vous, j'ignore où j'en serais.

— Merci, petit, ça fait plaisir à entendre.

— Mais dites-moi, tout cela est-il vraiment légal ? »

Il soupira en s'adossant à son fauteuil. « D'accord, petit, puisque tu me poses cette question, je vais te répondre en toute franchise. Notre opération comporte évidemment quelques démarches qui ne sont pas complètement casher. Mais bon Dieu, qui a jamais entendu parler de porc casher ? Vrai ou faux ? Laisse donc un peu tes SO au vestiaire. Quelquefois sur le champ de bataille — et jusque dans les épis de maïs — un soldat doit improviser, prendre quelques initiatives. Mais dans cette affaire, nous n'entreprenons rien qui n'ait déjà été pratiqué, et par les meilleurs. Et puis qui s'en apercevra ? Mais pour répondre à ta question, oui, nous allons négocier grâce à des informations internes à la compagnie — c'est-à-dire la fusion imminente Jane Doe-Sui —, mais ce genre de procédé n'a rien de nouveau. On ne peut pas gâcher les grandes occasions en pinaillant sur la morale de l'opération. Faut voir grand, petit ! Pense à Napoléon, pense à César, à Rothschild ! Bon Dieu, si tout se passe comme je m'y attends, ce sera un coup aussi fabuleux que ceux d'Ahasvérus. Je compte gagner ainsi mes galons d'authentiques J R — ce qui signifie évidemment Juif Rrant. Et tu seras dans le même bateau que moi, petit. Toute hésitation me paraît superflue. Tu es déjà dans le bain, maintenant nage ! A mon avis, ce coup est ton meilleur pari. Il promet d'être lucratif et expéditif. Je te promets que nous ne faisons rien qui n'ait été consacré de longue date par la tradition de Wall Street. Et puis rappelle-toi que j'ai tes intérêts à cœur. Nom de nom je ne te réclamerai même pas de commission. Et que sont cent actions ? On ne peut pas dire que ta participation soit décisive pour l'aventure. Sonny, j'essaie de te rendre service. Dois-je me justifier ?

— Très bien, Kahn, capitulai-je. Si vous m'assurez que tout vous semble correct, je vous crois. »

Il essuya son front. « Jésus Marie, petit ! C'est la vente la plus difficile que j'aie jamais faite. Merci quand même. J'apprécie ton vote de... (il sourit) Kahn-fiance... » Il me dévisagea. « Qu'y a-t-il, Sonny ?

— Je pensais à quelque chose.

— Quoi donc ? s'enquit-il.

— Vous connaissez la compagnie Sui Generis ? »

Il hocha la tête. « Évidemment. Quelle question !

— Eh bien, voici quelques jours j'ai consulté l'oracle pour savoir ce que je devais faire, et j'ai tiré l'hexagramme numéro dix-sept, "L'Attente".

— Et alors ?

— Eh bien, son nom chinois est *Sui*.

— Sans déconner ! » s'écria-t-il, impressionné. Je remarquai qu'il avait porté la main à son bracelet. « Tu te souviens de ce que je t'ai dit, petit ? Nous devrions utiliser ce truc, le *Yi king*. Ce serait un péché de se l'interdire ! »

Ainsi que Kahn l'avait prévu, l'introduction en Bourse se déroula sans anicroche. Mais ce qu'il n'avait pas prévu, ce qu'on ne pouvait raisonnablement lui reprocher, fut que l'offre d'achat des cinq cent mille actions de Jane Doe coïncida exactement avec les derniers soubresauts de l'euphorie financière estivale qui, telle une bête de somme harassée, s'écroula dans la poussière, où elle reçut le coup de grâce du gouvernement qui eut le toupet d'annoncer une récession économique imprévue touchant surtout le secteur agricole, où une récolte exceptionnelle avait entraîné des surplus et amené les prix à un niveau inférieur aux prévisions. Ce coup de malchance mit cependant du beurre dans le purin d'Olaf (si j'ose dire), lui permettant d'acheter sa matière première encore moins cher qu'auparavant. Dans l'enthousiasme qui suivit cette aubaine inespérée, il songea que l'heure de sa retraite n'avait peut-être pas encore sonné.

« Ne te ronge pas le sang, me rassura Kahn. Il suffit de rouvrir les négociations avec lui, de lui proposer quelques "adjuvants" supplémentaires. Cela prendra simplement un peu plus de temps que prévu. »

Le temps. Comme le lecteur ne l'ignore pas, c'était une denrée qui, du moins pour moi, se faisait rare. Il n'y avait pourtant rien à faire. Je dus attendre.

Pendant la journée, je faisais contre mauvaise fortune bon cœur. Mes activités de messager, relativement aisées mais absorbantes, occupaient mon esprit. Même en ce domaine, mon comportement subit quelques changements insidieux. Après la quasi-catatonie des premiers jours, due à mes Salamalecs Orientaux, j'avais adopté l'attitude du « lèche-cul modèle », pour reprendre l'expression de Kahn ; toujours gai et poli, je ne rechignais devant aucune demande inhabituelle (ainsi, quand un spécialiste me réclamait cinquante centimètres de papier-toilette pour se moucher et qu'il m'accordait l'insigne honneur de transporter jusqu'à une poubelle le tiède résidu de ses déjections nasales). Mais je me mis alors à adopter certains tics et attitudes du courtier — dangereuse et insupportable présomption chez un esclave de mon rang. Je restais parfois planté au milieu du parquet, hypnotisé par le ruban lumineux qui défilait au-dessus des têtes, annonçant au monde entier ses messages hiéroglyphiques que seuls les initiés savaient déchiffrer, par le spectacle grandiose et animé de l'avenir qui se déroulait sous mes yeux (avec une minute de retard). Jane Doe, bien sûr, était la légende que j'espérais voir divulguée au monde étonné. Malgré ma frustration, cela devint une sorte de plaisir abstrait. La Steel allait-elle gagner un huitième de point lors de la prochaine cotation, ou le perdre ? Bien que totalement désintéressé, du moins financièrement parlant, je ne pouvais résister à la tentation d'essayer de deviner. Quand je me trompais, je haussais les épaules avec fatalisme et me consolais de cette maxime éternelle : « Personne ne sait, n'a su et ne saura jamais ce qui va se passer sur le marché. » Quand mes prévisions se trouvaient confirmées, je haussai également les épaules. « Un coup de chance », me disais-je, mais en sentant le rouge me monter aux joues avec une bouffée de profonde satisfaction, intimement persuadé que par une dispense spéciale du destin dont les termes me demeuraient énigmatiques j'avais reçu le pouvoir de prédire l'avenir, un pouvoir qui me plaçait d'emblée dans une catégorie à part, m'exemptait des lois de fer de la gravitation qui régissaient la vie étriquée du commun des mortels. J'étais sans doute convaincu de jouir d'une intimité nouvelle avec le Dow, d'une connaissance parfaitement incommensurable avec tout ce que j'avais vécu auparavant quand, debout sur la touche, « j'observais sans participer ».

Kahn tolérait volontiers ces écarts. A l'heure du déjeuner dans son bureau, alors qu'avec une expression inquiète et concentrée je composais sans cesse le symbole DOE sur le clavier du Quotron, il arpentait silencieusement la pièce comme une mère de famille surveille sa fille enceinte dont l'époux est parti au front pour se battre dans les tranchées. J'étais cette jeune femme ; tous mes espoirs, toutes mes peurs se concentraient sur l'avenir ; Kahn incarnait mon aimable refuge, solide, sérieux, sympathique. Cette analogie provoqua chez moi une crispation d'angoisse. Je me demandai si je n'avais pas deviné l'état d'esprit de ma mère pendant les mois de son isolement et de sa grossesse. Je compris brusquement pourquoi Hsiao avait déclaré que les violentes alternances d'espoir et de peur — à l'origine de la mystérieuse parabole de la robe — s'étaient sûrement transmises par une sorte d'osmose spirituelle au fœtus qui grandissait et somnolait dans son ventre. Si tel était bien le cas, ce va-et-vient épuisant s'était gravé en moi et venait d'être réactivé après des années d'engourdissement. Car avant d'investir une chose qui m'appartînt, avant d'avoir quelque chose à perdre, je n'avais jamais compris la souffrance, tantôt insupportable, tantôt seulement triste, qui constitue le cœur de l'attente, dans l'espoir comme dans la peur.

Mais mon attente, mon désir était lié à une autre cause que la robe, et peut-être avec une intensité plus forte : à Li. Inséparables de ce tourment et aussi vifs, je ressentais remords et culpabilité envers Yin-mi. Voilà pourquoi les nuits étaient pour moi encore plus douloureuses que les jours, après que la sonnerie eut résonné et Wall Street expulsé ses hôtes. J'enviais les banlieusards, malgré leurs plaintes fort justifiées concernant leurs horaires draconiens et leurs longues heures harassantes de trajets quotidiens ; ils arrivaient chez eux épuisés, après la tombée de la nuit, mangeaient un dîner réchauffé, parcouraient un rapport, écoutaient les nouvelles, s'endormaient, puis le lendemain se levaient alors que toute la maison dormait encore, prenaient une douche, se hâtaient d'attraper leur train. Leur vie était solitaire, morne, vide, mais au moins, pensais-je, leur nuit n'était pas peuplée de mes terreurs. Leurs habitudes les protégeaient du vertige des temps morts, leur épargnaient les loisirs où l'âme échappe par nécessité sinon par choix à ses routines habituelles, où, se tournant vers elle-même, elle découvre qu'elle n'a plus de lieu, ayant détruit ou simplement perdu le chemin de son sanctuaire originel. Car telle était exactement ma situation. Ce lieu intérieur à moi-même, ces blocs de roc lentement usés par l'eau du torrent, cet espace frais ombragé par les arbres où les rayons adoucis du soleil filtraient à travers les branches jusqu'au tapis d'aiguilles de pin et faisaient scintiller les grains de poussière qui dansaient sur d'invisibles courants d'air, ce lieu où je m'étais autrefois retiré pour chanter... je le cherchais sans pouvoir le trouver. Car un tel endroit n'existe pas dans l'âme des financiers et des marchands (ce que j'étais devenu à ma modeste manière et par choix), ou s'il existe parfois dans une âme, celle-ci est aussi rare que le « juste » qu'Abraham cherchait à Sodome. Un tel endroit est en effet la marque d'une gratitude silencieuse envers la vie, et de toutes les passions engendrées par le Dow, c'est peut-être la plus rare.

D'abord, je ne me sentais pas reconnaissant, mais anxieux et insatisfait. Je me faisais pitié. Je voulais voir Li, mais savais que mon désir n'était pas partagé. De plus, chaque fois que je pensais à elle, l'image de Yin-mi se dressait devant moi comme un ange vengeur. Réciproquement, quand je désirais la consolation de sa compagnie comme par le passé, la pensée de

Li me paralysait, cela et la conviction d'avoir trahi la cadette. Dans les premiers jours de cette période d'attente, peu après notre conversation, Yinmi me laissa une fois un billet sur ma porte. « Comment pourrais-je comprendre si tu refuses de m'expliquer ? » Mais quelle explication aurais-je pu fournir ? C'était bien là le problème. Il n'y en avait tout bonnement pas. Et dans ces conditions, totalement coupable, totalement vulnérable, je ne pouvais me résoudre à lui faire face.

Je tentai de reprendre la méditation, mais mon esprit se révolta et je ne pus contrôler les nuées tourbillonnantes de visions accélérées qui, résultat d'un système particulier de hautes et basses pressions émotionnelles, jaillissaient du sol desséché de ma conscience comme les tornades du Kansas dont j'avais entendu parler et qui arrachent les maisons à leurs fondations avant de les réduire en miettes quand elles retombent à terre. Ce vortex de souffrances et de frustrations lançait à toute volée des morceaux de meubles brisés et de bruyants couvercles de poubelle contre les murs de mon cerveau jusqu'à ce que, moi-même emporté dans le cœur du cyclone, je ne pusse plus entendre le son de mon propre souffle.

Chaque matin en arrivant à Wall Street, je cherchais anxieusement Kahn dans l'espoir d'une bonne nouvelle. Mais à chaque fois, il m'adressait simplement un sourire de sympathie et haussait les épaules. « Pas encore, petit », disait-il.

Nous avions beau approcher rapidement de l'équinoxe d'automne, les journées semblaient s'allonger au parquet. Le Dow se languissait dans le pot au noir financier voisin de l'équateur. Tous les jours, les prophètes du marché prédisaient que le vent allait bientôt se lever et pousser les Indicateurs vers de nouvelles latitudes graphiques où simples matelots et officiers supérieurs découvriraient des climats plus hospitaliers et revigorants. Les investisseurs réagissaient à leurs prophéties par une apathie redoublée.

« Quand, Kahn ? Quand ? demandai-je continuellement.

— Que veux-tu que je fasse, petit ? me rétorquait-il en haussant les épaules, la bouche en cœur. Je suis infiniment plus mouillé que toi dans cette affaire, n'oublie pas ça. Mais vois-tu, une valeur nouvelle ne démarre pas sur les chapeaux de roue dans un marché aussi amorphe. Attention, elle ne va pas mourir ; elle somnole, c'est tout. Sois patient, petit. Sui viendra à notre rescousse. Et les dividendes seront généreux, ou bien devrais-je dire *Generis* ? » Il sourit. « De temps en temps, le marché est comme ça, ni ours ni taureau, mais entre les deux, un monstre saisi de vague à l'âme qui possède les pires défauts des deux animaux sus-cités, et aucune de leurs qualités, ni lard ni cochon, ni chair ni poisson. Moi, j'appelle ça un marché taurours.

— Un marché triste ?

— Ouais, triste et hybride, morose et monstrueux, dit-il en pouffant.

— Okay, Kahn, admis-je. J'espère seulement qu'il va bientôt se passer quelque chose. »

Il s'avéra que mon vœu fut exaucé. Mais j'aurais peut-être dû le préciser un peu. Quelque chose bougea pour de bon. Quittant sa léthargie, le marché manifesta un comportement ni ours ni taureau, même pas taurours, mais évoquant davantage la marmotte qui sort de son terrier à la fin de l'hiver, frotte ses yeux endormis avec la fourrure de ses pattes, regarde autour d'elle le paysage hivernal éclaboussé de lumière, bondit de frayeur en apercevant l'ombre de son corps sur la neige, puis retourne ventre à terre dans son terrier en poussant des glapissements paniqués, pour hiberner quelques semaines de plus. Ainsi du Dow. Avec un volume d'échanges relativement modeste, il dressa sa petite tête perverse hors de son trou, regarda la longue plaine monotone de sa récente somnolence, puis battit promptement en retraite de quinze points et se rendormit. Personne n'apprécia cette sortie sournoise, à l'exception des Techniciens qui profitèrent de l'occasion pour organiser une conférence et baptiser une nouvelle formation qu'avec un humour surprenant de leur part ils nommèrent « Le Chien de Prairie Renversé » (par contraste, je suppose, avec l'espèce domestique).

Des articles firent leur apparition dans tous les journaux importants, surmontés de titres comme « Le Dow est-il Mort (ou Seulement dans le Coma) ? » et « Possédez-Vous Trop d'Actions ? » Des courtiers au pourcentage s'inscrivirent au chômage. Dans toute l'Amérique, des milliers de ménagères penaudes abandonnèrent leurs clubs de femmes pour leurs fourneaux sous les sourires paternalistes de leurs maris narquois et leurs suffisants « Je te l'avais bien dit ! ». Les spécialistes organisèrent de discrètes parties de jacquet dans la grande salle de la Bourse où tombaient parfois d'horribles silences longs de plusieurs secondes entre la frappe d'une transaction sur le télétype et l'annonce de la suivante. Les avions à destination des Bahamas furent pris d'assaut ; en fin de journée les employés chargés du nettoiement poussèrent infiniment plus de paniers repas que d'habitude au bout de leurs balais.

Et Olaf tergiversait toujours. Cette situation dura tout le mois de septembre et jusqu'en octobre. Le temps me semblait se précipiter vers mon échéance, mais Jane Doe n'avait toujours pas doublé — ce dont j'avais besoin pour récupérer ma mise initiale et payer mes intérêts. En fait, la dernière et plus incroyable trouvaille de l'Amérique avait chuté de dix à huit dollars trois quarts. Même Kahn commençait à être nerveux. Quant à moi, j'étais au bord de la panique.

Parce qu'il me restait seulement deux semaines, je me résolus à l'expédient désespéré d'une visite à Mme Chin pour lui demander une prolongation. J'aurais mieux fait de m'abstenir ; mon acte était tout sauf rationnel.

De retour de mon travail, je me rasai, versai un peu d'eau de toilette sur mes joues, enfilai une chemise propre, faisant de mon faible mieux pour mettre toutes les chances de mon côté avant la désagréable confrontation.

Je les rencontrai, elle et Fan-ku, sur le palier, alors qu'ils sortaient pour la soirée. Quand elle m'aperçut, une lueur d'intuition — quelque chose de vieux, de rusé comme le Sphinx, le calcul mais aussi l'indifférence quant au résultat (presque de l'indifférence) — scintilla dans sa pupille. « Alors, Sun I, dit-elle, je suppose que tu m'apportes l'argent ? » Elle dit cela avec une gravité et une réserve qui interdisaient toute plaisanterie, qu'elle eût écartée comme une impertinence.

« J'aimerais justement discuter de cela avec vous », expliquai-je, mettant dans ma voix toute la confiance et l'entrain dont j'étais capable, espérant qu'ils seraient contagieux.

Elle me regarda sombrement (apparemment immunisée depuis belle lurette). « Qu'y a-t-il donc à discuter ? N'avons-nous pas conclu un marché ? C'était alors le moment de parler ; maintenant, place à l'action. Apporte-moi d'abord l'argent, ensuite nous pourrons parler tant que tu voudras. Mais jusque-là, nous sommes ennemis. N'essaie pas de me convaincre de faire une exception pour toi. Je suis dure, Sun I. Si tu l'ignores encore, apprends-le ce soir. Ma parole est de fer ; je ne la romprai pas. Je ne fais aucune exception. Jamais. Où serais-je donc si chaque client qui franchit ma porte pour m'apporter son bibelot "d'une valeur incalculable" parvenait à biaiser avec les termes de notre contrat ? Je vais te dire où je serais : je n'aurais pas quitté Shanghai ; j'y lirais encore les lignes de la main, j'y ferais encore le trottoir pour les marins. Non, aujourd'hui je porte de la soie comme une dame (elle haussa les sourcils, sa main lissa son flanc, prouvant fièrement ses dires), comme tu peux voir. Maintenant, c'est moi qui achète. » Avec un sourire figé, elle jeta un bref regard en direction de Fan-ku. « Voilà ce qui importe au bout du compte, Sun I. Et j'y suis arrivée à force de dureté. C'est une leçon qu'il te reste à apprendre. Ne me demande pas de modifier notre accord. C'est pure perte de temps. Mais je te prie de m'excuser. Nous avons rendez-vous et nous sommes pressés. Ne reviens pas sans l'argent. Il te reste encore deux semaines. Tu trouveras peut-être une solution. Sinon, considère la robe comme irrémédiablement perdue. Alors, si tu le désires, nous pourrons redevenir amis. Ou si ton cœur ne parvient pas à se défaire de cette possession, nous serons des voisins polis et distants. Ou bien tu pourras même partir. Cela ne me fait ni chaud ni froid. » Elle passa son bras à celui de son compagnon, puis ils s'éloignèrent, la douairière et son mignon, ce couple macabre qui me laissa muet et abattu, en proie à une frustration qui vira à la fureur, émit quelques bouffées sulfureuses avant de s'évaporer et de faire place au désespoir.

Quand le lendemain je parlai de cet incident à Kahn, il me donna une tape affectueuse dans le dos et dit : « C'est sans doute ce qu'on appelle "la discipline du marché". »

6

Le destin ou la chance voulut que ce jour-là quelques faveurs commencèrent à frémir dans le gréement supérieur de Wall Street parmi les haubans et les voiles de perroquet ; lentement, laborieusement, le Dow appareilla et retrouva un semblant de vitalité. En d'autres termes, le marché bougea timidement. Les négociants de tous les États et les grands investisseurs institutionnels dressèrent leur museau humide dans la brise pour la humer, certains attirés par le doux parfum d'un espoir naissant, d'autres par l'odeur du sang, quelques-uns, tels Kahn et moi, à l'affût de la moindre bouffée du purin de l'Illinois. Dix jours avant la date fatidique, alors que je m'étais déjà résolu, non sans douleur, à me détacher émotionnellement de la robe, Jane Doe connut un étrange soubresaut et ouvrit à un demi-point au-dessus de sa cotation de clôture de la veille. Était-ce le premier symptôme d'une santé retrouvée, ou bien le dernier sursaut spasmodique d'un cœur à l'agonie ? Malheureusement, je n'avais sous la main aucun cardiologue patenté pour me révéler le sens de cette fluctuation dans son électrocardiogramme, c'est-à-dire aucun Technicien pour interpréter les graphiques. Je n'eus cependant besoin d'aucun avis autorisé pour comprendre le sens des chiffres que je découvris soudain sur l'écran :

$$\text{DOE}$$
$$10\ 000 \text{ à } 9\ ^{1/4}$$

Dix mille actions à neuf dollars un quart ! Jane venait d'accéder à une notoriété instantanée ; son nom apparut en lettres de feu sur le Grand Tableau, comme celui d'une actrice célèbre sur la marquise d'un palace de Las Vegas ! Pendant que dans tout le pays les courtiers sirotaient leur deuxième tasse de café en lisant le *Wall Street Journal* et entre deux paragraphes soulignaient une cotation d'une main distraite, Jane Doe défia l'Amérique étonnée, s'exhiba impudemment devant un public médusé, se mêla vaillamment à l'aristocratie de la finance (Lady Jane en personne, maîtresse de maison distinguée et organisatrice de la fête !), s'imposa dans le club huppé qui réunissait les grands de ce monde sur le Tableau. Cinq minutes inoubliables sous les projecteurs de la Liste des Valeurs les plus Actives, avant que le cerbère intraitable ne la raccompagne dans l'air glacé de l'anonymat !

« Kahn ! Kahn ! » m'écriai-je en me ruant follement vers les ascenseurs à travers une foule de ronds-de-cuir et de courtiers apathiques qui me dévisagèrent comme si j'avais perdu la tête. « Vous avez vu ? » hurlai-je en pénétrant dans son bureau comme un ouragan. Je me campai devant lui, à bout de souffle.

Il était assis à sa table ; contrairement à mon attente, il n'était pas confortablement renversé dans son fauteuil tournant et ne tirait pas sur un cigare avec une mine réjouie — non, il avait le dos voûté comme un animal coupable qui attend la rebuffade de son maître. Il fixait son Quotron d'un regard inquiet en marmonnant entre ses dents. Il y avait une pile de papiers déchirés devant lui, des certificats de transactions bancaires qu'il avait réduits en minuscules confetti comme en prévision d'une fête. Mais à voir son expression lugubre, leur pile évoquait davantage le tas de détritus rassemblés par l'équipe de nettoyage après la fin des réjouissances.

« Vous n'avez pas vu la bande ? demandai-je. Un paquet de Doe a été annoncé à neuf un quart, une hausse de trois quarts de dollar par rapport à la clôture. »

Il leva les yeux avec un air amusé et sans joie, avec la morosité hypocondriaque et figée du lait caillé. « Sans blague ? rétorqua-t-il d'une voix sarcastique.

— Qu'y a-t-il, Kahn ? demandai-je, passant brusquement de l'exaltation à l'angoisse. C'est bien ce que nous attendions, n'est-ce pas ? Je veux dire, c'est seulement un début, nous sommes toujours dans la zone rouge. Mais il faut bien commencer quelque part, non ? »

Il fixait toujours sur moi son regard silencieux et caustique.

« Qu'y a-t-il ? Vous ne comprenez pas ce que ça veut dire ? »

Il eut un rire amer. « Oh, que si ! dit-il enfin. Ça veut dire que j'ai encore claqué six mille dollars, plus ou moins.

— Six mille dollars ? De quoi parlez-vous ?

— J'avais acheté ces actions moins de trois dollars. Hier, je les ai revendues à huit dollars et cinq huitièmes. Et quand je les ai rachetées ce matin, elles avaient encore grimpé de cinq huitièmes. Multiplie par dix mille, ça fait dans les six mille dollars, pas vrai ?

— Vous... ? éructai-je d'une voix de fausset dans l'intention de l'interroger et de l'accuser, tout en pointant machinalement l'index sur lui.

— Ne montre pas du doigt, me rabroua-t-il. Ça ne se fait pas. Je croyais te l'avoir déjà dit. »

Je regardai mon index, puis le repliai.

« Maintenant, si le BEV désire pinailler sur l'étiquette..., railla-t-il avec un gloussement amer.

— Ce n'est pas illégal ?

— Quoi donc ? Vendre mes propres actions, puis les racheter ? » Il rit. « Manipulation indiscutable. Manœuvre interdite par le Décret sur l'Echange des Valeurs de 1934. On appelle ça maquiller la bande — une vente fictive. Depuis quelques jours, je bidouillais des petits paquets d'actions, mais cette fois je n'y suis pas allé par quatre chemins. » L'ombre d'un sourire traversa son visage.

« Mais pourquoi ? l'implorai-je.

— Pourquoi ? *Pourquoi* ? C'est toi qui me demandes ça ? Depuis plusieurs semaines tu ne tiens pas en place, tu me demandes dix fois, vingt fois par jour : "Quand, Kahn ? Quand ?" Que veux-tu que je te dise ? J'en ai eu marre !

— Vous n'êtes pas sérieux ?

— Tout ce qu'il y a de plus sérieux, petit ! »

Mes lèvres se mirent à trembler. Je sentis que j'allais pleurer.

« Okay, okay — ce n'est pas seulement de ta faute. Jésus Marie ! Ne sois donc pas aussi nebbish, petit ! Mes emprunts touchent à leur terme. Mes créanciers commencent à s'impatienter. Si l'affaire Sui n'aboutit pas bientôt, je risque de perdre mon immeuble ainsi que mes autres biens, y compris celui sur lequel je pose mon honorable postérieur. Puisque je suis acculé, autant jouer mon va-tout, non ? Je veux dire : pas de gloire sans couilles. Il faut bien qu'un couillon se dévoue pour mettre la machine en branle, n'est-ce pas ? Mais trêve de métaphores érotiques ! » Il sourit en touchant son bracelet de cuivre. « Enfin, tu me comprends.

— Et si vous vous faites prendre ?

— Ne t'inquiète pas pour ça, m'assura-t-il. J'ai acheté par l'intermédiaire d'un compte numéroté de la Second Jersey Hi-Fidelity. Souviens-toi, petit, je suis peut-être un schlemiel, mais je ne suis pas un schlimazel. Je sais effacer mes traces. Personne ne pourra remonter jusqu'à moi.

— Mais...

— Foin de si et de mais ! » Comme la baguette d'un chef d'orchestre, sa main traça une virgule en l'air. « S'il te plaît un peu de confiance ! Tu veux voir ton capital fructifier, n'est-ce pas ? Tu veux récupérer la robe de mariée de ta maman — ou de fiançailles, je ne sais plus —, tu veux la retirer du mont de piété, oui ou non ? »

J'acquiesçai avec hésitation.

« Eh bien c'est la seule façon de procéder. Aussi évident que le nez au milieu du visage. »

Je scrutai stupidement l'appendice charnu susnommé, dont le volume en effet impressionnant semblait contenir dans le tréfonds de ses fosses, tel le précieux sperme renfermé dans le « foudre d'Heidelberg » du crâne de la baleine, la réponse qui attendait mon exhumation.

« Je sais bien que mes méthodes ne sont pas très orthodoxes, reconnut-il, mais elles produisent des résultats. Tu peux me croire, petit. »

A cet instant précis, des coups pressés retentirent à la porte. Kahn s'adossa dans son fauteuil, endossa son masque d'homme d'affaires. « Entrez, dit-il d'une voix sonore.

— Excuse-moi de te déranger, Aaron », dit un petit homme chauve en poussant la porte. Son front était presque aussi large — comparé à son menton et au bas de son visage — et brillant qu'un globe lumineux. Une paire de lourdes lunettes à monture de corne avait glissé le long de l'arête peu marquée de son nez minuscule, si bien qu'il regardait par-dessus avec une expression de moquerie vaniteuse dont il semblait parfaitement inconscient. « Je me demandais juste si tu savais quelque chose sur cette valeur, ah... comment est-ce déjà ? » Il jeta un coup d'œil à son bloc-notes. « Ah ouais (il ricana) Jane Doe. Mike Burnside, de la Morgan Guaranty, vient de me passer un coup de fil à ce sujet. J'ai promis de le renseigner.

— Jane Doe ? demanda Kahn en allumant calmement son cigare. Quel drôle de nom... » Il croisa mon regard tandis qu'il aspirait goulûment les premières bouffées et que ses bajoues se gonflaient et se creusaient comme celles du poisson embrasseur ; son œil, d'ailleurs, était aussi froid et inexpressif, du moins pour un observateur naïf, car moi j'y décelai aussitôt certaine lueur maîtrisée que j'avais appris à connaître.

Notre visiteur pouffa d'un rire nerveux. « Je trouve aussi le nom assez original, hasarda-t-il avec un sourire embarrassé.

— Peut-être l'est-il, peut-être l'est-il », opina Kahn d'un air patelin en éteignant son allumette. Il examina sa cendre sans la moindre hâte. « Tu sais, Piper, je crois me rappeler quelque chose à propos de cette valeur.

— Magnifique ! s'écria son interlocuteur en franchissant le seuil du bureau.

— Tu connais M. Piper, n'est-ce pas ? Il travaille à Merrill Lynch... » Il appuya légèrement les derniers mots en m'adressant un regard lourd de sous-entendus.

« Ravi de vous rencontrer, lui-dis-je en lui tendant la main.

— Moi aussi, moi aussi, répliqua Piper avec impatience et un bref hochement de tête dans ma direction.

— Tu allais sortir, n'est-ce pas petit ? me dit Kahn. Va donc nous chercher deux cafés. »

Piper prit son stylo et s'assit vivement au bord du fauteuil, près de la table de Kahn.

Je me glissai dans le rôle que m'avait donné Kahn. « Avec du lait et du sucre, M. Piper ? demandai-je d'une voix suave.

— Oui, *merci*, répondit-il avec agacement.

— Un café noir pour moi, dit Kahn, comme d'habitude. Et, oh, Sonny, me rappela-t-il, n'oublie pas de fermer la porte derrière toi. »

Je le regardai cyniquement ; il m'adressa alors le clin d'œil le plus appuyé que j'aie jamais vu.

« Okay, Aaron, entendis-je Piper commencer, alors pourquoi tout ce tintouin ?

— Ce "purin" mon cher, ce "purin", répondit Kahn en se vautrant dans son fauteuil et lançant vers le plafond un rond de fumée. Voilà le mot qui vaut un million de dollars. »

Je ne le reconnais pas sans honte, mais une fois dans le couloir je succombai à une crise de fou rire inextinguible. Plié en deux, je me frappai le genou en pensant à l'admirable fourberie de Kahn. Quelle chutzpah ! Quel pro ! Quel Kahn ! m'extasiai-je, en proie à une admiration idolâtre. Et quelle chance pour moi d'être tombé sur un maître si accompli ! Je me repris pourtant en songeant à la gravité de la situation ; mon enthousiasme subit une sorte de transmutation alchimique en son contraire, l'or se métamorphosa en plomb. Qu'avait-il fait ? Que manigançait-il ? Et moi-même, quel rôle jouais-je ? Je me reprochai violemment mon accès de démence, chassai impitoyablement tout plaisir et, le visage grave, allai chercher le café.

A mon retour, l'offre avait grimpé de cinq huitièmes, et la demande de sept huitièmes de dollar. A son poste dans l'annexe du parquet nommée le garage, le spécialiste suivait une formation accélérée de Jane Doe.

« Où en est Doe ? » entendis-je un courtier s'écrier en brandissant un ordre de transaction.

Avant que le spécialiste n'ait eu le temps de répondre, un autre courtier cria : « Cent Doe à sept huitièmes !

— Vendu ! » rétorqua aussitôt le premier.

Quelques secondes après, un plus gros poisson mordit à l'appât. La bande annonça une importante transaction.

DOE
1 000 à 10

Et voilà ! Jane Doe retournait dans la zone noire ! En fin de journée, elle avait grimpé à 12, après avoir brièvement atteint 12 1/2 avant de retomber. J'étais ravi. Fier ? *Fier ?* Je fus submergé d'une telle fierté que, renonçant temporairement à toute lucidité, je jurai sur-le-champ de rester fidèle à mon a-doe-rable chérie jusqu'à ce que la mort nous sépare. Ce fut ma première expérience de « gagnant », et je commençai à comprendre la satisfaction et le prestige immenses qui en découlaient, comme s'il se fût agi d'un signe objectif, quantifiable, de la faveur divine. Quelle extase ! Cette grande dame, l'Impératrice Dow-airière, avait croisé mon regard et opiné du chef ! Je compris pourquoi tant d'hommes renonçaient à tout, coupaient les ponts derrière eux, abandonnaient tous les plaisirs et les espoirs mineurs pour celui de se gagner les faveurs de la Grande Veuve Noire, et sans pouvoir se bercer de l'illusion consolatrice que la cruelle araignée les accepterait dans le soleil consolateur de sa bienveillance ou ferait par amour une exception pour eux, elle qui avait satisfait son appétit au fil des ans en dévorant leurs prédécesseurs. Emporté par la joie, je ressentis une extase inédite, une impression de pouvoir qui frisait l'omnipotence. Bizarrement, cela n'entama pas le nœud d'angoisse et de culpabilité qui m'avait serré la gorge lorsque Kahn m'avait avoué son forfait, et cela ne résolut pas davantage les contradictions grandissantes de ma vie personnelle. Tous ces éléments antagonistes coexistaient en moi, comme un feu de joie qui rugit sur une place publique et se nourrit des combustibles les plus hétéroclites.

Cette sensation devint plus fréquente et intense quand, les jours suivants, Doe accéléra son irrésistible ascension au parquet, atteignant la cote mirobolante de seize dollars à la fin de la semaine. Pendant le week-end, apparemment grisé par le succès de notre protégée, Olaf capitula enfin et donna carte blanche à Kahn ainsi qu'au cartel. Lundi matin, une semaine avant l'échéance, la fusion fut annoncée.

Ce matin-là, l'ouverture de Doe fut retardée d'une heure à cause des ordres de transactions hâtifs passés par les courtiers qui avaient bénéficié d'une fuite de l'information. Quand le spécialiste eut terminé ses comptes, il fixa la cote de Jane à dix-huit dollars. Kahn et moi débordions de joie. Négligeant nos devoirs respectifs au parquet, nous sablâmes le champagne dans son bureau en fumant des barreaux de chaise, dansâmes quelques gigues endiablées, entonnâmes des chants de victoire en *doe* majeur et triomphal. La semaine passa comme une apothéose prolongée. Nous suivions les événements d'heure en heure. Il y eut des moments de folie où tout semblait possible, d'autres de désespoir où la fièvre du lucre paraissait terrasser notre bien-aimée, l'abandonner lasse et apathique au bord de l'effondrement. Mais elle reprenait bientôt du poil de la bête, anéantissait les lignes de résistance ennemies, si bien que jeudi, à la veille de la date cruciale, elle atteignit pour la première fois, brièvement, la cote de vingt dollars, avant de battre en retraite à dix-neuf trois quarts à la fermeture.

« Alors, Kahn, croyez-vous que nous toucherons au but demain ? lui demandai-je avec un pincement de cœur tandis que nous sortions dans la rue.

— Je le crois, dit-il en soulignant les syllabes avec un calme paternel. Dans l'état actuel des choses, je ne vois pas ce qui pourrait nous en empêcher. » Il fouilla brièvement mon visage. « Mais si je ne me trompe, ce n'est pas ce qui doit te préoccuper, petit ? »

Je le regardai avec perplexité.

« Que vas-tu faire ? me demanda-t-il.

— Eh bien, récupérer la robe, évidemment ! répondis-je, surpris. C'est le but de toute l'opération, non ? »

Il acquiesça lentement, avec une moue paternaliste. « Bien sûr, bien sûr, que ferais-tu d'autre ?

— Kahn ?

— Hmmm ?

— Vous me cachez quelque chose. Quoi donc ? »

Il haussa les épaules d'un air faussement dégagé. « Oh, je ne sais pas.

— Kahn !

— Très bien, petit, dit-il en reprenant son sérieux. Je me disais en mon for intérieur : il se débarrasse de ses actions, il récupère sa sacrée robe, et après ?

— Que voulez-vous dire ?

— Ça t'avance à quoi ? Tu te retrouves à la case départ, non ? Bon, d'accord, tu auras eu ta petite histoire d'amour avec le Dow, ton aventure d'un soir. Mais es-tu naïf au point de croire que tu as tout compris de lui ?

— Non, bien sûr que non, concédai-je.

— Bon. Arrête-moi si je me trompe, mais n'était-ce pas ton but initial, "comprendre le Dow" — tes élucubrations sur le delta et tout le saint-frusquin ? »

Je le regardai sans mot dire.

« Ne le prends pas mal, petit. Tu as fait des progrès. Je te l'ai déjà dit, ces dernières semaines t'en ont plus appris sur le Dow que toutes les simagrées de ta phase d'approche. Mais le delta — tu crois vraiment y être ? »

Je me concentrai quelques instants pour chercher la vérité en moi-même. Quelques instants seulement, puis je secouai la tête. « Non, répondis-je. Je crois même que j'en suis encore plus éloigné qu'au début. »

Nous nous observâmes attentivement.

« J'admire ton honnêteté, Sonny, dit-il doucement. Je déteste jouer les rabat-joie, mais vu que je suis ton ami j'ai senti que je devais te poser cette question.

— Pour m'éviter de me vautrer dans mes SO, je suppose ? » le parodiai-je avec un sourire forcé.

Il haussa les épaules. « Et puis certains indices purement intrinsèques me disent que c'est sans doute le pire moment pour vendre. Notre chère Doe commence tout juste à s'échauffer, à prendre un peu de vitesse. Les vrais profits ne se matérialiseront que plus tard. Souviens-toi du vieil adage : "Minimise tes pertes et laisse ton profit suivre son bonhomme de chemin." Si tu vends maintenant, tu renonces à tous tes gains ultérieurs. D'accord, tu auras récupéré ta robe, mais une fois de plus tu seras raide comme un passe-lacet, et gros schmo comme devant. Il serait temps que tu te demandes ce qui compte le plus pour toi : la robe ou ta carrière d'investisseur ? » Il m'assena une tape amicale dans le dos puis s'éloigna. « Mais je ne veux pas t'influencer, ajouta-t-il en se retournant. Donne-moi ta réponse demain. Si tu décides de vendre, j'exécuterai ton ordre. Sinon... » Sur un signe de la main, il disparut dans la bouche du métro.

Tout en marchant vers Chinatown, je ruminai le problème qu'il avait soulevé. « Quelle chose comptait le plus... ? » Seul dans ma chambre en fin de soirée, je réfléchissais. La frénésie des cotations m'avait fait perdre de vue la question essentielle. Et maintenant la réponse ne me semblait pas aussi évidente qu'autrefois. J'avais eu tendance à y voir un simple choix entre, d'un côté, un objet artisanal porteur d'histoire et de sens, le seul héritage que ma mère m'eût légué ; et, de l'autre, l'argent, du « liquide », des « espèces ». Ces deux choses étaient évidemment incommensurables. Kahn avait pourtant jeté une lumière nouvelle sur mon dilemme : « ... la robe ou ta carrière d'investisseur. » Cela n'était pas aussi simple. Car ce n'était pas seulement ma carrière d'investisseur qui dépendait de ma décision, mais la mission plus vaste que j'étais venu remplir en Amérique et qui était devenue le centre de mon être. Je parle, bien sûr, de la preuve de la foi, de la quête du delta, du Tao dans le Dow, qui à Coney Island s'était indissolublement identifiée à la recherche de mon père, lequel était désormais pour moi le Dow par la loi de réciprocité. Ma quête m'avait déjà fait parcourir un long chemin. De nouveau, je devais choisir : renoncer ou aller de l'avant, m'enfoncer dans la toile, accroître les ambiguïtés. Mais, en un sens, cette décision n'avait-elle pas déjà été prise ? N'avais-je pas choisi, cet après-midi-là, à Coney Island ? Peut-être. Pourtant, gager la robe et m'en séparer définitivement — avec le plein acquiescement de ma volonté — constituaient deux choses différentes.

Tandis que je me débattais avec ce problème, l'ultimatum de Kahn me revint en mémoire : « Pour comprendre le Dow, tu dois investir, petit — une partie de toi-même. » N'était-il pas judicieux, cruellement judicieux, que le sort eût désigné mon bien le plus précieux pour le sacrifice nécessaire, l'holocauste requis ? Kahn avait déjà eu raison. Je n'avais pas encore tout donné. Mais quel terme de l'alternative était le bon : persévérer dans ma quête pour atteindre le delta (à moins qu'il ne se révélât parfaitement illusoire), ou bien m'accrocher à ce témoignage du passé ? Oui, mon dilemme avait désormais un sens plus profond.

Ou alors ce raisonnement élaboré était-il seulement une justification destinée à m'éviter de réfléchir à ma soif d'argent et à mon accoutumance aux angoisses boursières ? J'étais incapable d'envisager clairement cette question. A un moment, je décidai que je devais renoncer au bien matériel (à la robe) afin de poursuivre mon étude. Mais aussitôt l'ironie de cette décision me frappa de plein fouet ! Renoncer à mon « bien matériel » pour m'adosser dans un fauteuil en me curant nonchalamment les ongles tandis que mon capital de Jane Doe doublait ou triplait ? Quelle hypocrisie ! Et pourtant, me rappelai-je, tous les profits que je pourrais réaliser n'étaient pas une fin en soi, seulement le moyen d'accéder à une meilleure connaissance du Dow. Tant que ma conscience était pure, m'assurai-je, je ne pouvais mal agir. Mais ma conscience était-elle pure ? Bien sûr qu'elle l'était ! Cependant...

Tout cela se réduisit au bout du compte à une considération méthodologique fort prosaïque : le temps. Kahn m'avait fait remarquer à juste titre que, si je vendais maintenant à la veille de l'échéance, je sacrifiais irrévocablement tous mes bénéfices futurs, spirituels et éducatifs, dont les progrès allaient de pair avec la maximisation du profit. Et quand pareille occasion se présenterait-elle de nouveau ? A quand remontait le dernier gros coup de Kahn ? Il avait parlé de sept années de scoumoune. Je ne pouvais attendre aussi longtemps. Je devais à tout prix profiter de l'occasion. Je devais agir *maintenant*.

Après une nuit d'insomnie passée à me tourner et me retourner dans mon lit, au petit matin je me dégageai des draps qui s'étaient entortillés autour de moi comme les vrilles d'une vigne parasite, et je sus que pour le meilleur ou pour le pire j'avais décidé de rester fidèle à Jane Doe et de dire adieu à la robe de ma mère. Si je devenais extraordinairement riche, me consolai-je sans enthousiasme et avec une bonne dose d'ironie, je pourrais peut-être la racheter à Mme Chin à un prix exorbitant. (Non, lecteur, je n'y croyais pas.)

Toute la matinée je me sentis nauséeux et sillonnai le parquet sans entrain, plein d'angoisse, un fardeau pour moi-même et sans doute un piètre messager pour les autres. Parfois, je souhaitais presque que Doe dégringolât, redescendît au moins sous la barre des vingt dollars pour la journée, afin de pouvoir rendre le destin responsable de ma décision. Je n'eus évidemment pas cette chance. En milieu d'après-midi, Doe avait gagné un point de plus. Je dus assumer seul la responsabilité de mon acte. Ma décision était loin de me rendre heureux, mais sans cesse je me consolais en songeant que j'eusse été infiniment plus malheureux si j'avais vendu mes actions et renoncé à ma carrière d'« investisseur illuminé ». Toute ironie mise à part, étais-je parfaitement sincère ? Je l'ignore toujours. Peut-être aurais-je soulagé mon cœur du fardeau accablant des soucis et de l'angoisse si j'avais vendu mon modeste portefeuille et retrouvé volontairement ma position d'observateur sur la touche où je ne risquais aucune blessure spirituelle (c'est-à-dire de m'attacher à une somme d'argent, à un bien matériel). Mais que signifiait précisément « s'attacher à un bien matériel » ? Cette question débouchait sur une autre allée du labyrinthe moral où j'avais pénétré. Je me demandai si, dans mon cas, *wu-wei*, le non-agir, consistait à fixer un regard limpide, tranquille et sans passion sur les lointains pendant que la main s'activait et saisissait ce qu'elle pouvait ; ou bien, à l'inverse, si la main ne devait pas rester immobile tandis que le regard et l'esprit essayaient activement de comprendre, de posséder *intellectuellement* ? Mais cette possession abstraite était-elle moins coupable que la possession physique, matérielle ? Il me sembla qu'il valait mieux se salir les mains que l'esprit, mais je me demandai aussitôt s'il n'était pas naïf de croire qu'on pouvait se souiller les unes sans l'autre.

Malgré toute son habileté, Kahn ne m'aida nullement à résoudre mon dilemme. D'abord il n'aimait guère aborder ce genre de problème, et puis la passion de la chasse le rendait encore moins disponible que d'habitude. Je ne l'avais jamais vu aussi enthousiaste. Il y avait une tension nouvelle en lui, dans son apparence et son élocution, un côté incisif, tranchant, concentré. Il semblait avoir perdu quelques kilos et son penchant pour la plaisanterie cynique, l'extravagance et le délire intellectuels, rejetés comme autant de lest superflu. Son teint plombé s'était coloré de rose. Il bombait le torse, se dressait de toute sa taille. Je le surprenais parfois figé au milieu du parquet, les yeux levés vers la bande-annonce, un sourire subtil illuminant son visage, les joues rouges, une lueur dans l'œil, les narines frémissant de plaisir, tel un grand prédateur qui renifle dans l'air l'odeur du gibier. C'était là une attitude d'adolescent, ou bien de la plus intense profanation. Au fond, qu'attendais-je de lui ? Parce qu'il était Aaron Kahn et que sa vie était ce qu'elle était, il pouvait seulement me guider comme il me guidait. Je connaissais maintenant son attitude ultra-américaine « pas de gloire sans couilles », je savais qu'elle l'aveuglait à l'univers des valeurs que je cherchais. Et pourtant je choisissais de suivre son exemple. Pourquoi ? Par lâcheté ? Mauvaise foi ? Suivais-je simplement la ligne de moindre résistance ?

Je m'attribuerais volontiers ces motifs, voire de pires raisons, car je sais qu'à un niveau plus élevé je persévérais dans ma foi, cette foi que j'avais retrouvée sur la Grande Roue de Coney Island et qui m'assurait que la disparité entre son mode de vie et le mien, entre Ken Kuan et Wall Street, était simple apparence, que l'affluent turbulent et impétueux sur lequel je naviguais — le Dow — finirait un jour par déboucher sur le Tao. La saumure de cet océan était à mes yeux un solvant universel dans lequel toutes les différences s'annulaient, s'intégraient à la solution primordiale. Telle était ma foi ; j'avais quitté la Chine pour la mettre à l'épreuve de la réalité, pour vérifier que la réalité est Une, et le Tao la Réalité.

N'avais-je pas vu de mes propres yeux le Yang-tsê se dissoudre dans la mer de Chine, laquelle mêlait à son tour ses eaux au vaste océan oriental ; et l'Hudson se jeter dans l'Atlantique ? Je savais aussi qu'au large d'un cap dangereux et familier des tempêtes ces deux grands océans mêlaient leurs eaux, tout comme le *yin* et le *yang* finissaient par se confondre. Après avoir connu ce cap physique, il m'incombait maintenant de franchir le cap de mon Espérance intérieure, de suivre les vents et les marées de la vie jusqu'au lieu où le Dow américain, le fleuve du suprême intérêt personnel, contourne son propre promontoire avant de se jeter dans le grand Pacifique du Tao.

Je devais savoir si ce que je connaissais et aimais résisterait à l'épreuve de la dure réalité américaine, si la règle générale, le Tao, s'appliquait au cas particulier du Dow. Mais si le Dow constituait une exception, alors comment persévérer dans l'entreprise de mes jeunes années en sachant son immense et cruelle vanité ? Comment me consacrer de nouveau à la recherche du calme intérieur — me couler comme l'eau à travers les strates poreuses de l'ego jusqu'à la nappe souterraine du Tao — tout en sachant que cette nappe était en fait un égout ? Je ressemblais au savant qui a parcouru la moitié du monde pour voir l'éclipse de soleil, la seule exception momentanée à la règle générale. Le Dow était l'éclipse du Tao ; si, en examinant son disque noir, je ne pouvais m'assurer qu'en dessous le soleil brillait aussi intensément qu'auparavant, alors ma foi religieuse était une illusion, un espoir mensonger. S'il en était ainsi, j'étais dans la position de ce berger primitif dont on m'avait parlé en Chine et qui, voyant le ciel s'assombrir, crut la fin du monde arrivée ; préférant alors la vaste incertitude de la mort à un monde qu'il ne reconnaissait plus et dont il se méfiait, il se suicida en se pendant à un arbre fruitier tandis que son troupeau bêlait de terreur autour de ses jambes flasques.

7

Cet après-midi-là, je fus malgré tout soulagé quand la sonnerie retentit. Ma décision était désormais irrévocable. Après mon travail, je faillis aller demander à Mme Chin de m'accorder un dernier regard à mon trésor, mais je censurai cette impulsion avec une brusquerie et une intransigeance qui me surprirent moi-même, une dureté nouvelle dans mon répertoire émotionnel. Je comprenais maintenant, et en un sens je partageais même cette aversion pour le « schmaltz » que Kahn avait bien manifestée cent fois en ma présence. Non que j'eusse si aisément renoncé à la robe, mais une immense lassitude alliée à la totale futilité de ces « derniers hommages » me fit abandonner cette démarche qui bientôt me parut littéralement répugnante. Quand nous nous séparâmes en fin d'après-midi, Kahn me dit une chose étrange.

« Voilà, petit, je crois que tu as maintenant subi ton baptême du sang. » Il sourit sombrement. « C'est plutôt approprié, non ? Un baptême du sang avec la Biche*. »

Je compris seulement son allusion quand j'eus cherché le mot dans le dictionnaire : « Baptême du sang : initiation d'un novice qui a suivi la meute avec succès, de la découverte de la bête jusqu'à sa mise à mort, et qui consiste à marquer son visage avec le sang du gibier. » Brusquement je saisis. La mise en gage de la robe était la découverte du gibier. Mais aussi sa mise à mort.

Sur le chemin de Chinatown, je m'arrêtai devant l'église de Trinity. Derrière les grilles de fer, des feuilles dorées jonchaient les tombes, quelques-unes tombaient des arbres en virevoltant silencieusement dans les rayons de soleil qui striaient l'air frais de l'automne. Sur la façade noire de suie de l'église, je décelai une sagesse séculaire et triste, celle d'un être habitué depuis longtemps à une blessure et qui, en souffrant, a appris l'art ingrat de la patience, goûté par cette blessure même au vin d'une consolation plus intense que celles que ne connaîtront jamais les bien-portants. Dédaignant la fraîcheur de l'église, je passai mon chemin, non sans un hochement de tête et un léger soupir.

Comme la prospérité, ou du moins ma richesse future, devenait une réalité

---

* *Doe* signifie biche *(NdT)*.

de plus en plus tangible, je me mis à réfléchir à son utilisation quand tout serait terminé. Car enfin nous ne pouvions vivre éternellement la passion de la chasse ; le jour où nous aurions poursuivi la biche jusque dans ses derniers retranchements (à moins que nous ne fussions épuisés avant), il nous faudrait prendre la dure décision de précipiter les délices de l'hallali, de décocher la flèche pendant que le gibier était encore à portée, ou alors de risquer de le perdre à jamais. La biche deviendrait ensuite un simple trophée sur le mur, un souvenir évocateur, un sujet de conversation, mais plus jamais une raison d'aller de l'avant, ce que Jane la Biche était précisément pour l'instant. Qu'allait-il donc se passer ? Supposons que le scénario se développe exactement comme prévu et que je me retrouve submergé d'une montagne de doe-llars miraculeusement multipliés. Qu'aurais-je appris ? Et *que* serais-je ? Plus riche, indubitablement, mais plus sage ? Kahn ne s'était certes pas trompé : pour connaître le Dow, tu dois investir. Maintenant je le reconnaissais volontiers. Mais cette proposition qui m'avait paru douteuse, puis cruelle, me semblait maintenant insuffisante.

A mesure que les jours passaient et que Jane engraissait, un curieux corollaire de cette loi me vint à l'esprit. Selon cette prémisse que la fréquentation du Dow m'était bénéfique, il s'ensuivait que plus je me frottais à lui, plus j'avais de chances de le comprendre ; et plus ma connaissance du Dow était intime, plus je m'approchais de mon but : le delta, la confluence du Tao et du Dow. Bien. Mais la dernière étape du syllogisme m'étonnait, me déconcertait. En quoi consistait précisément une fréquentation assidue du Dow ? Et comment pouvait-on se gagner ses faveurs ? Eh bien, pour dire les choses crûment, grâce à l'argent. L'évidence des bénéfices que mon bien-être spirituel et ma santé mentale tireraient de l'accumulation de larges réserves de capital me frappa comme un éclair dans un ciel obscur. Je reculai évidemment de dégoût. Absurde ! me dis-je avec un rire méprisant, mais aussi légèrement hystérique. Quand j'y regardai de plus près, mes lèvres se figèrent. Où était la faille dans mon raisonnement ? Si j'acceptais les prémisses, la conclusion n'en découlait-elle pas avec une logique implacable ? Peut-être perdais-je le sens de la perspective, songeai-je. Mais je devais aussi considérer l'éventualité glaçante selon laquelle cette vérité s'imposerait peut-être un jour avec l'évidence élémentaire de l'ultimatum de Kahn.

Un après-midi (après une agréable matinée consacrée à regarder la bande-annonce et à ajuster mon équilibre mental aux hausses de huitièmes et de quarts de dollar), je retournai au bureau de Kahn avec nos déjeuners. L'ascenseur s'arrêta au Centre des Visiteurs, et je décidai brusquement d'aller sur la galerie pour jeter un coup d'œil en bas, en souvenir du bon vieux temps. Je contemplai la scène à mes pieds, soupirai de satisfaction en admirant la beauté imposante du spectacle, reniflai ce fort parfum de basse-cour. Après un moment, je remarquai comme une modeste émeute autour d'un des postes du garage. Tiens, c'était le poste de Jane Doe (« l'étendard de Jeanne d'Arc », ainsi que l'avait baptisé Kahn !). Les transactions étaient frénétiques ; en fait, je n'avais jamais vu une telle fièvre, même après l'annonce de la fusion avec Sui. Cette frénésie évoquait celle d'une fourmilière éventrée par un promeneur malveillant. Les courtier brandissaient leurs ordres au-dessus de leur tête et hurlaient à pleins poumons. Le spécialiste, qui tournait ses paumes vers eux comme pour les repousser, secouait sa tête inclinée en un geste de refus sympathique mais intraitable. Que leur refusait-il ? Essayaient-ils de vendre ou d'acheter ? Et où était Kahn ? Mon ami corpulent était ostensiblement absent de cette foule tapageuse et contestataire — je dis « ostensiblement » car tout se passait comme si la victime désignée avait eu l'audace de se dérober à la foule impatiente au moment du lynchage. En fait, la présence d'un officier de justice ne semblait guère superflue. En qualité de fidèle complice du gringo fautif, je n'avais pas la moindre envie de prendre sa place, si bien que je battis en retraite aussi rapidement et discrètement que possible vers son bureau, à la porte duquel je frappai.

« Foutez le camp ! grogna Kahn à l'intérieur.

— Aaron, c'est moi ! m'écriai-je. Ouvrez, j'apporte le déjeuner. »

N'entendant pas de réponse, je sortis ma clef et ouvris la porte.

Comme pour filer ma métaphore de western, Kahn était assis à sa table et contemplait d'un œil glauque, exorbité, ce qui s'avéra être un Colt 44. Il le rangea dans le tiroir de sa table, puis me regarda avec des pupilles dilatées, une expression craintive, vulnérable, contredite par son suave sourire de cinglé.

Je sentis mes poils se hérisser sur mes bras. L'anticipation d'un malheur me noua la gorge. « Kahn ? réussis-je à chuchoter.

— C'est fini, petit, dit-il en croisant mon regard. L'a-doe-rable Jane vient de nous lâcher. Un coup de poignard dans le Doe.

— Vous voulez dire... ? »

Il ferma les yeux, hocha la tête. « Ils ont interrompu les transactions au parquet. »

Je le regardai bouche bée, incapable de parler.

« Ils ont découvert le pot-aux-roses, petit. Je suis fini.

— Le pot-aux-roses ? »

Il opina. « Tout — le cartel, les achats, l'information interne, le maquillage de la bande — tout le tintouin. Tout le putain de megillah. »

J'étais abasourdi.

« Okay, je suis donc un schlimazel », dit-il en haussant les épaules. Puis il fondit en larmes.

Après quelques minutes, il sortit son mouchoir et se moucha bruyamment. « Excuse le schmaltz, me dit-il avec une légère ironie et un sourire plus mince encore.

— Mais comment ? » hasardai-je.

Il soupira en secouant la tête. « Je n'en sais rien, nom de Dieu ! Piper a dû me dénoncer. D'après ce que j'ai appris, tout a commencé par une enquête de routine. La hausse soudaine leur a mis la puce à l'oreille et ils ont voulu vérifier que tout était casher ; c'est alors que Piper a pondu son rapport. Lequel a provoqué une ruée sur notre valeur. Ils sont allés le voir et il m'a balancé. La crapule.

— Qui ça, "ils" ?

— Le BEV, petit. »

J'eus un hoquet de surprise.

« Exactement, Sonny, l'inspection générale. C'est un sport sanglant. Nous jouons pour de l'argent.

— Que va-t-il se passer maintenant ? »

Il haussa les épaules. « Tout dépend jusqu'où le Bureau des Gouverneurs voudra pousser le bouchon. En tout cas, je serai viré.

— Viré de la Bourse ? Pour de bon ? » m'écriai-je, paniqué.

Il opina du chef. « Mais la perte de mon siège est le cadet de mes problèmes potentiels. Tu connais aussi bien que moi l'idée que le public se fait du "négociant indélicat". Eh bien, pour tenir en laisse les hordes réformistes, les gars du BEV sont très soucieux de montrer qu'ils savent faire leur propre police. » Il me lança un coup d'œil lourd de sous-entendus.

« Et alors ? demandai-je.

— Alors ? Ils vont peut-être faire de moi un bouc émissaire.

— Ce qui veut dire ?

— Ils peuvent me traduire en justice. Et je ne crois pas que mes origines juives les porteront à la clémence, vois-tu... Voilà des années qu'ils essaient de se débarrasser de moi. Ils ont maintenant un prétexte tout trouvé. »

Le lendemain, les enquêteurs du BEV passèrent son dossier au peigne fin. Kahn cessa de quitter son bureau. Il acheta des cartouches pour son Colt, le chargea. Il se promena ostensiblement dans les couloirs en faisant des moulinets avec son arme, comme un homme de main. Dès que ses collègues le voyaient, ils rasaient les murs. Je le regardais avec consternation, avec désespoir. L'après-midi où ils vinrent enfin le chercher, j'étais là. Deux coups frappés à la porte — « division exécutive du BEV ». Mes genoux faillirent se dérober sous moi. Je ne conservai qu'à grand-peine le contrôle de mes intestins. Non seulement le danger immédiat — le péril encouru par Kahn (où j'étais sans doute aussi impliqué, bien que je fusse incapable d'estimer dans quelle mesure) — mais ma propre culpabilité d'étranger séjournant illégalement aux Etats-Unis assaillirent mon esprit terrifié.

A ma grande surprise, Kahn réagit par un sourire las, presque soulagé, et tendit la main vers la porte pour une présentation d'opérette en me regardant sous l'arc de ses sourcils comme pour dire : « Tu vois ? »

Tout cela fut implicite. Ce qu'il dit réellement, en sortant le revolver du tiroir de son bureau, fut : « Alors, petit, ce flingue contient six balles. Qu'en penses-tu ? Allons-nous les utiliser contre nous, ou préfères-tu une fusillade en bonne et due forme ?

— Kahn ! m'écriai-je en protestant avec véhémence. Ce n'est pas le moment de plaisanter ! »

Il haussa les épaules, sourit sombrement. « Qui plaisante, petit ?

— Ouvrez ! » Des poings martelèrent la porte.

Un sourire douloureux retroussa les commissures des lèvres de Kahn. Il me regarda droit dans les yeux en portant le canon de son arme à sa tempe.

« Que faites-vous, Aaron ? suppliai-je.

— Ida ne supportera jamais cette honte, dit-il avec un humour désenchanté, nihiliste, particulièrement terrifiant en les circonstances.

— Kahn ! », hurlai-je.

Il pressa lentement la détente ; le percuteur s'éloigna peu à peu de la culasse.

La porte s'ouvrit brusquement, une demi-douzaine de policiers envahirent le bureau. Deux tombèrent aussitôt à genoux en braquant sur nous leurs calibres 38 ; les autres se déployèrent derrière en brandissant à bout de bras leurs revolvers qu'ils tenaient à deux mains. « Pas un geste ! crièrent-ils.

— Faites comme chez vous, les gars, leur lança sarcastiquement Kahn.

— Ne bougez pas, ou nous tirons !

— Un peu de calme, messieurs », dit Kahn qui, de sa main libre, montra son Colt, comme pour expliquer à leurs cerveaux déficients la complexité de la situation. « Laissez simplement partir le gamin, stipula-t-il. Il n'a rien à voir là-dedans. Il se contente de m'apporter mon déjeuner. »

Le policier le plus proche fixa sur moi un regard dépourvu d'aménité. « Dehors ! », commanda-t-il en indiquant la porte d'un signe de tête.

Je regardai Kahn avec impuissance.

Sa bouche s'arrondit en une moue rassurante, il ferma les yeux, hocha paternellement la tête. « Ça va, petit. Fais ce qu'on te dit. »

Je me dirigeai vers la porte.

« Oh, Sonny, avant de partir…, me héla-t-il, allume-moi un cigare, veux-tu ? Je désire savourer mes derniers instants. » Il sollicita la permission des policiers. « Mon ultime requête, les amis ? » Le même policier qui m'avait fait signe de déguerpir, m'ordonna de revenir. « Vas-y », dit-il sèchement.

Kahn appliqua le canon du revolver à sa tempe gauche, puis fit tourner son barreau de chaise devant l'allumette que je tenais, pompant sur son cigare en utilisant ses joues comme un soufflet. Debout devant le bureau, je m'interposais entre lui et les policiers. Alors qu'au bord des larmes, je croyais accomplir les derniers rites avant le suicide de Kahn, il leva soudain les yeux vers moi et articula presque silencieusement : « T'in-qui-ète pas. Mon re-vol-ver est en plas-tique. »

Pétrifié de stupeur, je le dévisageai bouche bée jusqu'à ce que la flamme de l'allumette me brûlât les doigts et me fît sursauter.

« Maintenant tire-toi d'ici ou je tire ! grommela-t-il. Tu commences à m'énerver sérieusement !

— Vite ! Casse-toi ! » s'écrièrent les policiers en agitant leurs feux.

Je ne pris pas le temps de protester ni de poser de questions.

Quand je le revis en prison l'après-midi même, il m'expliqua qu'il s'était livré à toutes ces simagrées pour étoffer la thèse de la démence. « Après tout, si les terroristes du tiers monde et les blousons dorés de la bourgeoisie réussissent à s'en tirer après un meurtre, un viol, un incendie criminel, un assassinat politique, que sais-je encore, pourquoi pas les hors-la-loi en col blanc quand ils piétinent par mégarde les plates-bandes de l'illégalité ? C'est de la discrimination ! »

Pauvre Kahn, il plaisantait toujours alors même qu'on lui passait la corde au cou. Je crois qu'il n'avait pas encore bien réalisé ce qui était arrivé. Il était presque hilare — effronté, agressif, spirituel, mais ses plaisanteries me semblèrent un peu forcées. Au bout d'une semaine, j'eusse accueilli à bras ouverts la moindre idée aussi saugrenue que ses simagrées pour plaider la démence, tant était profonde la dépression qui s'était abattue sur sa vie comme un froid brouillard gris et menaçait de briser son cœur.

Je crois que l'attente humiliante de son avocat dans sa cellule, puis la comparution ignominieuse au banc des prévenus où on le conduisit comme un animal de foire, portèrent un coup fatal à son moral. Quand son avocat et le procureur se furent brièvement entretenus avec le juge, ce dernier le convoqua à la barre.

De l'endroit où j'étais assis dans la salle d'audience, j'entendis leurs répliques.

« Il m'arrive parfois de jouer en bourse, M. Kahn, dit le juge. Pour tout vous avouer, mon courtier m'a recommandé Jane Doe voici deux semaines.

— Rusé courtier, Votre Honneur, rétorqua Kahn en souriant avec une chutzpah légèrement déplacée. Traitez-le bien. Les hommes de valeur se font rares. »

Le juge fronça les sourcils puis regarda durement l'accusé par-dessus la monture de ses lunettes. « C'est le cas de le dire. Heureusement pour vous, je n'ai pas suivi son conseil. Vu la nature de l'infraction et parce que votre casier est vierge, je vous libère sans caution. Mais je tiens cependant à vous dire que je vous considère comme un parfait coquin.

— J'ai toujours été perfectionniste, Votre Honneur, renchérit Kahn. C'est plus fort que moi. Dans tout ce que je fais, je tiens à être le meilleur. »

Quand nous quittâmes la salle d'audience parmi une foule de journalistes avides, l'air suffisant de mon ami s'était évaporé, remplacé par une expression fantomatique d'absence et d'abattement.

Kahn et moi nous arrêtâmes machinalement à un carrefour pour prendre le journal de l'après-midi ; nous lûmes ce gros titre dans le *Daily News* :

UNE TENTATIVE DE SUICIDE INTERROMPT LES ACTIVITÉS DE WALL STREET
KAHN ACCUSÉ DE MANIPULATION

En dessous, en caractères plus petits, ce sous-titre :

LE FILS DE LOVE IMPLIQUÉ DANS LE SCANDALE

Peut-être le sais-tu, lecteur, mais il est étrange de constater avec quelle rapidité les choses peuvent se retourner contre soi et une situation glisser entre les mains. Oui, cela est fort étrange. Je suppose que c'est une des premières et dures leçons que le Dow enseigne à ses disciples, une leçon que je n'aurais jamais apprise en restant sur la touche. A Wall Street, apprendre est synonyme de perdre. Le Péché Impardonnable du négoce ? Le suprême faux pas du Dowiste ? Confondre les œufs avec les poulets, lecteur. Voilà ce que j'ai fait. C'est presque drôle. J'aurais dû être cent fois plus bouleversé. Mais je ressentis surtout un immense soulagement, une libération, comme si toutes mes erreurs avaient été réparées, et l'ardoise de mes transgressions effacée d'un coup. Mon cœur fut soulagé d'un énorme poids, dont j'avais à peine eu conscience avant d'en être débarrassé. Si Kahn n'avait pas été en si fâcheuse posture, j'aurais sauté de joie sans la moindre honte.

Mais ce « si » était incontournable. Mon ami faillit mourir. Je me sentis largement responsable de son malheur, comme si mes jérémiades incessantes l'avaient poussé hors de la légalité dans le domaine de l'escroquerie. Il s'avéra qu'hormis ses responsabilités financières, qui étaient considérables (il dut déclarer une banqueroute, article 13), les répercussions légales de l'affaire furent minimes. L'avocat de Kahn réussit à obtenir pour son client l'obligation de passer tous ses week-ends pendant six mois dans un pénitencier du nord de l'État de New York pour enseigner à des criminels endurcis — qui semblaient en avoir l'aptitude et le désir — les tenants et les aboutissants de « l'investissement classique » — le juge insista beaucoup sur le mot « classique ». Je crois que ce fut sa disgrâce qui, plus que tout autre chose, lui porta un coup fatal, non seulement le verdict de la cour, mais l'ostracisme de ses pairs et, peut-être plus encore, celui du Bureau des Gouverneurs. Kahn fut bel et bien chassé de la Bourse, son fauteuil vendu aux enchères pour contribuer au remboursement de ses dettes. Pire encore, on lui interdit de jamais remettre les pieds au parquet. Kahn encaissa presque tout comme un mensch — sauf cette dernière humiliation. Etre impitoyablement et sommairement banni de ce lieu qui pour lui était synonyme de la vie elle-même ! Ce fut le coup de grâce. Ce fut ce qui brisa sa volonté. Pauvre Kahn ! Comme je le plaignis ! Du jour au lendemain, on le relégua sur la touche, condamné à *observer sans participer*.

Toute plaisanterie mise à part, c'était littéralement pour lui l'équivalent de l'enfer sur terre. Il n'existait pas punition plus cruelle, plus absolue. C'était diabolique ! C'était sadique ! Se retrouver au piquet à la périphérie, ahanant et luttant comme un chien de meute enchaîné tandis que le renard filait sous son nez en le narguant, voilà ce qui l'abattit, le réduisit à l'ombre de lui-même. (Au sens figuré, car physiquement sa circonférence s'accrut. Il atteignit le poids record de cent vingt-cinq kilos.) Bien entendu, il était toujours libre de se livrer aux manœuvres dérisoires du boursicoteur à la petite semaine, comme n'importe quel pauvre crétin de cette triste fraternité qu'on nomme le Grand Public. Il pouvait ouvrir un compte chez un courtier de troisième zone, lui téléphoner ses ordres de transaction, qui atteindraient le parquet de la Bourse après plusieurs intermédiaires. La perspective de pareil avilissement lui fut intolérable, ainsi que le lecteur le comprendra aisément. Ne pas pouvoir exécuter ses ordres lui-même, en personne, *ipse homo* — c'était mortifiant, c'était impensable ! Si seulement il avait pu trouver un emploi de simple courtier au parquet, il se serait mis en cheville avec l'une des grandes sociétés fonctionnant à la commission. Bien que ce travail fût infiniment en deçà de ses compétences, il l'aurait accepté la tête haute, comme un aristocrate d'une vieille famille ruinée, pauvre mais au moins solvable quant à sa dignité, et, plus important encore, en contact direct avec la Source, avec le Dow. Mais non, rien à faire. Ils le clouèrent au pilori — eux qui n'étaient même pas dignes d'embrasser ses pieds ! Sa réputation était un stigmate ineffaçable. Les directeurs de société tremblaient de peur devant l'ivraie. Ah, pauvre Kahn ! Comme mon cœur saigna pour lui !

Et pourtant, savez-vous quelle fut son attitude, quelle position il maintint envers et contre tout ?

« Je regrette seulement que ça n'ait pas duré éternellement », me dit-il avec dans le regard une lueur fuligineuse, désenchantée. Sa voix était basse et voilée, frémissante de passion, comme s'il prenait congé de l'amour de sa vie, de la vie même. « Ça valait le coup, petit. Je ne regrette rien. » Une dignité triste, princière, s'affirmait à travers sa douleur. « C'était si beau. Si beau. » Il secoua la tête. « Tout est fini pour moi, petit. Je sais que je ne connaîtrai plus jamais une joie aussi profonde. J'y étais, petit. *J'y étais.* Tu comprends ? » Il m'adressa un regard brûlant.

« Ne dramatisez pas, Kahn, l'exhortai-je gravement. Après tout, votre vie est loin d'être terminée. »

Il me regarda attentivement en plissant les yeux, puis soupira, secoua encore la tête. « Tu ne vois donc toujours pas, hein ?

— Qu'y a-t-il à voir ?

— Qu'il s'agit justement de cela : ma vie *est* terminée.

— Mais vous pouvez faire tellement d'autres choses », protestai-je.

Il retroussa sombrement les lèvres. « J'ai déjà fait trop de choses. Mes semelles sont usées jusqu'à la corde, petit, mes semelles de Juif Errant. » Il sourit d'un air absent. « Les chaussures en crocodile de JR » Cette plaisanterie ne soulagea guère sa peine. « Pour moi, c'est fini. Je ne désire rien d'autre. »

J'eus du mal à l'admettre, mais je lui dis enfin avec sincérité : « Maintenant je crois que je comprends, Aaron. »

Une triste complicité brilla dans son regard, qui me rappela celui de Tsin. « Marqué par le sang », furent ses seules paroles.

« Quand un homme a connu le goût du sang, il ne l'oublie pas facilement. » Les paroles du soldat traversèrent mon esprit. Je regardai gravement Kahn, mais il souriait dans le vague, absorbé par son obsession comme le papillon autour de la lampe. « Tu sais, avec un peu plus de chance, un peu plus d'argent, nous aurions pu réussir le plus gros coup depuis la grande arnaque de Piggly Wiggly en 21. Nos noms en lettres d'or dans les livres d'histoire. » Il regarda dans le vide, puis éclata brusquement d'un rire tonitruant. « Et les deux fois dans le porc ! » Il secoua la tête. « Ça me rappelle un dicton : "Un taureau peut gagner de l'argent à Wall Street ; un ours peut gagner de l'argent à Wall Street ; mais un cochon finit toujours dans la mouise et la Sui." Je me suis fait baiser, petit. Des deux côtés ! » Il fit un geste obscène. « Par-devant et par-derrière ! » Il riait si fort que des larmes ruisselaient sur ses joues.

Je m'efforçai de lui cacher mon inquiétude, mais je commençai réellement à craindre pour sa santé mentale. Dans l'espoir de régler au moins le problème financier, je contactai les membres de feu le cartel pour leur demander d'organiser une souscription au bénéfice du bouc émissaire qu'on avait sacrifié en expiation de leurs péchés collectifs, mais ma tentative fut un échec. Leurs secrétaires notèrent mon numéro de téléphone, personne ne me rappela.

C'était assez clair : personne ne m'aiderait. La tâche reposait désormais sur mes seules épaules. Et je ne m'en plaignais pas. Comme je l'ai dit, je me sentais responsable du rôle d'instigateur. Eussé-je même été innocent, je n'aurais pu abandonner mon vieil ami à son sort. Oui, je le considérais maintenant comme un vieil ami, malgré le peu de temps écoulé depuis le fameux jour où je l'avais vu sortir d'une cabine de transactions en gobant des bonbons d'un air distrait. Je ne pouvais l'imaginer dans un autre paysage. Car, après tout, qu'est-ce qu'un éléphant sans une savane, un crocodile sans les eaux limoneuses d'un marigot, un ours sans une tanière pour hiberner, un taureau sans un pré ou une arène ? Oui, je me sentais moi aussi céder au schmaltz. Mais je me ressaisis en songeant à mes nouvelles responsabilités envers lui. Comment soulager sa peine ? Telle était la question. Et malheureusement je ne connaissais pas la réponse.

Quand le BEV déposa son rapport et interrompit les transactions, Jane Doe était cotée trente-deux dollars. Quand la valeur fut de nouveau négociable, l'offre était à trois dollars sept huitièmes. Olaf, qui avait pris soin de mettre ses billes à l'abri, abjura aussitôt et publiquement tout rapport avec Doe, ses propriétaires ou ses représentants. Il osa même suggérer que la direction avait fait circuler des rumeurs de fusion à son insu et sans son consentement, créant ainsi le spectre d'une nouvelle accusation pour information mensongère. Heureusement, plusieurs documents attestaient la fusion Jane Doe-Sui Generis, si bien que cette charge ne put être retenue contre Kahn. Mais les lâchetés d'Olaf n'aidèrent pas Doe, qui perdit aussitôt deux points puis continua de dégringoler régulièrement. La compagnie fut incapable de résister : deux semaines plus tard, Doe apparut sur la bande-annonce, précédée du « Q » de l'ignominie, la Lettre Ecarlate de Wall Street, le signe de Caïn, la marque de Kahn. Banqueroute. Faillite. Article 2.

QDOE
200 à 13/16

Deux cents actions à treize seizièmes. Ensuite, je cessai de regarder. Non par indifférence, mais parce que ce dénouement me rendait malade.

Si le fiasco avait un tel effet sur moi, imaginez l'état de Kahn. Mon ami dépérissait. Je le vis dégénérer peu à peu en une sorte de clochard élégant. Une gravité fatale (la gravité du sang ?) l'attirait chaque jour à la Bourse, où on le traitait en paria. Bien qu'il eût cessé de se raser chaque matin, il prenait toujours la peine de s'habiller, de mettre un costume et une cravate. Du moins au début. Ses vêtements de luxe semblaient plus fripés que jamais, à croire qu'il dormait habillé ; puis ils se mirent à exsuder une odeur positivement délétère qui rappelait l'arôme, non du piroshki bouilli, mais du piroshki pourri. Le jour où je remarquai qu'il ne portait plus de chaussettes sous ses chaussures à lacets, je compris que son état était critique.

Je l'apercevais souvent à l'étage sur la galerie des visiteurs, qu'il hantait avec la constance d'un spectre accusateur, fantôme d'une âme assassinée et inquiète qui planait au gré des vents, ses yeux globuleux et vides fixés sur le spectacle de la vie grouillante qu'il couvrait de muets anathèmes. Comme mon cœur compatissait ! Je montais aussi souvent que possible je lui apportais de modestes douceurs comme on fait avec un malade, témoignages de commisération et d'apaisement. Mais il refusait sombrement toute nourriture, désignant ainsi impitoyablement l'objet de sa faim véritable. Cédant à un irrésistible besoin de mortification, il ingérait seulement du pain et de l'eau. J'ignore comment il supportait d'entendre la voix enregistrée qui, heure après heure, répétait son interminable message, expliquait le fonctionnement du marché. « Supposons que vous, John D. Smith, Monsieur Tout le Monde, dans n'importe quelle ville des USA, décidiez de vendre cent actions de la compagnie X... » Comme ce petit gnome désincarné semblait gai en énumérant les chaînons de la transaction : du client au courtier de détail, du courtier au téléphoniste, du téléphoniste au négociant au parquet via le tableau d'annonces, et ainsi de suite avec le spécialiste, le rapporteur, sans oublier l'humble grouillot, avant que l'information enregistrée ne redescende tous les degrés fastidieux de cette échelle jusqu'au client lui-même. Quelle torture pour Kahn ! Autant ligoter Einstein sur une chaise et l'obliger à écouter un enregistrement des lois de Newton ! Mais mon malheureux ami semblait assoiffé de punition. A défaut de nourritures plus triviales, son appétit de mortifications semblait insatiable. Et puis, comme je l'ai suggéré, je craignais qu'un seul plat ne réussît à le satisfaire pour de bon. Le suicide. Non pas une répétition d'opérette, mais le passage à l'acte. Je devais agir.

Mais comment ? Malgré tous mes efforts, je ne trouvai rien qui pût soulager sa douleur. En désespoir de cause et comme je l'avais déjà fait si souvent en des situations où l'intellect se trouvait face à un cul-de-sac, je me tournai vers le *Yi king*. Saisissant mon exemplaire du livre (une fois encore couvert d'une légère couche de poussière), semblable au pêcheur du conte de fées qui convoque le poisson magique, je fis appel à lui en ces temps de détresse, espérant fermement qu'une réponse jaillirait des profondeurs insondables de son vaste cœur. Je redoutais simplement de voir une de mes craintes confirmée : à savoir que j'aie perdu la « pureté de cœur » indispensable pour l'interroger, à cause des actions que j'avais commises, des lieux que j'avais fréquentés, des choses que j'avais acceptées et permises.

L'oracle me répondit par le numéro cinquante-neuf, *Houan*, « Dispersion » ou « Dissolution », avec quatre traits faibles supérieurs. Cet hexagramme est composé des trigrammes *Sun*, ═══, ou le « Vent », au-dessus de *K'an*, ═══, l'« Eau ». A mesure que les traits s'organisaient, je fus frappé par une chose que je ne parvenais pas à définir clairement. Le Vent au-dessus de l'Eau. Qu'était-ce ? *Sun* au-dessus de *K'an*. *Sun* au-dessus de... *K'an* ? Sun au-dessus de Kahn ! L'homophone de mon nom était bien sûr une vieille connaissance, mais celui de mon ami ! C'était étrange ! Mais le plus étrange était peut-être que je n'y eusse pas pensé plus tôt.

Quand j'eus surmonté ma première excitation, ou le choc de la découverte, je me tournai vers le commentaire de *K'an* dans la partie du *Yi king* qui explicite le sens des trigrammes.

> L'insondable est l'eau, les fosses, le piège, ce qui se redresse et ce qui se courbe, l'arc et la flèche.
> Parmi les hommes, ce sont les mélancoliques, ceux qui ont des maladies de cœur, des maux d'oreilles.

C'est le signe du sang ; c'est le rouge.
Parmi les chevaux, ce sont ceux qui ont une belle croupe, une humeur farouche, ceux qui laissent pendre leur tête, ceux qui ont des sabots fins, ceux qui bronchent.
Parmi les chars, ce sont ceux qui ont beaucoup de défauts.
C'est la pénétration, c'est la lune.
Ce sont les voleurs.
Parmi les variétés de bois, ce sont ceux qui sont fermes avec beaucoup de marques.

Je me mis à pleurer. Ce fut pour moi comme une révélation. Il y avait tant de choses dans ce commentaire. N'était-ce pas l'homme lui-même ? L'Insondable ! Certes, cela s'appliquait admirablement à sa condition présente.

Je commençai de comprendre. *Sun au-dessus de K'an* : je sentis confirmée ma responsabilité envers mon ami. Et je compris soudain ce que l'oracle avait voulu dire à Coney Island : *Sui*, « Suivre ». « Ce n'est qu'en servant qu'on en vient à commander. » Servir avait signifié suivre le conseil de Kahn, obéir à son ultimatum. Je l'avais suivi vers Jane Doe, vers le Dow, afin de pouvoir le guider maintenant, hors de sa dépression. Mais comment ? L'hexagramme suggérait une réponse.

La célébration en commun des sacrifices solennels et des services divins... était le moyen employé par les grands souverains pour unifier les hommes. Les cœurs communiaient dans les grandes émotions grâce à la musique sacrée et à la pompe des cérémonies... Un autre moyen était le travail en commun à de grandes entreprises qui proposent un grand but à la volonté ; la concentration sur cet objectif fait tomber tout ce qui sépare, de même que dans un bateau qui traverse un large fleuve tous les passagers s'unissent dans le travail commun.
Toutefois seul est capable de faire fondre la dureté de l'égoïsme, celui qui est exempt de toute pensée égoïste et qui demeure dans la justice et la fermeté.

« Sacrifices solennels et services divins... musique sacrée et pompe des cérémonies. » Intéressant. Mais quel rapport avec ma mission ? Je n'en avais aucune idée. Car après tout, ces rites et ces rituels se référaient aux pratiques de la cour chinoise et au culte des ancêtres. Comment aujourd'hui interpréter ces indications ? L'oracle semblait pourtant prescrire ceci — une « grande entreprise » — en tant que cure thérapeutique pour mon ami au cœur malade. Dans l'espoir d'y voir plus clair, je me reportai au commentaire des traits :

Six à la troisième place signifie :
Il dissout son moi. Pas de remords.

Il est des circonstances où le travail est si pénible que l'on ne peut plus penser à soi-même. On doit laisser entièrement de côté sa propre personne et disperser tout ce que le moi voudrait rassembler autour de lui pour établir une barrière contre les autres. Ce n'est que sur la base d'un grand renoncement que l'on acquiert la force nécessaire à de grandes tâches. En plaçant notre but hors de nous dans une cause importante, nous pouvons atteindre ce point de vue.

Eh bien, certaines choses du moins étaient claires. J'étais celui à qui l'on enjoignait de « ne plus penser à lui-même » pour réaliser un but hors de lui, — la réhabilitation de Kahn. Mais qu'était-ce ce « grand renoncement » ? Je poursuivis ma lecture.

Six à la quatrième place signifie...
La dispersion mène à l'accumulation.
C'est là ce que les hommes ordinaires ne pensent pas.

« Dispersion... accumulation... un grand renoncement. » Le brouillard s'épaississait.

Neuf à la cinquième place signifie :
Ses grands cris dissolvent comme la sueur.
Dissolution ! Un roi séjourne sans blâme.

Aux époques de dispersion et de séparation générale, une grande pensée fournit le point autour duquel s'organise la guérison. Tout comme la sueur qui dissout marque la phase critique d'une maladie, de même, aux époques d'obstruction générale, des pensées stimulantes constituent une véritable libération. Les hommes ont ainsi un point autour duquel se rassembler.

« Aux époques d'obstruction générale, des pensées stimulantes constituent une véritable libération. » Certes ! Mais *quelles pensées* ? Etait-ce lié aux « rituels et cérémonies » mentionnés plus haut ?

Neuf en haut signifie :
Il dissout son sang.
S'en aller, se tenir à distance, sortir,
Cela est sans blâme.

Dissoudre le sang signifie dissoudre ce qui pouvait amener le sang et les blessures, c'est-à-dire éviter le danger. Toutefois cela n'implique pas que l'on évite les difficultés pour soi-même, mais que l'on délivre les êtres chers en les aidant à partir avant l'arrivée du danger, à se tenir à distance d'un danger déjà présent, à sortir d'un danger qui les a déjà assaillis.

La possibilité d'un suicide se trouvait malheureusement confirmée. Mais les mesures préventives n'étaient nullement exclues.
Parvenu au bout du commentaire, je revins en arrière et relus attentivement chaque phrase pour tenter d'en éclaircir le sens. En vain. Je ne fis que resserrer les nœuds déjà existants. Et toujours je retournais à ces rites et ces cérémonies si énigmatiques. Tout semblait converger vers eux. S'agissait-il d'une église, d'une synagogue ? Aucune de ces hypothèses ne

me parut particulièrement prometteuse. Je finis par renoncer et me rendre au conseil de l'oracle : « s'en aller, se tenir à distance, sortir ». Déprimé et inquiet, je remâchai mon problème en marchant dans les rues.

Laissant, selon mon habitude, le hasard ou mon inconscient me guider, je gravitai bientôt autour du quartier de la finance. Au moment de m'engager dans Wall Street, je sentis pourtant le signal décroître, aucune impulsion ne me poussa vers l'entrée de la Bourse. Bifurquant, je reconnus aussitôt en l'église de Trinity le but inconscient de mes déambulations. Une fois encore, sa gravité m'avait attiré. Mais quelle gravité ? Qu'allais-je y chercher ?

La messe de l'après-midi avait déjà commencé. Les derniers arrivants entraient dans l'église ; des femmes pressées vêtues de crêpe noir franchissaient les portes en silence. Aussi discrètement que possible, je me mêlai à elles. Je m'arrêtai dans le vestibule pour jeter un regard las à travers la nef. Un prêtre que je ne connaissais pas, en étole et aube, se tenait devant l'autel. Cela me décida. D'un pas furtif, je traversai l'arrière de l'église en direction de la nef latérale et me glissai vers un banc à l'ombre d'une des grandes colonnes cannelées qui jaillissaient vers la voûte, proliféraient en motifs floraux, alvéoles de pierre, dans ce vaste espace murmurant où j'entendais le soupir prolongé de la conque. Ma conviction d'être un intrus, de participer illégalement à des rites prohibés, ne fit qu'accentuer l'inexplicable excitation qui me coupait le souffle. Regardant autour de moi, je me grisais des souvenirs vivaces qui, avec le passage du temps et l'ébauche de ma modeste biographie, avaient pris une ampleur insoupçonnée. Pourquoi étais-je revenu ici ? Qu'étais-je venu chercher ?

Le prêtre se tourna vers les fidèles, leva les mains à hauteur des épaules, paumes tendues en une invitation apaisante, globale, qui semblait m'inclure moi aussi.

« Venez à moi », dit-il d'une voix forte au timbre grave qui, comme celle de Riley, s'accordait à la pénombre et aux harmoniques de l'église, une voix qui appartenait au rituel et non à l'homme, « vous tous qui êtes las et harassés, et je vous donnerai le repos ».

Ses paroles me firent l'effet d'une drogue ou de l'incantation d'un hypnotiseur. Une immense fatigue s'abattit sur moi, une lassitude spirituelle plus que physique. Je pris conscience d'une douleur intérieure, de pleurs qui s'épanchaient en deçà de ma conscience, comme la sirène devant l'appartement de Li, un gémissement que les gènes eux-mêmes avaient mémorisé. Je ne sus même pas quand cela commença. Autour de moi, les fidèles se relevaient et rejoignaient la travée centrale pour se rendre devant l'autel.

« Un festin princier pour un Dowiste. » Ces mots me revinrent en mémoire, et brusquement je compris. C'était ça. La gravité, la gravité du sang. Je ne saurais l'expliquer, lecteur, mais je fus saisi d'un désir si puissant que je faillis m'effondrer devant mon banc et pleurer toutes les larmes de mon corps. Je mordis ma langue pour garder contenance, je la mordis jusqu'au sang. Je me rappelle son goût amer, métallique, comme de pièces de monnaie dans ma bouche. Cela me soulagea, mais seulement quelques instants. Ensuite, ce fut comme une possession, une crise de delirium tremens, le manque du drogué, plus intense que sa volonté de vivre. Une seule gorgée — je n'en désirais pas plus — pour humecter mes lèvres du sang mystique. Cela m'aurait suffi. Mais c'était déjà trop. L'énormité du prix à payer dépassait de beaucoup mon capital spirituel au point que, ce prix, je parvins seulement à l'estimer par l'adjectif « démesuré ».

J'ignore combien de temps dura cet état. Je réussis enfin à maîtriser mon émotion, et quittai aussitôt mon banc. Je courais si vite quand j'atteignis le vestibule que je heurtai quelqu'un et faillis le renverser. « Excusez-moi, dis-je en saisissant un bras dans la pénombre. Pardonnez... » Deux yeux bleu pâle me fixèrent ; je crus les voir scintiller dans les ténèbres.

« Père Riley !
— Sun I, dit-il en hochant la tête. En voilà une surprise. »
Nous nous observâmes en silence.
« Je vous dois des excuses, dis-je enfin d'une voix tremblante, les yeux baissés.
— Pour la conférence ? m'interrompit-il. Ne sois pas stupide, je comprends maintenant. J'espère seulement ne pas t'avoir importuné dans cette tragédie. En tout cas, je compatis à ta perte. Je regrette de ne pas avoir pu voir la robe. Je suis navré de ce qui s'est passé, mais vu les circonstances tu as de la chance de ne pas avoir été plus gravement blessé. »

Avant qu'il ne parlât de la robe, je ne savais pas très bien à quoi il faisait allusion. Quelle « tragédie » était en cause ? Jane Doe ? Reprenant mes esprits, je compris qu'il évoquait mon agression. Je faillis rire. Puis je songeai que Yin-mi m'avait couvert. Elle avait menti à cet homme qu'elle admirait, qu'elle révérait, elle lui avait dit que mon agresseur m'avait volé la robe. Cette découverte déclencha en moi une douleur confuse, déchirante, mi-gratitude mi-honte, mais aussi une bouffée brûlante d'orgueil. Je crois que je rougis. Quand je me rappelai le fossé qui s'était creusé entre nous, je fus submergé d'un sentiment poignant de perte irrévocable.

« Tu te sens bien, Sun I ? demanda Riley.
— Bien sûr.
— Tu n'es pas fiévreux ?
— Non. Pourquoi ?
— Ton visage est si rouge, répondit-il. Et tes yeux si brillants. » Il posa sa main fraîche sur mon front. « Tu me parais un peu chaud.
— Vraiment ? »
Il acquiesça. « Viens, allons dans mon bureau. Je vais te préparer une tasse de thé bien fort. Rien de tel pour guérir une grippe. » Il partit sans me laisser le temps de protester, et je dus le suivre.

« Alors, pourquoi viens-tu ici cet après-midi ? me demanda-t-il en lavant les tasses. Tu n'as pas décidé de te convertir, j'imagine ? »
Je ris en me rappelant son zèle, ses plaisanteries.
« Non, je ne crois pas.
— Pas encore ? »
Je secouai la tête. « Pas encore. »
Il se retourna vers moi et croisa les bras en m'observant tandis que l'eau chauffait dans la bouilloire. Derrière lui, l'eau qui tombait goutte à goutte dans la cafetière attira mon attention. Je songeai à la clepsydre de Ken Kuan, aux « larmes du temps ». Un calme sinistre m'envahit et je soupirai.

« Tu as changé, sais-tu, me dit-il d'un air pensif.
— Quoi ? demandai-je, soudain tiré de ma rêverie.
— Je disais que tu avais changé. »
Je le regardai. « Comment ça ?
— C'est ce que j'essaie de définir. Je ne sais pas trop. »
Je souris. « Qu'est-ce qui vous fait dire que j'ai changé ?
— Ton apparence tout entière — ton visage, tes yeux, ton attitude, ta manière d'être. Par exemple, la dernière fois que je t'ai demandé si tu voulais te convertir, tu t'es raidi. Cette fois-ci, tu as souri. Pourquoi ? Que s'est-il passé entre-temps ? »
Je haussai les épaules. « Je n'en ai pas la moindre idée. Peut-être s'agit-il seulement d'un de vos fantasmes, un désir que vous aimeriez voir réalisé ? »
Il secoua la tête d'un air convaincu. « Non, je ne crois pas. On dirait que le noyau de dureté qui était en toi a commencé de s'effriter, comme un iceberg touché par des courants plus chauds en provenance de l'équateur. »
Il fouilla mon visage à la recherche de la vérité. « On distingue presque une sorte de halo autour de toi. Tu n'as pas trouvé le delta, par hasard ? »
L'ironie de sa question me fit rire tristement. « Loin de là, mon père. »
Il m'adressa un regard aigu. « Que veux-tu dire ?
— Je crois que je l'ai peut-être perdu, répondis-je en comprenant le sens de mes paroles à mesure que je les prononçais.
— Ah ! fit-il avec un léger cri de surprise. Ce n'est donc pas la lueur de l'illumination, seulement la souillure morale. »
Il posa sur moi un regard compréhensif, désenchanté.
L'eau était prête. Il se tourna vers la bouilloire pour préparer mon thé. Puis nous vidâmes lentement nos tasses en choisissant d'un commun accord de parler d'autre chose. Ainsi, la plus grande partie de notre conversation demeura tacite, inscrite en filigrane derrière les mots que nous utilisâmes pour évoquer des choses quotidiennes, triviales. Je lui racontai mon agression ; il m'écouta avec sympathie, sans me presser de questions. Une agréable intimité naquit entre nous, remplaçant la tension et la méfiance passées. Lui comme moi, je crois, nous en émerveillâmes secrètement. Craignant de la briser, nous nous traitions avec égards. Elle ressemblait à l'intimité que j'avais remarquée chez les frères de Ken Kuan en ces rares moments où leurs méditations leur laissaient un répit, quand ils buvaient paisiblement une tasse de thé ensemble, observaient le paysage, partageaient le silence particulier de la fraternité spirituelle, l'intimité des prêtres.

En le quittant, je me sentis heureux, apaisé. Mon bien-être se muait parfois en une joie immense, mais très calme, très intérieure, comme si j'eusse rectifié ce qui avait été faussé. Je songeai que je n'aurais pu connaître plus tôt cette joie, que ma débâcle seule — la perte de la robe, de Doe, de tout — l'avait rendue possible. Comme je marchais vers Chinatown, je ris en me rappelant le vieil adage : la merde fait pousser le maïs ! C'était vrai sur certaines terres. Et puisque j'avais trouvé un terrain d'entente avec Riley, pourquoi pas avec d'autres ? Mon espoir et ma confiance revinrent. Peu à peu, mon humeur allègre s'accentua. M'arrêtant devant la vitrine d'un magasin de spiritueux, je remarquai une rangée de bouteilles de Dry Sack, et derrière elles le brandy que j'avais vu Mme Chin boire l'après-midi où j'avais gagé la robe. « Oh, et puis zut ! » pensai-je en sortant mon portefeuille et comptant mon argent pour m'assurer que j'en avais assez. « Histoire de lui montrer que je ne suis pas rancunier. »

★

Ce fut la douairière en personne qui m'ouvrit. Derrière elle, l'appartement était plongé dans l'obscurité.

« Excusez-moi. J'espère que je ne vous ai pas réveillée.

— Chuut ! m'intima-t-elle avec un chuintement péremptoire. J'ai un client.

— Oh. » Locataire ? Ame perdue en quête de conseil spirituel ? me demandai-je en mon for intérieur. Ou bien un malheureux comme moi désireux de gager un pan inestimable de son passé ou de lui-même afin de payer ses factures mensuelles ou de satisfaire un vice dont il était l'esclave ?

« Que veux-tu ? » demanda-t-elle brusquement, méfiante. Je remarquai qu'elle portait sa tiare en plumes de paon ainsi qu'un châle de dentelle noire. Les bagues de ses doigts reflétaient la lumière du couloir, jetaient des miroitements liquides dans les ténèbres.

« Je repasserai plus tard.

— Si c'est pour la robe, tu ferais mieux de la chasser de ton esprit, m'avertit-elle. Elle est partie.

— Partie ? » répétai-je ; malgré moi, ma voix trembla de surprise et de déception.

« Je l'ai vendue. »

J'attendis en espérant une remise de peine. Mais le verdict demeura. Je poussai un profond soupir. « Eh bien, tant pis, acquiesçai-je en essayant de faire contre mauvaise fortune bon cœur. Il n'y a plus rien à faire.

— Absolument, renchérit-elle, presque joyeuse. J'en ai parlé à un ou deux de mes contacts, et au bout d'une semaine un homme s'est présenté, qui a accepté mon prix. Il n'a même pas marchandé. J'aurais sans doute pu en tirer bien davantage. »

Nous échangeâmes un regard.

« A propos... » Je plongeai la main dans ma poche.

Mme Chin sursauta, observa d'un œil inquiet ma main disparaître sous mon vêtement, comme si j'allais en sortir un revolver, un couteau, une arme contondante.

Magnanime jusqu'au bout, je refusai de rassurer sa méfiance, m'autorisant seulement un ton de vertu légèrement offensée : « Je vous ai apporté un modeste cadeau. » Je lui tendis la bouteille enveloppée de papier brun. « Pour vous montrer que je suis sans rancune. »

Retrouvant son aplomb, elle prit la bouteille avec un sourire écœurant de vanité. Elle saisit le goulot et vérifia rapidement la marque. « Mon brandy préféré ! » s'écria-t-elle avec ravissement. Elle m'adressa un sourire déliquescent d'oie blanche, particulièrement grotesque sur son visage fripé. « Tu apprends vite, me félicita-t-elle. Je dois avouer que je m'inquiétais pour toi, Sun I. Mais apparemment j'avais tort. Tu as sans doute des ressources cachées. Tu vas peut-être finir par t'en sortir. » Elle me fit don de son approbation amusée. « Pour une vieille femme comme moi, une bouteille d'alcool est un cadeau infiniment plus agréable que le précieux viatique de tes larmes, railla-t-elle en se retenant de pouffer, que tu semblais bien près de m'offrir lors de notre dernière rencontre. En retour, je peux t'assurer que la robe est entre de bonnes mains. L'acheteur est indubitablement un connaisseur. Il la maniait avec un réel respect — si tu l'avais rencontré, je suis sûre que cela aurait soulagé ton cœur — il l'examinait comme on examine un être humain. » Elle se perdit dans ses souvenirs.

« Comment s'appelait-il ? »

Elle se renfrogna. « Je ne lui ai pas demandé son nom. Il a payé en liquide.

— Alors comment était-il ? » insistai-je, non sans véhémence.

Elle haussa les épaules. « C'était un Blanc.

— C'est tout ce que vous pouvez me dire ? protestai-je.

— A quoi bon ? Un homme d'affaires, bien habillé, distingué, grand. Peut-être un banquier, ou un cadre supérieur. Comment veux-tu que je sache ?

— Et son visage ?

— Quoi, son visage ? rétorqua-t-elle, de plus en plus agressive.

— Pouvez-vous me le décrire ? De quelle couleur étaient ses yeux ? »

Elle haussa les épaules. « Je n'ai pas vu ses yeux.

— Pourquoi ? m'enquis-je.

— Il portait des lunettes de soleil.

— Des lunettes de soleil ? répétai-je. Vous avez bien dit des lunettes de soleil ?

— Oui, des lunettes de soleil, confirma-t-elle avec agacement. Qu'y a-t-il ? Tu deviens sourd ?

— Non, non, excusez-moi, dis-je. Simplement...

— Quoi ? »

Je secouai la tête. « Rien. Peu importe.

— Que t'arrive-t-il ? me demanda-t-elle. Tu es pâle.

— Tout va bien », la contredis-je.

Elle m'observa attentivement. « Ah, au fait, tu as bien failli me faire oublier. Il m'a demandé de te remettre quelque chose. C'était dans la poche de la robe. "Dites-lui qu'il a oublié ceci", telles furent ses paroles. »

Je crus entendre un rire fantomatique s'égrener dans le vent, un rire cinglant qui s'éloigna à une distance considérable quand la douairière posa l'objet sur ma paume. Oui, lecteur, la clef : la clef à la fine chaîne d'or et la patte de lapin porte-bonheur. Le charme provoqua la même aversion que le premier jour dans la cellule du maître, mais cette fois cela se mua en horreur. Pendant tout mon voyage je les avais rangées dans la poche de la robe, et dans la précipitation des récents événements je les y avais oubliées. Tandis que je les examinais à nouveau, le message de mon père s'empara une fois encore de mon esprit :

> D'un Dowiste à un autre,
> Une clef, une chaîne, un porte-bonheur :
> La patte de lapin pour la chance ;

La chaîne pour la nécessité ;
La clef, une clef majeure
(Puisse-t-elle t'assister),
Un rossignol qui ouvre les sombres
Secrets du cœur (car cette clef
Ouvre toutes les portes), et pour la congrégation
Des croyants (car nous sommes tous de la même foi,
N'est-ce pas ?) une clef d'église qui
T'enivrera d'extase, ou
Te fera entrer dans la Grande Cathédrale du Dow.

             Ton père,
             Love.

 Les aboiements de la meute, qui s'étaient éloignés au point de devenir presque inaudibles, plaintifs, hachés, pitoyables, et de me faire croire que les chiens avaient perdu la trace du gibier, que tout était fini, reprirent avec une frénésie et une vigueur nouvelles, plus proches que jamais. Etait-ce possible ? me demandai-je. Etait-ce vraiment possible ? Alors que j'avais perdu tout espoir de jamais le trouver, il surgissait brusquement dans les coulisses ! Les conséquences de son apparition s'approfondirent et se dilatèrent comme les cercles concentriques autour de la pierre jetée dans un bassin d'eau tranquille, prirent les proportions d'une vérité d'ordre général. Je me rappelai les paroles du maître : « Ce n'est parfois qu'en renonçant à une chose que nous pouvons la conserver. » Je pensai au panda géant de cette folle matinée sur la rive du Fleuve au Sable d'Or ; seulement quand j'avais accepté ma propre mort, il s'était détourné et m'avait laissé la vie sauve. Je pensai aussi au vitrail de Trinity figurant Abraham et Isaac ; Yin-mi m'avait expliqué que le père avait dû renoncer à ce qu'il aimait le plus au monde pour sanctifier Isaac et s'en montrer digne.

 Je me secouai violemment de mon rêve. Je n'osai pas lâcher la bride à mon imagination. C'était une coïncidence, certes troublante, mais surtout dangereuse, et rien de plus, me dis-je. En face de ce que je savais déjà — la quasi-certitude de la mort de Love —, elle ne faisait pas le poids sur la balance. Et puis, pouvais-je raisonnablement démentir le récit de Kahn qui prouvait... ? La description de Mme Chin s'appliquait à presque tous les hommes que je connaissais à Wall Street, ainsi qu'à une kyrielle d'autres citoyens de New York ! Comme s'il n'existait pas d'autres Américains connaisseurs de l'art chinois ! Absurde ! Et pourtant, ce détail des lunettes de soleil. A y réfléchir, même cela semblait dérisoire. Non, si je voulais rester lucide, je devais m'en tenir coûte que coûte à ma position première, à cette inévitable conclusion de la narration de Kahn : la mort d'Eddie Love. Tout le reste, mes conjectures à propos de ce mystérieux acquéreur, n'étaient que du vent, le fruit de la vanité et de la délusion.

 Mais la clef. Je la regardai encore. Quelle serrure ouvrait-elle ?

 Remarquant mon désarroi, Mme Chin avança les lèvres en haussant les sourcils, puis me lança avec négligence : « Une clef de coffre, non ? »

 Je la regardai stupidement.

 « Tu ne sais même pas ce que c'est, n'est-ce pas ? » demanda-t-elle avec une pitié méprisante.

Je ne répondis pas.

« Montre-la à un serrurier », suggéra-t-elle. Puis elle me ferma la porte au nez, m'abandonnant à la stupeur et au silence.

8

J'étais souvent passé devant une petite boutique située à la limite nord de Chinatown, une échoppe de serrurier installée sous une blanchisserie chinoise grouillante de monde, et à laquelle on accédait par une volée de marches. Le propriétaire, dont le nom était peint en caractères dorés sur la vitrine, s'appelait M. Har. Maintes fois je l'avais vu penché dans le halo de sa lampe, en train d'examiner quelque mécanisme compliqué avec une expression de concentration sereine, sondant les organes internes comme un chirurgien équipé d'instruments de précision. Les mots peints sur la vitrine m'avaient autant enchanté que l'aspect de l'artisan : Clefs Fabriquées / Serrures Ouvertes — ce que j'interprétais à chaque fois comme Solutions Proposées / Problèmes Résolus.

La journée était humide et fraîche ; une fine bruine automnale tombait par intermittence d'un ciel bas et gris. Les flaques d'eau luisaient dans la lumière argentée. Contrastant avec ces tonalités sombres, les jets tumultueux de vapeur blanche qui sortaient des orifices d'aération de la blanchisserie, ces cumulus ventrus et ondoyants prenaient une apparence magique rehaussée par l'odeur d'amidon bouillant qui planait, épaisse et gluante, dans l'air moite. Je respirai sa senteur douçâtre, légèrement âcre, en descendant les marches de ciment qui aboutissaient au domaine de M. Har.

Il s'occupait d'une cliente, une jeune mère d'apparence italienne, accompagnée d'un petit garçon de trois ou quatre ans qui, debout derrière elle, s'accrochait à l'un des pans du pardessus d'homme qu'elle portait, suçait son pouce et observait la scène avec une timidité silencieuse.

M. Har, les manches relevées sur ses bras glabres (ses muscles évoquaient de minces câbles ductiles, des cordes à piano reliées aux marteaux de ses doigts qui semblaient frapper une mélodie tâtonnante), examinait derrière ses lunettes à monture noire une boîte en bois placée sous la puissante lampe du comptoir. La boîte était d'un bois sombre et compact, peut-être celui d'un arbre fruitier, d'un cerisier ; le vernis jaunissant empêchait une identification immédiate. Au centre du couvercle, on avait incrusté une marqueterie beige figurant un chrysanthème où butinait une abeille dont les bandes jaunes et noires ainsi que l'aiguillon étaient admirablement rendus par des fragments alternés de bois de différentes couleurs. M. Har examinait le dessus, le dessous, les côtés de la boîte. Un feutre vert couvrait la face

inférieure. Aucune serrure n'était visible. Ils essayaient manifestement de l'ouvrir. Il sourit à la femme en tendant légèrement l'oreille vers la boîte, tel un médecin qui ausculte un patient. « Très fieux, dit-il.
— Fieux ? » demanda-t-elle.
Il opina du chef avec enthousiasme. « Peaucoup d'années.
— Ah, *vieux* ! interpréta-t-elle. Je l'ai trouvée l'autre jour au grenier avec des affaires de Mamma, des lettres, des vêtements. Mais les mites avaient fait de tels dégâts que j'ai dû presque tout jeter. Je n'avais jamais remarqué cette boîte, et elle était fermée. J'ai pensé qu'elle contenait peut-être quelque chose de précieux. Vous pouvez l'ouvrir ? »
M. Har la posa sur le comptoir. Alors qu'il faisait courir ses doigts minces le long du fond, le couvercle pivota soudain et un carillon entama une valse délicate, éthérée. A l'intérieur, deux danseurs, un homme et une femme vêtus en jeunes mariés, leurs visages de bois inexpressifs mais peints en un robuste rose vif, tourbillonnaient mécaniquement sur une trajectoire circulaire, sans rapport aucun avec la musique.
Le visage de la femme s'illumina un instant. Le garçonnet applaudit en criant de joie. Elle se baissa et le saisit sous les bras pour lui montrer la merveille. Leurs visages dont les joues se touchaient exprimaient ravissement et fascination, comme deux enfants qui entre les balustres dévorent des yeux le monde scintillant et enchanté des adultes dans la salle de bal inférieure.
M. Har aussi sourit en hochant la tête ; ses doigts tapotaient le comptoir en cadence avec la musique.
Alors, avec une brusque violence qui nous stupéfia tous, la femme tendit la main et rabattit brutalement le couvercle. « Mamma a toujours été une imbécile, déclara-t-elle avec un mélange de pitié et de mépris. Combien vaut-elle ?
— Che n'en feux pas. Pourquoi ne bas garder ? » demanda M. Har d'un ton plein de reproche, presque suppliant. Il regarda l'objet avec nostalgie. « Soufenir de famille. Faleur sentimendale.
— Gardez-la donc », proposa la femme qui saisit la main de l'enfant et pivota brusquement pour s'en aller.
« Attendez ! » s'écria le serrurier.
Elle se retourna.
Ouvrant le tiroir-caisse, il en sortit un billet de cinq dollars qu'il posa sur le comptoir.
« Merci », dit-elle, peut-être avec ironie, en glissant le billet dans la poche de son manteau. Puis elle prit le bras du petit garçon. « Viens, Joey. Nous ferions bien de préparer le dîner avant le retour de papa. »
Quand ils partirent, l'enfant ne cessa de regarder par-dessus son épaule, de lorgner la boîte avec la même expression de regret que j'avais vue dans les yeux du garçonnet à Coney Island.
Derrière le comptoir, M. Har, qui avait oublié ma présence, examinait sa nouvelle acquisition.
« Elle est très jolie », commentai-je en m'approchant.
Il leva les yeux. « Soufenir de famille », expliqua-t-il en la tendant vers moi comme pour me la présenter. Il secoua la tête. « Quel tommage. Les chens tefraient pas fentre.

— Devraient pas... ? demandai-je, n'ayant pas compris ses derniers mots.
— Fentre contre dollars, précisa-t-il.
— Ah, *vendre*. »
Il parut chercher mon approbation.
J'acquiesçai vigoureusement.
« Puis-che fous aider ? »
Je posai la clef sur le comptoir. « Pouvez-vous me dire de quoi il s'agit ?
— C'est une clef », répondit-il en s'inclinant avec un sourire.
Je lui retournai poliment son sourire. « Certes, mais de quoi ?
— Coffre perzonnel à la banque, m'informa-t-il sans hésitation. Ceci, numéro du coffre. » Il me montra les chiffres gravés sur l'anneau.
« Peut-on savoir de quelle banque il s'agit ? »
Il me regarda d'un air méfiant. « Où afez-fous troufé zet objet ? »
J'hésitai, mais une certaine fixité de son regard m'avertit qu'il ne servirait à rien de mentir. « Mon père me l'a laissé », répondis-je.
Il fouilla mon visage pendant quelques secondes, comme s'il y lisait une combinaison secrète, puis saisit la clef et l'examina plus attentivement sous la lampe. Il m'observa ensuite en plissant les yeux. « Fous êtes sûr ? »
J'acquiesçai.
« Che n'ai bas le droit de faire ça, fous safez. »
Sous le comptoir, il prit un lourd volume relié en vinyl noir, et le feuilleta quelques instants. Quand il eut trouvé ce qu'il cherchait, il décrocha le téléphone, puis me tourna le dos et parla à voix basse. Puis, sur une feuille de papier, il écrivit : « Boîte 1127, Chemicar Bank, Agence Principale. »
Mon bonheur fut tel que je faillis l'embrasser. Au lieu de quoi je sortis mon portefeuille. « Combien vous dois-je ? »
Il secoua la tête en fermant les yeux. « Rien. Soufenir de famille. »
Je cédai alors à une inspiration. « Accepteriez-vous dix dollars contre la boîte ? Cela vous fait un bénéfice de cent pour cent en cinq minutes. »
Il haussa les épaules en poussant la boîte vers moi.
Je me ruai hors de son échoppe, montai l'escalier quatre à quatre, regardai à gauche et à droite, puis courus en direction des deux silhouettes que je voyais au loin se diriger vers la Petite Italie.
J'étais à bout de souffle quand je les rattrapai. « Tiens », dis-je en tendant la boîte au garçonnet, que sa mère portait toujours sur ses épaules. Lorsqu'il vit mon merveilleux cadeau, son visage rayonna de bonheur et d'incrédulité. « Maman ! » s'écria-t-il.
Elle sursauta en entendant son cri. Me découvrant juste derrière elle, elle prit peur. « Que voulez-vous ? » demanda-t-elle d'une voix sourde, angoissée.
Je lui adressai un sourire béat, stupide ; elle comprit seulement mes intentions quand son fils brandit la boîte sous son nez. Elle la lui arracha des mains, puis me dévisagea avec une expression encore plus furieuse qui me stupéfia. Saisi d'une horreur impuissante, je la vis brandir la boîte au-dessus de sa tête, grimacer et fermer les yeux tandis que l'enfant hurlait et se débattait pour récupérer son bien, puis la jeter à toute volée sur le trottoir où elle se fracassa. Le visage cramoisi de colère, elle me foudroya

une dernière fois du regard, puis fit volte-face et s'éloigna d'un pas rapide en entraînant l'enfant inconsolable qui pleurait.

Quelques instants je regardai pensivement les fragments de la boîte — les mariés allongés à plat ventre dans l'eau du caniveau —, puis me dirigeai vers la bouche de métro pour aller à la banque.

Un éclair étoilé scintilla sur le bord de l'énorme porte d'acier et de chrome qui pivotait sur ses gonds en chuintant doucement ; l'espace d'un instant elle me révéla le royaume brillant et interdit de l'argent, puis elle se referma avec un long écho métallique quand l'employé en fut ressorti. Comme il marchait vers moi hors de cette mer de lumière éblouissante, avec la longue, étroite et profonde boîte de métal, je pensai seulement au vitrail de l'église de Trinity qui décrivait l'ange du Seigneur roulant la pierre et émergeant triomphalement de la tombe avec le linceul prouvant aux fidèles que le Christ était bel et bien ressuscité. J'y vis une expérience presque transcendante, un aperçu du paradis lui-même.

« Suivez-moi », dit-il. Je l'aurais suivi n'importe où.

Il m'emmena simplement dans une cabine exiguë meublée d'une table et d'une chaise fixées au sol, où chacun était libre d'inventorier ses richesses à l'abri des regards indiscrets.

Quand il ferma la porte, je m'assis et pris une profonde inspiration en regardant la boîte comme un enfant devant un cadeau de Noël, espérant deviner son contenu grâce à une sorte de rayon X magique. Je n'en suis plus si sûr aujourd'hui, mais je suppose que la question essentielle ne concernait pas tant le contenu de la boîte que celui de mes supputations. J'étais excité, plus excité que je ne l'ai jamais été, et puis aussi j'espérais. Je dois pourtant admettre qu'un vague pressentiment de malheur étreignait mon cœur.

Qu'aurais-je aimé découvrir ? Je ne saurais le dire au juste, simplement quelque chose de petit, de relativement digeste (émotionnellement et spirituellement digeste), un objet qui n'aurait pas bouleversé ma vie davantage qu'elle ne l'était. Vous savez, lecteur, ce dont je veux parler : une montre à gousset, une bague, une médaille de guerre, un signe de reconnaissance, la preuve qu'il avait pensé à moi et souhaité réparer, dans la mesure du possible, les torts qu'il avait infligés malgré lui à ma vie et à notre rapport.

Alors peut-être commencez-vous à imaginer ma surprise quand je soulevai le couvercle et découvris... ah, lecteur ! j'aimerais dire cela simplement, mais aujourd'hui encore, après toutes ces années, j'ai du mal à contrôler mon émotion face à une énormité si — eh bien oui : mirobolante ! Je découvris... découvris... Bon Dieu ! Je refuse de sombrer dans le mélodrame. Je le refuse ! Je découvris, d'abord, et pour être bref, de l'argent liquide. Non pas quelques billets rares, que j'aurais pu m'attendre à trouver dans cet œuf métallique, mais d'innombrables liasses de billets ! Des plaines fertiles de billets verts, semblables aux champs de laitues de Salinas, aux Champs Elysées eux-mêmes, et qui proliféraient avec une fécondité démentielle échappant aux lois de la nature. Perdant tout bon sens, je ris hystériquement, me mis à lancer des poignées de billets comme des confettis dans ma cabine. J'en couvris littéralement les murs.

Quand j'eus retrouvé un semblant de lucidité, je sombrai dans une longue méditation fascinée devant les billets. Bien que vieux selon les critères normaux (dans la brève demi-vie de cet isotope instable qu'est la richesse), ils semblaient aussi craquants et neufs que le jour de leur émission, conservés par l'air immortel et calibré du sous-sol de la banque. Avec une terreur muette, je passai en revue leurs diverses dénominations, totalement absorbé, hypnotisé par cette tâche. Jamais auparavant je n'avais remarqué les qualités artistiques de ces billets, ni le poids ou la qualité du papier sur lequel figurait la devise américaine. Après un examen méticuleux et lucide, je dus admettre que du seul point de vue esthétique le dollar méritait sa prééminence parmi les devises mondiales. En fait, il méritait d'être encadré. Léchant mon index à intervalles réguliers, je comptai les billets craquants, parfois écornés, ainsi que j'avais vu faire les caissiers dans les banques de Wall Street. « Argent », « fric », « flouze », « pèze », « pognon », « thunes », « oseille », « picaillon » — les noms génériques défilaient dans mon esprit, ceux que Kahn m'avait un jour récités, suivis rapidement par les dénominations d'espèce — « fafiot », « biffeton », « billet vert », « peau de grenouille », « feuille de laitue », « George », « simoléon » — toute la gamme des nuances américaines qui se résolvaient en un seul accord parfait, l'accord tonique universel de l'argent, le DOLLAR ! J'examinai les visages des divers saints patrons du liquide : George Washington, Père de la Nation ; Abe Lincoln, Émancipateur des Esclaves. Quelle trouvaille géniale de les avoir immortalisés sur une devise flottante circulant de main en main, eux qui semblaient intercéder pour réduire les dettes de leur postérité. Comme le cœur des Américains devait frémir d'orgueil, pensai-je, chaque fois qu'ils s'adonnaient à cet échange symbolique, livrant un Lincoln en esclavage volontaire au tiroir-caisse du boucher contre une livre de côte de bœuf ou quelques rognons de porc !

Ce ne fut que progressivement, à mesure que je comptabilisais et entassais tendrement mes liasses, que l'idée s'imposa à mon esprit : quelle pédagogie ! Non seulement la présence des présidents sur les billets servait de modèle, de noble exhortation aux financiers comme aux criminels pour qu'ils ne dérogent point aux principes les plus élevés de leurs transactions, mais en même temps elle éduquait les jeunes en identifiant à l'étude de l'histoire américaine cette activité fondamentale qui consiste à compter l'argent ! Une fois encore, je me sentis transi de terreur et d'admiration devant le spectacle de l'ingéniosité yankee ; je ressentis aussi, peut-être pour la première fois, un sentiment flatteur et presque anoblissant de ferveur patriotique — quel privilège d'être ici ! — tandis que le panorama de l'Amérique, Pays de Cocagne, Terre des Braves et des Hommes Libres, s'étalait devant moi entre mes piles de liasses. Le patriotisme me fit bomber le torse. Soudain, j'aimai mon pays d'adoption. Mes yeux s'emplirent de larmes de gratitude. L'Amérique ! Mon enthousiasme ne fut que légèrement entamé par le fait que j'étais un étranger séjournant illégalement, que je ne possédais aucun des droits et des privilèges des citoyens de ce pays mirifique et que, appréhendé, j'étais voué à une déportation immédiate et tyrannique, sans le moindre appel possible.

Comme le suggèrent peut-être ces remarques, mon émerveillement innocent et mon exaltation se compliquaient d'un élément plus sombre et amer, une sorte d'extase nihiliste, dirais-je, qui prenait un plaisir cynique à l'ironie de ma situation : mon soudain héritage suivait de si près l'« anéantissement de mes espoirs », mon « absolution ». « Tout allait bien se passer, l'ardoise serait effacée d'un coup » — mes propres phrases me revinrent en mémoire, accompagnées d'un chœur d'applaudissements du Bronx. Ah ! Quel idiot j'étais !

Mais je n'eus pas le temps de me vautrer dans la fange de ma culpabilité. Car je n'étais pas au bout de mes découvertes. Les billets cachaient d'autres trésors mystérieux qui, à l'examen, s'avérèrent être des bons de la défense nationale. Et en quantités considérables !

Enfin, des titres — plus beaux, même, que l'argent, avec leur liséré gravé et le symbole d'*American Power and Light*, l'Arbre de Vie (ou était-ce l'Arbre de la Connaissance du Bien et du Mal ?) flottant dans le chaos primordial, un énorme fruit vert indéterminé, aux formes de la Terre, pendant à une branche, et moi comme quelque Newton somnolant à l'ombre de ses frondaisons, sur le point d'être réveillé par sa chute, non pas avec une idée, mais une bosse sur le front ! Cent mille titres à mon nom ! Lecteur, trêve de circonvolutions : j'étais millionnaire en dollars ! Plusieurs fois millionnaire, en fait ! Dire que cette fortune *m'avait tout le temps attendu* depuis mon arrivée ! Je ris et pleurai avec une amertume violente, presque pathologique. Au moment précis où tout s'était réglé de soi-même, où ma vie était enfin redevenue simple. L'ironie de ma découverte était trop affreuse. Je ne pus la regarder en face. J'étais ébloui, aveuglé. Par bonheur les murs étaient insonorisés, car je dus éructer quelques jurons bien sentis. Peut-être auraient-ils dû être aussi capitonnés...

Maintenant je comprenais enfin le message. Mais alors que l'ambiguïté de ses allusions m'avait jusque-là fasciné, je décelai pour la première fois une sorte de malveillance dans ses insinuations : « car nous sommes de la même foi, n'est-ce pas ? » Mes pensées retournèrent de nouveau vers les vitraux de Trinity. Cette fois, l'homme au regard brillant et glacé me revint en mémoire, les champs de blé, les armées en marche, les vaisseaux aux voiles blanches qui naviguaient sur la mer bleue, tout cela présenté à son jeune compagnon d'un large geste du bras, comme pour lui signifier : « Ceci pourrait être à toi. » Car enfin étions-nous *vraiment* de la même foi, lui et moi ? Étais-je aussi un Dowiste ? Aussitôt, dans mon cœur je répondis non, avec une grande fermeté. Je refuserais cet héritage. Je le laisserais. Je me lèverais, quitterais la cabine, fermerais la porte derrière moi et m'en irais sans un regard de regret. Cette résolution m'apaisa. Je le ferais. Tout de suite.

Mais un nouvel ensemble d'associations, d'une autre provenance, m'assaillit alors. Quels prodiges Kahn n'accomplirait-il pas avec pareil héritage ! Cela suffirait largement à lui remettre le pied à l'étrier. Je secouai la tête. Rien à faire. Je le connaissais trop bien pour pouvoir me bercer de l'illusion flatteuse qu'il ravalerait son orgueil et accepterait ma charité.

Mais peut-être mon cadeau pouvait-il éviter l'apparence de la charité ? Un écho du passé, une bribe de phrase traversa mon esprit, d'abord trop flou pour que je pusse l'identifier. Il continua de se répercuter dans ma mémoire, gagnant en définition à chaque instant. Soudain le message fut clair : « sacrifices solennels et services divins... musique sacrée et pompe des cérémonies. » L'oracle. « Il est des circonstances où le travail est si pénible que l'on ne peut plus penser à soi-même. » Était-ce là le « grand renoncement » annoncé par le *Yi king* ? Je sentis comme une décharge électrique ; cette preuve indubitable de la valeur de l'oracle me fit frissonner. Je retournai le problème en tous sens. Ce devait être ça. Quelle autre interprétation donner de son verdict ? « Sacrifices solennels et services divins... musique sacrée et pompe des cérémonies » — qu'était-ce, sinon le marché, les rituels de l'investissement tels qu'ils étaient pratiqués par les grands prêtres de la haute finance ? Qu'était cette « musique sacrée » sinon le rythme claudiquant du télétype, le bourdonnement de la bande-annonce, le rugissement et le tohu-bohu des milliers de voix qui s'élèvent de la grande salle, psalmodient leur antienne répétitive et hypnotique, leur invocation rituelle à la divinité : le Dow ! Oui, il ne pouvait s'agir d'autre chose. Ce que j'avais perdu serait restauré ! Et mon mandat moral, ma mission, mon « grand but hors de moi-même » était la réhabilitation de Kahn, que je devais entreprendre quitte à conserver mon héritage ; entreprendre, aussi, *grâce* à mon héritage, en replongeant Kahn (et moi-même par la même occasion) dans son élément, le marché.

En d'autres termes, nous devions mettre nos ressources en commun — son savoir-faire, mon capital — et entrer en affaires ! L'étendue de ma richesse nouvelle allait nous permettre de signer une nouvelle traite sur la vie, de faire tout ce qui nous plairait, tout ce que voudrait mon Juif Rrant mélancolique. Oui, lecteur, quelle porte pourrait nous résister ?

« A Kahn, donc ! » me jurai-je comme on porte un toast.

L'étape suivante consistait à rameuter les énergies défaillantes, à réveiller l'enthousiasme là où il s'était assoupi, — chez Kahn. J'espérais seulement qu'il n'était pas trop tard. Le lendemain je profitai de mon heure de déjeuner pour me lancer à sa poursuite. Kahn laissait dans son sillage d'innombrables bouteilles de Dry Sack vides, accompagnées de petits cartons de lait éventrés (aussi touchants qu'un plateau de cantine d'écolier), qui me facilitèrent grandement la tâche. On l'avait aperçu au fin fond du quartier financier, errant d'un pas traînant dans son costume fripé, sans chaussettes, non rasé, le regard vitreux, les yeux rougis par les larmes, ses cernes de raton-laveur aussi visibles que des blessures. Avec son attaché-case — qu'il s'obstinait à transporter partout bien qu'il ne lui servît plus à rien, souvenir pathétique d'une gloire révolue —, il ressemblait à une grosse ménagère juive qui allait faire ses courses. Je le trouvai dans un petit bar proche de la Bourse, que nous avions autrefois fréquenté avant que nos affaires ne tournent au vinaigre, le café du Platane.

Les propriétaires de cet établissement, et ceux de quelques autres, prétendaient occuper le site de l'arbre légendaire du même nom sous les branches duquel le groupe désormais sanctifié des financiers hollandais, les pères fondateurs de Wall Street, avec leurs visages ronds, rubiconds et gonflés de bière plantés sur leurs cous massifs, tirant avec une ferveur religieuse sur leurs pipes en écume de mer, avaient atteint l'illumination à la Hollandaise et conçu leur utopie financière, la Bourse de New York, tout comme le Bouddha Gautama était entré au nirvana sous l'arbre de la Bodhi en Inde quelques siècles auparavant. Je songeai que Newton avait reçu son inspiration dans un cadre similaire. Peut-être ce genre de chose se passait-il toujours sous un arbre... Mais je m'étais promis de ne pas penser à moi. J'étais ici pour Kahn.

Le triste hère que je découvris vautré dans un recoin du bar sous une plante en pot qui évoquait irrésistiblement un Juif Errant, œuvrait à son salut d'une façon fort différente. Un seul coup d'œil suffisait pour comprendre que Kahn essayait d'atteindre le nirvana par l'alcool, ou plutôt par l'oubli que celui-ci lui procurait. Vu son état, je crois qu'il n'était pas en mesure de faire la différence. Des verres étaient empilés en une pyramide précaire sur sa table, comme un monument érigé à la gloire de son propre avilissement. A mon entrée, la serveuse, qui nous avait souvent vus ensemble auparavant, se précipita vers moi.

« Je ne sais pas quoi faire de M. Kahn, me confia-t-elle d'une voix plaintive. Il a passé là toute la matinée, sans parler de la journée d'hier et d'avant-hier. Je ne voudrais pas devoir appeler la police. Il a toujours été un bon client. Mais s'il ne s'en va pas bientôt, je n'aurai pas le choix. » Elle baissa la voix. « Je crois qu'il perd les pédales. Il refuse même que je nettoie sa table, il m'a dit qu'il essayait de reconstituer la captivité à Babylone, de reconstruire lui-même les pyramides, mais avec des verres à cocktail. »

Malgré la gravité de la situation, je ne pus m'empêcher de sourire. Je tentai de la rassurer, mais mes paroles eurent infiniment moins d'effet qu'un billet de dix sacs glissé dans sa paume consentante.

« Okay, Kahn, attaquai-je en m'essayant à une ironie légère, inoffensive, la Diaspora est terminée. »

Il leva la tête hors de ses bras pour m'adresser un regard glauque, sous-marin, comme un poisson maussade. « Va-t'en et laisse-moi souffrir en paix, grommela-t-il. C'est la seule chose qui me rende heureux.

— Ne soyez pas si difficile, le rabrouai-je.

— S'il y a une chose que je ne supporte pas, c'est bien les missionnaires, m'informa-t-il en laissant retomber sa tête dans ses bras. Je croyais que ce spécimen humain n'existait pas chez les Chinois. »

Comme je ne répondais pas, il releva les yeux. « Tu n'es pas venu ici pour me sauver, je suppose ?

— Qu'est-ce que vous prenez ? demandai-je d'un ton caustique. Peu importe. S'il vous plaît ! Une autre tournée de Dry Sack.

— Avec du lait, ajouta Kahn en rotant.

— Comme si je savais pas, gronda la serveuse, qui me fusilla du regard.

— Alors qu'est-ce que c'est que cette histoire de Diaspora terminée ? Tu te prends pour qui, petit, Moïse ? » Il gloussa. « Le p'tit Moïse, Moïse Sait-tung.

— Diaspora signifie dispersion, n'est-ce pas ?
— Ouais. Et alors ? »

Je lui souris d'un air mystérieux, incapable de ne pas lui faire endurer les affres de mon secret, histoire de lui rendre la monnaie de sa pièce.

« Alors, alors ? demanda-t-il en agitant les bras avec une exaltation irritée, comme pour attiser une flamme récalcitrante.

— J'ai consulté l'oracle pour vous, et c'est la réponse qu'il m'a donnée, le numéro cinquante-neuf, la "Dispersion". "Sacrifices solennels et services divins... musique sacrée et pompe des cérémonies." Ça ne vous évoque rien ? » Je lui adressai un regard perçant.

« La Pâque juive ? »

Je secouai la tête.

« Bon, okay, je donne ma langue au chat. Foin de subtilités et de mystères orientaux, d'accord, petit ? Je suis un type désespéré. Si tu as quelques chose à dire, accouche.

— Voilà, Kahn, en deux mots comme en cent — nous sommes riches !

— Formidable, répliqua-t-il d'un air abattu. Qui ça, "nous" ?

— Nous ! Vous et moi. » J'attendis un signe d'enthousiasme. « Qu'y a-t-il ? Vous ne semblez pas content ?

— Comprends-moi bien, petit. Je ne suis pas un ingrat. Mais nom de Dieu, peux-tu me dire de quoi tu parles ?

— J'ai hérité un million de dollars, Kahn ! Deux millions !

— Ne me raconte pas, dit-il sèchement, que ta riche vieille tante de Cleveland vient de passer l'arme à gauche et que...

— Non, Kahn. Eddie Love.

— Eddie Love ? » Il dressa l'oreille, sembla me prendre au sérieux pour la première fois.

J'acquiesçai.

« Parfait, plus que parfait ! Alors raconte. »

Et je lui racontai, très lentement et minutieusement, en faisant d'amples concessions à son ébriété. Il semblait suivre ; pourtant, alors que j'approchais de la fin de mon récit, son expression ne trahissait toujours aucun enthousiasme. « Qu'y a-t-il, vous ne me croyez pas ? demandai-je en terminant.

— Oh si, répondit-il. Pourquoi pas ? S'il y a une chose que j'ai apprise, c'est bien que tout peut arriver, et arrivera probablement, surtout si c'est désagréable. Il y a là une corrélation statistique sur laquelle les mathématiciens devraient un jour se pencher.

— C'est tout ce que vous trouvez à dire, demandai-je, exaspéré.

— Je sais, je sais, autant la boucler si l'on n'a rien de gentil à dire. Ne te méprends pas, petit. Je suis content pour toi. Sincèrement. Seulement, vu les exigences de ma culpabilité, je n'ai pas beaucoup de temps ni d'énergie à consacrer aux tapes dans le dos et aux marques de sympathie. Un petit malin comme toi devrait comprendre ça facilement.

— Mais justement ! m'écriai-je sans tenir compte de son ironie. Inutile désormais de vous complaire dans votre culpabilité, de vous vautrer dans vos humiliations.

— Et pourquoi pas ? demanda-t-il de but en blanc. Tu ne voudrais tout de même pas me priver de ma seule et unique consolation dans l'adversité ? » Une lueur moqueuse brilla dans son œil. « Tu ne serais pas venu m'apporter mes indemnités de chômage, par hasard ? »

Heureusement, comme le lecteur ne l'ignore pas, j'avais prévu cette impasse et mis au point une astuce pour m'en sortir. « Pas du tout, répondis-je. Au contraire, je suis venu vous demander un service. »

Il partit d'un grand rire débridé, qu'interrompit brusquement un rot. « Me demander un service, *à moi* ! C'est un comble. Pourquoi aurais-tu besoin de moi ? Tu as de l'argent et tu connais les ficelles. Comment t'aiderais-je ? Je suis le gars qui t'a fait perdre ta robe, tu te souviens ?

— Non, Kahn, le contredis-je. C'est ma propre décision qui est à l'origine de cette perte. Vous n'en êtes pas responsable. »

Mais il était déjà lancé dans une jérémiade où il s'accusait de tous les péchés du monde. « Tu n'as pas entendu les nouvelles, petit ? Je suis le type qui a craqué. Sept années de scoumoune, et j'ai paniqué. J'ai essayé de tricher, je me suis fait pincer. Manque de bol. Putain de malchance. Mais toi ! Tu as débarqué ici comme une fleur, ou plutôt comme un trèfle, un trèfle à quatre feuilles.

— Pourquoi n'oubliez-vous pas un peu tout ça ? » suggérai-je.

Il secoua la tête. « Moi qui espérais au moins t'avoir appris une chose, petit : "Minimise tes pertes et laisse ton profit suivre son bonhomme de chemin", tu te souviens ? Je suis un raté, petit. Un tocard de première bourre. Rends-toi un service, ne te mets pas en cheville avec un perdant.

— Vous m'avez également appris la valeur de l'opinion contraire, repris-je. Quand tout le monde vend, c'est le moment d'acheter. Et en ce moment, on dirait que tout le monde brade. »

D'un bref sourire triste, il me concéda ce point. Puis il secoua la tête en soupirant. « Tu sais, je ne comprends pas encore très bien comment ça s'est passé. C'est comme un rêve. Voici quelques semaines seulement, ne t'ai-je pas dit que le marché était "le test ultime de la personnalité" ? "L'épreuve du feu", je crois que j'ai utilisé cette expression. »

Je rougis d'embarras, pour lui comme pour moi.

« Suis-je un tel hypocrite ? » Il haussa les épaules. « Je suppose que oui. Mais quand je me suis retrouvé au pied du mur, je ne croyais pas que je le ferais — choisir l'argent contre... le reste, la rectitude, ma dignité, tout ça. Pourtant, c'est ce que j'ai fait. Sans même me poser la question. J'ai moi-même baissé ma culotte pour me baiser. Je sais pas ce qui s'est passé. C'est difficile à dire. Je crois qu'un jour je me suis réveillé et c'était là. Je n'ai même pas pris le temps d'y penser. C'est ça qui me tue. Cette démarche instinctive, tu vois ? J'ai lu un article à propos d'une jeune fille, une hippie de New York employée comme travailleur social dans une réserve indienne de l'Ouest. Elle a adopté un bébé loup, elle l'a ramené chez elle, a essayé de le domestiquer, de lui appliquer toutes les méthodes classiques destinées aux chiens. Et puis une nuit, le loup a vu la pleine lune par la fenêtre ; elle se levait derrière les montagnes, et il a poussé ce hurlement glaçant et désespéré qu'elle n'avait jamais entendu. Le lendemain, il était parti. En faisant péter le carreau de la fenêtre. Ce putain de mur de verre a volé en éclats. Voilà, petit : on ne peut pas transformer un loup en pacifiste ou en végétarien, même avec les meilleures intentions du monde. C'est tout bonnement un programme qu'il ne possède pas en lui. Je crois qu'en chacun de nous il y a un mur de verre — comme celui qui sépare la galerie de la grande salle. Certains réussissent à rester en sécurité derrière lui toute leur vie et ne quittent jamais la galerie ; d'autres brisent ce mur et atterrissent brutalement dans la grande salle de la Bourse, comme moi... » Il sourit avec une sagesse amère. « La gravité du sang, voilà ce qui m'a poussé à fracasser ce mur, petit. Tous mes aïeux, les guerriers ashkénazes, qui possédaient des monts de piété à Prague et Varsovie — leur faim insatiable, leurs dos voûtés, leurs âmes desséchées et leurs cœurs ratatinés, leur énorme cupidité comme une meule attachée à leur cou — tout cela, qui venait du fond des âges, a soudain éclaté en moi — "C'est ton héritage, petit goinfre ; tu y as droit ; sers-toi copieusement tant que tu peux", — et toutes mes bonnes intentions de modération, circonspection, honnêteté, altruisme, tout ça s'éparpilla au gré des vents comme autant de glumes. Ah, Sonny ! soupira-t-il en frottant vivement ses mains l'une contre l'autre. Tu ne trouves pas qu'il fait froid ici ? Mon hygroma !

— Allons, Kahn, l'exhortai-je. Cessez donc de vous plaindre. »

— Ah ah ! s'écria-t-il avec véhémence. Je le savais. Je savais que tu étais venu ici pour prêcher. Et pourquoi devrais-je m'arrêter ? Ça me fait du bien. Tu veux que je te dise un secret à propos des Juifs ? C'est ma mère qui me l'a appris, et je ne l'ai jamais oublié. (Je ne te l'aurais pas déjà dit, par hasard ? Je ne me souviens pas. Okay, je suis donc un peu shikker. Oh, et puis tant pis !) Nous excellons dans la souffrance. Elle permet à un Juif d'exprimer ses talents latents. C'est un produit de notre histoire. Nous avons si longtemps été traités comme de la merde que nous avons mis au point toute une panoplie de techniques compensatoires. Reconnais-le : aucune race ne nous arrive à la cheville question douleurs — y compris celles de l'âme, d'ailleurs —, à l'éventuelle exception des redoutables tu-sais-qui. Le seul problème est que nous nous barrons en couilles dans la prospérité, nous subissons tous les symptômes du manque, nous nous liquéfions. Regarde Israël. C'est pour ça que tant de Juifs ont cet air patelin que tu as sans doute remarqué. Parce qu'à un niveau probablement inconscient, chaque Juif sait qu'être, c'est souffrir. Il désire l'insulte ou l'affront, il t'y pousse le cas échéant, afin de s'assurer un bénéfice spirituel. C'est la seule voie qu'il connaisse vers l'illumination. Si un autre que moi disait cela, je l'accuserais aussitôt d'antisémitisme notoire. Le seul problème, c'est que c'est vrai.

— Eh bien, répondis-je, à vous voir, je dirais que vous n'êtes pas très fort. Votre souffrance ne semble avoir mis au jour aucun talent caché, sinon peut-être pour l'avilissement. S'agit-il d'une de ces "techniques compensatoires" que les Juifs en général, et Aaron Kahn en particulier, ont maîtrisées afin de s'ennoblir par la souffrance ? »

Kahn se renfrogna puis émit le sifflement d'une furtive créature nocturne surprise par un rai de lumière. « Tu sais, Sonny, dit-il, tu étais un gosse si candide quand tu es arrivé ici, facile à vivre, timide, débordant de zèle religieux. C'est ton manque de cynisme qui m'a attiré chez toi. C'était rafraîchissant. » Il fit une pause. « Que s'est-il passé ?

— Vous faites sans doute allusion à mes Salamalecs Orientaux, n'est-ce pas ? demandai-je ironiquement, un peu blessé par son portrait.
— Tu vois ? rétorqua-t-il. C'est exactement ça. Tu deviens blasé, petit, cynique. De plus en plus, je vois le Wasp se développer en toi. Je ne veux pas t'accabler de sermons, mais ça me paraît clair comme de l'eau de roche. Tu changes. Cette histoire que tu m'as racontée, comme quoi Eddie Love était ton père ? J'avoue que j'ai commencé par en douter. Mais plus maintenant. La ressemblance n'est que trop évidente. » Il soupira en secouant la tête. « Tu n'es pas différent de lui, petit. C'est la gravité du sang. Tôt ou tard, elle emporte le morceau. Personne n'y coupe. La récidive. Moi par exemple : je n'ai jamais voulu être juif ; mais peu à peu, comme un petit caillou, un grain de sable touché puis emporté par l'avance du glacier, je me suis retrouvé délesté de mes désirs personnels, balayé, emporté par des forces raciales et historiques. Et toi, petit, je te plains davantage que moi. Chez moi du moins, toutes ces forces tendaient dans la même direction, même si celle-ci était diamétralement opposée à celle que j'avais choisie. Mais toi ! Le Seigneur te vienne en aide ! A moitié Wasp, à moitié Chinois, comme un animal mythique, un satyre ou un triton, une tête d'homme sur un corps de bête, mi-Orient mi-Occident, mi-dragon mi-tigre, comme sur la robe de ta mère, prisonnier entre les opposés — comment les appelles-tu ? Je perds la mémoire. *Yin* et *yang* — ouais, c'est ça, coincé entre ton *yin* et ton *yang*. »

Kahn et moi échangeâmes un long regard, puis nous nous détournâmes, lui vers les glaçons qui flottaient au fond de son verre de lait, moi vers la fenêtre. Dans la rue, d'innombrables hommes jeunes à la démarche brusque et efficace, aux traits indubitablement anglo-saxons, marchaient d'un pas vif sur le trottoir, attaché-case à la main, trench-coat posé sur le bras. Ne serais-je pas mieux loti avec l'un d'eux, me demandai-je — un de ces jeunes gens volontaires, énergiques, pleins de santé, amateurs de jogging qui soignaient leur régime et surveillaient leur poids, séparaient radicalement leurs vies professionnelle et privée — ne serait-il pas plus raisonnable de choisir mon partenaire parmi leurs rangs ? Peut-être — sans doute, même. Mais ils ne m'intéressaient pas. Ils ressemblaient à autant de marionnettes et de pantins, comparés à ce Juif vieillissant aux yeux mélancoliques entourés de cernes semblables à deux cataplasmes bleus, trop bleus. Une force élémentaire nous attirait l'un vers l'autre, en partie, je crois, parce que nous appartenions tous deux à une vieille race qui avait souffert et survécu, et qui se connaissait elle-même. A l'inverse de ces Américains qui, comme l'avait dit mon oncle Hsiao, constituaient un peuple flambant neuf, à peine extrait du moule, un peuple qui n'avait pas fait ses preuves, que rien n'avait éprouvé. Et pourtant Kahn avait remarqué à juste titre que j'étais moi-même à moitié Wasp, un alliage, un métal inédit, un tempérament nouveau, l'incarnation d'un espoir sans limite, de l'énergie et de l'inexpérience, alliés à une souffrance immémoriale, au stoïcisme, à la résignation.

Certainement, songeai-je, il me serait plus facile de profiter de ma richesse nouvelle sans jeter le moindre regard en arrière vers Kahn. Cela me sembla surtout tentant en cet instant où il se montrait si difficile. Mais ma tâche consistait à « abandonner tout désir personnel » pour « placer mon but hors de moi ». Après tout, à quoi bon cet argent, sinon pour le mettre au service de Kahn ? Avec la véhémence du désespoir, je m'obligeai à graver ce fait dans ma mémoire, car je savais que si je le perdais de vue j'étais fini. De plus, malgré ses critiques malveillantes et ses lamentations, je sentis que Kahn avait mis le doigt sur une vérité fondamentale, qu'il l'avait énoncée sans peur des conséquences. Et cette vérité avait beau me blesser, j'avais beau haïr le mentor qui l'avait prononcée, j'appréciai en même temps sa sincérité. Après la valse-hésitation de l'amour et de la haine, la première émotion l'emporta. Je posai doucement ma main sur la sienne. « Vous êtes prêt à m'écouter maintenant ?

— Sonny, laisse tomber, veux-tu ? Ça ne m'intéresse plus, tu ne comprends pas ? » me supplia-t-il.

L'expression de son visage disait pourtant le contraire. « Non, répondis-je, je ne comprends pas. »

Il posa sa tête sur la table et se mit à pleurer.

« Allons-nous en. Sortons d'ici », dit-il enfin quand il eut maîtrisé ses sanglots, son visage empâté rouge de honte, son regard papillonnant çà et là, mais fuyant mes yeux.

Je payai la note pendant qu'il évitait la curiosité cruelle des patrons pour gagner l'anonymat de la rue.

Une fois encore, nous marchâmes en direction du fleuve. Notre pas était vif, nous ne parlions pas. Nous arrivâmes enfin au pont de Brooklyn. Suivant la rive, nous nous arrêtâmes pour regarder son arche monumentale qui enjambait l'eau à plusieurs dizaines de mètres au-dessus de nous. Dans la lente cristallisation de mon histoire personnelle, ce pont était devenu un symbole curieux, très américain, avec ses deux immenses piliers qui s'enfonçaient jusqu'au fond dans le limon et la vase du fleuve pollué, et au-dessus de l'eau les câbles qui luisaient au soleil comme les fils brillants d'une toile d'araignée, ou des cordes de harpe, une harpe éolienne bourdonnant près des toits, ou encore les fils presque invisibles du marionnettiste qui soutenaient le tablier. Que des torons aussi frêles et ténus réussissent à supporter une telle masse hideuse de puissance aveugle ne cessait de m'étonner et, comme je l'ai dit, me paraissait le symbole adéquat de l'Amérique elle-même, de son pouvoir gigantesque et des fils à peine visibles qui le manipulaient.

« Tu sais, dit Kahn d'une voix maintenant détendue, qu'on ne sentait plus sur le point de se briser, pendant ma première année à Mont-Nébo, je traversais ce pont tous les jours, dans un sens puis dans l'autre. Suite à un pacte que j'avais passé avec mon père. Vois-tu, il ne m'avait rien dit à propos d'Ahasvérus. Il me faisait même croire qu'il me suffisait de traverser ce pont par n'importe quel temps pour que mon inscription à Mont-Nébo fût une affaire entendue. "Tout privilège requiert un sacrifice, disait-il. Faut que tu assumes tes responsabilités." J'ai pris cela à cœur. Je trouvais formidable de me retrouver au milieu du pont en plein hiver et de regarder les tourbillons du courant. Cela me donnait une impression grisante de... je ne sais pas — de pouvoir, d'une destinée particulière — comme si j'avais été appelé à une tâche élevée et que ce sacrifice prouvait que j'en étais digne.

La vanité enfantine explique en partie mes prétentions, bien sûr, mais je fondais parfois en larmes quand je pensais à ma mission dans l'existence. Les larmes les plus douces que j'aie jamais versées. Mais je n'ai jamais trouvé ma mission, ce lieu qu'on m'avait réservé depuis le commencement du monde. J'ai schleppé de droite et de gauche. J'ai essayé de devenir un érudit. J'ai failli réussir. Peut-être aurais-je dû m'obstiner davantage, mais cela frustrait une partie de moi-même, une partie vile peut-être, mais bien réelle. Je mourais d'envie de participer à la mêlée, de me fondre dedans, de courir au-devant du risque et du danger, bref j'avais soif d'aventures.

« Tu sais, l'université m'a souvent manqué depuis que je suis arrivé à Wall Street, mais à la vérité — je te dis ça même maintenant, après tout ce qui s'est passé —, malgré la honte de tout ce que j'y ai fait, et bien que je m'interroge parfois sur les principes mêmes qui président aux activités de la Bourse, pourtant aussi loin que je me souvienne, je n'ai jamais ressenti cette inquiétude, cette angoisse, cette morsure d'impatience, tout le temps où j'ai travaillé à la Bourse. Car, quoi que j'en dise, quelque chose y satisfaisait mon appétit de vivre. » Kahn regarda au-delà du fleuve. « Je ne saurais nommer cette impression. Même si tu me payais. » Il eut un rire amer en saisissant l'ironie involontaire de sa remarque. « Non, même si tu me payais. » Puis il se tourna vers moi avec un sourire contraint. « Sacrée Kahn-fidence, pas vrai, petit ? » Son humeur s'assombrit. « Je ferais peut-être mieux de ne pas y penser. Tout ça est bel et bien terminé, autant mettre une croix dessus. Maintenant, il faut que je trouve autre chose. Je me demande où je vais atterrir cette fois. Les paris sont ouverts…

— Je vais vous dire ce que vous allez faire », répondis-je.

Surpris, il haussa les sourcils.

J'opinai gravement du chef. « Vous allez vous remettre en selle et repartir pour un tour. »

Il rit. « Le seul petit problème, Sonny, c'est qu'ils m'ont piqué ma selle.

— Façon de parler, Kahn, rétorquai-je d'un ton sarcastique.

— Tu sais, petit, je n'avais jamais remarqué que tu avais de l'humour. Pourtant, c'est très drôle : "vous remettre en selle et repartir pour un tour". Vraiment. Prends-le comme un compliment. Tu perds peut-être ton humanité, mais la bonne nouvelle est que je découvre chez toi un talent insoupçonné pour la gaudriole. » Il plissa le front, prit une pose d'histrion. « J'vâ met' mon ârmure et mes ép'rons, enfourcher mon bourrin, et gare à la casse ! "Tention les gars, j'dirai, feriez mieux d'laisser tomber 'vant que j'vous réduise en chair à pâté !" Non, Sonny, sincèrement, tu es en net progrès. Et puis quelle différence ça fait que je n'aie pas un sou vaillant, que je me sois fait blackbouler par le Bureau des Gouverneurs, que j'aie perdu ma réputation et mes amis ?

— Il vous reste moi », dis-je.

Je sentis une réplique cinglante chatouiller le bout de sa langue, mais il se retint *in extremis*. Avec un soupir de baudruche qui se dégonfle, il tapota mon bras. « Oui, petit, tu as raison. Et ça me fait plaisir.

— Vous savez, Aaron, dis-je, un vieux paradoxe taoïste compare la quête de l'illumination à la recherche d'un taureau sur lequel on est assis. Ce que nous cherchons désespérément se trouve parfois à l'endroit le plus improbable, juste sous notre nez.

— Quelle profondeur..., commenta-t-il avec une ironie lugubre.

— Profond ou pas, vous dites que vous devez décider quoi faire de votre vie, trouver un moyen de ramasser les morceaux. Et présomptueux ou pas, je crois que j'ai quelque chose à vous proposer. Du jour où je vous ai rencontré, je vous ai entendu vous plaindre de la profession, mais malgré cela — et ce que vous venez de dire me renforce dans ma conviction —, je suis persuadé que le marché est votre *tao*, votre voie personnelle pour le retour à la Source. Votre propre tension vers la grâce, Kahn. Vous avez subi un sérieux revers, d'accord, mais est-ce une excuse pour renoncer au voyage ? Pour moi, cela serait plus inexcusable que cette erreur de parcours. On peut tout pardonner, sauf cela.

— C'est très facile pour toi de dire ça, rétorqua-t-il avec passion, mais cela ne change rien aux faits. Comment précisément vais-je me remettre en selle, selon ton expression ? Je te l'ai dit, petit, je suis raide comme un passe-lacet. Mon nom remplace le mot de cinq lettres dans la bouche de tous les investisseurs américains. J'ai perdu tout mon crédit.

— J'ai envisagé le problème sous toutes les coutures, Kahn, le coupai-je. Je veux vous proposer d'entrer en affaires avec moi.

— En affaires ? demanda-t-il. Quel genre d'affaires ?

— Je ne sais pas. Voilà ce que j'espérais que vous me diriez. Un type de service financier, peut-être. Je suis ignare en la matière. Je vous fais entièrement confiance pour trouver. Voilà pourquoi j'ai besoin de vous. Et ce n'est pas de la charité. Mes fonds, votre savoir-faire — une mise en commun des ressources à cinquante-cinquante. Qu'en dites-vous ? »

Il m'adressa un regard suave, presque sentimental. « C'est terriblement gentil de ta part, petit — vouloir accorder un répit à ton vieux menteur — pardon, mentor ! Mais ne fais pas l'andouille. Je t'ai déjà ruiné une fois, pourquoi ne recommencerais-je pas ?

— Je vous l'ai déjà dit, Kahn, j'assume l'entière responsabilité de mes actes. Et puis, des deux, c'est moi qui vous ai fait le plus de mal.

— Quoi ! » Il me dévisagea avec incrédulité. « Tu es un petit futé, Sonny, mais j'aimerais voir comment tu vas justifier pareille absurdité. Alors ? Explique-moi un peu le mal que tu m'as fait...

— Je vous ai importuné, répondis-je. Je n'ai pas eu foi en vous. C'est écrit dans le *Tao-tö king* : "En ne croyant pas les gens, nous en faisons des menteurs." Les espoirs exorbitants que je plaçais en vous tout en me méfiant de vos capacités à y répondre ont exercé une pression injuste sur vous, qui vous a détourné de votre intention première — laquelle était bonne, j'en suis toujours convaincu. »

Kahn regarda le fleuve en refoulant un sanglot. « Elle l'était, petit. Crois-moi !

— Alors, demandai-je, marché conclu ? »

De nouveau il me regarda avec une moue dubitative, puis acquiesça en poussant un long soupir. « Okay, accepta-t-il, ajoutant aussitôt : J'espère seulement que tu ne le regretteras pas. » Il marqua un temps. « Et moi non plus. »

Nous rîmes tous deux, puis nous nous éloignâmes sans plus de cérémonie.

9

Mon modeste bienfait me procura une joie disproportionnée. Rentrant chez moi à travers les rues, je sentais parfois le rouge me monter aux joues, pas le rouge de la honte — celui du bonheur. Rempli de fierté, je me demandai si après tout Riley n'avait pas raison. Peut-être quelque chose fondait-il vraiment en moi, un noyau dur commençait-il à s'effriter sous l'action des courants chauds ? Était-ce le *tao* de l'amour ?

Une fois cette affaire réglée au mieux, je considérai d'un œil plus serein ma nouvelle richesse. C'était indiscutable : je l'avais sagement investie. Dans l'enthousiasme de la réussite, je songeai brièvement, presque par acquit de conscience, qu'elle était incompatible avec l'Humilité, le dernier de mes Trois Trésors. Si j'intervenais activement dans les affaires de Kahn, c'était par altruisme, n'est-ce pas ? Le *Yi king* lui-même n'avait-il pas conseillé de recourir à la puissance ? Non, la pédanterie et le pinaillage ne parviendraient pas à me détourner de mes bons offices. Car telle était précisément la lumière sous laquelle le dogme de non-intervention se présenta alors à mes yeux. Quelle chose était la plus importante, me demandai-je, la vie humaine ou la pureté doctrinale ? Un ressentiment bref mais violent contre mon éducation enflamma ma conscience. Que pouvait-on conclure d'un mode de vie qui laissait en suspens pareille question, pareille opposition ? Ne contenait-il pas une inhumanité fondamentale ? Mais que disais-je ! C'était un blasphème ! Ma girouette émotionnelle vira à cent quatre-vingts degrés, de l'ouest à l'est.

Néanmoins, plutôt que d'abdiquer le pouvoir conféré par ma nouvelle richesse, je préférai envisager d'autres utilisations. L'une en particulier me sembla extrêmement judicieuse. Elle rivalisait même en ingéniosité avec mon projet de réhabilitation de Kahn, bien qu'elle fût sans doute moins désintéressée. Mais sur ce chapitre, je n'étais pas d'humeur à couper les cheveux en quatre. Je parle bien sûr de Li. Je me rappelai une image qui était revenue sans cesse dans sa conversation : le Pays des Fées. En proie à une excitation nerveuse, à un espoir qui n'osait pas s'affirmer contre mes doutes habituels, je compris que j'étais maintenant en mesure de l'y mener. Non pas sur un tapis tissé de bonnes intentions, mais sur un tapis *magique*, lecteur, un tapis brodé de fils d'or !

Le problème était de savoir si elle me laisserait l'emmener. J'ignorais si mon plan réussirait. Pourtant, la devise d'Ahasvérus, « Pas de gloire sans couilles », semblait aussi valable dans ce contexte que dans celui de la Bourse, sinon plus. Peut-être couvrait-il d'ailleurs tout le spectre de la vie américaine !

    Quand je me fus décidé, je me sentis soudain plein de confiance. Je m'occupai aussitôt des préparatifs de cette rencontre. Je m'achetai d'abord un costume sur Canal Street, l'un de ces vêtements de luxe que j'avais vu les grands pontes chinois porter chez *Luck Fat*. J'achetai aussi une chemise, une cravate et un boxer short (en l'honneur de ma propre rébellion !), couronnant mes emplettes par une somptueuse paire de mocassins rouges achetée au libre service que j'avais remarqué depuis mon arrivée en ville. Dans la prodigalité de mon inspiration, j'en achetai douze paires !

    Sur le chemin du retour, je voulus réparer l'un des péchés de mon passé et m'arrêtai dans un magasin de spiritueux pour acheter la bouteille de Dry Sack que j'avais promise à Lo lors de notre dernière séance d'œnologie, puis j'obliquai vers le restaurant *Luck Fat*.

    Quand il m'aperçut dans l'entrebâillement de la porte de la ruelle, une expression surprise et douloureuse traversa son visage. Mais il se reprit aussitôt. « Le jeune dragon revient enfin de ses errances ! » proclama-t-il avec la malice affectueuse qui le caractérisait, souriant et s'inclinant tant et plus quand j'entrai dans son domaine privé.

    « Je passais dans les environs, commençai-je, et je me suis dit que trop de temps s'était écoulé depuis ma promesse. » Je lui montrai la bouteille de vin en souriant.

    Il la sortit du sac en papier, l'examina attentivement. « L'honorable cru dont nous avons discuté les mérites lors de notre dernière rencontre ? »

    Ravi, j'opinai du chef.

    « Je suis comblé, dit-il avec une profonde révérence.

    — Tout le plaisir est pour moi, insistai-je.

    — Non, non, protesta-t-il.

    — Si si », renchéris-je.

Nous éclatâmes de rire.

    « Je vois bien que vous être trop occupé pour le goûter maintenant, m'excusai-je, mais quand vous aurez un moment de loisir, peut-être condescendrez-vous à en boire une ou deux gorgées, ce qui nous permettrait de passer ensuite une heure agréable pour en parler comme autrefois.

    — Ah oui, que c'était plaisant ! soupira-t-il. Mon épouse me harcèle sans cesse, savez-vous. "Où est Sun I ? me demande-t-elle. Pourquoi ne vient-il plus jamais nous voir ? Nos aisselles seraient-elles nauséabondes ? Notre conversation trop terne ?" "Il nous délaisse à cause de tes insupportables tracasseries, femme !" je lui réponds. "Et chasser le jeune dragon ne te suffit apparemment pas ! En fait, si tu continues à me houspiller, je me verrai contraint de demander le divorce à l'empereur". » Il rit. « "Mais sérieusement, comment veux-tu que je sache ? Le dragon effectue maints vols lointains dans son exploration du globe, des vols inimaginables pour le commun des mortels comme toi et moi. Nous pouvons seulement être sûrs d'une chose : un jour, quand il sera bien fatigué, il reviendra pour se reposer et se nourrir. Et ce jour-là, nous serons là".

— Merci, Lo », dis-je pour répondre à la proposition sincère que masquaient ses remarques joviales.

Il sourit et s'inclina.

« Eh bien... » fis-je tout en m'exhortant à partir.

Il posa la main sur mon bras. « Attendez un peu. Avant votre départ, nous boirons une coupe ensemble. » Je fis mine de protester, il ne voulut rien savoir. « Non, non, j'insiste. La soirée est calme. Nous avons le temps. Et puis sinon vous me donnerez l'impression que je suis impoli. Juste une coupe.

— Bon, d'accord, concédai-je avec hésitation, si vous êtes sûr que je ne vous dérange pas.

— Parfaitement sûr. Tout est okay, *number one* ! »

Il chambra le vin, puis se tourna vers moi. « Vous savez, Sun I, bien qu'elle n'en parle jamais, je crois que Yin-mi plus que quiconque regrette vos visites. Ce n'est bien sûr pas à moi de le demander, mais j'espère qu'aucun nuage ne s'est levé entre vous. Je sais qu'elle pense souvent à vous, et nous avons cru comprendre que vous pensiez souvent à elle, n'est-ce pas ?

— Oh, oui. C'est que... Vous voyez, je suis passé il n'y a pas si longtemps, repris-je en décidant qu'il valait mieux éviter sa question, et elle n'était pas à l'appartement. En fait il n'y avait personne, sauf votre autre fille, Li.

— Ah, vous avez rencontré Li ! »

J'acquiesçai.

« Et qu'avez-vous pensé d'elle ?

— Je l'avais déjà vue auparavant, vous vous rappelez ? Au déjeuner de famille.

— Ah oui, bien sûr.

— Elle est très belle », déclarai-je avec une gravité involontaire.

Il m'observa attentivement en fronçant les sourcils. « Oui, très belle.

— Je n'ai pas vraiment eu l'occasion de la connaître, mentis-je en espérant rattraper ma gaffe et que Lo ne devinerait pas la vérité. Elle m'a paru très différente de Yin-mi. »

Il rit. « Aussi différentes que le jour et la nuit.

— Pourquoi ? demandai-je.

— Chacune a ses propres talents.

— Bien sûr.

— Depuis qu'elle était petite fille, Li a toujours su ce qu'elle voulait et s'est battue pour l'obtenir. Elle n'a quasiment pas eu besoin de nous pour trouver sa voie. Elle ressemble donc à un chat. Le chat a une intelligence particulière des choses, il agit selon des principes qui nous échappent. On ne peut rien apprendre au chat. Il sait ce qu'il sait. Essayez de forcer sa nature, et vous risquez de le rendre fou, voire de le tuer — il est impossible de le changer. Sa grande qualité est l'indépendance, tout comme celle du chien est la loyauté. De ce point de vue, Yin-mi ressemble à un chien. Elle a une nature noble, généreuse, elle vit à travers les autres. Elle est moins rusée et plus vulnérable que sa sœur. Elle aime le clair, l'élevé, le fort, tout comme sa sœur est attirée par le paradoxe, l'ambiguïté. » Il s'interrompit pour servir le vin. « Kan pei ! s'écria-t-il en trinquant avec moi.

— Kan pei, répondis-je.
— Mais je vous prie de pardonner mes divagations à propos de mes filles.
— Non non, protestai-je. Pas du tout. Cela m'intéresse. Continuez, s'il vous plaît.
— Vous ne dites pas cela par politesse ? »
Je secouai vigoureusement la tête.
« Eh bien, si cela vous intéresse, je vais vous confier une image qui pour moi résume magnifiquement leur différence. Puis-je ?
J'acquiesçai avec véhémence.
« Connaissez-vous les *Analectes* de Confucius ?
— Pas très bien, avouai-je.
— Je ne peux pas davantage me vanter d'une parfaite érudition concernant les paroles du maître, mais jeune homme déjà et parfois depuis je m'y suis intéressé. Vous avez certainement entendu parler des Danses Sacrées, la Danse de Succession et la Danse de Guerre ?
— Oui, elles ne me sont pas totalement inconnues.
— Eh bien, comme vous le savez sans doute, la Danse de Succession mime l'accession de l'Empereur Shun à la paix. Tout devint harmonie au ciel et sur la terre. A l'inverse, la Danse de Guerre décrit l'accession de l'Empereur belliqueux Wu, qui gagna son trône en renversant les Yin. » Il s'interrompit pour boire une gorgée de vin. « Il y a un passage dans le troisième livre... — il se racla la gorge — "Confucius parle de la Danse de Succession comme d'une parfaite beauté et d'une parfaite bonté." » Il m'adressa un regard appuyé. « "Au contraire, la Danse de Guerre est parfaite beauté, mais imparfaite bonté." Bien sûr, c'est pour moi le comble de la présomption que de comparer mon indigne progéniture aux Danses Sacrées, mais cette distinction m'a toujours paru fort pertinente pour mes filles. Vous ne trouvez pas ?
— Je n'en sais sincèrement rien », déclarai-je avec assurance, peu désireux de m'aventurer en terrain aussi glissant. Après un silence, je lui posai une question : « Quelle dynastie l'Empereur Wu a-t-il détrônée ?
— Les Yin », répondit-il.

Là-dessus, je m'élançai aussi courageusement que possible sur mes mocassins neufs. Je pris le métro omnibus pour me donner le temps de rassembler mes pensées. Je m'arrêtai chez un fleuriste du quartier de Li, où j'achetai un bouquet de chrysanthèmes, puis hélai un taxi pour qu'il me transportât jusqu'à chez elle, car je désirais soigner mon entrée en scène. Malheureusement, il n'y avait personne dans la cour pour me voir en descendre, même pas Ramon, que j'aperçus à travers les portes vitrées en train de téléphoner dans l'entrée de l'immeuble, le dos tourné à la rue. La porte extérieure était ouverte, et la deuxième coincée derrière une chaise si bien qu'il n'avait pas à se déranger à chaque nouvel arrivant. Je crus pouvoir atteindre les ascenseurs sans qu'il me remarquât, mais je n'eus pas cette chance ; il se retourna. « Momento, dit-il en plaquant sa paume contre le téléphone. Hey, mec, où tou crois qué tou vas, bordel ? »

Je pris un billet dans mon portefeuille et le tins ostensiblement entre pouce et index, comme une cape devant un taureau, mais avec l'intention opposée — amadouer.

Il regarda le billet, puis leva les yeux vers moi. Ses traits s'illuminèrent soudain d'un maigre sourire de bandit. « Oh, volountiers, mec, no problema. Tou vo qué ye sonne pour toi ? »

Je secouai la tête en lui donnant mon billet, puis filai pronto vers les ascenseurs tandis que Ramon reprenait ses interminables vitupérations.

Quand j'atteignis sa porte, je la fixai des yeux un long moment, puis soupirai et fis demi-tour. Je ne pouvais pas.

Je m'arrêtai. Je devais oser ! Je pris une profonde inspiration. Mon idée était stupide, pensai-je. J'aurais dû téléphoner d'abord. Elle allait me voir à travers le judas, elle appellerait la police. Je n'avais pas une chance sur mille. M'attendant au pire, avec une sorte de résignation stoïque, je frappai à sa porte.

Personne ne répondit. Je fus grandement soulagé. Je pivotai sur mes talons et courus presque vers les ascenseurs. Mais la porte s'ouvrit alors et j'entendis la chaîne glisser. Li se pencha dans le couloir, regarda d'abord dans la mauvaise direction, puis me vit. Nos regards se croisèrent en silence.

Elle portait une robe, qu'elle serrait contre sa gorge. Quand elle se pencha en avant, ses cheveux quittèrent son dos pour dessiner un long trait noir perpendiculaire au sol. Les portes de l'ascenseur se fermèrent sous mon nez.

« Alors, on prend la poudre d'escampette ? » demanda-t-elle d'une voix amusée, un peu moqueuse.

Je déglutis difficilement, secouai négativement la tête.

« Tant mieux, dit-elle, parce que je crois que tu viens de manquer le coche. » Elle rit, sortit dans le couloir, s'appuya négligemment contre le chambranle de sa porte en m'observant discrètement, impressionnée (du moins ma vanité le crut) par mes vêtements neufs. « Alors, qu'est-ce qui t'amène ? Je suis bien sûr flattée de ta visite, mais tu te rappelles ce que j'ai dit, ce dont nous étions convenus ?

— Je suis venu pour t'emmener... » Je reculai devant la suite de la tirade que j'avais préparée.

Étonnée, elle inclina la tête. « M'emmener où ?

— Au Pays des Fées », réussis-je à articuler, le schibboleth fissuré par le vibrato nerveux de ma voix.

Elle me regarda avec surprise, puis rit soudain en dévoilant ses dents blanches régulières et la peau soyeuse de sa gorge. Quand elle reprit son sérieux, son amusement se nuança de sympathie. « Mon pauvre garçon », dit-elle pour me consoler. Elle tendit la main vers moi.

« Tu peux donc maintenant te payer une nuit en ville, commença-t-elle quand nous fûmes entrés chez elle.

— Je peux me payer mille et une nuits, répondis-je.

— Il s'est passé quelque chose — ne me dis rien... Tu as changé de boulot ? »

Je secouai la tête.

« Tu travailles toujours au parquet ? »

J'acquiesçai, ajoutant aussitôt : « Oui, mais je n'en ai plus besoin. »

Elle haussa les sourcils.

« Je peux faire tout ce que je veux, *maintenant*.

— Vraiment ? » Elle m'examina de la tête aux pieds. « Tu ferais bien de commencer par t'acheter des vêtements neufs.

— Tu n'aimes pas mon costume ? demandai-je, blessé.

— Il est neuf ? »

J'opinai du chef.

Elle se mordit la lèvre. « Excuse-moi, dit-elle. Il n'est pas si moche que ça. Simplement, fais attention de ne pas fumer quand tu le portes. Si tu laisses tomber une cendre dessus, tu seras aussitôt brûlé vif. » Elle pouffa. « Mais tes chaussures sont vraiment hideuses.

— Je brûle déjà », lui dis-je en infligeant le même traitement aux étapes de mon discours et sans prendre garde à son avis négatif concernant mes chaussures.

Elle me lança un regard plein de défi, d'attente, de ruse.

« D'amour pour toi. »

Elle rit. « Hum... pas mal, concéda-t-elle. Tu as indubitablement acquis de l'expérience depuis notre dernière rencontre. Vas-tu me dire ce qui s'est passé ou préfères-tu me faire subir les affres du suspense ? »

Je la regardai sans répondre, comme un homme ivre.

« Très bien, ne me dis rien. Voyons, tu as gagné à la loterie ? »

Je secouai la tête. « Je suis entré en possession de... enfin, appelons ça un héritage.

— Je vois.

— Mais je ne veux pas te parler de ça, ajoutai-je aussitôt. L'argent importe peu. En fait, il me dégoûte. Toi seule comptes pour moi. Je veux te rendre heureuse. Je veux que tu m'aimes. Dis-moi quoi faire.

— Juste ciel ! Tu dois vraiment être riche ! Combien as-tu touché ?

— Est-ce si important ? implorai-je.

— Je ne sais pas, dit-elle. Peut-être.

— Beaucoup.

— Ça ne m'apprend pas grand-chose, se plaignit-elle. Mille dollars, c'est beaucoup, un million aussi. Tout est relatif. Quel nombre est plus près de la réalité ?

— Un million de dollars, répondis-je, mais c'est un peu faible. »

Elle écarquilla les yeux. « Voilà qui fera sans doute la différence.

— Quelle différence ?

— Ça dépend.

— Est-ce assez pour m'épouser ? proposai-je, fou d'amour, sans même prendre le temps de penser à ce que je disais.

— Ne sois pas stupide. Tu sais bien que je ne peux pas m'engager à cela. » Il y avait une trace de dégoût dans sa voix. Elle m'observa d'un air songeur. « Me dis-tu la vérité ? »

J'acquiesçai.

« Nous pourrions peut-être trouver un compromis, suggéra-t-elle.

— Je ne veux pas de compromis.

— Je sais, mais c'est tout ce que je peux te proposer. Parfois il faut accepter ce qu'on vous donne. » Elle haussa les épaules. « C'est un fait de la vie. »

J'acceptai, et de bon cœur. Ce fut bon. Incroyablement bon. Meilleur même dans l'accomplissement que dans son anticipation. Cette nuit-là, il ne fut pas question que je rentre chez moi. Allongé à côté d'elle, je la regardai dormir et respirer, j'écoutai les menus cris qu'elle poussait dans ses rêves. Elle s'endormit vite après l'amour, après la baise — selon son expression, mais elle employait ce mot avec naturel, sans provocation ni le moindre désir d'avilissement. Je l'avais pourtant redouté. Mais le mot avait une âpreté agréable, comme l'acte lui-même — « baiser »...

J'étais trop excité, trop exalté pour fermer les yeux. Je voulais savourer chaque instant, arracher à chaque seconde sa substance de bonheur, le baiser, baiser ma vie. Pour la première fois, je me sentis riche, immensément riche de vie et de potentialités, ivre, grisé, magnifiquement enivré de tous les possibles. Une fois encore, mon ressentiment s'enflamma contre mon ancien Mode de Vie qui m'avait privé de ce plaisir. Que je n'eusse pu le connaître plus tôt me parut un crime, un péché ! Car cette extase dépassait tout ce que j'avais pu imaginer. Les mots du *Tao-tö king* me revinrent en mémoire, frappés d'une ironie involontaire : « La saveur que procure le Tao... comme elle est mince et fade ! » Oui, vraiment ! Et comparée à quoi ? Comparée à *ceci* ! Tout était venu si vite, presque instantanément. Mon esprit était tellement bouleversé que je me rappelai à peine la succession des événements. Tant de choses s'étaient passées depuis la dernière fois où je m'étais allongé à côté d'elle. Mais quoi, précisément ? Quelle différence cruciale existait-il entre cette fois-là et maintenant ? A quoi attribuer ce bonheur impossible ?

A l'argent. N'était-ce pas là la raison ? Tout ne se ramenait-il pas à cela ? A mesure que je réfléchissais à ce problème, mon exaltation fit place à une humeur pensive, mesurée, un peu triste. Comme pour le Dow, l'argent n'était-il pas la « clef majeure », selon l'expression judicieuse de mon père, la condition *sine qua non* d'une participation fructueuse au jeu ? Mais s'agissait-il vraiment du tout dernier mot ? Pouvait-on acheter et vendre comme une marchandise la connaissance du Dow ou l'amour ? Peut-être en allait-il ainsi sur cette place du marché, dans ce monde souillé.

Il n'y avait donc rien en dehors de la portion de grâce relative à l'importance de mon compte en banque ? Quelle autre conclusion en tirer ? Rien n'avait fondamentalement changé en elle, ni en moi. Pourtant je me sentais maintenant ici en sécurité, et pour la première fois. « Un fait de la vie », avait-elle dit. L'expression me déroutait. Quel fait ? Et pourquoi de la vie ? La vie dans le monde tel qu'il est — là était peut-être l'explication. Suffisait-il de vivre dans le monde tel qu'il est ? Peut-être que non, mais existait-il autre chose ? Pouvais-je accepter cette vérité, cette vie, pouvais-je vivre selon ? Sans cesse je me rappelai le ton de Li quand elle prononça ces mots — son amoralité foncière. Un fait de la vie. Sa voix avait été étrangement pure, si assurée, limpide, évidente, avec une intonation qui me suggéra le rire de mon père, tel que je me l'imaginais.

Lo avait mis dans le mille. Elle ressemblait à un chat. Elle savait ce qu'elle voulait et, avec le pur instinct du prédateur, faisait ce qu'il fallait pour l'obtenir. Pas de culpabilité, pas de gcignardises ni de remords, pas de larmes de crocodile. Et ce qui pour moi aurait entraîné les plus grands débats de conscience n'impliquait pour elle aucune compromission. Comme l'eau, elle ne reculait devant aucun plongeon ; toujours fidèle à elle-même, elle suivait la ligne de moindre résistance et cherchait le niveau de la mer. Elle était plus taoïste que moi ! Cela me stupéfia. Je crois que son étrangeté radicale, la pureté — bien qu'équivoque —, l'abandon et l'intensité de sa vie intérieure piquèrent davantage ma curiosité que n'importe quel élément de sa personnalité, même sa beauté, même sa sexualité, oui, même la baise. Car tout cela, elle acceptait de le partager, mais cette autre chose, je savais qu'elle ne m'appartiendrait jamais — peu importaient ma richesse ou ce que je lui offrirais. Voilà comment je compris que, contrairement aux apparences, je ne pourrais jamais acheter Li. Non, à sa façon elle était aussi pure que Yin-mi. Mais d'une pureté différente ! Je songeai à la comparaison de Lo : la Danse de Guerre, parfaite beauté sans parfaite bonté ; l'Empereur Wu qui détrôna les Yin. Les Yin...

Mes pensées dérivèrent vers Yin-mi, s'y attardèrent avec mélancolie. La Danse de Succession : parfaite beauté, parfaite bonté. Avec une surprise peinée, je m'aperçus que je ne désirais plus cela, qui me semblait fade et incolore en regard de ce que me proposait sa sœur. Sa grâce était moins aboutie, moins polie et séduisante que celle de sa sœur, je devais reconnaître que Yin-mi possédait une candeur, une fraîcheur, un inachèvement délicieux, que l'expérience, la culture ou la promiscuité — on pouvait appeler cela comme on voulait — avaient usés et polis chez Li, raffinés jusqu'à l'inexistence. L'art et non la nature faisait la beauté de Li, ou plutôt l'art avait épuré sa nature. Un art que la nature façonne, n'était-ce pas là l'expression ? En comparaison, les charmes de Yin-mi étaient banals, son aura aussi prosaïque et grossière que le soleil pour un homme dont les yeux fragiles supportent seulement les pièces hautes de plafond, aux lambris sombres et aux lourdes draperies en velours, la pénombre perpétuelle d'un manoir uniquement éclairé par des chandeliers de cristal et les reflets de l'argenterie. Vraiment, cette image est appropriée, car plus que toute autre chose, je crois aujourd'hui que je désirais le crépuscule consolateur de la vie morale de Li, si différent de la lueur pénétrante et intransigeante des yeux de Yin-mi. Je savais que leur clarté implacable dévoilerait aussitôt mes contradictions. Trop souvent j'avais constaté les pouvoirs de sa grande solennité, cette énorme force passive qu'elle opposait à son père, à Wo, et enfin à moi. Non, je ne désirais plus cela.

Yin-mi constituait le dernier obstacle au fleuve de mon bonheur nouveau. Kahn, Riley, Mme Chin, Li, tous les fantômes fébriles et accusateurs avaient été apaisés, conciliés ; il ne restait plus qu'elle pour brasser follement les eaux de mon esprit. Mais n'était-elle pas le fleuve et moi le roc ? Car sa tournure d'esprit, ses réactions paraissaient incommensurables avec son âge, comme s'ils existaient depuis des siècles, usant lentement la force tenace et opiniâtre qui s'opposaient à eux. Elle était de ces rares personnes qu'on rencontre en une vie et qui semblent détenir l'énergie accumulée de maintes époques, de maintes vies.

En un sens, Li aussi malgré son âge évoquait la vieillesse. Mais le cours de ses réincarnations semblait plus décousu, il lui manquait la concentration sur un but unique qui animait Yin-mi, telle une vague parcourant les océans du temps et du destin, son cœur, son œil et son cerveau fixés sur leur but, l'instant où toutes les forces se rameutent, où jaillit la crête blanche avant que l'énorme masse liquide ne s'écrase sur la barre et ne rejoigne les eaux paisibles, claires et profondes de l'éternité. Possédée du génie de l'inaction, Li avait remis à plus tard l'accomplissement de sa destinée, lui préférant les plaisirs sensuels et transitoires de la terre. Elle me rappelait une incarnation plus jeune de Mme Chin, douée de la rage d'aimer. Elle avait appris à exciter sa sensibilité pour lui arracher les notes les plus exquises, les timbres et les harmonies les plus rares ; ainsi, Li avait perdu de vue sa destination, mais s'était trouvée.

Cette nuit-là je rêvai que j'errais dans le noir, non pas dans le vide, mais un espace que je me rappelais sans pouvoir immédiatement l'identifier. Des murs m'entouraient. J'allais de l'avant, avançant lentement dans un corridor courbe avec le sentiment de m'enfoncer dans un labyrinthe. Où étais-je ? S'agissait-il du dédale des ruelles derrière l'immeuble de Mulberry Street, dans lequel j'avais poursuivi Yin-mi sous la pluie ? Peut-être, mais les murs n'avaient pas cette texture visqueuse, membraneuse ; ils étaient pelucheux et rêches comme du bois brut. Une lumière rougeâtre tremblait au loin ; dans l'air planait une odeur bizarre, épaisse, douçâtre, un peu écœurante, comme celle de l'opium, mais avec une nuance supplémentaire. Je sus d'instinct ce que c'était : merde et sang. « Merde et sang » — où avais-je entendu cette expression ? Avant que je n'aie eu le temps de sonder ma mémoire, les murs disparurent brusquement et j'émergeai dans un espace ouvert semblable à une arène au sol composé d'un fin sable blanc. Je compris brusquement où j'étais : dans la cale du *Telemachos* ! Mais Scottie ne m'accompagnait pas, et la silhouette que je discernais dans un angle, faiblement éclairée par la lueur rougeâtre, n'était pas Manjusri, mais la Statue de la Liberté. Cette même lumière révéla à mes yeux les contours de la caisse brisée, qui ressemblait maintenant de façon frappante à un cercueil. M'approchant, je soulevai le couvercle. Il céda. Mais au moment précis où j'allais enfin savoir ce qu'elle contenait, à mon immense frustration quelque chose me fit sursauter et je me réveillai.
Eddie. Le chat avait bondi entre nous sur le matelas et marchait à pas feutrés sur la couverture vers Li, qui dormait paisiblement. D'un geste agacé je l'écartai du lit, puis tentai de retrouver le chemin de mon rêve. En vain. Le lendemain matin, au réveil, mes efforts avaient seulement abouti à une curiosité redoublée pour un incident que j'avais quasiment oublié. Qu'y avait-il dans la caisse ? Question absurde, je le savais, puisque je n'avais aucun espoir de jamais y répondre.
Ce matin-là sous la douche, je me mis à siffler machinalement un air. Je m'immobilisai sous l'eau pour essayer de retrouver son nom. Je haussai bientôt les épaules en désespoir de cause et continuai à me savonner. A midi, j'avais tout oublié de cet incident. Mais pendant des jours cette mélodie devait me revenir en mémoire aux moments les plus inattendus, mobiliser mes lèvres au point de m'agacer, voire de m'inquiéter.

Le lendemain, avant de retourner vers le centre ville, Li et moi fîmes un joyeux autodafé au coin de West End Avenue : nous jetâmes au feu mon costume neuf en polyester et mes mocassins. Je les regardai s'enflammer d'un air songeur, puis embrassai Li ; elle partit vers Columbia, moi vers la Bourse (dans un pantalon de cuir noir et des vêtements empruntés à la garde-robe de Peter), prêt à entrer dans la peau de mon nouvel avatar wall-streetien.

Kahn m'emmena chez son tailleur et fit prendre mes mesures pour une demi-douzaine de costumes à fines raies en laine peignée gris banquier. Profitant de l'occasion, je choisis une quantité similaire de chaussures en veau cousu main et songeai avec nostalgie à mes douze paires de mocassins rouges et à leur obsolescence prématurée. J'acquis aussi les chaussettes hautes de rigueur avec leurs fixe-chaussettes, ainsi que tous les accessoires indispensables et assortis, chemises, cravates, boutons de manchettes, etc. Durant cette expédition, Kahn se montra discret et déférent, imbu du sérieux excessif de qui vient de trouver un nouvel emploi et désire faire bonne impression, une sorte de majordome plus que le Kahn que je connaissais et aimais. Inutile de dire que ce fut extrêmement éprouvant — et pas du tout ce que j'avais escompté.

L'étape suivante consistait à assister à la vente aux enchères de son fauteuil, qui devait avoir lieu un matin pour rembourser une partie de ses dettes. Au milieu des enchères, je fus saisi d'une inspiration. Je me penchai pour chuchoter quelque chose à l'oreille de Kahn. Il me regarda avec une surprise qui se mua bientôt en joie, puis se leva vivement, provoquant les récriminations acerbes des acquéreurs potentiels, — ce qui eut la vertu de le faire jubiler. Alors que les autres clignaient des yeux, malmenaient le lobe de leur oreille, regardaient d'un air concentré par-dessus la monture de leurs lunettes, ou se perdaient en signes plus ou moins ésotériques, Kahn transmit discrètement son — notre — intention au commissaire priseur, accompagnant ses dires d'un large signe de tête qu'il généralisa illico presto à l'ensemble du public. Après cela, il parut nettement de meilleure humeur. Et quand nous eûmes loué un bureau dans le bâtiment de la Bourse — le numéro 2101 (là encore, ce fut mon idée) — il se mit à réintégrer son ancienne personnalité.

Mais les plaisirs des dépenses extravagantes adoucirent seulement sa blessure. Ce fut comme une anesthésie locale, qui rend la douleur supportable, mais ne dure qu'un temps. Quand l'effet en est passé, un traitement plus radical s'impose. Kahn avait besoin d'une victoire, d'un fait d'armes capable de lui rendre confiance. Nous devions monter un coup.

Mais il nous fallait d'abord ce qu'on appelle vulgairement un « créneau ». Oui, la question se posait, qu'allions-nous faire ? Comment utiliser mes nouvelles ressources ? Voilà où j'espérais qu'il se mouillerait, qu'il sortirait de sa coquille. Telle était la priorité dictée par « les sphères supérieures », mon premier mandat exécutif. Pourtant, un aspect des commentaires de l'oracle me demeurait obscur. Quel était « le grand but » à accomplir.

« Kahn, lui dis-je, apportez-moi une idée. »

Et c'est ce qu'il fit. Le caractère expéditif du processus me stupéfia. Je crois que la tragédie et l'ostracisme avaient si longtemps endigué son énergie que, lorsque je lui offris ce dérivatif, le torrent de son inspiration débridée jaillit de lui-même comme un raz de marée.

Quelques jours après ma question, un beau matin, il entra en trombe dans le bureau, pantelant, pourpre d'excitation, le regard fébrile. « Petit, je crois que je la tiens, dit-il d'une voix tremblante.

— Quoi donc ?

— *Elle*, petit, *elle*. La grande idée. »

Je me tus pour le laisser s'expliquer. Comme d'habitude, il ne le fit pas. « D'accord, cent fois d'accord, et alors ? le pressai-je en agitant les bras avec irritation.

— Je me demande encore comment je n'y ai pas pensé plus tôt. C'est tellement évident ! » Il secoua la tête puis sombra dans des spéculations grommelantes.

« *De quoi s'agit-il ?* répétai-je, de plus en plus excédé.

— Un projet que je rumine depuis des années. Mais je n'ai jamais eu assez de capital pour le réaliser.

— Kahn ! m'écriai-je. Expliquez-vous !

— D'accord, cent fois d'accord, dit-il sur un ton vexé. Un peu de patience. Je parle d'une société de management en investissements, petit.

— Une société de management en investissements ? » Je le regardai d'un œil perplexe.

« Oui, tu sais bien, une sorte de brain trust financier, où quelqu'un te paie une commission rondelette pour avoir le privilège de te laisser investir son fric à sa place.

— Mais pourquoi quelqu'un voudrait-il faire ça ? demandai-je.

— A cause de ta réputation, de tes performances passées. »

A la mention du mot « réputation », je crois que je blêmis.

« Je sais, je sais, anticipa-t-il. Tu te demandes quel connard me ferait confiance après l'histoire Jane Doe. Mais je ne parle de ma réputation, petit. Je parle de la *tienne*. » Une lueur malicieuse brilla dans son œil.

« La mienne ! m'écriai-je. Mais c'est ridicule, Kahn. Je ne possède même pas de réputation.

— Allons, allons, petit, contredit-il, ne sois donc pas si modeste. Ce n'est pas le moment des SO. Moi je dis : te connaître c'est t'aimer, et qui te connaît mieux que moi ? Et puis si tu n'as pas de réputation, eh bien il suffit de t'en confectionner une, pas vrai ?

— Confectionner ?

— Mais bien sûr ! Ce qui ne veut pas dire "t'en forger une de toutes pièces", ajouta-t-il.

— Mais comment ?

— Je suis content que me tu demandes ça. Voilà où commence ma "grande idée". Tu es prêt ?

— Je crois.

— Tu ferais mieux de t'accrocher à la rampe, petit, car je te garantis que l'idée d'Aaron Kahn va t'estomaquer. Assieds-toi, je t'en prie. » Il approcha un fauteuil, m'aida gentiment à m'y asseoir en me tenant par le coude comme si j'étais un convalescent ou un vieillard sénile. « Là. Laisse-moi t'apporter un verre d'eau. » Il se pencha au-dessus du distributeur, puis me tendit un gobelet en plastique. « Bon, dit-il, tu te demandes probablement quel atout je cache dans ma manche. Pourquoi une société de management ? N'y en a-t-il pas déjà une kyrielle qui se disputent la clientèle disponible, des types malins, parfois brillants, dotés d'une excellent CV et d'un passé blanc comme neige ? Comment rivaliser avec eux ? Pourquoi M. Tartempion s'adresserait-il à un Juif Rrant lessivé aux références morales douteuses et à un moine taoïste qui est descendu du Shanghai Express au mauvais arrêt avant d'atterrir à Wall Street ? Comment entrer dans la compétition ? Que possédons-nous qu'ils n'ont pas ? L'argent ? Cela ne suffit pas. L'intelligence ? Non, il y a plein de forts en thème rudement plus calés que toi et moi. L'intégrité ? Passons... Pas très brillant, hein, petit ? Réfléchis un peu à ce problème : qu'est-ce qui nous rend différent des autres ?

— Le cœur ? » suggérai-je.

Il fit papillonner ses mains au ras du plafond.

« Le courage alors ? » proposai-je.

Il haussa les épaules, retroussa ses lèvres en cul de poule.

« Okay, Kahn, je renonce. De quoi s'agit-il ?

— Voilà, petit, après que le Jane Doe fut retombé en nous éclaboussant copieusement — tu saisis le "Jane de mots" ? —, j'ai eu pas mal de temps pour réfléchir. J'ai retourné le problème dans tous les sens au moins cent mille fois. Je l'ai examiné du point de vue supérieur de l'oiseau de proie, du point de vue inférieur du ver de terre (surtout celui-ci, petit). Je l'ai considéré sous tous les angles, sous tous les éclairages, avec tous les grossissements possibles, et tu sais ce qui m'a paru le trait le plus remarquable de toute cette navrante détumescence ?

— Non, quoi ?

— *Sui*, dit-il.

— Sui Generis ? »

Il secoua la tête. « Non, *Sui*, le numéro dix-sept, petit. *Les Mutations.* »

Un frisson inquiet d'anticipation descendit le long de ma colonne vertébrale.

« Voilà ce qui me semble le trait saillant de l'affaire. Le *Yi king* avait choisi cette valeur avant même que tu ne connaisses son existence. Évidemment, tu as interprété cela à ta façon. Mais s'il n'avait tenu qu'à *moi*...

— Enfin, Kahn ! protestai-je. Vous oubliez tout ce qui s'est passé. Doe a été un désastre complet ! A supposer que l'oracle ait voulu me faire signe dans cette direction — mais je suis loin de l'admettre —, dans cette hypothèse, cela aura été l'un des pires faux lièvres jamais levés de toute l'histoire de Wall Street. »

Kahn gloussa. « "Le faux lièvre". Va falloir que j'ajoute cet animal à mon bestiaire de Wall Street.

— Admettez-le, insistai-je, j'ai raison.

— Une seconde. Pas si vite, objecta-t-il. D'accord, l'oracle nous a fourni

— t'a fourni, pour être exact — *Sui*, et ça n'a pas marché. D'un autre côté, l'oracle ne nous a pas demandé de saloper l'affaire comme des cochons, pas vrai ? Pour modifier légèrement la célèbre maxime, on peut conduire un cochon à *Sui*, mais on ne peut pas l'empêcher de manger. Non, petit, tu ne peux pas reprocher ça à l'oracle. Nous tenions une affaire en or et nous avons tout bousillé en nous montrant trop gourmands.

— Nous ! » protestai-je.

Il se renfrogna, mais poursuivit comme si de rien n'était. « L'oracle n'est pour rien dans ce qui s'est passé. La faillibilité humaine est seule responsable de notre échec. Ç'a été plus fort que nous. Ou, si tu préfères, ç'a été plus fort que *moi* — ou encore, je me suis laissé déborder par mon propre enthousiasme... Mais le plus important, c'est que l'oracle a prouvé qu'il savait choisir une valeur. Ce qui me ramène à mon point de départ. Tu te souviens ? Ce que nous possédons et que les autres n'ont pas ? » Il m'adressa un sourire triomphal.

« Mais Kahn ! m'écriai-je. Ce serait une grave profanation que d'utiliser l'oracle à des fins de gain personnel. Et puis, comment être sûr qu'il ne s'agit pas d'une simple coïncidence ? »

Il prit un air hautain, comme s'il eût déjà songé à mes objections et les eût déjà écartées. « Pour répondre à ton premier argument, dit-il en examinant ses ongles d'un air concentré, l'oracle aurait-il accepté de collaborer malgré ce soi-disant sacrilège ? L'instrument suprême de ta religion applaudirait-il à sa propre "profanation" ? déclama-t-il. Je pense que cette position trahit un manque de foi choquant de ta part, Sonny, dit-il, comme blessé. Si l'oracle suggère à l'évidence que nous l'utilisions comme une technique prévisionnelle, je crois qu'il serait sacrément stupide de notre part de décliner son offre.

« Quant à ta seconde objection, continua-t-il sans me laisser le temps de riposter, selon moi, une coïncidence est hautement improbable. Mais je reconnais que je ne peux l'exclure avec une *absolue* certitude.

— Dieu merci ! dis-je. Vous commencez enfin à retrouver un semblant de logique. »

Il ignora ma remarque. « Il y a un seul moyen de régler ce problème. »

Aïe, pensai-je, quelles élucubrations va-t-il encore trouver ? « Lequel ? demandai-je.

— L'interroger encore, répondit-il. Demander au *Yi king* son avis. S'il acquiesce, nous allons rouler sur l'or. Tous les investisseurs de ce pays vont venir frapper à notre porte pour nous supplier d'accepter leur capital excédentaire. » Il sourit.

Je fronçai les sourcils. « Et s'il n'acquiesce pas ? »

Il m'adressa un clin d'œil. « C'est là le coup de génie, petit, dit-il d'une voix de conspirateur qui exprimait l'intimité et le ravissement. Même si ça foire, tant que nous pourrons faire croire au GP — Grand Public — que ça marche, alors tous les investisseurs seront à genoux devant nous. Tu sais comment est la Bourse, petit. Tu as vu la psychologie grégaire à l'œuvre. Malgré sa froideur affectée, malgré toutes ces histoires de "verdict impartial", d'"œil calme et lucide", Wall Street est le lieu le plus superstitieux de la terre. Pas un seul négociant au parquet qui n'ait une cravate porte-bonheur, une chaîne de clef, une paire de boutons de manchettes ou de bretelles qui lui serve de fétiche grâce auquel il tente de suspendre les lois implacables de la gravité et des statistiques pour se concilier les faveurs du grand dieu Succès. Il préférerait se faire dévorer vivant plutôt que de partir de chez lui sans son gri-gri. Tout le monde se moque de ce phénomène, bien sûr, mais tout le monde y *croit*. Que désirer de plus, petit ? Rappelle-toi ce que je t'ai dit — un charme capable de maîtriser la vie. Voilà ce que tout le monde cherche. La technique infaillible. Le talisman. La ligne directe avec le sommet, avec le Très-Haut. Écarte la façade de rationalité, tu découvriras que nous sommes tous des sauvages en adoration devant des divinités animistes. Retire le costume trois-pièces, et tu trouveras de la fourrure, des griffes et des crocs. Nous vivons encore dans un monde de sacrifices sanglants, de rituels propitiatoires offerts à des dieux arbitraires et tout-puissants. Jamais je n'en ai eu autant la conviction que vers la fin de notre liaison avec Jane Doe. Je sentais dans l'air cette puanteur âcre, épaisse — l'odeur du sang qu'on boit dans des crânes humains avant la chasse pour se rendre invulnérable à la mort. Tu peux bien rire si tu veux, petit, mais tout cela n'est pas si ancien. Le pont existe toujours, qui nous relie au monde sauvage. C'est pour cela que nous n'aurons pas trop de mal à les convaincre. Car ils désireront croire. Ils riront pendant les cinq premières minutes ou les cinq premiers mois, mais les spectres obscurs finiront par remonter de l'abîme que nous sommes et d'où nous sortons, les hommes accourront vers nous en quête de notre charme. Comme les loups, petit, quand ils entendent le hurlement de la meute : ce sera plus fort qu'eux. » Son exaltation augmentait à mesure qu'il parlait.

« Mais Kahn, objectai-je, si ça ne marche pas, ce serait malhonnête. Tout recommencera comme avant, comme avec Doe. »

Il secoua la tête. « Je me contente d'ébaucher la suite des événements, petit, le pire scénario possible. Vois-tu, *moi je crois.* » Il fit tourner machinalement le bracelet de cuivre à son poignet. « C'est plutôt cocasse, tu ne trouves pas ? ajouta-t-il avec un léger rire.

— Quoi donc ?

— C'est toi qu'il faut convaincre de la validité de ta propre religion. »

L'ironie de sa remarque, même feinte, me plongea dans un étonnement désagréable.

« Alors, reprit-il, qu'en dis-tu ? »

Vous ne le croirez peut-être pas, lecteur, mais je jure que si la décision n'avait tenu qu'à moi, j'eusse sur-le-champ repoussé cette suggestion, cette tentation, avec une véhémence définitive. Mais je n'étais pas seul, je faisais tout cela pour lui ; là était mon problème. « Cela n'implique pas que l'on évite les difficultés pour soi-même, mais que l'on délivre les êtres chers — en les aidant... à se tenir à distance d'un danger déjà présent. »

« Très bien, acceptai-je gravement. Je suis loin d'être complètement rassuré, mais je suis d'accord. Pour vous, Kahn.

— Tu ne le regretteras pas, petit », me promit-il en touchant ma main ; ses yeux brillaient de gratitude comme des braises attisées par le vent. « Alors, comment nous y prenons-nous ? »

Le visage fermé, presque triste, je poussai le livre vers lui à travers le bureau.

Il se redressa en le dévorant des yeux et frottant ses mains d'un air excité. « Avons-nous besoin d'autre chose ?
— De baguettes d'achillée, répondis-je sur un ton volontairement froid.
— Baguettes d'achillée ?
— Ou de pièces de monnaie.
— Des pièces, ce sera parfait ! s'écria-t-il avec enthousiasme. Bien plus approprié à notre objectif, tu ne trouves pas ? Quoi d'autre ? »
J'hésitai avant de répondre. « Eh bien, il faut le *ling*.
— *Ling* ?
— Vous avez oublié ? demandai-je. La Pureté de Cœur. »
Kahn grimaça, puis repoussa vers moi les divers accessoires. « A toi de jouer, d'accord ? me pria-t-il presque timidement. Je ne me fais pas assez confiance. »
Son geste touchant me poussa à accepter malgré mes réticences. Je ne lui avouai pas que je doutais moi aussi du crédit de mon compte bancaire relatif à cette très précieuse marchandise spirituelle. Sans cesse l'avertissement me revenait en mémoire : « A ceux qui ne sont pas en contact avec le Tao, l'oracle ne retourne aucune réponse intelligible, car celle-ci ne servirait de rien. »
Pourtant, dans le cas présent, mes craintes étaient apparemment injustifiées. Car la réponse que me retourna l'oracle fut parfaitement et dramatiquement intelligible, du moins selon mon interprétation. L'hexagramme fut le numéro quatre, *Mong*, « La Folie Juvénile », avec un neuf à la deuxième place et un six à la quatrième. Cet hexagramme est composé du trigramme *Ken* (« L'Immobilisation », « La Montagne ») au-dessus de *K'an* (« L'Insondable », « L'Eau ») :

> L'attribut du signe supérieur est l'immobilité, celui du signe inférieur, le danger. S'arrêter plein de perplexité devant un dangereux abîme est également un symbole de la folie juvénile.

Aussitôt, même à ce niveau très élémentaire, j'aperçus une directive peu ambiguë : *Ken* évoquait l'image de Ken Kuan, le symbole de l'ancienne Voie, l'Immobilisation, *au-dessus de K'an*, comme dans Kahn, dont l'identification à l'eau dénotait un mouvement incessant. L'oracle semblait conseiller de donner préséance à l'ancienne Voie sur la nouvelle, au risque de commettre une folie juvénile. Le jugement disait :

> La folie juvénile possède la réussite.
> Ce n'est pas moi qui recherche le jeune fou,
> C'est le jeune fou qui me recherche.
> Au premier oracle, j'informe.
> S'il interroge deux, trois fois, c'est de l'importunité.
> S'il est importun, je n'informe pas.
>
> La réponse donnée par le maître aux questions du disciple doit être claire et précise comme celle qu'on attend de l'oracle ; elle doit alors être reçue comme résolution du doute et comme décision. Des questions supplémentaires provoquées par la méfiance ou le manque de réflexion

ne servent qu'à importuner le maître. Le mieux sera de garder le silence à leur sujet, de même que l'oracle ne donne qu'une réponse et refuse de se laisser tenter par des questions nées du doute.

Il y avait peu de doute dans mon esprit. J'en étais au « premier oracle ». J'allais recevoir une réponse intelligible. Mais si je persistais dans mon importunité, alors la conséquence que je redoutais serait inévitable. Je perdrais le contact avec le Tao, et la réponse de l'oracle « ne servirait de rien ».

Je me tournai enfin vers les traits :

> Neuf à la deuxième place signifie :
> Supporter avec douceur les insensés procure la fortune.
>
> L'oracle désigne ici un homme qui... possède la force spirituelle nécessaire pour porter la responsabilité de ce qui lui incombe. Il est doté de la supériorité et de la robustesse intérieures qui le rendent capable de supporter les lacunes de la folie humaine.

Jusque-là, l'oracle m'avait semblé opposé sans la moindre ambiguïté au projet proposé par Kahn et auquel j'avais accepté de participer à mon corps défendant. Ici, pourtant, surgissait l'ombre d'un doute. A la mention de la « responsabilité de ce qui lui incombe », je songeai immédiatement à mon obligation d'œuvrer à la réhabilitation de Kahn, indiquée auparavant par l'oracle. En ce cas, « supporter avec douceur les insensés » ne conseillait-il pas de se plier à son dessein certes extravagant d'utiliser *Les Mutations* en tant que technique prévisionnelle ? Je me tournai vers le dernier trait dans l'espoir d'élucider ce point :

> Six à la quatrième place signifie :
> Une folie juvénile limitée apporte l'humiliation.
>
> Dans la folie juvénile, l'attitude qui laisse le moins d'espoir consiste à se prendre dans des réseaux d'imagination vides. Plus on s'obstine dans de telles imaginations irréelles, plus on s'attire à coup sûr des humiliations.
> En face de ce dérèglement, le maître n'aura souvent d'autre ressource que de l'abandonner à lui-même pour un temps et de ne pas lui épargner l'humiliation qui s'ensuivra. Telle est souvent l'unique voie de salut.

Cela ne fit qu'accroître ma perplexité. Étais-je le maître indiqué ci-dessus, qui « en face de ce dérèglement, n'aura d'autre ressource que d'abandonner le fou (Kahn) à lui-même » dans l'espoir d'un salut ultérieur ? Ou bien, au contraire, le *Yi king* était-il lui-même le maître, et moi le jeune fou que l'on avertissait : si je persévérais dans ce projet bancal, je finirais par sombrer dans ma propre folie ? La réponse à cette question était bien sûr cruciale, car dans un cas l'oracle me conseillait d'aller de l'avant dans le projet de Kahn, et dans l'autre d'y renoncer.

Je me fis toutes ces réflexions en silence. Ce fut seulement au bout d'un certain temps que je dirigeai de nouveau mon attention vers Kahn. Il avait adopté une attitude qui suggérait une intensité similaire dans la concentration. Le coude posé sur le bureau, il soutenait sa tête dans la paume de sa main et répétait silencieusement, incessamment, l'expression « Folie juvénile ». Je l'observai avec une fascination pleine d'appréhension.

Brusquement, il se figea. « Ça y est », grommela-t-il pour lui-même. Retirant son bras, il leva les yeux. « J'ai trouvé, petit.

— Quoi ? demandai-je.

— Que t'évoque l'expression "Folie juvénile" ? »

Très brièvement, je lui annonçai les associations fournies par l'oracle, et lui fis part de ma perplexité quant à la marche à suivre.

« Non non, petit, fit-il sur un ton de dégoût indulgent, tu n'y es pas du tout. Tu interprètes l'oracle de travers. Il ne s'agit pas d'une mise en accusation ou d'une absolution, mais d'une indication relative au marché. Tu ne vois donc pas ? Folie juvénile... L'autre soir, je lisais un article là-dessus dans *Forbes*. "La révolution sexuelle et ses conséquences pour le profit des entreprises." Ça m'a tellement excité que les pages étaient toutes collées ensemble quand j'ai eu fini de lire. » Il sourit.

« Kahn ! protestai-je. C'est ridicule ! »

« Attends, laisse-moi finir. Je ne crois pas que tu aies idée des nouveaux marchés qui s'ouvrent grâce à la promiscuité croissante qui frappe ce pays. Savais-tu qu'il existait même un lobby à Washington pour promouvoir activement l'éducation sexuelle à l'école sous couvert d'un libéralisme désintéressé ? Petit ! Nous entrons dans une ère nouvelle ! Et c'est le business du Business que d'être à l'avant-garde de ce bouleversement des mœurs. Laisse-moi te donner un exemple. Es-tu jamais allé aux toilettes pour hommes d'une station-service ? Bon, tu as donc vu les distributeurs de capotes, pas vrai ? Tu as le choix : avec armature, réservoir d'embout, prélubrifiées an Sensitol, en parchemin (pour les talmudistes ?), sans parler des modèles les plus fantaisistes, comme la Chatouilleuse Française ou le Tourbillon Multicolore, et ça te coûte un *quarter* pièce. Un quart de dollar ! Bon Dieu, petit ! Enfin, à combien doit s'élever le coût de production à l'unité de la Vaillante modèle standard ? A peu près la même chose que pour les ballons à un sou, non ? Ce qui représente un bénéfice de deux mille cinq cents pour cent, nom de Dieu ! Voilà ce qu'on appelle une bonne affaire ! Et songe aussi au volume de production ! » Kahn arrondit sa main près de son oreille. « J'entends maintenant tous ces *quarters* tintinnabuler dans les fentes de l'Amérique entière, un flot incessant d'argent, exactement comme les machines à sous. Oui, un meilleur coup que les machines à sous, un coup fumant ! Les gens peuvent avoir faim, mais peu importe ce qui se passe, Sonny, récession, dépression, catastrophes naturelles ou guerre nucléaire, tu peux être sûr qu'un type voudra tirer son coup. Faut traire cette glande ! » Il fit rouler ses yeux, agita son doigt et ses bajoues en une parodie de Jimmy Durante. « Et je ne t'ai parlé que des capotes, petit ! Nous n'avons pas encore abordé le somptueux chapitre des diaphragmes et des stérilets, des émulsions et des gelées contraceptives, sans parler de la Pilule ! Voilà l'espoir du futur ! Regarde vers l'Ouest, jeune homme.

vers les cornues bouillonnantes de nos laboratoires pharmaceutiques ! Merde, nous avons inventé davantage de façons de saboter les fonctions naturelles du corps que je ne compte de poils sur ma queue ! Quelle merveille ! Et puis, bien sûr, les maladies vénériennes vont augmenter en proportion directe de cette flambée de sexualité prémaritale (que dis-je ? — préadolescente, *juvénile* !). Songe aux quantités de pénicilline et d'antibiotiques ingérées ou injectées chaque semaine dans les seules cliniques de New York ! C'est proprement époustouflant ! Le pain ne pourrit pas plus vite ! Je suis *sérieux*, petit. Je pourrais te parler encore pendant des heures, mais je crois que tu m'as compris.

— J'avoue que vous avez été éloquent, concédai-je, mais je ne vois toujours pas de quoi il s'agit.

— De Folie juvénile, petit ! Tu sais, la baisouille, le frotti-frotta. Je ne serais d'ailleurs pas autrement étonné que tu en aies tâté d'une façon ou d'une autre. »

Je rougis violemment.

« Ah ah, j'ai raison. Dans le mille ! s'écria-t-il, ravi. Laisse donc tomber tes affectations de pruderie taoïste. Tu ne vois donc pas, petit ? C'est un signe évident pour que nous investissions dans l'industrie pharmaceutique. Je le sens dans mes... — il m'adressa un sourire de ruse, fit un geste obscène — bourses ! »

Bien que vaguement déboussolé par ses simagrées, je réussis à lui faire entendre qu'il n'avait pas répondu à mes objections.

« Si ton interprétation était correcte, pourquoi dit-il : "la folie juvénile possède la réussite" ? fit-il remarquer à juste titre. Et puis, même si tu as raison, repense à ces phrases : "neuf à la deuxième place ; supporter avec douceur les insensés procure la fortune". » Il eut un sourire suave, affecta un charme quasiment enfantin. « Sois indulgent avec moi, petit. Donne-moi un bout de corde pour me pendre. Si je me trompe, mes erreurs seront relevées au fur et à mesure. Fais-moi ce seul plaisir, et je jure sur le sang de mon propre prépuce martyrisé que je ne te demanderai plus jamais un service tant que je vivrai et que mon outil se mettra au garde-à-vous. J'accepte même de coucher ça noir sur blanc, cinq ans de pénitence ou cinquante mille kilomètres à pied. »

Je le regardai avec une affection lugubre, exaspérée. Peut-être étais-je trop tendre, mais comment aurais-je pu lui refuser ce qu'il demandait ? Son exubérance, son charme, son brio étourdissant — comment résister à cela ? Et puis, me dis-je, ne devais-je pas laisser de côté ma propre personne pour placer mon but hors de moi ? Je soupirai. Si je me trompais, ce n'était pas la fin du monde... Cela me coûterait seulement un peu d'argent. Et l'argent n'était pas ce qui manquait. D'une main ferme, je signai un chèque de cinquante mille dollars à son ordre, que je lui tendis. Je craignis que Kahn, pris d'une crise d'euphorie exubérante, ne m'embrassât sur les deux joues. Retour à la compétition, de nouveau joueur ! Malgré mes réserves, je ne pus que sourire. Car il semblait au moins évident que je réussissais dans ma mission de réhabilitation.

Saisi d'une intuition, Kahn misa sur une petite entreprise dynamique, très récente et relativement inconnue à Wall Street, dont les actions se monnayaient pour une bouchée de pain. Deux jours après, la direction de l'entreprise annonça une nouvelle gamme de produits, des aphrodisiaques à base de ginseng, fabriqués « selon une ancienne recette chinoise », et qui « lors d'expériences indépendantes menées dans plusieurs grandes universités » avaient provoqué une satyriasis aiguë chez les souris. Les animaux de laboratoire s'étaient apparemment sacrifiés avec la ferveur des lemmings, s'adonnant à l'acte sexuel avec une telle énergie qu'ils ne s'interrompaient ni pour manger ni pour boire et se tuaient parfois littéralement à la tâche après avoir vaillamment lutté pour « rester en selle ». Il y eut une ruée sur tous les drugstores, telle qu'on n'en avait pas vu depuis que le Bureau des Narcotiques avait annoncé que la distribution illégale de substances mises au Tableau B — Quaaludes et Demerol — serait sévèrement punie, et que les pharmaciens devraient désormais remplir un carnet à souche. Presque du jour au lendemain, nos cinquante mille dollars devinrent cent cinquante mille. Je ne pus m'empêcher de penser au passage du *Chouo Koua* qui dans le *Yi king* explique le trigramme *Sun*. Juste après qu'il est dit que *Sun* concerne ceux qui « ont beaucoup de blanc dans l'œil », il développe les traits saillants de la personnalité concernée : « ceux qui sont âpres au gain, si bien qu'au marché ils reçoivent trois fois le prix ». C'était là une performance impressionnante, pour ne pas dire plus. J'avoue avoir été un peu émoustillé par ce succès. Car, après tout, si Kahn avait raison, n'étions-nous pas exactement dans la situation décrite par Julius Everstat lors de ses divagations sur le Chemin Aléatoire — ce que sa découverte aurait pu être, avant de révéler son amère conclusion — une bombe atomique financière, un marché parfaitement prévisible ? Oui, j'avoue que cela était excitant. Et peut-être aurait-on pu me convaincre assez facilement que mes doutes étaient déplacés. En tout cas, après ce triomphe, je remarquai qu'ils occupèrent de moins en moins souvent mes pensées.

Je signalerais que cela servit de modèle pour toutes les consultations ultérieures du *Yi king* touchant à des problèmes d'ordre financier. Tel l'Hermaphrodite du *Satyricon*, j'étais une sorte de demi-dieu de pacotille, sacro-saint en vertu de cette particularité assez douteuse de posséder les organes des deux sexes, et qui étais transporté dans un panier par ses zélateurs les grands prêtres (Kahn) qui interprétaient ses borborygmes incohérents pour les masses impatientes. Autrement dit, c'était une combinaison fructueuse de mon « toucher » (sacralisé par mon « *ling* » putatif) et de ses talents interprétatifs, dérivés d'une parfaite connaissance du manuel des *500 plus grandes entreprises*. Symbiose des plus profitables. Mais je ne dois pas laisser l'amertume anticiper sur les développements de l'intrigue, aussi déchirants fussent-ils.

Quand je lui confiai mes doutes relatifs à la légitimité de notre technique, Kahn me fusilla du regard et répliqua cyniquement : « Ouais, petit, je te permets de pleurnicher d'ici jusqu'à la banque. »

10

Ivre de succès, Kahn prit l'affaire en main ; il se mit à passer des ordres, transmettre des directives comme un général ou un administrateur de société. Les circulaires fusaient en feu d'artifice. Avec une terreur satisfaite, j'assistai à sa guérison miraculeuse.

« Okay, Kahn, et maintenant ? m'enquis-je timidement.

— Voilà, petit, me répondit-il, où nous en sommes : nous tenons une idée en or — le management en investissement ; nous avons notre angle personnel — le *Yi king*. Je suis convaincu ; tu es convaincu. Il nous suffit maintenant de convaincre le Grand Public. Ce qui implique un travail de promotion. Nous devons mettre sur pied une campagne de publicité du feu de Dieu. A ce propos, en ma qualité d'ancien rédacteur-concepteur, j'aimerais m'occuper de cela moi-même. »

J'acquiesçai naturellement avec la plus grande déférence.

« Mais avant même de songer à la promotion, nous devons définir le produit à promouvoir. Ainsi que tu le sais sans doute, la publicité dépend d'un grand symbole universel, une sorte de forme platonicienne ou de PPDC.

— PPDC ?

— Plus Petit Dénominateur Commun, expliqua-t-il. Le regard du publiciste doit être assez pur pour apercevoir les eidôlons de la consommation qui flottent au firmament du désir.

— Vous parlez du *ça* ? hasardai-je.

— Ne joue pas au plus fin, krechtza-t-il. Il faut quelque chose de facile à retenir, quelque chose de beau, capable de satisfaire le cœur et de convaincre l'esprit. Je sais que beaucoup de gens font la fine bouche devant la publicité, mais pour moi elle est digne de figurer à côté des plus beaux fleurons de la poésie américaine. Quel autre art exprime aussi bien le cœur et l'âme d'un peuple ? Quand une pub est vraiment de première bourre, elle s'incruste dans ton esprit comme une mélodie dont tu n'arrives pas à te débarrasser, une ritournelle intérieure, une sorte de tic bénin. Certaines accroches me touchent de plein fouet et m'obsèdent davantage que les vers les mieux ciselés de la poésie lyrique, elles rameutent les visions de ma jeunesse et me font pleurer sur le passé et mon innocence perdue.

— Allez, Kahn, dis-je avec scepticisme.

— Je suis sérieux, petit. Prends les *Rasoirs Burma* par exemple. Tu n'as probablement jamais entendu ça, mais à une époque tout le monde en Amérique avait ces slogans sur les lèvres, deux strophes de cinq ou six vers non rimés qui apparaissaient sur des panneaux le long de la route, un vers par panneau, et qui se terminaient à chaque fois par l'expression "Rasoirs Burma".

ÇA NE SE MANGE PAS
ÇA NE SE BOIT PAS
MAIS ATTENTION
ÇA S'IMITE
RASOIRS BURMA

« Je ne pense jamais à ces slogans sans me souvenir de papa. » Kahn sortit son mouchoir et se moucha. « Je n'oublierai jamais la première fois où je vis cette série de panneaux. Mon père nous avait emmenés en week-end dans les Adirondacks.

IL JOUAIT
DU SAX
IL SENTAIT BON
MAIS SES JOUES PIQUAIENT
ELLE L'A PLAQUÉ
RASOIRS BURMA

« Comme papa riait ! » Kahn se tamponna les yeux. « Le panorama romantique — cascades, feuilles d'automne mordorées, petits animaux adorables aux joues gonflées de noisettes et de baies sauvages — tout ça a disparu, mais ce slogan est resté. Rasoirs Burma... » Il secoua la tête. « Pour moi, on devrait le sacraliser comme une forme de versification typiquement nationale qui représente la quintessence de l'Amérique comme le haïku celle du japon. Je te laisse volontiers *Le corbeau* et *Annabel Lee*, pourvu que je puisse garder les *Rasoirs Burma* ! Un jour, dans une dissertation pour le cours de littérature américaine, j'ai fait une proposition dans ce sens, mais le prof — un vieux barbon — n'a même pas daigné me répondre.

« Ris donc si ça te chante, petit, mais laisse-moi te dire une bonne chose. Le publiciste n'a rien à voir avec le pékin de la Bourse qui est prêt à toutes les turpitudes pour gagner du fric. Non, les autres peuvent bien s'intéresser à l'argent, lui se passionne pour la vérité ou un concept encore plus élevé. D'ailleurs, les meilleurs esprits sont de mon avis. Crois-moi ou non, bien qu'on tienne cette vérité sous le boisseau, un bon concepteur-rédacteur est une denrée aussi rare dans le monde de la finance qu'un poète en herbe en milieu universitaire. Vraiment, petit, je te le dis, l'authentique publiciste est une race différente du commun des mortels.

« Et puis, Homère, Dante ou Shakespeare — oui, même le Barde Immortel ! — étaient-ils plus aptes à exprimer les valeurs de leur époque, à brandir un miroir devant leurs contemporains, que le publiciste aujourd'hui ? Son art intervient dans un travail d'équipe, comme pour les cathédrales du Moyen Age, il n'est pas souillé par l'arrogance de l'"artiste" qui désire la reconnaissance. Non, ces créateurs anonymes travaillent seulement pour l'amour et leur salaire, pas pour la gloire ; là réside le secret de la pureté de leur art. Comment, sinon, trouver des slogans aussi percutants que... tiens, "C'est la génération Pepsi !" pour citer un exemple qui m'est particulièrement cher ? Envisages-tu la portée de cette définition ? Elle embrasse toute une époque, elle la résume, elle nous offre une image qui nous permet de nous connaître et de nous reconnaître. Quand j'entends ça, petit, brusquement c'est l'été, sous les projecteurs du Yankee Stadium j'assiste au deuxième match de la soirée ; Micky Mantle vient de balancer une balle dans les gradins et trottine vers la troisième base en souriant et agitant sa casquette ; les spectateurs sont debout ; quand il touche au but, ses coéquipiers lui tendent une bouteille de Pepsi ; les gouttelettes glacées dégoulinent le long de son bras couvert de sueur, sur son menton et son gant de batteur, tandis que le public se déchaîne, l'ovationne, tape des pieds dans les tribunes, et que dans le stade délirant de bonheur mille bouteilles se lèvent pour porter un toast pétillant et sucré à la beauté de l'existence — l'Amérique à l'apogée du boum de l'après-guerre, avant le retour de bâton libéral, la plus grande nation du monde au sommet de sa prospérité, une seconde miraculeuse qui ne se produit peut-être qu'une fois par millénaire... Et tout cela cristallisé dans l'ambre, petit, par un génie inconnu — un publiciste ! »

Malgré tous mes doutes, l'espace d'un instant je vis ce qu'avait dû être le jeune Kahn, son intensité et sa passion transparaître dans la prison de la chair flasque. Et quoique parfaitement ignorant des faits qu'il évoquait, je le crus. Seule la vérité, pensai-je, a le pouvoir de transfigurer ainsi. L'image de Tsin me vint sinistrement en mémoire, comme pour me contredire, suivie de près par une autre image : le sourire de mon père, qui planait dans le vide comme le chat du Cheshire.

« Petit ?... Petit ? » J'entendis la voix de Kahn comme si elle venait de très loin.

« Hmm ? » J'émergeai lentement de ma rêverie ; la silhouette de Kahn se précisa sous mes yeux.

« Ça va ?
— Bien sûr, répondis-je. Pourquoi ?
— Tu viens d'avoir une absence qui a duré une bonne minute. »
Nous nous observâmes en silence.
« Alors, dit-il enfin, es-tu prêt ?
— Prêt ?
— A entendre mon idée.
— Kahn, répliquai-je, je crois que, *maintenant*, je suis prêt à tout. »

Il me lança un regard interloqué, puis ouvrit son attaché-case, en sortit une chemise pleine de papiers couverts de diagrammes tracés à la diable, de textes griffonnés, d'esquisses annotées de commentaires, de circulaires facétieuses ou inspirées.

« Vois-tu, petit, nous avons besoin d'un nom, d'un mot-valise pour faire prendre la mayonnaise dont tu connais maintenant les ingrédients. Je me suis creusé les méninges pour trouver quelque chose qui reflète parfaitement notre orientation unique et soit immédiatement compréhensible par le Grand Public. Nous devons suggérer le *Yi king*, toute la constellation de l'imagerie orientale, et en même temps rester fidèles au climat de la Bourse, inclure le symbolisme traditionnel du Dow — mi-Tao, mi-Dow, comme tu dis toujours, ou plutôt comme tu disais. »

La fin de sa phrase me fit tiquer.

Il poursuivit. « Alors que je retournais le problème dans mon esprit, deux choses me frappèrent : d'abord ton intention de me remettre en selle afin que je reparte pour un tour... » Je rougis. « Non, petit, vraiment, ça m'a inspiré, m'assura-t-il.

— Et la seconde ?

— Cette maxime taoïste qui compare la quête de l'illumination à la recherche d'un taureau égaré sur le dos duquel on est assis. » Il sourit, plein d'espoir.

« Alors ? lui dis-je.

— Tu ne vois pas, petit ? C'est ça !

— Quoi ?

— Le taureau !

— Le taureau ?

— Le parfait symbole de nos deux objectifs : d'un côté, le taureau de la prospérité, le taureau du Dow ; de l'autre, le taureau de l'illumination, le taureau du Tao et du *Yi king*. Sans oublier une perfide allusion au tarot qui, lui aussi, permet de prédire l'avenir. Tu vois ? C'est idéal ! » Il se tut. « Qu'y a-t-il, petit ? Tu fais une drôle de tête. Ça ne te plaît pas ? »

Je pensais à la mélodie qui depuis des jours, depuis mon rêve dans la cale du *Telemachos*, trottait dans ma tête. Je l'identifiai brusquement :

J'étreins la corde et m'y accroche désespérément !
Le Taureau est indiscipliné et dangereux.
Il galope vers les montagnes assiégées de nuages,
Ou se campe devant moi dans la vallée, écumant et tête
    baissée, prêt à charger.

Il m'a échappé dans les régions les plus sauvages, mais aujourd'hui je l'ai enfin capturé. Un long relâchement a produit de mauvaises habitudes : le taureau s'est habitué aux herbes tendres et aux néfastes fleurs sauvages ; il renâcle devant le foin et la bride. Pour le mater, je dois sortir le fouet.

C'était le quatrième chant, « La capture du taureau » !

« Alors, Sonny ?

— Rien, dis-je. Continuez.

— Eh bien j'en suis à peu près là, dit-il. Je comptais sur toi pour me renvoyer la balle avant de m'occuper des ultimes finitions, de serrer les derniers boulons, de procéder aux ajustages définitifs. Que dirais-tu d'appeler notre société, par exemple Pur Taureau ? Non, non, plutôt Vrai Taureau. Ou mieux encore, Vraitaureau en un seul mot — pour faire moderne. On pourrait ajouter quelque chose du genre : "Ne vous contentez pas de moins. Acceptez seulement le pur taureau non frelaté !" »

Mon opinion dut se lire sur mon visage.

« Okay, okay, dit-il d'un ton légèrement vexé. Ça ne te plaît donc pas.

Suffit de le dire. J'ai une autre idée ! Taureau Incorporated. Génial, non ? C'est simple ; c'est austère. Ça présente bien, ça possède même une certaine noblesse, tu ne trouves pas ? C'est chaleureux, sinon... Attends ! Une seconde ! Oui, taurride... Ça y est ! Je tiens notre slogan : "Rejoignez Taureau, Inc. pour des investissements taurrides."

— Kahn, l'interrompis-je, inquiété par la lueur fébrile de son regard qui m'annonçait que la situation serait bientôt incontrôlable. Nous devrions peut-être en rester à Taureau Inc., qu'en pensez-vous ?

— C'est ton bébé », rétorqua-t-il sur un ton de léger avertissement, haussant les épaules comme s'il refusait d'endosser la moindre responsabilité des éventuels désastres qui pourraient résulter de mon conservatisme impénitent et de mes indécrottables SO. « Nous sommes donc d'accord ? »

J'acquiesçai. « Tout à fait.

— Excellent ! » Il frotta ses mains l'une contre l'autre. « *Bon !* Nous disposons maintenant d'un produit éminemment vendable ; comment allons-nous le promouvoir ? »

Certain qu'il s'agissait d'une question purement rhétorique, j'attendis.

« Okay, petit, voilà mon plan. Ecoute attentivement, car il s'agit de la clef de voûte de toute notre entreprise, du coup de grâce taureau-magique, si j'ose dire. » Il s'interrompit un instant pour savourer son bon mot.

« Kahn !

— Une ordalie », rétorqua-t-il.

Je lui adressai un regard vide de toute expression.

« Une ordalie médiatique pour être plus précis, développa-t-il avec un large sourire.

— Je ne comprends pas. Qu'est-ce qu'une ordalie ?

— Ce terme désigne une épreuve rituelle qu'on imposait autrefois pour décider de l'intégrité d'un individu en l'exposant à un danger ou une souffrance. Ces pratiques survivent encore parmi certaines peuplades primitives, et se manifestent avec un mystérieux atavisme dans des contextes aussi modernes que, disons, la Bourse.

— Je suis perdu, Kahn.

— En d'autres termes, petit, c'est une cérémonie de légitimisation, un rite de passage comme la bar mitzvah, ou comme celui auquel se soumet un jeune homme pour prouver qu'il est digne de participer à la chasse et de s'asseoir avec ses aînés autour du feu — une sorte d'épreuve du feu en public, mais dans le cas présent, c'est une institution et non un individu qui devra s'y soumettre. Vois-tu où je veux en venir ?

— Franchement, non, répondis-je.

— Okay, petit, laisse-moi t'expliquer ça en détail. Le *Wall Street Journal*, tu connais ? Une pleine page. » Ses mains tracèrent en l'air des rangées de majuscules en caractères gras :

« Les Entreprises Kahn et Sun sont fières d'annoncer la création d'une société de management en investissements pas comme les autres

TAUREAU INCORPORATED

(« Désireux et Capable de répondre à Vos Besoins »)
Pour négocier votre capital excédentaire à la Bourse de New York sur la base d'une fantastique et inédite ARME SECRÈTE

Le *YI KING*

le tarot et la torah de la Chine ancestrale, une technique à 100 p. 100 infaillible pour choisir une valeur *quand il est manipulé par la personne adéquate*. Nous avons cette personne !

SONNY, fils d'EDDIE LOVE

l'autorité indiscutable en Amérique aujourd'hui dans le maniement du *Yi king*.

SCEPTIQUE ?

Tant mieux.
Vous pensez peut-être que ce n'est qu'un ramassis de

TAUREAUMONTADES ?

Parfait !
Nous allons miser notre propre argent sur l'avis de l'Oracle.
UN MILLION DE DOLLARS EN LIQUIDE !!!
qui seront investis sur une seule consultation de l'oracle manipulé par Sonny et interprété par son associé, Aaron Kahn.

INTÉRESSÉE, L'AMÉRIQUE ?

Vous êtes cordialement invités à la corrida ! Apportez vos pommes et vos tomates pourries si vous voulez, *mais n'oubliez surtout pas vos carnets de chèque !*
Amérique, prends garde à toi !

L'INVESTISSEMENT TAURRIDE EST A TES PORTES !!!

« Quelque chose comme ça, suggéra-t-il. Alors, qu'en dis-tu ?
— Un million de dollars ? » demandai-je.
Il haussa les épaules. « Ce n'est pas le moment de mégoter, petit. Nous essayons d'établir une image de marque. Enfin, quel est le nombre magique, la somme la plus agréable aux oreilles américaines ? Tu l'as dit, petit : la brique, les cent mille Hamilton. Y a pas à tortiller. Si nous risquons le coup, autant mettre le paquet. Pas de gloire sans couilles, comme disait Ahasvérus. Une seconde ! Ça y est ! Je l'ai trouvé ! Notre slogan !
— Pas de gloire sans couilles ?
— Pas de gloire sans *cornes*, petit. » Il sourit avec une satisfaction presque obscène. « Reconnais que c'est brillant.

— Terriblement, concédai-je, à demi convaincu.
— *Taur*riblement », corrigea-t-il.

Ainsi que Kahn l'avait prévu, l'annonce de l'ordalie provoqua quelques remous à Wall Street. Si je ne peux parler d'une authentique fureur, c'est simplement que la plupart des professionnels y virent une plaisanterie ou un cas d'aberration mentale. Après tout, Kahn avait sa réputation. Elle lui collait à la peau, bien qu'on l'eût spirituellement castré avec la bénédiction de la communauté. En tout cas, notre initiative fournit une rare occasion d'amusement et de jeu, une diversion dont ces êtres graves et sombres tenaient absolument à profiter. Chaque fois qu'on nous repérait sur le trottoir, dans les ascenseurs montant vers les bureaux des Entreprises Kahn et Sun, des rafales de signaux subreptices se déclenchaient sur notre passage, clins d'œil et coups de coude, raclements de gorge, roulements d'yeux et discrets tapotements contre la tempe. Mais derrière les moqueries et la dérision, je sentais un résidu de gratitude et d'affection, car nous fournissions cette denrée rarissime et *taur*riblement demandée en ces mornes lieux : de la distraction.

Les railleurs eurent un avant-goût du châtiment qui les attendait, lors du matin fatidique, quand à huit heures Kahn et moi nous installâmes sur la Chase Manhattan Plaza avec la sono et les caméras mobiles de location, sans oublier notre acolyte au triste visage, le représentant de la banque porteur du chèque certifié d'un million de dollars, dûment rempli à l'exception de l'ordre. Tandis que les foules de travailleurs défilaient devant nous en se rendant à leurs bureaux, Kahn leur servit un numéro ininterrompu de *public relations*, tel un journaliste radio annonçant quelque « prestigieuse inauguration ». En accord avec le protocole du grand rituel américain de la publicité, le clou du spectacle fut annoncé pour midi, pendant l'heure du déjeuner, afin d'attirer le plus de public possible et d'augmenter le suspense. Nous espérions, nous voulions à tout prix que notre modeste « happening » devînt le sujet de conversation de tous les bureaux du quartier de la finance pendant les quatre heures suivantes. *Bzz. Bzz.* « Vous avez entendu ? » « Non ! Sans blague ? » « Je vous jure ! » « Ils vont vraiment flamber ce fric ? » « Qui sait ? » « Allons vérifier. » « Exactement ! A tout à l'heure ! »

Notre plan fut couronné d'un tel succès que la municipalité dut dépêcher un détachement de la police montée afin de canaliser la foule. On eût dit un festival. Kahn avait tout prévu, jusqu'au moindre détail ! Il avait même fait imprimer sur des ballons le nom de notre société ainsi que notre devise, « Pas de gloire sans cornes ». En sa qualité de maître des cérémonies, il m'avait envoyé dans le public pour les distribuer. Je ne lui en tins pas rigueur. Mon seul désir était que le *Yi king* ne nous laisse pas tomber, mais montre une assurance aussi intraitable que mon mentor. Si je doutais, Kahn était ivre de confiance. Confronté au spectacle de sa foi, j'eus presque honte. Pourtant, que risquais-je de perdre ? La bagatelle d'un million de dollars. J'envisageai ce déficit avec une résignation courageuse — ma réaction la plus taoïste depuis quelques mois.

A douze heures quinze exactement, Kahn me convoqua solennellement devant la foule. Quand j'entendis les syllabes de mon nom résonner dans les haut-parleurs, je sursautai si violemment que je lâchai les ficelles des ballons. Ils s'envolèrent aussitôt dans le ciel bleu entre les gratte-ciel. Je les regardai rêveusement, en regrettant de ne pouvoir moi aussi m'échapper. Ma progression à travers la foule fut accompagnée du roulement d'un tambour que Kahn avait loué pour l'occasion, peut-être en souvenir de sa propre fête de bar mitzvah.

Quand j'atteignis l'estrade, il réclama le silence au micro et m'aida solennellement à enfiler la robe neuve qu'il avait tenu à ce que je portasse afin de conférer au spectacle une « touche d'authenticité ». J'eus le sentiment d'être un monstre en provenance d'une autre culture et d'une autre époque, exhibé devant une foule étonnée, assoiffée de nouveauté. Le silence se fit. La foule, qui avait envahi la rue, s'étendait à perte de vue à droite comme à gauche. La circulation était interrompue. Tous ces regards fixés sur moi ! Derrière moi sur l'estrade, Kahn, vêtu de sa propre robe, essaya à plusieurs reprises de s'asseoir en position du lotus, puis, après plusieurs tentatives infructueuses, se contenta de croiser les jambes « à l'indienne ». Il ferma les yeux, son visage devint solennel. Je le regardai, puis mes yeux se posèrent sur la mer de visages levés vers moi. Le ridicule de ma situation, la bassesse de l'imposture, la compromission de mes principes — si stupide qu'elle en devenait plus grotesque que condamnable —, tout cela me frappa brusquement et ce fut à grand-peine que je m'empêchai d'éclater de rire. Des vagues de fou rire malmenaient mon ventre. Retenant mon souffle, je tâchai de contenir cette bouffée d'hystérie. Mon visage s'empourpra. Heureusement, tout ce qui transpira de mon hilarité fut une expiration ambiguë, qu'on pouvait facilement interpréter comme un soupir méditatif ou un exercice respiratoire. Une fois passé ce paroxysme, j'eus l'impression de m'éveiller d'un rêve. Que m'arrivait-il donc ? Que faisais-je ici ?

Les cent mille paires d'yeux fixés sur moi ne me donnèrent guère le loisir de réfléchir plus avant à ces apories morales. Je devais jouer mon rôle coûte que coûte. Mon hystérie nerveuse s'intensifia quand je songeai que, si j'avais le malheur de décevoir leur désir de spectacle, ils m'étriperaient sans doute et jetteraient mon cadavre en pâture aux pigeons. Ce fut donc avec un mélange de gêne, de honte, de ressentiment envers Kahn et de mépris pour moi-même, que j'entamai la consultation. Alors que, tel un joueur de dés, je secouais les pièces dans mes mains moites, une image faillit me faire pleurer et me mortifier sur-le-champ, devant le public, afin de rectifier toutes mes erreurs passées. Je pensai au tigre danseur dont Hsiao avait parlé ! « Tigre et dresseur — peut-être y avait-il un peu des deux chez Love. » Oui, j'étais bel et bien son fils ! Avec une grimace, je mis mes lunettes de soleil. Ensuite, je soufflai dans mes mains jointes pour me porter chance, secouai de plus belle les dollars d'argent et les laissai tomber.

L'oracle choisit le numéro 48, *Tsing*, « Le Puits », avec un trait faible à la deuxième place. Aussitôt, je compris que son verdict serait aussi clair et net que la fois précédente, car Le Puits était composé du trigramme *K'an*, L'Insondable, au-dessus de *Sun*. Les mêmes que la dernière fois ! Mais inversés, avec Kahn en position ascendante. Je poussai un soupir de soulagement. Cela ne signifiait-il pas que j'avais eu raison de me ranger à son avis ? Ou bien était-ce une simple description de la situation ? Le jugement disait :

> On peut changer la ville
> Mais on ne peut pas changer le puits.
> Il ne diminue ni n'augmente.
> Ils vont, viennent et puisent au puits.
> Si l'on est presque arrivé à l'eau
> Mais que la corde soit légèrement trop courte
> Ou que la cruche se brise, cela apporte l'infortune.

Une vieille association me vint aussitôt à l'esprit : la comparaison, énoncée par Chong Fou, entre le *Yi king* et un puits construit par des ouvriers humains, mais qui contient les eaux froides et transparentes du Tao, tirées du pur réservoir de l'Etre qu'aucun homme ne saurait sonder. Ainsi, les deux premiers vers du jugement évoquaient mon voyage de Chine en Amérique, de Ken Kuan à New York. Certes, la ville avait changé, mais le puits — la Source, le Tao — demeurait éternellement identique. A la lumière des récents événements, je ne pouvais qu'y voir un reproche.
Le commentaire du jugement disait :

> Tout homme peut, au cours de sa formation, puiser à la fontaine intarissable de la nature divine qui est l'essence de l'homme. Mais deux dangers menacent : le premier est que l'homme ne pénètre pas jusqu'aux vraies racines de l'humanité ; le second, que l'on ne s'effondre brusquement en abandonnant la formation de son être.

L'impression d'avertissement fut encore renforcée par ce que je trouvai concernant les traits :

> Neuf à la deuxième place signifie :
> Dans le creux du puits, on tire sur les poissons.
> La cruche est brisée, et fuit.
>
> L'eau elle-même est claire, mais n'est pas utilisée. C'est pourquoi seuls les poissons vivent dans le puits, et si quelqu'un vient c'est seulement pour prendre du poisson...
> Cela décrit la situation où quelqu'un doté de bonnes qualités les néglige... Ainsi, il se dégrade intérieurement.

L'image d'un puits pollué ou négligé n'évoquait que trop bien notre présent usage, ou plutôt abus, de l'oracle. De même, la référence aux poissons sur lesquels on tire semblait une allusion à notre exploitation, à des fins de gains personnels, d'une ressource dont le seul usage légitime consistait à « boire de longues et fraîches gorgées de sagesse du seau » tiré, « lourd et rempli à ras bord, des profondeurs du cœur humain ». En d'autres termes, « tirer sur les poissons » signifiait « choisir des valeurs » — encore un exemple de la célèbre ironie de l'oracle qui dissimulait un profond sérieux.

En somme, selon mon interprétation, *Les Mutations* avait daigné m'avertir une deuxième fois de renoncer à mes plans. Comme on s'en doute, Kahn comprit différemment son verdict. Tandis que sa main bouchait le micro, nous discutâmes avec véhémence au fond de l'estrade.

« Pff ! Aaah ! explosa-t-il quand je lui eus exposé mes réserves. Tu es vraiment paranoïaque, petit. Il s'agit de puits de *pétrole*. C'est aussi évident que le nez au milieu de ton... enfin, de *mon* visage. » Il sourit. « Je surveille ce secteur depuis un moment. Il regorge de potentiels inexploités — surtout dans ses produits dérivés, l'exploration, le développement — tu vois, tout le saint-frusquin. Je pense en particulier à deux compagnies également prometteuses — en termes de profits présents et futurs rapportés au coût de l'action — bien que l'une soit un peu plus performante que l'autre. » Il eut un rire sinistre.

« Quelles compagnies ? demandai-je.

— Sun Oil et *Con*oco, répondit-il. Devine laquelle nous allons acheter. »

Kahn fit durer le suspense le plus longtemps possible, puis il prit le micro et, tel Bert Parks annonçant le résultat de la compétition pour le titre de Miss Amérique, révéla notre choix au public. Le chèque fut alors rempli avec toute la solennité requise en présence de témoins, des mains furent serrées, des félicitations échangées. L'ordre fut exécuté, les actions achetées. Des cigares circulèrent et l'on déboucha des milliers de bouteilles d'eau gazeuse à la place de champagne, qui était non seulement plus cher mais vivement déconseillé par la police. Puis la foule se dispersa. Dès lors, tout Wall Street attendit que le Dow rendît son arrêt, comme quelque grand empereur romain assis impassiblement au-dessus de l'arène du Colisée, observant d'un œil froid les gladiateurs se battre à mort. Pouce en l'air, pouce en bas — la Bourse tout entière attendait la sentence.

Les plus anxieux furent rapidement soulagés. Car l'après-midi même, moins d'un quart d'heure après la clôture de la séance (selon un scénario soigneusement étudié pour éviter, autant que possible, les ruées intempestives au parquet), la direction de *Conoco* (peut-être devrais-je dire *Kahn*-oco ?) annonça la découverte de réserves de gaz naturel dans la mer de Beaufort, au Canada, plus vastes que toutes les réserves connues à ce jour dans l'hémisphère occidental. La nouvelle frappa Wall Street comme un coup de tonnerre. Au lieu de se précipiter vers les taxis pour sauter dans les premiers trains à destination de Long Island ou du Connecticut, les courtiers s'attardèrent au parquet, s'agglutinèrent autour des machines, observèrent les développements de l'affaire dans un silence de mort, secouant la tête, échangeant des questions, des regards incrédules.

Pris d'une crise de folie, Kahn tomba à genoux au milieu du bureau, leva son visage vers le plafond et psalmodia des prières d'action de grâce tandis que les larmes ruisselaient sur ses joues. Moi aussi, je ressentis d'abord un accès de joie incontrôlée. Mais quand je vis mon ami, la même sensation d'horreur qui m'avait assailli sur l'estrade revint et j'eus le pressentiment d'un désastre. Pourtant, dans une autre partie de moi-même, je soupirai et laissai la situation suivre son cours. Cette deuxième réussite de Kahn m'obligeait à approuver en attendant la suite.

Cet après-midi-là, quand nous quittâmes le bâtiment, les airs de supériorité imbéciles qui nous avaient accueillis le matin étaient remplacés par des expressions troublées qui trahissaient des abîmes de doutes, comme si les vieilles certitudes eussent été ébranlées et qu'un ordre nouveau eût commencé d'émerger. Les négociants nous observaient comme si nos visages irradiaient une lumière surnaturelle, semblable à l'aura qui, paraît-il, nimbe le corps des Immortels.

Le Bureau d'Échange des Valeurs ouvrit aussitôt une enquête. Étions-nous de mèche avec la direction de la Conoco ? Encore un exemple flagrant d'information interne ? Mais ainsi que le lecteur ne l'ignore pas, nous étions cette fois blancs comme neige. Car si nous avions négocié sur la base d'informations internes, alors il s'agissait du tuyau ultime, d'une méthode de renseignements à la fois trop performante et trop subtile pour tomber sous le coup des règlements du BEV. Non, certains eurent beau parler de simple coïncidence, de coup de chance, d'autres, beaucoup d'autres crurent. Une fois de plus, Kahn avait habilement manœuvré et prouvé qu'il savait tirer les ficelles de la nature humaine. L'ordalie s'avéra un coup de maître. Du jour au lendemain, nous devînmes, sinon célèbres, du moins le point de mire de Wall Street. Nous avions ébloui la Bourse et l'Amérique elle-même, touché sa fibre intime en faisant appel à l'aspiration fondamentale, au désir d'« un charme capable de maîtriser la vie ». Si, suspendue au-dessus de ma tête, je sentais toujours l'épée de Damoclès de l'oracle, simplement retenue par un fil ténu, je n'y songeai pas. Car après tout l'oracle lui-même ne nous avait-il pas soutenus à deux reprises ? Non, lecteur, la ruée vers l'or avait bel et bien commencé. Le Taureau accompagné des aimables cow-boys et conducteur de bestiaux, Kahn et Sun, était lâché et se sentait d'humeur belliqueuse !

11

PERDU ?

Après une errance désespérée de 40 jours (ou 40 ans)
dans cette b-ourse
inhospitalière ?

PERPLEXE ?

déboursolé par les pias-pias, les cancans,
les fla-fla, les pronostics contradictoires
des pharisiens et des scribes,
les (blanches) hordes indistinctes des faux prophètes
du marché ?

NE DÉSESPÉREZ PAS !!!
LA CAVALERIE ARRIVE !!!
LES SECOURS SONT PROCHES !!!

(Ecoutez le tonnerre lointain des sabots...)

TAUREAU INCORPORATED A LA RESCOUSSE !!!

En selle, l'Amérique,
et laisse-nous t'emmener faire un tour !!!
Pour plus d'informations, téléphonez-nous. Notre numéro est

TAU RE AU

Les opératrices attendent ! (Et quelles opératrices !)

Cette publicité s'étala en pleine page du *Wall Street Journal*, du *New York Times*, du *Chicago Tribune*, du *Los Angeles Times*, du *Washington Post* et de plusieurs douzaines de journaux dans tout le pays. Le Grand Public marcha comme un seul homme. Inutile de dire que la fureur que nous avions échoué à soulever avec notre première publicité à cause de notre soi-disant manque de sérieux, se déchaîna avec une virulence redoublée. Presque aussitôt, nos concurrents lancèrent une contre-offensive.

NE VOUS LAISSEZ PAS ENC... ORNER PAR CE TAUREAU !!!

fut l'un des slogans les plus méchants. Dans tout Wall Street, on concocta des jeux de mots malicieux en sirotant la tasse de café matinale. On nous surnomma perfidement « Kahn et son caneton », ou, pire encore, « Kahn-a-Son ».

La virulence pathologique de la campagne de représailles médiatiques me scandalisa. En même temps, elle stimula mon agressivité.

Quant à Kahn, il était ravi sans la moindre arrière-pensée. Ainsi qu'il ne se lassait jamais de le souligner, la moindre bribe de publicité, même incendiaire et diffamatoire, apportait de l'eau à notre moulin. Son état s'améliorait de jour en jour, d'heure en heure. Il reprenait confiance. Une lueur de détermination, peut-être une trace de son ancienne conviction d'avoir été choisi par Dieu pour un destin hors pair, brillait maintenant sur son visage, expliquant sans doute ses fréquentes citations de l'Ancien Testament, qu'il connaissait sur le bout du doigt depuis l'enfance. Enthousiasmé par le succès de la phase un de notre campagne, il entreprit de trouver un logo pour notre opération. « Faut trouver une image percutante », m'assura-t-il en plissant le front avec sincérité.

Je lui avais montré des gravures d'un vieux sage taoïste aux épaules voûtées et à la robe déchirée, assis sur le dos d'un taureau. Il décida de l'utiliser pour concocter le logo de notre « marque ». Il modifia légèrement le sage, lui ajouta un superbe *Stetson*, un pantalon de cuir et des éperons en or à quatorze carats. Le taureau aussi subit une transformation : la douce et inoffensive bête de trait qui se soumet docilement aux ordres de son maître devint un monstre de rodéo féroce et écumant qui ruait avec une joyeuse énergie — bref, le bœuf de la version chinoise se métamorphosa en Longue-Corne musculeux du Texas. Cela, m'assura Kahn, permettrait de conserver intact le sens premier du symbole tout en l'accommodant au goût américain. Nos concurrents le surnommèrent le « Bronco de Brooklyn » ; ainsi nous assimila-t-on de plus en plus — péjorativement — aux investisseurs modestes, peu fortunés, par opposition aux princes de la haute finance. Mais Kahn réussit même à tourner cela à notre avantage : il identifia le Taureau au « Grand Véhicule » (comme dans le bouddhisme Mahayana) de la classe ouvrière. Et ce fut pour satisfaire cette fraction de notre clientèle que nous ouvrîmes une deuxième branche de nos services, une caisse mutuelle associée à notre société de management, entièrement placée sous l'égide des Entreprises Kahn et Sun : le Taureau Mutuel, « une division de Taureau Incorporated ».

C'en fut trop pour les grands manitous de l'institution. Ils avaient beau regarder de haut la lame de fond populaire que nous avions créée et que nous chevauchions, ils avaient beau ressentir quelques scrupules moraux à investir leurs ressources avec un intermédiaire aussi douteux que Kahn, ils firent alors la carpette pour palper leurs dividendes (ainsi que Kahn aurait pu le formuler) et ravalèrent leur morgue comme de gentils petits (vieux) garçons.

L'aspect le moins « révolutionnaire » de nos pratiques, surtout pour le « Taureau Mutuel » que Kahn dirigeait personnellement, n'était pas notre stratégie d'investissements originale qu'en l'honneur de sa jeunesse perdue, consacrée à poursuivre le fantôme impalpable de Mark Twain parmi les étagères de Columbia, il baptisa « l'Approche Pas de Quartier ». Elle consistait tout bonnement à « mettre tous nos œufs dans le même panier, *et à surveiller ce panier !* » Autrement dit, Kahn extrapolait une application boursière à partir de ma manipulation des pièces, puis il investissait promptement tout ce que nous possédions, l'intégralité de nos ressources, sur la valeur choisie. Bien que cela contrevînt scandaleusement à tous les principes élémentaires de l'investissement sain, sans parler du bon sens et de la logique, cette « approche » connut un succès phénoménal. Car si nous risquions à chaque fois l'annihilation totale, nos profits étaient de même « non diversifiés ». Et contre tout espoir, l'oracle continuait de nous soutenir. *Sze*, « L'Armée », nous fournit ainsi un indice particulièrement heureux pour un investissement dans le secteur militaire. Je pourrais multiplier les exemples, mais je crains qu'une prospérité aussi redondante ne paraisse obscène.

Naturellement, nous avions déjà « agrandi la boutique » en embauchant une bande de jeunes garçons vachers pour s'occuper des commandes, ainsi que les inévitables secrétaires et standardistes. Transgressant délibérément la mode et le modèle de Wall Street, nos employés arrivaient au travail en chapeaux et bottes de cow-boy, et portaient des cordons noués en rosette au lieu de la traditionnelle cravate.

Nous découvrîmes un curieux corollaire de l'Approche Pas de Quartier : quand nos ressources eurent augmenté, nous nous retrouvâmes parfois, involontairement mais avec plaisir, en mesure d'influer sur la masse de liquidités du marché. Surtout quand nous nous attaquions à de petites sociétés dynamiques que le *Yi king* semblait nous indiquer. Souvent, les actions disponibles étaient insuffisantes pour répondre à notre demande. Les premières fois où cela se produisit, nous renonçâmes magnanimement à acheter. Cela souleva le problème brûlant d'une expansion de notre société par la prise en main d'une autre. Kahn y était évidemment favorable. Quant à moi, je renâclais, car je ne m'étais pas encore habitué à la soudaineté et à l'ampleur de notre succès. Si nous devions nous diversifier, je tenais à rester prudent et rationnel, à ne pas me lancer dans une frénésie phagocytaire inconsidérée. Ce fut aussi à cette époque que nous choisîmes de nous introduire en Bourse.

Peu à peu, avec une admirable perspicacité, Kahn réussit à entamer mes réticences anti-expansionnistes. Ébloui par nos succès, pénétré de notre virtuelle omnipotence, il piaffait d'impatience et se sentait à l'étroit dans le cadre restreint de notre inspiration originelle. Pourquoi nous limiter à la simple gestion de portefeuilles, ou même à une caisse mutuelle ? Pourquoi ne pas créer une organisation générale de services financiers, placée sous la haute autorité de Kahn et Sun : courtage, investissements, arbitrages, opérations commerciales, peut-être un département de cartes de crédit (Taureau Furieux ?).

J'avais d'abord réagi avec fermeté, mais ses allusions continuelles à mes SO me piquaient au vif. Peut-être aurais-je résisté si, dans son ingéniosité, il n'avait avancé un argument qui, sans être vraiment original, me parut probant. Il s'agissait d'une version modifiée de l'apologie darwiniste de la lutte, adaptée à la Bourse, surtout aux fusions entre sociétés, et pimentée de quelques exemples frappants du style inimitable de Kahn. Patiemment, il m'expliqua qu'au lieu de servir une cause immorale ou, au mieux, amorale, en absorbant d'autres sociétés, nous allions contribuer concrètement à l'amélioration de l'écologie boursière américaine. En agissant comme « prédateurs des affaires », nous régulions efficacement le « patrimoine génétique de la finance », car nous assurions la survie des plus forts. Non, s'écria-t-il avec fougue, la compétition et le meurtre n'avaient pas pour fin la puissance ou l'intérêt personnel ; bien au contraire, ils fondaient une noble discipline spirituelle, profondément altruiste. Par un processus analogue à la sélection naturelle, où l'adaptabilité aux exigences et aux épreuves variées de la nature (« du Tao », ajouta-t-il) permet la survie individuelle tandis que les spécimens les plus faibles de l'espèce meurent, de même dans la sphère économique l'adaptabilité aux exigences de la compétition au sein de la libre concurrence assure la survie des affaires les plus saines et, ainsi, aide l'économie dans sa lente mais inévitable ascension vers la perfection.

Je fus stupéfait par les conséquences sublimes de sa vision, qui dépassaient de beaucoup le monde des affaires. Je repensai à ma première discussion avec Riley, me demandai si je ne tenais pas la réponse à la question qu'il m'avait posée : Comment les chrétiens conciliaient-ils l'existence du mal avec le caractère foncièrement bon de Dieu ? Ou encore, comment les taoïstes réconciliaient-ils l'existence de ce qui n'était pas le Tao avec l'unité primordiale de toutes choses *dans* le Tao ? Etait-ce enfin la réponse ? Dans l'affirmative, les deux objections étaient seulement dues à une étroitesse de vue. Dès qu'on apercevait le Grand Tout, les contradictions apparentes se résolvaient ; le mal devenait simplement le creuset où l'on prouvait et éprouvait le bien. La fièvre témoignait de la volonté de purification et de guérison du corps. Les plaies et les lieux corrompus de la sphère économique, — voilà où le Tao dépêchait ses légions, ses leucocytes, ses anticorps pour se débarrasser des expériences manquées, détruire les aberrations sanguines. La diversité était indispensable pour assurer la plus grande perfection possible, et si elle créait quelques monstres, elle veillait aussi à leur élimination par la sélection naturelle. C'était là le miracle ! Tout tendait vers le bien !

Telle était donc notre fonction à Taureau Incorporated : sélectionner (puis éliminer) les membres les plus faibles de notre industrie, les décomposer en éléments simples, les réduire en pièces détachées qui seraient ensuite absorbées, utilisées par les survivants les plus forts, nous ! Je ne saurais exagérer l'impact que cet argument eut sur moi. Il me frappa avec la force d'une révélation, l'articulation même d'une pensée qui me tenaillait depuis quelque temps, mais que je n'avais pas réussi à formuler clairement. Je la retournai en tous sens jusqu'à l'avoir parfaitement maîtrisée. Pour la première fois depuis la création de Taureau Inc., grâce à cette perspective morale inédite je m'impliquai à fond dans notre projet, bien au-delà du simple désir d'œuvrer à la réhabilitation de mon ami. Je cessai de freiner ses initiatives, me jetai à corps perdu dans notre entreprise, avec une énergie qui égalait, voire dépassait la sienne. Nous décidâmes alors d'un commun accord que, pour nous donner une assise solide en vue d'une éventuelle diversification, nous avions besoin d'une banque.

Dans le plus grand secret, nous commençâmes d'examiner les candidats dignes d'être absorbés. J'avoue que je pris plaisir à cette recherche. Notre intérêt me parut aussi voluptueux que le péché — on eût dit un couple de vieux noceurs examinant des danseuses de cabaret ; cela aurait pu me froisser si Kahn ne m'avait révélé le profond altruisme de notre tâche. Et puis, si l'exercice d'une fonction morale s'accompagnait d'un plaisir luxurieux, où était le mal ? Le taoïsme n'avait jamais fait bon ménage avec l'ascétisme, pensai-je ; sa philosophie consistait plutôt à prendre les choses comme elles venaient, dans leur flux et leur reflux, leur *yin* et leur *yang*. Tchouang-tseu avait souvent souligné que la pauvreté volontaire et les mortifications étaient aussi éloignées du libre exercice de la vie, de son va-et-vient entre abondance et pénurie, que la prodigalité excessive ou le laisser-aller. Je n'aurais pu être davantage d'accord avec lui !

Grâce à ces justifications, ma nouvelle richesse devint pour moi une bénédiction. Je m'exhortai à cesser de battre ma coulpe, à écarter tout remords, à jouir calmement de ma chance. De même que Kahn m'aidait dans ma vie professionnelle, je recevais conseils et encouragements de Li. A partir de cette époque, nous nous vîmes beaucoup : nous dînions souvent ensemble, nous allions au spectacle, au musée, à des fêtes, et même parfois dans une boîte de nuit. Elle m'initiait aux mystères du plaisir personnel, et bientôt nous louâmes un appartement dans un immeuble cossu — pierre de taille et façade couverte de lierre —, juste au-dessus de Washington Square. Je lui demandai d'emménager avec moi, et bien qu'elle insistât pour conserver son ancien appartement, elle accepta.

Je crois qu'elle assista à l'ascension de Taureau Inc. avec la même stupéfaction que les autres. Pourtant elle n'en parlait jamais sans une nuance amusée. Non qu'elle désapprouvât ; loin de là. Li ne jugeait jamais. Le crépuscule moral qui l'entourait était perpétuel. D'ailleurs, il calma, anesthésia ma conscience, alors que Yin-mi l'aurait sans doute mise à vif. Je réfléchis que le contact avec différentes cultures aux attitudes et aux valeurs extrêmement variées lui avait sans doute inculqué une sorte de relativisme moral ; mais peut-être, à l'inverse, était-ce son tempérament qui l'avait d'abord attirée vers ce type d'études.

Même la frénésie de notre brève liaison avec Jane Doe pâlit en comparaison de l'excitation de cette première absorption. Car en dernière analyse, ç'avait seulement été un beau spectacle (sinon pour Kahn, du moins pour moi), comme une course de chevaux où l'on parie sur un numéro avant d'assister à la bagarre avec un intérêt passionné mais sans connexion viscérale, en observant sans participer. Mais ceci était la chose elle-même, la Chasse. La soif de sang était seulement justifiée par les buts élevés de l'évolution ; les moyens tendaient vers une fin morale. « Surpassant cet art qui, selon vous, ajoute à la nature, existe un art que la nature façonne. » Tels furent les premiers vers de poésie occidentale que je compris jamais et que je sentis jusqu'au tréfonds de mon être. Ils modifièrent définitivement le cours de ma vie.

« Connexion viscérale », oui, cela traduit bien ma sensation d'alors. Car maintenant, contrairement à l'épisode Jane Doe, je sentais la présence d'une autre vie, d'une chose tapie dans l'épais feuillage de la jungle légale, une chose palpitante et craintive, au souffle lourd, mais aussi prête à bondir, fermement décidée à résister à notre attaque. Cette présence étrangère devint pour moi aussi palpable que celle d'un être humain, mais elle agissait contre moi, déclenchait une irritation subtile, semait dans mon esprit la graine d'un antagonisme irrévocable. A mesure que je me familiarisais avec cette sensation, une rage contrôlée se développa en moi, le désir de briser la nuque de sa résistance, de goûter le sang et la moelle tièdes, de sentir la chose se plier aux caprices de ma volonté. Si son assimilation n'était possible qu'au prix de sa vie, alors elle devait mourir.

De tout cela, je fus parfaitement conscient. Quand j'observais mes actes, quand je réfléchissais à mes décisions, je ne ressentais pas tant de l'horreur qu'une invincible terreur. Les prescriptions et autres proscriptions éculées de la moralité conventionnelle me revenaient en mémoire comme le disque rayé de conversations dépourvues de sens, les phrases apprises par cœur à l'école, un catéchisme vide. Tout cela ne s'appliquait pas à l'univers où nous attaquions et étions attaqués. Je crois que cette réaction s'explique en partie par l'inébranlable foi que j'avais en l'« altruisme supérieur » dont Kahn m'avait parlé. Mais plus encore, cette levée de ma censure fut un réflexe de ma conviction viscérale (encore ce mot) d'être dans mon bon droit et de progresser ainsi vers mon but : comprendre le Dow. Oui, quand Taureau Inc. absorba sa première société, je me sentis enfin en présence de la chose elle-même, sur le seuil du saint des saints du Dow. Mes yeux ne s'étaient pas encore habitués à l'obscurité de la chambre secrète, mais j'étais convaincu de fouler son sol.

Dans notre enthousiasme initial, nous n'écartâmes d'emblée aucune banque, aussi grosse ou formidable fût-elle. Chase, Chemical, Morgan Guaranty — aucune n'échappa à notre examen. Car bien que maintes de nos cibles potentielles eussent un capital plusieurs fois plus important que celui de Kahn et Sun, pour une fusion d'entreprises les banques n'étaient pas plus invulnérables que les brontosaures — ces doux herbivores, ces énormes, léthargiques et paisibles végétariens — assaillis par le Tyrannosaure Rex de Taureau Inc. Le prix croissant de nos actions, nos perspectives de développement et de rentabilité nous donnaient le poids nécessaire pour absorber des institutions infiniment plus grosses que nous, d'autant que nous envisagions le cas échéant — si la direction résistait, se vouant ainsi à une mort certaine (notre certitude, leur mort) — d'adopter la stratégie sanglante de l'offre publique d'achat, en proposant directement aux actionnaires de racheter leurs portefeuilles à un prix nettement plus élevé que le cours officiel du marché, quitte à les payer en obligations et en déclarations de dettes diverses, dont certaines « convertibles », ce qui rendait notre proposition extrêmement séduisante pour les investisseurs, qui pouvaient ainsi acquérir des actions de Kahn et Sun à des prix fort avantageux. Nous portâmes finalement notre choix sur une banque relativement modeste, la Second Jersey Hi-Fidelity, qui était malgré tout plusieurs fois plus grosse que nous.

Et notre crainte (ou notre désir ?) se réalisa. La direction résista. Lors d'un bref tête-à-tête, nous lui fîmes part de nos intentions et proposâmes une capitulation honorable. Ils refusèrent. Je n'oublierai jamais l'expression de tous ces directeurs lors de la conférence. C'étaient des hommes qu'en d'autres circonstances, dans un ascenseur ou dans la rue, je n'aurais peut-être pas remarqués. Car leurs visages ne portaient aucune trace de dignité ou de beauté. Mais ce matin-là, toute leur colère, toute leur peur, leur vulnérabilité, leur courage, leur volonté de résister luisaient sombrement sous la surface, donnant à leur regard un éclat et une profondeur inhabituels. Au risque de paraître impoli, je ne pus m'empêcher de les dévisager. Pourtant, toute politesse était déplacée en l'occurrence, car ils me fixaient aussi durement que je les observais. J'avais soigneusement préparé l'embuscade et maintenant que je les voyais se précipiter aveuglément dans le piège, mettant ainsi leur carrière — non, leur vie — en péril, je me découvris une certaine affection pour eux, une sorte de pitié, mais qui excluait tout désir de les épargner.

Alors que nous échangions des coups d'œil peu amènes de part et d'autre de la table de conférence, mon esprit s'absenta. Je songeai à cet après-midi passé en Chine au bord du Fleuve au Sable d'Or, quand, assis devant Tsin, je l'avais écouté avec une horreur fascinée décrire la bataille comme « la plus haute expression de l'aspiration humaine, la raison ultime de notre existence, qui nous fait dépasser nos limites pour accéder à la divinité ». « Nous tuons non pas à cause d'une regrettable nécessité, avait-il ajouté, mais pour nous rafraîchir et augmenter notre force, parce que notre esprit s'en repaît, parce que nous ne sommes réellement vivants que dans l'instant où nous enlevons la vie. » Maintenant je comprenais ses paroles ; mieux, je savais qu'il avait raison. Cette découverte me frappa si violemment que je faillis crier, au lieu de quoi je ris, peut-être un peu trop fort, de cette plaisanterie subtile que personne ne pouvait comprendre. Les autres me dévisagèrent comme si j'avais perdu tout bon sens. Peut-être avaient-ils raison. Je crois pourtant qu'à un niveau plus profond ils comprenaient, avec le plus intime des savoirs — celui de la proie en face du prédateur, qui le comprend mieux qu'il ne se comprend lui-même. Je sentis cela à l'expression de leurs visages — une seule et unique expression —, la souffrance sans l'apitoiement, l'acceptation sans la capitulation, le fatalisme sans la résignation ni le désespoir, une expression presque vide et cependant tellement parlante, hantée par la chose elle-même. Cela n'en finissait pas. J'aurais pu me perdre dans sa complexité. C'est peut-être d'ailleurs ce qui est arrivé.

Malgré la parfaite vivacité de ce souvenir, je le sens rogné par le flou du rêve. Tout allait tellement vite. Je me demande parfois si j'ai vraiment vécu cette période de ma vie. Je me rappelle que certains matins je me réveillais sans plus savoir où j'étais. Je ne reconnaissais plus le paysage. Un univers de merveilles naturelles s'offrait à moi : marécages préhistoriques et mers intérieures, volcans en éruption, vapeurs de solfatares et marais où des créatures se vautraient lourdement dans la fange ; des pics et des chaînes de montagnes se dressaient brusquement sous mes yeux, ou bien, à l'inverse, s'écroulaient et disparaissaient en une lente avalanche silencieuse — et tout cela décrivait mon paysage intérieur.

Néanmoins, d'autres sensations étaient parfaitement concrètes. La plus subtile fut une étrange altération dans ma perception de la lumière. Les couleurs me semblaient plus saturées, la lueur du jour prenait un éclat inhabituel, les ombres se détachaient plus nettement contre la pierre. A d'autres moments, j'avais une impression contraire de brume, comme un halo doré qui dissolvait le contour des choses. Avec un plaisir enfantin, j'agitais ma main devant mes yeux pour voir si le brouillard se mettrait à tourbillonner. Il le faisait parfois.

Encore plus tangibles bien que moins agréables, étaient ce que je me résolus à nommer « les animalcules », un mot que Li m'apprit. Les mages de l'Occident désignent ainsi les formes effilées qui se tortillent dans les gouttes d'eau qu'ils placent sous leurs microscopes. Dans mon cas, les animalcules planaient dans l'air comme des germes minuscules. Certains avaient même des formes de bactéries — coccus, spirillum, bacilles — mais la plupart étaient amorphes, invertébrés ; certains, pourtant, adoptaient une forme animale, mais de bêtes que je n'avais jamais vues, dont je n'avais jamais entendu parler, et aucune n'était plus grosse qu'une tête d'épingle. Quand j'en discutai avec Li pour la première fois, elle me confia qu'elle avait vécu une expérience similaire après avoir lu trop de livres dans la mauvaise lumière d'une bibliothèque ; sortant au grand jour, elle avait aperçu de petits alphabets qui s'étaient déployés devant ses yeux, comme si leurs lettres s'étaient gravées sur ses rétines. Peut-être devrais-je voir un ophtalmologue, suggéra-t-elle. Je commençai par refuser, mais quand le phénomène persista, je suivis son conseil.

J'y allai un samedi. Sans doute parce que Li avait évoqué son propre cas et que je portais des vêtements quelconques, le médecin me prit pour un étudiant ou un ouvrier. Sa politesse fut manifestement de pure forme ; tandis que je décrivais mes symptômes, il maîtrisait à grand-peine son impatience ; puis, sans le moindre commentaire, il m'examina. Comme il écartait mes paupières et se penchait au-dessus de moi avec un petit crayon lumineux, il restait silencieux et, selon moi, un peu brusque. Il rédigea ensuite une ordonnance pour des gouttes et me livra son verdict.

« Que vous est-il arrivé ? Vous avez reçu un produit toxique dans les yeux ? » Arrêtant d'écrire, il me dévisagea avec un bref intérêt.

Je lui retournai un regard interloqué. « Pas à ma connaissance.

— Cela ressemble fort à des brûlures d'origine chimique que j'ai déjà eu l'occasion de constater, ou à ce qui arrive aux soudeurs qui regardent directement leur chalumeau sans lunettes de protection. Vous n'êtes pas soudeur, par hasard ? »

Je souris en moi-même, songeant : « seulement d'une société à l'autre ». Je me contentai de secouer négativement la tête.

« Eh bien, quelle qu'en soit la cause, il y a une indéniable détérioration de la cornée, mais rien de grave... — il marqua un temps — à mon avis. Vous devez attendre et surveiller cela. » Il déchira la page de son bloc, puis me tendit l'ordonnance. « Ces gouttes devraient au moins calmer la sensation de brûlure. Vous avez bien dit que vos yeux vous brûlaient ?

— Non, répondis-je, je n'ai pas dit cela.

— Peu importe. Utilisez-les, me conseilla-t-il. Cela devrait venir à bout de vos calculs.

— Animalcules, corrigeai-je.

— Peu importe. »

Il me fit alors comprendre sans ambiguïté qu'il ne pouvait me consacrer davantage de temps. Je sortis de son bureau en bougonnant.

Je réfléchis ensuite que mon « baptême » dans l'East River était peut-être à l'origine de mon problème. Ma consultation chez l'ophtalmologue expliquait au moins la sensibilité à la lumière dont je souffrais depuis quelque temps, et mon besoin croissant des lunettes de soleil. Malgré ses assurances, les animalcules ne disparurent pas. Le collyre demeura sans effet. De toute façon, je doutais de son diagnostic. « Une détérioration progressive de la cornée. » Pourquoi était-il si sûr de lui ? Peut-être voyais-je simplement quelque chose que les autres ne remarquaient pas, ne pouvaient pas remarquer ? Peut-être les animalcules étaient-ils le résultat d'une amélioration, et non d'une détérioration de la vision ? Je me demandai si les formes noires que je voyais planer dans l'air étaient les molécules ou les atomes mêmes, qui se heurtaient et rebondissaient aléatoirement dans le vide.

Que l'augmentation plutôt que la baisse de mon acuité visuelle fût à l'origine de mes visions, j'en trouvai presque la confirmation dans un incident qui se produisit le matin avant notre conférence avec les directeurs de la banque. Alors que je nouais ma cravate devant le miroir de l'armoire dans la chambre de notre nouvel appartement, une impulsion bizarre me saisit. Je laissai tomber mes mains et, le front plissé sous l'effort de concentration, fixai obstinément ma cravate. D'abord, rien ne se produisit, bien qu'elle parût trembler légèrement. J'allais renoncer quand j'aperçus mon reflet dans le miroir. La cravate lévitait ! Allongée à l'horizontale devant moi, elle frémissait comme une flèche fichée dans un bloc de bois. J'étais si surpris, si ravi, que je poussai un cri de joie.

Li passa la tête par la porte de la salle de bains. « Tu as dit quelque chose ? » Avec un sourire de forban, je lui montrai ma cravate. Elle me retourna un regard perplexe.

Je baissai les yeux, et vis qu'elle était retombée. J'hésitai à lui confier ce qui venait de se passer, puis décidai de me taire. J'eus sans doute raison, car après son départ, aucun effort de concentration ne réussit à la faire se relever.

Pourtant j'avais bel et bien réussi une fois. Au diable le docteur pour les yeux — il s'agissait d'autre chose ! Et au cas, lecteur, où vous penseriez que j'ai imaginé tout cela, laissez-moi vous dire que le phénomène se reproduisit une deuxième fois. Ce matin-là, au bureau, alors que nous attendions l'heure de notre rendez-vous, Kahn et moi étions trop nerveux et excités pour travailler sérieusement, si bien que nous décidâmes de tuer le temps à notre façon habituelle : en lançant des pennies. Nous les jetions à tour de rôle vers le mur, comme des fers à cheval. Je m'aperçus qu'en me concentrant de toutes mes forces, je réussissais à infléchir leur trajectoire. Mon contrôle était grossier, incomplet, mais cependant efficace. Je pouvais même manipuler le côté sur lequel la pièce retombait, du moins une fois sur deux. Kahn n'avait rien remarqué : les distorsions étaient trop légères et se produisaient trop rapidement pour son œil, exactement comme les tours de passe-passe exécutés par un habile magicien. Et puis je ne tenais pas à vendre la mèche, pas tant que je gagnais de l'argent ! La joie que je ressentis fut d'autant plus délicieuse que sa cause restait secrète.

12

Notre victoire ne tarda pas. Les actionnaires de la *Second Jersey* se rallièrent en masse au Taureau. Le soir du jour où nous franchîmes la barre des cinquante et un pour cent, Kahn et moi sortîmes boire pour fêter notre victoire. Dans notre euphorie, nous étions affectueux et timides l'un envers l'autre. A maintes reprises nous répétâmes les mêmes formules et gestes de félicitation, les chargeant d'une émotion qui croissait à mesure de notre ébriété. Notre désir commun de mettre l'autre à l'aise en le faisant boire me rappela mes séances d'œnologie avec Lo, notre application scrupuleuse à suivre les règles de l'étiquette afin d'oublier nos pires intentions et notre principal objectif : nous soûler comme des cochons. Je crois que Kahn et moi tenions à marquer le coup d'une formule profonde ou d'une apostrophe exaltante, mais qu'aurions-nous pu ajouter ? Nous nous contentâmes de mines hilares et de grandes tapes dans le dos. Après quelques heures de cette beuverie chaleureuse, ivre mort et ravi, je pris un taxi pour rentrer à Washington Square.

Li m'attendait. Quand j'ouvris la porte, je la découvris debout sur la pointe des pieds dans l'entrée de l'appartement, en train d'arroser une fougère qu'elle avait apportée de chez elle, avec une bouteille achetée dans un magasin de diététique qui livrait aux chats leur ration quotidienne de lait caillé sucré. Elle la posa, puis avança vers moi en souriant, glissa un bras gracile autour de ma taille et m'embrassa de sa bouche tendre et chaude.

Aussitôt, sans raison, mon humeur changea. Ma gaieté disparut, remplacée par une étrange mélancolie douce-amère, une nostalgie incompréhensible. Je sentis que tout avait changé depuis cette première nuit passée avec Li, mais aussi que rien n'avait vraiment évolué. Après cette sortie au théâtre et notre promenade « ethnologique », je me sentais indigne, confondu, comme un cousin de province, ou pire, un amant de province, le péquenot qui courtise la princesse. Qu'avait-elle dit déjà ? « Dames de la cour payant fort cher le privilège de séduire les mendiants. » Elle ne me tenait plus ce discours désormais ; jusqu'à son attitude avait changé. Elle était douce, affable, attentive en toutes circonstances. Et pourtant, comment dire ? En sa présence, j'éprouvais encore une sorte de scrupule, comme si j'abusais de ses faveurs. Je crois qu'elle était profondément ancrée en moi, cette conviction d'occuper le strapontin de son cœur, d'où à tout moment la moindre saute de vent pouvait m'expulser sans espoir de retour. Je me demandai si l'habitude des lois implacables du marché n'expliquait pas ma réaction, l'intuition de la précarité et du caractère éphémère de nos entreprises les plus sûres, une paranoïa fondamentale, une réticence devant le monde matériel, due à ma participation au Dow — ce splendide principe féminin, l'index de la mortalité — qui enseignait aux néophytes l'art de monter en selle comme l'éclair et de se cramponner tant que durerait le rodéo.

Je réfléchis aux conséquences de cette pensée avec une grande tristesse. Puis je me reprochai mes réflexions en songeant que de tels amalgames entre ma vie professionnelle et ma vie privée étaient inadmissibles. Car le Dow était l'indicateur du destin matériel du monde, où toutes choses suivent inévitablement la pente qui mène à la ruine. Au contraire, dans le royaume de l'esprit, me dis-je, l'impossible devenait possible ; à l'inverse des métaux précieux, la richesse de l'amour ne rouillait pas, était à l'abri du temps et de ses vicissitudes ; les convictions du cœur résistaient à toutes les épreuves. Ce fut cet espoir qui m'apprit à lutter contre mes sentiments d'infériorité, à essayer de me considérer comme digne de l'amour de Li. Car je ne me demandais même plus si j'étais fou amoureux d'elle.

« Bonsoir, mon doux garçon, dit-elle avec indolence, en allongeant les syllabes. Tu m'as manqué aujourd'hui. Toute la journée, j'ai senti une sorte de douleur au creux de l'estomac. Ici. » Elle plaça mes mains sur son ventre, comme une future mère invite son époux à palper l'intimité du mystère, son secret, leur trésor, mais les mains de Li entouraient seulement le vide. « Depuis ce matin, je porte ton odeur sur ma robe, chuchota-t-elle à mon oreille en souriant, en se serrant contre moi. Comme un fantôme errant dans une maison abandonnée, qui hante le décor d'un amour défunt... — elle rit doucement — ou d'un crime. Je pense tout le temps à toi. C'est vrai. » Elle m'embrassa encore, cette fois sur le front. Puis elle posa sur moi ses yeux semblables à deux meurtrières donnant sur un monde de richesses secrètes — le scintillement voilé, liquide, des lumières qui signalent les corps-morts dans un port immobile, l'entrechoquement des coques, le doux lapement des vagues, l'eau si tranquille que les étoiles miroitent sur sa surface noire. Elle se tenait légèrement penchée, si bien que par sa chemise entrouverte j'aperçus ses seins qui oscillaient comme une marée attirée par la lune. Puis elle sourit et bâilla en montrant ses dents blanches. Le spectacle de cette tendresse voluptueuse fit disparaître ma méfiance, mes inhibitions, aussitôt remplacées par une langueur si intense qu'elle en était presque débilitante. Dieu, qu'elle savait aimer ! Elle me comblait de ses trésors. Elle était faite pour l'amour, elle était le cru le plus rare que j'eusse jamais goûté, si subtil et surprenant au palais que le cerveau commençait à peine de répertorier la palette de ses plaisirs, que déjà son goût avait quitté les lèvres. Mon splendide ange du sexe.

« Quand je te regarde, lui dis-je, m'abandonnant à l'ivresse, il me semble que tout est terminé. » J'examinai son visage. « Tu incarnes tellement mon désir, que plus rien ne me paraît réel. Voilà cinq minutes, j'étais fou de joie à cause d'une chose qui s'est passée aujourd'hui au bureau. Maintenant je me souviens à peine de quoi il s'agit — Dow, Tao — j'oublie le sens de ces mots quand je suis avec toi, et je m'en moque. » Je parlais avec passion, sans espérer qu'elle me comprendrait, qu'elle saisirait l'ampleur de mon trouble. « *Je m'en moque*, Li, comprends-tu ce que cela veut dire ? Je...

— Chut, dit-elle doucement en levant vers ses lèvres l'ongle parfait de son doigt mince. Tais-toi. Prends garde de ne pas l'effrayer.

— Quoi ? » demandai-je.

Elle sourit sans répondre.

Je faillis mordre mon poing pour résister à la soudaine langueur que ses paroles provoquèrent.

« Assieds-toi. » Je retirai ma veste, puis la laissai m'entraîner vers le sofa. Ses chaussettes bruissaient doucement sur le tapis. Elle prit une bouteille de vin blanc parmi les livres ouverts et les papiers étalés sur le secrétaire, remplit son verre, puis m'en servit un. « Tu sais, il s'est passé une drôle de chose aujourd'hui. » Les yeux baissés sur le verre pour ne pas renverser de vin, elle traversa la pièce vers moi. Elle me le tendit, puis s'assit à l'autre bout du sofa en repliant une jambe sous elle. Ensuite elle but une gorgée, retroussa un peu les lèvres en attendant ma question.

« Quoi donc ?

— J'ai vu Yin-mi.

— Où ? demandai-je vivement.

— Dans le parc. » Nous échangeâmes un regard. « J'ai failli paniquer. » Elle rit d'un air faussement dégagé.

« Alors ? »

Elle but encore une gorgée, secoua la tête. « Je suis presque sûre que c'était une coïncidence.

— Que faisait-elle ? »

Li haussa les épaules. « Comment veux-tu que je le sache ? Elle achetait probablement de la drogue.

— Yin-mi ? rétorquai-je, sceptique. Allez... »

Elle scruta mon visage. « Je plaisantais. Mais tu as l'air de penser qu'elle est trop pure pour ce genre de chose ? »

J'ignorai sa remarque. « Continue.

— C'est à peu près tout. J'ignore ce qu'elle faisait là. Je suis seulement convaincue que c'était parfaitement innocent.

— Pourquoi ? insistai-je.

— Sa réaction. Elle était contente de me voir. Nous avons un peu parlé. J'ai retrouvé ma confiance en moi. » Li eut un rire nerveux en se rappelant la scène. « J'ai bien failli tout lui avouer quand elle m'a demandé ce que je faisais là. J'ai rougi, je me suis troublée, perdue dans des explications confuses avant de réussir à bafouiller que j'allais voir une amie. Quand elle m'a demandé qui, le nom de Jane Doe m'a traversé l'esprit. J'ai oublié ce que je lui ai répondu. Jane quelque chose, peut-être Jane Dour. Elle m'a regardée bizarrement, mais je ne crois pas qu'elle a deviné mon mensonge. Pourtant, pendant une bonne minute, j'ai été terrifiée. C'est presque drôle, tu ne trouves pas, moi avoir peur d'elle ? »

Je haussai les épaules avec une neutralité un peu bougonne.

Elle me sourit malicieusement. « Je sais que c'est sans doute cruel, mais je n'ai pas pu m'empêcher de lui demander si elle t'avait vu.

— Pourquoi as-tu fait ça ? répliquai-je d'une voix brusque. Tu sais bien qu'elle ne m'a pas vu. »

Elle haussa les épaules presque joyeusement. « Je l'ignore. Je n'ai pas pu me retenir. Yin-mi a simplement secoué la tête avec tristesse, le regard perdu dans le vague. » Li fouilla mon visage, ce qui m'agaça un peu, me donna le sentiment d'une indiscrétion. « Elle est amoureuse de toi, ajouta-t-elle calmement.

— Et moi de toi », répondis-je tout à trac, comprenant soudain qu'elle était jalouse, aussitôt touché par la sincérité de son aveu.

« Chuut, fit-elle de nouveau en prenant ma main entre les siennes pour la poser contre sa joue. Ne dis pas cela, Sun I. A chaque fois, ça me fait peur.

— Pourquoi ? demandai-je, ma curiosité en partie émoussée par un vague malaise. Tu ne m'aimes pas ? Tu ne peux pas ? »

Li me regarda alors sans méchanceté mais avec cette distance que je connaissais si bien et redoutais tant. A la fois embrassé et exclu par son regard, j'imaginai une ressemblance entre Li et quelque déesse surnaturelle qui eût daigné baisser les yeux vers un mortel, attristée par le spectacle d'un suppliant dévoué que torturait la perspective de sa fin, presque bouleversée jusqu'à l'empathie par cette souffrance qu'elle ne pouvait partager, puis retenue par la gravité irrésistible de ses privilèges. Ce regard fut pour moi plus terrible que toute cruauté consciente, car il exprimait l'amoralité foncière qui était l'essence de son être, la chose que chez elle j'aimais plus que tout, mais dont aussi je désespérais, car j'y voyais l'ennemi implacable de mon but ultime. Je reconnus amèrement que jamais je ne partagerais cette amoralité. Alors je pensai aux yeux de Yin-mi, à cette grande solennité qui avait englobé mon être tout entier, et qui, à la lettre, ne le comprenait que trop bien.

« Tôt ou tard, elle découvrira la vérité, dit Li en me tirant de ma sombre rêverie, d'une façon ou d'une autre. Le mieux serait peut-être de la prévenir nous-mêmes. »

Cette proposition me surprit. Je me renfrognai.

« Préfères-tu t'en charger, ou que ce soit moi ? » demanda-t-elle.

Je détournai les yeux.

« Surtout ne montre pas trop d'enthousiasme, se moqua-t-elle avec un rire irrité.

— Tu trouves cela absolument nécessaire ? » demandai-je.

Elle haussa les épaules. « En tout cas, ce serait certainement plus honorable. »

J'acquiesçai. « Il vaudrait peut-être mieux que je m'en occupe. »

A ma grande surprise, elle grimaça. « Je n'en suis pas sûre. Je préférerais m'en charger moi-même.

— Alors pourquoi me demander ? lançai-je sans même essayer de dissimuler mon agacement.

— Je voulais voir ta réaction. » Après un silence, elle ajouta : « Elle ne te manque jamais ? »

J'hésitai à mentir, puis décidai de dire la vérité. « Parfois, admis-je. Un peu. »

Elle fronça les sourcils, plus sombrement cette fois. « Je préférerais que tu ne la voies pas. » Son ton était incisif, presque péremptoire.

« Tu sais bien que je ne l'ai pas vue, répliquai-je. Mais pourquoi ? Quelle différence cela fait-il ?

— Tu veux donc la voir. » Maintenant elle accusait, comme si elle venait de trouver la confirmation d'un vieux soupçon.

« Ce n'est pas ça, objectai-je. Je me demandais simplement pourquoi tu ne voulais pas.

— Eh bien, si j'ai rompu avec Peter, je ne vois pas pourquoi tu la fréquenterais, poursuivit-elle avec un mouvement d'humeur que je trouvai répugnant, insupportable.

— Mais alors, arrangeons-nous pour que les clauses du contrat soient absolument équitables, pour que les deux parties en aient pour leur argent, dis-je. Bon Dieu, Li, nous parlons de la voir pour lui annoncer que nous vivons ensemble ; ça n'a rien d'un rendez-vous d'amoureux ou d'une festivité quelconque, non ? Et puis, ajoutai-je, plein de ce que je considérai comme une juste indignation, je ne t'ai jamais rien demandé à propos de Peter. »

Son expression me prouva que j'avais fait mouche ; Li se durcit. « Très bien », dit-elle sèchement, d'une voix froide et volontairement énigmatique, volontairement cruelle. Elle croisa les bras, refusa de me regarder.

Je finis par céder. « Okay, je suis désolé. C'est sans importance. Occupe-t'en. Je m'en moque. »

Dire qu'elle accepta de bonne grâce ma capitulation serait exagéré. Tout cela avait un goût amer.

« Alors, reprit-elle avec une feinte gaieté, raconte-moi ta journée. En entrant, tu m'as dit que tu étais heureux. Que s'est-il passé ? Dis-moi combien de millions de dollars tu as gagnés, comment ton taureau a soulevé un nuage de poussière et laissé tout le monde derrière lui, aveuglé, éternuant et hurlant de rage. » Son image la fit rire, mais il y avait un peu de moquerie dans sa voix. « A moins que tu n'aies enlevé la douce Europe de la finance pour l'entraîner vers l'Asie, les seins nus et souriant avec un oubli complaisant tandis qu'elle tissait une guirlande de fleurs pour tes cornes.

— Tu te moques de moi, répondis-je sans animosité, résigné.

— Mais non ! protesta-t-elle avec un rire amusé.

— Suis-je si ridicule ?

Un instant, elle remit au fourreau l'arme aiguisée de son ironie, et s'adoucit tout en conservant un ton enjoué. « Ridicule ? répéta-t-elle. Je ne saurais dire. Peut-être un peu. Mais surtout étonnant. Ta réussite est une gageure, un miracle ! Un bébé parmi les loups — ou les ours — et qui les oblige à venir manger dans sa main. Qui l'eût cru ? Sun I — elle prit mon visage entre ses paumes —, tu es stupéfiant. Absolument. Mon beau kamikaze chinois, mon aigle qui bombarde Wall Street en piqué, plonge du haut des steppes tibétaines, fond sur New York à partir de son aire du toit du monde — qui aurait imaginé ça ? Si tu étais un personnage de roman, tous les lecteurs crieraient à l'invraisemblance. Et pourtant, tu es bien là, en chair et en os. Je le sais. Je sais au moins cela. » Elle embrassa brièvement mes lèvres, peut-être pour y apposer le sceau de son approbation.

Toute ma rancœur et ma souffrance s'évaporèrent comme la rosée au soleil de sa générosité, aussi extravagante fût-elle. Elle était ainsi. Je ne pouvais y résister, et pas davantage à elle.

« Allez, viens, dit-elle, la table est mise et j'ai gardé le dîner au chaud pour toi. » Elle dénoua ma cravate, déboutonna mon gilet.

Pendant le dîner, elle me laissa parler. Je lui appris les récents développements de la prise en main de la banque, le dernier épisode du drame qu'elle avait suivi tout du long avec intérêt. A mesure que je parlais et buvais, ma bonne humeur revint. L'exaltation aussi, inévitablement suivie par la loquacité. Je parlais toujours quand nous allâmes nous coucher et une fois que nous eûmes fait l'amour, quand nous allumâmes une cigarette pour la fumer ensemble. Pris d'un enthousiasme sans doute un peu pompeux, je me lançai dans une longue digression pédante sur l'« altruisme supérieur ». Ce fut seulement alors qu'elle m'interrompit, et par un rire. Bouche bée, l'index encore dressé vers le plafond, je me tournai vers elle en clignant des yeux. « Quoi ? »

Elle se contenta de sourire en silence avec une expression amusée et provocante.

« Alors ? persistai-je d'une voix presque indignée.

— Rien, dit-elle en levant les mains avec une humilité feinte, comme pour s'excuser. Enfin... tu ne crois pas vraiment ce que tu dis, n'est-ce pas ?

— Et pourquoi pas ? » la défiai-je.

Elle haussa les épaules. « Oh, je ne sais pas, sauf que bien sûr tout cela est du baratin pompeux, vaniteux, hypocrite et autosatisfait. »

Stupéfait, je la regardai bouche bée. Pour la première fois, elle jugeait mes activités professionnelles.

« Mais ne te méprends pas, continua-t-elle. Je ne désapprouve nullement que tu absorbes une banque. Je trouve merveilleux que tu réussisses aussi bien. Pourtant, tu devrais avoir l'honnêteté de reconnaître tes vrais motifs, non ? Je veux dire, si tu veux baiser quelqu'un, aies au moins la décence de ne pas essayer de le convaincre que c'est pour son bien.

— Bon, disons alors pour le bien du système dans son ensemble, dis-je.

— Tss, tss, fit-elle en secouant la tête. Même si ta comparaison avec l'évolution tient (et je n'en suis pas sûre ; les animaux tuent par instinct alors que l'homme est censé posséder le libre arbitre), elle ne t'exonère pas *personnellement*. Quand tu t'empares de la société d'un autre contre sa volonté, le premier organisme qui en profite est ton compte en banque. » Elle rit. « A propos, m'accorderais-tu une procuration pour tirer des chèques sur ton compte ? »

Je la regardai avec une douloureuse incrédulité. « Malgré tout ce que je t'ai dit sur les raisons de ma venue aux Etats-Unis et de mon travail à la Bourse, tu penses vraiment que je suis seulement motivé par l'intérêt personnel ?

— Eh bien, appelons ça les intérêts composés, si tu préfères.

— Je suis sérieux, Li ! Ce n'est pas drôle. Tu penses vraiment que je pourrais trahir mes principes au point de chercher le profit pour lui-même sans avoir d'objectif plus élevé ? »

Elle plissa les yeux, puis m'adressa son sourire narquois en haussant les épaules. « Pourquoi pas ? Tout le monde fait ça, moi comprise. Pourquoi serais-tu si spécial ? Allez, Sun I, tu vis dans le monde réel maintenant. Tu as mûri, tu es un grand garçon. D'ailleurs, n'était-ce pas le but de Taureau Inc. et de cette fameuse ordalie — un rite de passage, l'abandon de l'enfance ?

— Mais c'était l'idée de Kahn, protestai-je. J'ai tout accepté pour lui. »

Une lueur dure brilla dans ses yeux. Elle sourit sans joie. « Au fond de ton cœur, tu as consenti à tout. »

Je fus si blessé, si abasourdi que je n'essayai même pas de me défendre.

« Je ne veux pas te vexer, Sun I, poursuivit-elle, mais je ne marche pas quand tu prends un air vertueux pour me parler de pure et simple prédation capitaliste. Non que je désapprouve la pure et simple prédation capitaliste, loin de là. Mais n'essaie pas de te faire passer pour un doux agneau bêlant. Ce que tu as fait, ce que tu fais, est incroyable, mais ça n'a rien à voir avec un combat moral désintéressé, du moins pas pour moi. Je crois que tu fais ça parce que tu aimes ça, à cause de ce que tu y gagnes ; aucun de tes arguments ne pourra me convaincre du contraire. C'est tout ce que j'ai à dire.

— Et qu'est-ce que j'y gagne ? » demandai-je sur un ton cynique, abattu.

Levant les mains, elle imita parfaitement le geste du prêtre qui invite les fidèles à la communion. « Tout ça », dit-elle en tournant la tête pour montrer la chambre, l'appartement.

Je franchis le dernier pas. « Y compris toi ? »

Elle rougit violemment. « Peut-être, dit-elle avec cette voix qui semblait me défier de la prendre au mot. Si tu veux. »

Je restai assis en silence, secouant la tête, essayant de cacher mon trouble.

« C'est tout bonnement un fait de la vie, Sun I. »

Encore cette expression. « Comme la mort ? » demandai-je.

Elle eut un sourire las. « Oui. Comme la mort. Et comme la mort, mieux vaut l'accepter sans trop rechigner.

— Tu te contentes toujours d'observer sans prendre parti, attaquai-je. Depuis le début, tu n'as que mépris pour tout ce que je fais.

— Loin de là, me contredit-elle. J'ai été profondément impressionnée. J'admire ce que tu as accompli. Sincèrement. Mais je ne peux croire que tu as réalisé tout cela par altruisme.

— C'est pourtant le cas ! m'écriai-je en m'enflammant de nouveau. Si tu ne le crois pas, alors tu ne crois pas en moi — pas vraiment, pas pour ce qui importe. »

Elle ne broncha pas. Je détournai les yeux en poussant un soupir.

« Tu as tort, tu sais, reprit-elle calmement. Je crois vraiment en toi. J'en ai douté lors de nos premières rencontres, mais maintenant je commence vraiment à avoir la foi. Mais sans doute pas de la façon dont toi, tu crois en toi. Je ne crois pas à ton sacerdoce, à cette image d'Epinal du pèlerin, à ta quête religieuse du Graal. Pur et simple fantasme d'adolescent. Tu en as peut-être eu besoin pour rassembler tes forces, pour t'aiguillonner. Mais tu as grandi depuis ce temps-là. Le moment est venu de laisser tomber cette mythologie. » Elle tendit le bras vers moi — j'étais assis au bord du lit — et posa doucement sa main sur mon épaule. « Je crois que tu es vraiment beaucoup plus fort que cela, et meilleur. »

Me tournant vers elle, je lui adressai un regard ironique. « Meilleur ?

— Meilleur pour moi. »

Je posai mes coudes sur mes genoux, croisai les doigts en fixant mes pieds sans penser à rien, seulement conscient d'une douleur triste et lointaine. La vue de mes orteils me rappela les soirées d'été passées sur le toit avec Yin-mi quand, nos pieds pendant dans le vide, je lui racontais mon histoire, mes espoirs, tandis que le soleil sombrait lentement dans les terres sauvages derrière l'Hudson. *Elle* avait cru. Je fus submergé d'un insupportable sentiment de perte. Jamais auparavant je ne l'avais regrettée, pas depuis que j'avais rencontré Li. Maintenant j'avais envie de pleurer.

« Tu as l'air si triste, dit-elle tendrement, d'une voix vibrante. Viens ici. » Elle m'attira vers elle, posa mon visage sur sa poitrine. « Que puis-je faire ? »

Je fermai les yeux sans répondre, seulement désireux de me dissoudre.

« Veux-tu que je te raconte une histoire ? proposa-t-elle en caressant mes cheveux. Voyons... » Elle réfléchit, puis : « Je sais — Phaéton. Tu as entendu parler de lui ? »

Je secouai la tête comme un enfant boudeur en quête de cajoleries, mais qui refuse de reconnaître son désir.

« C'est un personnage de la mythologie grecque, expliqua-t-elle.

— Comme Œdipe ?

— Comme Œdipe, confirma-t-elle. Sa mère, Clyméné, était une mortelle, mais son père était Hélios, le dieu du soleil. A partir du deuxième mois de la grossesse de Clyméné, Phaéton tambourina contre la matrice de sa mère en hurlant pour sortir à l'air libre, "poussé par le destin", comme Enée, comme tous les autres. Sa curiosité et son désir étaient insatiables. On dit de lui qu'il avait les yeux "fixés sur les étoiles". » Li m'observa curieusement avant de poursuivre. « Sa mère l'éduqua, mais il n'en faisait qu'à sa tête. Doutant d'être vraiment le fils du dieu du soleil, voulant une preuve à tout prix, il chercha son père dans le palais des dieux du mont Olympe, puis supplia Hélios de le laisser conduire le char du soleil à travers les cieux pendant une journée afin de mettre à l'épreuve leur parenté — une sorte d'ordalie que lui-même s'imposa. Hélios tenta de l'en dissuader. Il décrivit les monstres qu'il devrait affronter : le Scorpion, le Lion, la Grande Ourse, Ursa Major, le Taureau... une horde de "lions, de tigres et d'ours". Mais Phaéton fut implacable. Tu sais ce qui arriva ? »

Je secouai la tête.

« Les chevaux trop fougueux s'emballèrent. Phaéton fut aveuglé par la lumière de mille soleils, de mille galaxies. Les mains ensanglantées par les rênes du pouvoir, il paniqua et perdit le contrôle du char qui incendia les cieux, creusa le sillon de la Voie Lactée, jusqu'à ce que l'univers tout entier fût menacé d'une conflagration générale. Zeus dut intervenir. Il déchaîna la foudre et frappa à mort l'imprudent. Phaéton tomba en chute libre dans les eaux du fleuve Eridan et disparut loin du regard des hommes.

— Il a péché par orgueil, commentai-je, plus pour moi-même que pour Li.

— Oui, par orgueil, arrogance, présomption. Les Grecs ont un mot pour désigner toute cette constellation de sens : hubris.

— Hubris », répétai-je soigneusement en essayant cette combinaison inédite de syllabes.

Elle serra mon visage entre ses mains. « Toi aussi, tu as des "yeux fixés sur les étoiles", dit-elle.
— Tu penses donc que l'orgueil figure parmi tous mes défauts ? » demandai-je.
Elle sourit en hochant la tête. « Oui, je crois. L'orgueil, et peut-être aussi un peu d'hypocrisie.
— D'hypocrisie ?
— "D'hypocrisie ?" m'imita-t-elle pour me narguer. Je crois que tu vois très bien ce que je veux dire. »
Je clignai les yeux.
« Reconnais, dit-elle, que tu apprécies les belles choses, tout ce que ta nouvelle existence t'a apporté.
— Mais je peux vivre sans elles, affirmai-je. J'ai passé presque toute mon existence sans elles.
— C'était avant de me rencontrer », ajouta-t-elle en me laissant tirer mes propres conclusions.
Je ne répondis rien.
« Tu sais que tu es toujours libre de retrouver ce mode de vie, remarqua-t-elle avec un fatalisme vaguement admonitoire. Tu pourrais même solliciter la complicité de ma petite sœur dans cette entreprise.
— Je t'en prie. » Je sentis le vortex de son agressivité m'aspirer. « Je croyais que nous avions réglé ce problème.
— Il faut que tu comprennes une chose, Sun I, poursuivit-elle comme si je n'avais rien dit. Tout ceci n'est pas gratuit. *Je* ne suis pas gratuite. » Elle écarquilla les yeux, me regarda avec une expression cynique de défi. « Exactement. Ne prends pas cet air surpris. Tu l'as dit toi-même. Mais si tu n'as pas encore compris, tu ferais mieux de regarder la vérité en face. Tu soutiens mordicus que ton but ultime est une sorte de connaissance, que tu es venu ici en pèlerinage pour chercher la pureté et la vérité. Mais en même temps, tu dis que je suis le symbole même de ton désir. Tu ne vois donc pas ? C'est contradictoire ! Tu ne peux pas avoir deux désirs suprêmes.
— Qu'est-ce que tu racontes ? gémis-je, partagé entre l'angoisse et la frustration.
— Je me pose simplement une question : à l'heure du choix — et cette heure vient toujours, Sun I, tôt ou tard —, quel désir sacrifieras-tu ?
— Pourquoi poses-tu toujours des questions aussi terribles ? » J'eus l'impression qu'on m'écartelait. « Pourquoi insistes-tu toujours sur ce point ? J'ai déjà rompu mon vœu pour toi, ça ne te suffit pas ? Que désires-tu de plus ?
— Je veux simplement que tu n'oublies pas, Sun I, que malgré tes protestations d'altruisme supérieur et de quête religieuse, sans l'argent tu ne pourrais pas avoir tout cela... Et sans cela, tu ne pourrais pas m'avoir. »
Je me réfugiai dans mon exil au bord du lit, m'accrochant à l'image de Yin-mi comme à un talisman capable de me protéger contre toute cette laideur.
Li se pencha vers moi, releva de nouveau mon visage. Son regard était tendre, plein de remords. Ma propre indifférence me surprit.

« Ne sois pas triste, Sun I », murmura-t-elle.
Je ne lui répondis pas.
« Il n'y a pas que cela. Ce n'est pas seulement un problème d'argent. Je voulais simplement dire que, malgré mes sentiments pour toi, je ne pourrais jamais être heureuse sans certaines... "choses". Est-ce tellement détestable ? L'argent n'est qu'une condition nécessaire, aucunement une valeur sacro-sainte. Pense à la pièce que nous avons vue. Peu importent la beauté et la grandeur du drame, pour créer une bonne mise en scène il faut de l'argent, afin de montrer la pièce sous son meilleur jour. C'est un fait de la vie. » Ses dernières paroles me firent tiquer, alors même que j'étais sur le point de céder. « Tu voudrais que l'esprit accomplisse tout, remue des montagnes. Comme ce serait bien ! Mais c'est une pure utopie, Sun I. Crois-moi, choisis la réalité. Elle ne te laissera pas pantois, bouche bée en permanence, abasourdi, éberlué... (elle reprit son souffle entre chaque mot, mimant avec humour la stupéfaction) mais il y a toujours de bonne choses à manger et du vin à boire. » Elle prit son verre, porta un toast en mon honneur. « Nous pouvons toujours faire l'amour jusqu'à ce que nos corps s'écroulent d'épuisement. » Son regard était à la fois sensuel et vulnérable. « Ça va mieux, n'est-ce pas ? »
Des larmes brûlaient maintenant mes yeux. Je ne fis rien pour les cacher.
Elle sourit avec une tristesse tendre, comme si elle prenait une profonde inspiration, puis le dos de sa main caressa mon visage. « Tu es bon, Sun I, dit-elle, trop bon. »
Je fondis en larmes.
Elle soupira puis s'éloigna, m'abandonnant à ma peine. Quand je me retournai, elle était adossée aux oreillers avec, sur le visage, une expression rêveuse et concentrée. Elle jouait avec une mèche de cheveux qu'elle cardait comme de la laine ; son poignet exécutait les mêmes gestes que lorsqu'elle tordait dans un sens puis dans l'autre sa chaîne d'or. Je ne saurais dire pourquoi, mais ce geste machinal me choqua davantage que toutes ses paroles, peut-être à cause du profond oubli dont il témoignait. Dans la pénombre, une étrange aura, aussi froide que l'éclat du marbre, luisait autour d'elle. Au bout d'un moment, elle remarqua que je l'observais et ses doigts quittèrent la mèche. Tous les sens en éveil, je ne quittai pas ses cheveux des yeux. La mèche tomba le long de ses seins, noire contre la blancheur de sa peau nue, épousa les contours de son corps. Soudain, elle frémit, se balança comme une queue. Quand je levai les yeux, le sourire de Li s'inscrivait sur le visage d'une renarde.
« Que veux-tu ? demandai-je en chinois, d'une voix prudente et terrifiée, comme si j'eusse parlé à un esprit.
— Tout ceci, répondit-elle. Toi. Toi tout entier, avec tes contradictions, surtout tes contradictions. Je désire ton ambivalence, ton paradoxe. » Elle me sourit encore, mais la renarde avait disparu ; l'illusion, ma vision prémonitoire, appelez cela comme vous voudrez, s'était envolée.
L'air siffla entre mes dents, je soupirai avec une exaspération résignée.
« Li, Li — je secouai la tête — je désespère parfois de ton amour. "Ambivalence", "paradoxe" — que veux-tu que je fasse de ces mots ? Je ne les connais même pas.

« — Je n'en suis pas si sûre, dit-elle. J'ai parfois l'impression que tu n'as pas la moindre idée de qui tu es. Peut-être ai-je eu tort de parler d'hypocrisie à ton propos. Tu es aussi véridique que tu le peux. Simplement, tu ne te connais pas. On dirait qu'en toi deux âmes habitent un seul corps, deux âmes diamétralement opposées, mais enfantines, qui dans leur innocence cherchent à se réconcilier. Peut-être ta mère et ton père, la foi et le doute, la volonté de vivre et la pulsion de mort ? J'ignore la réponse. Pourtant je te vois clamer la pureté de tes intentions alors que tu chasses dans cette jungle et que tes mains sont pleines de sang. Si la pureté est ce que tu désires vraiment, tu n'aurais jamais dû quitter ton monastère. Pourquoi es-tu parti ? La pureté n'existe pas ici, alors que des lieux comme Ken Kuan ont pour seule fonction de la maintenir en vie. Les hommes tels que ceux que tu as connus là-bas ont pour mission d'empêcher sa disparition définitive. Je respecte leur tâche. Mais tu n'es pas l'un d'eux, Sun I. Tu as passé de nombreuses années parmi eux, je sais ; tu as du mal à tirer un trait. Mais tu es fait pour ce monde-ci. Je crois que ton maître t'a laissé partir pour cette raison, parce qu'il savait que ton destin était de ce monde, dans le Dow. Et peut-être ton ami Kahn a-t-il raison de dire que, dans son acception la plus large, le Dow est le monde. Tu peux te frapper la tête contre ce mur, t'y briser le cœur, mais tu es ici chez toi et c'est pour cette raison que tu es venu en Amérique. Parce que ce pays est son apothéose, l'apothéose du Dow, de même que la Chine est peut-être celle du Tao. Quant au reste — le Tao dans le Dow — autant oublier ces balivernes. Tu ne le trouveras jamais. Il n'y a rien de tel ici. Ton "delta" n'existe nulle part, sinon peut-être sur l'arc-en-ciel de tes rêves et de ton cœur, mais ce lieu n'est pas réel.
— Vraiment ? »
Elle secoua la tête avec assurance. « Les deux sont irréconciliables, Sun I, à jamais. Le "delta", "le Tao dans le Dow" — ce sont les formules de ta propre absolution, conçues pour apaiser la tension qui règne en toi entre le bien et le mal. La réconciliation que tu cherches est une illusion, un tour de passe-passe irréalisable. Et puis, même si tu trouvais ce trésor, il te répugnerait. Ta félicité te rendrait complètement flasque. » Elle tendit le bras, ses doigts se refermèrent autour de mon pénis flaccide, elle eut presque un sourire d'excuse. « Tu cesserais d'être un homme pour devenir un saint. Tu n'aurais plus aucun intérêt, Sun I, du moins pour moi. »
Elle s'interrompit pour laisser ses paroles faire leur effet. « Mon pauvre garçon, me consola-t-elle en touchant mon visage du bout de ses doigts frais. Tu penses encore que par miracle, dans une éternité mathématique à laquelle tu veux absolument croire, les deux parallèles de tes destins incompatibles, de tes ambitions contradictoires, finiront par se rejoindre et que tous tes tourments se résoudront comme par magie. » Elle chuchotait. « Les choses ne sont pas ainsi, Sun I. »
Quand elle se tut, je m'aperçus que depuis quelque temps j'écoutais autre chose, la mélodie plaintive, incohérente, de la harpe qu'elle avait apportée de son appartement pour la fixer sur le rebord de la fenêtre de notre chambre. « Tu as peut-être raison, capitulai-je d'une voix épuisée, atone. Je ne sais plus. »
Contournant le lit, elle s'agenouilla à mes pieds, posa sa tête sur ma

cuisse, qu'elle berça doucement. « Ne t'inquiète pas, murmura-t-elle. Tout ira bien. »

Quand je baissai les yeux vers sa chevelure noire, j'eus le sentiment d'une blessure irrémédiable. Elle avait atteint un lieu si profond en moi que rien ne pourrait plus jamais être comme avant ; elle avait à jamais blessé mon cœur, volontairement mais, je crois, sans méchanceté. Et pourtant je n'éprouvais ni amertume ni ressentiment. En fait, ma tendresse pour elle était plus profonde que jamais, un amour plus intense que je n'avais cru possible d'en vivre. Mon regard se brouilla. Je caressai rêveusement ses cheveux. Soudain, je pris conscience d'un immense vide calme en moi, d'une libération. Après l'explosion, la virulence de la passion, après la bataille, je me sentais purifié, entier. J'étais en paix.

Cette nuit-là, allongé dans le lit, je pensai à Yin-mi. Mon esprit dériva sombrement vers le passé, évoquant mille incidents, le plaisir innocent que nous prenions ensemble, la douceur avec laquelle nous l'acceptions. Tout cela devenait poignant, presque déchirant à la lumière des événements ultérieurs qui jetait les ombres de catastrophes que nous n'avions pas prévues sur les pans lumineux de la mémoire. Je songeai à l'expression de Yin-mi le premier soir, dans la cuisine de son père, cette même expression que j'avais remarquée le dernier matin quand j'étais passé devant elle pour sortir de ma chambre. Ce regard liait le commencement et la fin, fermait le cercle de notre intimité. Je me rappelai aussi son animation, l'étincelle d'intérêt qui avait brillé dans ses yeux, les petits signes de tête encourageants qu'elle m'avait adressés pendant que je parlais à Wo (en fait à elle) dans le salon des Ha-p'i. Oui, elle avait cru à mon but supérieur, elle y avait cru et s'y était identifiée si intensément qu'elle avait découvert le cristal qui figurait la véritable intention de mon cœur, elle l'avait extrait comme un joyau hors du torrent écumant de mon discours, pour me l'offrir entre ses mains tremblantes. Le delta — elle m'avait donné cela ; Li venait de me le retirer.

Li reposait endormie sur les oreillers. Elle était si belle. Mon merveilleux ange du sexe... Elle m'avait donné cela, fait cadeau de ma sexualité. C'était là son présent, son delta. (« Voilà le delta, mon doux garçon, le seul qui importe. ») Et je l'avais désiré. Mais l'autre, le Tao dans le Dow — « Ta félicité te rendrait complètement flasque ». Je touchai mon sexe sous les draps. Saisi d'une paix lugubre, je fermai les yeux.

Soudain un éclat de rire jaillit du plus profond de moi-même, un bref et violent *ah !* Je pensais à ce que Kahn m'avait dit au café du Platane : « Coincé entre ton *yin* et ton *yang*. » Yin-mi, *yang*... Ma main se crispa. Il n'avait bien sûr pas voulu dire cela, mais peu importait. C'était parfait. Tout aussi brusquement, une bouffée de remords et de douleur m'assaillit quand je me rappelai cette nuit sous la pluie, la folle poursuite dans les ruelles. Si seulement j'avais alors connu ma sexualité ; et si Yin-mi avait connu la sienne... Mais connaissait-elle l'amour ? Peut-être... Pour moi, mon désir s'était bizarrement transmuté en aversion et en méfiance. Cela, et non la débâcle à Trinity, avait marqué le début de notre séparation. Je la revis debout dans l'entrée de l'immeuble, les mains derrière elle, ses seins à travers la chemise trempée. Je sentis ma gorge se nouer et j'eus une érection en me souvenant de son regard quand je l'avais soulevée, un regard presque triste, puis la pression de ses lèvres sur ma bouche, leur goût. Inconsolable, je fermai les yeux et, pour l'éphémère soulagement que cela me procurerait avant que la morsure d'impatience ne tenaillât de nouveau mon ventre, je me masturbai. Le visage de Tsin, celui de mon père, le mystérieux animal cornu dans la cale du *Telemachos*, toutes ces images traversèrent mes rêves, ainsi qu'un éclat de rire moqueur et désincarné qui, l'espace d'un instant, accompagna la musique de la harpe.

13

Ce fut notre première dispute. Et la dernière. Et toutes celles entre les deux. Elles se résumaient toujours à ceci : son relativisme ethnologique exemplaire, mon besoin d'absolu. Le matin qui suivit notre altercation, j'eus l'impression d'avoir été battu à mort, roué de coups de matraque — une humiliation si violente que j'en eus physiquement mal. A cause de mon affrontement avec Li, mais aussi de l'absorption de la banque, de mon « plaisir solitaire ». Je me sentais profondément souillé, dégoûté de moi-même et de la vie. Était-ce cela que Tsin avait nommé « le contrecoup de la bataille » ?

L'exaltation de la veille possédait toujours Kahn, qui fanfaronnait et passait des ordres par douzaines. Je l'évitais comme on fuit un individu peu recommandable ; je rasais les murs, me terrais dans les coins obscurs. Je quittai le bureau de bonne heure. Dans le taxi qui me ramena chez moi, je caressai un instant l'idée de rompre avec Li, de la mettre à la porte, tout en sachant que je ne le ferais jamais. Je ne pouvais vivre sans elle. Mais bizarrement, cette dernière phrase n'évoquait nullement les images romantiques habituelles. Mon rapport avec Li ressemblait davantage à la dépendance vis-à-vis d'une drogue. Une autre association remonta vers ma conscience, où elle explosa comme une bulle : « une parodie insidieuse et débilitante de la joie profonde de l'illumination », les mots que le maître avait adressés à Hsiao. Il avait parlé de l'opium, mais je me demandai si cela ne s'appliquait pas aussi à Li, à son amour comparé à celui de Yin-mi. « Coincé entre ton *yin* et ton *yang*. » Je ris amèrement. J'étais donc un drogué.

Ma générosité d'esprit fut amplement récompensée quand j'arrivai à l'appartement. Assise par terre au milieu du salon, Li feuilletait rapidement un magazine tiré d'une pile. Elle portait encore sa chemise de nuit et sa robe de chambre ; elle n'avait apparemment pas assisté à ses cours. J'aurais juré qu'elle avait pleuré, car dans ses yeux les larmes brillaient encore. Mais dès qu'elle me vit, une lueur d'espoir inonda son visage.

« Tu es là ! » Elle bondit sur ses pieds, jeta ses bras autour de mon cou, se pelotonna contre moi. Puis, prenant mon visage entre ses mains, elle se pencha en arrière pour me regarder. Elle semblait paisible, grave, plus tendre et sensible que jamais.

« J'ai pensé à toi toute la journée », dit-elle d'une voix qui tremblait un peu. Elle m'étreignit encore, posa son visage sur ma poitrine. « Excuse-moi pour hier soir. Je regrette sincèrement ce que je t'ai dit. Je ne sais pas ce qui m'a prise. » Elle se pencha encore en arrière pour me dévisager. « Je te demande pardon.

— Tu n'es pas allée à tes cours ? » Ce brusque accès de tendresse avait quelque chose de langoureux et de pleurnichard qui m'emplit d'un vague dégoût. Je me demandai en silence si elle ne craignait pas tout bonnement de perdre sa nouvelle richesse, « tout cela ». Puis je me méprisai à cause d'une supposition aussi vile.

« Si, j'ai assisté à un cours, répondit-elle. Mais c'était insupportable. Ton sperme ne cessait de couler dans mes vêtements — si froid que j'ai eu envie de pleurer. Quand je suis rentrée ici, j'ai fondu en larmes. Et dormi. Et pleuré encore.

— Qu'est-ce que c'est ? dis-je en montrant les magazines qui jonchaient le sol.

— Oh, je suis passée chez moi et j'ai ramené quelques revues. » Elle se dégagea, marcha vers elles, s'agenouilla. Avec une expression rêveuse, elle se remit à les feuilleter. « J'ai vu quelque chose — je ne sais pas si je vais le retrouver — une photo qui m'a fait penser à toi. » Elle chercha quelques instants, puis ferma le magazine avec un soupir résigné. « Bah, autant que je te le raconte moi-même. C'était un reportage sur l'Amérique du Sud, le Chili, je crois, plein de photos superbes : des soudeurs et leurs flammes bleues et blanches, entourés de gerbes d'étincelles ; un cratère monstrueux dans le désert, l'Atacama, avec de gros camions jaunes et des bulldozers qui ressemblaient à des jouets ; des chalutiers rentrant au port sous une nuée de mouettes ; les gratte-ciel de Santiago qui se détachent sur un arrière-plan de montagnes, la pleine lune est en partie cachée par une tour de verre. Et parmi toutes ces illustrations du "progrès", de la "modernisation", l'étrange photo d'un petit garçon assis dans la neige, le menton posé sur ses genoux relevés — elle imita son attitude —, son minuscule visage légèrement incliné comme s'il avait du mal à dormir. Sa peau sombre, la configuration de ses traits, ses longs cheveux noirs nattés révèlent sa race : c'est un Indien.

« Je suis restée longtemps à le regarder, quelque chose me frappait en lui. Il était vêtu de peaux et de plumes ; autour de lui dans la neige, on voyait les jouets avec lesquels il avait joué avant de s'endormir : une chienne et ses chiots, un lama en or battu, une cuiller à cocaïne. » A chaque mot, elle touchait légèrement le tapis, comme pour disposer autour d'elle ces objets imaginaires. « Il portait un bandeau noué avec un lacet de cuir. Au milieu de son front, comme un troisième œil, un assemblage de perles représentait le soleil et ses rayons centrifuges, mais colorés de noir.

« L'expression de son visage me frappa surtout, une sorte de moue avec la lèvre inférieure retroussée, une irritation partiellement absorbée par le sommeil. Il plissait le front, mais le bas de son visage était parfaitement détendu, les lèvres légèrement disjointes. On eût dit qu'il s'était endormi en boudant, mais qu'il n'avait pu rester fidèle à sa résolution de haïr celui qui l'avait abandonné là.

« Un examen plus attentif de la photo me fit remarquer que ses bras étaient couverts d'une étrange fourrure brune. Par endroits, sa peau se desquamait ; on voyait presque les os en dessous. Alors je lus la légende : "Le garçon inca." D'abord je ne parvins pas à y croire — un Inca ! Comprends-tu ce que cela veut dire ? Il fut découvert dans l'exacte position de la photo par une équipe de météorologues tout en haut de la Cordillère, sur une montagne nommée El Plomo, à six mille mètres d'altitude. Ils aperçurent son bras qui sortait d'une congère, en pleine tempête de neige. Il était là depuis *quatre cents ans.* » Elle se tut quelques instants.

« Sa coiffure, le signe du bandeau, la présence des objets de cérémonie autour du cadavre, tout cela convainquit les savants qu'on l'avait choisi pour un sacrifice. Le soleil noir, selon eux, fait allusion à une éclipse. D'ailleurs, vers cette époque, toute l'Europe observa une éclipse presque totale. La tribu l'interpréta sans doute comme un signe de colère du soleil et sacrifia cet enfant pour apaiser le dieu.

« J'ai pleuré en lisant cela, et j'ai pensé à toi.

— Pourquoi ? demandai-je.

— Parce que tu me fais penser à ce petit Inca, Sun I, un innocent sacrifié, abandonné par une culture disparue, qui se réveille brusquement dans un paysage moderne et tente d'appliquer les principes qu'on lui a inculqués au Nouveau Monde qu'il découvre, croyant toujours à ces dieux sauvages, impitoyables, primitifs que nous avons perdus (que j'ai perdus, Sun I), le regard brillant encore de quelque terrible certitude que nos instruments ne peuvent détecter et que nous repoussons comme une superstition. J'ai pensé à toi, à tes robes de cérémonie consacrées à un dieu que le progrès, la science ont déposé, à toi, figé dans tes souffrances, exhibé dans la vitrine d'un musée, offert en pâture à la curiosité des touristes, contraint de rejouer éternellement le rituel de ton agonie, sans espoir de salut ni de libération. » Elle me fixait d'un regard fiévreux, implorant.

J'étais si ému, si blessé, que je ne pus parler. Cela n'annulait pas ses paroles de la veille au soir, mais touchait la blessure d'un coup de baguette magique, recouvrait de flocons de neige la chair à vif. Li me parut brusquement si profonde, si intuitive. Mieux que quiconque, elle comprenait mes ténèbres et ma peine, même si Yin-mi connaissait ma lumière et mon intégrité. Le passé fut balayé. Nous étions réconciliés. J'étais de nouveau amoureux.

Elle aussi était amoureuse, je crois, pour la première fois. Ce fut peut-être le seul soir où elle m'aima réellement, où elle m'aima au point de ne plus calculer. Le lendemain matin, on ressortirait les livres de compte pour les épousseter et les rouvrir à la page où on les avait fermés.

« C'est donc vrai ? » demanda-t-elle joyeusement quand elle eut observé — et compris — ma réaction.

Je lui retournai son regard.

« Je n'ai pas voulu dire autre chose hier soir, affirma-t-elle vivement. Mais je me suis mal exprimée ; plus j'essayais de t'expliquer, plus mes mots sonnaient faux. »

Je savais que ce n'était pas vrai, mais ne la contredis pas. Peu importait. J'étais heureux. Et elle aussi. Nous étions ensemble, nous partagions ce moment de bonheur, le plus parfait que nous devions vivre. (Tu as été mon premier amour, Li. Si j'ai ensuite trouvé quelque chose de plus sûr, de plus sain et de plus calme, cela ne posséda jamais ce noyau incandescent de lumière blanche.)

Puis nous fîmes l'amour, dans les sanglots, les cris, les violences de la baise. Nous sortîmes ensuite pour dîner à la lueur des bougies dans un petit bistro du quartier. « Habillons-nous », avait-elle proposé gaiement. Après le repas, nous descendîmes Sullivan Street vers les bars de Soho. Devant Bleecker Street, nous remarquâmes l'affiche d'un cinéma : *AUJOURD'HUI : LE MAGICIEN D'OZ*. Nous nous regardâmes, puis sans un mot, rejoignîmes la file d'attente. Et ce fut là, en attendant, que nous vîmes Yin-mi.

Elle était avec deux amies chinoises, probablement des camarades de lycée, entre elles. Calme et attentive, elle parlait tantôt à l'une, tantôt à l'autre, souriait parfois — belle, gracieuse, digne et jeune.

Quand elle nous aperçut sur le trottoir d'en face, elle s'arrêta ; ses amies poursuivirent comme si de rien n'était. Comme dans un cauchemar, il était trop tard pour faire quoi que ce fût. Notre secret transparaissait sur nous. Tels deux blocs de marbre issus de la même carrière, nous partagions une aura, un éclat — froid comme la pierre — qui nous entouraient d'un halo de lumière surnaturelle. Avec nos vêtements élégants, nous devions ressembler à deux êtres enchantés revenant d'une fête pour retrouver leur enfer, le Pays des Fées ou la Cité d'Émeraude, surpris par deux yeux mortels que notre spectacle pétrifiait. Nous la regardâmes ; je ne regardai jamais Li. L'appréhension et la honte durent marquer nos traits ; mais ce ne fut rien en comparaison de la souffrance nue, atemporelle, qui apparut sur le visage de Yin-mi. Elle aurait pu ébranler la pierre, se graver dans le métal. Pendant une seconde, pendant l'éternité, elle nous fixa, nous absorba. Je songeai au bœuf le long du fleuve, à ses yeux bleu-noir quand il leva la tête après avoir bu, l'eau, les arbres, le monde lui-même disparaissant un instant dans leur globe, aspirés par la puissance même de sa passivité. Les yeux de Yin-mi étaient ainsi — et nous, deux infimes poussières tourbillonnant au bord du grand vortex de sa condamnation qui menaçait de nous engloutir à jamais dans les ténèbres.

Puis elle avança vers nous. Quand elle traversa la rue, elle ne prit même pas garde à la circulation, pas un instant elle ne nous quitta des yeux.

Ni Li ni moi ne bougeâmes. Li passa brusquement son bras au mien et se serra contre moi. Moi aussi je me raidis avant d'affronter l'épreuve. A quoi pensais-je donc ? Allait-elle nous attaquer, nous cracher au visage ?

Yin-mi s'arrêta devant nous. Se tournant vers Li, elle posa ses mains sur les épaules de sa sœur, puis pressa doucement ses lèvres contre son front en un baiser silencieux. Moi, elle me fixa un peu plus longtemps avant de se dresser sur la pointe des pieds pour m'embrasser sur les lèvres. Avant de s'éloigner, elle toucha ma main (elle ne la serra pas, l'effleura à peine) puis chuchota quelque chose : « Je comprends », ou « Maintenant je comprends » ; je ne saisis pas exactement, bien que la différence fût énorme entre ces deux phrases. Après quoi elle rejoignit ses amies.

★

Mon cœur se brisa pendant tout le film, même quand je riais ; surtout quand je riais. Et comme j'ai ri, essuyant mes larmes avec mon mouchoir. (Il aurait certes fallu un mouchoir de magicien pour effacer ma peine.) J'avais alors lu le livre deux ou trois fois, et trouvai le film meilleur à maints points de vue. J'admirai surtout la façon dont le réalisateur avait donné une résonance et un contexte à l'histoire en faisant du Pays d'Oz une merveilleuse transfiguration du Kansas, en conservant tous les personnages, mais légèrement modifiés, créant ainsi une atmosphère de rêve qui n'existait pas dans le livre. J'aimai aussi la manière dont ils s'endormaient dans les champs de pavots pour être réveillés par la neige de Glinda. Je me rappelai que Li avait comparé Yin-mi à Glinda, et cela me plut, la fraîcheur et la pureté de la neige, l'aiguisement des sens qu'elle procurait. Je ne regrettai pas la Reine des Souris des Champs, même si sans elle pour sauver le Lion, le Bûcheron de Fer-Blanc ne pouvait dire : « Nous devons l'abandonner ici où il dormira éternellement, et peut-être rêvera-t-il qu'il a enfin trouvé le courage de se lever. » Car c'était là ma réplique préférée. Mais à la fin, ils le sauvent. J'étais heureux qu'il fût sauvé, même si cela modifiait beaucoup de choses.

Après le film, réunis par une tonalité paisible, plongés en nous-mêmes, nous entrâmes dans le labyrinthe des rues au sud de Houston, presque jusqu'à Chinatown (d'un accord tacite revenant sur nos pas avant d'entrer dans le quartier chinois), une promenade sereine, nostalgique. J'ai souvent tenté de retrouver l'itinéraire que nous empruntâmes ce soir-là, mais toujours à un moment le fil se rompt et le dédale nous avale.

J'ai surtout essayé de me rappeler l'emplacement exact d'une petite boutique où nous entrâmes. Aujourd'hui, je me souviens seulement d'un halo jaune, rassurant, qui débordait sur le trottoir d'une rue sombre et déserte, jonchée d'ordures et silencieuse à l'exception de l'écho sec de nos pas et des miaulements de deux chats qui se battaient ou copulaient dans une venelle, une succession de gémissements plaintifs, étranges, qui culminaient en des quintes de sifflements violents. Il devait être minuit passé ; je fus surpris de trouver une échoppe ouverte dans une rue aussi vide. Mais nous fûmes contents, car nous avions un peu froid et n'étions pas vraiment sûrs de notre chemin. A l'intérieur, un Vietnamien d'origine chinoise était penché au-dessus d'un cageot renversé, occupé à faire ses comptes sur un boulier. Il nous regarda entrer, puis retourna à ses calculs, nous laissant flâner dans sa boutique.

L'endroit ressemblait autant à un entrepôt qu'à un magasin, rempli par des piles de paniers qui dégageaient une odeur de chanvre et de rotin, des éventails, des fauteuils en osier, la plupart bon marché et fabriqués en série, qui s'entassaient le long des murs des étroits couloirs que nous empruntions. Au fond, pourtant, le caractère de la boutique changeait ; elle se transformait en magasin d'antiquités, dont les pièces précieuses et fort chères étaient soigneusement disposées dans des vitrines de verre. Il y avait de merveilleux ensembles de porcelaine en terre d'os peinte à la main, aussi fine et translucide que des pétales de cornouiller ; de magnifiques poupées et marionnettes, des éventails en papier décorés avec une minutie affolante ; accrochées au plafond, des lanternes créaient une atmosphère de fête. Ce qui attira aussitôt mon œil, et celui de Li, fut une série de netsuke. Il y en avait une douzaine seulement, mais très beaux : un animal étrange issu de la mythologie japonaise et que je ne reconnus pas, doté d'une tête de dragon et d'un corps de lion ; des exemplaires plus naturalistes — une truie allaitant sa portée ; une cigale, ses antennes, ses yeux à facettes, son tympan, les stigmates de son ventre, son ovipositeur, méticuleusement observés et sculptés. Après un bref examen, nous concentrâmes notre attention fascinée sur une sculpture figurant un moine — du moins, d'un côté, ressemblait-elle à un moine. Car l'autre profil révélait un être entièrement différent. Au lieu de sa robe, il portait un vêtement fait de poils emmêlés, émaillés de feuilles pourries et de brins de paille, mais ce n'était pas un manteau (ou bien de ces manteaux qu'on n'enlève jamais), comme on s'en apercevait en regardant le pied qui, contrairement au membre opposé — une jambe humaine nue, un pied chaussé d'une sandale de corde — était une patte couverte de fourrure, dotée de quatre griffes et d'un ergot. Son visage aussi se fondait imperceptiblement en celui d'un animal, peut-être un blaireau ou un ours.

« L'enfant des fées, dit une voix derrière nous, en cantonais. Tous reviennent vers cet exemplaire. Je ne sais pas ce qu'il signifie. » Le propriétaire contourna son comptoir, prit une clef de son trousseau et ouvrit la vitrine. Posant le netsuke sur le verre, il le fit lentement pivoter pour nous permettre de l'examiner. « Celui-ci est censé représenter un bonze défroqué qui a vendu son âme aux fées pour obtenir des pouvoirs surnaturels. Aux enfants des fées, on reprochait la disparition d'animaux domestiques, les grossesses des jeunes filles, et ainsi de suite. » Il me vit rougir quand Li me regarda. « Oui, ce sont de sacrés séducteurs, aucune jeune fille n'est à l'abri.

— Vous êtes sûr qu'il est bouddhiste ? demanda malicieusement Li en continuant de me regarder. Son crâne n'est pas rasé. Est-il vraiment impossible qu'il soit taoïste ? »

Le propriétaire haussa les épaules avec indifférence. « En ce qui me concerne, j'aimerais autant m'en débarrasser. C'est un excellent travail, mais... je ne sais pas. Il ne m'a jamais plu. » Son poing se referma autour du netsuke, puis il me regarda avec un vague sourire. « Vous désirez l'acheter ?

— Je ne crois pas que je l'aime beaucoup, moi non plus, répondis-je.
— Oh, mais il me plaît, à moi ! » protesta Li.

Ses yeux étincelaient d'un tel plaisir que je fus ébranlé. Je sortis mon portefeuille, levai les sourcils pour m'enquérir du prix.

Nous retrouvâmes enfin notre chemin jusqu'à une grande artère et prîmes un taxi. Pelotonnés l'un contre l'autre sur la banquette arrière, nous examinâmes notre achat avec une fascination émerveillée.

« Synchronisme, dit seulement Li à voix basse, davantage pour elle que pour moi. Trouver cet objet comme ça. »

Quant à moi, je ne cessai de repenser au film. Le pied animal pouvait être celui d'un lion ou d'une autre bête. J'imaginai le valet de ferme Hank figé au milieu de sa métamorphose, mi-homme mi-animal, enfourchant le miroir magique entre Oz et le Kanzas. « Bizarre, songeai-je, que dans ce monde onirique plus pur, Hank devienne un animal, alors qu'au Kansas il était un homme. Je ne peux m'empêcher de penser que l'inverse eût été plus vraisemblable.
— Peut-être est-ce la clef de l'énigme », suggéra Li.
Nous restâmes silencieux jusqu'à l'appartement.

Pour retrouver notre entrain, nous décidâmes de prendre une douche ensemble. Li s'agenouilla, lava mes cuisses et mes mollets au savon parfumé, creusant lentement et profondément mes muscles tandis que les jets d'eau chaude éclaboussaient mon dos. De fines gouttelettes tourbillonnaient autour de mes épaules, mouillaient sa lourde chevelure rassemblée en un vague chignon. Quelques mèches pendaient sur sa nuque. Ses vertèbres évoquaient un chemin de pierres au milieu de deux ruisseaux d'eau argentée qui couraient parallèlement jusqu'à ses reins et se rejoignaient avant de se glisser dans le ravin encaissé de ses fesses. Elle travaillait d'une main experte, comme une masseuse ; quand elle eut fini, elle saisit mon pénis entre ses doigts savonneux, faisant glisser chacune de ses mains vers sa base, avec la langueur du chat qui aiguise lentement ses griffes contre un meuble.

Après la douche, elle me frotta avec de l'huile jusqu'à ce que la sueur perlât sur ma peau, puis me permit de l'oindre pareillement. Son corps était doux, comme imbibé d'une chaleur moite, tropicale, légèrement mais fermement musclé, svelte, ramassé. Je frottai ses seins avec un appétit à peine dissimulé, deux plénitudes fertiles dans le désert de sa minceur. Quand elle se pencha vers moi pour essuyer ses pieds, je remarquai le léger renflement de son pelvis qui obliquait à l'aine et s'incurvait vers le genou, ce lieu vide où le reflet du dallage s'interrompait, devenait une clarté argentée semblable à celle d'une lame qui mettait en valeur la touffe de poils emmêlés entre ses jambes. Mes anciennes idées concernant la chasteté me frappèrent alors comme vaguement risibles, des conventions extraites de la poésie médiévale. A quoi devaient-elles donc servir ? Je me rappelais tout sauf cela.

Pourtant je redoutais parfois de lui faire l'amour, je me sentais intimidé par son expérience, mais plus encore par la désolation qui suivait son assouvissement, une sorte de perversité qui annonçait le retrait de Li en un lieu où régnait une souffrance inconsolable. Ce soir-là, ce ne fut pas différent. Assise contre la tête du lit, une jambe pliée, elle se rongeait l'ongle du pouce quand elle ne tirait pas sur la cigarette que je lui tendais. Partagé entre l'angoisse et la tendresse, incapable de réagir à cette humeur introspective, je l'observais avec impuissance.

« Qu'y a-t-il, Li ? lui demandai-je doucement au bout d'un moment. Quand tu te retires en toi, j'ai peur, je me sens mal. Parle-moi, s'il te plaît. Dis-moi ce que je peux faire pour te rendre heureuse.

— Je pense justement à ça, grommela-t-elle en examinant d'un œil critique l'ongle de son pouce pour éviter de croiser mon regard.
— A quoi ?
— La façon dont elle t'a regardé, le baiser qu'elle a posé sur tes lèvres, répondit-elle avec amertume.
— Oublie tout ça », l'implorai-je.
Elle haussa les épaules, se remit à ronger son ongle. « Comme tu voudras.
— Parlons d'autre chose », suggérai-je.
Elle sourit pour elle-même. « D'accord, je te propose une devinette. » Elle laissa tomber ses mains sur ses cuisses, prit cet air provocant que je connaissais si bien. « L'Épouvantail veut un cerveau, commença-t-elle. Le Bûcheron de Fer-Blanc veut un cœur. Le Lion veut du courage. Auquel des trois ressembles-tu le plus ? »
Je faillis répondre le Lion, mais réfléchis et changeai d'avis. « Peut-être à Dorothy, proposai-je.
— Qui voulait seulement retourner au Kansas, fit-elle observer en fronçant les sourcils.
— Ce n'est pas ce que je voulais dire.
— Ou à Oz, continua-t-elle en suivant le fil de ses pensées, Oz qui voulait tout. » Elle scruta mon visage. « Oz aussi était un enfant des fées, en un sens, non ? Rappelle-toi dans le livre, "La Grande Arnaque" ?
— Je ne comprends pas, dis-je.
— Vraiment ? railla-t-elle. Je veux simplement dire que l'enfant des fées est un meilleur modèle, plus véridique en tout cas.
— Plus véridique que quoi ?
— Que le garçon inca, par exemple. » La bassesse et le mépris apparurent fugitivement sur son visage, rapidement remplacés par la fureur. « Séducteur des jeunes filles. Tu ferais mieux de ne pas toucher à elle (sa voix se mua en un murmure glacé), *bâtard*. »
« Bâtard » — le mot perça mon cœur comme la pointe froide d'un pic à glace. L'intensité de sa haine était presque pathologique. Elle glaça mon sang. Toute la poésie, la générosité, l'intimité silencieuse de cette longue soirée... tout cela vola en éclats sous l'impact d'un seul mot.
Sans répondre, je me recroquevillai en chien de fusil et m'endormis. Je rêvai d'un soleil vert qui se levait sur Oz, du Lion endormi parmi les pavots écarlates, les fleurs ensanglantées, et qui plus jamais ne devait se réveiller.

14

Si ma vie privée sombrait dans l'insatisfaction et le malheur, mes affaires n'avaient jamais autant prospéré. Notre position à Wall Strett s'était consolidée. Dès l'annonce officielle de sa création, le Taureau Mutuel fut pris d'assaut par les actionnaires déchaînés. Notre service de gestion de portefeuilles enregistra un succès similaire. Les Entreprises Kahn et Sun étaient devenues la coqueluche de Wall Street. En partie bien sûr grâce à Kahn, dont la campagne de publicité fut couronnée de succès. La communauté financière attendait nos pleines pages hebdomadaires avec la même avidité que les ménagères guettent la création d'un nouveau produit de beauté. Mon grand et gros ami avait prouvé ses talents de publiciste et de poète capitaliste. Mais surtout, chapeau bas devant le témoignage irréfutable du bilan de notre société, qui en dernière analyse constitue l'argument le plus éloquent de la santé d'une entreprise.
Chaque semaine, nos coffres engrangeaient des millions de dollars. Une atmosphère euphorique régnait dans nos bureaux. Nous les avions d'ailleurs agrandis, au point d'occuper tout le vingt et unième étage de la Bourse avec les nouveaux chefs comptables, secrétaires et autres opératrices, lesquelles travaillaient désormais selon les trois huit. Cela devint nécessaire à cause du volume des appels que nous recevions, mais aussi parce que notre clientèle couvrait maintenant l'ensemble des États-Unis. Nous dûmes nous plier aux horaires des investisseurs de Rocky Mountain ou de la côte du Pacifique. Ces nouveaux services donnèrent lieu à un autre slogan promotionnel : « Maintenant Vous Pouvez Avoir le Taureau au Corne-t 24 heures sur 24 !!! »
Vu l'immense popularité de nos opérations sur la côte Ouest, nous dûmes ouvrir une succursale à Los Angeles. L'hystérie qu'elle déchaîna dans cette ville dépassa encore la passion provoquée à New York. Une pléthore d'autocollants déferlèrent sur les pare-chocs des Mercedes-Benz de Los Angeles : « Les Taureaux ont de plus grosses cornes ! » ; « Hou, les Cornes ! (klaxonnez une fois si vous avez compris, deux fois pour tous renseignements sur Taureau Inc.) » ; « Tarot, Torah, Taureau font un tabac ! » Les rédacteurs-concepteurs s'en donnèrent à cœur joie ; les tics de Kahn mirent dans le mille.
Les plus importants hebdomadaires d'information — *Time, Life,*

Newsweek, US News and World Report — « couvrirent » Kahn et moi. (La presse financière — *Fortune, Forbes, Business Week* — était depuis longtemps venue et repartie.) Un matin, un journaliste arriva dans nos bureaux, un grand vieillard étique vêtu d'une veste en madras froissée et d'un nœud papillon à pois, aux joues caves et aux lunettes à montures d'acier. Il souffla sur ses verres, puis les essuya avec son mouchoir en regardant autour de lui avec une expression de surprise bilieuse. Quand Kahn l'aperçut dans la glace sans tain qui séparait la salle d'attente de notre bureau, il cessa de commenter avec moi les rapports du jour, poussa mon coude avec la liasse des papiers qu'il tenait, puis baissa la voix malgré lui. « Tu vois ce type ? »

J'acquiesçai.

« Regarde-le bien. C'est Ernest "le Squelette" Hackless, l'éminence grise de la presse financière.

— Hackless, répétai-je rêveusement. L'homme qui a écrit tous ces articles sur mon grand-père et mon père. »

Kahn opina sombrement du chef. « Petit, c'est le chroniqueur de la fortune des Love depuis le commencement ; il est toujours en avance, comme le poisson-pilote, ou légèrement en retard comme le vautour. On dirait qu'aujourd'hui il est venu te voir. »

Je déglutis difficilement. « Peut-être ignore-t-il ma parenté.

— Peut-être, dit Kahn sceptique.

— Que me veut-il selon vous ? demandai-je.

— A ton avis ? répliqua Kahn en faisant mine de se retirer.

— Non, attendez, Kahn ! m'écriai-je. Ne me laissez pas seul avec lui. »

Kahn haussa les épaules. « Puisque tu me trouves indispensable, petit... Mais je ne crois pas que je vais servir à grand-chose. »

Je restai à me tortiller dans mon fauteuil pendant que Kahn allait le chercher. « Ne lui dites rien ! » avait été ma dernière requête avant sa sortie.

« J'ai vu pas mal de choses dans ma vie, Kahn, disait Hackless quand ils entrèrent, mais ceci est vraiment *saignant*. » Il prononça ce dernier mot avec une emphase ironique, puis me fixa.

Je sentis le sang me monter au visage.

« Ne dites jamais "saignant", M. Hackless, plaisanta Kahn, dites plutôt "à point". A Taureau Incorporated, nous aimons le taureau à point ! »

Hackless salua le jeu de mots d'une brève grimace, puis traversa le bureau vers moi. « Ainsi, vous êtes le petit prince, dit-il, l'héritier des Love, le dernier rejeton de la lignée. » Tendant vers moi une main osseuse, il me sourit comme une tête de mort. « J'ai toujours dit qu'Eddie Love ne ferait jamais rien de bon en Asie. Vous avez une sacrée paire de chaussures noires à remplir, mon petit. »

Tout en serrant la main tendue, j'adressai un regard suppliant à Kahn, paniqué à la seule mention du nom de mon père.

Comme chagriné de devoir m'abandonner à mon sort, Kahn haussa les épaules pour s'excuser. « Navré, petit, j'ai lâché le morceau. Ç'a été plus fort que moi. »

Hackless s'assit dans le fauteuil à côté de mon bureau, puis, sortant un canif de sa poche, entreprit de tailler la pointe de son crayon. Au bout d'un moment, il leva les yeux et dit à Kahn par-dessus son épaule. « Si cela ne vous fait rien, votre patron et moi aimerions échanger quelques mots en privé. »

Bien qu'il rougît au mot « patron », Kahn allait obtempérer sans rechigner quand je saisis férocement son poignet. « Nous sommes associés à part entière, M. Hackless, affirmai-je. Nous n'avons aucun secret l'un pour l'autre.

— Eh bien, je ne voulais humilier personne, répliqua Hackless en haussant les sourcils.

— D'autre part, poursuivis-je sur un ton plus conciliant, vous savez sans doute que je suis arrivé en Amérique il y a peu de temps. Kahn doit parfois me servir d'interprète.

— Ça me paraît un anglais assez courant, maugréa-t-il.

— Excusez je vous prie, pouvez-vous répéter ? »

Il haussa les épaules, puis, quand il eut achevé l'intervention chirurgicale sur son crayon, essaya sa pointe en la fichant d'un geste sec dans le bloc-notes jaune posé sur ses genoux. « Alors messieurs, dit-il, quelles explications allez-vous fournir au grand public ? »

L'entretien couvrit un grand nombre de sujets (j'eus le sentiment d'évoluer en terrain miné). Le plus traumatisant — en dehors de ses allusions à mon père, des sous-entendus où le mot hideux et haï de « bâtard » faillit apparaître plusieurs fois — fut peut-être ses questions répétées concernant notre utilisation du *Yi king*, qu'il devinait être une épine à mon pied.

« Vous prétendez posséder avec ce *Yi king* l'outil dont rêvent tous les spéculateurs depuis Babylone, dit-il en des termes qui apparurent tels quels dans la mouture définitive de son article, une méthode infaillible, une sorte de mouvement perpétuel spéculatif, la pierre philosophale des Dowistes, *une façon de choisir des valeurs qui ne saurait échouer*. Eh bien, messieurs, pouvez-vous m'expliquer pourquoi le premier venu ne peut pas l'employer ? Pourquoi les gens accepteraient-ils de payer fort cher vos services, s'ils peuvent s'en passer, acheter un exemplaire du livre et accomplir tous ces rituels chez eux sans bourse délier ? Bref, quel est votre secret ? »

Je secouai gravement la tête. « Nous n'avons pas de secret. »

Il me sourit avec indulgence. « Vous voulez me faire croire que n'importe qui, avec deux sous et un exemplaire de ce bouquin, peut devenir millionnaire à Wall Street du jour au lendemain, comme vous ? Allez...

— Théoriquement, oui, répondis-je, à condition d'avoir un capital de départ. » Je soutins son regard, opposai toute ma franchise à son expression dégoûtée.

Kahn, debout juste derrière mon fauteuil, décida que le moment d'intervenir était venu. « Vous savez déjà l'essentiel, M. Hackless, dit-il, mais vous négligez un détail fondamental. Voyez-vous, réussir à utiliser le *Yi king* pour choisir des valeurs ne s'explique par aucun secret, mais seulement par une condition que doit remplir le consultant. Voilà pourquoi Sonny ici présent est tellement qualifié pour ce rituel. » Il posa fièrement la main sur mon épaule.

« Et quelle est cette condition ? demanda Hackless en regardant non pas Kahn mais moi.

— La pureté de cœur », répliqua mon interprète sans sourciller ni la moindre trace d'ironie.

Je sentis le sang quitter mon visage.

« Sonny ? » demanda Hackless, qui réussit à placer une pointe d'ironie jusque dans la prononciation de mon nom.

En face d'un autre, j'eusse peut-être réussi à nier, détourner la question ou répondre à côté, mais cette tête de mort grimaçante m'emplit d'une telle rage que j'opinai laconiquement puis, m'excusant, allai aux toilettes où je vomis mon petit déjeuner.

A mon retour, je découvris avec agacement qu'il était toujours là, vautré dans son fauteuil, envoyant des ronds de fumée au plafond en souriant mystérieusement. Kahn avait disparu.

« Excusez-moi, M. Hackless, mais je vous ai accordé tout le temps dont je dispose, lui dis-je froidement.

— Oh, c'est parfait, répondit-il gaiement en rassemblant ses affaires. J'ai découvert tout ce que j'avais besoin de savoir. » Il marqua un temps. « Une dernière question, cependant. » Nos regards se croisèrent. « Et maintenant ?

— Nous n'avons aucun projet d'expansion dans un avenir prévisible, répliquai-je, si c'est à cela que vous faites allusion. A Kahn et Sun, nous sommes très heureux de ce que nous avons déjà accompli.

— Allons donc, cela ne ressemble pas au fils d'Eddie Love », railla-t-il avec un sourire qui, malgré son tranchant, était presque affectueux.

J'ignore pourquoi, mais je lui retournai son sourire — avec toute la discrétion requise. « Bonne journée, M. Hackless », le congédiai-je. Et il partit.

La semaine suivante, mon visage apparut sur la couverture de *Your Money and Your Life* (Votre Argent et Votre Vie), accompagné de ce gros titre :

UN NOUVEAU SOLEIL SE LÈVE SUR WALL STREET : LE FILS DE LOVE (EDDIE LOVE)

Dans un style que Kahn qualifia de « ramassis de bruits de chiottes », Hackless jetait en pâture les détails de ma parenté comme des morceaux de viande fraîche aux mâchoires américaines affamées de scandales en tout genre. Pourtant, son article ne m'emplit pas tant de honte que d'orgueil et de défi. Qu'ils jasent donc. Ils ne pouvaient m'atteindre. J'étais hors de portée de la prose boueuse d'Ernest Hackless. Voilà pourquoi le Grand Public avait faim de nouvelles, de bulletins du front, de la frontière, des derniers combats. Là, Kahn et moi chassions, et c'est pourquoi, loin de compromettre notre pouvoir, les coups de griffe de Hackless le rehaussaient. Car il faisait de nous des êtres magiques, différents, hors d'atteinte de la loi.

Les seules phrases de son article qui me piquèrent au vif furent celles de sa conclusion : « Ce Sun, ce Soleil fera-t-il pâlir celui de son père, ou s'avérera-t-il être simplement la lueur éphémère d'une planète éclairée par l'astre du jour ? » Cela ressemblait à un murmure insinuant destiné à mes seules oreilles. « Restez fidèles à M & L ! ajoutait-il. Car nous parions *Votre argent et votre vie* qu'il s'agit seulement du premier épisode d'une longue histoire. La suite au prochain numéro ! »

« "Ce Soleil fera-t-il pâlir celui de son père ?" » Pour une raison que je m'expliquai mal, cette question devint une obsession, d'abord un faible écho résonnant de temps à autre dans une pièce désaffectée de mon cerveau, puis, au fil du temps, une sorte de tic mécanique et inconscient, un disque rayé répétant sans fin la même note. Je crus au début que la sincérité de ma piété filiale était en cause, mais je sentis cette explication insuffisante, incapable d'apaiser mon angoisse.

Je n'eus pourtant pas le loisir de m'appesantir. Nos manœuvres financières étaient trop absorbantes. A cette époque déjà, nos opérations étaient devenues si importantes que nos prédictions d'investissement faisaient souvent figure de prophéties infaillibles. Non seulement nous étions en mesure d'imposer concrètement nos choix au marché en utilisant le levier puissant de notre capital (on ne peut cependant abuser de cet argument), mais psychologiquement notre impact était devenu quasiment illimité et dépassait les extrapolations les plus folles, puisant à la source même de la peur et de la cupidité humaines. Ceux qui osaient contrarier nos plans étaient fort rares. Car, protégés par la puissance magique de notre fétiche, nous ne nous étions jusque-là jamais trompés. Dès que nous désignions une victime ou une favorite, Wall Street obtempérait et nous tendait respectueusement la hache ou les lauriers. Curieuse conséquence de cet état de fait, le *Yi king*, qui nous avait accordé notre puissance, devint quasiment obsolète, comme pour se conformer au septième chant des *Dix Taureaux* :

> Seulement sur le Taureau pouvait-il Revenir.
> Mais hélas, le Taureau a désormais disparu ;
> Le bouvier solitaire entame le long labeur de l'oubli.
> Le soleil a atteint le zénith d'un ciel venteux.
> Une fois la tâche accomplie, le bouvier rêve un rêve sans nuage.
> Le fouet et la bride gisent abandonnés dans la hutte vide.

> Le collet devient inutile quand on a attrapé le lapin. Quand le saumon repose dans l'éclat doré du plat, à quoi bon le filet ? L'or s'est écoulé de la gangue brûlante ; la lune a percé les nuages ; un rayon de lumière virginal inonde le monde.

Oui, *Les Mutations* avait été l'instrument, le sombre grillage du tamis dans lequel nous avions piégé l'éclat argenté, fascinant et fugace de l'aspiration fondamentale de Wall Street, et cet instrument était désormais inutile ; nous possédions la chose elle-même. Il y avait là une ironie délicieuse que Kahn refusait de reconnaître. Quand je suggérai que nous cessions de consulter l'oracle, il devint grave et intraitable — l'envers de l'histrion spirituel que je connaissais. Tournant et retournant les bracelets de ses poignets, il insista pour que nous nous en tenions « religieusement » au rituel. Je remarquai avec amusement qu'il était désormais plus taoïste que moi. Bien que par égard pour lui je continuasse d'accomplir les gestes nécessaires, au fond de moi-même j'avais perdu tout intérêt pour le résultat. Car celui-ci était désormais superflu.

Et cela non seulement à cause de notre impact psychologique ; une autre raison rendait caduque l'utilisation des pièces. Depuis ce jour crucial où, dans le bureau de Kahn, j'avais remarqué pour la première fois que je pouvais infléchir la trajectoire des pennies, mon contrôle s'était accru. Les dernières consultations que nous avions exécutées furent pour moi une banalité. Car je prévoyais la récolte alors même que je semais le grain ; mieux, je la provoquais moi-même par un acte de volonté consciente. Kahn, bien sûr, ignora tout de cela, du seuil que j'avais franchi en moi-même et dont je choisis de ne pas lui parler.

J'essayai non seulement d'exercer mon pouvoir sur des valeurs particulières, mais sur la Bourse elle-même. Hormis certains moments de grâce, la concentration indispensable excédait mes forces. Mais les rares fois où je réussis ! Comment expliquer aux non-initiés l'effet que ce pouvoir eut sur moi ? Imaginez : toute la trajectoire de la création distillée sur un graphique financier en la seule et unique tendance du Dow, la ligne anthracite sécrétée par les filières de la Grande Veuve Noire tandis qu'elle construit la grille orthogonale de sa toile, l'univers lui-même... Se concentrer et par un effort de volonté conscient la faire, *le faire changer de direction* — infléchir le Dow ! Je songe parfois que c'était un plaisir délicieux, trop doux pour les mortels, que de poser sa tête contre les seins fertiles et consentants de cette femelle primordiale et d'*entendre réellement battre le cœur du monde*, une sensation dont je n'ai jamais retrouvé l'équivalent.

Quand je redescendais de ces hauteurs grisantes, impossibles, je me sentais à chaque fois plus méprisable, noir et souillé. Je renonçais à ces plaisirs troubles, multipliais les serments et les larmes. De plus en plus souvent, j'étais sujet à des visions. Un jour, alors que je me rendais à mon travail, je regardai dans la fontaine du parc, et vis sept pièces de monnaie qui dessinaient très précisément la constellation de l'Ourse ; l'espace d'un instant, le puits qu'elles formaient traversa le centre de la terre, déboucha dans la nuit chinoise, la tache aveugle de l'Amérique, l'Amérique, le *yang* de l'univers ! Fermant les yeux, je me sentis soulevé au-dessus de la terre comme par une tornade, puis tournoyer dans des éternités sifflantes d'espace et de temps, alors que les larmes froides de la vitesse mouillaient mes tempes. J'entendis les sons, je sentis les odeurs, un instant je fus pour de bon en Chine. Mais ma joie fut de courte durée. Car lorsque j'ouvris les yeux, tout disparut sauf les larmes. Un jour, me promis-je, je ne les rouvrirai pas, et comme le Lion je dormirai éternellement.

Même l'excitation des opérations boursières ne dura pas. Tout allait de plus en plus vite. Nous dûmes bientôt opérer d'autres diversifications « synergiques » sur des marchés financiers inédits. Nous débloquâmes d'abord des fonds pour un secteur de recherche et publiâmes une lettre bimensuelle intitulée « L'abécé taureau-magique », qui examinait la stratégie boursière à la lumière de la sagesse taoïste. Puis nous nous lançâmes dans l'arbitrage, nommant notre département de devises étrangères « John Bull* » à la demande de Kahn. Enfin nous pénétrâmes le marché de l'or, important de Zurich une équipe de spécialistes pour diriger nos opérations sous le label « Cornes Dorées, Unlimited ». Et chacune de ces expansions

---

* *John Bull* (John Taureau) : terme générique désignant l'Anglais typique *(NdT)*.

requit l'absorption de nouvelles entreprises, petites ou grandes, dirigées par des hommes de faibles, moyennes ou exceptionnelles compétences et détermination, qui avaient passé le plus clair de leur vie à servir ou bâtir ces affaires que nous phagocytions sauvagement et en toute impunité.

Je ressemblais à un ours géant qui s'attaque à une ruche, brise le sceau en cire de ses précieux alvéoles et enduit ses pattes de miel sombre et doré. Malgré leur fureur, les abeilles industrieuses ne pouvaient me blesser, même si certaines enragées réussissaient parfois à me piquer, audace qu'elles payaient ensuite fort cher. Non, quand la rage de la destruction s'emparait de moi, rien ne pouvait les sauver, pas même leur capitulation. D'un seul geste de mon énorme patte, je réduisais à néant leurs existences imperceptibles.

Quand à haute altitude je lâchais la bombe impitoyable de notre puissance inouïe sur les cités qu'ils habitaient, je regardais avec une fascination sereine leurs minuscules maisons de poupée, leurs usines et leurs fermes soufflées comme des fétus de paille par le vent nucléaire. Je voyais la conflagration se répandre dans les rues, j'observais l'agitation frénétique de ces infimes points noirs (eux), j'entendais de très loin le hurlement strident des sirènes, mais à mon altitude aucune horreur, aucune tragédie personnelle ne pouvait m'émouvoir. De là-haut, comme à travers un kaléidoscope aux images changeantes et toujours surprenantes, je voyais un ordre se dessiner à une échelle plus vaste, qui englobait leurs vies et leurs misères, la fleur noire s'épanouir miraculeusement hors du centre calciné de la terre. Tout cela était si beau, si étrange, presque irréel. Peut-être aurais-je dû y lire un avertissement. Car je sais aujourd'hui qu'en ces instants de visions désincarnées, hallucinées, tandis que je flottais comme un dieu au-dessus de la terre, je saisis pour la première fois — non, *enfin* — l'hostie de la communion noire entre mes lèvres et bus le sang du péché, qui est seulement le sang non consacré issu du cruel sacrifice du meurtre. Il ne requiert aucun Antéchrist pour le souiller d'un blasphème, mais porte en lui-même sa propre malédiction, que Dieu lui-même ne saurait effacer — impardonnable dans les siècles des siècles, un enfer sans fin.

Mais à d'autres moments, tout aussi intenses, je me réjouissais d'avoir enfin trouvé mon salut. Je me rappelle le matin où cette conviction m'assaillit pour la première fois, totalement à l'improviste. Depuis quelque temps déjà, Kahn montrait des signes, sinon de véritable régression, du moins d'une lassitude et d'une irritabilité nouvelles que j'étais bien en peine d'expliquer. Ce jour-là, dans mon bureau, il se plaignait d'une de nos nouvelles filiales, quand je songeai que je le négligeais depuis quelques semaines, et qu'il me demandait peut-être seulement un peu d'attention.

« Venez, Kahn, lui proposai-je, sortons d'ici cinq minutes et allons nous promener quelque part, comme au bon vieux temps. »

Le promptitude avec laquelle il accepta me convainquit que je ne m'étais pas trompé.

« C'est bien simple, maugréa-t-il alors que les portes de l'ascenseur s'ouvraient au troisième étage et que nous nous mêlions à la foule de la salle, nous sommes tellement écrasés de tâches en tous genres, obsédés par ces succursales et ces filiales, que nous n'avons jamais le temps de rien. Enfin quoi, si j'avais voulu faire des mômes, je me serais marié, pas vrai ? Pourtant, je me retrouve dans la même situation : j'ai l'impression d'élever une flopée de bambins. Faut toujours passer derrière eux pour ramasser les couches sales. Ne crois pas que je me plains ni rien, tout ça est formidable, toutes ces absorptions et autres expansions. Mais par moments, toi-même tu n'en as pas marre ? »

J'opinai paternellement tandis que nous arpentions la galerie.

« Tu sais ce qui me plairait vraiment, juste une fois ? dit-il, aussi excité qu'un gosse. Retourner au parquet comme au bon vieux temps, balancer toute la sauce sur un outsider. » Il baissa rêveusement les yeux, puis se tourna vers moi avec une brusque véhémence. « Bon Dieu, petit, je ne suis pas un homme d'affaires, je suis un négociant. Tu le sais bien. Et l'on n'apprend pas de nouveaux tours à un vieux singe, ni à un vieux loup d'ailleurs, même si nous avons réussi à faire du fric neuf avec un vieux bouquin. » Il sourit, puis se renfrogna. « Pour dire les choses autrement, on peut mener une vieille tique vers de nouveaux chiens, mais on ne peut pas l'obliger à boire, pas vrai ? Et pour moi, certaines de nos opérations sont des chiens auxquels je n'ai pas envie de sucer le sang, car j'en suis rassasié. J'en ai jusque-là, petit. Je n'ai plus faim, je suis repu. Et puis, ce qui me rebute, c'est cette vigilance continuelle. On dirait un mariage, "jusqu'à ce que la mort nous sépare". J'ai toujours eu un faible pour les contrats avec porte de sortie. C'est le principal attrait du boulot de négociant au parquet. Pour l'instant, nous les baisons, puis nous passons tout notre temps à les retaper, les bichonner, les briquer. Cinq minutes de plaisir sous le soleil et une éternité de blouses de ménage, de bigoudis et de rouleaux à pâtisserie (Jane Doe était presque plus palpitante...) » Il haussa les épaules pour s'excuser. « Je suis sûrement un incorrigible Juif Errant, petit, avec un E majuscule, plus rien à voir avec J.R. Je n'y peux rien, c'est comme ça. Petit ? Hé, petit ! Tu m'écoutes ?

— Hmm ? fis-je, émergeant de la transe où m'avait plongé le grouillement du parquet. Mais oui, Kahn, dis-je, je vous écoute. »

En fait, je ne l'écoutais pas, bien que j'eusse dû le faire. Car alors que je regardais la foule s'agiter à mes pieds, une étrange sensation s'empara de moi. Peut-être fut-ce seulement une aberration visuelle, mais je fus certain de ne plus contempler les images familières que Wall Street m'avait enseignées ; ce n'était plus la prairie sauvage de l'Ouest, ni les insectes sociaux, ni la pantomime de la vie humaine, mais quelque chose d'infiniment plus profond — la chose elle-même, pour tout dire. Par une soudaine résolution de l'image comme sous un microscope — une mise au point qui en même temps accroissait le flou, comme sur une photo à long temps de pose — les visages se fondirent les uns dans les autres, les corps fusionnèrent en un unique torrent rugissant. Cette activité ressemblait à la contraction et la dilatation d'un cœur mystique et matériel — la circulation du sang d'oreillette à ventricule dans le vaste cœur de l'Amérique elle-même. Ensuite, même ces mouvements concrets disparurent, et tel Dieu, je baissai les yeux vers le majestueux va-et-vient métaphysique du Tao, la Bourse devint une pure essence spirituelle. Ce fut alors que je me posai la question pour la première fois : étais-je réellement arrivé au bout du voyage ? Était-ce le delta ? Y étais-je vraiment ?

Certains signes le suggéraient. Je me rappelai les mots du *Tao-tö king*

> Sans franchir sa porte,
> On connaît le monde entier.
> Sans regarder par la fenêtre,
> On voit la voie du ciel.
> Plus on va loin
> Moins on connaît.
> Le sage connaît sans voyager,
> Définit sans voir,
> Accomplit sans agir.

« Le sage accomplit sans agir » — cela ne décrivait-il pas parfaitement la maîtrise que je possédais sur le marché ? De quoi s'agissait-il au juste sinon du *wu-wei* taoïste, le non-agir du sage, *wu-wei* qui dans sa plus haute réalisation devient enfin le *tö* lui-même, le *tö* du *Tao-tö king*, la Voie et sa *Puissance*, *tö*, la preuve et la justification de la longue pénitence du taoïste, le gage de l'illumination, le signe extérieur visible d'une grâce intérieure et spirituelle, le triomphe sur la mort elle-même ?

Et pourtant il manquait quelque chose. La modification n'était pas aussi radicale que je l'avais espéré, pas aussi tranchée. Dans l'accalmie du combat, je regardai autour de moi, et le monde me parut identique, inchangé. Le doute se remit à me tenailler, je m'interrogeai sur ma réussite. Car j'aspirais à une certitude qu'aucun doute n'entacherait, à un lieu où tout serait métamorphosé, transmuté à jamais, à un cadran du ciel où mon âme était désormais attirée comme une sombre flèche pointée sur le soleil.

Après la pléthore des absorptions, je commençai de ressentir une impatience similaire à celle de Kahn. Mais je ne voulais pas retourner au parquet de la Bourse. Au contraire, une rage instinctive militait en moi contre toute autosatisfaction, me poussait furieusement à chercher un motif de stimulation supérieure, quelque affirmation plus intense de la vie.

Je me mis à faire le même rêve que celui qui m'avait poursuivi en Chine avant ma décision de quitter Ken Kuan. Mais cette fois, c'était un cauchemar hideux qui se déroulait dans un cadre urbain : New York. Et maintenant, aussi, j'apercevais parfois la bête, qui levait les yeux vers moi à travers la grille d'un égout ou qui guettait mon reflet dans la vitrine d'un magasin. Cette créature protéiforme ressemblait tantôt à un tigre, tantôt à un ours, parfois encore à un ours à tête de tigre. Et en certaines occasions particulièrement terrifiantes, elle avait un visage humain. Me réveillant en sursaut au milieu de la nuit, je la décrivis à Li.

A ma grande surprise, elle rit. « Un Kalidah, dit-elle.
— Un quoi ?
— Un Kalidah, le monstre issu du *Magicien d'Oz* — le livre, pas le film — tu ne te souviens pas ? » Elle tendit la main vers la table de chevet et ouvrit l'exemplaire que je lisais moi-même avant de m'endormir. « "Les Kalidahs les poursuivirent sur un tronc d'arbre qui enjambait un ravin où

la Route de Brique Jaune s'interrompait brusquement dans la forêt", lut-elle. Tu te rappelles ? Le Bûcheron de Fer-Blanc les sauva en l'abattant quand ils eurent traversé. Les voilà — "des bêtes monstrueuses aux corps d'ours et aux têtes de tigre". » Elle ferma le livre avec assurance. « Il faut simplement que tu changes de livre de chevet. » Elle sourit. « Ce livre est réservé aux adultes. »

Mais mon Kalidah s'obstina à me poursuivre. Quelques jours après, j'étais devenu si angoissé que je ne trouvais plus le sommeil. Li prit alors mon problème au sérieux. Elle me raconta une histoire.

« C'est un professeur qui nous en a parlé, commença-t-elle. Je l'avais complètement oubliée, mais j'ai consulté mes notes, et je l'ai retrouvée. Il étudiait cette tribu malaise — les Senoï, je crois — qui possède un culte centré sur le rêve et l'interprétation des rêves. L'un de ses exemples, un cas authentique, ce qui le rend d'autant plus intéressant pour toi, évoquait un petit garçon qui rêvait qu'un tigre le poursuivait. Une nuit, il se réveille en hurlant. Le lendemain matin, sa mère l'emmène voir le chaman, et le vieillard dit au garçon qu'il a commis une grave erreur en n'affrontant pas le tigre, car l'animal va sentir sa peur et revenir chaque nuit hanter ses rêves jusqu'à ce que le garçon ait maîtrisé sa peur et l'affronte. Le vieillard dit au garçon de faire appel à ses amis si le tigre s'avère trop fort, mais de ne jamais cesser de lutter, car le moindre relâchement de la concentration risquerait d'être fatal. S'il soumettait l'ennemi du rêve, dit le chaman au garçon, il devrait lui demander un gage — un poème, une danse, la réponse à une énigme — n'importe quoi, à condition que cela soit utile dans la vie éveillée, sinon personne ne le croirait.

« Pourquoi n'essaies-tu pas ? suggéra-t-elle d'une voix paisible. Tu n'as rien à perdre. » Elle sourit. « Et n'oublie pas de réclamer ton gage au Kalidah. »

Je suivis son conseil. Pendant plusieurs nuits, je me battis et me débattis contre lui dans des rêves terrifiants qui se terminaient régulièrement par le pat de l'aube, quand nous nous séparions et qu'il retournait dans la forêt pour lécher ses blessures. Mes amis du rêve me relayaient : Wu arriva avec son gros bambou, Scottie décocha des coups de ses tennis dans les flancs du monstre, versa du rhum sur sa tête, puis essaya de l'enflammer ; le Lion Pleutre vint aussi, mais se contenta d'observer la scène à bonne distance ; j'appelai aussi mon père, mais les morts ne nous entendent apparemment pas. La troisième nuit, un peu avant l'aube, je pris enfin le dessus. Le Kalidah m'adressa un regard soumis, docile. « Que désires-tu ? » me demanda-t-il, et je répondis « Le bonheur et la vérité ». Mais il ne pouvait m'offrir qu'une seule chose si bien qu'après avoir hésité, je choisis la vérité. Le Kalidah disparut alors longtemps dans la forêt, puis revint en tenant une pomme dans sa gueule, qu'il posa délicatement à mes pieds. Puis il s'évapora comme le chat du Cheshire, laissant seulement dans l'air son sourire, les rangées de ses crocs semblables à ceux peints sur le nez du P-40, exactement superposés à la morsure imprimée dans le fruit, lequel — je le découvris en l'examinant — grouillait de vers et de mouches bourdonnantes qui s'immobilisaient quelques instants pour déféquer et pondre leurs œufs.

Et voilà comment l'idée m'est d'abord venue de m'emparer d'American

Power and Light, « LA PupiLLe de l'œil américain ». La beauté de l'association me ravit. « Ce Soleil fera-t-il pâlir celui de son père ? » Ce serait l'épreuve ultime, l'assaut final contre le sommet.

Quand j'en parlai à Kahn, il éclata de rire. « APL ? Tu plaisantes ? Dis-moi, petit, tu te prends pour qui, le Roi Soleil, Louis Quatorze ? » Il sourit. « Ou plutôt le Môme Soleil. Petit Louis, Sonny Quatorzio, le mafioso supremo, SAS le Môme Soleil, armé de pied en cap, la terreur des entreprises. Voilà ton nouveau surnom, le Môme Soleil.

— Je suis sérieux, Kahn, dis-je d'une voix glaciale.

— "Je suis *sérieux*" ! se moqua-t-il. Arrête de me faire rire, veux-tu ? Je vais attraper une hernie si ça continue. Et toi, si tu continues, tu vas bientôt te pavaner en costume Prince de Galles et crier sur tous les toits que tu es l'empereur de Wall Street. »

Ses railleries me mirent dans une colère noire. Kahn refusait de m'entendre. Je découvris que je le méprisais. Contenant ma rage, je réussis pourtant à lui expliquer posément mon point de vue. Et il retrouva enfin un peu de la gravité qui convenait à la situation.

« Petit, je te demande de tout reprendre à zéro. Enfin, tu ne te rends pas compte de ce que tu dis ? APL. Sais-tu à quel point c'est *gros* ? Ce n'est pas un peu plus gros, ni même beaucoup plus gros que nous. C'est *énorme*, formidable, colossal — *grooos* ! Je veux dire, Taureau est gros, mais pas dans la même catégorie.

— D'accord, APL est gros, "formidable", si vous voulez, répondis-je. Mais dans le passé nous avons déjà absorbé des entreprises plus grosses que nous. La banque, par exemple, fournit une bonne analogie. Comme la banque, APL est gros, lent, léthargique, éléphantesque. La cote de l'action fluctue dans une fourchette très étroite. Elle rapporte un bon dividende, mais c'est une valeur pour grand-mères, comme les livrets de caisse d'épargne ou les bons du Trésor. Supposons que nous attaquions bille en tête et proposions le double de la cote de l'action, payable en obligations et garanties, dont une fraction convertible. N'importe qui doué d'un peu de jugeote sautera sur l'occasion. Même les grand-mères. Ça a déjà marché ; pourquoi pas cette fois ? »

Il secoua la tête. « Nous parlons maintenant de magnitudes incompatibles, petit. Même Taureau Inc. ne réussirait pas une absorption de cette envergure.

— Nous le devons, dis-je.

— Nous ne pouvons pas, répondit-il.

— Nous le ferons, insistai-je.

— Je t'en supplie, Sonny, m'implora-t-il. A genoux. Sors-toi ça de l'esprit. Nous avons fait du bon boulot jusqu'ici, mais nous ne sommes pas invulnérables. APL est la plus grosse entreprise d'Amérique...

— "Et donc du monde", dis-je avec ironie.

— C'est... c'est... c'est de la folie pure, voilà ce que c'est ! Si tu insistes je...

— Oui ? demandai-je.

— Je vais... »

Je le regardai d'un œil noir.

« Je démissionnerai !
— Certainement pas. »

Il eut un sourire provocant. « Ah, tu crois ça ?

— Kahn, le priai-je tout en l'avertissant, ne me faites pas cela. Je ne vous ai jamais rien demandé jusqu'ici. Mais cette fois, je vous le demande.

— Pourquoi ? siffla-t-il, comme si l'objet de notre conversation le dépassait complètement.

— Parce que je n'ai pas le choix. »

Une expression de rare tendresse apparut sur ses traits. « Tu es donc si malheureux ? »

Je reculai sous le coup de la surprise. « Qu'est-ce que le malheur vient faire ici ? Nous parlons seulement affaires. »

Il secoua la tête. « Il ne s'agit pas d'affaires, petit. C'est autre chose, même si je ne sais pas exactement quoi. Mais tu ne peux pas me demander ça. »

Je le regardai avec incrédulité. « Je ne peux pas ? Je ne peux pas ? Après tout ce que j'ai fait pour vous ? »

Il rougit, puis aussitôt blêmit. Ses lèvres tremblaient quand il parla. « Tu as été bon avec moi, petit, je le reconnais. Je te dois une fière chandelle. Demande-moi n'importe quoi, mais pas ça. Je t'en supplie. Je ferai ce que tu veux, mais je refuse de grimper sur ton bûcher funéraire pour me transformer en torche humaine. C'est peut-être une coutume orientale fort respectable, mais ainsi que je te l'ai déjà dit, un protocole différent est en vigueur à Manhattan.

— Mais pourquoi considérer cela comme un autodafé suicidaire ? protestai-je. Ce pourrait tout à fait être un triomphe. »

Kahn devint brusquement lugubre. Il toucha machinalement son bracelet de cuivre. « Que veux-tu que je te dise, petit ? Ma modeste voix dit non. »

Je le narguai. « Votre modeste voix est un couinement, Kahn, le cri plaintif de la souris. Vous avez donc perdu toute audace ? Où est votre shutzpah ? Qu'est-il arrivé à "pas de gloire sans couilles" — le cri de guerre des soldats ashkénazes ? Qu'est-ce que ceci, les Salamalecs Hassidiques, SH ?

— Tu peux rire si tu veux, petit, dit-il tristement, mais ma position est claire et nette. Si tu persistes dans ton idée, je démissionne. Sans blague.

— Après tout ce que... ? »

Il opina solennellement. « Essaie un peu.

— Et si en effet j'étais malheureux ? demandai-je. Si je vous disais que je suis prêt à tout miser là-dessus ? Comment réagiriez-vous ?

— Ah, petit, petit, soupira-t-il en secouant la tête, ne me fais pas payer pour le passé. Ne me fais pas ça. Ne te fais pas ça.

— Je suis malheureux, Kahn », dis-je.

Il sourit avec une sympathie sans joie. « Ton angoisse est si raffinée, si subtile qu'il n'y a pas une demi-douzaine d'hommes sur terre capables de l'apprécier. Ne la rejette pas. Elle est encore nouvelle pour toi ; apprends à la faire mûrir.

— Kahn...
— Non.

— Je ne vous le pardonnerai jamais.
— Peut-être, dit-il, mais un jour tu m'en seras reconnaissant. »
Je renonçai donc momentanément. Mais sa résistance ne fit qu'affirmer ma décision. Je bouillai intérieurement et commençai de comploter. Dans le plus grand secret, je recrutai quelques complices de toute confiance pour entamer des reconnaissances en vue d'une stratégie d'attaque cohérente. J'ouvris un dossier top-secret sur APL, que nous baptisâmes du nom de code « La Douairière ».

Mes ambitions ainsi contrecarrées, ma frustration et mon impatience se reportèrent sur ma vie privée, ou plutôt y trouvèrent un terrain propice à leur épanouissement. Depuis quelque temps, Li se comportait curieusement. J'avais déjà senti ses réticences pendant l'absorption de la première entreprise, mais, trop occupé pour y prendre garde, je les avais écartées non sans un léger agacement. Pourtant, dans la présente accalmie, elles me frappèrent chaque jour davantage. J'observais attentivement Li. Elle restait parfois taciturne et silencieuse pendant des jours. Puis son humeur changeait, et avec une véhémence qui créait sa propre onde de choc émotionnelle, elle m'agressait, m'accusait avec incohérence, affirmant d'abord que je la négligeais, puis se plaignant de ce que mon incessante proximité l'importunait. La phase de la lune changeant de nouveau, elle m'accablait de tendresse ou bien devenait possessive et tyrannique. Un matin où je la rejoignis pour le petit déjeuner, elle était assise devant sa tasse de café qu'elle tenait à deux mains et sur laquelle elle soufflait légèrement en regardant à travers la vapeur qui en montait. Elle semblait plus calme et plus posée que je ne l'avais vue depuis quelque temps. « Je rentrerai tard ce soir, dit-elle. Ne m'attends pas. »

Je lui adressai un regard interrogateur.

« J'ai une échéance à respecter pour ma thèse, dit-elle en baissant les yeux vers sa tasse. Je n'ai quasiment rien fait depuis quelques semaines.
— Tu vas à la bibliothèque ? »
Elle acquiesça en soufflant sur son café.

J'étais couché et je ne dormais pas quand elle rentra. Pour ne pas me réveiller, elle arriva sur la pointe des pieds au bord du lit, puis se pencha au-dessus de moi. « Tu dors ? » chuchota-t-elle.

Je ne bronchai pas.

Elle me regarda longtemps, puis j'entendis le bruit feutré de ses pas sur le tapis. La porte de la salle de bain se ferma. Je vis un rai de lumière jaune apparaître au ras du sol. J'entendis le bruit de la chasse d'eau. Elle ouvrit le robinet de la douche. Je me retournai vers le mur, malade d'angoisse et de soupçons.

Le lendemain matin, elle partit de bonne heure, et je fouillai dans la corbeille à papiers comme un voleur, avec une curiosité avide, obsessionnelle, désespérée. J'y trouvai l'emballage en carton d'une poire vaginale, qui montrait une femme en sous-vêtements dansant joyeusement dans une lumière diaphane. « Vinaigre et eau, disait la notice, recommandé par la plupart des médecins. » Je fus pris de nausée : « vinaigre et eau, songeai-je amèrement, salope ». Je sentis la résignation sourdre derrière la panique, comme si j'avais déjà renoncé, déjà tout perdu et tout oublié. Je m'obligeai à réagir contre le fatalisme, à éviter la conclusion de ma découverte.

Le lendemain soir, je ne pus dormir. J'arpentai furieusement la chambre, comme un tigre en cage, en l'attendant. Cédant à une impulsion subite, j'enfilai mon manteau et sortis. Je hélai un taxi au carrefour, donnai au chauffeur l'adresse de son appartement. J'examinai mon trousseau de clefs. Oui, je possédais toujours le double qu'elle avait fait faire pour moi.

Quand Ramon quitta des yeux le cadran du téléphone et me vit à la porte de l'immeuble, une expression inquiète traversa fugitivement son visage. Il se reprit aussitôt, mais je l'avais remarquée. Abandonnant le récepteur pendu au bout du fil, il vint m'ouvrir.

« Hé, mec, ça fait oun bail, dit-il avec son air moqueur de fausse camaraderie. Comment va ?

— Elle est là ? demandai-je en vrillant mon regard dans ses yeux.

— Hé, mec, dit-il en reculant d'un pas et levant vers moi les paumes de ses mains, yé sais rien, pigé ? Rien de rien. Nada. »

Je me dirigeai vers l'ascenseur sans lui répondre.

Avançant à pas de loup dans le couloir, je baissai la tête comme si je suivais une piste, à l'affût de la moindre voix, du moindre indice. Rien. Je m'immobilisai devant sa porte, respirant à peine. Mon cœur battait la chamade. Le plus doucement possible, je glissai la clef dans la serrure, puis la tournai. La porte s'ouvrit, puis se bloqua presque aussitôt. La chaîne de sécurité. Li était là. Forcément. Peut-être travaillait-elle. « Li », fis-je doucement. Pas de réponse. Elle dormait peut-être. « Li », appelai-je de nouveau, plus fort. Toujours pas de réponse. Une rage subite s'empara de moi. « *Li !* criai-je. Ouvre la porte. Je sais que tu es là. » Haletant et furieux, je m'arrêtai pour écouter. J'entendis des verrous cliqueter de gauche et de droite dans le couloir. Des portes s'entrebâillèrent autour de moi.

« Qui est là ? chuchota une voix de femme.

— Que regardez-vous ? hurlai-je en faisant mine de bondir vers elle. Occupez-vous de vos oignons ! » Je secouai violemment la porte de Li entre le chambranle et l'arrêt de la chaîne de sécurité, je donnai des coups de pied dedans, la claquai, puis retournai vers les ascenseurs sans me donner la peine de la fermer à clef. Puis je rentrai l'attendre à la maison.

Quand elle arriva, je l'observai en la fusillant du regard. « Salope, éructai-je à voix basse.

— Tu as dit quelque chose ? » Elle leva les yeux, alors qu'elle cherchait quelque chose dans son sac.

« J'ai dit "salope" », répétai-je.

Elle regarda par-dessus son épaule, comme si je parlais à une femme derrière elle, puis me dévisagea avec surprise. « C'est à moi que tu parles ? » Elle porta la main à sa poitrine.

« "C'est à moi que tu parles ?" minaudai-je d'une voix de fausset. Inutile de me dire des conneries. Je sais que tu étais là-bas.

— Qu'est-ce que tu racontes ? » Elle posa son sac par terre, prit un air ennuyé. « Où, là-bas ? »

Sa mauvaise foi évidente m'écœura. Je détournai les yeux, refusant de lui parler ou de reconnaître sa présence.

« On dirait que tu as eu une rude journée, mon garçon, commenta-t-elle avec hostilité.

— Infernale, répondis-je en lui jetant un regard mauvais. Vinaigre et eau, recommandé par la plupart des médecins. »

Elle plissa les yeux, me regarda avec une expression bizarre. « Tu as perdu l'esprit ?

— J'ai, semble-t-il, perdu davantage.

— *Mais de quoi parles-tu ?* » s'écria-t-elle.

Je ricanai. « De poire vaginale.

— De quoi ?

— Un emballage de poire vaginale — je l'ai trouvé ce matin dans la corbeille.

— Et alors ? dit-elle

— Je ne l'ai tout de même pas imaginé ?

— Non, reconnut-elle. Je l'y ai mis hier soir. J'ai eu mes règles hier. »

Je lui lançai un regard soupçonneux.

« Quoi ? demanda-t-elle. Quelque chose m'échapperait-il ? A-t-on voté une loi qui fait des règles un crime capital ? » Elle marqua un temps. « Passible d'une scène conjugale en bonne et due forme ?

— Montre-moi, fis-je.

— Tu veux que je te montre quoi ?

— Le sang. »

Elle m'adressa un regard incrédule, puis ses traits se tordirent en une grimace dégoûtée. « Tu es infect, siffla-t-elle.

— Très bien, concédai-je à contrecœur. A supposer que tu me dises la vérité, comment expliques-tu la chaîne de sécurité ?

— Quelle chaîne de sécurité ?

— Allez, Li, ne fais pas l'innocente. La chaîne de sécurité de ton appartement.

— Et alors ?

— Comment se fait-il qu'elle était fermée *de l'intérieur ?* »

Elle haussa les épaules. « Que veux-tu que je te réponde ?

— Tu plaisantes ?

— Bien sûr que non, affirma-t-elle. Comment veux-tu que je le sache ?

— Tu le sais parfaitement, dis-je. C'est toi qui l'avais fermée. »

Elle secoua la tête. « Je crois que je commence à comprendre.

— A comprendre quoi ? »

Son visage était rose vif, ses yeux lançaient des éclairs. « Voilà deux semaines qu'une amie à moi habite mon appartement.

— Qui ? demandai-je.

— Kay Ellis, qui suit les mêmes cours de doctorat que moi. Tu veux lui téléphoner ? Ne te gêne surtout pas. Tu connais le numéro. »

Je sentis mon estomac se contracter. Je regardai le téléphone, douloureusement tenté de décrocher.

« Tu es allé là-bas, n'est-ce pas ? demanda-t-elle, furieuse. Qu'as-tu fait ? Tu as essayé d'enfoncer la porte ?

Pris d'un brusque abattement, je fus incapable de lui répondre.

Elle rit avec amertume. « Tu veux savoir pourquoi la chaîne de sécurité était en place ? Je vais te le dire. Mon amie s'est probablement barrée par l'escalier d'incendie en se croyant attaquée par un cinglé, — et elle n'avait pas tort. Espèce de bâtard ! Salaud ! » Cherchant frénétiquement une échappatoire à sa colère, elle cracha par terre, puis fondit en larmes ; saisissant son manteau au passage, elle courut vers la porte, qu'elle fit claquer derrière elle.

J'étais effondré. Mais peut-être mentait-elle. Non, personne n'aurait pu feindre aussi bien. Et pourtant ? Non ! Non ! Non ! Que m'arrivait-il ?

Quand elle revint, c'était presque l'aube. Échevelée, pâle, elle me regarda d'un air grave.

« Je suis désolé », dis-je d'une voix qui tremblait. Puis je m'écroulai, enfouis mon visage entre mes mains, fondis en larmes.

Li sortit une main de la poche de son manteau pour la poser sur ma tête, sans la caresser, sans jouer avec mes cheveux, sans rien faire. Très lointaine, très absente, très douce et froide, elle me sourit.

Plusieurs jours durant, je la submergeai de tendresse. Je la cajolai, je la servis. Je lui offris des cadeaux. Elle accepta tout avec ce même sourire froid et lointain.

Puis, un jour, alors qu'assise à la table de la cuisine elle soufflait sur son café, d'une voix neutre, sans même lever les yeux, elle me demanda : « Tu te rappelles le soir où tu m'as dit que tu voulais m'emmener au Pays des Fées ? »

J'acquiesçai.

« Tu m'as demandé autre chose. » Elle me lança un regard furtif au-dessus de sa tasse, puis but une gorgée avec précaution.

« Je t'ai demandé de m'épouser », ajoutai-je d'une voix qui frémissait d'excitation.

Elle leva les yeux vers moi. « Et maintenant, le désires-tu toujours ?

— Oui, murmurai-je, ravi. Oui, oui, oui. »

Elle but lentement son café. « Très bien, dit-elle calmement. Tu le penses vraiment ?

— Absolument. »

Je fus aux anges pendant plusieurs jours. Seul le souvenir de Yin-mi, comme une mélodie plaintive issue d'une autre pièce, me troublait parfois. Tout cela semblait incompréhensible. J'avais assisté à la lente détérioration de mon rapport avec Li ; je l'avais crue perdue et maintenant, brusquement... Et elle se comportait si bizarrement, avec une telle distance, une telle froideur. Mais qu'avais-je espéré ? C'était sans importance. Plus rien n'avait d'importance !

Avec elle, néanmoins, rien n'avait changé. Son indifférence s'était installée comme une nouvelle saison, comme l'hiver. Ses absences se prolongèrent.

Je voulais échafauder des projets, annoncer notre mariage au monde entier, mais elle me demanda d'attendre. Elle avait besoin de régler certaines choses. Elle ne m'en dit pas plus et je ne lui posai pas de question, désireux de lui prouver ma confiance. Car je lui faisais confiance. Elle me demanda seulement ceci : « Je crois qu'ensuite j'aimerais sans doute déménager.

— Où ? » m'enquis-je.

Elle haussa les épaules. « Je ne sais pas. Peut-être à la campagne. En avons-nous les moyens ? » Elle m'interrogeait avec une tendre réticence, presque avec timidité.

« Bien sûr », dis-je en prenant sa main et plongeant mes yeux dans les siens avec une expression douloureuse, comme si je l'eusse privée de quelque chose, « bien sûr ».

Ce fut seulement un peu plus tard que la perspective de nous installer au domaine de Sands Point m'effleura. Il faudrait évidemment faire beaucoup de travaux, mais... Mais peut-être la maison ne lui plairait-elle pas. En tout cas je pouvais toujours l'emmener là-bas et voir sa réaction. Ce serait agréable, pensai-je. Li devait visiter le domaine des Love

15

Cette fois, un parallélisme : l'heureux bouleversement de ma vie privée présagea un regain d'intérêt pour mon travail ; car peu à peu les Cornes du Taureau — nom de code de ma cellule de cadres fidèles sélectionnés parmi la plus vaste Agence de Renseignements de Kahn et Sun (baptisée du sigle τρ) — réussirent à rassembler une image claire de l'histoire et du fonctionnement d'American Power and Light. Bien que les origines de la plus grande entreprise d'Amérique (et donc, bien sûr, du monde) fussent aussi mystérieuses que les origines de la nation elle-même avec sa hache et son cerisier mythiques, je sentis tous mes doutes s'envoler, fasciné par la vision que me révélèrent leurs recherches, d'un véritable Pays des Fées financier, un Oz industriel. La vieille plaisanterie revint à la mode : « Et Dieu dit : "Que la lumière soit" ; et la lumière fut », la Puissance et la Lumière de l'Amérique *(American Power and Light)*.

Je ne sais ce qui m'enthousiasma le plus : la perspective de mon futur mariage avec Li, ou celle de convoler en justes noces avec APL. Là aussi, je jouai l'amant jaloux, téléphonant tous les quarts d'heure pour m'assurer de l'humeur de la Douairière sur le Grand Tableau. Je savais que je ne pouvais espérer être payé de retour, car APL était un Sphinx, aussi vieux et rusé que le temps lui-même — deux siècles, à vrai dire — et qui posait à ses doux prétendants écervelés une devinette à laquelle peu répondaient adéquatement. Moyennant quoi elle avait souvent connu le veuvage, si souvent même qu'on l'avait baptisée la Grande Veuve Noire du Dow. Hélas, mon père avait été l'une de ses plus récentes victimes. Mais quelles profondes bouffées de plaisir enivrant il avait certainement goûtées !

L'une des rares entreprises existant aujourd'hui et qui sévissait déjà à l'aube de la république, née avec l'Amérique, sa sœur jumelle et son fer de lance, APL qu'aucun ventre mortel n'avait procréé était le fruit de l'immaculée conception ; certains soutenaient même que la Douairière avait jailli, parfaitement formée, du front crevassé d'Alexander Hamilton en personne, telle Minerve du cerveau de Jupiter. Selon cette version, Hamilton accoucha de ce projet pendant une heure de loisir, et le peaufina toujours davantage au fil des ans, au point qu'APL devint pour lui une passion dévorante. Beaucoup plus que des œuvres mineures telles que la Banque nationale, la dette publique, ou encore la bonne foi et la solvabilité de la nouvelle république, cette corporation bénéficia de toute l'énergie d'Hamilton dans ses vieux jours, qu'il passa dans un état de contemplation abstraite, comme un homme saisi d'un rêve éveillé ou un savant fou — un politicien délirant — obsédé par l'ébauche de sa charte et de sa vocation. Mais l'entreprise nouveau-née n'était pas morte avec Hamilton, oh non ! Elle lui survécut, comme survivent toutes les idées vraies et belles, sous la protection du grand ami et patron de Hamilton, George Washington, Père de la Nation (et Oncle de la Corporation), qui veilla à son développement, bien que sous un nom différent. Cœur et foie des États récemment unis, cette entreprise ne pouvait mourir ni faire faillite tant que durerait l'Amérique. Car aussi indestructible que la matière, aussi substantielle et pure qu'elle, elle contenait un minimum d'excroissances métaphysiques et de gaz spirituels délétères.

Enfin, après maintes réincarnations, façonnée par les Love, elle atteignit la perfection qu'on lui connaissait désormais sous son présent nom. American Power and Light : que ces mots sonnaient bien ! Oui, « aussi bien que n'importe quel vers de poésie jamais écrit au Nouveau Monde », ainsi que Hackless l'avait un jour déclaré. Le parangon de l'industrie ! Là et nulle part ailleurs s'était exercé le génie le plus original de l'Amérique ! Hsiao avait raison. Les arts valaient à peine mieux que de grossiers gribouillages néolithiques peints par des sauvages sur les murs des cavernes, comparés à sa fabuleuse, à son incomparable technologie !

Mais assez d'emphase ! Je me suis laissé aller au souvenir de l'extase que mon rêve, mon obsession, suscita alors. Étrange, après tout ce qui s'est passé, que cette vision ait encore un tel pouvoir sur moi. Étais-je alors inspiré, ou me leurrais-je ?

Mais peut-être, lecteur, faut-il t'initier brièvement aux rites mystérieux de la haute finance américaine ? Peut-être t'interroges-tu sur la nature de cette lumière éblouissante qui m'aveugla en effet ? Quels étaient l'actif et le passif de la corporation (ce dernier, quasiment inexistant), ses sources de revenus, ses profits passés et envisagés, ses perspectives de développement ? Question pertinente et fondamentale, de celles qui convoquent davantage l'histoire américaine tout entière que la place restreinte de mon pauvre paragraphe. Néanmoins, ton humble serviteur va tenter d'éclairer ta lanterne.

American Power and Light est bien plus qu'une simple entreprise de services publics. Elle explora en pionnier le concept de conglomérat, cette diversification omnivore. Dans les services publics, elle fut tout sauf paresseuse ; en fait, elle cumule toutes les ressources énergétiques, elle est la source de cette incandescence divine qui illumine la nation de l'intérieur, fait de l'Amérique un fanal et un phare pour le monde. Après la lumière, la chaleur, cette chaleur qui réchauffe le sang même du pays. Actuellement, les générateurs d'APL sont partout ; certains fonctionnent au charbon, d'autres au pétrole, d'autres encore avec le combustible nucléaire.

Mais les holdings d'APL vont bien au-delà des traditionnels services publics. Longtemps avant l'invention de l'électricité, alors que l'Amérique s'éclairait encore avec des bougies au blanc de baleine, APL entreprit de se diversifier, investit massivement dans l'industrie baleinière de New

Bedford et du Nantucket, puis se développa synergiquement dans les chantiers navals. Sur la terre, afin de s'assurer un approvisionnement régulier en matières premières, elle acheta des mines de charbon en Pennsylvanie et en Virginie occidentale, et des chemins de fer pour accéder à ces mines. L'acquisition de terrains et de couloirs stratégiques la rendit propriétaire d'immenses étendues de forêts, de puits de pétrole et de mines supplémentaires — or et argent, tungstène, cuivre, fer. Plus récemment, APL a fait de gros investissements dans l'exploration pétrolière. Ses forages offshore sondent les fonds marins en des régions aussi éloignées que la mer de Beaufort au nord du Canada, ou les eaux boueuses du golfe du Mexique. Extrapolant à partir de ses premiers chantiers navals, elle construit aussi les super-tankers indispensables à nos quotas de pétrole moyen-oriental, qui vont mouiller dans les ports en eau profonde du golfe Persique. Et comme la production d'acier est une composante vitale de l'industrie des chantiers navals, les eaux des Grands Lacs reflètent les lueurs fuligineuses des hauts fourneaux de Buffalo et de Gary, où les filiales d'APL travaillent nuit et jour, quand elles ne sont pas en grève, pour produire l'acier indispensable.

Avec ses holdings de ressources naturelles, sa puissante industrie de transformation, sa production d'acier et de navires de tous tonnages, il n'était que naturel qu'American Power and Light se diversifiât dans l'armement pour produire non seulement des bateaux mais des avions, des chars, des véhicules blindés, sans parler de l'artillerie, des explosifs, des armes à feu et des munitions, ainsi que ces autres armes de génocide et de destruction qui, au cours de la seconde guerre mondiale, firent florès et permirent à la corporation de devenir la plus importante du monde.

Après la guerre, la production d'équipement militaire lourd poussa APL à fabriquer des voitures et des camions, qui concurrencèrent, puis supplantèrent les chemins de fer, transportèrent les marchandises les plus diverses aux quatre coins de l'Amérique grâce aux autoroutes inter-États, elles-mêmes construites par des sociétés filiales de la maison mère. Métamorphosant les étendues sauvages en terres cultivables, American Power and Light se lança dans l'agronomie, achemina les troncs d'arbres vers ses propres scieries, débita les forêts américaines en planches calibrées. Ce qui lui mit le pied à l'étrier pour pénétrer le marché de l'industrie du logement. Élargissant une fois encore le champ de ses activités, elle entreprit de fabriquer la panoplie affolante des outils du charpentier. Ses filiales automobiles produisirent des camionnettes et des véhicules à quatre roues motrices pour transporter le bois et les outils jusqu'aux sites isolés auparavant déboisés, dont les rondins servaient à construire des maisons. American Power and Light produisait donc les camions qui transportaient les outils qu'elle fabriquait et les billes de bois qu'elle coupait puis transformait ; ces camions recevaient l'essence qu'elle importait ou raffinait, puis elle alla encore plus loin, acquérant les usines textiles pour habiller ses ouvriers, les grandes surfaces indispensables pour leur vendre le nécessaire, les banques commerciales, les services de prêt et de caisse d'épargne pour que le travailleur pût emprunter de l'argent afin d'investir dans ces mêmes camions, outils, billes de bois, maisons, vêtements. Elle récupérait ainsi le fruit de son labeur et le nourrissait des produits de ses fermes, après quoi elle créa les Loisirs pour le soulager de sa peine et le renvoyer au travail avec des forces neuves.

Et les Loisirs — cette géniale trouvaille américaine dont l'apothéose fut l'invention du week-end — ouvrirent de nouveaux horizons aux grands manitous et imprésarios visionnaires de la libre entreprise qui siégeaient au conseil d'administration de cette corporation tentaculaire, leur révélèrent des marchés mirobolants, inouïs !

Il y eut d'abord les livres, lourdes bibles et traités de commerce, austères manuels et recueils de prières, néanmoins assez distrayants pour soutirer un maigre sourire aux lèvres minces d'un Père Puritain assis sur sa chaise à dos droit par une soirée d'hiver bostonienne, comptabilisant l'actif et le passif dans le vaste registre de son salut, à la lumière parcimonieuse d'une unique bougie au blanc de baleine (elle aussi fournie par APL). Mais cette période balbutiante fut bientôt suivie par la douce éclosion de la poésie lyrique, une fleur de serre importée d'Europe, dont les graines éparses de pollen doré essaimèrent dans l'air vierge du Nouveau Monde, se mêlèrent à des espèces plus rudes, au pin et au cèdre de la mélancolie, pour produire les accents sauvages et robustes du chant inaugural, la nouvelle et la romance. Ce bâtard qui tenait du chien fou, des générations successives l'améliorèrent, le domestiquèrent pour lui faire engendrer le fruit pulpeux et délicieux, généreux et prolixe, du Roman Américain, capable de satisfaire les goûts les plus éclectiques d'un public démocratique, forme vigoureuse et aboutie qu'on ne put ensuite qu'émasculer, arracher à son environnement naturel pour le réintroduire dans la serre monstrueuse de l'imagination urbaine dépravée où elle perdit la fermeté de sa chair et sa sauvage spontanéité, le mordant et la causticité qui la caractérisaient quand elle croissait librement dans les forêts.

Alors les genres proliférèrent. Quelque part le long de la chaîne — la chaîne de production, s'entend —, naquit l'institution de la presse, un droit aussi inaliénable que la vie, la liberté, la recherche du bonheur. Le mot fait chair — et quelle chair ! Les journaux se divisèrent bientôt en douze tribus et s'éparpillèrent aux quatre coins de la terre (aujourd'hui encore, certains errent sans le moindre repère), et parmi eux votre *Times* et votre *Tribune*, vos *Sun*, *Globe*, *Dispatches*, *Gazette*, *Courier*, *Journal*, *Sentinel*, *Observer*, *Post*, *Constitution*, et autres *Constitutionals* avec toutes leurs formules et dans tous leurs états, quotidiens du matin ou du soir, bi-hebdomaires ou hebdomadaires (certains plus chameaux que doux-amers), mensuels, trimestriels, semestriels, annuels, saisonniers, décennaux, millénaires ou merveilleusement occasionnels. Avec eux, la population apprit à lire, se fit les dents et se prépara à l'initiation fondamentale.

A cette époque, la gent féminine, qui ne possédait aucun moyen d'expression adéquat, devait se contenter de cet expédient frustrant qu'est le bouche à oreille, le ragot, la rumeur, un mode de communication fastidieux, primitif, irrationnel, un véritable affront à la dignité de la femme moderne. Ainsi naquit le magazine, qui pourvut enfin aux désirs de cette fraction de la population, et dont tous les successeurs copièrent avec plus ou moins de succès les techniques d'infiltration et de propagande. Le mouvement de libération des femmes connut alors son premier triomphe !

Les hommes furent-ils ébaubis ? Certes oui ! Pestant et maugréant, amidonnant leurs propres cols de chemise et repassant avec moult plis leurs sous-vêtements à jambes longues, ils se mirent au travail et piratèrent bientôt les idées de leurs épouses pour créer leurs propres publications professionnelles ou sportives, ainsi que des revues qui présentaient la Femme dans une incarnation plus nostalgique, idéale et charnelle, c'est-à-dire séduisante, désirable et largement dévêtue. Mais effectuons un saut dans le temps et l'espace jusqu'à la Quarante-deuxième rue et ses cinémas à vingt-cinq *cents*, ses cabines privées peuplées de grognements, d'ahanements, qui exhalent une odeur de sueur et parfois une puanteur plus âcre, jusqu'à ses rayons de perversions exotiques aussi variées que les plantes du fleuriste. Les enfants refusèrent bien sûr de rester sur la touche ; aussitôt les penseurs d'American Power and Light inventèrent la bande dessinée, *Mad Magazine* pour les cinglés, *Les fondements de la mécanique* pour les forts en thème et autres apprentis garagistes, sans oublier *Toi et Moi* pour les amoureux transis des deux sexes.

Mais le mot imprimé ne pouvait satisfaire éternellement l'appétit grandissant de distractions dû à l'accroissement des Loisirs. Les livres étaient trop intellectuels, demandaient trop de concentration, de réflexion, d'efforts. Après tout, les week-ends étaient faits pour s'amuser ! Pourquoi ne pas inventer une distraction populaire qui satisfît l'être tout entier (sans fatiguer le cerveau) ? Comme d'habitude, American Power and Light trouva la solution. La radio, les films muets et enfin, quand la technologie le permit, le parlant ! Hollywood ! Fred Astaire et Ginger Rogers, Marlene Dietrich, Garbo, Bette Davis, Citizen Kane et Capra, Cukor, Griffith, Garland, Cary Grant, Gary Cooper et les milliers d'autres qu'on ne saurait citer sans d'impardonnables omissions !

Et les grands studios, RKO et MGM, sans parler du tissu social, engendrèrent enfin, l'ultime, le *nec plus ultra* des distractions américaines, sans doute le témoignage le plus abouti de la créativité et du génie de la nation — la boîte, le petit écran, la télé !

On hésite humblement à aborder un sujet aussi vaste. Que dire ? On en reste pantois, abasourdi ! Il suffit de remarquer qu'heure après heure, soir après soir, nous restons assis avec un visage de marbre (mais intérieurement ravis), baignant comme de monstrueux légumes hydropiques dans la lueur bleutée de notre TV à écran panoramique, peu soucieux des rayons que nous absorbons et qui irradient nos testicules et nos ovaires avec toutes les couleurs de l'arc-en-ciel radioactif, assurant la viabilité des générations futures en veillant à l'évolution de notre capital génétique afin qu'il continue de produire d'étranges et merveilleux mutants qui, en accord avec les enseignements de Darwin, seront décimés dans la lutte impitoyable pour la survie, ou bien produiront une espèce plus performante, un Surhomme qui, débarrassé des angoisses de la mort, s'élèvera sur les ailes d'un aigle vers le clair empyrée, et dans un acte glorieux — un sourire complice, un clin d'œil, un « OK » adressé aux parents restés à la maison — triomphera instantanément et deviendra ce que nous ne pouvons même pas commencer d'imaginer. Ô jour de gloire ! Aurons-nous la chance d'assister à ce prodige de notre vivant ? L'*Homo sapiens*, ayant enfin touché le jackpot, transcende la mesquinerie de son destin historique. Encore ce vieux leitmotiv grec, lecteur, le deus ex machina (la machine, la télé). L'homme, ce pauvre infirme, ne se met-il pas toujours dans un mauvais pas d'où ses dieux, qui descendent lourdement des cintres grinçants de son théâtre, couronnes et auréoles légèrement de guingois, suspendus à des poulies rouillées, le tirent. *nous* tirent en effaçant magiquement les lois de la gravité ?

La télévision fut bien sûr le coup de maître et l'apothéose de la campagne séculaire d'APL pour frayer de nouvelles voies étincelantes dans les étendues sauvages de la conscience américaine (bâtir des motels économiques, des restaurants familiaux, des grands magasins, des chaînes de fast-food, aménager des débouchés à ses produits, organiser les soldes et les ventes de voitures d'occasion).

Mais la télévision fut agrémentée d'autres sources de plaisir, en particulier la radio. Quel Américain n'a pas, à un moment ou à un autre, tué les longues heures d'ennui estival sur les plages situées entre Malibu et Coney Island à l'aide de son fidèle transistor dans son étui noir similicuir ? Pourtant, à l'heure où j'écris, cette grande institution américaine a subi le sort de toutes les bonnes choses, devenant un dinosaure technologique avant son temps. Le transistor a perdu dans la compétition implacable qui l'a opposé à la radio-cassette high-tech, digitale, Dolby-compatible, mieux connue sous le nom d'Attaché-Case du tiers monde, qu'on voit aujourd'hui porté en bandoulière ou sur l'épaule dans les rues ou le métro de New York, un accessoire indispensable à ceux qui considèrent comme intolérable de faire cent mètres sur le trottoir sans musique pour les distraire et court-circuiter la moindre introspection ressemblant à l'oppression de la pensée. Car la pensée est apparemment devenue synonyme d'impérialisme intellectuel inventé par les classes supérieures pour asservir les pauvres, les défavorisés, les minorités. Renonçant à toute activité rationnelle et aux valeurs prônées par la mentalité agressive, impérialiste, de l'Occident, les membres les plus radicaux de ces groupes se sont branchés sur les fiches de leur radio-cassette en attendant que leurs cortex cérébraux se ramollissent peu à peu et les affranchissent définitivement de toute pensée.

Les progrès de l'électronique qui ont permis cette invention excitante ont aussi engendré la chaîne stéréo, laquelle a évolué à partir du Victrola préhistorique au point de devenir un accessoire aussi important de la vie domestique américaine que la plomberie ou le four General Electric (filiale d'APL). Car on ne saurait nier que les Américains sont un peuple qui aime la musique. Après tout, Orphée n'a-t-il pas dompté les bêtes fauves avec sa lyre (bien qu'on ignore s'il utilisa son instrument pour leur jouer une sérénade ou les assommer) ? American Power and Light encourage les artistes du Nouveau Monde à jouer de l'instrument qui correspond le mieux à leur génie, synthétiseur moog, tympanon, triangle, basse Fender ou guitare Stratocaster, tuba, pédale wha-wha, Wurlitzer ou Flentrop, banjo, violon, piano, et naturellement cet albatros national qu'est l'hélicon ! La corporation finance l'industrie du disque, engage des producteurs, des ingénieurs du son, et bien sûr (devinez qui ?) les hyènes de l'entreprise (toujours ricanants, l'Amérique — car ils se moquent de *toi* !), les publicistes.

Dans un genre moins commercial et afin d'apaiser sa conscience capitaliste (à défaut d'obtenir un acquittement en bonne et due forme), elle investit une part de ses profits pour embaucher des archivistes qui récoltent et pressent dans le vinyle la riche moisson sauvage de la musique ethnique américaine : *bluegrass* dans les vallées pierreuses des Appalaches avec son parfum de gigues irlandaises et de branles écossais qui rappelle la morsure d'un vieux cidre râpeux, *blues* plus sombre du Sud, joué avec un cure-dents au Texas et à mains nues en Caroline du Nord, musique créée par des musiciens aveugles comme Will McTell qui suivait le circuit poussiéreux des églises et des foires, à peine présentable avec son costume luisant élimé et sa casquette, ses chaussures sans chaussettes ni lacets, assis au bord de sa chaise et fixant droit devant lui son regard laiteux tout en grattant et chantant, perdu dans quelque folle parabole de péché et de ténébreuse rédemption. Alors le *blues* leva les yeux vers le ciel et vit la lumière du protestantisme évangélique américain, avec pour résultat le *gospel*, qui s'établit à Nashville, ainsi que la *country music*, Hank Williams, Wailin' Waylon Jennings, Tammy (« Lâche Pas Ton Pote ») Whine-ette. De La Nouvelle-Orléans, via Chicago, New York et San Juan vint le jazz, qui se combina à maints autres éléments pour donner naissance à la Grande Synthèse Universelle du Rock 'n' Roll, lequel connut une brève mais fastueuse Renaissance (aussi courte qu'une génération de mouches de laboratoire) pendant les années soixante, peu de temps après mon arrivée sur ces rivages, avant de dégénérer rapidement en maniérisme avec le Punk et la New Wave, sans oublier le clinquant décérébré, exhibitionniste du disco et son rythme haletant, palpitant, métronomique de copulation dans une lapinière. Grâce à APL, tout ceci est disponible sur la simple pression d'un bouton, et chez vous !

Ensuite, pour nous aider à sortir de ces bulles de plaisir qu'elle avait créées afin de nous distraire, American Power and Light créa la vie nocturne : clubs et bars, discothèques et salles de concert, autant de lieux où s'échapper de nos heureux foyers pour trouver soulagement et nous reposer de nos Loisirs si absorbants, écouter en direct nos musiques préférées, danser, boire un coup de trop, coucher ensemble —, et contracter une kyrielle de maladies vénériennes qui ouvrirent un nouveau marché à l'industrie pharmaceutique qu'Eddie Love avait déjà explorée en son temps et avec la fortune qu'on sait, anesthésiant les forces armées pendant la dure épreuve de la deuxième guerre mondiale.

Le champ d'application des produits pharmaceutiques était naturellement illimité. La corporation se mit à produire des médicaments miracles comme la pénicilline, ainsi que tous les accessoires indispensables au contrôle des naissances. Puis son horizon s'élargit. Car avec l'extraordinaire développement de la vie nocturne, l'Amérique eut grand besoin de drogues, surtout d'amphétamines, pour les noctambules qui éprouvaient quelque difficulté à rester éveillés pendant et après les festivités. Conséquence logique, on mit au point les barbituriques pour annuler les effets du *speed* et nous aider à retrouver le sommeil. Il fallut ensuite ouvrir des centres pour drogués dans les hôpitaux ; APL mit sur pied des cliniques réservées aux toxicomanes, embaucha travailleurs sociaux, psychiatres, psychologues, infirmières, conseillers, tous gens bien intentionnés et dispensateurs d'avis judicieux, qui montraient magnifiquement à leurs patients l'exemple d'une vie saine et d'une utilisation constructive du temps.

Puis l'insatiable appétit américain de bonnes et saines distractions se jeta sur les sports comme la pauvreté sur le monde ! APL veilla à ce que tous les quartiers de Harlem eussent leur anneau métallique et leur panneau de bois en séquoia, sapin Douglas ou *redwood* géant, et fussent ainsi reliés symboliquement à la campagne, la forêt, la frontière, représentant ainsi les possibilités illimitées de mobilité sociale et géographique de l'Amérique, sous-entendant presque que n'importe quel petit gars pouvait, avec un peu de pratique, devenir sinon président des États-Unis, du moins champion de basket ! Tout cela suscita une forte demande d'équipements sportifs : chaussures de jogging et carabines pour la chasse à l'éléphant, sacs à dos, arcs et flèches, cannes à pêche et moulinets, piolets et mousquetons, pitons et cordes de rappel pour descendre à flanc de montagne (ou bon Dieu à flanc de n'importe quoi !), clubs de golf, raquettes de tennis, équipements de plongée, ballons ovales de football américain, crosses, palets et patins à glace de hockey, chevrotine pour les petites espèces à fourrure ou à plumes, lunettes télescopiques pour le gros gibier (ou pour les flâneurs des cours d'immeuble !), et bien d'autres choses, lecteur, car les Américains cherchent à se distraire sur terre, sur mer et dans les airs, ils pratiquent le motocross, la lutte dans la boue, le surf, le ski, la voile, ils glissent, coulent, nagent, planent, volent, bavent, suent, jouent avec des modèles réduits, des cerfs-volants, des B-52, des hélicoptères de combat, balancent napalm, bombes incendiaires, giclées de balles de calibre 50, sautent en parachute afin de razzier et terroriser, semer la mort, l'holocauste et la destruction sur tout ce qui bouge ! *Hourra !*

Mais afin qu'on ne pense pas qu'American Power and Light dilapide une fraction indue de son capital dans la poursuite de Loisirs frivoles, je me hâte d'ajouter que selon la plupart des dirigeants du monde de la finance (bien placés pour avoir une juste opinion en la matière), les frontières les plus prometteuses pour les affaires se situent à l'intérieur de l'esprit humain lui-même, ultime marché à explorer. Car les Américains dépensent davantage pour rêver, s'amuser, échapper au quotidien que pour l'acquisition de biens directement utiles. APL se contente de suivre le mouvement, de se laisser porter par cette lame de fond qui nous emmène tous vers l'aube bénie d'industries nouvelles et de lendemains qui chantent.

Tel fut le rapport que mes Cornes acérées me soumirent peu à peu, et que je réactualise pour la convenance du lecteur. A l'époque, dans mon innocence, je fus transporté par mes découvertes. Plus je réfléchissais, plus j'étais séduit à l'idée de piller ces trésors, de rafler ce trophée — moi qui étais jadis content (dupé, lecteur, on m'avait dupé — que Dieu maudisse à jamais les salamalecs et le mysticisme, cette sorcellerie qui avait sapé mes aspirations naturelles au confort matériel !) avec « du riz brut à manger, l'eau froide du puits et le creux d'un coude en guise d'oreiller ». Mais cinquante pour cent de sang américain coulait dans mes veines, garantis à cent pour cent comme le whisky de maïs ou le supercarburant, lesquels, alliés à mon instinct atavique chinois pour le jeu, produisaient un mélange hautement volatil et explosif, semblable au combustible qui propulsa les astronautes de la mission Apollo vers la lune. Et moi aussi je rêvais secrètement de m'élancer hors des royaumes de l'existence sublunaire pour atteindre l'orbite lumineuse de la Réalisation Ultime, enfin libéré, enfin illuminé, assis à la place du navigateur, sur le fauteuil tournant du président du conseil d'administration et PDG d'American Power and Light, tout l'univers s'étalant devant mes yeux ravis, et le véhicule capable de sillonner son immensité bourdonnant régulièrement entre mes jambes, prêt à décoller pour voyager à la vitesse de la pensée, pour le suivre, *lui*, mon père, jusqu'à l'ultime règlement de comptes dans le trou noir où il avait sombré sans laisser de trace, ce lieu dont j'avais sombrement rêvé, mais où je n'avais pu le suivre par manque de technologie spirituelle. Bientôt j'allais l'y retrouver !

Ce fut seulement alors, je crois, que je compris que tout du long, sans vraiment le savoir (mais poussé par la certitude de l'instinct), je m'étais approché de plus en plus près de mon but ultime, et que d'une manière imprévisible et inimaginable j'étais désormais à portée, sur le seuil. Car je compris brusquement que cette dernière conquête financière, la prise en main d'American Power and Light, constituait l'ultime assaut vers le sommet de l'Illumination elle-même. Toutes les distinctions se résorbaient. Le monde devenait Un. J'abordais l'épreuve ultime. Au-delà du voile, par-delà le septième sceau de ma carrière d'investisseur, se trouvait le delta dont j'avais rêvé, le lieu magique où le Dow se jetait enfin dans le vaste Pacifique du Tao, mêlant ses eaux troublées à l'immensité limpide et silencieuse. La route touchait au but, et j'étais presque chez moi ! Non, il ne pouvait en être autrement !

Les joies de la méditation (« le profond bien-être qu'engendre la quiétude »), même le sexe n'étaient rien comparés à mon exaltation, aux frémissements exquis qui annoncent l'extase, à ce pouvoir insensé qui me permettrait d'acheter ou de vendre des univers entiers. Christophe Colomb dut ressentir la même émotion en débarquant au Nouveau Monde pour la première fois ; le continent vierge qui s'offrait à mes yeux me semblait un nouveau commencement pour l'humanité. Sur le point de réaliser mon rêve, je m'arrêtai pour contempler le panorama, tel Moïse au sommet du Mont-Nébo, les yeux fixés sur le dernier kilomètre d'étendues stériles et de désert qui me séparait du paradis, de la Terre Promise, après un si long et si douloureux voyage.

Mais un obstacle me barrait encore la route ; Moïse et le Mont-Nébo me le remirent en mémoire. Kahn. Qu'allais-je faire de lui ? Pouvais-je vraiment me résoudre à couper les ponts ? S'il refusait de céder, je n'aurais pas le choix. D'ailleurs, cela ne pourrait vraiment pas passer pour une trahison, me consolai-je. Sa réhabilitation était désormais totale. Et mon amitié pour lui ? Elle ne comptait plus, me dis-je. Plus maintenant. Seules importaient les affaires.

16

Informé par ma secrétaire que je désirais le voir pour affaires urgentes, Kahn entra, me jeta un coup d'œil et s'arrêta net. Secouant la tête, il émit un susurrement à mi-chemin entre rire et soupir, puis arbora un sourire éclatant — infiniment trop éclatant. « Alors ? dit-il.

— Alors quoi ? demandai-je, légèrement agacé quand je compris qu'il n'allait pas continuer. Je suppose que vous savez pourquoi je vous ai fait venir.

— Évident, non ? répliqua-t-il. Toute cette gravité et ce mystère — c'est clair comme de l'eau de roche. Suffit de regarder ton visage. On jurerait un condamné à mort. »

L'ironie de sa remarque me fit sombrement sourire. « Qui êtes-vous donc, un prophète ? »

Il haussa encore les épaules. « J'appartiens à un peuple de prophètes, Sonny. Mais je n'ai besoin d'aucun talent particulier pour deviner ce qui t'agite depuis quelques semaines. On dirait un gamin qui découvre son cadeau de Noël.

— Ne jouez pas au professeur avec moi, Kahn », dis-je.

Il me sourit tristement. « Ne rendons pas ce tête-à-tête plus désagréable que nécessaire, petit. Je n'ai pas envie de me battre avec toi. » Il y avait de la résignation et de la prière dans sa voix.

« Moi non plus », soupirai-je. Je réfléchis à ses paroles. « Je suppose que vous avez raison ; vous avez deviné le motif de notre entrevue. »

Il haussa les épaules comme pour dire : « Qu'y puis-je si je suis un putain de génie ? »

Je souris. « Alors ? »

Nous nous observâmes cruellement, chacun bien décidé à ne pas dévier d'un iota de ses résolutions. Mais pendant que je regardais Kahn, les cernes mélancoliques qui semblaient supporter ses yeux, ses bajoues flasques, je sentis se dissoudre l'irritation latente qui avait commencé d'empoisonner notre rapport, emportée comme des alluvions par le courant de notre ancienne amitié.

« Eh oui, petit, dit-il (sans doute en proie à la même émotion), ça fait un moment qu'il y a de l'eau dans le gaz, pas vrai ? Mais nous n'avons jamais pris le temps d'en parler. Ce n'est pas seulement l'histoire d'APL.

Malgré mes mises en garde, j'ai écouté attentivement ton plan de bataille. Je ne suis pas d'accord avec tes arguments, mais je peux me tromper. Car je crois que tu as une chance de t'en tirer. Si quelqu'un peut réussir cette gageure, c'est bien toi. Mais tout ce shtick n'est pas pour moi. Absorption, gestion, administration — je te l'ai déjà dit, je suis un négociant, pas un homme d'affaires. J'ai le mal du pays, petit, le mal du parquet, tu ne comprends donc pas ? Le jour où nous avons discuté sur la galerie, je l'entendais presque, vois-tu ? Comme le loup qui entend le bruissement des montagnes. Je veux rentrer chez moi, petit. Ils m'accepteront maintenant, sinon à bras ouverts, du moins à portefeuilles ouverts. Tu sais aussi bien que moi que l'argent peut tout acheter. Voilà un moment que j'essaie de t'annoncer ma décision à doses homéopathiques, mais tu étais trop absorbé par ton projet pour m'entendre. Je ne t'en veux pas. Nous sommes tous deux très occupés. Nous avons raté maintes occasions d'éclaircir la situation. Mais les signes cryptiques sont désormais du passé. Je m'en vais. Je ne vois pas comment dire ça plus clairement. Tu n'as plus besoin de moi. D'ailleurs, tu n'as peut-être jamais eu besoin de moi, sauf au début, pour que je te donne un petit coup de pouce. Je t'ai appris tout ce que je savais. J'espère que ça suffira. »

Il secoua la tête. « Non, il y a belle lurette que tu m'as dépassé, Sonny. Maintenant, personne ne peut plus t'aider ni te blesser, sinon toi-même. Si je restais, je deviendrais un boulet à ton pied. Le guide t'a emmené aussi loin qu'il le peut ; tu dois accomplir la dernière étape tout seul. Ce n'est que justice.

« Et tu sais quoi ? » Je secouai négativement la tête. « Moi non plus, je n'ai plus besoin de toi. Mais ne te méprends pas, je ne suis pas un ingrat. Je sais ce que tu as fait pour moi. Je veux dire, sans toi... » Sa voix se brisa, ses yeux brillèrent d'une tendresse presque féroce. « Enfin, tu comprends. Je te dois tout. Tu m'as remis sur pied. Je ne l'oublierai jamais. Je t'en remercie. » Ses traits se durcirent brusquement. « Mais je ne compte pas me perdre en courbettes devant toi, ni m'étouffer de culpabilité. Car je sais, même si tu l'ignores... (il plissa les yeux comme pour aiguiser sa vision) mais je crois que tu le sais aussi : tu as aussi fait ça pour toi-même, je dirais même : surtout pour toi-même. C'était ta chance de pénétrer les arcanes, le saint des saints. » Il sourit. « Et maintenant tu y es. Ça n'a pas été vraiment difficile, n'est-ce pas ? *Facilis descensus averno*, tu te souviens ? Je t'avais dis qu'un jour tu comprendrais. Ai-je raison ?

— Peut-être, dis-je. Mais ceci n'est pas l'enfer.

— Non, concéda-t-il avec une moue pensive, ce n'est pas encore l'enfer. » Puis il me défia d'un sourire prédateur. « Mais peut-être quelque chose d'équivalent. »

Nos regards se croisèrent longtemps. « Alors ? dis-je.

— "Alors ?" » Il haussa les épaules. « Je crois que c'est la fin, non ?

— Je le crois aussi. »

Il rit. « Je suis quand même déçu.

— Désolé.

— Oh non, pas que nos chemins se séparent, dit-il. Après tout, c'est moi qui démissionne, n'est-ce pas ? Même si tu comptais me virer ou m'aiguiller sur une voie de garage. Je m'attendais seulement à ce que tu protestes un peu plus vigoureusement, voilà tout. Suis-je vraiment aussi facilement remplaçable ? Qui va interpréter l'oracle pour toi ?

— Je n'ai plus besoin de ça », répondis-je.

Il fronça les sourcils.

Je fermai les yeux, secouai la tête. « L'oracle est superflu depuis longtemps. J'ai seulement continué pour ne pas vous contrarier.

— Ah bon ? »

Je pris sur mon bureau le gobelet où je conservais les pièces, et les agitai au creux de ma main. « Maintenant, quand je les tiens, murmurai-je d'une voix rauque, je vois déjà les pièces immobiles avant de les avoir lancées. » Je me préparai à affronter le regard incrédule qui, je le savais, me serait opposé.

« Tu veux dire... ? »

J'acquiesçai. « Avant même de lancer les pièces. »

Son regard était sceptique, mais surtout inquiet. « Tu plaisantes, hein ? »

Je secouai la tête. « Je suis sérieux, Kahn. »

Il ne sourit pas.

« Je savais que vous ne me croiriez pas.

— Eh bien tu as raison, je ne te crois pas.

— Alors à quoi bon tergiverser ? Nous avons perdu notre synergie, Kahn. Vous ne croyez plus en moi, et je ne... » Je m'arrêtai à temps.

« Vas-y, continue, insista-t-il avec un sourire amer. Termine. Tu ne crois plus en moi. Qu'y a-t-il ? Tu me trouves trop vieux pour réagir au quart de tour ? Ou peut-être nos démêlés avec Jane Doe m'ont-ils usé, peut-être ai-je perdu de mon ressort ? »

Je ne fis aucun commentaire, me contentant de répondre avec une froide cruauté : « C'est vous qui le dites, pas moi.

— Ouais, je l'ai dit. » Vexé, il se leva.

« C'est peut-être mieux ainsi, Aaron, repris-je. Maintenant, je n'ai plus à me soucier que de moi. Si je tombe, je ne vous entraînerai pas dans ma chute. Vous n'aurez pas à partager les blâmes et les remords.

— Et pas davantage les profits, rétorqua-t-il cyniquement.

— Exact.

— Très bien, dit-il plus calmement. Tu as enfin craché le morceau. La situation est claire. Je crois qu'il n'y a rien à ajouter.

— Ne partez pas en colère, dis-je.

— Quelle importance ? demanda-t-il en faisant volte-face. Tu as peur que je te mette des bâtons dans les roues ? » Il me foudroya du regard, puis se reprit. « Désolé, petit. Tu ne mérites pas ça. Il est inutile que tu t'inquiètes. Je me désolidariserai discrètement de *Kahn et Sun* (ça va devenir *Sun Enterprises*, pas vrai ?) pour ne pas flanquer la trouille aux actionnaires. Une cote en baisse est la pire vacherie qui puisse t'arriver.

— J'apprécie votre geste, dis-je.

— Je pense que tu ne rachèteras pas personnellement mes actions ? »

Je secouai la tête. « Impossible. Je vais devoir mettre le paquet sur APL si je veux avoir une chance de coincer mon pied dans leur porte. Mais j'aimerais savoir dans quelles mains elles vont tomber.

— Bien sûr, promit-il. Ne t'inquiète pas. Je vais même faire mieux que ça. Je les céderai lentement, par petits paquets. Je te dois bien ça.

— Merci. Kahn. »

N'ayant rien d'autre à nous dire, mais hésitant à nous séparer sur une note aussi triviale, nous sombrâmes dans un silence tendu.

« Qu'allez-vous faire maintenant ? »

Il haussa les épaules. « Qui sait ? Prendre des vacances. Lire quelques bouquins. Peut-être aller en Israël pour chercher Herschel. Il est probablement quelque part sur le Jourdain, un petit vieux ben Torah à longue barbe et rondelle en tricot sur le crâne, à la tête d'une bande d'Herschels miniatures dotés de barbichettes et de nattes tressées qui passent le plus clair de leur temps à plancher sur l'exégèse talmudique. Peut-être entrerai-je même dans un kibboutz. Tu me vois ? Le nouveau Kahn repenti grâce à la vie claire. Le retour à la nature. Bon Dieu, petit, tant que j'y suis, pourquoi n'entrerais-je pas dans un monastère taoïste pour consacrer quelques années à l'étude du *Yi king* ? » Il remarqua mon expression sceptique et amusée. « D'accord, c'est une hypothèse un peu farfelue. Mais tu m'en crois incapable ? Écoute bien, petit, me confia-t-il avec un air de conspirateur, si tu réussis à devenir dowiste, je peux devenir taoïste.

— Une fois taoïste, toujours dowiste, affirmai-je avec ambiguïté.

— Exact, répliqua-t-il. Et vice versa. »

Je ris.

« En tout cas, il y a une chose que je vais faire, dit-il rêveusement.

— Quoi donc ? »

Il passa la paume de sa main sur son crâne. « Une greffe de cheveux. » Il semblait prêt à fondre sur n'importe quelle objection.

« Une greffe de cheveux ? demandai-je d'une voix aussi neutre que possible.

— Ouais, tu sais, pour ma tête.

— Oh. » Je grimaçai un sourire.

« Qu'y a-t-il ? C'est trop artificiel pour ton goût ?

— Eh bien..., hésitai-je.

— Ne tourne pas autour du pot. Profitons de l'occasion pour nous dire les choses en face. Alors ? Je veux connaître ton avis.

— Bon, puisque vous y tenez, commençai-je, j'ai toujours pensé que vous seriez plus "distingué" si vous cessiez de cacher votre calvitie. Après tout, c'est un phénomène naturel. Je ne comprends pas pourquoi vous y attachez une telle importance. »

Il répéta ma dernière phrase en opinant du chef. « Pourquoi j'y attache une telle importance... Tu veux savoir pourquoi j'y attache "une telle importance"? Parce que c'est une partie de moi-même qui meurt, voilà pourquoi. » De son pouce, il poignarda sa poitrine. « De moi, petit. Pas de toi. De moi. C'est la mort en marche, voilà tout. Et elle entre en scène prématurément. Je ne suis pas prêt à mourir.

— Mais cela fait partie de la vie, non ? lui demandai-je calmement.

— Oh, quelle profondeur, commenta-t-il cyniquement. On croirait entendre la pythie. C'est sans doute un joyau de la sagesse taoïste, une perle rare ? Tiens — il se pencha vers mon bureau — passe-moi donc un crayon et du papier. Je veux noter cet aphorisme pour ne pas l'oublier. "La mort fait partie de la vie." Hmmm, éblouissant.

— Navré, Kahn, m'excusai-je. J'ignorais que vous étiez aussi susceptible sur le sujet.

— Susceptible ! Je ne suis pas susceptible ! Qu'est-ce qui te fait croire que je suis susceptible ? » Il ne put retenir un léger sourire.

« Je l'ai constaté, insistai-je.

— Et alors, que sommes-nous censés faire ? poursuivit-il comme si de rien n'était. Nous horizontaliser, écarter les jambes et nous laisser enculer par l'entropie ? L'illumination, c'est donc ça ? Hein ? C'est ça, pas vrai ? Reconnais-le. En dernière analyse, quand les jeux sont faits, le Tao se résume à ça — à l'entropie. Et la devise taoïste est : "Tu ne peux pas gagner, *ergo* n'essaie pas", et ensuite, "Aime ça", "Le bonheur consiste à se vautrer dans sa propre dégradation, à bénir le viol thermodynamique." » Il ricana. « Tu essaies encore de me vendre cette salade, petit ? *Toi ? Maintenant ?* Un peu de sérieux, que diable ! Je pensais qu'il y avait belle lurette que tu avais laissé tomber toutes ces fredaines. Mais non, tu y crois toujours dur comme fer, c'est une partie de toi-même, tu es encore convaincu d'agir pour un but supérieur.

— Je sais que vous en doutez, Kahn, alors laissons tomber, d'accord ?

— Tu as fichtrement raison de dire que je n'y crois pas. C'est une plaisanterie. Et de mauvais goût.

— Et les greffes de cheveux sont artificielles, répliquai-je du tac au tac.

— Artificielles ? » Il sourit de toutes ses dents. « Comme les greffes du rein, les injections d'insuline, les dentiers — il se pencha vers moi pour frotter son pouce contre le revers de mon veston — ou les costumes à huit cents dollars. Le problème avec toi, petit, c'est que tu te prends pour un empereur. » Il secoua la tête d'un air dégoûté. « Je ne voulais pas m'engueuler avec toi, Sonny. J'espère que tout ira bien. Sincèrement. »

« Merci, Kahn, grondai-je.

— Eh bien, je crois que nous avons fait le tour du problème, non ? » Il se leva, puis se dirigea brusquement vers la porte. « A la prochaine, petit, dit-il sans se retourner.

— Aaron... »

Il s'arrêta, pivota sur ses talons.

Dans un suprême effort, je lui tendis la main. « Souhaitez-moi bonne chance », l'implorai-je avec un sourire forcé.

Il s'avança vers moi et saisit ma main en me regardant droit dans les yeux. « Que dirais-tu d'un mazeltov à la place ? me lança-t-il. Ça ne mange pas de pain et ça tient mieux la route... Espèce de con. » Puis il se retourna, marcha jusqu'à la porte, l'ouvrit et sortit.

Je fus presque soulagé de le voir traverser la salle d'attente, puis sortir dans le couloir, disparaître à jamais. Je poussai un soupir, me détendis, oubliai Kahn et notre entrevue.

Ce fut seulement alors, quand j'eus pris ma décision et entamé l'exécution (de Kahn, de mon projet), seulement quand je compris la marche à suivre, qu'un sentiment semblable à la paix m'envahit, pour la première fois depuis... je ne savais même plus quand. Depuis la Chine, me sembla-t-il.

Je ressentis même une certaine légèreté de cœur, une sorte de gaieté, en me jetant à corps perdu dans le torrent écumant du Dow, totalement soumis à la gravité inexorable de mon destin.

Car j'éprouvais maintenant une impression de fatalité, comme si dans mon voyage j'avais franchi la dernière frontière qui me séparait du monde sauvage. J'avais suivi les traces de mon père, la piste jalonnée de miettes de pain qui s'enfonçait vers le cœur du Dow — le sentier vertigineux qui courait le long des berges du cours d'eau impétueux — et il n'était désormais plus question de faire demi-tour. J'avais coupé les ponts derrière moi. Suivant les courbes et les méandres du torrent, j'avais parié que mon voyage finirait par me conduire à la Source, par me ramener au calme océan du Tao. Le fleuve disparaissait maintenant derrière la base du plus gros obstacle placé sur ma route, American Power and Light. Au-delà de ce virage, déboucherait-il enfin sur la mer scintillante de mon désir, ou bien allait-il plonger, comme la cataracte occidentale, dans le vide qui marque la fin du monde ?

Je persistai à croire. Et pourtant, à dire vrai, l'ultime destination de ce torrent en crue ne m'importait plus réellement. Car je n'avais plus le choix ; j'avais pris ma décision depuis longtemps, depuis le début peut-être ; j'avais cessé de m'en inquiéter. Je devais désormais aller de l'avant sans me soucier du but, mais seulement du voyage. Le tumulte et la vitesse, le mouvement pur avaient pris possession de mon âme. J'étais grisé, hypnotisé par le paysage qui défilait sous mes yeux le long du torrent dans les contreforts montagneux qui aboutissaient au seuil invisible au-delà duquel il n'y a plus de retour possible (mais où aurais-je pu revenir en arrière ? Autant s'interroger sur l'origine de la vie), tandis qu'une gravité impérieuse m'entraînait vers le cœur mystique et matériel de l'Amérique. Oui, je pouvais seulement aller de l'avant ! Tout conspirait à accélérer ma progression. Et je la désirais follement, elle et le but qui s'annonçait. Je n'avais pas oublié la raison pour laquelle j'avais quitté la Chine — voilà si longtemps, me semblait-il ! Comment l'aurais-je pu ? Mais elle me paraissait maintenant un rêve, un précieux vestige d'une époque révolue, une relique dont on a perdu l'usage, pourtant sanctifié par le temps et la mémoire. Je pouvais seulement espérer qu'en suivant la voie tracée par le destin, j'aboutirais à mon point de départ, à la Voie. Mais c'était un simple souhait ; je laissais cette décision à la vie elle-même, à la vie réelle, la vie dans le monde tel qu'il est. Parce que je n'avais pas le choix.

Quand je me fus débarrassé de Kahn comme de l'ultime lest, ma première décision fut de convoquer les Cornes en vue de définir une stratégie d'absorption. Cette réunion s'avéra extrêmement fructueuse. Je m'initiai un peu plus aux mystères d'American Power and Light et surtout à ceux de son organisation interne. Car il y avait des mystères, du moins des bizarreries, la moindre n'étant pas qu'après la disparition de mon père le conseil d'administration avait subi une refonte radicale d'où il était sorti radicalement identique. En effet, personne n'avait succédé à Love au poste de président, une décision qui, selon certains, fut prise pour permettre à tous ses membres d'exercer le pouvoir suprême sans en être individuellement responsable, éviter ainsi la prééminence d'un seul, et par là même les tares qui avaient provoqué la chute de mon père. Il s'agissait bien sûr de pures spéculations, comme pour tout ce qui touchait aux motifs, méthodes ou manœuvres des membres du conseil, lesquels se protégeaient derrière un ensemble d'écrans de fumée, de précautions et autres dispositifs de sécurité particulièrement sophistiqués même selon les critères de Wall Street. Pour le Grand Public, l'équilibre du pouvoir résultant fut présenté comme une tentative révolutionnaire de « démocratisation » de l'entreprise, de « républicanisme fiduciaire », système censé éviter les abus de pouvoir dont Eddie Love s'était rendu coupable. « Plus jamais nous ne pâtirons de semblables errements. » Oui, le conseil d'administration avait bel et bien répudié mon père, même si la plupart de ses membres, sinon tous, lui devaient leur position, même s'ils avaient reconnu sa loi et respecté sa règle en figeant l'état de l'entreprise tel qu'il était à sa mort, exception faite de la tête décapitée. Je m'emparai aussitôt de ce fait. Le flagrant délit d'ingratitude constitué par la répudiation de mon père renforça ma résolution, y ajouta le miel de la revanche. C'était l'occasion de réhabiliter sa mémoire, me dis-je, de restaurer l'honneur de la famille. Ainsi, je marcherais dans ses pas.

En tout cas, APL était dirigé par une sorte de politburo financier qui prenait ses décisions à la majorité de ses membres, une structure quasiment sans précédent dans le monde des affaires américain. Cette junte, ainsi que l'appelait parfois la presse, comptait d'habitude onze membres. Ç'avait été une surprise considérable à Wall Street que ces hommes arrivés au pouvoir dans le sillage de mon père, pour la plupart jeunes et sans expérience des affaires, eussent réussi à se maintenir au sommet, car on les considérait comme de simples hommes de paille, des marionnettes totalement soumises à Eddie Love. Néanmoins, ils avaient survécu — non seulement survécu, mais prospéré.

Le comité exécutif d'APL, responsable de la gestion au jour le jour de l'entreprise, comptait trois hommes, tous membres du conseil d'administration. Comme pour ce dernier, ils formaient un triumvirat, chacun présidant un secteur d'activités particulier, mais responsable de ses décisions devant les deux autres. Malgré l'impartialité de ce système de contrôles et d'équilibres, les analystes de Wall Street estimaient qu'un homme, David Bateson, avait réussi à affirmer sa suprématie, sinon *de jure*, du moins *de facto*. Il était le porte-parole et l'intermédiaire d'APL dans ses rapports avec le monde. Je dressai l'oreille quand j'entendis son nom, car Bateson avait servi avec mon père sous les ordres de Chennault en Chine. Plusieurs membres du conseil avaient aussi appartenu aux Tigres Volants, mais seul Bateson avait été l'ailier de mon père. Ils avaient combattu ensemble. A mes yeux, cet homme possédait donc une aura particulière et indubitablement diabolique. Avoir vécu sur un tel pied d'égalité avec Eddie Love, avoir volé à ses côtés dans la bataille, lui devoir sa position dans le monde, pour ensuite souiller activement la mémoire de mon père, cela me parut le comble de la trahison. Selon les informations que je reçus, Bateson semblait un individu fort banal, sans charisme ni talent particulier. « Un bon joueur d'équipe », « un homme organisé », tel fut le profil que dégagèrent mes Cornes : une sorte de bluffeur bon enfant. Et sa bonhomie ne me le fit haïr que davantage.

Depuis l'époque de mon père et comme la direction, la corporation elle-même avait changé en restant quasiment statique. A un examen plus attentif, il apparut qu'APL n'était pas aussi dynamique et innovateur que dans le passé. L'état réel de la société était loin d'être aussi rose que le suggérait son bilan. L'augmentation ininterrompue des bénéfices au cours des dernières années était dû non pas tant à une productivité accrue résultant d'investissements judicieux qu'à des envolées fantaisistes de la part des comptables d'APL. Des abattements fiscaux dus à de nombreuses absorptions ou fusions d'entreprises furent transmutés en « profits » dans les creusets plus ou moins propres des comptables. Ils exercèrent une magie (noire) similaire en encourageant les fusions avec des sociétés dont le rapport prix / bénéfices était inférieur à celui d'APL, un processus qui par une obscure logique nécromantique assurait automatiquement à APL une hausse de ses bénéfices par action, même si ni elle ni la société absorbée n'augmentait sa productivité, ses investissements ou son chiffre d'affaires. La magie de la combinaison avait un effet sacramentel sur le bilan de la maison mère et créait de toutes pièces des « profits » et des « bénéfices » qui tombaient du ciel comme la manne céleste !

Les preuves réitérées de cette comptabilité « créative » ressemblaient à une pellicule de boue qui masquait une stagnation globale de l'initiative, cachée ou excusée par une lâcheté doublement coupable. Je commençai à comprendre que la corporation hésitait régulièrement à investir à long terme pour moderniser ses industries de base et préférait chercher des bénéfices faciles dans les secteurs plus récents et non productifs, tels que les loisirs et les jeux. Au lieu du capitalisme forcené que j'avais vu à l'œuvre au parquet de la Bourse, qui reconnaissait la seule loi de la jungle, la survie du plus fort, nous découvrîmes un marécage bureaucratique peuplé de créatures timorées, dont le moindre pas, le moindre geste était minutieusement programmé afin d'éviter tout risque. Pas de cow-boys ni d'hommes de main dans ces parages ; la fondrière remplaçait l'Ouest sauvage. Non seulement leur politique était timide et méprisable, sans panache ni grandeur, mais à force de jérémiades ils avaient réussi à obtenir les subsides du gouvernement, dont les décrets maintenaient les prix à un niveau artificiellement élevé dans maints secteurs d'activité. Quand les rares risques pris par APL se soldaient par un échec, le gouvernement épongeait le déficit résultant en accordant une déduction d'impôts à la société. Et de toute façon, les abattements fiscaux dont bénéficiait APL étaient si énormes qu'ils équivalaient à une aide gouvernementale. Il y avait aussi, bien sûr, les contrats passés avec l'État, surtout dans le domaine de la défense. Finalement, je trouvai ce portrait profondément déprimant.

Non que j'eusse été naïf en la matière. Kahn et Sun avaient souvent utilisé ces trucages comptables pour ses propres absorptions, mais seulement afin d'éviter des taxes trop élevées. La vigoureuse expansion qui caractérisait notre carrière contrastait violemment avec le marasme d'APL. Le pire était que la Douairière tentait de cacher sa décrépitude réelle derrière un maquillage de vieille pute. Cela dénotait un esprit tortueux, un cynisme sous-jacent qui était presque choquant. Je fus même tenté de renoncer à mon projet. Mais finalement, le malaise structurel d'APL ne fit que m'aiguillonner. Car je réfléchis qu'une fusion avec Rising Sun Enterprises (Les Entreprises du Soleil Levant, le nouveau nom de la compagnie) serait bénéfique pour les deux parties : pour nous, car elle nous fournirait de grosses réserves de capital ; et pour les actionnaires d'APL, car la politique et le style de gestion qui avaient fait la fortune de Taureau Inc. donneraient un coup de fouet à la Douairière apathique et marqueraient le début d'une période de réformes. Elle avait surtout besoin d'une transfusion de sang neuf, et c'était précisément ce que j'avais à lui offrir.

Ainsi, au-delà de mes motifs personnels, l'absorption prit des allures de croisade, un argument que les Cornes et moi comptions bien utiliser en temps voulu dans une campagne promotionnelle pour convaincre les actionnaires d'APL que la fusion aurait lieu dans leur intérêt même. Avec la direction, cependant, ce serait une autre paire de manches. Ses membres méritaient de perdre. Les dirigeants d'APL avaient laissé péricliter des investissements décidés par mon père et ses prédécesseurs dans la famille, récoltant les bénéfices de leur travail sans semer à nouveau ni labourer la terre. Des champs autrefois situés sur la frontière étaient maintenant touchés par les fléaux urbains. Aux dépens de la corporation, la direction avait confirmé cette vieille scie de Wall Street, à savoir que l'immobilisme est la façon la plus sûre de changer — la plus sûre et la pire. Oui, ils méritaient de perdre. Mais je n'étais pourtant pas naïf au point de croire que les dirigeants d'APL abdiqueraient facilement leur pouvoir, même dans l'intérêt des actionnaires. Car les actionnaires et eux avaient des intérêts divergents, et je savais que les capitalistes, même de l'espèce la plus outrageusement conservatrice (surtout ceux-là) combattraient pied à pied pour préserver leur apanage, préférant s'immoler par le feu dans leur propre maison, se livrer à un autodafé suicidaire plutôt que de se rendre à l'adversaire.

Ce fait, ajouté à la trahison de la mémoire de mon père, m'inspira une haine quasiment pathologique pour ces hommes que je n'avais jamais vus. Leurs crimes m'emplissaient d'une indignation vertueuse, me convainquaient du but moral que je croyais avoir perdu. Mi-chevalier errant, mi-pieux fils chinois à la mode confucéenne, je voyais l'Orient et l'Occident se fondre indissolublement dans ma quête et ma personne, tandis que je constituais mon propre comité de salut public et me lançais dans une croisade vengeresse essentielle à l'« honneur » des deux parties, afin d'un côté de sauver la face, et de l'autre de servir Dieu et mon pays.

Quel était donc mon plan ? Après les succès rencontrés par nos offres publiques d'achat, je décidai en accord avec les Cornes qu'il serait stupide de modifier une formule gagnante, à moins bien sûr qu'APL ne capitulât sans combattre, auquel cas nous serions contraints à la clémence — perspective que je jugeai extrêmement improbable. D'ailleurs, les holdings que possédait la Second Jersey Hi-Fi — la banque que nous avions absorbée — dans APL, ainsi que mon propre portefeuille d'actions (que je vendis à la corporation pour consolider nos comptes) nous permirent de progresser vers notre but.

L'étape suivante consistait à acquérir en secret un grand nombre d'actions d'APL par paquets relativement modestes, allant de quelques centaines à huit ou neuf mille ; pour cela, nous comptions suivre l'exemple de Kahn et les acheter par le biais de comptes numérotés pour éviter d'être identifiés, cette fois non par le BEV, mais par APL elle-même. Nous tenions absolument à conserver l'avantage de la surprise le plus longtemps possible, à éviter que la Douairière apathique ne s'ébroue et n'adopte des mesures défensives. Les Cornes calculèrent que l'achat de quatre pour cent des actions d'APL nous donnerait le poids suffisant pour annoncer l'offre publique. Mais ces quatre pour cent n'avaient rien d'une bagatelle, d'autant qu'il fallait payer les actions sur le marché en espèces sonnantes et trébuchantes. Afin d'emprunter les sommes nécessaires, Rising Sun Enterprises dut se délester d'une part importante de son capital, deuxième excellente raison pour garder le plus grand secret, car cette situation nous rendait vulnérable aux attaques extérieures. Mais dès que nous aurions coincé notre pied (ou notre sabot) dans leur porte et pourrions procéder à l'OPA, notre position serait consolidée, car, comme par le passé, nous comptions proposer des titres de dette aux actionnaires d'APL à la place d'un argent liquide que nous ne possédions pas.

Nous avions ensuite l'intention d'acquérir cinquante et un pour cent de toutes les actions d'American Power and Light en proposant *deux fois* leur valeur cotée en Bourse. L'hystérie d'achat qui nous entourait et notre rapport bénéfices / prix beaucoup plus élevé que celui d'APL devaient nous permettre d'absorber cette compagnie infiniment plus grosse que nous. Et comme si un profit de cent pour cent n'était pas un argument suffisant, nous décidâmes d'allécher les actionnaires d'APL en leur donnant une chance d'acquérir nos actions avec un rabais substantiel.

L'un dans l'autre, notre proposition était quasiment irrésistible, un véritable pactole pour les actionnaires d'American Power and Light. Notre générosité, pensions-nous, compenserait plus que largement le fait qu'ils seraient payés, non pas en liquide, mais en titres, bons et obligations. La santé florissante de Rising Sun Enterprises rendait ces titres presque aussi intéressants que du liquide — plus en fait, car leur valeur augmenterait proportionnellement à celle de notre action. L'ultime raffinement du projet, son coup de maître, était une méthode conçue par les Cornes pour nous permettre, après l'absorption, de transférer son coût aux livres de comptes d'American Power and Light. L'idée me ravit, car elle signifiait que la Douairière financerait elle-même sa propre sujétion.

Le début de notre plan se déroula avec une précision d'horloger. Pensant que nous procédions à nos achats anonymes sur le marché, j'ordonnai de commencer à transférer aussi discrètement que possible les réserves de Taureau Inc.

Nous avions acquis un peu plus de deux pour cent des actions d'APL quand survint le premier contretemps. Je n'ai jamais su s'il s'agissait d'une fuite dans notre système de sécurité ou d'infiltration de leur part, mais APL découvrit le pot-aux-roses. Le nom de Kahn fut cité par les Cornes, qui avaient conservé une vieille dent contre lui, de l'époque où ils avaient œuvré en secret contre les propres forces de Kahn regroupées sous le sigle τρ. Je préférai écarter l'hypothèse de sa trahison, car en tout état de cause il était trop tard pour y remédier. Quand nous eûmes réexaminé notre position, il apparut que cette anicroche ne constituait aucunement un obstacle insurmontable pour les phases suivantes de notre plan. Simplement, APL déciderait sans doute d'acheter ses propres actions pour se défendre, rendant ainsi l'absorption un peu plus coûteuse que prévu. Nous avions voulu acquérir quatre pour cent des actions avant d'annoncer officiellement notre offre publique d'achat. Nous fûmes tentés d'aborder aussitôt cette phase cruciale, mais après discussion nous décidâmes qu'il serait plus sage d'attendre tout en continuant d'améliorer notre position en achetant le plus d'actions possible.

Le lendemain du jour où nous découvrîmes qu'ils nous avaient découverts, l'intrigue se compliqua. Bateson me téléphona.

« Bonjour, Sun I. Ici David Bateson, d'APL.

— Oui, répondis-je d'une voix neutre, que puis-je faire pour vous ? »

Il rit. « Le problème est plutôt : qu'êtes-vous en train de *me* faire, n'est-ce pas ? » Cela semblait le réjouir au plus haut point.

« J'ignorais que je vous faisais quelque chose *personnellement*, dis-je, ravi de l'intelligence avec laquelle j'avais paré sa question sans mentir.

— A nous alors, rectifia-t-il platement d'une voix qui avait perdu son entrain. Il va de soi que je suis seulement un rouage de la machine. Oui, "à nous". Non que cela me gêne — "nous" gêne, pardon ! poursuivit-il en retrouvant son aplomb. Je tiens à ce que vous le sachiez : l'intérêt que vous semblez porter à la bonne santé de notre entreprise nous flatte. » Ce fut à son tour de rire. « Oui, nous sommes très heureux de nous gagner le respect et la confiance de la génération montante, surtout d'un individu aussi exceptionnel que vous. Nous avons suivi avec beaucoup d'intérêt votre... "ascension". Nous vous avons toujours soutenu moralement, exactement comme l'un des nôtres. Car enfin, étant donné votre parenté, vous faites quasiment partie des nôtres. Comme si nos entreprises étaient des sœurs consanguines. Quel dommage, si un nuage venait assombrir ce ciel serein. Pourquoi ne pas venir faire un tour ici, au sommet. Non que je veuille jouer les personnages hautains, mais le fait est que nous sommes tout en haut de l'immeuble. Ça ne vous coûtera même pas le prix d'un taxi. Nous pourrions discuter tranquillement autour d'un déjeuner, voir si nous pouvons régler à l'amiable nos petits différends. Qu'en dites-vous ? Demain par exemple ?

— Très bien, M. Bateson.

— David, David, je vous en prie ! A demain donc ! »

Je raccrochai et appelai ma secrétaire. « Je n'ai rien de prévu pour le déjeuner de demain, n'est-ce pas ?

— Une réunion avec les administrateurs du Metropolitan Museum à propos de la collection chinoise, me dit-elle sur un ton de reproche.

— Zut ! Eh bien il faudra de nouveau annuler. Convoquez-les pour la semaine prochaine. »

Je raccrochai, ravi de ma performance. Ils s'étaient sentis contraints de bouger les premiers. Cela signifiait qu'ils avaient peur. Ils s'étaient montrés conciliants. Cela prouvait qu'ils ne savaient comment réagir. Oui, j'étais très content. Je n'avais rien révélé, rien reconnu. C'était la politique idéale en la circonstance. Laisser venir. Moins j'en disais, mieux cela valait, moins je risquais de commettre d'erreur. Je décidai de suivre la même ligne de conduite lors de la réunion du lendemain.

17

Malgré ma nervosité, je ressentis un plaisir imprévu en entrant dans les bureaux d'American Power and Light. J'eus l'impression de pénétrer dans une autre époque. Contrairement à nos bureaux récemment décorés, où tout jusqu'au moindre détail répondait aux exigences d'une esthétique minimaliste, je découvris ici un éclectisme chaleureux, une sorte de bariolage feutré, une profusion de meubles hétéroclites. Mais c'étaient presque tous des pièces de collection. Le bureau de la secrétaire particulière de Bateson était d'une beauté lourde, sculpté dans un acajou du Honduras que le temps avait couvert d'une patine presque noire. Je remarquai la galerie finement ciselée qui courait autour du plateau, les pieds décorés de griffes et de boules. Son poids et sa matière exprimaient le luxe et l'élégance d'une époque plus opulente. Sur la plaque de verre supérieure étaient posés une lampe Tiffany et un précieux vase chinois qui contenait un somptueux bouquet de chrysanthèmes jaune pâle semblables à des soleils explosés. Tandis que je les regardais en attendant qu'on m'annonçât, une humeur rêveuse s'empara de moi, presque aussi intense que ce que j'avais ressenti à Sands Point — la conviction que le passé vivait à nouveau.

« Vous aimez les fleurs ? »

Debout sur le seuil de son bureau, Bateson souriait en m'observant attentivement. Son apparence me surprit. Malgré ses cheveux argentés et clairsemés, il paraissait plus jeune que je ne me l'étais imaginé. Cela me fit songer que mon père, eût-il été vivant, aurait encore été un homme relativement jeune, âgé d'une cinquantaine d'années. Bateson avait des yeux bleus, brillants et froids où se lisait une gaieté dépourvue de toute aménité. Les Cornes m'avaient appris qu'il portait un sonotone à une oreille, un souvenir de guerre. De temps à autre, son index l'enfonçait dans son pavillon, comme pour améliorer la qualité de l'écoute. Mais l'appareil le démangeait peut-être.

Il avança vers moi et, avant même de me serrer la main, sectionna nettement la tige d'une fleur avec un canif. « Auriez-vous une épingle, Anne ? » demanda-t-il à sa secrétaire en plissant le front comme il soulevait le revers de mon veston pour passer la tige à travers la boutonnière. Anne ouvrit un tiroir, puis lui tendit une épingle, qu'il piqua dans la fleur et le tissu avant de lisser par deux fois mon revers. « Là, dit-il en souriant. C'est très joli. » Il se tourna vers la jeune femme. « Vous ne trouvez pas ? »

Elle me sourit aussi.

« Les fleurs sont merveilleuses, n'est-ce pas ? Elles ajoutent vraiment une touche unique. » Il me fit alors poliment passer dans son bureau, puis se retourna vers sa secrétaire. « Nous ne voulons pas être dérangés. » Il ferma la porte.

« Asseyez-vous, asseyez-vous, me dit-il en m'indiquant un fauteuil. Oui, nous avons toujours des fleurs ici. C'est une tradition qui, je crois, remonte à Arthur Love. Et que votre père a maintenue. Mais il était assez partial à leur égard, savez-vous ? A notre modeste façon, nous essayons de conserver les apparences. Ici, nous sommes très soucieux des traditions familiales. » Il s'assit et s'adossa à son fauteuil. « Vous retrouverez ici l'esprit de maints défunts, des Love, de votre père surtout. Ils ont fait de ce lieu ce qu'il est. C'est indéniable. En un sens, je suis — *nous sommes*, excusez-moi — seulement leurs exécuteurs testamentaires, les mandataires qui poursuivent leur œuvre. »

A première vue, Bateson était plus charmant que je ne l'avais cru, d'un charme presque désarmant. Si j'avais ignoré la mauvaise foi patente de ses protestations de loyauté et de fidélité à la tradition, il m'aurait sans doute plu. Je commençai même à me demander si l'homme capable de mentir à ce point ne tenait pas du monstre. Désireux d'établir mon autorité avant qu'il ne me privât de ma position d'adversaire et donc d'égal, je choisis d'abandonner la stratégie prévue et de le défier d'entrée de jeu.

« Je ne comprends pas comment vous osez mentionner le nom de mon père », l'accusai-je d'une voix amère.

Il parut surpris. « Mais, Sun I, votre père et moi étions très liés. Nous étions ensemble avec Chennault en Chine. Vous l'ignoriez ? J'étais...

— Oui, oui, l'interrompis-je, je sais. Vous étiez son ailier. C'est cela qui est inexcusable. Je ne vois pas comment vous avez le culot d'en parler après la façon dont vous l'avez trahi. »

Il sembla sincèrement soucieux. « Comment l'ai-je trahi ?

— "Républicanisme fiduciaire", répliquai-je d'un ton cinglant. Vous lui avez fait porter le chapeau, vous l'avez spolié, vous avez même manigancé une campagne de presse contre lui.

— C'est là ce qui vous gêne ? » Il s'adossa de nouveau à son fauteuil. « Ne soyez pas naïf, Sun I. Quel choix avions-nous ? La corporation dut se dissocier du scandale. Ce fut une décision professionnelle, un point c'est tout. Vous avez vous-même parlé d'une campagne de presse. Votre père aurait fait la même chose. Je sais qu'il n'aurait pas agi autrement. Pourtant, dans l'intimité de nos bureaux, nous restons fidèles à sa mémoire, ainsi que vous l'avez sans doute constaté. Regardez autour de vous. Rien n'a changé depuis son époque. Les fleurs ne sont qu'un exemple. Il y en a maints autres. Vous allez vous en rendre compte. » Il se leva. « Ainsi, dans la salle de réunion où les autres directeurs nous attendent. » Il m'aida poliment à me lever de mon fauteuil. « Saviez-vous que quand votre père fut... enfin, quand nous le perdîmes, en signe de respect le conseil d'administration décida de laisser définitivement vide son fauteuil situé au centre des autres ? » Il hocha solennellement la tête, comme désireux d'éclaircir à tout prix ce malentendu. « C'est une des raisons pour lesquelles nous n'avons plus jamais nommé de président. Qui aurait pu occuper sa place, ou son fauteuil ? » demanda-t-il avec une grimace navrée.

Bien que silencieux, je ne fus pas impressionné par cette démonstration de loyauté qui me parut hypocrite. Je ne savais pas au juste à quoi jouait Bateson. Il semblait sincèrement désolé, au point que je l'eusse volontiers plaint si je n'avais su qu'il simulait. C'était un excellent acteur ; mais il croyait peut-être à son laïus, auquel cas il méritait réellement ma pitié.

Quand nous entrâmes, les dix autres membres du conseil d'administration, tous assis à l'extrémité opposée d'une table de conférence ovale, massive et couverte d'une plaque de marbre noir veiné, se levèrent pour nous accueillir. Puis ce furent les poignées de main rituelles et les sourires de circonstance, certains sévères, d'autres sincères ou appréciateurs, presque sympathiques, sans oublier les inévitables protestations de familiarité : « Non, non, appelez-moi... » suivi du prénom adéquat. L'absence de toute animosité me surprit. Mais ils avaient bien sûr tout intérêt à cacher leurs véritables sentiments.

Bateson n'avait pas menti à propos du fauteuil. Pour être exact, deux sièges étaient vacants — l'un, supputai-je, étant le sien. Les membres du conseil se rassirent, cinq à gauche des fauteuils vides, cinq à droite. La table était immense ; assis, les directeurs auraient à peine pu se toucher la main. Bateson m'indiqua ma place — j'étais seul devant eux —, puis se mit à marcher autour de la table.

« Messieurs, j'étais justement en train de parler à Sun I de notre quasi-vénération envers son père. » Une idée lui vint et il sourit. « On pourrait presque dire que nous sommes des modèles de piété filiale confucéenne. » Il s'assit autour de la table, puis se pencha pour tapoter le dos du fauteuil central avec une confiance pateline. Mais brusquement, une expression de surprise horrifiée apparut sur ses traits ; suivant son regard, je découvris, qui fumait dans le cendrier posé devant le « fauteuil vénéré », hors d'atteinte de Bateson ou de l'homme assis de l'autre côté de la « place du mort », une cigarette allumée qui se terminait par deux bons centimètres de cendre grise.

Je ricanai avec un sincère plaisir. « En effet, on dirait qu'il est définitivement vide depuis au moins cinq minutes. » Je lui adressai un regard cynique. « Vous savez, je ne suis pas sûr de ce que vous désirez prouver avec votre petit numéro de charme, mais vous ne devriez pas tenir compte de moi. Vous ne vous attendez tout de même pas à ce que, ému par votre piété, je renonce à mes intentions ? Mettons un terme à cette mascarade. Je vous promets que je ne serai pas le moins du monde choqué si vous tenez à vous asseoir dans le "fauteuil mystique du pouvoir". »

Les membres du conseil échangèrent de sombres regards.

« Mais non, vous vous méprenez, dit Bateson. Quand je suis allé vous chercher, je venais de cette pièce. J'ai tout simplement oublié ma cigarette ici. Regardez, il n'y a pas d'autre cendrier sur la table. » D'un large geste du bras, il m'invita à vérifier ses dires. Il tira une bouffée en grimaçant, toussa, puis, rougissant copieusement, écrasa la cigarette dans le cendrier et se hâta de s'asseoir.

Tout cela me parut extraordinairement bizarre. J'aurais juré que Bateson n'avait jamais fumé une cigarette de sa vie. J'observai l'arabesque blanc grisâtre de la fumée qui montait encore de la cigarette, et la même impression d'irréalité me submergea que devant les chrysanthèmes du bureau de la secrétaire. La pièce elle-même renforçait mon sentiment d'étrangeté, voire de légère ivresse. Le confort élégant et luxueux qui m'avait séduit dans les deux pièces que j'avais traversées manquait absolument ici. En fait, cette salle ressemblait davantage à Rising Sun Enterprises, à son austérité lucide, implacable. Extrêmement nue, elle contenait seulement cette table massive, installée en diagonale. Les deux murs latéraux étaient couverts de miroirs du sol jusqu'au plafond, tout comme le mur dans lequel la porte se découpait, l'ensemble produisant un effet déroutant de reflets qui se multipliaient à l'infini. Du coup, je me sentis mal à l'aise, exposé, exhibé comme dans une vitrine, d'autant que je savais que les directeurs pouvaient voir mon dos, avantage dont j'étais moi-même privé : car le mur du fond, qui se dressait à deux ou trois mètres derrière leurs sièges, était constitué d'une grande tenture en velours vert foncé. Je trouvai l'ensemble plutôt décevant, aussi anonyme et sans âme que la réception d'un motel.

« Je vois que vous examinez la salle, dit Bateson, qui avait retrouvé son assurance. Encore une idée de votre père. »

Je le regardai avec une légère surprise.

Il acquiesça. « Il s'est occupé de sa conception. Mais en ce moment, elle n'apparaît pas sous son meilleur jour. » Il passa la main sous la table et j'entendis un déclic. Les rideaux s'écartèrent automatiquement à partir du centre du mur. Une lueur aveuglante se rua aussitôt entre les pans du tissu, se refléta sur le marbre, rebondit indéfiniment sur les miroirs, tourbillonna vertigineusement dans la pièce avec l'ivresse démoniaque d'un djinn soudain libéré d'une bouteille hermétiquement close. Entre les deux voiles qui semblaient se recroqueviller sur eux-mêmes, apparut le panorama le plus somptueux des gratte-ciel de New York et de l'East River que j'aie jamais vu. Je compris brusquement l'intention de mon père, l'astuce éblouissante du dispositif. Le résultat était affolant, stupéfiant. Tout avait été impitoyablement sacrifié à ce spectacle. La nudité des miroirs me donna l'impression de me tenir au bord d'un abîme, de regarder dans le vide, ou plutôt de flotter dedans. C'était vertigineux et grandiose. Nous étions si haut que le sommet des piliers du pont de Brooklyn apparaissait à mi-distance sous nos yeux. Le fleuve ressemblait à une sombre veine de lapis-lazuli pas plus large que mon bras et mouchetée des ombres grises des nuages. Un remorqueur qui avançait à contre-courant me fit songer à l'arête pointue d'un ciseau de sculpteur qui progresse en laissant derrière elle un sillage de copeaux blancs. A l'extrémité méridionale de Roosevelt Island, une conduite d'eau, qui semblait avoir éclaté, lançait vers le ciel une fantastique gerbe de gouttelettes haute de plusieurs dizaines de mètres, qui retombaient en un brillant rideau cristallin où le soleil hivernal dessinait des arcs-en-ciel. Et loin au sud, dans l'angle inférieur du cadre, la Statue de la Liberté nous tournait le dos, cet ange exterminateur dont une main serrait le rôle des élus du Jugement dernier, et l'autre la torche de la désolation. Je me rappelai l'instant où j'avais ouvert les yeux sur la Grande Roue et découvert l'orbe majestueux de l'horizon terrestre. Mais maintenant mon exaltation s'était affranchie de toute peur. Je contemplais l'objet de mon désir. Je tenais presque la récompense de mes ambitions.

« Qu'en pensez-vous ? demanda Bateson.
— Je ne m'étais pas attendu à cela. »

Il rit. « Vous aviez prévu de la fumée de cigare et des manches de chemise relevées ? » Il secoua la tête. « Non, Sun I, l'air est vif au sommet du monde. Comme dans les Alpes, c'est un air raréfié, immortel. » Il s'exprimait avec une passion tranquille, un savoir légèrement désabusé. « Votre père aimait beaucoup cette salle de réunion. Il avait l'impression de voler, disait-il. »

Je ris en comprenant la justesse de l'image. Mais pour moi, le plus surprenant fut que le soleil ne blessait plus mes yeux. Je souris intérieurement à la pensée de l'ophtalmologue. Oui, il se passait quelque chose, mais ce n'était pas une détérioration. Au contraire, ma vue s'améliorait. En face de moi, le visage de Bateson semblait auréolé par la couronne solaire, et alors que je l'observais avec émerveillement, sa peau se mit à luire, à devenir translucide. Soudain, comme dans une radiographie, son crâne apparut à travers la chair, entouré d'un fin réseau de veines et d'artères frémissantes qui irriguaient la masse sombre du cerveau. Mon ravissement se mua en horreur. J'eus un haut-le-cœur, je sentis le picotement de millions de pores qui se dilataient. Mais cette vision ne dura qu'un instant ; je cillai et elle disparut, me laissant désorienté, vaguement nauséeux. Avec une grimace, je portai la main à mon front pour protéger mes yeux.

« Trop brillant pour vous ? demanda Bateson. Attendez, je vais refermer la tenture. »

Alors que le moteur bourdonnait en ramenant les deux pans de tissu l'un vers l'autre, l'un des membres du conseil assis à l'extrémité opposée de la table entama la conférence. « Nous avons suivi vos progrès avec beaucoup d'admiration », dit-il.

Je souris poliment en regardant le panorama se réduire peu à peu à mesure que les pans le rognaient de part et d'autre comme l'obturateur à rideau d'un appareil de photo ou la pupille d'un œil qui se contracte.

« Et y avons même modestement contribué », renchérit un autre.

Les bords des tentures se touchèrent, frémirent ; l'une se coinça dans un tuyau de chauffage et laissa filtrer un rai de lumière qui papillonna dans la salle.

« Pas de doléances à formuler, j'espère ? » persiflai-je. Je m'obligeai à quitter des yeux l'interstice lumineux pour regarder mon interlocuteur. « Nous essayons de plaire au public.

— Le public ! protesta un autre directeur d'une voix enjouée. Sincèrement, Sun I, j'espère que nous sommes davantage à vos yeux. Surtout compte tenu des liens familiaux.

— C'est justement là où le bât blesse, Ted, intervint Bateson. Sun I s'obstine à nous considérer comme des outsiders. Contre toute évidence, il persiste à croire que notre bonne volonté est feinte. »

Des murmures de protestation s'élevèrent autour de la table.

« Non, rectifia l'un pour m'endoctriner, nous espérons jouer un rôle paternel... — il remarqua ma grimace — bon, disons avunculaire, oui, un rôle d'oncle vis-à-vis de vous.

— Ce qui veut dire, explicita Bateson, que nous avions espéré un règlement à l'amiable. »

Le rai de lumière issu de la fente des rideaux dansait dans mes yeux. Je me penchai pour regarder Bateson. « Rien ne me ferait plus plaisir, dis-je en souriant avec une joie perverse. Mes termes sont simples. »

Des commentaires approbateurs et soulagés parcoururent la table.

« Et que sont-ils ? demanda Bateson avec un optimisme plus nuancé que les autres.

— Je veux le contrôle exécutif.

— Quoi ! éructa l'un.

— Impossible ! » s'écria un autre.

La table se mit à bourdonner tandis que, penchés l'un vers l'autre, ils conféraient à voix basse. Parfaitement froid, ravi de la sensation que je venais de créer, je fixais Bateson dont le visage exprimait pour la première fois la gravité. Il était blême, presque gris.

« Réfléchissez à ce que cela impliquerait, dit l'un en essayant de me raisonner. Comme vous le constatez sans doute, la corporation n'a quasiment pas évolué depuis l'époque de votre père.

— C'est bien là le problème, répliquai-je aussitôt. Elle a stagné. Elle a besoin de nouvelles initiatives. Cette corporation est un marécage.

— Un marécage ! s'indigna-t-il. American Power and Light est une entité historique, jeune homme, me rabroua-t-il, et, au-delà, un monument vivant à la mémoire de votre père. Voulez-vous détruire tout cela ?

— Je ne veux pas le détruire, répondis-je, je veux seulement injecter un sang neuf dans la corporation.

— En l'absorbant dans Rising Sun Enterprises, je présume ? » poursuivit-il d'une voix mordante.

J'acquiesçai. « Exactement.

— Mais vous ne comprenez donc pas que cela reviendrait précisément à la détruire ? dit un autre. La corporation en tant que telle cesserait d'exister. American Power and Light une subdivision de Rising Sun Enterprises ! » Il rit avec mépris. « Absurde !

— Impensable ! s'écria un autre.

— Aberrant ! railla un troisième.

— C'est précisément ce que j'ai tenté de lui expliquer, intervint Bateson. Absorber APL reviendrait non seulement à violenter une vénérable institution publique, et ainsi semer la discorde sur le marché, mais ce serait une sorte de parricide fiduciaire. »

Ce sophisme me fit sourire. « Parricide », répétai-je. Pardonnez ma lenteur d'esprit, mais comment peut-on tuer un homme qui est déjà mort ? »

Bateson plissa les yeux. « Vous pouvez assassiner sa mémoire, Sun I.

— Sa mémoire ! Après l'excellent travail que vous avez réalisé en ce domaine, il ne reste plus grand-chose à assassiner. »

Bateson s'adossa dans son fauteuil et se renfrogna. « Je vous ai déjà expliqué que notre reniement est dû à des raisons purement professionnelles. En privé, nous continuons à vénérer Eddie Love. Si vous ne pouvez pas voir ça... » Il leva les mains vers le plafond. « Non, Sun I, la mémoire de votre père survit parmi nous, et, plus importante encore que sa mémoire, son œuvre. Car cette corporation est son œuvre. Si vous la démantelez, vous détruirez son esprit. Voilà ce que j'appelle un parricide. »

Nullement convaincu, je haussai les épaules. « Je vois les choses différemment. Je considère cette absorption comme une réhabilitation de sa mémoire, une restauration de l'honneur familial. »

Bateson secoua la tête, riva sur moi un regard sévère. « Vous vous trompez dangereusement sur ce point ; si vous persistez dans votre erreur, je redoute qu'elle ne nous oppose irrévocablement. Auquel cas je crains pour vous comme pour nous. Nous n'oublions pas votre puissance, mais ne sous-estimez pas la nôtre. Je ne vous cacherai pas que nous nous sentons menacés par votre démonstration de force. La raideur de votre attitude m'inquiète, personnellement, et je crois pouvoir parler au nom de tous les directeurs. Vous nous mettez en position difficile. Nous ne sommes plus aussi agiles qu'autrefois, ou que vous aujourd'hui. Mais cette souplesse perdue, nous la compensons largement par notre puissance. Le poids de cette corporation, si nous choisissons, si nous sommes contraints de le jeter dans la balance, est énorme. Si vous tentez de nous forcer la main, je ne doute pas que nous puissions organiser une campagne formidable. Nous avons déjà mis des gens au travail. Nous trouverons les biais adéquats, car ils existent toujours ; toute cuirasse a son défaut.

— Quels biais ? demandai-je avec mépris. Moi aussi, j'ai mis des gens au travail, et puis je ne crois pas que vous ayez une telle liberté de manœuvre.

— Allez, se moqua l'homme assis au bout de la table, vous ne pensez pas sérieusement que nous allons vous révéler notre stratégie, n'est-ce pas ?

— Pas davantage que nous nous attendons à ce que vous divulguiez la vôtre, ajouta un autre.

— La surprise est l'argument clef, déclara Bateson. C'était le point fort de votre père, la surprise. »

Le rayon de soleil issu de la fente des rideaux caressait mon visage et mes yeux comme une plume, m'agaçait avec une constance sadique, me faisait loucher et me tortiller sur mon fauteuil.

« Je vous dirai néanmoins une chose, continua Bateson. Nous savons que vous avez l'intention de payer nos actionnaires avec des titres convertibles, du moins en partie. » Il scruta mon visage à la recherche d'un acquiescement ou d'une dénégation.

Mais je grimaçais toujours en essayant d'éviter le rai de lumière.

Il poursuivit, menaçant. « Vous comprenez bien sûr qu'une telle mesure serait injuste envers vos propres actionnaires de Rising Sun Enterprises

— Je crois qu'ils ne seraient pas particulièrement enchantés de l'apprendre, suggéra un autre.

— Je n'ai pas l'intention de leur cacher cette information, contre-attaquai-je sèchement.

— Certes, mais je suppose que vous ne vous en vanterez pas, fit remarquer Bateson.

— Vous voulez dire... », fis-je en comprenant son stratagème.

Il sourit sans répondre.

« Quoi ? Une lettre ouverte envoyée à mes actionnaires ? me moquai-je. Quelle crédibilité croyez-vous qu'ils accorderont à vos allégations ?

— Ce sera la vérité », dit-il.

Je fronçai les sourcils. « Eh bien, je pense que les avantages à long terme dont bénéficieront les actionnaires de Rising Sun Enterprises l'emporteront sur ce désagrément temporaire. »

Il haussa les épaules d'un air suffisant. « Il y a aussi le petit problème de la récente incursion de Taureau Mutuel dans APL.

— Tout cela a été rendu public, répondis-je. Où est le problème ? »

Il retroussa les lèvres en une moue de fausse courtoisie. « Oh, nous avons trouvé cela très intéressant, voilà tout.

— Nous sommes loin de nous en plaindre, intervint quelqu'un.

— Ravis de constater que vous prisez à ce point nos actions, renchérit un autre.

— Simplement, jusqu'ici, vous avez préféré acheter des valeurs plus volatiles, plus risquées, avec des perspectives de croissance prometteuses. A l'inverse, APL est une valeur stable, dont l'intérêt tient aux seuls dividendes. Comment vont réagir vos actionnaires si leurs avoirs sont liés à ce que vous-même qualifiez de "marécage capitaliste", soit à American Power and Light ? Comment cette décision va-t-elle modifier le comportement de votre valeur ? »

J'avais cette fois une réponse toute prête. « Avez-vous songé que, quand l'absorption sera chose faite, ...

— Si absorption il y a, rectifia quelqu'un.

— *Quand* elle sera chose faite, répétai-je avec emphase, APL jouira d'une hausse... — je faillis donner un chiffre, mais décidai de réserver cette surprise pour plus tard — ... considérable. Et instantanée. Je ne suis pas en mesure de vous donner une évaluation exacte, mais je crois pouvoir apaiser vos inquiétudes ; cela constituera ce que nous appelons dans le métier "une bonification sensible". »

Ils échangèrent des regards soucieux.

« Cela me paraît assez clair, observai-je caustiquement. Les ressources de Taureau Mutuel et de Taureau Inc. nous fourniront le poids nécessaire à l'absorption ; puis les deux Taureaux enregistreront une hausse notable de leurs actions, simultanée à la hausse d'APL dont ils auront financé l'absorption. »

Plus personne ne souriait, sauf moi. Je ris. « Vous constatez donc, messieurs, que malgré vos menaces de "biais à trouver", je ne vois pas quelle parade vous pourriez opposer à ma stratégie. Et puis, nous n'avons même pas évoqué ce qui devrait être votre première préoccupation : l'immense bénéfice que vos actionnaires tireront de cette opération. Remarquez que j'ai bien dit *"devrait* être", car je devine qu'en l'occurrence et de votre point de vue, c'est le cadet de vos soucis.

— Absolument pas, riposta Bateson. Vos jugements de valeur ne concernent que vous. De plus, nous sommes certainement mieux placés que vous pour connaître les intérêts de nos actionnaires. Après tout, nous avons consacré notre vie à cette tâche.

— Vous préférez peut-être le croire, rétorquai-je, mais je ne suis pas de cet avis. Et je vais vous dire autre chose, poursuivis-je avec passion, une hausse instantanée de cent pour cent de la valeur de leur investissement servira indiscutablement les intérêts de vos actionnaires. Si vous pensez pouvoir les en dissuader, je vous prie d'essayer.

— Cent pour cent ! » lâcha l'un des directeurs.

Bateson me regarda sombrement.

« Absolument, dis-je en me tournant vers l'homme qui avait parlé. Nous avons l'intention de proposer le double de la cote actuelle de votre action sur le marché.

— Payable en argent de Monopoly, dit un autre avec mépris.

— En vulgaires déclarations de dette ! railla un troisième.

— Autant dire en papier tue-mouches ! »

Je souris, refusant de m'abaisser à répondre à des attaques aussi grossières. « Appelez ça comme vous voudez, messieurs. Si vous avez la moindre raison de douter de la santé financière de *Rising Sun Enterprises* ou de la valeur de nos titres, je serai ravi de les entendre.

— Etes-vous vraiment certain de vos réserves ? » demanda un homme avec mépris.

Bateson lui adressa un regard de reproche.

« Tout à fait, répondis-je sur un ton dégagé. C'est faible, messieurs, vraiment faible. Vous bluffez. »

Bateson avança brusquement au bord de son fauteuil. « Très bien, dit-il. Mettons un terme à ces escarmouches avant que la situation ne s'envenime. Désirons-nous vraiment une effusion de sang ? N'y a-t-il pas une autre façon de procéder ?

— Votre capitulation sans conditions, exigeai-je, emporté par ma passion.

— Impertinent ! s'écria un directeur outragé. Croyez-vous qu'un poisson d'agrément comme le cyprin doré puisse avaler le Léviathan ? Nous vous écraserons !

— Assez ! intima Bateson en haussant la voix. Laissez-moi finir, pour l'amour du ciel ! » Il se tourna vers moi. « Voyons, Sun I, vous savez aussi bien que moi que c'est hors de question. Nous pouvons cependant envisager votre proposition comme un point de départ à la discussion. Cela vous semble-t-il équitable ? »

Je lui adressai une moue hautaine.

« Ne me répondez pas tout de suite. Réfléchissez-y. Le déjeuner est prêt. Laissons les esprits se calmer et la température redescendre de quelques degrés. »

A ce moment précis, des maîtres d'hôtel entrèrent pour nous installer autour de la table, presque aussitôt suivis par d'autres qui poussaient des tables roulantes chargées de plats somptueux.

« Nous aimons parfois déjeuner ici, expliqua Bateson, surtout dans les grandes occasions. Et à nos yeux, contrairement à ce que vous semblez penser, il s'agit d'une grande occasion. » Il m'adressa un sourire engageant. « Pour fêter notre rencontre, poursuivit-il, nous avons préparé quelque chose d'un peu spécial en votre honneur, Sun I. J'espère que cela vous plaira. Mais auparavant, prenez donc un peu de pain. » Il me passa la corbeille. Quand je soulevai la serviette qui la couvrait, un nuage de vapeur parfumée s'en dégagea. « Ces petits pains croustillants cuits à la française sortent tout droit du four, dit-il. Pierre est un merveilleux boulanger. Un peu de vin ? »

Il se leva pour prendre la bouteille des mains du sommelier, puis me servit lui-même en me présentant l'étiquette. « Château lafite-rothschild, quarante-deux, annonça-t-il. Le préféré de votre père. Au-delà de l'excellence du cru, je crois qu'Eddie Love avait un faible pour ce vin qui lui rappelait l'époque de son séjour en Chine. Un jour, il en acheta plusieurs caisses lors d'une vente aux enchères. Cette bouteille est l'une des dernières. » Bateson soupira en se souvenant. « Eddie l'appelait "Le Vite Roussi" en imitant l'outrecuidance d'un nouveau riche du Texas. Ce jeu de mots devint l'une de nos plaisanteries préférées. » Il rit doucement en hochant la tête. « Il en réclamait toujours pour les grandes occasions. Ce fut le vin que nous bûmes au déjeuner des directeurs quand nous accédâmes au pouvoir. Je l'ai souvent goûté depuis, mais il ne cesse de me surprendre. » Ses yeux s'embrumèrent sous le coup de la passion du connaisseur ; j'y vis une lueur que je connaissais bien pour l'avoir souvent remarquée dans le regard de Lo quand il discutait les subtilités du vin. « Tout cela le rend doublement approprié à notre rencontre aujourd'hui, à notre "réunion", si vous préférez. » Il leva son verre entre nous. « Kan pei, dit-il en m'adressant un regard de connivence.

— Santé », répondis-je sombrement en faisant tinter mon verre contre le sien.

Jamais je n'avais goûté de vin comparable. Il avait la complexité et l'épaisseur d'une personnalité humaine, d'un être extraordinaire, peut-être un peu excentrique, qui à peine entré dans une pièce focalise sur lui l'attention générale, laisse les autres invités pantois et bouche bée, non par un calcul prémédité, mais par le seul effet d'une vitalité peu commune. Je fus ivre après une seule gorgée, ou plutôt je vécus un état modifié de la conscience, modifié par la concentration qu'exigeait le vin pour se laisser apprécier. J'eus envie de discourir sur sa subtilité à la manière de Lo, mais quand je remarquai l'expression unanime de contemplation absorbée, satisfaite et sobre sur les visages de mes hôtes, je réussis à me retenir.

Le plat principal du repas était une côte de bœuf saignante au jus. Le spectacle de la viande rouge baignant dans son sang et la graisse fondue qui brillait avec des irisations nacrées, me mit légèrement mal à l'aise. Mais je ne pus détacher mon regard de sa beauté ineffable, obscène.

A mesure que le repas s'acheminait vers sa conclusion, l'impression rêveuse d'irréalité que j'avais ressentie depuis le début, s'approfondit. Après m'avoir « caressé dans dans le sens du poil », Bateson tapota ses lèvres avec sa serviette et se prépara à reprendre la discussion, tandis que les garçons desservaient. « Maintenant que nous nous sentons mieux j'aimerais vous faire une proposition, Sun I, commença-t-il. Nous en avons décidé avant cette réunion ; nous pensons qu'il s'agit pour vous d'un compromis acceptable. Si vous doutez encore de nos bons offices, j'espère que ceci vous convaincra. Bon. Vous possédez déjà un pourcentage d'APL, peut-être un et demi.

— Plus de deux pour cent », rectifiai-je gaiement.

Il haussa les sourcils. Certains directeurs échangèrent des regards perplexes.

« Très bien, disons deux, concéda-t-il. Nous en avons parlé, et nous considérons que cela vous donne droit à un siège au conseil d'administration. Mais il ne s'agit pas simplement d'une question de droit : nous sommes *très désireux* de vous avoir parmi nous. C'est d'ailleurs notre intention depuis longtemps. Certains de vos arguments sont sans doute fondés. Nous sommes devenus un peu suffisants, nous avons pris de l'embonpoint. Une intraveineuse nous sera peut-être profitable. Mais nous avons encore quelques tours dans notre sac, que vous serez certainement intéressé d'apprendre. Une initiation approfondie aux mystères de la corporation est une expérience passionnante, Sun I. » Il m'adressa un large sourire, puis se rembrunit brusquement. « Mais vous devrez abandonner toute prétention au contrôle exécutif. » Il fit claquer ses mains sur le marbre de la table. « Alors, Sun I, qu'en dites-vous ? Un siège au conseil — vous ne nierez pas que c'est là une proposition généreuse.

— Je suppose que c'est *votre* point de départ à la discussion », le narguai-je.

Son visage devint gris. « Non, Sun I, répondit-il d'une voix calme, c'est notre première et notre dernière proposition. Soit vous l'acceptez, soit vous vous préparez à subir les conséquences de votre refus.

— Un ultimatum, autrement dit », rétorquai-je.

Il haussa les épaules. « Appelez ça comme vous voudrez. »

J'hésitai. Ce n'était pas une offre négligeable, loin de là, et elle avait l'avantage d'éviter toute effusion de sang. Le pinceau lumineux frémissait entre les rideaux, dansait dans mes yeux. Je ne réfléchis pas longtemps.

« Eh bien, messieurs, dis-je en repoussant mon fauteuil, je pense que cela clôt notre discussion. Vous me pardonnerez si je dois m'éclipser aussi vite, mais vous connaissez les habitudes des prédateurs de la haute finance, n'est-ce pas ? » Je leur adressai à tous un sourire radieux. « Bonne journée. »

Je quittai la réunion en proie au triomphe, à la joie, à la fièvre, sans oublier la légère ivresse du vin. « Ce sont des imposteurs, des imposteurs, me répétais-je sans cesse, en gloussant avec un plaisir malicieux. Ils n'ont même pas un atout dans leur jeu, rien. "Nous trouverons les biais adéquats." » Je répétais cette phrase avec mépris. C'était du bluff. « Imposteurs ! » Ce mot me rassurait comme un talisman.

Pourtant un ensemble de choses m'avait vaguement perturbé. Pas tant leurs paroles ; sur ce chapitre, la réunion s'était à peu près déroulée conformément à *mon* plan. J'avais atteint mes objectifs. Non, c'était l'accumulation des détails troublants qui me tracassaient : les fleurs, le repas, l'incident de la cigarette, la salle de conférence elle-même, sa beauté presque surréelle, l'impression d'apesanteur que j'avais ressentie comme si toute gravitation eût soudain été annulée, cette sensation de « vol », et puis la disposition des fauteuils ! Il y avait aussi leurs déclarations de loyauté stupides et réitérées, tellement spécieuses, et puis ce rayon de soleil agaçant qui perçait entre les rideaux. Que signifiait tout cela ? Mon imagination me jouait-elle un tour ? Ou avait-on soigneusement mis en scène tous ces détails ? Essayaient-ils de miner ma confiance et ma détermination par un subtil travail de sape psychologique, par des manœuvres d'intimidation subliminale ? Le fait est que cela eut sur moi un effet diabolique. Mais qu'y avait-il de tangible dans tout cela ? Rien. Strictement rien. Peut-être avaient-ils drogué le vin ?

« Imposteurs ! » conclus-je avec une joyeuse assurance que je ne ressentais pas vraiment. Je décidai de passer à l'attaque, d'annoncer officiellement et le plus tôt possible l'offre publique d'achat. Ils m'avaient soumis un ultimatum ? Ma riposte leur apprendrait les bonnes manières ! Je n'étais pas homme à me laisser intimider. On ne badinait pas avec moi !

Malheureusement, nous étions vendredi. Les Cornes me convainquirent de ne pas céder à la précipitation, alors que tout Wall Street attendait impatiemment la clôture de la séance et que maints habitués avaient déjà entamé leur pèlerinage du week-end vers le nord de l'État de New York ou les Hamptons ; il valait mieux attendre et jeter le quartier de viande premier choix de l'OPA dans l'arène rugissante des lions affamés du lundi matin, quand leurs regards brilleraient de convoitise. J'obtempérai à contrecœur, redoutant la perspective de deux jours d'inactivité forcée à remâcher mon obsession.

18

Cette nuit-là, je dormis à peine. Je ne cessai de me retourner et de réveiller Li, qui me suggéra finalement de prendre une douche chaude ou de faire le tour du pâté de maisons. Je suivis ses deux conseils, sans résultat. Ensuite, je me préparai du thé et m'assis à la table de la cuisine, mains serrées autour de ma tasse, pour tramer, comploter, supputer. Le lendemain matin, longtemps après que la lumière eut commencé d'envahir les pièces, Li apparut en robe de chambre sur le seuil de la cuisine, où elle s'arrêta pour bâiller en lançant ses poings fermés vers le plafond. Son visage encore endormi exprimait un bonheur paisible.

« Bonjour », me dit-elle d'une voix pâteuse.

Je rivai sur elle un regard menaçant.

« Humm, fit-elle en cambrant ses reins pour se gratter le haut du dos, on dirait que tu t'es levé du pied gauche.

— Exactement », répondis-je.

Elle m'observa attentivement. « Qu'y a-t-il ? Tu m'as empêchée de dormir toute la nuit. »

J'eus un sourire sarcastique. « On ne le dirait pas. »

Elle fit claquer sa langue avec agacement. « Tu aurais peut-être voulu que je reste éveillée pour te tenir la main ? » Elle posa la bouilloire sur la cuisinière. « C'est ton histoire avec APL, n'est-ce pas ?

— Je les ai rencontrés hier pour la première fois », dis-je en sautant sur l'occasion.

« Tu as besoin de te changer les idées, de te distraire », me conseilla-t-elle, refusant la perche que je lui tendais.

Mon enthousiasme tomba, je rentrai dans ma coquille.

« Je devrais travailler aujourd'hui, poursuivit-elle, plus pour elle que pour moi, comme si elle hésitait, mais je pourrais reporter ça... » Elle pivota vers moi. « Que dirais-tu de partir en expédition ?

— En expédition ? »

Elle sourit. « Mais oui, comme au bon vieux temps, une enquête ethnologique sur le terrain. Sauf que cette fois, c'est toi qui me guideras.

— Où ça ? demandai-je sans passion.

— Nous pourrions louer une voiture et aller à Long Island, suggéra-t-elle. Pour que tu me montres la maison. »

Je sursautai. « Sands Point ? »

Elle acquiesça, ravie de son idée.

« D'accord, dis-je en dissimulant mon enthousiasme. Pourquoi pas ? »

Sur la route, je profitai de la captivité de mon public pour me soulager du poids de mes soucis. J'avais bien sûr informé Li de mes projets, mais nous n'avions jamais discuté à fond l'absorption d'APL. Un flot de paroles se déversait maintenant par ma bouche. Je décrivis la réunion, m'attardai sur les détails, fouillai son visage en quête d'une quelconque réaction, peu désireux de l'interroger directement. Elle ne semblait pas particulièrement intriguée ; son indifférence me porta à me demander une fois de plus si je n'avais pas tout imaginé. Un détail qui me semblait mineur retint cependant son attention.

Je citai avec mépris la remarque de Bateson à propos du « parricide fiduciaire », ajoutant que je l'avais habilement esquivée en la qualifiant de sophisme. J'attendis un signe d'approbation de la part de Li. Il ne vint pas.

« Alors ? demandai-je avec irritation. Es-tu d'accord qu'il s'agissait d'un sophisme ? »

Elle observa mon visage, puis détourna les yeux. « Je crois que c'était assez astucieux de sa part, affirma-t-elle platement.

— Que veux-tu dire ? » Je faillis enfoncer la pédale des freins au milieu de l'autoroute pour qu'elle dît le fond de sa pensée, et déchaîner sur elle toute la violence de ma frustration.

Elle haussa les épaules. « Il n'y a pas de quoi s'exciter. C'est une réaction parfaitement normale.

— Quoi donc, assassiner son propre père ?

— Sa mémoire, rectifia-t-elle calmement. C'est bien ce qu'il a dit, non ?

— J'aimerais savoir où tu veux en venir », rétorquai-je avec agacement.

Elle se tourna vers moi. Elle ne souriait pas vraiment, mais une lueur amusée brillait dans son regard. « Tu te souviens d'Œdipe ? »

Sa question me frappa de plein fouet. « Mais Œdipe n'a pas consciemment voulu...

— C'est rarement conscient, me coupa-t-elle. Il n'y a pas de quoi en avoir honte, Sun I. La haine entre pères et fils dure depuis plusieurs millénaires. Au moins depuis Zeus et Cronos, Jupiter et Saturne si tu préfères. Rappelle-toi Saturne. Dans la rage de l'ébriété, il tenta de dévorer ses enfants, mais Jupiter, protégé par sa mère Rhéa, échappa au massacre. Rhéa trompa son époux en lui présentant une pierre à la place du fils qu'il voulait dévorer. Il devait être rudement soûl, car il ne remarqua pas la substitution. Un épisode vraiment macabre, surtout pour Jupiter. A mon avis, c'est une des images les plus glaçantes de la mythologie grecque, qui n'est pourtant pas avare d'horreurs en tous genres. »

Elle développa à sa manière habituelle. « J'imagine le garçon recroquevillé dans l'ombre, la sueur froide qui dégouline sur son visage ; il ose à peine respirer, ses mains moites serrent le manche lisse de la faux, et il écoute les hurlements de bête fauve de son père dans la pièce voisine. Suivent les cris de ses frères et sœurs, l'affreux bruit mat de leurs crânes qui éclatent contre le mur, puis les craquements de leurs os entre les dents du monstre. Jupiter attend que la fureur de son père se calme et qu'il s'endorme pour lui ouvrir le ventre d'un grand coup de faux, arracher l'organe qui symbolise son pouvoir, et le déposer. » Elle me regarda pour voir ma réaction.

« Plutôt horrible, n'est-ce pas, mais aussi vieux que le péché, et tout aussi naturel. Le père en veut au fils parce que celui-ci menace son pouvoir ; le fils en veut au père parce que le père l'entrave dans son désir de domination et d'expression. D'habitude, le combat s'engage autour de la figure de la mère. Tu trouveras tout ça dans Freud. Si je me souviens bien, il affirme même quelque part que notre quête inconsciente d'immortalité, due à notre peur de la mort, implique nécessairement que nous souhaitions la mort du père qui, comme dernier maillon de la chaîne de la mortalité, en vient à représenter la chaîne elle-même, la mortalité — un memento mori qui rappelle au fils son destin inéluctable, si bien qu'il a pour seul choix de tuer son père symboliquement afin d'oblitérer l'ensemble du cycle de la mort et trouver ainsi l'immortalité en devenant *son propre père*, se régénérant lui-même sans fin. C'est assez fascinant quand on y pense. » Le plaisir qu'elle avait pris à son exposé faisait rosir ses joues.

« Peut-être, dis-je avec un peu d'acrimonie. Mais quel rapport avec moi ? Je ne déteste pas mon père. Je n'ai aucune raison de le haïr.

— Allez, Sun I, me reprit-elle, tous les enfants ont des griefs envers leurs parents. Mais *toi* — ton cas est classique. Par où veux-tu que je commence ? Bâtardise, abandon, exil dans un monastère... » Elle les compta sur ses doigts, pouce, index, majeur, touchant chacun du pouce de son autre main.

« Il n'a rien désiré de tout cela, protestai-je ingénument. Ce sont les circonstances. »

Elle sourit sans plaisir, son regard fixé droit devant elle. « C'est toujours comme ça. »

Je décidai de regarder moi aussi le paysage, pour lui cacher les larmes qui me montaient aux yeux. « Peut-être a-t-il voulu m'épargner », hasardai-je.

Elle m'observa avec étonnement. « T'épargner quoi ? »

Je lui retournai un sourire malicieux. « Tout cela. »

Elle éclata d'un rire cassant, aussi sec et violent qu'une gifle. « Voilà une chose charmante à dire à sa fiancée. »

Je ne répondis pas.

« Comprends-moi bien, Sun I, continua-t-elle. Je ne juge ni lui ni toi.

— Tu ne juges jamais, observai-je amèrement.

— A ta place, je réagirais probablement comme toi, dit-elle en ignorant ma remarque. Tout être normal réagirait ainsi.

— J'aime mon père », dis-je en regardant les lignes blanches de l'autoroute se rejoindre au loin, puis l'autoroute elle-même disparaître vers un horizon que ni Li ni moi ne connaîtrions jamais, que je ne désirais même pas connaître.

« Bien sûr, répondit-elle. Mais toute médaille a son envers, que tu préfères sans doute ignorer.

— Pourquoi prétends-tu connaître mes motifs inconscients ? lui demandai-je avec une brusque véhémence. Si tu les trouves si méprisables, pourquoi veux-tu te marier avec moi ?

— Je ne pense pas que tes motifs soient mauvais, protesta-t-elle avec un calme olympien. Je n'ai jamais dit ça. Je les trouve normaux et sains.

— En d'autres termes, "ambivalents", la parodiai-je cyniquement.

— Oui, si tu veux. Ambivalents. »

Nous restâmes quelques instants silencieux, puis je lui demandai enfin d'une voix tendue : « Pourquoi plaides-tu toujours la cause de l'adversaire ? » C'était presque une supplication.

La tendresse adoucit ses traits. « Ce n'est pas mon intention, dit-elle doucement. Je ne prends pas parti.

— Exactement, poursuivis-je avec rancœur, tu ne prends jamais parti. Tu n'es jamais ni pour l'un ni pour l'autre, tu t'installes tranquillement au milieu et tu envoies promener le reste. Que désires-tu de moi, Li ? mon argent ?

— Tu es injuste, dit-elle froidement, mais ses yeux jetaient des éclairs. Si tu n'as pas le courage de tes opinions, si tu ne crois pas assez en toi, ne t'attends pas à ce que je te serve de prothèse.

— Très bien, concédai-je. D'accord. Mais est-ce trop te demander que de considérer parfois mon point de vue, de m'aider à croire en moi ? Pourquoi vois-tu toujours le pire de moi-même ?

— Je ne savais pas que c'était le cas, répondit-elle, étonnée. Je suis désolée que tu aies cette impression. Je n'ai jamais voulu t'humilier ni te vexer. Quand tu me demandes mon avis, je te le donne. Je t'ai dit la vérité. » Elle m'adressa un sourire amer. « C'est peut-être là le problème. »

Je continuai de regarder devant moi.

« Si tu as ce sentiment, dit-elle enfin, très calmement, nous commettons peut-être une erreur.

— Peut-être », reconnus-je, prêt à jeter l'enfant avec l'eau du bain.

Après quelques minutes d'un silence déchirant, je n'y tins plus. « Li, suppliai-je en cherchant anxieusement son regard, je suis désolé. Oublie tout ce que j'ai dit. Ce bras de fer avec APL me fait perdre la tête. Je ne suis plus moi-même aujourd'hui. »

Elle posa les yeux sur moi, me regarda sans étonnement, sans reproche ni approbation ; puis elle tourna la tête pour fixer le paysage qui défilait, ses mains résolument croisées sur son ventre.

Notre dispute pesait sur nous comme une lourde chape quand nous atteignîmes la maison et commençâmes notre exploration. Toute la joie que j'avais anticipée pour notre expédition — je jouais cette fois le rôle du cicerone qu'elle avait adopté avec moi le premier soir, dans le West Side — s'était envolée. Dans ces conditions, faire le guide me parut vide de sens, ridicule. Comme pour refléter mon humeur maussade, le ciel était d'un gris métallique et plombé, et l'après-midi hivernal, sombre, froid et sans vent. Quand elle sortit de la voiture, Li enfila un chandail à capuche et m'en tendit un autre en silence.

Personne ne répondit aux coups que nous frappâmes à la porte. Chiang Po n'était nulle part visible, ni dans la maison, ni dans le jardin. Je considérai cela comme une chance, car je n'aurais su quoi lui dire après la conclusion désastreuse de notre première entrevue, quand il m'avait interdit de remettre les pieds dans cette maison, sinon peut-être en tant qu'acquéreur potentiel — mon argent seul justifiant alors ma présence. Je doutais pourtant que cet argument l'eût impressionné ; et moi-même, la main posée sur le heurtoir de bronze, je n'en étais pas complètement convaincu.

« C'est assez mal entretenu, commenta Li.

— Oui, c'est le moins qu'on puisse dire », renchéris-je d'une voix lugubre.

Comme personne ne vint nous ouvrir, nous nous engageâmes sur la longue pelouse qui aboutissait à la mer et à l'étroite bande de la plage. En un contraste frappant avec sa splendeur estivale, le gazon était à l'abandon, brun, flétri. Des tiges mortes de pissenlits montaient la garde çà et là, semblables aux filaments d'ampoules électriques explosées. J'escaladai le mur de pierre gris-noir et, une fois assis dessus, tendis la main à Li.

Une sorte d'état second s'empara de moi pendant que nous nous promenions sur la plage, une étrange extase visuelle qui s'attachait aux objets triviaux que je trouvais sur mon chemin. La mer était basse, d'énormes rochers sombres émergeaient de l'eau, grotesques concrétions striées de sable, auxquelles des grappes de moules s'accrochaient sous le niveau de la marée haute signalé par un trait noir et gras. Autour des rochers, des mollusques pointaient leurs doigts morts vers le soleil, quittaient leur univers de vase pour se balancer lentement en une prière fantomatique et décousue, sans espoir ni passion. La puanteur douçâtre, âcre et forte de la putréfaction océanique planait sur toute la plage dans l'air figé. La mer était d'huile ; on eût dit un miroir argenté dont le bord se relevait près du rivage en courtes vaguelettes qui claquaient contre la pierre comme un coup de fouet trop bruyant dans le silence et l'immobilité environnants. Dans les flaques résiduelles d'eau verdâtre couverte des diaprures nacrées de l'essence, des fragments roses et argentés de coquillages et de quartz scintillaient avec l'éclat de joyaux. La plage était jonchée de détritus rejetés par la mer : bois flottant lisse et pétrifié dans ses gracieuses contorsions ; morceaux de fils de pêche brisés ; coquilles de buccins incurvées, effilées comme de minuscules vertèbres humaines, qui contenaient d'autres coquillages parfaitement formés, à peine plus gros qu'une tête d'épingle.

Je m'arrêtai pour ramasser la poche à œufs d'une raie, semblable à la bourse de soie noire que mon père m'avait donnée, et, pris d'une humeur fantasque, je me demandai si elle n'abritait pas une clef majeure capable d'ouvrir les mystères de cette plage. Car il y avait bel et bien un mystère à déchiffrer, des formules cryptiques écrites dans les ordures, de minces joncs creux comme le chaume après la moisson, mais plus petits, articulés comme du bambou, brisés et noircis par la décomposition. Ils jaillissaient du sol selon des configurations étranges, un ordre qui semblait exclure le hasard. Ils évoquaient les courbes adoptées par la limaille de fer, qui révèlent la présence d'une énergie invisible et insoupçonnée à travers les lignes de force magnétique du jusant. D'où venaient-ils ? Il n'y avait dans les environs ni roseaux ni marais. A quelle loi obéissait leur disposition ? Que signifiaient-ils ? Je l'ignorais. Je sentais simplement leur présence. Ils ressemblaient aux baguettes d'achillée, aux os de l'oracle, aux traits forts ou faibles, six et neuf, choisir un œuf, sept et huit, ouvrir l'huître. Mais pour y trouver quoi ? Une perle ou un monstre ? Il y avait seulement cette phrase que mon esprit répétait inlassablement : « formules cryptiques écrites dans les ordures ». Au bout de quelques minutes, je remarquai que Li partageait la même concentration, la même contemplation. « Comment te sens-tu ? » lui demandai-je, choisissant une autre formule codée qui renvoyait à une autre question, plus profonde.

Elle comprit. Avec un sourire mélancolique, elle regarda l'horizon vide. « Cela me fait penser à Stephen Dedalus sur la plage de Dublin, dit-elle rêveusement : "inéluctable modalité du visible, signatures de toutes choses qu'ici je dois lire". » Puis elle me regarda avec une légère moue dubitative.

« Qu'est-ce que ça veut dire ?

— "Inéluctable", expliqua-t-elle en se détournant, contre quoi il est impossible de lutter, inévitable. "Modalité"... » Elle serra les lèvres. « C'est plus difficile. Il s'agit peut-être d'une autre façon de dire "faculté", "capacité". Auquel cas cela signifie que nous ne pouvons échapper à ce que nous voyons, au sens de la vue. Mais "signatures de toutes choses qu'ici je dois lire" — signature, lecture — cela suggère quelque chose de plus complexe. En philosophie, un "mode" est la façon dont une substance invisible se manifeste concrètement. »

Ses derniers mots suscitèrent une association. « Un signe extérieur et visible d'une grâce spirituelle invisible, récitai-je.

— Oui, c'est ça, comme un sacrement. La vision ressemble à un sacrement que nous célébrons afin de participer au mystère plus profond et toujours invisible. Voilà pourquoi cette phrase de Joyce a quelque chose de pathétique : le sacrement que nous célébrons est aussi une peine que nous purgeons. Nous sommes condamnés à lire continuellement le monde, comme un code fascinant mais peut-être indéchiffrable, pour tenter de rejoindre l'origine elle-même par-delà tous les codes, ce lieu où le sens est synonyme d'être. La vie : voilà notre peine ; chercher le signataire à travers la signature, lire sans cesse...

— Mais qui est ce signataire ? » demandai-je.

Elle haussa les épaules. « Dieu, je suppose. Il est le tueur tapi dans notre roman d'horreur, dit-elle, puis elle sourit en passant à la parodie, il sème des indices à chaque page de nos vies, que nous devons tourner pour le trouver, lui. » Elle rit doucement. « Oui, jusqu'au dernier paragraphe de la dernière page, nous devons lire, lire sans cesse.

— Formules cryptiques écrites dans les ordures », songeai-je, répétant mon mantra personnel qui s'accordait étrangement aux réflexions de Li. Synchronicité. Connexion mystique.

Un peu plus loin, nous découvrîmes une sterne morte, et je m'agenouillai près de l'oiseau. Plusieurs mouches, que l'arrière-saison énervait, s'étaient posées sur la charogne. Avançant brusquement de quelques pas, s'arrêtant soudain, repartant dans une autre direction, elles ressemblaient aux victimes traumatisées d'une catastrophe qui errent sans but dans le paysage de leur désolation. A l'inverse, l'oiseau semblait maître de lui, comme apaisé par le deuil. A travers les plumes ébouriffées et clairsemées de son cou, on apercevait la peau noire comme du goudron. Ses ailes étaient étendues sur le sable en une maladroite parodie du vol alors même que la lente décomposition bactériologique liquéfiait sa chair. Sa pose avait l'élégance d'une calligraphie ; figé dans son vol, il abordait les sombres mystères de la corruption, retournait à la poussière — voilà ce qu'annonçait son hiéroglyphe. Son visage ne trahissait rien, seulement peut-être une sorte de paix souriante, même si les mouches s'installaient au fond de ses orbites pour sucer sa viande.

Un coup de tonnerre vrilla soudain le silence. Le paysage trembla.

« Qu'est-ce que c'est ? m'écriai-je, le cœur battant.

— Un avion qui a franchi le mur du son », répondit Li sans se troubler. Elle quitta sa posture agenouillée dans le sable, comme une vache qui se relève lourdement ; elle fit tomber le sable de son pantalon, puis mit la capuche de son chandail. Il faisait de plus en plus froid. « Regarde, tu vois les traînées blanches ? » Mettant sa main en visière, elle tendit l'autre vers le ciel. Je remarquai alors son ongle effilé, élégant et sinistre, aussi pointu et tranchant qu'une lame. Peut-être fut-ce le hurlement de l'avion, mais quand elle allongea son index, je crus entendre le crissement strident du morceau de craie sur le tableau noir, mais amplifié dix mille fois, comme si elle gravait une rune sur une ardoise vaste comme le ciel — « signatures de toutes choses qu'ici je dois lire ». Je pensai au Pays d'Oz, au message que la Sorcière Maléfique traçait en lettres cursives sur le ciel d'émeraude.

Il se passait quelque chose. Le ciel se mit à fondre comme de la glace, à tournoyer et se transformer. D'étranges choses gelées au cœur du glacier en émergèrent, se métamorphosèrent douloureusement. Dans un autre cadran du ciel, j'aperçus ce qui ressemblait à un nuage grouillant d'abeilles. Je crus d'abord à une tornade, mais vis bientôt plus clairement de quoi il s'agissait. « Regarde », dis-je en tendant le bras à mon tour.

La main toujours en visière, Li leva les yeux.

— Là ! » Je dépliai plusieurs fois mon bras avec véhémence.

Elle plissa les yeux pour mieux voir.

« Tu ne les vois donc pas ? »

Alors elle se tourna vers moi, me regarda bizarrement. « Je ne vois rien. » Sa voix s'était calmée.

Je levai de nouveau les yeux pour m'assurer que je ne me trompais pas.

« Que vois-tu au juste ?

— Les animalcules ! hurlai-je en lançant plusieurs fois mon index vers eux. Là, je ne rêve pas ! »

Leur essaim commença de monter comme une montgolfière ; sombre et opalescent, il se dirigea vers le soleil, où il se dispersa pour former des rayons autour du disque solaire, comme une couronne d'épines ou les traits qui s'échappaient du cercle noir du soleil inca. J'entendis de nouveau le coup de tonnerre du mur du son. Les angles du détroit frémirent comme de la gélatine. Un visage apparut dans le soleil ; les ondes de chaleur faisaient trembler ses traits. Ce visage ressemblait à celui du Grand Oz, à la fois tête énorme et terrifiante boule de feu. Ses lèvres remuaient, parlaient, mais je ne distinguais pas leurs paroles. Je retirai mes lunettes de soleil pour mieux voir.

« Que fais-tu ? demanda Li.

— Je lis, dis-je sans la regarder, en souriant pour moi-même, je lis sur les lèvres.

— Arrête ! m'ordonna-t-elle sèchement en luttant contre moi pour couvrir mes yeux. Tu vas t'aveugler ! »

Je maintins fermement ses poignets en continuant de fixer le soleil. « Il ne peut pas me blesser, lui dis-je pour la rassurer, comme on calme un enfant incapable de comprendre. Le soleil aveugle seulement ceux qui voient déjà, mais il rend la vue aux aveugles.

— Ce n'est pas d'un ophtalmologue que tu as besoin, dit-elle en se débattant violemment pour se dégager, tu as besoin d'un psy ! »

Déconcentré, je la foudroyai du regard en la repoussant loin de moi. Elle trébucha et tomba à genoux dans le sable. Quand je relevai les yeux, le visage avait disparu. Il y avait seulement le ciel vide.

Je me tournai vers elle. « Salope ! m'écriai-je, furieux. A cause de toi, je l'ai perdu. »

Elle se tenait à quatre pattes, le visage tourné vers le sable. Lentement, elle leva la tête : ce fut une gueule de renarde qui apparut sous la capuche pointue du chandail, un long museau aux petites dents blanches effilées, des yeux où brillait une malice féroce. Dans sa gueule elle tenait l'oiseau mort, qu'elle secoua une fois ou deux d'un brusque mouvement de tête, avec une hilarité silencieuse. Je sentis une porte s'ouvrir en moi et un vent glacé souffler à une distance insondable. L'ombre noire de l'aile de la folie fila sur le sol devant moi, puis m'enveloppa dans son obscurité avant d'envahir la terre entière.

Je ne me souviens pas d'être rentré chez moi. Je me réveillai au lit avec une migraine atroce et une sensation de brûlure aux yeux. La douche coulait dans la salle de bain. Je ressentis un besoin urgent de me rappeler ce qu'Oz avait dit à Dorothy en se matérialisant devant elle comme une énorme tête sur le trône de marbre vert. Quelle condition avait-il donc posée à son retour au Kansas ? Je ne me le rappelais plus, bien que ce fût essentiel. Je pris donc le livre sur la table de nuit et l'ouvris pour chercher le passage ; mais aussitôt les lettres s'animèrent sur la page, elles se mirent à grouiller, proliférer et se tordre comme des vers noirs — ou des animalcules. Je refermai violemment le livre avant qu'elles ne se répandent sur les draps. Des heures ou quelques instants passèrent. L'eau coulait toujours quand je m'endormis.

Dans mon rêve j'ouvrais les yeux dans une pénombre verte et veloutée où l'on ne discernait rien. Un pinceau de lumière incandescente apparut brusquement par une fente verticale. Puis ce fut une lueur éblouissante, qui contrairement à mon attente ne provenait pas du soleil, mais d'un projecteur à pinceau focalisé, et les ténèbres qui se déchiraient étaient un rideau qui s'ouvrait sur une scène, la salle de réunion d'American Power and Light. A l'extrémité opposée de la table en marbre noir, onze personnages étaient assis autour d'un fauteuil vide, cinq d'un côté et six de l'autre, tandis que moi, le douzième homme, étais installé en face d'eux, dans une position qui me permettait de participer au drame tout en l'observant avec le public. Un soleil jaune satiné aux rayons grossièrement peints pendait des cintres au-dessus d'une vaste toile qui représentait Manhattan, et encadrait ma tête comme une auréole un peu terne.

Les personnages présents sur scène semblaient attendre quelque chose. De temps à autre, l'un d'eux se grattait le crâne avec un geste mécanique, saccadé, puis tournait brusquement la tête à droite et à gauche, ou bien Bateson se levait maladroitement pour arranger les chrysanthèmes dans le vase, tenter de leur donner du volume comme une femme avec sa coiffure, réussissant seulement à les flétrir davantage. Ce manège se poursuivit pendant un temps démesuré. J'entendais les spectateurs bâiller ou se trémousser sur leurs sièges. Soudain, un hurlement à glacer le sang, comme celui d'un loup, sortit des coulisses. Mes cheveux se dressèrent sur ma nuque. Ensuite, le hurlement monta d'une octave et se mua en aboiement, le yap-yap d'un roquet furieux. Un terrier à poil dur bondit sur scène côté cour, puis freina en s'arc-boutant sur ses pattes comme dans un dessin animé en pantelant joyeusement face au public dont il attendit les applaudissements. « Toto ! » s'écrièrent les spectateurs. La vedette canine se dressa sur ses pattes arrière, décrivit un cercle dans cette posture, puis sauta sur la table de marbre noir. Mais Toto n'avait pas une taille normale ; il était aussi gros que les hommes assis, presque aussi vaste que la table elle-même, moyennant quoi ses gestes étaient un peu pataud. Au cours de son numéro, il renversa le vase, lequel explosa en mille fragments et répandit un liquide rouge et visqueux sur le marbre noir. Bateson bondit sur ses pieds en lançant ses bras en l'air, dansa une courte gigue éplorée qui attira l'attention de Toto ; le molosse inclina bizarrement la tête, puis décapita le directeur et allongea le cou pour gober cette grosse bouchée de chair et d'os. Le public ravi trépigna. Toto baissa alors la tête et entreprit de laper joyeusement cet étrange liquide en remuant la queue, chacun de ses robustes coups de langue assenant une gifle mouillée aux membres du conseil d'administration d'American Power and Light, dont les crânes s'entrechoquaient avec un bruit mat de boules de bowling. Le public rugit. Nullement échaudé par sa précédente mésaventure, le cadavre mutilé de Bateson fit magiquement apparaître une miche de pain français croustillant « tout droit sortie du four » qui lui permit d'absorber le fluide rouge, et que le directeur me tendit ensuite. Je la façonnai en une bouteille verte qui portait l'étiquette « Château Huile de Serpent ». Au lieu de l'appellation du cru, je lus « Vie Eternelle ».

Intrigué par ce détail, je remarquai à peine l'étrange métamorphose de Toto. A mesure qu'il lapait, son corps grossissait par endroits et s'affinait à d'autres. Il enflait et rétrécissait en même temps. J'entendis un roulement de tambour, un coup de cymbales, et quand je levai les yeux, Toto avait disparu, remplacé par le chien de Tsin. Son œil de verre scintillait d'un éclat aussi froid que Sirius dans un ciel d'hiver. Le public pétrifié de stupeur retint son souffle quand l'énorme bête se dressa sur ses pattes arrière pour accomplir son numéro avec encore moins d'élégance que Toto. A la fin de sa pénible révolution, l'animal avait de nouveau changé, comme façonné par un tour de magie : je découvris une renarde souriante qui portait des vêtements féminins.

Alors les cymbales résonnèrent de nouveau, et une fois encore ce fut Toto.

Les soupirs du public s'échappèrent comme des gaz. Épuisés par le suspense mais heureux, les spectateurs applaudirent puis se mirent à hurler de joie quand le petit Toto, toujours debout sur ses pattes arrière, arpenta le devant de la scène en saluant de droite et de gauche. Il bondit brusquement pour le clou de son numéro, un terrifiant double saut périlleux ! Oh non ! Les spectateurs fermèrent les yeux, l'air siffla entre leurs dents. Mais si ! La toile du décor se désintégra dans un grand bruit de tissu déchiré, et Toto disparut dans le soleil !

Malades d'angoisse, nous attendîmes. Rien ne se passait. Il était parti ! Un petit garçon se mit à geindre au fond de la salle. Alors, comme dans un film projeté à l'envers, le roquet réapparut par le trou du décor, jappant de plaisir, en équilibre sur le fil invisible de son trapèze volant ! Le public se déchaîna ! Les mères mirent deux doigts dans leur bouche pour siffler, les pères fondirent en larmes. Les enfants sautèrent sur leurs fauteuils jusqu'à ce que les ressorts percent le capitonnage avec un long chuintement extatique de guimbarde en folie, et que le royaume du Ciel parût à portée de main.

Alors une petite main se leva, et l'un après l'autre les spectateurs se turent. Derrière la toile du décor déchirée, parmi les fils et les poulies, essayant surtout de passer inaperçu, se trouvait un homme ! Un géant ! Et nous comprîmes soudain que nous venions de voir des marionnettes, sauf Toto, que toute la scène, le rideau et les accessoires faisaient partie d'un théâtre de marionnettes ! Moi aussi, j'étais une poupée de chiffons ! Le géant rassembla ses affaires, démonta l'échafaudage qui avait soutenu notre monde magique, et tous les acteurs, moi inclus, s'effondrèrent comme Guignol et Gendarme, visages contre la table, bustes affaissés entre les jambes raides suspendues en l'air. Les chuchotements se muèrent en horions. Le marionnettiste sourit d'un air gêné comme pour s'excuser, toucha le rebord de son haut-de-forme en soie noire tout en rangeant ses accessoires dans son sac à malices qui débordait comme un volcan et laissait derrière lui une piste de menus objets, telles des miettes de pain qui ne menaient nulle part.

Maintenant d'humeur belliqueuse, les spectateurs le conspuèrent copieusement, lancèrent des avions en papier sur la scène en criant : « Imposteur ! Imposteur ! » au point que j'eus presque pitié de lui. Mais j'aurais dû me douter que cela aussi faisait partie de son numéro. Car après un roulement de tambour, le géant toucha son haut-de-forme et se métamorphosa en un tigre aux yeux verts émeraude et aux pupilles verticales, dont la queue noire et orange sortait par la fente de son frac. Quand il rugit, la terre entière trembla avec un gémissement strident, comme une scie électrique ou un P-40 en piqué, moteur lancé à fond. Les femmes s'évanouirent, leurs enfants les calmèrent. Les hommes se ruèrent vers les sorties. Les cymbales retentirent, il toucha de nouveau son chapeau et se métamorphosa en ours, en panda géant au visage blême semblable à un crâne, les cernes anthracite de l'onanisme entourant ses yeux couleur de miel. Agitant son haut-de-forme, il entama une gigue frénétique, rejoignit les coulisses à fond de train, revint aussitôt, puis répéta ce manège plusieurs fois sous les applaudissements déchaînés du public.

Quand les spectateurs furent presque aphones à force de hurler leur joie, il revint saluer une dernière fois, et quand il se redressa, je découvris bien sûr mon père, Eddie Love, qui portait ses lunettes d'aviateur aux verres en forme de larmes vert foncé et souriait de son mystérieux sourire, que soudain je compris. Dans un éclair de lumière aveuglante, il disparut derrière un nuage de fumée multicolore, laissant dans l'air un parfum immanquable de fleurs sauvages mêlées de crottin, la puanteur de la putréfaction sur la plage, et une vague odeur de soufre. Les éclairagistes éteignirent les lumières, la salle s'obscurcit, je m'éveillai en proie à des sueurs froides.

L'eau coulait toujours dans la salle de bain. Je tendis machinalement la main pour prendre une cigarette. Mes doigts tremblaient, mais mon esprit était clair — pour la première fois depuis des mois, me sembla-t-il — plus clair qu'il ne l'avait jamais été. Maintenant je comprenais. Ce rêve fit tout exploser. La clef tourna dans la serrure, la clef majeure ; la porte s'ouvrit en grinçant ; à l'intérieur, tout était en place : le parachute vide, le mystérieux acheteur de Mme Chin, les détails incongrus de la conférence avec APL — la cigarette, les fleurs — tout était une farce ! Il était toujours là ! Il vivait ! Il avait été là tout du long, comme le marionnettiste qui tirait les ficelles derrière le décor, comme le faux Oz, le Grand Imposteur qui manipulait les touches de son splendide stéréopticon, sa lanterne magique. Le Hun dans le Soleil de Wall Street, vraiment ! Tout cela avait été une monstrueuse plaisanterie dont je faisais les frais depuis le début, depuis avant le début, spermatozoïde souriant, fonçant tête baissée vers l'ovule, soûl comme un cosaque, en proie à la *rigor mortis* d'une hilarité incontinente.

Oui, j'avais été le dindon de sa farce, même quand je l'adorais comme Dieu, même quand je renonçais à mon propre salut pour le suivre dans son mystère putride. Oui, j'étais perdu. Bel et bien, définitivement perdu. Un enfer sans fin. Il m'avait mené par le bout du nez dans sa « *descensus averno* ». Qui aurait pu dire pourquoi ? Le fils suit les traces de son père, non pas pour sortir de la forêt enchantée, mais pour s'y enfoncer toujours davantage, toucher de plus près le délicieux mystère. Et quel était ce mystère ? Le péché, lecteur, le péché, le compromis et l'apostasie, le sacrifice de l'innocence, des principes et de l'espoir — toutes choses qui flétrissent notre âme dans le monde tel qu'il est. Mais je l'avais suivi de mon plein gré, ramassant pieusement chaque miette derrière lui, chaque fragment, chaque lambeau sanglant, me jetant dessus pour les dévorer avant de me lécher les doigts ! Ah ! Quel crétin j'avais été ! Comme je me méprisais ! Comme je *le* méprisais ! Oui, *lui*. Li avait raison, je le comprenais maintenant. Ma haine, endiguée par mes réticences, déconnectée par un circuit que je reniais maintenant violemment, explosa dans ma conscience avec le rugissement des eaux de retenue du barrage de Grand Coulee pulvérisant le béton et menaçant d'engloutir le monde sous un nouveau déluge. Oui, la haine bouillonnait en moi.

Pourtant il y avait aussi de la joie dans mon cœur, car il était vivant, il se cachait toujours derrière le miroir ! Ces miroirs dans la salle de réunion ; était-ce des glaces sans tain ? Bien sûr ! Et il avait observé toute la scène de son point de vue privilégié ! Il existait néanmoins une chose qu'il n'avait pas vue, qu'il ne pouvait avoir vue. Il ne savait pas que je savais. « La surprise était son point fort. » Eh bien, j'avais suivi ses traces jusque-là, tel un fils respectueux sous tous rapports, et sous celui-là aussi, nom de Dieu ! J'allais me venger. « Car aujourd'hui nous voyons comme dans un miroir, confusément ; alors nous verrons face à face. » Oui, exactement, face à face. Alors je tiendrai ma revanche. Les feux de joie brûlaient si fort avec ma peine que je fus pris de frissons et de tremblements. Je sentis de nouveau le vent froid monter en moi d'une distance insondable, je vis l'ombre approcher incroyablement vite sur le sol. Je fermai les yeux et luttai, grinçant des dents, serrant les poings, et elle passa. Quand je rouvris les yeux, je tremblais de tous mes membres comme un chien qui émerge d'une mer glacée, ayant au péril de sa vie récupéré le jouet bondissant de ma propre santé mentale.

La porte de la salle de bain s'ouvrit, Li apparut en robe de chambre. Elle essuyait ses cheveux. « Tu es réveillé ! » Elle scruta anxieusement mon visage. « Comment te sens-tu ?

— Magnifiquement, répondis-je avec une bonne dose d'ironie.

— Hmm, fit-elle. On dirait que ça va mieux. Je me suis fait beaucoup de souci pour toi là-bas. Tu t'es comporté si bizarrement.

— Bah, un épisode psychotique mineur, lui répondis-je, pas de quoi s'inquiéter. Cela arrive tout le temps. »

Elle avança vers le lit en riant. Debout au-dessus de moi, elle leva mon menton. « Tu as repris des couleurs, constata-t-elle. Te sens-tu vraiment rétabli ?

— Bien sûr, lui assurai-je en écartant la tête avec agacement.

— Je crois que tu devrais voir quelqu'un, dit-elle calmement. En fait, j'insiste pour que tu voies quelqu'un.

— Oh mais j'en ai tout à fait l'intention ! la narguai-je en pensant avec plaisir à un rendez-vous bien précis.

— Que veux-tu dire ?

— Rien, répondis-je. Laisse tomber.

— Pas question, Sun I. Ce qui s'est passé sur la plage est grave. Tu as eu une crise de quelque chose. Tu t'es brusquement évanoui, et ta crise a duré plusieurs minutes. Tu t'en souviens ?

— Comment sommes-nous rentrés à la maison ?

— *Tu nous as ramenés en voiture*, m'apprit-elle avec une incrédulité exaspérée. Ô Seigneur, nous avons de la chance d'être en vie ! Dès que tu es arrivé ici, tu t'es écroulé sur le lit et dix secondes après tu dormais. » Elle regarda sa montre. « Il y a trois heures de cela.

— Très bien, concédai-je, je verrai quelqu'un, d'accord ?

— D'accord. » Elle me regarda d'un air préoccupé. « Tu sais, ce qui t'est arrivé sur la plage m'a rappelé quelque chose. Sur le chemin du retour, j'ai trouvé quoi. » Elle alla dans l'autre pièce et revint avec un livre. « J'aimerais que tu lises quelque chose. » Elle avait placé un repère dans le livre.

« Lis-le-moi », dis-je, car j'appréhendais un peu d'être confronté à des signes typographiques.

« Tu te souviens que nous avons parlé de Freud ? Ce passage concerne l'un de ses cas cliniques, un certain Schreber. Freud parle du soleil comme d'un symbole sublimé du père. Voici :

> Le soleil lui parlait (à Schreber) un langage humain et se révélait donc à lui en tant qu'être vivant. Schreber avait pour habitude de l'injurier et de lui hurler des menaces ; de plus, il déclare que, lorsqu'il se campait devant lui pour lui parler, ses rayons pâlissaient. Après sa « guérison », il se vante de pouvoir le fixer sans la moindre difficulté et en souffrant seulement d'un léger éblouissement, chose dont jusque-là il avait naturellement été incapable.
> Ce privilège fantasmatique — pouvoir regarder le soleil sans en être aveuglé — évoque une association mythologique. Nous lisons dans Reinach que les historiens de l'antiquité attribuaient ce pouvoir au seul aigle, lequel, en tant qu'habitué des plus hautes régions atmosphériques, entretenait une relation particulièrement intime avec les cieux, le soleil et la foudre. De plus, les mêmes sources nous apprennent que l'aigle soumet sa progéniture à une épreuve avant de la reconnaître comme légitime. Les aiglons incapables de regarder le soleil sans ciller sont précipités hors de l'aire (...)
> Ce rituel imposé par l'aigle à sa descendance est une *ordalie* (Li m'adressa un regard appuyé), une épreuve de filiation que l'on retrouve parmi les races les plus différentes de l'antiquité.

« Intéressant, n'est-ce pas ? » Elle ferma son livre. « Alors ? » demanda-t-elle avec gravité.

Je ne répondis rien. J'étais trop absorbé par le spectacle de ses mains. Lovées autour du dos du livre fermé qu'elles pressaient comme des serres, ses ongles parfaits d'un blanc éblouissant, la pulpe du bout de ses doigts, ridée, fripée à cause de l'eau. Je me rappelai aussitôt la phrase que j'avais cherchée un peu plus tôt, l'ultimatum d'Oz aux pèlerins : « Tuez la Sorcière », voilà ce qu'il leur disait. « Tuez la Sorcière Maléfique de l'Ouest » ; et ensuite ses hurlements quand Dorothy l'arrosait d'eau froide et qu'elle se liquéfiait en une flaque fumante sur le sol. Je me ramassai sur moi-même avec une haine implacable, surveillant les gestes de Li. « Tout cela n'est qu'un jeu pour toi, n'est-ce pas ? sifflai-je.

— Que veux-tu dire ? demanda-t-elle avec inquiétude. Pourquoi me regardes-tu ainsi ? » Elle recula d'un pas, serra inconsciemment le livre contre elle pour se défendre.

Ce ne fut pas la face de la renarde que je vis alors, mais une chose aussi répugnante. Elle me fit penser à Mme Chin, elle regardait le monde et me regardait avec un appétit maladif et glouton (ou raffiné, peu importe). J'étais pour elle un simple objet d'étude, je l'avais toujours été. Elle était aussi distante et froide que lors de notre première nuit, lointaine et glacée comme une statue, une version restaurée de la Vénus de Milo dotée d'une souriante et cynique tête de mort, et qui invitait lascivement à goûter aux plaisirs de sa chair parfaite. « Tu te rappelles la première nuit où nous avons fait l'amour, murmurai-je, tu m'avais dit que je te haïrais pour ça ? »

Elle me dévisageait bouche bée, stupéfaite et angoissée.

« Eh bien, tu avais raison, continuai-je, je te hais.

— Que dis-tu ? s'écria-t-elle soudain. Bon Dieu, mais tu dérailles complètement ? »

Je ne lui livrai pas mon secret. Je ne répondis rien, ne la poursuivis pas davantage dans l'autre pièce où elle se réfugia aussitôt. Je savais qu'elle complotait contre moi, contre ma vie. Mais c'était sans importance. La vraie sorcière n'était pas Li, mais American Power and Light, la Douairière. Et ce n'était pas la sorcière que je désirais vraiment. C'était Oz.

Je restai quelque temps assis au bord du lit pour réfléchir. Après la frénésie incontrôlable qui avait suivi mon rêve, ma fureur s'était passablement calmée, ou plutôt, comme par un coup de baguette magique, transformée en une chose aussi désespérée, froide et perverse que la cité où je séjournais — et où je m'étais perdu. Car je n'avais plus le moindre doute à ce sujet. J'étais perdu. Bel et bien perdu. A jamais et à jamais. Un enfer sans fin. Je souris. Le fleuve qui m'avait porté tout du long venait de disparaître dans les entrailles de la terre, et s'écoulait maintenant dans d'humides cavernes crayeuses où d'énormes stalactites s'écroulaient dans l'eau verdâtre et phosphorescente avec un fracas irréel dont les échos semblaient se répercuter sans fin. Jadis, j'avais sincèrement cru que ce cours d'eau finirait par ressortir au soleil, par retrouver la clarté du grand jour. Plus maintenant. Je savais désormais avec certitude que j'avais commis une terrible erreur. Je savais que le fleuve qui m'emportait se nommait Phlégéthon et débouchait au cœur de l'enfer dans une citerne noire, émeraude et rouge, bouillonnante et putride, où les âmes sont baptisées avant une éternité de souffrances. Oui, j'avais commis une terrible erreur, aussi terrible que l'enfer, et désormais je savais. J'avais joué, et perdu. Je devais maintenant payer et renoncer à mon âme elle-même. A jamais et à jamais. Un enfer sans fin.

Je ris en songeant qu'il ne me restait plus rien, en songeant à l'étendue de ma déchéance et de ma chute. J'avais goûté au sang, peut-être un festin princier pour un dowiste, mais un crime impardonnable pour un taoïste. Oui, j'étais perdu.

Pourtant, la joie de savoir qu'il vivait encore me consolait perversement. Je me rappelai une fois encore le passage de l'Epître aux Corinthiens : « Quand j'étais enfant, je parlais comme un enfant, je pensais comme un enfant, je raisonnais comme un enfant. En devenant homme, j'ai éliminé tout ce qu'il y avait de puéril. » Oui, il était grand temps d'éliminer toutes les puérilités. L'enfant était mort dans mon cœur. Tel était le prix que j'avais dû payer. Mais j'allais maintenant le connaître comme il me connaissait, j'allais vivre cette intimité que seul Tsin avait osé goûter, « cette intimité plus profonde que toute autre qui lie le chasseur à sa proie ». Maintenant je comprenais. J'étais l'Adversaire, j'étais le Chasseur de la métaphore de Chong Fou, je l'avais suivi à travers la terre, pistant ses traces sanglantes jusqu'au cul-de-sac de cet ultime sanctuaire, American Power and Light. Là nous nous rencontrerions bientôt sur le champ de bataille, nous partagerions le seul cadeau qui nous restait, l'extase du combat. Je réfléchis que tout du long, au nom de la réhabilitation, j'avais inconsciemment comploté une revanche subtile mais meurtrière contre lui, contre son nom et sa mémoire. Bateson avait raison. Et il savait parce que mon père savait. La perspective s'élargit et je compris qu'enfant déjà je le haïssais et que, telle une Furie vengeresse, je l'avais suivi à travers la moitié du monde, attendant le moment opportun de lui faire payer ma bâtardise. Je compris seulement alors qu'au-delà de toutes les transcendances spécieuses qui avaient pourtant exalté mon âme et bouleversé mes croyances, seule restait cette question insidieuse et exaspérante : « Ce soleil fera-t-il pâlir celui de son père ? » Et je me jurai que oui, même au prix d'une éternité de souffrances ; non pas comme une « ordalie » ni pour me montrer digne de lui, pas davantage pour restaurer sa mémoire ou l'honneur de la famille, mais pour la simple joie du meurtre. Oui, c'était Oz que je désirais et le meurtre était dans mon cœur.

« Parricide fiduciaire. » Je ris en me rappelant l'indignation vertueuse avec laquelle j'avais nié cette interprétation. Maintenant, elle me semblait curieusement en deçà de la réalité. Non, « parricide fiduciaire » était insuffisant. Je voulais le sang. Je voulais la chose elle-même. Je voulais tremper mes mains dedans, dépecer son cadavre, en arracher son cœur et ses viscères palpitants pour les dévorer crus. Je voulais... Mais de nouveau je vis l'aile sombre tournoyer, s'approcher, et je me retins. Je dirais seulement que mon cœur débordait de joie.

19

De bonne heure le lendemain matin, Li, qui semblait nerveuse et inquiète, m'annonça qu'elle allait en bibliothèque. « Je préférerais rester, mais je dois aller travailler à ma thèse », me dit-elle en penchant un peu la tête pour mettre une boucle d'oreille.

Je remarquai qu'elle était maquillée.

« Tu crois que ça va aller ? » demanda-t-elle.

Avec un sourire ambigu j'opinai du chef en l'observant à la dérobée. Ses traits dansaient dans les vagues de chaleur de ma haine. Je savais où elle allait. Tout cela était enfin clair en moi. Elle m'avait trompé une fois. J'avais été stupide de la croire. Mais je ne me laisserais plus duper. Trop souvent j'avais joué ce rôle devant trop de clowns et d'imposteurs qui dissimulaient leur vice derrière le maquillage. Je savais qu'elle le voyait de nouveau. Le pédé. Peter. Ils complotaient, mais il n'était pas difficile de voir à quoi. « Le mariage, la sainte vie conjugale. » Sur mes lèvres, ces mots devenaient un sacrement empoisonné. Je savais ce qui suivrait, et ce n'était pas « jusqu'à ce que mort s'ensuive ». Ou peut-être que si. Mais je ne pensais pas qu'ils iraient aussi loin. Ils n'avaient pas assez de cran. Contrairement à moi — et cette pensée me flatta. Et puis c'était pour eux superflu. Il existait d'autres biais. Je voyais ce qu'ils tramaient. Un divorce. A l'amiable. Cela les ravirait. Ou bien elle allait tenter de me faire enfermer. Comme Schreber... La machination avait déjà commencé ; les engrenages tournaient. Mais je devais d'abord tomber dans leur piège.

Je souriai sombrement en songeant que j'allais déjouer leurs manigances. Peut-être trouverais-je même l'occasion de les détruire sans risque pour moi-même. Ici aussi j'avais l'avantage de la surprise. Mais je ne comptais pas leur sacrifier mon objectif essentiel. C'étaient seulement des personnages secondaires.

Après son départ, je continuai frénétiquement d'alimenter la fournaise, engouffrant par sa porte de grandes pelletées de rage et de souffrance, poussant les feux de ma haine jusqu'à ce que le métal virât au rouge. Je ne pus soutenir longtemps cette cadence infernale ; la soif du sang était trop épuisante. Il y eut une baisse brutale de température. Une résolution froide comme la mort se répandit lentement à partir des extrémités jusqu'au centre, jusqu'au cœur. Elle s'accompagna d'une panique grandissante où je discernai faiblement, comme une musique lointaine, les trilles perçants et sans âme de l'hystérie.

Je fouillai dans l'armoire à pharmacie et pris un somnifère. Mais il ne fit que m'abrutir. Plusieurs fois je sombrai dans le sommeil et me réveillai désorienté, en proie à une terreur croissante. Allongé sur le lit, je levais les yeux vers le plâtre uniforme du plafond et me perdais dans son étendue blanche. Je me sentais terriblement seul, comme une minuscule voile perdue sur l'océan, sans la moindre terre en vue, et qui naviguait obstinément. Je désirai désespérément être couvert, enveloppé ; je me tournai vers les draps et les couvertures. Je m'agenouillai, les tirai sur moi, enfouis mon visage dans les oreillers en me balançant d'avant en arrière avec un gémissement grave, inarticulé.

Comment en étais-je arrivé là ? me demandai-je. Comment ? Les motifs de ma quête avaient-ils été impurs ? Non, je ne pouvais m'accuser de cela. J'avais eu raison de partir. Mais le delta ? Le Tao dans le Dow — une graine maléfique s'était-elle glissée dans l'objet de ma recherche ? Tout cela était trop loin... beaucoup trop loin. Comment en étais-je arrivé là ? Comment un homme — un enfant — parti avec un cœur pur arrive-t-il à une telle dégradation dans un monde soumis aux lois du Tao ?

Il n'y avait pas de réponse. Seulement la voile qui progressait péniblement. Mais la voile était maintenant noire, et elle naviguait sur un océan rouge. Car le fleuve du Dow était rouge de sang et ici enfin, au delta, il se jetait dans une mer de sang.

Mon esprit s'emplit de sang. Dans un rêve éveillé, j'inventoriai des fûts et des tonneaux de sang, des barriques et des foudres, des fleuves et des lacs, de vastes étendues liquides couvertes de sang dans lesquelles je nageais sans espoir, désespérément las. Le sang était trop épais (infiniment plus épais que l'eau), je savais que j'allais me noyer. Mon menton toucha sa surface, puis baigna dedans. Je sentis la chaleur monter du liquide visqueux comme une brise à la puanteur écœurante. Je me débattis, mais ma tête s'enfonça de plus en plus jusqu'à ce que des bulles poisseuses se forment autour de mes lèvres, et bientôt il couvrit mes yeux, et mes cheveux se dressèrent sur mon crâne en oscillant doucement comme les mollusques effilés de la plage de Sands Point.

Je me réveillai en hurlant de terreur. Ce n'était pas ce que j'avais désiré. Ce n'était pas ce que j'avais cherché. Pas cela. Je ne voulais pas cela.

Comme je me balançais en gémissant, je perçus un murmure lointain qui parlait dans mon oreille interne, un chuchotement remémoré, une voix du passé. Je me figeai pour me concentrer. D'abord inarticulée, la voix s'amplifia, franchit le seuil de ma conscience, et je la reconnus. C'était celle de Riley ; il disait : « Ceci est mon sang du Nouveau Testament, qui est versé pour vous, et pour maints autres, pour la rémission des péchés. » Cela recommençait aussitôt, comme une boucle enregistrée. Parfaitement immobile, sans même respirer, hypnotisé comme un animal nocturne pris dans le pinceau des phares, je fixai cette voix tandis que mon cœur s'emballait.

« Pour la rémission des péchés », répétai-je d'une voix incrédule et si étouffée qu'on eût dit que ces mots fragiles risquaient de se briser sur ma langue, comme l'hostie, comme le corps, et avec eux leur promesse. Une excitation terrible s'empara de moi, terrible car je redoutais qu'à la plus légère pression la promesse disparaisse, éclate comme une bulle.

Alors, brusquement, la merveille me submergea, déferla sur moi telle une vague de lumière. Si j'étais perdu et damné, le sang pouvait peut-être aussi me sauver. « Un festin princier pour un dowiste » — cette expression dont l'ironie m'avait frappé plus tôt m'emplissait maintenant d'un espoir gigantesque. C'était le seul festin concevable, mon unique espoir. Le taoïsme ne pouvait plus m'offrir son salut. J'avais dilapidé tous mes trésors. Peut-être le christianisme pouvait-il me sauver ? Il n'était peut-être pas trop tard. Il me restait sans doute une chance. Qu'avais-je à perdre ? J'étais déjà tombé dans tous les pièges du dowiste, je pouvais bien essayer la religion. L'adoration du sang devant l'autel sanglant. La conversion me semblait une simple formalité. N'avais-je pas déjà goûté au sacrement ? « La rémission des péchés. »

Je voulais laver mon âme dans le sang très précieux du Christ, comme disait le livre de prières de Riley. Oui, voilà ce que je désirais. Cesser de me noyer dans le liquide visqueux, mais être purifié par le sang du saint sacrifice. Le meurtre sacré. Cette idée m'apporta la paix. Me nourrir de lui et l'en remercier. Oh oui. Oui. Je désirais communier.

Je m'habillai en toute hâte et pris un taxi. L'avenue des Amériques était presque déserte. Passant la tête par la fenêtre, je laissai le vent froid aplatir mes cheveux sans prendre garde aux larmes qui coulaient sur mes joues. Je levai les yeux vers la bande bleue qui semblait couler entre les bâtiments, regardai les éclaboussures jaunes du soleil sur le trottoir entre les ombres noires et blanches du matin, et me sentis heureux. Ce spectacle me réconforta, me rendit à moi-même.

Mais devant l'église je perdis courage. La logique de ma décision m'échappa brusquement, mon projet me parut désespéré, ou pire encore, dément. Je ne m'éloignai pourtant pas. Non sans honte j'entrai, je me glissai furtivement par la porte, ainsi que je l'avais déjà fait, puis me cachai sur un banc du fond. Et quand l'huissier, arrivant à ma hauteur, me fit signe de me joindre aux autres, je me levai pour rejoindre les fidèles qui marchaient vers l'autel. Riley officiait avec un autre prêtre ; ils se séparèrent pour administrer la communion, commençant par l'extrémité de la rangée et se rapprochant peu à peu. Parmi les derniers, je m'arrangeai pour tomber du côté de Riley. Abandonnant toute dignité et toute prudence, je me mis à jouer des coudes à travers la foule en m'excusant. Je gagnai ainsi un temps considérable. Puis je m'agenouillai avec les autres, je levai les mains en une attitude de prière, inclinai ma tête sur le velours cramoisi de la balustrade tout en examinant la trame élimée du tapis. Je les entendis approcher ; leurs voix qui se synchronisaient puis se dissociaient eurent pour moi un effet hallucinatoire, comme d'une voix unique réverbérée à l'octave supérieure par son propre écho.

L'hostie chatouilla ma paume. C'était l'autre prêtre. Riley était à côté de lui, presque assez près pour que je pusse toucher l'ourlet de son aube, mais il fit volte-face. Mon cœur cognait dans ma poitrine ; je soupirai. Je la laissai se dissoudre lentement sur ma langue, dans ma salive. « Quel goût imperceptible et fade ! » songeai-je, et je faillis rire en me rappelant la subtile apologie de Lao-tseu à propos de la saveur du Tao. Mais le vin arriva bientôt. C'était lui que je désirais. Je les entendais converger de nouveau vers le centre en murmurant la secrète antiphonie qui réjouissait mon cœur : « Ceci est mon sang *(sang)* du Nouveau Testament *(ament)* qui est versé pour vous, et pour maints autres *(autres),* pour la rémission des péchés *(péchés).* » Cela chuintait comme une vague. Fermant les yeux, je répétai en silence les syllabes avec eux ; je me guidai sur la voix de Riley tout en écoutant avec plaisir le deuxième prêtre qui lui faisait écho, distillait ce message vers une blancheur immaculée. Brusquement, il n'y eut plus que ma voix. Riley s'était tu. Quand j'ouvris les yeux, je le vis debout immobile devant moi, tenant le calice au niveau de mon visage ; l'or brillait entre ses mains devant les plis de son vêtement. Il l'inclina un peu, et le vin d'un pourpre presque noir scintilla dans la pénombre des bougies. Je levai alors mon visage vers Riley et lui montrai toute ma souffrance. Une tendresse troublée apparut sur ses traits. Il tendit le calice à l'autre prêtre (qui, immobile à côté de lui, scrutait tantôt mon visage, tantôt celui de Riley), passa de l'autre côté de la balustrade de cuivre, me releva doucement par le bras, puis m'entraîna vers la sacristie.

J'avais d'abord cru que la chance me souriait. Mais je déchantai vite. Sa tendresse demeura, mais comme un condiment sucré servi avec un plat amer. Son visage s'empourpra de colère et d'embarras. Ses yeux se mirent à scintiller comme des éclats de verre brisé. Il ferma soigneusement la porte, puis explosa en exhalant longuement et avec une véhémence qui interdisait d'appeler cela un soupir. Il se mit à arpenter la sacristie d'un pas rageur.

« C'est donc ce que tu étais venu faire ici, dit-il comme s'il venait de comprendre, l'après-midi où tu as failli me renverser dans le vestibule. » Il s'éloigna en secouant la tête comme si sa propre naïveté le stupéfiait. « Je ne peux pas y croire. Comment oses-tu ? » Plein d'une indignation vertueuse, il se tourna soudain vers moi. « *Comment oses-tu ?* Et nous faisions ami-ami autour d'une tasse de thé, hein ? L'Orient rencontre l'Occident ?

— Pardonnez-moi, mon père, dis-je en baissant la tête.

— "Mon père" ? répéta-t-il en souriant d'un air presque amusé. Mon père ? Ne joue pas à ce jeu-là, Sun I. N'essaie pas de singer l'humble pénitent. Ça ne marchera pas, mon garçon. Je ne suis pas ton "père". Ceci n'est pas ton église. Mais qui es-tu, une sorte de pervers religieux ? Tu portes un slip en dentelle noire et une ceinture de barbelé à même la peau ? Oui, qui es-tu ? Tu devrais comprendre mieux que quiconque la gravité de ton acte. N'ai-je pas passé une soirée à te sermonner sur ce chapitre ? Es-tu stupide ? Ou débile ? Hein ? » Il se frappa le front. « Que mijotes-tu ? Le coup du papillon de nuit et de la flamme ? Es-tu un poivrot ? Le vin rouge te donnerait-il des ailes ? Ou bien as-tu complètement oublié ce que je t'ai dit ? "Car si le bénéfice est grand, quand avec une foi authentique et un cœur vraiment contrit on reçoit le saint sacrement ; de même le danger quand on reçoit le même sacrement lorsqu'on en est indigne." Alors ? Ça te rappelle quelque chose ? Ou as-tu perdu la mémoire ?

— Je m'en souviens, mon père, répondis-je sincèrement sans broncher sous ses piques. C'est parce que je m'en souviens que je suis revenu. Je ne suis pas sûr de me rappeler exactement ces mots que vous venez de répéter, mais peu importe. J'y souscris totalement. Oui, ils sont justes. Et je suis prêt. Je désire endosser le vêtement rituel et m'approcher de l'autel. »

Il parut abasourdi. « Au nom du ciel, que dis-tu ? Tu as perdu la tête ?

— Je suis prêt à me convertir, mon père », dis-je. Comme il ne répondait toujours pas, je croisai mes mains avec violence, inclinai la tête et me mis à prier avec ferveur. « Accorde-nous, Seigneur... »

Quand je relevai les yeux, Riley me regardait avec stupéfaction et pleurait. Cachant d'une main son visage, il se détourna. « Pardonne-moi, Sun I, dit-il d'une voix suppliante. J'ai commis une erreur terrible. »

Je souris gravement. « Moi aussi, mon père. Moi aussi.

— Je suis tellement ému. » Il leva un regard embué vers le plafond, puis sanglota entre ses mains.

« Cela ne vous rend pas malheureux ?

— Non, non, dit-il en essuyant ses larmes sur sa manche. Ce n'est pas ça. Simplement, je suis si heureux pour toi. Sais-tu que cela ne m'est jamais arrivé ? Et pourtant... — il me dévisagea en plissant les yeux, comme si ma décision lui semblait par trop invraisemblable — je ne m'y attendais pas. Pas de ta part. Tu paraissais si ferme dans ta foi, si déterminé. » Il secoua la tête en soupirant. « Mais oublions cela. Aujourd'hui il y a de la joie dans cette église. » Il se figea brusquement. « Bon Dieu, je dois faire le sermon ! Il faut que je retourne là-bas, Sun I. Le père Davis sera furieux. Retrouve-moi ici après le service, et je te présenterai personnellement aux instructeurs. » Rayonnant de bonheur, il saisit mes mains. « Je suis si ému, Sun I, vraiment.

— Et la communion, mon père ? lui rappelai-je alors qu'il faisait mine de partir. Le calice ? »

Il pivota sur ses talons. « Il faut d'abord que tu sois baptisé, Sun I », m'expliqua-t-il doucement, comme on répète une interdiction à un enfant bien-aimé mais étourdi.

« Je comprends bien, mon père, dis-je. Mais ne pouvons-nous accélérer les formalités, ou les différer, juste pour cette fois, pour aujourd'hui ?

— Pourquoi es-tu si désireux de communier ? demanda-t-il. Quelque chose te gêne ? »

Baissant la tête, j'acquiesçai en silence.

« Sun I, je te répondrai une fois encore par les textes sacrés. » Il prit un ton inflexible, mais paternel. « "Pour s'approcher de la sainte communion, une conscience sans tache et une foi inébranlable en la miséricorde du Seigneur sont indispensables." Il faut donc que tu te prépares, Sun I. Ce qui t'a amené ici aujourd'hui t'y ramènera demain et après-demain, car il faut éclaircir la nature de ton trouble — il sourit — pour que tu puisses "te présenter pur et sanctifié devant le Festin". Et puis on ne franchit pas cette étape à la va-vite. Vers Pâques, quand l'évêque baptisera et confirmera, tu devrais être prêt. J'admire ton enthousiasme, mais tu dois attendre jusque-là. Crois-moi, cela aura encore plus de sens pour toi.

— Cela n'aura plus aucun sens, le contredis-je durement. A Pâques il sera trop tard. Même demain il sera trop tard. Ce doit être maintenant, mon père. Aujourd'hui même.

— Mais pourquoi ? » demanda-t-il en retrouvant sa perplexité exaspérée.

Je secouai la tête. « Je ne sais pas. Sincèrement, je ne sais pas. » Je gardai la tête baissée. Comme il ne disait rien, je continuai de supplier. « Cela étanche une soif en moi, lui confiai-je d'une voix que la passion rendait rauque. Cela me donne la paix.

— Mais c'était alors un péché mortel, dit-il. En tout cas, c'en serait un maintenant. »

Je le regardai droit dans les yeux en concentrant sur lui toute ma conviction, toute ma sincérité. « Je sais. »

Il recula d'un pas ; la répulsion fit trembler son visage. Il parut m'interroger en silence, puis dit : « Tu le savais, n'est-ce pas, en venant aujourd'hui, que c'était un péché mortel ? Et pourtant tu as communié — au moins essayé ? »

Je ne répondis pas.

Une rougeur monta de son cou pour envahir son visage comme un brusque coup de soleil. « Maintenant je crois que je commence à comprendre. » Un sourire méprisant tordit ses traits. « Tu pensais donc pouvoir te sauver en redoublant ta damnation ? Ou bien t'en moquais-tu ? Tu t'en moquais, n'est-ce pas ? Tu désirais seulement une consolation — et au diable les conséquences ? En venant ici, tu cherchais ta damnation ; la conversion n'était qu'un prétexte. Ô mon Dieu... » Il rit. « J'ai bel et bien commis une terrible erreur. » Je crus qu'il allait me cracher au visage. « Tu me dégoûtes. Tu ressembles à un chien qui salive devant un quartier de viande, à un vieil obsédé qui lorgne une belle jeune fille chaste et tente de coucher avec elle en lui promettant de l'épouser alors qu'il n'en a pas l'intention. Est-ce ainsi que tu t'y es pris avec Yin-mi ? » ajouta-t-il vicieusement.

Ce fut à mon tour de rougir ; mais je ne bronchai pas, refoulant la rage qu'avaient fait naître ses paroles. « Je sais seulement que mon âme est en train de mourir, dis-je d'une voix tremblante, et je vous demande de m'aider. » Je ne pus réprimer un sanglot, puis j'enfouis mon visage entre mes mains. « Et je tiendrai parole », déclarai-je sauvagement entre mes larmes.

Il s'adoucit. « Je t'ai déjà aidé, Sun I, dit-il, autant que je le pouvais.

— Aujourd'hui ? » demandai-je.

Il secoua sombrement la tête en retroussant les lèvres.

« Ce n'est pas suffisant.

— Alors va-t'en, commanda-t-il. Si cela ne te suffit pas, va-t'en. Dehors ! » Il s'approcha de moi en gesticulant, comme s'il voulait me frapper.

Un calme glacé saisit soudain mon cœur, comme si j'avais plongé dans un bassin d'eau froide. Je me retournai, marchai vers la porte.

« Et ne reviens pas », lâcha-t-il d'une voix rageuse.

Je m'arrêtai sur le seuil de la sacristie. « Ne vous inquiétez pas, je ne reviendrai pas, rétorquai-je haineusement.

— Si ton besoin, ou ta lubie, persiste, cherche un autre prêtre, une autre paroisse. Ne remets plus les pieds ici. J'espère seulement que tu trouveras le pardon. Mais ne reviens pas. Je ne peux plus rien pour toi. Pas après cela. » Il plissa les yeux. « Tu es perdu, Sun I, chuchota-t-il. Perdu.

— Je sais, dis-je avec un sourire pervers, et c'est à vous que je le dois. » Je lui lançai un dernier coup d'œil furieux, puis sortis.

Sur le trottoir, je m'arrêtai pour regarder le cimetière. Le fer forgé glacé de la grille mordit mes doigts. La douleur me fit le serrer plus fort. La douleur : cela était réel quand plus rien ne l'était. Elle courait dans mes veines comme la brûlure de l'électricité. Un sourire s'épanouit lentement sur mon visage quand je compris que de façon oblique, inattendue, j'avais atteint mon objectif. Tout danger était écarté. Je n'avais plus peur. J'avais retrouvé ma haine. Une haine implacable.

20

A l'ouverture de la séance du lundi matin, Rising Sun avait perdu un point, baisse plutôt étrange compte tenu de nos récentes performances. Il n'y avait cependant pas lieu de s'inquiéter. Les Cornes supputèrent — et je me rangeai à leur avis — que Kahn s'était sans doute montré trop impatient de se débarrasser de ses actions. Rien de bien grave. Nous décidâmes d'annoncer notre offre publique d'achat le jour même à midi, prévoyant que cette nouvelle provoquerait une hausse brutale, non seulement de la cote d'American Power and Light, qui en serait principalement affectée, mais aussi, dans une moindre mesure, de la cote de nos actions. Ce matin-là il y eut parmi nos rangs d'innombrables frottements de mains satisfaits, clins d'œil complices et autres claquements de langue réjouis en anticipation de la fureur et de la confusion que notre coup de main allait immanquablement provoquer. Je me glissai subrepticement jusqu'à la Galerie des Visiteurs afin d'assister à la scène et de jouir de mon triomphe.

Les échanges continuèrent à se dérouler normalement pendant les dix premières minutes qui suivirent mon arrivée. puis un homme sortit en courant de la Salle des Courtiers réservée aux fumeurs, avec une cigarette à la main. Il fit plusieurs foulées avant de remarquer sa présence, s'arrêta brusquement, la considéra avec agacement, fit aussitôt volte-face comme pour sortir, loucha de nouveau vers elle, pivota sur ses talons, aspira une bouffée, puis la jeta et l'écrasa rageusement sous sa chaussure. Alors seulement il s'élança vers le premier poste. En chemin, il rencontra une connaissance qu'il accompagna pendant quelques instants en agitant fébrilement les mains. Manifestement pressé et distrait, l'autre hocha la tête comme pour se débarrasser de son interlocuteur et lui échappa bientôt. Le premier homme se retourna aussitôt pour saisir le bras du courtier le plus proche. Le visage cramoisi, il lança les mains en l'air. L'individu ainsi interpellé le dévisagea comme on regarde un fou. L'essentiel du message dut cependant être transmis, car le courtier devint attentif, secoua la tête avec véhémence et remua les lèvres — « Tu es sûr ? »

Le premier acquiesça avec volubilité. Un troisième homme se joignit à leur conversation. Alors, sous mes yeux, les dominos se mirent à dégringoler. L'onde de choc, qui se propageait séquentiellement, dessinait d'étranges paraphes, arabesques et spirales autour des postes d'échanges, sur le seuil du garage, devant la Salle des Courtiers ou celle réservée au public, et au-delà des portes jusque dans la rue. Quand la nouvelle et les dominos tombaient, un profond silence s'ensuivait. Ceux qui l'avaient entendue se figeaient en une attitude de stupéfaction hagarde. Les comptables posaient leur stylo et oubliaient d'inscrire les derniers ordres dans leurs registres, les standardistes sombraient dans une hébétude catatonique et les ampoules clignotaient vainement devant leurs yeux morts. Le tube pneumatique lui-même se mit à siffler de faim et, privé de son aliment vital, le cœur gigantesque de l'organisme frissonna, hoqueta et fut saisi d'un infarctus foudroyant. La mort du cerveau s'ensuivit ; pendant quelques secondes, la bande-annonce bourdonna sans message, vide ! Peut-être pour la première et seule fois dans l'histoire de Wall Street, le parquet fut immobile ; il y régnait un tel silence qu'on eût entendu le crissement du stylo d'un rond-de-cuir notant un ordre, mais aucun n'écrivait. Spécialistes, courtiers, négociants, comptables, employés, rapporteurs, messagers, grouillots et saute-ruisseau, tous semblaient pétrifiés par une terreur primitive. Alors un rugissement assourdissant s'éleva vers le plafond. Il aurait pu annoncer le jaillissement des missiles hors de leurs silos, ou l'envol vers le ciel de milliers de ballons multicolores lors d'une grande fête mondiale pour la paix et la fraternité humaine, car personne ne sut d'abord si le monde touchait à sa fin ou si le miracle du millénaire s'était accompli. Simplement, il se passait quelque chose d'énorme, un événement sans précédent — de cela seulement ils étaient sûrs.

Alors, brusquement, ils se mirent à courir en tous sens comme des bêtes terrifiées par la foudre et qui fuient follement en l'absence du berger, qui fuient vers le précipice. Des courtiers cramoisis jouaient des coudes et se ruaient vers les pneumatiques pour passer leurs ordres en premier, semant la panique parmi les spécialistes et les employés de la Bourse qui tentaient de canaliser leur assaut furieux. Quelques petits malins réglaient leurs affaires à l'écart du parquet devant le tableau d'affichage du Dow Jones, tandis que des visages désespérés s'agglutinaient pour essayer d'absorber le déluge des communiqués de presse qui jaillissaient des télex. Et c'était moi, moi seul, qui avais émis l'impulsion initiale qui faisait choir ces rangées innombrables de dominos ; d'un léger coup de pouce, j'avais tout mis en branle.

« Monsieur... monsieur... » dit une voix timide qui interrompit désagréablement ma méditation.

Fronçant les sourcils, je baissai les yeux vers une jeune fille inquiète et surmenée, qui semblait tirer sur ma manche depuis un certain temps. Je reconnus la réceptionniste du Centre des Visiteurs. « Oui ? l'interrogeai-je d'une voix sévère.

— Je suis désolée, monsieur, s'excusa-t-elle. Mais la galerie est temporairement fermée au public. Vous devez partir.

— "Au public" ? Mademoiselle, dis-je en adoptant un ton d'autorité stertoreuse, avez-vous la moindre idée de la personne à qui vous parlez ? »

Elle m'adressa un regard interloqué, mais, désirant éviter tout ennui à elle comme à moi, se contenta de répéter : « Excusez-moi, monsieur, je suis une simple employée, je ne suis pas responsable du règlement. Nous fermons toujours la galerie quand il y a une panique. Les ordres viennent d'en haut, ou plutôt d'en bas — en tout cas du sommet.

— Une panique, hé ? » Je louchai d'un œil vers le parquet, largement dédommagé par le mot lui-même. « La panique. » Oui, cela avait de l'ampleur et du panache. « Très bien, concédai-je, vous faites votre métier. Je ne voudrais pas vous causer d'ennuis. Je me rappelle moi-même ce que c'est que de travailler pour un salaire. »

Et à son grand soulagement, je quittai pacifiquement la galerie, avec une sorte de joie même, car je venais d'avoir l'idée brillante d'observer cette « panique », *ma* panique, du point de vue privilégié du parquet lui-même, à la lueur des explosions, des déflagrations et des bombes incendiaires qui embrasaient l'air.

Ainsi, entre des piles de papier de plus en plus hautes, semblables aux cendres qui recouvrirent les villes d'Herculanum et Pompéi, mais ici roses, jaunes et bleu azur, comme des pétales de fleur jetés sur le chemin d'un conquérant, je fis mon entrée au parquet livré à la panique et au tumulte que j'avais créés. Au milieu des hommes et des femmes bouleversés qui hurlaient, pleuraient, gémissaient ou grinçaient des dents, je planais comme un esprit invisible au cœur de la tourmente que je survolais mentalement, comme si je foulais toujours le sol de la galerie (oui, enfoui dans la galerie la plus profonde de ma mine intime), et je baissais les yeux vers le spectacle de la cupidité débridée, de la passion amok, que je contemplais avec la mélancolie la plus exquise et une sorte d'intérêt scientifique, tel un observateur d'une autre planète ou un dieu parfaitement étranger aux us et coutumes de l'humanité. Si ce sentiment vaguement désenchanté, cette satiété lointaine et détachée qui ressemblait presque à une absence ne correspondaient nullement à mon attente, ils n'en étaient pas désagréables pour autant. L'astronaute devait ressentir la même chose, conjecturai-je, quand il se retourne vers la terre tandis que son vaisseau traverse la froide nuit de l'espace à grande vitesse.

Je me rappelai l'exultation qui s'était emparée de moi le premier jour, et tant de fois depuis, à observer le spectacle époustouflant du parquet, l'un des plus excitants qui soient, de ceux qui bouleversent celui qui le contemple, l'initié comme le néophyte. Mais cette exultation s'était maintenant dissoute, évaporée, laissant seulement derrière elle le parfum de l'expérience, ou plutôt son bouquet. Et de fait, ce bouquet était tout ce que je désirais, car j'écartai sans regret ce vin trop rude, trop violent, trop charnel pour le palais d'un aussi fin connaisseur. Pendant que je méditais ces pensées, je me retournai pour regarder avec nostalgie la galerie, tellement plus élevée que le parquet, cette galerie où je m'étais arrêté le premier matin, et je soupirai en sachant que plus jamais le marché ne m'apparaîtrait comme il m'était alors apparu, à la lumière de mon innocence perdue. Il semblait approprié que cet étroit corridor ombreux d'où l'on observait sans participer, peut-être charmé mais à l'abri de la passion, demeurât vide si *moi* je ne pouvais y être, approprié que tout le monde se trouvât réuni ici au parquet pour s'entre-dévorer comme une bande de requins aveugles. Tout le monde, moi compris : car si j'avais bouclé la boucle, si maintenant j'observais de nouveau sans participer, c'était seulement parce que j'avais porté la participation à son point le plus aigu, parce que j'avais rassasié et été rassasié.

Mais à mieux y regarder, je m'aperçus que je me trompais. Il y avait bel et bien quelqu'un là-haut ! Dans les reflets des plafonniers qui éclaboussaient d'une douzaine de soleils équidistants la paroi de Plexiglas, un visage brouillé apparut. Était-ce la réceptionniste ? D'abord je ne distinguai pas ses traits, car le visiteur avançait et reculait, se fondait et disparaissait dans les halos de lumière — mais il s'agissait apparemment d'un homme. Tel celui qui regarde une toile dans un musée et tente de trouver le bon endroit pour éviter les reflets sur la surface brillante de la peinture, je fis quelques pas par-ci, quelques pas par-là en essayant de trouver l'emplacement idéal. Quand enfin je l'eus atteint, je me figeai et un frisson glacé descendit le long de mon dos.

C'était lui. Face à face pour la première fois, lecteur : je me campai devant mon père et adversaire — Eddie Love. Il n'y avait pas d'erreur possible. Du visage plus empâté de l'âge mûr, que le temps avait alourdi d'un quart de siècle, comme d'une prison de chair, le visage du jeune homme de la photographie me regardait. Je le reconnus aussi sûrement que j'eusse reconnu mon propre visage, comme dans un miroir confus ou un Palais des Glaces. Et peut-être pour m'enlever mes derniers doutes, il portait les mêmes lunettes de soleil aux verres en forme de larmes vert foncé que moi, et il souriait de ce mystérieux sourire que je n'avais jamais pu élucider. Mais maintenant je le comprenais, je comprenais parfaitement son sourire, et donc mon père. Car il exprimait la satiété lointaine d'un homme qui a perdu tout appétit pour la vie, qui l'a transformée en jeu, et qui tue le temps qui lui reste à vivre, l'utilise aux seules fins de son propre amusement et pour conjurer le désespoir toujours prêt à sourdre, la morsure d'inquiétude qu'engendrent le savoir définitif, le pouvoir sans partage, la saveur du sang de l'adversaire, le péché originel et ultime, sans rédemption ni espoir de pardon, à jamais et à jamais, un enfer sans fin. Je compris son sourire parce qu'il reflétait le mien, parce que nous étions les deux derniers joueurs du grand jeu ; chacun connaissait l'autre comme il se connaissait lui-même, lisait dans les pensées de son adversaire, anticipait chaque geste, si bien que chacun devait se reposer sur une chose plus profonde, sur la plus profonde des choses, pour espérer gagner. Cela, nous nous le confirmâmes à travers la distance qui nous séparait, nous aimant et nous haïssant, partageant cet ultime sourire secret. D'un commun accord, nous retirâmes nos lunettes de soleil pour nous dévisager dans une intimité silencieuse dans laquelle le mystère et la beauté indicibles de l'univers firent mouche en chacun de nous. Et comme les pêcheurs, nous rejetâmes dans l'océan du monde nos poissons magiques — chacun pêcheur, chacun poisson — dans l'attente du jour où nous lutterions pour de bon.

Je pris peu à peu conscience de voix qui chuchotaient autour de moi. « C'est lui, c'est lui », disaient-elles, en répercutant ma propre découverte.

Agacé par cette évidence, j'acquiesçai, puis fondis sur la victime la plus proche. « Savez-vous qui est cet homme ? demandai-je en indiquant la galerie derrière moi.

— Quel homme ? rétorqua-t-il innocemment.

— Là-haut ! » J'agitai la main. « Sur la galerie ! »

Mon interlocuteur et son compagnon échangèrent un regard perplexe.

« C'est mon père ! m'écriai-je en pivotant sur mes talons pour leur prouver ma bonne foi. Vous voyez... ? » Ma question mourut sur mes lèvres.

« Il n'y a personne là-haut », remarqua-t-il calmement. Eddie Love avait disparu. Mais ce n'était que trop normal. Le contraire m'eût surpris.

Des voix sans cesse plus nombreuses reprirent le refrain en chœur, psalmodièrent l'antienne : « C'est lui, c'est lui. » Jetant par curiosité un dernier regard par-dessus mon épaule, je fis volte-face et compris qu'ils parlaient de moi.

Ébranlé par l'incident, je pris congé ; à mesure que je me frayais un chemin, la foule se séparait comme les eaux de la mer Rouge quand Moïse leva le bras, et il y avait de la crainte et de la stupéfaction dans leurs yeux. Car pendant cette brève demi-heure et pour l'investisseur ordinaire de Wall Street, j'avais accompli mon ascension vers le firmament de la haute finance, l'Excalibur mystique et fiduciaire m'avait métamorphosé en une sorte de dieu qu'il fallait supplier, apaiser, adorer comme les paysans de la Chine adorent le Yang-tsê, implorent la divinité capricieuse d'inonder leurs rizières à la bonne saison, d'apporter « la vigueur au riz et les poissons aux filets », et de leur épargner les effets catastrophiques de sa colère. Je n'étais plus désormais un simple type brillant, la dernière coqueluche ou le phénomène du trimestre. Non, j'avais pris place dans la constellation des grands spéculateurs qui — que cela plaise ou non — constitue le seul panthéon que Wall Street reconnaîtra jamais. J'avais accompli ce que Gould, Harriman ou Jessie Livermore lui-même, le Grand Ours, ce que Diamond Jim et Fisk et tous les Love à leur tour, en commençant par A.E. Senior, pour descendre leur lignée sans oublier Arthur, par son abdication, et enfin Eddie, par son assomption, avaient accompli : j'avais créé une panique. Tel était l'ultime compliment que la vieille Garce pouvait faire à un homme : prendre la mouche, répondre par l'hystérie à une manœuvre imprévue de son courtisan, jeter toute dignité aux orties et battre en retraite devant lui. « Ce soleil fera-t-il pâlir celui de son père ? » Cela restait encore à voir. mais au moins, j'avais déjà égalé son éclat.

Et quelle panique ! La première réaction du Dow à la nouvelle de l'attaque menée contre son pilier le plus solide, le cœur et l'âme de l'Indicateur, fut tout simplement une terreur mortelle. En deux heures il perdit cinquante points. Déjà la bande-annonce accusait un retard de quarante minutes. Il semblait certain qu'avant la fin de la journée, cent millions d'actions auraient changé de main. Le plongeon de l'Indicateur fut même accéléré par la prédiction désastreuse d'un des plus éminents analystes de Wall Street, Joseph Pettyville, qui déclara que l'absorption d'American Power and Light par Rising Sun Enterprises entraînerait peut-être « la fin du capitalisme américain et du système de la libre entreprise tels que nous les connaissons », pronostic qui apparut sur les télex précédé d'une épigraphe de Yeats : « Les choses se défont ; le centre ne peut résister. »

Mais à l'heure la plus sombre, un autre gourou aux disciples également fervents, également féroces, fit savoir qu'à son avis la fusion envisagée était la meilleure chose qui pût arriver à l'économie américaine depuis l'achat de la Louisiane, qu'elle injecterait un sang neuf dans les veines de la maison mère de l'Amérique, la secouerait de sa torpeur, l'obligerait à quitter son autosatisfaction béate pour retrouver le feu et la flamme qui avaient fait d'elle la plus grande entreprise d'Amérique — en d'autres termes, le mariage du soleil levant et du soleil couchant (« Extinction des Feux » était le surnom d'APL à New York où, par le biais d'une filiale, elle possédait et entretenait le réseau électrique ; « Vieille Coupure » était un autre sobriquet moins respectueux). Sur cet avis contradictoire, l'Indicateur toucha le fond et rebondit. En fin d'après-midi, le marché avait regagné les cinquante points perdus, et grimpé de trente autres pour faire bonne figure. Cela rendit le deuxième analyste célèbre en quelques heures, et constitua une claque monumentale pour Pettyville, qu'on brûla en effigie dans les métropoles du monde entier.

Car ces soubresauts ne se limitèrent nullement à Wall Street ou aux rives du Nouveau Monde. A Londres, l'indicateur financier chuta de plus de quarante points, mais la séance s'acheva trop tôt pour enregistrer le retournement de tendance, si bien qu'à la réouverture du lendemain on assista à une frénésie telle qu'on n'en avait pas vu depuis la fin de la deuxième guerre mondiale. A Hong Kong, l'indicateur Hang Seng se haussa de dix points sur la crête du tsunami financier avec un aplomb encore plus impudent qu'à l'ordinaire. Une folie plus conservatrice se manifesta dans les mouvements du Crédit Suisse de Zurich, de la Commerzbank de Francfort, de l'ANPCBS d'Amsterdam ou de la Bourse de Paris. A Singapour et Sydney, Oslo, Milan et Toronto, les Indicateurs enregistrèrent des séismes similaires, sans parler du Nikkei-Dow de Tokyo où l'on dégaina les sabres ancestraux en poussant de sonores banzaï !

Et au milieu de ces folles fluctuations globales, les valeurs individuelles aussi parurent atteintes de tarentisme et de danse de Saint-Guy. A Wall Street, APL, telle une vieille rombière sur le Grand Huit, mi-indignée mi-terrifiée, coula comme une pierre, puis ses seins rebondissants et son corset claquant au vent, remonta en chandelle en retenant son bonnet d'une main et s'accrochant à la barre de sécurité de l'autre, finissant la journée sur une hausse de trois points et demi. Quant à Rising Sun Enterprises, sa curieuse écurie de Taureaux prit le mors aux dents, rua des quatre fers comme les bêtes de rodéo du même nom. Mais bizarrement, Rising Sun enregistra une baisse de deux points à la fermeture, phénomène étrange en les circonstances. De plus en plus curieux. Néanmoins, ce léger repli fut porté au compte du chaos momentané provoqué par notre offre publique ; cette baisse creusait seulement une imperceptible dépression dans la ligne montante de la tendance à long terme du Taureau de notre félicité, la mienne et celle des Cornes. Mes hommes de confiance suggérèrent — et je me rangeai à leur avis — qu'il ne fallait pas s'inquiéter de pareille broutille quand notre campagne avait été couronnée d'un succès aussi total et grandiose.

Car lorsque la poussière et les papiers usagés se furent posés à terre, et que les huissiers les eurent balayés pour les envoyer à l'incinérateur, un ordre nouveau avait commencé d'émerger de ces cendres, une configuration d'une ampleur inédite, si vaste et magnifique qu'elle dépassait l'entreprise, la corporation, la multinationale — *Novus Ordo Seculorum*, l'Ordre des Temps Nouveaux, tel que l'avaient prophétisé les Pères Fondateurs ! Un concept si vaste que l'esprit reculait devant lui comme devant l'infini ! Ce monolithe industriel, que je proposai d'appeler *American Sun* — Soleil Américain ; ou mieux encore, Soleil de Toutes les Amériques — serait à la science économique ce que la première boule de feu était aux astronomes et aux physiciens : l'état originel indifférencié, l'unité, l'Un et, oui, inutile désormais de feindre la modestie, le Tao ! Le Tao qui, ainsi que Riley et moi en avions un jour discuté, avait autrefois explosé pour une raison inconnue, donnant naissance aux dix mille choses projetées dans l'espace de plus en plus loin les unes des autres, comme les galaxies expulsées de la boule de feu primitive et dont le rayonnement émis se déplaçait toujours vers le rouge. Cette explosion était le mystère central qui avait engendré toutes les religions ; et maintenant je comprenais enfin qu'il m'incombait de suturer la plaie, de rendre au monde son intégrité. Perdu ? Ah ! Quel crétin j'avais été ! J'étais sauvé ! Libéré ! Délivré ! Guidé par la foi et l'intuition taoïstes, je n'avais cessé de croire que le Tao finirait par émerger du labyrinthe du Dow. Et la vie avait confirmé mon intuition ! C'était le destin choisi pour moi par Dieu que, malgré ma bâtardise, je dusse réintégrer les hordes hurlantes dans l'unité originelle, raccompagner les dix mille choses vers le sein nourricier, maternel et indulgent du Tao ; et le moyen pour accomplir cela était la fusion de Rising Sun Enterprises, le *yang* dynamique des corporations, avec le *yin* apathique mais toujours fertile d'American Power and Light ! Ce but donnait un sens nouveau à mes actes. Tous les motifs secondaires — le pouvoir, le lucre, la revanche elle-même — seraient englobés et pardonnés par mon apostolat. Ainsi conjecturai-je, et les Cornes se rangèrent à mon avis. J'étais si ravi que je leur accordai des primes substantielles pour leur bon travail et les invitai à dîner au Lutèce.

Je rentrai chez moi assez tard et passablement éméché, prêt à pardonner à Li toutes ses incartades et plein de désir pour elle. Malheureusement, mes perspectives de conquête et de reddition ne se confirmèrent pas. Quand, l'œil embrumé par la boisson et la passion, je pénétrai dans notre chambre à coucher, je découvris étendue sur mon matelas grand format non pas l'objet prévu de ma concupiscence, mais une valise dans laquelle mon seul et unique amour lançait en vrac l'ensemble de ses biens terrestres.

« Que fais-tu ? » demandai-je en entrant derrière le chat Eddie dont j'imitai les mouvements de tête de droite et de gauche tandis qu'il suivait des yeux la trajectoire des déshabillés et autres accessoires affriolants de lingerie intime qui avaient figuré dans mes récents fantasmes et décrivaient maintenant d'aussi gracieuses paraboles que le volant emplumé du badminton.

« Comme si tu ne le savais pas », me répondit-elle d'une voix mordante.

Ses mots me frappèrent à l'estomac. Baissant les yeux, je découvris que je tenais un panda en peluche qu'elle venait de me jeter.

« Qu'est-ce que c'est que ça ? me demanda-t-elle. Une offrande propitiatoire ? Un pot-de-vin pour me faire rester ?

— De quoi parles-tu ? répliquai-je, de plus en plus troublé. Je n'ai jamais vu ce jouet de ma vie. » Je la regardai de nouveau. Hmm... peut-être que si, après tout.

« Tu ne me l'as pas envoyé ? »

Je secouai la tête en toute innocence.

« Eh bien, je suis contente que tu n'aies pas été jusque-là. » Elle se remit à remplir sa valise. « Il est arrivé ce matin. C'est peut-être une plaisanterie. »

Je lâchai l'animal en peluche et m'approchai d'elle.

« Reste où tu es, m'avertit-elle en reculant. Ne me touche pas. Je ne me laisserai pas intimider.

— Mais de quoi parles-tu ? Qu'est-ce que ça veut dire ? l'implorai-je.

— Ça veut dire que je te quitte, dit-elle d'une voix ferme en me défiant brièvement du regard avant de reprendre son activité.

— Mais pourquoi ?

— Pourquoi ! répéta-t-elle, incrédule. Après ce que tu m'as dit hier soir ? La façon dont tu m'as regardée ? » Elle frissonna au seul souvenir de sa terreur. « J'ai eu peur de toi, Sun I, j'ai craint pour ma vie.

— Tu as craint *pour ta vie* ? demandai-je en riant. Tu as eu peur de *moi* ? »

Elle me retourna un regard sans expression.

« Mais c'est ridicule ! m'écriai-je. Tu as peur de moi maintenant ? »

Elle secoua la tête, pas tant pour répondre à ma question qu'afin de déplorer la naïveté de mon attitude. « Aujourd'hui est aujourd'hui, hier était hier, dit-elle. C'est exactement ça. Tu n'es pas le même d'un jour à l'autre, ni même d'une minute à l'autre. Tu as changé. Tu perds les pédales. Tu as besoin d'aide.

— Si j'ai besoin d'aide, qui mieux que toi pourrait m'en donner ? rétorquai-je. Tu es ma fiancée, non ? »

Elle vrilla son regard dans mes yeux. « D'une aide qualifiée, précisa-t-elle. Tu n'es pas bien, Sun I. Il faut que tu voies quelqu'un. J'aimerais t'aider, mais — elle secoua la tête — je ne veux pas courir de risque inconsidéré, mettre ma vie en danger. » Puis elle se mura dans un silence buté.

« Parle-moi, suppliai-je. Nous ne pouvons donc même pas en discuter ? »

Elle secoua la tête en pliant un chandail. « Il n'y a rien à ajouter. J'ai pris ma décision. Rien de ce que tu pourras dire ne m'en fera changer. Si tu vois quelqu'un, alors nous pourrons peut-être parler de nouveau. » Elle ferma brusquement la valise et la verrouilla. Elle la souleva du lit avec difficulté, puis prit sous le bras son manteau posé sur une chaise et se campa devant moi au seuil de la chambre. « Ecarte-toi de mon chemin, m'intima-t-elle d'une voix menaçante. Je ne plaisante pas. S'il te plaît, ne rends pas mon départ plus pénible que nécessaire. »

Tremblant de rage et de désespoir, je lui fis face. Le sol se déroba sous mes pieds, toute ma confiance disparut, je ne pus me raccrocher à rien pour affronter la fermeté de son attitude, de sa résolution. Je m'écartai, la laissai partir.

« Je sais où tu vas », lui lançai-je, au bord des larmes.

Elle s'arrêta.

« Tu vas le retrouver », ajoutai-je.

Elle se retourna vers moi. « C'est vraiment ce que tu penses ? »

Je soutins son regard sans broncher. « Vous n'aurez pas un sou, sifflai-je.

— Tu es malade, Sun I. Vraiment malade. » Elle jeta ses clefs vers ma poitrine, sortit en courant, claqua la porte derrière elle. Je sentis sa décision irrévocable, aussi définitive qu'une preuve de culpabilité.

C'était ce qui pouvait m'arriver de mieux, me dis-je aussitôt. Son départ était sans importance. Allongé sur le lit, je fermai les yeux et me masturbai en évoquant l'image de son corps derrière mes paupières closes. Je jouis en sanglotant, puis me tournai vers son côté du lit où je respirai son odeur — parfum et sueur mêlés, ainsi que nos humeurs — et je m'endormis en pleurant. Mon merveilleux ange du sexe.

Mais il est infiniment plus facile de haïr que de porter le deuil, et sur le principe d'une telle économie mon inconscient échafauda sa stratégie. Bien que haïssant Li et ses infidélités, je persistai dans mon diagnostic optimiste, continuai de penser que tout finirait par s'arranger, que je verrais « quelqu'un », qu'elle s'apaiserait, renoncerait à Peter et reviendrait vers moi. En fait, le travail fut ma planche de salut. Car pour utiliser une métaphore éculée mais adéquate dans les circonstances, ma haine pour Li ressemblait à une bougie au soleil, comparée à la haine dévorante que je nourrissais envers *lui*, Eddie Love.

Et comme si cela ne suffisait pas, une divinité compatissante m'envoya quelques soucis en guise de diversion. L'éminence grise de la presse jaune s'était tapie dans l'ombre pour observer, avec son horrible rictus de chacal, les récents événements de ma vie privée. La semaine suivante, une édition spéciale de *Votre argent et votre vie* publia un article de Hackless, qui avait réussi à découvrir ma visite à Trinity et s'en gaussait en ces termes :

> *Après avoir annoncé publiquement son OPA aux actionnaires d'American Power and Light, ce dernier week-end, Sonny, alias le Pape Mandarin, vient d'aborder la deuxième phase de son plan global de domination financière et religieuse du monde en lançant un assaut pacifique contre l'Église épiscopale. Comptant apparemment sur une convergence d'intérêts et de doctrines pour pousser le conseil d'administration anglican à la fusion, Sonny fut échaudé et surpris de recevoir un « non merci » poli mais ferme de la part du Révérend et Très Honorable Archevêque de Canterbury, qui déclina sa proposition « avec tous ses regrets ».*

Hackless semait ensuite la graine du doute sur le montant des dividendes qu'allaient toucher les actionnaires de Rising Sun Enterprises lors du prochain trimestre.

Comment les fidèles actionnaires de Rising Sun réagiront-ils à l'eau qu'on verse ainsi dans leur vin, en proposant des obligations convertibles aux infidèles d'APL pour les pousser à la conversion et au salut (ou à la damnation) ? Porteront-ils leur croix avec une humilité toute chrétienne ? Ou bien le nuage noir de la Réforme plane-t-il à l'horizon de l'église du Soleil Levant ?
Et puis qu'arrive-t-il à Taureau Inc. et au Taureau Mutuel ? Selon un rapport relatif aux dividendes et publié aujourd'hui, les profits du trimestre dernier enregistraient seulement une hausse de 28 % et 32 % respectivement, comparée aux 290 % et 360 % des trois mois précédents. Espérons que leurs dirigeants ne s'empêtrent pas trop dans leurs transactions avec APL !

Ces évidentes calomnies et leur histrionisme haineux nous poussèrent à nous demander si Hackless n'avait pas été attiré dans le camp adverse moyennant espèces sonnantes et trébuchantes. En tout cas, ses affirmations furent matraquées par une campagne de lettres et de coups de téléphone orchestrée par APL, qui contacta et mit en garde tant ses actionnaires que les nôtres, d'abord à propos d'une prétendue « fragilité » de nos obligations convertibles, et ensuite contre l'injustice qui frappait nos actionnaires du premier jour. Cette manœuvre ne fut qu'une des innombrables stratégies défensives de harcèlement et d'intimidation que Bateson et son équipe utilisèrent pour menacer nos flancs. Ils tentèrent même de couper nos lignes de communication en soudoyant les principales firmes spécialisées dans les procurations à Wall Street ; mais nous éventâmes leur complot avant qu'ils n'aient eu le temps de le mettre en œuvre. Ensuite, le bruit courut qu'ils cherchaient frénétiquement un « cavalier blanc » susceptible de les absorber avant nous et de coincer ainsi dans nos roues le bâton de la loi antitrust ; ou alors, à défaut d'un cavalier blanc, ils espéraient s'en tirer en absorbant à leur tour une organisation de services financiers comparable à Rising Sun Enterprises, et obtenir un résultat similaire. Mais ce n'étaient là que forfanteries, vantardises, supercheries de tigres de papier. Ces manœuvres dérisoires accusaient le désespoir d'hommes déboussolés qui scrutaient vainement l'horizon en espérant l'arrivée d'un navire ou de la cavalerie. Presque pathétiques, leurs efforts nous firent davantage de bien en consolidant notre confiance, que de mal en détruisant celle de nos actionnaires.

Beaucoup plus inquiétant que leurs pitoyables simagrées était le déclin continu et inexplicable de notre propre valeur sur le marché. Comme par une fuite mystérieuse dans un puits, ou une hémorragie interne dans le corps fiduciaire, impossible à arrêter parce que d'origine inconnue, les actions de Rising Sun continuaient de s'affaiblir, de s'effriter lentement mais sûrement, un quart ou un huitième de dollar par jour, puis un demi-dollar, baisse qui fut suivie d'une légère reprise, insuffisante à regagner le terrain déjà perdu. Nous n'étions certes pas menacés dans notre existence, ni même dans notre but majeur — la prise en main d'APL. Car notre position bénéficiait d'un avantage tel que nous calculâmes (les Cornes calculèrent, je me rangeai à leur avis) que même dans le pire et inconcevable scénario d'une chute de

25 ou même 30 % de cote de notre action, notre offre resterait séduisante pour les actionnaires d'American Power and Light. En fait, un certain nombre d'entre eux avaient déjà rejoint nos rangs ; après la première semaine, nous possédions déjà 15 % de leurs actions — un bon début. Et jusque-là, notre déclin avait seulement entamé 5 p. 100 de notre capital. Cependant nous ne pouvions être trop prudents, car à long terme la viabilité de l'absorption reposait sur trois facteurs : notre prix élevé comparé à celui d'APL, nos excellentes perspectives de profits, et, argument essentiel, l'aura magique d'infaillibilité qui entourait nos succès phénoménaux. Notre séduction tenait à un substrat plus subtil que le simple jugement froid et rationnel ; c'était là notre atout majeur.

Après de longues délibérations, nous décidâmes que la meilleure façon d'atteindre nos objectifs — renflouer la cote de notre valeur, rassurer nos actionnaires et inciter ceux d'APL à palper le pactole offert sur notre plateau — consistait à orchestrer un investissement aussi spectaculaire qu'avant le départ de Kahn et nos transferts de fonds dans APL, lesquels avaient indubitablement entamé nos dividendes. En d'autres termes, une consultation du *Yi king* semblable à l'ordalie initiale, dûment montée en épingle par les média. Un grand succès nous remettrait définitivement à flot et ferait de l'absorption d'APL une simple formalité. Une large publicité servirait évidemment nos objectifs, car avec la pression psychologique que nous continuions d'exercer sur le marché, le moindre signal d'achat émis par nous provoquerait une ruée des investisseurs sur la compagnie que nous aurions sélectionnée et assurerait du même coup une brusque hausse de sa cote en Bourse. Cela ferait à son tour fructifier nos capitaux investis dans cette compagnie et contribuerait à renflouer Rising Sun.

Mais cette fois, comme je le savais parfaitement, toute consultation en bonne et due forme était superflue. J'avais déjà montré, et les événements l'avaient confirmé, que je contrôlais totalement l'oracle, au point que les pièces et même les baguettes étaient devenues obsolètes, une sorte d'accessoire gênant dans sa matérialité triviale. Non, ce devait être un acte purement mental. Purement. Il réaliserait, consacrerait la vision du but élevé que j'avais eue ce matin-là au parquet, un but situé au-delà de l'« altruisme supérieur », un altruisme ultime dont les pièces se mettaient peu à peu en place et que, tout du long, j'avais porté en moi.

Les Cornes, tous convaincus de l'efficacité du *Yi king*, émirent certaines réserves quant à la prudence de cette acrobatie en solo que l'un d'eux baptisa « consultation sans culottes ». Mais je passai résolument outre leurs réticences. Je soutins que le succès non seulement rassurerait les fidèles, mais transformerait les croyants en fanatiques, créerait un raz de marée hystérique qui balaierait tous les obstacles devant lui, devant nous. Cela constituerait mon apothéose indiscutable devant les investisseurs médusés. Ce serait un miracle.

Ainsi, sans plus tergiverser, la date du lundi suivant fut fixée. Je me sentis nerveux, étrangement triste, durant toute la matinée et même pendant les moments cruciaux de la consultation. Ce fut ainsi que je m'expliquai ensuite que, contre toute attente, contre toute certitude, cette fois cela ne marcha pas. Oh oui, je fermai les yeux et un à un les traits apparurent, s'inscrivant sur la rétine de mon œil intérieur (formules cryptiques écrites dans les ordures). L'hexagramme qui en résultat fut *Kou*, le numéro dix-huit, « Le Travail sur ce qui est Corrompu », ou simplement « La Corruption ». Le caractère *kou* est un pictogramme qui montre un bol contenant de la nourriture avariée et dans lequel grouillent les vers. Le seul trait faible était ainsi commenté :

> Supporter ce qui a été corrompu par le père.
> En continuant on voit l'humiliation.
>
> Ici est montrée la situation où, par faiblesse, on ne s'oppose pas à la corruption, fruit du passé, qui se déclare maintenant, mais où on la laisse suivre son cours. Si l'on continue ainsi, il s'ensuivra une humiliation.

Après cette lecture, je crus émerger d'un rêve. Je regardai les flashes des appareils de photo, les journalistes qui fouillaient mon visage à la recherche d'un indice, les stylos suspendus au-dessus des blocs-notes, mais je ne pus me rappeler ce que je faisais ici, la raison de cette réunion. L'espace d'un instant, je redevins le garçon marqué par les étoiles, le Bloc de Bois Brut que j'avais été en arrivant de Chine, le jour où je débarquai sur ces rivages. Etait-il possible que le petit garçon ne fût pas complètement mort en moi ?

Je fus pris d'une peur terrible, car alors même que je la voyais encore palpiter, cette part de moi-même commença de s'éloigner, puis diminua au point de n'être plus qu'une tache minuscule ; le bureau derrière lequel j'étais assis, la salle, les projecteurs et les caméras, Rising Sun Enterprises elles-mêmes, devinrent une sorte d'affreuse excroissance, un cancer qui s'était développé autour et aux dépens de l'unique cellule saine de l'être que j'avais été, un parasite animé d'une lourde vie pulsatile dont le seul but était d'étouffer ma nature originelle. Oui, il était trop tard pour faire machine arrière. La petite tache disparut avec un cri ténu, comme un flocon de neige qui se dissout dans la mer.

Retrouvant brusquement le sens de la réalité, je pris une profonde inspiration, contractai les muscles de ma mâchoire et achevai la consultation. Après discussion, nous portâmes notre choix sur une firme pharmaceutique qui avais mis au point un procédé bon marché pour produire des cultures bactériologiques d'où l'on tirait la pénicilline et les antibiotiques dérivés, bien que le procédé fût encore au stade expérimental et que le marché des médicaments traversât une période de récession.

Notre apport de capital eut des effets encourageants, mais à la fin de la semaine une catastrophe survint : on découvrit chez plusieurs chercheurs de la firme de graves et irréversibles lésions chromosomiques dues aux expérimentations en cours, et le procédé fut interdit par le ministère de la Santé. La cote de l'action chuta vertigineusement. Un désastre sans précédent. Quand nous vendîmes, Taureau Mutuel et Taureau Inc. avaient perdu plus de 15 pour 100 de leurs avoirs combinés — soit ceux de nos clients. Du jour au lendemain, Rising Sun chuta de plusieurs points.

J'étais désespéré. Un vent de rébellion souffla parmi les Cornes. Mes fidèles bras droits vitupérèrent l'imprudence avec laquelle j'avais abandonné les techniques éprouvées de la consultation. Je devins apathique, je me perdis en jérémiades, battis ma coulpe, pris sur moi toute la faute. Oui, j'avais procédé trop cavalièrement. Oui, tout se serait bien passé si je n'avais pas transgressé le rituel. Mais que faire maintenant ? La situation était critique. Les actionnaires nous désertaient massivement. Le flux des transfuges d'APL se tarit d'un coup, et nous n'avions pas encore atteint la barre des 20 pour 100. La chute de la cote de notre action s'expliquait maintenant parfaitement. Des mesures énergiques s'imposaient. Mais lesquelles ?

Ce fut alors que nous échafaudâmes le plan extraordinaire qui mit Wall Street dans tous ses états, le plan que Hackless brocarda en ces termes, avec les événements qui le précédaient :

LE DOGME DE L'INFAILLIBILITÉ RECONNU
PAR UNE BULLE PAPALE !
Le Canard Pékinois de Sun I Sent le Roussi
Baisse de Régime — et de Pression sur APL !

Le Pape Mandarin — facétieusement surnommé « La Pâle Mandarine » par ses anciens collègues messagers au parquet de la Bourse de New York —, suite à une colossale erreur de jugement qui, selon certaines rumeurs, aurait provoqué une chute de 25 pour 100 des avoirs nets des holdings de Rising Sun Enterprises, vient de prendre une mesure sans précédent dans l'histoire de Wall Street : renversant le rapport traditionnel qui lie le pasteur à son troupeau, il réclame à sa propre congrégation une indulgence pour la rémission de ses péchés qui, reconnaît-il, ont pris des proportions affolantes.

Temporairement possédé d'une crise épique autant qu'épileptique de mégalomanie galopante, il propose maintenant d'engager tous ses biens personnels, y compris ses propres holdings de Rising Sun (le plus gros portefeuille d'actions, selon certains) pour indemniser ses actionnaires, si une deuxième consultation, qui doit avoir lieu dans un avenir proche, s'avérait aussi désastreuse.

Cette fois il promet de suivre à la lettre les prescriptions du rituel et d'abandonner l'approche catastrophique rien-dans-les-mains je-vois-tout-avant-vous. La direction a même proposé de « réhabiliter » son ancien camarade, le Président Kahn, qui cire actuellement le parquet de la Bourse de New York, afin qu'il aide à déchiffrer l'oracle selon la procédure originelle de la séparation des pouvoirs.

En un mot comme en cent, une nouvelle épreuve ! Le Pape va-t-il redorer son blason ou mordre la poussière ? Les fidèles vont-ils se réunir autour de la croix ? Et le cas échéant, avec les baumes adéquats, ou bien les piques, sarcasmes et autres pointes acérées ? Restez branchés ! L'oracle répondra — ou se taira —, mais le marché tranchera ! Comme toujours !

Dans l'état de prostration et de culpabilité qui était le mien, la dérision du sieur Hackless me fit presque plaisir. Quant à cette deuxième consultation, qu'il décrivait avec extravagance mais en des termes plus ou moins adéquats, j'avais peu d'espoir. Brutalement descendues des sommets fiévreux des jours précédents, après les revers tant publics que privés que j'avais subis, ma détermination et ma confiance étaient quasiment anéanties. S'il y eut jamais un moment, un lieu, une chance de tout reconsidérer et d'envisager un retrait ou une démission de ma part, ce fut bien là. La brève intuition d'un minuscule fragment de mon âme épargné par la ruine générale et le naufrage de ma vie — cette vision presque instantanée qui m'avait bouleversé lors de la précédente consultation —, l'espoir de sauver cela me tenailla constamment à l'époque. Il me semblait que le destin, ou le ciel, m'offrait un répit dans la furieuse conflagration qui faisait rage en moi, calmait mon esprit torturé avec la brise d'un souvenir mélancolique. Ce fut alors que, sur cette même brise, Yin-mi vint vers moi.

21

Bien que perplexe, je ne fus pourtant pas vraiment étonné quand ma secrétaire m'annonça par l'interphone la présence de Yin-mi dans la salle d'attente. Je levai les yeux et m'oubliai totalement, le doigt toujours appuyé sur la touche « parlez ».

« Monsieur ? » Mary avait entrouvert la porte et me considérait avec une expression inquiète et vexée. « Que dois-je lui dire ? chuchota-t-elle comme si elle redoutait les oreilles indiscrètes. Voulez-vous que je la fasse entrer ? »

Alors la panique me submergea.

« Monsieur ? insista-t-elle d'une voix tremblante.

— D'accord, murmurai-je.

— D'accord *quoi* ? » demanda-t-elle mi-implorante mi-agacée.

Je pris une profonde inspiration puis soupirai. « Faites-la entrer.

— Mademoiselle... » dit Mary d'une voix forte et soulagée, en regardant par-dessus son épaule. Tenant la porte ouverte derrière elle, elle s'effaça, puis sourit machinalement quand Yin-mi entra dans mon bureau. Mary haussa légèrement les sourcils, comme étonnée, avec un air un peu désapprobateur.

« Bonjour », dit Yin-mi.

Elle était debout devant moi, et je réussis à ne pas la voir jusqu'à ce que sa voix résonnât dans mon souvenir.

Son visage, tellement différent de celui auquel je m'étais attendu, me stupéfia. Elle souriait, elle rayonnait de plaisir, comme si nous étions deux vieux amis qui se retrouvaient après une longue séparation, sans qu'aucun nuage n'eût jamais obscurci leurs rapports. Rien du tranchant aiguisé de la douleur ou d'une trahison pas plus oubliée que pardonnée ne brillait dans son regard, contrairement à celui de Li le soir où elle m'avait quitté. Cette absence ouvrait une large brèche par où l'on me proposait d'entrer.

« Tu as perdu ta langue ? Tu l'as donnée au chat ? » demanda-t-elle malicieusement.

Cette allusion aux chats me fit grimacer ; elle brisa le charme. « Excuse-moi. Assieds-toi, je t'en prie », lui dis-je avec une courtoisie machinale dont je compris aussitôt le ridicule.

Elle eut un rire clair, heureux. « Mon Dieu, que de formalités. » Elle choisit le fauteuil (si proche de moi !), ramena ses mains vers son estomac, et son visage s'anima. « Je suppose que les présentations sont superflues, n'est-ce pas ? » me taquina-t-elle d'un air espiègle.

Je ne répondis rien.

« Tu te souviens de moi ?

— Yin-mi, répondis-je avec une sincérité stupide.

— Bravo ! » Elle pouffa. « Et vous vous appelez Sun I. » Elle tendit le bras pour toucher mes lèvres avec l'extrémité de son index frais ; je fermai les yeux et faillis fondre en larmes.

Quand je les rouvris, elle posait sur moi la grande solennité de son regard. J'essuyai mon visage contre la manche de ma veste et une étrange impression de légèreté s'empara de moi. « Alors, comment vas-tu ? » lui demandai-je gaiement en me levant pour me diriger vers les baies vitrées.

« Comment vas-tu, *toi* ? » rétorqua-t-elle sur un ton beaucoup plus grave que le mien.

Je reniflai, pris une longue inspiration, puis lui fis de nouveau face en ignorant sa question. « Laisse-moi te regarder. »

Le léger embarras avec lequel elle accepta mon examen avait quelque chose de merveilleusement touchant ; elle baissa les yeux en rougissant un peu, puis les releva, sourit presque douloureusement.

Je l'observai sans désir — il n'y avait plus la moindre trace de désir en moi, *d'aucune sorte* —, mais avec une joie profonde et néanmoins délicieuse, comme lorsqu'on passe tôt le matin près d'un massif de fleurs sauvages qui poussent au bord de la route et qu'on se penche pour inhaler leur parfum et l'humidité froide de la rosée.

Magiquement, comme pour confirmer mon image, sa main se leva vers moi. « Je t'ai apporté quelque chose », dit Yin-mi avec un beau sourire. Elle me tendait un chrysanthème dont elle faisait aller et venir la tige entre son pouce et son index comme un minuscule parasol.

Je ressentis une dissonance déchirante, une amertume très douce. Prenant la fleur, j'observai ses pétales avec une mélancolie songeuse, puis la posai soigneusement au bord de mon bureau. Yin-mi la saisit et ses doigts se mirent à faire tourner nerveusement la tige dans un sens puis dans l'autre.

Au bout d'un moment l'association cessa de résonner dans mon esprit, et je l'oubliai. Mais je ne pouvais oublier Yin-mi — sa présence physique. Elle portait une jupe de cuir noir, des collants et des chaussures élégantes qui lui allaient bien. Elle avait mûri et semblait une variante plus chaste et classique de maintes jeunes femmes à la mode qu'on voyait à Wall Street. Mais son visage n'était pas maquillé et son cardigan s'ouvrait sur un simple corsage blanc à col rond boutonné jusqu'au cou, qui accordait à sa personne une certaine fragilité. Elle était assise au bord de son fauteuil, le dos très droit, les genoux serrés, les mains posées en haut des cuisses. Je remarquai une grâce tendue dans sa posture, qui me rappela un arc bandé, prêt à décocher sa flèche, et je me souvins que j'avais découvert Yin-mi dans cette attitude lors du premier déjeuner de famille à l'appartement de ses parents.

Je me remémorai son visage, comparai chacun de ses traits à l'image que j'en avais conservée. Ses cheveux avaient poussé. Ils étaient beaux et altéraient son visage, contribuaient à lui donner de la maturité. Ses yeux n'avaient pas changé ; ils ne changeraient jamais. Les minuscules paillettes dorées de ses iris, ses dents légèrement de guingois me firent rire intérieurement de joie, comme si je venais de retrouver par hasard un objet précieux que j'avais d'abord cru perdu avant de l'oublier définitivement, englouti dans les soucis de la vie quotidienne. Pourtant elle était là. Sa présence me donna le sentiment de redécouvrir un souvenir inestimable dans une boîte où il était peut-être resté pendant des années, de l'examiner à nouveau, d'un œil neuf. Je reconnaissais chacun de ses traits, mais les voyais aussi pour la première fois ; et au-delà de ses traits, outrepassant leur somme, une qualité nouvelle, totalement inédite, qui semblait enfouie au plus profond de son visage et de sa présence, une chose neuve et inconnue que je ne parvenais pas à définir ou à déchiffrer.

« Tu as changé, dis-je.

— Tu trouves ? » Elle porta la main à ses cheveux, fit passer une mèche derrière son oreille.

Je hochai la tête, puis souris en me rappelant.

Elle rougit. « Toi aussi. » Sa remarque était parfaitement transparente ; elle me retourna mon sourire. Mais je pivotai vers les baies vitrées, regardai sombrement les immeubles qui me faisaient face.

« J'ai pensé que tu aurais peut-être faim, reprit-elle après un silence. Je t'ai apporté à déjeuner. » Elle saisit le sac de papier blanc qu'elle avait posé par terre à côté du fauteuil, puis me le tendit pour que j'examine son contenu. « En fait, c'est mon père qui te l'envoie.

— Lo ? » demandai-je avec surprise.

Elle acquiesça en souriant.

« Comment va-t-il ?

— Comme d'habitude, rétorqua-t-elle. Il m'a demandé de transmettre ses amitiés au jeune dragon. » Elle pouffa.

Je la dévisageai. « Tu lui as dit que tu venais ici ? »

Elle opina. « Il a approuvé ma décision.

— Tu lui as parlé de... » Je n'achevai pas.

Elle me regarda sans répondre.

« Et ta mère ? »

Son visage s'assombrit, elle secoua la tête.

Je détournai les yeux ; quelque chose allait de travers. La fleur, le déjeuner — sa générosité et son tact me touchaient, me stupéfiaient. Elle ne faisait aucune allusion désagréable ou amère, comme si nous venions de reprendre notre conversation après une brève interruption due à une cause extérieure. C'était peut-être cela : je ne pouvais accepter sa proposition silencieuse. Je ne la méritais pas, et pourtant elle me l'offrait. Je sentis une mystérieuse ulcération croître dans mon cœur, comme des cristaux de glace qui se forment sur une vitre. Oui, c'était bien ça. Avec Yin-mi, tout était offert. Elle proposait toujours sa commisération. Alors que je désirais la justice. Je voulais *subir* les effets de la justice. Du coup, le pardon qui transparaissait dans son regard et sur son visage m'agaça. Non que je ne ressentisse une immense tendresse pour elle. Plus même que de la tendresse, un désir sauvage de protection. Mais je tenais surtout à la protéger contre moi-même. Je ne lui voulais bien sûr aucun mal, mais je désirais la prémunir du passé. Je voulais payer à cause d'elle et à cause du passé, bien qu'il n'y eût désormais plus rien à réparer. Cela me paraissait mérité. Je le méritais. Et j'allais payer. Payer au centuple.

« Pourquoi es-tu venue ? lui demandai-je sèchement.

— Dois-je avoir une raison ? »

J'éclatai d'un rire narquois. « Moi, j'ai besoin d'une raison.

— Cela fait longtemps, dit-elle.

— Combien de temps ?

— Trop longtemps.

— Bah ! Le printemps ne dure qu'un temps, dis-je méchamment.

— Qu'y a-t-il, Sun I ? » Je décelai dans sa voix un désespoir discret qui m'effraya, qui m'effraya plus que je ne saurais dire. « Si je te fais de la peine — sans le vouloir —, je préfère m'en aller.

— Ne pars pas, dis-je en me tournant vivement vers elle avec un air suppliant que je me reprochai aussitôt. Ne pars pas, Yin-mi. »

Elle battit des paupières. « J'ai parlé avec le père Riley.

— Ah. » Je m'assis dans mon fauteuil, posai mes coudes sur le bureau et dressai mes mains jointes devant mon visage. « Il t'a parlé de notre petite entrevue ?

— Il m'a dit que tu as essayé de communier. »

L'air s'échappa violemment de mes narines — rire, soupir, ricanement. « Le voleur honteux, commentai-je en mordant les ongles et la première phalange de mes index. Le monte-en-l'air du Saint Sacrement. » Je lui souris de toutes mes dents.

« Ce n'est pas drôle, me rabroua-t-elle. Il m'a dit que tu lui avais demandé de te convertir. »

Je fronçai les sourcils en détournant les yeux. « C'était une blague, expliquai-je d'une voix haineuse sans me soucier qu'elle me crût ou non, une mauvaise plaisanterie.

— J'ignorais que tu étais un blagueur », rétorqua-t-elle, s'aventurant plus loin qu'elle n'aurait dû.

Je lui retournai un sourire sarcastique. « Tu ignores beaucoup de choses sur moi.

— Je sais », concéda-t-elle en rougissant ; elle baissa les yeux vers la fleur qu'elle couvrit spontanément d'une main, puis prit doucement au creux de sa paume pour la protéger comme avec un bouclier.

De nouveau, je ressentis de l'irritation. « Tout ceci... » dis-je en faisant pivoter mon fauteuil et changeant mon fusil d'épaule. Je levai les deux mains vers le plafond, paumes ouvertes — le geste de Riley invitant les communiants à approcher de l'autel. « Cela ne t'impressionne pas ? »

Elle ne regarda ni à gauche ni à droite, riva ses yeux sur mon visage. « C'est beau », reconnut-elle.

Je reniflai avec mépris. « Ce n'est rien, la contredis-je avec une insatisfaction amère.

— Puisque tu le sais... » Elle ne termina pas sa phrase.

Je secouai la tête. « Balivernes. Savoir ne sert à rien. Je ne désire pas seulement ça, en tout cas. » Je lui adressai un regard sauvage, accusateur. « Tu devrais le savoir. »

Elle baissa les yeux en rougissant.

« Je suis perdu, Yin-mi », dis-je.

Elle posa sur moi un regard intense, dénégateur, noyé de larmes.

Je secouai la tête avec lucidité en sachant qu'elle se trompait. « C'est la vérité. Elle ne me fait pas peur. » Je regardai d'un air absent par la fenêtre. « La seule chose qui m'importe désormais, c'est lui.

— Qui ? demanda-t-elle.

— Mon père, répondis-je, étonné qu'elle n'ait pas deviné. Tu te rappelles Coney Island ?

— Comment pourrais-je oublier ? dit-elle tendrement.

— Je t'avais dit qu'il était mort ? »

Elle acquiesça.

Je la fixai en faisant peser sur elle tout le poids des mots que j'allais prononcer. « Je l'ai vu.

— Ton père ? » Elle se pencha brusquement vers moi.

Je fermai les yeux et opinai du chef.

« Où ?

— Sur la galerie.

— Tu lui as parlé ?

— J'étais au parquet, expliquai-je.

— Quand ?

— Pendant la panique. Après l'annonce de notre OPA. »

Elle cilla sans comprendre. « Tu es sûr de ne pas avoir tout imaginé ? »

Je la foudroyai du regard. « Toi aussi, tu me crois cinglé, n'est-ce pas ? lui rétorquai-je d'une voix perçante. Exactement comme Li. Tu penses que je devrais "voir quelqu'un". » Je crachai ces mots avec un sourire haineux. « Tu es venue me sauver, hein ?

— J'aimerais le pouvoir, dit-elle sincèrement, douloureusement. Je ferais n'importe quoi. N'importe quoi. » Elle soupira en secouant la tête. « Je crois simplement que tu souffres, poursuivit-elle calmement en examinant mon visage comme un texte qu'elle eût essayé de déchiffrer. D'une douleur terrible. Et je désire t'aider. »

Le sanglot s'arrêta net dans ma gorge, comme un éternuement contenu ; je me détournai en attendant qu'il passât. « Je n'ai pas besoin de ton aide, refusai-je d'une voix froide et plate, je n'en veux pas. »

La tristesse de son regard sembla reculer de plus en plus loin. Je ressentis un brusque accès de panique et de désespoir. « Et puis pourquoi veux-tu m'aider ? » demandai-je en détournant les yeux, désireux de la récupérer sans renier ce que j'avais déjà fait pour la repousser. « Je ne le mérite pas, dis-je en oubliant un instant Yin-mi.

— Comment cela — tu ne le mérites pas ? demanda-t-elle tendrement en s'approchant de nouveau.

— Après... tout, expliquai-je. La façon dont je t'ai traitée.

— Je ne crois pas que tu aies jamais voulu me faire du mal, Sun I », affirma-t-elle sauvagement, comme un point sur lequel elle ne transigerait pas. En un éclair, je vis sa tache aveugle, sa faiblesse, et je compris aussitôt que c'était précisément sa plus grande force, le filament incandescent de son intimité même.

« Tu t'es laissé prendre par un ensemble de circonstances qui te dépassaient », dit-elle, et ce fut comme l'écho d'une autre phrase.

« Tu me crois donc innocent ? demandai-je, incrédule et accusateur.
— Pas complètement. Mais pas davantage entièrement coupable. »
Je ressentis le frisson du déjà-vu. « Alors à qui attribuer le reste de la faute ? » demandai-je, répétant ma réplique comme un vieil acteur qui connaît son rôle par cœur, est incapable de l'oublier bien que la pièce elle-même lui soit sortie de la mémoire.
Elle ferma les yeux, secoua la tête avec un sourire douloureux.
« Au monde, murmurai-je pour moi-même, lui volant sa réplique.
— Je ne sais pas — Yin-mi me surprit —, aux autres. »
L'écho s'empara encore de mon esprit. Incapable de retrouver son origine, je le laissai se répercuter dans les couloirs obscurs de la mémoire, puis rejoindre la zone opaque d'où il avait jailli.
« Depuis le premier jour où je t'ai vu..., reprit-elle d'une voix qui tremblait un peu, une voix que je connaissais.
— Je t'en prie, la suppliai-je doucement, les yeux toujours clos, l'esprit obnubilé par les dernières vibrations de l'écho.
— Bronzé, plein de santé, décrivit-elle sans tenir compte de moi, tes mains calleuses à cause des semaines passées en mer, tes yeux clairs, ton visage tel que je m'en souviens, tel que je le connais, sérieux et intense, cependant calme et serein, pas comme il est aujourd'hui, nerveux, amer, désespéré, avec ce masque de peur et ces cernes bleutés sous tes yeux... » Elle se pencha pour effleurer ma joue, passa doucement son pouce sous mes yeux. « Te voir ainsi me donne presque envie de pleurer, murmura-t-elle tandis que ses traits se crispaient.
— "Depuis le premier jour..." » répétai-je.
Sa main tomba, Yin-mi se rassit. « Ton cœur voulait extraire une vérité inimaginable du centre de la terre où on l'avait oubliée. Je comprenais mal sa nature, je savais seulement que tu avais besoin de cette vérité pour te comprendre toi-même et que tu aurais affronté n'importe quelle épreuve pour la trouver.
— Depuis le premier jour..., insistai-je avec lassitude.
— Depuis le premier jour, reprit-elle, j'ai su que je t'aimais et que je devais t'aider. Et que tu m'aimerais. Un jour. »
Je la dévisageai comme je m'étais retourné pour regarder la petite fille à l'orée de la forêt, en sachant qu'elle était mon seul espoir de bonheur et que je devais y renoncer. La vie ne le permettrait pas, je ne me le permettrais pas. Et j'avais vu mon avenir tracé devant moi : des années et des années passées à la rechercher, la retrouver, la quitter, la laisser partir, puis la pleurer, l'ensemble du cycle se résumant enfin au terrible succédané de la douleur. Encore et toujours.
« Renonce, Yin-mi, dis-je en proie à une terrible pitié pour nous deux.
— Je ne peux pas », répondit-elle au bord des larmes.
J'eus un sourire sans joie. « Tu n'as jamais pu. »
Elle couvrit son visage avec le dos de sa main et pleura.
« Tu dis cela, même après Li. » Je souris. « Autrefois, tu m'accusais de ne pas être de ce monde. Tu disais que j'étais un rêveur. Mais c'est toi qui rêves, Yin-mi, pas moi », dis-je en riant.
Elle essuya son nez sur sa manche. « Mes rêves aspirent à la réalité, répondit-elle. Les tiens, à l'illusion. »

— Tu ne pourrais jamais me pardonner, dis-je avec ambiguïté, et pire encore — je détournai les yeux —, je ne pourrais jamais me pardonner.

— Quoi qu'il y ait à pardonner, dit-elle d'une voix hachée, s'il y a jamais eu quelque chose, je le pardonne maintenant. Comme je t'avais d'avance tout pardonné. Le premier soir. A jamais et à jamais.

— Un enfer sans fin », ajoutai-je avec une ironie désespérée.

Puis mon humeur changea, je me sentis étrangement allègre et enjoué. « Cesse donc de pleurer, la grondai-je avec l'insouciance affectueuse qu'on a pour un vieil ami. Pourquoi pleures-tu ? »

Le visage baissé, elle secoua la tête comme si les larmes l'empêchaient de parler. « Je ne sais pas », répondit-elle enfin entre deux sanglots.

Nos regards se croisèrent. Une belle lumière brillait sur son visage à travers les pleurs. « Quelque chose dans mon cœur. »

Bouleversé par le souvenir, je souris douloureusement.

« Écoute, Sun I.

— Je t'en prie, Yin-mi, l'implorai-je. Si tu continues, tu vas me faire pleurer. Et je ne peux pas pleurer. Je ne peux plus. »

Elle me retourna un regard de détresse et de sympathie.

« Je n'ai plus de larmes.

— Que puis-je faire ? demanda-t-elle. Dis-moi ce dont tu as besoin. »

Je secouai la tête. « Je désire seulement payer, lui dis-je. Rien d'autre. Pas toi. Rien. Seulement cela. Payer et en finir. Rembourser ma dette, le prix. En finir. Terminer.

— Tu es si fatigué, remarqua-t-elle. Je n'ai jamais vu quelqu'un d'aussi fatigué.

— Oui, dis-je seulement.

— Un jour tu te sentiras autrement, continua-t-elle. Tu seras comme avant. La vie te donnera cela. Tu te sentiras mieux, régénéré.

— Il n'y a plus rien à régénérer, la contredis-je sans la moindre trace d'apitoiement sur moi-même. Il ne reste que des cendres et quelques braises. » Je secouai tristement la tête. « Et tu sais quoi ? Je ne désire même pas me sentir mieux. » Je compris la vérité de ces mots en les prononçant. « Je désire seulement payer. Payer le prix fixé.

— Mais quel est ce prix, Sun I ? demanda-t-elle en penchant un peu la tête, les yeux mi-clos.

— Qui sait ? répondis-je avec un haussement d'épaules. Tout. » Soudain je trouvai cela drôle et je ris.

« Je ne te crois pas, me contredit-elle, brusquement perdue, commettant ainsi une autre erreur.

— Merci. » Je regardai ailleurs. « Mais tu te trompes.

— Que t'est-il arrivé ? demanda-t-elle. C'est à cause d'elle ?

— De Li ? » J'éclatai de rire. « Crois-tu vraiment qu'elle aurait pu ?

— Le soir où je vous ai vus — son regard fixe traversait sauvagement mon visage —, ça m'a brisé le cœur. Tu ressemblais à un cheval sauvage qu'on aurait domestiqué, maté, vendu à un cirque et obligé de faire des tours d'animal savant avec un haut-de-forme planté sur les oreilles. »

Je fronçai les sourcils. « Ce n'est pas très gentil. Plutôt méprisant. Ça ne te ressemble pas.

— Excuse-moi, dit-elle en baissant les yeux.

— Tu sais que je l'aimais », dis-je en laissant la colère m'envahir, sans faire un effort pour refermer la porte de la fournaise. Cruel, j'ajoutai : « *Elle*.

— Elle t'aimait ? » répondit-elle en rougissant.

Je ris. « Nous voilà maintenant au cœur du débat, pas vrai ? Nous abordons les choses sérieuses. Elle s'est donnée à moi, dis-je en me tournant vers Yin-mi avec une fureur haineuse, et je l'ai baisée, ajoutai-je méchamment. Je lui ai tout donné.

— Quoi ? demanda-t-elle en me suppliant du regard et de la voix de retrouver mon calme. Le joyau secret de ta vie ? »

Son allusion fit mouche, un filet de sang coula de l'ancienne blessure. « J'ai essayé, je crois, dis-je, peiné mais reconnaissant. Pourtant Li n'a jamais désiré cela. Elle n'a jamais cru en moi, Yin-mi, contrairement à toi.

— Je crois toujours en toi », murmura-t-elle.

Je secouai la tête avec amertume. « Cela n'a plus d'importance. Il est trop tard.

— Pourquoi ? demanda-t-elle. Pourquoi trop tard ?

— Parce que je ne crois plus en moi. »

Elle se contenta de me regarder sans mot dire. Car il n'y avait rien à dire. L'incendie fit de nouveau rage. « Elle m'a donné son corps, dis-je. Contrairement à toi.

— Tu ne l'as jamais demandé », répondit-elle aussitôt, comme si tout le temps elle avait tenu sa réponse prête. Elle m'adressa un sourire tendre, un peu blessé, presque gai et terriblement direct. Sa sincérité me choqua, me scandalisa. Je fus surpris qu'on pût encore me choquer. Oui, sa jeunesse, sa beauté, son innocence, son courage étaient choquants.

« Et si je te le demandais maintenant ? suggérai-je soudain, l'irritation revenant une fois encore.

— Non, Sun I, supplia-t-elle.

— Pourquoi pas ? insistai-je. Je te demande ton corps. Tu m'as bien dit que tu voulais me sauver, que tu étais prête à tout pour cela ? Et si c'était là le prix à payer ? *Ton* prix ? »

Elle secoua la tête. « Ça ne marcherait pas.

— Comment le sais-tu ? Et si moi, je pensais le contraire ? Si je te le disais ? »

Elle cilla sans acquiescer ni se révolter. Je ne la quittai pas des yeux et appuyai sur une touche de l'interphone avec un sourire vaniteux. « Mary, pas d'appels. Nous ne voulons pas être dérangés pendant... — je repoussai ma manche de chemise, regardai ma montre, puis, avec une cruelle bonhomie — disons un quart d'heure ? Non, plutôt une demi-heure. » Je sus à cet instant qu'il y avait quelque chose de monstrueux dans mon cœur, que j'étais perdu au-delà de toute rédemption. Jamais auparavant je n'avais perçu la présence active du mal en moi, mais je le sentis alors palpiter, et j'adorai cela. C'était enivrant, grisant et terrifiant comme un tour de manège, comme la Grande Roue.

« Qu'y a-t-il ? la brusquai-je, tu as peur ?

— Oui, répondit-elle d'une voix dont le calme m'étonna, j'ai peur pour toi. »

Je plissai les lèvres en une moue de dérision. Je l'observai par-dessus l'arche de mes doigts, mordant mes index avec une froide énergie nerveuse, fasciné par l'attente.

La pitié et la résignation traversèrent son visage. De grosses larmes roulèrent sur ses joues. Puis elle baissa les yeux sur sa main qui montait lentement vers le cou et qu'elle regardait comme un objet étranger, sur son poignet si mince, si blanc et souple qui se plia pour ouvrir le bouton supérieur de son corsage. Je ne parviens jamais à oublier son sourire. Je ne peux pas oublier qu'elle souriait. Mais pourquoi ce sourire ? Stupéfait, bouleversé, je sanglotai brusquement, enfouis mon visage entre mes mains. « Va-t'en, m'écriai-je en m'effondrant sur mon sous-main pour donner libre cours à mes larmes. C'était seulement une plaisanterie, une mauvaise plaisanterie. » Cédant à l'hystérie, je me mis à rire et à pleurer.

Quand je relevai les yeux, elle était partie. Sur le fauteuil gisait la tige verte du chrysanthème qu'elle avait mis en pièces et dont les pétales froissés jonchaient le cuir du siège et la laine sombre du tapis.

Je me sentais étrangement calme. Je remarquai le sac de papier blanc et l'ouvris pour examiner son contenu. Il y avait deux gaufrettes porte-bonheur posées sur une pile de serviettes en papier par-dessus les boîtes blanches aux poignées métalliques. Je pris les gaufrettes et les brisai. La première disait : « Même les heureuses surprises commencent souvent par nous paraître étranges. » Je reconnus les mots du *Yi king*. Sur la deuxième, je lus : « Méfie-toi de tes désirs ; ils se réalisent parfois. » Je souris et me demandai laquelle était destinée à Yin-mi laquelle à moi. Je le devinai assez vite.

Portant machinalement un morceau de gaufrette à ma bouche, je retirai les dernières miettes sur mon bureau, les jetai dans la corbeille à papier, puis me concentrai sur autre chose et oubliai complètement la visite de Yin-mi.

22

La perspective de la deuxième consultation me rendit presque joyeux. Je m'inquiétai à peine de ses conséquences possibles pour le déroulement ultérieur de l'absorption, l'avenir de Rising Sun Enterprises, sans parler de mon propre destin. Non que j'eusse perdu tout espoir ou tout intérêt, ou que je fusse incapable de comprendre la précarité de la situation ; quand les Cornes, évidemment terrifiées par mon attitude, me sermonnèrent individuellement et à plusieurs sur ce chapitre, j'opinai solennellement du chef à la pertinence de leurs arguments, j'acquiesçai à toutes leurs initiatives et leur promis de m'amender. Mais pour dire la vérité, l'économie restreinte de ma vie intérieure m'interdisait de consacrer mes loisirs à pareilles futilités, car j'étais totalement mobilisé par une priorité infiniment plus urgente : l'existence, l'existence elle-même dont j'avais hérité franco de port, sans la réclamer et d'un donneur anonyme, cadeau et fardeau qui réclamait maintenant, brusquement, un investissement à cent pour cent de mon temps, de mon attention et de mon énergie. Pourtant je n'étais ni désespéré ni malheureux ; aucune difficulté, aucun obstacle insurmontable ne me barrait la route ; je ne souffrais pas spécialement, mais tout simplement la vie sous sa forme la plus triviale — tourner un bouton de porte, traverser mon bureau jusqu'à mon fauteuil, m'asseoir, trouver un crayon bien taillé — tâches sur lesquelles je me concentrais profondément pendant plusieurs minutes et qui me procuraient une satisfaction disproportionnée — cela m'absorbait totalement, au point de rejeter le passé et le futur dans des régions aussi lointaines que la métaphysique ou la lune.

Mais cet état ne dura qu'un temps. Je crois que mon esprit se reposait instinctivement en vue de la glorieuse apothéose à venir ; le feu couvait toujours sous le poids des cendres de ce qui avait déjà été consumé ; la gravité de la destruction déclencherait bientôt la combustion spontanée de l'ultime combustible.

J'eus plaisir à revoir Kahn. Sa présence me rassura ; il me sembla qu'il ramenait l'ancienne sécurité, cette sécurité relative qui avait existé durant ces jours lointains et pleins d'espoir où nous avions conçu notre plan avant de le baptiser Taureau Inc., et où mon ami s'épanouissait au soleil de nos idées comme une fleur flétrie qui renaît lentement à la vie. Ce fut bon de le retrouver, même s'il m'observait sans cesse avec dans les yeux la même lueur que pendant les semaines éprouvantes qui avaient suivi son ultimatum et sa narration de l'histoire d'Eddie Love après son séjour en Chine, des semaines qui m'avaient vu désespérer de ma vie et de mon avenir, sombrer dans des tourments dont l'innocence et la candeur me touchaient rétrospectivement. « Quand j'étais enfant, je raisonnais comme un enfant » — souffrais comme un enfant. Je fis de mon mieux pour me concentrer sur mon bien-être personnel et celui de Rising Sun, mais sans grand résultat. Kahn s'inquiétait beaucoup plus que moi du succès de mon entreprise.

Cette deuxième consultation bénéficia d'une mise en scène encore plus tapageuse que la première, que l'ordalie elle-même, peut-être parce que son enjeu parut crucial. Le public de Wall Street avait perçu l'ordalie comme une plaisanterie, les gens étaient venus avec des œufs et des pommes pourris. La consultation précédente, *Kou*, aurait dû s'inscrire dans une série de succès qui étaient devenus monotones et banals, du moins avant sa conclusion désastreuse. Mais la chaîne était désormais rompue, et cette fois les hordes de la finance convergèrent sur nous avec les yeux rouges et affamés des charognards fondant sur un animal blessé qui se débat dans les broussailles. Non, cela n'avait plus rien de drôle. L'odeur du sang chaud empestait l'air, les rapaces rôdaient autour de nous avec un appétit obscène, attendant pour se repaître le signe ultime, l'intonation révélatrice d'un grognement, un silence plus pesant. Cela réveilla ma colère, me rendit une partie de mes moyens. Je me rappelai les visages de tous les hommes que nous avions broyés, leur désespoir sourd, leur haine sinistre ; j'essayai de ne pas y penser, j'essayai même d'en sourire, mais je savais que la même expression s'était désormais gravée sur mes traits. Eux aussi avaient souri, je m'en souvenais, en me maudissant entre leurs dents serrées tout comme à présent je maudissais d'autres prédateurs. Et pourtant cela me redonna courage. Je me rappelai les paroles de Yin-mi — « Un jour tu te sentiras mieux, régénéré » — et je souris avec une ironie morbide. « La vie te donnera cela », avait-elle promis. La haine m'avait régénéré. La haine était peut-être la même chose que la vie. Plus je considérai cette proposition, plus je la trouvai profonde : la vie comme une rage tempérée contre la matière inanimée, contre l'entropie. Une rage de perdant.

Après ma manipulation — cette fois avec le livre et selon le rituel ; je n'utilisai même pas les pièces, mais les baguettes —, l'oracle me retourna l'hexagramme *Ming Yi*, *K'ouen* au-dessus de *Li*, « La Terre » au-dessus du « Feu », « L'obscurcissement de la Lumière ».

> Le soleil s'est enfoncé sous la terre et s'est donc obscurci. Le nom de l'hexagramme signifie proprement le fait de « blesser ce qui est lumineux », et c'est pourquoi les différents traits parlent souvent de blessure.

Il y avait des traits faibles à la quatrième et la sixième place :

Six à la quatrième place signifie :
Il pénètre dans le côté gauche du ventre.
On parvient au cœur de l'obscurcissement de la lumière,
Et l'on quitte la porte et la cour.

On se trouve dans le voisinage du chef de l'obscurité et l'on découvre ainsi ses pensées les plus secrètes. On se rend compte par là qu'il n'y a plus d'amélioration à espérer.

Six en haut signifie :
Non la lumière mais l'obscurité.
Tout d'abord il s'est élevé au ciel,
Puis il a plongé dans les profondeurs de la terre.

L'obscurité parvient ici à son comble. La force ténébreuse était d'abord placée si haut qu'elle pouvait blesser toutes les puissances bonnes et lumineuses. A la fin pourtant elle périt par sa propre obscurité, car la chute du mal doit se produire au moment même où il a complètement vaincu le bien et, par suite, consumé la force à laquelle il devait jusque-là son existence.

Après la menace initiale de désastre, le commentaire du dernier trait — six en haut — me fit de nouveau espérer. Car qui était cette « force ténébreuse » sinon mon père, Eddie Love, que j'avais d'abord « placé si haut », mais qui aujourd'hui, à cause de ma propre ascension, était enfin à portée ? Et vraiment, « dans le voisinage du chef de l'obscurité », j'avais « découvert ses pensées les plus secrètes », moi qui avais toujours été du côté des « puissances bonnes et lumineuses ». Il finit par périr dans ses propres ténèbres, « car la chute du mal doit se produire au moment même où il a complètement vaincu le bien et, par suite, consumé la force à laquelle il devait jusque-là son existence ». Cette prophétie me procura une satisfaction délicieuse, je me réjouis par avance de son accomplissement.

A l'inverse, Kahn, qui était là pour en tirer une application boursière, fut nettement moins optimiste que moi. En fait, après une demi-heure de tâtonnements infructueux, nous décidâmes de congédier la presse et de reporter au lendemain l'annonce de notre choix afin de lui donner le temps de réfléchir.

« J'arrive tout bonnement à rien, petit, dit-il en secouant la tête d'un air perplexe. L'oracle me laisse froid comme la banquise. » Il leva les yeux. « A moins qu'il ne nous conseille d'acheter des options de vente sur American Power and Light. » Il sourit. « Tu me suis ? L'obscurcissement de la Lumière ?

— Je vous suis, Kahn, répondis-je. Mais croyez-vous qu'il serait sage d'acheter des options de vente sur une valeur dont notre OPA fait monter la cote ?

— Je blaguais, petit. Prends donc pas la mouche et ne t'inquiète pas, je vais trouver quelque chose. Je tiens à explorer quelques pistes avant de m'engager. Je te donnerai ma réponse vers huit ou neuf heures ce soir. »

Mais Kahn ne me fit pas signe avant neuf heures passées le lendemain matin. Il restait seulement quelques minutes avant l'ouverture de la séance. Les Cornes paniquaient. Toute la nuit j'avais essayé de mettre la main sur mon ami introuvable.

Quand il entra dans mon bureau, je crus qu'il avait passé la nuit à boire. Il tenait sa veste accrochée à un doigt sur son épaule, ses manches de chemise étaient relevées, sa cravate desserrée pendait de travers. Le chaume bleu de sa barbe couvrait ses joues jusqu'à ses pommettes, ses yeux cernés étaient rouges. Mais il souriait comme un forban.

« Kahn, vous êtes ivre ! » lui reprochai-je avec indignation.

Une expression de vertu offusquée apparut sur ses traits. « Nullement, Armand, railla-t-il en jetant sa veste devant moi sur mon bureau.

— Où étiez-vous ? demandai-je. Je vous ai cherché toute la nuit.

— A Columbia, dit-il laconiquement afin de profiter le plus longtemps possible de son avantage.

— Columbia ! »

Il opina du chef, bâilla, tapota sa bouche du dos de la main avec une feinte et exaspérante nonchalance. « A la bibliothèque. J'ai eu envie d'aller voir si ma vieille turne était toujours là.

— Kahn ! » menaçai-je.

Il prit sa veste, en sortit un journal plié, sans oublier un paquet de bonbons qu'il tendit alentour et dont personne ne voulut.

« Sans regrets ? Tant mieux ! » s'écria-t-il avec satisfaction. Il lança ensuite le journal sur mon sous-main, d'une légère et adroite torsion du poignet le fit atterrir dans le bon sens devant moi, puis il se pencha en avant et se mit à le lire à l'envers tout en piochant dans son paquet de bonbons.

C'était la page financière du *London Times*.

« Pourquoi Londres ? » demandai-je.

Il acquiesça. « Tu me dois une fière chandelle, Sonny, dit-il. Ou plutôt...
— il haussa les sourcils — nous sommes quittes. »

Un sigle incompréhensible était entouré d'un cercle de feutre noir : « DMUCHA.

— Une renaissance de l'art-nouveau ? demandai-je.

— Non, petit, dit-il sèchement. D-M-U-CH-A.

— Oh », fis-je.

Il sortit autre chose de sa poche, une sorte de brochure promotionnelle, peut-être un rapport annuel, qu'il jeta devant moi. Sur la couverture, au-dessus de la photographie d'une douzaine de femmes arabes en tchador, assises côte à côte devant autant de machines à coudre, je lus : « Deux Mille Un : les Chevaliers Arabes. Habits de Soirée pour Hommes Cheiks.

— Qu'est-ce que c'est, Kahn, une plaisanterie ? lui lançai-je d'un ton cinglant.

— Est-ce le moment de plaisanter ? rétorqua-t-il aussitôt. Je ne blague pas, petit. Ce truc est l'affaire la plus juteuse en Angleterre depuis Cecil Rhodes — quasiment la seule affaire, d'ailleurs.

— Qui la dirige ?

— Yassuh Gamal Hassan Abdullah Tinbad Mohammed Fahd Ali el-Ararat de-Sadat, dit Kahn, également connu sous le nom de Lumière du Désert, l'Artiste Tailleur de Suez, le Dandy du Coran, le Canard Boiteux d'Assouan, le Pied Soyeux de l'Orient, le Protège-Coudes de l'Imam, l'Aisselle de l'Univers, l'Empereur de l'Empeigne, le Pape de la Popeline, le Cinglé de la Singer, le Point de Feston des Rires et des Sourires Damnés, le Pharaon du Veston, le Cheik du Chic, également président-directeur général et président du conseil d'administration de Deux Mille Un : les Chevaliers Arabes, "le Cartel de la Mode Future".

« Il a acheté la propriété d'un baronnet du Sussex et l'a transformée en usine (la presse appelle ça "l'Atelier des Deux Mille et Une Nuits") pour produire les habits de soirée de haute couture — tu piges ? L'Obscurcissement de la Lumière ? — à des prix défiant toute concurrence à cause de la main-d'œuvre immigrée bon marché. Il a quitté le Sud-Yémen avec ses douze sœurs, qui sont maintenant contremaîtres dans l'usine. Après leur lancement réussi, ils ont attiré d'autres ouvrières en leur faisant miroiter des mariages arrangés avec des étrangers travaillant en Angleterre. Au bout de sept brèves années d'un apprentissage quasiment esclavagiste, Yassuh réussit à garder ses arpettes d'une façon ou d'une autre, car notre homme a aussi la réputation de diriger un réseau de prostitution islamique.

— Mais Kahn, protestai-je, cette opération est-elle valable ? Je veux dire, assez grosse ? »

Il pencha la tête en haussant un seul sourcil. « *Grosse*, répéta-t-il sombrement. C'est sans doute le plus gros coup depuis Rolls-Royce. Je suis sérieux, petit. Ce type incarne la vraie camelote, le véritable entrepreneur du Tiers-Monde — la pure laine vierge cardée à la main — il sourit — pour ainsi dire. Un peu fadasse à première vue, il vend pourtant aux meilleures boîtes. Tu es allé chez Macy's dernièrement ? Tu peux aujourd'hui acheter des smokings, des ceintures turbans, des fracs produits par tu sais qui.

— Vous croyez que c'est vraiment ça ? demandai-je.

— L'obscurcissement de la Lumière, dit-il en haussant les épaules.

— Deux Mille Un : les Chevaliers Arabes, répétai-je afin d'éprouver les sonorités de l'expression. Habits de Soirée pour Hommes Cheiks.

— Il y a une plaisanterie en vogue actuellement, petit, reprit Kahn. Le spécialiste des chemises de nuit blanche et des smokings blindés pour rois du pétrole arabes en voyage à l'étranger. »

Je le foudroyai du regard.

« Tu y es ? Chemise de nuit blanche : Habits de Soirée ? Smokings blindés : Chevaliers Arabes ?

— J'y suis, Kahn, rétorquai-je sèchement. Si vous voulez mon avis, tout cela est une plaisanterie. Et d'un goût exécrable.

— Ah mais excuse-moi ! se vexa-t-il. J'ai passé toute la nuit à essayer de sortir de la mouise ton sale petit cul oriental, et voilà comment tu me remercies ? Rappelle-moi à l'avenir de m'en tenir à l'onanisme. C'est moins fatigant et plus distrayant.

— D'accord, Kahn, dis-je sur un ton plus conciliant, ne prenez donc pas la mouche. J'apprécie vos efforts. Sincèrement. »

Il hocha la tête avec une moue boudeuse.

Je me tournai vers les Cornes. « Okay, les gars, vous avez entendu notre homme. Maintenant, à vos téléphones ! »

Et cette fois, contre tout espoir, cela marcha. Dans la demi-heure suivante, je reçus un appel téléphonique d'un Yassuh excité qui me jura que sa descendance m'adorerait pendant « cent dix-sept générations » et que lui-même, malgré son « handicap physique » sur la nature duquel il n'épilogua point (et je ne l'interrogeai pas davantage), se prosternerait dorénavant dix fois par jour en direction de Wall Street, avant et après La Mecque. Plus important encore, il m'annonça dans la même matinée que cette injection de capital inespérée allait lui permettre l'importation globale et l'installation forcée de deux villages de nomades, ainsi que l'acquisition d'une chaîne de châteaux hôteliers le long de la Tamise. Avant la fin de l'après-midi, DMUCHA enregistrait, ainsi que nos investissements, une hausse mirobolante de vingt-deux pour cent. A la fin de la semaine, aidé par un retrait de la livre sterling devant le dollar, Rising Sun Enterprises avait regagné presque tout le terrain perdu, les transfuges d'APL séduits par notre offre publique d'achat se pressaient de nouveau à nos portes, et j'avais réussi à éviter le pire à mes capitaux personnels. Le lundi suivant, j'offris à Kahn et aux Cornes un banquet islamique. Mais notre convivialité trébucha sur une fausse note quand les troupes restées au fort par mesure de sécurité nous annoncèrent au téléphone qu'à la clôture de la séance Rising Sun avait perdu un point, reprenant ainsi son déclin. Tous nous enlevâmes nos turbans de location, nous assîmes sombrement autour de la table, où nous demeurâmes silencieux jusqu'à ce que Kahn prît la parole.

« Écoutez, dit-il, je ferais peut-être mieux de me mêler de mes oignons, mais vous êtes tous des jeunes types d'après la Réforme. Vous ne pouvez donc pas vous rappeler l'époque paradisiaque — infernale conviendrait sans doute mieux — interrompue par l'adoption de la Charte d'Échange des Valeurs en trente-quatre, cette époque bénie où le parquet ressemblait au Jardin d'Éden. Moi non plus je ne m'en rappelle pas. Mais je l'ai vécue indirectement, par procuration, grâce à mon oncle Ahasvérus. » Il marqua un temps pour donner du poids à ses paroles et reprendre son souffle.

« Et alors ? Que voulez-vous dire ?

— Une seule chose, petit, répondit-il. Cette fuite qui vous tracasse tant, elle présente toutes les caractéristiques d'un classique raid d'ours.

— Un raid d'ours, répéta l'une des Cornes. Je sais ce que c'est. J'ai étudié ça pour un cours d'histoire des affaires.

— C'est complètement démodé, dit un deuxième.

— C'est illégal, renchérit un troisième.

— Il parle d'une vente à tout crin », supputa un quatrième.

Je songeai au panda en peluche que j'avais trouvé chez moi après la conférence avec APL ; un frisson glacé descendit le long de mon dos. « Qu'est-ce qu'un raid d'ours, Kahn ? demandai-je calmement.

— C'est une attaque contre la cote d'une valeur par le biais de ventes répétées à court terme pendant une longue période, expliqua-t-il.

— Une inondation du marché, une vente à tout crin, réitéra la même Corne. Cela engendre un excès d'actions disponibles et un effondrement de sa cote, car l'offre est infiniment plus grande que la demande.

— Est-ce illégal ? interrogeai-je.

— Et comment ! répondit violemment l'une des Cornes.

— Manipulation d'une valeur ! dit un deuxième.

— C'est légal tant qu'on ne se fait pas prendre, dit Kahn avec un sourire de weltzschmerz sage et désabusé.

— C'est ça, fis-je, en proie à une brusque rage froide. Les salauds ! » Je fixai mon regard sur Kahn. « Très bien, comment se défend-on contre un raid d'ours ? »

Il retroussa les lèvres en secouant la tête. « Je vois une seule chose à faire :

stimuler la demande en achetant tes propres actions pour te défendre. Soit cela, soit trouver la preuve de leur fraude.

— Comment faire pour les démasquer ?

— C'est difficile », répondit-il. Il regarda les Cornes. « Mets donc quelques-uns de ces petits génies au boulot. Ils dénicheront peut-être quelque chose.

— Le problème, poursuivis-je, plus pour moi-même que pour lui, en réfléchissant à la première option qui consistait à acheter nos propres actions, c'est que la quasi-totalité de nos capitaux sont investis dans l'absorption.

— Il faut que tu empruntes encore, dit-il. Tu possèdes une banque, non ?

— Dois-je emprunter beaucoup ?

— Plutôt trop que pas assez, répondit-il. Et à ta place, je jetterais dans la balance tous mes avoirs personnels. »

Je l'interrogeai du regard.

« Ils te serviront de garantie pour obtenir un prêt, développa-t-il. Ça fera un peu baisser la pression qui s'exerce sur la compagnie. Tu ne veux pas que Rising Sun devienne une véritable pieuvre ; il ne pourrait rien t'arriver de pire.

— Que voulez-vous dire ?

— Soyez sur vos gardes, répondit-il d'un air mystérieux. Faites attention à ce qu'ils ne se glissent pas par la porte de derrière.

— Vous craignez qu'ils ne nous absorbent ? »

Il opina vigoureusement.

« Mais s'ils entreprennent un raid d'ours, comment peuvent-ils essayer de nous absorber en même temps ? le contredit l'une des Cornes. Ils ne peuvent pas vendre nos actions à tire-larigot et en même temps nous acheter ?

— Hmm, réfléchit Kahn. Un point pour vous. Je constate avec plaisir que vous avez quelque chose dans le crâne. » Il se tourna vers moi en désignant son interlocuteur du menton. « Tu as embauché un crack. Je voulais simplement m'assurer que vous aviez encore les yeux en face des trous. »

Mon protégé rougit en bombant le torse.

« Okay, j'ai donc mis mon grain de sel et le moment est venu de nous quitter. Vous autres, prenez bien soin de mon protégé. » Il se tourna vers moi. « A la prochaine, petit. Et mazel tov *one more time* et à fortiori. »

Le lendemain matin, l'une des Cornes apporta un lourd volume muni d'un vieux fermoir et d'une reliure en cuir noir moisi qui dégageait une forte odeur. Ce volume empli de grandes pages jaunissantes et cassantes imprimées en caractères gothiques avec de grosses lettrines et de lourds empattements ornementaux, où tous les *s* s'écrivaient comme des *f*, s'intitulait : *Wall Street avant la Chute : Usque ad annum Domini MCMXXXIV*. Quand je l'ouvris, son dos craqua et le cuir hurla comme une âme en peine. A l'intérieur nous découvrîmes l'équivalent d'une salle de tortures médiévale parfaitement équipée de cercueils à pointes, fouets à neuf queues, vis à ailettes, chevalet et roue, ainsi que tous les autres dispositifs ingénieux qu'on utilisait quotidiennement avant 1934 (et, si Kahn avait raison, contre nous en ce moment même). Nous apprîmes le fonctionnement intime des ventes fictives et des monopoles ; nous nous initiâmes aux manipulations des trusts : le premier et le second trust des Chemins de Fer Harlem, les raids téléguidés par Drew, Fisk et Gould, le trust de la Northern Pacific, l'affaire de Stutz et Piggly Wiggly dont les prouesses enchantaient encore Wall Street. Parmi tous ces trésors, nous trouvâmes une analyse succincte mais lumineuse de la technique connue sous le nom de raid d'ours, et nous fûmes plus que jamais convaincus que c'était là le chevalet de torture où l'on nous avait ligotés, la roue sur laquelle nous tournions, une version améliorée, modernisée, du supplice moyenâgeux, la vente à tout crin, avec commande à crémaillère pour des contorsions plus souples et silencieuses.

Nous nous mobilisâmes aussitôt afin d'échafauder une stratégie de défense. Je commençai par choisir quelques-unes des Cornes les plus acérées dont l'unique mission consisterait à découvrir ou exhumer les preuves de manœuvres illégales de la part des membres du conseil d'administration d'APL, sans négliger les liaisons extra-maritales ni les perversions sexuelles, qui me paraissaient hautement probables. Ensuite, et plus important encore, je téléphonai à la direction du Groupe Bancaire du Taureau (anciennement Second Jersey Hi-Fi) pour contacter un homme dont la réputation de droiture et de probité en matière fiduciaires lui avait permis de conserver son poste après la guerre et notre absorption, malgré son amertume et son inimitié évidente envers Kahn, une inimitié dont j'étais désormais le seul bénéficiaire depuis le départ de mon compagnon. Je lui expliquai brièvement la situation et fus attristé de voir un sourire vindicatif illuminer ses traits. Il fit grincer ses molaires avec une satisfaction de prédateur. Je lui dis que Rising Sun aurait besoin de prêts supplémentaires pour se défendre en achetant ses propres actions, et que j'aurais personnellement besoin de fonds pour lutter dans le même sens. Il me rétorqua que, de son point de vue, la banque était déjà trop impliquée dans l'absorption et que d'autres engagements constitueraient une concentration imprudente des ressources, un pari qui, en cas de contretemps imprévisible, pouvait s'avérer désastreux, voire aboutir à la faillite de la banque. Déjà, se plaignit-il, les organismes de crédit d'APL commençaient à exercer des pressions sur la banque et à faire de lui un paria, la brebis galeuse de la communauté financière. S'échauffant, il poursuivit en insistant sur cette évidence qu'en tant que P-DG de la maison mère, j'étais bien sûr libre de le renvoyer pour installer dans son fauteuil un individu plus malléable, mais que je ne l'obligerais jamais à déroger à ce qu'il considérait comme les principes inaltérables de la finance. S'étant ainsi soulagé de son credo, il continua en concédant à contrecœur qu'on pouvait en effet envisager quelques prêts supplémentaires à la corporation, et que, dans mon cas personnel, lui-même serait ravi de définir des prêts aux conditions de crédit que la banque accordait à ses meilleurs partenaires commerciaux, mais que, si j'attendais de lui qu'il mît sa réputation en jeu en recourant à la moindre pratique illicite, eh bien je me fourvoyais complètement, et que de surcroît...

Je l'arrêtai là et lui assurai que je désirais simplement le traitement préférentiel classique ; puis, comme il me semblait amadoué, je lui demandai combien je pouvais espérer contre la garantie de mes actions, et il me répondit promptement et sans ambiguïté soixante cents pour un dollar. Quand je lui fis part de ma stupéfaction, il me rétorqua que c'étaient là les termes habituels et que la banque devait se protéger contre tout investissement peu judicieux. Je lui demandai alors, non sans un certain énervement, s'il considérait un investissement dans Rising Sun Enterprises comme peu judicieux, et il me répondit que son travail ne consistait pas à juger du bien-fondé d'un investissement, qu'il était banquier et non spéculateur. Je lui demandai aussitôt s'il comprenait que l'avenir même de cette banque, qu'il dirigeait si brillamment, et, espérais-je, continuerait à diriger, était lié, intimement et inextricablement lié à la bonne santé de la valeur Rising Sun, et que de surcroît son propre poste de président-directeur général de ladite banque dépendait également de la tenue de la valeur Rising Sun et qu'il ferait fichtrement mieux d'avoir foi en elle, sur quoi il conclut avec un froncement de sourcils que, puisque tout le monde attendait de savoir si le récent et indéniable effritement de Rising Sun était dû à des facteurs intrinsèques ou artificiellement provoqué par un éventuel et illégal raid d'ours, une vente tous azimuts, il était prêt à me faire une faveur en me proposant le chiffre généreux et sans précédent de soixante-cinq cents pour un dollar, à condition naturellement que les prêts soient à très court terme, sur des périodes n'excédant pas une semaine, et agrémentés de taux d'intérêts substantiels afin de compenser le risque couru par la banque. Selon cet arrangement, qui reçut le beau nom d'« accord à l'amiable entre les parties concernées », j'acceptais qu'au cas où les stratégies défensives échoueraient à rendre toute sa vigueur à Rising Sun avant, disons, une semaine, et dans l'éventualité fort improbable où Rising Sun continuerait (temporairement) de décliner, j'aurais le droit de rembourser ma dette non pas en argent liquide, mais en déposant comme garantie toutes les nouvelles actions Rising Sun achetées, et que, de plus, le remboursement du principal pourrait être indéfiniment repoussé par moi-même, jusqu'au moment qui m'agréerait pour donner entière satisfaction aux termes de l'accord initial, le tout signé et dûment notarié ce jour du... etc., etc.

23

Nous découvrîmes l'ampleur de l'attaque lancée contre nous par APL quand nous eûmes commencé à nous défendre. Malgré les ressources considérables que nous engageâmes dans notre contre-attaque, le répit fut seulement temporaire. L'effritement de la cote de notre action se poursuivit, la fuite devint un ruisseau, puis un torrent, et rien de ce que nous entreprîmes ne réussit à le tarir. Les transfuges d'APL décrurent une fois encore et nous n'avions réussi à amasser que 28 pour 100 de leurs actions. Rising Sun continuait de chuter. Après l'expiration du terme initial de mon prêt, incapable d'en rembourser les intérêts grâce au rétablissement attendu mais inexistant de Rising Sun, je dus remettre en gage une fraction des actions que je venais d'acheter.

Une fois de plus, je me trouvai non seulement professionnellement mais personnellement en butte à l'érosion de mon capital, bref en péril. Je ne courais bien sûr pas le risque de perdre mes actions suite à l'engagement d'une procédure pour non-paiement, car la banque était sinon directement du moins ultimement sous ma juridiction, et je savais, oui, *je savais* que l'érosion de notre valeur n'était nullement le résultat du « froid verdict du marché », mais celui des manipulations ourdies par APL, c'est-à-dire par *lui*, et ne pouvait se prolonger indéfiniment. Non, dès que nous aurions découvert le point caché sur lequel ils appliquaient leur levier malfaisant (et illégal), Rising Sun exploserait inévitablement en balayant toutes les lignes de résistance artificielles sur les graphiques, tel un geyser colmaté par un obstacle qui augmente lentement la pression de sa nappe souterraine et finit par jaillir en une fontaine spectaculaire qui ferait ma fortune et rendrait à Rising Sun sa juste valeur. Aucune autre issue n'était possible, ni même concevable.

Mais nous étions encore loin de cette radieuse conclusion, et il était peu probable que la justice immanente restaurât d'elle-même un équilibre plus fidèle à la réalité des choses. C'était la guerre. Nous étions maintenant au milieu de notre offensive majeure, les deux camps subissaient de lourdes pertes, appliquaient de furieuses et implacables mesures de représailles. La Chasse était bel et bien entamée ; chacun était proie et chasseur ; chacun était blessé et saignait abondamment.

Il y avait de la joie dans la bataille ; la lutte était tantôt belle et subtile, tantôt profondément obscène. Car pour la première fois depuis notre naissance, nos pillages et autres razzias d'entreprises, nous nous sentions menacés ; pour la première fois nous luttions contre un adversaire de notre calibre dans le feu du combat, selon l'expression de Tsin, et nous entrions « dans les ultimes parages du mystère ». Car ils étaient vraiment nos égaux. *Il* était mon égal. La maîtrise et l'audace de sa campagne, son impénétrabilité étaient affolantes ; elles portaient sa signature, la surprise fondant hors du soleil, la faux noire qui s'abattait pour le massacre.

Sa signature. Comme je désirais la lire dans le registre ouvert de mes dettes, là, à côté de mon propre parafe. Des égaux. La moindre fibre de mon être aspirait à cet ultime règlement de comptes. A payer le prix. Régler les dernières dettes. Tirer le trait définitif qui équilibrerait l'actif et le passif, clore à jamais les registres. Ne demander aucun pardon pour mes dettes et ne rien pardonner. Car ce lieu ne tolérait aucune compassion. Et ce savoir — le montant exorbitant du prix à payer — transformait l'épreuve en plaisir, le plaisir le plus doux que j'eusse jamais goûté, aussi doux que le vin de messe, aussi doux que le sang d'un enfant, l'enfant que je portais dans mon cœur et sacrifiais maintenant avec le plein accord de ma volonté, l'enfant que Love avait porté, ces deux enfants réunis, le mien et le sien, que nous allions maintenant retrancher impitoyablement de nos livres de comptes respectifs. Car il n'y aurait aucune pitié là-bas, et pas davantage de remords ou de différence entre la joie et l'obscénité, l'obscénité et la religion, tout cela laissé loin derrière, très loin en dessous de nous, demi-vérités qui permettent à un monde approximatif de fonctionner, mais dont les valeurs sonnaient creux dans l'atmosphère limpide des sommets dont j'approchais alors, de ce lieu où il avait toujours séjourné en m'attendant depuis le commencement du monde. Et voici un secret, lecteur, que j'offre comme une aumône à celui qui m'a suivi jusqu'à la sombre antichambre du mystère : cet enfer n'est pas un abîme, mais un sommet.

Tsin m'accompagna sans cesse pendant ces jours (ce jour, cette heure, cet instant). Je me remémorai toutes ses paroles ; elles jouaient dans mon esprit comme un enregistrement qui ne cessait de m'émouvoir, de me terrifier. J'avais dépassé tous les autres maîtres, leurs mots ne me touchaient plus à l'endroit où je désirais être touché ; mais sa voix à lui résonnait toujours, elle faisait vibrer mes nerfs avec les frissons et les fièvres de l'authenticité indiscutable. Il avait séjourné en ce lieu qui était mon but, où je me tenais désormais ; je le considérais maintenant comme mon mentor et mon guide pour pénétrer au cœur du mystère, dans le saint des saints. « C'est un sentiment de réalité et de présence qui nous dispense des dieux. Il sature et rassasie, convainc l'esprit de l'existence d'une vérité absolue. Les consolations de la religion, le sens de la vie, les incertitudes de l'avenir — tous ces problèmes et ces dilemmes nous apparaissent alors sous leur vrai jour : spécieux, et s'évanouissent. L'insatisfaction qui tenaille notre ventre disparaît elle aussi. Nous cessons d'être divisés avec nous-mêmes. La réalité trouve son apothéose quand, dans la mêlée, nous affrontons un seul adversaire. » Face à face. « Notre science est imparfaite, nos prophéties sont imparfaites. Mais quand sera venue la perfection, alors disparaîtra ce qui est imparfait... Aujourd'hui, nous voyons comme dans un miroir, confusément ; alors nous verrons face à face. Aujourd'hui, je ne connais que partiellement ; alors je connaîtrai comme je suis connu. »

Oui, je savais. Maintenant je savais. Tsin avait raison : la damnation est un prix modique à payer pour la douceur d'une telle extase, pour un tel savoir. Toute discussion me semblait futile. Non que je fusse aveugle au péril où je me trouvais. A chaque seconde, je goûtais aux sombres fruits de la perdition, partagé entre une intolérable souffrance et une exaltation impossible. Par-delà toute incertitude, au-delà de tout espoir, je vivais la réalité de ma damnation, de ma perte irrévocable ; et pourtant, elle ne m'importait pas. Je m'en moquais. J'étais tombé amoureux de ma propre mort morale, amoureux de la féroce beauté des flammes. Et ainsi, sans amertume ni regret, j'acceptai la vanité de ma quête, son errance stupide, car il n'y avait pas de delta, le torrent écumant du Dow ne rejoignait jamais la destination que je lui avais assignée et à laquelle j'avais cru de tout mon cœur. Il n'existait aucun lieu pour cela, lecteur, pour cette rage animale primitive et immaculée, ou plutôt, pour cette quintessence de la violence humaine, cette joie de tuer dans le sang — non pas afin de se nourrir ou de se défendre, pour aucune raison de survie ou de nécessité, mais comme une forme de jeu, oui, un jeu semblable à celui des dieux, où l'on accédait un instant à l'ineffable, où l'on faisait l'expérience de sa splendeur et de sa puissance à travers la destruction volontaire de la vie d'autrui (ainsi, dans le déchaînement de la furie atomique, la nature révèle ses ultimes secrets, livre, contrainte et forcée, ses vérités dernières) — non, pour cela aucun lieu n'existait, pour cette chose que Tsin avait définie avec la magie glaçante d'un talisman par l'expression « extase du combat », il n'y avait pas place pour cela dans le Tao. Ainsi, sans amertume ni regret, comme je l'ai dit, j'ouvris la main et laissai s'envoler le frêle et timide papillon de ma dernière illusion, de mon dernier espoir, et je me sentis incroyablement propre et exposé, rendu à la nudité animale, réduit au brutal noyau humain débarrassé de toutes ses scories.

La cote des actions ne cessait de tomber, de plus en plus vite. Mes apports semblaient s'engouffrer dans un puits sans fond, alimenter une faim insatiable, un monstre dont la voracité semblait seulement aiguiser l'appétit. En quelques semaines, en quelques *jours*, le prix de Rising Sun avait perdu 25 pour 100 et atteint la ligne rouge fixée par les Cornes, la ligne de partage des eaux au-delà de laquelle l'absorption était menacée, puis elle chuta à 30 pour 100 sous sa valeur d'avant le raid, atteignant ainsi la ligne de dernière résistance, toucha même brièvement les 35 pour 100 de perte, soit soixante-cinq cents contre le dollar initial, et à ce moment, après une diatribe furibonde de mon banquier, je dus déposer en gage l'intégralité des nouvelles actions de Rising Sun que je venais d'acheter grâce au prêt bancaire afin de réapprovisionner ma garantie originelle. Il n'y avait plus rien à faire. Je touchais le fond. La première stratégie — acheter nos propres actions pour nous défendre — s'était révélée un échec. Si nous n'avions pas autant manqué de capital au début, elle aurait pu réussir. Mais ce raisonnement constituait une maigre consolation. Notre dernière chance consistait à démasquer l'adversaire.

Et ce fut alors, in extremis, que je trouvai la parade. Tandis que les

Cornes s'évertuaient à découvrir la trace de transferts de fonds sur des comptes suisses numérotés, je tombai brusquement sur la solution. Son évidence me fit rire de joie et de dégoût. C'était si évident. Dire que cette réponse avait toujours été là, dissimulée par sa banalité même, comme les lunettes de soleil sur le présentoir tournant. Les directeurs d'APL eux-mêmes l'avaient suggérée. Le fauteuil qu'ils me proposaient dans leur conseil. *Mon* fauteuil. Bien sûr ! Et à l'époque, quand ils me l'avaient offert, je possédais seulement 2 pour 100. Maintenant, j'avais près de 28 pour 100 des actions d'APL ! Je pouvais exiger trois sièges dans leur petit politburo intime, certainement deux, au moins deux, plus une voix pour choisir le troisième, un candidat de compromis, un tiers neutre, qui servirait aussi bien ma cause. Je pouvais les miner *de l'intérieur*, sinon par la voie du scrutin majoritaire, du moins en participant à leur conseil. Oui ! Je ris de plaisir à cette perspective. C'était tellement évident ! Alors, si cela marchait, rien ne serait perdu. La cote de Rising Sun remonterait bientôt en flèche. Et sur cette inspiration, je sus immédiatement ce que je devais faire. Je téléphonai à Bateson.

« Ah, Sun I, dit-il de sa charmante voix totalement dépourvue de charme, en voilà une surprise.

— Je crois que nous avons besoin de nous rencontrer, l'informai-je sombrement.

— Vraiment ? » Il se tut.

« Alors ? le relançai-je avec impatience.

— Désolé, répondit-il comme si pendant quelques secondes il avait oublié ma présence. J'essayais simplement de me rappeler. La dernière fois, c'est moi qui vous ai appelé, si je ne m'abuse. » J'entendis dans ses mots une joie contenue à grand-peine. « C'est gentil de me rendre ma politesse, poursuivit-il, à deux doigts d'éclater de rire. Sacrée délicatesse ! Un déjeuner ? »

Ses insinuations me mirent en rage, mais je me retins et goûtai une satisfaction délicieuse, empoisonnée et délicieuse, en songeant à la revanche que j'allais prendre sur lui. « Je saisis vos sous-entendus, Bateson, lui dis-je d'une voix que la haine faisait frémir. Vous croyez que la situation est inversée, que la dernière fois, quand j'avais tous les atouts en main, vous êtes venu vers moi, mais qu'aujourd'hui c'est moi qui viens vers vous. » Il ne répondit rien, mais je l'entendis presque ricaner. « C'est bien ça, non ? insistai-je avec colère.

— C'est vous qui le dites, répliqua-t-il d'une voix soudain calme et grave.

— Je vous réserve une grosse surprise, mon ami, l'avertis-je.

— Vraiment ? J'adore les cadeaux, persifla-t-il. Et puis, quelle coïncidence ! J'en ai — pardon ! — *nous* en avons une pour vous.

— Je sais déjà tout de votre petit secret, Bateson. L'envoi du panda manque de subtilité — rien de plus qu'un tour pendable. Vous copiez les Siciliens avec leur poisson, ou quoi ? Mais bien sûr, ce n'est pas votre idée, n'est-ce pas ? C'est la *sienne*.

— Le panda ? Les Siciliens ? *La sienne ?* Excusez-moi, mais je crains de ne pas vous suivre. De quoi et de qui parlez-vous ?

— Ça suffit, Bateson, je n'espère pas que vous vous trahirez. Laissez-moi seulement vous dire que je sais tout, et depuis un certain temps.

— Excusez-moi, mais que savez-vous ?

— Votre "petite surprise" n'est qu'un secret de Polichinelle ; je suis informé de vos manœuvres.

— Ah, je commençais à penser que nous étions sur des longueurs d'onde différentes. Mais si vous connaissez tout de nos activités, à quoi bon nous rencontrer ?

— N'espérez surtout pas que j'abatte mon jeu aujourd'hui, Bateson, dis-je. Vous devrez attendre notre rencontre.

— Eh bien, je l'attends avec impatience ; je compte les minutes, comme on dit.

— A demain donc, proposai-je.

— Demain, absolument ! Une heure ?

— D'accord. » J'allais raccrocher, mais il ne put résister au plaisir d'une ultime pique.

« Ah, Sun I, une dernière question avant de nous séparer. J'adore les cadeaux, mais je déteste les surprises. Si vous connaissez tout de nos "manœuvres", et depuis un certain temps déjà, il me semble que vos informations n'ont pas vraiment modifié la physionomie de la situation, si je ne me trompe ?

« Voyons, où en sont vos actions aujourd'hui ? » Je l'entendis tapoter les touches du Quotron que j'avais vu dans son bureau. « Ah la la, toujours à la baisse. *Quel dommage*, Sun I.

— Vous réalisez bien sûr que vous venez de vous trahir en reconnaissant implicitement vos manipulations ?

— Manipulations ! » Il rit. « Croyez-vous vraiment que nous nous amusions à ça ici ?

— Vous venez de l'avouer, Bateson, triomphai-je, puis une idée perverse me vint à l'esprit. Et cette conversation est enregistrée », mentis-je.

Sa voix devint brusquement sévère. « Je n'ai rien reconnu, me contredit-il. Et pour votre information, les enregistrements téléphoniques sont illégaux. »

Ce fut à mon tour de rire. « Vous voilà soudain bien à cheval sur le règlement, Bateson. Vous étiez plus coulant autrefois.

— Très bien, Sun I, conclut-il. Cette conversation n'a plus de raison d'être. Je vous attends demain A une heure.

— Je compte les minutes ! le narguai-je en retournant contre lui ses propres sarcasmes. Ah, Bateson, avant de nous séparer, une dernière chose. » Je me tus en attendant sa réaction.

« Oui ?

— Non seulement je vais vous absorber, non seulement je vais vous virer, vous et votre régime fantoche, mais je vais foutre votre cul en prison. »

Il fut si abasourdi qu'il en resta coi. « En prison ! répéta-t-il enfin avec une légèreté qui sonnait faux, une parodie dérisoire de son ancienne assurance. Juste ciel ! Vos paroles dépassent votre pensée, n'est-ce pas ? Vous n'exagérez pas un peu ?

— Nullement.

— Très bien donc ! dit-il. Je souhaite néanmoins croiser le fer de nos fourchettes et de nos couteaux demain midi. A une heure donc.

— Bateson ? insistai-je, profitant de mon avantage Je compte sur vous pour nous servir des miches de pain croustillant "tout droit sorties du four", n'est-ce pas ? Et ce vin — comment s'appelait-il ? Le Vite Roussi. Je crois qu'en les circonstances, il sera tout à fait approprié.

— Comptez sur moi », dit-il sèchement, puis il raccrocha.

J'appelai immédiatement ma secrétaire. « Mary ? Déjeuner demain à une heure dans les bureaux d'APL.

— Je suis désolée, monsieur, répondit-elle, vous devez déjeuner avec les administrateurs du Metropolitan Museum. Vous avez déjà reporté trois fois cette réunion.

— Merde ! jurai-je. Très bien. Arrangez-vous pour que ce soit tôt. Midi — si possible avant. Je suis un homme pressé. Mon temps est précieux.

— Bien, monsieur, dit-elle, je sais. »

Que Bateson aille au diable, songeai-je en raccrochant. De toute façon, je n'avais aucune envie de déjeuner avec lui.

Le repas au Metropolitan Museum se déroula pour moi dans un état de profonde absence dû à l'anticipation de ma rencontre avec Bateson. Une absence néanmoins pas assez profonde pour que je pusse continuer d'ignorer qu'on m'avait choisi comme bienfaiteur ou mécène potentiel en vue de l'aménagement des salles d'art chinois qui devaient s'ajouter au musée dans un avenir plus ou moins proche qui dépendait naturellement des généreuses donations attendues d'amis des arts aussi honorables que moi. Naturellement. J'écoutais leurs plaidoiries d'une oreille distraite, m'obligeant pour la forme à regarder de temps à autre mon interlocuteur, et faisant des efforts surhumains pour ne pas trop souvent relever ma manche afin de vérifier l'heure. Ces hommes étaient assez subtils vraiment, et sophistiqués — des hommes charmants. De plus, ils avaient bien appris leur leçon. Ils savaient qui j'étais, d'où je venais, ce que j'avais fait. J'eus même droit à une allusion amusée à la « fusion », que je relevai avec un sourire glacé qui coupa net l'herbe sous le pied de l'orateur, lui fit lâcher ce sujet comme on lâche une pomme de terre brûlante. Ils savaient éviter les questions épineuses et ramener la conversation à une réserve et un tact qui me convenaient davantage. Oui, ces hommes étaient réellement charmants. Je n'avais jamais rencontré leurs émules. En tout cas certainement pas à Wall Street, bien que j'y connusse quelques esprits cultivés. Avec une précision chirurgicale ils me couvrirent de flatteries extravagantes, mais sans la moindre trace d'obséquiosité ni, à l'inverse, de condescendance. Pourtant eux aussi étaient humains, et ils commirent une erreur.

« Vous comprenez, bien sûr », disait l'un des plus jeunes membres de la réunion, un homme aux cheveux clairsemés et aux joues rougissantes comme celles d'une jeune fille, un peu plus ardent que ses aînés, celui-là même qui m'avait adressé la remarque à propos de l'absorption, « qu'un grand nombre d'objets de culte prendront place dans ces salles, à condition évidemment qu'elles soient construites. » Les administrateurs sourirent, ou bien rirent avec modération. « Prenez notre exposition qui a lieu en ce moment. L'avez-vous vue ? »

Il me surprit la main sur la manche de ma chemise. Je levai les yeux, grimaçai un sourire contraint, secouai négativement la tête.

« Peut-être pourrions-nous organiser une visite ? suggéra-t-il. Personnellement, j'aimerais...

— Une autre fois, le coupai-je. Je suis terriblement pressé aujourd'hui.

— Bien sûr, concéda-t-il comme un bon génie prêt à servir son maître, ou plutôt à réintégrer son flacon après avoir été congédié. Je tenais néanmoins à dire qu'il me semblait, qu'il nous semblait — il s'énervait, rougissait à mesure — que vous seriez particulièrement intéressé par le fait que, — par les objets de culte, je veux dire. » Il s'interrompit ; non sans une certaine cruauté, je restai muet. Ses pairs échangèrent des regards discrètement étonnés.

« Comme vous étiez, insista-t-il non sans véhémence, si je ne me trompe, autrefois bouddhiste, c'est bien cela, n'est-ce pas ? » Son regard, celui d'un homme fier habitué aux hommages, m'implorait de façon obscène.

Pour la première fois depuis le début du déjeuner, son erreur me secoua de ma torpeur et me rendit toute mon attention, cela et son emploi de l'imparfait suivi du mot « autrefois », comme si ma carte était périmée — ce qu'en un sens elle était sans doute en effet, mais cela ne regardait pas ce jeune fat, ce chiot maladroit (bien qu'il fût plus âgé que moi), ne lui donnait aucun droit de m'importuner ainsi.

« Taoïste, rectifiai-je d'un ton cassant en regardant ostensiblement ma montre. Messieurs, — je me levai avec un sourire figé — je vous prie de m'excuser. J'ai un rendez-vous extrêmement important à treize heures. Ce déjeuner m'a ravi. Je vous donnerai de mes nouvelles. » Je faillis ajouter : « Ne me contactez pas, je vous appellerai », me retins à temps.

Plutôt que de prendre la limousine avec chauffeur qu'ils m'avaient envoyée, je hélai un taxi sur la Cinquième Avenue. « A Wall Street », dis-je au chauffeur. Mais alors que je pivotais en me laissant tomber sur la banquette, mon œil fut soudain attiré par l'immense bannière qui pendait de l'entablement du musée au-dessus des colonnes. Malgré les trous espacés qu'on y avait percés pour réduire sa prise au vent, elle se gonflait comme un spinnaker dans la bourrasque. « Une seconde, arrêtez-vous », commandai-je. Je levai les yeux en attendant qu'elle faseillât.

Je ne m'étais pas trompé. Je l'avais déjà vue. « Tenez », dis-je en tendant au chauffeur davantage d'argent que je ne lui en devais, puis je descendis du taxi.

J'ai déjà dit que le monde contient une myriade de signes, autant de signes qu'il y avait d'étoiles dans le ciel nocturne au large de la sombre côte de Sumatra cet été-là, voilà si longtemps, ou de Bornéo, je ne sais plus, pendant ces nuits où Scottie m'avait enseigné la carte du ciel ainsi que mes premiers rudiments d'anglais, ces nuits où j'avais cru lire mon destin écrit en runes de craie scintillante sur l'ardoise noire de l'univers, un alphabet cryptique qui brûlait d'une lueur aussi froide et tranchante que celle du diamant. Dès que je le vis, je fus certain que ce Manjusri était le même que celui aperçu par Scottie et moi dans la cale du *Telemachos*. Car tous sont légèrement différents, à cause de ces précieux et subtils détails dus au travail de l'artisan anonyme ; malgré la reproduction approximative en vastes pièces de tissus semblables à des taches de couleur cousues sur une grand-voile, malgré l'immensité de cette bannière qui défiait toute échelle, quelque chose dans les yeux, je crois, ces deux yeux humains souriants et le Troisième Œil de la sagesse transcendante au milieu du front, quelque chose me convainquit qu'il s'agissait de la statue que nous avions vue. « La Religion Perdue du Tibet », annonçait la banderole. Et à côté de lui, à côté de Manjusri, équilibrant la composition, un personnage, un gigantesque personnage cornu...

Je gravis les marches en courant.

Je suivis le flot des visiteurs et achetai le catalogue de l'exposition, que je feuilletai distraitement en marchant. Mais à peine l'avais-je ouvert que je franchissais déjà le seuil de l'exposition, où je n'en eus plus besoin, où les descriptions, les mots devinrent superflus, car je fus en présence de la chose elle-même, du signataire en personne, qui rendait la signature dérisoire. Face à face.

A côté de Manjusri, le Bodhisattva de la Sagesse Transcendantale qui tenait le lotus et le livre dans ses mains blessées (ah, mais cela disait tout, le Livre du Savoir sur la blessure) ainsi qu'une épée nouvellement forgée par le restaurateur, à côté de lui et équilibrant la composition, haut de cinq mètres et sans doute lourd de plusieurs tonnes, effrayant à regarder même en image, se dressait un personnage noir doté de deux grandes cornes de bronze, aussi grosses à leur base que la taille d'un homme et qui s'effilaient jusqu'à la pointe acérée d'une lance (dans la pénombre je vis presque le lambeau de ma vieille veste empalé sur l'une d'elles, la gauche, un trophée parmi tant d'autres), des cornes décorées non de fleurs, comme celles qu'Europe tissa pour les cornes de Zeus, mais de crânes humains, de vrais crânes humains. Une énorme érection noire, un sexe de pierre aux veines aussi saillantes et noueuses que celles de l'avant-bras d'un drogué, se dressait presque jusqu'à son plexus solaire. Parmi d'innombrables objets, qui tous avaient sans doute une signification ésotérique pour moi obscure, le personnage tenait le sablier dont je me souvenais, jadis rempli d'un sable si étrange (une poudre magique pour un sommeil et des rêves magiques, le monstre était sans doute le Marchand de Sable Magique), il le tenait dans l'une de ses nombreuses mains, chacune exhibant un mudra particulier et sacrilège, un mudra de puissance et d'obscénité que je n'avais jamais vu. Et dans ses quatre mains centrales, dont chacune exhibait les quatre griffes du dragon, il serrait la Roue de la Vie elle-même, l'Œuf du Chaos, la Grande Opposition Primordiale, *T'ai Chi T'u*, *yin* et *yang*, le symbole du Tao. Inscrit sur la couronne extérieure de la Roue, je lus le mantra universel : « Om Mani Padme Hum », le Joyau dans le Lotus. Mais ce fut surtout le visage qui me fascina, car c'était la gueule écumante d'un taureau furieux, ses yeux exorbités — les trois — en une expression de surprise et de plaisir obscènes, comme un personnage de bande dessinée pornographique qui se frotte les mains et se pourlèche les babines devant une vierge de huit ans, la bouche entrouverte, la langue incurvée sur les incisives supérieures, presque timide, quasiment hilare, une langue rouge sang, tandis que la bête ouvre ses bras, tous ses bras, en un geste d'invite déjà vu, celui de Riley, mais pour inciter à une communion plus sombre que celles jamais célébrées par le prêtre, à un mystère plus noir que le plus noir de ses rêves.

Yama, le Seigneur Noir de la Mort, la contrepartie tibétaine de Yen Lo Wang, mais à une différence près, un détail crucial qui faisait toute la différence. Yama, l'autre pilier de la composition, Yama, avec la tête noire d'un taureau. Oui, ici enfin et par hasard, je m'engageais dans l'ultime corridor, je pénétrais au cœur même du labyrinthe et découvrais mon souriant Minotaure prêt à m'étreindre comme un amant. Yama, le Seigneur de la Mort. Yama. Le Taureau. L'illumination définitive. L'éclipse totale. Illumination définitive, éclipse totale. « Le Samsara égale le Nirvana. » Je me rappelai ce précepte et souris sombrement. Ainsi, le Nirvana égale le Samsara. Souvenez-vous de la loi commutative. Le Nirvana est le Samsara. Formules cryptiques écrites dans les ordures.

L'écriteau sur le mur bouclait la boucle :

Extrait de La voie des nuages blancs *par le lama Anagarika Govinda :*
« *Le Dieu de la Mort (Yama) est représenté sous sa forme terrible par une divinité à tête de taureau...* »

« Tête de taureau » — j'éclatai de rire. Plusieurs visiteurs me dévisagèrent.

Selon une légende populaire, un saint ermite qui avait passé toute son existence à méditer dans une caverne solitaire était sur le point d'atteindre l'illumination ultime quand des voleurs entrèrent dans sa caverne avec un taureau qu'ils avaient volé, et qu'ils tuèrent en lui tranchant la tête, sans remarquer la présence de l'ermite. Quand ils découvrirent que ce dernier avait assisté à leur forfait, ils le tuèrent également en le décapitant. Mais ils n'avaient pas tenu compte de son pouvoir surnaturel acquis durant sa longue réclusion. A peine eurent-ils décapité l'ermite que son cadavre se dressa, saisit la tête du taureau et la plaqua sur son cou, se transformant ainsi en la forme terrifiante de Yama. Empêché d'atteindre le but le plus élevé de la réalisation, et saisi d'une fureur insatiable, il décapita à son tour les voleurs, dont il accrocha les têtes en guirlande autour de son cou, puis erra de par le monde en y semant la mort, jusqu'au jour...

Je ne lus pas la suite. Aussi léger qu'une plume, flottant à quelques kilomètres au-dessus du sol, j'eus à peine besoin d'un taxi pour rejoindre Wall Street. Car je sortis du musée comme Yama, « saisi d'une fureur insatiable », un Troisième Œil scintillant au milieu de mon front et rivé sur les onze hommes — les douze hommes, oui, les douze, je ne devais surtout pas oublier le fauteuil vide, lui seul importait — qui m'avaient volé le fruit de ma propre pénitence, douze étoiles qui allaient bientôt briller autour de mon cou, figurer une nouvelle constellation. Yama, la Mort. Car j'avais été bon, infiniment bon, mais je serais désormais terrifiant.

24

Bien que cela ne me surprît guère (rien n'aurait pu me surprendre), l'humeur de Bateson contredit mon attente. Quand il m'accueillit, ses manières étaient empreintes d'une sorte de gravité mélancolique, je crus discerner au fond de ses yeux froids une vague lueur de tendresse. C'était étrange, comme si la conversation de la veille n'avait jamais eu lieu, et d'autant plus étrange que je souffris de la même illusion. Nous parlâmes quelques minutes dans son bureau, je ne sais plus de quoi, de la pluie et du beau temps, oui, de la neige. Il s'était mis à neiger tandis que le taxi roulait, lui dis-je. Il releva les stores vénitiens et nous restâmes côte à côte, absorbés par le mystère de sa chute feutrée, silencieuse. Puis nous nous assîmes et il m'offrit une cigarette avant d'en prendre une, à ma grande surprise. Il fumait vraiment. Peut-être, lors de notre dernière entrevue, s'était-il tout simplement énervé. Mais il avait retrouvé son calme. Moi aussi. Nous fumâmes sans mot dire, partageant l'intimité de notre éloignement, convaincus de l'inutilité de toute parole, tels des soldats avant la bataille. Car lui et moi étions ennemis, et la bataille ferait bientôt rage entre nous. Posant la tête contre mon dossier pour exhaler la fumée, je repensai à la cigarette qui s'était consumée dans le cendrier devant le fauteuil vide lors de notre dernière réunion. Une hilarité inexplicable s'empara de moi, j'éclatai de rire. Bateson, qui ressentit la même chose au même instant, se joignit à moi. Ainsi, songeant à cette cigarette et à toutes celles qui, avant elle, formaient comme une chaîne passant par la table de nuit de Li avant de rejoindre la Création elle-même et le repos du Seigneur lors du septième jour, je ris si fort que les larmes coulèrent sur mes joues, et Bateson rit avec moi tout du long, bien qu'il ne pût jamais se douter de la raison première de mon hilarité. Quand je le regardais, plié de rire (à la fois présent dans son bureau et infiniment plus haut, voyeur de moi-même), j'avais l'étrange impression d'observer mon reflet dans un miroir. Cédant à une impulsion subite, je me levai de mon fauteuil en riant toujours, et passai la main sur sa tête comme pour le bénir ou me réchauffer à une flamme de Pentecôte qui eût brûlé au centre de son crâne.

Il recula légèrement, comme si j'eusse voulu le frapper. « Pour l'amour du ciel... ? lâcha-t-il, stupéfait mais toujours souriant.

— Simple vérification, dis-je en pouffant, savourant une plaisanterie que je pouvais seul comprendre.

— Pour vérifier quoi ? demanda-t-il alors avec un sourire de connivence.
— Pour voir s'il n'y a pas de fil qui dépasse », répondis-je en éclatant de rire ; et il rit aussi, maudit soit-il, il rit aussi.

Je me souviens presque mieux de ce détail trivial que du reste de la réunion. Il m'obsède encore. Pourquoi Bateson riait-il ? Il ne pouvait deviner mes pensées, mon rêve du marionnettiste. Je n'avais rien dit de particulier. Non, la vraie raison se cachait derrière les mots. Obligatoirement.

Je ne trouvai certes pas l'homme plus séduisant que lors de notre rencontre précédente, mais je sentis une intimité plus grande entre nous, comme si nous nous connaissions depuis toujours, presque de la tendresse, une estime qui ne pouvait s'enraciner que dans la haine. La présence de Bateson me frappa presque aussi intensément que celle qui m'avait stupéfait voilà si longtemps sur le toit, celle de Yin-mi lorsque l'infime couture de la réalité s'était ouverte et que j'avais aperçu son âme, la chose elle-même, qui détalait timidement dans la forêt de son paysage intérieur, bondissait comme une biche, chacun de ses minuscules sabots indéfiniment figé en l'air avant de toucher terre, puis s'agenouillait gracieusement pour boire à l'étang miroitant de nos espoirs communs. En présence de Yin-mi, tous mes autres désirs avaient disparu. Mais devant Bateson, j'étais le chasseur guettant au bord d'un étang plus sombre, j'attendais la tuerie, et la chose qui émergeait de sa jungle mentale, la chose qui m'observait, m'épiait, n'était pas une biche ni un cerf, mais un prédateur de la même espèce que moi, dans les yeux duquel je lus le calme, la science et le désir de mort. Il voulait me tuer. Chacun reconnut la détermination de l'autre, rendant du même coup le dénouement presque banal, comme si cet ultime rite de ténèbres pouvait engendrer la lumière, et se sacrilège définitif déboucher sur une nouvelle innocence.

Nous rejoignîmes la salle de conférence où je sentis une inexplicable atmosphère de fête, aussi inexplicable que notre récente hilarité, une fébrilité contenue, un bouillonnement maîtrisé qui risquait à tout moment de déraper vers l'hystérie, une hystérie due non au désespoir mais à la confiance et au pouvoir, et qui miroitait comme des ondes de chaleur dans un air brûlant.

Je fus heureux de les trouver rayonnants de confiance, aussi allègres que moi. Cela retirait à la mise à mort son odeur putride, cela ôtait de ma bouche l'amertume laissée par les regards noirs et désespérés des autres absorptions. Tout était brillant et tendu, les conséquences connues, acceptées, pardonnées d'avance, justifiées par l'exaltation du jeu. C'était tellement mieux ainsi. Vraiment, l'atmosphère était légère, enjouée. Un observateur extérieur eût tout à fait pu croire à une fête d'entreprise le jour de Noël, à l'heure de la remise des primes. Il y avait néanmoins une tension semblable à un coup de fouet dans chaque sourire, dans chaque regard. Les remarques les plus banales ouvraient des abîmes ; nous nous arrêtions pour les contempler, pour contempler *cela*, comme Bateson et moi avions contemplé la chute de neige silencieuse, unis devant elle, émus et respectueux, bien que *cela* fût seulement l'inexorable fatalité de ce que nous devions accomplir, la destruction qu'il nous incombait de mener à terme, comme des amants, l'un donnant et l'autre acceptant, dans l'étrange coït de la guerre où la consommation apporte non le repos mais la mort.

« Bien, messieurs », dit enfin Bateson en serrant ses mains devant lui ; son expression, son attitude étaient celles de l'hôte qui a consacré beaucoup de temps et de soin à la préparation d'un banquet, et qui, à l'heure de réunir les invités autour de la table, éprouve une sorte de tristesse résignée en comprenant que le repas, aussi bon soit-il, sera infiniment moins délicieux que les heures passées à le préparer. « Je pense que nous devrions nous mettre au travail — même si, je l'avoue, j'ignore la nature précise de notre ordre du jour. » Tous les autres rirent. « Il me semble que l'atmosphère est plus à la fête qu'aux affaires, vous ne trouvez pas ? Tout le monde a apporté des surprises ! Sun I a des surprises. Nous avons des surprises. Il nous en a promis une de taille. Et à notre modeste façon, nous espérons ne pas déchoir, n'est-ce pas, messieurs ? » Il hocha la tête de droite et de gauche. Les autres se glissaient peu à peu vers lui, se regroupaient insensiblement autour et derrière lui, formaient leurs lignes comme en dansant, eux d'un côté de la table, moi de l'autre, selon un rituel déjà éprouvé. « Oui, nous avons quelques surprises en réserve. » Il sourit, puis céda à la vanité. « De fait, quand je songe à elles, à nos surprises, à vos surprises, il me semble que nous en avons tant qu'on ne sait vraiment pas par où commencer ! »

Il haussa les épaules en tournant ses paumes vers le plafond, fronça les sourcils, écarquilla les yeux, adoptant à son insu la mimique du clown perplexe. Oui, exactement. Comme au cirque. Je crus entendre les rugissements hilares du public, le tonnerre des applaudissements. Mais où était Monsieur Loyal, le maître des cérémonies, l'homme en haut de forme et smoking noir ? Les miroirs se moquaient de moi, qui me renvoyaient ma propre image indéfiniment redoublée en une cascade de reflets vertigineux de taille décroissante qui creusaient un espace ambigu. Là-bas, au point de fuite, derrière la glace sans tain, il était tapi. Je sentais sa présence, j'entendais presque son souffle.

« Puisque je connais déjà les vôtres, dis-je en me portant au secours de Bateson mais regardant le miroir, mes yeux, et les siens derrière les miens, je suppose que cette tâche m'incombe. »

Il acquiesça avec une moue qui se voulait magnanime.

« J'ai été ravi de recevoir votre cadeau par la poste, commençai-je ainsi que je l'avais prévu depuis longtemps. Le panda. Je l'ai beaucoup fréquenté ces temps derniers ; à vrai dire il ne me quitte presque jamais — je souris dans le vague —, d'ailleurs il m'a fait reconsidérer un certain nombre de choses, réviser mon jugement sur quelques points, dont notre dernière réunion ; je crois m'être fourvoyé à votre sujet en doutant de votre bonne foi et de vos professions de loyauté envers lui — j'adressai un sourire au miroir — envers mon père, Eddie Love. Je tiens à vous présenter mes excuses, car j'ai compris à quel point je me trompais, à quel point je vous sous-estimais, dis-je en leur adressant un sourire féroce, vous et la profondeur de votre sincérité. Un numéro fort impressionnant de pres-ti-di-gi-ta-tion, messieurs — je ris —, votre dissimulation — dans les deux sens du terme, tant pour le corps physique que pour les comptes —, oui, un numéro unique au monde. » Je dévisageai les directeurs l'un après l'autre en savourant mes insinuations. « Mais pour en revenir au cadeau, repris-je, j'apprécie la satisfaction que votre petite plaisanterie vous a sans doute procurée, je l'apprécie profondément. D'un autre côté, je dois ajouter que j'apprécie au moins autant le manque de discipline qui en est à l'origine — malheureusement pour vous, heureusement pour moi, car il m'a permis de découvrir votre complot, votre petite "surprise", comme vous l'appelez. Bref, messieurs, dis-je d'une voix soudain cassante, le raid d'ours que vous menez contre la cote de l'action qui m'appartient. Je suis venu vous dire que cela doit cesser. *Maintenant.* »

Des murmures éclatèrent autour de la table. Ils se penchèrent les uns vers les autres pour conférer à voix basse. « Raid d'ours », entendis-je fuser çà et là sur un ton de surprise ou d'indignation.

Bateson s'assit au bord de son fauteuil, poussa un soupir presque soulagé. « Éclaircissons ce point, Sun I, commença-t-il. Est-ce là votre "surprise" ? » Il regarda brièvement les autres directeurs. « Vous êtes venu nous dire que cela doit cesser ? » Il ricana en dévisageant ses collègues avec incrédulité ; puis il me fixa attentivement. « A supposer que l'effritement de votre valeur soit dû à une manipulation — comment avez-vous appelé ça, un raid d'ours ? C'est un peu vieillot, vous ne trouvez pas ? — et pas simplement au libre jeu des forces du marché, ce que je crois, et à supposer que nous soyons derrière cette prétendue manipulation, quelle raison aurions-nous de modifier notre stratégie ? Votre demande ? Vous n'êtes tout de même pas venu nous supplier ? » Il faillit pouffer de rire.

— Exact. Je ne suis pas venu vous supplier de quoi que ce soit. » Je posai mes coudes sur la table, me penchai en avant, vrillai mon regard sur le sien. « Je suis venu prendre, Bateson — je crachai presque son nom — prendre ce qui est mien.

— Et de quoi parlez-vous ? » demanda-t-il d'une voix sourde et haineuse, en grimaçant un sourire.

Je le dévisageai quelques instants, puis m'adossai pour bander mon arc. « Ce que vous m'avez proposé lors de notre première réunion, dis-je calmement en haussant les sourcils afin d'examiner mes ongles. Vous vous rappelez ? » Je lui souris. « Mon fauteuil. » Je m'interrompis pour regarder le trait sombre de la flèche traverser l'espace. J'entendis presque son sifflement doux, plaisant, avant l'éclatement brutal et sec, l'horrible craquement de l'os fracassé quand sa pointe s'enfonça dans la cible.

« C'était fort généreux de votre part à l'époque, poursuivis-je en savourant les plus infimes changements d'expression de son regard, car je possédais seulement deux pour cent des actions d'APL. » Je souris, puis cessai de sourire. « Aujourd'hui, comme vous le savez très certainement, j'ai plus de vingt-huit pour cent de ces mêmes actions. Ce n'est qu'un début, bien sûr. Je ne possède pas encore la majorité. Mais ma position a changé. A quoi bon attendre ? Je veux prendre possession de ce qui m'appartient déjà. Je ne vois pas ce que vous pourriez redire à cela. Après tout, je ne fais que me conformer aux mœurs américaines, n'est-ce pas ? Vingt-huit pour cent, voyons... » Je levai les yeux au plafond et serrai les lèvres comme si je calculais. « Cela me donne droit à trois sièges, si je ne m'abuse. Non, messieurs, je ne vous supplierai pas de m'accorder ce qui m'appartient de droit. » Ravi de mon triomphe, je leur adressai un sourire rayonnant.

« Et pourquoi ce brusque désir de vous joindre à nous, Sun I, demanda Bateson, alors que la dernière fois, vous avez aussitôt rejeté notre proposition ? » Il regarda ses acolytes avec une expression qui disait « comme si je ne le savais pas ».

« Disons simplement que je désire travailler à l'intérieur du système, expliquai-je joyeusement. Je veux bénéficier de votre excellent conseil, le narguai-je.

— Vous voulez découvrir nos méthodes de travail, renchérit-il.

— Exact, dis-je. Et naturellement exercer mon droit de vote.

— Vous réalisez que ce droit implique aussi des responsabilités, bien sûr.

— Bien sûr.

— Nous avons toujours partagé une certaine unicité de point de vue ici, parce que nous l'avons forgée nous-mêmes. Et parce que nous avons tous les mêmes buts en tête : la prospérité de la corporation et les intérêts de nos actionnaires.

— Je vous prie de ne pas insister, répliquai-je. Je croyais vous avoir déjà fait part de mon opinion à ce sujet.

— Nous exigerons certaines preuves de votre bonne foi, naturellement. »

Je me renfrognai. « Je ne pense pas que vous soyez en mesure d'exiger quoi que ce soit. »

Il m'observa, puis secoua la tête comme s'il parvenait à une décision. « Je crains que nous ne soyons loin du compte, Sun I. A moins, bien sûr, que vous renonciez à cette idée d'absorption. Auquel cas nous pourrions envisager un arrangement. Mais sinon, je crois que de graves conflits d'intérêt surviendraient rapidement entre nous. Un poste de directeur au conseil — même deux — ne vous avancerait pas à grand-chose. Car nous travaillons démocratiquement, comme vous le savez...

— Oui, "républicanisme fiduciaire", répliquai-je sarcastiquement.

— ... et vous ne pourriez imposer vos vues contre l'avis de la majorité — il hocha la tête de droite et de gauche — si nous pensons que cette absorption va contre les intérêts de la corporation.

— Si je ne peux vous soumettre démocratiquement, je vous démasquerai, attaquai-je. En tant que directeur, je dois être informé de tous les secrets de la corporation, n'est-ce pas ? Eh bien, je vais dévoiler vos sales petites manigances, votre tour de passe-passe, et si vous ne démissionnez pas...

— Vous réunirez une conférence de presse, dit-il, achevant ma phrase. C'est exactement ce que je veux dire, Sun I, quand je parle de conflit d'intérêts. Le directeur qui sabote sa propre compagnie devient un traître. Je crains que nous ne le tolérions pas.

— Dommage, Bateson, raillai-je. Pourtant, vous devrez vous y faire, n'est-ce pas ? Vous n'avez pas le choix. » Je lui adressai un large sourire.

« Comment cela : "pas le choix" ?

— Allez, Bateson, ne soyez donc pas si obtus, insistai-je cruellement. Vous me gâchez mon plaisir. Vous savez aussi bien que moi que vous ne pouvez pas me laisser sur la touche. Acceptez-le de bonne grâce. C'est un fait de la vie, comme la mort. *Vous perdez.* » Je ris.

« Deviendrais-je stupide ? » demanda-t-il en regardant autour de lui. Puis ses yeux se fixèrent sur moi. « Il y a quelque chose qui cloche dans votre argumentation, Sun I. Vous n'êtes *pas* directeur.

— Ne me racontez pas d'histoire, Bateson. Vous savez comme moi que c'est une simple formalité. Vous ne pouvez pas me laisser sur la touche. Je contrôle vingt-huit pour cent de vos actions. Bon Dieu, *je serai directeur* ; mieux encore, je nommerai deux autres directeurs de mon choix et je ferai ce qui me plaira quand je siégerai.

— Vous ne cessez de dire "je", Sun I. "Je possède", "je contrôle", "je nommerai". Arrêtez-moi si je me trompe, mais il me semblait que Rising Sun Enterprises possédait ces actions.

— *Je suis Rising Sun !* tonnai-je en frappant la table du plat de la main.

— Je vous prie de ne pas élever la voix. » Il secoua la tête en soupirant. « Dire que tout cela avait si bien commencé. Nous devrions peut-être marquer une pause en déjeunant pour laisser les esprits se calmer. Cette méthode a fait une fois ses preuves, pourquoi pas une deuxième ?

— Allez vous faire voir, Bateson (j'étais furieux), je ne veux pas de votre déjeuner. Je tiens à régler cela immédiatement.

— Ne me privez pas, ne *nous* privez pas de ce plaisir, Sun I, répondit-il avec une moue que je trouvai ridicule. Si vous y tenez absolument, nous poursuivrons cette discussion pendant le déjeuner ; mais ne serait-il pas plus agréable de profiter de cette parenthèse pour manger ? Soyez conciliant. D'autant que nous avons fait préparer quelque chose de très particulier en votre honneur.

— Ah oui, dis-je avec colère en m'adossant violemment à mon fauteuil, vos déjeuners sont toujours un peu particuliers, n'est-ce pas ? Je vous l'accorde. Qu'allez-vous me proposer au dessert, des figues à l'arsenic ? »

Il ricana. « Oh, nous avons tout le temps de penser au dessert. » Il changea de sujet. « Nous déjeunerons de nouveau ici, si cela vous convient. Voulez-vous que j'ouvre les rideaux pour que nous regardions la neige ? » Il appuya sur le bouton, les tentures de velours vert s'écartèrent lentement, entraînées par le moteur au bourdonnement feutré. Il neigeait moins fort que tout à l'heure. Un pan de ciel bleu dominait le fleuve. Le soleil hivernal ressemblait à une énorme lanterne de papier blanc suspendue au-dessus de Brooklyn parmi des nuées qu'il tentait de dissiper, un embrasement blême et fiévreux dans un ciel glacé.

J'étais fiévreux moi aussi, et vaguement déçu. Je compris que j'avais eu tort de croire qu'ils capituleraient aussitôt mon jeu abattu. Bien sûr, Bateson n'avait d'autre choix que de continuer à bluffer. Je ne lui en voulais pas de cela. Simplement je désirais en finir, cesser de jouer au plus fin. Je voulais les faire payer. Je voulais ma place parmi eux.

Bateson s'excusa, soi-disant pour informer la cuisine que nous étions prêts à déjeuner. Peut-être allait-il au rapport ? Cela faisait sans doute partie du jeu. Il gagnait du temps, attendait de nouvelles consignes. Mais à quoi bon ces simagrées ? La bataille était terminée ; j'avais gagné. Je scrutai les miroirs à la recherche d'une fissure, d'une écaillure du tain qui m'eût permis de voir de l'autre côté, comme on essuie les traces de condensation sur une glace de salle de bain afin d'apercevoir le visage qui se cache derrière. Et tandis que j'examinai l'argenture, je me demandai, le temps d'un éclair, s'il se cachait réellement derrière. Et s'il n'y avait personne ? Pour la première fois depuis mon rêve, depuis Coney Island en fait, j'en doutai.

L'éventualité de son absence m'effraya davantage que celle de sa présence. Je fus pris d'un brusque vertige. Coney Island à l'envers, un passage à vide de la foi : je réalisai que, de même que j'avais eu besoin de lui auparavant pour l'aimer, au moins dans son « incarnation mystique », à travers « l'alchimie plus subtile qui se produit dans le cœur du croyant grâce à la foi », de même j'avais désormais besoin de lui pour le haïr. Cette pensée m'attrista ; je me demandai si j'avais vraiment renoncé à tout, si je parviendrais à renoncer, si c'était possible. Mais je me rappelai alors la cigarette, je ris comme Bateson et moi avions ri, puis je songeai à Yama, et une détermination implacable s'empara de moi.

On servit alors le repas, apporté sur des tables roulantes comme la dernière fois, sur lesquelles tintaient les énormes cloches argentées qui couvraient les plats. Des maîtres d'hôtel en livrée blanche, deux de leur côté de la table, un pour moi seul, s'activaient. Quand tout fut en place, Bateson adressa un signe de tête à mon maître d'hôtel qui souleva la cloche étincelante avec une serviette blanche.

Un énorme nuage de vapeur tourbillonnante s'éleva du plat, à travers lequel deux yeux laiteux me regardèrent.

« Oh mon Dieu, dis-je en grimaçant de dégoût, mais m'approchant pour mieux voir, qu'est-ce donc ? »

Bateson me considéra avec une expression vaguement blessée, comme si ma réaction le surprenait. « Tête de veau au beurre noir, annonça-t-il en français et d'une voix peinée. Avec des pommes de terre nouvelles, des petites carottes, des cœurs de céleri. » Les contractions spasmodiques des muscles de son menton, dues à sa déception, lui donnaient un air sénile. « Ne me dites pas que vous n'aimez pas ça.

— C'en est, n'est-ce pas ?
— Quoi donc ? rétorqua-t-il, stupéfait.
— *De la vache !*
— Du veau, rectifia-t-il, vexé. Une tête de veau. »

Je le dévisageai bouche bée, sceptique, convaincu qu'il plaisantait. Quelle parfaite expression de stupéfaction il arborait ! Il avait dû s'entraîner devant un miroir. Après réflexion, je décidai de ne pas lui accorder le bénéfice du doute et d'adopter le ton de l'indignation vertueuse. « Décidément, vous avez un faible pour les symboles. Encore un exemple de terrorisme gastronomique ? » Je ne pouvais détourner mon regard des yeux bouillis qui semblaient me fixer.

« "Terrorisme gastronomique" — vous exagérez un peu, vous ne trouvez pas ? me demanda-t-il sur un ton enjoué, mais encore un peu froissé. Je ne nierai pas que j'ai commandé ce plat en pensant à vous, Sun I, comme une sorte de tribut. Taureau Inc. ... ?

— Oui, Bateson, répondis-je sèchement, je crois que j'ai compris.

— D'un autre côté, souligna-t-il, c'est une des spécialités de notre chef, peut-être son plat le plus fin. » Il chercha l'approbation de ses collègues. « Ce n'est pas quelque chose que nous mangeons tous les jours, poursuivit-il avec l'indignation qu'on manifeste à un enfant qui a mal nettoyé son assiette, vous pouvez me croire.

— Vous avez bien raison, dis-je. Moi non plus, je n'en mangerais pas tous les jours. »

Il prit un air outré, qu'imitèrent bientôt les autres.

Brusquement, cela m'apparut presque drôle. Avec une grimace j'enfonçai les dents de ma fourchette dans l'œil bouilli. « Croyez-vous pouvoir me soutirer des concessions en m'obligeant à jeûner ? » L'œil éclata, l'humeur vitreuse s'écoula en une larme gélatineuse qui glissa sur le museau. Je renversai la tête, partis d'un grand rire nerveux qui se mua en frisson de dégoût. « Enlevez ça », ordonnai-je ; je fermai les yeux et détournai la tête en repoussant mon assiette. « J'ai bien fait de manger avant de venir. » Bateson ne sembla pas m'entendre, occupé qu'il était à vérifier la cuisson de la viande avec sa fourchette. « Très bien, Bateson, maintenant que vous avez fait votre petite plaisanterie, reprenons notre discussion.

— Mmm », fit-il, la bouche pleine, en hochant la tête. Il déglutit avec difficulté. « Cela ne vous dérange pas, n'est-ce pas ? » De son couteau, il désigna son assiette. « Continuez. Vous disiez ? » Il se tourna vers son voisin de table. « Délicieux. » Les deux hommes opinèrent vigoureusement du chef.

« Oui, sublime, répondit enfin l'autre, incapable de trouver un compliment plus flatteur.

— Nous aimons le veau et le bœuf, commenta Bateson. La viande nous garde en forme et — il s'autorisa un demi-sourire — entretient notre instinct carnivore. Je suis navré que ce plat ne vous plaise pas. A voir votre réaction, on eût cru que nous vous présentions une tête de mort, et non une tête de veau. » Il pouffa avec les autres de cette bonne plaisanterie.

Je les observais pendant qu'ils mangeaient, j'écoutais le bruit cristallin de l'argenterie contre la porcelaine, le cliquetis des plats, la rumeur indistincte de leurs voix qui évoquaient les borborygmes de la digestion. Leur appétit me fascinait et me terrifiait. Bateson surtout prenait un grand plaisir à manger. Avec un sentiment assez proche de l'horreur, je le regardai s'attaquer aux deux embryons de corne bouillis qui saillaient à travers la chair tendre du front. Il les fit sauter d'un coup de couteau, les éventra sur son assiette, puis les saisit entre ses doigts pour en sucer la moelle. Remarquant mon intérêt, il en tendit une vers moi comme pour un toast, souriant et opinant du chef avec une affreuse bonhomie.

« Nous parlions de mes vingt-huit pour cent », repris-je enfin d'une voix faible. Je m'obligeai à détourner les yeux.

« Oui ! acquiesça-t-il en levant le menton pour avaler et son couteau pour rectifier. Les vingt-huit pour cent de Rising Sun. » Il eut un sourire suave.

« Où est la différence, Bateson ? Mes actions, celles de Rising Sun ? Nous avons déjà réglé ce problème. Je vous l'ai dit, je suis Rising Sun.

— Bah, concéda-t-il en continuant de mastiquer. En effet, vous l'avez déjà dit. » Il tamponna ses lèvres avec sa serviette, puis héla le maître d'hôtel. « Servez le deuxième plat, commanda-t-il à voix basse.

— Vous savez, Sun I, dit-il en pliant sa serviette sans me regarder, je trouve que vous avez une attitude très cavalière envers votre position dans votre compagnie, envers vos actionnaires. » Il me lança un regard aigu. « Peut-être procède-t-on ainsi à Taureau Incorpored, à Rising Sun, mais très sincèrement, cette attitude me choque — *nous* choque. Voilà une autre raison pour laquelle ça ne marcherait pas — je veux dire, faire équipe joindre nos forces. Ici, personne n'aurait l'idée d'amalgamer "nos" ressources avec celles de la corporation. » Il fronça les sourcils en secouant gravement la tête. « Non, vraiment, cela me paraît un peu irresponsable, un peu léger.

— Laissons Rising Sun en dehors de la discussion, voulez-vous ? demandai-je avec une politesse acide. La façon dont je dirige ma compagnie ne vous regarde en rien. Le problème n'est pas là. Nous sommes ici pour parler de vous. »

Pliant toujours sa serviette d'un air soucieux, il secoua la tête. « Non, Sun I, vous avez tort. Tout le problème est là. Servez, dit-il au maître d'hôtel qui s'était immobilisé à ma gauche avec un plat.

— Je n'en veux pas, déclinai-je d'une voix adoucie, en secouant la tête avec un sourire.

— Mais vous n'avez même pas vu de quoi il s'agit, protesta Bateson.

— Je ne tiens nullement à le voir.

— Je vais devoir insister, dit-il sombrement. Allez-y », intima-t-il au maître d'hôtel avec un geste du poignet, avant que je n'aie eu le temps de protester. L'homme souleva la cloche, et sur le plat, au milieu de brins de persil vert, je découvris une épaisse pile de certificats d'actions. Le logo gravé montrait un demi-soleil en équilibre sur l'horizon — un motif que j'avais emprunté à la robe de ma mère. *Rising Sun.*

Mon cœur s'emballa. « Qu'est-ce que c'est ? demandai-je calmement.

— Le dessert, répondit-il en souriant. *Juste* le dessert.

— Très drôle, Bateson, le complimentai-je avec un mépris glacé. Et que suis-je censé comprendre ? »

Il haussa les épaules avec une moue fataliste. « Simplement que nous aussi, Sun I, nous sommes actionnaires dans *votre* corporation, et qu'à ce titre nous nous intéressons à la bonne marche de la compagnie, et particulièrement au comportement et à la mentalité de ses directeurs, à *votre* comportement et à *votre* mentalité, Sun I, tout comme vous vous préoccupez des nôtres. »

C'était donc ça ? Je sentis la flèche passer en sifflant devant mon visage et poursuivre sa course dans l'espace. Elle m'avait manqué. Une bouffée de joie sauvage me submergea, je tournai les yeux vers la baie panoramique : le ciel s'était brusquement dégagé, le soleil brillait.

« C'était donc ça, demandai-je, votre surprise ? »

Il hocha la tête. « C'est ça. »

Je lui ris au visage.

Les directeurs échangèrent des regards graves. « Je ne crois pas que le rire soit approprié en la circonstance, Sun I, me rabroua-t-il.

— Non, non, vous avez raison, concédai-je en essuyant avec le dos de mon poignet les larmes qui perlaient aux coins de mes yeux. Simplement, je suis tellement soulagé. Vous m'avez fait peur. Un moment, j'ai cru... » Je secouai la tête. « Mais il va de soi, messieurs, que vous avez votre mot à dire à Rising Sun. Après tout, moi aussi je dirige mon affaire démocratiquement. C'est le prix à payer pour être coté en Bourse, n'est-ce pas ? » Ils ne réagirent pas à mes tentatives de weltzschmerz fiduciaire. « Vous bénéficiez naturellement des mêmes droits que les autres actionnaires », déclarai-je enfin en imitant la réserve polie des administrateurs du Metropolitan Museum.

Bateson leva l'index pour m'interrompre. « Pas tout à fait les mêmes droits, Sun I, rectifia-t-il. Je pense que vous n'avez pas encore bien compris.

— Que voulez-vous dire ?

— Vous feriez bien de les compter. »

Jaillie de nulle part, la flèche revint. L'univers se déroba sous mes pieds, je me sentis tomber à grande vitesse, chuter vertigineusement. « Pourquoi ne m'annoncez-vous pas leur nombre ? leur dis-je en essayant de ne pas paniquer.

— Cinquante-trois, répondit-il.

— Cinquante-trois mille ?

Il eut un sourire de pitié. « Pour cent. »

La flèche fit mouche. Je fermai les yeux. Réveille-toi, pensai-je. « Impossible, dis-je à haute voix. Vous ne pouvez pas établir une position aussi solide — du menton, je désignai les certificats d'actions — et en même temps vendre tous azimuts, vendre au point de nous mettre en situation difficile. » Je secouai la tête avec véhémence. « Que manigancez-vous ? Une autre plaisanterie ? Quoi, ce sont des faux ? Encore du terrorisme psychologique ?

— Vérifiez vous-même, suggéra-t-il. Allez-y. »

Je pris le premier rectangle de papier crissant, un certificat pour dix mille actions, et le levai vers la lumière. Je vis le filigrane. Je regardai en transparence les gratte-ciel de Manhattan. Chutant toujours, j'entendais le vent siffler dans mes oreilles. Des larmes froides coulaient de mes yeux et remontaient vers mon front. Cédant à la panique, je me mis à rire, renversai la tête et hurlai. Et au-dessus de mon rire, par-delà le sifflement du vent, je discernai un autre rire, plus aigu, plus étrange que le mien, comme un cri d'orfraie, ténu, nasillard et perçant, pas vraiment humain, et avec lui le vrombissement d'un moteur. A travers le papillonnement de mes cils, je vis un minuscule point noir apparaître au centre du soleil, puis grossir. Mais quand je l'eus reconnu, il était trop tard. J'étais déjà mort.

« Vous avez déjà remarqué, Sun I, disait Bateson en désignant le certificat que je tenais à la main, ce dessin étonnant ? On ne sait pas si le soleil se lève ou s'il se couche. Un motif ambigu.

— Le soleil de Rising Sun se lève, affirmai-je machinalement avant de comprendre que j'étais perdu.

— C'est un soleil couchant, dit-il, pour vous. »

Puis l'aiguille retomba dans le sillon, le bon sillon du disque, et la mélodie reprit. Je secouai la tête. « Impossible, dis-je. Vous n'avez pas pu accumuler nos actions, vous les vendiez, vous vendiez à court terme. Comment auriez-vous pu les acheter sur cette échelle en même temps ?

— C'est la question à soixante-quatre mille dollars, n'est-ce pas, Sun I ? Mais soixante-quatre millions de dollars serait sans doute plus près de la vérité, bien qu'encore un peu faible.

— C'est de la poudre aux yeux, un tour de passe-passe. »

Je crachai mes accusations au miroir. « Comment auriez-vous pu mettre la main sur autant d'actions ? Dites-moi simplement cela. Cinquante-trois pour cent. » Je foudroyai du regard les certificats.

Il haussa les épaules. « Question facile. Il y a eu votre offre d'achat initiale. Nous avons investi beaucoup d'argent à ce moment-là. Je tiens pourtant à vous dire que nos motifs étaient parfaitement innocents. *Alors.* Vous ne le croirez peut-être pas — à cause de ce que vous nous avez obligés à faire ensuite —, mais au début nous vous souhaitions le plus grand bien. Sincèrement. » Il rentra ses lèvres, m'adressa un regard accusateur et plein d'excuse.

« Menteur ! lui criai-je.

— Comme vous voudrez, dit-il. Ensuite, bien sûr, il y a eu les achats sur le marché. Des achats massifs. Et puis votre ami Kahn.

— Kahn ? » Je fus abasourdi. « Je ne vous crois pas. »

Il hocha la tête. « Eh si. Bien sûr, il ignorait à qui il vendait. Nous avons acheté par l'intermédiaire de courtiers ayant pignon sur rue, de comptes numérotés, par paquets relativement modestes. Il n'a jamais été notre complice objectif, encore qu'il n'ait pas montré de scrupules superflus quant aux acquéreurs de son portefeuille. En fin de compte, nous avons réussi à rafler presque toutes les actions dont il s'est débarrassé. C'est à peu près tout, je crois. » Il sourit. « Oh attendez — j'ai failli oublier la meilleure. Les derniers petits pour cent qui nous manquaient.

— Et alors ?

— Vous nous les avez donnés, Sun I. » Il rayonnait.

Je touchai ma poitrine malgré moi. « Moi ? »

Il opina du chef. « Votre offre si alléchante de convertibilité, vous vous rappelez ? Nous avons décidé d'en profiter nous-mêmes. »

Je le regardai avec stupéfaction. « Vous m'avez vendu vos propres actions alors que j'essayais de vous absorber ?

— Exactement. Pour devenir majoritaires dans votre corporation. Inutile de vous dire que ces derniers pour cent furent les plus agréables. Cette fois je crois n'avoir rien oublié. »

Je secouai la tête. « Si. Cela laisse la question centrale sans réponse. A supposer que vous ne mentiez pas, comment avez-vous pu acheter des actions, acheter sur cette échelle, tout en faisant *baisser* la cote ? »

Bateson eut un sourire paternel. « C'est là le nœud du problème, n'est-ce pas, Sun I ? *Bon.* Nous contrôlons désormais Rising Sun Enterprises, ce qui signifie, entre autres, que nous contrôlons indirectement ces fameux vingt-huit pour cent de nos actions que vous vous êtes donné tant de mal pour acquérir bien inutilement et dans le seul but de nous les restituer, des actions que par étourderie vous prétendiez tout à l'heure posséder, ce qui signifie en outre que vous n'avez plus droit à rien, à très exactement rien — pas un siège à notre conseil, pas de privilèges de vote, pas d'information confidentielle — bref, zéro. Vous comprenez ? Qui plus est, nous vous relevons de vos fonctions de P-DG de Rising Sun Enterprises, mesure applicable immédiatement.

— Mais vous ne pouvez pas, protestai-je faiblement en tendant la main pour essayer d'arrêter l'avalanche. Je possède toujours mes intérêts initiaux dans la corporation. Je suis Rising Sun. C'est moi qui ai créé cette entreprise.

— Faux, une fois encore, dit-il. Nous ne pouvons pas vous relever de vos fonctions ? Vu que nous possédons cinquante-trois pour cent des actions, nous sommes libres de faire tout ce qui nous chante. » Des rires fusèrent autour de la table. Leurs mains frappèrent le marbre.

« Quant au deuxième point, poursuivit-il, vos intérêts initiaux : bien qu'ils ne fassent pas le poids en face des nôtres, je dois vous rappeler que toutes vos actions servent actuellement de garantie pour des prêts que vous avez sollicités afin de renforcer votre position dans APL. Comme la cote de Rising Sun n'a cessé de chuter, nous savons que vous n'avez pu honorer vos échéances, que vous avez dû gager ces nouvelles actions, voire reporter un certain nombre de fois le remboursement du principal.

— Ce sont des informations confidentielles, explosai-je. Comment les avez-vous obtenues ? »

Il sourit. « Nous avons nos sources. Il y a toujours moyen de savoir.

— Peu importe, dis-je. Garantie ou pas, gagées ou non, je possède toujours ces actions. Vous ne pouvez pas maintenir artificiellement la cote de Rising Sun aussi bas. Finalement je pourrai rembourser mes dettes. » J'eus un sourire caustique. « A moins qu'en tant que nouveaux directeurs, vous n'envisagiez de saboter Rising Sun ? Ce serait une trahison, vous le savez. » Je leur offris cette platitude en pâture.

Bateson secoua la tête. « Faux une fois encore, Sun I. Totalement faux. Nous n'avons pas besoin de saboter Rising Sun pour mener à bien nos projets. En fait, ce que nous avons en tête — un petit émondage indispensable, qui ne traîne que trop — devrait accorder à la corporation une croissance jamais vue. Quant à votre "finalement", je crains que dans votre cas, ce "finalement" ne soit trop tard. Car *aujourd'hui*, nous contrôlons le Groupe Bancaire du Taureau ainsi que tous les autres avoirs de Rising Sun Enterprises, nous vous déclarons en cessation de paiement et confisquons votre garantie originelle ainsi que la totalité des actions gagées ultérieurement par vous, tant pour consolider votre garantie initiale que pour rembourser les intérêts de vos dettes, le tout s'élevant à... » D'un geste brusque, il sortit de sa poche une paire de lunettes de lecture, les ouvrit sèchement d'une main et parcourut d'un air soucieux une feuille de papier posée sur la table. Puis il les rangea tout aussi brusquement et m'examina avec une lueur dure dans le regard. « Le tout s'élevant à, eh bien je crois que cela équivaut à une faillite, Sun I », triompha-t-il en feignant la surprise. (Aucune pitié en ce lieu.) Il échangea des regards de sombre satisfaction avec ses acolytes. « Oui, il s'agit bel et bien d'une faillite. Votre compte présente un léger débit, parfaitement épongeable par vos deux semaines d'indemnités, et puis j'imagine que vous avez un petit pécule de côté. » Il sourit. « Vous voyez ? Vous échappez malgré tout aux poursuites légales. Il ne vous reste pas grand-chose, c'est entendu, sans doute moins que vous ne l'espériez. En tout cas, le problème d'une haute position dans Rising Sun Enterprises ne se pose pas. La situation est claire comme de l'eau de roche : vous n'avez plus ni responsabilités ni actions dans la corporation. Nu comme un nouveau-né, selon l'expression consacrée.

— Rien, répétai-je, stupéfait par l'ampleur de la catastrophe, incapable de réaliser son étendue. Rien. » Je levai les yeux vers lui. « Rien ?

— Pas rien, Sun I. Un modeste actif. Mais bien sûr, nous parlons seulement de la corporation et de ses avoirs. Un homme d'affaires comme vous possède certainement d'autres biens personnels, de quoi se renflouer en cas de pépin. Ne vous inquiétez pas. Nous n'avons aucune visée sur vos biens privés.

— J'ai engagé tous mes biens personnels pour garantir les prêts, expliquai-je, tous — jusqu'à mes économies. »

Bateson secoua la tête ; l'espace d'un instant, une lueur de sympathie brilla dans ses yeux. « Quelle imprudence, mon garçon, me lança-t-il doucement. Vous auriez dû y réfléchir à deux fois. Que cela vous serve de leçon à l'avenir. »

Je ris. « L'avenir. » Je restai assis, bouche bée. L'avenir. Rien. Tellement énorme. Brusquement, un écho se réverbéra dans mon oreille interne. « Une faillite, avez-vous dit. » Je cherchai une confirmation sur ses traits. « Vous avez bien parlé de faillite ? »

Il fronça les sourcils. « Oui, il me semble. Mais ce n'était qu'une figure de style.

— C'est ça, dis-je, plongé dans une soudaine contemplation. Voilà comment vous avez fait pour renforcer votre position chez nous tout en faisant baisser notre cote. » Ma découverte me procura une consolation momentanée dans la débâcle générale. J'entendis la reliure de cuir grincer alors que le tome s'ouvrait. Le chapitre sur les faillites suivait celui consacré aux ventes fictives. « Une vente fictive. Vous n'avez jamais réellement vendu nos actions, n'est-ce pas ? Comment avez-vous procédé ? » Je hochai la tête. « Ne me dites rien. Je devine. Une sorte de navette entre vos filiales, pas vrai ? Pas une action n'échappe à la corporation. Tout reste chez APL. Un travail en famille. La caisse de retraite d'une de vos holdings vend à perte des Rising Sun à l'une de vos filiales. Le prix baisse, mais le portefeuille reste sous le contrôle d'APL. Vous perdez de l'argent sur vos Rising Sun, mais ça en vaut la peine. Vous *devez* perdre cet argent pour vous protéger. C'était là le prix à payer. *Votre* prix. C'est bien ça, non ? Ventes fictives entre les filiales du groupe APL, dans un sens puis dans l'autre, ventes redoublées et à perte, mais sans jamais cesser de contrôler une seule action. Raids d'ours et vente fictive combinés. Ingénieux.

— Très ingénieux, renchérit Bateson non sans rougir de fierté. Mais farfelu. Quelle imagination, Sun I. Vous devriez entrer dans la publicité ou écrire un roman. »

J'éclatai de rire. « C'est illégal, Bateson, dis-je. Vous ne vous en tirerez pas comme ça. Je veillerai à ce que vous soyez dénoncé.

— A vous de prouver ce que vous avancez, Sun I, remarqua-t-il. Mais il me semble que vous avez épuisé toutes vos ressources. Les vôtres comme les nôtres. Celles de Rising Sun, j'entends. Vous avez une équipe valable, là-bas. Comment les appelez-vous déjà, les Cornes ? Bien sûr, vous continuerez votre enquête sans leur collaboration, en tant que "privé", citoyen lambda, membre émérite et à part entière du Grand Public. En d'autres termes, vous êtes seul, Sun I. Si vous tenez à poursuivre votre petite vendetta contre nous, grand bien vous fasse. Mais cela en vaut-il vraiment la peine ? Pensez-vous sincèrement que si vos Cornes n'ont rien découvert, vous trouverez quelque chose tout seul ? S'il y avait quoi que ce soit à découvrir, ils l'auraient fait. » Il secoua la tête. « Renoncez, mon garçon. Attelez-vous à une autre tâche. Il n'y a rien de plus pitoyable qu'un homme déterminé à se martyriser sur la croix d'une souffrance personnelle. Surtout quand lui-même est responsable de cette souffrance, ce qui — pardonnez-moi — est sans conteste votre cas.

— Il n'en reste pas moins que c'est illégal, Bateson, persistai-je en ignorant ses conseils sentencieux. Vous avez peut-être effacé proprement vos foutues traces — c'est possible, je le sais —, mais c'est illégal. »

Il soupira comme devant un cas irrécupérable. « Ça toujours été votre faiblesse en tant qu'adversaire, Sun I, votre faiblesse et notre atout. Vous avez joué *de jure* et non pas *de facto* dans un monde qui reconnaît seulement le *de facto*. Il n'existe pas de loi. Pas en ce lieu. Pas *ici*.

— C'est *lui* qui vous a dit cela ? »

Mais il n'entendit pas ou feignit de ne pas entendre. « Avez-vous vraiment cru que nous vous laisserions batifoler ici comme un Méphisto, une sorte de Méphisto taoïste en chaussures à semelles craquantes, et nous absorber comme on enlève une jeune fille, que nous ne trouverions pas un biais quelconque, légal... » Il se tut.

« Ou illégal ? »

Il ferma les yeux, presque pour approuver, puis soupira par le nez. « Je crois vraiment que vous ne l'avez pas, mon garçon.

— Quoi donc ?

— L'instinct du tueur. »

Je ne répondis pas. Il rit.

« J'ai presque pitié de vous.

— Rendez-moi ce qui m'appartient, alors, dis-je avec véhémence. J'ai créé Rising Sun. Rendez-moi mes actions.

— Ah ! » Il haussa les sourcils, eut un sourire attristé. « Vous me faites pitié, mais ma pitié ne va pas jusque-là. »

Nous restâmes silencieux.

« Laissez-moi le voir », dis-je sans regarder son visage.

Il pencha un peu la tête. « Voir qui ?

— Vous savez *qui*, répliquai-je. *Lui*. A quoi bon continuer ces feintes et ces simagrées ? Je sais qu'il est derrière tout ça. Je l'ai vu, ce jour-là, sur la galerie. Dites-moi la vérité. »

Bateson secoua la tête. « Navré, Sun I, mais je crains de ne pas comprendre. Je ne vois pas de qui vous voulez parler.

— Love. » Je tendis le doigt vers le miroir. Quand je vis mon reflet tendre le doigt vers moi, mon bras tomba brusquement. « S'il vous plaît, Bateson, l'implorai-je, soudain très las, écrasé par le poids des ruines qu'il avait accumulées sur mes épaules, ou que j'y avais entassées — peu importait. Je vous en supplie.

— Vous parlez de votre père, n'est-ce pas ? *Eddie* Love. »

Il échangea des regards étonnés avec les autres directeurs.

J'acquiesçai, épuisé.

« Vous voulez dire que, selon vous, il vit *toujours* ? »

Je le regardai sans répondre.

Il renifla. « Absurde ! Vous perdez la tête. Où avez-vous pêché une idée aussi saugrenue ? »

Je réunis tristement mes affaires.

« Eddie Love ! » répéta Bateson en un chuchotement stupéfait, confidentiel, destiné à son voisin. Tous deux éclatèrent de rire. Les onze hommes éclatèrent de rire.

Mon pardessus posé sur le bras, je ramassai le catalogue de l'exposition, puis me dirigeai vers la porte sans un mot.

« Vous recevrez vos deux semaines d'indemnités, Sun I, me cria Bateson en s'étranglant presque de rire. Déduction faite de vos dernières dettes. Oh, Sun I, si vous cherchez du travail ? »

Je me retournai vers lui.

« Ma femme me tanne depuis un moment pour que je lui trouve un domestique chinois. Elle croit que ça fait "aristocrate", minauda-t-il. Je sais que vous avez une expérience de cuisinier. Peut-être cela vous conviendrait-il ? Après tout, mieux vaut diriger une cuisine que rien du tout. »

Tous éclatèrent de rire, hurlèrent comme des loups.

« Bâtard », l'injuriai-je à voix basse, sans même le haïr.

Il ricana. « Autant pour vous, Sun I. »

25

Je touchais donc au bout du voyage. L'expression de leurs visages m'apprit l'ultime et terrible vérité. Non seulement la vérité, mais tout simplement le dessillement de la dernière illusion. Malgré leurs sarcasmes et leur dérision, je n'avais plus le moindre doute. Pas sur ce sujet. Ils n'avaient pas compris mes allusions relatives à mon père. Il n'avait jamais été là. Jamais. Je n'en revenais pas. Chaque chose, chaque événement était pure surface. Simple apparence. Et ce face à face tant désiré, un pur fantasme. Aucun Dieu dans les coulisses pour tirer les ficelles. Personne derrière le rideau. Pas de mystère, pas de sacrement, seulement les signes extérieurs et visibles. Pas de signataire, seulement les signatures. Pas de deus ex machina, seulement les grincements désincarnés de la machinerie. Cette banalité, cette médiocrité étaient infiniment plus horribles que mon rêve de tuerie rédemptrice, ce rêve que j'avais fait dans le profond mystère du péché. Pas de mystère. Pas même de péché. Même pas cela. Bateson au cœur du labyrinthe. Bateson, le Minotaure. C'était presque grotesque. C'était grotesque. Horriblement grotesque, et hilarant. Je n'en revenais pas. Je ne parvenais pas à comprendre. Love n'existait pas. Il n'avait jamais été là. Même pas dans son « incarnation mystique ». Même pas à travers « l'alchimie plus subtile qui se produit dans le cœur du croyant grâce à la foi », cette imposture. Jamais présent, sous quelque forme que ce fût. Bateson avait raison. J'étais fou. J'avais tout le temps été fou. Depuis le premier instant dans la cellule du maître quand j'avais sottement scellé mon destin et ouvert la bouche pour demander à Hsiao de me raconter mon histoire. Fou même alors. Fou de croire. Fou d'espérer. Fou d'aimer.

« L'ampleur de la catastrophe. » L'expression obsédait mon esprit comme un disque rayé, comme un tic. Je faillis rire. Mais je n'osai me laisser aller au rire par crainte du silence qui le suivrait inévitablement et qui, s'ouvrant, risquait de déboucher sur un paysage inconnu.

Ainsi, peu à peu, j'assimilai la nouvelle, ce que j'avais perdu. C'est-à-dire tout. Oui, maintenant enfin, tout. Je compris que je l'avais perdu, lui. Et ensuite, que l'ardoise était effacée d'un coup. Mon compte définitivement clos. Totalement exposé, dévêtu. Rendu à bien autre chose qu'à la nudité animale. A la chose elle-même. Mais cela, ce deuil, n'avait aucune dignité, rien d'anoblissant dans la souffrance ou le sacrifice. Il ne restait qu'une étendue morne et laide qui s'offrait devant et derrière moi, sans grandeur ni caractère. Seulement ce moment et ce lieu. Ici et maintenant. Le lieu où je me tenais. Et je me résolvais difficilement à l'envisager, à regarder autour de moi, à observer le monde. Ce Nouveau Monde. Ce qui me restait. Ce qui avait toujours été là. Identique à soi-même. Le monde tel qu'il est. Face à face. Un spectacle trop horrible.

M'obligeant malgré tout à l'ingurgiter comme un médicament, je regardai autour de moi, frémis à ce spectacle, et bientôt ne voulus plus regarder. Plus jamais. J'en avais assez vu. Trop vu.

Je touchais donc au but. Nirvana, Samsara, le monde tel qu'il est, une seule et même chose. Empalé sur les cornes de l'ultime équation, du dilemme final, par la loi commutative, je me trouvai, moi, Sun I. Face à face. « Alors je connaîtrai comme je suis connu. » Je me connus moi-même, enfin. Et à travers moi-même, je connus le reste, le monde tel qu'il est. Ni sommet ni abîme, pas davantage le cri du maître que celui de l'être subjugué, ni un chant, un rire ou des larmes, mais comme moi un ensemble de choses pitoyables, morcelées, cobayes de laboratoire tremblant sous la lumière aseptisée d'un soleil fluorescent, créatures étiolées, les pierres aussi vivantes que les yeux humains, et le tout presque moribond.

Je pensai au visage de la sterne morte sur la plage de Sands Point, à l'expression presque souriante de son regard. L'oiseau souriait alors même que les mouches frottaient leurs ailes et se posaient pour se nourrir de sa chair. Ce sourire. Je ne pouvais l'oublier. Le savoir se résumait donc à cela. Le savoir ultime et définitif qu'était l'illumination. Et tout le monde pouvait l'obtenir. Sans la moindre pénitence. Tout le monde. Ce savoir sauvage.

Cela fondit sur moi d'un coup, cela m'écrasa instantanément, l'ampleur de la découverte, son énormité, ce que j'avais fait et perdu — ma fierté, ma paix, mon espoir et mon bonheur, ma jeunesse, mon innocence, mon âme — tout cela sacrifié à une cause perdue, pour payer une dette inexistante. Car tel était le prix à payer pour vivre dans le monde tel qu'il est. L'énormité du prix. Tout. Et jamais je n'entrerais dans ces régions glorieuses, dans ce Royaume des Délices dont j'avais rêvé, auquel j'avais tout sacrifié (tous mes Trésors gaspillés, à jamais dissipés), je ne verrais jamais le lieu utopique où les lignes parallèles de mes deux ambitions incompatibles, de mes deux destins inconciliables, se rencontraient enfin, ce point fantasmé où les rails d'acier s'éprenaient l'un de l'autre. Je ne le verrais jamais. Car la voie s'arrêtait là. Terminus. Tout le monde descend

J'étais au bout du voyage. J'avais atteint le terminus de la ligne. La destination ultime. Impossible d'aller plus loin. J'étais arrivé. J'y étais. Il me restait seulement à découvrir le monde tel qu'il est.

Je regardai autour de moi : ce "terminus" était un ascenseur. Ce lieu me parut aussi judicieux qu'un autre. J'étais devant avec le groom ; quand nous nous arrêtâmes, je fus expulsé, éjecté de la cabine avec la foule, le troupeau, le Grand Public, dans la salle du Centre des Visiteurs au troisième étage. Entraîné par le groupe, je n'offris aucune résistance, car je n'en avais plus. J'avais épuisé toutes mes réserves. Pourquoi ne pas suivre les touristes ?

Ce fut étrangement agréable d'être là avec le bétail, étrange et plaisant d'accompagner ce troupeau, de sentir son contact. Ce côtoiement me fit du bien. Souvenir après souvenir, cercle après cercle, je descendis l'échelle qui menait du brillant paradis du désespoir jusqu'à la tristesse banale, humaine, celle de l'homme du commun qui vit dans le monde tel qu'il est et qui a payé le prix d'entrée — tout — exactement comme les autres, mais pour une visite non guidée.

Sur la galerie, je pleurai. Je ressentis d'abord du soulagement, comme une libération. Puis, quand mes larmes furent taries, la futilité de toute libération. La souffrance nue. Je laissai tomber mon manteau par terre et enfouis mon visage entre mes mains pour pleurer. Mon groupe s'éloigna sans moi, un autre arriva. Je continuai de pleurer là où j'étais, tout au bout, sans honte, tandis que l'un après l'autre les groupes défilaient devant moi comme autant de générations, fils après pères, pères après fils, fils devant leur père, à l'infini dans les deux sens, jusqu'au début du monde et la fin des temps, et je pleurais pour eux tous et pour moi-même, je pleurais sans apaisement ni douceur. Je pleurais là, devant le spectacle de mon existence, la vie au-delà du miroir et derrière la paroi de Plexiglas, la vie exemptée de tout mystère. Je pleurais parce que je m'y perdais pour la première fois, anonyme et peureux comme tous les autres, peureux parce que perdu, perdu parce que banal, exactement comme les autres. Je pleurais parce que j'avais cru jadis être différent et qu'un destin particulier m'attendait, que je ne mourrais jamais. Je pleurais parce que j'avais perdu tout espoir, perdu ma foi, mon amour, tout perdu. L'énormité du prix, l'ampleur de la découverte.

Une main toucha légèrement mon épaule, une main humaine. Je levai les yeux à travers mes larmes, remerciai d'un hochement de tête, d'un regard absent qui ne vit rien, qui n'avait même pas besoin de voir car je savais qui c'était, un homme comme moi, anonyme et peureux, qui un instant dominait sa crainte pour se montrer aimable. Il remit doucement mon manteau sur mon bras, puis le tapota.

« Ne pleure pas, fils, me consola-t-il d'une voix paisible et triste. Ça n'en vaut pas la peine. »

J'acquiesçai en essayant de me maîtriser. « Non, concédai-je, vous avez raison. Ça n'en vaut pas la peine.

— Mais parfois c'est plus fort que soi. »

J'entendis le sourire dans sa voix ; je souris aussi à travers mes larmes. « Oui, admis-je. Parfois.

— Je ne crois pas que nous sommes ici pour être heureux », dit-il.

Je secouai la tête, d'accord avec lui.

« Je pensais autrefois que c'était un de nos droits fondamentaux, que le bonheur était garanti. Plus maintenant.

— Moi aussi je le croyais, dis-je.

— Et pourtant, nous sommes parfois heureux. »

Cette fois je ne répondis pas, car j'ignorais si je le croyais.

« Tu le seras encore, me promit-il avec le même sourire derrière ses mots.

— J'ai tout perdu, lui dis-je, la seule vérité que je connaissais.

— Je sais, répondit-il. Ça se voit. Je suis désolé. » Puis il resta longtemps silencieux, respectueux de mon désespoir, de son ampleur.

« Était-ce si important ? » demanda-t-il enfin.

D'abord la question me scandalisa, mais je me forçai à y réfléchir. Je

faillis trouver le recoin de mon cœur qui répondait non, ce n'est pas si important. Mais je changeai d'avis et dis : « Oui, bien sûr.
— D'accord, concéda-t-il, c'était important. » Cette fois, son silence semblait presque perplexe. « Mais perdre fait partie du jeu, n'est-ce pas ? demanda-t-il comme s'il posait lui-même la question.
— Oui, répondis-je. Certainement.
— Je pense parfois que c'est le secret du jeu, poursuivit-il. Peut-être même le sens du jeu. » Le sourire revint dans sa voix. « Gagner me paraît mesquin et futile, comparé à cela ; ce bonheur est banal, presque trivial, comparé à la souffrance et au deuil. Un mystère, affirma-t-il avec dans la voix un sourire différent, plus froid, plus lumineux et détaché. Et puis Dieu est compatissant. Au revoir, jeune homme. Bonne chance. »

De nouveau, il effleura doucement mon épaule, et je ressentis un frisson, une faible décharge électrique — la même que devant Chong Fou quand il avait posé sa main sur ma poitrine, puis par un mystérieux tour de magie extrait la cigale du temple de mon cœur, avant de la lâcher dans la salle de prières en riant ; et aussi lorsqu'il m'avait touché à la porte du monastère quand je l'avais vu pour la dernière fois et que j'étais parti dans le monde, dans ce monde, le monde tel qu'il est.

Quand j'eus séché mes larmes, essuyé mes yeux et que je lui prêtai vraiment attention, il s'éloignait dans le couloir. Le groupe qui s'en allait l'entoura et l'entraîna avec lui comme un morceau de bois flotté.

« Au revoir ! » m'écriai-je en levant le bras, pris du désir de l'arrêter, de le faire revenir, troublé par quelque chose, sans doute par l'envie de mieux l'examiner.

« Merci ! » criai-je encore pour qu'il se retournât.

Il ne le fit pas, se contenta de lever la main par-dessus son épaule, et accéléra le pas. Ce fut alors que je remarquai qu'il boitait. Mon cœur faillit s'arrêter, puis s'emballa. Je me sentis pris de faiblesse, malade d'excitation, malade d'un espoir impossible.

« Attendez ! hurlai-je. Une minute ! »

Quand il atteignit le seuil, il s'arrêta, se retourna et leva la main.

Un léger cri monta de ma gorge, désespoir et bonheur. C'était lui. C'était Love. Il portait les lunettes d'aviateur aux verres en forme de larmes vert foncé.

Puis il disparut à travers la porte comme par un goulot d'étranglement, entraîné par le poids de la foule qui le poussait telle une masse liquide, comme les eaux de la terre.

« Attendez ! » criai-je en courant vers lui. Mais le groupe suivant arriva comme un changement de marée. Jouant des coudes et des épaules, je me frayai un chemin à travers les visiteurs. Je franchis enfin le seuil, puis m'élançai vers lui, vers les ascenseurs.

Debout dans l'encadrement de la porte, il était le seul occupant de la cabine. Les mains serrées devant lui, il levait les yeux vers le panneau lumineux qui clignotait au-dessus de la porte.

Je faillis l'atteindre, faillis le toucher. Il me regarda au dernier moment, droit dans les yeux, tandis que les plaques métalliques coulissaient, que le rideau se fermait, et il me sourit. Je ne réussis jamais à oublier ce sourire. Je ne peux l'oblitérer.

Je regardai les voyants s'allumer jusqu'au sommet. Il ne s'arrêta pas au dernier étage, pas davantage à APL. Je savais d'ailleurs qu'il irait jusqu'au bout. Au sommet. Sur le toit. Le plus haut possible. Et je l'y suivis. Là-bas. Je le suivis sur cet ultime terrain sauvage, dans le monde tel qu'il est.

Une bouffée d'air froid, un jaillissement de lumière m'accueillirent quand les portes de l'ascenseur s'ouvrirent au niveau du toit. Je ressentis une excitation presque insupportable, mêlée de tristesse. La dernière traque. A jamais et à jamais. La neige, qui avait commencé de fondre, formait des flaques et des mares dans le gravier. Aucune trace. Il restait invisible. Pourtant je sentais sa présence, je l'entendais presque respirer. Je marchai d'un pas rapide vers le centre du toit et, plissant les yeux dans le vent, scrutai l'espace. L'espace du monde. De la terre. D'un horizon à l'autre. Mais il n'y avait plus d'horizon. Plus de terre. Il ne restait que le ciel. Un bleu illimité qui s'étendait à perte de vue dans chaque direction. Le vent, le ciel et la lumière, aussi diaphane qu'un bloc de glace, et les ombres bleutées, comme de la fumée sur le gravier, comme les ombres dans un bloc de glace. Je sentais sa présence mais il n'était pas là. Bien que convaincu de son absence, je me mis à sa recherche, sans espoir ni désespoir.

J'entendais le bourdonnement des moteurs, le grincement désincarné de la machinerie, un sifflement comme celui du fil de nylon qui s'échappe du moulinet, le crissement des freins d'une locomotive. Des bruits de gare de triage. Des poulies et des engrenages tournaient. Des roues. Je le cherchai parmi elles. Dans la coupole de l'ascenseur. La porte était ouverte. Il faisait plus chaud à l'intérieur. Le sol de ciment était très propre, balayé. Une salle aussi vaste qu'une usine. Les énormes câbles luisants de graisse allaient et venaient, les tambours pivotaient et s'arrêtaient, frémissaient puis repartaient, comme s'ils pêchaient dans le Puits des Soupirs. Le cœur de la machine. Le cabinet d'Oz. C'était tellement cohérent avec le reste. Je fouillai chaque recoin en sachant qu'il n'était pas là, en sachant à chaque instant qu'il ne pouvait être là. Alors je me penchai pour scruter le puits, en me demandant s'il n'y était pas retourné, au cœur de la machine. Un instant, un seul instant, je sentis cela revenir, je sentis cela s'infiltrer dans mon esprit, goutte à goutte, un vide semblable à un poison administré en intraveineuse. Je sentis l'attirance de la gravité, la gravité de la ruine, l'ampleur de la débâcle, qui m'intimait de le suivre tout en bas, jusqu'au cœur de la machine. Je caressai la pensée de tomber, et mon esprit fut pris d'un long vertige délicieux. Mais au lieu d'y céder, je fouillai dans ma poche, en sortis un penny et le lâchai dans le Puits en regrettant de ne pas mourir. Parce qu'il n'était pas là. Et nulle part ailleurs. Parce que j'y étais. A jamais et à jamais. L'ampleur de la débâcle. Ma présence, son absence. Il n'y avait rien d'autre. Rien d'autre. Rien. Ces quatre mots disaient tout. Je vis brusquement le seau remonter, remonter vers la lumière, émerger du Puits des Soupirs. Et débordant de mystère. Le monde tel qu'il est. Et je ris parce que je compris. Tant de choses. Je me souvenais de tant de choses. Je me rappelais la réponse de ma mère à Hsiao quand il lui avait annoncé le départ de Love. « Je sais, dit-elle, tu ne vois donc pas ? Je l'ai toujours su. » Il n'avait pas compris cela, que maintenant je comprenais. Je réalisai que, même à la fin, elle avait été heureuse. Et moi aussi j'étais heureux, parce que je savais, parce que j'avais toujours su, comme elle. Bien sûr, il n'était pas là. Cela allait de soi. Et je renversai la tête pour éclater de rire. J'essuyai ensuite les larmes de mes yeux avant de quitter l'immense salle.

De retour à l'extérieur sous le ciel froid dans le vent et la lumière, à l'intérieur d'une ombre bleutée inscrite sur le gravier comme une photographie, je vis la cigarette. Jetée dans une flaque. Une simple cigarette. Mais mon cœur accéléra de nouveau. Et au-delà, plus près du bord du toit, sur une plaque de neige, l'empreinte d'un pas, une seule empreinte. Une simple empreinte. Dirigée vers le vide. Vers le bleu illimité qui circonscrivait le monde. Je suivis cette piste et regardai à mes pieds la cité qui s'étendait vers l'horizon puis le ciel. Alors je la vis. La trace de vapeur qui longeait les rayons de lumière, le clin d'œil argenté, l'étincelle. Je vis cette trace de vapeur comme le vol ralenti d'une flèche décochée vers le soleil, et qui s'éternisait dans sa course, je l'observai avec joie jusqu'à ce que j'eusse froid. J'avisai alors mon manteau toujours sur mon bras ainsi qu'il l'avait posé, et quand je le secouai j'aperçus quelque chose voleter, un morceau de papier, un fragment de ticket déchiré — le prix d'entrée, le prix exorbitant de l'entrée — une chose qui tournoyait, voltigeait de-ci de-là comme une feuille morte, une feuille d'automne. Un déchet. Bizarrement, cela montait. Et soudain j'aperçus la phalène. Ce ne pouvait être qu'une phalène. Avec une stupéfaction ravie, j'observai ses acrobaties. Et alors qu'elle tourbillonnait vers le ciel, le soleil embrasa ses ailes qui s'incendièrent comme des vitraux, et la phalène se transforma en papillon. Quand je baissai les yeux vers mon manteau, j'y découvris, glissée là par quelque mystérieux tour de magie, la robe de ma mère.

De retour dans les rues, je marchai comme un somnambule, en proie à une transe joyeuse, vers le fleuve, vers l'East River, attiré par l'ancienne gravité, cette même gravité qui entraînait la neige fondue vers le caniveau, et je poussais le cri du maître et celui de l'être subjugué, je riais, je riais devant l'eau qui coulait, l'eau de tous les fleuves, l'eau qui irriguait les cellules, les flux du sang, les fleuves de sang et tous leurs affluents qui convergeaient vers le cours principal, puis vers la mer, l'océan mystique, entraînés par l'ancienne gravité de la ruine et de l'espoir, par la gravité de la perte et de l'entropie. Je baissai les yeux vers l'eau qui tourbillonnait à mes pieds ; il y avait du sang dedans, une nuance rose pâle qui venait sans doute du marché aux poissons, cela et les radeaux précaires de détritus, les fleurs exposées dans la rue devant la boutique du fleuriste, lancées sur les fleuves de neige, comme une flottille, comme un défilé, les suivant dans le caniveau puis dans l'égout. Tout se précipitait de concert avec moi, aspiré par l'entropie. Brindilles et fragments de roseaux dérivaient dans le courant qui les emportait, baguettes et rameaux comme ceux qui jonchaient la plage de Sands Point. Formules cryptiques écrites dans les ordures, les champs de force du jusant. Maintenant je comprenais. Ce flot se consumait lui-même, il effaçait ses traces dans cette extase sauvage où il disparaissait, où Eddie Love disparaissait, et il nous restait seulement cela — des formules cryptiques écrites dans les ordures, les miettes de pain pour sortir du labyrinthe, les lignes du champ magnétique de la marée basse, de l'entropie, de tout ce qui fuit. Alors le mystère s'approfondit et j'entrevis le joyau dans le lotus, et je pleurai encore parce que je compris que j'y étais, que je touchais au but, au delta — la Perte, l'Entropie — et que les choses comme les êtres s'y dirigeaient, même le torrent écumant du Dow, même les fleuves de sang, tout retournait vers ce lieu, au delta, au Confluent Majeur, à la perte, l'Entropie, l'océan primordial, le Tao. Le retour à la Source. Le retour au monde tel qu'il est.

Les paroles du neuvième chant, « Le Retour à la Source » montèrent vers mes lèvres, et je chantai.

> *Trop long le chemin qui m'a amené ici,*
> *A la Source de Toutes Choses.*
> *Aveugle et sot depuis le début,*
> *Pourquoi ai-je fait le premier pas ?*
> *Assis jambes croisées dans la cellule de ma Nature Originelle,*
> *Indifférent au monde extérieur,*
> *Le fleuve coule paisiblement où il doit couler ;*
> *Et les fleurs sont rouges dans l'aube nouvelle.*

Oui, lecteur, elles le sont. Car les fleurs aussi sont ensanglantées.

Collection « Les romans étrangers »

dirigée par Tony Cartano

Déjà parus :

La mort d'un apiculteur, par Lars Gustafsson. Traduit du suédois par C.G. Bjurström et Lucie Albertini.

Une mère et ses deux filles, par Gail Godwin. Traduit de l'anglais par Françoise Cartano.

Ararat, par D.M. Thomas. Traduit de l'anglais par Claire Malroux.

Le club, par Leonard Michaels. Traduit de l'anglais par Françoise Cartano.

Voyages intermédiaires, par Ted Mooney. Traduit de l'américain par Robert Pépin.

Journée d'adieu, par John McGahern. Traduit de l'anglais par Alain Delahaye.

La joueuse de flûte, par D.M. Thomas. Traduit de l'anglais par Suzanne Mayoux.

Rencontre d'été, par Steve Tesich. Traduit de l'américain par Janine Hérisson

Speranza, par Sven Delblanc. Traduit du suédois par Jean-Baptiste Brunet-Jailly.

Strindberg et l'ordinateur, par Lars Gustafsson. Traduit du suédois par Marc de Gouvenain.

Lumière pâle sur les collines, par Kazuo Ishiguro. Traduit de l'anglais par Sophie Mayoux.

In memoriam, par Rodney Hall. Traduit de l'anglais par Françoise Cartano.

Le centaure dans le jardin, par Moacyr Scliar. Traduit du brésilien par Rachel Uziel et Salvatore Rotolo.

Sempreviva, par Antonio Callado. Traduit du brésilien par Jacques Thiériot.

Musique funèbre, par Lars Gustafsson. Traduit du suédois par Marc de Gouvenain.

Folie d'une femme séduite, par Suzan Fromberg Schaeffer. Traduit de l'américain par Eléonore Bakhtadzé.

Poupées russes, par D.M. Thomas. Traduit de l'anglais par Brice Matthieussent.

La nuit de Jérusalem, par Sven Delblanc. Traduit du suédois par Jean-Baptiste Brunet-Jailly.

Cet ouvrage a été composé par Facompo
et imprimé par la S.E.P.C. à Saint-Amand-Montrond (Cher)
pour le compte des éditions Presses de la Renaissance

Achevé d'imprimer en mars 1986